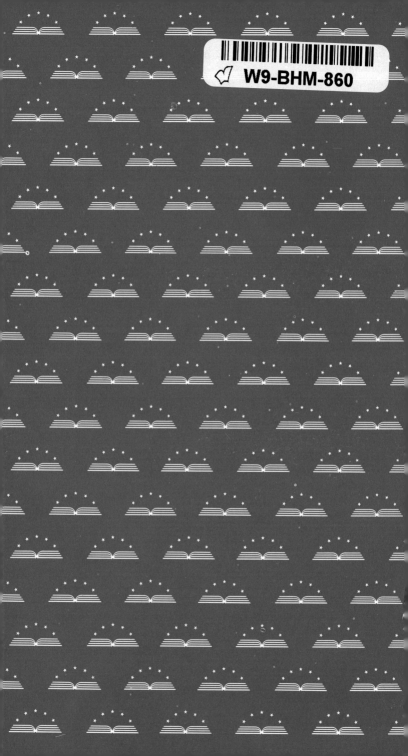

WILLIAM FAULKNER

WILLIAM FAULKNER

NOVELS 1957–1962

The Town
The Mansion
The Reivers

THE LIBRARY OF AMERICA

The Town © 1957 by William Faulkner; copyright renewed 1985
by Jill Faulkner Summers.
The Mansion © 1955, 1959 by William Faulkner; copyright
renewed 1983, 1987 by Jill Faulkner Summers.
The Reivers © 1962 by William Faulkner; copyright renewed
1990 by Jill Faulkner Summers.
Reprinted by arrangement with Random House.

The paper used in this publication meets the
minimum requirements of the American National Standard for
Information Sciences—Permanence of Paper for Printed
Library Materials, ANSI Z39.48—1984.

Distributed to the trade in the United States
by Penguin Putnam Inc.
and in Canada by Penguin Books Canada Ltd.

Library of Congress Catalog Number: 99–18348
For cataloging information, see end of Notes.
ISBN 1–883011–69–8

First Printing
The Library of America—112

Manufactured in the United States of America

JOSEPH BLOTNER AND NOEL POLK
WROTE THE NOTES AND EDITED THE TEXTS
FOR THIS VOLUME

The publishers wish to thank Mrs. Paul D. Summers, Jr.,
and the Alderman Library of the University of Virginia
for the use of archival materials,
and the University of Southern Mississippi
for technical assistance.

The texts of The Town, The Mansion, *and* The Reivers,
have been established by Noel Polk.

Contents

THE TOWN

VOLUME TWO

Snopes

To PHIL STONE

He did half the laughing for thirty years

ONE

C HARLES MALLISON
I wasn't born yet so it was Cousin Gowan who was
there and big enough to see and remember and tell me afterward when I was big enough for it to make sense. That is, it
was Cousin Gowan plus Uncle Gavin or maybe Uncle Gavin
rather plus Cousin Gowan. He—Cousin Gowan—was thirteen. His grandfather was Grandfather's brother so by the
time it got down to us, he and I didn't know what cousin to
each other we were. So he just called all of us except Grandfather 'cousin' and all of us except Grandfather called him
'cousin' and let it go at that.

They lived in Washington, where his father worked for the
State Department, and all of a sudden the State Department
sent his father to China or India or some far place, to be gone
two years; and his mother was going too so they sent Gowan
down to stay with us and go to school in Jefferson until they
got back. 'Us' was Grandfather and Mother and Father and
Uncle Gavin then. So this is what Gowan knew about it until
I got born and big enough to know about it too. So when I
say 'we' and 'we thought' what I mean is Jefferson and what
Jefferson thought.

At first we thought that the water tank was only Flem
Snopes's monument. We didn't know any better then. It
wasn't until afterward that we realised that that object low on
the sky above Jefferson, Mississippi, wasn't a monument at all.
It was a footprint.

One day one summer he drove up the southeast road into
town in a two-mule wagon containing his wife and baby and
a small assortment of house-furnishings. The next day he was
behind the counter of a small back-alley restaurant which belonged to V. K. Ratliff. That is, Ratliff owned it with a partner, since he—Ratliff—had to spend most of his time in his
buckboard (this was before he owned the Model T Ford)
about the county with his demonstrator sewing machine for
which he was the agent. That is, we thought Ratliff was still

3

the other partner until we saw the stranger in the other greasy apron behind the counter—a squat uncommunicative man with a neat minute bow tie and opaque eyes and a sudden little hooked nose like the beak of a small hawk; a week after that, Snopes had set up a canvas tent behind the restaurant and he and his wife and baby were living in it. And that was when Ratliff told Uncle Gavin:

"Just give him time. Give him six months and he'll have Grover Cleveland" (Grover Cleveland Winbush was the partner) "out of that café too."

That was the first summer, the first Summer of the Snopes, Uncle Gavin called it. He was in Harvard now, working for his M.A. After that he was going to the University of Mississippi law school to get ready to be Grandfather's partner. But already he was spending the vacations helping Grandfather be City Attorney; he had barely seen Mrs Snopes yet so he not only didn't know he would ever go to Germany to enter Heidelberg University, he didn't even know yet that he would ever want to: only to talk about going there someday as a nice idea to keep in mind or to talk about.

He and Ratliff talked together a lot. Because although Ratliff had never been to school anywhere much and spent his time travelling about our county selling sewing machines (or selling or swapping or trading anything else for that matter), he and Uncle Gavin were both interested in people—or so Uncle Gavin said. Because what I always thought they were mainly interested in was curiosity. Until this time, that is. Because this time it had already gone a good deal further than just curiosity. This time it was alarm.

Ratliff was how we first began to learn about Snopes. Or rather, Snopeses. No, that's wrong: there had been a Snopes in Colonel Sartoris's cavalry command in 1864—in that part of it whose occupation had been raiding Yankee picket-lines for horses. Only this time it was a Confederate picket which caught him—that Snopes—raiding a Confederate horse-line and, it was believed, hung him. Which was evidently wrong too, since (Ratliff told Uncle Gavin) about ten years ago Flem and an old man who seemed to be his father appeared suddenly from nowhere one day and rented a little farm from Mr Will Varner who just about owned the whole settlement and district called Frenchman's Bend about twenty miles from Jefferson. It was a farm so poor and small and already worn-out that only the most trifling farmer would undertake it, and even they stayed only one year. Yet Ab and Flem rented it and evidently (this is Ratliff) he or Flem or both of them together found it——

"Found what?" Uncle Gavin said.

"I dont know," Ratliff said. "Whatever it was Uncle Billy and Jody had buried out there and thought was safe."—because that winter Flem was the clerk in Uncle Billy's store. And what they found on that farm must have been a good one, or maybe they didn't even need it anymore; maybe Flem found something else the Varners thought was hidden and safe under the counter of the store itself. Because in another year old Ab had moved into Frenchman's Bend to live with his son and another Snopes had appeared from somewhere to take over the rented farm; and in two years more still another Snopes was the official smith in Mr Varner's blacksmith shop. So there were as many Snopeses in Frenchman's Bend as there were Varners; and five years after that, which was the year Flem moved to Jefferson, there were even more Snopeses than Varners because one Varner was married to a Snopes and was nursing another small Snopes at her breast.

Because what Flem found that last time was inside Uncle Billy's house. She was his only daughter and youngest child, not just a local belle but a belle throughout that whole section. Nor was it just because of old Will's land and money. Because I saw her too and I knew what it was too, even if she was grown and married and with a child older than I was and I only eleven and twelve and thirteen. ("Oh ay," Uncle Gavin said. "Even at twelve dont think you are the first man ever chewed his bitter thumbs for that like reason such as her.") She wasn't too big, heroic, what they call Junoesque. It was that there was just too much of what she was for any just one human female package to contain and hold: too much of white, too much of female, too much of maybe just glory, I dont know: so that at first sight of her you felt a kind of shock of gratitude just for being alive and being male at the same instant with her in space and time, and then in the next second and forever after a kind of despair because you knew that there never would be enough of any one male to match and hold and deserve her; grief forever after because forever after nothing less would ever do.

That was what he found this time. One day, according to Ratliff, Frenchman's Bend learned that Flem Snopes and Eula Varner had driven across the line into the next county the night before and bought a license and got married; the same day, still according to Ratliff, Frenchman's Bend learned that three young men, three of Eula's old suitors, had left the country suddenly by night too, for Texas it was said, or anyway west, for enough west to be longer than Uncle Billy or Jody Varner could have reached if they had needed to try. Then a month later Flem and Eula also departed for Texas (that bourne, Uncle Gavin said, in our time for the implicated the insolvent or the merely hopeful), to return the next summer with a girl baby a little larger than you would have expected at only three months——

"And the horses," Uncle Gavin said. Because we did know about that, mainly because Flem Snopes had not been the first to import them. Every year or so someone brought into the county a string of wild unbroken plains ponies from somewhere in the west and auctioned them off. This time the ponies arrived, in the charge of a man who was obviously from Texas, at the same time that Mr and Mrs Snopes returned home from that state. This string however seemed to be uncommonly wild, since the resultant scattering of the untamed and untameable calico-splotched animals covered not just Frenchman's Bend but the whole east half of the county too. Though even to the last, no one ever definitely connected Snopes with their ownership. "No no," Uncle Gavin said. "You were not one of the three that ran from the smell of Will Varner's shotgun. And dont tell me Flem Snopes traded you one of those horses for your half of that restaurant because I wont believe it. What was it?"

Ratliff sat there with his bland brown smoothly-shaven face and his neat tieless blue shirt and his shrewd intelligent gentle eyes not quite looking at Uncle Gavin. "It was that old house," he said. Uncle Gavin waited. "The Old Frenchman place." Uncle Gavin waited. "That buried money." Then Uncle Gavin understood: not an old pre-Civil War plantation house in all Mississippi or the South either but had its legend of the money and plate buried in the flower garden from Yankee raiders;—in this particular case, the ruined mansion which in the old time had dominated and bequeathed its name to the whole section known as Frenchman's Bend, which the Varners now owned. "It was Henry Armstid's fault, trying to get even with Flem for that horse that Texas man sold him that broke his leg. No," Ratliff said, "it was me too as much as anybody else, as any of us. To figger out what Flem was doing owning that old place that anybody could see wasn't worth nothing. I dont mean why Flem bought it. I mean, why he even taken it when Uncle Billy give it to him and Eula for a wedding gift. So when Henry taken to following and watching Flem and finally caught him that night digging in that old flower garden, I dont reckon Henry had to persuade me very hard to go back the next night and watch Flem digging myself."

"So when Flem finally quit digging and went away, you and Henry crawled out of the bushes and dug too," Uncle Gavin said. "And found it. Some of it. Enough of it. Just exactly barely enough of it for you to hardly wait for daylight to swap Flem Snopes your half of that restaurant for your half of the Old Frenchman place. How much longer did you and Henry dig before you quit?"

"I quit after the second night," Ratliff said. "That was when I finally thought to look at the money."

"All right," Uncle Gavin said. "The money."

"They was silver dollars me and Henry dug up. Some of them was pretty old. One of Henry's was minted almost twenty years ago."

"A salted goldmine," Uncle Gavin said. "One of the oldest tricks in the world, yet you fell for it. Not Henry Armstid: you."

"Yes," Ratliff said. "Almost as old as that handkerchief Eula Varner dropped. Almost as old as Uncle Billy Varner's shotgun." That was what he said then. Because another year had passed when he stopped Uncle Gavin on the street and said, "With the court's permission, Lawyer, I would like to take a exception. I want to change that-ere to 'still'."

"Change what-ere to 'still'?" Uncle Gavin said.

"Last year I said 'That handkerchief Miz Flem Snopes dropped'. I want to change that 'dropped' to 'still dropping'. They's one feller I know still following it."

Because in six months Snopes had not only eliminated the partner from the restaurant, Snopes himself was out of it, replaced behind the greasy counter and in the canvas tent too by another Snopes accreted in from Frenchman's Bend into the vacuum behind the first one's next advancement by that same sort of osmosis by which, according to Ratliff, they had covered Frenchman's Bend, the chain unbroken, every Snopes in Frenchman's Bend moving up one step, leaving that last slot at the bottom open for the next Snopes to appear from nowhere and fill, which without doubt he had already done though Ratliff had not yet had time to go out there and see.

And now Flem and his wife lived in a small rented house in a back street near the edge of town, and Flem was now superintendent of the town power-plant which pumped the water and produced the electricity. Our outrage was primarily shock; shock not that Flem had the job, we had not got that far yet, but shock that we had not known until now that the job existed; that there was such a position in Jefferson as superintendent of the power-plant. Because the plant—the boilers and the engines which ran the pump and dynamo—was operated by an old saw mill engineer named Harker, and the dynamos and the electric wiring which covered the town were cared for by a private electrician who worked on a retainer from the town;—a condition which had been completely satisfactory ever since running water and electricity first came to Jefferson. Yet suddenly and without warning, we needed a superintendent for it. And as suddenly and simultaneously and with that same absence of warning, a country man who had not been in town two years now and (we assumed) had probably never seen an electric light until that first night two years ago when he drove in, was that superintendent.

That was the only shock. It wasn't that the country man was Flem Snopes. Because we had all seen Mrs Snopes by now, what few times we did see her which was usually behind the counter in the restaurant in another greasy apron, frying the hamburgers and eggs and ham and the tough pieces of steak on the grease-crusted kerosene griddle, or maybe once a week on the Square, always alone; not, as far as we knew, going anywhere: just moving, walking in that aura of decorum and modesty and solitariness ten times more immodest and a hundred times more disturbing than one of the bathing suits young women would begin to wear about 1920 or so, as if in the second just before you looked, her garments had managed in one last frantic pell mell scurry to overtake and cover her. Though only for a moment because in the next one, if only you followed long enough, they would wilt and fail from that mere plain and simple striding which would shred them away like the wheel of a constellation through a wisp and cling of trivial scud.

And we had known the mayor, Major de Spain, longer than that. Jefferson, Mississippi, the whole South for that matter, was still full at that time of men called General or Colonel or Major because their fathers or grandfathers had been generals or colonels or majors or maybe just privates, in Confederate armies, or who had contributed to the campaign funds of successful state governors. But Major de Spain's father had been a real major of Confederate cavalry, and De Spain himself was a West Pointer who had gone to Cuba as a second lieutenant with troops and came home with a wound—a long scar running from his hair through his left ear and down his jaw, which could have been left by the sabre or gun-rammer we naturally assumed some embattled Spaniard had hit him with, or by the axe which political tactics during the race for mayor claimed a sergeant in a dice game had hit him with.

Because he had not been long at home and out of his blue Yankee coat before we realised that he and Jefferson were incorrigibly and invincibly awry to one another, and that one of them was going to have to give. And that it would not be him: that he would neither flee Jefferson nor try to alter himself to fit Jefferson, but instead would try to wrench Jefferson until the town fitted him, and—the young people hoped—would succeed.

Until then, Jefferson was like all the other little Southern towns: nothing had happened in it since the last carpetbagger had given up and gone home or been assimilated into another unregenerate Mississippian. We had the usual mayor and board of aldermen who seemed to the young people to have been in perpetuity since the Ark or certainly since the last Chickasaw departed for Oklahoma in 1820, as old then as now and even now no older: old Mr Adams the mayor with a long patriarchial white beard, who probably seemed to young people like Cousin Gowan older than God Himself, until he might actually have been the first man; Uncle Gavin said there were more than just boys of twelve and thirteen like Cousin Gowan that referred to him by name, leaving off the last s, and to his old fat wife as 'Miss Eve Adam', fat old Eve long since free of the danger of inciting a snake or anything else to tempt her.

So we were wondering just what axe Lieutenant de Spain would use to chop the corners off Jefferson and make it fit him. One day he found it. The city electrician (the one who kept the town's generators and dynamos and transformers working) was a genius. One afternoon in 1904 he drove out of his back yard into the street in the first automobile we had ever seen, made by hand completely, engine and all, from magneto coil to radius rod, and drove into the Square at the moment when Colonel Sartoris the banker's surrey and blooded matched team were crossing it on the way home. Although Colonel Sartoris and his driver were not hurt and the horses when caught had no scratch on them and the electrician offered to repair the surrey (it was said he even offered to put a gasoline engine in it this time), Colonel Sartoris appeared in person before the next meeting of the board of aldermen, who passed an edict that no gasoline-propelled vehicle should ever operate on the streets of Jefferson.

That was De Spain's chance. It was more than just his. It was the opportunity which that whole contemporary generation of young people had been waiting for, not just in Jefferson but everywhere, who had seen in that stinking noisy little home-made self-propelled buggy which Mr Buffaloe (the electrician) had made out of odds and ends in his back yard in his spare time, not just a phenomenon but an augury, a promise of the destiny which would belong to the United States. He—De Spain—didn't even need to campaign for mayor: all he needed was to announce. And the old dug-in city fathers saw that too, which was why they spooked to the desperate expedient of creating or exhuming or repeating (whichever it was) the story of the Cuban dice game and the sergeant's axe. And De Spain settled that once and for all not even as a politician; Caesar himself couldn't have done it any neater.

It was one morning at mail-time. Mayor Adams and his youngest son Theron who was not as old as De Spain and not even very much bigger either, mainly just taller, were coming out of the post office when De Spain met them. That is, he was already standing there with a good crowd watching, his finger already touching the scar when Mr Adams saw him. "Good morning, Mister Mayor," he said. "What's this I hear about a dice game with an axe in it?"

"That's what the voters of the city of Jefferson would like to ask you, sir," Mr Adams said. "If you know of any proof to the contrary nearer than Cuba, I would advise you to produce it."

"I know a quicker way than that," De Spain said. "Your Honor's a little too old for it, but Theron there's a good-sized boy now. Let him and me step over to McCaslin's hardware store and get a couple of axes and find out right now if you are right."

"Aw now, Lieutenant," Theron said.

"That's all right," De Spain said. "I'll pay for both of them."

"Gentlemen," Theron said. And that was all of that. In June De Spain was elected mayor. It was a landslide because more than just he had won, been elected. The new age had entered Jefferson; he was merely its champion, the Godfrey de Bouillon, the Tancred, the Jefferson Richard Lion-heart of the twentieth century.

He wore that mantle well. No: it wasn't a mantle: it was a banner, a flag and he was carrying it, already out in front before Jefferson knew we were even ready for it. He made Mr Buffaloe City Electrician with a monthly salary, though his first official act was about Colonel Sartoris's edict against automobiles. We thought of course that he and his new aldermen would have repealed it for no other reason than that one old mossback like Colonel Sartoris had told another old mossback like Mayor Adams to pass it, and the second old mossback did.

But they didn't do that. Like I said, it was a landslide that
elected him; it was like that axe business with old Mayor
Adams and Theron in front of the post office that morning
had turned on a light for all the other young people in
Jefferson. I mean, the ones who were not yet store- and gin-
owners and already settled lawyers and doctors, but were only
the clerks and book-keepers in the stores and gins and offices,
trying to save enough to get married on, who all went to work
to get De Spain elected mayor. And not only did that, but
more: before they knew it or even intended it, they had displaced the old dug-in aldermen and themselves rode into
office as the city fathers on Manfred de Spain's coat-tails or
anyway axe. So you would have thought the first thing they
would have done would be to throw out forever that automobile law. Instead, they had it copied out on a piece of parch-
ment like a diploma or a citation and framed and hung on the
wall in a lighted glass case in the hall of the Courthouse, where
pretty soon people were coming in automobiles from as far
away as Chicago to laugh at it. Because Uncle Gavin said this
was still that fabulous and legendary time when there was still
no paradox between an automobile and mirth, before the time
when every American had to have one and they were killing
more people than wars did.

He—De Spain—did even more than that. He himself had
brought into town the first real automobile—a red E.M.F.
roadster, and sold the horses out of the livery stable his father
had left him and tore out the stalls and cribs and tack-rooms
and established the first garage and automobile agency in
Jefferson, so that now all his aldermen and all the other
young people to whom neither of the banks would lend one
cent to buy a motor vehicle with, no matter how solvent they
were, could own them too. Oh yes, the motor age had
reached Jefferson and De Spain led it in that red roadster:
that vehicle alien and debonair, as invincibly and irrevocably
polygamous and bachelor as De Spain himself. And would
ever be, living alone in his late father's big wooden house
with a cook and a houseman in a white coat; he led the
yearly cotillion and was first on the list of the ladies' german;
if café society—not the Social Register nor the Four Hundred: Café Society—had been invented yet and any of it had

come to Jefferson, he would have led it; born a generation too soon, he would have been by acclamation ordained a high priest in that new national religious cult of Cheesecake as it translated still alive the Harlows and Grables and Monroes into the hierarchy of American cherubim.

So when we first saw Mrs Snopes walking in the Square giving off that terrifying impression that in another second her flesh itself would burn her garments off, leaving not even a veil of ashes between her and the light of day, it seemed to us that we were watching Fate, a fate of which both she and Mayor de Spain were victims. We didn't know when they met, laid eyes for the first time on one another. We didn't need to. In a way, we didn't want to. We assumed of course that he was slipping her into his house by some devious means or method at night, but we didn't know that either. With any else but them, some of us—some boy or boys or youths—would have lain in ambush just to find out. But not with him. On the contrary, we were on his side. We didn't want to know. We were his allies, his confederates; our whole town was accessory to that cuckolding—that cuckolding which for any proof we had, we had invented ourselves out of whole cloth; that same cuckoldry in which we would watch De Spain and Snopes walking amicably together while (though we didn't know it yet) De Spain was creating, planning how to create, that office of power-plant superintendent which we didn't even know we didn't have, let alone needed, and then get Mr Snopes into it. It was not because we were against Mr Snopes; we had not yet read the signs and portents which should have warned, alerted, sprung us into frantic concord to defend our town from him. Nor were we really in favor of adultery, sin: we were simply in favor of De Spain and Eula Snopes, for what Uncle Gavin called the divinity of simple unadulterated uninhibited immortal lust which they represented; for the two people in each of whom the other had found his single ordained fate; each to have found out of all the earth that one match for his mettle; ours the pride that Jefferson would supply their battleground.

Even Uncle Gavin; Uncle Gavin also. He said to Ratliff: "This town aint that big. Why hasn't Flem caught them?"

"He dont want to," Ratliff said. "He dont need to yet."

Then we learned that the town—the mayor, the board of aldermen, whoever and however it was done—had created the office of power-plant superintendent, and appointed Flem Snopes to fill it.

At night Mr Harker, the veteran saw mill engineer, ran the power-plant, with Tomey's Turl Beauchamp, the Negro fireman, to fire the boilers as long as Mr Harker was there to watch the pressure gauges, which Tomey's Turl either could not or would not do, apparently simply declining to take seriously any connection between the firebox below the boiler and the little dirty clock-face which didn't even tell the hour, on top of it. During the day the other Negro fireman, Tom Tom Bird, ran the plant alone, with Mr Buffaloe to look in now and then though as a matter of routine since Tom Tom not only fired the boilers, he was as competent to read the gauges and keep the bearings of the steam engine and the dynamos cleaned and oiled as Mr Buffaloe or Mr Harker were: a completely satisfactory arrangement since Mr Harker was old enough not to mind or possibly even prefer the night shift, and Tom Tom—a big bull of a man weighing two hundred pounds and sixty years old but looking about forty and married about two years ago to his fourth wife: a young woman whom he kept with the strict jealous seclusion of a Turk in a cabin about two miles down the railroad track from the plant—declined to consider anything but the day one. Though by the time Cousin Gowan joined Mr Harker's night shift, Mr Snopes had learned to read the gauges and even fill the oil cups too.

This was about two years after he became superintendent. Gowan had decided to go out for the football team that fall and he got the idea, I dont reckon even he knew where, that a job shovelling coal on a power-plant night shift would be the exact perfect training for dodging or crashing over enemy tacklers. Mother and Father didn't think so until Uncle Gavin took a hand. (He had his Harvard M.A. now and had finished the University of Mississippi law school and passed his bar and Grandfather had begun to retire and now Uncle Gavin really was the city attorney; it had been a whole year now—this was in June, he had just got home from the University and he hadn't seen Mrs Snopes yet this summer—since he had even talked of Heidelberg as a pleasant idea for conversation.)

"Why not?" he said. "Gowan's going on thirteen now; it's time for him to begin to stay out all night. And what better place can he find than down there at the plant where Mr Harker and the fireman can keep him awake?"

So Gowan got the job as Tomey's Turl's helper and at once Mr Harker began to keep him awake talking about Mr Snopes, talking about him with a kind of amoral amazement with which you would recount having witnessed the collision of a planet. According to Mr Harker, it began last year. One afternoon Tom Tom had finished cleaning his fires and was now sitting in the gangway smoking his pipe, pressure up and the safety-valve on the middle boiler blowing off, when Mr Snopes came in and stood there for a while, chewing tobacco and looking up at the whistling valve.

"How much does that whistle weigh?" he said.

"If you talking about that valve, about ten pounds," Tom Tom said.

"Solid brass?" Mr Snopes said.

"All except that little hole it's what you call whistling through," Tom Tom said. And that was all then, Mr Harker said; it was two months later when he, Mr Harker, came on duty one evening and found the three safety-valves gone from the boilers and the vents stopped with one-inch steel screw plugs capable of a pressure of a thousand pounds and Tomey's Turl still shovelling coal into the fireboxes because he hadn't heard one of them blow off yet.

"And them three boiler heads you could poke a hole through with a sody straw," Mr Harker said. "When I seen the gauge on the first boiler I never believed I would live to reach the injector.

"So when I finally got it into Turl's head that that 100 on that dial meant where Turl wouldn't only lose his job, he would lose it so good wouldn't nobody never find the job nor him again neither, I finally got settled down enough to in-quire where them safety-valves had went to.

"'Mr Snopes took um off,' he says.

"'What in hell for?'

"'I dont know. I just telling you what Tom Tom told me. He say Mr Snopes say the shut-off float in the water tank aint heavy enough. Say that tank start leaking some day, so he going to fasten them three safety-valves on the float and weight it heavier.'

"'You mean,' I says. That's as far as I could get. 'You mean—'

"'That's what Tom Tom say. I dont know nothing about it.'

"Anyhow they was gone; whether they was in the water tank or not, was too late to find out now. Until then, me and Turl had been taking it pretty easy after the load went off and things got kind of quiet. But you can bet we never dozed none that night. Me and him spent the whole of it time about on the coal pile where we could watch them three gauges all at once. And from midnight on, after the load went off, we never had enough steam in all them three boilers put together to run a peanut parcher. And even when I was home in bed, I couldn't go to sleep. Time I shut my eyes I would begin to see a steam gauge about the size of a washtub, with a red needle big as a coal scoop moving up toward a hundred pounds, and I would wake myself up hollering and sweating.

"So come daylight enough to see; and I never sent Turl neither: I clumb up there myself and looked at that float. And there wasn't no safety-valves weighting it neither and maybe he hadn't aimed for them to be fastened to it where the first feller that looked in could a reached them. And even if that tank is forty-two foot deep I still could a opened the cock and dreened it. Only I just work there, Mr Snopes was the superintendent, and it was the day shift now and Tom Tom could answer whatever questions Joe Buffaloe would want to know in case he happened in and seen them thousand-pound screw plugs where safety-valves was supposed to been.

"So I went on home and that next night I couldn't hardly get Turl to run them gauge needles up high enough to turn the low-pressure piston, let alone move the dynamos; and the next night, and the next one, until about ten days when the express delivered a box; Tom Tom had waited and me and him opened the box (It was marked C.O.D. in big black paint but the tag itself had been wrenched off and gone temporarily. 'I know where he throwed it,' Tom Tom said.) and taken them screw plugs out of the vents and put the three new safety-valves back on; and sho enough Tom Tom did have the crumpled-up tag: Mister Flem Snopes Power-plant Jefferson Miss C.O.D. twenty-three dollars and eighty-one cents."

And now there was some of it which Mr Harker himself didn't know until Uncle Gavin told him after Tom Tom told Uncle Gavin: how one afternoon Tom Tom was smoking his pipe on the coal pile when Mr Snopes came in carrying in his hand what Tom Tom thought at first was a number three mule shoe until Mr Snopes took it into a corner behind the boilers where a pile of discarded fittings—valves, rods, bolts and such—had been accumulating probably since the first light was turned on in Jefferson; and, kneeling (Mr Snopes), tested every piece one by one into two separate piles in the gangway behind him. Then Tom Tom watched him test with the magnet every loose piece of metal in the whole boiler room, sorting the mere iron from the brass. Then Snopes ordered Tom Tom to gather up the separated brass and bring it to the office.

Tom Tom gathered the brass into a box. Snopes was waiting in the office, chewing tobacco. Tom Tom said he never stopped chewing even to spit. "How do you and Turl get along?" he said.

"I tend to my business," Tom Tom said. "What Turl does with his aint none of mine."

"That aint what Turl thinks," Mr Snopes said. "He wants me to give him your day shift. He claims he's tired of firing at night."

"Let him fire as long as I is, and he can have it," Tom Tom said.

"Turl dont aim to wait that long," Mr Snopes said. Then he told Tom Tom: how Turl was planning to steal iron from the plant and lay it on Tom Tom and get him fired. That's right. That's what Tom Tom told Uncle Gavin Mr Snopes called it: iron. Maybe Mr Snopes hadn't heard of a magnet himself until just yesterday and so he thought that Tom Tom had never heard of one and so didn't know what he was doing. I mean, not of magnets nor brass either and couldn't tell brass from iron. Or maybe he just thought that Tom Tom, being a Negro, wouldn't care. Or maybe that, being a Negro, whether he knew or not or cared or not, he wouldn't have any part of what a white man was mixed up in. Only we had to imagine this part of it of course. Not that it was hard to do: Tom Tom standing there about the size and shape and color (disposition too) of a Black Angus bull, looking down at the white man. Turl on the contrary was the color of a saddle and even with a scoop full of coal he barely touched a hundred and fifty pounds. "That's what he's up to," Mr Snopes said. "So I want you to take this stuff out to your house and hide it and dont breathe a word to nobody. And soon as I get enough evidence on Turl, I'm going to fire him."

"I knows a better way than that," Tom Tom said.

"What way?" Snopes said. Then he said: "No no, that wont do. You have any trouble with Turl and I'll fire you both. You do like I say. Unless you are tired of your job and want Turl to have it. Are you?"

"Aint no man complained about my pressure yet," Tom Tom said.

"Then you do like I tell you," Snopes said. "You take that stuff home with you tonight. Dont let nobody see you, even your wife. And if you dont want to do it, just say so. I reckon I can find somebody that will."

So Tom Tom did. And each time the pile of discarded fittings accumulated again, he would watch Snopes test out another batch of brass with his magnet for Tom Tom to take home and hide. Because Tom Tom had been firing boilers for forty years now, ever since he became a man, and these three for the twenty they had been there, since it was he who built the first fires beneath them. At first he had fired one boiler and he had got five dollars a month for it. Now he had the three and he got sixty dollars a month, and now he was sixty and he owned his little cabin and a little piece of corn land and a mule and wagon to ride to church in twice each Sunday, with a gold watch and the young wife which was the last new young wife he would probably have too.

Though all Mr Harker knew at this time was that the junked metal would accumulate slowly in the corner behind the boilers, then suddenly disappear overnight; now it became his nightly joke to enter the plant with his busy bustling air and say to Turl: "Well, I notice that-ere little engine is still running. There's a right smart of brass in them bushings and wrist-pins, but I reckon they're moving too fast to hold that magnet against. But I reckon we're lucky, at that. I reckon he'd sell them boilers too if he knowed any way you and Tom Tom could keep up steam without them."

Though he—Mr Harker—did tell what came next, which was at the first of the year, when the town was audited: "They come down here, two of them in spectacles. They went over the books and poked around ever where, counting ever thing in sight and writing it down. Then they went back to the office and they was still there at six oclock when I come on. It seems there was something a little out; it seems there was some old brass fittings wrote down in the books, except that that brass seemed to be missing or something. It was on the books all right, and the new valves and truck that had replaced it was there. But be durn if they could find a one of them old fittings except one busted bib that had done got mislaid beyond magnet range you might say under a work bench some way or other. It was right strange. So I went back with them and held the light while they looked again in all the corners, getting a right smart of sut and grease and coal-dust on them white shirts. But that brass just naturally seemed to be plumb gone. So they went away.

"And the next morning they come back. They had the city clerk with them this time and they beat Mr Snopes down here and so they had to wait until he come in in his check cap and his chew of tobacco, chewing and looking at them while they hemmed and hawed until they told him. They was right sorry; they hemmed and hawed a right smart being sorry, but there wasn't nothing else they could do except come back on him being as he was the superintendent; and did he want me and Turl and Tom Tom arrested right now or would tomorrow do? And him standing there chewing, with his eyes looking like two gobs of cup grease on a hunk of raw dough, and them still telling him how sorry they was.

"'How much does it come to?' he says.

"'Two hundred and eighteen dollars and fifty-two cents, Mr Snopes.'

" 'Is that the full amount?'

" 'We checked our figgers twice, Mr Snopes.'

" 'All right,' he says. And he reaches down and hauls out the money and pays the two hundred and eighteen dollars and fifty-two cents in cash and asks for a receipt."

Only by the next summer Gowan was Turl's student fireman, so now Gowan saw and heard it from Turl at first hand; it was evening when Mr Snopes stood suddenly in the door to the boiler room and crooked his finger at Turl and so this time it was Turl and Snopes facing one another in the office.

"What's this trouble about you and Tom Tom?" he said.

"Me and which?" Turl said. "If Tom Tom depending on me for his trouble, he done quit firing and turned waiter. It takes two folks to have trouble and Tom Tom aint but one, I dont care how big he is."

"Tom Tom thinks you want to fire the day shift," Mr Snopes said.

Turl was looking at everything now without looking at anything. "I can handle as much coal as Tom Tom," he said.

"Tom Tom knows that too," Mr Snopes said. "He knows he's getting old. But he knows there aint nobody else can crowd him for his job but you." Then Mr Snopes told him how for two years now Tom Tom had been stealing brass from the plant and laying it on Turl to get him fired; how only that day Tom Tom had told him, Mr Snopes, that Turl was the thief.

"That's a lie," Turl said. "Cant no nigger accuse me of stealing something I aint, I dont care how big he is."

"Sho," Mr Snopes said. "So the thing to do is to get that brass back."

"Not me," Turl said. "That's what they pays Mr Buck Conner for." Buck Connors was the town marshal.

"Then you'll go to jail sho enough," Snopes said. "Tom Tom will say he never even knowed it was there. You'll be the only one that knew that. So what you reckon Mr Conner'll think? You'll be the one that knowed where it was hid at, and Buck Conner'll know that even a fool has got more sense than to steal something and hide it in his own corn crib. The only thing you can do is, get that brass back. Go out there in the daytime, while Tom Tom is here at work, and get that brass and bring it to me and I'll put it away to use as evidence on Tom Tom. Or maybe you dont want that day shift. Say so, if you dont. I can find somebody else."

Because Turl hadn't fired any boilers forty years. He hadn't done anything at all that long, since he was only thirty. And if he were a hundred, nobody could accuse him of having done anything that would aggregate forty years net. "Unless tom-catting at night would add up that much," Mr Harker said. "If Turl ever is unlucky enough to get married he would still have to climb in his own back window or he wouldn't even know what he come after. Aint that right, Turl?"

So, as Mr Harker said, it was not Turl's fault so much as Snopes's mistake. "Which was," Mr Harker said, "when Mr Snopes forgot to remember in time about that young light-colored new wife of Tom Tom's. To think how he picked Turl out of all the Negroes in Jefferson, that's prowled at least once—or tried to—every gal within ten miles of town, to go out there to Tom Tom's house knowing all the time how Tom Tom is right here under Mr Snopes's eye wrastling coal until six oclock a m and then with two miles to walk down the railroad home, and expect Turl to spend his time out there" (Gowan was doing nearly all the night firing now. He had to; Turl had to get some sleep, on the coal pile in the bunker after midnight. He was losing weight too, which he could afford even less than sleep.) "hunting anything that aint hid in Tom Tom's bed. And when I think about Tom Tom in here wrastling them boilers in that-ere same amical cuckolry like what your uncle says Miz Snopes and Mayor de Spain walks around in, stealing brass so he can keep Turl from get-ting his job away from him, and all the time Turl is out yon-der tending by daylight to Tom Tom's night homework, sometimes I think I will jest die."

He was spared that; we all knew it couldn't last much longer. The question was, which would happen first: if Tom Tom would catch Turl, or if Mr Snopes would catch Turl, or if Mr Harker really would burst a blood vessel. Mr Snopes won. He was standing in the office door that evening when Mr Harker, Turl and Gowan came on duty; once more he crooked his finger at Turl and once more they stood facing

each other in the office. "Did you find it this time?" Mr
Snopes said.

"Find it which time?" Turl said.

"Just before dark tonight," Mr Snopes said. "I was standing at the corner of the crib when you crawled out of that
corn patch and climbed in that back window." And now indeed Turl was looking everywhere fast at nothing. "Maybe
you are still looking in the wrong place," Mr Snopes said. "If
Tom Tom had hid that iron in his bed, you ought to found it
three weeks ago. You take one more look. If you dont find it
this time, maybe I better tell Tom Tom to help you." Turl
was looking fast at nothing now.

"I'm gonter have to have three or four extra hours off tomorrow night," he said. "And Tom Tom gonter have to be
held right here unto I gets back."

"I'll see to it," Snopes said.

"I mean held right here unto I walks in and touches him,"
Turl said. "I dont care how late it is."

"I'll see to that," Snopes said.

Except that it had already quit lasting any longer at all;
Gowan and Mr Harker had barely reached the plant the next
evening when Mr Harker took one quick glance around. But
before he could even speak Mr Snopes was standing in the
office door, saying, "Where's Tom Tom?" Because it wasn't
Tom Tom waiting to turn over to the night crew: it was Tom
Tom's substitute, who fired the boilers on Sunday while Tom
Tom was taking his new young wife to church; Gowan said
Mr Harker said,

"Hell fire," already moving, running past Mr Snopes into
the office and scrabbling at the telephone. Then he was out of
the office again, not even stopping while he hollered at
Gowan: "All right, Otis"—his nephew or cousin or something who had inherited the saw mill, who would come in
and take over when Mr Harker wanted a night off—"Otis'll
be here in fifteen minutes. Jest do the best you can until
then."

"Hold up," Gowan said. "I'm going too."

"Durn that," Mr Harker said, still running, "I seen it first:"
on out the back where the spur track for the coal cars led back
to the main line where Tom Tom would walk every morning

and evening between his home and his job, running (Mr Harker) in the moonlight now because the moon was almost full. In fact, the whole thing was full of moonlight when Mr Harker and Turl appeared peacefully at the regular hour to relieve Tom Tom's substitute the next evening:

"Yes sir," Mr Harker told Gowan, "I was jest in time. It was Turl's desperation, you see. This would be his last go-round. This time he was going to have to find that brass, or come back and tell Mr Snopes he couldn't, in either case that country picnic was going to be over. So I was jest in time to see him creep up out of that corn patch and cross the moonlight to that back window and tomcat through it; jest exactly time enough for him to creep across the room to the bed and likely fling the quilt back and lay his hand on meat and say, 'Honeybunch, lay calm. Papa's done arrived.'" And Gowan said how even twenty-four hours afterward he partook for the instant of Turl's horrid surprise, who believed that at that moment Tom Tom was two miles away at the power plant waiting for him (Turl) to appear and relieve him of the coal scoop;—Tom Tom lying fully dressed beneath the quilt with a naked butcher knife in his hand when Turl flung it back.

"Jest exactly time enough," Mr Harker said. "Jest exactly as on time as two engines switching freight cars. Tom Tom must a made his jump jest exactly when Turl whirled to run, Turl jumping out of the house into the moonlight again with Tom Tom and the butcher knife riding on his back so that they looked jest like—What do you call them double-jointed half-horse fellers in the old picture books?"

"Centaur," Gowan said.

"—looking jest like a centawyer running on its hind legs and trying to ketch up with itself with a butcher knife about a yard long in one of its extry front hoofs until they run out of the moonlight again into the woods. Yes sir, Turl aint even half as big as Tom Tom, but he sho toted him. If you'd a ever bobbled once, that butcher knife would a caught you whether Tom Tom did or not, wouldn't it?"

"Tom Tom a big buck man," Turl said. "Make three of me. But I toted him. I had to. And whenever I would fling my eye back and see the moon shining on that butcher knife I could a picked up two more like him without even slowing down."

Turl said how at first he just ran; it was only after he found himself—or themself—among the trees that he thought about trying to rake Tom Tom off against the trunk of one. "But he helt on so tight with that one arm that whenever I tried to bust him against a tree I busted myself too. Then we'd bounce off and I'd catch another flash of moonlight on that nekkid blade and all I could do was just run.

"'Bout then was when Tom Tom started squalling to let him down. He was holding on with both hands now, so I knowed I had done outrun that butcher knife anyway. But I was good started then; my feets never paid Tom Tom no more mind when he started squalling to stop and let him off than they done me. Then he grabbed my head with both hands and started to wrenching it around like I was a runaway bareback mule, and then I seed the ditch too. It was about forty foot deep and it looked a solid mile across but it was too late then. My feets never even slowed up. They run as far as from here to that coal pile yonder out into nekkid air before we even begun to fall. And they was still clawing moonlight when me and Tom Tom hit the bottom."

The first thing Gowan wanted to know was, what Tom Tom had used in lieu of the dropped butcher knife. Turl told that. Nothing. He and Tom Tom just sat in the moonlight on the floor of the ditch and talked. And Uncle Gavin explained that: a sanctuary, a rationality of perspective, which animals, humans too, not merely reach but earn by passing through unbearable emotional states like furious rage or furious fear, the two of them sitting there not only in Uncle Gavin's amicable cuckoldry but in mutual and complete federation too: Tom Tom's home violated not by Tomey's Turl but by Flem Snopes; Turl's life and limbs put into frantic jeopardy not by Tom Tom but by Flem Snopes.

"That was where I come in," Mr Harker said.

"You?" Gowan said.

"He holp us," Turl said.

"Be durn if that's so," Mr Harker said. "Have you and Tom Tom both already forgot what I told you right there in that ditch last night? I never knowed nothing and I dont aim to know nothing, I dont give a durn how hard either one of you try to make me?"

"All right," Gowan said. "Then what?" Turl told that: how he and Tom Tom went back to the house and Tom Tom untied his wife where he had tied her to a chair in the kitchen and the three of them hitched the mule to the wagon and got the brass out of the corn crib and loaded it to haul it away. There was near a half-ton of it; it took them the rest of the night to finish moving it.

"Move it where?" Gowan said. Only he said he decided to let Mr Snopes himself ask that; it was nearing daylight now and soon Tom Tom would come up the spur track from the main line, carrying his lunch pail to take over for the day shift; and presently there he was, with his little high hard round intractable cannon ball head, when they all turned and there was Mr Snopes too standing in the boiler room door. And Gowan said that even Mr Snopes seemed to know he would just be wasting his time crooking his finger at anybody this time; he just said right out to Turl:

"Why didn't you find it?"

"Because it wasn't there," Turl said.

"How do you know it wasn't there?" Mr Snopes said.

"Because Tom Tom said it wasn't," Turl said.

Because the time for wasting time was over now. Mr Snopes just looked at Tom Tom a minute. Then he said: "What did you do with it?"

"We put it where you said you wanted it," Tom Tom said.

"We?" Mr Snopes said.

"Me and Turl," Tom Tom said. And now Mr Snopes looked at Tom Tom for another minute. Then he said:

"Where I said I wanted it when?"

"When you told me what you aimed to do with them safety-valves," Tom Tom said.

Though by the time the water in the tank would begin to taste brassy enough for somebody to think about draining the tank to clean it, it wouldn't be Mr Snopes. Because he was no longer superintendent now, having resigned, as Mr de Spain would have said when he was still Lieutenant de Spain, "for the good of the service". So he could sit all day now on the gallery of his little back street rented house and look at the shape of the tank standing against the sky above the Jefferson roof-line,—looking at his own monument, some might have thought. Except that it was not a monument: it was a foot-print. A monument only says *At least I got this far* while a footprint says *This is where I was when I moved again.*

"Not even now?" Uncle Gavin said to Ratliff.

"Not even now," Ratliff said. "Not catching his wife with Manfred de Spain yet is like that twenty-dollar gold piece pinned to your undershirt on your first maiden trip to what you hope is going to be a Memphis whorehouse. He dont need to unpin it yet."

TWO

G AVIN STEVENS
He hadn't unpinned it yet. So we all wondered what he was using to live on, for money, sitting (apparently) all day long day after day through the rest of that summer on the flimsy porch of that little rented house, looking at his water tank. Nor would we ever know, until the town would decide to drain the tank and clean it and so rid the water of the brassy taste, exactly how much brass he had used one of the Negro firemen to blackmail the other into stealing for him and which the two Negroes, confederating for simple mutual preservation, had put into the tank where he could never, would never dare, recover it.

And even now we dont know whether or not that brass was all. We will never know exactly how much he might have stolen and sold privately (I mean before he thought of drafting Tom Tom or Turl to help him) either before or after someone—Buffaloe probably, since if old Harker had ever noticed those discarded fittings enough to miss any of them he would probably have beat Snopes to the market; very likely, for all his pretence of simple spectator enjoyment, his real feeling was rage at his own blindness—notified somebody at the city hall and had the auditors in. All we knew was that one day the three safety-valves were missing from the boilers; we had to assume, imagine, what happened next: Manfred de Spain—it would be Manfred —sending for him and saying, "Well, Bud," or Doc or Buster or whatever Manfred would call his . . . you might say foster husband; who knows? maybe even Superintendent: "Well, Superintendent, this twenty-three dollars and eighty-one cents worth of brass"— naturally he would have looked in the catalogue before he sent for him—"was missing during your regime, which you naturally wish to keep spotless as Caesar's wife: which a sim-ple C.O.D. tag addressed to you will do." And that, accord-ing to Harker, the two auditors hemmed and hawed around the plant for two days before they got up nerve enough to tell

Snopes what amount of brass they thought to the best of their knowledge was missing, and that Snopes took the cash out of his pocket and paid them.

That is, disregarding his salary of fifty dollars a month, the job cost Snopes two hundred and forty-two dollars and thirty-three cents out of his own pocket or actual cash money you might say. And even if he had saved every penny of his salary, less that two-hundred-plus dollar loss, and assuming there had been two hundred dollars more of brass for him to have stolen successfully during that time, that was still not enough for him to support his family on very long. Yet for two years now he had been sitting on that little front gallery, looking (as far as we knew) at that water tank. So I asked Ratliff.

He's farming, Ratliff said. "Farming?" I said (all right, cried if you like). "Farming what? Sitting there on that gallery from sunup to sundown watching that water tank?"

Farming Snopeses, Ratliff said. Farming Snopeses: the whole rigid hierarchy moving intact upward one step as he vacated ahead of it except that one who had inherited into the restaurant was not a Snopes. Indubitably and indefensibly not a Snopes; even to impugn him so was indefensible and outrageous and forever beyond all pale of pardon, whose mother, like her incredible sister-by-marriage a generation later, had, must have, as the old bucolic poet said, cast a leglin girth herself before she married whatever Snopes was Eck's titular father.

That was his name: Eck. The one with the broken neck; he brought it to town when he moved in as Flem's immediate successor, rigid in a steel brace and leather harness. Never in the world a Snopes. Ratliff told it; it happened at the saw mill. (You see, even his family—Flem—knew he was not a Snopes: sending, disposing of him into a saw mill where even the owner must be a financial genius to avoid bankruptcy and there is nothing for a rogue at all since all to steal is lumber, and to embezzle a wagon-load of planks is about like embezzling an iron safe or a—yes: that damned water tank itself.)

So Flem sent Eck to Uncle Billy Varner's saw mill (it was that I suppose or chloroform or shoot him as you do a sick bird dog or a wornout mule) and Ratliff told about it: one day, and Eck made the proposition that for a dollar each, he and one of the Negro hands (one of the larger ones and of course the more imbecilic) would pick up a tremendous cypress log and set it onto the saw-carriage. And they did (didn't I just say that one was not even a Snopes and the other already imbecile), had the log almost safely on, when the Negro slipped, something, anyway went down; whereupon all Eck had to do was let go his end and leap out from under. But not he: no Snopes nor no damned thing else, bracing his shoulder under and holding his end up and even taking the shock when the Negro's end fell to the ground, still braced under it until it occurred to someone to drag the nigger out.

And still without sense enough to jump, let alone Snopes enough, not even knowing yet that even Jody Varner wasn't going to pay him anything for saving even a Varner Negro: just standing there holding that whole damned log up, with a little blood already beginning to run out of his mouth, until it finally occurred again to them to shim the log up with another one and pull him from under too, where he could sit hunkered over under a tree, spitting blood and complaining of a headache. ("Dont tell me they gave him the dollar," I said—all right: cried—to Ratliff. "Dont tell me that!")

Never in this world a Snopes: himself and his wife and son living in the tent behind the restaurant and Eck in his turn in the greasy apron and the steel-and-leather neck harness (behind the counter, frying on the crusted grill the eggs and meat which, because of the rigid brace, he couldn't even see to gauge the doneness, cooking, as the blind pianist plays, by simple ear), having less business here than even in the saw mill since at the saw mill all he could do was break his own bones where here he was a threat to his whole family's long tradition of slow and invincible rapacity because of that same incredible and innocent assumption that all people practise courage and honesty for the simple reason that if they didn't everybody would be frightened and confused; saying one day, not even privately but right out loud where half a dozen strangers not even kin by marriage to Snopeses heard him: "Aint we supposed to be selling beef in these here hamburgers? I dont know jest what this is yet but it aint no beef."

So of course they—when I say 'they' I mean Snopeses; when you say 'Snopeses' in Jefferson you mean Flem Snopes—fired him. They had to; he was intolerable there. Only of course the question rose immediately: where in Jefferson, not in the Jefferson economy but in the Snopes (oh yes, when you say Snopes in Jefferson you mean Flem Snopes) economy would he not be intolerable, would Snopeses be safe from him? Ratliff knew that too. I mean, everybody in Jefferson knew because within twenty-four hours everybody in Jefferson had heard about that hamburger remark and naturally knew that something would have to be done about Eck Snopes and done quick and so of course (being interested) as soon as possible, almost as soon in fact as Flem himself knew, what and where. I mean, it was Ratliff who told me. No: I mean it had to be Ratliff who told me: Ratliff with his damned smooth face and his damned shrewd bland innocent intelligent eyes, too damned innocent, too damned intelligent:

"He's night watchman now down at Renfrow's oil tank at the deepo. Where it wont be no strain on his neck like having to look down to see what that was he jest smelled burning. He wont need to look up to see whether the tank's still there or not, he can jest walk up and feel the bottom of it. Or even set there in his chair in the door and send that boy to look. That horse boy," Ratliff said.

"That what boy?" I said, cried.

"That horse boy," Ratliff said. "Eck's boy. Wallstreet Panic. The day that Texas feller arctioned off them wild Snopes ponies, I was out there. It was jest dust-dark and we had done et supper at Miz Littlejohn's and I was jest undressing in my room to go to bed when Henry Armstid and Eck and that boy of hisn went in the lot to ketch their horses; Eck had two: the one the Texas feller give him to get the arction started off, and the one Eck felt he had to at least bid on after having been give one for nothing, and won it. So when Henry Armstid left the gate open and the whole herd stampeded over him and out of it, I reckon the hardest instantaneous decision Eck ever had to make in his life was to decide which one of them horses to chase: the one the Texas man give him, which represented the most net profit if he caught it, or the one that he already had five or six dollars of his own money invested in; that is, was a hundred-plus percent. of a free horse worth more than just a hundred percent. of a six-dollar horse? That is, jest how far can you risk losing a horse that no matter what you get for him you will still have to subtract six dollars from it, to jest catch one that will be all net profit?

"Or maybe he decided him and that boy better split up after both of them while he figgered it out. Anyway, the first I knowed, I had done took off my britches and was jest leaning out the window in my shirt-tail trying to see what was going on, when I heerd a kind of sound behind me and looked over my shoulder and there was one of them horses standing in the door looking at me and standing in the hall behind him with a piece of plow-line was that boy of Eck's. I reckon we both moved at the same moment: me out the window in my shirt-tail and the horse swirling to run on down the hall, me realising I never had no britches on and running around the house toward the front steps jest about the time the horse met Miz Littlejohn coming onto the back gallery with a arm-ful of washing in one hand and the washboard in the other; they claimed she said 'git out of here you son of a bitch' and split the washboard down the center of its face and throwed the two pieces at it without even changing hands, it swirling again to run back up the hall jest as I run up the front steps, and jumped clean over that boy still standing in the hall with his plow-line without touching a hair, on to the front gallery again and seen me and never even stopped: jest swirled and run to the end of the gallery and jumped the railing and back into the lot again, looking jest like a big circus-colored hawk, sailing out into the moonlight and across the lot again in about two jumps and out the gate that still hadn't nobody thought to close yet; I heerd him once more when he hit the wooden bridge jest this side of Bookright's turn-off. Then that boy come out of the house, still toting the plow-line. 'Howdy, Mr Ratliff,' he says. 'Which way did he go?'—Except you're wrong."

Horse boy, dog boy, cat boy, monkey boy, elephant boy: anything but Snopes boy. And then suppose, just suppose; suppose and tremble: one generation more removed from Eck Snopes and his innocence; one generation more until that innocent and outrageous belief that courage and honor are practical, has had time to fade and cool so that merely the habit of courage and honor remain; add to that then that generation's natural heritage of cold rapacity as instinctive as breathing, and tremble at that prospect: the habit of courage and honor compounded by rapacity or rapacity raised to the absolute *nth* by courage and honor: not horse boy but a lion or tiger boy: Genghis Khan or Tamerlane or Attila in the defenseless midst of indefensible Jefferson. Then Ratliff was looking at me. I mean, he always was. I mean I discovered with a kind of terror that for a second I had forgot it. "What?" I said. "What did you say?"

"That you're wrong. About Eck's night watchman job at the oil tank. It wasn't Manfred de Spain this time. It was the Masons."

"What?" I said, cried.

"That's right. Eck was one of the biggest ones of Uncle Billy Varner's Frenchman's Bend Masons. It was Uncle Billy sent word in to the Masons in Jefferson to find Eck a good light broke-neck job."

"That bad?" I said. "That bad? The next one in the progression so outrageous and portentous and terrifying that Will Varner himself had to use influence twenty-two miles away to save Frenchman's Bend?" Because the next one after Eck behind the restaurant counter was I.O., the blacksmith-cum-schoolmaster-cum-bigamist, or -times bigamist, multiplied by bigamy—a thin undersized voluble weasel-faced man talking constantly in a steady stream of worn saws and proverbs usually having no connection with one another nor application to anything else, who even with the hammer would not have weighed as much as the anvil he abrogated and dispossessed; who (Ratliff of course, Ratliff always) entered Frenchman's Bend already talking, or rather appeared one morning already talking in Varner's blacksmith shop which an old man named Trumbull had run man and boy for fifty years.

But no blacksmith, I.O. He merely held the living. It was the other one, our Eck, his cousin (whatever the relationship was, unless simply being both Snopes was enough until one proved himself unworthy, as Eck was to do, like two Masons from that moment to apostasy like Eck's, forever sworn to show a common front to life), who did the actual work. Until one day, one morning, perhaps the curate, Eck, was not there or perhaps it simply occurred to the vicar, the high priest, for the first time that his actually was the right and the authority to hold a communion service and nobody could really prevent him: that morning, Zack Houston with his gaited stallion until Snopes quicked it with the first nail; whereupon Houston picked Snopes up and threw him hammer and all into the cooling tub and managed somehow to hold the plunging horse and wrench the shoe off and the nail out at the same time, and led the horse outside and tied it and came back and threw Snopes back into the cooling tub again.

And no schoolmaster either. He didn't merely usurp that as a position among strangers, he actually stole it as a vocation from his own kin. Though Frenchman's Bend didn't know that yet. They knew only that he was hardly out of the blacksmith shop (or dried again out of the cooling tub where Houston had flung him) when he was installed as teacher ('Professor', the teacher was called in Frenchman's Bend, provided of course he wore trousers) in the one-room schoolhouse which was an integer of old Varner's princedom—an integer not because old Varner or anyone else in Frenchman's Bend considered that juvenile education filled any actual communal lack or need, but simply because his settlement had to have a going schoolhouse to be complete as a freight train has to have a caboose to be complete.

So I.O. Snopes was now the schoolmaster; shortly afterward he was married to a Frenchman's Bend belle and within a year he was pushing a homemade perambulator about the village and his wife was already pregnant again; here, you would have said, was a man not merely settled but doomed to immobilization, until one day in the third year a vast gray-colored though still young woman, accompanied by a vast gray-colored five-year-old boy, drove up to Varner's store in a buggy—

"It was his wife," Ratliff said.

"His wife?" I said, cried. "But I thought—"

"So did we," Ratliff said. "Pushing that-ere homemade buggy with two of them in it this time, twins, already named Bilbo and Vardaman, besides the first one, Clarence. Yes sir, three chaps already while he was waiting for his other wife with that one to catch up with him—a little dried-up feller not much bigger than a crawfish, and that other wife—no, I mean the one he had now in Frenchman's Bend when that-ere number one one druv up—wasn't a big girl neither—Miz Vernon Tull's sister's niece by marriage she was—yet he got onto her too them same big gray-colored kind of chaps like the one in the buggy with his ma driving up to the store and saying to whoever was setting on the gallery at the moment: 'I hear I.O. inside.' (He was. We could all hear him.) 'Kindly step in and tell him his wife's come.'

"That was all. It was enough. When he come to the Bend that day three years ago he had a big carpet-bag, and in them three years he had probably accumulated some more stuff; I mean besides them three new chaps. But he never stopped for none of it. He jest stepped right out the back door of the store. And Flem had done long since already sold old man Trumbull back to Varner for the blacksmith, but now they was needing a new professor too or anyhow they would as soon as I.O. could get around the first corner out of sight where he could cut across country. Which he evidently done; never nobody reported any dust-cloud travelling fast along a road nowhere. They said he even stopped talking, though I doubt that. You got to draw the line somewhere, aint you?"

You have indeed. Though I.O. didn't. That is, he was already talking when he appeared in his turn behind the restaurant counter in the greasy apron, taking your order and cooking it wrong or cooking the wrong thing not because he worked so fast but simply because he never stopped talking long enough for you to correct or check him, babbling that steady stream of confused and garbled proverbs and meta-phors attached to nothing and going nowhere.

And the wife. I mean the number one wife, what might be called the original wife, who was number one in the cast even though she was number two on the stage. The other one, the number two in the cast even though she was num-ber one on the stage, the Tull's wife's sister's niece wife, who foaled the second set of what Ratliff called gray-colored chaps, Clarence and the twins Vardaman and Bilbo, remained in Frenchman's Bend. It was the original one, who appeared in Frenchman's Bend sitting in the buggy and left French-man's Bend in the buggy, still sitting, and appeared in Jefferson five years later still sitting, translated, we knew not how, and with no interval between from the buggy where Ratliff had seen her twenty-two miles away that day five years ago, to the rocking chair on the front gallery of the boarding house where we saw her now, still at that same right angle enclosing her lap as if she had no movable hinge at the hips at all—a woman who gave an impression of specific density and immobility like lead or uranium, so that whatever force had moved her from the buggy to that chair had not been merely human, not even ten I.O.'s.

Because Snopes was moving his echelons up fast now. That one—I.O. and the vast gray-colored sitting wife and that vast gray-colored boy (his name was Montgomery Ward)—did not even pause at the tent behind the restaurant where Eck and his wife and two sons now ("Why not?" Ratliff said. "There's a heap of more things besides frying a hamburger you dont really have to look down for.") were still living. They—the I.O.'s—by-passed it completely, the wife already sitting in the rocking chair on the boarding house's front gallery—a big more-or-less unpainted square building just off the Square where itinerant cattle drovers and horse- and mule-traders stopped and where were incarcerated, boarded and fed, juries and important witnesses during court term, where she would sit rocking steadily—not doing anything, not reading, not particularly watching who passed in or out of the door or along the street: just rocking—for the next five years while and then after the place changed from a boarding house to a warren, with nailed to one of the front veranda posts a pine board lettered terrifically by hand, with both S's reversed:

ƧNOPEƧ HOTEL

And now Eck, whose innocence or honesty or both had long since eliminated him from the restaurant into his night watchman's chair beside the depot oil tank, had vacated his wife and sons (Wallstreet Panic: oh yes, I was like Ratliff: I couldn't believe that one either, though the younger one, Admiral Dewey, we both could) from the tent behind it. In fact, the restaurant was not sold lock stock barrel and good-will, but gutted, moved intact even to the customers and without even a single whole day's closure, into the new boarding house where Mrs Eck was now the landlady; moved intact past the rocking figure on the gallery which continued to rock there through mere legend and into landmark like the effigy signs before the old-time English public houses, so that country men coming into town and inquiring for the Snopes hotel were told simply to walk in that direction until they came to a woman rocking, and that was it.

And now there entered that one, not whose vocation but at least the designation of whose vocation, I.O. Snopes had usurped. This was the actual Snopes schoolmaster. No: he looked like a schoolmaster. No: he looked like John Brown with an ineradicable and unhideable flaw: a tall gaunt man in a soiled frock coat and string tie and a wide politician's hat, with cold furious eyes and the long chin of a talker: not that verbal diarrhea of his cousin (whatever kin I.O. was; they none of them seemed to bear any specific kinship to one another; they were just Snopeses, like colonies of rats or termites are just rats and termites) but a kind of unerring gift for a base and evil ratiocination in argument, and for correctly reading the people with whom he dealt: a demagogue's capacity for using people to serve his own appetites, all clouded over with a veneer of culture and religion; the very names of his two sons, Byron and Virgil, were not only instances but warnings.

And no schoolmaster himself either. That is, unlike his cousin, he was not even with us long enough to have to prove he was not. Or maybe, coming to us in the summer and then gone before the summer was, he was merely between assignments. Or maybe taking a busman's holiday from a busman's holiday. Or maybe in and about the boarding house and the Square in the mere brief intervals from his true bucolic vocation whose stage and scene were the scattered country churches and creeks and horse-ponds where during the hot summer Sundays revival services and baptisings took place: himself (he had a good baritone voice and probably the last working pitch pipe in north Mississippi) setting the tune and lining out the words, until one day a posse of enraged fathers caught him and a fourteen-year-old girl in an empty cotton house and tarred and feathered him out of the country. There

had been talk of castration also though some timid conservative dissuaded them into holding that as a promise against his
return.

So of him there remained only the two sons, Byron and
Virgil. Nor was Byron with us long either, gone to Memphis
now to attend business college. To learn book-keeping; we
learned with incredulity that Colonel Sartoris himself was behind that: Colonel Sartoris himself in the back room of the
bank which was his office;—an incredulity which demanded,
compelled inquiry while we remembered what some of us,
the older ones, my father among them, had not forgot: the
original Ab Snopes, the (depending on where you stand) pa-
triot horse raider or simple horse thief who had been hanged
(not by a Federal provost-marshal but by a Confederate one,
the old story was) while a member of the cavalry command of
old Colonel Sartoris, the real colonel, father of our present
banker-honorary colonel who had been only an uncommis-
sioned A.D.C. on his father's staff, back in that desperate twilight of 1864–65 when more people than men named Snopes
had to choose not survival with honor but simply between
empty honor and almost as empty survival.

The horse which came home to roost. Oh yes, we all said
that, all us wits: we would not have missed that chance. Not
that we believed it or even disbelieved it, but simply to defend
the old Colonel's memory by being first to say aloud among
ourselves what we believed the whole Snopes tribe was long
since chortling over to one another. Indeed, no Confederate
provost-marshal hanged that first Ab Snopes, but Snopeses
themselves had immolated him in that skeleton, to put, as the
saying is, that monkey on the back of Ab's commander's descendant as soon as the lineage produced a back profitable to
the monkey; in this case, the new bank which our Colonel
Sartoris established about five years ago.

Not that we really believed that, of course. I mean, our
Colonel Sartoris did not need to be blackmailed with a skeleton. Because we all in our country, even half a century after,
sentimentalise the heroes of our gallant lost irrevocable unreconstructible debacle, and those heroes were indeed ours because they were our fathers and grandfathers and uncles and
great-uncles when Colonel Sartoris raised the command right

here in our contiguous counties. And who with more right to sentimentalise them than our Colonel Sartoris, whose father had been the Colonel Sartoris who had raised and trained the command and saved its individual lives when he could in battle and even defended them or at least extricated them from their own simple human lusts and vices while idle between engagements; Byron Snopes was not the first descendant of those old company and battalion and regimental names who knew our Colonel Sartoris's bounty.

But the horse which at last came home to roost sounded better. Not witty, but rather an immediate unified irrevocably scornful front to what the word Snopes was to mean to us, and to all others, no matter who, whom simple juxtaposition to the word irrevocably smirched and contaminated. Anyway, he (it: the horse come to roost) appeared in good time, armed and girded with his business college diploma; we would see him through, beyond, inside the grillework which guarded our money and the complex records of it whose custodian Colonel Sartoris was, bowed (he, Snopes, Byron) over the book-keepers' desk in an attitude not really of prayer, obeisance; not really of humility before the shine, the blind glare of the blind money, but rather of a sort of respectful unhumble insistence, a deferent invincible curiosity and inquiry into the mechanics of its recording; he had not entered crawling into the glare of a mystery so much as, without attracting any attention to himself, he was trying to lift a corner of its skirt.

Using, since he was the low last man in that hierarchy, a long cane fishing-pole until he could accrete close enough for the hand to reach; using, to really mix, really confuse our metaphor, an humble cane out of that same quiver which had contained that power-plant superintendency, since Colonel Sartoris had been of that original group of old Major de Spain's bear and deer hunters when Major de Spain established his annual hunting camp in the Big Bottom shortly after the war; and when Colonel Sartoris started his bank five years ago, Manfred de Spain used his father's money to become one of the first stockholders and directors.

Oh yes: the horse home at last and stabled. And in time of course (we had only to wait, never to know how of course even though we watched it, but at least to know more or less when) to own the stable, Colonel Sartoris dis-stabled of his byre and rick in his turn as Ratliff and Grover Cleveland Winbush had been dis-restauranted in theirs. We not to know how of course since that was none of our business; indeed, who to say but there was not one among us but did not want to know: who, already realising that we would never defend Jefferson from Snopeses, let us then give, relinquish Jefferson to Snopeses, banker mayor aldermen church and all, so that, in defending themselves from Snopeses, Snopeses must of necessity defend and shield us, their vassals and chattels, too.

The quiver borne on Manfred de Spain's back, but the arrows drawn in turn by that hand, that damned incredible woman, that Frenchman's Bend Helen, Semiramis——No: not Helen nor Semiramis: Lilith: the one before Eve herself whom earth's Creator had perforce in desperate and amazed alarm in person to efface, remove, obliterate, that Adam might create a progeny to populate it; and we were in my office now where I had not sent for him nor even invited him: he had just followed, entered, to sit across the desk in his neat faded tieless blue shirt and the brown smooth bland face and the eyes watching me too damned shrewd, too damned intelligent.

"You used to laugh at them too," he said.

"Why not?" I said. "What else are we going to do about them? Of course you've got the best joke: you dont have to fry hamburgers anymore. But give them time; maybe they have got one taking a correspondence school law course. Then I wont have to be acting city attorney anymore either."

"I said 'too'," Ratliff said.

"What?" I said.

"At first you laughed at them too," he said. "Or maybe I'm wrong, and this here is still laughing?"—looking at me, watching me, too damned shrewd, too damned intelligent. "Why dont you say it?"

"Say what?" I said.

"'Get out of my office, Ratliff'," he said.

"Get out of my office, Ratliff," I said.

THREE

CHARLES MALLISON
Maybe it was because Mother and Uncle Gavin were twins, that Mother knew what Uncle Gavin's trouble was just about as soon as Ratliff did.

We were all living with Grandfather then. I mean Grandfather was still alive then and he and Uncle Gavin had one side of the house, Grandfather in his bedroom and what we all called the office downstairs, and Uncle Gavin on the same side upstairs, where he had built an outside stairway so he could go and come from the side yard, and Mother and Father and Cousin Gowan on the other side while Gowan was going to the Jefferson high school while he was waiting to enter the prep school in Washington to get ready for the University of Virginia.

So Mother would sit at the end of the table where Grandmother used to sit, and Grandfather opposite at the other end, and Father on one side and Uncle Gavin and Gowan (I wasn't born then and even if I had been I would have been eating in the kitchen with Aleck Sander yet) on the other and, Gowan said, Uncle Gavin not even pretending anymore to eat: just sitting there talking about Snopeses like he had been doing now through every meal for the last two weeks. It was almost like he was talking to himself, like something wound up that couldn't even run down, let alone stop, like there wasn't anybody or anything that wished he would stop more than he did. It wasn't snarling. Gowan didn't know what it was. It was like something Uncle Gavin had to tell, but it was so funny that his main job in telling it was to keep it from being as funny as it really was, because if he ever let it be as funny as it really was, everybody and himself too would be laughing so hard they couldn't hear him. And Mother not eating either now: just sitting there perfectly still, watching Uncle Gavin, until at last Grandfather took his napkin out of his collar and stood up and Father and Uncle Gavin and Gowan stood up too and Grandfather said to Mother like he did every time:

"Thank you for the meal, Margaret," and put the napkin on the table and Gowan went and stood by the door while he went out like I was going to have to do after I got born and got big enough. And Gowan would have stood there while Mother and Father and Uncle Gavin went out too. But not this time. Mother hadn't even moved, still sitting there and watching Uncle Gavin; she was still watching Uncle Gavin when she said to Father:

"Dont you and Gowan want to be excused too?"

"Nome," Gowan said. Because he had been in the office that day when Ratliff came in and said,

"Evening, Lawyer. I just dropped in to hear the latest Snopes news," and Uncle Gavin said:

"What news?" and Ratliff said:

"Or do you jest mean what Snopes?" and sat there too looking at Uncle Gavin, until at last he said, "Why dont you go on and say it?" and Uncle Gavin said,

"Say what?" and Ratliff said,

"Git out of my office, Ratliff." So Gowan said,

"Nome."

"Then maybe you'll excuse me," Uncle Gavin said, putting his napkin down. But still Mother didn't move.

"Would you like me to call on her?" she said.

"Call on who?" Uncle Gavin said. And even to Gowan he said it too quick. Because even Father caught on then. Though I dont know about that. Even if I had been there and no older than Gowan was, I would have known that if I had been about twenty-one or maybe even less when Mrs Snopes first walked through the Square, I not only would have known what was going on, I might even have been Uncle Gavin myself. But Gowan said Father sounded like he had just caught on. He said to Uncle Gavin:

"I'll be damned. So that's what's been eating you for the past two weeks." Then he said to Mother: "No, by Jupiter. My wife call on that——"

"That what?" Uncle Gavin said, hard and quick. And still Mother hadn't moved: just sitting there between them while they stood over her.

"'Sir'," she said.

"What?" Uncle Gavin said.

"'That what, sir?'" she said. "Or maybe just 'sir' with an inflection."

"You name it then," Father said to Uncle Gavin. "You know what. What this whole town is calling her. What this whole town knows about her and Manfred de Spain."

"What whole town?" Uncle Gavin said. "Besides you? You and who else? the same ones that probably rake Maggie here over the coals too without knowing any more than you do?"

"Are you talking about my wife?" Father said.

"No," Uncle Gavin said. "I'm talking about my sister and Mrs Snopes."

"Boys, boys, boys," Mother said. "At least spare my nephew." She said to Gowan: "Gowan, dont you really want to be excused?"

"Nome," Gowan said.

"Damn your nephew," Father said. "I'm not going to have his aunt——"

"Are you still talking about your wife?" Uncle Gavin said. This time Mother stood up too, between them while they both leaned a little forward, glaring at each other across the table.

"That really will be all now," Mother said. "Both of you apologise to me." They did. "Now apologise to Gowan." Gowan said they did that too.

"But I'll still be damned if I'm going to let——" Father said.

"Just the apology, please," Mother said. "Even if Mrs Snopes is what you say she is, as long as I am what you and Gavin both agree I am since at least you agree on that, how can I run any risk sitting for ten minutes in her parlor? The trouble with both of you is, you know nothing about women. Women are not interested in morals. They aren't even interested in unmorals. The ladies of Jefferson dont care what she does. What they will never forgive is the way she looks. No: the way the Jefferson gentlemen look at her."

"Speak for your brother," Father said. "I never looked at her in her life."

"Then so much the worse for me," Mother said, "with a mole for a husband. No: moles have warm blood; a Mammoth Cave fish——"

"Well, I *will* be damned," Father said. "That's what you

want, is it? a husband that will spend every Saturday night in Memphis chasing back and forth between Gayoso and Mulberry street——"

"Now I will excuse you whether you want to be or not," Mother said. So Uncle Gavin went out and on upstairs toward his room and Mother rang the bell for Guster and Gowan stood at the door again for Mother and Father and then Mother and Gowan went out to the front gallery (it was October, still warm enough to sit outside at noon) and she took up the sewing basket again and Father came out with his hat on and said,

"Flem Snopes's wife, riding into Jefferson society on Judge Lemuel Stevens's daughter's coat-tail," and went on to town to the store; and then Uncle Gavin came out and said:

"You'll do it, then?"

"Of course," Mother said. "Is it that bad?"

"I intend to try to not let it be," Uncle Gavin said. "Even if you aren't anything but just a woman, you must have seen her. You must have."

"Anyway, I have watched men seeing her," Mother said.

"Yes," Uncle Gavin said. It didn't sound like an out-breathe, like talking. It sounded like an in-breathe: "Yes."

"You're going to save her," Mother said, not looking at Uncle Gavin now: just watching the sock she was darning.

"Yes!" Uncle Gavin said, fast, quick: no in-breathe this time, so quick he almost said the rest of it before he could stop himself, so that all Mother had to do was say it for him:

"—from Manfred de Spain."

But Uncle Gavin had caught himself by now; his voice was just harsh now. "You too," he said. "You and your husband too. The best people, the pure, the unimpugnable. Charles who by his own affirmation has never even looked at her; you by that same affirmation not only Judge Stevens's daughter, but Caesar's wife."

"Just what—" Mother said, then Gowan said she stopped and looked at him. "Dont you really want to be excused a little while? as a personal favor?" she said.

"Nome," Gowan said.

"You cant help it either, can you?" she said. "You've got to be a man too, haven't you?" She just talked to Uncle Gavin then: "Just what is it about this that you cant stand? That Mrs Snopes may not be chaste, or that it looks like she picked Manfred de Spain out to be unchaste with?"

"Yes!" Uncle Gavin said. "I mean no! It's all lies—gossip. It's all——"

"Yes," Mother said. "You're right. It's probably all just that. Saturday's not a very good afternoon to get in the barbershop, but you might think about it when you pass."

"Thanks," Uncle Gavin said. "But if I'm to go on this crusade with any hope of success, the least I can do is look wild and shaggy enough to be believed. You'll do it, then?"

"Of course," Mother said.

"Thank you," Uncle Gavin said. Then he was gone.

"I suppose I could be excused now," Gowan said.

"What for now?" Mother said. She was still watching Uncle Gavin, down the walk and into the street now. "He should have married Melisandre Backus," she said. Melisandre Backus lived on a plantation about six miles from town with her father and a bottle of whiskey. I dont mean he was a drunkard. He was a good farmer. He just spent the rest of his time sitting on the gallery in summer and in the library in winter with the bottle, reading Latin poetry. Miss Melisandre and Mother had been in school together, at high school and the Seminary both. That is, Miss Melisandre was always four years behind Mother. "At one time I thought he might; I didn't know any better then."

"Cousin Gavin?" Gowan said. "Him married?"

"Oh yes," Mother said. "He's just too young yet. He's the sort of man doomed to marry a widow with grown children."

"He could still marry Miss Melisandre," Gowan said.

"It's too late," Mother said. "He didn't know she was there."

"He sees her every day she comes in to town," Gowan said.

"You can see things without looking at them, just like you can hear things without listening," Mother said.

"He sure didn't just do that when he saw Mrs Snopes that day," Gowan said. "Maybe he's waiting for her to have another child besides Linda and for them to grow up?"

"No no," Mother said. "You dont marry Semiramis: you just commit some form of suicide for her. Only gentlemen with as little to lose as Mr Flem Snopes can risk marrying Semiramis.—It's too bad you are so old too. A few years ago I could have made you come with me to call on her. Now you'll have to admit openly that you want to come; you may even have to say 'Please'."

But Gowan didn't. It was Saturday afternoon and there was a football game and though he hadn't made the regular team yet you never could tell when somebody that had might break a leg or have a stroke or even a simple condition in arithmetic. Besides, he said Mother didn't need his help anyway, having the whole town's help in place of it; he said they hadn't even reached the Square the next morning on the way to church when the first lady they met said brightly:

"What's this I hear about yesterday afternoon?" and Mother said just as brightly:

"Indeed?" and the second lady they met said (she belonged to the Byron Society and the Cotillion Club too):

"I always say we'd all be much happier to believe nothing we dont see with our own eyes, and only half of that," and Mother said still just as brightly:

"Indeed?" They—the Byron Society and the Cotillion Club, both when possible of course though either alone in a pinch—seemed to be the measure. Now Uncle Gavin stopped talking about Snopeses. I mean, Gowan said he stopped talking at all. It was like he didn't have time anymore to concentrate on talk in order to raise it to conversation, art, like he believed was everybody's duty. It was like he didn't have time to do anything but wait, to get something done that the only way he knew to get it done was waiting. More than that, than just waiting: not only never missing a chance to do things for Mother, he even invented little things to do for her, so that even when he would talk a little, it was like he was killing two birds with the same stone.

Because when he talked now, in sudden spells and bursts of it that sometimes never had any connection at all with what Father and Mother and Grandfather might have been talking about the minute before, it wouldn't even be what he called BB gun conversation. It would be the most outrageous praise, praise so outrageous that even Gowan at just thirteen years old could tell that. It would be of Jefferson ladies that

he and Mother had known all their lives, so that whatever
ideas either one of them must have had about them, the other
must have known it a long time by now. Yet all of a sudden
every few days during the next month Uncle Gavin would
stop chewing fast over his plate and drag a fresh one of them
by the hair you might say into the middle of whatever
Grandfather and Mother and Father had been talking about,
talking not to Grandfather or Father or Gowan, but telling
Mother how good or pretty or intelligent or witty somebody
was that Mother had grown up with or anyway known all her
life.

Oh yes, members of the Byron Society and the Cotillion
Club or maybe just one of them (probably only Mother knew
it was the Cotillion Club he was working for) at a pinch, so
that each time they would know that another new one had
called on Mrs Flem Snopes. Until Gowan would wonder how
Uncle Gavin would always know when the next one had
called, how to scratch her off the list that hadn't or add her
onto the score that had or whatever it was he kept. So Gowan
decided that maybe Uncle Gavin watched Mrs Snopes's
house. And it was November now, good fine hunting weather,
and since Gowan had finally given up on the football team, by
rights he and Top (Top was Aleck Sander's older brother except that Aleck Sander wasn't born yet either. I mean, he was
Guster's boy and his father was named Top too so they called
him Big Top and Top Little Top) would have spent every afternoon after school with the beagles Uncle Gavin gave them
after rabbits. But instead, Gowan spent every afternoon for almost a week in the big ditch behind Mr Snopes's house, not
watching the house but to see if Uncle Gavin was hid somewhere in the ditch too watching to see who called on Mrs
Snopes next. Because Gowan was only thirteen then: he was
just watching for Uncle Gavin; it wasn't until later that he said
how he realised that if he had tried harder or longer, he might
have caught Mr de Spain climbing in or out of the back window like most of Jefferson was convinced he was doing, and
then he really would have had something he could have sold
for a dollar or two to a lot of people in town.

But if Uncle Gavin was hid somewhere in that ditch too,
Gowan never caught him. Better still, Uncle Gavin never

caught Gowan in it. Because if Mother had ever found out
Gowan was hiding in that ditch behind Mr Snopes's house
because he thought Uncle Gavin was hidden in it too, Gowan
didn't know what she might have done about Uncle Gavin
but he sure knew what would have happened to him. And
worse: if Mr Snopes had ever found out Gowan thought
Uncle Gavin might be hiding in that ditch spying on his
house. Or worse still: if the town ever found out Gowan was
hiding in that ditch because he thought Uncle Gavin was.

Because when you are just thirteen you dont have sense
enough to realise what you are doing and shudder. Because
even now I can remember some of the things Aleck Sander
and I did for instance and never think twice about it, and I
wonder how any boys ever live long enough to grow up. I remember, I was just twelve; Uncle Gavin had just given me my
shotgun; this was after (this is how Father put it) Mrs Snopes
had sent him to Heidelberg to finish his education and he had
been in the War and then come back home and got himself
elected County Attorney in his own right; there were five of
us: me and three other white boys and Aleck Sander, hunting
rabbits one Saturday. It was cold, one of the coldest spells we
ever had; when we came to Harrykin Creek it was frozen over
solid and we begun to talk about how much we would take
to jump into it. Aleck Sander said he would do it if each one
of us would give him a dollar so we said we would and sure
enough, before we could have stopped him, Aleck Sander
hauled off and jumped into the creek, right through the ice,
clothes and all.

So we got him out and built a fire while he stripped off and
wrapped up in our hunting coats while we tried to dry his
clothes before they froze solid too and got him dressed again
at last and then he said, "All right. Now pay me my money."

We hadn't thought about that. Back then, no Jefferson,
Mississippi boy or anywhere else in Mississippi that I know of,
ever had a whole dollar at one time very often, let alone four
at the same time. So we had to trade with him. Buck Connors
and Aleck Sander traded first: if Buck jumped through the ice,
Aleck Sander would let him off his dollar. So Buck did, and
while we dried him off I said,

"If that's what we got to do, let's all jump in at once and

get it over with," and we even started for the creek when
Aleck Sander said No, that we were all white boys taking advantage of him because he was a Negro by asking him to let
us do the same thing he did. So we had to trade again. Ashley
Holcomb was next. He climbed up a tree until Aleck Sander
said he was high enough and shut his eyes and jumped out of
it, and Aleck Sander let him off his dollar. Then I was next,
and somebody said how, because Aleck Sander's mother was
our cook and Aleck Sander and I had more or less lived together ever since we were born, that Aleck Sander would
probably let me off light. But Aleck Sander said No, he had
thought of that himself and for that very reason he was going
to have to be harder on me than on Ashley and so the tree I
would jump out of would be over a brier patch. And I did; it
was like jumping into cold fire streaking my hands and face
and tearing my britches though my hunting coat was brand
new almost (Uncle Gavin had mailed it to me from Germany
the day he got Mother's cable that I was born; it was the best
hunting coat in Jefferson everybody said when I finally got
big enough to wear it) so it didn't tear except for one pocket.

So that left only John Wesley Roebuck and maybe all of a
sudden Aleck Sander realised that here was his last dollar
going because John Wesley suggested everything but Aleck
Sander still said No. Finally John Wesley offered to do all of
them: jump through the ice then out of Ashley's tree and
then out of mine but Aleck Sander still said No. So this is
how they finally traded though in a way that still wasn't fair
to Aleck Sander because old man Ab Snopes had already shot
John Wesley in the back once about two years ago and so
John Wesley was used to it, which may have been one of the
reasons why he agreed to the trade. This was it. John Wesley
borrowed my hunting coat to put on top of his because we
had already proved that mine was the toughest, and he borrowed Ashley's sweater to wrap around his head and neck,
and we counted off twenty-five steps for him and Aleck
Sander put one shell in his gun and somebody, maybe me,
counted One Two Three slow and when whoever it was said
One John Wesley broke and ran and when whoever it was
said Three Aleck Sander shot John Wesley in the back and
John Wesley gave me and Ashley back the sweater and my

hunting coat and (it was late by then) we went home. Except that I had to run all the way (it was cold, the coldest spell I ever remember) because we had to burn up my hunting coat because it would be easier to explain no hunting coat at all than one with the back full of Number Six shot.

Then we found out how Uncle Gavin would find out which one called next. It was Father did the scoring for him. I dont mean Father was Uncle Gavin's spy. The last thing Father was trying to do was to help Uncle Gavin, ease Uncle Gavin's mind. If anything, he was harder against Uncle Gavin even than he had thought he was that first day against Mother going to call on Mrs Snopes; it was like he was trying to take revenge on Mother and Uncle Gavin both: on Uncle Gavin for even wanting Mother to call on Mrs Snopes, and on Mother for saying right out loud in front of Uncle Gavin and Gowan both that she not only was going to do it, she didn't see any harm in it. In fact, Gowan said it was Father's mind that Mrs Snopes seemed to stay on now, more than on Uncle Gavin's. Almost any time now Father would walk in rubbing his hands and saying "oh you kid" or "twenty-three skiddoo" and they knew that he had just seen Mrs Snopes again on the street or had just heard that another Cotillion or Byron Society member had called on her; if they had invented wolf whistles then, Father would have been giving one.

Then it was December; Mother had just told how the Cotillion Club had finally voted to send Mr and Mrs Snopes an invitation to the Christmas Ball and Grandfather had got up and put his napkin down and said, "Thank you for the meal, Margaret," and Gowan went and held the door for him to go out, then Father said:

"Dance? Suppose she dont know how?" and Gowan said,

"Does she have to?" and now they all stopped; he said they all stopped at exactly the same time and looked at him and he said that even if Mother and Uncle Gavin were brother and sister one was a woman and the other was a man and Father wasn't any kin to either one of them. Yet he said they all three looked at him with exactly the same expression on their faces. Then Father said to Mother:

"Hold him while I look at his teeth again. You told me he wasn't but thirteen."

"What have I said now?" Gowan said.

"Yes," Father said. "What were we saying? Oh yes, dancing, the Christmas Cotillion." He was talking to Uncle Gavin now. "Well by godfrey, that puts you one up on Manfred de Spain, dont it? He's a lone orphan; he hasn't got a wife or a twin sister who was one of the original founders of Jefferson literary and snobbery clubs; all he can do to Flem Snopes's wife is——" Gowan said how until now Mother was always between Father and Uncle Gavin, with one hand on each of their chests to hold them apart. He said that now Mother and Uncle Gavin were both at Father, with Mother holding one hand on Father's mouth and reaching for his, Gowan's, ears with the other, and she and Uncle Gavin both saying the same thing, only Uncle Gavin was just using another set of words for it:

"Dont you dare!"

"Go on. Say it."

So Father didn't. But even he didn't anticipate what Uncle Gavin would do next: try to persuade Mother to make the Cotillion committee not invite Mr de Spain to the ball at all. "Hell fire," Father said. "You cant do that."

"Why cant we?" Mother said.

"He's the mayor!" Father said.

"The mayor of a town is a servant," Mother said. "He's the head servant of course: the butler. You dont invite a butler to a party because he's a butler. You invite him in spite of it."

But Mayor de Spain got his invitation too. Maybe the reason Mother didn't stop it like Uncle Gavin wanted her to, was simply for that reason she had already given, explained, described: that she and the Cotillion Club didn't have to invite him because he was Mayor, and so they invited him just to show it, prove it. Only Father didn't think that was the reason. "No sir," he said. "You damned gals aint fooling me or anybody else. You want trouble. You want something to happen. You like it. You want two red-combed roosters strutting at one another, provided one of you hens is the reason for it. And if there's anything else you can think of to shove them in to where one of them will have to draw blood in self defense, you'll do that too because every drop of that blood or every black eye or every public-torn collar or split or muddy britches is another item of revenge on that race of menfolks that hold you ladies thralled all day long day after day with nothing to do between meals but swap gossip over the telephone. By godfrey," he said, "if there wasn't any club to give a Christmas dance two weeks from now, you all would probably organise one just to invite Mrs Snopes and Gavin and Manfred de Spain to it. Except you are wasting your time and money this trip. Gavin dont know how to make trouble."

"Gavin's a gentleman," Mother said.

"Sure," Father said. "That's what I said: it aint that he dont want to make trouble: he just dont know how. Oh I dont mean he wont try. He'll do the best he knows. But he just dont know how to make the kind of trouble that a man like Manfred de Spain will take seriously."

But Mr de Spain did the best he could to teach Uncle Gavin how. He began the day the invitations were sent out and he got his after all. When he bought that red E.M.F. the first thing he did was to have a cut-out put on it and until he got elected mayor the first time you could hear him all the way to the Square the moment he left home. And soon after that Lucius Hogganbeck got somebody (it was Mr Roth Edmonds and maybe Mr de Spain too since Lucius's father, old Boon Hogganbeck, had been Mr Roth's father's, Mr McCaslin Edmonds, and his uncle's, Uncle Ike McCaslin, and old Major de Spain's huntsman-doghandler-manFriday back in the time of Major de Spain's old hunting camp) to sign a note for him to buy a Model T Ford and set up in the jitney passenger-hauling business, and he had a cut-out too and on Sunday afternoons half the men in Jefferson would slip off from their wives and go out to a straight stretch of road about two miles from town (even two miles back in town you could hear them when the wind was right) and Mr de Spain and Lucius would race each other. Lucius would charge his passengers a nickel a head to ride in the race, though Mr de Spain carried his free.

Though the first thing Mr de Spain did after he got to be mayor was to have an ordinance passed that no cut-out could be opened inside the town limits. So it had been years now since we had heard one. Then one morning we did. I mean we—Grandfather and Mother and Father and Uncle Gavin and Gowan—did, because it was right in front of our house. It was just about the time everybody would be going to school or to work and Gowan knew which car it was even before he got to the window because Lucius's Ford made a different sound, and besides nobody but the mayor would have risked that cut-out with the cut-out law in force. It was him: the red car just going out of sight and the cut-out off again as soon as he had passed the house; and Uncle Gavin still sitting at the table finishing his breakfast just as if there hadn't been any new noise at all.

And as Gowan reached the corner on the way home from school at noon, he heard it again; Mr de Spain had driven blocks out of his way to rip past our house again in second gear with the cut-out wide open; and again while Mother and Father and Grandfather and Uncle Gavin and he were still sitting at the table finishing dinner, with Mother sitting right still and not looking at anything and Father looking at Uncle Gavin and Uncle Gavin sitting there stirring his coffee like there wasn't a sound anywhere in the world except maybe his spoon in the cup.

And again about half-past five, about dark, when the storekeepers and doctors and lawyers and mayors and such as that would be going home at the end of the day to eat supper all quiet and peaceful, without having to go back to town until tomorrow morning; and this time Gowan could even see Uncle Gavin listening to the cut-out when it passed the house. I mean, this time Uncle Gavin didn't mind them seeing that he heard it, looking up from the paper a little and holding the paper in front of him until the sound went on and then quit off when Mr de Spain passed the end of our yard and picked up his foot; Uncle Gavin and Grandfather both looking up while it passed though all Grandfather did yet was just to frown a little and Uncle Gavin not even doing that: just waiting, almost peaceful, so that Gowan could almost hear him saying *That's all at last. He had to make the fourth run past to get back home.*

And so it was all, through supper and afterward when they went to the office where Mother would sit in the rocking chair always sewing something though it seemed to be mostly darning socks and Gowan's stockings and Grandfather and

Father would sit across the desk from one another playing checkers and sometimes Uncle Gavin would come in too with his book when he wouldn't feel like trying again to teach Mother to play chess until I got born next year and finally got big enough so he could begin to try to teach me. And now it was already past the time when the ones going to the picture show would have gone to it, and the men just going back to town after supper to loaf in Christian's drugstore or to talk with the drummers in the Holston House lobby or drink some more coffee in the café, and anybody would have thought he was safe. Only this time it wasn't even Father. It was Grandfather himself jerking his head up and saying:

"What the devil's that? That's the second time today."

"It's the fifth time today," Father said. "His foot slipped."

"What?" Grandfather said.

"He was trying to mash on the brake to go quiet past the house," Father said. "Only his foot slipped and mashed on the cut-out instead."

"Telephone Connors," Grandfather said. That was Mr Buck Connors. "I wont have it."

"That's Gavin's job," Father said. "He's the acting City Attorney when you're in a checker game. He's the one to speak to the marshal. Or better still, the mayor. Aint that right, Gavin?" And Gowan said they all looked at Uncle Gavin, and that he himself was ashamed, not of Uncle Gavin: of us, the rest of them. He said it was like watching somebody's britches falling down while he's got to use both hands trying to hold up the roof: you are sorry it is funny, ashamed you had to be there watching Uncle Gavin when he never even had any warning he would need to try to hide his face's nakedness when that cut-out went on and the car ripped slow in second gear past the house again after you would have thought that anybody would have had the right to believe that other time before supper would be the last one at least until tomorrow, the cut-out ripping past and sounding just like laughing, still sounding like laughing even after the car had reached the corner where Mr de Spain would always lift his foot off the cut-out. Because it was laughing: it was Father sitting at his side of the checker board, looking at Uncle Gavin and laughing.

"Charley!" Mother said. "Stop it!" But it was already too late. Uncle Gavin had already got up, quick, going toward the door like he couldn't quite see it, and on out.

"What the devil's this?" Grandfather said.

"He rushed out to telephone Buck Connors," Father said. "Since this was the fifth time today, he must have decided that fellow's foot never slipped at all." Now Mother was standing right over Father with the stocking and the darning egg in one hand and the needle in the other like a dagger.

"Will you please hush, dearest?" she said. "Will you please shut your gee dee mouth?—I'm sorry, Papa," she said to Grandfather. "But he—" Then she was at Father again: "Will you? Will you now?"

"Sure, kid," Father said. "I'm all for peace and quiet too." Then Mother was gone too and then it was bed time and then Gowan told how he saw Uncle Gavin sitting in the dark parlor with no light except through the hall door, so that he couldn't read if he tried. Which Gowan said he wasn't: just sitting there in the half-dark, until Mother came down the stairs in her dressing gown and her hair down and said,

"Why dont you go to bed? Go on now. Go on," and Gowan said,

"Yessum," and she went on into the parlor and stood beside Uncle Gavin's chair and said,

"I'm going to telephone him," and Uncle Gavin said,

"Telephone who?" and Mother came back and said,

"Come on now. This minute," and waited until Gowan went up the stairs in front of her. When he was in bed with the light off she came to the door and said Goodnight and all they would have to do now would be just to wait. Because even if five was an odd number and it would take an even number to make the night whole for Uncle Gavin, it couldn't possibly be very long because the drugstore closed as soon as the picture show was out, and anybody still sitting in the Holston House lobby after the drummers had all gone to bed would have to explain it to Jefferson some time or other, no matter how much of a bachelor he was. And Gowan said he thought how at least Uncle Gavin and he had their nice warm comfortable familiar home to wait in, even if Uncle Gavin was having to sit up in the dark parlor by himself, instead of having to use the drugstore or the hotel to put off finally having to go home as long as possible.

And this time Gowan said Mr de Spain opened the cut-out as soon as he left the Square; he could hear it all the way getting louder and louder as it turned the two corners into our street, the ripping loud and jeering but at least not in second gear this time, going fast past the house and the dark parlor where Uncle Gavin was sitting, and on around the other two corners he would have to turn to get back into the street he belonged in, dying away at last until all you could hear was just the night and then Uncle Gavin's feet coming quiet up the stairs. Then the hall light went out, and that was all.

All for that night, that day I mean. Because even Uncle Gavin didn't expect it to be completely all. In fact, the rest of them found out pretty quick that Uncle Gavin didn't aim for it to be all; the next morning at breakfast it was Uncle Gavin himself that raised his head first and said: "There goes Manfred back to our salt-mine," and then to Gowan: "Mr de Spain has almost as much fun with his automobile as you're going to have with one as soon as your Cousin Charley buys it, doesn't he?" Whenever that would be because Father said almost before Uncle Gavin could finish getting the words out:

"Me own one of those stinking noisy things? I wouldn't dare. Too many of my customers use horses and mules for a living." But Gowan said that if Father ever did buy one while he was there, he would find something better to do with it besides running back and forth in front of the house with the cut-out open.

And again while he was on the way home at noon to eat dinner, and again while they were sitting at the table. Nor was it just Gowan who found out Uncle Gavin didn't aim for that to be all because Mother caught Gowan almost before Uncle Gavin turned his back. Gowan didn't know how she did it. Aleck Sander always said that his mother could see and hear through a wall (when he got bigger he said Guster could smell his breath over the telephone) so maybe all women that were already mothers or just acting like mothers like Mother had to while Gowan lived with us, could do that too and that was how Mother did it: stepping out of the parlor just as Gowan put his hand in his pocket.

"Where is it?" Mother said. "What Gavin just gave you. It was a box of tacks; wasn't it a box of tacks? to scatter out there in the street where he will run over them? Wasn't it? Acting just like a high school sophomore. He should marry Melisandre Backus before he ruins the whole family."

"I thought you said it's too late for that," Gowan said. "That the one that marries Cousin Gavin will have to be a widow with four children."

"Maybe I meant too early," Mother said. "Melisandre hasn't even got the husband yet." Then she wasn't seeing Gowan. "Which is exactly what Manfred de Spain is acting like," she said. "A high school sophomore." Gowan said she was looking right at him but she wasn't seeing him at all, and all of a sudden he said she was pretty, looking just like a girl. "No: exactly what we are all acting like," and now she was seeing him again. "But dont you dare let me see you doing it, do you hear? Dont you dare!"

"Yessum," Gowan said. It was no trouble. All he and Top had to do after school was just divide the tacks into their hands and kind of fool around out in the middle of the street like they were trying to decide what to do next while the tacks dribbled down across the tracks of the automobile; Mr de Spain had made nine trips by now so Gowan said he almost had two ruts. Only he and Top had to stay out in the cold now because they wanted to see it. Top said that when the wheels blew up, they would blow the whole automobile up. Gowan didn't think so, but he didn't know either and Top might be partly right, enough right anyway to be worth watching.

So they had to stand behind the big jasmine bush and it began to get dark and it got colder and colder and Guster opened the kitchen door and begun to holler for Top then after a while she came to the front door and hollered for both of them; it was full dark and good and cold now when at last they saw the lights coming, it reached the corner of the yard and the cut-out went on and the car ripped slow and loud past and they listened and watched both but nothing happened, nothing at all, it just went on and even the cut-out went back off; Gowan said how maybe it would take a little time for the tacks to finally work in and blow the wheels up and they waited for that too but nothing happened. And now it had been long enough for him to be home.

And after supper, all of them in the office again, but not anything at all this time, not even anything passed the house so Gowan thought maybe it hadn't blown up until after he was home and now Uncle Gavin never would know when it would be safe to come out of the dark parlor and go upstairs to bed; so that he, Gowan, made a chance to whisper to Uncle Gavin: "Do you want me to go up to his house and look?" Only Father said,

"What? What're you whispering about?" so that didn't do any good either. And the next morning nothing happened either, the cut-out ripping slow past the house like next time it was coming right through the dining room itself. And twice more at noon and that afternoon when Gowan got home from school Top jerked his head at him and they went to the cellar; Top had an old rake-head with a little of the handle still in it so they built a fire behind the stable and burned the handle out and when it was dark enough Gowan watched up and down the street while Top scraped a trench across the tire-rut and set the rake teeth-up in it and scattered some leaves over to hide it and they watched from behind the jasmine bush again while the car ripped past. And nothing happened though when the car was gone they went and saw for themselves where the wheels had mashed right across the rake.

"We'll try it once more," Gowan said. And they did: the next morning: and nothing. And that afternoon Top worked on the rake a while with an old file and then Gowan worked on it a while even after they both knew they would still be working on it that way when the Cotillion Club would be planning next year's Christmas Ball. "We need a grindstone," Gowan said.

"Unk Noon," Top said.

"We'll take the gun like we are going rabbit hunting," Gowan said. So they did: as far as Uncle Noon Gatewood's blacksmith shop on the edge of town. Uncle Noon was big and yellow; he had a warped knee that just seemed to fit exactly into the break of a horse's forearm and pastern; he would pick up a horse's hind leg and set the foot inside the knee and reach out with one hand and take hold of the nearest post and if the post held, the horse could jerk and plunge all it wanted to and Uncle Noon and the horse might sway back and forth but the foot wouldn't move. He let Gowan and Top use his rock and while Top turned and tilted the water-can Gowan held the teeth one by one to the stone until they would have gone through almost anything that mashed against them, let alone an automobile.

And Gowan said they sure did have to wait for dark this time. For dark and late too, when they knew nobody would see them. Because if the sharpened rake worked, the car might not blow up so bad that Mr de Spain wouldn't have time to wonder what caused it and start looking around and find the rake. And at first it looked like it was going to be a good thing it was a long December night too because the ground was frozen that they had to dig the trench through, not just a short trench like before to set the rake in but one long enough so they could tie a string to the rake and then snatch the rake back into the yard between the time the wheel blew up and Mr de Spain could begin to hunt for what caused it. But Gowan said at least tomorrow was Saturday so they would have all day to fix the rake so they could be behind the jasmine bush and see it by daylight.

So they were: already behind the bush with the rake-head fixed and the end of the string in Gowan's hand when they heard it coming and then saw it, then the cut-out came on and it came ripping past with the cut-out like it was saying HAhaHAhaHAha until they were already thinking they had missed this time too when the wheel said BANG and Gowan said he didn't have time to snatch the string because the string did the snatching, out of his hand and around the jasmine bush like the tail of a snake, the car saying HAha-HAhaclankHAhaHAhaclank every time the rake that seemed to be stuck to the wheel would wham against the mudguard again, until Mr de Spain finally stopped it. Then Gowan said the parlor window behind them opened, with Mother and Father standing in it until Mother said:

"You and Top go out and help him so you both will learn something about automobiles when your Cousin Charley buys one."

"Me buy one of those noisy stinking things?" Father said. "Why, I'd lose every horse and mule customer I've got—"

"Nonsense," Mother said. "You'd buy one today if you thought Papa would stand for it.—No," she said to Gowan. "Just you help Mr de Spain. I want Top in the house."

So Top went into the house and Gowan went out to the car where Mr de Spain was standing beside the crumpled wheel holding the rake-head in his hand and looking down at it with his lips poked out like he was kind of whistling a tune to himself Gowan said. Then he looked around at Gowan and took out his knife and cut the string loose and put the rake-head into his overcoat pocket and begun to roll the string up, watching the string where it came jerking out of our yard, his mouth still pursed out like he was whistling to himself. Then Top came up. He was wearing the white jacket he wore when Mother would try to teach him to wait on the table, carrying a tray with a cup of coffee and the cream and sugar bowl. "Miss Maggie say would you care for a cup of coffee while you resting in the cold?" he said.

"Much obliged," Mr de Spain said. He finished rolling the string up and took the tray from Top and set it on the mud-guard of the car and then handed the rolled-up string to Top. "Here's a good fish line for you," he said.

"It aint none of mine," Top said.

"It is now," Mr de Spain said. "I just gave it to you." So Top took the string. Then Mr de Spain told him to take off that clean white coat first and then he opened the back of the automobile and showed Gowan and Top the jack and tire tool and then he drank the coffee while Top crawled under the car and set the jack in place and he and Gowan wound up the wheel. Then Mr de Spain put down the empty cup and took off his overcoat and hunkered down by the crumpled wheel with the tire tool. Except that from then on Gowan said all he and Top learned was some curse-words they never had heard before, until Mr de Spain stood up and threw the tire tool at the wheel and said, to Gowan this time: "Run in the house and telephone Buck Connors to bring Jabbo here double quick." Only Father was there by that time.

"Maybe you've got too many experts," he said. "Come on

in and have a drink. I know it's too early in the morning but this is Christmas."

So they all went into the house and Father telephoned Mr Connors to bring Jabbo. Jabbo was Uncle Noon Gatewood's son. He was going to be a blacksmith too until Mr de Spain brought that first red automobile to town and, as Uncle Noon said, 'ruint him'. Though Gowan said that never made much sense to him because Jabbo used to get drunk and wind up in jail three or four times a year while he was still only a blacksmith, while now, since automobiles had come to Jefferson, Jabbo was the best mechanic in the county and although he still got drunk and into jail as much as ever, he never stayed longer than just overnight anymore because somebody with an automobile always needed him enough to pay his fine by morning.

Then they went into the dining room, where Mother already had the decanter and glasses set out. "Wait," Father said. "I'll call Gavin."

"He's already gone," Mother said right quick. "Sit down now and have your toddy."

"Maybe he hasn't," Father said, going out anyway.

"Please dont wait on them," Mother said to Mr de Spain.

"I dont mind waiting," Mr de Spain said. "It's too early in the morning to start drinking for the next few minutes." Then Father came back.

"Gavin says to please excuse him," Father said. "He seems to have heart-burn these days."

"Tell him salt is good for heart-burn," Mr de Spain said.

"What?" Father said.

"Tell him to come on," Mr de Spain said. "Tell him Maggie will set a salt-cellar between us." And that was all then. Mr Connors came with a shotgun and Jabbo in handcuffs and they all went out to the car while Mr Connors handed the shotgun to Jabbo to hold while he got out the key and unlocked the handcuffs and took the shotgun back. Then Jabbo picked up the tire tool and had the tire off in no time.

"Why dont you," Father said, "if you could just kind of embalm Jabbo a little—you know: so he wouldn't get cold or hungry—tie him on the back of the car like he was an extra wheel or engine, then every time you had a puncture or it wouldn't start, all you'd have to do would be to untie Jabbo and stand him up and unbalm him—is that the word? unbalm?"

"When you get it patched," Mr de Spain said to Jabbo, "bring it on to my office."

"Yessir," Jabbo said. "Mr Buck can bring the fining paper along with us."

"Thank your aunt for the coffee," Mr de Spain said to Gowan.

"She's my cousin," Gowan said. "And the toddy."

"I'll walk to town with you," Father said to Mr de Spain. That was Saturday. The Cotillion Ball would be Wednesday. On Monday and Tuesday and Wednesday Jefferson had the biggest run on flowers the town ever had, even when old General Compson died, who had not only been a Confederate brigadier, but for two days he had been Governor of Mississippi too. It wasn't through any of us that Mr de Spain found out what Uncle Gavin was planning to do, and decided that he—Mr de Spain—had better do it too. And it would be nice to think that the same notion occurred to Uncle Gavin and Mr de Spain at the same time. But that was too much to expect either.

So it was Mrs Rouncewell. She ran the flower shop; not, Uncle Gavin said, because she loved flowers nor even because she loved money but because she loved funerals; she had buried two husbands herself and took the second one's insurance and opened the flower shop and furnished the flowers for every funeral in Jefferson since; she would be the one that told Mr de Spain how Uncle Gavin had wanted to send Mrs Snopes a corsage to wear to the ball until Mother told him that Mrs Snopes already had a husband and he couldn't send one to her alone and Uncle Gavin said All right, did Mother want him to send one to Mr Snopes too? and Mother said he knew what she meant and Uncle Gavin said All right, he would send one to each one of the Cotillion ladies. Until Mr de Spain had to do the same thing, so that not just Mrs Snopes but all the ladies of the Cotillion Club were going to get two corsages apiece.

Not to mention the rest of the town: not just the husbands

and beaus of the ladies in the Club, but the husbands and
beaus of all the other ladies who were invited; especially the
husbands who were already married because they wouldn't
have had to send their wives a corsage at all because their
wives wouldn't have expected one except for Uncle Gavin and
Mr de Spain. But mainly Uncle Gavin since he started the
whole thing; to listen to them around the barbershop getting
their hair cut for the dance, and in Mr Kneeland's tailor shop
renting the dress suits, you would have thought they were going to lynch Uncle Gavin.

And one was more than just cussing Uncle Gavin: Mr
Grenier Weddel and Mrs Maurice Priest. But all that came out
later; we didn't hear about that until the day after the Ball. All
we knew about now was the corsage-run on Mrs Rouncewell,
what Father called the Rouncewell panic. ("I had to make
that one myself," Father said. "It was Gavin's by right; he
should have done it but right now he aint even as faintly close
to humor as that one was." Because he was cussing Uncle
Gavin too since now he would have to send Mother a corsage
that he hadn't figured on doing since Uncle Gavin was, which
would make three she would get—that is, if the rest of the
men aiming to attend the Ball didn't panic too and decide
they would all have to send the members a separate corsage.)
Because by Monday night Mrs Rouncewell had run clean out
of flowers; by the time the north-bound train ran Tuesday
afternoon all the towns up and down the road from Jefferson
had been milked dry too; and early Wednesday morning a
special hired automobile made a night emergency run from
Memphis with enough flowers to make out so Mrs Rouncewell could begin to deliver the corsages, using her own delivery boy and Lucius Hogganbeck's jitney and even renting
Miss Eunice Habersham's home-made truck that she peddled
vegetables from to finish the deliveries in time, delivering five
of them at our house which they all thought were for Mother
until she read the names on the boxes and said:

"This one's not for me. It's for Gavin." And they all stood
watching Uncle Gavin while he stood right still looking down
at the box, his hand already raised toward the box and then
his hand stopped too in midair. Until at last he broke the
string and lifted the lid and moved the tissue paper aside and

then—Gowan said it was all of a sudden yet it wasn't fast either—moved the tissue paper back and put the lid back on
and picked up the box. "Aren't you going to let us see it?"
Mother said.

"No," Uncle Gavin said. But Gowan had already seen. It
was the rake-head, with two flowers like a bouquet, all bound
together with a band or strip of something that Gowan knew
was thin rubber but it was another year or two until he was a
good deal bigger and older that he knew what the thing was;
and at the same time he realised what it was, he said he knew
it had already been used; and at the same time he knew at
least how Uncle Gavin was supposed to believe it had been
used, which was the reason Mr de Spain sent it to him: that
whether Uncle Gavin was right or not about how it had been
used, he would never be sure and so forever afterward would
have no peace about it.

And Gowan was just thirteen then; until that one, he
wouldn't have thought that anybody could have paid him or
even dragged him to a Cotillion Ball. But he said he had already had to see too much by now; he had to be there if there
was going to be anything else, any more to it, even if he
couldn't imagine what else there could be after this, what
more could happen at just a dance. So he put on his blue
Sunday suit and watched Mother with her hair all primped
and Grandmother's diamond ear-rings trying to make Father
say which one of her four corsages to carry: the one he gave
her or to agree with the one of the other three that she
thought went best with her dress; then he went across to
Uncle Gavin's room where Uncle Gavin got out another
white bow tie like his and put it on Gowan and a flower for
his buttonhole too and they all went downstairs, the hack was
waiting and they drove through the cold to the Square and
the Opera House where the other hacks and now and then a
car were pulling up for the other guests to get out crimped
and frizzed in scarves and ear-rings and perfume and long
white gloves like Mother or in claw-hammer coats and boiled
shirts and white ties and yesterday's haircuts like Father and
Uncle Gavin and (the white tie at least) Gowan, with the
loafers, Negro and white boys too, hanging around the door
to hear the music after the band started to play.

It was Professor Handy, from Beale Street in Memphis. His band played at all the balls in north Mississippi and Gowan said how the hall was all decorated for Christmas and the Cotillion Club ladies and their escorts all lined up to receive the guests; he said you could smell all the corsages even before you began to climb the stairs and that when you got inside the ballroom it looked like you should have been able to see the smell from them too like mist in a swamp on a cold morning. And he said how Mr Snopes was there too, in a rented dress suit, and Jefferson probably thought at first that that rented dress suit was just the second footprint made on it, until they had time to realise that it wasn't anymore just a footprint than that water tank was a monument: it was a red flag. No: it was that sign at the railroad crossing that says Look Out For The Locomotive.

And Gowan said how, since Mother was President of the Club that year, everybody (once Mrs Rouncewell finally realised that floral goldmine she had fallen into, there wasn't anybody in Jefferson in the dark any longer about Mr de Spain and Uncle Gavin and Mrs Snopes) expected her to give Uncle Gavin the first dance with Mrs Snopes. But she didn't. She sent Grenier Weddel; he was a bachelor too. And even after that she still kept the dances equal between Uncle Gavin and Mr de Spain until Mr de Spain ruined it. Because he was a bachelor. I mean, like Uncle Gavin said: that there are some men who are incorrigibly and invincibly bachelor no matter how often they marry, just as some men are doomed and emasculate husbands if they never find a woman to take them. And Mr de Spain was one of them. I mean the first kind: incorrigibly and invincibly bachelor and threat no matter what happened to him because Uncle Gavin said things, circumstance and conditions, didn't happen to people like Mr de Spain: people like him happened to circumstances and conditions.

This time he had help. I wasn't there to see it and I know now that Gowan didn't know what he was seeing either. Because after a while I got born and then big enough to see Mrs Snopes myself, and after a while more I was old enough to feel what Uncle Gavin and Mr de Spain (and all the other men in Jefferson, and Frenchman's Bend and everywhere else that ever saw her I reckon, the little cautious men who were not as brave and unlucky as Uncle Gavin and brave and lucky as Mr de Spain, though they probably called it being more sensible) felt just looking at her. And after a while more still and she was dead and Mr de Spain had left town wearing public mourning for her as if she had been his wife and Jefferson finally quit talking about her, my bet is there was more than me in Jefferson that even just remembering her could feel it still and grieve. I mean, grieve because her daughter didn't have whatever it was that she had; until you realised that what you grieved for wasn't that the daughter didn't have it too; grieved not that we didn't have it anymore, but that we couldn't have it anymore: that even a whole Jefferson full of little weak puny frightened men couldn't have stood more than one Mrs Snopes inside of just one one-hundred years. And I reckon there was a second or two at first when even Mr de Spain had time to be afraid. I reckon there was a second when even he said Hold on here; have I maybe blundered into something not just purer than me but even braver than me, braver and tougher than me because it is purer than me, cleaner than me? Because that was what it was.

Gowan said it was the way Mrs Snopes and Mr de Spain began to dance together. That is, the way that Mr de Spain all of a sudden began to dance with Mrs Snopes. Up to that time, Gowan said, Uncle Gavin and Mr de Spain and the other men Mother sent to write their names on Mrs Snopes's program had been taking turns all calm and peaceful. Then all of a sudden Gowan said everybody else stopped dancing and kind of fell back and he said he saw Mrs Snopes and Mr de Spain dancing together alone in a kind of aghast circle of people. And when I was old enough, fourteen or fifteen or sixteen, I knew what Gowan had seen without knowing what he was seeing: that second when Mr de Spain felt astonishment, amazement and unbelief and terror too at himself because of what he found himself doing without even knowing he was going to:—dancing like that with Mrs Snopes to take revenge on Uncle Gavin for having frightened him, Mr de Spain, enough to make him play the sophomore tricks like the cut-out and the rake-head and the used rubber thing in a corsage; frightened at himself at finding out that he couldn't possibly be only what he had thought for all those years he was, if he could find himself in a condition capable of playing tricks like that; while Mrs Snopes was dancing that way, letting Mr de Spain get her into dancing that way in public, simply because she was alive and not ashamed of it like maybe right now or even for the last two weeks Mr de Spain and Uncle Gavin had been ashamed; was what she was and looked the way she looked and wasn't ashamed of it and not afraid or ashamed of being glad of it, nor even of doing this to prove it since this appeared to be the only way of proving it, not being afraid or ashamed, that the little puny people fallen back speechless and aghast in a shocked circle around them, could understand; all the other little doomed mean cowardly married and unmarried husbands looking aghast and outraged in order to keep one another from seeing that what they really wanted to do was cry, weep because they were not that brave, each one knowing that even if there was no other man on earth, let alone in that ball room, they still could not have survived, let alone matched or coped with, that splendor, that splendid unshame.

It should have been Mr Snopes of course because he was the husband, the squire, the protector in the formal ritual. But it was Uncle Gavin and he wasn't any husband or squire or knight or defender or protector either except simply and quickly his own: who didn't really care even how badly Mrs Snopes got battered and bruised in the business provided there was enough of her left when he finally got the last spark of life trampled out of Mr de Spain. Gowan said how he stepped in and grabbed Mr de Spain by the shoulder and jerked, and now a kind of sound went up and then he said all the men were streaming across the floor toward the back stairs that led down into the back alley and now the ladies were screaming good only Gowan said that a lot of them were streaking after the men too so that he had to kind of burrow along among skirts and legs, down the back stairs; he said he could see Uncle Gavin through the legs just getting up from the alley and he, Gowan, pushed on through to the front and saw Uncle Gavin just getting up from the alley again with his face all bloody and two men helping him or anyway trying to, because he flung them off and ran at Mr de Spain again: and when I was older I knew that too: that Uncle Gavin wasn't trying anymore to destroy or even hurt Mr de Spain because he had already found out by that time that he couldn't. Because now Uncle Gavin was himself again. What he was doing was simply defending forever with his blood the principle that chastity and virtue in women shall be defended whether they exist or not.

"Damn it," Mr de Spain said, "hold him, some of you fellows, and let me get out of here." So Father held Uncle Gavin and somebody brought Mr de Spain's hat and coat and he left; and Gowan said this was the time he expected to hear that cut-out again for sure. But he didn't. There was nothing: just Uncle Gavin standing there wiping the blood from his face on his handkerchief then on Father's.

"You fool," Father said. "Dont you know you cant fight? You dont know how."

"Can you suggest a better way to learn than the one I just tried?" Uncle Gavin said.

And at home too, in his bathroom, where he could take off his vest and collar and tie and shirt and hold a wet towel against the bleeding, when Mother came in. She had a flower in her hand, a red rose from one of the corsages. "Here," she said. "She sent it to you."

"You lie," Uncle Gavin said. "You did it."

"Lie yourself!" Mother said. "She sent it!"

"No," Uncle Gavin said.

"Then she should have!" Mother said; and now Gowan said she was crying, half way holding to Uncle Gavin and half way beating him with both fists, crying: "You fool! You fool! They dont deserve you! They aren't good enough for you! None of them are, no matter how much they look and act like a—like a—like a god damn whorehouse! None of them! None of them!"

Only Mr Snopes left more footprints than them on Jefferson that night; he left another bloody nose and two black eyes. That fourth corsage Mother got that night was from Grenier Weddel. He was a bachelor like Mr de Spain. I mean, he was the kind of bachelor that Uncle Gavin said would still be one no matter how many times who married him. Maybe that was why Sally Hampton turned him down.

Anyway, she sent his ring back and married Maurice Priest instead and so when Uncle Gavin and Mr de Spain started what Father called the Mrs Rouncewell panic that day, Grenier saw his chance too and sent Mrs Priest not just what Father called a standard panic-size corsage, but a triple one. Maybe that was why she didn't wear it to the ball that night: it was too big to carry. Anyway she didn't but anyway after Uncle Gavin and Mr de Spain got through with the alley, Grenier and Maurice Priest went back there and Grenier came out with one of the black eyes and Maurice went home with the bloody nose and the next morning when Sally Priest came to town she had the other black eye. And maybe she didn't wear the corsage in public but she sure did that eye. She was not only around town all that morning, she came back that afternoon so everybody in Jefferson would have a chance to see it or at least hear about it. Gowan said you would even have thought she was proud of it.

Except that Flem Snopes wasn't the first Snopes in Jefferson neither.

FOUR

V. K. RATLIFF

She was. His aunt (not his two uncles nor his grand-paw, but any of his womenfolks) could have told him why: proud she still had a husband that could and would black her eye; proud her husband had a wife that could still make him need to.

And he was right about Flem not being the first Snopes in Jefferson too. The first one was Mink, that spent two and a half months in the Jefferson jail on his way to his permanent residence in the penitentiary at Parchman for killing Zack Houston. And he spent them two and a half months laboring under a mistake.

I dont mean a mistake in killing Houston. He knowed what he aimed to do then. Zack was a proud man to begin with, and he had just lost his young wife that he had had a considerable trouble persuading her folks to let her marry him—she was old man Cal Bookright's youngest child, a school teacher, and although Zack owned his place and was a good farmer, that's all he was: just a farmer without no special schooling, besides being a hard liver when he was a young man and even right up to when he got serious about Letty Bookright and found out that old Cal was serious too. Then when he, or both of them together I reckon, finally beat old Cal down and they was married, he never even had her a whole year before he lost her. And even then he had to lose her hard, the hardest way: that same blood stallion killed her with his feet in the stall one day that Mink shot him off of that morning—and that made him a little extra morose because he was unhappy. So between being proud to begin with and then unhappy on top of that, he was a little overbearing. But since most of the folks around Frenchman's Bend knowed he was proud and knowed how hard he had had to work to persuade old Cal to let Letty marry him, he would a still been all right if he hadn't tangled with Mink Snopes.

Because Mink Snopes was mean. He was the only out-and-out mean Snopes we ever experienced. There was mad short-tempered barn-burners like old Ab, and there was the mild innocent ones like Eck that not only wasn't no Snopes, no matter what his maw said, he never had no more business being born into a Snopes nest than a sparrow would have in a hawk's nest; and there was the one pure out-and-out fool like I.O. But we never had run into one before that was just mean without no profit consideration or hope atall.

Maybe that was why he was the only mean Snopes: there wasn't no sign of any profit in it. Only he was bound or anyway must a had a little of his cousin I.O.'s foolishness too or he wouldn't have made his mistake. I mean, the mistake not of shooting Houston but of when he picked out to do it; picking out the time to do it while Flem was still off on his Texas honeymoon. Sholy he knowed that Flem hadn't got back yet. Or maybe the night before he had got the Snopes grapevine word that he had been waiting for, that Flem would reach Frenchman's Bend tomorrow, and it was only then that he taken that old wore-out ten gauge britch-loader and hid in that thicket and bushwhacked Houston off the horse when he rid past. But then I dont know. Maybe by that time nothing else mattered to him but seeing Houston over the end of them barrels then feeling that stock jolt back against his shoulder.

Anyhow, that's what he done. And likely it wasn't until Houston was laying in the mud in the road and that skeered stallion with the loose reins and the empty saddle and flapping stirrups already tearing on to Varner's store to spread the news, that he realised with whatever horror it was, that he had done too soon something it was long since too late to undo. Which was why he tried to hide the body and then dropped the gun into that slough and come on to the store, hanging around the store ever day while the sheriff was still hunting for Houston, not to keep up with whether the sheriff was getting warm or not but waiting for Flem to get back from Texas and save him; right up to the time when Houston's hound led them to the body and some fish-grabblers even found the gun in the slough that ever body knowed was hisn because wouldn't nobody else own it.

And that was when the rage and the outrage and the injustice and the betrayal must a got unbearable to him, when he decided or realised or whatever it was, that Flem by now must a heard about the killing and was deliberately keeping away from Frenchman's Bend or maybe even all Mississippi so he wouldn't have to help him, get him out of it. Not even despair: just simple anger and outrage: to show Flem Snopes that he never give a durn about him neither: handcuffed now and in the sheriff's surrey on the way in to the jail when he seen his chance right quick and wedged his neck tight into the V of the top stanchion and tried to fling his legs and body over the side until they caught him back.

But it was just the initial outrage and hurt and disappointment; it couldn't last. Which likely his good sense told him it wouldn't, and probably he was glad in a way he had got shut of it so calm good sense could come back. Which it did, since now all he had to do was just to be as comfortable as he could in jail and wait until Flem did get home since even Flem Snopes couldn't stay forever even on a honeymoon even in Texas.

So that's what he done. Up there on the top floor of the jail (since he was a authentic topclass murderer, he wouldn't have to go out and work on the streets like just a nigger crapshooter), not even impatient for a long time: just standing there with his hands laying in the crossbars where he could watch the street and the sidewalk that Flem would come walking up from the Square; not impatient during all that first month and not even bad worried in the second one after the Grand Jury indicted him: just hollering down now and then to somebody passing if Flem Snopes was in town yet; not even until the end of the second month that he begun to think that maybe Flem hadn't got back yet and he would holler down to folks to send word out to Frenchman's Bend for Will Varner to come in and see him.

So it wasn't until just them two last weeks before Court and no Will Varner nor nobody else had come in to see him that he probably found out he simply could not believe that Flem Snopes hadn't got back to Frenchman's Bend; he just could not believe that; he dassent to believe that: only that the grown folks he had been hollering down to hadn't never delivered his message, not sleeping much at night now so that (that-ere top

floor behind the barred window would be dark and with the
street light shining on it you could see the white blob of his
face and the two blobs of his hands gripping the bars) he had
plenty of time to stand there all night if necessary waiting for
somebody to pass that he could trust would deliver his message: boys, a boy like that Stevens boy, Lawyer Stevens's visiting nephew, that hadn't been spoiled and corrupted yet by the
world of growed-up men into being his enemies, whispering
down to them until they would stop and look up at him; still
whispering down at them even after they had done broke and
run: "Boys! Fellers! You, there. You want ten dollars? Get
word out to Frenchman's Bend, tell Flem Snopes his cousin
Mink Snopes says to hurry in here, hurry——"

And right up to that morning in court. As soon as they
brung him in the door, handcuffed, he started to craning his
neck, looking at all the faces, still craning his neck around at
the folks still crowding in long after they had run out of anything to set on and still at it while they was choosing the jury,
even trying to stand up on a chair to see better until they
would shove him down; still craning and darting his head
while the clerk read the indictment and then said, "Guilty or
not guilty?" Only this time he had already stood up before
they could stop him, looking out over the crowd toward the
last faces at the clean back of the room and says:

"Flem!"

And now the Judge was banging his little mallet and the
lawyer the Court had appointed was up too and the bailiff
hollering, "Order! Order in the court!"

And Mink says again, "Flem! Flem Snopes!" Only this time
the Judge his-self leaned down toward him across the Bench
and says,

"You there! Snopes!" until Mink finally turned and looked
at him. "Are you guilty or not guilty?"

"What?" Mink says.

"Did you kill Zack Houston or didn't you?" the Judge says.

"Dont bother me now," Mink says. "Cant you see I'm
busy?" turning his head again toward the faces come to see if
maybe they wouldn't hang him anyhow, no matter who said
he was crazy, since that was what he seemed to want his-self,
having already tried it once and so the Law wouldn't be

doing no more than just accommodating him, saying: "Somebody there! Anybody with a car. To run out to Varner's
store quick and get Flem Snopes. He will pay you, whatever
you charge and whatever extry—ten dollars extry—twenty
extry——"

Last summer Lawyer had to do something, he didn't know
what. Now he had to do something, he didn't care what. I
dont even think he especially hunted around for something. I
think he just reached his hand and snatched something, the
first nearest thing, and it just happened to be that old quick-
vanishing power-plant brass that ever body in Jefferson, including Flem Snopes—sholy including Flem Snopes—had
been trying out of pure and simple politeness to forget about.
When as acting City Attorney he drawed up the suit against
Mayor de Spain's bonding company, charging malfeasance in
office and criminal connivance or however they put it, naturally ever body thought all he aimed to do then was to walk
in and lay the papers on Manfred de Spain's desk. But they
was wrong; he never no more wanted to buy anything from
De Spain than he did that night in the alley behind that
Christmas ball, when his brother-in-law told him he couldn't
fight because he never knowed how—a piece of information
already in Lawyer's possession, having already lived with his-
self for more or less twenty-two or maybe twenty-three years.
He didn't want nothing from De Spain because the only
thing De Spain had that he wanted, Lawyer didn't know his-
self that was what he wanted until his paw told him that last
afternoon.
So Lawyer filed the suit. And the first thing was the pleasant young feller from the bonding company in his nice city
suit getting off the morning train with his nice city suitcase,
saying "Now fellers lets all have a drink of this-here nice city
whiskey and see if we can jest all get together on this thing,"
then spending one quick horrified day, mostly on the long
distance telephone between talking with them two Negro
firemen, Tom Tom Bird and Tomey's Turl Beauchamp, while
waiting for Flem to get back from where he had went suddenly on a visit into the next county.
So on the third day the one come from the bonding

company that was big enough in it to have the gray hair and come in a Pullman in striped britches and a gold watch chain big enough to boom logs with and gold eyeglasses and even a gold toothpick and the pigeon-tailed coat and the plug hat until by nightfall you couldn't even a got a glass of water in the Holston Hotel for ever porter and waiter hanging around his door to wait on him and he could a owned ever other Negro in Jefferson too by tomorrow if he had had anything he could a done with them, saying "Gentlemen. Gentlemen. Gentlemen." and the mayor coming in where they was all setting around the table, to stand there laughing at them for a while and then saying,

"You'll have to excuse me. Even the mayor of just Jefferson, Mississippi has got to do a little work now and then." And Lawyer Stevens setting there calm and white in the face and looking exactly like he done that night when he told his brother-in-law: "Can you suh-jest a better way for me to learn how to fight than the one I just tried?"

And Flem Snopes hadn't got back yet and in fact they couldn't even locate him, like he had evidently went on a camping trip in the woods where there wasn't no telephone; and the big boss one, the one with the white vest and the gold toothpick, says: "I'm sure Mr de Spain would resign. Why dont we jest let him resign and forget all this here unhappiness?" and Lawyer Stevens says, "He's a good mayor. We dont want him to resign," and the white vest says, "Then what do you want? You will have to prove our client's representative stole any brass and all you have is the word of them two nigras because Mr Snopes his-self has went out of town."

"That water tank aint went out of town," Lawyer says. "We can drain that water tank."

So what they called was a special meeting of the board of aldermen. What they got was like one of them mass carcasses to vote between two beauty queens, the courthouse bell beginning to ring about eight oclock like it actively was some kind of a night session of court, and the folks coming up the streets and gathering in the Square, laughing and making jokes back and forth, until they decided right quick that the mayor's office wouldn't hold even the start of it so they moved into the courtroom upstairs like it was Court.

Because this was just January; that Christmas ball wasn't barely three weeks old yet. Even when they chose sides it was still jest fun, because most of them had jest come to watch and listen anyhow, even after somebody beat the Judge's mallet on the table until they quit laughing and joking and hushed and one of the aldermen said, "I dont know how much it will cost to drain that tank, but I for one will be damned——"

"I do," Lawyer Stevens says. "I already asked. It will cost three hundred and eighty dollars to rig a auxiliary tank long enough to drain and then fill the other one up again and then dismantle the auxiliary and get shut of it. It wont cost nothing to send somebody down inside of it to look because I'll do that myself."

"All right," the alderman says. "Then I will still be damned——"

"All right," Lawyer says. "Then I will pay for it myself," and the old bonding feller, the white vest one, saying "Gentlemen. Gentlemen. Gentlemen." and the young one, the first one, standing up now and hollering:

"Dont you see, Mr Stevens? Dont you see, Mr Stevens? If you find brass in the tank, there wont be no crime because the brass already belongs to the city?"

"I already thought of that too," Lawyer says. "The brass still belongs to the city even if we dont drain the tank. Only, where is it at?" and the little bonding feller saying:

"Wait! Wait! That aint what I meant. I mean if the brass aint missing there aint no crime because it wasn't never stole."

"Tom Tom Bird and Tomey's Turl Beauchamp says it was because they stole it," Lawyer says. Now they was two aldermen talking at once, saying,

"Hold up here; hold up here," until finally the loudest one, Henry Best, won:

"Then who are you charging, Gavin? Are them nigras under Manfred's bond too?"

"But there aint no crime! We know the brass is in that tank because that's where the nigras said they put it!" the little bonding feller was hollering and all this time the big one, the white vest one, still saying "Gentlemen. Gentlemen. Gentlemen." like a big bass drum a far piece off that never nobody paid any attention to nohow; until Henry Best hollered,

"Wait, god damn it," so loud that they did hush and Henry said: "Them nigras confessed they stole that brass, but there aint no evidence of theft until we drain that tank. So right now, they didn't steal no brass. And if we drain that damn tank and find brass in it, they did steal brass and are guilty of theft. Only, as soon as we find brass in that tank, they never stole any brass because the brass is not just once more in the possession of the city: it aint never been out of it. God damn it, Gavin, is that what you are trying to tell us? Then what the hell do you want? What in hell do you want?"

And Lawyer Stevens setting there calm and still, with his face still white and still as paper. And maybe he hadn't learned how to fight yet neither. But he still hadn't heard about no rule against trying. "That's right," he says. "If there is brass in that tank—valuable property of the city unlawfully con-strained into that tank by the connivance and condonance of a employee of the city, a crime has been committed. If we find brass in that tank—valuable property belonging to the city unlawfully constrained into that tank with the connivance or condonance of a employee of the city, even if it is recovered, a attempt at a crime has been condoned by a employee of the city. But that tank *per se* and what brass may or may not *per se* be in it, is beside the point. What we have engaged the at-tention of this honorable bonding company about is, jest which malfeasance did our honorable mayor commit? Jest which crime by who did our chief servant of our city con-done?" Because he didn't know either what he wanted. And even when next day his paw told him what his behavior acted like he wanted and for a minute Lawyer even agreed, that still wasn't it.

Because that was all they got then, which wasn't nothing to be settled jest off-hand by a passel of amateurs like a alderman board. It was something for a professional, a sho-enough ac-tive judge; whether they aimed to or not, they had done got themselves now to where they would have to have a court. Though I didn't know Judge Dukinfield was in the crowd un-til Henry Best stood up and looked out at us and hollered: "Judge Dukinfield, is Judge Dukinfield still here?" and Judge Dukinfield stood up in the back and says,

"Yes, Henry?"

"I reckon we'll have to have help, Judge," Henry says. "I reckon you heard as much of this as we done, and we all hope you made more sense out of it than we done—"

"Yes; all right," Judge Dukinfield says. "We will hold the hearing here in chambers tomorrow morning at nine. I dont believe either plaintiff or defendant will need more counsel than are represented tonight but they are welcome to bring juniors if they like—or should we say seconds?"

Then we all got up to leave, still laughing and talking and joking back and forth, still not taking no sides but just mainly enjoying it, jest being in principle on whichever other side from them two foreign bonding fellers for the simple reason that they was foreigners, not even paying no attention to Lawyer's twin sister standing there by him now until you could almost hear her telling Henry Best: "Now you're satisfied; maybe you can let him alone now;" not even paying no attention when a boy—I didn't recognise who he was—come burrowing through and up to the table and handed Lawyer something and Lawyer taken it; not realising until tomorrow that something had happened between that meeting that night and the next morning that we never knowed about and it's my opinion we aint going to, just going on home or about our business until the Square was empty except for that one light in his and his paw's office over the hardware store where he was setting alone—provided it was him of course and providing he was alone—how does the feller say it? inviting his soul?

FIVE

GAVIN STEVENS
The poets are wrong of course. According to them I should even have known the note was on the way, let alone who it was from. As it was, I didn't even know who it was from after I read it. But then, poets are almost always wrong about facts. That's because they are not really interested in facts: only in truth: which is why the truth they speak is so true that even those who hate poets by simple natural instinct are exalted and terrified by it.

No: that's wrong. It's because you dont dare to hope, you are afraid to hope. Not afraid of the extent of hope of which you are capable, but that you—the frail web of bone and flesh snaring that fragile temeritous boundless aspirant sleepless with dream and hope—cannot match it; as Ratliff would say, Knowing always you wont never be man enough to do the harm and damage you would do if you were just man enough.—and, he might add, or maybe I do it for him, thank God for it. Ay, thank God for it or thank anything else for it that will give you any peace after it's too late; peace in which to coddle that frail web and its unsleeping ensnared anguish both on your knee and whisper to it: There, there, it's all right; I know you are brave.

The first thing I did on entering the office was to turn on all the lights; if it hadn't been January and the thermometer in the low thirties I would have propped the door to stand open too for that much more of a Mississippi gentleman's tender circumspection toward her good name. The second thing I did was to think *My God all the lights on for the whole town to see* because now I would have Grover Winbush (the night marshal) up the stairs as surely as if I had sent for him since with the usual single desk lamp on he would have thought I was merely working and would let me alone, where with all of them burning like this he would come up certainly, not to surprise the intruder but to participate in the conversation.

So I should have leaped to turn them off again, knowing

that once I moved, turned loose the chair arms I would probably bolt, flee, run home to Maggie who has tried to be my
mother ever since ours died and someday may succeed. So I
just sat there thinking how if there were only time and means
to communicate, suggest, project onto her wherever she
might be at this moment between her home and here, the
rubber soles for silence and the dark enveloping night-blend-
ing cloak and scarf for invisibility; then in the next second
thinking how the simple suggestion of secret shoes and con-
cealing cloak would forever abrogate and render null all need
for either since although I might still be I, she must forever
be some lesser and baser other to be vulnerable to the base insult of secrecy and fearfulness and silence.

So when I heard her feet on the stairs I didn't even think
For God's sake take off your shoes or at least tiptoe. What I
thought was How can you move and make that little noise,
with only the sound of trivial human feet: who should have
moved like Wagner: not with but *in* the sonorous sweep of
thunder or brass music, even the very limbs moving in tune
with the striding other in a sound of tuned wind and storm
and mighty harps. I thought *Since making this more or less secret date to meet me here at this hour of night is her idea, at
least she will have to look at me.* Which she had never done yet.
If she had ever even seen me yet while I was too busy playing
the fool because of her to notice, buffoon for her, playing
with tacks in the street like a vicious boy, using not even honest bribery but my own delayed vicious juvenility to play on
the natural and normal savagery (plus curiosity; dont forget
that) of an authentic juvenile—to gain what? for what? what
did I want, what was I trying for: like the child striking
matches in a hay-stack yet at the same time trembling with
terror lest he does see holocaust.

You see? terror. I hadn't even taken time to wonder what in
hell she wanted with me: only the terror after the boy put the
note in my hand and I found privacy to open and read it and
still (the terror) in the courage, desperation, despair—call it
whatever you like and whatever it was and wherever I found
it—to cross to the door and open it and think as I always had
each time I was that near, either to dance with her or merely
to challenge and give twenty or thirty pounds to an impugner

of her honor: *Why, she cant possibly be this small, this little*, apparently standing only inches short of my own six feet yet small, little; too small to have displaced enough of my peace to contain this much unsleep, to have disarranged this much of what I had at least thought was peace. In fact I might have said she stood almost eye to eye with me if she had looked at me that long, which she did not: that one quick unhasting blue (they were dark blue) envelopment and then no more; no more needing to look—if she ever had—at me, but rather instead one single complete perception to which that adjective complete were as trivial as the adjective dampness to the blue sea itself; that one single glance to add me up and then subtract and then dispense as if that calm unhasting blueness had picked me up whole and palped me over front and back and sides and set me down again. But she didn't sit down herself. She didn't even move yet. Then I realised suddenly that she was simply examining the office as women examine a room they have never seen before.

"Wont you sit down?" I said.

"All right," she said. And, sitting in that ordinary chair across the desk, she was still too small to hold, compass without one bursting seam all that unslumber, all that chewed anguish of the poet's bitter thumbs which were not just my thumbs but all male Jefferson's or actually all male earth's by proxy, that thumb being all men's fate who had earned or deserved the right to call themselves men; too small, too little to contain, bear those . . . I had, must have, seen her at least five years ago though it was only last summer that I must have looked at her; say only since last summer since until then I had been too busy passing bar examinations to have had time to prone and supine myself for proper relinquishment; call it two hundred for round numbers from June to January with some (not much) out for sleeping—two hundred nights of fevered projection of my brother's mantle to defend and save her honor from its ravisher.

You see? It still had not once occurred to me to ask her what she wanted. I was not even waiting for her to tell me. I was simply waiting for those two hundred nights to culminate as I had spent at least some of them or some small part of them expecting when this moment came, if it did, would, was fated: I to be swept up as into storm or hurricane or tornado itself and tossed and wrung and wrenched and consumed, the light last final spent insentient husk to float slowing and weightless, for a moment longer during the long vacant rest of life, and then no more.

Only it didn't happen, no consumption to wrench wring and consume me down to the ultimate last proud indestructible grateful husk, but rather simply to destroy me as the embalmer destroys with very intactness what was still life, was still life even though it was only the living worm's. Because she was not examining the office again because I realised now that she had never stopped doing it, examining it rapidly once more with that comprehensive female glance.

"I thought it would be all right here," she said. "Better here."

"Here?" I said.

"Do it here. In your office. You can lock the door and I dont imagine there'll be anybody high enough up this late at night to see in the window. Or maybe—" Because she was already up and probably for a moment I couldn't have moved, just watching as she went to the window and had already begun to pull down the shade.

"Here?" I said again, like a parrot. "Here? In here?" Now she was looking at me over her shoulder. That's right. She didn't even turn: just her head, her face to look back at me across her shoulder, her hands still drawing the shade down across the window in little final tucking tugs against the sill. No: not again. She never had looked at me but that once as she entered. She simply confronted me across her shoulder with that blue envelopment like the sea, not questioning nor waiting, as the sea itself doesn't need to question or wait but simply to be the sea. "Oh," I said. "And be quick, hurry too maybe since you haven't got much time since you really ought to be in bed this minute with your husband, or is this one of Manfred's nights?" and she still watching me though turned now, standing, perhaps leaning a little against the window-sill behind her, watching me quite grave, just a little curious. "But of course," I said. "Naturally it's one of Manfred's nights since it's Manfred you're saving: not Flem.—No, wait," I said. "Maybe I'm wrong; maybe it is both of them;

maybe they both sent you: both of them that scared, that desperate; their mutual crisis and fear so critical as to justify even this last desperate gambit of your woman's—their mutual woman's—all?" And still she just watched me: the calm unfathomable serenely waiting blue, waiting not on me but simply on time. "I didn't mean that," I said. "You know I didn't. I know it's Manfred. And I know he didn't send you. Least of all, he." Now I could get up. "Say you forgive me first," I said.

"All right," she said. Then I went and opened the door. "Goodnight," I said.

"You mean you dont want to?" she said.

Now I could laugh too.

"I thought that was what you wanted," she said. And now she was looking at me. "What did you do it for?" Oh yes, I could laugh, with the door open in my hand and the cold dark leaning into the room like an invisible cloud and if Grover Winbush were anywhere on the Square now (which he would not be in this cold since he was not a fool about everything) he would not need merely to see all the lights. Oh yes, she was looking at me now: the sea which in a moment more would destroy me, not with any deliberate and calculated sentient wave but simply because I stood there in its insentient way. No: that was wrong too. Because she began to move.

"Shut the door," she said. "It's cold"—walking toward me, not fast. "Was that what you thought I came here for? because of Manfred?"

"Didn't you?" I said.

"Maybe I did." She came toward me, not fast. "Maybe at first. But that doesn't matter. I mean, to Manfred. I mean that brass. He doesn't mind it. He likes it. He's enjoying himself. Shut the door before it gets so cold." I shut it and turned quickly, stepping back a little.

"Dont touch me," I said.

"All right," she said. "Because you cant . . . ." Because even she stopped then; even the insentient sea compassionate too but then I could bear that too; I could even say it for her:

"Manfred wouldn't really mind because just I cant hurt him, harm him, do him any harm; not Manfred, not just me, no matter what I do. That he would really just as soon resign as not and the only reason he doesn't is just to show me I cant make him. All right. Agreed. Then why dont you go home? What do you want here?"

"Because you are unhappy," she said. "I dont like unhappy people. They're a nuisance. Especially when it can—"

"Yes," I said, cried, "this easy, at no more cost than this. When nobody will even miss it, least of all Manfred since we both agree that Gavin Stevens cant possibly hurt Manfred de Spain even by cuckolding him on his mistress. So you came just from compassion, pity: not even from honest fear or even just decent respect. Just compassion. Just pity." Then I saw all of it. "Not just to prove to me that having what I think I want wont make me happy, but to show me that what I thought I wanted is not even worth being unhappy over. Does it mean that little to you? I dont mean with Flem: even with Manfred?" I said, cried: "Dont tell me next that this is why Manfred sent you: to abate a nuisance!"

But she just stood there looking at me with that blue serene terrible envelopment. "You spend too much time expecting," she said. "Dont expect. You just are, and you need, and you must, and so you do. That's all. Dont waste time expecting," moving again toward me where I was trapped not just by the door but by the corner of the desk too.

"Dont touch me!" I said. "So if I had only had sense enough to have stopped expecting, or better still, never expected at all, never hoped at all, dreamed at all; if I had just had sense enough to say *I am, I want, I will and so here goes* ——If I had just done that, it might have been me instead of Manfred? But dont you see? cant you see? I wouldn't have been me then?" No: she wasn't even listening: just looking at me: the unbearable and unfathomable blue, speculative and serene.

"Maybe it's because you're a gentleman and I never knew one before."

"So is Manfred!" I said. "And that other one, that first one—your child's father——" *the only other one* I thought because, yes, oh yes, I knew now: Snopes himself was impotent. I even said it: "The only other one besides Manfred. Back there in Frenchman's Bend, that Ratliff told me about, that fought off the five or six men who tried to ambush you in the buggy that night, fought them off with the buggy whip and one hand because he had to use the other to shield you with, whipped them all off even with one arm broken where I couldn't even finish the fight I started myself with just one opponent?" And still not moving: just standing there facing me so that what I smelled was not even just woman but that terrible, that drowning envelopment. "Both alike," I said. "But not like me. All three gentlemen but only two were men."

"Lock the door," she said. "I've already drawn the shade. Stop being afraid of things," she said. "Why are you afraid?"

"No," I said, cried. I might—would—have struck her with my out-flung arm, but there was room: out of the trap now and even around her until I could reach the door knob and open it. Oh yes, I knew now. "I might buy Manfred from you but I wont buy Flem," I said. "Because it is Flem, isn't it? Isn't it?" But there was only the blue envelopment and the fading Wagner, trumpet and storm and rich brasses diminuendo toward the fading arm and hand and the rainbow-fading ring. "You told me not to expect; why dont you try it yourself? We've all bought Snopeses here, whether we wanted to or not; you of all people should certainly know that. I dont know why we bought them. I mean, why we had to: what coin and when and where we so recklessly and improvidently spent that we had to have Snopeses too. But we do. But nothing can hurt you if you refuse it, not even a brass-stealing Snopes. And nothing is of value that costs nothing so maybe you will value this refusal at what I value it cost me." She moved then and only then did I notice that she had evidently brought nothing with her: none of the scatter of gloves, bags, veils, this and that which women bring into a room with them so that the first minute of their quitting it is a problem resembling scavenging. "Dont worry about your husband," I said. "Just say I represent Jefferson and so Flem Snopes is my burden too. You see, the least I can do is to match you: to value him as highly as your coming here proves you do. Goodnight."

"Goodnight," she said. The cold invisible cloud leaned in again. Again I closed it.

SIX

V. K. RATLIFF

So next morning first thing we heard was that Judge
Dukinfield had recused his-self and designated Judge Stevens,
Lawyer's paw, to preside in his stead. And they ought to rung
the courthouse bell this time sholy, because whether or not it
was a matter of communal interest and urgency last night, it
was now. But it was to be in chambers this time and what
Judge Dukinfield called his chambers wouldn't a helt us. So
all we done this time was just to happen to be somewhere
about the Square, in the store doors or jest looking by chance
and accident out of the upstairs doctors' and suches' windows
while old man Job, that had been Judge Dukinfield's janitor
for longer than anybody in Jefferson, including Job and
Judge Dukinfield too, knowed, in a old cast-off tailcoat of
Judge Dukinfield's that he wore on Sundays, bustled in and
out of the little brick house back of the courthouse that Judge
Dukinfield called his chambers, sweeping and dusting it until
it suited him enough to let folks in it.

Then we watched Judge Stevens cross the Square from his
office and go through the door and then we watched the two
bonding fellers come out of the hotel and cross the Square
with their little lawyers' grips, the young one toting his own
grip but Samson, the hotel porter, walking behind the white
vest one toting his, and Samson's least boy walking behind
Samson toting what I reckon was the folded Memphis paper
the white vest one had been reading while they et breakfast
and they, except Samson and his boy, went in too. Then
Lawyer come up by his-self and went in, and sho enough before extra long we heard the car and then Mayor de Spain
druv up and parked and got out and says,

"Morning, Gentlemen. Any of you fellers looking for me?
Excuse me a minute while I step inside and pass good morning with our out-of-town guests and I'll be right with you."
Then he went in too and that was about all: Judge Stevens
setting behind the desk with his glasses on and the paper

open in his hand, and the two bonding fellers setting quiet and polite and anxious across from him, and Lawyer setting at one end of the table and Manfred de Spain that hadn't even set down: jest leaning against the wall with his hands in his pockets and that-ere dont-give-a-durn face of hisn already full of laughing even though it hadn't moved yet. Until Judge Stevens folded the paper up slow and deliberate and laid it to one side and taken off his glasses and folded them too and then laid his hands one in the other on the desk in front of him and says:

"The plaintiff in this suit has of this date withdrawn his charge and his bill of particulars. The suit—if it was a suit— no longer exists. The litigants—plaintiff, defendant and prisoner—if there was a prisoner—are discharged. With the Court's apologies to the gentlemen from Saint Louis that their stay among us was marred, and its hope and trust that their next one will not be. Court is adjourned. Good morning, gentlemen," and the two bonding fellers got up and begun to thank Judge Stevens for a little spell, until they stopped and taken up their grips and kind of tiptoed out; and now there wasn't nobody but just Lawyer still setting with his paper-colored face bent a little and Judge Stevens still setting there not looking at nothing in particular yet and Manfred de Spain still leaning with his feet crossed against the wall and his face still full of that laughing that was still jest waiting for a spell too. Then Judge Stevens was looking at him.

"Manfred," he says. "Do you want to resign?"

"Certainly, sir," De Spain says. "I'll be glad to. But not for the city: for Gavin. I want to do it for Gavin. All he's got to do is say Please."

And still Lawyer didn't move: jest setting there with that still paper-colored face like it was froze stiff and his hands too laying on the table in front of him: not clenched one inside the other like his paw's: jest laying there. Then Manfred begun to laugh, not loud, not even in no hurry: jest standing there laughing with his feet still crossed and his hands still in his pockets, jest laughing even while he turned and went across to the door and opened it and went out and closed it behind him. Which jest left Lawyer and his paw and that was when Lawyer said it.

"So you dont want him not to be mayor," Judge Stevens says. "Then what is it you do want? for him not to be alive? Is that it?"

That was when Lawyer said it: "What must I do now, Papa? Papa, what can I do now?"

So something happened somewhere between that board of aldermen meeting last night and that special court session this morning. Except that if we ever knowed what it was, it wasn't going to be Lawyer's fault. I mean, we might a knowed or anyway had a good idea what happened and where while them lights was burning in that upstairs office long after ever body else in Jefferson had done went home to bed; some day Lawyer his-self might tell it, probably would, would have to tell it to somebody jest to get some rest from it. What we wouldn't know would be jest how it happened. Because when Lawyer come to tell it, he wouldn't be having to tell what happened: he would be having to tell, to say, it wouldn't much matter what, to somebody, anybody listening, it wouldn't much matter who.

The only one of the whole three of them that understood her, was Flem. Because needing or expecting to understand one another hadn't never occurred between her and Manfred de Spain. All the understanding one another they needed was you might say for both of them to agree on when and where next and jest how long away it would have to be. But apart from that, they never no more needed to waste time understanding one another than sun and water did to make rain. They never no more needed to be drawed together than sun and water needed to be. In fact, most of Manfred's work had already been done for him by that boy back in Frenchman's Bend—McCarron, who except that he come first, could a been Manfred's younger brother; who never even lived in Frenchman's Bend and nobody in Frenchman's Bend ever seen or heard of him before that summer, like he had been sent through Frenchman's Bend at the one exact moment to see her, like you might say Manfred de Spain had been sent through Jefferson at the one exact moment to see her.

And a heap of McCarron's work already done for him too because she done it: that night when them five Frenchman's

Bend boys laid for them and bushwacked them in the buggy
to drag him out of it and maybe beat him up or anyhow skeer
him out of Frenchman's Bend. And gradually the tale come
out how, even with one arm broke, he fought them all off and
got the buggy turned around and got her back home all safe
except for a natural maiden swoon. Which aint quite right.
Because them five boys (I knowed two of them) never told it,
which you might say is proof. That after they broke his arm it
was her that taken the loaded end of the buggy-whip and finished the last one or maybe two, and her that turned the
buggy around in the road and got it away from there. Jest far
enough; not back home yet: jest far enough; to as the feller
says crown the triumph on the still-hot field of the triumph;
right there on the ground in the middle of the dark road because somebody had to still hold that skeered horse, with the
horse standing over them and her likely having to help hold
him up too off of that broke arm; not jest her first time but
the time she got that baby. Which folks says aint likely to happen jest the first time but between what did happen and what
ought to happened, I dont never have trouble picking ought.

But Lawyer Stevens never understood her and never would:
that he never had jest Manfred de Spain to have to cope with,
he was faced with a simple natural force repeating itself under
the name of De Spain or McCarron or whatever into ever gap
or vacancy in her breathing as long as she breathed; and that
wouldn't never none of them be him. And he never did realise that she understood him because she never had no way
of telling him because she didn't know herself how she done
it. Since women learn at about two or three years old and
then forget it, the knowledge about their-selves that a man
stumbles on by accident forty-odd years later with the same
kind of startled amazement of finding a twenty-five cent piece
in a old pair of britches you had started to throw away. No,
they dont forget it: they jest put it away until ten or twenty or
forty years later the need for it comes up and they reach
around and pick it out and use it and then hang it up again
without no more remembering just which one it was than she
could remember today which finger it was she scratched with
yesterday: only that tomorrow maybe she will itch again but
she will find something to scratch that one with too.

Or I dont know, maybe he did understand all that and maybe he did get what he wanted. I mean, not what he wanted but what he knew he could have, the next best, like any thing is better than nothing, even if that anything is jest a next-best anything. Because there was more folks among the Helens and Juliets and Isoldes and Guineveres than jest the Launcelots and Tristrams and Romeos and Parises. There was them others that never got their names in the poetry books, the next-best ones that sweated and panted too. And being the next-best to Paris is jest a next-best too, but it aint no bad next-best to be. Not ever body had Helen, but then not ever body lost her neither.

So I kind of happened to be at the deepo that day when Lucius Hogganbeck's jitney drove up and Lawyer got out with his grips and trunk and his ticket to Mottstown junction to catch the express from Memphis to New York and get on the boat that would take him to that German university he had been talking for two years now about what a good idea it would be to go to it providing you happened to want to go to a university in Germany like that one; until that morning yesterday or maybe it was the day before when he told his paw: "What must I do now, Papa? Papa, what can I do now?" It was still cold so he taken his sister on into the waiting room and then he come back out where I was.

"Good," he says, brisk and chipper as you could want. "I was hoping to see you before I left, to pass the torch on into your active hand. You'll have to hold the fort now. You'll have to tote the load."

"What fort?" I says. "What load?"

"Jefferson," he says. "Snopeses. Think you can handle them till I get back?"

"Not me nor a hundred of me," I says. "The only thing to do is get completely shut of them, abolish them."

"No no," he says. "Say a herd of tigers suddenly appears in Yoknapatawpha County; wouldn't it be a heap better to have them shut up in a mule-pen where we could at least watch them, keep up with them, even if you do lose a arm or a leg ever time you get within ten feet of the wire, than to have them roaming and strolling loose all over ever where in the entire country? No, we got them now; they're ourn now; I dont know jest what Jefferson could a committed back there whenever it was, to have won this punishment, gained this right, earned this privilege. But we did. So it's for us to cope, to resist; us to endure, and (if we can) survive."

"But why me?" I says. "Why out of all Jefferson pick on me?"

"Because you're the only one in Jefferson I can trust," Lawyer says.

Except that that one dont really ever lose Helen, because for the rest of her life she dont never actively get rid of him. Likely it's because she dont want to.

SEVEN

C HARLES MALLISON
I remember how Ratliff once said that the world's Helens never really lose forever the men who once loved and lost them; probably because they—the Helens—dont want to.

I still wasn't born when Uncle Gavin left for Heidelberg so as far as I know his hair had already begun to turn white when I first saw him. Because although I was born by then, I couldn't remember him when he came home from Europe in the middle of the War, to get ready to go back to it. He said that at first, right up to the last minute, he believed that as soon as he finished his Ph.D. he was going as a stretcher-bearer with the German army; almost up to the last second before he admitted to himself that the Germany he could have loved that well had died somewhere between the Liège and Namur forts and the year 1848. Or rather, the Germany which had emerged between 1848 and the Belgian forts he did not love since it was no longer the Germany of Goethe and Bach and Beethoven and Schiller. This is what he said hurt, was hard to admit, to admit even after he reached Amsterdam and could begin to really ask about the American Field Service of which he had heard.

But he said how we—America—were not used yet to European wars and still took them seriously; and there was the fact that he had been for two years a student in a German university. But the French were different: to whom another Germanic war was just the same old chronic nuisance; a nation of practical and practising pessimists who were willing to let anyone regardless of his politics, who wanted to, do any-thing—particularly one who was willing to do it free. So he—Uncle Gavin—spent those five months with his stretcher just behind Verdun and presently was himself in a bed in an American hospital until he got over the pneumonia and could come home, in Jefferson again, waiting, he said, until we were in it, which would not be long.

And he was right: the Sartoris boys, Colonel Sartoris's twin

grandsons, had already gone to England into the Royal Flying
Corps and then it was April and then Uncle Gavin had his appointment as a Y.M.C.A. secretary, to go back to France with
the first American troops; when suddenly there was Montgomery Ward Snopes, the first of what Ratliff called "them
big gray-colored chaps of I.O.'s", the one whose mamma was
still rocking in the chair in the front window of the Snopes
Hotel because it was still too cold yet to move back onto the
front gallery. And Jackson McLendon had organised his
Jefferson company and had been elected captain of it and
Montgomery Ward could have joined them. But instead he
came to Uncle Gavin, to go to France with Uncle Gavin in
the Y.M.C.A.; and that was when Ratliff said what he did
about sometimes the men that loved and lost Helen of Troy
just thought they had lost her. Only he could have added, All
her kinfolks too. Because Uncle Gavin did it. I mean, took
Montgomery Ward.

"Confound it, Lawyer," Ratliff said. "It's a Snopes."

"Certainly," Uncle Gavin said. "Can you suggest a better
place for a Snopes today than north-western France? as far
west of Amiens and Verdun as you can get him?"

"But why?" Ratliff said.

"I thought of that too," Uncle Gavin said. "If he had said
he wanted to go in order to defend his country, I would have
had Hub Hampton handcuff him hand and foot in jail and sit
on him while I telephoned Washington. But what he said was,
'They're going to pass a law soon to draft us all anyhow, and
if I go with you like you're going, I figger I'll get there first
and have time to look around'."

"To look around," Ratliff said. He and Uncle Gavin looked
at one another. Ratliff blinked two or three times.

"Yes," Uncle Gavin said. Ratliff blinked two or three times
again.

"To look around," he said.

"Yes," Uncle Gavin said. And Uncle Gavin took Montgomery Ward Snopes with him and that was the exact
time when Ratliff said about the folks that thought they had
finally lost Helen of Troy. But Gowan was still living with us;
maybe because of the war in Europe the State Department
still hadn't let his mother and father come back from China

or wherever it was yet; at least once every week on the way home across the Square he would meet Ratliff, almost like Ratliff was waiting for him, and Gowan would tell Ratliff the news from Uncle Gavin and Ratliff would say:

"Tell him to watch close. Tell him I'm doing the best I can here."

"The best you can what?" Gowan said.

"Holding and toting," Ratliff said.

"Holding and toting what?" Gowan said. That was when Gowan said he first noticed that you didn't notice Ratliff hardly at all, until suddenly you did or anyway Gowan did. And after that, he began to look for him. Because the next time, Ratliff said:

"How old are you?"

"Seventeen," Gowan said.

"Then of course your aunt lets you drink coffee," Ratliff said. "What do you say——"

"She's not my aunt, she's my cousin," Gowan said. "Sure. I drink coffee. I dont specially like it. Why?"

"I like a occasional ice cream cone myself," Ratliff said.

"What's wrong with that?" Gowan said.

"What say me and you step in the drugstore here and have a ice cream cone?" Ratliff said. So they did. Gowan said Ratliff always had strawberry when they had it, and that he could expect Ratliff almost any afternoon now and now Gowan said he was in for it, he would have to eat the cone whether he wanted it or not, he and Ratliff now standing treat about, until finally Ratliff said, already holding the pink-topped cone in his brown hand:

"This here is jest about as pleasant a invention as any I know about. It's so pleasant a feller jest dont dare risking getting burnt-out on it. I cant imagine no tragedy worse than being burnt-out on strawberry ice cream. So what you say we jest make this a once-a-week habit and the rest of the time jest swapping news?"

So Gowan said all right and after that they would just meet in passing and Gowan would give Ratliff Uncle Gavin's last message: "He says to tell you he's doing the best he can too but that you were right: just one aint enough. One what?" Gowan said. "Aint enough for what?" But then Gowan was

seventeen; he had a few other things to do, whether grown
people believed it or not, though he didn't object to delivering the messages Mother said Uncle Gavin sent in his letters
to Ratliff, when he happened to see Ratliff, or that is when
Ratliff saw, caught him, which seemed to be almost every day
so that he wondered just when Ratliff found time to earn a
living. But he didn't always listen to all Ratliff would be saying at those times, so that afterward he couldn't even say just
how it was or when that Ratliff put it into his mind and he
even got interested in it like a game, a contest or even a
battle, a war, that Snopeses had to be watched constantly like
an invasion of snakes or wild cats and that Uncle Gavin and
Ratliff were doing it or trying to because nobody else in
Jefferson seemed to recognise the danger. So that winter
when the draft finally came and got Byron Snopes out of
Colonel Sartoris's bank, Gowan knew exactly what Ratliff was
talking about when he said:

"I dont know how he will do it but I will lay a million to
one he dont never leave the United States; I will lay a hundred to one he wont get further away from Mississippi than
that first fort over in Arkansas where they first sends them;
and if you will give me ten dollars I will give you eleven if he
aint back here in Jefferson in three weeks." Gowan didn't do
it but he said later he wished he had because Ratliff would
have lost by two days and so Byron was back in the bank
again. But we didn't know how and even Ratliff never found
out how he did it until after he had robbed the bank and escaped to Mexico, because Ratliff said the reason Snopeses
were successful was that they had all federated unanimously to
remove being a Snopes from just a zoological category into a
condition composed of success by means of the single rule
and regulation and sacred oath of never to tell anybody how.
The way Byron did it was to go to bed every night with a
fresh plug of chewing tobacco taped into his left armpit until
it ran his heart up to where the army doctors finally discharged him and sent him home.

So at least there was some fresh Snopes news to send Uncle
Gavin, which was when Ratliff noticed that it had been
months since Uncle Gavin had mentioned Montgomery Ward
Snopes. Though by the time Uncle Gavin's letter got back

saying *Dont mention that name to me again. I wont discuss it. I will not* we had some fresh Snopes news of our own to send him.

This time it was Eck. "Your uncle was right," Ratliff said.

"He's my cousin, I tell you," Gowan said.

"All right, all right," Ratliff said. "Eck wasn't a Snopes. That's why he had to die. Like there wasn't no true authentic room for Snopeses in the world and they made their-selves one by that pure and simple mutual federation, and the first time one slips or falters or fails in being Snopes, it dont even need the rest of the pack like wolves to finish him: simple environment jest watched its chance and taken it."

Eck was the one with the steel brace where a log broke his neck one time, the night watchman of the oil company's storage tank at the depot; I knew about this myself because I was almost four years old now. It was just dust-dark; we were at supper when there came a tremendous explosion, the loudest sound at one time that Jefferson ever heard, so loud that we all knew it couldn't be anything else but that German bomb come at last that we—Mayor de Spain anyway—had been looking for ever since the Germans sank the Lusitania and we finally had to get into the war too. That is, Mayor de Spain had gone to West Point and had been a lieutenant in Cuba and when this one started he wanted to get into it too. But he couldn't maybe so he tried to organise a Home Guard company, except that nobody but him took it very seriously. But at least he had an alarm system to ring the courthouse bell when a German attack came.

So when that tremendous big sound went off and the bell began to ring, we all knew what it was and we were all waiting for the next one to fall, until the people running out into the street hollering "Which way was it?" finally located it down toward the depot. It was the oil storage tank. It was a big round tank, about thirty feet long and ten feet deep, sitting on brick trestles. That is, it had been there because there wasn't anything there now, not even the trestles. Then about that time they finally got Mrs Nunnery to hush long enough to tell what happened.

She was Cedric Nunnery's mamma. He was about five years old. They lived in a little house just up the hill from the depot

and finally they made her sit down and somebody gave her a
drink of whiskey and she quit screaming and told how about
five oclock she couldn't find Cedric anywhere and she came
down to where Mr Snopes was sitting in his chair in front of
the little house about the size of a privy that he called the office where he night watched the tank, to ask him if he had
seen Cedric. He hadn't but he got up right away to help her
hunt, in all the box cars on the side track and in the freight
warehouse and everywhere, hollering Cedric's name all
around; only Mrs Nunnery didn't remember which of them
thought of the oil tank first. Likely it was Mr Snopes since he
was the one that knew it was empty, though probably Mrs
Nunnery had seen the ladder too still leaning against it where
Mr Snopes had climbed up to open the manhole in the top to
let fresh air come in and drive the gas out.

And likely Mr Snopes thought all the gas was out by now,
though they probably both must have figured there would
still be enough left to fix Cedric when he climbed down inside. Because Mrs Nunnery said that's where they both
thought Cedric was and that he was dead; she said she was so
sure that she couldn't even bear to wait and see, she was
already running—not running anywhere: just running—when
Mr Snopes came out of his little office with the lighted
lantern and still running while he was climbing up the ladder
and still running when he swung the lantern over into the
manhole; that is she said she was still running when the explosion (she said she never even heard it, she never heard anything, or she would have stopped) knocked her down and the
air all around her whizzing with pieces of the tank like a
swarm of bumble bees. And Mr Harker from the power-plant
that got there first and found her, said she begun to try to run
again as soon as he picked her up, shrieking and screaming
and thrashing around while they held her, until she sat down
and drank the whiskey and the rest of them walked and
hunted around among the scattered bricks from the trestles,
still trying to find some trace of Cedric and Mr Snopes, until
Cedric came at a dead run up the track from where he had
been playing in a culvert about a half a mile away when he
heard the explosion.

But they never did find Mr Snopes until the next morning

when Tom Tom Bird, the day fireman at the power-plant, on his way in to work from where he lived about two miles down the track, saw something hanging in the telegraph wires about two hundred yards from where the tank had been and got a long pole and punched it down and when he showed it to Mr Harker at the plant, it was Mr Snopes's steel neck-brace though none of the leather was left.

But they never did find anything of Mr Snopes, who was a good man, everybody liked him, sitting in his chair beside the office door where he could watch the tank or walking around the tank when he would let the coal oil run into the cans and drums and delivery tanks, with his neck and head stiff in the steel brace so he couldn't turn his head at all: he would have to turn all of himself like turning a wooden post. All the boys in town knew him because pretty soon they all found out that he kept a meal sack full of raw peanuts from the country and would holler to any of them that passed and give them a handful.

Besides, he was a Mason too. He had been a Mason such a long time that he was a good one even if he wasn't very high up in it. So they buried the neck-brace anyway, in a coffin all regular, with the Masons in charge of the funeral, and more people than you would have thought sent flowers, even the oil company too although Mr Snopes had ruined their tank for nothing because Cedric Nunnery wasn't even in it.

So they buried what they did have of him; there was the Baptist preacher too, and the Masons in their aprons dropping a pinch of dirt into the grave and saying "Alas my brother", and covered the raw red dirt with the flowers (one of the flower pieces had the Mason signs worked into it); and the tank was insured so when the oil company got through cussing Mr Snopes for being a grown man with no more sense than that, they even gave Mrs Snopes a thousand dollars to show they were sorry for her even if she had married a fool. That is, they gave the money to Mrs Snopes because their oldest boy, Wallstreet, wasn't but sixteen then. But he was the one that used it.

But that came later. All that happened now was that Mayor de Spain finally got to be a commanding officer long enough to ring his alarm bell at least, and we had some more fresh

Snopes news to send Uncle Gavin. By 'we' I mean me now.
Gowan's mother and father had finally got home from China
or wherever it was and now Gowan was in Washington (it was
fall) for the last year anyway at the prep school getting ready
for the University of Virginia next year and one afternoon
Mother sent for me, into the parlor, and there was Ratliff in
his neat faded blue tieless shirt and his smooth brown face, in
the parlor like company (there was a tea tray and Ratliff had a
teacup and a cucumber sandwich and I know now there were
a lot of people in Jefferson, let alone in the county where
Ratliff came from, that wouldn't have known what to do with
a cup of tea at four oclock in the afternoon and maybe Ratliff
never saw one before then either but you couldn't have told
it by watching him) and Mother said,

"Make your manners to Mister Ratliff, bub. He's come to
call on us," and Ratliff said,

"Is that what you call him?" and Mother said,

"No, we just call him whatever is handy yet," and Ratliff
said,

"Sometimes fellers named Charles gets called Chick when
they gets to school." Then he said to me: "Do you like strawberry ice cream cones?" and I said,

"I like any kind of ice cream cones," and Ratliff said:

"Then maybe your cousin—" and stopped and said to
Mother: "Excuse me, Miz Mallison; I done been corrected so
many times that it looks like it may take me a spell yet." So
after that it was me and Ratliff instead of Gowan and Ratliff,
only instead of two cones it cost Ratliff three now because
when I went to town without Mother, Aleck Sander was with
me. And I dont know how Ratliff did it and of course I cant
remember when because I wasn't even five yet. But he had put
into my mind too, just like into Gowan's, that idea of
Snopeses covering Jefferson like an influx of snakes or varmints
from the woods and he and Uncle Gavin were the only ones
to recognise the danger and the threat and now he was having
to tote the whole load by himself until they would finally stop
the war and Uncle Gavin could get back home and help. "So
you might just as well start listening now," he said, "whether
you aint but five or not. You're going to have to hear a heap
of it before you get old enough or big enough to resist."

It was November. Then that day, the courthouse bell rang again and all the church bells too this time, wild and frantic too in the middle of the week from the Sunday steeples and a few shotguns and pistols too like the old veterans that were still alive when they unveiled the Confederate monument that day except that the ones this time hadn't been to a war yet so maybe what they were celebrating this time was that this one finally got over before they had to go to it. So now Uncle Gavin could come home where Ratliff himself could ask him what Montgomery Ward Snopes had done that his name must not be mentioned or discussed. That was when Ratliff told me, "You might as well get used to hearing it even if you aint but five." That was when he said: "What do you reckon it was he done? Your cousin has been watching Snopeses for going on ten years now; he even taken one all the way to France with him to keep his-self abreast and up-to-date. What you reckon a Snopes could a done after ten years to shock and startle him so much he couldn't bear even to discuss it?"

Or this was when he meant it because when Uncle Gavin came home it was for only two weeks. He was out of the uniform, the army, the Y.M.C.A. now but as soon as he was out they put him into some kind of board or committee or bureau for war rehabilitation in Europe because he had lived in Europe all that time, especially the two years as a student in Germany. And possibly the only reason he came home at all was that Grandfather had died during the last year of the war and he came home to see us as people do in bereavement. Though I believed then that the reason he came was to tell Ratliff what it was about Montgomery Ward Snopes that was too bad to write on paper. Which was when Ratliff said about all the listening I would have to do, meaning that with him, Ratliff, alone again to tote the load, anyway I could do that much.

It was one day; sometimes Mother let me go to town by myself now. I mean, when she wasn't noticing enough to say Come back here. No: I mean, when she found out I had now she didn't jump on me too hard.—it was one day, Ratliff's voice said, "Come here." He had traded off his buckboard and team and now he had a Model T, with the little painted house with the sewing machine in it fastened to the back in place of a back seat; what they call pickup trucks now though Ratliff and Uncle Noon Gatewood had made this one. He was sitting in it with the door already open and I got in and he shut the door and we drove right slow along the back streets around the edge of town. "How old did you say you was?" he said. I told him again: five. "Well, we cant help that, can we?"

"Cant help what?" I said. "Why?"

"Come to think of it, maybe you're right at that," he said. "So all we got to do now is jest take a short ride. So what happened to Montgomery Ward Snopes was, he quit the fighting army and went into business."

"What business?" I said.

"The . . . canteen business. Yes, the canteen business. That's what he done while he was with your cousin. They was at a town named Châlons, only your cousin had to stay in the town to run the office, so he give Montgomery Ward, since he had the most spare time, the job of running the canteen at another little town not far away that would be more convenient for the soldiers—a kind of a shack with counters like a store where soldiers could buy the candy bars and sody pop and hand-knitted socks like your cousin told us about that time last week when they wasn't busy fighting, you remember? Except that after a while Montgomery Ward's canteen got to be jest about the most popular canteen the army or even the Y.M.C.A. either ever had in France or anywhere else; it got so popular that finally your cousin went his-self and looked at it and found that Montgomery Ward had cut off the back end and fixed it up as a new fresh entertainment room with a door in the back and a young French lady he happened to know in it, so that any time a soldier got tired of jest buying socks or eating chocolate bars he could buy a ticket from Montgomery Ward and go around through the back door and get his-self entertained.

"That was what your cousin found out. Only the army and the Y.M.C.A. had some kind of a rule against entertainment; they figgered that a soldier ought to be satisfied jest buying socks and sody pop in a canteen. Or maybe it was your cousin; likely it was him. Because if the army and the Y.M.C.A. had found out about that back room, they would a

fired Montgomery Ward so hard he would likely a come back
to Jefferson in handcuffs—providing he never stopped off at
Leavenworth, Kansas, first. Which reminds me of something I
may have said to your other cousin Gowan once when likely
you wasn't present: about how some of the folks that lost
Helen of Troy might someday wish they hadn't never found
her to begin with."

"Why?" I said. "Where was I if I wasn't there then?"

"It was your cousin. Montgomery Ward might have even
saved enough out of the back-room entertainment tickets to
bought his-self out of it. But he never needed to. He had
your cousin. He was the hair-shirt of your cousin's lost love
and devotion, whether he knowed it or not or cared or not.
Or maybe it was Jefferson. Maybe your cousin couldn't bear
the idea of Jefferson being represented in Leavenworth prison
even for the reward of one Snopes less in Jefferson itself. So
likely it was him, and afterwards saying, 'But dont never let
me see your face again in France.'

"That is, dont never bring your face to me again. Because
Montgomery Ward was the hair-shirt; likely your cousin taken
the same kind of proud abject triumphant submissive horror
in keeping up with his doings that them old hermits setting
on rocks out in the hot sun in the desert use to take watching their blood dry up and their legs swivelling, keeping up
from a distance while Montgomery Ward added more and
more entertaining ladies to that-ere new canteen he set up in
Paris—"

"They have chocolate bars and soda pop in canteens," I
said. "Uncle Gavin said so. Chewing gum too."

"That was the American army," Ratliff said. "They had
been in the war such a short time that likely they hadn't got
used to it yet. This new canteen of Montgomery Ward's was
you might say a French canteen, with only private American
military connections. The French have been in enough wars
long enough to find out that the best way to get shut of one
is not to pay too much attention to it. In fact the French
probably thought the kind of canteen Montgomery Ward was
running this time was just about the most solvent and eco-
nomical and you might say self-perpetuating kind he could a
picked out, since, no matter how much money you swap for

ice cream and chocolate candy and sody pop, even though the money still exists, that candy and ice cream and sody pop dont anymore because it has been consumed and will cost some of that money to produce and replenish, where in jest strict entertainment there aint no destructive consumption at all that's got to be replenished at a definite production labor cost: only a normal natural general overall depreciation which would have took place anyhow."

"Maybe Montgomery Ward wont come back to Jefferson," I said.

"If I was him, I wouldn't," Ratliff said.

"Unless he can bring the canteen with him," I said.

"In that case I sholy wouldn't," Ratliff said.

"Is it Uncle Gavin you keep on talking about?" I said.

"I'm sorry," Ratliff said.

"Then why dont you say so?" I said.

"I'm sorry," Ratliff said. "Your uncle. It was your cousin Gowan (I'm right this time, aint I?) got me mixed up but I'll remember now. I promise it."

Montgomery Ward didn't come home for two years. Though I had to be older than that before I understood what Ratliff meant when he said Montgomery Ward had done the best he knew to bring an acceptable Mississippi version of his Paris canteen back home with him. He was the last Yoknapatawpha soldier to return. One of Captain McLendon's company was wounded in the first battle in which American troops were engaged and was back in uniform with his wound stripe in 1918. Then early in 1919 the rest of the company except two dead from flu and a few in hospital, were all home again to wear their uniforms too around the Square for a little while. Then in May one of Colonel Sartoris's twin grandsons (the other one had been shot down in July last year) got home from the British Air Force though he didn't have on a uniform at all: just a big low-slung racing car that made the little red E.M.F. that Mayor de Spain used to own look like a toy, driving it fast around town between the times when Mr Connors would have to arrest him for speeding, but mostly about once a week back and forth to Memphis while he was getting settled down again. That is, that's what Mother said he was trying to do.

Only he couldn't seem to either, like the war had been too much for him too. I mean, Montgomery Ward Snopes couldn't seem to settle down enough from it to come back home, and Bayard Sartoris came home all right but he couldn't settle down, driving the car so fast between Sartoris Station and Jefferson that finally Colonel Sartoris, who hated automobiles almost as much as Grandfather did, who wouldn't even lend the bank's money to a man who was going to buy one, gave up the carriage and the matched team, to ride back and forth into town with Bayard in the car, in hopes that maybe that would make Bayard slow it down before he killed himself or somebody else.

So when Bayard finally did kill somebody, as we (all Yoknapatawpha County grown folks) all expected he would, it was his grandfather. Because we didn't know that either: that Colonel Sartoris had a heart condition; Doctor Peabody had told him that three years ago, and that he had no business in an automobile at all. But Colonel Sartoris hadn't told anybody else, not even his sister, Mrs Du Pre that kept house for him: just riding in that car back and forth to town every day to keep Bayard slowed down (they even managed somehow to persuade Miss Narcissa Benbow to marry him in hopes maybe that would settle him down) until that morning they came over a hill at about fifty miles an hour and there was a Negro family in a wagon in the road and Bayard said, "Hold on, Grandfather," and turned the car off into the ditch; it didn't turn over or even wreck very bad: just stopped in the ditch with Colonel Sartoris still sitting in it with his eyes still open.

So now his bank didn't have a president anymore. Then we found out just who owned the stock in it: that Colonel Sartoris and Major de Spain, Mayor de Spain's father until he died, had owned two of the three biggest blocks, and old man Will Varner out in Frenchman's Bend owned the other one. So we thought that maybe it wasn't just Colonel Sartoris's father's cavalry command that got Byron Snopes his job in the bank, but maybe old Will Varner had something to do with it too. Except that we never really believed that since we knew Colonel Sartoris well enough to know that any single one of those old cavalry raids or even just one night around a bivouac fire would have been enough.

Of course there was more of it, that much again and even more scattered around in a dozen families like the Compsons and Benbows and Peabodys and Miss Eunice Habersham and us and a hundred others that were farmers around in the county. Though it wasn't until Mayor de Spain got elected president of it to succeed Colonel Sartoris (in fact, because of that) that we found out that Mr Flem Snopes had been buying the stock in lots anywhere from one to ten shares for several years; this, added to Mr Varner's and Mayor de Spain's own that he had inherited from his father, would have been enough to elect him up from vice president to president (There was so much going on that we didn't even notice that when the dust finally settled Mr Flem Snopes would be vice president of it too.) even if Mrs Du Pre and Bayard's wife (Bayard had finally got himself killed testing an aeroplane at an Ohio testing field that they said nobody else would fly and that Bayard himself didn't have any business in) hadn't voted theirs for him.

Because Mayor de Spain resigned from being mayor and sold his automobile agency and became president of the bank just in time. Colonel Sartoris's bank was a national bank because Ratliff said likely Colonel Sartoris knew that would sound safer to country folks with maybe an extra ten dollars to risk in a bank, let alone the female widows and orphans since females never had much confidence in menfolks' doings about anything, let alone money, even when they were not widows too. So with a change of presidents like that, Ratliff said the government would have to send somebody to inspect the books even if the regular inspection wasn't about due; the two auditors waiting in front of the bank at eight oclock that morning for somebody to unlock the door and let them in, which would have been Byron Snopes except that he didn't show up. So they had to wait for the next one with a key: which was Mr de Spain.

And by fifteen minutes after eight, which was about thirteen minutes after the auditors decided to start on the books that Byron kept, Mr de Spain found out from the Snopes hotel that nobody had seen Byron since the south-bound train at nine twenty-two last night, and by noon everybody knew that Byron was probably already in Texas though he probably wouldn't reach Mexico itself for another day yet. Though it was not until two days later that the head auditor was ready to commit himself roughly as to how much money was missing; by that time they had called a meeting of the bank's board of directors and even Mr Varner that Jefferson never saw once in twelve months, had come in and listened to the head auditor for about a minute and then said, "Police hell. Send somebody out home for my pistol, then show me which way he went."

Which wasn't anything to the uproar Mr de Spain himself was making, with all this time all Jefferson watching and listening, until on the third day Ratliff said, though I didn't know what he meant then: "That's how much it was, was it? At least we know now jest how much Miz Flem Snopes is worth. Now your uncle wont need to worry about how much he lost when he gets home because now he can know exactly to the last decimal how much he saved." Because the bank itself was all right. It was a national bank so whatever money Byron stole would be guaranteed whether they caught Byron or not. We were watching Mr de Spain. Since his father's money had helped Colonel Sartoris start it and Mr de Spain had himself been vice president of it, even if he had not been promoted president of it just ahead of when the auditors decided to look at Byron Snopes's books, we believed he would still have insisted on making good every cent of the money. What we expected to hear was that he had mortgaged his home, and when we didn't hear that, we just thought that he had made money out of his automobile agency that was saved up and put away that we didn't know about. Because we never expected anything else of him; when the next day they called another sudden meeting of the board of directors and announced the day after that that the stolen money had been made good by the voluntary personal efforts of the president, we were not even surprised. As Ratliff said, we were so unsurprised in fact that it was two or three days before anybody seemed to notice how at the same time they announced that Mr Flem Snopes was now the new vice president of it.

And now, it was another year, the last two Jefferson soldiers came home for good or anyway temporarily for good: Uncle Gavin finally come back from rehabilitating war-torn Europe

to get elected County Attorney, and a few months later,
Montgomery Ward Snopes too except that he was the temporarily for good one. Like Bayard Sartoris, he wasn't in uniform either but in a black suit and a black overcoat without
any sleeves and a black thing on his head kind of drooping
over one side like an empty cow's bladder made out of black
velvet, and a long limp-ended bow tie; and his hair long and
he had a beard and now there was another Snopes business in
Jefferson. It had a name on the window that Ratliff didn't
know either and when I went up to the office where Uncle
Gavin was waiting for the first of the year to start being
County Attorney and told him, he sat perfectly still for a good
two seconds and then got up already walking. "Show me," he
said.

So we went back to where Ratliff was waiting for us. It was
a store on the corner by an alley, with a side door on the alley; the painter was just finishing the curlicue letters on the
glass window that said

Atelier Monty

and inside, beyond the glass, Montgomery Ward still wearing
the French cap (Uncle Gavin said it was a Basque beret) but
in his shirt sleeves. Because we didn't go in then; Uncle Gavin
said, "Come on now. Let him finish it first." Except Ratliff.
He said,

"Maybe I can help him." But Uncle Gavin took hold of my
arm that time.

"If atelier means just a studio," I said, "why dont he call it
that?"

"Yes," Uncle Gavin said. "That's what I want to know
too." And even though Ratliff went in, he hadn't seen anything either. And he sounded just like me.

"Studio," he said. "I wonder why he dont just call it that?"

"Uncle Gavin didn't know either," I said.

"I know," Ratliff said. "I wasn't asking nobody yet. I was
jest kind of looking around for a place to jump." He looked at
me. He blinked two or three times. "Studio," he said. "That's
right, you aint even up that far yet. It's a photographing studio." He blinked again. "But why? His war record has done
already showed he aint a feller to be satisfied with no jest dull

run-of-the-mill mediocrity like us stay-at-homes back here in Yoknapatawpha County has to get used to."

But that was all we knew then. Because the next day he had newspapers fastened on the window so you couldn't see inside and he kept the door locked and all we ever saw would be the packages he would get out of the post office from Sears and Roebuck in Chicago and unlock the door long enough to take them inside.

Then on Thursday when the Clarion came out, almost half of the front page was the announcement of the formal opening, saying *Ladies Especially Invited*, and at the bottom: *Tea*. "What?" I said. "I thought it was going to be a studio."

"It is," Uncle Gavin said. "You get a cup of tea with it. Only he's wasting his money. All the women in town and half the men will go once just to see why he kept the door locked." Because Mother had already said she was going.

"Of course you wont be there," she told Uncle Gavin.

"All right," he said. "Most of the men then." He was right. Montgomery Ward had to keep the opening running all day long to take care of the people that came. He would have had to run it in sections even with the store empty like he rented it. But now it wouldn't have held hardly a dozen at a time, it was so full of stuff, with black curtains hanging all the way to the floor on all the walls that when you drew them back with a kind of pulley it would be like you were looking through a window at outdoors that he said one was the skyline of Paris and another was the Seine river bridges and ks whatever they are and another was the Eiffel tower and another Notre Dame, and sofas with black pillows and tables with vases and cups and something burning in them that made a sweet kind of smell; until at first you didn't hardly notice the camera. But finally you did, and a door at the back and Montgomery Ward said, he said it quick and he kind of moved quick, like he had already begun to move before he had time to decide that maybe he better not:

"That's the dark room. It's not open yet."

"I beg pardon?" Uncle Gavin said.

"That's the dark room," Montgomery Ward said. "It's not open yet."

"Are we expected to expect a dark room to be open to the

public?" Uncle Gavin said. But Montgomery Ward was already giving Mrs Rouncewell another cup of tea. Oh yes, there was a vase of flowers too; in the Clarion announcement of the opening it said *Flowers by Rouncewell* and I said to Uncle Gavin, where else in Jefferson would anybody get flowers except from Mrs Rouncewell? and he said she probably paid for half the advertisement, plus a vase containing six overblown roses left over from another funeral, that she will probably take out in trade. Then he said he meant her trade and he hoped he was right. Now he looked at the door a minute, then he looked at Montgomery Ward filling Mrs Rouncewell's cup. "Beginning with tea," he said.

We left then. We had to, to make room. "How can he afford to keep on giving away tea?" I said.

"He wont after today," Uncle Gavin said. "That was just bait, ladies' bait. Now I'll ask you one: why did he have to need all the ladies in Jefferson to come in one time and look at his joint?" And now he sounded just like Ratliff; he kind of happened to be coming out of the hardware store when we passed. "Had your tea yet?" Uncle Gavin said.

"Tea," Ratliff said. He didn't ask it. He just said it. He blinked at Uncle Gavin.

"Yes," Uncle Gavin said. "So do we. The dark room aint open yet."

"Ought it to be?" Ratliff said.

"Yes," Uncle Gavin said. "So did we."

"Maybe I can find out," Ratliff said.

"Do you even hope so?" Uncle Gavin said.

"Maybe I will hear about it," Ratliff said.

"Do you even hope so?" Uncle Gavin said.

"Maybe somebody else will find out about it and maybe I will be standing where I can hear him," Ratliff said.

And that was all. Montgomery Ward didn't give away any more cups of tea but after a while photographs did begin to appear in the show window, faces that we knew—ladies with and without babies and high school graduating classes and the prettiest girls in their graduation caps and gowns and now and then a couple just married from the country looking a little stiff and uncomfortable and just a little defiant and a narrow white line between his haircut and his sunburn; and now and then a couple that had been married fifty years that we had known all the time without really realising it until now how much alike they looked, not to mention being surprised, whether at being photographed or just being married that long.

And even when we begun to realise that not just the same faces but the same photographs of them had been in the same place in the window for over two years now, as if all of a sudden as soon as Montgomery Ward opened his atelier folks stopped graduating and getting married or staying married either, Montgomery Ward was still staying in business, either striking new pictures he didn't put in the window or maybe just selling copies of the old ones, to pay his rent and stay open. Because he was and maybe it was mostly dark room work because it was now that we begun to realise that most of his business was at night like he did need darkness, his trade seeming to be mostly men now, the front room where he had had the opening dark now and the customers going and coming through the side door in the alley; and them the kind of men you wouldn't hardly think it had ever occurred to them they might ever need to have their picture struck. And his business was spreading too; in the second summer we begun to find out how people—men, the same kind of usually young men that his Jefferson customers were—were beginning to come from the next towns around us to leave or pick up their prints and negatives or whatever it was, by that alley door at night.

"No no," Uncle Gavin told Ratliff. "It cant be that. You simply just cant do that in Jefferson."

"There's folks would a said you couldn't a looted a bank in Jefferson too," Ratliff said.

"But she would have to eat," Uncle Gavin said. "He would have to bring her out now and then for simple air and exercise."

"Out where?" I said. "Bring who out?"

"It cant be liquor," Ratliff said. "At least that first suh-jestion of yours would a been quiet, which you cant say about peddling whiskey."

"What first suggestion?" I said. "Bring who out?" Because it wasn't whiskey or gambling either; Grover Cleveland Winbush (the one that owned the other half of Ratliff's café until Mr Flem Snopes froze him out too. He was the night marshal now.) had thought of that himself. He came to Uncle Gavin before Uncle Gavin had even thought of sending for him or Mr Buck Connors either, and told Uncle Gavin that he had been spending a good part of the nights examining and watching and checking on the studio and he was completely satisfied there wasn't any drinking or peddling whiskey or dice-shooting or card-playing going on in Montgomery Ward's dark room; that we were all proud of the good name of our town and we all aimed to keep it free of any taint of big-city corruption and misdemeanor and nobody more than him. Until for hours at night when he could have been sitting comfortably in his chair in the police station waiting for the time to make his next round, he would be hanging around that studio without once hearing any suspicion of dice or drinking or any one of Montgomery Ward's customers to come out smelling or even looking like he had had a drink. In fact, Grover Cleveland said, once during the daytime while it was not only his legal right but his duty to his job to be home in bed asleep, just like it was right now while he was giving up his rest to come back to town to make this report to Uncle Gavin as County Attorney, even though he had no warrant, not to mention the fact that by rights this was a job that Buck Connors himself should have done, he—Grover Cleveland—walked in the front door with the aim of walking right on into the dark room even if he had to break the door to do it since the reason the people of Jefferson appointed him night marshal was to keep down big-city misdemeanor and corruption like gambling and drinking, when to his surprise Montgomery Ward not only didn't try to stop him, he didn't even wait to be asked but instead opened the dark room door himself and told Grover Cleveland to walk right in and look around.

So Grover Cleveland was satisfied, and he wanted the people of Jefferson to be too, that there was no drinking or gambling or any other corruption and misdemeanor going on in that back room that would cause the christian citizens of Jefferson to regret their confidence in appointing him night marshal which was his sworn duty to do even if he didn't take any more pride in Jefferson's good name than just an ordinary citizen, and any time he could do anything else for Uncle Gavin in the line of his sworn duty, for Uncle Gavin just to mention it. Then he went out, pausing long enough in the door to say:

"Howdy, V.K.," before going on. Then Ratliff came the rest of the way in.

"He come hipering across the Square and up the stairs like maybe he had found something," Ratliff said. "But I reckon not. I dont reckon Montgomery Ward Snopes would have no more trouble easing him out of that studio than Flem Snopes done easing him out of the rest of our café."

"No," Uncle Gavin said. He said: "What did Grover Cleveland like for fun back then?"

"For fun?" Ratliff said. Then he said: "Oh. He liked excitement."

"What excitement?" Uncle Gavin said.

"The excitement of talking about it," Ratliff said.

"Of talking about what?" Uncle Gavin said.

"Of talking about excitement," Ratliff said. He didn't quite look at me. No: he didn't quite not look at me. No, that's wrong too because even watching him you couldn't have said that he had ever stopped looking at Uncle Gavin. He blinked twice. "Female excitement," he said.

"All right," Uncle Gavin said. "How?"

"That's right," Ratliff said. "How?"

Because I was only eight now, going on nine, and if Uncle Gavin and Ratliff who were three times that and one of them had been all the way to Europe and back and the other had left at least one footprint in every back road and lane and turnrow too probably in Yoknapatawpha County, didn't know what it was until somebody came and told them, it wasn't any wonder that I didn't.

There was another what Ratliff called Snopes industry in town now too, though Uncle Gavin refused to call it that because he still refused to believe that Eck was ever a Snopes. It was Eck's boy, Wallstreet Panic, and from the way he began to act as soon as he reached Jefferson and could look around and I reckon find out for the first time in his life that you didn't actually have to act like a Snopes in order to breathe, whether his father was a Snopes or not he sure wasn't.

Because they said (he was about nine too when they moved in from Frenchman's Bend) how as soon as he got to town and found out about school, he not only made his folks let him go to it but he took his brother, Admiral Dewey who wasn't but six, with him, the two of them starting out together in the kindergarten where the mothers brought the little children who were not big enough yet to stay in one place more than just half a day, with Wallstreet Panic sticking up out of the middle of them like a horse in a duck-pond.

Because he wasn't ashamed to enter the kindergarten: he was just ashamed to stay in it, not staying in it himself much longer than a half a day because in a week he was in the first grade and by Christmas he was in the second and now Miss Vaiden Wyott who taught the second grade began to help him, telling him what Wallstreet Panic meant and that he didn't have to be named that, so that when she helped him pass the third grade by studying with her the next summer, when he entered the fourth grade that fall his name was just Wall Snopes because she told him that Wall was a good family name in Mississippi with even a general in it and that he didn't even need to keep the Street if he didn't want to. And he said from that first day and he kept right on saying it when people asked him why he wanted to go to school so hard: "I want to learn how to count money," so that when he heard about it, Uncle Gavin said:

"You see? That proves what I said exactly: no Snopes wants to learn how to count money because he doesn't have to because you will do that for him—or you had damn well better."

He, I mean Wall, was going to need to learn to count it. Even during that first winter while he was making up two grades he had a job. The store next to the Snopes café that they lived behind in the tent was a grocery store about the same class as the Snopes café. Every morning Wall would get up before schooltime, as the days got shorter he would get up in the dark, to build a fire in the iron stove and sweep out the store and as soon as he got back after school in the afternoon he would be the delivery boy too, using a wheel barrow until finally the owner of the store bought him a second-hand bicycle and took the money out of his pay each week.

And on Saturdays and holidays he would clerk in the store too, and all that summer while Miss Wyott was helping him pass the third grade; and even that wasn't enough: he got enough recommendations around the Square to get the delivery route for one of the Memphis papers, only by that time he was so busy with his other affairs that he made his brother the paper boy. And the next fall while he was in the fourth grade he managed to get a Jackson paper too and now he had two more boys besides Admiral Dewey working for him, so that by that time any merchant or stock-trader or revival preacher or candidate that wanted handbills put out always went to Wall because he had an organization already set up.

He could count money and save it too. So when he was sixteen and that empty oil tank blew his father away and the oil company gave Mrs Snopes the thousand dollars, about a month later we found out that Mrs Snopes had bought a half interest in the grocery store and Wall had graduated from high school by now and he was a partner in the store. Though he was still the one that got up before daylight on the winter mornings to start the fire and sweep. Then he was nineteen years old and his partner had sold the rest of the store to Mrs Snopes and retired, and even if because of Wall's age the store still couldn't be in his name, we knew who it really belonged to, with a hired boy of his own now to come before daylight on the winter mornings to build the fire and sweep.

And another one too, except that another Snopes industry wouldn't be the right word for this one, because there wasn't any profit in it. No, that's wrong; we worked at it too hard and Uncle Gavin says that anything people work at as hard as all of us did at this, has a profit, is for profit whether you can convert that profit into dollars and cents or not or even want to.

The last Snopes they brought into Jefferson didn't quite make it. I mean, this one came just so far, right up to in sight of the town clock in fact, and then refused to go any further; even, they said, threatening to go back to Frenchman's Bend, like an old cow or a mule that you finally get right up to the open gate of the pen, but not a step more.

He was the old one. Some folks said he was Mr Flem's father but some said he was just his uncle: a short thick dirty old man with fierce eyes under a tangle of eyebrows and a neck that would begin to swell and turn red before, as Ratliff said, you had barely had time to cross the first word with him. So they bought a little house for him about a mile from town, where he lived with an old maid daughter and the twin sons named Vardaman and Bilbo that belonged to I.O. Snopes's other wife, the one that Uncle Gavin called the Number Two wife that was different from the Number One one that rocked all day long on the front gallery of the Snopes hotel.

The house had a little piece of ground with it, that old man Snopes made into a truck garden and water-melon patch. The water-melon patch was the industry. No, that's wrong. Maybe I mean the industry took place because of the water-melon patch. Because it was like the old man didn't really raise the water-melons to sell or even just to be eaten, but as a bait for the pleasure or sport or contest or maybe just getting that mad, of catching boys robbing it; planting and cultivating and growing water-melons just so he could sit ambushed with a loaded shotgun behind a morning glory vine on his back gallery until he could hear sounds from the melon patch and then shooting at it.

Then one moonlight night he could see enough too and this time he actually shot John Wesley Roebuck with a load of squirrel shot, and the next morning Mr Hub Hampton, the sheriff, rode out there and told old Snopes that if he ever again let that shotgun off he would come back and take it away from him and throw him in jail to boot. So after that, old Snopes didn't dare use the gun. All he could do now was to stash away piles of rocks at different places along the fence, and just sit behind the vine with a heavy stick and a flashlight.

That was how the industry started. Mr Hampton had passed the word around town to all the mothers and fathers to tell their sons to stay out of that damned patch now; that any time they wanted a water-melon that bad, he, Mr Hampton, would buy them one, because if they kept on making old man Snopes that mad, someday he would burst a blood vessel and die and we would all be in jail. But old Snopes didn't know that because Vardaman and Bilbo didn't tell him. They would wait until he was in the house, lying down maybe to take a nap after dinner, when they would run in and wake him, yelling, hollering that some boys were in the patch, and he would jump up yelling and cursing and grab up the oak cudgel and go tearing out to the patch, and nobody in it or near it except Vardaman and Bilbo behind the corner of the house dying laughing, then dodging and running and still laughing while the old man scrabbled up his piled rocks to throw at them.

Because he never would catch on. No, that's wrong too: he always caught on. The trouble was, he didn't dare risk doing nothing when they would run in hollering "Grampaw! Grampaw! Chaps in the melon patch!" because it might be true. He would have to jump up and grab the stick and run out, knowing before hand he probably wouldn't find anybody there except Vardaman and Bilbo behind the corner of the house that he couldn't even catch, throwing the rocks and cursing them until he would give out of rocks and breath both, then standing there gasping and panting with his neck as red as a turkey gobbler's and without breath anymore to curse louder than whispering. That's what we—all the boys in Jefferson between six and twelve years old and sometimes even older—would go out there to hide behind the fence and watch. We never had seen anybody bust a blood vessel and die and we wanted to be there when it happened to see what it would look like.

This was after Uncle Gavin finally got home from rehabilitating Europe. We were crossing the Square when she passed us. I never could tell if she had looked at Uncle Gavin, though I know she never looked at me, let alone spoke when we passed. But then, that was all right; I didn't expect her either to or not to; sometimes she would speak to me but sometimes she never spoke to anybody and we were used to it. Like she did this time: just walking on past us exactly like a pointer dog walks just before it freezes onto the birds. Then I saw that Uncle Gavin had stopped and turned to look after her. But then I remembered he had been away since 1914 which was eight years ago now so she was only about five or six when he saw her last.

"Who is that?" he said.

"Linda Snopes," I said. "You know: Mr Flem Snopes's girl." And I was still watching her too. "She walks like a pointer," I said. "I mean, a pointer that's just——"

"I know what you mean," Uncle Gavin said. "I know exactly what you mean."

EIGHT

GAVIN STEVENS
I knew exactly what he meant. She was walking steadily toward us, completely aware of us, yet not once had she looked at either of us, the eyes not hard and fixed so much as intent, oblivious; fixed and unblinking on something past us, beyond us, behind us, as a young pointer will walk over you if you dont move out of the way, during the last few yards before the actual point, since now it no longer needs depend on clumsy and fumbling scent because now it is actually looking at the huddled trigger-set covey. She went past us still walking, striding, like the young pointer bitch, the maiden bitch of course, the virgin bitch, immune now in virginity, not scorning the earth, spurning the earth, because she needed it to walk on in that immunity: just intent from earth and us too, not proud and not really oblivious: just immune in intensity and ignorance and innocence as the sleepwalker is for the moment immune from the anguishes and agonies of breath.

She would be thirteen, maybe fourteen now and the reason I did not know her and would not have known her was not because I had possibly not seen her in eight years and human females change so drastically in the years between ten and fifteen. It was because of her mother. It was as though I—you too perhaps—could not have believed but that a woman like that must, could not other than, produce an exact replica of herself. That Eula Varner—You see? Eula *Varner*. Never Eula Snopes even though I had—had had to—watched them in bed together. Eula Snopes it could never be simply because it must not simply because I would decline to have it so.—that Eula Varner owed that much at least to the simple male hunger which she blazed into anguish just by being, existing, breathing; having been born, becoming born, becoming a part of Motion;—that hunger which she herself could never assuage since there was but one of her to match with all that hungering. And that single *one* doomed to fade; by the fact of that mortality doomed not to assuage nor even negate the hunger; doomed never to efface the anguish and the hunger from Motion even by her own act of quitting Motion and so fill with her own absence from it, the aching void where once had glared that incandescent shape.

That's what you thought at first, of course: that she must of necessity repeat herself, duplicate herself if she reproduced at all. Because immediately afterward you realised that obviously she must not, must not duplicate: very Nature herself would not permit that to occur, permit two of them in a place no larger than Jefferson, Mississippi in one century, let alone in overlapping succession, within the anguished scope of a single generation. Because even Nature, loving concupiscent uproar and excitement as even Nature loves it, insists that it at least be reproductive of fresh fodder for the uproar and the excitement. Which would take time, the time necessary to produce that new crop of fodder, since she—Eula Varner—had exhausted, consumed, burned up that one of hers. Whereupon I would remember what Maggie said once to Gowan back there in the dead long time ago when I was in the throes of my own apprenticeship to holocaust: "You dont marry Helen and Semiramis; you just commit suicide for her."

Because she—the child—didn't look at all like her mother. And then in that same second I knew exactly who she did resemble. Back there in that time of my own clowning belated adolescence (none the less either for being both), I remember how I could never decide which of the two unbearables was the least unbearable; which (as the poet has it) of the two chewed bitter thumbs was the least bitter for chewing. That is, whether Manfred de Spain had seduced a chaste wife, or had simply been caught up in passing by a rotating nympholept. This was my anguish. If the first was right, what qualities of mere man did Manfred have that I didn't? If the second, what blind outrageous fortune's lightning-bolt was it that struck Manfred de Spain that mightn't, shouldn't, couldn't, anyway didn't, have blasted Gavin Stevens just as well? Or even also (oh yes, it was that bad once, that comical once) I would even have shared her if I had to, couldn't have had her any other way.

That was when (I mean the thinking why it hadn't been me in Manfred's place to check that glance's idle fateful swing that day whenever that moment had been) I would say that she must be chaste, a wife true and impeachless. I would think *It's that damned child, that damned baby*—that innocent infant which, simply by innocently being, breathing, existing, lacerated and scoriated and reft me of peace: if there had only been no question of the child's paternity; or better still, no child at all. Thus I would even get a little relief from my chewed thumbs since I would need both of them for the moment to count with. Ratliff had told me how they departed for Texas immediately after the wedding and when they returned twelve months later, the child was already walking. Which (the walking at least) I did not believe, not because of the anguish, the jealousy, the despair, but simply because of Ratliff. In fact, it was Ratliff who gave me that ease of hope— or if you like, ease from anguish; all right: tears too, peaceful tears but tears, which are the jewel-baubles of the belated adolescence's clown-comedian—to pant with. Because even if the child had been only one day old, Ratliff would have invented the walking, being Ratiff. In fact, if there had been no child at all yet, Ratliff would have invented one, invented one already walking for the simple sake of his own paradox and humor, secured as he was from checkable facts by this much miles and time between Frenchman's Bend and Jefferson two years later. That was when I would rather believe it was Flem's own child; rather defilement by Manfred de Spain than promiscuity by Eula Varner—whereupon I would need only to taste that thumb again to realise that any other thumb was less bitter, no matter which: let her accept the whole earth's Manfred de Spains and refuse Gavin Stevens, than to accept one Flem Snopes and still refuse him.

So you see how much effort a man will make and trouble he will invent, to guard and defend himself from the boredom of peace of mind. Or rather perhaps the pervert who deliberately infests himself with lice, not just for the simple pleasure of being rid of them again, since even in the folly of youth we know that nothing lasts; but because even in that folly we are afraid that maybe Nothing will last, that maybe Nothing will last forever, and anything is better than Nothing, even lice. So now, as another poet sings, That Fancy passed me by And nothing will remain; which, praise the gods, is a damned lie

since, praise, O gods! Nothing cannot remain anywhere since
nothing is vacuum and vacuum is paradox and unbearable
and we will have none of it even if we would, the damned-
fool poet's Nothing steadily and perennially full of perennially
new and perennially renewed anguishes for me to measure my
stature against whenever I need reassure myself that I also am
Motion.

Because the second premise was much better. If I was not
to have her, then Flem Snopes shall never have. So instead of
the poet's Fancy passes by And nothing remaining, it is
Remaining which will always remain, never to be completely
empty of that olden anguish. So no matter how much more
the blood will slow and remembering grow more lascerant,
the blood at least will always remember that once it was that
capable, capable at least of anguish. So that girl-child was not
Flem Snopes's at all, but mine; my child and my grandchild
both since the McCarron boy who begot her (oh yes, I can
even believe Ratliff when it suits me) in that lost time, was
Gavin Stevens in that lost time; and, since remaining must remain or quit being remaining, Gavin Stevens is fixed by his
own child forever at that one age in that one moment. So
since the son is father to the man, the McCarron fixed forever
and timeless in that dead youth as Gavin Stevens, is of necessity now the son of Gavin Stevens's age, and McCarron's
child is Gavin Stevens's grandchild.

Whether Gavin Stevens intended to be that father-grand-
father or not, of course. But then neither did he dream that
that one idle glance of Eula Varner's eye which didn't even
mark him in passing, would confer on him foster-uncleship
over every damned Snopes wanting to claim it out of that
whole entire damned connection she married into. I mean
foster-uncleship in the sense that simple enragement and outrage and obsession *per se* take care of their own just as simple
per se poverty and (so they say) virtue do of theirs. But foster-
uncleship only to *he*: never *she*. So this was not the first time
I ever thought how apparently all Snopeses are male, as if the
mere and simple incident of woman's divinity precluded
Snopesishness and made it paradox. No: it was rather as if
Snopes were some profound and incontrovertible hermaph-
roditic principle for the furtherance of a race, a species, the

principle vested always physically in the male, any anonymous conceptive or gestative organ drawn into that radius to conceive and spawn, repeating that male principle and then vanishing; the Snopes female incapable of producing a Snopes and hence harmless like the malaria-bearing mosquito of whom only the female is armed and potent, turned upside down and backward. Or even more than a mere natural principle: a divine one: the unsleeping hand of God Himself, unflagging and constant, else before now they would have owned the whole earth, let alone just Jefferson Mississippi.

Because now Flem Snopes was vice president of what we still called Colonel Sartoris's bank. Oh yes, our banks have vice presidents the same as anybody else's bank. Only nobody in Jefferson ever paid any attention to just the vice president of a bank before; he—a bank vice president—was like someone who had gained the privilege of calling himself major or colonel by having contributed time or money or influence to getting a governor elected, as compared to him who had rightfully inherited his title from a father or grandfather who had actually ridden a horse at a Yankee soldier, like Manfred de Spain or our Colonel Sartoris.

So Flem was the first actual living vice president of a bank we had ever seen to notice. We heard he had fallen heir to the vice presidency when Manfred de Spain moved up his notch, and we knew why: Uncle Billy Varner's stock plus the odds and ends which (we now learned) Flem himself had been picking up here and there for some time, plus Manfred de Spain himself. Which was all right; it was done now; too late to help; we were used to our own Jefferson breed or strain of bank vice presidents and we expected no more of even a Snopes bank vice president than simple conformation to pattern.

Then to our surprise we saw that he was trying to be what he—a Snopes or anyway a Flem Snopes—thought a bank vice president was or should be. He began to spend most of the day in the bank. Not in the back office where Colonel Sartoris had used to sit and where Manfred de Spain now sat, but in the lobby, standing a little back from the window watching the clients coming and going to leave their money or draw it out, still in that little cloth cap and the snap-on-behind bow tie he had come to town in thirteen years ago and his jaw still moving faintly and steadily as if he were chewing something though I anyway in my part of those thirteen years had never seen him spit.

Then one day we saw him at his post in the lobby and we didn't even know him. He was standing where he always stood, back where he would be out of the actual path to the window but where he could still watch it (watching how much money was going in or how much was coming out, we didn't know which; whether perhaps what held him thralled there was the simple solvency of the bank which in a way—by deputy, by proxy—was now his bank, his pride: that no matter how much money people drew out of it, there was always that one who had just deposited that zero-plus-one dollar into it in time; or whether he actually did believe in an inevitable moment when De Spain or whoever the designated job would belong to, would come to the window from the inside and say "Sorry, folks, you cant draw out any more money because there aint any more", and he—Flem—simply wanted to prove to himself that he was wrong).

But this time we didn't know him. He still wore the little bow tie and his jaw was still pulsing faintly and steadily, but now he wore a hat, a new one of the broad black felt kind which country preachers and politicians wore. And the next day he was actually inside the cage where the money actually was and where the steel door opened into the concrete vault where it stayed at night; and now we realised that he was not watching the money any longer; he had learned all there was to learn about that. Now he was watching the records of it, how they kept the books.

And now we—some of us, a few of us—believed that he was preparing himself to show his nephew or cousin Byron how to really loot a bank. But Ratliff (naturally it was Ratliff) stopped that quick. "No no," he said, "he's jest trying to find out how anybody could think so light of money as to let a feller no brighter than Byron Snopes steal some of it. You boys have got Flem Snopes wrong. He's got too much respect and reverence not jest for money but for sharpness too, to outrage and debase one of them by jest crude robbing and stealing the other one."

And as the days followed, he—Snopes—had his coat off too, in his galluses now like he actually worked there, was paid money every Saturday to stay inside the cage, except that he still wore the new hat, standing now right behind the book-keepers while he found out for himself how a bank was run. And now we heard how always when people came in to pay off notes or the interest on them, and sometimes when they came to borrow the money too (except the old short-tempered ones, old customers from back in Colonel Sartoris's time, who would run Flem out of the back room without waiting for De Spain to do it or even asking his—De Spain's —leave) he would be there too, his jaw still faintly pulsing while he watched and learned; that was when Ratliff said that all he—Snopes—needed to learn now was how to write out a note so that the fellow borrowing the money couldn't even read when it was due, let alone the rate of interest, like Colonel Sartoris could write one (the tale, the legend was that once the colonel wrote out a note for a countryman cus-tomer, a farmer, who took the note and looked at it, then turned it upside down and looked at it, then handed it back to the colonel and said, "What does it say, Colonel? I cant read it," whereupon the colonel took it in his turn, looked at it, turned it upside down and looked at it, then tore it in two and threw it in the waste basket and said, "Be damned if I can either, Tom. We'll try another one."), then he—Snopes— would know all there was to learn about banking in Jefferson, and could graduate.

Evidently he learned that too. One day he was not in the bank anymore, and the day after that, and the day after that. On the day the bank first opened about twenty years ago Mrs Jennie Du Pre, Colonel Sartoris's sister, had put a tremen-dous great rubber plant in the corner of the lobby. It was taller than a man, it took up as much room as a privy; it was in everybody's way and in summer they couldn't even open the front door all the way back because of it. But she wouldn't let the colonel nor the board of directors either re-move it, since she belonged to that school which believed that any room inhabited by people had to have something green in it to absorb the poison from the air. Though why it had to be that monstrous rubber plant, nobody knew, unless perhaps she believed that nothing less than rubber and that much of it would be tough and durable and resilient enough to cope with air poisoned by the anxiety or exultation over as much money as her brother's, a Sartoris, old Colonel Sartoris's son's, bank would naturally handle.

So when the days passed and Snopes was no longer to be seen taking up room in the lobby while he watched the borrowing and the lending and the paying in and the drawing out (or who did each, and how much of each, which according to Ratliff was the real reason he was there, was what he was really watching), it was as if Mrs Du Pre's rubber tree had vanished from the lobby, abandoned it. And when still more days passed and we finally realised he was not coming back anymore, it was like hearing that the rubber tree had been hauled away somewhere and burned, destroyed for ever. It was as if the single aim and purpose of that long series of interlocked circumstances—the bank which a sentimentalist like Colonel Sartoris founded in order that, as Ratliff said, a feller no brighter than Byron Snopes could steal from it; the racing car which Bayard Sartoris drove too fast for our country roads (the Jefferson ladies said because he was grieving so over the death in battle of his twin brother that he too was seeking death though in my opinion Bayard liked war and now that there was no more war to go to, he was faced with the horrid prospect of having to go to work) until his grandfather took to riding with him in the hope that he would slow down: as a result of which, the normal check-up of the bank for reorganization revealed the fact that Byron Snopes had been robbing it: as a result of which, to save the good name of the bank which his father had helped to found, Manfred de Spain had to allow Flem Snopes to become vice president of it;— the single result of all this apparently was to efface that checked cap from Flem Snopes and put that hot-looking black politician-preacher's hat on him in its stead.

Because he still wore the hat. We saw that about the Square every day. But never again in the bank, his bank, the one in which he was not only a director but in whose hierarchy he had an official designated place, second-in-command. Not even to deposit his own money in it. Oh yes, we knew that; we had Ratliff's word for that. Ratliff had to know a fact like that by now. After this many years of working to establish and maintain himself as what he uniquely was in Jefferson, Ratliff could not afford, he did not dare, to walk the streets and not have the answer to any and every situation which was not really any of his business. Ratliff knew: that not only was Flem Snopes no longer a customer of the bank of which he was vice president, but that in the second year he had transferred his account to the other rival bank, the old Bank of Jefferson.

So we all knew the answer to that. I mean, we had been right all along. All except Ratliff of course, who had dissuaded us before against our mutually combined judgments. We had watched Flem behind the grille of his bank while he taught himself the intricacies of banking in order to plumb laboriously the crude and awkward method by which his cousin or nephew Byron had made his petty and unambitious haul; we had seen him in and out of the vault itself while he learned the tide-cycle, the rise and fall of the actual cash against the moment when it would be most worth pillaging; we believed now that when that moment came, Flem would have already arranged himself for his profit to be one hundred percent., that he himself was seeing to it in advance that he would not have to steal even one forgotten penny of his own money.

"No," Ratliff said. "No."

"In which case, he will defeat himself," I said. "What does he expect to happen when the other depositors, especially the ignorant ones that know too little about banks and the smart ones that know too much about Snopeses, begin to find out that the vice president of the bank doesn't even keep his own loose change in it?"

"No, I tell you," Ratliff said. "You folks—"

"So he's hoping—wishing—dreaming of starting a run on his own bank, not to loot it but to empty it, abolish it. All right. Why? For revenge on Manfred de Spain because of his wife?"

"No no, I tell you!" Ratliff said. "I tell you, you got Flem all wrong, all of you have. I tell you, he aint just got respect for money: he's got active" (he always said active for actual, though in this case I believe his choice was better than Webster's) "reverence for it. The last thing he would ever do is hurt that bank. Because any bank whether it's hisn or not

stands for money, and the last thing he would ever do is to insult and degrade money by mishandling it. Likely the one and
only thing in his life he is ashamed of is the one thing he wont
never do again. That was that-ere power-plant brass that time.
Likely he wakes up at night right now and writhes and squirms
over it. Not because he lost by it because dont nobody know
yet, nor never will, whether he actively lost or not because
dont nobody know yet jest how much of that old brass he
might a sold before he made the mistake of trying to do it
wholesale by using Tom Tom Bird and Tomey Beauchamp.
He's ashamed because when he made money that-a-way, he
got his-self right down into the dirt with the folks that waste
money because they stole it in the first place and aint got
nowhere to put it down where they can risk turning their
backs on it."

"Then what is he up to?" I said. "What is he trying to do?"

"I dont know," Ratliff said. And now he not only didn't
sound like Ratliff, answering he didn't know to any question,
he didn't even look like Ratliff: the customary bland smooth
quizzical inscrutable face not quite baffled maybe but certainly questioning, certainly sober. "I jest dont know. We got
to figger. That's why I come up here to see you: in case you
did know. Hoping you knowed." Then he was Ratliff again,
humorous, quizzical, invincibly . . . maybe the word I want
is not optimism or courage or even hope, but rather of sanity
or maybe even of innocence. "But naturally you dont know
neither. Confound it, the trouble is we dont never know
beforehand, to anticipate him. It's like a rabbit or maybe a
bigger varmint, one with more poison or anyhow more teeth,
in a patch or a brake: you can watch the bushes shaking but
you cant see what it is or which-a-way it's going until it
breaks out. But you can see it then, and usually it's in time.
Of course you got to move fast when he does break out, and
he's got the advantage of you because he's already moving
because he knows where he's going, and you aint moving
yet because you dont. But it's usually in time."

That was the first time the bushes shook. The next time
was almost a year later; he came in, he said "Good morning,
Lawyer," and he was Ratliff again, bland, smooth, courteous,
a little too damned intelligent. "I figgered you might like to

hear the latest news first, being as you're a member of the family too by simple bad luck and exposure, you might say. Being as so far dont nobody know about it except the directors of the Bank of Jefferson."

"The Bank of Jefferson?" I said.

"That's right. It's that non-Snopes boy of Eck's, that other non-Snopes that blowed his-self up in that empty oil tank back while you was away at the war, wasting his time jest hunting a lost child that wasn't even lost, jest his maw thought he was——"

"Yes," I said. "Wallstreet Panic." Because I already knew about that: the non-Snopes son of a non-Snopes who had had the good fortune to discover (or be discovered by) a good woman early in life: the second grade teacher who, obviously recognising that un-Snopes anomaly, not only told him what Wallstreet Panic meant, but that he didn't really have to have it for his name if he didn't want to; but if he thought a too-violent change might be too much, then he could call himself simply Wall Snopes since Wall was a good name, having been carried bravely by a brave Mississippi general at Chickamauga and Lookout Mountain, and though she didn't think that, being a non-Snopes, he would particularly need to remember courage, remembering courage never hurt anyone.

And how he had taken the indemnity money the oil company paid for his father's bizarre and needless and un-Snopesish death and bought into the little back street grocery store where he had been the afterschool-and-Saturday clerk and errand boy, and continued to save his money until, when the old owner died at last, he, Wallstreet, owned the store. And how he got married who was never a Snopes, never in this world a Snopes: doomed damned corrupted and self-convicted not merely of generosity but of taste; holding simple foolish innocent rewardless generosity, not to mention taste, even higher than his own repute when the town should learn he had actually proposed marriage to a woman ten years his senior.

That's what he did, not even waiting to graduate—the day, the moment when in the hot stiff brand new serge suit, to walk sweating through the soundless agony of the cut flowers, across the highschool rostrum and receive his diploma from the hand of the principal—but only for the day when he knew he was done with the school, forever more beyond the range of its help or harm (he was nineteen. Seven years ago he and his six-year-old brother had entered the same kindergarten class. In this last year his grades had been such that they didn't even ask him to take the examinations.)—to leave the store of which he was now actual even if not titular proprietor, just in time to be standing at the corner when the dismissal bell rang, standing there while the kindergarten then the first grade children streamed past him, then the second grade, standing there while the Lilliputian flow divided around them like a brook around two herons, while without even attempting to touch her in this all juvenile Jefferson's sight, he proposed to the second grade teacher and then saw her, as another teacher did from a distance, stare at him and partly raise one defending hand and then burst into tears, right there in plain view of the hundred children who at one time within the last three or four years had been second graders too, to whom she had been mentor, authority, infallible.

Until he could lead her aside, onto the vacating playground, himself to screen her while she used his handkerchief to regain composure, then, against all the rules of the school and of respectable decorum too, back into the empty room itself smelling of chalk and anguished cerebration and the dry inflexibility of facts, she leading the way, but not for the betrothing kiss, not to let him touch her even and least of all to remind him that she had already been twenty-two years old that day seven years ago and twelve months from now he would discover that all Jefferson had been one year laughing at him. Who had been divinitive enough to see seven years beyond that wallstreet panic, but was more, much more than that: a lady, the tears effaced now and she once more the Miss Wyott, or rather the 'Miss Vaiden' as Southern children called their teacher, telling him, feeding him none of those sorry reasons: saying simply that she was already engaged and some day she wanted him to know her fiancé because she knew they would be friends.

So that he would not know better until he was much older and had much more sense. Nor learning it then when it was too late because it was not too late since didn't I just say that she was wise, more than just wise: divinitive? Also, remember her own people had come from the country (her own branch of it remained there where they had owned the nearest ford, crossing, ferry before Jefferson even became Jefferson) so without doubt she even knew in advance the girl, which girl even since she seems to have taken him directly there, within the week, almost as though she said "This is she. Marry her" and within the month he didn't even know probably that he had not remarked that Miss Vaiden Wyott had resigned from the Jefferson school where she had taught the second grade for a decade, to accept a position in a school in Bristol, Virginia, since when that fall day came he was two months husband to a tense fierce not quite plain-faced girl with an ambition equal to his and a will if anything even more furious against that morass, that swamp, that fetid seethe from which her husband (she naturally believed) had extricated himself by his own suspenders and boot straps, herself clerking in the store now so that the mother-in-law could now stay at home and do the cooking and housework; herself, although at that time she didn't weigh quite a hundred pounds, doing the ap-prentice chores—sweeping, wrestling the barrels of flour and molasses, making the rounds of the town on the bicycle in which the telephone orders were delivered until they could afford to buy the second-hand Model T Ford—during the hours while the younger one, Admiral Dewey, was in school where it was she now, his sister-in-law, who made him go whether he would or not.

Yes, we all knew that; that was a part of our folklore, or Snopeslore, if you like: how Flem himself was anyway the sec-ond one to see that here was a young man who was going to make money by simple honesty and industry, and tried to buy into the business or anyway lend Wallstreet money to expand it; and we all knew who had refused the offer. That is, we liked to believe, having come to know Wallstreet a little now, that he would have declined anyway. But since we had come to know his wife, we knew that he was going to decline. And how he had learned to be a clerk and a partner the hard way, and he would have to learn to be a proprietor the hard way too: and sure enough in time he overbought his stock; and how he went to Colonel Sartoris's bank for help.

That was when we first realised that Flem Snopes actually was a member of the board of directors of a Jefferson bank. I mean, that a Flem Snopes actually could be. Oh, we had seen his name among the others on the annual bank report above the facsimile of Colonel Sartoris's illegible signature as president, but we merely drew the logical conclusion that that was simply old man Will Varner's voting proxy to save him a trip to town; all we thought was, "That means that Manfred de Spain will have Uncle Billy's stock too in case he ever wants anything."

And obviously we knew, believed, that Flem had tried again to buy into Wallstreet's business, save him with a personal private loan before he, as a director, blocked the loan from the bank. Because we thought we saw it all now; all we seemed to have missed was, what hold he could have had over the drummer to compel him to persuade Wallstreet to overbuy, and over the wholesale house in St Louis to persuade it to accept the sale;—very likely the same sign or hoodoo-mark he planned to use on the other bank, the Bank of Jefferson, to prevent them lending Wallstreet money after Colonel Sartoris's bank declined.

But there was never any question about which one of the Wallstreet Snopeses had turned Flem down. Anybody could have seen her that morning, running, thin, not so much tense as fierce, still weighing less than a hundred pounds, even after six months of marriage looking still not so much like a nymph as like a deer, not around the Square as pedestrians walked but across it, through it, darting among the automobiles and teams and wagons, toward and into the bank (and how she knew, divined so quickly that he had been refused the loan we didn't know either, though on second thought that was obvious too: that simple automatic fierce Snopes antipathy which had reacted as soon as common sense told her it should not have taken the bank that long to say Yes, and that Flem Snopes was on the board of directors of it);—darting into the lobby already crying: "Where is he? Where is Wall?" and out again when they told her Gone, not at all desperate: just fierce and hurried, onto the street where someone else told her he went that way: which was the street leading to the back street leading to the rented house where Flem lived, who had no office nor other place of business, running now until she overtook him, in time. And anyone there could have seen that too: clinging to him in broad daylight when even sweethearts didn't embrace on the street by daylight and no lady any-where at any time said God damn in public, crying (weeping too but no tears, as if the fierce taut irreconcilable face blis-tered and evaporated tears away as fast as they emerged onto it): "Dont you dare! Them damn Snopes! God damn them! God damn them!"

So we thought of course that her father, a small though thrifty farmer, had found the money somehow. Because Wallstreet saved his business. And he had not only learned about solvency from that experience, he had learned some-thing more about success too. In another year he had rented (then bought it) the store next door and converted it into a warehouse, stock room, so he could buy in larger wholesale lots for less money; another few years and he had rented what had been the last livery stable in Jefferson for his warehouse and knocked down the wall between the two stores and now we had in Jefferson the first self-service grocery store we had ever seen, built on the pattern which the big chain grocery stores were to make nation-wide in the purveying of food; the street his store faced on made an L with the alley where the old Snopes restaurant had been so that the tent in which he had passed his first night in Jefferson was directly behind his store too; he either bought or rented that lot (there were more automobiles in Jefferson now) and made a parking lot and so taught the housewives of Jefferson to come to town and seek his bargains and carry them home themselves.

That is, we—or that is, I—thought that it was his father-in-law who had found the money to save him, until now. "Well, I'll be damned," I said. "So it was you."

"That's right," Ratliff said. "All I wanted was just a note for it. But he insisted on making me a partner. And I'll tell you something else we're fixing to do. We're fixing to open a wholesale."

"A what?" I said.

"A wholesale company like the big ones in St Louis, right here in Jefferson, so that instead of either having to pay high freight on a little shirt-tail full of stuff, or risk overloading on something perishable to save freight, a merchant anywhere in the county can buy jest what he needs at a decent price without having to add no freight a-tall."

"Well I'll be damned," I said. "Why didn't you think of that yourself years ago?"

"That's right," Ratliff said. "Why didn't you?"

"Well I'll be damned," I still said. Then I said: "Hell fire, are you still selling stock? Can I get in?"

"Why not?" he said. "Long as your name aint Snopes. Maybe you could even buy some from him if your name wasn't jest Flem Snopes. But you got to pass that-ere little gal first. His wife. You ought to stop in there sometime and hear her say Them goddamn Snopes once. Oh sho, all of us have thought that, and some of us have even said it out loud. But she's different. She means it. And she aint going to never let him change neither."

"Yes," I said. "I've heard about that. I wonder why she never changed their name."

"No no," he said. "You dont understand. She dont want to change it. She jest wants to live it down. She aint trying to drag him by the hair out of Snopes, to escape from Snopes. She's got to purify Snopes itself. She's got to beat Snopes from the inside. Stop in there and listen sometimes."

"A wholesale house," I said. "So that's why Flem——" But that was foolish, as Ratliff himself saw even before I said it.

"—why Flem changed his account from his own bank to the other one? No no. We aint using the banks here. We dont need them. Like Flem was the first feller in Jefferson to find out that. Wall's credit is too good with the big wholesalers and brokers we deal with. The way they figger, he aint cutting into nobody's private business: he's helping all business. We dont need no bank. But we—he—still aims to keep it home-made. So you see him if you want to talk about stock."

"I will," I said. "But what is Flem himself up to? Why did he pull his money out of De Spain's bank as soon as he got to be vice president of it? Because he's still that, so he still owns stock in it. But he doesn't keep his own money in it. Why?"

"Oh," he said, "is that what you're worried about? Why, we aint sho yet. All we're doing now is watching the bushes shake." Between the voice and the face there was always two

Ratliffs: the second one offering you a fair and open chance to divine what the first one really meant by what it was saying, provided you were smart enough. But this time that second Ratliff was trying to tell me something which for whatever reason the other could not say in words. "As long as that little gal lives, Flem aint got no chance to ever get a finger-hold on Wall. So Eck Snopes is out. And I.O. Snopes never was in because I.O. never was worth nothing even to I.O., let alone for anybody else to take a cut of the profit. So that jest about exhausts all the Snopes in reach that a earnest hardworking feller might make a forced share-crop on."

"There's that—" I said.

"All right," he said. "I'll say it for you. Montgomery Ward. The photograph gallery. If Flem aint been in that thing all the time from the very first, he dont never aim to be. And the fact that there aint been a new photograph in his show window in over a year now, let alone Jason Compson collecting his maw's rent prompt on time since the second month after Montgomery Ward opened up, is proof enough that Flem seen from the first day that there wasn't nothing there for him to waste his time on. So I cant think of but one Snopes object that he's got left."

"All right," I said. "I'll bite."

"That-ere twenty-dollar gold piece."

"What twenty-dollar gold piece?"

"Dont you remember what I said that day, about how when a country boy makes his first Sad-dy night trip to Memphis, that-ere twenty-dollar bill he wears pinned inside his undershirt so he can at least get back home?"

"Go on," I said. "You cant stop now."

"What's the one thing in Jefferson that Flem aint got yet? The one thing he might want. That maybe he's been working at ever since they taken Colonel Sartoris out of that wrecked car and he voted Uncle Billy Varner's stock to make Manfred de Spain president of that bank?"

"To be president of it himself," I said. "No!" I said. "It cant be! It must not be!" But he was just watching me. "Nonsense," I said.

"Why nonsense?" he said.

"Because, to use what you call that twenty-dollar gold

piece, he's got to use his wife too. Do you mean to tell me you believe for one moment that his wife will side with him against Manfred de Spain?" But still he just looked at me. "Dont you agree?" I said. "How can he hope for that?"

Yes, he was just looking at me. "That would jest be when he finally runs out of the bushes," he said. "Out to where we can see him. Into the clearing. What's that clearing?"

"Clearing?" I said.

"That he was working toward?—All right," he said. "That druv him to burrow through the bushes to get out of them?"

"Rapacity," I said. "Greed. Money. What else does he need? want? What else has ever driven him?"

But he just looked at me, and now I could actually watch that urgency fade until only the familiar face remained, bland, smooth, impenetrable and courteous. He drew out the dollar watch looped on a knotted shoelace between his button hole and his breast pocket. "I be dog if it aint almost dinner time," he said. "Jest about time to walk to it."

NINE

V. K. RATLIFF
Because he missed it. He missed it completely.

TEN

C HARLES MALLISON
They finally caught Montgomery Ward Snopes. I mean,
they caught Grover Cleveland Winbush. Like Ratliff said, anybody bootlegging anything that never had any more sense
than to sell Grover Cleveland Winbush some of it, deserved
to be caught.

Except Uncle Gavin said that, even without Grover
Cleveland, Montgomery Ward was bound to be caught
sooner or later, since there simply wasn't any place in Jefferson, Mississippi culture for a vocation or hobby or interest
like the one Montgomery Ward had tried to establish among
us. In Europe, yes; and maybe among the metropolitan rich
or bohemians, yes too. But not in a land composed mainly of
rural Baptists.

So they caught Grover Cleveland. It was one night, not
very late. I mean, the stores were all closed but folks were still
going home from the second running of the picture show;
and some of them, I reckon anybody that passed and happened to look inside, saw the two fellows inside Uncle Willy
Christian's drug store working at the prescription case where
Uncle Willy kept the medicines; and even though they were
strangers—that is, nobody passing recognised them—the ones
that looked in and saw them said the next day that they never
thought anything of it, being that early and the lights on and
Grover Cleveland not having anything to do as night marshal
except to walk around the Square and look in the windows,
that sooner or later he would have to see them if they never
had any business there.

So it wasn't until the next morning when Uncle Willy
opened up for business, that he found out somebody had unlocked the store and not only unlocked the safe and took
what money he had in it, they had broke open his pharmacy
cabinet and stole all his morphine and sleeping pills. That's
what caused the trouble. Ratliff said they could have taken
the money or for that matter all the rest of the store too

except that prescription case, including the alcohol because Walter Christian, the Negro janitor, had been taking that a drink at a time ever since he and Uncle Willy both were boys and first started in the store, and Uncle Willy would have cussed and stomped around of course and even had the Law in, but that was all. But whoever touched that prescription cabinet with the morphine in it raised the devil himself. Uncle Willy was a bachelor, about sixty years old, and if you came in at the wrong time of day he even snarled at children too. But if you were careful to remember the right time of day he supplied the balls and bats for our baseball teams and after a game he would give the whole teams ice cream free whether they won or not. I mean, until one summer some of the church ladies decided to reform him. After that it was hard to tell when to speak to him or not. Then the ladies would give up for a while and it would be all right again.

Besides that, the federal drug inspectors had been nagging and worrying at him for years about keeping the morphine in that little flimsy wooden drawer that anybody with a screw-driver or a knife blade or maybe just a hair pin could prize open, even though it did have a key to it that Uncle Willy kept hidden under a gallon jug marked *Nux Vomica* on a dark shelf that nobody but him was even supposed to bother because it was so dark back there that even Walter never went back there since Uncle Willy couldn't have seen whether he had swept there or not even if he had; and each time Uncle Willy would have to promise the inspectors to lock the morphine up in the safe from now on.

So now he was going to have more trouble than ever explaining to the inspectors why he hadn't put the morphine in the safe like he promised; reminding them how, even if he had, the robbers would still have got it and it wasn't going to do any good now because, like Ratliff said, federal folks were not interested in whether anything worked or not, all they were interested in was that you did it exactly like their rules said to do it.

So Uncle Willy was the real cause of them catching Montgomery Ward Snopes. He was good and wild at first. He was so wild for a while that nobody could find out how much had been stolen or even what he was talking about, with more folks coming in from the street not so much to see where the robbery was but to watch Uncle Willy; until finally, it was Ratliff of course, said: "Uncle Willy dont need no sheriff yet. What he needs first is Doc Peabody."

"Of course," Uncle Gavin said to Ratliff. "Why does it always have to be you?" He went back to where Skeets McGowan, Uncle Willy's clerk and soda-jerker, and two other boys were standing with their heads inside the open safe looking at where the money had been stolen from, and pulled Skeets out and told him to run upstairs quick and tell Doctor Peabody to hurry down. Then Uncle Gavin and the others kind of crowded Uncle Willy more or less quiet without actually holding him until Doctor Peabody came in with the needle already in his hand even and ran most of them out and rolled up Uncle Willy's sleeve then rolled it back down again and then Uncle Willy settled down into being just mad.

So he was the one responsible for catching Montgomery Ward. Or the two fellows that stole his morphine were. By this time we knew that several people passing from the picture show had seen the two fellows in the store, and now Uncle Willy wanted to know where Grover Cleveland Winbush was all that time. Yes sir, he wasn't wild now. He was just mad, as calm and steady and deadly about it as a horsefly. By that time, nine oclock in the morning, Grover Cleveland would be at home in bed asleep. Somebody said they would telephone out and wake him up and tell him to get on back to the Square fast as he could.

"Hell," Uncle Willy said. "That'll take too long. I'll go out there myself. I'll wake him up and get him back to town. He wont need to worry about quick because I'll tend to that. Who's got a car?"

Only Mr Buck Connors, the marshal, the chief of police, was there by this time. "Hold up now, Uncle Willy," he said. "There's a right way and a wrong way to do things. We want to do this one the right way. These folks have probably done already trompled up most of the evidence. But at least we can make an investigation according to police procedure regulations. Besides, Grover Cleveland was up all last night on duty. He's got to stay up again all night tonight. He's got to get his sleep."

"Exactly," Uncle Willy said. "Egg-zackly. Up all night, but not far enough up to see two damn scoundrels robbing my store in full view of the whole damn town. Robbed me of three hundred dollars' worth of valuable medicine, yet Grover Winbush—"

"How much cash did they get?" Mr Connors said.

"What?" Uncle Willy said.

"How much money was in the safe?"

"I dont know," Uncle Willy said. "I didn't count it.—yet Grover Winbush that we pay a hundred and twenty-five a month just to wake up once an hour during the night and look around the Square, has got to get his sleep. If nobody's got a car here, get me a taxi. That son of a bitch has already cost me three hundred dollars; I aint going to stop at just one more quarter."

But they still held him hemmed off while somebody telephoned Grover Cleveland. And at first we thought that whoever telephoned and woke him up had scared him good too, until we learned the rest of it and realised all he needed for his scare was to hear that anything had happened anywhere in Jefferson last night that he would have seen if he had been where he was supposed to be or where folks thought he was. Because it wasn't hardly any time before Ratliff said:

"There he was. I jest seen him."

"Where?" somebody said.

"He jest snatched his head back in the alley yonder," Ratliff said. We all watched the alley. It led from a side street onto the Square where Grover Cleveland could have cut across lots from his boarding house. Then he stepped out of it, already walking fast. He didn't wear a uniform like Mr Connors, he wore ordinary clothes with usually his coat-tail hiked up over the handle of the pistol and the blackjack in his hip pocket, coming up the street fast, picking his feet up quick like a cat on a hot stove. And if you thought it would have been Mr Connors or even Mr Hampton, the sheriff, that did the investigating, you would have been wrong. It was Uncle Willy himself. At first Grover Cleveland tried to bluff. Then he fell back on lying. Then he just fell back.

"Howdy, son," Uncle Willy said. "Sorry to wake you up in the middle of the night like this, just to answer a few questions. The first one is, just where were you, roughly, more or less, at exactly half-past ten oclock last night, more or less?"

"Who, me?" Grover Cleveland said. "Where I'm always at at that time of night: standing right across yonder in the station door where if anybody after the last picture show might need anything, like maybe losing their car key or maybe they find out they got a flat tire—"

"Well, well," Uncle Willy said. "And yet you never saw a light on in my store, and them two damned scoundrels——"

"Wait," Grover Cleveland said. "I'm wrong. When I seen the last picture show beginning to let out, I noticed the time, half past ten or maybe twenty-five to eleven, and I decided to go down and close up the Blue Goose and get that out of the way while I had time." The Blue Goose was a Negro café below the cotton gin. "I'm wrong," Grover Cleveland said. "That's where I was."

Uncle Willy never said anything. He just turned his head enough and hollered "Walter!" Walter came in. His grandfather had belonged to Uncle Willy's grandfather before the Surrender and he and Uncle Willy were about the same age and a good deal alike, except that instead of morphine Walter would go into the medicinal alcohol every time Uncle Willy put the key down and turned his back, and if anything Walter was a little more irascible and short-tempered. He came in from the back and said,

"Who calling me?"

"I am," Uncle Willy said. "Where were you at half past ten last night?"

"Who, me?" Walter said, exactly like Grover Cleveland did, except he said it like Uncle Willy had asked him where he was when Dr Einstein first propounded his theory of relativity. "You talking about last night?" he said. "Where you reckon? At home in bed."

"You were at that damned Blue Goose café, where you are every night until Grover Winbush here comes in and runs all you niggers out and closes it up," Uncle Willy said.

"Then what you asking me, if you know so much?" Walter said.

"All right," Uncle Willy said. "What time last night did Mr Winbush close it?" Walter stood there, blinking. His eyes were always red. He made in an old fashioned hand freezer the ice cream which Uncle Willy sold over his soda fountain. He made it in the cellar: a dark cool place with a single door opening onto the alley behind the store, sitting in the gloom and grinding the freezer, so that when you passed about all you saw was his red eyes, looking not malevolent, not savage but just dangerous if you blundered out of your element and into his, like a dragon or a crocodile. He stood there, blinking. "What time did Grover Winbush close up the Blue Goose?" Uncle Willy said.

"I left before that," Walter said. Now suddenly, and we hadn't noticed him before, Mr Hampton was there, doing some of the looking too. He didn't blink like Walter. He was a big man with a big belly and little hard pale eyes that didn't seem to need to blink at all. They were looking at Grover Cleveland now.

"How do you know you did?" he said to Walter.

"Hell fire," Uncle Willy said. "He aint never left that damned place before they turned the lights out since they first opened the door."

"I know that," Mr Hampton said. He was still looking at Grover Cleveland with his little hard pale unblinking eyes. "I've been marshal and sheriff both here a long time too." He said to Grover Cleveland: "Where were you last night when folks needed you?" But Grover Cleveland still tried; you'll have to give him that, even if now even he never believed in it:

"Oh, you mean them two fellers in Uncle Willy's store about half past ten last night. Sure, I seen them. I naturally thought, taken for granted it was Uncle Willy and Skeets. So I . . . ."

"So you what?" Mr Hampton said.

"I . . . stepped back inside and . . . taken up the evening paper," Grover Cleveland said. "Yes, that's where I was: setting right there in the station reading the Memphis evening paper . . . ."

"When Whit Rouncewell saw them two fellows in here, he went back to the station looking for you," Mr Hampton said. "He waited an hour. By that time the lights were off in here but he never saw anybody come out the front door. And you never showed up. And Walter there says you never showed up at the Blue Goose either. Where were you last night, Grover?"

So now there wasn't anywhere for him to go. He just stood there with his coat-tail hiked up over the handle of his pistol and blackjack like a little boy's shirt-tail coming out. Maybe that's what it was: Grover Cleveland was too old to look like a boy. And Uncle Willy and Mr Hampton and all the rest of us looking at him until all of a sudden we were all ashamed to look at him anymore, ashamed to have to find out what we were going to find out. Except that Mr Hampton wasn't ashamed to. Maybe it was being sheriff so long had made him that way, learned him it wasn't Grover Cleveland you had to be ashamed of: it was all of us.

"One night Doc Peabody was coming back from a case about one oclock and he saw you coming out of that alley side door to what Montgomery Ward Snopes calls his studio. Another night I was going home late myself, about midnight, and I saw you going into it. What's going on in there, Grover?"

Grover Cleveland didn't move now either. It was almost a whisper: "It's a club."

Now Mr Hampton and Uncle Gavin were looking at each other. "Dont look at me," Uncle Gavin said. "You're the law." That was the funny thing: neither one of them paid any attention to Mr Connors, who was the marshal and ought to have been attending to this already. Maybe that was why.

"You're the County Attorney," Mr Hampton said. "You're the one to say what the law is before I can be it."

"What are we waiting for then?" Uncle Gavin said.

"Maybe Grover wants to tell us what it is and save time," Mr Hampton said.

"No, dammit," Uncle Gavin said. "Take your foot off him for a minute anyway." He said to Grover Cleveland: "You go on back to the station until we need you."

"You can read the rest of that Memphis paper," Mr Hampton said. "And we wont want you either," he said to Mr Connors.

"Like hell, Sheriff," Mr Connors said. "Your jurisdiction's just the county. What goes on in Jefferson is my jurisdiction. I got as much right——" he stopped then but it was already too late. Mr Hampton looked at him with the little hard pale eyes that never seemed to need to blink at all.

"Go on," Mr Hampton said. "Got as much right to see what Montgomery Ward Snopes has got hid as me and Gavin have. Why didn't you persuade Grover to take you into that club then?" But Mr Connors could still blink. "Come on," Mr Hampton said to Uncle Gavin, turning. Uncle Gavin moved too.

"That means you too," he said to me.

"That means all of you," Mr Hampton said. "All of you get out of Uncle Willy's way now. He's got to make a list of what's missing for the narcotics folks and the insurance too."

So we stood on the street and watched Mr Hampton and Uncle Gavin go on toward Montgomery Ward's studio. "What?" I said to Ratliff.

"I dont know," he said. "That is, I reckon I know. We'll have to wait for Hub and your uncle to prove it."

"What do you reckon it is?" I said.

Now he looked at me. "Let's see," he said. "Even if you are nine going on ten, I reckon you still aint outgrowed ice cream, have you. Come on. We wont bother Uncle Willy and Skeets now neither. We'll go to the Dixie Café." So we went to the Dixie Café and got two cones and stood on the street again.

"What?" I said.

"My guess is, it's a passel of French postcards Montgomery Ward brought back from the war in Paris. I reckon you dont know what that is, do you?"

"I dont know," I said.

"It's kodak pictures of men and women together, experimenting with one another. Without no clothes on much." I dont know whether he was looking at me or not. "Do you know now?"

"I dont know," I said.

"But maybe you do?" he said.

That's what it was. Uncle Gavin said he had a big album of them, and that he had learned enough about photography to have made slides from some of them so he could throw them magnified on a sheet on the wall with a magic lantern in that back room. And he said how Montgomery Ward stood there laughing at him and Mr Hampton both. But he was talking mostly to Uncle Gavin.

"Oh sure," he said. "I dont expect Hub here——"

"Call me Mister Hampton," Mr Hampton said.

"—to know any better—"

"Call me Mister Hampton, boy," Mr Hampton said.

"Mister Hampton," Montgomery Ward said. "—but you're a lawyer; you dont think I got into this without reading a little law first myself, do you? You can confiscate these—all you'll find here; I dont guess Mister Hampton will let a little thing like law stop him from that——"

That was when Mr Hampton slapped him. "Stop it, Hub!" Uncle Gavin said. "You damned fool!"

"Let him go ahead," Montgomery Ward said. "Suing his bondsmen is easier than running a magic lantern. Safer too. Where was I? Oh yes. Even if they had been sent through the mail, which they haven't, that would just be a federal charge, and I dont see any federal dicks around here. And even if you tried to cook up a charge that I've been making money out of them, where are your witnesses? All you got is Grover Winbush, and he dont dare testify, not because he will lose his job because he'll probably do that anyway, but because the God-fearing christian holy citizens of Jefferson wont let him because they cant have it known that this is what their police do when they're supposed to be at work. Let alone the rest of my customers not to mention any names scattered around in banks and stores and gins and filling stations and farmers too two counties wide in either direction—Sure: I just thought of this too: come on, put a fine on me and see how quick it will be paid . . . ." and stopped and said with a kind of hushed amazement: "Sweet Christ." He was talking fast now: "Come on, lock me up, give me a thousand stamped envelopes and I'll make more money in three days than I made in the whole two years with that damned magic lantern." Now he was talking to Mr Hampton: "Maybe that's what you wanted, to begin with: not the postcards but the list of customers; retire from sheriff and spend all your time on the collections. Or no: keep the star to bring pressure on the slow payers——"

Only this time Uncle Gavin didn't have to say anything because this time Mr Hampton wasn't going to hit him. He just stood there with his little hard eyes shut until Montgomery Ward stopped. Then he said to Uncle Gavin:

"Is that right? We've got to have a federal officer? There's nothing on our books to touch him with? Come on, think. Nothing on the city books even?" Now it was Uncle Gavin who said By God.

"That automobile law," he said. "That Sartoris law," while Mr Hampton stood looking at him. "Hanging right there in that frame on the wall by your own office door? Didn't you ever look at it? that you cant drive an automobile on the streets of Jefferson—"

"What?" Montgomery Ward said.

"Louder," Uncle Gavin said. "Mr Hampton cant hear you."

"But that's just inside the city!" Montgomery Ward said. "Hampton's just County Sheriff; he cant make an arrest on just a city charge."

"So you say," Mr Hampton said; now he did put his hand on Montgomery Ward's shoulder; Uncle Gavin said if he had been Montgomery Ward, he'd just as soon Mr Hampton had slapped him again. "Tell your own lawyer, not ours."

"Wait!" Montgomery Ward said to Uncle Gavin. "You own a car too! So does Hampton!"

"We're doing this alphabetically," Uncle Gavin said. "We've passed the H'es. We're in S now, and S-n comes before S-t. Take him on, Hub."

So Montgomery Ward didn't have anywhere to go then, he had run completely out; he just stood there now and Uncle Gavin watched Mr Hampton take his hand off Montgomery Ward and pick up the album of pictures and the envelopes that held the rest of them and carry them to the sink where Montgomery Ward really would develop a film now and then, and tumble them in and then start hunting among the bottles and cans of developer stuff on the shelf above it.

"What are you looking for?" Uncle Gavin said.

"Alcohol—coal oil—anything that'll burn," Mr Hampton said.

"Burn?" Montgomery Ward said. "Hell, man, those things are valuable. Look, I'll make a deal: give them back to me and I'll get to hell out of your damned town and it'll never see me again.—All right," he said. "I've got close to a hundred bucks in my pocket. I'll lay it on the table here and you and Stevens turn your backs and give me ten minutes——"

"Do you want to come back and hit him again?" Uncle Gavin said. "Dont mind me. Besides, he's already suggested we turn our backs so all you'll have to do is just swing your arm." But Mr Hampton just took another bottle down and took out the stopper and smelled it. "You cant do that," Uncle Gavin said. "They're evidence."

"All we need is just one," Mr Hampton said.

"That depends," Uncle Gavin said. "Do you just want to convict him, or do you want to exterminate him?" Mr Hampton stopped, the bottle in one hand and the stopper in the other. "You know what Judge Long will do to the man that just owns one of these pictures." Judge Long was the Federal Judge of our district. "Think what he'll do to the man that owns a wheelbarrow full of them."

So Mr Hampton put the bottle back and after a while a deputy came with a suitcase and they put the album and the envelopes into it and locked it and Mr Hampton locked the suitcase in his safe to turn over to Mr Gombault, the U.S. marshal, when he got back to town, and they locked Montgomery Ward up in the county jail for operating an automobile contrary to law in the city of Jefferson, with Montgomery Ward cussing a while then threatening a while then trying again to bribe anybody connected with the jail or the town that would take the money. And we wondered how long it would be before he sent for Mr de Spain because of that connection. Because we knew that the last person on earth he would hope for help from would be his uncle or cousin Flem, who had already got shut of one Snopes through a murder charge so why should he balk at getting rid of another one with just a dirty postcard.

So even Uncle Gavin, that Ratliff said made a kind of religion of never letting Jefferson see that a Snopes had surprised him, didn't expect Mr Flem that afternoon when he walked into the office and laid his new black hat on the corner of the desk and sat there with the joints of his jaws working faint and steady like he was trying to chew without unclamping his teeth. You couldn't see behind Mr Hampton's eyes because they looked at you too hard; you couldn't pass them like you couldn't pass a horse in a lane that wasn't big enough for a horse and a man both but just for the horse. You couldn't see behind Mr Snopes's eyes because they were not really looking at you at all, like a pond of stagnant water is not looking at you. Uncle Gavin said that was why it took him a minute or two to realise that he and Mr Snopes were looking at exactly the same thing: it just wasn't with the same eye.

"I'm thinking of Jefferson," Mr Snopes said.

"So am I," Uncle Gavin said. "Of that damned Grover Winbush and every other arrested adolescent between fourteen and fifty-eight in half of north Mississippi with twenty-five cents to pay for one look inside that album."

"I forgot about Grover Winbush," Mr Snopes said. "He wont only lose his job but when he does folks will want to know why and this whole business will come out." That was Mr Snopes's trouble. I mean, that was our trouble with Mr Snopes: there wasn't anything to see even when you thought he might be looking at you. "I dont know whether you know it or not. His ma lives out at Whiteleaf. He sends her a dollar's worth of furnish by the mail rider every Saturday morning."

"So to save one is to save both," Uncle Gavin said. "If Grover Winbush's mother is to keep on getting that dollar's worth of fatback and molasses every Saturday morning, somebody will have to save your cousin, nephew—which is he, anyway?—too."

Like Ratliff said, Mr Snopes probably missed a lot folks said to him behind his back, but he never missed what folks didn't say to him to his face. Anyway, irony and sarcasm were not one of them. Or anyway it wasn't this time. "That's how I figgered it," he said. "But you're a lawyer. Your business is to know how to figger different."

Uncle Gavin didn't miss much of what wasn't quite said to his face either. "You've come to the wrong lawyer," he said. "This case is in federal court. Besides, I couldn't take it anyway; I draw a monthly salary to already be on the other side. Besides," he said (while he was just City Attorney he talked Harvard and Heidelberg. But after that summer he and I spent travelling about the county running for County Attorney, he began to talk like the people he would lean on fences or squat against the walls of country stores with, saying 'drug' for 'dragged' and 'me and you' instead of 'you and I' just like they did, even saying figgered just like Mr Snopes just said it), "let's you and me get together on this. I want him to go to the penitentiary."

And that's when Uncle Gavin found out that he and Mr Snopes were looking at exactly the same thing: they were just standing in different places because Mr Snopes said, as quick and calm as Uncle Gavin himself: "So do I." Because Montgomery Ward was his rival just like Wallstreet was, both of them alike in that there just wasn't room in Jefferson for either one of them and Mr Snopes too. Because according to Ratliff, Uncle Gavin was missing it. "So do I," Mr Snopes said. "But not this way. I'm thinking of Jefferson."

"Then it's just too bad for Jefferson," Uncle Gavin said. "He will get Judge Long and when Judge Long sees even one of those pictures, let alone a suitcase full of them, I will almost feel sorry even for Montgomery Ward. Have you forgotten about Wilbur Provine last year?"

Wilbur Provine lived in Frenchman's Bend too. Ratliff said he was really a Snopes; that when Providence realised that Eck Snopes was going to fail his lineage and tradition, it hunted around quick and produced Wilbur Provine to plug the gap. He ran a still in the creek bottom by a spring about a mile and a half from his house, with a path worn smooth as a ribbon and six inches deep from his back door to the spring where he had walked it twice a day for two years until they caught him and took him to federal court before Judge Long, looking as surprised and innocent as if he didn't even know what the word 'still' meant while the lawyer questioned him, saying No, he never had any idea there was a still within ten miles, let alone a path leading from his back door to it because he himself hadn't been in that creek bottom in ten years, not even to hunt and fish since he was a christian and he believed that no christian should destroy God's creatures, and he had burned out on fish when he was eight years old and hadn't been able to eat it since.

Until Judge Long himself asked him how he accounted for that path, and Wilbur blinked at Judge Long once or twice and said he didn't have any idea, unless maybe his wife had worn it toting water from the spring; and Judge Long (he had the right name, he was six and a half feet tall and his nose looked almost a sixth of that) leaning down across the Bench with his spectacles at the end of his nose, looking down at Wilbur for a while, until he said: "I'm going to send you to the penitentiary, not for making whiskey but for letting your wife carry water a mile and a half from that spring." That was who Montgomery Ward would get when he came up for trial and you would have thought that everybody in Yoknapatawpha County, let alone just Jefferson, had heard the story by now. But you would almost thought Mr Snopes hadn't. Because now even the hinges of his jaws had quit that little faint pumping.

"I heard Judge Long gave him five years," he said. "Maybe them extra four years was for the path."

"Maybe," Uncle Gavin said.

"It was five years, wasn't it?" Mr Snopes said.

"That's right," Uncle Gavin said.

"Send that boy out," Mr Snopes said.

"No," Uncle Gavin said.

Now the hinges of Mr Snopes's jaws were pumping again. "Send him out," he said.

"I'm thinking of Jefferson too," Uncle Gavin said. "You're vice president of Colonel Sartoris's bank. I'm even thinking of you."

"Much obliged," Mr Snopes said. He wasn't looking at anything. He didn't waste any time but he wasn't hurrying either: he just got up and took the new black hat from the desk and put it on and went to the door and opened it and didn't quite stop even then, just kind of changing feet to step around the opening door and said, not to anybody anymore than he had ever been looking at anybody: "Good day," and went out and closed the door behind him.

Then I said, "What—" and then stopped, Uncle Gavin and I both watching the door as it opened again, or began to, opening about a foot with no sound beyond it until we saw Ratliff's cheek and one of his eyes, then it opened on and Ratliff came in, eased in, sidled in, still not making any sound.

"Am I too late, or jest too soon?" he said.

"Neither," Uncle Gavin said. "He stopped, decided not to. Something happened. The pattern went wrong. It started out all regular. You know: this is not just for me, and least of all for my kinsman. Do you know what he said?"

"How can I yet?" Ratliff said. "That's what I'm doing now."

"I said 'You and I should get together. I want him to go to the penitentiary.' And he said, 'So do I'."

"All right," Ratliff said. "Go on."

"'—not for me, my kinsman'," Uncle Gavin said. "'For Jefferson'. So the next step should have been the threat. Only he didn't—"

"Why threat?" Ratliff said.

"The pattern," Uncle Gavin said. "First the soap, then the threat, then the bribe. As Montgomery Ward himself tried it."

"This aint Montgomery Ward," Ratliff said. "If Montgomery Ward had been named Flem, them pictures wouldn't a never seen Jefferson, let alone vice versa. But we dont need to worry about Flem being smarter than Montgomery Ward; most anybody around here is that. What we got to worry about is, who else around here may not be as smart as him too. Then what?"

"He quit," Uncle Gavin said. "He came right up to it. He even asked me to send Chick out. And when I said No, he just picked up his hat and said Much obliged and went out as if he had just stopped in here to borrow a match."

Ratliff blinked at Uncle Gavin. "So he wants Montgomery Ward to go to the penitentiary. Only he dont want him to go under the conditions he's on his way there now. Then he changed his mind."

"Because of Chick," Uncle Gavin said.

"Then he changed his mind," Ratliff said.

"You're right," Uncle Gavin said. "It was because he knew that by refusing to send Chick out I had already refused to be bribed."

"No," Ratliff said. "To Flem Snopes, there aint a man breathing that cant be bought for something; all you need to do is jest to find it. Only, why did he change his mind?"

"All right," Uncle Gavin said. "Why?"

"What was the conversation about jest before he told you to send Chick out?"

"About the penitentiary," Uncle Gavin said. "I just told you."

"It was about Wilbur Provine," I said.

Ratliff looked at me. "Wilbur Provine?"

"His still," I said. "That path and Judge Long."

"Oh," Ratliff said. "Then what?"

"That's all," Uncle Gavin said. "He just said 'Send that boy out' and I said—"

"That wasn't next," I said. "The next was what Mr Snopes said about the five years, that maybe the extra four years was for the path, and you said Maybe and Mr Snopes said again, 'It was five years, wasn't it?' and you said Yes and then he said to send me out."

"All right, all right," Uncle Gavin said. But he was looking at Ratliff. "Well?" he said.

"I dont know neither," Ratliff said. "All I know is, I'm glad I aint Montgomery Ward Snopes."

"Yes," Uncle Gavin said. "When Judge Long sees that suitcase."

"Sho," Ratliff said. "That's jest Uncle Sam. It's his Uncle Flem that Montgomery Ward wants to worry about, even if he dont know it yet. And us too. As long as all he wanted was jest money, at least you knowed which way to guess even if you knowed you couldn't guess first. But this time——" He looked at us, blinking.

"All right," Uncle Gavin said. "How?"

"You mind that story about how the feller found his strayed dog? he jest set down and imagined where he would be if he was that dog and got up and went and got it and brung it home. All right. We're Flem Snopes. We got a chance to get shut of our—what's that old-timey word? unsavory—unsavory nephew into the penitentiary. Only we're vice president of a bank now and we cant afford to have it knowed even a unsavory nephew was running a peep show of French postcards. And the judge that will send him there is the same judge that told Wilbur Provine he was going to Parchman not for making whiskey but for letting his wife tote water a mile and a half." He blinked at Uncle Gavin. "You're right. The question aint 'what' a-tall: it's jest 'how'. And since you wasn't interested in money, and he has got better sense than to offer it to Hub Hampton, we dont jest know what that 'how' is going to be. Unless maybe since he got to be a up-and-coming feller in the Baptist church, he is depending on Providence."

Maybe he was. Anyway, it worked. It was the next morning, about ten oclock; Uncle Gavin and I were just leaving the office to drive up to Wyott's Crossing where they were having some kind of a squabble over a drainage tax suit, when Mr Hampton came in. He was kind of blowing through his teeth, light and easy like he was whistling except that he wasn't making any noise and even less than that of tune. "Morning," he said. "Yesterday morning when we were in that studio and I was hunting through them bottles on that shelf for alcohol or something that would burn."

"All right," Uncle Gavin said.

"How many of them bottles and jugs did I draw the cork or unscrew the cap and smell? You were there. You were watching."

"I thought all of them," Uncle Gavin said. "Why?"

"So did I," Mr Hampton said. "I could be wrong." He looked at Uncle Gavin with his hard little eyes, making that soundless whistling between his teeth.

"You've prepared us," Uncle Gavin said. "Got us into the right state of nervous excitement. Now tell us."

"About six this morning, Jack Crenshaw telephoned me." (Mr Crenshaw was the Revenue field agent that did the moonshine still hunting in our district.) "He told me to come on to that studio as soon as I could. They were already inside, two of them. They had already searched it. Two of them gallon jugs on that shelf that I opened and smelled yesterday that never had nothing but kodak developer in them, had raw corn whiskey in them this morning, though like I said I could have been wrong and missed them. Not to mention five gallons more of it in a oil can setting behind the heater, that I hadn't got around to smelling yesterday when you stopped me for the reason that I never seen it there when I looked behind the heater yesterday or I wouldn't been smelling at the bottles on that shelf for something to burn paper with. Though, as you say, I could be wrong."

"As *you* say," Uncle Gavin said.

"You may be right," Mr Hampton said. "After all, I've been having to snuff out moonshine whiskey in this county ever since I first got elected. And since 1919, I have been so in practice that now I dont even need to smell: I just kind of feel it the moment I get where some of it aint supposed to be. Not to mention that five-gallon coal oil can full of it setting where you would have thought I would have fell over it reaching my hand to that shelf."

"All right," Uncle Gavin said. "Go on."

"That's all," Mr Hampton said.

"How did he get in?" Uncle Gavin said.

"He?" Mr Hampton said.

"All right," Uncle Gavin said. "Take 'they' if you like it better."

"I thought of that too," Mr Hampton said. "The key. I said THE key because even that fool would have more sense than to have a key to that place anywhere except on a string around his neck."

"That one," Uncle Gavin said.

"Yep," Mr Hampton said. "I dropped it into the drawer where I usually keep such, handcuffs and a extra pistol. Anybody could have come in while me and Miss Elma" (she was the office deputy, widow of the sheriff Mr Hampton had succeeded last time) "was out, and taken it."

"Or the pistol either," Uncle Gavin said. "You really should start locking that place, Hub. Some day you'll leave your star in there and come back to find some little boy out on the street arresting people."

"Maybe I should," Mr Hampton said. "All right," he said. "Somebody took that key and planted that whiskey. It could have been any of them—any of the folks that that damned Grover Winbush says was coming from four counties around to sweat over them damn pictures at night."

"Maybe it's lucky you at least had that suitcase locked up. I suppose you've still got that, since Mr Gombault hasn't got back yet?"

"That's right," Mr Hampton said.

"And Jack Crenshaw and his buddy are just interested in whiskey, not photography. Which means you haven't turned that suitcase over to anybody yet."

"That's right," Mr Hampton said.

"Are you going to?" Uncle Gavin said.

"What do you think?" Mr Hampton said.

"That's what I think too," Uncle Gavin said.

"After all, the whiskey is enough," Mr Hampton said. "And even if it aint, all we got to do is show Judge Long just any one of them photographs right before he pronounces sentence. Damn it," he said, "it's Jefferson. We live here. Jefferson's got to come first, even before the pleasure of cru-cifying that damned——"

"Yes," Uncle Gavin said. "I've heard that sentiment." Then Mr Hampton left. And all we had to do was just to wait, and not long. You never had to wonder about how much Ratliff had heard because you knew in advance he had heard all of it. He closed the door and stood just inside it.

"Why didn't you tell him yesterday about Flem Snopes?" he said.

"Because he let Flem Snopes or whoever it was walk right in his office and steal that key. Hub's already got about all the felonious malfeasance he can afford to compound," Uncle Gavin said. He finished putting the papers into the brief case and closed it and stood up.

"You leaving?" Ratliff said.

"Yes," Uncle Gavin said. "Wyott's Crossing."

"You aint going to wait for Flem?"

"He wont come back here," Uncle Gavin said. "He wont dare. What he came here yesterday to try to bribe me to do, is going to happen anyway without the bribe. But he dont dare come back here to find out. He will have to wait and see like anybody else. He knows that." But still Ratliff didn't move from the door.

"The trouble with us is, we dont never estimate Flem Snopes right. At first we made the mistake of not estimating him a-tall. Then we made the mistake of over-estimating him. Now we're fixing to make the mistake of under-estimating him again. When you jest want money, all you need to do to satisfy yourself is count it and put it where cant nobody get it, and forget about it. But this-here new thing he has done found out it's nice to have, is different. It's like keeping warm in winter or cool in summer, or peace or being free or content-ment. You cant jest count it and lock it up somewhere safe and forget about it until you feel like looking at it again. You got to work at it steady, never to forget about it. It's got to be out in the open, where folks can see it, or there aint no such thing."

"No such thing as what?" Uncle Gavin said.

"This-here new discovery he's jest made," Ratliff said. "Call it civic virtue."

"Why not?" Uncle Gavin said. "Were you going to call it something else?" Ratliff watched Uncle Gavin, curious, intent; it was as if he were waiting for something. "Go on," Uncle Gavin said. "You were saying."

Then it was gone, whatever it had been. "Oh yes," Ratliff said. "He'll be in to see you. He'll have to, to make sho you recognise it too when you see it. He may kind of hang around until middle of the afternoon, to kind of give the dust a chance to settle. But he'll be back then, so a feller can at least see jest how much he missed heading him off."

So we didn't drive up to Wyott's then, and this time Ratliff was the one who under-estimated. It wasn't a half an hour until we heard his feet on the stairs and the door opened and he came in. This time he didn't take off the black hat: he just said "Morning, gentle-men" and came on to the desk and dropped the key to Montgomery Ward's studio on it and was going back toward the door when Uncle Gavin said:

"Much obliged. I'll give it back to the sheriff. You're like me," he said. "You dont give a damn about truth either. What you are interested in is justice."

"I'm interested in Jefferson," Mr Snopes said, reaching for the door and opening it. "We got to live here. Morning, gentle-men."

ELEVEN

V. K. RATLIFF
And still he missed it, even set—sitting right there in his own office and actively watching Flem rid Jefferson of Montgomery Ward. And still I couldn't tell him.

TWELVE

CHARLES MALLISON

Whatever it was Ratliff thought Mr Snopes wanted, I dont reckon that what Uncle Gavin took up next helped it much either. And this time he didn't even have Miss Melisandre Backus for Mother to blame it on because Miss Melisandre herself was married now, to a man, a stranger, that everybody but Miss Melisandre (we never did know whether her father, sitting all day long out there on that front gallery with a glass of whiskey-and-water in one hand and Horace or Virgil in the other—a combination which Uncle Gavin said would have insulated from the reality of rural north Mississippi harder heads than his—knew or not) knew was a big rich New Orleans bootlegger. In fact she still refused to believe it even when they brought him home with a bullet hole neatly plugged up in the middle of his forehead, in a bullet-proof hearse leading a cortege of Packards and Cadillac limousines that Hollywood itself, let alone Al Capone, wouldn't have been ashamed of.

No, that's wrong. We never did know whether she knew it or not too, even years after he was dead and she had all the money and the two children and the place which in her childhood had been just another Mississippi cotton farm but which he had changed with white fences and weather-vanes in the shape of horses so that it looked like a cross between a Kentucky country club and a Long Island race track, and plenty of friends who felt they owed it to her that she should know where all that money actually came from; and still, as soon as they approached the subject, she would change it— the slender dark girl still, even though she was a millionairess and the mother of two children, whose terrible power was that defenselessness and helplessness which conferred knighthood on any man who came within range, before he had a chance to turn and flee;—changing the entire subject as if she had never heard her husband's name or, in fact, as though he had never lived.

I mean, this time Mother couldn't even say "If he would only marry Melisandre Backus, she would save him from all this", meaning Linda Snopes this time like she had meant Mrs Flem Snopes before. But at least she thought about saying it because almost at once she stopped worrying. "It's all right," she told Father. "It's the same thing again: dont you remember? He never was really interested in Melisandre. I mean . . . . you know: really interested. Books and flowers. Picking my jonquils and narcissus as fast as they bloomed, to send out there where that whole two-acre front yard was full of jonquils, cutting my best roses to take out there and sit in that hammock reading poetry to her. He was just forming her mind: that's all he wanted. And Melisandre was only five years younger, where with this one he is twice her age, practically her grandfather. Of course that's all it is."

Then Father said: "Heh heh heh. Form is right, only it's on Gavin's mind, not hers. It would be on mine too if I wasn't already married and scared to look. Did you ever take a look at her? You're human even if you are a woman." Yes, I could remember a heap of times when Father had been born too soon, before they thought of wolf whistles.

"Stop it," Mother said.

"But after all," Father said, "maybe Gavin should be saved from those sixteen-year-old clutches. Suppose you speak to him; tell him I am willing to make a sacrifice of myself on the family altar——"

"Stop it! Stop it!" Mother said. "Cant you at least be funny?"

"I'm worse than that, I'm serious," Father said. "They were at a table in Christian's yesterday afternoon. Gavin just had a saucer of ice cream but she was eating something in a dish that must have set him back twenty or thirty cents. So maybe Gavin knows what he's doing after all; she's got some looks of her own, but she still aint quite up with her mother: you know——" using both hands to make a kind of undulating hourglass shape in the air in front of him while Mother stood watching him like a snake. "Maybe he's concentrating on just forming her form first you might say, without bothering too much yet about her mind. And who knows? maybe some day she'll even look at him like she was looking at that banana split or whatever it was when Skeets McGowan set it down in front of her."

But by that time Mother was gone. And this time she sure needed somebody like Miss Melisandre, with all her friends (all Jefferson for that matter) on the watch to tell her whenever Uncle Gavin and Linda stopped in Christian's drugstore after school while Linda ate another banana split or ice cream soda, with the last book of poetry Uncle Gavin had ordered for her lying in the melted ice cream or spilled coca cola on the marble table top. Because I reckon Jefferson was too small for a thirty-five-year-old bachelor, even a Harvard M.A. and a Ph.D. from Heidelberg and his hair already beginning to turn white even at just twenty-five, to eat ice cream and read poetry with a sixteen-year-old high school girl. Though if it had to happen, maybe thirty-five was the best age for a bachelor to buy ice cream and poetry for a sixteen-year-old girl. I told Mother that. She didn't sound like a snake because snakes cant talk. But if dentists' drills could talk she would have sounded just like one.

"There's no best or safe age for a bachelor anywhere between three and eighty to buy ice cream for a sixteen-year-old girl," she said. "Forming her mind," she said. But she sounded just like cream when she talked to Uncle Gavin. No: she didn't sound like anything because she didn't say anything. She waited for him to begin it. No: she just waited because she knew he would have to begin it. Because Jefferson was that small. No, I mean Uncle Gavin had lived in Jefferson or in little towns all his life so he not only knew what Jefferson would be saying about him and Linda Snopes and those banana splits and ice cream sodas and books of poetry by now, but that Mother had too many good friends to ever miss hearing about it.

So she just waited. It was Saturday. Uncle Gavin walked twice in and out of the office (we still called it that because Grandfather had, except when Mother could hear us. Though after a while even she stopped trying to call it the library) where Mother was sitting at the desk adding up something, maybe the laundry; he walked in and out twice and she never moved. Then he said:

"I was thinking—" Because they were like that. I mean, I

thought the reason they were like that was because they were twins. I mean, I assumed that because I didn't know any other twins to measure them against. She didn't even stop adding.

"Of course," she said. "Why not tomorrow?" So he could have gone out then since obviously both of them knew what the other was talking about. But he said:

"Thank you." Then he said to me: "Aint Aleck Sander waiting for you outside?"

"Fiddlesticks," Mother said. "Anything he will learn about sixteen-year-old girls from you will probably be a good deal more innocent than what he will learn someday from sixteen-year-old girls. Shall I telephone her mother and ask her to let her come for dinner tomorrow, or do you want to?"

"Thank you," Uncle Gavin said. "Do you want me to tell you about it?"

"Do you want to?" Mother said.

"Maybe I'd better," Uncle Gavin said.

"Do you have to?" Mother said. This time Uncle Gavin didn't say anything. Then Mother said: "All right. We're listening." Again Uncle Gavin didn't say anything. But now he was Uncle Gavin again. I mean, until now he sounded a good deal like I sounded sometimes. But now he stood looking at the back of Mother's head, with his shock of white hair that always needed cutting and the stained bitt of the corncob pipe sticking out of his breast pocket and the eyes and the face that you never did quite know what they were going to say next except that when you heard it you realised it was always true, only a little cranksided; that nobody else would have said it quite that way.

"Well, well," he said, "if that's what a mind with no more aptitude for gossip and dirt than yours is inventing and thinking, just imagine what the rest of Jefferson, the experts, have made of it by now. By Cicero, it makes me feel young already; when I go to town this morning I believe I will buy myself a red necktie." He looked at the back of Mother's head. "Thank you, Maggie," he said. "It will need all of us of good will. To save Jefferson from Snopeses is a crisis, an emergency, a duty. To save a Snopes from Snopeses is a privilege, an honor, a pride."

"Especially a sixteen-year-old female one," Mother said.
"Yes," Uncle Gavin said. "Do you deny it?"

"Have I tried to?" Mother said.

"Yes, you have tried." He moved quick and put his hand on the top of her head, still talking. "And bless you for it. Tried always to deny that damned female instinct for uxorious and rigid respectability which is the backbone of any culture not yet decadent, which remains strong and undecadent only so long as it still produces an incorrigible unreconstructable with the temerity to assail and affront and deny it—like you—" and for a second both of us thought he was going to bend down and kiss her; maybe all three of us thought it. Then he didn't, or anyway Mother said:

"Stop it. Let me alone. Make up your mind: do you want me to telephone her, or will you do it?"

"I'll do it," he said. He looked at me. "Two red ties: one for you. I wish you were sixteen too. What she needs is a beau."

"Then if by being sixteen I'd have to be her beau, I'm glad I'm not sixteen," I said. "She's already got a beau. Matt Levitt. He won the Golden Gloves up in Ohio or somewhere last year. He acts like he can still use them. Would like to, too. No, much obliged," I said.

"What's that?" Mother said.

"Nothing," Uncle Gavin said.

"You never saw him box then," I said. "Or you wouldn't call him nothing. I saw him once. With Preacher Birdsong."

"And just which of your sporting friends is Preacher Birdsong?" Mother said.

"He aint sporting," I said. "He lives out in the country. He learned to box in France in the war. He and Matt Levitt—"

"Let me," Uncle Gavin said. "He—"

"Which he?" Mother said. "Your rival?"

"—is from Ohio," Uncle Gavin said. "He graduated from that new Ford mechanic's school and the company sent him here to be a mechanic in the agency garage—"

"He's the one that owns that yellow cut-down racer," I said. "And Linda rides in it?" Mother said.

"—and since Jefferson is not that large and he has two eyes," Uncle Gavin said, "sooner or later he saw Linda

Snopes, probably somewhere between her home and the school house; being male and about twenty-one, he naturally lost no time in making her acquaintance; the Golden Gloves reputation which he either really brought with him or invented somewhere en route, has apparently eliminated what rivals he might have expected——"

"Except you," Mother said.

"That's all," Uncle Gavin said.

"Except you," Mother said.

"He's maybe five years her senior," Uncle Gavin said. "I'm twice her age."

"Except you," Mother said. "I dont think you will live long enough to ever be twice any woman's age, I dont care what it is."

"All right," Uncle Gavin said. "What was it I just said? to save Jefferson from a Snopes is a duty; to save a Snopes from a Snopes is a privilege."

"An honor, you said," Mother said. "A pride."

"All right," Uncle Gavin said. "A joy then. Are you pleased now?" That was all, then. After a while Father came home but Mother didn't have much to tell him he didn't already know, so there wasn't anything for him to do except to keep on needing the wolf whistle that hadn't been invented yet; not until the next day after dinner in fact.

She arrived a little after twelve, just about when she could have got here after church if she had been to church. Which maybe she had, since she was wearing a hat. Or maybe it was her mother who made her wear the hat on account of Mother, coming up the street from the corner, running. Then I saw that the hat was a little awry on her head as if something had pulled or jerked at it or it had caught on something in passing, and that she was holding one shoulder with the other hand. Then I saw that her face was mad. It was scared too, but right now it was mostly just mad as she turned in the gate, still holding her shoulder but not running now, just walking fast and hard, the mad look beginning to give way to the scared one. Then they both froze into something completely different because then the car passed, coming up fast from the corner—Matt Levitt's racer because there were other stripped-down racers around now but his was the only one with that big double-barrel brass horn on the hood that played two notes when he pressed the button, going past fast; and suddenly it was like I had smelled something, caught a whiff of something for a second that even if I located it again I still wouldn't know whether I had ever smelled it before or not; the racer going on and Linda still walking rigid and fast with her hat on a little crooked and still holding her shoulder and still breathing a little fast even if what was on her face now was mostly being scared, on to the gallery where Mother and Uncle Gavin were waiting.

"Good morning, Linda," Mother said. "You've torn your sleeve."

"It caught on a nail," Linda said.

"I can see," Mother said. "Come on up to my room and slip it off and I'll tack it back for you."

"It's all right," Linda said. "If you've just got a pin."

"Then you take the needle and do it yourself while I see about dinner," Mother said. "You can sew, cant you?"

"Yessum," Linda said. So they went up to Mother's room and Uncle Gavin and I went to the office so Father could say to Uncle Gavin:

"Somebody been mauling at her before she could even get here? What's the matter, boy? Where's your spear and sword? where's your white horse?" Because Matt didn't blow the two-toned horn when he passed that first time so none of us knew yet what Linda was listening for, sitting at the dinner table with the shoulder of her dress sewed back all right but looking like somebody about ten years old had done it and her face still looking rigid and scared. Because we didn't re-alise it then. I mean, that she was having to do so many things at once: having to look like she was enjoying her din-ner and having to remember her manners in a strange house and with folks that she didn't have any particular reason to think were going to like her, and still having to wonder what Matt Levitt would do next without letting anybody know that's what was mainly on her mind. I mean, having to expect what was going to happen next and then, even while it was happening, having to look like she was eating and saying Yessum and Nome to what Mother was saying, and that cut-down racer going past in the street again with that two-toned horn blowing this time, blowing all the way past the house, and Father suddenly jerking his head up and making a loud snuffing noise, saying, "What's that I smell?"

"Smell?" Mother said. "Smell what?"

"That," Father said. "Something we haven't smelled around here in . . . how long was it, Gavin?" Because I knew now what Father meant, even if I wasn't born then and Cousin Gowan just told me. And Mother knew too. I mean, she remembered, since she had heard the other one when it was Mr de Spain's cut-out. I mean, even if she didn't know enough to connect that two-toned horn with Matt Levitt, all she had to do was look at Linda and Uncle Gavin. Or maybe just Uncle Gavin's face was enough, which is what you get for being twins with anybody. Because she said,

"Charley," and Father said:

"Maybe Miss Snopes will excuse me this time." He was talking at Linda now. "You see, whenever we have a pretty girl to eat with us, the prettier she is, the harder I try to make jokes so they will want to come back again. This time I just tried too hard. So if Miss Snopes will forgive me for trying too hard to be funny, I'll forgive her for being too pretty."

"Good boy," Uncle Gavin said. "Even if that one wasn't on tiptoe, at least it didn't wear spikes like the joke did. Let's go out to the gallery where it's cool, Maggie."

"Let's," Mother said. Then we were all standing there in the hall, looking at Linda. It wasn't just being scared in her face now, of being a sixteen-year-old girl for the first time in the home of people that probably had already decided not to approve of her. I didn't know what it was. But Mother did, maybe because it was Mother she was looking at it with.

"I think it will be cooler in the parlor," Mother said. "Let's go there." But it was too late. We could hear the horn, not missing a note: da DA da DA da DA getting louder and louder then going past the house still not missing a note as it faded on, and Linda staring at Mother for just another second or two with the desperation. Because it—the desperation— went too; maybe it was something like despair for a moment, but then that was gone too and her face was just rigid again.

"I've got to go," she said. "I . . . excuse me, I've got . . ." Then at least she kind of got herself together. "Thank you for my dinner, Mrs Mallison," she said. "Thank you for my dinner, Mr Mallison. Thank you for my dinner, Mr Gavin," already moving toward the table where she had put the hat and her purse. But then I hadn't expected her to thank me for it.

"Let Gavin drive you home," Mother said. "Gavin—"

"No no," she said. "I dont—he dont—" Then she was gone, out the front door and down the walk toward the gate, almost running again, then through the gate and then she was running, desperate and calm, not looking back. Then she was gone.

"By Cicero, Gavin," Father said. "You're losing ground. Last time you at least picked out a Spanish-American war hero with an E.M.F. sportster. Now the best you can do is a Golden Gloves amateur with a home-made racer. Watch yourself, bud, or next time you'll have a boy scout defying you to mortal combat with a bicycle."

"What?" Mother said.

"What would you do," Father said, "if you were a twenty-one-year-old garage mechanic who had to work until six p.m., and a white-headed old grandfather of a libertine was waylaying your girl on her way home from school every afternoon and tolling her into soda dens and plying her with ice cream? Because how could he know that all Gavin wants is just to form her mind?"

Only it wasn't every afternoon anymore. It wasn't any afternoon at all. I dont know what happened, how it was done: whether she sent word to Uncle Gavin not to try to meet her after school or whether she came and went the back way where he wouldn't see her, or whether maybe she stopped going to school at all for a while. Because she was in high school and I was in grammar school so there was no reason for me to know whether she was still going to school or not.

Or whether she was still in Jefferson, for that matter. Because now and then I would see Matt Levitt in his racer after the garage closed in the afternoon, when Linda used to be with him, and now and then at night going to and from the picture show. But not anymore now. He would be alone in the racer, or with another boy or man. But as far as I knew, Matt never saw her any more than Uncle Gavin did.

And you couldn't tell anything from Uncle Gavin. It used to be that on the way home from school I would see him and Linda inside Christian's drugstore eating ice cream and when he or they saw me he would beckon me in and we would all have ice cream. But that—the fact that there was no longer any reason to look in Christian's when I passed—was the only difference in him. Then one day—it was Friday—he was sitting at the table inside waiting and watching to beckon me inside, and even though there was no second dish on the table I thought that Linda had probably just stepped away for a moment, maybe to the perfume counter or the magazine rack, and even when I was inside and he said, "I'm having peach. What do you want?" I still expected Linda to step out from behind whatever for the moment concealed her.

"Strawberry," I said. On the table was the last book—it was John Donne—he had ordered for her.

"It will cost the same dime to mail it to her here in Jefferson that it would cost if she were in Memphis," he said. "Suppose I stand the ice cream and give you the dime and you take it by her house on the way home."

"All right," I said. When Mr Snopes first came to Jefferson he rented the house. Then he must have bought it because since he became vice president of the bank they had begun to fix it up. It was painted now and Mrs Snopes I reckon had had the wistaria arbor in the side yard fixed up and when I came through the gate Linda called me and I saw the hammock under the arbor. The wistaria was still in bloom and I remember how she looked with her black hair under it because her eyes were kind of the color of wistaria and her dress almost exactly was: lying in the hammock reading and I thought *Uncle Gavin didn't need to send this book because she hasn't finished the other one yet.* Then I saw the rest of her school books on the ground beneath the hammock and that the one she was reading was geometry and I wondered if knowing she would rather study geometry than be out with him would make Matt Levitt feel much better than having her eat ice cream with Uncle Gavin.

So I gave her the book and went on home. That was Friday. The next day, Saturday, I went to the baseball game and then I came back to the office to walk home with Uncle Gavin. We heard the feet coming up the outside stairs, more than two of them, making a kind of scuffling sound and we could even hear hard breathing and something like whispering, then the door kind of banged open and Matt Levitt came in, quick and fast, holding something clamped under his arm, and shoved the door back shut against whoever was trying to follow him inside, holding the door shut with his braced knee until he fumbled at the knob until he found how to shoot the bolt and lock it. Then he turned. He was good-looking. He didn't have a humorous or happy look, he had what Ratliff called a merry look, the merry look of a fellow that hadn't heard yet that they had invented doubt. But he didn't even look merry now and he took the book—it was the John Donne I had taken to Linda yesterday—and kind of shot it onto the desk so that the ripped and torn pages came scuttering and scattering out across the desk and some of them even on down to the floor.

"How do you like that?" Matt said, coming on around the desk where Uncle Gavin had stood up. "Dont you want to put up your dukes?" he said. "But that's right, you aint much of a fighter, are you. But that's O.K.; I aint going to hurt you much anyway: just mark you up a little to freshen up your memory." He didn't, he didn't seem to hit hard, his fists not travelling more than four or five inches it looked like, so that it didn't even look like they were drawing blood from Uncle Gavin's lips and nose but just instead wiping the blood onto them; two or maybe three blows before I could seem to move and grab up Grandfather's heavy walking stick where it still stayed in the umbrella stand behind the door and raise it to swing at the back of Matt's head as hard as I could.

"You, Chick!" Uncle Gavin said. "Stop! Hold it!" Though even without that, I wouldn't have thought Matt could have moved that fast. Maybe it was the Golden Gloves that did it. Anyway he turned and caught the stick and jerked it away from me almost before I knew it and naturally I thought he was going to hit me or Uncle Gavin or maybe both of us with it so I had already crouched to dive at his legs when he dropped the point of the stick like a bayoneted rifle, the point touching my chest just below the throat as if he were not holding me up but had really picked me up with the stick like you would a rag or a scrap of paper.

"Tough luck, kid," he said. "Nice going almost; too bad your uncle telegraphed it for you," and threw the stick into the corner and stepped around me toward the door, which was the first time I reckon that any of us realised that whoever it was he had locked out was still banging on it, and shot the bolt back and opened it then stepped back himself as Linda came in, blazing; yes, that's exactly the word for it: blazing: and without even looking at Uncle Gavin or me, whirled onto her tiptoes and slapped Matt twice, first with her left hand and then her right, panting and crying at the same time:

"You fool! You ox! You clumsy ignorant ox! You clumsy ignorant stupid son of a bitch!" Which was the first time I ever heard a sixteen-year-old girl say that. No: the first time I ever heard any woman say that, standing there facing Matt and crying hard now, like she was too mad to even know what to do next, whether to slap him again or curse him again, until Uncle Gavin came around the desk and touched her and said,

"Stop it. Stop it now," and she turned and grabbed him, her face against his shirt where he had bled onto it, still crying hard, saying,

"Mister Gavin, Mister Gavin, Mister Gavin."

"Open the door, Chick," Uncle Gavin said. I opened it. "Get out of here, boy," Uncle Gavin said to Matt. "Go on." Then Matt was gone. I started to close the door. "You too," Uncle Gavin said.

"Sir?" I said.

"You get out too," Uncle Gavin said, still holding Linda where she was shaking and crying against him, his nose bleeding onto her too now.

THIRTEEN

GAVIN STEVENS

"Go on," I said. "You get out too." So he did, and I stood there holding her. Or rather, she was gripping me, quite hard, shuddering and gasping, crying quite hard now, burrowing her face into my shirt so that I could feel my shirt front getting wet. Which was what Ratliff would have called tit for tat, since what Victorians would have called the claret from my nose had already stained the shoulder of her dress. So I could free one hand long enough to reach around and over her other shoulder to the handkerchief in my breast pocket and do a little emergency work with it until I could separate us long enough to reach the cold water tap.

"Stop it," I said. "Stop it now." But she only cried the harder, clutching me, saying,

"Mister Gavin. Mister Gavin. Oh, Mister Gavin."

"Linda," I said. "Can you hear me?" She didn't answer, just clutching me; I could feel her nodding her head against my chest. "Do you want to marry me?" I said.

"Yes!" she said. "Yes! All right! All right!"

This time I got one hand under her chin and lifted her face by force until she would have to look at me. Ratliff had told me that McCarron's eyes were gray, probably the same hard gray as Hub Hampton's. Hers were not gray at all. They were darkest hyacinth, what I have always imagined that Homer's hyacinthine sea must have had to look like.

"Listen to me," I said. "Do you want to get married?" Yes, they dont need minds at all, except for conversation, social intercourse. And I have known some who had charm and tact without minds even then. Because when they deal with men, with human beings, all they need is the instinct, the intuition before it became battered and dulled, the infinite capacity for devotion untroubled and unconfused by cold moralities and colder facts.

"You mean I dont have to?" she said.

"Of course not," I said. "Never if you like."

"I dont want to marry anybody!" she said, cried; she was clinging to me again, her face buried again in the damp mixture of blood and tears which seemed now to compose the front of my shirt and tie. "Not anybody!" she said. "You're all I have, all I can trust. I love you! I love you!"

FOURTEEN

CHARLES MALLISON
When he got home, his face was clean. But his nose and his lip still showed, and there wasn't anything he could have done about his shirt and tie. Except he could have bought new ones, since on Saturday the stores were still open. But he didn't. Maybe even that wouldn't have made any difference with Mother; maybe that's one of the other things you have to accept in being a twin. And yes sir, if dentists' drills could talk, that's exactly what Mother would have sounded like after she got done laughing and crying both and saying Damn you, Gavin, damn you damn you, and Uncle Gavin had gone up stairs to put on a clean shirt and tie for supper.

"Forming her mind," Mother said.

It was like he could stand just anything except getting knocked down or getting his nose bloodied. Like if Mr de Spain hadn't knocked him down in the alley behind that Christmas dance, he could have got over Mrs Snopes without having to form Linda's mind. And like if Matt Levitt hadn't come into the office that afternoon and bloodied his nose again, he could have stopped there with Linda's mind without having to do any more to it.

So he didn't stop because he couldn't. But at least he got rid of Matt Levitt. That was in the spring, it was her last year in high school; she would graduate in May and any school afternoon I could see her walking along the street from school with a few books under her arm. But if any of them was poetry now I didn't know it, because when she came to Christian's drugstore now she wouldn't even look toward the door, just walking on past with her face straight in front and her head up a little like the pointer just a step or two from freezing on the game; walking on like she saw people, saw Jefferson, saw the Square all right because at the moment, at any moment she had to walk on and among and through something and it might as well be Jefferson and Jefferson people and the Jefferson Square as anything else, but that was all.

Because Uncle Gavin wasn't there somewhere around like an accident any more now. But then, if Uncle Gavin wasn't sitting on the opposite side of that marble-topped table in Christian's watching her eating something out of a tall glass that cost every bit of fifteen or twenty cents, Matt Levitt wasn't there either. Him and his cut-down racer both because the racer was empty now except for Matt himself after the garage closed on week days, creeping along the streets and across the Square in low gear, parallelling but a little behind where she would be walking to the picture show now with another girl or maybe two or three of them, her head still high and not once looking at him while the racer crept along at her elbow almost, the cut-out going chuckle-chuckle-chuckle, right up to the picture show and the two or three or four girls had gone into it. Then the racer would dash off at full speed around the block, to come rushing back with the cut-out as loud as he could make it, up the alley beside the picture show and then across in front of it and around the block and up the alley again, this time with Otis Harker, who had succeeded Grover Cleveland Winbush as night marshal after Grover Cleveland retired after what Ratliff called his eye trouble, waiting at the corner yelling at Matt at the same time he was jumping far enough back not to be run over.

And on Sunday through the Square, the cut-out going full blast and Mr Buck Connors, the day marshal now, hollering after him. And now he—Matt—had a girl with him, a country girl he had found somewhere, the racer rushing and roaring through the back streets into the last one, to rush slow and loud past Linda's house, as if the sole single symbol of frustrated love or anyway desire or maybe just frustration possible in Jefferson was an automobile cut-out; the sole single manifestation which love or anyway desire was capable of assuming in Jefferson, was rushing slow past the specific house with the cut-out wide open, so that he or she would have to know who was passing no matter how hard they worked at not looking out the window.

Though by that time Mr Connors had sent for the sheriff

himself. He—Mr Connors—said his first idea was to wake up Otis Harker to come back to town and help him but when Otis heard that what Mr Connors wanted was to stop that racer, Otis wouldn't even get out of bed. Later, afterward, somebody asked Matt if he would have run over Mr Hampton too and Matt said—he was crying then, he was so mad—"Hit him? Hub Hampton? have all them god-damn guts splashed over my paint job?" Though by then even Mr Hampton wasn't needed for the cut-out because Matt went right on out of town, maybe taking the girl back home; anyway about midnight that night they telephoned in for Mr Hampton to send somebody out to Caledonia where Matt had had a bad fight with Anse McCallum, one of Mr Buddy McCallum's boys, until Anse snatched up a fence rail or something and would have killed Matt except that folks caught and held them both while they telephoned for the sheriff and brought them both in to town and locked them in the jail and the next morning Mr Buddy McCallum came in on his cork leg and paid them both out and took them down to the lot behind I.O. Snopes's mule barn and told Anse:

"All right. If you cant be licked fair without picking up a fence rail, I'm going to take my leg off and whip you with it myself."

So they fought again, without the fence rail this time, with Mr Buddy and a few more men watching them now, and Anse still wasn't as good as Matt's Golden Gloves but he never quit until at last Mr Buddy himself said, "All right. That's enough," and told Anse to wash his face at the trough and then go and get in the car and then said to Matt: "And I reckon the time has come for you to be moving on too." Except that wasn't necessary now either; the garage said Matt was already fired and Matt said,

"Fired, hell. I quit. Tell the son of a bitch to come down here and say that to my face." And Mr Hampton was there too by then, tall, with his big belly and his little hard eyes looking down at Matt. "Where the hell is my car?" Matt said.

"It's at my house," Mr Hampton said. "I had it brought in this morning."

"Well well," Matt said. "Too bad, aint it? McCallum came

in and sprung me before you had time to sell it and stick the money in your pocket, huh? What are you going to say when I walk over there and get in it and start the engine?"

"Nothing, son," Mr Hampton said. "Whenever you want to leave."

"Which is right now," Matt said. "And when I leave your . . . .ing town, my foot'll be right down to the floor board on that cut-out too. And you can stick that too, but not in your pocket. What do you think of that?"

"Nothing, son," Mr Hampton said. "I'll make a trade with you. Run that cut-out wide open all the way to the county line and then ten feet past it, and I wont let anybody bother you if you'll promise never to cross it again."

And that was all. That was Monday, trade day; it was like the whole county was there, had come to town just to stand quiet around the Square and watch Matt cross it for the last time, the paper suitcase he had come to Jefferson with on the seat by him and the cut-out clattering and popping; nobody waving goodbye to him and Matt not looking at any of us: just that quiet and silent suspension for the little gaudy car to rush slowly and loudly through, blatant and noisy and defiant yet at the same time looking as ephemeral and innocent and fragile as a child's toy, a birthday favor, so that looking at it you knew it would probably never get as far as Memphis, let alone Ohio; on across the Square and into the street which would become the Memphis highway at the edge of town, the sound of the cut-out banging and clattering and echoing between the walls, magnified a thousand times now beyond the mere size and bulk of the frail little machine which produced it; and we—some of us—thinking how surely now he would rush slow and roaring for the last time at least past Linda Snopes's house. But he didn't. He just went on, the little car going faster and faster up the broad street empty too for the moment as if it too had vacated itself for his passing, on past where the last houses of town would give way to country, the vernal space of woods and fields where even the defiant uproar of the cut-out would become puny and fade and be at last absorbed.

So that was what Father called—said to Uncle Gavin—one down. And now it was May and already everybody knew that

Linda Snopes was going to be the year's Number One student, the class's valedictorian; Uncle Gavin slowed us as we approached Wildermark's and nudged us in to the window, saying, "That one. Just behind the green one."

It was a lady's fitted travelling case.

"That's for travelling," Mother said.

"All right," Uncle Gavin said.

"For travelling," Mother said. "For going away."

"Yes," Uncle Gavin said. "She's got to get away from here. Get out of Jefferson."

"What's wrong with Jefferson?" Mother said. The three of us stood there. I could see our three reflections in the plate glass, standing there looking at the fitted feminine case. She didn't talk low or loud: just quiet. "All right," she said. "What's wrong with Linda then?"

Uncle Gavin didn't either. "I dont like waste," he said. "Everybody should have his chance not to waste."

"Or his chance to the right not to waste a young girl?" Mother said.

"All right," Uncle Gavin said. "I want her to be happy. Everybody should have the chance to be happy."

"Which she cant possibly do of course just standing still in Jefferson," Mother said.

"All right," Uncle Gavin said. They were not looking at one another. It was like they were not even talking to one another but simply at the two empty reflections in the plate glass, like when you put the written idea into the anonymous and even interchangeable empty envelope, or maybe into the sealed empty bottle to be cast into the sea, or maybe two written thoughts sealed forever at the same moment into two bottles and cast into the sea to float and drift with the tides and the currents on to the cooling world's end itself, still immune, still intact and inviolate, still ideas and still true and even still facts whether any eye ever saw them again or any other idea ever responded and sprang to them, to be elated or validated or grieved.

"The chance and duty and right to see that everybody is happy, whether they deserve it or not or even want it or not," Mother said.

"All right," Uncle Gavin said. "Sorry I bothered you.

Come on. Let's go home. Mrs Rouncewell can send her a dozen sunflowers."

"Why not?" Mother said, taking his arm, already turning him, our three reflections turning in the plate glass, back toward the entrance and into the store, Mother in front now across to the luggage department.

"I think the blue one will suit her coloring, match her eyes," Mother said. "It's for Linda Snopes—her graduation," Mother told Miss Eunice Gant, the clerk.

"How nice," Miss Eunice said. "Is Linda going on a trip?"

"Oh yes," Mother said. "Very likely. At least probably to one of the eastern girls' schools next year perhaps. Or so I heard."

"How nice," Miss Eunice said. "I always say that every young boy and girl should go away from home for at least one year of school in order to learn how the other half lives."

"How true," Mother said. "Until you do go and see, all you do is hope. Until you actually see for yourself, you never do give up and settle down, do you?"

"Maggie," Uncle Gavin said.

"Give up?" Miss Eunice said. "Give up hope? Young people should never give up hope."

"Of course not," Mother said. "They dont have to. All they have to do is stay young, no matter how long it takes."

"Maggie," Uncle Gavin said.

"Oh," Mother said, "you want to pay cash for it instead of charge? All right; I'm sure Mr Wildermark wont mind." So Uncle Gavin took two twenty dollar bills from his wallet and took out one of his cards and gave it to Mother.

"Thank you," she said. "But Miss Eunice probably has a big one, that will hold all four names." So Miss Eunice gave her the big card and Mother held out her hand until Uncle Gavin uncapped his pen and gave it to her and we watched her write in the big sprawly hand that still looked like somebody thirteen years old in the ninth grade:

Mr and Mrs Charles Mallison
Charles Mallison Jr
Mr Gavin Stevens

and capped the pen and handed it back to Uncle Gavin and

took the card between the thumb and finger of one hand and waved it dry and gave it to Miss Eunice.

"I'll send it out tonight," Miss Eunice said. "Even if the graduation isn't until next week. It's such a handsome gift, why shouldn't Linda have that much more time to enjoy it."

"Yes," Mother said. "Why shouldn't she?" Then we were outside again, our three reflections jumbled into one walking now across the plate glass; Mother had Uncle Gavin's arm again.

"All four of our names," Uncle Gavin said. "At least her father wont know a white-headed bachelor sent his seventeen-year-old daughter a fitted travelling case."

"Yes," Mother said. "One of them wont know it."

FIFTEEN

GAVIN STEVENS

The difficulty was, how to tell her, explain to her. I mean, why. Not the deed, the act itself, but the reason for it, the *why* behind it—say point blank to her over one of the monstrous synthetic paradoxes which were her passion or anyway choice in Christian's drugstore, or perhaps out on the street itself: "We wont meet anymore from now on because after Jefferson assimilates all the details of how your boyfriend tracked you down in my office and bloodied my nose one Saturday, and eight days later, having spent his last night in Jefferson in the county jail, shook our dust forever from his feet with the turbulent uproar of his racer's cut-out;—after that, for you to be seen still meeting me in ice cream dens will completely destroy what little was left of your good name."

You see? That was it: the very words *reputation* and *good name*. Merely to say them, speak them aloud, give their existence vocal recognition, would irrevocably soil and besmirch them, would destroy the immunity of the very things they represented, leaving them not just vulnerable but already doomed; from the inviolable and proud integrity of principles they would become, reduce to, the ephemeral and already doomed and damned fragility of human conditions; innocence and virginity become symbol and postulant of loss and grief, evermore to be mourned, existing only in the past tense *was* and *now is not, no more no more.*

That was the problem. Because the act, the deed itself, was simple enough. Luckily the affair happened late on a Saturday afternoon, which would give my face thirty-six hours anyway before it would have to make a public appearance. (It wouldn't have needed that long except for the ring he wore—a thing not quite as large as a brass knuckle and not really noticeably unlike gold if you didn't get too close probably, of a tiger's head gripping between its jaws what had been—advisedly—a ruby; advisedly because the fact that the stone was missing at the moment was a loss only to my lip.)

Besides, the drugstore meetings were not even a weekly affair, let alone daily, so even a whole week could pass before
(1) it would occur to someone that we had not met in over a
week, who (2) would immediately assume that we had something to conceal was why we had not met in over a week, and
(3) the fact that we had met again after waiting over a week
only proved it.

By which time I was even able to shave past my cut lip. So
it was very simple; simple indeed in fact, and I the simple one.
I had planned it like this: the carefully timed accident which
would bring me out the drugstore door, the (say) tin of pipe
tobacco still in plain sight on its way to the pocket, at the
exact moment when she would pass on her way to school:
"Good morning, Linda—" already stepping on past her and
then already pausing: "I have another book for you. Meet me
here after school this afternoon and we'll have a coke over it."

Which would be all necessary. Because I was the simple
one, to whom it had never once occurred that the blow of
that ruby-vacant reasonably almost-gold tiger's head might
have marked her too even if it didn't leave a visible cut; that
innocence is innocent not because it rejects but because it
accepts; is innocent not because it is impervious and invulnerable to everything, but because it is capable of accepting
anything and still remaining innocent; innocent because it
foreknows all and therefore doesn't have to fear and be afraid;
the tin of tobacco now in my coat pocket because by this time
even it had become noticeable, the last book-burdened stragglers now trotting toward the sound of the first strokes of the
school bell and still she had not passed; obviously I had
missed her somehow: either taken my post not soon enough
or she had taken another route to school or perhaps would
not leave home for school at all today, for whatever reasons
no part of which were the middleaged bachelor's pandering
her to Jonson and Herrick and Thomas Campion; crossing—
I—the now-unchildrened street at last, mounting the outside
stairs since tomorrow was always tomorrow; indeed, I could
even use the tobacco tin again, provided I didn't break the
blue stamp for verity, and opened the screen door and entered
the office.

She was sitting neither in the revolving chair behind the

desk nor in the leather client's one before it but in a straight
hard armless one against the book-case as though she had
fled, been driven until the wall stopped her, and turned then,
her back against it, not quite sitting in the chair nor quite
huddled in it because although her legs, knees were close and
rigid and her hands were clasped tight in her lap, her head
was still up watching the door and then me with the eyes the
McCarron boy had marked her with which at a distance
looked as black as her hair until you saw they were that blue
so dark as to be almost violet.

"I thought . . ." she said. "They—somebody said Matt quit
his job and left—went yesterday. I thought you might . . . ."

"Of course," I said. "I always want to see you," stopping
myself in time from *I've been waiting over there on the corner
until the last bell rang, for you to pass* though this is what I
really stopped from *Get up. Get out of here quick. Why did you
come here anyway? Dont you see this is the very thing I have been
lying awake at night with ever since Saturday?* So I merely said
that I had bought the can of tobacco which I must now find
someone capable or anyway willing to smoke, to give it to, to
create the chance to say: "I have another book for you. I forgot to bring it this morning, but I'll bring it at noon. I'll wait
for you at Christian's after school and stand you a soda too.
Now you'll have to hurry; you're already late."

I had not even released the screen door and so had only to
open it again, having also in that time in which she crossed
the room, space to discard a thousand frantic indecisions: to
remain concealed in the office as though I had not been there
at all this morning, and let her leave alone; to follow to the
top of the stairs and see her down them, avuncular and fond;
to walk her to the school itself and wait to see her through
the actual door: the family friend snatching the neighbor's
child from the rife midst of truancy and restoring it to duty—
family friend to Flem Snopes who had no more friends than
Blackbeard or Pistol, to Eula Varner who no more had friends
than man or woman either would have called them that
Messalina and Helen had.

So I did all three: waited in the office too long, so that I
had to follow down the stairs too fast, and then along the
street beside her not far enough either to be un-noticed or

forgotten. Then there remained only to suborn my nephew with the dollar bill and the book: I dont remember which one, I dont believe I even noticed.

"Sir?" Chick said. "I meet her in Christian's drugstore after school and give her the book and tell her you'll try to get there but not to wait. And buy her a soda. Why dont I just give her the book at school and save time?"

"Certainly," I said. "Why dont you just give me back the dollar?"

"And buy her a soda," he said. "Do I have to pay for that out of the dollar?"

"All right," I said. "Twenty-five cents then. If she takes a banana split you can drink water and make a nickel more."

"Maybe she'll take a coke," he said. "Then I can have one too and still make fifteen cents."

"All right," I said.

"Or suppose she dont want anything."

"Didn't I say all right?" I said. "Just dont let your mother hear you say 'she dont'."

"Why?" he said. "Father and Ratliff say 'she dont' all the time, and so do you when you are talking to them. And Ratliff says 'taken' for 'took' and 'drug' for 'dragged' and so do you when you are talking to country people like Ratliff."

"How do you know?" I said.

"I've heard you. So has Ratliff."

"Why? Did you tell him to?"

"No sir," he said. "Ratliff told me."

My rejoinder may have been Wait until you get as old as Ratliff and your father and me and you can too, though I dont remember. But then, inside the next few months I was to discover myself doing lots of things he wasn't old enough yet for the privilege. Which was beside the point anyway now; now only the afternoon remained: the interminable time until a few moments after half-past-three filled with a thousand indecisions which each fierce succeeding harassment would revise. You see? She had not only abetted me in making that date with which I would break, wreck, shatter, destroy, slay something, she had even forestalled me in it by the simplicity of directness.

So I had only to pass that time. That is, get it passed, live it down; the office window as good as any for that and better than most since it looked down on the drugstore entrance so I had only to lurk there. Not to hear the dismissal bell of course this far away but rather to see them first: the little ones, the infantile inflow and scatter of primer- and first-graders, then the middle-graders boisterous and horsing as to the boys, then the mature ones, juniors and seniors grave with weight and alien with puberty; and there she was, tall (no: not for a girl that tall but all right then: tall, like a heron out of a moil of frogs and tadpoles), pausing for just one quick second at the drugstore entrance for one quick glance, perhaps at the empty stairway. Then she entered, carrying three books any one of which might have been that book and I thought *He gave it to her at school; the damned little devil has foxed me for that odd quarter.*

But then I saw Chick; he entered too, carrying the book and then I thought how if I had only thought to fill a glass with water, to count off slowly sixty seconds say to cover the time Skeets McGowan, the soda squirt, would need to tear his fascinations from whatever other female junior or senior and fill the order, then drink the water slowly to simulate the coke; thinking *But maybe she did take the banana split; maybe there is still time,* already across the office, the screen door already in my hand before I caught myself: at least the county attorney must not be actually *seen* running down his office stairs and across the street into a drugstore where a sixteen-year-old high school junior waited.

And I was in time but just in time. They had not even sat down, or if they had she had already risen, the two of them only standing beside the table, she carrying four books now and looking at me for only that one last instant and then no more with the eyes you thought were just dark gray or blue until you knew better.

"I'm sorry I'm late," I said. "I hope Chick told you."

"It's all right," she said. "I have to go on home anyway."

"Without a coke even?" I said.

"I have to go home," she said.

"Another time then," I said. "What they call a rain check."

"Yes," she said. "I have to go home now." So I moved so

she could move, making the move first to let her go ahead, toward the door.

"Remember what you said about that quarter," Chick said.

And made the next move first too, opening the screen for her then stopping in it and so establishing severance and separation by that little space before she even knew it, not even needing to pause and half-glance back to prove herself intact and safe, intact and secure and unthreatened still, not needing to say Mister Stevens nor even Mister Gavin nor Goodbye nor even anything to need to say Thank you for, nor even to look back then although she did. "Thank you for the book," she said; and gone.

"Remember what you said about that quarter," Chick said.

"Certainly," I said. "Why the bejesus dont you go somewhere and spend it?"

Oh yes, doing a lot of things Chick wasn't old enough yet himself to do. Because dodging situations which might force me to use even that base shabby lash again was fun, excitement. Because she didn't know (Must not know, at least not now, not yet: else why the need for that base and shabby lash?), could not be certainly sure about that afternoon, that one or two or three (whatever it was) minutes in the drugstore; never sure whether what Chick told her was the truth: that I actually was going to be late and had simply sent my nephew as the handiest messenger to keep her company until or when or if I did show up, I so aged and fatuous as not even to realise the insult either standing her up would be, or sending a ten-year-old boy to keep her company and believing that she, a sixteen-year-old high school junior, would accept him; or if I had done it deliberately: made the date then sent the ten-year-old boy to fill it as a delicate way of saying *Stop bothering me.*

So I must not even give her a chance to demand of me with the temerity of desperation which of these was right. And that was the fun, the excitement. I mean, dodging her. It was adolescence in reverse, turned upside down: the youth, himself virgin and—who knew?—maybe even more so, at once drawn and terrified of what draws him, contriving by clumsy and timorous artifice the accidental encounters in which he still would not and never quite touch, would not even hope to

touch, really want to touch, too terrified in fact to touch; but
only to breathe the same air, be laved by the same circumambience which laved the mistress's moving limbs; to whom the
glove or the handkerchief she didn't even know she had lost,
the flower she did even know she had crushed, the very
ninth- or tenth-grade arithmetic or grammar or geography
bearing her name in her own magical hand on the flyleaf, are
more terrible and moving than ever will be afterward the
gleam of the actual naked shoulder or spread of unbound hair
on the pillow's other twin.

That was me: not to encounter; continuously just to miss
her yet never be caught at it. You know: in a little town of
three thousand people like ours, the only thing that could
cause more talk and notice than a middleaged bachelor meeting a sixteen-year-old maiden two or three times a week,
would be a sixteen-year-old maiden and a middleaged bachelor just missing each other two or three times a week by darting into stores or up alleys. You know: a middleaged lawyer,
certainly the one who was county attorney too, could always
find enough to do even in a town of just three thousand to
miss being on the one street between her home and the
school house at eight-thirty and twelve and one and three-
thirty oclock when the town's whole infant roster must come
and go, sometimes, a few times even, but not forever.

Yet that's what I had to do. I had no help, you see; I couldn't
stop her suddenly on the street one day and say, "Answer
quickly now. Exactly how much were you fooled or not
fooled that afternoon in the drugstore? Say in one word exactly what you believe about that episode." All I could do was
leave well-enough alone, even when the only well-enough I
had wasn't anywhere that well.

So I had to dodge her. I had to plan not just mine but
Yoknapatawpha County's business too ahead in order to
dodge a sixteen-year-old girl. That was during the spring. So
until school was out in May it would be comparatively simple,
at least for five days of the week. But in time vacation would
arrive, with no claims of regimen or discipline on her; and
observation even if not personal experience had long since
taught me that anyone sixteen years old not nursing a child or

supporting a family or in jail, could be almost anywhere at any time during the twenty-four hours.

So when the time came, which was that last summer before her final year in high school when she would graduate, I didn't even have the catalogues and brochures from the alien and outland schools sent first to me in person, to be handed by me to her, but sent direct to her, to Miss Linda Snopes, Jefferson, Mississippi, the Mississippi to be carefully spelt out in full else the envelope would go: first, to Jefferson, Missouri; second, to every other state in the forty-eight which had a Jefferson in it, before: third, it would finally occur to somebody somewhere that there might be someone in Mississippi capable of thinking vaguely of attending an eastern or northern school or capable of having heard of such or anyway capable of enjoying the pictures in the catalogues or even deciphering the one-syllable words, provided they were accompanied by photographs.

So I had them sent direct to her—the shrewd suave snob-enticements from the Virginia schools at which Southern mothers seemed to aim their daughters by simple instinct, I dont know why, unless because the mothers themselves did not attend them, and thus accomplishing by proxy what had been denied them in person since they had not had mothers driven to accomplish vicariously what they in their turn had been denied.

And not just the Virginia ones first but the ones from the smart 'finishing' schools north of Mason's and Dixon's too. I was being fair. No: we were being fair, she and I both, the two of us who never met anymore now for the sake of her good name, in federation and cahoots for the sake of her soul; the two of us together saying *in absentia* to her mother: *There they all are: the smart ones, the snob ones. We have been fair, we gave you your chance. Now, here is where we want to go, where you can help us go, if not by approval, at least by not saying No;* arranging for the other catalogues to reach her only then: the schools which would not even notice what she wore and how she walked and used her fork and all the rest of how she looked and acted in public because by this time all that would be too old and fixed to change, but mainly because it had not

mattered anyway since what did matter was what she did and
how she acted in the spirit's inviolable solitude.

So now—these last began to reach her about Christmas
time of that last year in high school—she would have to see
me, need to see me, not to help her decide which one of
them but simply to discuss, canvass the decision before it
became final. I waited, in fact quite patiently while it finally
dawned on me that she was not going to make the first gesture to see me again. I had avoided her for over six months
now and she not only knew I had been dodging her since in
a town the size of ours a male can no more avoid a female
consistently for that long by mere accident than they can
meet for that long by what they believed or thought was discretion and surreption, even she realised by this time that
that business in Christian's drugstore that afternoon last April
had been no clumsy accident. (Oh yes, it had already occurred to me also that she had no reason whatever to assume
I knew she had received the catalogues, let alone had instigated them. But I dismissed that as immediately as you will
too if we are to get on with this.)

So I must make that first gesture. It would not be quite as
simple now as it had used to be. A little after half-past-three
on any weekday afternoon I could see her from the office
window (if I happened to be there) pass along the Square in
the school's scattering exodus. Last year, in fact during all the
time before, she would be alone, or seemed to be. But now,
during this past one, particularly since the Levitt troglodyte's
departure, she would be with another girl who lived on the
same street. Then suddenly (it began in the late winter, about
St Valentine's day) instead of two there would be four of
them: two boys, Chick said the Rouncewell boy and the
youngest Bishop one, the year's high school athletic stars.
And now, after spring began, the four of them would be on
almost any afternoon in Christian's drugstore (at least there
harbored apparently there no ghosts to make her blush and
squirm and I was glad of that), with coca colas and the
other fearsome (I was acquainted there) messes which young
people, young women in particular, consume with terrifying
equanimity not only in the afternoon but at nine and ten in
the morning too: which—the four of them—I had taken to

be two pairs, two couples in the steadfast almost uxorious fashion of high school juniors and seniors, until one evening I saw (by chance) her going toward the picture show squired by both of them.

Which would make it a little difficult now. But not too much. In fact, it would be quite simple (not to mention the fact that it was already May and I couldn't much longer afford to wait): merely to wait for some afternoon when she would be without her convoy, when the Bishop and the Rouncewell would have to practise their dedications or maybe simply be kept in by a teacher after school. Which I did, already seeing her about a block away but just in time to see her turn suddenly into a street which would by-pass the Square itself: obviously a new route home she had adopted to use on the afternoons when she was alone, was already or (perhaps) wanted to be.

But that was simple too: merely to back-track one block then turn myself one block more to the corner where the street she was in must intercept. But quicker than she, faster than she, so that I saw her first walking fast along the purlieus of rubbish and ashcans and loading platforms until she saw me at the corner and stopped in dead midstride and one quick fleeing half-raised motion of the hand. So that, who knows? at that sudden distance I might not have even stopped, being already in motion again, raising my hand and arm in return and on, across the alley, striding on as you would naturally expect a county attorney to be striding along a side street at forty-two minutes past three in the afternoon; one whole block more for safety and then safe, inviolate still the intactness, unthreatened again.

There was the telephone of course. But that would be too close, too near the alley and the raised hand. And *grüss Gott* they had invented the typewriter; the Board of Supervisors could subtract the letterhead from my next pay check or who knows they might not even miss it; the typewriter and the time of course were already mine:

Dear Linda:
  When you decide which one you like the best, let's have a talk. I've seen some of them myself and can tell you more than the

*catalogue may have. We should have a banana split too; they
may not have heard of them yet at Bennington and Bard and
Swarthmore and you'll have to be a missionary as well as a
student.*

Then in pencil, in my hand:

*Saw you in the alley the other afternoon but didn't have time to
stop. Incidentally, what were you doing in an alley?*

You see? *the other afternoon* so that it wouldn't matter when
I mailed it: two days from now or two weeks from now; two
whole weeks in which to tear it up, and even addressed the
stamped envelope, knowing as I did so that I was deliberately
wasting two—no, three, bought singly—whole cents, then
tore them neatly across once and matched the torn edges
and tore them across again and built a careful small tepee
on the cold hearth and struck a match and watched the burn
and uncreaked mine ancient knees and shook my trousers
down.

Because it was May now; in two weeks she would graduate.
But then Miss Eunice Gant had promised to send the dressing case yesterday afternoon and *grüss Gott* they had invented
the telephone too. So once more (this would be the last one,
the last lurk) to wait until half-past-eight oclock (the bank
would not open until nine but then even though Flem was
not president of it you simply declined to imagine him hanging around the house until the last moment for the chance to
leap to the ringing telephone) and then picked it up:

"Good morning, Mrs Snopes. Gavin Stevens. May I speak
to Linda if she hasn't already . . . I see, I must have missed
her. But then I was late myself this morning . . . Thank you.
We are all happy to know the dressing case pleased her.
Maggie will be pleased to have the note . . . . If you'll give
her the message when she comes home to dinner. I have some
information about a Radcliffe scholarship which might interest her. That's practically Harvard too and I can tell her about
Cambridge . . . Yes, if you will: that I'll be waiting for her in
the drugstore after school this afternoon. Thank you."

And goodbye. The sad word, even over the telephone. I

mean, not the word is sad nor the meaning of it, but that you really can say it, that the time comes always in time when you can say it without grief and anguish now but without even the memory of grief and anguish, remembering that night in this same office here (when was it? ten years ago? twelve years?) when I had said not just Goodbye but Get the hell out of here to Eula Varner, and no hair bleached, no bead of anguished sweat or tear sprang out, and what regret still stirred a little was regret that even if I had been brave enough not to say No then, even that courage would not matter now since even the cowardice was only thin regret.

At first I thought I would go inside and be already sitting at the table waiting. Then I thought better: it must be casual but not taken-for-granted casual. So I stood at the entrance, but back, not to impede the juvenile flood or perhaps rather not to be trampled by it. Because she must not see me from a block away waiting, but casual, by accident outwardly and chance: first the little ones, first- and second- and third-grade; and now already the larger ones, the big grades and the high school; it would be soon now, any time now. Except that it was Chick, with a folded note.

"Here," he said. "It seems to be stuck."

"Stuck?" I said.

"The record. The victrola. This is the same tune it was playing before, aint it? just backward this time." Because she probably had insisted he read it first before she released it to him. So I was the second, not counting her:

> Dear Mr Stevens
>   *I will have to be a little late if you can wait for me*
>   *Linda*

"Not quite the same," I said. "I dont hear any dollar now."

"Okay," he said. "Neither did I. I reckon you aint coming home now."

"So do I," I said. So I went inside then and sat down at the table; I owed her that much anyway; the least I could give her was revenge so let it be full revenge; full satisfaction of watching from wherever she would be watching while I sat still waiting for her long after even I knew she would not come;

let it be the full whole hour then since 'finis' is not 'goodbye'
and has no cause to grieve the spring of grief.

So when she passed rapidly across the plate glass window, I
didn't know her. Because she was approaching not from the
direction of the school but from the opposite one, as though
she were on her way to school, not from it. No: that was not
the reason. She was already in the store now, rapidly, the
screen clapping behind her, at the same instant and in the
same physical sense both running and poised motionless,
wearing not the blouse and skirt or print cotton dress above
the flat-heeled shoes of school; but dressed, I mean 'dressed',
in a hat and high heels and silk stockings and makeup who
needed none and already I could smell the scent: one poised
split-second of immobilised and utter flight in bizarre and
paradox panoply of allure, like a hawk caught by a speed lense.

"It's all right," I said. Because at least I still had that much
presence.

"I cant," she said. At least that much presence. There were
not many people in the store but even one could have been
too many so I was already up now, moving toward her.

"How nice you look," I said. "Come on; I'll walk a way
with you," and turned her that way, not even touching her
arm, on and out, onto the pavement, talking (I presume I
was; I usually am), speaking: which was perhaps why I did not
even realise that she had chosen the direction, not in fact
until I realised that she had actually turned toward the foot of
the office stairs, only then touching her: her elbow, holding it
a little, on past the stairs so that none (one hoped intended
must believe) had marked that falter, on along the late spring
store-fronts—the hardware and farm-furnish stores cluttered
with garden and farm tools and rolls of uncut plowline and
sample sacks of slag and fertilizer and even the grocery ones
exposing neat cases of seed packets stencilled with gaudy and
incredible vegetables and flowers—talking (oh ay, trust me always) sedate and decorous: the young girl decked and scented
to go wherever a young woman would be going at four
oclock on a May afternoon, and the gray-headed bachelor,
avuncular and what old Negroes called 'settled', incapable
now of harm, slowed the blood and untroubled now the flesh
by turn of wrist or ankle, faint and dusty-dry as memory now

the hopes and anguishes of youth—until we could turn a corner into privacy or at least room or anyway so long as we did not actually stop.

"I cant," she said.

"You said that before," I said. "You cant what?"

"The schools," she said. "The ones you . . . . the catalogues. From outside Jefferson, outside Mississippi."

"I'm glad you cant," I said. "I didn't expect you to decide alone. That's why I wanted to see you: to help you pick the right one."

"But I cant," she said. "Dont you understand? I cant."

Then I—yes, I—stopped talking. "All right," I said. "Tell me."

"I cant go to any of them. I'm going to stay in Jefferson. I'm going to the Academy next year." Oh yes, I stopped talking now. It wasn't what the Academy was that mattered. It wasn't even that the Academy was in Jefferson that mattered. It was Jefferson itself which was the mortal foe since Jefferson was Snopes.

"I see," I said. "All right. I'll talk to her myself."

"No," she said. "No. I dont want to go away."

"Yes," I said. "We must. It's too important. It's too important for even you to see now. Come on. We'll go home now and talk to your mother—" already turning. But already she had caught at me, grasping my wrist and forearm with both hands, until I stopped. Then she let go and just stood there in the high heels and the silk stockings and the hat that was a little too old for her or maybe I was not used to her in a hat or maybe the hat just reminded me of the only other time I ever saw her in a hat which was that fiasco of a Sunday dinner at home two years ago which was the first time I compelled, forced her to do something because she didn't know how to refuse; whereupon I said suddenly: "Of course I dont really need to ask you this, but maybe we'd better just for the record. You dont really want to stay in Jefferson, do you? You really do want to go up East to school?" then almost immediately said: "All right, I take that back. I cant ask you that; I cant ask you to say outright you want to go against your mother.—All right," I said, "you dont want to be there yourself when I talk to her: is that it?" Then I said: "Look at me," and she did, with the eyes that were not blue or gray either but hyacinthine, the two of us standing there in the middle of that quiet block in full view of at least twenty discreet window-shades; looking at me even while she said, breathed, again:

"No. No."

"Come on," I said. "Let's walk again," and she did so, docile enough. "She knows you came to meet me this afternoon because of course she gave you my telephone message.—All right," I said. "I'll come to your house in the morning then, after you've left for school. But it's all right; you dont need to tell her. You dont need to tell her anything —say anything—" Not even No No again, since she had said nothing else since I saw her and was still saying it even in the way she walked and said nothing. Because now I knew why the clothes, the scent, the makeup which belonged on her no more than the hat did. It was desperation, not to defend the ingratitude but at least to palliate the rudeness of it: the mother who said *Certainly, meet him by all means. Tell him I am quite competent to plan my daughter's education, and we'll both thank him to keep his nose out of it;* the poor desperate child herself covering, trying to hide the baseness of the one and the shame of the other behind the placentae of worms and the urine and vomit of cats and cancerous whales. "I'll come tomorrow morning, after you've gone to school," I said. "I know. I know. But it's got too important now for either of us to stop."

So the next morning: who—I—had thought yesterday to have seen the last of lurking. But I had to be sure. And there was Ratliff.

"What?" he said. "You're going to see Eula because Eula wont let her leave Jefferson to go to school? You're wrong."

"All right," I said. "I'm wrong. I dont want to do it either. I'm not that brave—offering to tell anybody, let alone a woman, how to raise her child. But somebody's got to. She's got to get away from here. Away for good from all the very air that ever heard or felt breathed the name of Snopes——"

"But wait, I tell you! wait!" he said. "Because you're wrong—"

But I couldn't wait. Anyway, I didn't. I mean, I just deferred, marked time until at least nine oclock. Because even on a hot Mississippi May morning, when people begin to get up more or less with the sun, not so much in self defense as to balance off as much as possible of the day against the hours between noon and four, a housewife would demand a little time to prepare (her house and herself or perhaps most of all and simply, her soul) for a male caller not only uninvited but already unwelcome.

But she was prepared, self house and soul too; if her soul was ever in her life unready for anything that just wore pants or maybe if any woman's soul ever needed pre-readying and pre-arming against anything in pants just named Gavin Stevens, passing through the little rented (still looking rented even though the owner or somebody had painted it) gate up the short rented walk toward the little rented veranda and onto it, my hand already lifted to knock before I saw her through the screen, standing there quite still in the little hallway watching me.

"Good morning," she said. "Come in," and now with no screen between us still watching me. No: just looking at me, not brazenly, not with welcome, not with anything. Then she turned, the hair, where all the other women in Jefferson, even Maggie, had bobbed theirs now, still one heavy careless yellow bun at the back of her head, the dress which was not a morning gown nor a hostess gown nor even a house dress but just a simple cotton dress that was simply a dress and which, although she was thirty-five now—yes: thirty-six now by Ratliff's counting from that splendid fall—like that one when she first crossed the Square that day sixteen years ago, appeared not so much as snatching in desperate haste to hide them but rather to spring in suppliance and adulation to the moving limbs, the very flowing of the fabric's laving folds crying *Evoe! Evoe!*

Oh yes, it was a sitting room, exactly like the hall and both of them exactly like something else I had seen somewhere but didn't have time to remember. Because she said, "Will you have some coffee?" and I saw that too: the service (not silver but the stuff the advertisements dont tell you is better than silver but simply newer. New: inf. silver is quite all right and even proper for people still thrall to gaslight and horse-and-buggy) on a low table, with two chairs already drawn up and I thought *I have lost* even if she had met me wearing a barrel or a feed sack. Then I thought *So it really is serious* since this—the coffee, the low table, the two intimate chairs—was an assault not on the glands nor even just the stomach but on the civilised soul or at least the soul which believes it thirsts to be civilised.

"Thank you," I said and waited and then sat too. "Only, do you mind if I wonder why? We dont need an armistice, since I have already been disarmed."

"You came to fight then," she said, pouring.

"How can I, without a weapon?" I said, watching: the bent head with the careless, almost untidy bun of hair, the arm, the hand which could have rocked a warrior-hero's cradle or even caught up its father's fallen sword, pouring the trivial (it would probably not even be very good coffee) fluid from the trivial spurious synthetic urn—this, in that room, that house; and suddenly I knew where I had seen the room and hallway before. In a photograph, the photograph from say *Town and Country* labelled *American Interior*, reproduced in color in a wholesale furniture catalogue, with the added legend: *This is neither a Copy nor a Reproduction. It is our own Model scaled to your individual Requirements.* "Thank you," I said. "No cream. Just sugar.—Only it doesn't look like you."

"What?" she said.

"This room. Your house." And that was why I didn't even believe at first that I had heard her.

"It wasn't me. It was my husband."

"I'm sorry," I said.

"My husband chose this furniture."

"Flem?" I said, cried. "Flem Snopes?"—and she looking at me now, not startled, amazed: not anything or if anything, just waiting for my uproar to reach its end: nor was it only from McCarron that Linda got the eyes, but only the hair from him. "Flem Snopes!" I said. "Flem Snopes!"

"Yes. We went to Memphis. He knew exactly what he wanted. No, that's wrong. He didn't know yet. He only knew he wanted, had to have. Or does that make any sense to you?"

"Yes," I said. "Terribly. You went to Memphis."

"Yes," she said. "That was why: to find somebody who could tell him what he had to have. He already knew which store he was going to. The first thing he said was, 'When a man dont intend to buy anything from you, how much do you charge him just to talk?' Because he was not trading now, you see. When you're on a trade, for land or stock or whatever it is, both of you may trade or both of you may not, it all depends; you dont have to buy it or sell it; when you stop trading and part, neither of you may be any different from when you began. But not this time. This was something he had to have and knew he had to have: he just didn't know what it was and so he would not only have to depend on the man who owned it to tell him what he wanted, he would even have to depend on the man selling it not to cheat him on the price or the value of it because he wouldn't know that either: only that he had to have it. Do you understand that too?"

"All right," I said. "Yes. And then?"

"It had to be exactly what it was, for exactly what he was. That was when the man began to say, 'Yes, I think I see. You started out as a clerk in a country store. Then you moved to town and ran a café. Now you're vice president of your bank. A man who came that far in that short time, is not going to stop just there, and why shouldn't everybody that enters his home know it, see it? Yes, I know what you want.' And Flem said No. 'Not expensive,' the man said. 'Successful.' And Flem said No. 'All right,' the man said. 'Antique then,' and took us into a room and showed us what he meant. 'I can take this piece here for instance and make it look still older.' And Flem said, 'Why?' and the man said, 'For background. Your grandfather.' And Flem said, 'I had a grandfather because everybody had. I dont know who he was but I know that whoever he was he never owned enough furniture for a room, let alone a house. Besides, I dont aim to fool anybody. Only a fool would try to fool smart people, and anybody that needs to fool fools is already one.' And that was when the man said wait while he telephoned. And we did, it was not long before a woman came in. She was his wife. She said to me: 'What are your ideas?' and I said, 'I dont care,' and she said 'What?' and I said it again and then she looked at Flem and I watched them looking at one another, a good while. Then she said, not loud like her husband, quite quiet: 'I know,' and now it was Flem that said, 'Wait. How much will it cost?' and she said, 'You're a trader. I'll make a trade with you. I'll bring the stuff down to Jefferson and put it in your house myself. If you like it, you buy it. If you dont like it, I'll load it back up and move it back here and it wont cost you a cent.'"

"All right," I said. "And then?"

"That's all," she said. "Your coffee's cold. I'll get another cup—" and began to rise until I stopped her.

"When was this?" I said.

"Four years ago," she said. "When he bought this house."

"Bought the house?" I said. "Four years ago? That's when he became vice president of the bank!"

"Yes," she said. "The day before it was announced. I'll get another cup."

"I dont want coffee," I said, sitting there saying *Flem Snopes Flem Snopes* until I said, cried: "I dont want anything! I'm afraid!" until I finally said "What?" and she repeated:

"Will you have a cigarette?" and I saw that too: a synthetic metal box also and there should have been a synthetic matching lighter but what she had taken from the same box with the cigarette was a kitchen match. "Linda says you smoke a corncob pipe. Smoke it if you want to."

"No," I said again. "Not anything.—But Flem Snopes," I said. "Flem Snopes."

"Yes," she said. "It's not me that wont let her go away from Jefferson to school."

"But why?" I said. "Why? When she's not even his—he's not even her—I'm sorry. But you can see how urgent, how we dont even have time for . . . . ."

"Politeness?" she said. Nor did I make that move either: just sitting there watching while she leaned and scratched the match on the sole of her side-turned slipper and lit the cigarette.

"For anything," I said. "For anything except her. Ratliff tried to tell me this this morning, but I wouldn't listen. So maybe that's what you were telling me a moment ago when I wouldn't or didn't listen? The furniture. That day in the store. Didn't know what he wanted because what he wanted didn't matter, wasn't important: only that he did want it, did need it, must have it, intended to have it no matter what cost or who lost or who anguished or grieved. To be exactly what he needed to exactly fit exactly what he was going to be to-morrow after it was announced: a vice president's wife and child along with the rest of the vice president's furniture in the vice president's house? Is that what you tried to tell me?"

"Something like that," she said.

"Just something like that," I said. "Because that's not enough. It's nowhere near enough. We wont mention the money because everybody who ever saw that bow tie would know he wouldn't pay out his own money to send his own child a sleeper-ticket distance to school, let alone another man's ba—" and stopped. But not she, smoking, watching the burning tip of the cigarette.

"Say it," she said. "Bastard."

"I'm sorry," I said.

"Why?" she said.

"I'm trying," I said. "Maybe I could, if only you were. Looked like you were. Or even like you were trying to be."

"Go on," she said. "Not the money."

"Because he—you—could get that from Uncle Will proba-bly, not to mention taking it from me as a scholarship. Or is that it? he cant even bear to see the money of even a mortal enemy like old man Will Varner probably is to him, wasted on sending a child out of the state to school when he pays taxes every year to support the Mississippi ones?"

"Go on," she said again. "Not the money."

"So it is that furniture catalogue picture after all, scaled in cheap color from the Charleston or Richmond or Long Island or Boston photograph, down to that one which Flem Snopes holds imperative that the people of Yoknapatawpha County must have of him. While he was just owner of a back-alley café it was all right for all Frenchman's Bend (and all Jefferson and the rest of the county too after Ratliff and a few others like him got through with it) to know that the child who bore his name was really a——"

"Bastard," she said again.

"All right," I said. But even then I didn't say it: "—and even when he sold the café for a nice profit and was superin-tendent of the power-plant, it still wouldn't have mattered.

And even after that when he held no public position but was
simply a private usurer and property-grabber quietly minding
his own business; not to mention the fact that ten or twelve
years had now passed, by which time he could even begin to
trust Jefferson to have enough tenderness for a twelve- or
thirteen-year-old female child not to upset her life with that
useless and gratuitous information. But now he is vice president of a bank and now a meddling outsider is persuading the
child to go away to school, to spend at least the three months
until the Christmas holidays among people none of whose
fathers owe him money and so must keep their mouths shut,
any one of whom might reveal the fact which at all costs he
must now keep secret. So that's it," I said, and still she
wasn't looking at me: just smoking quietly and steadily while
she watched the slow curl and rise of the smoke. "So it's you,
after all," I said. "He forbade her to leave Jefferson, and
blackmailed you into supporting him by threatening you with
what he himself is afraid of: that he himself will tell her of her
mother's shame and her own illegitimacy. Well, that's a blade
with three edges. Ask your father for the money, or take it
from me, and get her away from Jefferson or I'll tell her myself who she is—or is not."

"Do you think she will believe you?" she said.

"What?" I said. "Believe me? Believe me? Even without a
mirror to look into, nothing to compare with and need to repudiate from, since all she needed was just to live with him
for the seventeen years which she has. What more could she
want than to believe me, believe anyone, a chance to believe
anyone compassionate enough to assure her she's not his
child? What are you talking about? What more could she ask
than the right to love the mother who by means of love saved
her from being a Snopes? And if that were not enough, what
more could anybody want than this, that most never have the
chance to be, not one in ten million have the right to be, deserve to be: not just a love child but one of the elect to share
cousinhood with the world's immortal love-children—fruit of
that brave virgin passion not just capable but doomed to
count the earth itself well lost for love, which down all the
long record of man the weak and impotent and terrified and
sleepless that the rest of the human race calls its poets, have

dreamed and anguished and exulted and amazed over—" and she watching me now, not smoking: just holding the poised cigarette while the last blue vapor faded, watching me through it.

"You dont know very much about women, do you?" she said. "Women aren't interested in poets' dreams. They are interested in facts. It doesn't even matter whether the facts are true or not, as long as they match the other facts without leaving a rough seam. She wouldn't even believe you. She wouldn't even believe him if he were to tell her. She would just hate you both—you most of all because you started it."

"You mean she will take . . . this—him—in preference to nothing? will throw away the chance for school and everything else? I dont believe you."

"To her, this isn't nothing. She will take it before a lot of things. Before most things."

"I dont believe you!" I said, cried, or thought I did. But only thought it, until I said: "So there's nothing I can do."

"Yes," she said. And now she was watching me, the cigarette motionless, not even seeming to burn. "Marry her."

"What?" I said, cried. "A gray-headed man more than twice her age? Dont you see, that's what I'm after: to set her free of Jefferson, not tie her down to it still more, still further, still worse, but to set her free? And you talk about the reality of facts."

"The marriage is the only fact. The rest of it is still the poet's romantic dream. Marry her. She'll have you. Right now, in the middle of all this, she wont know how to say No. Marry her."

"Goodbye," I said. "Goodbye."

And Ratliff again, still in the client's chair where I had left him an hour ago.

"I tried to tell you," he said. "Of course it's Flem. What reason would Eula and that gal have not to jump at a chance to be shut of each other for nine or ten months for a change?"

"I can tell you that now myself," I said. "Flem Snopes is vice president of a bank now with a vice president's house with vice president's furniture in it and some of that vice president's furniture has got to be a vice president's wife and child."

"No," he said.

"All right," I said. "The vice president of a bank dont dare have it remembered that his wife was already carrying somebody else's bastard when he married her, so if she goes off to school some stranger that dont owe him money will tell her who she is and the whole playhouse will blow up."

"No," Ratliff said.

"All right," I said. "Then you tell a while."

"He's afraid she'll get married," he said.

"What?" I said.

"That's right," he said. "When Jody was born, Uncle Billy Varner made a will leaving half of his property to Miz Varner and half to Jody. When Eula was born, he made a new will leaving that same first half to Miz Varner and the other half split in two equal parts, one for Jody and one for Eula. That's the will he showed Flem that day him and Eula was married and he aint changed it since. That is, Flem Snopes believed him when he said he wasn't going to change it, whether anybody else believed him or not—especially after Flem beat him on that Old Frenchman place trade."

"What?" I said. "He gave that place to them as Eula's dowry."

"Sho," Ratliff said. "It was told around so because Uncle Billy was the last man of all that would have corrected it. He offered Flem the place but Flem said he would rather have the price of it in cash money. Which was why Flem and Eula was a day late leaving for Texas: him and Uncle Billy was trading, with Uncle Billy beating Flem down to where he never even thought about it when Flem finally said all right, he would take that figger provided Uncle Billy would give him a option to buy the place at the same amount when he come back from Texas. So they agreed, and Flem come back from Texas with them paint ponies and when the dust finally settled, me and Henry Armstid had done bought that Old Frenchman place from Flem for my half of that restaurant and enough of Henry's cash money to pay off Uncle Billy's option, which he had done forgot about. And that's why Flem Snopes at least knows that Uncle Billy aint going to change that will. So he dont dare risk letting that girl leave Jefferson and get married, because he knows that Eula will leave him too then. It was

Flem started it by saying No, but you got all three of them against you, Eula and that girl too until that girl finds the one she wants to marry. Because women aint interested——"

"Wait," I said, "wait. It's my time now. Because I dont know anything about women because things like love and morality and jumping at any chance you can find that will keep you from being a Snopes are just a poet's romantic dream and women aren't interested in the romance of dreams; they are interested in the reality of facts, they dont care what facts, let alone whether they are true or not if they just dovetail with all the other facts without leaving a saw-tooth edge. Right?"

"Well," he said, "I might not a put it jest exactly that way."

"Because I dont know anything about women," I said. "So would you mind telling me how the hell you learned?"

"Maybe by listening," he said. Which we all knew, since what Yoknapatawphian had not seen at some time during the past ten or fifteen years the tin box shaped and painted to re-semble a house and containing the demonstrator machine, in the old days attached to the back of a horse-drawn buckboard and since then to the rear of a converted automobile, hitched or parked beside the gate to a thousand yards on a hundred back-country roads, while, surrounded by a group of four or five or six ladies come in sunbonnets or straw hats from any-where up to a mile along the road, Ratliff himself with his smooth brown bland inscrutable face and his neat faded tie-less blue shirt, sitting in a kitchen chair in the shady yard or on the gallery, listening. Oh yes, we all knew that.

"So I didn't listen to the right ones," I said.

"Or the wrong ones neither," he said. "You never listened to nobody because by that time you were already talking again."

Oh yes, easy. All I had to do was stand there on the street at the right time, until she saw me and turned, ducked with that semblance of flight, into the side street which would by-pass the ambush. Nor even then to back-track that one block but merely to go straight through the drugstore itself, out the back door, so that no matter how fast she went I was in the alley first, ambushed again behind the wall's angle in ample time to hear her rapid feet and then step out and grasp her arm just above the wrist almost before it began to rise in that reflex of flight and repudiation, holding the wrist, not hard, while she wrenched, jerked faintly at it, saying, "Please. Please."

"All right," I said. "All right. Just tell me this. When you went home first and changed before you met me in the drug-store that afternoon. It was your idea to go home first and change to the other dress. But it was your mother who insisted on the lipstick and the perfume and the silk stockings and the high heels. Isn't that right?" And she still wrenching and jerking faintly at the arm I held, whispering:

"Please. Please."

SIXTEEN

C HARLES MALLISON
This is what Ratliff said happened up to where Uncle
Gavin could see it.

It was January, a gray day though not cold because of the
fog. Old Het ran in Mrs Hait's front door and down the hall
into the kitchen, already hollering in her strong bright happy
voice, with strong and childlike pleasure:

"Miss Mannie! Mule in the yard!"

Nobody knew just exactly how old old Het really was.
Nobody in Jefferson even remembered just how long she had
been in the poorhouse. The old people said she was about
seventy, though by her own counting, calculated from the
ages of various Jefferson ladies from brides to grandmothers
that she claimed to have nursed from infancy, she would be
around a hundred and, as Ratliff said, at least triplets.

That is, she used the poorhouse to sleep in or anyway pass
most or at least part of the night in. Because the rest of the
time she was either on the Square or the streets of Jefferson
or somewhere on the mile-and-a-half dirt road between town
and the poorhouse; for twenty-five years at least ladies, seeing
her through the front window or maybe even just hearing her
strong loud cheerful voice from the house next door, had
been locking themselves in the bathroom. But even this did
no good unless they had remembered first to lock the front
and back doors of the house itself. Because sooner or later
they would have to come out and there she would be, tall,
lean, of a dark chocolate color, voluble, cheerful, in tennis
shoes and the long rat-colored coat trimmed with what forty
or fifty years ago had been fur, and the purple toque that old
Mrs Compson had given her fifty years ago while General
Compson himself was still alive, set on the exact top of her
headrag (at first she had carried a carpetbag of the same color
and apparently as bottomless as a coal mine, though since the
ten cent store came to Jefferson the carpetbag had given place
to a successsion of the paper shopping bags which it gave

away), already settled in a chair in the kitchen, having established already upon the begging visitation a tone blandly and incorrigibly social.

She passed that way from house to house, travelling in a kind of moving island of alarm and consternation as she levyed her weekly toll of food scraps and castoff garments and an occasional coin for snuff, moving in an urbane uproar and as inescapable as a tax-gatherer. Though for the last year or two since Mrs Hait's widowing, Jefferson had gained a sort of temporary respite from her because of Mrs Hait. But even this was not complete. Rather, old Het had merely established a kind of local headquarters or advanced foraging post in Mrs Hait's kitchen soon after Mr Hait and five mules belonging to Mr I.O. Snopes died on a sharp curve below town under the fast north-bound through freight one night and even the folks at the poorhouse heard that Mrs Hait had got eight thousand dollars for him. She would come straight to Mrs Hait's as soon as she reached town, sometimes spending the entire forenoon there, so that only after noon would she begin her implacable rounds. Now and then when the weather was bad she spent the whole day with Mrs Hait. On these days her regular clients or victims, freed temporarily, would wonder if in the house of the man-charactered and man-tongued woman who as Ratliff put it had sold her husband to the railroad company for eight thousand percent. profit, who chopped her own firewood and milked her cow and plowed and worked her own vegetable garden;—they wondered if maybe old Het helped with the work in return for her entertainment or if even now she still kept the relationship at its social level of a guest come to divert and be diverted.

She was wearing the hat and coat and was carrying the shopping bag when she ran into Mrs Hait's kitchen, already hollering: "Miss Mannie! Mule in the yard!"

Mrs Hait was squatting in front of the stove, raking live ashes from it into a scuttle. She was childless, living alone now in the little wooden house painted the same color that the railroad company used on its stations and boxcars—out of respect to and in memory of, we all said, that morning three years ago when what remained of Mr Hait had finally been sorted from what remained of the five mules and several feet of new manila rope scattered along the right-of-way. In time the railroad claims adjuster called on her, and in time she cashed a check for eight thousand five hundred dollars, since (as Uncle Gavin said, these were the halcyon days when even the railroad companies considered their southern branches and divisions the rightful legitimate prey of all who dwelt beside them) although for several years before Mr Hait's death single mules and pairs (by coincidence belonging often to Mr Snopes too; you could always tell his because every time the railroad killed his mules they always had new strong rope on them) had been in the habit of getting themselves killed on that same blind curve at night, this was the first time a human being had—as Uncle Gavin put it—joined them in mutual apotheosis.

Mrs Hait took the money in cash; she stood in a calico wrapper and her late husband's coat sweater and the actual felt hat he had been wearing (it had been found intact) on that fatal morning and listened in cold and grim silence while the bank teller then the cashier then the president (Mr de Spain himself) tried to explain to her about bonds, then about savings accounts, then about a simple checking account, and put the money into a salt sack under her apron and departed; that summer she painted her house that serviceable and time-defying color which matched the depot and the boxcars, as though out of sentiment or (as Ratliff said) gratitude, and now she still lived in it, alone, in the calico wrapper and the sweater coat and the same felt hat which her husband had owned and wore until he no longer needed them; though her shoes by this time were her own: men's shoes which buttoned, with toes like small tulip bulbs, of an archaic and obsolete pattern which Mr Wildermark himself ordered especially for her once a year.

She jerked up and around, still clutching the scuttle, and glared at old Het and said—her voice was a good strong one too, immediate too—

"That son of a bitch," and, still carrying the scuttle and with old Het still carrying the shopping bag and following, ran out of the kitchen into the fog. That's why it wasn't cold: the fog: as if all the sleeping and breathing of Jefferson during that whole long January night was still lying there imprisoned between the ground and the mist, keeping it from quite freezing, lying like a scum of grease on the wooden steps at the back door and on the brick coping and the wooden lid of the cellar stairs beside the kitchen door and on the wooden planks which led from the steps to the wooden shed in the corner of the back yard where Mrs Hait's cow lived; when she stepped down onto the planks, still carrying the scuttle of live ashes, Mrs Hait skated violently before she caught her balance. Old Het in her rubber soles didn't slip.

"Watch out!" she shouted happily. "They in the front!" One of them wasn't. Because Mrs Hait didn't fall either. She didn't even pause, whirling and already running toward the corner of the house where, with silent and apparition-like suddenness, the mule appeared. It belonged to Mr. I.O. Snopes too. I mean, until they finally unravelled Mr Hait from the five mules on the railroad track that morning three years ago, nobody had connected him with Mr Snopes's mule business, even though now and then somebody did wonder how Mr Hait didn't seem to need to do anything steady to make a living. Ratliff said the reason was that everybody was wondering too hard about what in the world I.O. Snopes was doing in the livestock business. Though Ratliff said that on second thought maybe it was natural: that back in French-man's Bend I.O. had been a blacksmith without having any business at that, hating horses and mules both since he was deathly afraid of them, so maybe it was natural for him to take up the next thing he wouldn't have any business in or sympa-thy or aptitude for, not to mention being six or eight or a dozen times as scared since now, instead of just one horse or mule tied to a post and with its owner handy, he would have to deal alone with eight or ten or a dozen of them running loose until he could manage to put a rope on them.

That's what he did though—bought his mules at the Memphis market and brought them to Jefferson and sold them to farmers and widows and orphans black and white, for whatever he could get, down to some last irreducible figure, after which (up to the night when the freight train caught Mr Hait too and Jefferson made the first connection between Mr Hait and Mr Snopes's livestock business) single mules and pairs and gangs (always tied together with that new strong manila rope which Snopes always itemised and listed in his claim) would be killed by night freight trains on that same blind curve of Mr Hait's exit; somebody (Ratliff swore it wasn't him but the depot agent) finally sent Snopes through the mail a printed train schedule for the division.

Though after Mr Hait's misfortune (miscalculation, Ratliff said; he said it was Mr Hait the agent should have sent the train schedule to, along with a watch) Snopes's mules stopped dying of sudden death on the railroad track. When the adjuster came to adjust Mrs Hait, Snopes was there too, which Ratliff said was probably the most terrible decision Snopes ever faced in his whole life: between the simple prudence which told him to stay completely clear of the railroad company's investigation, and his knowledge of Mrs Hait which had already told him that his only chance to get any part of that indemnity would be by having the railroad company for his ally.

Because he failed. Mrs Hait stated calmly that her husband had been the sole owner of the five mules; she didn't even have to dare Snopes out loud to dispute it; all he ever saw of that money (oh yes, he was there in the bank, as close as he dared get, watching) was when she crammed it into the salt bag and folded the bag into her apron. For five or six years before that, at regular intervals he had passed across the peaceful and somnolent Jefferson scene in dust and uproar, his approach heralded by forlorn shouts and cries, his passing marked by a yellow cloud of dust filled with the tossing jug-shaped heads and the clattering hooves, then last of all Snopes himself at a panting trot, his face gaped with forlorn shouting and wrung with concern and terror and dismay.

When he emerged from his conference with the adjuster he still wore the concern and the dismay but the terror was now blended into an incredulous, a despairing, a shocked and passionate disbelief which still showed through the new overlay of hungry hope it wore during the next three years (again, Ratliff said, such a decision and problem as no man should be faced with: who—Snopes—heretofore had only to unload the mules into the receiving pen at the depot and then pay a Negro to ride the old bell mare which would lead them across town to his sales stable-lot, while now and single-handed he had to let them out of the depot pen and then force, herd them into the narrow street blocked at the end by Mrs Hait's small unfenced yard) when the uproar—the dust-cloud filled with plunging demonic shapes—would seem to be translated in one single burst across the peaceful edge of Jefferson and into Mrs Hait's yard, where the two of them, Mrs Hait and Snopes—Mrs Hait clutching a broom or a mop or whatever weapon she was able to snatch up as she ran out of the house cursing like a man, and Snopes, vengeance for the moment sated or at least the unbearable top of the unbearable sense of impotence and injustice and wrong taken off (Ratliff said he had probably long since given up any real belief of actually extorting even one cent of that money from Mrs Hait and all that remained now was the raging and baseless hope) who would now have to catch the animals somehow and get them back inside a fence—ducked and dodged among the thundering shapes in a kind of passionate and choreographic pantomime against the backdrop of that house whose very impervious paint Snopes believed he had paid for and within which its very occupant and chatelaine led a life of queenly and sybaritic luxury on his money (which according to Ratliff was exactly why Mrs Hait refused to appeal to the law to abate Snopes as a nuisance: this too was just a part of the price she owed for the amazing opportunity to swap her husband for eight thousand dollars);—this, while that whole section of town learned to gather—the ladies in the peignoirs and boudoir caps of morning, the children playing in the yards, and the people Negro and white who happened to be passing at the moment—and watch from behind neighboring shades or the security of adjacent fences.

When they saw it, the mule was running too, its head high too in a strange place it had never seen before, so that coming suddenly out of the fog and all it probably looked taller than a giraffe rushing down at Mrs Hait and old Het with the halter-rope whipping about its ears.

"Dar hit!" old Het shouted, waving the shopping bag, "Hoo! Scat!" She told Ratliff how Mrs Hait whirled and skidded again on the greasy planks as she and the mule now ran parallel with one another toward the cowshed from whose open door the static and astonished face of the cow now

looked out. To the cow, until a second ago standing peacefully in the door chewing and looking at the fog, the mule
must have looked taller and more incredible than any giraffe,
let alone looking like it aimed to run right through the shed
as if it were straw or maybe even pure and simple mirage.
Anyway, old Het said the cow snatched her face back inside
the shed like a match going out and made a sound inside the
shed, old Het didn't know what sound, just a sound of pure
shock and alarm like when you pluck a single string on a harp
or a banjo, Mrs Hait running toward the sound old Het said
in a kind of pure reflex, in automatic compact of female with
female against the world of mules and men, she and the mule
converging on the shed at top speed, Mrs Hait already swinging the scuttle of live ashes to throw at the mule. Of course it
didn't take this long; old Het said she was still hollering "Dar
hit! Dar hit!" when the mule swerved and ran at her until she
swung the shopping bag and turned it past her and on around
the next corner of the house and back into the fog like a
match going out too.

That was when Mrs Hait set the scuttle down on the edge
of the brick coping of the cellar entrance and she and old Het
turned the corner of the house in time to see the mule coincide with a rooster and eight white leghorn hens coming out
from under the house. Old Het said it looked just like something out of the Bible, or maybe out of some kind of hoodoo
witches' bible: the mule that came out of the fog to begin
with like a hant or a goblin, now kind of soaring back into the
fog again borne on a cloud of little winged ones. She and Mrs
Hait were still running; she said Mrs Hait was now carrying
the worn-out stub of a broom though old Het didn't remember when she had picked it up.

"There's more in the front!" old Het hollered.

"That son of a bitch," Mrs Hait said. There were more of
them. Old Het said that little handkerchief-sized yard was full
of mules and I.O. Snopes. It was so small that any creature
with a stride of three feet could have crossed it in two paces,
yet when they came in sight of it it must have looked like
watching a drop of water through a microscope. Except that
this time it was like being in the middle of the drop of water
yourself. That is, old Het said that Mrs Hait and I.O. Snopes

were in the middle of it because she said she stopped against
the house where she would be more or less out of the way
even though nowhere in that little yard was going to be safe,
and watched Mrs Hait still clutching the broom and with a
kind of sublime faith in something somewhere, maybe in just
her own invulnerability though old Het said Mrs Hait was
just too mad to notice, rush right into the middle of the
drove, after the one with the flying halter-rein that was still
vanishing into the fog still in that cloud of whirling loose
feathers like confetti or the wake behind a speed boat.

And Mr Snopes too, the mules running all over him too, he
and Mrs Hait glaring at each other while he panted:

"Where's my money? Where's my half of it?"

"Catch that big son of a bitch with the halter," Mrs Hait
said. "Get that big son of a bitch out of here," both of them,
old Het and Mrs Hait both, running on so that Snopes's
panting voice was behind them now:

"Pay me my money! Pay me my part of it!"

"Watch out!" old Het said she hollered. "He heading for
the back again!"

"Get a rope!" Mrs Hait hollered back at Snopes.

"Fore God, where is ere rope?" Snopes hollered.

"In the cellar, fore God!" old Het hollered. She didn't wait
either. "Go round the other way and head him!" she said.
And she said that when she and Mrs Hait turned that corner,
there was the mule with the flying halter once more seeming
to float lightly onward on a cloud of chickens with which,
since the chickens had been able to go under the house and
so along the chord while the mule had to go around on the
arc, it had once more coincided. When they turned the next
corner, they were in the back yard again.

"Fore God!" Het hollered, "he fixing to misuse the cow!"
She said it was like a tableau. The cow had come out of the
shed into the middle of the back yard; it and the mule were
now facing each other about a yard apart, motionless, with
lowered heads and braced legs like two mismatched book-
ends, and Snopes was half in and half out of the now-open
cellar door on the coping of which the scuttle of ashes still sat,
where he had obviously gone seeking the rope; afterward old
Het said she thought at the time an open cellar door wasn't a

very good place for a scuttle of live ashes, and maybe she did.
I mean, if she hadn't said she thought that, somebody else
would since there's always somebody handy afterward to
prove their foresight by your hindsight. Though if things
were going as fast as she said they were, I dont see how anybody there had time to think anything much.

Because everything was already moving again; when they
went around the next corner this time, I.O. was leading, carrying the rope (he had found it), then the cow, her tail raised
and rigid and raked slightly like the flagpole on a boat, and
then the mule, Mrs Hait and old Het coming last and old
Het told again how she noticed the scuttle of live ashes sitting
on the curb of the now-open cellar with its accumulation of
human refuse and Mrs Hait's widowhood—empty boxes for
kindling, old papers, broken furniture—and thought again
that wasn't a very good place for the scuttle.

Then the next corner. Snopes and the cow and the mule
were all three just vanishing on the cloud of frantic chickens
which had once more crossed beneath the house just in
time. Though when they reached the front yard there was
nobody there but Snopes. He was lying flat on his face, the
tail of his coat flung forward over his head by the impetus of
his fall, and old Het swore there was the print of the cow's
split foot and the mule's hoof too in the middle of his white
shirt.

"Where'd they go?" she shouted at him. He didn't answer.
"They tightening on the curves!" she hollered at Mrs Hait.
"They already in the back again!" They were. She said maybe
the cow had aimed to run back into the shed but decided she
had too much speed and instead whirled in a kind of desperation of valor and despair on the mule itself. Though she said
that she and Mrs Hait didn't quite get there in time to see it:
only to hear a crash and clash and clatter as the mule swerved
and blundered over the cellar entrance. Because when they
got there, the mule was gone. The scuttle was gone from the
cellar coping too but old Het said she never noticed it then:
only the cow in the middle of the yard where she had been
standing before, her fore legs braced and her head lowered
like somebody had passed and snatched away the other book-
end. Because she and Mrs Hait didn't stop either, Mrs Hait

running heavily now old Het said, with her mouth open and her face the color of putty and one hand against her side. In fact she said they were both run out now, going so slow this time that the mule overtook them from behind and she said it jumped clean over them both: a brief demon thunder rank with the ammonia-reek of sweat, and went on (either the chickens had finally realised to stay under the house or maybe they were worn out too and just couldn't make it this time); when they reached the next corner the mule had finally succeeded in vanishing into the fog; they heard its hooves, brief, staccato and derisive on the hard street, dying away.

Old Het said she stopped. She said, "Well. Gentlemen, hush," she said. "Aint we had—" Then she smelled it. She said she stood right still, smelling, and it was like she was actually looking at that open cellar as it was when they passed it last time without any coal scuttle setting on the coping. "Fore God," she hollered at Mrs Hait, "I smell smoke! Child, run in the house and get your money!"

That was about nine oclock. By noon the house had burned to the ground. Ratliff said that when the fire engine and the crowd got there, Mrs Hait, followed by old Het carrying her shopping bag in one hand and a framed crayon portrait of Mr Hait in the other, was just coming out of the house carrying an umbrella and wearing the army overcoat which Mr Hait had used to wear, in one pocket of which was a quart fruit jar packed with what remained of the eighty-five hundred dollars (which would be most of it, according to how the neighbors said Mrs Hait lived) and in the other a heavy nickel-plated revolver, and crossed the street to a neighbor's house, where with old Het beside her in a second rocker, she had been sitting ever since on the gallery, the two of them rocking steadily while they watched the volunteer fire-fighters flinging her dishes and furniture up and down the street. By that time Ratliff said there were plenty of them interested enough to go back to the Square and hunt up I.O. and keep him posted.

"What you telling me for?" I.O. said. "It wasn't me that set that-ere scuttle of live fire where the first thing that passed would knock it into the cellar."

"It was you that opened the cellar door though," Ratliff said.

"Sho," Snopes said. "And why? To get that rope, her own rope, right where she sent me to get it."

"To catch your mule, that was trespassing on her yard," Ratliff said. "You cant get out of it this time. There aint a jury in the county that wont find for her."

"Yes," Snopes said. "I reckon not. And just because she's a woman. That's why. Because she is a durned woman. All right. Let her go to her durned jury with it. I can talk too; I reckon it's a few things I could tell a jury myself about——" Then Ratliff said he stopped. Ratliff said he didn't sound like I.O. Snopes anyway because whenever I.O. talked what he said was so full of mixed-up proverbs that you stayed so busy trying to unravel just which of two or three proverbs he had jumbled together that you couldn't even tell just exactly what lie he had told you until it was already too late. But right now Ratliff said he was too busy to have time for even proverbs, let alone lies. Ratliff said they were all watching him.

"What?" somebody said. "Tell the jury about what?"

"Nothing," he said. "Because why, because there aint going to be no jury. Me and Miz Mannie Hait? You boys dont know her if you think she's going to make trouble over a pure acci-dent couldn't me nor nobody else help. Why, there aint a fairer, finer woman in Yoknapatawpha County than Mannie Hait. I just wish I had a opportunity to tell her so." Ratliff said he had it right away. He said Mrs Hait was right behind them, with old Het right behind her, carrying the shopping bag. He said she just looked once at all of them generally. After that she looked at I.O.

"I come to buy that mule," she said.

"What mule?" I.O. said. He answered that quick, almost automatic, Ratliff said. Because he didn't mean it either. Then Ratliff said they looked at one another for about a half a minute. "You'd like to own that mule?" he said. "It'll cost you a hundred and fifty, Miz Mannie."

"You mean dollars?" Mrs Hait said.

"I dont mean dimes nor nickels neither, Miz Mannie," Snopes said.

"Dollars," Mrs Hait said. "Mules wasn't that high in Hait's time."

"Lots of things is different since Hait's time," Snopes said. "Including you and me, Miz Mannie."

"I reckon so," she said. Then she went away. Ratliff said she turned without a word and left, old Het following.

"If I'd a been you," Ratliff said, "I dont believe I'd a said that last to her."

And now Ratliff said the mean harried little face actually blazed, even frothing a little. "I just wisht she would," Snopes said. "Her or anybody else, I dont care who, to bring a court suit about anything, jest so it had the name mule and the name Hait in it—" and stopped, the face smooth again. "How's that?" he said. "What was you saying?"

"That you dont seem to be afraid she might sue you for burning down her house," Ratliff said.

"Sue me?" Snopes said. "Miz Hait? If she was fixing to try to law something out of me about that fire, do you reckon she would a hunted me up and offered to pay me for it?"

That was about one oclock. Then it was four oclock; Aleck Sander and I had gone out to Sartoris to shoot quail over the dogs that Miss Jenny Du Pre still kept, I reckon until Benbow Sartoris got big enough to hold a gun. So Uncle Gavin was alone in the office to hear the tennis shoes on the outside stairs. Then old Het came in; the shopping bag was bulging now and she was eating bananas from a paper sack which she clamped under one arm, the half-eaten banana in that hand while with the other she dug out a crumpled ten-dollar bill and gave it to Uncle Gavin.

"It's for you," old Het said. "From Miss Mannie. I done already give him hisn"—telling it: waiting on the corner of the Square until it looked like sure to God night would come first, before Snopes finally came along, and she handed the banana she was working on then to a woman beside her and got out the first crumpled ten-dollar bill. Snopes took it.

"What?" he said. "Miz Hait told you to give it to me?"

"For that mule," old Het said. "You dont need to give me no receipt. I can be the witness I give it to you."

"Ten dollars?" Snopes said. "For that mule? I told her a hundred and fifty dollars."

"You'll have to contrack that with her yourself," old Het said. "She just give me this to hand to you when she left to get the mule."

"To get the— She went out there herself and taken that mule out of my lot?" Snopes said.

"Lord, child," old Het said she said. "Miss Mannie aint skeered of no mule. Aint you done found that out?—And now here's yourn," she said to Uncle Gavin.

"For what?" Uncle Gavin said. "I dont have a mule to sell."

"For a lawyer," old Het said. "She fixing to need a lawyer. She say for you to be out there at her house about sundown, when she had time to get settled down again."

"Her house?" Uncle Gavin said.

"Where it use to be, honey," old Het said. "Would you keer for a banana? I done et about all I can hold."

"No much obliged," Uncle Gavin said.

"You're welcome," she said. "Go on. Take some. If I et one more, I'd be wishing the good Lord hadn't never thought banana One in all His life."

"No much obliged," Uncle Gavin said.

"You're welcome," she said. "I dont reckon you'd have nothing like a extra dime for a little snuff."

"No," Uncle Gavin said, producing it. "All I have is a quarter."

"That's quality," she said. "You talk about change to qual-ity, what you gets back is a quarter or a half a dollar or some-times even a whole dollar. It's just trash that cant think no higher than a nickel or ten cents." She took the quarter; it vanished somewhere. "There's some folks thinks all I does, I tromps this town all day long from can-see to cant, with a hand full of gimme and a mouth full of much oblige. They're wrong. I serves Jefferson too. If it's more blessed to give than to receive like the Book say, this town is blessed to a fare-you-well because it's steady full of folks willing to give anything from a nickel up to a old hat. But I'm the onliest one I knows that steady receives. So how is Jefferson going to be steady blessed without me steady willing from dust-dawn to dust-dark, rain or snow or sun, to say much oblige? I can tell Miss Mannie you be there?"

"Yes," Uncle Gavin said. Then she was gone. Uncle Gavin

sat there looking at the crumpled bill on the desk in front of him. Then he heard the other feet on the stairs and he sat watching the door until Mr Flem Snopes came in and shut it behind him.

"Evening," Mr Snopes said. "Can you take a case for me?"

"Now?" Uncle Gavin said. "Tonight?"

"Yes," Mr Snopes said.

"Tonight," Uncle Gavin said again. "Would it have anything to do with a mule and Mrs Hait's house?"

And he said how Mr Snopes didn't say What house? or What mule? or How did you know? He just said, "Yes."

"Why did you come to me?" Uncle Gavin said.

"For the same reason I would hunt up the best carpenter if I wanted to build a house, or the best farmer if I wanted to share-crop some land," Mr Snopes said.

"Thanks," Uncle Gavin said. "Sorry," he said. He didn't even have to touch the crumpled bill. He said that Mr Snopes had not only seen it the minute he entered, but he believed he even knew at that same moment where it came from. "As you already noticed, I'm already on the other side."

"You going out there now?" Mr Snopes said.

"Yes," Uncle Gavin said.

"Then that's all right." He began to reach into his pocket. At first Uncle Gavin didn't know why; he just watched him dig out an old-fashioned snap-mouth wallet and open it and separate a ten-dollar bill and close the wallet and lay the bill on the desk beside the other crumpled one and put the wallet back into the pocket and stand looking at Uncle Gavin.

"I just told you I'm already on the other side," Uncle Gavin said.

"And I just said that's all right," Mr Snopes said. "I dont want a lawyer because I already know what I'm going to do. I just want a witness."

"And why me for that?" Uncle Gavin said.

"That's right," Mr Snopes said. "The best witness too."

So they went out there. The fog had burned away by noon and Mrs Hait's two blackened chimneys now stood against what remained of the winter sunset; at the same moment Mr Snopes said, "Wait."

"What?" Uncle Gavin said. But Mr Snopes didn't answer so

they stood, not approaching yet; Uncle Gavin said he could already smell the ham broiling over the little fire in front of the still-intact cowshed, with old Het sitting on a brand new kitchen chair beside the fire turning the ham in the skillet with a fork, and beyond the fire Mrs Hait squatting at the cow's flank, milking into a new tin bucket.

"All right," Mr Snopes said, and again Uncle Gavin said What? because he had not seen I.O. at all: he was just suddenly there as though he had materialised, stepped suddenly out of the dusk itself into the light of the fire (there was a brand new galvanised coffee pot sitting in the ashes near the blaze and now Uncle Gavin said he could smell that too), to stand looking down at the back of Mrs Hait's head, not having seen Uncle Gavin and Mr Flem yet. But old Het had, already talking to Uncle Gavin while they were approaching:

"So this coffee and ham brought you even if them ten dollars couldn't," she said. "I'm like that, myself. I aint had no appetite in years it seems like now. A bird couldn't live on what I eats. But just let me get a whiff of coffee and ham together, now.—Leave that milk go for a minute, honey," she said to Mrs Hait. "Here's your lawyer."

Then I.O. saw them too, jerking quickly around over his shoulder his little mean harassed snarling face; and now Uncle Gavin could see inside the cowshed. It had been cleaned and raked and even swept, the floor was spread with fresh hay. A clean new kerosene stable lantern burned on a wooden box beside a pallet bed spread neatly on the straw and turned back for the night and now Uncle Gavin saw a second wooden box set out for a table beside the fire, with a new plate and knife and fork and spoon and cup and saucer and a still-sealed loaf of machine-made bread.

But Uncle Gavin said there was no alarm in I.O.'s face at the sight of Mr Flem though he said the reason for that was that he, Uncle Gavin, hadn't realised yet that I.O. had simply reached that stage where utter hopelessness wears the mantle of temerity. "So here you are," I.O. said. "And brung your lawyer too. I reckon you come now to get that-ere lantern and them new dishes and chair and that milk bucket and maybe the milk in too soon as she's done, hey? That's jest fine. It's even downright almost honest, coming right out in the open here where it aint even full dark yet. Because of course your lawyer knows all the rest of these here recent mulery and arsonery circumstances; likely the only one here that aint up to date is old Aunt Het there, and sholy she should be learned how to reco-nise a circumstance that even if she was to get up and run this minute, likely she would find she never had no shirt nor britches left neither by the time she got home, since a stitch in time saves nine lives for even a cat, as the feller says. Not to mention the fact that when you dines in Rome you durn sho better watch your overcoat.

"All right then. Now, jest exactly how much of them eight thousand and five hundred dollars the railroad company paid Miz Hait here for that husband of hern and them five mules of mine, do you reckon Miz Hait actively" (Uncle Gavin said he said actively for actually too, just like Ratliff. And Uncle Gavin said they were both right) "got? Well, in that case you will be jest as wrong as everybody else was. She got half of it. The reason being that the vice presi-dent here handled it for her. Of course, without a fi-nancial expert like the vice president to handle it for her, she wouldn't a got no more than that half nohow, if as much, so by rights she aint got nothing to complain of, not to mention the fact that jest half of even that half was rightfully hern, since jest Lonzo Hait was hern because them five mules was mine.

"All right. Now, what do you reckon become of the other half of them eight thousand and five hundred dollars? Then you'll be jest as wrong this time as you was that other one. Because the vice presi-dent here taken them. Oh, it was done all open and legal; he explained it: if Miz Hait sued the railroad, a lone lorn widder by herself, likely she wouldn't get more than five thousand at the most, and half of that she would have to give to me for owning the mules. And if me and her brought the suit together, with a active man on her side to compel them cold hard millionaire railroad magnits to do a lone woman justice, once I claimed any part of them mules, due to the previous bad luck mules belonging to me had been having on that-ere curve, the railroad would smell a rat right away and wouldn't nobody get nothing. While with him, the vice presi-dent, handling it, it would be seventy-five hundred or maybe a even ten thousand, of which he would not only guarantee her a full half, he would even take out of his half the hundred dollars he would give me. All legal and open: I could keep my mouth shut and get a hundred dollars, where if I objected, the vice presi-dent his-self might acci-dent-ly let out who them mules actively belonged to, and wouldn't nobody get nothing, which would be all right with the vice presi-dent since he would be right where he started out, being as he never owned Lonzo Hait nor the five mules neither.

"A pure and simple easy choice, you see: either a feller wants a hundred dollars, or either he dont want a hundred dollars. Not to mention, as the vice presi-dent his-self pointed out, that me and Miz Hait was fellow townsmen and you might say business acquaintances and Miz Hait a woman with a woman's natural tender gentle heart, so who would say that maybe in time it wouldn't melt a little more to where she might want to share a little of her half of them eight thousand and five hundred dollars. Which never proved much except that the vice presi-dent might know all there was to know about railroad companies and eight thousand and five hun-dred dollars but he never knowed much about what Miz Hait toted around where other folks totes their hearts. Which is neither here nor there; water that's still under a bridge dont fill no oceans, as the feller says, and I was simply outvoted two to one, or maybe eight thousand and five hundred dollars to one hundred dollars; or maybe it didn't even take that much: jest Miz Hait's half of them eight thousand and five hundred, against my one hundred since the only way I could a out-voted Miz Hait would a been with four thousand and two hundred and fifty-one dollars of my own, and even then I'd a had to split that odd dollar with her.

"But never mind. I done forgot all that now; that spilt milk aint going to help no ocean neither." Now Uncle Gavin said he turned rapidly to Mrs Hait with no break in the snarling and outraged babble: "What I come back for was to have a little talk with you. I got something that belongs to you, and I hear you got something that belongs to me. Though natu-rally I expected to a-just it in private."

"Lord, honey," old Het said. "If you talking at me. Dont you mind me. I done already had so much troubles myself that listening to other folks' even kind of rests me. You gawn talk what you wants to talk; I'll just set here and mind this ham."

"Come on," he said to Mrs Hait. "Run them all away for a minute."

Mrs Hait had turned now, still squatting, watching him. "What for?" she said. "I reckon she aint the first critter that ever come in this yard when it wanted and went or stayed when it liked." Now Uncle Gavin said I.O. made a gesture, brief, fretted, and restrained.

"All right," he said. "All right. Let's get started then. So you taken the mule."

"I paid you for it," Mrs Hait said. "Het brought you the money."

"Ten dollars," I.O. said. "For a hundred-and-fifty-dollar mule."

"I dont know anything about hundred-and-fifty-dollar mules," Mrs Hait said. "All I know about mules is what the railroad pays for them. Sixty dollars a head the railroad paid that other time before that fool Hait finally lost all his senses and tied himself to that track too——"

"Hush!" I.O. said. "Hush!"

"What for?" Mrs Hait said. "What secret am I telling that you aint already blabbed to anybody within listening?"

"All right," I.O. said. "But you just sent me ten."

"I sent you the difference," Mrs Hait said. "The difference between that mule and what you owed Hait."

"What I owed Hait?" I.O. said.

"Hait said you paid him fifty dollars a trip, each time he got mules in front of the train in time, and the railroad had paid you sixty dollars a head for the mules. That last time, you never paid him because you never would pay him until afterward and this time there wasn't no afterward. So I taken a mule instead and sent you the ten dollars difference with Het here for the witness." Uncle Gavin said that actually stopped him. He actually hushed; he and Mrs Hait, the one standing and the other still squatting, just stared at one another while again old Het turned the hissing ham in the skillet. He said they were so still that Mr Flem himself spoke twice before they even noticed him.

"You through now?" he said to I.O.

"What?" I.O. said.

"Are you through now?" Mr Flem said. And now Uncle Gavin said they all saw the canvas sack—one of the canvas sacks stamped with the name of the bank which the bank itself used to store money in the vault—in his hands.

"Yes," I.O. said. "I'm through. At least I got one ten dollars out of the mule business you aint going to touch." But Mr Flem wasn't even talking to him now. He had already turned toward Mrs Hait when he drew a folded paper out of the sack.

"This is the mortgage on your house," he said. "Whatever the insurance company pays you now will be clear money; you can build it back again. Here," he said. "Take it."

But Mrs Hait didn't move. "Why?" she said.

"I bought it from the bank myself this afternoon," Mr Flem said. "You can drop it in the fire if you want to. But I want you to put your hand on it first." So she took the paper then, and now Uncle Gavin said they all watched Mr Flem reach into the sack again and this time draw out a roll of bills, I.O. watching too now, not even blinking.

"Fore God," old Het said. "You could choke a shoat with it."

"How many mules have you got in that lot?" Mr Flem said to I.O. Still I.O. just watched him. Then he blinked, rapid and hard.

"Seven," he said.

"You've got six," Mr Flem said. "You just finished selling one of them to Mrs Hait. The railroad says the kind of mules you deal in are worth sixty dollars a head. You claim they are worth a hundred and fifty. All right. We wont argue. Six times a hundred and fifty is—"

"Seven!" I.O. said, loud and harsh. "I aint sold Mrs Hait nor nobody else that mule. Watch." He faced Mrs Hait. "We aint traded. We aint never traded. I defy you to produce ara man or woman that seen or heard more than you tried to hand me this here same ten-dollar bill that I'm a handing right back to you. Here," he said, extending the crumpled bill, then jerking it at her so that it struck against her skirt and fell to the ground. She picked it up.

"You giving this back to me?" she said. "Before these wit-nessess?"

"You durn right I am," he said. "I jest wish we had ten times this many witnesses." Now he was talking to Mr Flem. "So I aint sold nobody no mule. And seven times a hundred and fifty dollars is ten hundred and fifty dollars——"

"Nine hundred dollars," Mr Flem said.

"Ten hundred and fifty," I.O. said.

"When you bring me the mule," Mr Flem said. "And on the main condition."

"What main condition?" I.O. said.

"That you move back to Frenchman's Bend and never own a business in Jefferson again as long as you live."

"And if I dont?" I.O. said.

"I sold the hotel this evening too," Mr Flem said. And now even I.O. just watched him while he turned toward the light of the fire and began to count bills—they were mostly fives and ones, with an occasional ten—from the roll. I.O. made one last effort.

"Ten hundred and fifty," he said.

"When you bring me the mule," Mr Flem said. So it was still only nine hundred dollars which I.O. took and counted for himself and folded away into his hip pocket and buttoned the pocket and turned to Mrs Hait.

"All right," he said, "where's Mister Vice Presi-dent Snopes's other mule?"

"Tied to a tree in the ravine ditch behind Mr Spilmer's house," Mrs Hait said.

"What made you stop there?" I.O. said. "Why didn't you take it right on up to Mottstown? Then you could a really enjoyed my time and trouble getting it back." He looked around again, snarling, sneering, indomitably intractable. "You're right fixed up here, aint you? You and the vice presi-dent could both save money if he jest kept that mortgage which aint on nothing now noway, and you didn't build no house a-tall. Well, good night, all. Soon as I get this-here missing extry mule into the lot with the vice presi-dent's other six, I'll do myself the honor and privilege of calling at his residence for them other hundred and fifty dollars since cash on the barrel-head is the courtesy of kings, as the feller says, not to mention the fact that beggars' choices aint even choices when he aint even got a roof to lay his head in no more. And if Lawyer Stevens has got ara thing loose about him the vice presi-dent might a taken a notion to, he better hold onto it since as the feller says even a fool wont tread where he jest got through watching somebody else get bit. Again, good night all." Then he was gone. And this time Uncle Gavin said that Mr Flem had to speak to him twice be-fore he heard him.

"What?" Uncle Gavin said.

"I said, how much do I owe you?" Mr Flem said. And Uncle Gavin said he started to say One dollar, so that Mr Flem would say One dollar? Is that all? and then Uncle Gavin could say Yes, or your knife or pencil or just anything so that when I wake up tomorrow I'll know I didn't dream this. But he didn't. He just said:

"Nothing. Mrs Hait is my client." And he said how again Mr Flem had to speak twice. "What?" Uncle Gavin said.

"You can send me your bill."

"For what?" Uncle Gavin said.

"For being the witness," Mr Snopes said.

"Oh," Uncle Gavin said. And now Mr Snopes was going and Uncle Gavin said how he expected he might even have said Are you going back to town now? or maybe even Shall we walk together? or maybe at least Goodbye. But he didn't. He didn't say anything at all. He simply turned and left and was gone too. Then Mrs Hait said:

"Get the box."

"That's what I been aiming to do soon as you can turn loose all this business and steady this skillet," old Het said. So Mrs Hait came and took the chair and the fork and old Het went into the shed and set the lantern on the ground and brought the box and set it at the fire. "Now, honey," she said to Uncle Gavin, "set down and rest."

"You take it," Uncle Gavin said. "I've been sitting down all day. You haven't." Though old Het had already begun to sit down on the box before he declined it; she had already for-gotten him, watching now the skillet containing the still hiss-ing ham which Mrs Hait had lifted from the fire.

"Was it you mentioned something about a piece of that

ham," she said, "or was it me?" So Mrs Hait divided the ham
and Uncle Gavin watched them eat, Mrs Hait in the chair
with the new plate and knife and fork, and old Het on the
box eating from the skillet itself since Mrs Hait had apparently purchased only one of each new article, eating the ham
and sopping the bread into the greasy residue of its frying,
and old Het had filled the coffee cup from the pot and produced from somewhere an empty can for her own use when
I.O. came back, coming up quietly out of the darkness (it was
full dark now), to stand holding his hands to the blaze as
though he were cold.

"I reckon I'll take that ten dollars," he said.

"What ten dollars?" Mrs Hait said. And now Uncle Gavin
expected him to roar, or at least snarl. But he did neither, just
standing there with his hands to the blaze; and Uncle Gavin
said he did look cold, small, forlorn somehow since he was so
calm, so quiet.

"You aint going to give it back to me?" he said.

"Give what back to you?" Mrs Hait said. Uncle Gavin said
he didn't seem to expect an answer nor even to hear her: just
standing there musing at the fire in a kind of quiet and unbelieving amazement.

"I bear the worry and the risk and the agoment for years
and years, and I get sixty dollars a head for them. While you,
one time, without no trouble and risk a-tall, sell Lonzo Hait
and five of my mules that never even belonged to him, for
eighty-five hundred dollars. Of course most of that-ere
eighty-five hundred was for Lonzo, which I never begrudged
you. Cant nere a man living say I did, even if it did seem a
little strange that you should get it all, even my sixty standard
price a head for them five mules, when he wasn't working for
you and you never even knowed where he was, let alone even
owned the mules; that all you done to get half of that money
was just to be married to him. And now, after all them years
of not actively begrudging you it, you taken the last mule I
had, not didn't jest beat me out of another hundred and forty
dollars, but out of a entire another hundred and fifty."

"You got your mule back, and you aint satisfied yet?" old
Het said. "What does you want?"

"Justice," I.O. said. "That's what I want. That's all I want: justice. For the last time," he said. "Are you going to give me my ten dollars back?"

"What ten dollars?" Mrs Hait said. Then he turned. He stumbled over something—Uncle Gavin said it was old Het's shopping bag—and recovered and went on. Uncle Gavin said he could see him for a moment—he could because neither Mrs Hait nor old Het were watching him any longer—as though framed between the two blackened chimneys, flinging both clenched hands up against the sky. Then he was gone; this time it was for good. That is, Uncle Gavin watched him. Mrs Hait and old Het had not even looked up.

"Honey," old Het said to Mrs Hait, "what did you do with that mule?" Uncle Gavin said there was one slice of bread left. Mrs Hait took it and sopped the last of the gravy from her plate.

"I shot it," she said.

"You which?" old Het said. Mrs Hait began to eat the slice of bread. "Well," old Het said, "the mule burnt the house and you shot the mule. That's what I calls more than justice: that's what I calls tit for tat." It was full dark now, and ahead of her was still the mile-and-a-half walk to the poorhouse with the heavy shopping bag. But the dark would last a long time on a winter night, and Uncle Gavin said the poorhouse too wasn't likely to move any time soon. So he said that old Het sat back on the box with the empty skillet in her hand and sighed with peaceful and happy relaxation. "Gentlemen, hush," she said. "Aint we had a day."

And there, as Uncle Gavin would say, was Ratliff again, sitting in the client's chair with his blue shirt neat and faded and quite clean and still no necktie even though he was wearing the imitation leather jacket and carrying the heavy black policeman's slicker which were his winter overcoat; it was Monday and Uncle Gavin had gone that morning over to New Market to the supervisors' meeting on some more of the drainage canal business and I thought he would have told Ratliff that when Ratliff came to see him yesterday afternoon at home.

"He might a mentioned it," Ratliff said. "But it dont matter. I didn't want nothing. I jest stopped in here where it's quiet to laugh a little."

"Oh," I said. "About I.O. Snopes's mule that burned down Mrs Hait's house. I thought you and Uncle Gavin laughed at that enough yesterday."

"That's right," he said. "Because soon as you set down to laugh at it, you find out it aint funny a-tall." He looked at me. "When will your uncle be back?"

"I thought he would be back now."

"Oh well," he said. "It dont matter." He looked at me again. "So that's two down and jest one more to go."

"One more what?" I said. "One more Snopes for Mr Flem to run out of Jefferson, and the only Snopes left will be him; or—"

"That's right," he said. "—one more uncivic ditch to jump like Montgomery Ward's photygraph studio and I.O.'s railroad mules, and there wont be nothing a-tall left in Jefferson but Flem Snopes." He looked at me. "Because your uncle missed it."

"Missed what?" I said.

"Even when he was looking right at it when Flem his—himself come in here the morning after them—those federals raided that studio and give your uncle that studio key that had been missing from the sheriff's office ever since your uncle and Hub found them—those pictures; and even when it was staring him in the face out yonder at Miz Hait's chimbley Saturday night when Flem give—gave her that mortgage and paid I.O. for the mules, he still missed it. And I cant tell him."

"Why cant you tell him?" I said.

"Because he wouldn't believe me. This here is the kind of a thing you—a man has got to know his—himself. He has got to learn it out of his own hard dread and skeer. Because what somebody else jest tells you, you jest half believe, unless it was something you already wanted to hear. And in that case, you dont even listen to it because you had done already agreed, and so all it does is make you think what a sensible feller it was that told you. But something you dont want to hear is something you had done already made up your mind against, whether you knowed—knew it or not; and now you can even insulate against having to believe it by resisting or maybe even getting even with that-ere scoundrel that meddled in and told you."

"So he wouldn't hear you because he wouldn't believe it because it is something he dont want to be true. Is that it?"

"That's right," Ratliff said. "So I got to wait. I got to wait for him to learn it his—himself, the hard way, the sure way, the only sure way. Then he will believe it, enough anyhow to be afraid."

"He is afraid," I said. "He's been afraid a long time."

"That's good," Ratliff said. "Because he had purely better be. All of us better be. Because a feller that jest wants money for the sake of money, or even for power, there's a few things right at the last that he wont do, will stop at. But a feller that come—came up from where he did, that soon as he got big enough to count it he thought he discovered that money would buy anything he could or would ever want, and shaped all the rest of his life and actions on that, trompling when and where he had to but without no—any hard feelings because he knowed—knew that he wouldn't ask nor expect no—any quarter his—himself if it had been him;—to do all this and then find out at last, when he was a man growed—grown and it was maybe already too late, that the one thing he would have to have if there was to be any meaning to his life or even peace in it, was not only something that jest money couldn't buy, it was something that not having money to begin with or even getting a holt of all he could count or imagine or even dream about and then losing it, couldn't even hurt or harm or grieve or change or alter;—to find out when it was almost too late that what he had to have was something that any child was born having for free until one day he growed—grew up and found out when it was maybe too late that he had throwed—thrown it away."

"What?" I said. "What is it he's got to have?"

"Respectability," Ratliff said.

"Respectability?"

"That's right," Ratliff said. "When it's jest money and power a man wants, there is usually some place where he will stop; there's always one thing at least that ever—every man

wont do for jest money. But when it's respectability he finds
out he wants and has got to have, there aint nothing he wont
do to get it and then keep it. And when it's almost too late
when he finds out that's what he's got to have, and that even
after he gets it he cant jest lock it up and set—sit down on top
of it and quit, but instead he has got to keep on working with
ever—every breath to keep it, there aint nothing he will stop
at, aint nobody or nothing within his scope and reach that
may not anguish and grieve and suffer."

"Respectability," I said.

"That's right," Ratliff said. "Vice president of that bank
aint enough anymore. He's got to be president of it."

"*Got* to be?" I said.

"I mean soon, that he dont dare risk waiting, putting it off.
That girl of Miz Snopes's—Linda. She's going on—"

"She'll be nineteen the twelfth of April," I said.

"—nineteen now, over there——How do you know it's the
twelfth?"

"That's what Uncle Gavin says," I said.

"Sho, now," Ratliff said. Then he was talking again. "—at
the University at Oxford where there's a thousand extry
young fellers all new and strange and interesting and male and
nobody a-tall to watch her except a hired dormitory matron
that aint got no wife expecting to heir half of one half of
Uncle Billy Varner's money, when it was risky enough at the
Academy right here in Jefferson last year before your uncle or
her maw or whichever it was or maybe both of them together,
finally persuaded Flem to let her quit at the Academy and go
to the University after Christmas where he couldn't his—himself supervise her masculine acquaintance down to the same
boys she had growed—grown up with all her life so at least
their folks might have kinfolks that owed him money to help
handle them; not to mention having her home ever—every
night where he could reach out and put his hand on her
ever—every time the clock struck you might say. So he cant,
he dassent, risk it; any time now the telegram or the telephone might come saying she had jest finished running off to
the next nearest town with a j.p. in it that never give a hoot
who Flem Snopes was, and got married. And even if he located them ten minutes later and dragged her——"

"Drug," I said.

"—back, the—What?" he said.

"Drug," I said. "You said 'dragged'."

Ratliff looked at me a while. "For ten years now, whenever he would stop talking his-self long enough that is, and for five of them I been listening to you too, trying to learn—teach myself to say words right. And, jest when I call myself about to learn and I begin to feel a little good over it, here you come, of all people, correcting me back to what I been trying for ten years to forget."

"I'm sorry," I said. "I didn't mean it that way. It's because I like the way you say it. When you say it, 'taken' sounds a heap more took than just 'took', just like 'drug' sounds a heap more dragged than just 'dragged'."

"And not jest you neither," Ratliff said. "Your uncle too: me saying 'dragged' and him saying 'drug' and me saying 'dragged' and him saying 'drug' again, until at last he would say, 'In a free country like this, why aint I got as much right to use your *drug* for my *dragged* as you got to use my *dragged* for your *drug*?'"

"All right," I said. " 'Even if he drug her back'."

"—even if he drug—dragged—drug— You see?" he said. "Now you done got me so mixed up until even I dont know which one I dont want to say?"

" '—it would be too late and the damage'—" I said.

"Yes," Ratliff said. "And at least even your Uncle Gavin knows this; even a feller as high- and delicate-minded as him must know that the damage would be done then and Miz Snopes would quit Flem too and he could kiss goodbye not jest to her share of Uncle Billy's money but even to the voting weight of his bank stock too. So Flem's got to strike now, and quick. He's not only got to be president of that bank to at least keep that much of a holt on that Varner money by at least being president of where Uncle Billy keeps it at, he's got to make his lick before the message comes that Linda's done got married or he'll lose the weight of Uncle Billy's voting stock."

SEVENTEEN

GAVIN STEVENS
At last we knew why he had moved his money. It was as a bait. Not putting it into the other bank, the old Bank of Jefferson, as the bait, but for the people of Jefferson and Yoknapatawpha County to find out that he had withdrawn his own money from the bank of which he himself was vice president, and put it somewhere else.

But that wasn't first. At first he was simply trying to save it. Because he knew no better then. His association with banks had been too brief and humble for the idea even to have occurred to him that there was a morality to banking, an inevictable ethics in it, else not only the individual bank but banking as an institution, a form of social behavior, could not endure.

His idea and concept of a bank was that of the Elizabethan tavern or a frontier inn in the time of the opening of the American wilderness: you stopped there before dark for shelter from the wilderness; you were offered food and lodging for yourself and horse, and a bed (of sorts) to sleep in; if you waked the next morning with your purse rifled or your horse stolen or even your throat cut, you had none to blame but yourself since nobody had compelled you to pass that way nor insisted on you stopping. So when he realised that the very circumstances which had made him vice president of a bank had been born of the fact that the bank had been looted by an oaf with no more courage or imagination than he knew his cousin Byron to possess, his decision to remove his money from it as soon as he could was no more irrational than the traveller who, unsaddling in the inn yard, sees a naked body with its throat cut being flung from an upstairs window and recinches his saddle with no loss of time and remounts and rides on again, to find another inn perhaps or if not, to pass the night in the woods, which after all, Indians and bears and highwaymen to the contrary, would not be a great deal more unsafe.

It was simply to save his money—that money he had worked so hard to accumulate, too hard to accumulate, sacrificed all his life to gather together from whatever day it had been on whatever worn-out tenant farm his father had moved from, onto that other worn-out one of old Will Varner's at Frenchman's Bend which nobody else except a man who had nothing, would undertake, let alone hope, to wrest a living from;—from that very first day when he realised that he himself had nothing and would never have more than nothing unless he wrested it himself from his environment and time, and that the only weapon he would ever have to do it with would be just money.

Oh yes, sacrificed all his life for, sacrificed all the other rights and passions and hopes which make up the sum of a man and his life. Perhaps he would never, could never, have fallen in love himself and knew it: himself constitutionally and generically unfated ever to match his own innocence and capacity for virginity against the innocence and virginity of who would be his first love. But, since he was a man, to do that was his inalienable right and hope. Instead, his was to father another man's bastard on the wife who would not even repay him with the passion of gratitude, let alone the passion of passion since he was obviously incapable of that passion, but merely with her dowry.

Too hard for it, all his life for it, knowing at the same time that as long as life lasted he could never for one second relax his vigilance, not just to add to it but simply to keep, hang on to, what he already had, had so far accumulated. Amassing it by terrible and picayune nickel by nickel, having learned soon, almost simultaneously probably, that he would never have any other method of gaining it save simple ruthless antlike industry, since (and this was the first time he ever experienced humility) he knew now that he not only had not the education with which to cope with those who did have education, whom he must outguess and outfigure and despoil, but that he never would have that education now since there was no time now since his was the fate to have first the need for the money before he had opportunity to acquire the means to get it. And, even having acquired some of the money, he still had no place to put it down in safety while he did acquire the education which would enable him to defend it from those with the education who would despoil him of it in their turn.

Humility, and maybe a little even of regret—what little time there was to regret in—but without despair, who had nothing save the will and the need and the ruthlessness and the industry and what talent he had been born with, to serve them; who never in his life had been given anything by any man yet and expected no more as long as life should last; who had no evidence yet that he could cope with and fend off that enemy which the word Education represented to him, yet had neither qualm nor doubt that he was going to try.

So at first his only thought was to save that money which had cost him so dear, had in fact cost him everything since he had sacrificed his whole life to gain it and so it was his life, from the bank which his cousin had already proved vulnerable. That was it: a bank so vulnerable that someone like the one he himself knew his cousin Byron to be could have robbed it—an oaf without courage or even vision in brigandage to see further than the simple temptation of a few temporarily unguarded nickels and dimes and dollar bills of the moment, a feller, as Ratliff would have said, hardly bright enough to be named Snopes even, not even bright enough to steal the money without having to run immediately all the way to Texas before he could stop long enough to count it; having in fact managed to steal just about enough to buy the railroad ticket with.

Because remember, he didn't merely know that banks could be looted (*vide* his cousin Byron which he had witnessed himself), he believed, it was a tenet of his very being, that they were constantly looted; that the normal condition of a bank was a steady and decorous embezzlement, its solvency an impregnable illusion like the reputation of a woman who everybody knows has none yet which is intact and invulnerable because of the known (maybe proven) fact that every one of her male connections will spring as one man, not just to repudiate but to avenge with actual gunfire the slightest whisper of a slur on it. Because that—the looting of them—was the reason for banks, the only reason why anybody would go to the trouble and expense of organising one and keeping it running.

That was what Colonel Sartoris had done (he didn't know how yet, that was the innocence, but give him time) while he was president, and what Manfred de Spain would do as long as he in his turn could or did remain on top. But decently, with decorum, as they had done and would do: not rieved like a boy snatching a handful of loose peanuts while the vendor's back was turned, as his cousin Byron had done. Decently and peacefully and even more: cleverly, intelligently; so cleverly and quietly that the very people whose money had been stolen would not even discover it until after the looter was dead and safe. Nor even then actually, since by that time the looter's successor would have already shouldered the burden of that yet-intact disaster which was a natural part of his own heritage. Because, to repeat, what other reason was there to establish a bank, go to all the work and trouble to start one to be president of, as Colonel Sartoris had done; and to line up enough voting stock, figure and connive and finagle and swap and trade (not to mention digging into his own pocket —Ratliff always said De Spain borrowed some if not all of it on his personal note from old Will Varner—to replace the sum which Byron Snopes had stolen) to get himself elected president after the Colonel's death, as Manfred de Spain had done: who—De Spain—would have to be more clever even than the Colonel had been, since he—De Spain—must also contrive to cover up the Colonel's thievery in order to have any bank to loot himself.

He didn't—to repeat again—know how Colonel Sartoris had done it and how De Spain would continue to do it of course—how Colonel Sartoris had robbed it for twelve years yet still contrived to die and be buried in the odor of unimpugnable rectitude; and how De Spain would carry on in his turn and then quit his tenure (whenever that would be) not only with his reputation unimpaired but somehow even leaving intact that bubble of the bank's outward solvency. Or not yet, anyway. Which may have been when he first really tasted that which he had never tasted before—the humility of not knowing, of never having had any chance to learn the rules and methods of the deadly game in which he had gauged his life; whose fate was to have the dreadful need and the will and the ruthlessness, and then to have the opportunity itself thrust upon him before he had had any chance to learn how to use it.

So all he knew to do was to move his money out of the bank of which he was only vice president: not high enough in rank to rob it himself in one fell swoop which would net him enough to make it worth while fleeing beyond extradition for the rest of his life, nor even high enough in its hierarchy to defend himself from the inevitable next Byron Snopes who would appear at the book-keeper's desk, let alone from the greater hereditary predator who already ranked him.

And then he had nowhere to put it. If he could withdraw it from his own bank in utter secrecy, with no one ever to know it, he could have risked hiding it in his house or burying it in the back yard. But it would be impossible to keep it a secret; if no one else, the very book-keeper who recorded the transaction would be an automatic threat. And if word did spread that he had withdrawn his money from the bank in cash, every man and his cousin in the county would be his threat and enemy until every one of them was incontrovertibly convinced that the actual money actually was somewhere else, and exactly where that somewhere else was.

So he had no choice. It would have to be another bank, and done publicly. Of course he thought at once of the best bank he could find, the strongest and safest one: a big Memphis bank for instance. And here he had a new thought: a big bank where his (comparative) widow's mite would be safe because of its very minuscularity; but, believing as he did that money itself, cash dollars, possessed an inherent life of its mutual own like cells or disease, his minuscule sum would increment itself by simple parasitic osmosis like a leech or a goitre or cancer.

And even when he answered that thought immediately with *No. That wont do. The specific whereabouts of the money must be indubitably and incontrovertibly known. All Jefferson and Yoknapatawpha County must know by incontrovertible evidence that the money still is and will remain in Jefferson and Yoknapatawpha County, or I wont even dare leave my home long enough to go to the postoffice, for my neighbors and fellow citizens waiting to climb in the kitchen window to hunt for the sock inside the mattress or the coffee can beneath the hearth,* he did not yet realise what his true reason for moving the money was going to be. And even when he thought how by trans-ferring it to the other Jefferson bank, he would simply be moving it from the frying pan into the fire itself by laying it vulnerable to whatever Byron Snopes the Bank of Jefferson contained, not to mention that one's own Colonel Sartoris or Manfred de Spain, and immediately rejected that by remind-ing himself that the Bank of Jefferson was older, had had a whole century since 1830 or so to adjust itself to the natural and normal thieving of its officers and employees which was the sole reason for a bank, and so by now its very unbroken longevity was a protection, its very unaltered walls themselves a guarantee, as the simple edifice of the longtime standing church contains diffuses and even compels a sanctity invul-nerable to the human frailties and vices of parson or vestry or choir;—even when he told himself this, his eyes had still not seen the dazzling vista composed not only of civic rectitude but of personal and private triumph and revenge too which the simple withdrawing of that first dollar had opened before him.

He was too busy; his own activity blinded him. Not just getting the money from one bank to the other, but seeing to it, making sure, that everyone in the town and the county knew that he was doing so, laboring under his preconception that the one universal reaction of every man in the county to the news that he had withdrawn his money from the Sartoris bank, would be the determined intention of stealing it as soon as he put it down and turned his back; not for the county to know he had withdrawn it from a bank, but that he had put every cent of it into a bank.

It was probably days afterward, the money safe again or at least still again or at least for the moment still again; and I like to imagine it: one still in the overalls and the tieless shirt and still thrall, attached irrevocably by the lean umbilicus of bare livelihood which if it ever broke he would, solvently speaking, die, to the worn-out tenant farm which—the farm and the tieless shirt and the overalls—he had not wrenched free of yet as Snopes himself had, nor ever would probably and who for that very reason had watched the rise of one exactly like him-self, from the overalls and the grinding landlord to a white shirt and a tie and the vice presidency of a bank; watched this not with admiration but simply with envy and respect (ay, hatred too), stopping Snopes on the street one day, calling him mister, servile and cringing because of the white shirt and the tie but hating them also because they were not his:

"Likely hit aint a thing to it, but I heerd tell you taken your money outen your bank."

"That's right," Snopes said. "Into the Bank of Jefferson."

"Outen the bank that you yourself are vice president of."

"That's right," Snopes said. "Into the Bank of Jefferson."

"You mean, the other one aint safe?" Which to Snopes was to laugh, to whom no bank was safe; to whom any bank was that clump of bushes at the forest's edge behind the one-room frontier cabin, which the pioneer had to use for out-house since he had no other: the whole land, the whole dark wilderness (which meant the clump of bushes too) infested with Indians and brigands, not to mention bears and wolves and snakes. Of course it was not safe. But he had to go there. Because not until then did that vista, prospect containing the true reason why he moved his money, open before him. "Then you advise me to move mine too."

"No," Snopes said. "I just moved mine."

"Outen the bank that you yourself air vice president of."

"That's right," Snopes said. "That I myself am vice president of."

"I see," the other said. "Well, much oblige."

Because he saw it then, whose civic jealousy and pride four years later would evict and eliminate from Jefferson one of his own kinsmen who had set up a pay-as-you-enter peep show with a set of imported pornographic photographs, by planting in his place of business several gallons of untaxed home-made whiskey and then notifying the federal revenue people; the same civic jealousy and pride which six years later would evict and eliminate from Jefferson another (and the last) objectional member of his tribe who had elevated into a profession the simple occupation of hitching mules between the rails at a strategic curve of the railroad where engine drivers couldn't see them in time, by the direct expedient of buying the kinsman's remaining mules at his—the kinsman's—own figure on condition that the kinsman never show his face in Jefferson again.

Civic jealousy and pride which you might say only discovered civic jealousy and pride at the same moment he realised that, in the simple process of saving his own private money from rapine and ravagement, he could with that same stroke evict and eliminate from his chosen community its arch-fiend among sinners too, its supremely damned among the lost infernal seraphim: a creature who was a living mockery of virtue and morality because he was a paradox: lately mayor of the town and now president of one of its two banks and a warden of the Episcopal church, who was not content to be a normal natural Saturday-night whoremonger or woman chaser whom the town could have forgiven for the simple reason that he was natural and human and understandable and censurable, but instead must set up a kind of outrageous morality of adultery, a kind of flaunted uxoriousness in *par amours* based on an unimpugnable fidelity which had already lasted flagrant and unimpugnable ever since the moment the innocent cuckolded husband brought the female partner of it into town twelve years ago and which promised, bade or boded, whichever side you are on, to last another twelve unless the husband found some way to stop it, and twice twelve probably if he—the husband—waited for the town itself to do anything about it.

Civic virtue which, like all virtue, was its own reward also. Because in that same blinding flash he saw his own vengeance and revenge too, as if not just virtue loved virtue but so did God since here He was actually offering to share with virtue that quality which He had jealously reserved solely to Himself: the husband's vengeance and revenge on the man who had presented him with the badge of his championship; vengeance and revenge on the man who had not merely violated his home but outraged it—the home which in all good faith he had tried to establish around a woman already irrevocably soiled and damaged in the world's (Frenchman's Bend's, which was synonymous enough then) sight, and so give her bastard infant a name. He had been paid for it, of course. That is, he had received her dowry: a plantation of barely accessible worn-out land containing the weed-choked ruins of a formal garden and the remains (what the neighbors had not pulled down plank by plank for firewood) of a columned colonial house—a property so worthless that Will Varner gave it away since even as ruthless an old pirate as Will Varner had failed in a whole quarter-century of ownership to evolve any way to turn a penny out of it; so worthless in fact that even he, Snopes, had been reduced to one of the oldest and hoariest expedients man ever invented: the salted gold-mine: in order to sell the place to Henry Armstid and V. K. Ratliff, one of whom, Ratliff anyhow, should certainly have known better, for which reason he, Snopes, had no pity on him.

So in return for that worthless dowry (worthless since what value it had he had not found in it but himself had brought there) he had assumed the burden not only of his wife's moral fall and shame, but of the nameless child too; giving his name to it. Not much of a name maybe, since like what remained of the Old Frenchman's plantation, what value he found in it he himself had brought there. But it was the only name he had, and even if it had been Varner (ay, or Sartoris or De Spain or Compson or Grenier or Habersham or McCaslin or any of the other cognomens long and splendid in the annals of Yoknapatawpha County) he would have done the same.

Anyway, he gave the child a name and then moved the mother herself completely away from that old stage and scene and milieu of her shame, onto, into a new one, where at least no man could say *I saw that fall* but only *This is what gossip said*. Not that he expected gratitude from her, anymore than he did from old Will Varner, who by his (Varner's) lights had already paid him. But he did expect from her the simple sense and discretion taught by hard experience: not gratitude toward him but simple sensibleness toward herself, as you neither expect nor care that the person you save from burning is grateful for being saved but at least you expect that from now on that person will stay away from fire.

But that was not the point, that maybe women are no more capable of sensibleness than they are of gratitude. Maybe women are capable only of gratitude, capable of nothing else but gratitude. Only, since the past no more exists for them than morality does, they have nothing which might have taught them sensibility with which to deal with the future and gratitude toward what or who saved them from the past; gratitude in them is a quality like electricity: it has to be produced projected and consumed all in the same instant to exist at all.

Which was simply saying what any and every man whose fate—doom, destiny, call it whatever you will—finally led him into marriage, long since and soon learned the hard way: his home had been violated not because his wife was ungrateful and a fool, but simply because she was a woman. She had no more been seduced from the chastity of wifehood by the incorrigible bachelor flash and swagger of Manfred de Spain than she had been seduced from that of maidenhood by that same quality in that boy—youth—man—McCarron—back there in her virginity which he was convinced she no longer even remembered. She was seduced simply by herself: by a nymphomania not of the uterus: the hot unbearable otherwise unreachable itch and burn of the mare or heifer or sow or bitch in season, but by a nymphomania of a gland whose only ease was in creating a situation containing a recipient for gratitude, then supplying the gratitude.

Which still didn't exculpate Manfred de Spain. He didn't expect Manfred de Spain to have such high moral standards that they would forbid him seducing somebody else's wife. But he did expect him to have enough sense not to, since he wasn't a woman; to have too much sense this time, enough sense to look a little ahead into the future and refrain from seducing this wife anyway. But he hadn't. Worse: De Spain had even tried to recompense him for the privilege of that violation and defilement; out of base fear to pay him in base and niggling coin for what he, De Spain, juxtaposing De Spain against Snopes, considered his natural and normal *droit de seigneur*. True, old Will Varner had paid him for marrying his damaged daughter, but that was not the same. Old Will wasn't even trying to cover up, let alone liquidate, his daughter's shame. The very fact of what he offered for it—that ruined and valueless plantation of which even he, with a quarter of a century to do it in, had been able to make nothing, revealed what value he held that honor at; and as for liquidating the shame, he—old Will—would have done that himself with his pistol, either in his hand or in that of his oafish troglodyte son Jody, if he had ever caught McCarron. He—old Will—had simply used that forthrightness to offer what

he considered a fair price to get out of his house the daughter who had already once outraged his fireside peace and in
time would very likely do it again.

But not De Spain, who without courage at all had tried to
barter and haggle, using his position as mayor of the town to
offer the base coinage of its power-plant superintendency and
its implied privileges of petty larceny, not only to pay for the
gratification of his appetite but to cover his reputation, trying
to buy at the same time the right to the wife's bed and the security of his good name from the husband who owned them
both;—this, for the privilege of misappropriating a handful of
brass which he—Snopes—had availed himself of not for the
petty profit it brought him but rather to see what depth De
Spain's base and timorous fear would actually descend to.

He saw. They both did. It was not his—Snopes's—shame
anymore than it was De Spain's pride that when the final crisis of the brass came which could have destroyed him, De
Spain found for ally his accuser himself. The accuser, the city
official sworn and—so he thought until that moment—dedicated too, until he too proved to be vulnerable (not competent: merely vulnerable) to that same passion from which
derived what should have been his—De Spain's—ruin and
desolation; the sworn and heretofore dedicated city official
who found too dangerous for breathing too that same air
simply because she had breathed it, walked in it while it laved
and ached; the accuser, the community's civic champion likewise blasted and stricken by that same lightning-bolt out of
the old passion and the old anguish. But for him (the accuser)
only the grieving without even the loss; for him not even ruin
to crown the grieving: only the desolation, who was not competent for but merely vulnerable to, since it was not even for
him to hold her hand.

So De Spain brazened that through too, abrogating to
courage what had merely been his luck. And as if that were
not temerity enough, effrontery enough: Colonel Sartoris
barely dead of his heart attack in his grandson's racing automobile (almost as though he—De Spain—had suborned the
car and so contrived the accident) and the presidency of the
bank barely vacant, when here he—De Spain—was again not
requesting or suggesting but with that crass and brazen gall

assuming, taking it for granted that he, Snopes, was down-right panting for the next new chance not merely to re-com-pound but publicly affirm again his own cuckolding, that mutual co-violating of his wife's bed,—ay, publicly affirming her whoredom; the last clod still echoing as it were on Colonel Sartoris's coffin when De Spain approaches, figura-tively rubbing his hands, already saying, "All right, let's get going. That little shirt-tail full of stock you own will help some of course. But we need a big block of it. You step out to Frenchman's Bend tomorrow—tonight if possible—and sew up Uncle Billy before somebody else gets to him. Get moving now." Or maybe even the true explicit words: *Your kinsman—cousin—has destroyed this bank by removing a link, no matter how small or large, in the chain of its cash integrity. Which means not just the value of the stock you own in it, but the actual dollars and cents which you worked so hard to acquire and deposit in it, and which until last night were available to you on demand, were still yours. The only way to anneal that chain is to restore that link to the last penny which your cousin stole. I will do that, but in return for it I must be president of the bank; anyone who restores that money will insist on being president in return, just as anyone to become president will have to restore that money first. That's your choice: keep the par of your stock and the full value of your deposit through a president that you know exactly how far you can trust him, or take your chance with a stranger to whom the value of your stock and de-posit may possibly mean no more than they did to your cousin Byron.*

He obeyed. He had no choice. Because there was the in-nocence; ignorance, if you like. He had naturally taught him-self all he could about banking since he had to use them or something equivalent to keep his money in. But so far his only opportunities had been while waiting in line at a win-dow, to peer through the grilled barricade which separated the money and the methods of handling it from the people to whom it belonged, who brought it in and relinquished it on that simple trust of one human being in another, since there was no alternative between that baseless trust and a vulner-able coffee can buried under a bush in the back yard.

Nor was it only to save his own money that he obeyed. In

going out to Frenchman's Bend to solicit the vote of old Will Varner's stock for Manfred de Spain, he not only affirmed the fact that simple baseless unguaranteed unguaranteeable trust between man and man was solvent, he defended the fact that it not only could endure: it must endure since the robustness of a nation was in the solvency of its economy, and the solvency of an economy depended on the rectitude of its banks and the sacredness of the individual dollars they contained, no matter to whom the dollars individually belonged, and that rectitude and sanctity must in the last analysis depend on the will of man to trust and the capacity of man to be trusted; in sacrificing the sanctity of his home to the welfare of Jefferson, he immolated the chastity of his wife on the altar of mankind.

And at what added price: not just humbling his pride but throwing it completely away to go out there and try to persuade, perhaps even plead and beg with that old pirate in his dingy country store at Varner's Crossroads—that tall lean choleric outrageous old brigand with his grim wife herself not church-ridden but herself running the local church she belonged to with the cold high-handedness of a ward-boss, and his mulatto concubines (Ratliff said he had three: the first Negroes in that section of the county and for a time the only ones he would permit there, by whom he now had grand-children, this—the second—generation already darkening back but carrying intact still the worst of the new white Varner traits grafted onto the worst of their fatherless or two-fathered grandmothers' combined original ones), who was anything in the world but unmoral since his were the strictest of simple moral standards: that whatever Will Varner decided to do was right, and anybody in the way had damned well better beware.

Yet he went, to deal with the old man who despised him for having accepted an already-dishonored wife for a price no greater than what he, Varner, considered the Old Frenchman place to be worth; and who feared him because he, Snopes, had been smart enough to realise from it what he, Varner, had not been able to in twenty-five years; who feared him for what that smartness threatened and implied and therefore hated him because he had to fear.

And dealt with him too, persuaded or tricked or forced.

Even Ratliff, whose Yoknapatawpha County reputation and good name demanded that he have an answer to everything, did not have that one, Ratliff himself knowing no more than the rest of us did. Which was, one day there was a rumored coalition De Spain-Varner-Snopes; on the second day De Spain's own personal hand restored the money which Byron Snopes had absconded to Texas with; on the third day the stock-holders elected De Spain president of the bank and Flem Snopes vice president.

That was all. Because there was the innocence. Not ignorance; he didn't know the inner workings of banks not because of ignorance but simply because he had not had opportunity and time yet to teach himself. Now he had only the need, the desperate necessity of having to save the entire bank in order to free his own deposit in it long enough to get the money out and into safety somewhere. And now that he was privileged, the actual vice president of it, from whom all the most secret mechanisms and ramifications of banking and the institution of banks, not only the terror and threat of them but the golden perquisites too, could no longer be hidden, he had less than ever of time. He had in fact time only to discover how simple and easy it was to steal from a bank since even a courageless unimaginative clod like his cousin Byron, who probably could not even conceive of a sum larger than a thousand or two dollars, had been able to do it with impunity; and to begin to get his own money out of it before all the rest of the employees, right on down to the Negro janitor who swept the floor every morning, would decide that the dust and alarm had settled enough to risk (or perhaps simply that the supply of loose money had built up enough again to make it worth while) emulating him.

That was it: the rush, the hurry, the harassment; it was probably with something very like shame that he remembered how it was not his own perspicuity at all but the chance meeting with an ignorant country man alarmed over his own (probably) two-figure bank balance, which opened to him that vista, that dazzling opportunity to combine in one single stroke security for himself and revenge on his enemy—that vengeance which had apparently been afoot for days and even weeks since a well-nigh nameless tenant farmer who probably

never came to town four times a year, had been his first notice
of its existence; that revenge which he was not only unaware
of which he himself had not even planned and instigated, as if
the gods or fates—circumstance—something—had taken up
the cudgel in his behalf without even asking his permission,
and naturally would some day send him a bill for it.

But he saw it now. Not to destroy the bank itself, wreck it,
bring it down about De Spain's ears like Samson's temple;
but simply to move it still intact out from under De Spain.
Because the bank stood for money. A bank was money, and as
Ratliff said, he would never injure money, cause to totter for
even one second the parity and immunity of money; he had
too much veneration for it. He would simply move the bank
and the money it represented and stood for, out from under
De Spain, intact and uninjured and not even knowing it had
been moved, into a new physical niche in the hegemony and
economy of the town, leaving De Spain high and dry with
nothing remaining save the mortgage on his house which (according to Ratliff) he had given old Will Varner for the
money with which to restore what Byron Snopes had stolen.

Only, how to do it. How to evict De Spain from the bank
or remove the bank from under De Spain without damaging
it—snatch it intact from under De Spain by persuading or
frightening enough more of the depositors into withdrawing
their money; how to start the avalanche of dollars which
would suck it dry; persuade enough of the depositors and
stock-holders to move their stock and funds bodily out of this
one and into a new set of walls across the Square, or perhaps
even (who knew) into the set of walls right next door to De
Spain's now empty ones without even breaking the slumber
of the bank's solvency.

Because even if every other one-gallused share-cropper in
the county whose sole cash value was the October or November sale of the single bale of cotton which was his tithe of his
year's work, withdrew his balance also, it would not be
enough. Nor did he have nature, biology, nepotism, for his
weapon. Although there were probably more people named
Snopes or married to a Snopes or who owed sums ranging
from twenty-five cents to five dollars to a Snopes, than any
other name in that section of Mississippi, with one exception

not one of them represented the equity of even one bale of share-crop cotton, and that exception—Wallstreet Panic, the grocer—already banked with the other bank and so could not have been used even if he—Flem—could have found any way to cope with the fierce implacable enmity of his—Wallstreet's —wife.

And less than any did he possess that weapon which could have served him best of all: friendship, a roster of people whom he could have approached without fear or alarm and suggested or formed a cabal against De Spain. He had no friends. I mean, he knew he didn't have any friends because he had never (and never would) intended to have them, be cluttered with them, be constantly vulnerable or anyway liable to the creeping sentimental parasitic importunity which his observation had shown him friendship meant. I mean, this was probably when he discovered, for the first time in his life, that you needed friends for the simple reason that at any time a situation could—and in time would, no matter who you were—arise when you could use them; could not only use them but would have to since nothing else save friendship, someone to whom you could say "Dont ask why; just take this mortgage or lien or warrant or distrainer or pistol and point it where I tell you, and pull the trigger", would do. Which was the innocence again: having had to scratch and scrabble and clutch and fight so soon and so hard and so un-flaggingly long to get the money which he had to have, that he had had no time to teach himself how to hold onto it, de-fend and keep it (and this too with no regret either, since he still had no time to spend regretting). Yes, no regret for lack of that quantity which his life had denied him the opportunity to teach himself that he would need, not because he had no time for regret at this specific moment, but because that des-perate crisis had not yet risen where even friendship would not have been enough. Even Time was on his side now; it would be five years yet before he would be forced to the last desperate win-all lose-all by the maturation of a female child.

Though he did have his one tool, weapon, implement—that nethermost stratum of unfutured, barely-solvent one-bale tenant farmers which pervaded, covered thinly the whole county and on which in fact the entire cotton-economy of the county was founded and supported; he had that at least, with running through his head probably all the worn platitudinous saws about the incrementation of the mere enoughs: enough grains of sand and single drops of water and pennies saved. And working underground now. He had always worked submerged each time until the mine was set and then blew up in the unsuspecting face. But this time he actually consorted with the moles and termites—not with Sartorises and Benbows and Edmondses and Habershams and the other names long in the county annals, which (who) owned the bank stock and the ponderable deposits, but with the other nameless tenants and croppers like his first interlocutor who as that one would have put it: "Knowed a rat when he smelt one."

He didn't proselytise among them. He was simply visible, depending on that first one to have spread the word, the idea, letting himself be seen going and coming out of the other bank, the Bank of Jefferson, himself biding until they themselves would contrive the accidental encounter for corroboration, in pairs or even groups, like a committee, straight man and clown, like this:

"Mawnin, Mister Snopes. Aint you strayed off the range a little, over here at this bank?"

"Maybe Mister Flem has done got so much money now that jest one bank wont hold it."

"No, boys, it's like my old pappy used to say: Two traps will hold twice as many coons as one trap."

"Did your pappy ever ask that smart old coon which trap he would ruther be in, Mister Snopes?"

"No, boys. All that old coon ever said was, Just so it aint the wrong trap."

That would be all. They would guffaw; one might even slap the faded blue of his overalled knee. But that afternoon (or maybe they would even wait a day or two days or even a week) they would appear singly at the teller's window of the old long-established Bank of Jefferson, the gnarled warped sunburned hands relinquishing almost regretfully the meagre clutch of banknotes; never to transfer the account by a simple check at the counter but going in person first to the bank which because of a whispered word supported by a clumsy parable they were repudiating, and withdraw the thin laborious sum in its actual cash and carry it across the Square to the other bank which at that same cryptic anonymous source-less breath they would repudiate in its turn.

Because they were really neither moles nor termites. Moles can undermine foundations and the termites can reduce the entire house to one little pile of brown dust. But these had neither the individual determination of moles nor the com-munal determination of the termites even though they did resemble ants in numbers. Because like him, Snopes, they simply were trying to save their meagre individual dollars, and he—Flem—knew it: that another breath, word, would alarm them back into the other bank; that if De Spain himself only wanted to, with the judicious planting of that single word he could recover not merely his own old one-bale clients, but the Bank of Jefferson's entire roster too. Which he nor any other sane banker would want, since it would mean merely that many more Noes to say to the offers of galled mules and wornout farm- and household-gear as security to make down payments on second-hand and wornout automobiles.

It was not enough. It would be nowhere near enough. He recast his mind, again down the diminishing vain roster of names which he had already exhausted, as though he had never before weighed them and found them all of no avail: his nephew or cousin Wallstreet Panic the grocer, who less than ten years ago, by simple industry and honesty and hard work, plus the thousand-dollar compensation for his father's violent death, had gained an interest in a small side-street grocery store and now, in that ten years, owned a small chain of them scattered about north Mississippi, with his own wholesale warehouse to supply them; who—Wallstreet—would alone have been enough to remove De Spain's bank from under him except for two insurmountable obstacles: the fact that he already banked and owned stock in the other bank, and the implacable enmity of his wife toward the very word Snopes, who, it was said in Jefferson, was even trying to persuade her husband to change his own by law. Then the rest of his tribe of Snopes, and the other Snopeses about the county who were not Snopeses nor tenant farmers either, who had been paying him the usury on five or ten or twenty-dollar loans for that many years, who, even if he could have enrolled them at the price of individual or maybe lump remission, would have added no weight to his cause for the simple reason that anyone with any amount of money in a public institution anywhere would never have dared put his signature on any piece of paper to remain in his, Flem's, possession.

Which brought him back to where he had started, once more to rack and cast his mind down the vain and diminishing list, knowing that he had known all the while that one name to which he would finally be reduced, and had been dodging it. Old man Will Varner, his father-in-law, knowing all the time that in the end he would have to eat that crow: go back to the choleric irascible old man who never had and never would forgive him for having tricked him into selling him the Old Frenchman place for five hundred dollars, which he, Flem, sold within two weeks for a profit of three or four hundred percent.; go back again to the old man whom only five years ago he had swallowed his pride and approached and persuaded to use the weight of his stock and money to make president of the bank the same man he must now persuade Varner to dispossess.

You see? That was his problem. Probably, except for the really incredible mischance that the bastard child he had given his name to happened to be female, he would never have needed to surmount it. He may have contented himself with the drowsy dream of his revenge, himself but half awake in the long-familiar embrace of his cuckoldry as you recline in a familiar chair with a familiar book, if his wife's bastard had not been a girl.

But she was. Which fact (oh yes, men are interested in facts too, even ones named Flem Snopes) must have struck him at last, whatever the day, moment, was, with an incredible unanticipated shock. Here was this thing, creature, which he had almost seen born you might say, and had seen, watched, every day of its life since. Yet in all innocence, unsuspecting, unforewarned. Oh he knew it was female, and, continuing to remain alive, it must inevitably mature; and, being a human creature, on maturing it would have to be a woman. But he had been too busy making money, having to start from scratch (scratch? scratch was euphonism indeed for where he started from) to make money without owning or even hoping for anything to make it with, to have had time to learn or even to discover that he might need to learn anything about women. You see? a little thing, creature, is born; you say: It will be a horse or a cow, and in time it does become that horse or that cow and fits, merges, fades into environment with no seam, juncture, suture. But not that female thing or creature which becomes (you cannot stop it; not even Flem Snopes could) a woman—woman who shapes, fits herself to no environment, scorns the fixitude of environment and all the behavior patterns which had been mutually agreed on as being best for the greatest number; but on the contrary just by breathing, just by the mere presence of that fragile and delicate flesh, warps and wrenches milieu itself to those soft unangled rounds and curves and planes.

That's what he had. That's what happened to him. Because by that time he had probably resigned himself to no more than the vain and hopeless dream of vengeance and revenge on his enemy. I mean, to canvass and canvass, cast and recast, only to come always back to that one-gallused one-bale residuum which, if all their resources, including the price of the second-hand overalls too, could have been pooled, the result would not have shaken the economy of a country church, let alone a county-seat bank. So he probably gave up, not to the acceptance of his horns, but at least to living with them.

Then the bastard child to whom in what you might call all innocence he had given his name, not satisfied with becoming just *a* woman, must become or threaten to become this particular and specific woman. Being female, she had to become a woman, which he had expected of her and indeed would not have held against her, provided she was content to become merely an ordinary woman. If he had had choice, he naturally would have plumped for a homely one, not really insisting on actual deformity, but one merely homely and frightened from birth and hence doomed to spinsterhood to that extent that her coeval young men would as one have taken one glance at her and then forgot they had ever seen her; and the one who would finally ask for her hand would have one eye, probably both, on her (purported) father's money and so would be malleable to his hand.

But not this one, who was obviously not only doomed for

marriage from the moment she entered puberty, but as obviously doomed for marriage with someone beyond his control,
either because of geography or age or, worst, most outrageous of all: simply because the husband already had money
and would neither need nor want his. *Vide* the gorilla-sized
bravo drawn from as far away as Ohio while she was still only
fifteen years old, who with his Golden Gloves fists or maybe
merely his Golden Gloves reputation intimidated into a male
desert except for himself her very surrounding atmosphere;
until he was dispossessed by a fact which even his Golden
Gloves could not cope with: that she was a woman and hence
not just unpredictable: incorrigible.

You see? the gorilla already destined to own at least a Ford
agency if not an entire labor union, not dispossessed by nor
even superseded by, because they overlapped: the crown
prince of the motor age merely on the way out because his
successor was already in: the bachelor lawyer twice her age
who, although apparently now fixed fast and incapable of
harm in the matrix of the small town, bringing into her life
and her imagination that same deadly whiff of outland, meeting her in the afternoon at soft-drink stands, not just to en-
tice and corrupt her female body but far worse: corrupting
her mind, inserting into her mind and her imagination not
just the impractical and dreamy folly in poetry books but the
fatal poison of dissatisfaction's hopes and dreams.

You see? the middleaged (whiteheaded too even) small-
town lawyer you would have thought incapable and therefore
safe, who had actually served as his, Flem's, champion in the
ejection of that first, the Ohio gorilla, threat, had now himself
become even more of a danger since he was persuading the
girl herself to escape beyond the range of his control, not only
making her dissatisfied with where she was and should be, but
even showing her where she could go to seek images and
shapes she didn't know she had until he put them in her
mind.

That was his problem. He couldn't even solve it by choosing, buying for her a husband whom he could handle and
control. Because he dared not let her marry anybody at all
until God or the devil or justice or maybe simple nature herself, wearied to death of him, removed old Will Varner from

the surface at least of the earth. Because the moment she married, the wife who had taken him for her husband for the single reason of providing her unborn child with a name (a little perhaps because of old Will's moral outrage and fury, a good deal maybe just to escape the noise he was probably making at the moment, but mostly, almost all, for the child) would quit him too, either with her present lover or without; in any case, with her father's will drawn eighteen years before she married Flem Snopes and ten or twelve before she ever heard of him, still unchanged.

She must not marry at all yet. Which was difficult enough to prevent even while she was at home in Jefferson, what with half the football and baseball teams escorting her home from school in the afternoon and squiring her in gangs to the picture show during her junior and senior high school years. Because at least she was living at home where her father could more or less control things either by being her father (oh yes, her father; she knew no different and in fact would have denied, repudiated the truth if anyone had tried to tell her it since women are not interested in truth or romance but only in facts whether they are true or not, just so they fit all the other facts, and to her the fact was that he was her father for the simple fact that all the other girls (boys too of course) had fathers unless they were dead beneath locatable tombstones) or by threatening to call in or foreclose a usurious note or mortgage bearing the signature of the father or kin of the would-be bridegroom, or—if he, Flem, were lucky—that of the groom himself.

Then who must appear but this meddling whiteheaded outsider plying her with ice cream sodas and out-of-state college catalogues and at last convincing her that not only her pleasure and interest but her duty too lay in leaving Jefferson, getting out of it the moment she graduated from high school. Upon which, she would carry that rich female provocation which had already drawn blood (ay, real blood once anyway) a dozen times in Jefferson, out into a world rifely teeming with young single men vulnerable to marriage whether they knew it or not before they saw her. Which he forestalled or rather stalled off for still another year which compelled, persuaded (I dont know what he used; tears even perhaps;

certainly tears if he could have found any to use) her to waste
at the Academy (one of the last of those gentle and stubbornly fading anachronisms called Miss So-and-So's or The
So-and-So Female Academy or Institute whose curriculum included deportment and china-painting, which continue to
dot the South though the rest of the United States knows
them no more); this, while he racked his brain for how to
eliminate this menace and threat to his wife's inheritance
which was the middleaged country lawyer with his constant
seduction of out-of-state school brochures. The same middleaged lawyer in fact who had evicted the preceding menace of
the Ohio garage mechanic. But none appeared to eliminate
the lawyer save he, the embattled father, and the only tool he
knew was money. So I can imagine this: Flem Snopes during
all that year, having to remain on constant guard against any
casual stranger like a drummer with a line of soap or hardware
stopping off the train overnight, and at the same time wring
and rack his harassed imagination for some means of compelling me to accept a loan of enough money at usurious
enough interest, to be under his control.

Which was what I expected of course. I had even reached
the point of planning, dreaming what I would do with the
money, what buy with the money for which I would continue
to betray him. But he didn't do that. He fooled me. Or perhaps he did me that honor too: not just to save my honor for
me by withholding the temptation to sully it, but assuming
that I would even sell honor before I would sully it and so
temptation to do the one would be automatically refused because of the other. Anyway, he didn't offer me the bribe. And
I know why now. He had given up. I mean, he realised at last
that he couldn't possibly keep her from marriage even though
he kept her in Jefferson, and that the moment that happened,
he could kiss goodbye forever to old Will Varner's money.

Because sometime during that last summer—this last summer or fall rather, since school had opened again and she had
begun her second year at the Academy, wasting another year
within the fading walls where Miss Melissa Hogganbeck still
taught stubbornly to the dwindling few who were present,
that not just American history but all history had not yet
reached Christmas Day, 1865, since although General Lee (and

other soldiers too, including her own grandfather) had surrendered, the war itself was not done and in fact the next ten
years would show that even those token surrenders were mistakes—he sat back long enough to take stock. Indeed, he—or
any other male—had only to look at her to know that this
couldn't go on much longer, even if he never let her out of
the front yard—that girl (woman now; she will be nineteen
this month) who simply by moving, being, promised and demanded and would have not just passion, not her mother's
fierce awkward surrender in a roadside thicket at night with a
lover still bleeding from a gang fight; but love, something
worthy to match not just today's innocent and terrified and
terrifying passion, but tomorrow's strength and capacity for
serenity and growth and accomplishment and the realisation
of hope and at last the contentment of one mutual peace and
one mutual conjoined old age. It—the worst, disaster, catastrophe, ruin, the last irrevocable chance to get his hands on
any part of old Will Varner's money—could happen at any
time now; and who knows what relief there might have been
in the simple realization that at any moment now he could
stop worrying not only about the loss of the money but having to hope for it, like when the receptionist opens the door
to the dentist's torture-chamber and looks at you and says
"Next" and it's too late now, simple face will not let you leap
up and flee.

You see? Peace. No longer to have to waste time hoping or
even regretting, having canvassed all the means and rejected
all, since who knows too if during that same summer while he
racked his harassed and outraged brain for some means to
compel me to accept a loan at a hundred percent. interest, he
had not also toyed with the possibility of finding some dedicated enthusiast panting for martyrdom in the simple name of
Man who would shoot old Will some night through his
kitchen window and then rejected that too, relinquishing not
hope so much as just worry.

And not just peace, but joy too since, now that he could relinquish forever that will-o-the-wisp of his father-in-law's
money, he could go back to his original hope and dream of
vengeance and revenge on the man responsible for the situation because of which he must give over all hope of his wife's

inheritance. In fact he knew now why he had deferred that vengeance so long, dodged like a coward the actual facing of old Will's name in the canvass of possibilities. It was because he had known instinctively all the time that only Will could serve him, and once he had employed Will for his vengeance, by that same stroke he himself would have destroyed forever any chance of participating in that legacy.

But now that was all done, finished, behind him. He was free. Now there remained only the method to compel, force, cajole, persuade, trick—whichever was handiest or quickest or most efficient—the voting power of old Will's stock, plus the weight of that owned by others who were too afraid of old Will to resist him, in addition to his—Flem's—own stock and his corps of one-gallused depositors and their whispering campaign, to remove De Spain's bank from under him by voting him out of its presidency.

All that remained was how, how to handle—in a word, lick—Will Varner. And who to dispute that he already knew that too, that plan already tested and retested back in the very time while he was still dodging the facing of old Will's name. Because, apparently once his mind was made up and he had finally brought himself to cut out and cauterise with his own hand that old vain hope of his wife's inheritance, he didn't hesitate. Here was the girl, the one pawn which could wreck his hopes of the Varner money, whom he had kept at home where he could delay to that extent at least the inevitable marriage which would ruin him, keeping her at home not only against her own wishes but against those of her mother too (not to mention the meddling neighbor); keeping her at home even when to him too probably it meant she was wasting her time in that anachronistic vacuum which was the Female Academy. This for one entire year and up to the Christmas holidays in the second one; then suddenly, without warning, overnight, he gives his permission for her to go, leave Jefferson and enter the State University; only fifty miles away to be sure, yet they were fifty miles, where it would be impossible for her to report back home every night and where she would pass all her waking hours among a thousand young men, all bachelors and all male.

Why? It's obvious. Why did he ever do any of the things he

did? Because he got something in return more valuable to him than what he gave. So you dont really need to imagine this: he and his wife talking together (of course they talked sometimes; they were married, and you have to talk sometime to someone even when you're not married)—or four of them that is since there would be two witnesses waiting in the synthetic hall until she should take up the pen: *Sign this document guaranteeing me one half of whatever you will inherit under your father's will, regardless of whatever your and my status in respect to one another may be at that time, and I will give my permission for Linda to go away from Jefferson to school.* All right, granted it could be broken, abrogated, set aside, would not hold. She would not know that. And even if she had never doubted it would hold, had the actual inheritance in her hand at the moment, would she have refused to give him half of it for that in return? Besides, it wasn't her it was to alarm, spook out of the realm of cool judgment.

That was the 'how'. Now remained only the 'when'; the rest of the winter and she away at the University now and he still about town, placid, inscrutable, unchanged, in the broad black planter's hat and the minute bow tie seen somewhere about the Square at least once during the day as regular as the courthouse clock itself; on through the winter and into the spring, until yesterday morning.

That's right. Just gone. So you will have to imagine this too since there would be no witnesses even waiting in a synthetic hall this time: once more the long, already summer-dusty gravel road (it had been simple dirt when he traversed it that first time eighteen years ago) out to Varner's store. And in an automobile this time, it was that urgent, 'how' and 'when' having at last coincided. And secret; the automobile was a hired one. I mean, an imported hired one. Although most of the prominent people in Jefferson and the county too owned automobiles now, he was not one of them. And not just because of the cost, of what more men than he in Yoknapatawpha County considered the foolish, the almost criminal immobilisation of that many dollars and cents in something which, even though you ran it for hire, would not pay for itself before it wore out, but because he was not only not a prominent man in Jefferson yet, he didn't even want to be: who would have defended as he did his life the secret even of exactly how solvent he really was.

But this was so urgent that he must use one for speed, and so secret that he would have hired one, paid money for the use of one, even if he had owned one, so as not to be seen going out there in his own; too secret even to have ridden out with the mail carrier, which he could have done for a dollar; too secret even to have commandeered from one of his clients a machine which he actually did own since it had been purchased with his money secured by one of his myriad usurious notes. Instead, he hired one. We would never know which one nor where: only that it would not bear Yoknapatawpha County license plates, and drove out there in it, out to Varner's Crossroads once more and for the last time, dragging, towing a fading cloud of yellow dust along the road which eighteen years ago he had travelled in the mule-drawn wagon containing all he owned: the wife and her bastard daughter, the few sticks of furniture Mrs Varner had given them, the deed to Ratliff's half of the little back-street Jefferson restaurant and the few dollars remaining from what Henry Armstid (now locked up for life in a Jackson asylum) and his wife had scrimped and hoarded for ten years, which Ratliff and Armstid had paid him for the Old Frenchman place where he had buried the twenty-five silver dollars where they would find them with their spades.

For the last time, completing that ellipsis which would contain those entire eighteen years of his life since Frenchman's Bend and Varner's Crossroads and Varner's store would be one, perhaps *the* one, place to which he would never go again as long as he lived since, win or lose he would not need to, and win or lose he certainly would not dare to. And who knows? thinking even then what a shame that he must go to the store and old Will instead of to Varner's house where at this hour in the forenoon there would be nobody but Mrs Varner and the Negro cook,—must go to the store and beard and beat down by simple immobility and a scrap of signed and witnessed paper, that violent and choleric old brigand instead. Because women are not interested in romance or morals or sin and its punishment, but only in facts, the immutable facts necessary to the living of life while you are in it and which they are going to damned well see themselves dont fiddle and fool and back and fill and mutate. How simple to have gone straight to her, a woman (the big hard cold gray woman who never came to town anymore now, spending all her time between her home and her church, both of which she ran exactly alike: herself self-appointed treasurer of the collections she browbeat out of the terrified congregation, herself selecting and choosing and hiring the ministers and firing them too when they didn't suit her; legend was that she chose one of them out of a cotton field while passing in her buggy, hoicked him from between his plow-handles and ordered him to go home and bathe and change his clothes and followed herself thirty minutes later and ordained him).

How simple to ride up to the gate and say to the hired driver: "Wait here. I wont be long," and go up the walk and enter his ancestral halls (all right, his wife's; he was on his way now to dynamite his own equity in them) and on through them until he found Mrs Varner wherever she was, and say to her: "Good morning, Ma-in-law. I just found out last night that for eighteen years now our Eula's been sleeping with a feller in Jefferson named Manfred de Spain. I packed up and moved out before I left town but I aint filed the divorce yet because the judge was still asleep when I passed his house. I'll tend to that when I get back tonight," and turn and go back to the car and say to the driver: "All right, son. Back to town," and leave Mrs Varner to finish it, herself to enter the lair where old Will sat among the symbolical gnawed bones— the racks of hames and plow-handles, the rank side meat and flour and cheap molasses and cheese and shoes and coal oil and work gloves and snuff and chewing tobacco and fly-specked candy and the liens and mortgages on crops and plow-tools and mules and horses and land—of his fortune. There would be a few loungers though not many since this was planting time and even the ones there should have been in the field, which they would realise, already starting in an alarmed surge of guilt when they saw her, though not fast enough.

"Get out of here," she would say while they were already moving. "I want to talk to Will.—Wait. One of you go to the sawmill and tell Jody I want his automobile and hurry." And they would say "Yessum Miz Varner," which she would not hear either, standing over old Will now in his rawhide-bottomed chair. "Get up from there. Flem has finally caught Eula, or says he has. He hasn't filed the suit yet so you will have time before the word gets all over the county. I dont know what he's after, but you go in there and stop it. I wont have it. We had enough trouble with Eula twenty years ago. I aint going to have her back in my house worrying me now."

But he couldn't do that. It wasn't that simple. Because men, especially one like old Will Varner, were interested in facts too, especially a man like old Will in a fact like the one he, Flem, had signed and witnessed and folded inside his coat pocket. So he had to go, walk himself into that den and reach his own hand and jerk the unsuspecting beard and then stand while the uproar beat and thundered about his head until it spent itself temporarily to where his voice could be heard: "That's her signature. If you dont know it, them two witnesses do. All you got to do is help me take that bank away from Manfred de Spain—transfer your stock to my name, take my post-dated check if you want, the stock to be yourn again as soon as Manfred de Spain is out, or you to vote the stock yourself if you had druther—and you can have this paper. I'll even hold the match while you burn it."

That was all. And here was Ratliff again (oh yes, Jefferson could do without Ratliff, but not I—we—us; not I nor the whole damned tribe of Snopes could do without him), all neat and clean and tieless in his blue shirt, blinking a little at me. "Uncle Billy rid into town in Jody's car about four oclock this morning and went straight to Flem's. And Flem aint been to town today. What you reckon is fixing to pop now?" He blinked at me. "What do you reckon it was?"

"What what was?" I said.

"That he taken out there to Miz Varner yesterday that was important enough to have Uncle Billy on the road to town at four oclock this morning?"

"To *Mrs* Varner?" I said. "He gave it to Will."

"No no," Ratliff said. "He never seen Will. I know. I taken him out there. I had a machine to deliver to Miz Ledbetter at Rockyford and he suh-jested would I mind going by French-man's Bend while he spoke to Miz Varner a minute and we did, he was in the house about a minute and come back out and we went on and et dinner with Miz Ledbetter and set up the machine and come on back to town." He blinked at me. "Jest about a minute. What do you reckon he could a said or handed to Miz Varner in one minute that would put Uncle Billy on the road to Jefferson that soon after midnight?"

EIGHTEEN

V. K. RATLIFF

No no, no no, no no. He was wrong. He's a lawyer, and to a lawyer, if it aint complicated it dont matter whether it works or not because if it aint complicated up enough it aint right and so even if it works, you dont believe it. So it wasn't that—a paper phonied up on the spur of the moment, that I dont care how many witnesses signed it, a lawyer not nowhere near as smart as Lawyer Stevens would a been willing to pay the client for the fun he would have breaking it wide open.

It wasn't that. I dont know what it was, coming up to me on the Square that evening and saying, "I hear Miz Ledbetter's sewing machine come in this morning. When you take it out to her, I'll make the run out and back with you if you wont mind going by Frenchman's Bend a minute." Sho. You never even wondered how he heard about things because when the time come around to wonder how he managed to hear about it, it was already too late because he had done already made his profit by that time. So I says,

"Well, a feller going to Rockyford could go by Frenchman's Bend. But then, a feller going to Memphis could go by Birmingham too. He wouldn't have to, but he could."—You know: jest to hear him dicker. But he fooled me.

"That's right," he says. "It's a good six miles out of your way. Would four bits a mile pay for it?"

"It would more than pay for it," I says. "To ride up them extra three dollars, me and you wouldn't get back to town before sunup Wednesday. So I'll tell you what I'll do. You buy two cigars, and if you'll smoke one of them yourself, I'll carry you by Frenchman's Bend for one minute jest for your company and conversation."

"I'll give them both to you," he says. So we done that. Oh sho, he beat me out of my half of that little café me and Grover Winbush owned, but who can say jest who lost then? If he hadn't a got it, Grover might a turned it into a French

260

postcard peepshow too, and then I'd be out there where Grover is now: nightwatchman at that brick yard.

So I druv him by Frenchman's Bend. And we had the conversation too, provided you can call the monologue you have with Flem Snopes a conversation. But you keep on trying. It's because you hope to learn. You know silence is valuable because it must be, there's so little of it. So each time you think *Here's my chance to find out how a expert uses it.* Of course you wont this time and never will the next neither, that's how come he's a expert. But you can always hope you will. So we druv on, talking about this and that, mostly this of course, with him stopping chewing ever three or four miles to spit out the window and say "Yep" or "That's right" or "Sounds like it" until finally—there was Varner's Crossroads jest over the next rise—he says, "Not the store. The house," and I says,

"What? Uncle Billy wont be home now. He'll be at the store this time of morning."

"I know it," he says. "Take this road here." So we taken that road; we never even seen the store, let alone passed it, on to the house, the gate.

"You said one minute," I says. "If it's longer than that, you'll owe me two more cigars."

"All right," he says. And he got out and went on, up the walk and into the house, and I switched off the engine and set there thinking *What? What? Miz Varner. Not Uncle Billy: MIZ Varner.* That Uncle Billy jest hated him because Flem beat him fair and square, at Uncle Billy's own figger, out of that Old Frenchman place, while Miz Varner hated him like he was a Holy Roller or even a Baptist because he had not only condoned sin by marrying her daughter after somebody else had knocked her up, he had even made sin pay by getting the start from it that wound him up vice president of a bank. Yet it was *Miz* Varner he had come all the way out here to see, was willing to pay me three extra dollars for it. (I mean, offered. I know now I could a asked him ten.)

No, not thinking *What? What?* because what I was thinking was *Who,* who ought to know about this, trying to think in the little time I would have, since he his-self had volunteered that-ere one minute so one minute it was going to be, jest which who that was. Not me, because there wasn't no more loose dangling Ratliff-ends he could need; and not Lawyer Stevens and Linda and Eula and that going-off-to-school business that had been the last what you might call Snopes uproar to draw attention on the local scene, because that was ended too now, with Linda at least off at the University over at Oxford even if it wasn't one of them Virginia or New England colleges Lawyer was panting for. I didn't count Manfred de Spain because I wasn't on Manfred de Spain's side. I wasn't against him neither; it was jest like Lawyer Stevens his-self would a said: the feller that already had as much on his side as Manfred de Spain already had or anyway as everybody in Jefferson whose business it wasn't neither, believed he had, didn't need no more. Let alone deserve it.

Only there wasn't time. It wasn't one minute quite but it wasn't two neither when he come out the door in that-ere black hat and his bow tie, still chewing because I doubt if he ever quit chewing any more than he probably taken off that hat while he was inside, back to the car and spit and got in and I started the engine and says, "It wasn't quite a full two, so I'll let you off for one," and he says,

"All right," and I put her in low and set with my foot on the clutch and says,

"In case she was out, you want to run by the store and tell Uncle Billy you left a message on the hatrack for her?" and he chewed a lick or two more and balled up the ambeer and leaned to the window and spit again and set back and we went on to Rockyford and I set up the machine for Miz Ledbetter and she invited us to dinner and we et and come home and at four oclock this morning Uncle Billy druv up to Flem's house in Jody's car with his Negro driver and I know why four oclock because that was Miz Varner.

I mean Uncle Billy would go to bed soon as he et his supper, which would be before sundown this time of year, so he would wake up anywhere about one or two oclock in the morning. Of course he had done already broke the cook into getting up then to cook his breakfast but jest one Negro woman rattling pans in the kitchen wasn't nowhere near enough for Uncle Billy, ever body else hadn't jest to wake up then but to get up too: stomping around and banging doors and hollering for this and that until Miz Varner was up and dressed too. Only Uncle Billy could eat his breakfast then set in a chair until he smoked his pipe out and then he would go back to sleep until daylight. Only Miz Varner couldn't never go back to sleep again, once he had done woke her up good.

So this was her chance. I dont know what it was Flem told her or handed her that was important enough to make Uncle Billy light out for town at two oclock in the morning. But it wasn't no more important to Miz Varner than her chance to go back to bed in peace and quiet and sleep until a decent Christian hour. So she jest never told him or give it to him until he woke up at his usual two a.m.; if it was something Flem jest handed her that she never needed to repeat, likely she never had to get up a-tall but jest have it leaning against the lamp when Uncle Billy struck a match to light it so he could see to wake up the rest of the house and the neighbors.

So I dont know what it was. But it wasn't no joked-up piece of paper jest in the hopes of skeering Uncle Billy into doing something that until now he hadn't aimed to do. Because Uncle Billy dont skeer, and Flem Snopes knows it. It had something to do with folks, people, and the only people connected with Jefferson that would make Uncle Billy do something he hadn't suspected until this moment he would do, are Eula and Linda. Not Flem; Uncle Billy has knowed for twenty years now exactly what he will do to Flem the first time Flem's eye falters or his hand slips or his attention wanders.

Let alone going to Uncle Billy his-self with it. Because anything in reference to that bank that Flem would know in advance that jest by handing it or saying it to Miz Varner, would be stout enough to move Uncle Billy from Frenchman's Bend to Jefferson as soon as he heard about it, would sooner or later have to scratch or leastways touch Eula. And maybe Uncle Billy Varner dont skeer and Flem Snopes knows it, but Flem Snopes dont skeer neither and most folks knows that too. And it dont take no especial coward to not want to walk into that store and up to old man Will Varner and tell him his daughter aint reformed even yet, that she's been sleeping around again for eighteen years now with a feller she aint married to, and that her husband aint got guts enough to know what to do about it.

NINETEEN

CHARLES MALLISON
It was like a circus day or the County fair. Or more: it was like the District or even the whole State field meet because we even had a holiday for it. Only it was more than just a fair or a field day because this one was going to have death in it too though of course we didn't know that then.

It even began with a school holiday that we didn't even know we were going to have. It was as if time, circumstance, geography, contained something which must, anyway was going to, happen and now was the moment and Jefferson, Mississippi was the place, and so the stage was cleared and set for it.

The school holiday began Tuesday morning. Last week some new people moved to Jefferson, a highway engineer, and their little boy entered the second grade. He must have been already sick when his mother brought him because he had to go home, they sent for her and she came and got him that same afternoon and that night they took him to Memphis. That was Thursday but it wasn't until Monday afternoon that they got the word back that what he had was polio and they sent word around that the school would be closed while they found out what to do next or what to not do or whatever it was while they tried to learn more about polio or about the engineer's little boy or whatever it was. Anyhow it was a holiday we hadn't expected or even hoped for, in April; that April morning when you woke up and you would think how April was the best, the very best time of all not to have to go to school, until you would think *Except in the fall* with the weather brisk and not-cold at the same time and the trees all yellow and red and you could go hunting all day long; and then you would think *Except in the winter* with the Christmas holidays over and now nothing to look forward to until summer; and you would think how no time is the best time to not have to go to school and so school is a good thing after all because without it there wouldn't be any holidays or vacations.

Anyhow we had the holiday, we didn't know how long; and that was fine too because now you never had to say *Only two days left* or *Only one day left* since all you had to do was just be holiday, breathe holiday, today and tomorrow too and who knows? tomorrow after that and, who knows? still tomorrow after that. So on Wednesday when even the children who would have been in school except for the highway engineer's little boy, began to know that something was happening, going on inside the president's office of the bank—not the old one, the Bank of Jefferson, but the other, the one we still called the new bank or even Colonel Sartoris's bank although he had been dead seven years now and Mr de Spain was president of it—it was no more than we expected, since this was just another part of whatever it was time or circumstance or whatever it was had cleared the stage and emptied the school so it could happen.

No, to say that the stage was limited to just one bank; to say that time, circumstance, geography, whatever it was, had turned school out in the middle of April in honor of something it wanted to happen inside just one set of walls, was wrong. It was all of Jefferson. It was all the walls of Jefferson, the ground they stood on, the air they rose up in; all the walls and air in Jefferson that people moved and breathed and talked in; we were already at dinner except Uncle Gavin, who was never late unless he was out of town on county business, and when he did come in something was already wrong. I mean, I didn't always notice when something was wrong with him and it wasn't because I was only twelve yet, it was because you didn't have to notice Uncle Gavin because you could always tell from Mother since she was his twin; it was like when you said "What's the matter?" to Mother, you and she and everybody else knew you were saying What's wrong with Uncle Gavin.

But we could always depend on Father. Uncle Gavin came in at last and sat down and unfolded his napkin and said something wrong and Father glanced at him and then went back to eating and then looked at Uncle Gavin again.

"Well," he said, "I hear they got old Will Varner out of bed at two this morning and brought him all the way in to town to promote Manfred de Spain. Promote him where?"

"What?" Uncle Gavin said.

"Where do you promote a man that's already president of the bank?" Father said.

"Charley," Mother said.

"Or maybe promote aint the word I want," Father said. "The one I want is when you promote a man quick out of bed—"

"Charley!" Mother said.

"—especially a bed he never had any business in, not to mention having to send all the way out to Frenchman's Bend for your pa-in-law to pronounce that word—"

"Charles!" Mother said. That's how it was. It was like we had had something in Jefferson for eighteen years and whether it had been right or whether it had been wrong to begin with didn't matter anymore now because it was ours, we had lived with it and now it didn't even show a scar, like the nail driven into the tree years ago that violated and outraged and anguished that tree. Except that the tree hasn't got much choice either: either to put principle above sap and refuse the outrage and next year's sap both, or accept the outrage and the sap for the privilege of going on being a tree as long as it can, until in time the nail disappears. It dont go away; it just stops being so glaring in sight, barked over; there is a lump, a bump of course, but after a while the other trees forgive that and everything else accepts that tree and that bump too until one day the saw or the axe goes into it and hits that old nail.

Because I was twelve then. I had reached for the second time that point in the looping circles children—boys anyway—make growing up when for a little while they enter, live in, the same civilisation that grown people use, when it occurs to you that maybe the sensible and harmless things they wont let you do really seem as silly to them as the things they seem either to want to do or have to do, seem to you. No: it's when they laugh at you and suddenly you say, *Why, maybe I am funny,* and so the things they do are not outrageous and silly or shocking at all: they're just funny; and more than that, it's the same funny. So now I could ask. A few more years and I would know more than I knew then. But the loop, the circle, would be swinging on away out into space again where you cant ask grown people because you cant talk to anybody, not even the others your age because they too are rushing on out into space where you cant touch anybody, you dont dare try, you are too busy just hanging on; and you know that all the others out there are just as afraid of asking as you are, nobody to ask, nothing to do but make noise, the louder the better, then at least the other scared ones wont know how scared you are.

But I could still ask now, for a little while. I asked Mother. "Why dont you ask Uncle Gavin?" she said.

She wanted to tell me. Maybe she even tried. But she couldn't. It wasn't because I was only twelve. It was because I was her child, created by her and Father because they wanted to be in bed together and nothing else would do, nobody else would do. You see? If Mrs Snopes and Mr de Spain had been anything else but people, she could have told me. But they were people too, exactly like her and Father; and it's not that the child mustn't know that the same magic which made him was the same thing that sent an old man like Mr Will Varner into town at four oclock in the morning just to take something as sorry and shabby as a bank full of money away from another man named Manfred de Spain: it's because the child couldn't believe that. Because to the child, he was not created by his mother's and his father's passion or capacity for it. He couldn't have been because he was there first, he came first, before the passion; he created the passion, not only it but the man and the woman who served it; his father is not his father but his son-in-law, his mother not his mother but his daughter-in-law if he is a girl.

So she couldn't tell me because she could not. And Uncle Gavin couldn't tell me because he wasn't able to, he couldn't have stopped talking in time. That is, that's what I thought then. I mean, that's what I thought then was the reason why they—Mother—didn't tell me: that the reason was just my innocence and not Uncle Gavin's too and she had to guard both since maybe she was my mother but she was Uncle Gavin's twin and if a boy or a girl really is his father's and her mother's father-in-law or mother-in-law, which would make the girl her brother's mother no matter how much younger she was, then a girl with just one brother and him a twin at that, would maybe be his wife and mother too.

So maybe that was why: not that I wasn't old enough to accept biology, but that everyone should be, deserves to be, must be, defended and protected from the spectators of his own passion save in the most general and unspecific and impersonal terms of the literary and dramatic lay-figures of the protagonists of passion in their bloodless and griefless posturings of triumph or anguish; that no man deserves love since nature did not equip us to bear it but merely to endure and survive it, and so Uncle Gavin's must not be watched where she could help and fend him, while it anguished on his own unarmored bones.

Though even if they had tried to tell me, it would have been several years yet, not from innocence but from ignorance, before I would know, understand, what I had actually been looking at during the rest of that Wednesday afternoon while all of Jefferson waited for the saw to touch that buried nail. No: not buried, not healed or annealed into the tree but just cysted into it, alien and poison; not healed over but scabbed over with a scab which merely renewed itself, incapable of healing, like a signpost.

Because ours was a town founded by Aryan Baptists and Methodists, for Aryan Baptists and Methodists. We had a Chinese laundryman and two Jews, brothers with their families, who ran two clothing stores. But one of them had been trained in Russia to be a rabbi and spoke seven languages including classic Greek and Latin and worked geometry problems for relaxation and he was absolved, lumped in the same absolution with old Doctor Wyott, president emeritus of the Academy (his grandfather had founded it) who could read not only Greek and Hebrew but Sanskrit too, who wore two foreign decorations for (we, Jefferson, believed) having been not just a professing but a militant and even boasting atheist for at least sixty of his eighty years and who had even beaten the senior Mr Wildermark at chess; and the other Jewish brother and his family and the Chinaman all attended, were members of, the Methodist church and so they didn't count either, being in our eyes merely non-white people, not actually colored. And although the Chinese was definitely a colored man even if not a Negro, he was only he, single peculiar and barren; not just kinless but even kindless, half the world or anyway half the continent (we all knew about San Francisco's Chinatown) sundered from his like and therefore as threatless as a mule.

There is a small Episcopal church in Jefferson, the oldest extant building in town (It was built by slaves and called the best, the finest too, I mean by the Northern tourists who passed through Jefferson now with cameras, expecting—we dont know why since they themselves had burned it and blown it up with dynamite in 1863—to find Jefferson much older or anyway older looking than it is and faulting us a little because it isn't.) and a Presbyterian congregation too, the two oldest congregations in the county, going back to the old days of Issetibbeha, the Chickasaw chief, and his sister's son Ikkemotubbe whom they called Doom, before the county was a County and Jefferson was Jefferson. But nowadays there wasn't much difference between the Episcopal and Presbyterian churches and Issetibbeha's old mounds in the low creek bottoms about the county because the Baptists and Methodists had heired from them, usurped and dispossessed; ours a town established and decreed by people neither Catholics nor Protestants nor even atheists but incorrigible Nonconformists, nonconformists not just to everybody else but to each other in mutual accord; a nonconformism defended and preserved by descendants whose ancestors hadn't quitted home and security for a wilderness in which to find freedom of thought as they claimed and oh yes, believed, but to find freedom in which to be incorrigible and unreconstructible Baptists and Methodists; not to escape from tyranny as they claimed and believed, but to establish one.

And now, after eighteen years, the saw of retribution which we of course called that of righteousness and simple justice, was about to touch that secret hidden unhealed nail buried in the moral tree of our community—that nail not only corrupted and unhealed but unhealable because it was not just sin but mortal sin—a thing which should not exist at all, whose very conception should be self-annihilative, yet a sin which people seemed constantly and almost universally to commit with complete impunity; as witness these two for eighteen years, not only flouting decency and morality but even compelling decency and morality to accept them simply by being discrete: nobody had actually caught them yet; outraging morality itself by allying economics on their side since the very rectitude and solvency of a bank would be involved in their exposure.

In fact, the town itself was divided into two camps, each split in turn into what you might call a hundred individual nonconforming bivouacs: the women who hated Mrs Snopes for having grabbed Mr de Spain first or hated Mr de Spain for having preferred Mrs Snopes to them, and the men who were jealous of De Spain because they were not him or hated him for being younger than they or braver than they (they called it luckier of course); and those of both sexes—no: the same sour genderless sex—who hated them both for having found or made together something which they themselves had failed to make, whatever the reason; and in consequence of which that splendor must not only not exist, it must never have existed—the females of it who must abhor the splendor because it was, had to be, barren; the males of it who must hate the splendor because they had set the cold stability of currency above the wild glory of blood: they who had not only abetted the sin but had kept alive the anguish of their own secret regret by supporting the sinners' security for the sake of De Spain's bank. Two camps: the one that said the sin must be exposed now, it had already lasted eighteen years too long; the other which said it dare not be exposed now and so reveal our own baseness in helping to keep it hidden all this long time.

Because the saw was not just seeking that nail. As far as Jefferson was concerned it had already touched it; we were merely waiting now to see in what direction the fragments of that particular tree in our wood (not the saw itself, never the saw: if that righteous and invincible moral blade flew to pieces at the contact, let us all dissolute too since the very fabric of Baptist and Methodist life were delusion, nothing) would scatter and disintegrate.

That was that whole afternoon while old Mr Varner still stayed hidden or anyway invisible in Mr Snopes's house. We

didn't even know definitely that he was actually in town, nobody had seen him; we only had Ratliff's word that he had
come in in his son's automobile at four oclock this morning,
and we didn't know that for sure unless Ratliff had sat up all
night watching the Snopes's front door. But then Mr Varner
was there, he had to be or there wouldn't be any use for the
rest of it. And Mr de Spain's bank continued its ordinary
sober busy prosperous gold-aura-ed course to the closing
hour at three oclock, when almost at once the delivery boy
from Christian's drugstore knocked at the side door and was
admitted with his ritual tray of four coca colas for the two girl
book-keepers and Miss Killebrew the teller and Mr Hovis the
cashier. And presently, at his ordinary hour, Mr de Spain came
out and got in his car as usual and drove away to look at one
of the farms which he now owned or on which the bank held
a mortgage, as he always did: no rush, no panic to burst upon
the ordered financial day. And some time during the day,
either forenoon or afternoon, somebody claimed to have seen
Mr Snopes himself, unchanged too, unhurried and un-
alarmed, the wide black planter's hat still looking brand new
(the tiny bow tie which he had worn for eighteen years now
always did), going about his inscrutable noncommunicable
affairs.

Then it was five oclock and nothing had happened; soon
now people would begin to go home to eat supper and then
it would be too late and at first I thought of going up to the
office to wait for Uncle Gavin to walk home, only I would
have to climb the stairs and then turn around right away and
come back down again and I thought how what a good name
spring fever was to excuse not doing something you didn't
want to do, then I thought how maybe spring fever wasn't an
excuse at all because maybe spring fever actually was.

So I just stood on the corner where he would have to pass,
to wait for him. Then I saw Mrs Snopes. She had just come
out of the beauty parlor and as soon as you looked at her you
could tell that's where she had been and I remembered how
Mother said once she was the only woman in Jefferson that
never went to one because she didn't need to since there was
nothing in a beauty shop that she could have lacked. But she
had this time, standing there for a minute and she really did

look both ways along the street before she turned and started toward me and then she saw me and came on and said, "Hello, Chick," and I tipped my cap, only she came up and stopped and I took my cap off; she had a bag on her arm like ladies do, already opening it to reach inside.

"I was looking for you," she said. "Will you give this to your uncle when you go home?"

"Yessum," I said. It was an envelope.

"Thank you," she said. "Have they heard any more about the little Riddell boy?"

"I dont know'm," I said. It wasn't sealed. It didn't have any name on the front either.

"Let's hope they got him to Memphis in time," she said. Then she said Thank you again and went on, walking like she does, not like a pointer about to make game like Linda, but like water moves somehow. And she could have telephoned him at home and I almost said *You dont want me to let Mother see it* before I caught myself. Because it wasn't sealed. But then, I wouldn't have anyway. Besides, I didn't have to. Mother wasn't even at home yet and then I remembered: Wednesday, she would be out at Sartoris at the meeting of the Byron Society though Mother said it had been a long time now since anybody listened to anybody read anything because they played bridge now but at least she said that when it met with Miss Jenny Du Pre they had toddies or juleps instead of just coffee or coca colas.

So nothing had happened and now it was already too late, the sun going down though the pear tree in the side yard had bloomed and gone a month ago and now the mocking bird had moved over to the pink dogwood, already beginning where he had sung all night long all week until you would begin to wonder why in the world he didn't go somewhere else and let people sleep. And nobody at home at all yet except Aleck Sander sitting on the front steps with the ball and bat. "Come on," he said. "I'll knock you out some flies." Then he said, "All right, you knock out and I'll chase um."

So it was almost dark inside the house; I could already smell supper cooking and it was too late now, finished now: Mr de Spain gone out in his new Buick to watch how much money his cotton was making, and Mrs Snopes coming out of the beauty shop with her hair even waved or something or whatever it was, maybe for a party at her house tonight so maybe it hadn't even begun; maybe old Mr Varner wasn't even in town at all, not only wasn't coming but never had aimed to and so all the Riddell boy did by catching polio was just to give us a holiday we didn't expect and didn't know what to do with; until I heard Uncle Gavin come in and come up the stairs and I met him in the upstairs hall with the envelope in my hand: just the shape of him coming up the stairs and along the hall until even in that light I saw his face all of a sudden and all of a sudden I said:

"You're not going to be here for supper."

"No," he said. "Will you tell your mother?"

"Here," I said and held out the envelope and he took it.

TWENTY

GAVIN STEVENS
Though you have to eat. So after I went back and unlocked the office and left the door on the latch, I drove out
to Seminary Hill, to eat cheese and crackers and listen to old
Mr Garraway curse Calvin Coolidge while he ran the last loaf-
ing Negroes out of the store and closed it for the night.

Or so I thought. Because you simply cannot go against
a community. You can stand singly against any temporary
unanimity of even a city-full of human behavior, even a mob.
But you cannot stand against the cold inflexible abstraction
of a long-suffering community's moral point of view. Mr
Garraway had been one of the first—no: the first—to move
his account from Colonel Sartoris's bank to the Bank of
Jefferson, even before Flem Snopes ever thought or had reason to think of his tenant-farmer panic. He had moved it in
fact as soon as we—the town and county—knew that Manfred
de Spain was definitely to be president of it. Because he—Mr
Garraway—had been one of that original small inflexible unreconstructible puritan group, both Baptist and Methodist, in
the county who would have moved their fiscal allegiance also
from Jefferson while De Spain was mayor of it, to escape the
moral contamination and express their opinion of that liaison
which he represented, if there had been another fiscal town in
the county to have moved it to. Though later, a year or two
afterward, he moved the account back, perhaps because he
was just old or maybe he could stay in his small dingy store
out at Seminary Hill and not have to come to town, have to
see with his own eyes and so be reminded of his county's
shame and disgrace and sin if he didn't want to be. Or maybe
once you accept something, it doesn't really matter anymore
whether you like it or not. Or so I thought.

The note said ten oclock. That was all: *Please meet me at
your office at ten tonight.* Not *if convenient,* let alone *when
could you see me at your office?* but simply *at ten tonight please.*
You see. Because in the first place, Why me? *Me?* To say that

to all of them, all three of them—no, all four, taking De Spain with me: *Why cant you let me alone? What more can you want of me than I have already failed to do?* But there would be plenty of time for that; I would have plenty of time to eat the sardines and crackers and say What a shame to the account of whatever the recent outrage the President and his party had contrived against Mr Garraway, when he—Mr Garraway—said suddenly (an old man with an old man's dim cloudy eyes magnified and enormous behind the thick lenses of his iron-framed spectacles): "Is it so that Will Varner came in to town this morning?"

"Yes," I said.

"So he caught them." Now he was trembling, shaking, standing there behind the worn counter which he had inherited from his father, racked with tins of meat and spools of thread and combs and needles and bottles of cooking extract and malaria tonic and female compound some of which he had probably inherited too, saying in a shaking voice: "Not the husband! The father himself had to come in and catch them after eighteen years!"

"But you put your money back," I said. "You took it out at first, when you just heard at second hand about the sin and shame and outrage. Then you put it back. Was it because you saw her too at last? She came out here one day, into your store, and you saw her yourself, got to know her, to believe that she at least was innocent? Was that it?"

"I knew the husband," he said, cried almost, holding his voice down so the Negroes couldn't hear what we—he was talking about. "I knew the husband! He deserved it!"

Then I remembered. "Yes," I said, "I thought I saw you in town this afternoon." Then I knew. "You moved it again to-day, didn't you? You drew it out again and put it back into the Bank of Jefferson today, didn't you?" and he standing there, shaking even while he tried to hold himself from it. "Why?" I said. "Why again today?"

"She must go," he said. "They must both go—she and De Spain too."

"But why?" I said, muttered too, not to be overheard: two white men discussing in a store full of Negroes a white woman's adultery. More: adultery in the very top stratum of a white man's town and bank. "Why only now? It was one thing as long as the husband accepted it; it became another when somebody—how did you put it?—catches them, blows the gaff? They become merely sinners then, criminals then, lepers then? nothing for constancy, nothing for fidelity, nothing for devotion, unpoliced devotion, eighteen years of devotion?"

"Is that all you want?" he said. "I'm tired. I want to go home." Then we were on the gallery where a few of the Negroes still lingered, the arms and faces already fading back into the darkness behind the lighter shades of shirts and hats and pants as if they were slowly vacating them, while his shaking hands fumbled the heavy padlock through the hasp and fumbled it shut; until suddenly I said, quite loud:

"Though if anything the next one will be worse because the next president will probably be Governor Smith and you know who Governor Smith is of course: a Catholic," and would have stopped that in time in very shame but could not, or maybe should have stopped it in time in very shame but would not. Since who was I, what anguish's missionary I that I must compound it blindly right and left like some blind unrational minor force of nature? who had already spoiled supper and ruined sleep both for the old man standing there fumbling with his clumsy lock as if I had actually struck him,—the old man who in his fashion, in a lot of people's fashion, really was a kindly old man who never in his life wittingly or unwittingly harmed anyone black or white, not serious harm: not more than adding a few extra cents to what it would have been for cash, when the article went on credit; or selling to a Negro for half-price or often less (oh yes, at times even giving it to him) the tainted meat or rancid lard or weevilled flour or meal he would not have permitted a white man—a Protestant gentile white man of course—to eat at all out of his store; standing there with his back turned fumbling at the giant padlock as though I had actually struck him, saying,

"They must go. They must go, both of them."

There is a ridge; you drive on beyond Seminary Hill and in time you come upon it: a mild unhurried farm road presently mounting to cross the ridge and on to join the main highway leading from Jefferson to the world. And now, looking back and down, you see all Yoknapatawpha in the dying last of day beneath you. There are stars now, just pricking out as you watch them among the others already coldly and softly burning; the end of day is one vast green soundless murmur up the northwest toward the zenith. Yet it is as though light were not being subtracted from earth, drained from earth backward and upward into that cooling green, but rather had gathered, pooling for an unmoving moment yet, among the low places of the ground so that ground, earth itself is luminous and only the dense clumps of trees are dark, standing darkly and immobile out of it.

Then, as though at signal, the fireflies—lightning-bugs of the Mississippi child's vernacular—myriad and frenetic, random and frantic, pulsing; not questing, not quiring, but choiring as if they were tiny incessant appeaseless voices, cries, words. And you stand suzerain and solitary above the whole sum of your life beneath that incessant ephemeral spangling. First is Jefferson, the center, radiating weakly its puny glow into space; beyond it, enclosing it, spreads the County, tied by the diverging roads to that center as is the rim to the hub by its spokes, yourself detached as God himself for this moment above the cradle of your nativity and of the men and women who made you, the record and annal of your native land proffered for your perusal in ring by concentric ring like the ripples on living water above the dreamless slumber of your past; you to preside unanguished and immune above this miniature of man's passions and hopes and disasters—ambition and fear and lust and courage and abnegation and pity and honor and sin and pride—all bound, precarious and ramshackle held together, by the web, the iron-thin warp and woof of his rapacity but withal yet dedicated to his dreams.

They are all here, supine beneath you, stratified and superposed, osseous and durable with the frail dust and the phantoms:—the rich alluvial river-bottom land of old Issetibbeha, the wild Chickasaw king, with his Negro slaves and his sister's son called Doom who murdered his way to the throne and, legend said (record itself said since there were old men in the county in my own childhood who had actually seen it), stole an entire steamboat and had it dragged intact eleven miles

overland to convert into a palace proper to aggrandise his
state; the same fat black rich plantation earth still synonymous
of the proud fading white plantation names whether we—
I mean of course they—ever actually owned a plantation or
not: Sutpen and Sartoris and Compson and Edmonds and
McCaslin and Beauchamp and Grenier and Habersham and
Holston and Stevens and De Spain, generals and governors
and judges, soldiers (even if only Cuban lieutenants) and
statesmen failed or not, and simple politicians and over-reach-
ers and just simple failures, who snatched and grabbed and
passed and vanished, name and face and all. Then the road-
less, almost pathless perpendicular hill-country of McCallum
and Gowrie and Frazier and Muir translated intact with their
pot stills and speaking only the old Gaelic and not much of
that, from Culloden to Carolina, then from Carolina to
Yoknapatawpha still intact and not speaking much of anything
except that they now called the pots 'kettles' though the
drink (even I can remember this) was still usquebaugh; then
and last on to where Frenchman's Bend lay beyond the
south-eastern horizon, cradle of Varners and ant-heap for the
north-east crawl of Snopes.

And you stand there—you, the old man, already white-
headed (because it doesn't matter if they call your gray hairs
premature because life itself is always premature which is why
it aches and anguishes) and pushing forty, only a few years
from forty—while there rises up to you, proffered up to you,
the spring darkness, the unsleeping darkness which, although
it is of the dark itself declines the dark since dark is of the
little death called sleeping. Because look how, even though
the last of west is no longer green and all of firmament is now
one unlidded studded slow-wheeling arc and the last of earth-
pooled visibility has drained away, there still remains one faint
diffusion since everywhere you look about the dark panorama
you still see them, faint as whispers: the faint and shapeless
lambence of blooming dogwood returning loaned light to
light as the phantoms of candles would.

And you, the old man, standing there while there rises to
you, about you, suffocating you, the spring dark peopled and
myriad two and two seeking never at all solitude but simply
privacy, the privacy decreed and created for them by the

spring darkness, the spring weather, the spring which an American poet, a fine one, a woman and so she knows, called girls' weather and boys' luck. Which was not the first day at all, not Eden morning at all because girls' weather and boys' luck is the sum of all the days: the cup, the bowl proffered once to the lips in youth and then no more; proffered to quench or sip or drain that lone one time and even that sometimes premature, too soon. Because the tragedy of life is, it must be premature, inconclusive and inconcludable, in order to be life; it must be before itself, in advance of itself, to have been at all.

And now for truth was the one last chance to choose, decide: whether or not to say *Why me? Why bother me? Why cant you let me alone? Why must it be my problem whether I was right and your husband just wants your lover's scalp, or Ratliff is right and your husband doesn't care a damn about you or his honor either and just wants De Spain's bank?*—the Square empty beneath the four identical faces of the courthouse clock saying ten minutes to ten to the north and east and south and west, vacant now beneath the arclight-stippled shadows of fledged leaves like small bites taken out of the concrete paving, the drugstores closed and all still moving now were the late last homeward stragglers from the second running of the picture show. Or better still, what she herself should have thought without my needing to say it: *Take Manfred de Spain in whatever your new crisis is, since you didn't hesitate to quench with him your other conflagration eighteen years ago. Or do you already know in advance he will be no good this time, since a bank is not a female but neuter?*

And of course Otis Harker. "Evening, Mr Stevens," he said. "When you drove up I almost hoped maybe it was a gang come to rob the postoffice or the bank or something to bring us a little excitement for a change."

"But it was just another lawyer," I said, "and lawyers dont bring excitement: only misery?"

"I dont believe I quite said that, did I?" he said. "But leastways lawyers stays awake so if you're going to be around a while, maybe I'll jest mosey back to the station and maybe take a nap while you watch them racing clock-hands a spell for me." Except that he was looking at me. No: he wasn't looking at me at all: he was watching me, deferent to my white hairs as a well-'raised' Mississippian should be, but not my representative position as his employer; not quite servile, not quite impudent, waiting maybe or calculating maybe.

"Say it," I said. "Except that—"

"Except that Mr Flem Snopes and Mr Manfred de Spain might cross the Square any time now with old Will Varner chasing them both out of town with that pistol."

"Good night," I said. "If I dont see you again."

"Good night," he said. "I'll likely be somewhere around. I mean around awake. I wouldn't want Mr Buck himself to have to get up out of bed and come all the way to town to catch me asleep."

You see? You cant beat it. Otis Harker too, who, assuming he does keep awake all night as he is paid to do, should have been at home all day in bed asleep. But of course, he was there; he actually saw old Varner cross the Square at four this morning on his way to Flem's house. Yes. You cant beat it: the town itself officially on record now in the voice of its night marshal; the county itself had spoken through one of its minor clowns; eighteen years ago when Manfred de Spain thought he was just bedding another loose-girdled bucolic Lilith, he was actually creating a piece of buffoon's folklore.

Though there were still ten minutes, and it would take Otis Harker at least twenty-five to "round up" the gin and compress and their purlieus and get back to the Square. And I know now that I already smelled tobacco smoke even before I put my hand on what I thought was an unlocked door for the reason that I myself had made a special trip back to leave it unlocked, still smelling the tobacco while I still tried to turn the knob, until the latch clicked back from inside and the door opened, she standing there against the dark interior in what little there was of light. Though it was enough to see her hair, that she had been to the beauty parlor: who according to Maggie had never been to one, the hair not bobbed of course, not waved, but something, I dont know what it was except that she had been to the beauty parlor that afternoon.

"Good for you for locking it," I said. "We wont need to risk a light either. Only I think that Otis Harker already—"

"That's all right," she said. So I closed the door and locked it again and turned on the desk lamp. "Turn them all on if you want to," she said. "I wasn't trying to hide. I just didn't want to have to talk to somebody."

"Yes," I said, and sat behind the desk. She had been in the client's chair, sitting in the dark smoking; the cigarette was still burning in the little tray with two other stubs. Now she was sitting again in the client's chair at the end of the desk where the light fell upon her from the shoulder down but mostly on her hands lying quite still on the bag on her lap. Though I could still see her hair—no makeup, lips or nails either: just her hair that had been to the beauty shop. "You've been to the beauty shop," I said.

"Yes," she said. "That's where I met Chick."

"But not inside," I said, already trying to stop. "Not where water and soap are coeval, conjunctive," still trying to stop. "Not for a few years yet," and did. "All right," I said. "Tell me. What was it he took out there to your mother yesterday that had old Will on the road to town at two oclock this morning?"

"There's your cob pipe," she said. They were in the brass bowl beside the tobacco jar. "You've got three of them. I've never seen you smoke one. When do you smoke them?"

"All right," I said. "Yes. What was it he took out there?"

"The will," she said.

"No no," I said. "I know about the will; Ratliff told me. I mean, what was it Flem took out there to your mother yesterday morning—"

"I told you. The will."

"Will?" I said.

"Linda's will. Giving her share of whatever she would inherit from me, to her—him." And I sat there and she too, opposite one another across the desk, the lamp between us low on the desk so that all we could really see of either probably was just the hands: mine on the desk and hers quite still, almost like two things asleep, on the bag in her lap, her voice almost like it was asleep too so that there was no anguish, no alarm, no outrage anywhere in the little quiet dingy mausoleum of human passions, high and secure, secure even from any random exigency of what had been impressed on Otis Harker as his duty for which he was paid his salary, since he already knew it would be me in it: "The will. It was her idea. She did it herself. I mean, she believes she thought of it, wanted to do it, did it, herself. Nobody can tell her otherwise. Nobody will. Nobody. That's why I wrote the note."

"You'll have to tell me," I said. "You'll have to."

"It was the . . . school business. When you told her she wanted to go, get away from here; all the different schools to choose among that she hadn't even known about before, that it was perfectly natural for a young girl—young people to want to go to them and to go to one of them, that until then she hadn't even thought about, let alone known that she wanted to go to one of them. Like all she needed to do to go to one of them was just to pick out the one she liked the best and go to it, especially after I said Yes. Then her—he said No.

"As if that was the first time she ever thought of No, ever heard of No. There was a . . . scene. I dont like scenes. You dont have to have scenes. Nobody needs to have a scene to get what you want. You just get it. But she didn't know that, you see. She hadn't had time to learn it maybe, since she was just seventeen then. But then you know that yourself. Or maybe it was more than not knowing better. Maybe she knew too much. Maybe she already knew, felt even then that he had already beat her. She said: 'I will go! I will! You cant stop me! Damn your money; if Mamma wont give it to me, Grandpa will—Mr Stevens (oh yes, she said that too) will—' While he just sat there—we were sitting then, still at the table; only Linda was standing up—just sat there saying, 'That's right. I cant stop you.' Then she said, 'Please.' Oh yes, she knew she was beaten as well as he did. 'No,' he said. 'I want you to stay at home and go to the Academy.'

"And that was all. I mean . . . nothing. That was just all. Because you—a girl anyway—dont really hate your father no matter how much you think you do or should or should want to because people expect you to or that it would look well to because it would be romantic to—"

"Yes," I said, "—because girls, women, are not interested in romance but only facts. Oh yes, you were not the only one: Ratliff told me that too, that same day in fact."

"Vladimir too?" she said.

"No: Ratliff," I said. Then I said, "Wait." Then I said:

"Vladimir? Did you say Vladimir? V.K. Is his name Vladimir?" And now she did sit still, even the hands on the bag that had been like things asleep and breathing their own life apart, seemed to become still now.

"I didn't intend to do that," she said.

"Yes," I said. "I know: nobody else on earth knows his name is Vladimir because how could anybody named Vladimir hope to make a living selling sewing machines or anything else in rural Mississippi? But he told you: the secret he would have defended like that of insanity in his family or illegitimacy. Why?—No, dont answer that. Why shouldn't I know why he told you; didn't I breathe one blinding whiff of that same liquor too? Tell me. I wont either. Vladimir K. What K?"

"Vladimir Kyrilytch."

"Vladimir Kyrilytch what? Not Ratliff. Kyrilytch is only his middle name; all Russian middle names are itch or ovna. That's just son or daughter of. What was his last name before it became Ratliff?"

"He doesn't know. His . . . six or eight or ten times grandfather was . . . not lieutenant—"

"Ensign."

"—in a British army that surrendered in the Revolution—"

"Yes," I said. "Burgoyne. Saratoga."

"—and was sent to Virginia and forgotten and Vla—his grandfather escaped. It was a woman of course, a girl, that hid him and fed him. Except that she spelled it R-a-t-c-l-i-f-f-e and they married and had a son or had the son and then married. Anyway he learned to speak English and became a Virginia farmer. And his grandson, still spelling it with a c and an e at the end but with his name still Vladimir Kyrilytch though nobody knew it, came to Mississippi with old Doctor Habersham and Alexander Holston and Louis Grenier and started Jefferson. Only they forgot how to spell it Ratcliffe and just spelled it like it sounds but one son is always named Vladimir Kyrilytch. Except that like you said, nobody named Vladimir Kyrilytch could make a living as a Mississippi country man—"

"No," I said, cried. "Wait. That's wrong. We're both wrong. We're completely backward. If only everybody had known his name was really Vladimir Kyrilytch, he would be a millionaire by now since any woman anywhere would have bought anything or everything he had to sell or trade or swap. Or maybe they already do?" I said, cried. "Maybe they already do?—All right," I said. "Go on."

"But one in each generation still has to have the name because Vla—V.K. says the name is their luck."

"Except that it didn't work against Flem Snopes," I said. "Not when he tangled with Flem Snopes that night in that old Frenchman's garden after you came back from Texas.— All right," I said. "'So that was all because you dont really hate your father—'"

"He did things for her. That she didn't expect, hadn't even thought about asking for. That young girls like, almost as though he had put himself inside a young girl's mind even before she thought of them. He gave me the money and sent us both to Memphis to buy things for her graduation from high school—not just a graduating dress but one for dancing too, and other things for the summer; almost a trousseau. He even tried—offered, anyway told her he was going to—to have a picnic for her whole graduating class but she refused that. You see? He was her father even if he did have to be her enemy. You know: the one that said 'Please' accepting the clothes, while the one that defied him to stop her refused the picnic.

"And that summer he gave me the money and even made the hotel reservation himself for us to go down to the coast— you may remember that—"

"I remember," I said.

"—to spend a month so she could swim in the ocean and meet people, meet young men; he said that himself: meet young men. And we came back and that fall she entered the Academy and he started giving her a weekly allowance. Would you believe that?"

"I do now," I said. "Tell me."

"It was too much, more than she could need, had any business with, too much for a seventeen-year-old girl to have every week just in Jefferson. Yet she took that too that she didn't really need just like she took the Academy that she didn't want. Because he was her father, you see. You've got to remember that. Can you?"

"Tell me," I said.

"That was the fall, the winter. He still gave her things—clothes she didn't need, had no business with, seventeen years old in Jefferson; you may have noticed that too; even a fur coat until she refused to let him, said No in time. Because you see, that was the You cant stop me again; she had to remind him now and then that she had defied him; she could accept the daughter's due but not the enemy's bribe.

"Then it was summer, last summer. That was when it happened. I saw it, we were all at the table again and he said, 'Where do you want to go this summer? The coast again? or maybe the mountains this time? How would you like to take your mother and go to New York?' And he had her; she was already beat; she said, 'Wont that cost a lot of money?' and he said, 'That doesn't matter. When would you like to go?' and she said, 'No. It will cost too much money. Why dont we just stay here?' Because he had her, he had beat her. And the . . . terrible thing was, she didn't know it, didn't even know there had been a battle and she had surrendered. Before, she had defied him and at least she knew she was defying him even if she didn't know what to do with it, how to use it, what to do next. Now she had come over to his side and she didn't even know it.

"And that's all. Then it was fall, last October, she was at the Academy again and this time we had finished supper, we were in the living room before the fire and she was reading, sitting on one of her feet I remember and I remember the book too, the John Donne you gave her—I mean, the new one, the second one, to replace the one that boy—what was his name? the garage mechanic, Matt Something, Levitt—tore up that day in your office—when he said, 'Linda,' and she looked up, still holding the book (that's when I remember seeing what it was) and he said, 'I was wrong. I thought the Academy ought to be good enough, because I never went to school and didn't know any better. But I know better now, and the Academy's not good enough anymore. Will you give up the Yankee schools and take the University at Oxford?'

"And she still sat there, letting the book come down slow onto her lap, just looking at him. Then she said, 'What?'

" 'Will you forget about Virginia and the northern schools for this year, and enter the University after Christmas?' She

threw the book, she didn't put it down at all: she just threw
it, flung it as she stood up out of the chair and said:

"'Daddy.' I had never seen her touch him. He was her
father, she never refused to speak to him or to speak any way
except respectfully. But he was her enemy; she had to keep
him reminded always that although he had beaten her about
the schools, she still hadn't surrendered. But I had never seen
her touch him until now, sprawled, flung across his lap,
clutching him around the shoulders, her face against his collar, crying, saying, 'Daddy! Daddy! Daddy! Daddy!'"

"Go on," I said.

"That's all. Oh, that was enough; what more did he need
to do than that? have that thing—that piece of paper—drawn
up himself and then twist her arm until she signed her name
to it? He didn't have to mention any paper. He probably
didn't even need to see her again and even if he did, all he
would have needed—she already knew about the will, I mean
Papa's will leaving my share to just Eula Varner without even
mentioning the word Snopes—all he would need would be
just to say something like 'Oh yes, your grandfather's a fine
old gentleman but he just never did like me. But that's all
right; your mother will be taken care of no matter what happens to me myself; he just fixed things so I nor nobody else
can take her money away from her before you inherit it'—
something like that. Or maybe he didn't even need to do
that much, knew he didn't have to. Not with her. He was her
father, and if he wouldn't let her go off to school it was because he loved her since that was the reason all parents
seemed to have for the things they wont let their children
do; then for him to suddenly turn completely around and almost order her to do the thing she wanted, which he had
forbidden her for almost two years to do, what reason could
that be except that he loved her still more: loved her enough
to let her do the one thing in her life he had ever forbidden
her?

"Or I dont know. He may have suggested it, even told her
how to word it; what does it matter now? It's done, there:
Papa storming into the house at four this morning and flinging it down on my bed before I was even awake—Wait," she

said, "I know all that too; I've already done all that myself. It was legal, all regular—What do they call it?"

"Drawn up," I said.

"—drawn up by a lawyer in Oxford, Mr Stone—not the old one: the young one. I telephoned him this morning. He was very nice. He—"

"I know him," I said. "Even if he did go to New Haven."

"—said he had wanted to talk to me about it, but there was the . . ."

"Inviolacy," I said.

"Inviolacy.—between client and lawyer. He said she came to him, it must have been right after she reached Oxford— Wait," she said. "I asked him that too: why she came to him and he said—He said she was a delightful young lady who would go far in life even after she ran out of—of—"

"Contingencies," I said.

"—contingencies to bequeath people—she said that she had just asked someone who was the nicest lawyer for her to go to and they told her him. So she told him what she wanted and he wrote it that way; oh yes, I saw it: 'my share of what-ever I might inherit from my mother, Eula Varner Snopes, as distinct and separate from whatever her husband shall share in her property, to my father Flem Snopes'. Oh yes, all regular and legal though he said he tried to explain to her that she was not bequeathing a quantity but merely devising a—what was it? contingency, and that nobody would take it very seri-ously probably since she might die before she had any inheri-tance or get married or even change her mind without a husband to help her or her mother might not have any inher-itance beyond the one specified or might spend it or her fa-ther might die and she would inherit half of his inheritance from herself plus the other half which her mother would in-herit as her father's relict, which she would heir in turn back to her father's estate to pass to her mother as his relict to be inherited once more by her; but she was eighteen years old and competent and he, Mr Stone, was a competent lawyer or at least he had a license saying so, and so it was at least in le-gal language and on the right kind of paper. He—Mr Stone— even asked her why she felt she must make the will and she told him: Because my father has been good to me and I love and admire and respect him—do you hear that? Love and admire and respect him. Oh yes, legal. As if that mattered, legal or illegal, contingency or incontingency—"

Nor did she need to tell me that either: that old man seething out there in his country store for eighteen years now over the way his son-in-law had tricked him out of that old ruined plantation and then made a profit out of it, now wild with rage and frustration at the same man who had not only out-briganded him in brigandage but since then had even out-usury-ed him in sedentary usury, and who now had used the innocence of a young girl, his own grand-daughter, who could repay what she thought was love with gratitude and generosity at least, to disarm him of the one remaining weapon which he still held over his enemy. Oh yes, of course it was worth nothing except its paper but what did that matter, legal or valid either. It didn't even matter now if he destroyed it (which of course was why Flem ever let it out of his hand in the first place); only that he saw it, read it, comprehended it: took one outraged incredulous glance at it, then came storming into town—

"I couldn't make him hush," she said. "I couldn't make him stop, be quiet. He didn't even want to wait until daylight to get hold of Manfred."

"De Spain?" I said. "Then? At four in the morning?"

"Didn't I tell you I couldn't stop him, make him stop or hush? Oh yes, he got Manfred there right away. And Manfred attended to everything. It was quite simple to him. That is, when I finally made him and Papa both believe that in another minute they would wake up, rouse the whole neighborhood and before that happened I would take Papa's—Jody's—car and drive to Oxford and get Linda and none of them would ever see us again. So he and Papa hushed then—"

"But Flem," I said.

"He was there.—for a little while, long enough—"

"But what was he doing?" I said.

"Nothing," she said. "What was he supposed to do? What did he need to do now?"

"Oh," I said. " 'long enough to—' "

"—enough for Manfred to settle everything: we would

simply leave, go away together, he and I, which was what we should have done eighteen years ago—"

"What?" I said, cried. "Leave—elope?"

"Oh yes, it was all fixed; he stopped right there with Papa still standing over him and cursing him—cursing him or cursing Flem; you couldn't tell now which one he was talking to or about or at—and wrote out the bill of sale. Papa was . . . what's that word? neutral. He wanted both of them out of the bank, intended to have both of them out of it, came all the way in from home at four oclock in the morning to fling both of them out of Jefferson and Yoknapatawpha County and Mississippi all three—Manfred for having been my lover for eighteen years, and Flem for waiting eighteen years to do anything about it. Papa didn't know about Manfred until this morning. That is, he acted like he didn't. I think Mamma knew. I think she has known all the time. But maybe she didn't. Because people are really kind, you know. All the people in Yoknapatawpha County that might have made sure Mamma knew about us, for her own good, so she could tell Papa for his own good. For everybody's own good. But I dont think Papa knew. He's like you. I mean, you can do that too."

"Do what?" I said.

"Be able to not have to believe something just because it might be so or somebody says it is so or maybe even it is so."

"Wait," I said. "Wait. What bill of sale?"

"For his bank stock. Manfred's bank stock. Made out to Flem. To give Flem the bank, since that was what all the trouble and uproar was about.—and then the check for Flem to sign to buy it with, dated a week from now to give Flem time to have the money ready when we cashed the check in Texas —when people are not married, or should have been married but aren't yet, why do they still think Texas is far enough? or is it just big enough?—or California or Mexico or wherever we would go."

"But Linda," I said. "Linda."

"All right," she said. "Linda."

"Dont you see? Either way, she is lost? Either to go with you, if that were possible, while you desert her father for another man; or stay here in all the stink without you to protect

her from it and learn at last that he is not her father at all and
so she has nobody, nobody?"

"That's why I sent the note. Marry her."

"No. I told you that before. Besides, that wont save her.
Only Manfred can save her. Let him sell Flem his stock, give
Flem the damned bank; is that too high a price to pay for
what—what he—he—"

"I tried that," she said. "No."

"I'll talk to him," I said. "I'll tell him. He must. He'll have
to; there's no other—"

"No," she said. "Not Manfred." Then I watched her
hands, not fast, open the bag and take out the pack of cigarettes and the single kitchen match and extract the cigarette
and put the pack back into the bag and close it and (no, I
didn't move) strike the match on the turned sole of her shoe
and light the cigarette and put the match into the tray and
put her hands again on the bag. "Not Manfred. You dont
know Manfred. And so maybe I dont either. Maybe I dont
know about men either. Maybe I was completely wrong that
morning when I said how women are only interested in facts
because maybe men are just interested in facts too and the
only difference is, women dont care whether they are facts or
not just so they fit, and men dont care whether they fit or not
just so they are facts. If you are a man, you can lie uncon-
scious in the gutter bleeding and with most of your teeth
knocked out and somebody can take your pocketbook and
you can wake up and wash the blood off and it's all right; you
can always get some more teeth and even another pocketbook
sooner or later. But you cant just stand meekly with your head
bowed and no blood and all your teeth too while somebody
takes your pocketbook because even though you might face
the friends who love you afterward you never can face the
strangers that never heard of you before. Not Manfred. If I
dont go with him, he'll have to fight. He may go down fighting and wreck everything and everybody else, but he'll have
to fight. Because he's a man. I mean, he's a man first. I mean,
he's got to be a man first. He can swap Flem Snopes his bank
for Flem Snopes's wife, but he cant just stand there and let
Flem Snopes take the bank away from him."

"So Linda's sunk," I said. "Finished. Done. Sunk." I said,

cried: "But you anyway will save something! To get away yourself at least, out of here, never again to . . . . never again Flem Snopes, never again, never—"

"Oh, that," she said. "You mean that. That doesn't matter. That's never been any trouble. He . . . cant. He's—what's the word? impotent. He's always been. Maybe that's why, one of the reasons. You see? You've got to be careful or you'll have to pity him. You'll have to. He couldn't bear that, and it's no use to hurt people if you dont get anything for it. Because he couldn't bear being pitied. It's like V.K.'s Vladimir. Ratliff can live with Ratliff's Vladimir, and you can live with Ratliff's Vladimir. But you mustn't ever have the chance to, the right to, the choice to. Like he can live with his impotence, but you mustn't have the chance to help him with pity. You promised about the Vladimir, but I want you to promise again about this."

"I promise," I said. Then I said: "Yes. You're going tonight. That's why the beauty parlor this afternoon: not for me but for Manfred. No: not even for Manfred after eighteen years: just to elope with, get on the train with. To show your best back to Jefferson. That's right, isn't it? You're leaving tonight."

"Marry her, Gavin," she said. I had known her by sight for eighteen years, with time out of course for the war; I had dreamed about her at night for eighteen years including the war. We had talked to one another twice: here in the office one night fourteen years ago, and in her living room one morning two years back. But not once had she ever called me even Mister Stevens. Now she said Gavin. "Marry her, Gavin."

"Change her name by marriage, then she wont miss the one she will lose when you abandon her."

"Marry her, Gavin," she said.

"Put it that I'm not too old so much as simply discrepant; that having been her husband once, I would never relinquish even her widowhood to another. Put it that way then."

"Marry her, Gavin," she said. And now I stopped, she sitting beyond the desk, the cigarette burning on the tray, balancing its muted narrow windless feather where she had not touched it once since she lit it and put it down, the hands still quiet on the bag and the face now turned to look at me out of the half-shadow above the rim of light from the lamp—the big broad simple still unpainted beautiful mouth, the eyes not the hard and dusty blue of fall but the blue of spring blooms all one inextricable mixture of wistaria cornflowers larkspur bluebells weeds and all, all the lost girls' weather and boys' luck and too late the grief, too late.

"Then this way. After you're gone, if or when I become convinced that conditions are going to become such that something will have to be done, and nothing else but marrying me can help her, and she will have me. But have me, take me. Not just give up, surrender."

"Swear it then," she said.

"I promise. I have promised. I promise again."

"No," she said. "Swear."

"I swear," I said.

"And even if she wont have you. Even after that. Even if she w—you cant marry her."

"How can she need me then?" I said. "Flem—unless your father really does get shut of the whole damned boiling of you, runs Flem out of Jefferson too—will have his bank and wont need to swap, sell, trade her anymore; maybe he will even prefer to have her in a New England school or even further than that if he can manage it."

"Swear," she said.

"All right," I said. "At any time. Anywhere. No matter what happens."

"Swear," she said.

"I swear," I said.

"I'm going now," she said and rose and picked up the burning cigarette and crushed it carefully out into the tray and I rose too.

"Of course," I said. "You have some packing to do even for an elopement, dont you. I'll drive you home."

"You dont need to," she said.

"A lady, walking home alone at—it's after midnight. What will Otis Harker say? You see, I've got to be a man too; I cant face Otis Harker otherwise since you wont stop being a lady to him until after tomorrow's south-bound train; I believe you did say Texas, didn't you?" Though Otis was not in sight this time though with pencil paper and a watch I could have calculated about where he would be now. Though the figures could have been wrong and only Otis was not in sight, not we, crossing the shadow-bitten Square behind the flat rapid sabre-sweep of the headlights across the plate glass store-fronts, then into the true spring darkness where the sparse street lights were less than stars. And we could have talked if there had been more to talk about or maybe there had been more to talk about if we had talked. Then the small gate before the short walk to the small dark house not rented now of course and of course not vacant yet with a little space yet for decent decorum, and I wondered, thought *Will Manfred sell him his house along with his bank or just abandon both to him— provided of course old Will Varner leaves him time to collect either one* and stopped.

"Dont get out," she said and got out and shut the door and said, stooping a little to look at me beneath the top: "Swear again."

"I swear," I said.

"Thank you," she said. "Good night," and turned and I watched her, through the gate and up the walk, losing dimension now, onto or rather into the shadow of the little gallery and losing even substance now. And then I heard the door and it was as if she had not been. No, not that; not *not been,* but rather no more *is,* since *was* remains always and forever, inexplicable and immune, which is its grief. That's what I mean: a dimension less, then a substance less, then the sound of a door and then, not *never been* but simply *no more is* since always and forever that *was* remains, as if what is going to happen to one tomorrow already gleams faintly visible now if the watcher were only wise enough to discern it or maybe just brave enough.

The spring night, cooler now, as if for a little while, until tomorrow's dusk and the new beginning, somewhere had suspired into sleep at last the amazed hushed burning of hope and dream two-and-two engendered. It would even be quite cold by dawn, daybreak. But even then not cold enough to chill, make hush for sleep the damned mocking bird for three nights now keeping his constant racket in Maggie's pink dogwood just under my bedroom window. So the trick of course would be to divide, not him but his racket, the having to listen to him: one Gavin Stevens to cross his dark gallery too and into the house and up the stairs to cover his head in the bedclothes, losing in his turn a dimension of Gavin Stevens, an ectoplasm of Gavin Stevens impervious to cold and hearing too to bear its half of both, bear its half or all of any other burdens anyone wanted to shed and shuck, having only this moment assumed that one of a young abandoned girl's responsibility.

Because who would miss a dimension? who indeed but would be better off for having lost it, who had nothing in the first place to offer but just devotion, eighteen years of devotion, the ectoplasm of devotion too thin to be crowned by scorn, warned by hatred, annealed by grief. That's it: unpin, shed, cast off the last clumsy and anguished dimension, and so be free. Unpin: that's the trick, remembering Vladimir Kyrilytch's "He aint unpinned it yet"—the twenty-dollar gold piece pinned to the undershirt of the country boy on his first trip to Memphis, who even if he has never been there before, has as much right as any to hope he can be, may be, will be tricked or trapped into a whorehouse before he has to go back home again. *He has unpinned it now* I thought.

TWENTY ONE

C HARLES MALLISON
You know how it is, you wake in the morning and you know at once that it has already happened and you are already too late. You didn't know what it was going to be, which was why you had to watch so hard for it, trying to watch in all directions at once. Then you let go for a second, closed your eyes for just one second, and bang! it happened and it was too late, not even time to wake up and still hold off a minute, just to stretch and think *What is it that makes today such a good one?* then to let it come in, flow in: *Oh yes, there's not any school today.* More: *Thursday and in April and still there's not any school today.*

But not this morning. And halfway down the stairs I heard the swish of the pantry door shutting and I could almost hear Mother telling Guster: "Here he comes. Quick. Get out," and I went into the dining room and Father had already had breakfast, I mean even when Guster has moved the plate and cup and saucer you can always tell where Father has eaten something; and by the look of his place Uncle Gavin hadn't been to the table at all and Mother was sitting at her place just drinking coffee, with her hat already on and her coat over Uncle Gavin's chair and her bag and gloves by her plate and the dark glasses she wore in the car whenever she went beyond the city limits as if light didn't have any glare in it except one mile from town. And I reckon she wished for a minute that I was about three or four because then she could have put one arm around me against her knee and held the back of my head with the other hand. But now she just held my hand and this time she had to look up at me. "Mrs Snopes killed herself last night," she said. "I'm going over to Oxford with Uncle Gavin to bring Linda home."

"Killed herself?" I said. "How?"

"What?" Mother said. Because I was only twelve then, not yet thirteen.

"What did she do it with?" I said. But then Mother remembered that too by that time. She was already getting up.

"With a pistol," she said. "I'm sorry, I didn't think to ask whose." She almost had the coat on too. Then she came and got the gloves and bag and the glasses. "We may be back by dinner, but I dont know. Will you try to stay at home, at least stay away from the Square, find something to do with Aleck Sander in the back yard? Guster's not going to let him leave the place today, so why dont you stay with him?"

"Yessum," I said. Because I was just twelve; to me that great big crepe knot dangling from the front door of Mr de Spain's bank signified only waste: another holiday when school was suspended for an indefinite time; another holiday piled on top of one we already had, when the best, the hardest holiday user in the world couldn't possibly use two of them at once, when it could have been saved and added on to the end of the one we already had when the little Riddell boy either died or got well or anyway they started school again. Or better still: just to save it for one of those hopeless days when Christmas is so long past you have forgotten it ever was, and it looks like summer itself has died somewhere and will never come again.

Because I was just twelve; I would have to be reminded that the longest school holiday in the world could mean nothing to the people which that wreath on the bank door freed for one day from work. And I would have to be a lot older than twelve before I realised that that wreath was not the myrtle of grief, it was the laurel of victory; that in that dangling chunk of black tulle and artificial flowers and purple ribbons was the eternal and deathless public triumph of virtue itself proved once more supreme and invincible.

I couldn't even know now what I was looking at. Oh yes, I went to town, not quite as soon as Mother and Uncle Gavin were out of sight, but close enough. So did Aleck Sander. We could hear Guster calling us both a good while after we had turned the corner, both of us going to look at the wreath on the closed bank door and seeing a lot of other people too, grown people, come to look at it for what I know now was no braver reason than the one Aleck Sander and I had. And when Mr de Spain came to town as he always did just before nine oclock and got his mail from the postoffice like he always did and let himself into the back door of the bank with his key like he always did because the back door always stayed locked, we—I couldn't know that the reason he looked exactly like nothing had happened was because that was exactly the way he had to come to town that morning to have to look. That he had to get up this morning and shave and dress and maybe practise in front of the mirror a while in order to come to the Square at the time he always did so everybody in Jefferson could see him doing exactly as he always did, like if there was grief and trouble anywhere in Jefferson that morning, it was not his grief and trouble, being an orphan and unmarried; even to going on into the closed bank by the back door as if he still had the right to.

Because I know now that we—Jefferson—all knew that he had lost the bank. I mean, whether old Mr Will Varner ran Mr Flem Snopes out of Jefferson too after this, Mr de Spain himself wouldn't stay. In a way, he owed that not just to the memory of his dead love, his dead mistress; he owed that to Jefferson too. Because he had outraged us. He had not only flouted the morality of marriage which decreed that a man and a woman cant sleep together without a certificate from the police, he had outraged the economy of marriage which is the production of children, by making public display of the fact that you can be barren by choice with impunity; he had outraged the institution of marriage twice: not just his own but the Flem Snopes's too. So they already hated him twice: once for doing it, once for not getting caught at it for eighteen years. But that would be nothing to the hatred he would get if, after his guilty partner had paid with her life for her share of the crime, he didn't even lose that key to the back door of the bank to pay for his.

We all knew that. So did he. And he knew we knew. And we in our turn knew he knew we did. So that was all right. He was finished, I mean, he was fixed. His part was set. No: I was right the first time; and now I know that too. He was done, ended. That shot had finished him too and now what he did or didn't do either didn't matter any more. It was just Linda now; and when I was old enough I knew why none of us expected that day that old Mr Varner would come charging out of Mr Snopes's house with the same pistol maybe seeking more blood, if for no other reason than that there would have been no use in it. Nor were we surprised when (after a discreet interval of course, for decorum, the decorum of bereavement and mourning) we learned that 'for business reasons and health' Mr de Spain had resigned from the bank and was moving out West (he actually left the afternoon of the funeral, appeared at the grave—alone and nobody to speak to him except to nod—with a crape armband which was of course all right since the deceased was the wife of his vice president, and then turned from the grave when we all did except that he was the first one and an hour later that afternoon his Buick went fast across the Square and into the Memphis highway with him in it and the back full of baggage) and that his bank stock—not his house; Ratliff said that even Flem Snopes didn't have that much nerve: to buy the house too the same day he bought the bank stock—was offered for sale, and even less surprised that (even more discreetly) Mr Snopes had bought it.

It was Linda now. And now I know that the other people, the grown people, who had come to look at that wreath on the bank door for exactly the same reason that Aleck Sander and I had come to look at it, had come only incidentally to look at the wreath since they had really come for exactly the same reason Aleck Sander and I had really come: to see Linda Snopes when Mother and Uncle Gavin brought her home even if mine and Aleck Sander's reason was to see how much Mrs Snopes's killing herself would change the way Linda looked so that we would know how we would look if Mother and Guster ever shot themselves. It was Linda because I know now what Uncle Gavin believed then (not knew: believed: because he couldn't have known because the only one that could have told him would have been Mrs Snopes herself and if she had told him in that note she gave me that afternoon before she was going to commit suicide, he would have stopped her or tried to because Mother anyway would have known it if he had tried to stop her and failed), and not just Uncle Gavin but other people in Jefferson too. So now they even forgave Mrs Snopes for the eighteen years of carnal sin, and now they could even forgive themselves for condoning adultery by forgiving it, by reminding themselves (one another too I reckon) that if she had not been an abomination before God for eighteen years, she wouldn't have reached the point where she would have to choose death in order to leave her child a mere suicide for a mother instead of a whore.

Oh yes, it was Linda. She had the whole town on her side now, the town and the county and everybody who ever heard of her and Mr de Spain or knew or even suspected or just guessed anything about the eighteen years, to keep any part of the guessing or suspecting or actual knowing (if there was any, ever was any) from ever reaching her. Because I know now that people really are kind, they really are; there are lots of times when they stop hurting one another not just when they want to keep on hurting but even when they have to; even the most Methodist and Baptist of the Baptists and Methodists and Presbyterians—all right, Episcopals too:—the car coming at last with Linda in the front seat between Mother and Uncle Gavin; across the Square and on to Linda's house so that Aleck Sander and I had plenty of time to be waiting at the corner to flag Uncle Gavin when he came back.

"I thought Guster and your mother told both of you to stay home this morning," he said.

"Yes sir," we said. We went home. And he didn't eat any dinner either: just trying to make me eat, I dont know why. I mean, I dont know why all grown people in sight believe they have to try to persuade you to eat whether you want to or not or even whether they really want to try to persuade you or not, until at last even Father noticed what was going on.

"Come on," he told me. "Either eat it or leave the table. I dont want to lie to your mother when she comes home and asks me why you didn't eat it and I can always say you left suddenly for Texas." Then he said, "What's the matter, you too?" because Uncle Gavin had got up, right quick, and said,

"Excuse me," and went out; yes, Uncle Gavin too; Mr de Spain was finished now as far as Jefferson was concerned and now we—Jefferson—could put all our mind on who was next in sight, what else the flash of that pistol had showed up like when you set off a flashlight powder in a cave; and one of them was Uncle Gavin. Because I know now there were people in Jefferson then who believed that Uncle Gavin had been her lover too, or if he hadn't he should have been or else not just the whole Jefferson masculine race but the whole masculine race anywhere that called itself a man, ought to be ashamed.

Because they knew about that old Christmas ball older ago than I was then, and the whole town had seen and then heard about it so they could come, pass by accident and see for themselves Uncle Gavin and Linda drinking ice cream sodas in Christian's with a book of poetry on the table between them. Except that they knew he really hadn't been Mrs Snopes's lover too, that not only if he had really wanted her, tried for her, he would have failed there too for simple consistency, but that even if by some incredible chance or accident he had beat Mr de Spain's time, it would have showed on the outside of him for the reason that Uncle Gavin was incapable of having a secret life which remained secret; he was, Ratliff said, "a feller that even his in-growed toe-nails was on the outside of his shoes."

So, since Uncle Gavin had failed, he was the pure one, the only pure one; not Mr Snopes, the husband, who if he had been a man, would have got a pistol even if he, Flem Snopes, had to buy one and blown them both, his wife and her fancy banker both, clean out of Jefferson. It was Uncle Gavin. He was the bereaved, the betrayed husband forgiving for the sake of the half-orphan child. It was that same afternoon, he had left right after he went out of the dining room, then Mother came back alone in the car, then about three oclock Uncle Gavin came back in a taxi and said (Oh yes, Aleck Sander and I stayed at home after Guster got hold of us, let alone Mother.):

"Four gentlemen are coming to see me. They're preachers so you'd better show them into the parlor." And I did: the Methodist, the Baptist, the Presbyterian and ours, the Episcopal, all looking like any other bankers or doctors or storekeepers except Mr Thorndyke and the only thing against him was his hind-part-before dog collar; all very grave and long in the face, like horses; I mean, not looking unhappy: just looking long in the face like horses, each one shaking hands with me and kind of bumbling with each other while they were getting through the door, into the parlor where Uncle Gavin was standing too, speaking to each of them by name while they all shook hands with him too, calling them all Doctor, the four of them bumbling again until the oldest one, the Presbyterian, did the talking: they had come to offer themselves singly or jointly to conduct the service; that Mr Snopes was a Baptist and Mrs Snopes had been born a Methodist but neither of them had attended, been a communicant of, any church in Jefferson; that Mr Stevens had assumed— offered his— that is, they had been directed to call on Mr Stevens in regard to the matter, until Uncle Gavin said:

"That is, you were sent. Sent by a damned lot of damned old women of both sexes, including none. Not to bury her: to forgive her. Thank you, gentlemen. I plan to conduct this service myself." But that was just until Father came home for supper and Mother could sick him on Uncle Gavin too. Because we had all thought, taken it for granted, that the Varners (maybe Mr Flem too) would naturally want her buried in Frenchman's Bend; that Mr Varner would pack her up too when he went back home along with whatever else he had brought to town with him (Ratliff said it wouldn't be much since the only thing that travelled lighter than Uncle Billy Varner was a crow) and take her back with him. But Uncle Gavin said No, speaking for Linda—and there were people enough to say Gavin Stevens said No speaking *to* the daughter. Anyway, it was No, the funeral to be tomorrow after Jody Varner's car could get back in from Frenchman's Bend with Jody and Mrs Varner; and now Uncle Gavin had Father at him too.

"Dammit, Gavin," he said. "You cant do it. We all admit you're a lot of things but one of them aint an ordained minister."

"So what?" Uncle Gavin said. "Do you believe that this town believes that any preacher that ever breathed could get her into heaven without having to pass through Jefferson, and that even Christ Himself could get her through on that route?"

"Wait," Mother said. "Both of you hush." She was looking at Uncle Gavin. "Gavin, at first I thought I would never understand why Eula did it. But now I'm beginning to believe that maybe I do. Do you want Linda to have to say afterward that another bachelor had to bury her?"

And that was all. And tomorrow Mrs Varner and Jody came in and brought with them the old Methodist minister who had christened her thirty-eight years ago—an old man who had been a preacher all his adult life but would have for the rest of it the warped back and the wrenched bitter hands of a dirt farmer—and we—the town—gathered at their little house, the women inside and the men standing around the little front yard and along the street, all neat and clean and wearing coats and not quite looking at each other while they talked quietly about crops and weather; then to the graveyard and the new lot empty except for the one raw excavation and even that not long, hidden quickly, rapidly beneath the massed flowers, themselves already doomed in the emblem-shapes—wreaths and harps and urns—of the mortality which they de-stingered, euphemised; and Mr de Spain standing there not apart: just solitary, with his crape armband and his face looking like it must have when he was a lieutenant in Cuba back in that time, day, moment after he had just led the men that trusted him or anyway followed him because they were supposed to, into the place where they all knew some of them wouldn't come back for the reason that all of them were not supposed to come back which was all right too if the lieutenant said it was, provided old Mayor Adams had been wrong that day in front of the postoffice and Mr de Spain really had been a lieutenant in Cuba.

Then we came home and Father said, "Dammit, Gavin, why dont you get drunk?" and Uncle Gavin said,

"Certainly, why not?"—not even looking up from the paper. Then it was supper time and I wondered why Mother didn't nag at him about not eating. But at least as long as she didn't think about eating, her mind wouldn't hunt around and light on me. Then we—Uncle Gavin and Mother and I—went to the office. I mean that for a while after Grandfather died Mother still tried to make us all call it the library but now even she called it the office just like Grandfather did, and Uncle Gavin sitting beside the lamp with a book and even turning a page now and then, until the door bell rang.

"I'll go," Mother said. But then, nobody else seemed to intend to or be even curious. Then she came back down the hall to the office door and said, "It's Linda. Come in, honey,"

and stood to one side and beckoned her head at me as Linda
came in and Uncle Gavin got up and Mother jerked her head
at me again and said, "Chick," and Linda stopped just inside
the door and this time Mother said, "Charles!" so I got up
and went out and she closed the door after us. But it was all
right. I was used to it by this time. As soon as I saw who it
was I even expected it.

TWENTY TWO

GAVIN STEVENS
    Then Maggie finally got Chick out and closed the door. I said, "Sit down, Linda." But she just stood there. "Cry," I said. "Let yourself go and cry."

"I cant," she said. "I tried." She looked at me. "He's not my father," she said.

"Of course he's your father," I said. "Certainly he is. What in the world are you talking about?"

"No," she said.

"Yes," I said. "Do you want me to swear? All right. I swear he's your father."

"You were not there. You dont know. You never even saw her until she—we came to Jefferson."

"Ratliff did. Ratliff was there. He knows. He knows who your father is. And I know from Ratliff. I am sure. Have I ever lied to you?"

"No," she said. "You are the one person in the world I know will never lie to me."

"All right," I said. "I swear to you then. Flem Snopes is your father." And now she didn't move: it was just the tears, the water, not springing, just running quietly and quite fast down her face. I moved toward her.

"No," she said, "dont touch me yet," catching, grasping both my wrists and gripping, pressing my hands hard in hers against her breast. "When I thought he wasn't my father, I hated her and Manfred both. Oh yes, I knew about Manfred: I have . . . seen them look at each other, their voices when they would talk to each other, speak one another's name, and I couldn't bear it, I hated them both. But now that I know he is my father, it's all right. I'm glad. I want her to have loved, to have been happy.—I can cry now," she said.

304

TWENTY THREE

V. K. RATLIFF

It was liken a contest, like Lawyer had stuck a stick of dynamite in his hind pocket and lit a long fuse to it and was interested now would or wouldn't somebody step in in time and tromple the fire out. Or a race, like would he finally get Linda out of Jefferson and at least get his-self shut forever of the whole tribe of Snopes first, or would he jest blow up his-self beforehand first and take ever body and ever thing in the neighborhood along with him.

No, not a contest. Not a contest with Flem Snopes anyway because it takes two to make a contest and Flem Snopes wasn't the other one. He was a umpire, if he was anything in it. No, he wasn't even a umpire. It was like he was running a little mild game against his-self, for his own amusement, like solitaire. He had ever thing now that he had come to Jefferson to get. He had more. He had things he didn't even know he was going to want until he reached Jefferson because he didn't even know they was until then. He had his bank and his money in it and his-self to be president of it so he could not only watch his money from ever being stole by another twenty-two calibre rogue like his cousin Byron, but nobody could ever steal from him the respectability that being president of one of the two Yoknapatawpha County banks toted along with it. And he was going to have one of the biggest residences in the county or maybe Mississippi too when his carpenters got through with Manfred de Spain's old home. And he had got rid of the only two downright arrant outrageous Snopeses when he run Montgomery Ward and I.O. finally out of town so that now, for the time being at least, the only other Snopes actively inside the city limits was a wholesale grocer not only as respectable but maybe even more solvent than jest a banker. So you would think he would a been satisfied now. But he wasn't. He had to make a young girl (woman now) that wasn't even his child, say "I humbly thank you, papa, for being so good to me."

That's right, a contest. Not even against Linda, and last of all against Lawyer Stevens since he had already milked out of Lawyer Stevens all he needed from him, which was to get his wife buried all right and proper and decorous and respectable, without no uproarious elements making a unseemly spectacle in the business. His game of solitaire was against Jefferson. It was like he was trying to see jest exactly how much Jefferson would stand, put up with. It was like he knowed that his respectability depended completely on Jefferson not jest accepting but finally getting used to the fact that he not only had evicted Manfred de Spain from his bank but he was remodeling to move into it De Spain's birthsite likewise, and that the only remaining threat now was what might happen if that-ere young gal that believed all right so far that he was her paw, might stumble onto something that would tell her different. That she might find out by accident that the man that was leastways mixed up somehow in her mother's suicide, whether he actively caused it or not, wasn't even her father, since if somebody's going to be responsible why your maw killed herself, at least let it be somebody kin to you and not jest a outright stranger.

So you would a thought that the first thing he would do soon as the dust settled after that funeral, would be to get her clean out of Jefferson and as far away as he could have suhjested into her mind she wanted to go. But not him. And the reason he give was that monument. And naturally that was Lawyer Stevens too. I mean, I dont know who delegated Lawyer into the monument business, who gave it to him or if he jest taken it or if maybe by this time the relationship between him and anybody named Snopes, or anyway maybe jest the Flem Snopeses (or no: it was that for him Eula Varner hadn't never died and never would because oh yes, I know about that too) was like that one between a feller out in a big open field and a storm of rain: there aint no being give nor accepting to it: he's already got it.

Anyway it was him—Lawyer—that helped Linda hunt through that house and her mother's things until they found the right photograph and had it—Lawyer still—enlarged, the face part, and sent it to Italy to be carved into a . . . yes, medallion to fasten onto the front of the monument, and him that the practice drawings would come back to to decide and change here and there and send back. Which would a been his right by his own choice even if Flem had tried to interfere in and stop him because he wanted that monument set up where Flem could pass on it more than anybody wanted it because then Flem would let her go. But it was Flem's monument; dont make no mistake about that. It was Flem that paid for it, first thought of it, planned and designed it, picked out what size and what was to be wrote on it—the face and the letters—and never once mentioned price. Dont make no mistake about that. It was Flem. Because this too was a part of what he had come to Jefferson for and went through all he went through afterward to get it.

Oh yes, Lawyer had it all arranged for Linda to leave, get away at last; all they was hung on was the monument because Flem had give his word he would let her go then. It was to a place named Greenwich Village in New York; Lawyer had it all arranged, friends he knowed in Harvard to meet the train at the depot and take care of her, get her settled and ever thing.

"Is it a college?" I says. "Like out at Seminary Hill?"

"No no," he says. "I mean, yes. But not the kind you are talking about."

"I thought you was set on her going to a college up there."

"That was before," he says. "Too much has happened to her since. Too much, too fast, too quick. She outgrew colleges all in about twenty-four hours two weeks ago. She'll have to grow back down to them again, maybe in a year or two. But right now, Greenwich Village is the place for her."

"What is Greenwich Village?" I says. "You still aint told me."

"It's a place with a few unimportant boundaries but no limitations where young people of any age go to seek dreams."

"I never knowed before that place had no particular geography," I says. "I thought that-ere was a varmint you hunted anywhere."

"Not always. Not for her, anyway. Sometimes you need a favorable scope of woods to hunt, a place where folks have already successfully hunted and found the same game you want.

Sometimes, some people, even need help in finding it. The particular quarry they want to catch, they have to make first. That takes two."

"Two what?" I says.

"Yes," he says. "Two."

"You mean a husband," I says.

"All right," he says. "Call him that. It dont matter what you call him."

"Why, Lawyer," I says. "You sound like what a heap, a right smart in fact, jest about all in fact, unanimous in fact of our good God-fearing upright embattled christian Jeffersons and Yoknapatawphas too that can proudly affirm that never in their life did they ever have one minute's fun that the most innocent little child couldn't a stood right there and watched, would call a deliberate incitement and pandering to the Devil his-self."

Only Lawyer wasn't laughing. And then I wasn't neither. "Yes," he says. "It will be like that with her. It will be difficult for her. She will have to look at a lot of them, a long time. Because he will face something almost impossible to match himself against. He will have to have courage, because it will be doom, maybe disaster too. That's her fate. She is doomed to anguish and to bear it, doomed to one passion and one anguish and all the rest of her life to bear it, as some people are doomed from birth to be robbed or betrayed or murdered."

Then I said it. "Marry her. Naturally you never thought of that."

"I?" he says. It was right quiet: no surprise, no nothing. "I thought I had just been talking about that for the last ten minutes. She must have the best. It will be impossible even for him."

"Marry her," I says.

"No," he says. "That's my fate: just to miss marriage."

"You mean escape it?"

"No no," he says. "I never escape it. Marriage is constantly in my life. My fate is constantly to just miss it or it to, safely again, once more safe, just miss me."

So it was all fixed, and now all he needed was to get his carved marble face back from Italy, nagging by long distance telephone and telegraph dispatch ever day or so in the most courteous affable legal manner you could want, at the Italian consul in New Orleans, so he could get it fastened onto the monument and then (if necessary) take a holt on Flem's coat collar and shove him into the car and take him out to the cemetery and snatch the veil offen it, with Linda's ticket to New York (he would a paid for that too except it wasn't necessary since the last thing Uncle Billy done before he went back home after the funeral was to turn over to the bank— not Flem: the bank, with Lawyer as one of the trustees—a good size chunk of what would be Eula's inheritance under that will of hisn that he hadn't never changed to read Snopes) in his other hand.

So we had to wait. Which was interesting enough. I mean, Lawyer had enough to keep him occupied worrying the I-talian government, and all I ever needed was jest something to look at, watch, providing of course it had people in it. They—Flem and Linda—still lived in the same little house that folks believed for years after he bought it that he was still jest renting it. Though pretty soon Flem owned a automobile. I mean, presently, after the polite amount of time after he turned up president of the bank; not to have Santy Claus come all at once you might say. It wasn't a expensive car: jest a good one, jest the right unnoticeable size, of a good polite unnoticeable black color and he even learned to drive it because maybe he had to because now ever afternoon after the bank closed he would have to go and watch how the carpenters was getting along with his new house (it was going to have colyums across the front now, I mean the extry big ones so even a feller that never seen colyums before wouldn't have no doubt a-tall what they was, like in the photographs where the Confedrit sweetheart in a hoop skirt and a magnolia is saying goodbye to her Confedrit beau jest before he rides off to finish tending to General Grant) and Flem would have to drive his-self because, although Linda could drive it right off and done it now and then and never mind if all women are naturally interested in the house-building or -remodeling occupation no matter whose it is the same as a bird is interested in the nesting occupation, although she druv him there the first afternoon to look at the house, she wouldn't go inside to look at it and after that one time she never even drove him back anymore.

But like I said we was all busy or anyway occupied or at least interested, so we could wait. And sho enough, even waiting ends if you can jest wait long enough. So finally the medallion came. It was October now, a good time of year, one of the best. Naturally it was Lawyer went to the depot and got it though I'm sho Flem paid the freight on it for no other reason than Lawyer wouldn't a waited long enough for the agent to add it up, herding the two Negroes toting it all wrapped up in straw and nailed up in a wooden box, across the platform to his car like he was herding two geese. And for the next three days when his office seen him it was on the fly you might say, from a distance when he happened to pass it. Which was a good thing there wasn't no passel of brigands or highwaymen or contractors or jest simple lawyers making a concerted financial attack on Yoknapatawpha County at that time because Yoknapatawpha would a jest had to rock along the best it could without no help from its attorney. Because he had the masons already hired and waiting with likely even the mortar already mixed, even before the medallion come; one morning I even caught him, put my hand on the car door and says,

"I'll ride out to the cemetery with you," and he jest reached across, the car already in gear and the engine already racing, and lifted my hand off and throwed it away and says,

"Get out of the way," and went on and so I went up to the office, the door never was locked nohow even when he was jest normal and jest out of it most of the time, and opened the bottom drawer where he kept the bottle but it never even smelled like he used to keep whiskey in it. So I waited on the street until school let out and finally caught that boy, Chick, and says,

"Hasn't your uncle got some whiskey at home some-where?" and he says,

"I dont know. I'll look. You want me to pour up a drink in something and bring it?" and I says,

"No. He dont need a drink. He needs a whole bottle, pro-viding it's big enough and full enough. Bring all of it; I'll stay with him and watch."

Then the monument was finished, ready for Flem to pass on it, and he—Lawyer—sent me the word too, brisk and lively as a general jest getting ready to capture a town: "Be at the office at three-thirty so we can pick up Chick. The train leaves Memphis at eight oclock so we wont have any time to waste."

So I was there. Except it wasn't in the office at all because he was already in the car with the engine already running when I got there. "What train at eight oclock to where and whose?" I says.

"Linda's," he says. "She'll be in New York Saturday morning. She's all packed and ready to leave. Flem's sending her to Memphis in his car as soon as we are done."

"Flem's sending her?" I says.

"Why not?" he says. "She's his daughter. After all you owe something to your children even if it aint your fault. Get in," he says. "Here's Chick."

So we went out to the cemetery and there it was—another colyum not a-tall saying what it had cost Flem Snopes because what it was saying was exactly how much it was worth to Flem Snopes, standing in the middle of that new one-grave lot, at the head of that one grave that hadn't quite healed over yet, looking—the stone, the marble—whiter than white itself in the warm October sun against the bright yellow and red and dark red hickories and sumacs and gums and oaks like splashes of fire itself among the dark green cedars. Then the other car come up with him and Linda in the back seat, and the Negro driver that would drive her to Memphis in the front seat with the baggage (it was all new too) piled on the seat by him; coming up and stopping, and him setting there in that black hat that still looked brand new and like he had borrowed it, and that little bow tie that never had and never would look anything but new, chewing slow and steady at his tobacco; and that gal setting there by him, tight and still and her back not even touching the back of the seat, in a kind of dark suit for travelling and a hat and a little veil and her hands in white gloves still and kind of clenched on her knees and not once, not never once ever looking at that stone monument with that marble medallion face that Lawyer had picked out and selected that never looked like Eula a-tall you thought at first, never looked like nobody nowhere you thought at first, until you were wrong because it never looked like all women because what it looked like was one woman that ever man that was lucky enough to have been a man would say, "Yes, that's her. I knowed her five years ago or ten years ago or fifty years ago and you would a thought that by now I would a earned the right not to have to remember her anymore," and under it the carved letters that he his-self, and I dont mean Lawyer this time, had picked out:

EULA VARNER SNOPES
1889   1927
A virtuous Wife is a Crown to her Husband
Her Children rise and call Her Blessed

and him setting there chewing, faint and steady, and her still and straight as a post by him, not looking at nothing and them two white balls of her fists on her lap. Then he moved. He leant a little and spit out the window and then set back in the seat.

"Now you can go," he says.

TWENTY FOUR

C HARLES MALLISON
So the car went on. Then I turned and started walking
back to ours when Ratliff said behind me: "Wait. You got a
clean handkerchief?" and I turned and saw Uncle Gavin
walking on away from us with his back to us, not going anywhere: just walking on, until Ratliff took the handkerchief
from me and we caught up with him. But he was all right
then, he just said:

"What's the matter?" Then he said, "Well, let's get on
back. You boys are free to loaf all day long if you want to but
after all I work for the County so I have to stay close enough
to the office so that anybody that wants to commit a crime
against it can find me."

So we got in the car and he started it and we drove back to
town. Except that he was talking about football now, saying
to me: "Why dont you wake up and get out of that kindergarden and into high school so you can go out for the team?
I'll need somebody I know on it because I think I know
what's wrong with football the way they play it now;" going
on from there, talking and even turning loose the wheel with
both hands to show us what he meant: how the trouble with
football was, only an expert could watch it because nobody
else could keep up with what was happening; how in baseball
everybody stood still and the ball moved and so you could
keep up with what was happening. But in football, the ball
and everybody else moved at the same time and not only that
but always in a clump, a huddle with the ball hidden in the
middle of them so you couldn't even tell who did have it, let
alone who was supposed to have it; not to mention the ball
being already the color of dirt and all the players thrashing
and rolling around in the mud and dirt until they were all
that same color too; going on like that, waving both hands
with Ratliff and me both hollering, "Watch the wheel! Watch
the wheel!" and Uncle Gavin saying to Ratliff, "Now you
dont think so," or "You claim different of course," or "No

313

matter what you say," and Ratliff saying, "Why, I never," or "No I dont," or "I aint even mentioned football," until finally he—Ratliff—said to me:

"Did you find that bottle?"

"No sir," I said. "I reckon Father drank it. Mr Gowrie wont bring the next kag until Sunday night."

"Let me out here," Ratliff said to Uncle Gavin. Uncle Gavin stopped talking long enough to say,

"What?"

"I'll get out here," Ratliff said. "See you in a minute."

So Uncle Gavin stopped long enough for Ratliff to get out (we had just reached the Square) then we went on, Uncle Gavin talking again or still talking since he had only stopped long enough to say What? to Ratliff, and parked the car and went up to the office and he was still talking that same kind of foolishness that you never could decide whether it didn't make any sense or not, and took one of the pipes from the bowl and begun to look around the desk until I went and shoved the tobacco jar up and he looked at the jar and said, "Oh yes, thanks," and put the pipe down, still talking. Then Ratliff came in and went to the cooler and got a glass and the spoon and sugar-bowl from the cabinet and took a pint bottle of white whiskey from inside his shirt, Uncle Gavin still talking, and made the toddy and came and held it out.

"Here," he said.

"Why, much obliged," Uncle Gavin said. "That looks fine. That sure looks fine." But he didn't touch it. He didn't even take it while Ratliff set it down on the desk where I reckon it was still sitting when Clefus came in the next morning to sweep the office and found it and probably had already started to throw it out when he caught his hand back in time to smell it or recognise it or anyway drink it. And now Uncle Gavin took up the pipe again and filled it and fumbled in his pocket and then Ratliff held out a match and Uncle Gavin stopped talking and looked at it and said, "What?" Then he said, "Thanks," and took the match and scratched it carefully on the underside of the desk and blew it carefully out and put it into the tray and put the pipe into the tray and folded his hands on the desk and said to Ratliff:

"So maybe you can tell me because for the life of me, I cant figure it out. Why did she do it? Why? Because as a rule women dont really care about facts just so they fit; it's just men that dont give a damn whether they fit or not, who is hurt, how many are hurt, just so they are hurt bad enough. So I want to ask your opinion. You know women, travelling around the country all day long right in the middle of them, from one parlor to another all day long all high and mighty, as dashing and smooth and welcome as if you were a damned rush—" and stopped and Ratliff said,

"What? What rush? Rush where?"

"Did I say rush?" Uncle Gavin said. "No no, I said Why? a young girl's grief and anguish when young girls like grief and anguish and besides, they can get over it. Will get over it. And just a week from her birthday too of course but after all Flem is the one to get the zero for that: for missing by a whole week anything as big as a young girl's nineteenth birthday. Besides, forget all that; didn't somebody just say that young girls really like grief and anguish? No no, what I said was, Why?" He sat there looking at Ratliff. "Why? Why did she have to? Why did she? The waste. The terrible waste. To waste all that, when it was not hers to waste, not hers to destroy because it is too valuable, belonged to too many, too little of it to waste, destroy, throw away and be no more." He looked at Ratliff. "Tell me, V.K. Why?"

"Maybe she was bored," Ratliff said.

"Bored," Uncle Gavin said. Then he said it again, not loud: "Bored." And that was when he began to cry, sitting there straight in the chair behind the desk with his hands folded together on the desk, not even hiding his face. "Yes," he said. "She was bored. She loved, had a capacity to love, for love, to give and accept love. Only she tried twice and failed twice to find somebody not just strong enough to deserve, earn it, match it, but even brave enough to accept it. Yes," he said, sitting there crying, not even trying to hide his face from us, "of course she was bored."

And one more thing. One morning—it was summer again now, July—the north-bound train from New Orleans stopped and the first man off was usually the Negro porter—not the pullman porters, they were always back down the track at the end; we hardly ever saw them, but the one from the day coaches at the front end—to get down and strut a little while he talked to the section hands and the other Negroes that were always around to meet the passenger trains. But this time it was the conductor himself, almost jumping down before the train stopped, with the white flagman at his heels, almost stepping on them; the porter himself didn't get off at all: just his head sticking out a window about half way down the car.

Then four things got off. I mean, they were children. The tallest was a girl though we never did know whether she was the oldest or just the tallest, then two boys, all three in overalls, and then a little one in a single garment down to its heels like a man's shirt made out of a flour- or meal-sack or maybe a scrap of an old tent. Wired to the front of each one of them was a shipping tag written in pencil:

> From: Byron Snopes, El Paso, Texas
> To: Mr Flem Snopes, Jefferson, Mississippi

Though Mr Snopes wasn't there. He was busy being a banker now and a deacon in the Baptist church, living in solitary widowerhood in the old De Spain house which he had remodeled into an ante-bellum Southern mansion; he wasn't there to meet them. It was Dink Quistenberry. He had married one of Mr Snopes's sisters or nieces or something out at Frenchman's Bend and when Mr Snopes sent I.O. Snopes back to the country the Quistenberrys came in to buy or rent or anyway run the Snopes Hotel, which wasn't the Snopes Hotel anymore now but the Jefferson Hotel though the people that stayed there were still the stock traders and juries locked up by the Circuit Court. I mean, Dink was old enough to be Mr Snopes's brother-in-law or whatever it was but he was the kind of man it just didn't occur to you to say Mister to.

He was there; I reckon Mr Snopes sent him. And when he saw them I reckon he felt just like we did when we saw them, and like the conductor and the flagman and the porter all looked like they had been feeling ever since the train left New Orleans, which was evidently where they got on it. Because they didn't look like people. They looked like snakes. Or maybe that's too strong too. Anyway, they didn't look like children; if there was one thing in the world they didn't look like it was children, with kind of dark pasty faces and black hair that looked like somebody had put a bowl on top of their heads and then cut their hair up to the rim of the bowl with a dull knife, and perfectly black perfectly still eyes that nobody in Jefferson (Yoknapatawpha County either) ever afterward claimed they saw blink.

I dont know how Dink talked to them because the conductor had already told everybody listening (there was a good crowd by that time) that they didn't talk any language or anything else that he had ever heard of and that to watch them because one of them had a switch knife with a six-inch blade, he didn't know which one and he himself wasn't going to try to find out. But anyway Dink got them into his car and the train went on.

Maybe it was the same thing they used in drugstores or at least with Skeets McGowan in Christian's because it wasn't a week before they could go into Christian's, all four of them (it was always all four of them, as if when the medicine man or whoever it was separated each succeeding one from the mother, he just attached the severed cord to the next senior child. Because by that time we knew who they were: Byron Snopes's children out of a Jicarilla Apache squaw in Old Mexico), and come out two minutes later all eating ice cream cones.

They were always together and anywhere in town or near it at any time of day, until we found out it was any time of night too; one night at two oclock in the morning when Otis Harker caught them coming in single file from behind the coca cola bottling plant; Otis said he didn't know how in the world they got into it because no door was open nor window broken, but he could smell warm coca cola syrup spilled down the front of the little one's nightshirt or dressing-sacque or whatever it was from five or six feet away. Because that was as close as he got; he said he hollered at them to go on home to the Snopes, I mean the Jefferson Hotel but they just stood there looking at him and he said he never intended anything: just to get them moving since maybe they didn't understand what he meant yet. So he sort of flung his arms out and was just kind of jumping at them, hollering again, when he stopped himself just in time, the knife already in one of their hands with the blade open at least six inches long; so fast that he never even saw where it came from and in the next minute gone so fast he still didn't even know which one of the three in overalls—the girl or the two boys—had it; that was when Mr Connors went to Dink Quistenberry the next morning and told him he would have to keep them off the streets at night.

"Sure," Dink said. "You try it. You keep them off the streets or off anywhere else. You got my full permission. You're welcome to it!"

So when the dog business happened, even Mr Hub Hampton himself didn't get any closer than that to them. This was the dog business. We were getting paved streets in Jefferson now and so more new families, engineers and contractors and such like the little Riddell boy's that gave us that holiday two years ago, had moved to Jefferson. One of them didn't have any children but they had a Cadillac and his wife had a dog that they said cost five hundred dollars, the only dog higher than fifty dollars except a field-trial pointer or setter (and a part Airedale bear dog named Lion that Major de Spain, Mr de Spain's father, owned once that hunting people in north Mississippi still talked about) that Jefferson ever heard of, let alone saw—a Pekinese with a gold name-plate on its collar that probably didn't even know it was a dog, that rode in the Cadillac and sneered through the window not just at other dogs but at people too, and even ate special meat that Mr Wall Snopes's butcher ordered special from Kansas City because it cost too much for just people to buy and eat it.

One day it disappeared. Nobody knew how, since the only time it wasn't sneering out through the Cadillac window, it was sneering out through a window in the house where it—they—lived. But it was gone and I dont think anywhere else ever saw a woman take on over anything like Mrs Widrington did, with rewards in all the Memphis and north Mississippi and west Tennessee and east Arkansas papers and Mr Hampton and Mr Connors neither able to sleep at night for Mrs Widrington ringing their telephone, and the man from the insurance company (its life was insured too so maybe there were more people insured in Jefferson than there were dogs but then there was more of them not insured in Jefferson than there was dogs too) and Mrs Widrington herself likely at almost any time day or night to be in your back yard calling what Aleck Sander and I thought was Yow! Yow! Yow! until Uncle Gavin told us it was named Lao T'se for a Chinese poet. Until one day the four Snopes Indians came out of Christian's drugstore and somebody passing on the street pointed his finger and hollered "Look!"

It was the collar with the gold name-plate. The little one was wearing it around its neck above the nightshirt. Mr Connors came quick and sent about as quick for Mr Hampton. And that was when Mr Hampton didn't come any closer either and I reckon we all were thinking about what he was: what a mess that big gut of his would make on the sidewalk if he got too close to that knife before he knew it. And the four Snopes Indians or Indian Snopeses, whichever is right, standing in a row watching him, not looking dangerous, not looking anything; not innocent especially and nobody would have called it affectionate, but not dangerous in the same sense that four shut pocket knives dont look threatening. They look like four shut pocket knives but they dont look lethal. Until Mr Hampton said:

"What do they do when they aint eating ice cream up here or breaking in or out of that bottling plant at two oclock in the morning?"

"They got a kind of camp or reservation or whatever you might call it in a cave they dug in the big ditch behind the school house," Mr Connors said.

"Did you look there?" Mr Hampton said.

"Sure," Mr Connors said. "Nothing there but just some trash and bones and stuff they play with."

"Bones?" Mr Hampton said. "What bones?"

"Just bones," Mr Connors said. "Chicken bones, spare ribs, stuff like that they been eating I reckon."

So Mr Hampton went and got in his car and Mr Connors went to his that had the red light and the sireen on it and a few others got in while there was still room, and the two cars went to the school house, the rest of us walking because we wanted to see if Mr Hampton with his belly really would try to climb down into that ditch and if he did how he was going to get out again. But he did it, with Mr Connors showing him where the cave was but letting him go first since he was the sheriff, on to where the little pile of bones was behind the fireplace and turned them over with his toe and then raked a few of them to one side. Because he was a hunter, a woodsman, a good one before his belly got too big to go through a thicket. "There's your dog," he said.

And I remember that time, five years ago now, we were all at the table and Matt Levitt's cut-out passing in the street and Father said at Uncle Gavin: "What's that sound I smell?" Except that Mr Snopes's brass business at the power-plant was before I was even born: Uncle Gavin's office that morning and Mrs Widrington and the insurance man because the dog's life had been insured only against disease or accident or acts of God, and the insurance man's contention (I reckon he had been in Jefferson long enough to have talked with Ratliff; any stranger in town for just half a day, let alone almost a week, would find himself doing that) was that four half-Snopeses and half-Jicarilla Apache Indians were none of them and so Jefferson itself was liable and vulnerable to suit. So I had only heard about Mr Snopes and the missing brass from Uncle Gavin, but I thought about what Father said that day because I had been there then: "What's that sound I smell?" when Mr Snopes came in, removing his hat and saying "Morning" to everybody without saying it to anybody; then to the insurance man: "How much on that dog?"

"Full pedigree value, Mr Snopes. Five hundred dollars," the insurance man said and Mr Snopes (the insurance man himself got up and turned his chair around to the desk for him) sat down and took a blank check from his pocket and filled in the amount and pushed it across the desk in front of Uncle Gavin and got up and said "Morning" without saying it to anybody and put his hat on and went out.

Except that he didn't quite stop there. Because the next day Byron Snopes's Indians were gone. Ratliff came in and told us.

"Sho," he said. "Flem sent them out to the Bend. Neither of their grandmaws, I mean I.O.'s wives, would have them but finally Dee-wit Binford"—Dewitt Binford had married

another of the Snopes girls. They lived near Varner's store—
"taken them in. On a contract, the Snopeses all clubbing together pro rata and paying Dee-wit a dollar a head a week on
them, providing of course he can last a week. Though naturally the first four dollars was in advance, what you might call
a retainer you might say."

It was. I mean, just about a week. Ratliff came in again; it
was in the morning. "We jest finished using up Frenchman's
Bend at noon yesterday, and that jest about cleans up the
county. We're down at the dee-po now, all tagged and the
waybill paid, waiting for Number Twenty-Three southbound
or any other train that will connect more or less or there-
abouts for El Paso, Texas"—telling about that too: "A combination you might say of scientific interest and what's that
word?" until Uncle Gavin told him anthropological "anthropological coincidence; them four vanishing Americans coming
durn nigh taking one white man with them if Clarence
Snopes's maw and a few neighbors hadn't got there in time."

He told it: how when Dewitt Binford got them home he
discovered they wouldn't stay in a bed at all, dragging a quilt
off onto the floor and lying in a row on it and the next morning he and his wife found the bedstead itself dismantled and
leaned against the wall in a corner out of the way; and that
they hadn't heard a sound during the process. He—Dewitt—
said that's what got on his mind even before he began to
worry about the little one: you couldn't hear them; you
didn't even know they were in the house or not, when they
had entered it or left it; for all you knew, they might be right
there in your bedroom in the dark, looking at you.

"So he tried it," Ratliff said. "He went over to Tull's and
borrowed Vernon's flashlight and waited until about midnight and he said he never moved quieter in his life, across the
hall to the door of the room, trying to not even breathe if he
could help it; he had done already cut two sighting notches in
the door-frame so that when he laid the flashlight into them
by feel it would be aimed straight at where the middle two
heads would be on the pallet; and held his breath again, listening until he was sho there wasn't a sound, and snapped on
the light. And them four faces and them eight black eyes already laying there wide open looking straight at him.

"And Dee-wit said he would like to a give up then. But by that time that least un wouldn't give him no rest a-tall. Only he didn't know what to do because he had done been warned about that knife even if he hadn't never seen it. Then he remembered them pills, that bottle of knock-out opium pills that Doc Peabody had give Miz Dee-wit that time the brooder lamp blowed up and burnt most of her front hair off so he taken eight of them and bought four bottles of sody pop at the store and put two capsules into each bottle and druv the caps back on and hid the bottles jest exactly where he figgered they would have to hunt jest exactly hard enough to find them. And by dark the four bottles was gone and he waited again to be sho it had had plenty of time to work and taken Vernon's flashlight and went across the hall and got on his hands and knees and crawled across to the pallet—he knowed by practice now exactly where on the pallet that least un slept or anyway laid—and reached out easy and found the hem of that nightshirt with one hand and the flashlight ready to snap on in the other.

"And when he told about it, he was downright crying, not with jest skeer so much as pure and simple unbelief. 'I wasn't doing nothing,' he says. 'I wasn't going to hurt it. All in the world I wanted was jest to see which it was—'"

"Which is it?" Uncle Gavin said.

"That's what I'm telling you," Ratliff said. "He never even got to snap the flashlight on. He jest felt them two thin quick streaks of fire, one down either cheek of his face; he said that all that time he was already running backward on his hands and knees toward the door he knowed there wouldn't even be time to turn around, let alone get up on his feet to run, not to mention shutting the door behind him; and when he run back into his and Miz Dee-wit's room there wouldn't be no time to shut that one neither except he had to, banging it shut and hollering for Miz Dee-wit now, dragging the bureau against it while Miz Dee-wit lit the lamp and then come and holp him until he hollered at her to shut the windows first; almost crying, with them two slashes running from each ear, jest missing his eye on one side, right down to the corners of his mouth like a great big grin that would bust scab and all if he ever let his face go, telling how they would decide that the best thing would be to put the lamp out too and set in the dark until he remembered how they had managed somehow to get inside that locked-up coca cola plant without even touching the patented burglar alarm.

"So they jest shut and locked the windows and left the lamp burning, setting there in that air-tight room on that hot summer night, until it come light enough for Miz Dee-wit to at least jump and dodge on the way back to the kitchen to start a fire in the stove and cook breakfast. Though the house was empty then. Not safe of course: jest empty except for themselves while they tried to decide whether to try to get word in to Flem or Hub Hampton to come out and get them, or jest pack up themselves without even waiting to wash up the breakfast dishes, and move over to Tull's. Anyhow Dee-wit said him and Miz Dee-wit was through and they knowed it, four dollars a week or no four dollars a week; and so, it was about nine oclock, he was on his way to the store to use the telephone to call Jefferson, when Miz I.O. Snopes, I mean the Number Two one that got superseded back before she ever had a chance to move to town, saved him the trouble."

We knew Clarence Snopes ourselves. He would be in town every Saturday, or every other time he could get a ride in, according to Ratliff—a big hulking man now, eighteen or nineteen, who was all a gray color: a graying tinge to his tow-colored hair, a grayish pasty look to his flesh, which looked as if it would not flow blood from a wound but instead a pallid fluid like thin oatmeal; he was the only Snopes or resident of Frenchman's Bend or Yoknapatawpha County either for that matter, who made his Texas cousins welcome. "You might say he adopted them," Ratliff said. "Right from that first day. He even claimed he could talk to them and that he was going to train them to hunt in a pack; they would be better than any jest pack of dogs because sooner or later dogs always quit and went home, while it didn't matter to them where they was.

"So he trained them. The first way he done it was to set a bottle of sody pop on a stump in front of the store with a string running from it to where he would be setting on the gallery, until they would maneuver around and finally bushwack up to where one of them could reach for it, when he would snatch it off the stump with the string and drag it out of their reach. Only that never worked but once so then he would have to drink the bottles empty and then fill them again with muddy water or some such, or another good training method was to gather up a few throwed-away candy bar papers and wrap them up again with mud inside or maybe jest not nothing a-tall because it taken them a good while to give up then, especially if now and then he had a sho enough candy bar or a sho enough bottle of strawberry or orange shuffled into the other ones.

"Anyhow he was always with them, hollering at them and waving his arms to go this way or that way when folks was watching, like dogs; they even had some kind of a play house or cave or something in another ditch about half a mile up the road. That's right. What you think you are laughing at is the notion of a big almost growed man like Clarence, playing, until all of a sudden you find out that what you're laughing at is calling anything playing that them four things would be interested in.

"So Dee-wit had jest reached the store when here come Clarence's maw, down the road hollering 'Them Indians! Them Indians!' jest like that: a pure and simple case of mother love and mother instinct. Because likely she didn't know anything yet and even if she had, in that state she couldn't a told nobody: jest standing there in the road in front of the store wringing her hands and hollering Them Indians until the men squatting along the gallery begun to get up and then to run because about that time Dee-wit come up. Because he knowed what Miz Snopes was trying to say. Maybe he never had no mother love and mother instinct but then neither did Miz Snopes have a last-night's knife-slash down both cheeks.

"'Them Indians?' he says. 'Fore God, men, run. It may already be too late.'

"But it wasn't. They was in time. Pretty soon they could hear Clarence bellowing and screaming and then they could line him out and the fastest ones run on ahead and down into the ditch to where Clarence was tied to a blackjack sapling with something less than a cord of wood stacked around him jest beginning to burn good.

"So they was in time. Jody telephoned Flem right away and in fact all this would a formally took place yesterday evening except that Clarence's hunting pack never reappeared in sight until this morning when Dee-wit lifted the shade enough to see them waiting on the front gallery for breakfast. But then his house was barred in time because he hadn't never unbarred it from last night. And Jody's car was already standing by on emergency alert as they say and it wasn't much trouble to toll them into it since like Clarence said one place was jest like another to them.

"So they're down at the dee-po now. Would either of you gentlemen like to go down with me and watch what they call the end of a erea, if that's what they call what I'm trying to say? The last and final end of Snopes out-and-out unvarnished behavior in Jefferson, if that's what I'm trying to say?"

So Ratliff and I went to the station while he told me the rest of it. It was Miss Emily Habersham; she had done the telephoning herself: to the Travellers' Aid in New Orleans to meet the Jefferson train and put them on the one for El Paso, and to the El Paso Aid to get them across the border and turn them over to the Mexican police to send them back home, to Byron Snopes or the reservation or wherever it was. Then I noticed the package and said, "What's that?" but he didn't answer. He just parked the pickup and took the cardboard carton and we went around onto the platform where they were: the three in the overalls and what Ratliff called the least un in the nightshirt, each with the new shipping tag wired to the front of its garment, but printed in big block capitals this time, like shouting this time:

> From: Flem Snopes, Jefferson, Miss.
> To: BYRON SNOPES
>   EL PASO, TEXAS

There was a considerable crowd around them, at a safe distance, when we came up and Ratliff opened the carton; it contained four of everything: four oranges and apples and candy bars and bags of peanuts and packages of chewing gum.

"Watch out, now," Ratliff said. "Maybe we better set it on the ground and shove it up with a stick or something." But he didn't mean that. Anyway, he didn't do it. He just said to me, "Come on; you aint quite growed so they may not snap at you," and moved near and held out one of the oranges, the eight eyes not once looking at it nor at us nor at anything that we could see; until the girl, the tallest one, said something, something quick and brittle that sounded quite strange in the treble of a child; whereupon the first hand came out and took the orange, then the next and the next, orderly, not furtive: just quick, while Ratliff and I dealt out the fruit and bars and paper bags, the empty hand already extended again, the objects vanishing somewhere faster than we could follow, except the little one in the nightshirt which apparently had no pockets: until the girl herself leaned and relieved the overflow.

Then the train came in and stopped; the day coach vestibule clanged and clashed open, the narrow steps hanging downward from the orifice like a narrow dropped jaw. Evidently, obviously, Miss Habersham had telephoned a trainmaster or a superintendent (maybe a vice president) somewhere too because the conductor and the porter both got down and the conductor looked rapidly at the four tags and motioned, and we—all of us; we represented Jefferson—watched them mount and vanish one by one into that iron impatient maw: the girl and the two boys in overalls and Ratliff's least un in its ankle-length single garment like a man's discarded shirt made out of flour- or meal-sacking or perhaps the remnant of an old tent. We never did know which it was.

Oxford–Charlottesville–Washington–New York
November 1955–September 1956.

THE MANSION

VOLUME THREE

Snopes

To PHIL STONE

CONTENTS

THE MANSION

This book is the final chapter of, and the summation of, a work conceived and begun in 1925. Since the author likes to believe, hopes that his entire life's work is a part of a living literature, and since "living" is motion, and "motion" is change and alteration and therefore the only alternative to motion is un-motion, stasis, death, there will be found discrepancies and contradictions in the thirty-four-year progress of this particular chronicle; the purpose of this note is simply to notify the reader that the author has already found more discrepancies and contradictions than he hopes the reader will—contradictions and discrepancies due to the fact that the author has learned, he believes, more about the human heart and its dilemma than he knew thirty-four years ago; and is sure that, having lived with them that long time, he knows the characters in this chronicle better than he did then.

W. F.

MINK

One

THE JURY said "Guilty" and the Judge said "Life" but he didn't hear them. He wasn't listening. In fact, he hadn't been able to listen since that first day when the Judge banged his little wooden hammer on the high desk until he, Mink, dragged his gaze back from the far door of the courtroom to see what in the world the man wanted, and he, the Judge, leaned down across the desk hollering: "You, Snopes! Did you or didn't you kill Zack Houston?" and he, Mink, said, "Dont bother me now. Cant you see I'm busy?" then turned his own head to look again toward the distant door at the back of the room, himself hollering into, against, across the wall of little wan faces hemming him in: "Snopes! Flem Snopes! Anybody here that'll go and bring Flem Snopes! I'll pay you—Flem'll pay you!"

Because he hadn't had time to listen. In fact, that whole first trip, handcuffed to the deputy, from his jail cell to the courtroom, had been a senseless, a really outrageously foolish interference with and interruption, and each subsequent daily manacled trip and transference, of the solution to both their problems—his and the damned law's both—if they had only waited and let him alone: the watching, his dirty hands gripping among the grimed interstices of the barred window above the street, which had been his one, his imperious need during the entire two months between his incarceration and the opening of the Court.

At first, during the first few days behind the barred window, he had simply been impatient with his own impatience and—yes, he admitted it—his own stupidity. Long before the moment came when he had had to aim the gun and fire the shot, he knew that his cousin Flem, the only member of his clan with the power to and the reason to, or at least to be expected to, extricate him from its consequences, would not be there to do it. He even knew why Flem would not be there for at least a year; Frenchman's Bend was too small: everybody in it knew everything about everybody else; they would all have seen through that Texas trip even without the hurrah and hulla-baloo that Varner girl had been causing ever since she (or whoever else it was) found the first hair on her bump, not to mention just this last past spring and summer while that durn McCarron boy was snuffing and fighting everybody else off exactly like a gang of rutting dogs.

So that long before Flem married her, he, Mink, and every-body else in ten miles of the Bend knew that old Will Varner was going to have to marry her off to somebody, and that quick, if he didn't want a woods-colt in his back yard next grass. And when it was Flem that finally married her, he, Mink, anyway was not surprised. It was Flem, with his usual luck. All right, more than just luck then: the only man in Frenchman's Bend that ever stood up to and held his own with old Will Varner; that had done already more or less elim-inated Jody, old Will's only son, out of the store, and now was fixing to get hold of half of all the rest of it by being old Will's only son-in-law. That just by marrying her in time to save her from dropping a bastard, Flem would not only be the rightful husband of that damn girl that had kept every man under eighty years old in Frenchman's Bend in an uproar ever since she was fifteen years old by just watching her walk past, but he had got paid for it to boot: not only the right to fum-ble his hand every time the notion struck him under that dress that rutted a man just thinking even about somebody else's hand doing it, but was getting a free deed to that whole Old Frenchman place for doing it.

So he knew Flem would not be there when he would need him, since he knew that Flem and his new wife would have to stay away from Frenchman's Bend at least long enough for what they would bring back with them to be able to call itself only twelve months old without everybody that looked at it dying of laughing. Only, when the moment finally came, when the instant finally happened when he could no longer defer having to aim the gun and pull the trigger, he had for-got that. No, that was a lie. He hadn't forgot it. He simply could wait no longer: Houston himself would not let him wait longer—and that too was one more injury which Zack Houston in the very act of dying, had done him: compelled him, Mink, to kill him at a time when the only person who had the power to save him and would have had to save him whether he wanted to or not because of the ancient immutable laws of simple blood kinship, was a thousand miles away; and this time it was an irreparable injury because in the very act of committing it, Houston had escaped forever all retribution for it.

He had not forgotten that his cousin would not be there. He simply couldn't wait any longer. He had simply had to trust *them*—the *Them* of whom it was promised that not even a sparrow should fall unmarked. By *them* he didn't mean that whatever-it-was that folks referred to as Old Moster. He didn't believe in any Old Moster. He had seen too much in his time that, if any Old Moster existed, with eyes as sharp and power as strong as was claimed He had, He would have done something about. Besides, he, Mink, wasn't religious. He hadn't been to a church since he was fifteen years old and never aimed to go again—places which a man with a hole in his gut and a rut in his britches that he couldn't satisfy at home, used, by calling himself a preacher of God, to get conveniently together the biggest possible number of women that he could tempt with the reward of the one in return for the job of the other—the job of filling his hole in payment for getting theirs plugged the first time the husband went to the field and she could slip off to the bushes where the preacher was waiting; the wives coming because here was the best market they knowed of to swap a mess of fried chicken or a sweet potato pie; the husbands coming not to interrupt the trading because he knowed he couldn't interrupt it or even keep up with it, but at least to try and find out if his wife's name would come to the head of the waiting list today or if maybe he could still finish scratching that last forty before he would have to tie her to the bedpost and hide behind the door watching; and the young folks not even bothering to enter the church a-tall for already running to be the first couple behind the nearest handy thicket-bush.

He meant, simply, that *them—they—it*, whichever and whatever you wanted to call it, who represented a simple fundamental justice and equity in human affairs, or else a man might just as well quit; the *they, them, it*, call them what you like, which simply would not, could not harass and harry a man forever without someday, at some moment, letting him get his own just and equal licks back in return. They could harass and worry him, or They could even just sit back and watch everything go against him right along without missing a lick, almost like there was a pattern to it; just sit back and watch and—all right, why not? he—a man—didn't mind, as long as he was a man and there was a justice to it—enjoy it too; maybe in fact They were even testing him, to see if he was a man or not, man enough to take a little harassment and worry and so deserve his own licks back when his turn came. But at least that moment would come when it was his turn, when he had earned the right to have his own just and equal licks back, just as They had earned the right to test him and even to enjoy the testing; the moment when They would have to prove to him that They were as much a man as he had proved to Them that he was; when he not only would have to depend on Them but had won the right to depend on Them and find Them faithful; and They dared not, They would not dare, to let him down, else it would be as hard for Them to live with themselves afterward as it had finally become for him to live with himself and still keep on taking what he had taken from Zack Houston.

So he knew that morning that Flem was not going to be there. It was simply that he could wait no longer; the moment had simply come when he and Zack Houston could, must, no longer breathe the same air. And so, lacking his cousin's presence, he must fall back on that right to depend on *them* which he had earned by never before in his life demanding anything of them.

It began in the spring. No, it began in the fall before. No, it began a long time before that even. It began at the very instant Houston was born already shaped for arrogance and intolerance and pride. Not at the moment when the two of them, he, Mink Snopes also, began to breathe the same north Mississippi air, because he, Mink, was not a contentious man. He had never been. It was simply that his own bad luck had all his life continually harassed and harried him into the constant and unflagging necessity of defending his own simple rights.

Though it was not until the summer before that first fall that Houston's destiny had actually and finally impinged on his, Mink's, own fate—which was another facet of the outrage: that nothing, not even *they*, least of all *they*, had vouchsafed him any warning of what that first encounter would end in. This was the year after Houston's young wife had gone into the stallion's stall hunting a hen-nest and the horse had killed her and any decent man would have thought that any decent husband would have destroyed the horse as fast as he could have run to the house and got his pistol. But not Houston. Houston was not only rich enough to own a blooded stallion capable of killing his wife, but arrogant and intolerant enough to defy all decency afterward and keep the horse: supposed to be so grieving over his wife that even the neighbors didn't dare knock on his front door anymore, yet two or three times a week ripping up and down the road on that next murderer of a horse, with that big Bluetick hound running like a greyhound or another horse along beside it, right up to Varner's store and not even getting down: the three of them just waiting there in the road—the arrogant intolerant man and the bad-eyed horse and the dog that bared its teeth and raised its hackles any time anybody went near it—while Houston ordered whoever was on the front gallery to step inside and fetch him out whatever it was he had come for like they were Negroes.

Until one morning when he, Mink, was walking to the store (he had no horse to ride when he had to go for a tin of snuff or a bottle of quinine or a piece of meat); he had just come over the brow of a short hill when he heard the horse behind him, coming fast and hard, and he would have given Houston the whole road if he had had time, the horse already on top of him until Houston wrenched it savagely off and past, the damn hound leaping so close it almost brushed his chest, snarling right into his face, Houston whirling the horse and holding it dancing and plunging, shouting down at him: "Why in hell didn't you jump when you heard me coming? Get off the road! Do you still want him to beat your brains out too before I can get him down again?"

Well, maybe that was what they call grieving for the wife that maybe you didn't actually kill her yourself but at least you were either too fond of the horse or rich enough to afford to be too stingy to get rid of what did kill her. Which was all right with him, Mink, especially since all anybody had to do was just wait until sooner or later the son of a bitching horse would kill Houston too; until the next thing happened which he had not counted on, planned on, not even anticipated.

It was his milk cow, the only one he owned, not being a rich man like Houston but only an independent one, asking no favors of any man, paying his own way. She—the cow—had missed someway, failed to freshen; and there he was, not only having gone a winter without milk and now faced with another whole year without it, he had also missed out on the calf for which he had had to pay a fifty-cents cash bull fee since the only bull in reach he could get for less than a dollar was the scrub bull belonging to a Negro who insisted on cash at the gate.

So he fed the cow all that winter, waiting for the calf which wasn't even there. Then he had to lead the cow the three miles back to the Negro's house, not to claim the return of the fifty cents but only to claim a second stand from the bull, which the Negro refused to permit without the payment in advance of another fifty cents, he, Mink, standing in the yard cursing the Negro until the Negro went back into the house and shut the door, Mink standing in the empty yard cursing the Negro and his family inside the blank house until he had exhausted himself enough to lead the still-barren cow the three miles again back home.

Then he had to keep the barren and worthless cow up inside fence while she exhausted his own meagre pasture, then he had to feed her out of his meagre crib during the rest of that summer and fall, since the local agreement was that all stock would be kept up until all crops were out of the field. Which meant November before he could turn her out for the winter. And even then he had to divert a little feed to her from his winter's meat-hogs, to keep her in the habit of coming more or less back home at night; until she had been missing three or four days and he finally located her in Houston's pasture with his beef herd.

In fact, he was already in the lane leading to Houston's

house, the coiled plowline in his hand, when without even knowing he was going to and without even pausing or breaking stride he had turned about, already walking back toward home, rapidly stuffing the coiled rope inside his shirt where it would be concealed, not to return to the paintless repairless tenant cabin in which he lived, but simply to find privacy in which to think, stopping presently to sit on a log beside the road while he realised the full scope of what had just dawned before him.

By not claiming the worthless cow yet, he would not only winter her, he would winter her twice—ten times—as well as he himself could afford to. He would not only let Houston winter her (Houston, a man not only rich enough to be able to breed and raise beef cattle, but rich enough to keep a Negro to do nothing else save feed and tend them—a Negro to whom Houston furnished a better house to live in than the one that he, Mink, a white man with a wife and two daughters, lived in) but when he would reclaim the cow in the spring she would have come in season again and, running with Houston's beef herd bull, would now be carrying a calf which would not only freshen her for milk but would itself be worth money as grade beef where the offspring of the Negro's scrub bull would have been worth almost nothing.

Naturally he would have to be prepared for the resulting inevitable questions; Frenchman's Bend was too little, too damn little for a man to have any privacy about what he did, let alone about what he owned or lacked. It didn't even take four days. It was at Varner's store, where he would walk down to the crossroads and back every day, giving them a chance to go ahead and get it over with. Until finally one said—he didn't remember who; it didn't matter: "Aint you located your cow yet?"

"What cow?" he said. The other said,

"Zack Houston says for you to come and get that bone-rack of yours out of his feed-lot; he's tired of boarding it."

"Oh, that," he said. "That aint my cow anymore. I sold that cow last summer to one of the Gowrie boys up at Caledonia Chapel."

"I'm glad to hear that," the other said. "Because if I was

you and my cow was in Zack Houston's feed-lot, I would take my rope and go and get it, without even noticing myself doing it, let alone letting Zack Houston notice me. I dont believe I would interrupt him right now even to say Much obliged." Because all Frenchman's Bend knew Houston: sulking and sulling in his house all alone by himself since the stallion killed his wife two years ago. Like nobody before him had ever lost a wife, even when, for whatever incomprehensible reason the husband could have had, he didn't want to get shut of her. Sulking and sulling alone on that big place with two nigger servants, the man and the woman to cook, and the stallion and the big Bluetick hound that was as high-nosed and intolerant and surly as Houston himself—a durn surly sullen son of a bitch that didn't even know he was lucky: rich, not only rich enough to afford a wife to whine and nag and steal his pockets ragged of every dollar he made, but rich enough to do without a wife if he wanted: rich enough to be able to hire a woman to cook his victuals instead of having to marry her. Rich enough to hire another nigger to get up in his stead on the cold mornings and go out in the wet and damp to feed not only the beef cattle which he sold at the top fat prices because he could afford to hold them till then, but that blooded stallion too, and even that damn hound running beside the horse he thundered up and down the road on, until a fellow that never had anything but his own two legs to travel on, would have to jump clean off the road into the bushes or the son of a bitching horse would have killed him too with its shod feet and left him laying there in the ditch for the son of a bitching hound to eat before Houston would even have reported it.

All right, if Houston was in too high and mighty a mood to be said much obliged to, he, Mink, for one wasn't going to break in on him uninvited. Not that he didn't owe a much obliged to something somewhere. This was a week later, then a month later, then Christmas had passed and the hard wet dreary winter had set in. Each afternoon, in the slicker held together with baling wire and automobile tire patching which was the only winter outer garment he owned over his worn patched cotton overalls, he would walk up the muddy road in the dreary and fading afternoons to watch Houston's pedigreed beef herd, his own sorry animal among them, move, not even hurrying, toward and into the barn which was warmer and tighter against the weather than the cabin he lived in, to be fed by the hired Negro who wore warmer clothing than any he and his family possessed, cursing into the steamy vapor of his own breathing, cursing the Negro for his black skin inside the warmer garments than his, a white man's, cursing the very rich feed devoted to cattle instead of humans even though his own animal shared it; cursing above all the unawares white man through or because of whose wealth such a condition could obtain, cursing the fact that his very revenge and vengeance—what he himself called simple justice and inalienable rights—could not be done at one stroke but instead must depend on the slow incrementation of feed converted to weight, plus the uncontrollable, even un-predictable, love-mood of the cow and the long subsequent nine months of gestation; cursing his own condition that the only justice available to him must be this prolonged and pas-sive one.

That was it. Prolongation. Not only the anguish of hope deferred, not even the outrage of simple justice deferred, but the knowledge that, even when the blow fell on Houston, it would cost him, Mink, eight dollars in cash—the eight dollars which he would have to affirm that the imaginary purchaser of the cow had paid him for the animal in order to make good the lie that he had sold it, which, when he reclaimed the cow in the spring, he would have to give to Houston as an earnest that until that moment he really believed he had sold the animal—or at least had established eight dollars as its value—when he went to Houston and told him how the purchaser had come to him, Mink, only that morning and told him the cow had escaped from the lot the same night he had bought it and brought it home, and so reclaimed the eight dollars he had paid for it, thus establishing the cow not only in Houston's arrogant contempt but in the interested curiosity of the rest of Frenchman's Bend too, as having now cost him, Mink, sixteen dollars to reclaim his own property.

That was the outrage: the eight dollars. The fact that he could not even have wintered the cow for eight dollars, let alone put on it the weight of flesh he could see with his own eyes it now carried, didn't count. What mattered was, he would have to give Houston, who didn't need it and wouldn't even miss the feed the cow had eaten, the eight dollars with which he, Mink, could have bought a gallon of whiskey for Christmas, plus a dollar or two of the gew gaw finery his wife and his two daughters were forever whining at him for.

But there was no help for it. And even then, his pride was that he was not reconciled. Not he to be that meagre and niggling and puny as meekly to accept something just because he didn't see yet how he could help it. More, since this too merely bolstered the anger and rage at the injustice: that he would have to go fawning and even cringing a little when he went to recover his cow; would have to waste a lie for the privilege of giving eight dollars which he wanted, must sacrifice to spare, to a man who didn't even need them, would not even miss their lack, did not even know yet that he was going to receive them. The moment, the day at last at the end of winter when by local custom the livestock which had run loose in the skeletoned cornfields since fall, must be taken up by their owners and put inside fences so the land could be plowed and planted again; one afternoon, evening rather, waiting until his cow had received that final feeding with the rest of Houston's herd before he approached the feed-lot, the worn plowline coiled over his arm and the meagre lump of worn dollar bills and nickels and dimes and quarters wadded into his overall pocket, not needing to fawn and cringe yet because only the Negro with his hayfork would be in the lot now, the rich man himself in the house, the warm kitchen, with in his hand a toddy not of the stinking gagging home-made corn such as he, Mink, would have had to buy with his share of the eight dollars if he could have kept them, but of good red chartered whiskey ordered out of Memphis. Not having to fawn and cringe yet: just saying, level and white-man, to the nigger paused in the door to the feeding shed to look back at him:

"Hidy. I see you got my cow there. Put this rope on her and I'll get her outen your way," the Negro looking back at him a second longer then gone, on through the shed toward the house; not coming back to take the rope, which he, Mink, had not expected anyway, but gone first to tell the white man, to know what to do. Which was exactly what he, Mink, had expected, leaning his cold-raw, cold-reddened wrists which even the frayed slicker sleeves failed to cover, on the top rail of the white-painted fence. Oh yes, Houston with the toddy of good red whiskey in his hand and likely with his boots off and his stocking feet in the oven of the stove, warming for supper, who now, cursing, would have to withdraw his feet and drag on again the cold wet muddy rubber and come back to the lot.

Which Houston did: the very bang of the kitchen door and the squish and slap of the gum boots across the back yard and into the lot sounding startled and outraged. Then he came on through the shed too, the Negro about ten feet behind him. "Hidy, Zack," Mink said. "Too bad to have to roust you out into the cold and wet again. That nigger could have tended to it. I jest learned today you wintered my cow for me. If your nigger'll put this plowline on her, I'll get her out of your way."

"I thought you sold that cow to Nub Gowrie," Houston said.

"So did I," Mink said. "Until Nub rid up this morning on a mule and said that cow broke out of his lot the same night he got her home and he aint seen her since, and collected back the eight dollars he paid me for her," already reaching into his pocket, the meagre wad of frayed notes and coins in his hand. "So, since eight dollars seems to be the price of this cow, I reckon I owe you that for wintering her. Which makes her a sixteen-dollar cow now, dont it, whether she knows it or not. So here. Take your money and let your nigger put this plowline on her and I'll—"

"That cow wasn't worth eight dollars last fall," Houston said. "But she's worth a considerable more now. She's eaten more than sixteen dollars' worth of my feed. Not to mention my young bull topped her last week. It was last week wasn't it, Henry?" he said to the Negro.

"Yes sir," the Negro said. "Last Tuesday. I put it on the book."

"If you had jest notified me sooner I'd have saved the strain on your bull and that nigger and his pitchfork too," Mink said. He said to the Negro: "Here. Take this rope—"

"Hold it," Houston said; he was reaching into his pocket too. "You yourself established the price of that cow at eight dollars. All right. I'll buy her."

"You yourself jest finished establishing the fact that she has done went up since then," Mink said. "I'm trying right now to give the rest of sixteen for her. So evidently I wouldn't take sixteen, let alone jest eight. So take your money. And if your nigger's too wore out to put this rope on her, I'll come in and do it myself." Now he even began to climb the fence.

"Hold it," Houston said again. He said to the Negro: "What would you say she's worth now?"

"She'd bring thirty," the Negro said. "Maybe thirty-five."

"You hear that?" Houston said.

"No," Mink said, still climbing the fence. "I dont listen to niggers: I tell them. If he dont want to put this rope on my cow, tell him to get outen my way."

"Dont cross that fence, Snopes," Houston said.

"Well well," Mink said, one leg over the top rail, the coil of rope dangling from one raw-red hand, "dont tell me you bring a pistol along ever time you try to buy a cow. Maybe you even tote it to put a cotton seed or a grain of corn in the ground too?" It was tableau: Mink with one leg over the top rail, Houston standing inside the fence, the pistol hanging in one hand against his leg, the Negro not moving either, not looking at anything, the whites of his eyes just showing a little. "If you had sent me word, maybe I could a brought a pistol too."

"All right," Houston said. He laid the pistol carefully on the top of the fence post beside him. "Put that rope down. Get over the fence at your post. I'll back off one post and you can count three and we'll see who uses it to trade with."

"Or maybe your nigger can do the counting," Mink said. "All he's got to do is say Three. Because I aint got no nigger with me neither. Evidently a man needs a tame nigger and a pistol both to trade livestock with you." He swung his leg back to the ground outside the fence. "So I reckon I'll jest step over to the store and have a word with Uncle Billy and the constable. Maybe I ought to done that at first, saved a walk up here in the cold. I would a suh-gested leaving my plowline here, to save toting it again, only likely you would be charging me thirty-five dollars to get it back, since that seems to be your bottom price for anything in your lot that dont belong to you." He was leaving now. "So long then. In case you do make any eight-dollar stock deals, be sho you dont take no wooden nickels."

He walked away steadily enough but in such a thin furious rage that for a while he couldn't even see, and with his ears ringing as if someone had fired a shotgun just over his head. In fact he had expected the rage too and now, in solitude and privacy, was the best possible time to let it exhaust itself. Because he knew now he had anticipated something like what had happened and he would need his wits about him. He had known by instinct that his own outrageous luck would invent something like this, so that even the fact that going to Varner, the justice of the peace, for a paper for the constable to serve on Houston to recover the cow would cost him another two dollars and a half, was not really a surprise to him: it was simply *them* again, still testing, trying him to see just how much he could bear and would stand.

So, in a way, he was not really surprised at what happened next either. It was his own fault in a way: he had simply underestimated *them:* the whole matter of taking the eight dollars to Houston and putting the rope on the cow and leading it back home had seemed too simple, too puny for Them to bother with. But he was wrong; They were not done yet. Varner would not even issue the paper; whereupon two days later there were seven of them, counting the Negro—himself, Houston, Varner and the constable and two professional cattle-buyers—standing along the fence of Houston's feed-lot while the Negro led his cow out for the two experts to examine her.

"Well?" Varner said at last.

"I'd give thirty-five," the first trader said.

"Bred to a paper bull, I might go to thirty-seven and a half," the second said.

"Would you go to forty?" Varner said.

"No," the second said. "She might not a caught."

"That's why I wouldn't even match thirty-seven and a half," the first said.

"All right," Varner said—a tall, gaunt, narrow-hipped heavily-moustached man who looked like what his father had been:

one of Forrest's cavalrymen. "Call it thirty-seven and a half then. So we'll split the difference then." He was looking at Mink now. "When you pay Houston eighteen dollars and seventy-five cents, you can have your cow. Only you haven't got eighteen dollars and seventy-five cents, have you?"

He stood there, his raw red wrists which the slicker did not cover lying quiet on the top rail of the fence, his eyes quite blind again and his ears ringing again as though somebody had fired a shotgun just over his head, and on his face that expression faint and gentle and almost like smiling. "No," he said.

"Wouldn't his cousin Flem let him have it?" the second trader said. Nobody bothered to answer that at all, not even to remind them that Flem was still in Texas on his honeymoon, where he and his wife had been since the marriage last September.

"Then he'll have to work it out," Varner said. He was talking to Houston now. "What have you got that he can do?"

"I'm going to fence in another pasture," Houston said. "I'll pay him fifty cents a day. He can make thirty-seven days and from light till noon on the next one digging post holes and stringing wire. What about the cow? Do I keep her, or does Quick" (Quick was the constable) "take her?"

"Do you want Quick to?" Varner said.

"No," Houston said. "She's been here so long now she might get homesick. Besides if she's here Snopes can see her every day and keep his spirits up about what he's really working for."

"All right, all right," Varner said quickly. "It's settled now. I dont want any more of that now."

That was what he had to do. And his pride still was that he would not be, would never be, reconciled to it. Not even if he were to lose the cow, the animal itself to vanish from the entire equation and leave him in what might be called peace. Which—eliminating the cow—he could have done himself. More: he could have got eighteen dollars and seventy-five cents for doing it, which, with the eight dollars Houston had refused to accept, would have made practically twenty-six dollars, more cash at one time than he had seen in he could not remember when since even with the fall sale of his bale or two of cotton, the subtraction of Varner's landlord's share, plus his furnish bill at Varner's store, barely left him that same eight or ten dollars in cash with which he had believed in vain that he could redeem the cow.

In fact, Houston himself made that suggestion. It was the second or third day of digging the post holes and setting the heavy locust posts in them; Houston came up on the stallion and sat looking down at him. He didn't even pause, let alone look up.

"Look," Houston said. "Look at me." He looked up then, not pausing. Houston's hand was already extended; he, Mink, could see the actual money in it. "Varner said eighteen-seventy-five. All right, here it is. Take it and go on home and forget about that cow." Now he didn't even look up any longer, heaving onto his shoulder the post that anyway looked heavier and more solid than he did and dropping it into the hole, tamping the dirt home with the reversed shovel-handle so that he only had to hear the stallion turn and go away. Then it was the fourth day; again he only needed to hear the stallion come up and stop, not even looking up when Houston said,

"Snopes," then again, "Snopes," then he said, "Mink," he—Mink—not even looking up, let alone pausing while he said:

"I hear you."

"Stop this now. You got to break your land for your crop. You got to make your living. Go on home and get your seed in the ground and then come back."

"I aint got time to make a living," he said, not even pausing. "I got to get my cow back home."

The next morning it was not Houston on the stallion but Varner himself in his buckboard. Though he, Mink, did not know yet that it was Varner himself who was suddenly afraid, afraid for the peace and quiet of the community which he held in his iron usurious hand, buttressed by the mortgages and liens in the vast iron safe in his store. And now he, Mink, did look up and saw money in the closed fist resting on Varner's knee.

"I've put this on your furnish bill for this year," Varner said. "I just come from your place. You aint broke a furrow yet. Pick up them tools and take this money and give it to Zack and take that damn cow on home and get to plowing."

Though this was only Varner; he could pause and even lean on the post-hole digger now. "Have you heard any complaint from me about that-ere cow court judgment of yourn?" he said.

"No," Varner said.

"Then get out of my way and tend to your business while I tend to mine," he said. Then Varner was out of the buckboard—a man already old enough to be called Uncle Billy by the debtors who fawned on him, yet agile too: enough so to jump down from the buckboard in one motion, the lines in one hand and the whip in the other.

"God damn you," he said, "pick up them tools and go on home. I'll be back before dark, and if I dont find a furrow run by then, I'm going to dump every sorry stick you've got in that house out in the road and rent it to somebody else to-morrow morning."

And he, Mink, looking at him, with on his face that faint gentle expression almost like smiling. "Likely you would do jest exactly that," he said.

"You're God-damned right I will," Varner said. "Get on. Now. This minute."

"Why, sholy," he said. "Since that's the next court judgment in this case, and a law-abiding feller always listens to a court judgment." He turned.

"Here," Varner said to his back. "Take this money."

"Aint it?" he said, going on.

By midafternoon he had broke the better part of an acre. When he swung the plow at the turn-row he saw the buckboard coming up the lane. It carried two this time, Varner and the constable, Quick, and it was moving at a snail's pace because, on a lead rope at the rear axle, was his cow. He didn't hurry; he ran out that furrow too, then unhitched the traces and tied the mule to the fence and only then walked on to where the two men still sat in the buckboard, watching him.

"I paid Houston the eighteen dollars and here's your cow," Varner said. "And if ever again I hear of you or anything belonging to you on Zack Houston's land, I'm going to send you to jail."

"And seventy-five cents," he said. "Or maybe them six bits evaporated. That cow's under a court judgment. I cant accept it until that judgment is satisfied."

"Lon," Varner said to the constable in a voice flat and almost gentle, "put that cow in the lot yonder and take that rope off it and get to hell back in this buggy."

"Lon," Mink said in a voice just as gentle and just as flat, "if you put that cow in my lot I'll get my shotgun and kill her."

Nor did he watch them. He went back to the mule and untied the lines from the fence and hooked up the traces and ran another furrow, his back now to the house and the lane, so that not until he swung the mule at the turnrow did he see for a moment the buckboard going back down the lane at that snail's pace matched to the plodding cow. He plowed steadily on until dark, until his supper of the coarse fatback and cheap molasses and probably weevilly flour which, even after he had eaten it, would still be the property of Will Varner until he, Mink, had ginned and sold the cotton next fall which he had not even planted yet.

An hour later, with a coal oil lantern to light dimly the slow lift and thrust of the digger, he was back at Houston's fence. He had not lain down nor even stopped moving, working, since daylight this morning; when daylight came again he would not have slept in twenty-four hours; when the sun did rise on him he was back in his own field with the mule and plow, stopping only for dinner at noon, then back to the field again—or so he thought until he waked to find himself lying in the very furrow he had just run, beneath the canted handles of the still-bedded plow, the anchored mule still standing in the traces and the sun just going down.

Then supper again like last night's meal and this morning's breakfast too, and carrying the lighted lantern he once more crossed Houston's pasture toward where he had left the posthole digger. He didn't even see Houston sitting on the pile of waiting posts until Houston stood up, the shotgun cradled in his left arm. "Go back," Houston said. "Dont never come on my land again after sundown. If you're going to kill yourself, it wont be here. Go back now. Maybe I cant stop you from working out that cow by daylight but I reckon I can after dark."

But he could stand that too. Because he knew the trick of it. He had learned that the hard way; himself taught that to himself through simple necessity: that a man can bear anything by simply and calmly refusing to accept it, be reconciled to it, give up to it. He could even sleep at night now. It was not so much that he had time to sleep now, as because he now had a kind of peace, freed of hurry and haste. He broke the rest of his rented land now, then opened out the middles while the weather held good, using the bad days on Houston's fence, marking off one day less which meant fifty cents less toward the recovery of his cow. But with no haste now, no urgency; when spring finally came and the ground warmed for the reception of seed and he saw before him a long hiatus from the fence because of the compulsion of his own crop, he faced it calmly, getting his corn- and cotton-seed from Varner's store and planting his ground, making a better job of sowing than he had ever done before since all he had to do now was to fill the time until he could get back to the fence and with his own sweat dissolve away another of the half-dollars. Because patience was his pride too: never to be reconciled since by this means he could beat Them; They might be stronger for a moment than he but nobody, no man, no nothing could wait longer than he could wait when nothing else but waiting would do, would work, would serve him.

Then the sun set at last on the day when he could put down patience also along with the digger and the stretchers and what remained of the wire. Houston would know it was the last day too of course. Likely Houston had spent the whole day expecting him to come trotting up the lane to get the cow the minute the sun was below the western trees; likely Houston had spent the whole day from sunrise on in the kitchen window to see him, Mink, show up for that last day's work already carrying the plowline to lead the cow home with. In fact, throughout that whole last day while he dug the last holes and tamped into them not the post at all but the last of that outrage which They had used old Will Varner himself as their tool to try him with, to see how much he really could stand, he could imagine Houston hunting vainly up and down the lane, trying every bush and corner to find where he must have hidden the rope.

Which—the rope—he had not even brought yet, working steadily on until the sun was completely down and no man could say the full day was not finished and done, and only then gathering up the digger and shovel and stretchers, to carry them back to the feed lot and set them neatly and carefully in the angle of the fence where the nigger or Houston or anybody else that wanted to look couldn't help but see them, himself not glancing even once toward Houston's house, not even glancing once at the cow which no man could now deny was his, before walking on back down the lane toward his cabin two miles away.

He ate his supper, peacefully and without haste, not even listening for the cow and whoever would be leading it this time. It might even be Houston himself. Though on second thought, Houston was like him; Houston didn't scare easy either. It would be old Will Varner's alarm and concern sending the constable to bring the cow back, now that the judgment was worked out to the last penny, he, Mink, chewing his fatback and biscuits and drinking his coffee with that same gentle expression almost like smiling, imagining Quick cursing and stumbling up the lane with the lead-rope for having to do the job in the dark when he too would rather be at home with his shoes off eating supper; Mink was already rehearsing, phrasing what he would tell him: "I worked out eighteen and a half days. It takes a light and a dark both to make one of them, and this one aint up until daylight tomorrow morning. Just take that cow back where you and Will Varner put it eighteen and a half days ago, and I'll come in the morning and get it. And remind that nigger to feed early, so I wont have to wait."

But he heard nothing. And only then did he realise that he had actually expected the cow, had counted on its return you might say. He had a sudden quick light shock of fear, terror, discovering now how spurious had been that peace he thought was his since his run-in with Houston and the shotgun at the fence-line that night two months ago; so light a hold on what he had thought was peace that he must be constantly on guard now, since almost anything apparently could throw him back to that moment when Will Varner had told him he would have to work out eighteen dollars and seventy-five cents at fifty cents a day to gain possession of his own cow. Now he would have to go to the lot and look to make sure Quick hadn't put the cow in it unheard and then run, fled; he would have to light a lantern and go out in the dark to look for what he knew he would not find. And if that was not enough, he would have to explain to his wife where he was going with the lantern. Sure enough, he had to do it, using the quick hard unmannered word when she said, "Where you going? I thought Zack Houston warned you,"—adding, not for the crudeness but because she too would not let him alone:

"Lessen of course you will step outside and do it for me."

"You nasty thing!" she cried. "Using words like that in front of the girls!"

"Sholy," he said. "Or maybe you could send them. Maybe both of them together could make up for one a-dult. Though from the way they eat, ara one of them alone ought to do hit."

He went to the barn. The cow was not there of course, as he had known. He was glad of it. The whole thing—realising that even if one of them brought the cow home, he would still have to go out to the barn to make sure—had been good for him, teaching him, before any actual harm had been done, just exactly what They were up to: to fling, jolt, surprise him off balance and so ruin him: who couldn't beat him in any other way: couldn't beat him with money or its lack, couldn't outwait him; could beat him only by catching him off balance and so topple him back into that condition of furious blind earless rage where he had no sense.

But he was all right now. He had actually gained; when he took his rope tomorrow morning and went to get his cow, it wouldn't be Quick but Houston himself who would say, "Why didn't you come last night? The eighteenth and a half day was up at dark last night"; it would be Houston himself to whom he would answer:

"It takes a light and a dark both to make a day. That ere eighteen-and-a-half day is up this morning—providing that delicate nigger of yourn has done finished feeding her."

He slept. He ate breakfast; sunrise watched him walk without haste up the lane to Houston's feed-lot, the plowline coiled on his arm, to lean his folded arms on the top rail of the fence, the coiled rope loosely dangling, watching the Negro with his pitchfork and Houston also for a minute or two before they saw him. He said:

"Mawnin, Zack. I come by for that-ere court-judgment cow if you'll kindly have your nigger to kindly put this-here rope on her if he'll be so kindly obliging," then still leaning there while Houston came across the lot and stopped about ten feet away.

"You're not through yet," Houston said. "You owe two more days."

"Well well," he said, easily and peacefully, almost gently. "I reckon a man with a lot full of paper bulls and heifers, not to mention a half a mile of new pasture fence he got built free for nothing, might get mixed up about a little thing not no more important than jest dollars, especially jest eighteen dollars and seventy-five cents of them. But I jest own one eight-dollar cow, or what I always thought was jest a eight-dollar cow. I aint rich enough not to be able to count up to eighteen-seventy-five."

"I'm not talking about eighteen dollars," Houston said. "I'm——"

"And seventy-five cents," Mink said.

"—talking about nineteen dollars. You owe one dollar more."

He didn't move; his face didn't change; he just said: "What one dollar more?"

"The pound-fee," Houston said. "The law says that when anybody has to take up a stray animal and the owner dont claim it before dark that same day, the man that took it up is entitled to a one-dollar pound-fee."

He stood quite still; his hand did not even tighten on the coiled rope. "So that was why you were so quick that day to save Lon the trouble of taking her to his lot," he said. "To get that extra dollar."

"Damn the extra dollar," Houston said. "Damn Quick too. He was welcome to her. I kept her instead to save you having to walk all the way to Quick's house to get her. Not to mention I have fed her every day, which Quick wouldn't have done. The digger and shovel and stretchers are in the corner yonder where you left them last night. Any time you want to——"

But he had already turned, already walking, peacefully and steadily, carrying the coiled rope, back down the lane to the road, not back toward his home but in the opposite direction toward Varner's store four miles away. He walked through the bright sweet young summer morning between the burgeoning woodlands where the dogwood and red bud and wild plum had long since bloomed and gone, beside the planted fields sprouting strongly with corn and cotton, some of it almost as good as his own small patches (obviously the people who planted these had not had the leisure and peace he had thought he had to sow in); treading peacefully the rife and vernal earth boiling with life—the frantic flash and glint and crying of birds, a rabbit bursting almost beneath his feet, so young and thin as to have but two dimensions, unless the third one could be speed—on to Varner's store.

The gnawed wood gallery above the gnawed wood steps would be vacant now. The overalled men who after laying-by would squat or stand all day against the front wall or inside the store itself, would be in the field too today, ditching or mending fences or running the first harrows and shovels and cultivators among the tender sprouts. The store was too empty in fact. He thought *If Flem was jest here*—his cousin who had been Varner's clerk for four years now, until last August when he and Varner's daughter were suddenly married and the two of them were still in Texas on their honeymoon. Because Flem was not there; he, Mink, knew if anyone did that that honeymoon would have to last until they could come back home and tell Frenchman's Bend that the child they would bring with them hadn't been born sooner than this past May at the earliest, and at least nobody would laugh out loud. But even if it hadn't been that, it would have been something else; his cousin's absence when he was needed was just one more test, harassment, enragement They tried him with, not to see if he would survive it because They had no doubt of that, but simply for the pleasure of watching him have to do something extra there was no reason whatever for him to have to do.

Only Varner was not there either. Mink had not expected that. He had taken it for granted that They would not miss this chance: to have the whole store crammed with people

who should have been busy in the field—loose idle ears all
strained to hear what he had come to say to Will Varner. But
even Varner was gone; there was nobody in the store but Jody
Varner and Lump Snopes, the clerk Flem had substituted in
when he quit to get married last summer.

"If he went in to town, he wont be back before night,"
Mink said.

"Not to town," Jody said. "He went over to look at a mill
on Punkin Creek. He said he'll be back by dinner time."

"He wont be back until night," Mink said.

"All right," Jody said. "Then you can go back home and
come back tomorrow."

So he had no choice. He could have walked the five miles
back home and then the five more back to the store in just
comfortable time before noon, if he had wanted a walk. Or he
could stay near the store until noon and wait there until old
Varner would finally turn up just about in time for supper,
which he would do, since naturally They would not miss that
chance to make him lose a whole day. Which would mean he
would have to put in half of one night digging Houston's
post holes since he would have to complete the two days by
noon of day after tomorrow in order to finish what he would
need to do since he would have to make one trip in to town
himself.

Or he could have walked back home just in time to eat his
noon meal and then walk back, since he would already have
lost a whole day anyway. But They would certainly not miss
that chance; as soon as he was out of sight, the buckboard
would return from Punkin Creek and Varner would get out of
it. So he waited, through noon when, as soon as Jody left to
go home to dinner, Lump hacked off a segment of hoop
cheese and took a handful of crackers from the barrel.

"Aint you going to eat no dinner?" Lump said. "Will wont
miss it."

"No," Mink said.

"I'll put it on your furnish then, if you're all that tender
about one of Will Varner's nickels," Lump said.

"I'm not hungry," he said. But there was one thing he
could be doing, one preparation he could be making while he
waited, since it was not far. So he went there, to the place

he had already chosen, and did what was necessary since he already knew what Varner was going to tell him, and returned to the store and yes, at exactly midafternoon, just exactly right to exhaust the balance of the whole working day, the buckboard came up and Varner got out and was tying the lines to the usual gallery post when Mink came up to him.

"All right," Varner said. "Now what?"

"A little information about the Law," he said. "This-here pound-fee law."

"What?" Varner said.

"That's right," he said, peaceful and easy, his face quiet and gentle as smiling. "I thought I had finished working out them thirty-seven and a half four-bit days at sundown last night. Only when I went this morning to get my cow, it seems like I aint done quite yet, that I owe two more days for the pound-fee."

"Hell fire," Varner said. He stood over the smaller man, cursing. "Did Houston tell you that?"

"That's right," he said.

"Hell fire," Varner said again. He dragged a huge worn leather wallet strapped like a suitcase from his hip pocket and took a dollar bill from it. "Here," he said.

"So the Law does say I got to pay another dollar before I can get my cow."

"Yes," Varner said. "If Houston wants to claim it. Take this dollar——"

"I dont need it," he said, already turning. "Me and Houston dont deal in money, we deal in post-holes. I jest wanted to know the Law. And if that's the Law, I reckon there aint nothing for a law-abiding feller like me to do but jest put up with it. Because if folks dont put up with the Law, what's the use of all the trouble and expense of having it?"

"Wait," Varner said. "Dont you go back there. Dont you go near Houston's place. You go on home and wait. I'll bring your cow to you as soon as I get hold of Quick."

"That's all right," he said. "Maybe I aint got as many post-holes in me as Houston has dollars, but I reckon I got enough for just two more days."

"Mink!" Varner said. "Mink! Come back here!" But he was gone. But there was no hurry now; the day was already

ruined; until tomorrow morning, when he was in Houston's
new pasture until sundown. This time he hid the tools under
a bush as he always did when he would return tomorrow, and
went home and ate the sowbelly and flour gravy and undercooked biscuits; they had one time-piece, the tin alarm clock
which he set for eleven and rose again then; he had left coffee in the pot and some of the meat cold in the congealed
skillet and two biscuits so it was almost exactly midnight
when the savage baying of the Bluetick hound brought the
Negro to his door and he, Mink, said, "Hit's Mister Snopes.
Reporting for work. Hit's jest gone exactly midnight for the
record." Because he would have to do this in order to quit at
noon. And They—Houston—were still watching him because
when the sun said noon and he carried the tools back to the
fence corner, his cow was already tied there in a halter, which
he removed and tied his plowline around her horns and this
time he didn't lead her but, himself at a trot, drove her trotting before him by lashing her across the hocks with the end
of the rope.

Because he was short for time, to get her back home and
into the lot. Nor would he have time to eat his dinner, again
today, with five miles still to do, even straight across country,
to catch the mail carrier before he left Varner's store at two
oclock for Jefferson, since Varner did not carry ten-gauge
buckshot shells. But his wife and daughters were at the table,
which at least saved argument, the necessity to curse them
silent or perhaps even to have actually to strike, hit his wife,
in order to go to the hearth and dig out the loose brick and
take from the snuff tin behind it the single five-dollar bill
which through all vicissitudes they kept there as the boat-
owner will sell or pawn or lose all his gear but will still cling
on to one life-preserver or ring buoy. Because he had five
shells for the ancient ten-gauge gun, ranging from bird-shot
to one Number Two for turkey or geese. But he had had
them for years, he did not remember how long; besides, even
if he were guaranteed that they would fire, Houston deserved
better than this.

So he folded the bill carefully into the fob pocket of his
overalls and caught the mail carrier and by four that afternoon
Jefferson was in sight across the last valley and by simple

precaution, a simple instinctive preparatory gesture, he thrust his fingers into the fob pocket, then suddenly dug frantically, himself outwardly immobile, into the now vacant pocket where he knew he had folded and stowed carefully the bill, then sat immobile beside the mail carrier while the buckboard began to descend the hill. *I got to do it* he thought *So I might as well* and then said quietly aloud, "All right. I reckon I'll take that-ere bill now."

"What?" the carrier said.

"That-ere five-dollar bill that was in my pocket when I got in this buggy back yonder at Varner's."

"Why, you little son of a bitch," the carrier said. He pulled the buckboard off to the side of the road and wrapped the lines around the whip-stock and got out and came around to Mink's side of the vehicle. "Get out," he said.

Now I got to fight him Mink thought. *And I aint got no knife and likely he will beat me to ere a stick I try to grab. So I might jest as well get it over with* and got out of the buckboard, the carrier giving him time to get his puny and vain hands up. Then a shocking blow which Mink didn't even feel very much, aware instead rather merely of the hard ungiving proneness of the earth, ground against his back, lying there, peaceful almost, watching the carrier get back into the buckboard and drive on.

Then he got up. He thought *I not only could a saved a trip, I might still had them five dollars* But for only a moment; he was already in the road, already walking steadily on toward town as if he knew what he was doing. Which he did, he had already remembered: two, three years ago it was when Solon Quick or Vernon Tull or whoever it was had seen the bear, the last bear in that part of the county, when it ran across Varner's mill-dam and into the thicket, and how the hunt had been organised and somebody rode a horse in to Jefferson to get hold of Ike McCaslin and Walter Ewell, the best hunters in the county, and they came out with their buckshot big-game shells and the bear and deer hounds and set the standers and drove the bottom where the bear had been seen but it was gone by then. So he knew what to do, or at least where to try, until he crossed the Square and entered the hardware store where McCaslin was junior partner and saw McCaslin's eyes. Mink thought quietly *Hit wont do no good. He has done spent too much time in the woods with deer and bears and panthers that either are or they aint, right quick and now and not no shades between. He wont know how to believe a lie even if I could tell him one.* But he had to try.

"What do you want with two buckshot shells?" McCaslin said.

"A nigger come in this morning and said he seen that bear's foot in the mud at Blackwater Slough."

"No," McCaslin said. "What do you want with buckshot shells?"

"I can pay you soon as I gin my cotton," Mink said.

"No," McCaslin said. "I aint going to let you have them. There aint anything out there at Frenchman's Bend you need to shoot buckshot at."

It was not that he was hungry so much, even though he hadn't eaten since midnight: it was simply that he would have to pass the time some way until tomorrow morning when he would find out whether the mail carrier would take him back to Varner's store or not. He knew a small dingy back-street eating-place owned by the sewing machine agent, Ratliff, who was well known in Frenchman's Bend, where, if he had a half a dollar or even forty cents, he could have had two hamburgers and a nickel's worth of bananas and still had twenty-five cents left.

For that he could have had a bed in the Commercial Hotel (an unpainted two-storey frame building on a back street also; in two years his cousin Flem would own it though of course Mink didn't know that now. In fact, he had not even begun to think about his cousin yet, not once again after that moment when he entered Varner's store yesterday morning, where until his and his wife's departure for Texas last September, the first object he would have seen on entering it would have been Flem) but all he had to do was to pass time until eight oclock tomorrow morning and if it cost cash money just to pass time he would have been in the poorhouse years ago.

Now it was evening, the lights had come on around the Square, the lights from the drugstores falling outward across the pavement, staining the pavement with dim rose and green from the red and green liquid-filled jars in the windows; he could see the soda fountains and the young people, young men and girls in their city clothes eating and drinking the gaudy sweet concoctions, and he could watch them, the couples, young men and girls and old people and children, all moving in one direction. Then he heard music, a piano, loud. He followed also and saw in a vacant lot the big high plank stockade with its entrance beside the lighted ticket window: the Airdome they called it; he had seen it before from the outside by day while in town for Saturdays, and three times at night too, lighted as now. But never the inside because on the three previous times he had been in Jefferson after dark he had ridden a mule in from Frenchman's Bend with companions of his age and sex to take the early train to a Memphis brothel with in his pocket the few meagre dollars he had wrenched as though by main strength from his bare livelihood, as he had likewise wrenched the two days he would be gone from earning the replacement of them, and in his blood a need far more urgent and passionate than a moving picture show.

Though this time he could have spared the dime it would cost. Instead he stood a little aside while the line of patrons crept slowly past the ticket window until the last one passed inside. Then the glare and glow of light from beyond the fence blinked out and into a cold flickering; approaching the fence and laying his eye to a crack he could see through the long vertical interstice a section, a fragment—the dark row of motionless heads above which the whirring cone of light burst, shattered into the passionate and evanescent posturings where danced and flickered the ephemeral hopes and dreams, tantalising and inconsequent since he could see only his narrow vertical strip of it, until a voice spoke from the ticket window behind him: "Pay a dime and go inside. Then you can see."

"No much obliged," he said. He went on. The Square was empty now, until the show would let out and once more the young people, young men and girls, would drink and eat the confections which he had never tasted either, before strolling home. He had hoped maybe to see one of the automobiles; there were two in Jefferson already: the red racer belonging to the mayor, Mr de Spain, and the White Steamer that the president of the old bank, the Bank of Jefferson, owned (Colonel Sartoris, the other rich bank president, president of the new bank, not only wouldn't own an automobile, he even had a law passed three years ago that no motor-driven vehicle could operate on the streets of Jefferson after the home-made automobile a man named Buffaloe had made in his back yard frightened the colonel's matched team into running away). But he didn't see either one; the Square was still empty when he crossed it. Then the hotel, the Holston House, the drummers sitting in leather chairs along the sidewalk in the pleasant night; one of the livery stable hacks was already there, the Negro porter loading the grips and sample cases in it for the south-bound train.

So he had better walk on, to be in time, even though the four lighted faces of the clock on top of the courthouse said only ten minutes past eight and he knew by his own experience that the New Orleans train from Memphis Junction didn't pass Jefferson until two minutes to nine. Though he knew too that freight trains might pass at almost any time, let alone the other passenger train, the one his experience knew too, going north at half past four. So just by spending the night, without even moving, he would see certainly two and maybe five or six trains before daylight.

He had left the Square, passing the dark homes where some of the old people who didn't go to the picture show either sat in dim rocking chairs in the cool dark of the yards, then a section all Negro homes, even with electric lights too, peaceful, with no worries, no need to fight and strive single-handed, not to gain right and justice because they were already lost, but just to defend the principle of them, his rights to them, but instead could talk a little while and then go even into a nigger house and just lay down and sleep in place of walking all the way to the depot just to have something to look at until the durn mail carrier left at eight oclock tomorrow. Then the depot: the red and green eyes of the signal lamps, the hotel bus and the livery stable hacks and Lucius Hogganbeck's automobile jitney, the long electric-lighted shed already full of the men and boys come down to see the train pass, that were there the three times he had got off of it, looking at him also like he had come from a heap further than a Memphis whore house.

Then the train itself: the four whistle-blasts for the north crossing, then the headlight, the roar, the clanging engine, the engineer and the fireman crouched dim and high above the hissing steam, slowing, the baggage and day coaches then the dining car and the cars in which people slept while they rode. It stopped, a Negro even more uppity than Houston's getting out with his footstool, then the conductor, and the rich men and women getting gaily aboard where the other rich ones were already asleep, followed by the nigger with his footstool and the conductor, the conductor leaning back to wave at the engine, the engine speaking back to the conductor, to all of them, with the first deep short ejaculations of starting.

Then the twin ruby lamps on the last car diminished rapidly together in one last flick! at the curve, the four blasts came fading back from the south crossing and he thought of distance, of New Orleans where he had never been and perhaps never would go, with distance even beyond New Orleans, with Texas somewhere in it; and now for the first time he began really to think about his absent cousin: the one Snopes of them all who had risen, broken free, had either been born with or had learned, taught himself, the knack or the luck to cope with, hold his own, handle the They and Them which he, Mink, apparently did not have the knack or the luck to do. *Maybe I ought to waited till he got back* he thought, turning at last back to the now empty and vacant platform, noticing only then that he had thought, not *should* wait for Flem, but should *have* waited, it already being too late.

The waiting room was empty too, with its hard wooden benches and the cold iron tobacco-spattered stove. He knew about signs in depots against spitting but he never heard of one against a man without a ticket sitting down. Anyhow, he would find out—a small man anyway, fleshless, sleepless and more or less foodless too for going on twenty-two hours now, looking in the empty barren room beneath the single un-shaded bulb as forlorn and defenseless as a child, a boy, in faded patched overalls and shirt, sockless in heavy worn iron-hard brogan shoes and a sweat-and-grease stained black felt hat. From beyond the ticket window he could hear the intermittent clatter of the telegraph, and two voices where the night operator talked to somebody now and then, until the voices ceased and the telegraph operator in his green eyeshade was looking at him through the window. "You want something?" he said.

"No much obliged," Mink said. "When does the next train pass?"

"Four twenty-two," the operator said. "You waiting for it?"

"That's right," he said.

"That's six hours off yet. You can go home and go to bed and then come back."

"I live out at Frenchman's Bend," he said.

"Oh," the operator said. Then the face was gone from the window and he sat again. It was quiet now and he even began to notice, hear the katydids in the dark trees beyond the tracks buzzing and chirring back and forth, interminable and peaceful, as if they might be the sound of the peaceful minutes and seconds themselves of the dark peaceful summer night clicking to one another. Then the whole room shook and trembled, filled with thunder; the freight train was already passing and even now he couldn't seem to get himself awake enough to get outside in time. He was still sitting on the hard bench, cramped and cold while the ruby lights on the caboose flicked across the windows then across the open door, sucking the thunder behind them; the four crossing blasts came back and died away. This time the operator was in the room with him and the overhead bulb had been switched off. "You were asleep," he said.

"That's right," Mink said. "I nigh missed that un."

"Why dont you lay down on the bench and be comfortable?"

"You aint got no rule against it?"

"No," the operator said. "I'll call you when they signal Number Eight."

"Much obliged," he said, and lay back. The operator went back into the room where the telegraph was already chattering again and Mink sat up and removed the two hard buckshot shells from his hip pocket and put them in a side pocket where he wouldn't lie on them and lay down again. *Yes* he thought peacefully *if Flem had been here he could a stopped all this on that first day before it ever got started. Working for Varner like he done, being in with Houston and Quick and all the rest of them. He could do it now if I could jest a waited. Only it wasn't me that couldn't wait. It was Houston his-self that wouldn't give me time.* Then immediately he knew that that was wrong too, that no matter how long he had waited They themselves would have prevented Flem getting back in time. He must drain this cup too: must face, accept this last ultimate useless and reasonless risk and jeopardy too just to show how much he could stand before They would let his cousin come back where he could save him. This same cup also contained Houston's life but he wasn't thinking about Houston. In a way, he had quit thinking about Houston at the same moment when Varner told him he would have to pay the pound-fee. "All right," he said peacefully, aloud this time, "if that's what They want, I reckon I can stand that too."

At half-past seven he was standing in the small lot behind the postoffice where the RFD carriers' buckboards would stand until the carriers came out the back door with the bags of mail. He had already discerned the one for Frenchman's Bend and he stood quietly, not too near: simply where the carrier could not help but see him, until the man who had knocked him down yesterday came out and saw, recognised, him, a quick glance, then came on and stowed the mail pouch into the buckboard, Mink not moving yet, just standing there, waiting, to be refused or not refused, until the carrier got in and released the wrapped lines from the whip-stock and said, "All right. I reckon you got to get back to your crop. Come on," and Mink approached and got in.

It was just past eleven when he got down at Varner's store and said Much obliged and began the five-mile walk home. So he was home in time for dinner, eating steadily and quietly while his wife nagged and whined at him (evidently she hadn't noticed the disturbed brick) about where he was last night and why, until he finished, drank the last of his coffee and rose from the table and with vicious and obscene cursing drove the three of them, his wife and the two girls, with the three hoes out to the patch to chop out his early cotton, while he lay on the floor in the cool draft of the dogtrot hall, sleeping away the afternoon.

Then it was tomorrow morning. He took from its corner behind the door the tremendous ten-gauge double-barrelled shotgun which had belonged to his grandfather, the twin hammers standing above the receiver almost as tall as the ears of a rabbit. "Now what?" his wife said, cried. "Where you fixing to go with that?"

"After a rabbit," he said. "I'm burnt out on sowbelly," and with two of the heaviest loads out of his meagre stock of Number Two and -Five and -Eight shot shells, he went not even by back roads and lanes but by hedgerows and patches of woods and ditches and whatever else would keep him private and unseen, back to the ambush he had prepared two days ago while waiting for Varner to return, where the road from Houston's to Varner's store crossed the creek bridge— the thicket beside the road, with a log to sit on and the broken-off switches not yet healed over where he had opened a sort of port to point the gun through, with the wooden planks of the bridge fifty yards up the road to serve as an alert beneath the stallion's hooves in case he dozed off.

Because sometimes a week would pass before Houston would ride in to the store. But sooner or later he would do so. And if all he, Mink, needed to beat Them with was just waiting, They could have given up three months ago and saved Themselves and everybody else trouble. So it was not the first day nor the second either that he would go home with no rabbit, to eat his supper in quiet and inflexible silence while his wife nagged and whined at him about why there was none, until he would push away his empty plate and in a cold level vicious monotone curse her silent.

And it might not have been the third day either. In fact, he couldn't remember how many days it had been, when at last he heard the sudden thunder of the hooves on the bridge and then saw them: the stallion boring, frothing a little, wrenching its arrogant vicious head at the snaffle and curb both with which Houston rode it, the big lean hound bounding along beside it. He cocked the two hammers and pushed the gun through the port-hole, and even as he laid the sight on Houston's chest, leading him just a little, his finger already taking up the slack in the front trigger, he thought *And even now; They still aint satisfied yet*, thinking how if there had only been time, space, between the roar of the gun and the impact of the shot, for him to say to Houston and for Houston to have to hear it: "I aint shooting you because of them thirty-seven and a half four-bit days. That's all right; I done long ago forgot and forgive that. Likely Will Varner couldn't do nothing else, being a rich man too and all you rich folks has got to stick together or else maybe some day the ones that aint rich might take a notion to raise up and take hit away from you. That aint why I shot you. I killed you because of that-ere extry one-dollar pound fee."

Two

So THE JURY said "guilty" and the Judge said "life" but he wasn't even listening. Because something had happened to him. Even while the sheriff was bringing him in to town that first day, even though he knew that his cousin was still in Texas he believed that at every mile-post Flem or a messenger from him would overtake them or step into the road and stop them, with the money or the word or whatever it would be that would make the whole thing dissolve, vanish like a dream.

And during all the long weeks while he waited in jail for his trial, he would stand at the barred little window of his cell, his grimed hands gripped among them and his face craned and pressed against them, to watch a slice of the street before the jail and the slice of the Square which his cousin would have to cross to come to the jail and abolish the dream, free him, get him out. "Which is all I want," he would tell himself. "Jest to get out of here and go back home and farm. That dont seem like a heap to ask."

And at night too still standing there, his face invisible but his wan hands looking almost white, almost clean in the grimed interstices against the cell's darkness, watching the free people, men and women and young people who had nothing but peaceful errands or pleasures as they strolled in the evening cool toward the Square, to watch the picture show or eat ice cream in the drug store or maybe just stroll peaceful and free because they were free, he beginning at last to call down to them, timidly at first, then louder and louder, more and more urgent as they would pause, almost as though startled, to look up at his window and then seem almost to hurry on, like they were trying to get beyond where he could see them; finally he began to offer, promise them money: "Hey! Mister! Missus! Somebody! Anybody that will send word out to Varner's store to Flem Snopes! He will pay you! Ten dollars! Twenty dollars!"

And even when the day finally came and they brought him handcuffed into the room where he would face his jeopardy, he had not even looked once toward the Bench, the dais which could well be his Golgotha too, for looking, staring out

over the pale identical anonymous faces of the crowd for that
of his cousin or at least the messenger from him; right up to
the moment when the Judge himself had to lean down from
his high desk and say, "You, Snopes! Look at me. Did you or
didn't you kill Zack Houston?" and he answered:

"Dont bother me now. Cant you see I'm busy?"

And the next day too, while the lawyers shouted and wrangled and nagged, he hearing none of it even if he could have
understood it, for watching the door at the rear where his
cousin or the messenger would have to enter; and on the way
back to the cell, still handcuffed, his unflagging glance which
at first had been merely fretted and impatient but which now
was beginning to be concerned, a little puzzled and quite
sober, travelling rapid and quick and searching from face to
face as he passed them or they passed him, to stand again at
his cell window, his unwashed hands gripping the grimed bars
and his face wrenched and pressed against them to see as
much as possible of the street and the Square below where his
kinsman or the messenger would have to pass.

So when on the third day, handcuffed again to the jailor, he
realised that he had crossed the Square without once looking
at one of the faces which gaped at him, and had entered the
courtroom and taken his accustomed place in the dock still
without once looking out over the massed faces toward that
rear door, he still did not dare admit to himself that he knew
why. He just sat there, looking as small and frail and harmless
as a dirty child while the lawyers ranted and wrangled, until
the end of the day when the jury said Guilty and the Judge
said Life and he was returned, handcuffed, to his cell, and the
door clanged to and he sitting now, quiet and still and composed on the mattress-less steel cot, this time only looking at
the small barred window where for months now he had stood
sixteen or eighteen hours a day in quenchless expectation and
hope.

Only then did he say it, think it, let it take shape in his
mind: *He aint coming. Likely he's been in Frenchman's Bend
all the time. Likely he heard about that cow clean out there in
Texas and jest waited till the word come back they had me safe
in jail, and then come back to make sho they would do ever thing
to me they could now that they had me helpless. He might even*

been hid in the back of that room all the time, to make sho wouldn't nothing slip up before he finally got rid of me for good and all.

So now he had peace. He had thought he had peace as soon as he realised what he would have to do about Houston, and that Houston himself wasn't going to let him wait until Flem got back. But he had been wrong. That wasn't peace then; it was too full of too many uncertainties: such as if any-body would send word to Flem about his trouble at all, let alone in time. Or even if the word was sent in time, would the message find Flem in time. And even if Flem got the message in time, there might be a flood or a wreck on the railroad so he couldn't get back in time.

But all that was finished now. He didn't have to bother and worry at all now since all he had to do was wait, and he had already proved to himself that he could do that. Just to wait: that's all he needed; he didn't even need to ask the jailor to send a message since the lawyer himself had said he would come back to see him after supper.

So he ate his supper when they brought it—the same side-meat and molasses and undercooked biscuits he would have had at home; this in fact a little better since the meat had more lean in it than he could afford to eat. Except that his at home had been free, eaten in freedom. But then he could stand that too if that was all *they* demanded of him now. Then he heard the feet on the stairs, the door clashed, letting the lawyer in, and clashed again on both of them—the lawyer young and eager, just out of law school they told him, whom the Judge had appointed for him—commanded rather, since even he, Mink, busy as he was at the time, could tell that the man didn't really want any part of him and his trouble—he never did know why then because then he still thought that all the Judge or anybody else needed to do to settle the whole business was just to send out to Frenchman's Bend and get hold of his cousin.

Too young and eager in fact, which was why he—the lawyer—had made such a hash of the thing. But that didn't matter now either; the thing now was to get on to what came next. So he didn't waste any time. "All right," he said. "How long will I have to stay there?"

"It's Parchman—the penitentiary," the lawyer said. "Cant you understand that?"

"All right," he said again. "How long will I have to stay?"

"He gave you life," the lawyer said. "Didn't you even hear him? For the rest of your life. Until you die."

"All right," he said for the third time, with that peaceful, that almost compassionate patience: "How long will I have to stay?"

By that time even this lawyer understood. "Oh. That depends on you and your friends—if you have any. It may be all your life, like Judge Brummage said. But in twenty or twenty-five years you will be eligible under the Law to apply for pardon or parole—if you have responsible friends to support your petition, and your record down there at Parchman dont hold anything against you."

"Suppose a man aint got friends," he said.

"Folks that hide in bushes and shoot other folks off their horses without saying Look out first or even whistling, dont have," the lawyer said. "So you wont have anybody left except you to get you out."

"All right," he said, with that unshakable, that infinite patience, "that's what I'm trying to get you to stop talking long enough to tell me. What do I have to do to get out in twenty or twenty-five years?"

"Not to try to escape yourself or engage in any plot to help anybody else escape. Not to get in a fight with another prisoner or a guard. To be on time for whatever they tell you to do, and do it without shirking or complaining or talking back, until they tell you to quit. In other words, to start right now doing all the things that, if you had just been doing them all the time since that day last fall when you decided to let Mr Houston winter your cow for nothing, you wouldn't be sitting in this cell here trying to ask somebody how to get out of it. But mainly, dont try to escape."

"Escape?" he said.

"Break out. Try to get away."

"Try?" he said.

"Because you cant," the lawyer said with a kind of seething yet patient rage. "Because you cant escape. You cant make it. You never can. You cant plan it without some of the others catching on to it and they always try to escape with you and so you all get caught. And even if they dont go with you, they tell the Warden on you and you are caught just the same. And even if you manage to keep everybody else from knowing about it and go alone, one of the guards shoots you before you can climb the fence. So even if you are not in the dead house or the hospital, you are back in the penitentiary with twenty-five more years added onto your sentence. Do you understand now?"

"That's all I got to do to get out in twenty or twenty-five years. Not try to escape. Not get in no fights with nobody. Do whatever they tell me to do, as long as they say to do it. But mainly not try to escape. That's all I got to do to get out in twenty or twenty-five years."

"That's right," the lawyer said.

"All right," he said. "Now go back and ask that judge if that's right, and if he says it is, to send me a wrote-out paper saying so."

"So you dont trust me," the lawyer said.

"I dont trust nobody," he said. "I aint got time to waste twenty or twenty-five years to find out whether you know what you're talking about or not. I got something I got to attend to when I get back out. I want to know. I want a wrote-out paper from that judge."

"Maybe you never did trust me then," the lawyer said. "Maybe you think I made a complete bust of your whole case. Maybe you think that if it hadn't been for me, you wouldn't even be here now. Is that it?"

And he, Mink, still with that inflexible and patient calm: "You done the best you knowed. You jest wasn't the man for the job. You're young and eager, but that wasn't what I needed. I needed a trader, a smart trader, that knowed how to swap. You wasn't him. Now you go get that paper from that judge."

Now he, the lawyer, even tried to laugh. "Not me," he said. "The Court discharged me from this case right after he sentenced you this afternoon. I just stopped in to say good-bye and to see if there was anything else I could do for you. But evidently folks that dont have friends dont need well-wishers either."

"But I aint discharged you yet," Mink said, rising now, without haste, the lawyer already on his feet, springing, leaping back against the locked door, looking at the small figure moving toward him as slight and frail and harmless-looking as a child and as deadly as a small viper—a half-grown asp or cobra or krait. Then the lawyer was shouting, bellowing, even while the turnkey's feet galloped on the stairs and the door clashed open and the turnkey stood in it with a drawn pistol.

"What is it?" the turnkey said. "What did he try to do?"

"Nothing," the lawyer said. "It's all right. I'm through here. Let me out." Only he was not through; he only wished he were. He didn't even wait until morning. Instead, not fifteen minutes later he was in the hotel room of the Circuit Judge who had presided on the case and pronounced the sentence, he, the lawyer, still breathing hard, still incredulous at his recent jeopardy and still amazed at his escape from it.

"He's crazy, I tell you!" he said. "He's dangerous! Just to send him to Parchman, where he will be eligible for parole and freedom in only twenty or twenty-five years, let alone if some of his kin—God knows he has enough—or someone with an axe to grind or maybe just some bleeding-heart meddler with access to the Governor's ear, doesn't have him out before that time even! He must go to Jackson, the asylum, for life, where he'll be safe. No: we'll be safe."

And ten minutes after that the District Attorney who had prosecuted the case was in the room too, saying (to the lawyer): "So now you want a suspended sentence, and a motion for a new trial. Why didn't you think of this before?"

"You saw him too," the lawyer said, cried. "You were in that courtroom with him all day long for three days too!"

"That's right," the District Attorney said. "That's why I'm asking you why now."

"Then you haven't seen him since!" the lawyer said. "Come up to that cell and look at him now, like I did thirty minutes ago!"

But the Judge was an old man, he wouldn't go then so it was the next morning when the turnkey unlocked the cell and let the three of them in where the frail-looking fleshless small figure in the patched and faded overalls and shirt and the sockless iron-stiff brogans got up from the cot. They had shaved him this morning and his hair was combed too, parted and flattened down with water across his skull.

"Come in, gentle-men," he said. "I aint got no chair but likely you aint fixing to stay long enough to set nohow. Well, Judge, you not only brought me my wrote-out paper, you brought along two witnesses to watch you hand it to me."

"Wait," the lawyer said rapidly to the Judge. "Let me." He said to Mink: "You wont need that paper. They—the Judge—is going to give you another trial."

Now Mink stopped. He looked at the lawyer. "What for?" he said. "I done already had one that I never got much suption out of."

"Because that one was wrong," the lawyer said. "That's what we've come to tell you about."

"If that un was wrong, what's the use of wasting time and money having another one? Jest tell that feller there to bring me my hat and open that door and I'll go back home and get back to my crop. I done already lost two months like it is."

"No, wait," the lawyer said. "That other trial was wrong because it sent you to Parchman. You wont have to go to Parchman now, where you'll have to work out in the hot sun all day long in a crop that isn't even yours." And now, with the pale faded gray eyes watching him as if they were not only incapable of blinking but never since birth had they ever needed to, the lawyer found himself babbling, not even able to stop it: "Not Parchman: Jackson, where you'll have a nice room to yourself—nothing to do all day long but just rest—doctors——" and stopped then; not he that stopped his babbling but the fixed unwinking pale eyes that did it.

"Doctors," Mink said. "Jackson." He stared at the lawyer. "That's where they send crazy folks."

"Hadn't you rather," the District Attorney began. That was as far as he got too. He had been an athlete in college and still kept himself fit. Though even then he managed to grasp the small frantic creature only after it had hurled itself on the lawyer and both of them had gone to the floor. And even then it took him and the turnkey both to drag Mink up and away and hold him, frantic and frothing and hard to hold as a cat, panting,

"Crazy, am I? Crazy, am I? Aint no son a bitch going to call me crazy, I dont care how big he is or how many of them."

"You damn right, you little bastard," the District Attorney panted. "You're going to Parchman. That's where they've got the kind of doctors you need."

So he went to Parchman, handcuffed to a deputy sheriff, the two of them transferring from smoking car to smoking car of local trains, this one having left the hills which he had known all his life, for the Delta which he had never seen before—the vast flat alluvial swamp of cypress and gum and brake and thicket lurked with bear and deer and panthers and snakes, out of which man was still hewing savagely and violently the rich ragged fields in which cotton stalks grew ranker and taller than a man on a horse, he, Mink, sitting with his face glued to the window like a child.

"This here's all swamp," he said. "It dont look healthy."

"It aint healthy," the deputy said. "It aint intended to be. This is the penitentiary. I cant imagine no more unhealth a man can have than to be locked up inside a bobwire pen for twenty or twenty-five years. Besides, a good unhealthy place ought to just suit you; you wont have to stay so long."

So that's how he saw Parchman, the penitentiary, his destination, doom, his life the Judge had said; for the rest of his life as long as he lived. But the lawyer had told him different, even if he couldn't really trust him: only twenty-five, maybe only twenty years, and even a lawyer a man couldn't trust could at least be trusted to know his own business that he had even went to special law school to be trained to know it, where all a judge had to do to get to be a judge was just to win a election vote-race for it. And even if the Judge hadn't signed a paper saying only twenty or twenty-five years, that didn't matter either since the Judge was on the other side and would naturally lie to a man coming up against him, where a lawyer, a man's own lawyer, wouldn't. More: he couldn't lie to him, because there was some kind of rule somebody had told him about that if the client didn't lie to his lawyer, the Law itself wouldn't let the lawyer lie to his own client.

And even if none of that was so, that didn't matter either because he couldn't stay in Parchman all his life, he didn't have time, he would have to get out before then. And looking at the tall wire stockade with its single gate guarded day and night by men with shotguns, and inside it the low grim brick buildings with their barred windows, he thought, tried to remember, with a kind of amazement of the time when his only reason for wanting to get out was to go back home and farm, remembering it only for a moment and then no more, because now he had to get out.

He had to get out. His familiar patched faded blue overalls and shirt were exchanged now for the overalls and jumper of coarse white barred laterally with black which, according to the Judge, would have been his fate and doom until he died, if the lawyer hadn't known better. He worked now—gangs of them—in the rich black cotton-land while men on horses with shotguns across the pommels watched them, doing the only work he knew how to do, had done all his life, in a crop which would never be his for the rest of his life if the Judge had his way, thinking *And that's all right too. Hit's even better. If a feller jest wants to do something, he might make it and he might not. But if he's GOT to do something, cant nothing stop him.*

And in the wooden bunk at night too, sheetless, with a cheap coarse blanket and his rolled-up clothing for a pillow, thinking, dinning it into himself since he was now having to change overnight and forever for twenty or twenty-five years his whole nature and character and being: *To do whatever they tell me to do. Not to talk back to nobody. Not to get into no fights. That's all I got to do for jest twenty-five or maybe even jest twenty years. But mainly not to try to escape.*

Nor did he even count off the years as they accomplished. Instead, he simply trod them behind him into oblivion beneath the heavy brogan shoes in the cotton middles behind the mule which drew the plow and then the sweep, then with the chopping and thinning hoe and at last with the long dragging sack into which he picked, gathered the cotton. He didn't need to count them; he was in the hands of the Law now and as long as he obeyed the four rules set down by the Law for his side, the Law would have to obey its single rule of twenty-five years or maybe even just twenty.

He didn't know how many years it had been when the letter came, whether it was two or three as he stood in the

Warden's office, turning the stamped pencil-addressed envelope in his hand while the Warden watched him. "You cant
read?" the Warden said.

"No," he said.

"You want me to open it?" the Warden said.

"All right," he said. So the Warden did.

"It's from your wife. She wants to know when you want
her to come to see you, and if you want her to bring the
girls."

Now he held the letter himself, the page of foolscap out of
a school writing pad, pencilled over, spidery and hieroglyph,
not one jot less forever beyond him than Arabic or Sanscrit.
"Yettie cant read and write neither," he said. "Miz Tull must
a wrote it for her."

"Well?" the Warden said. "What do you want me to tell
her?"

"Tell her it aint no use in her coming all the way here because I'll be home soon."

"Oh," the Warden said. "You're going to get out soon, are
you?" He looked at the small frail creature not much larger
than a fifteen-year-old boy, who had been one of his charges
for three years now without establishing an individual entity
in the prison's warp. Not a puzzle, not an enigma: he was not
anything at all; no record of run-in or reprimand with or from
any guard or trusty or official, never any trouble with any
other inmate. A murderer, in for life, who in the Warden's experience fell always into one of two categories: either an irreconcilable, with nothing more to lose, a constant problem
and trouble to the guards and the other prisoners; or a syco-
phant, sucking up to whatever of his overlords who could
make things easiest for him. But not this one: who assumed
his assigned task each morning and worked steady and unflagging in the cotton as if it was his own crop he was bringing to fruit. More: he worked harder for this crop from which
he would not derive one cent of profit than, in the Warden's
experience, men of his stamp and kind worked in their own.
"How?" the Warden said.

Mink told him; it was automatic now after three years; he
had only to open his mouth and breathe: "By doing what

they tell me to. Not talking back and not fighting. Not to try to escape. Mainly that: not to try to escape."

"So in either seventeen or twenty-two years you'll go home," the Warden said. "You've already been here three."

"Have I?" he said. "I aint kept count.—No," he said. "Not right away. There's something I got to attend to first."

"What?" the Warden said.

"Something private. When I finish that, then I'll come on home. Write her that." *Yes sir,* he thought. *It looks like I done had to come all the way to Parchman jest to turn right around and go back home and kill Flem.*

Three

V. K. RATLIFF

Likely what bollixed Montgomery Ward at first, and for the next two or three days too, was exactly why Flem wanted him specifically in Parchman. Why wouldn't no other equally secure retired place do, such as Atlanta or Leavenworth or maybe even Alcatraz two thousand miles away out in California, where old Judge Long would a already had him on the first train leaving Jefferson while he was still looking at the top one of them French postcards; jest exactly why wouldn't no other place do Flem to have Montgomery Ward sent to but Parchman, Missippi.

Because even in the initial excitement, Montgomery Ward never had one moment's confusion about what was actively happening to him. The second moment after Lawyer and Hub walked in the door, he knowed that at last something was happening that he had been expecting ever since whenever that other moment was when Flem found out or suspected that whatever was going on up that alley had a money profit in it. The only thing that puzzled him was, why Flem was going to all that extra trouble and complication jest to usurp him outen that nekkid picture business. That was like the story about the coon in the tree that asked the name of the feller aiming the gun at him and when the feller told him, the coon says, "Hell fire, is that who you are? Then you dont need to waste all this time and powder jest on me. Stand to one side and I'll climb down."

Not to mention reckless. Having Flem Snopes take his business away from him was all right. He had been expecting that: that sooner or later his turn would come too, running as he did the same risk with ever body else in Yoknapatawpha County owning a business solvent enough for Flem to decide he wanted it too. But to let the county attorney and the county sheriff get a-holt of them pictures, the two folks of all the folks in Yoknapatawpha County that not even Grover Winbush would a been innocent enough to dream would ever turn them loose again—Lawyer Stevens, so dedicated to civic improvement and the moral advancement of folks that his purest notion of duty was brow-beating twelve-year-old boys into running five-mile foot-races when all they really wanted to do was jest to stay at home and set fire to the barn; and Hub Hampton, a meat-eating hard-shell Baptist deacon whose purest notion of pleasure was counting off the folks he personally knowed was already bound for hell.

Why, in fact, Montgomery Ward had to go anywhere, if all his uncle or cousin wanted was jest to take his business away from him, except maybe jest to stay outen sight for a week or maybe a month or two to give folks time to forget about them nekkid pictures, or anyway that anybody named Snopes was connected with them, Flem being a banker now and having to deal not jest in simple usury but in respectability too.

No, what really should a puzzled Montgomery Ward, filled him in fact with delighted surprise, was how he had managed to last even this long. It never needed the Law nor Flem Snopes neither to close out that studio, pull the blinds down (or rather up) for good and all on the French postcard industry in Jefferson, Missippi. Grover Winbush done that when he let whoever it was ketch him slipping outen that alley at two oclock that morning. No: Grover Winbush had done already wrecked and ruined that business in Jefferson at the same moment when he found out there was a side door in a Jefferson alley with what you might call a dry whorehouse behind it. No, that business was wrecked in Jefferson the same moment Grover got appointed night marshal, Grover having jest exactly enough sense to be a night policeman providing the town wasn't no bigger and never stayed awake no later than Jefferson, Missippi, since that would be the one job in all paid laborious endeavor—leaning all night against a lamp-post looking at the empty Square—you would have thought he could a held indefinitely, providing the influence of whoever got it for him or give it to him lasted that long, without stumbling over anything he could do any harm with, to his-self or the job or a innocent bystander or maybe all three; and so naturally he would be caught by somebody, almost anybody, the second or third time he come slipping outen that alley.

Which was jest a simple unavoidable occupational hazard of running a business like that in the same town where Grover

Winbush was night marshal, which Montgomery Ward
knowed as well as anybody else that knowed Grover. So when
the business had been running over a year without no unto-
ward interruption, Montgomery Ward figgered that whoever
had been catching Grover slipping in and out of that alley after midnight once a month for the last nine or ten of them,
was maybe business acquaintances Grover had made raiding
crap games or catching them with a pint of moonshine whiskey
in their hind pockets. Or who knows? maybe even Flem his-
self had got a holt of each one of them in time, protecting not
so much his own future interests and proposed investments,
because maybe at that time he hadn't even found out he
wanted to go into the a-teelyer (that's what Montgomery
Ward called it; he had the name painted on the window:
Atelier Monty) business, but simply protecting and defending
solvency and moderate profit itself, not jest out of family loyalty to another Snopes but from pure and simple principle,
even if he was a banker now and naturally would have to
compromise, to a extent at least, profit with respectability,
since any kind of solvency redounds to the civic interest providing it dont get caught, and even respectability can go hand
in hand with civic interest providing the civic interest has got
sense enough to take place after dark and not make no loud
noise at it.

So when the county attorney and the county sheriff walked
in on him that morning, Montgomery Ward naturally believed that pure and simple destiny was simply taking its natural course, and the only puzzling thing was the downright
foolhardy, let alone reckless way Flem Snopes was hoping to
take advantage of destiny. I mean, getting Lawyer Stevens and
Sheriff Hampton into it, letting them get one whiff or flash of
them nekkid pictures. Because of what you might call the late
night shift his business had developed into, the Square never
seen Montgomery Ward before noon. So until Lawyer and
Hub told him about it, he hadn't had time yet to hear about
them two fellers robbing Uncle Willy Christian's drug cabinet
last night, that none of the folks watching the robbers
through the front window could find hide nor hair of Grover
Winbush to tell him about it until Grover finally come slipping back outen Montgomery Ward's alley, by which time

even the robbers, let alone the folks watching them, had done all went home.

I dont mean Montgomery Ward was puzzled that Lawyer and Hub was the first ones there. Naturally they would a been when his a-teeler business finally blowed up, no matter what was the reason for the explosion. He would a expected them first even if Yoknapatawpha County hadn't never heard the word Flem Snopes—a meal-mouthed sanctimonious Harvard- and Europe-educated lawyer that never even needed the excuse of his office and salaried job to meddle in anything providing it wasn't none of his business and wasn't doing him no harm; and old pussel-gutted Hampton that could be fetched along to look at anything, even a murder, once somebody remembered he was Sheriff and told him about it and where it was. No. What baffled Montgomery Ward was, what in creation kind of a aberration could Flem Snopes been stricken with to leave him believing he could use Lawyer Stevens and Hub Hampton to get them pictures, and ever dream of getting them away from them.

So for a moment his faith and confidence in Flem Snopes his-self wavered and flickered you might say. For that one horrid moment he believed that Flem Snopes could be the victim of pure circumstance compounded by Grover Winbush, jest like anybody else. But only a moment. If that durn boy that seen them two robbers in Uncle Willy's drug cabinet had to pick out to go to the late picture show that same one night in that whole week that Grover picked out to take jest one more slip up that alley to Montgomery Ward's back room; if Flem Snopes was subject to the same outrageous misfortune and coincidence that the rest of us was, then we all might jest as well pack up and quit.

So even after Lawyer and Hub told him about them two robbers in Uncle Willy's store, and that boy that his paw ought to burned his britches off for not being home in bed two hours ago, Montgomery Ward still never had one second's doubt that it had been Flem all the time—Flem his-self, with his pure and simple nose for money like a preacher's for sin and fried chicken, finding out fast and quick that profit of some degree was taking place at night behind that alley door, and enough of it to keep folks from as far away as three county seats sneaking up and down that alley at two and three oclock in the morning.

So all Flem needed now was to find out exactly what was going on up that alley that was that discreet and that profitable, setting his spies—not that Grover Winbush would a needed anybody calling his-self a respectable spy with pride in his profession to ketch him, since any little child hired with a ice cream cone would a done for that—to watch who come and went around that corner; until sooner or later, and likely sooner than later, one turned up that Flem could handle. Likely a good deal sooner than later; even spread over four counties like that business was, there wasn't many among the set Montgomery Ward drawed his clientele from that hadn't at least offered to put his name onto a piece of paper to Flem at forty or fifty percent. of three or four dollars, so that Flem could say to him: "About that-ere little note of yourn. I'd like to hold the bank offen you myself, but I aint only vice president of it, and I cant do nothing with Manfred de Spain."

Or maybe it was Grover his-self that Flem caught, catching Grover his-self in the active flesh on that second or third time which was the absolute outside for Grover to slip outen that alley without somebody ketching him, long in fact before them two fellers robbing Uncle Willy Christian's store exposed him by rifling that prescription desk in plain sight of half Jefferson evidently going home from the late picture show except that couldn't nobody locate Grover to tell him about it. Anyway, Flem caught somebody he could squeeze enough to find out jest what Montgomery Ward was selling behind that door. So now all Flem had to do was move in on that industry too, move Montgomery Ward outen it or move it out from under Montgomery Ward the same way he had been grazing on up through Jefferson ever since he eased me and Grover Winbush outen that café we thought we owned back there when I never had no more sense neither than to believe I could tangle with Flem.

Only, a banker now, a vice president, not to mention being the third man, after the Negro that fired the furnace and the preacher his-self, inside the Baptist church ever Sunday morning and the rest of his career in Jefferson doomed to respectability like a feller in his Sunday suit trying to run

through a field of cuckleburrs and beggarlice, naturally Flem
not only couldn't show in it, it couldn't even have no connection with the word Snopes. So as far as Jefferson was concerned the Atelier Monty would be closed out, cleaned up
and struck off the commercial register forevermore and the
business moved into another alley that hadn't never heard of
it before and under a management that, if possible, couldn't
even spell Snopes. Or likely, if Flem had any sense, clean to
another town in Montgomery Ward's old district, where it
would be clean outen Grover Cleveland's reach until at least
next summer when he taken his next two-week's vacation.

So all Montgomery Ward had to do, all he could do in fact,
was jest to wait until Flem decided the moment was ripe to
usurp him outen his a-teelyer or usurp that a-teelyer out from
under him, whichever Flem seen fittest. Likely Montgomery
Ward had at least one moment or two of regretful musing
that his business wasn't the kind where he could a held some
kind of a quick fire-sale before Flem would have time to hear
about it. But his stock in trade being such a nebulous quantity that it never had no existence except during the moment
when the customer was actively buying and consuming it, the
only thing he could a sold would be his capital investment itself, which would not only be contrary to all the economic
laws, he wouldn't even have no nebulous stock in trade to sell
to nobody during whatever time he would have left before
Flem foreclosed him, which might be weeks or even months
yet. So all he could do was to apply whatever methods and
means of speed-up and increased turn-over was available
while waiting for Flem to move, naturally speculating on jest
what method Flem would finally use—whether Flem had
done found some kind of handle or crowbar in his, Montgomery Ward's, own past to prize him out, or maybe would
do something as crude and unimaginative as jest offering him
money for it.

So he expected Flem. But he never expected Hub
Hampton and Lawyer Stevens. So for what you might call a
flashing moment or two after Hub and Lawyer busted in that
morning, Montgomery Ward figgered it was this here new respectability Flem had done got involved with: a respectability
that delicate and tetchous that wouldn't nothing else suit it

but it must look like the Law itself had purified the Snopes a-teelyer industry outen Jefferson, and so Flem was jest using Lawyer Stevens and Hub Hampton for a cat'spaw. Of course another moment of thoughtful deliberation would a suhjested to him that once a feller dedicated to civic improvement and the moral advancement of youth like Lawyer Stevens, and a meat-eating Hardshell Baptist deacon like Hub Hampton got a holt of them nekkid photographs, there wouldn't be nothing left of that business for Flem to move nowhere except the good will. Though them little hard pale-colored eyes looking down at him across the top of Hub Hampton's belly wasn't hardly the time for meditation and deliberation of any kind, thoughtful or not. In fact Montgomery Ward was so far from being deliberate or even thinking a-tall for that matter, that it aint surprising if in that same flashing moment he likely cast on his cousin Flem the horrid aspersion that Flem had let Lawyer Stevens and Hub Hampton outfigger him; that Flem had merely aimed to close him, Montgomery Ward, out, and was innocent enough to believe he could get them nekkid pictures back outen Hub Hampton's hands once Hub had seen them, and that that cat'spaw's real name was Flem Snopes.

Though even in his extremity Montgomery Ward had more simple sense and judgment, let alone family pride and loyalty, than to actively believe that ten thousand Lawyer Stevenses and Hub Hamptons, let alone jest one each of them, could a diddled Flem Snopes. In fact, sooner than that foul aspersion, he would believe that Flem Snopes was subject to bad luck too, jest like a human being—not the bad luck of misreading Grover Winbush's character that Grover could slip up and down that alley two or three times a week for seven or eight months without ever body in Yoknapatawpha County ketching him at least once, but the bad luck of being unable to anticipate that them two robbers would pick out the same night to rob Uncle Willy Christian's drugstore that that Rouncewell boy would to climb down the drain pipe and go to the late picture show.

So all Montgomery Ward had to do now was set in his jail cell where Hub taken him and wait with what you might call almost professional detachment and interest to see how Flem was going to get them pictures back from Hub. It would take time of course; even with all his veneration and family pride for Flem Snopes, he knowed that even for Flem it wouldn't be as simple as picking up a hat or a umbrella. So when the rest of that day passed and hadn't nothing more happened, it was exactly as he had anticipated. Naturally he had toyed with the notion that, took by surprise too, Flem might call on him, Montgomery Ward, to pick up whatever loose useful ends of information he might have without even knowing he had none. But when Flem never showed up nor sent word, if anything his admiration and vindication for Flem jest increased that much more since here was active proof that Flem wasn't going to need even what little more, even if it wasn't no more than encouragement and moral support, that Montgomery Ward could a told him.

And he anticipated right on through that night and what you might call them mutual Yoknapatawpha County bedbugs, on into the next morning too. So you can imagine his interested surprise—not alarm yet nor even astonishment: jest interest and surprise—when whatever thoughtful acquaintance (it was Euphus Tubb, the jailor; he was a interested party too, not to mention having spent most of his life being surprised) come in that afternoon and told him how Hub Hampton had went back to the studio that morning jest in case him and Lawyer had overlooked any further evidence yesterday, and instead captured five gallons of moonshine whiskey setting in the bottles on the shelf that Montgomery Ward his-self assumed never held nothing but photograph developer. "Now you can go to Parchman instead of Atlanta," Euphus says. "Which wont be so fur away. Not to mention being in Missippi, where a native Missippi jailor can get the money for your keep instead of these durn judges sending our Missippi boys clean out of the country where folks we never even heard of before can collect on them."

Not alarm, not astonishment: jest interest and surprise and even that mostly jest interest. Because Montgomery Ward knowed that them bottles never had nothing but developer in them when him and Hub and Lawyer left the a-teelyer yesterday morning, and he knowed that Hub Hampton and Lawyer Stevens both knowed that was all that was in them, because for a feller in the nekkid photograph business in Jefferson, Missippi, to complicate it up with peddling whiskey, would be jest pleading for trouble, like the owner of a roulette wheel or a crap table dreaming of running a counterfeiting press in the same basement.

Because he never had one moment's doubt it was Flem that planted that whiskey where Hub Hampton would have to find it; and this time his admiration and veneration notched right up to the absolute top because he knowed that Flem, being a banker now and having to be as tender about respectability as a unescorted young gal waking up suddenly in the middle of a drummers' convention, not only couldn't a afforded to deal with no local bootlegger and so probably had to go his-self back out to Frenchman's Bend or maybe even all the way up into Beat Nine to Nub Gowrie to get it, he even had to pay twenty-five or thirty dollars of his own cash money to boot. And indeed for a unguarded fraction of the next moment the thought might a occurred to him how them twenty-five or thirty dollars revealed that Flem too in the last analysis wasn't immune neither to the strong and simple call of blood kinship. Though that was jest a fraction of a moment, if as much as that even, because even though Flem too at times might be victim of weakness and aberration, wouldn't none of them ever a been paying even twenty dollars for a Snopes.

No, them twenty-five or thirty dollars simply meant that it was going to be a little harder than Flem had expected or figgered. But the fact that he hadn't hesitated even twenty-four hours to pay it, showed that Flem anyhow never had no doubts about the outcome. So naturally Montgomery Ward never had none neither, not even needing to anticipate no more but jest to wait, because by that time about half of Jefferson was doing the anticipating for him and half the waiting too, not to mention the watching. Until the next day we watched Flem cross the Square and go up the street to the jail and go into it and a half a hour later come out again. And the next day after that Montgomery Ward was out too with Flem for his bond. And the next day after that one Clarence Snopes was in town—Senator Clarence Egglestone Snopes of the state legislature now, that used to be Constable Snopes of

Frenchman's Bend until he made the mistake of pistol-whip-
ping in the name of the Law some feller that was spiteful and
vindictive enough to object to being pistol-whipped jest because the one doing the whipping was bigger than him and
wore a badge. So Uncle Billy Varner had to do something
with Clarence so he got a holt of Flem and both of them got
a holt of Manfred de Spain at the bank and all three of them
got a holt of enough other folks to get Clarence into the legislature in Jackson where he wouldn't even know nothing to
do until somebody Uncle Billy and Manfred could trust
would tell him when to mark his name or hold up his hand.

Except that, as Lawyer Stevens said, he seemed to found his
true vocation before that: finally coming in to town from
Frenchman's Bend one day and finding out that the country
extended even on past Jefferson, on to the north-west in fact
until it taken in Mulberry and Gayoso and Pontotoc streets in
Memphis, Tennessee, so that when he got back three days
later the very way his hair still stood up and his eyes still
bugged out seemed to be saying, "Hell fire, hell fire, why
wasn't I told about this sooner? How long has this been going on?" But he was making up fast for whatever time he had
missed. You might say in fact he had done already passed it
because now ever time he went or come between Frenchman's Bend and Jackson by way of Jefferson he went by way
of Memphis too, until now he was what Lawyer Stevens called
the apostolic venereal ambassador from Gayoso Avenue to the
entire north Missippi banloo.

So when on the fourth morning Montgomery Ward and
Clarence got on Number Six north-bound, we knowed Clarence was jest going by Memphis to Jackson or Frenchman's
Bend. But all we thought about Montgomery Ward was, jest
what could he a had in that a-teelyer that even Hub never
found, that was worth two thousand dollars of bond money
to Flem Snopes to get him to Mexico or wherever Montgomery Ward would wind up. So ours wasn't jest interested
surprise: ours was interested all right but it was astonishment
and some good hard fast thinking too when two days later
Clarence and Montgomery Ward both got off of Number
Five south-bound and Clarence turned Montgomery Ward
back over to Flem and went on to Jackson or Frenchman's

Bend or wherever he would have to go to leave from to come back by Gayoso Street, Memphis, next time. And Flem turned Montgomery Ward back over to Euphus Tubb, back into the cell in the jail, that two-thousand dollar bond of Flem's rescinded or maybe jest withdrawed for all time like you hang your Sunday hat back on the rack until the next wedding or funeral or whenever you might need it again.

Who—I mean Euphus—apparently in his turn turned Montgomery Ward over to Miz Tubb. We heard how she even hung a old shade over the cell window to keep the morning sun from waking him up so early. And how any time Lawyer Stevens or Hub Hampton or any other such members of the Law would want a word with Montgomery Ward now, the quickest place to look for him would be in Miz Tubbziz kitchen with one of her aprons on, shelling peas or husking roasting-ears. And we—all right, me then—would kind of pass along the alley by the jail and there Montgomery Ward would be, him and Miz Tubb in the garden while Montgomery Ward hoed out the vegetable rows, not making much of a out at it maybe, but anyhow swinging the hoe as long as Miz Tubb showed him where to chop next.

"Maybe she's still trying to find out about them pictures," Homer Bookwright says.

"What?" I says. "Miz Tubb?"

"Of course she wants to know about them," Homer says. "Aint she human too, even if she is a woman?"

And three weeks later Montgomery Ward stood up in Judge Long's court and Judge Long give him two years in the state penitentiary at Parchman for the possession of one developer jug containing one gallon of moonshine whiskey herewith in evidence.

So ever body was wrong. Flem Snopes hadn't spent no two thousand dollars worth of bond money to purify Montgomery Ward outen the U.S.A. America, and he hadn't spent no twenty-five or thirty dollars worth of white mule whiskey jest to purify the Snopes family name outen Atlanta, Georgia. What he had done was to spend twenty-five or thirty dollars to send Montgomery Ward to Parchman when the government would a sent him to Georgia free. Which was a good deal more curious than jest surprising, and a good deal more interesting than all three. So the next morning I happened to be on the deepo platform when Number Eleven south-bound was due and sho enough, there was Montgomery Ward and Hunter Killegrew, the deputy, and I says to Hunter: "Dont you need to step into the wash-room before you get on the train for such a long trip? I'll watch Montgomery Ward for you. Besides, a feller that wouldn't run off three weeks ago under a two-thousand dollar bond aint likely to try it now with nothing on him but a handcuff."

So Hunter handed me his half of the handcuff and moved a little away and I says to Montgomery Ward:

"So you're going to Parchman instead. That'll be a heap better. Not only you wont be depriving no native-born Missippi grub contractor outen his rightful and natural profit on the native-born Missippi grub they'll be feeding a native-born Missippi convict, you wont be lonesome there neither, having a native-born Missippi cousin or uncle to pass the time with when you aint otherwise occupied with field work or something. What's his name? Mink Snopes, your uncle or cousin that got in that little trouble a while back for killing Zack Houston and kept trying to wait for Flem to come back from Texas in time to get him outen it, except that Flem was otherwise occupied too and so Mink acted kind of put out about it? Which was he, your uncle or your cousin?"

"Yeah?" Montgomery Ward says.

"Well, which?" I says.

"Which what?" Montgomery Ward says.

"Is he your uncle or is he your cousin?" I says.

"Yeah?" Montgomery Ward says.

Four

MONTGOMERY WARD SNOPES

So the son of a bitch fooled you," I said. "You thought they were going to hang him but all he got was life."

He didn't answer. He just sat there in the kitchen chair—he had toted it up himself from Tubb's kitchen. For me, there wasn't anything in the cell but the cot; for me and the bedbugs that is—he just sat there with the shadow of the window bars crisscrossing that white shirt and that damn little ten-cent snap-on bow tie; they said the same one he had worn in from Frenchman's Bend sixteen years ago. No: they said not the same one he took out of Varner's stock and put on the day he came in from that tenant farm and went to work as Varner's clerk and married Varner's whore of a daughter in and wore to Texas while the bastard kid was getting born and then wore back again; that was when he wore the cloth cap about the size for a fourteen-year-old child. And the black felt hat somebody told him was the kind of hat bankers wore, that he didn't throw away the cap: he sold it to a nigger boy for a dime that he took out in work and put the hat on for the first time three years ago and they said had never taken it off since, not even in the house, except in church, that still looked new. No, it didn't look like it belonged to anybody, even after day and night for three years, not even sweated, which would include while he was laying his wife too which would be all right with her probably since the sort of laying she was used to they probably didn't even take off their gloves, let alone their hats and shoes and overcoats.

And chewing. They said when he first came in to Frenchman's Bend as Varner's clerk it was tobacco. Then he found out about money. Oh, he had heard about money and had even seen a little of it now and then. But now he found out for the first time that there was more of it each day than you could eat up each day if you ate twice as much fried sowbelly and white gravy. Not only that, but that it was solid, harder than bones and heavy like gravel and that if you could shut your hands on some of it, there was no power anywhere that

could make you let go of more of it than you had to let go
of, so he found out that he couldn't afford to chew up ten
cents' worth of it every week because he had discovered
chewing gum by then that a nickel's worth of would last five
weeks, a new stick every Sunday. Then he came to Jefferson
and he really saw some money, I mean all at one time, and
then he found out that the only limit to the amount of money
you could shut your hands on and keep and hold, was just
how much money there was, provided you had a good safe
place to put that other handful down and empty your fists
again. And then was when he found out he couldn't afford to
chew even one cent a week. When he had nothing, he could
afford to chew tobacco; when he had a little, he could afford
to chew gum; when he found out he could be rich provided
he just didn't die before hand, he couldn't afford to chew
anything, just sitting there in that kitchen chair with the
shadow of the cell-bars crisscrossing him, chewing that and
not looking at me or not anymore anyway.

"Life," I said. "That means twenty years, the way they figure it, unless something happens between now and then.
How long has it been now? Nineteen-eight, wasn't it, when
he hung all day long maybe in this same window here, watching the street for you to come on back from Texas and get
him out, being as you were the only Snopes then that had
enough money and influence to help him as he figured it, hollering down to anybody that passed to get word out to
Varner's store for you to come in and save him, then standing
up there in that courtroom on that last day and giving you
your last chance, and you never came then either? Nineteen-
eight to nineteen-twenty-three from twenty years, and he'll
be out again. Hell fire, you've only got five more years to live,
haven't you? All right. What do you want me to do?"

He told me.

"All right," I said. "What do I get for it?"

He told me that. I stood there for a while leaning against
the wall, laughing down at him. Then I told him.

He didn't even move. He just quit chewing long enough to
say, "Ten thousand dollars."

"So that's too high," I said. "All your life is worth to you
is about five hundred, mostly in trade, on the installment

plan." He sat there in that cross-barred shadow, chewing his mouthful of nothing, watching me or at least looking toward me. "Even if it works, the best you can do is get his sentence doubled, get twenty more years added onto it. That means that in nineteen-forty-three you'll have to start all over again worrying about having only five years more to live. Quit sucking and smouching around for bargains. Buy the best; you can afford it. Take ten grand cash and have him killed. From what I hear, for that jack you could have all Chicago bidding against each other. Or ten grand, hell, and Chicago, hell too; for one you could stay right here in Mississippi and have a dozen trusties right there in Parchman drawing straws for him, for which one would shoot him first in the back."

He didn't even quit chewing this time.

"Well well," I said. "So there's something that even a Snopes wont do. No, that's wrong; Uncle Mink never seemed to have any trouble reconciling Zack Houston up in front of that shotgun when the cheese begun to bind. Maybe what I mean is, every Snopes has one thing he wont do to you—provided you can find out what it is before he has ruined and wrecked you. Make it five then," I said. "I wont haggle. What the hell, aint we cousins or something?"

This time he quit chewing long enough to say, "Five thousand dollars."

"Okay, I know you haven't got five grand cash either now," I said. "You dont even need it now. That lawyer says you got two years to raise it in, hock or sell or steal whatever you'll have to hock or sell or steal."

That got to him—or so I thought then. I'm a pretty slow learner myself sometimes, now and then, mostly now in fact. Because he said something: "You wont have to stay two years. I can get you out."

"When?" I said. "When you're satisfied? When I have wrecked the rest of his life by getting twenty more years hung onto it? Not me, you wont. Because I wont come out. I wouldn't even take the five grand; I was kidding you. This is how we'll do it. I'll go on down there and fix him, get him whatever additional time the traffic will bear. Only I wont come out then. I'll finish out my two years first; give you a little more time of your own, see. Then I'll come out and come

on back home. You know: start a new life, live down that old
bad past. Of course I wont have any job, business, but after
all there's my own father's own first cousin every day and
every way getting to be bigger and bigger in the bank and the
church and local respectability and civic reputation and what
the hell, aint blood thicker than just water even if some of it
is just back from Parchman for bootlegging, not to mention
at any minute now his pride might revolt at charity even from
his respectable blood kin banker cousin and he might decide
to set up that old unrespectable but fairly damned popular
business again. Because I can get plenty more stock-in-trade
and the same old goodwill will still be here just waiting for
me to tell them where to go and maybe this time there wont
be any developer-fluid jugs sitting carelessly around. And suppose they are, what the hell? it's just two years and I'll be back
again, already reaching to turn over that old new leaf——"

He put his hand inside his coat and he didn't say "Yep" in
that tone because he didn't know how yet but if he had
known he would. So he said, "Yep, that's what I figgered,"
and drew out the envelope. Oh sure, I recognised it. It was
one of mine, with *Atelier Monty Jefferson Miss* in the left corner, all stamped and showing the cancellation clear as an etch-
ing and addressed to *G.C. Winbush, City* so I already knew
what was in it before he even took it out: the photo that
Winbush had insisted on buying for five bucks for his private
files as they call it that I hadn't wanted to let him have it because anybody associating with him in anything was already in
jeopardy. But what the hell, he was the Law, or what passed
for it in that alley at one or two in the morning anyway. And
oh yes, it had been through the mail all right even though I
never mailed it and it hadn't been any further than through
that damn cancelling machine inside the Jefferson postoffice.
And with the trouble Winbush was already in from being in
my back room instead of getting what he called his brains
beaten out by old dope-eating Will Christian's burglars, it
wouldn't have taken any Simon Legree to find out he had the
picture and then to get it away from him; nor anything at all
to make him swear or perjure to anything anybody suggested
to him regarding it. Because he had a wife and all you'd need
would be just to intimate to Winbush you were going to

show it to her since she was the sort of wife that no power on earth would unconvince her that the girl in the photo—she happened to be alone in this one and happened not to be doing anything except just being buck-naked—was not only Winbush's private playmate but that probably only some last desperate leap got Winbush himself out of the picture without his pants on. And it wouldn't take any Sherlock Holmes to discern what that old sanctimonious lantern-jawed son of a bitch up there on that Federal bench would do when he saw that cancelled envelope. So I said,

"So it looks like I've been raised. And it looks like I wont call. In fact, it looks like I'm going to pass. After I go down there and get him fixed, you get me out. Then what?"

"A railroad ticket to wherever you want, and a hundred dollars."

"Make it five," I said. Then I said, "All right. I wont haggle. Make it two-fifty." And he didn't haggle either.

"A hundred dollars," he said.

"Only I'm going to cut the pot for the house kitty," I said. "If I've got to spend at least a year locked up in a goddamned cotton farm—" No, he didn't haggle; you could say that for him.

"I figgered that too," he said. "It's all arranged. You'll be out on bond tomorrow. Clarence will pick you up on his way through town to Memphis. You can have two days." And by God he had even thought of that too. "Clarence will have the money. It will be enough."

Whether what he would call enough or what I would call enough. So nobody was laughing at anybody anymore now. I just stood there looking down at him where he sat in that kitchen chair, chewing, not looking at anything and not even chewing anything, that everybody that knew him said he never took a drink in his life yet hadn't hesitated to buy thirty or forty dollars' worth of whiskey to get me into Parchman where I could wreck Mink, and evidently was getting ready to spend another hundred (or more likely two if he intended to pay for Clarence too) to reconcile me to staying in Parchman long enough to do the wrecking that would keep Mink from getting out in five years; and all of a sudden I knew what it was that had bothered me about him ever since I got

big enough to understand about such and maybe draw a
conclusion.

"So you're a virgin," I said. "You never had a lay in your
life, did you? You even waited to get married until you found
a woman who not only was already knocked up, she wouldn't
even have let you run your hand up her dress. Jesus, you do
want to stay alive, dont you? Only, why?" And still he said
nothing: just sitting there chewing nothing. "But why put
out money on Clarence too? Even if he does prefer nigger
houses where the top price is a dollar, it'll cost you something
with Clarence as the operator. Give me all the money and let
me go by myself." But as soon as I said it I knew the answer
to that too. He couldn't risk letting me get one mile out of
Jefferson without somebody along to see I came back, even
with that cancelled envelope in his pocket. He knew better,
but he couldn't risk finding out he was right. He didn't dare.
He didn't dare at his age to find out that all you need to handle nine people out of ten is just to trust them.

Tubb knew about the bond so he was all for turning me
out that night so he could put the cost of my supper in his
pocket and hope that in the confusion it wouldn't be noticed
but I said Much obliged. I said: "Dont brag. I was in (on the
edge of it anyway) the U.S. army; if you think this dump is
lousy, you should have seen some of the places I slept in,"
with Tubb standing there in the open cell door with the key-
ring in one hand and scratching his head with the other. "But
what you can do, go out and get me a decent supper; Mr
Snopes will pay for it; my rich kinfolks have forgiven me now.
And while you're about it, bring me the Memphis paper." So
he started out until this time I hollered it: "Come back and
lock the door! I dont want all Jefferson in here; one son of a
bitch in this kennel is enough."

So the next morning Clarence showed up and Flem gave
him the money and that night we were in Memphis, at the
Teaberry. That was me. Clarence knew a dump where he was
a regular customer, where we could stay for a dollar a day
even when it wasn't even his money. Flem's money, that you
would have thought anybody else named Snopes would have
slept on the bare ground provided it just cost Flem twice as
much as anywhere else would.

"Now what?" Clarence said. It was what they call rhetorical. He already knew what, or thought he did. He had it all lined up. One thing about Clarence: he never let you down. He couldn't; everybody that knew him knew he would have to be a son of a bitch, being my half-brother.

Last year Virgil (that's right. Snopes. You guessed it: Uncle Wesley's youngest boy—the revival song-leader that they caught after church that day with the fourteen-year-old girl in the empty cotton house and tar-and-feathered him to Texas or anyway out of Yoknapatawpha County; Virgil's gift was inherited) and Fonzo Winbush, my patient's nephew I believe it is, came up to Memphis to enter a barbers' college. Somebody—it would be Mrs Winbush; she wasn't a Snopes—evidently told them never to rent a room to live in unless the woman of the house looked mature and Christian, but most of all motherly.

So they were probably still walking concentric circles around the railroad station, still carrying their suitcases, when they passed Reba Rivers's at the time every afternoon when she would come out her front door to exercise those two damn nasty little soiled white dogs that she called Miss Reba and Mr Binford after Lucius Binford who had been her pimp until they both got too old and settled down and all the neighborhood—the cop, the boy that brought the milk and collected for the paper, and the people on the laundry truck—called him landlord until he finally died.

She looked mature all right in anything, let alone the wrappers she wore around that time in the afternoon, and she would probably sound Christian all right whether religious or not, to anybody near enough to hear what she would say to those dogs at times when she had had a little extra gin; and I suppose anybody weighing two hundred pounds in a wrapper fastened with safety pins would look motherly even while she was throwing out a drunk, let alone to two eighteen-year-old boys from Jefferson, Mississippi.

Maybe she was motherly and Virgil and Fonzo, in the simple innocence of children, saw what us old long-standing mere customers and friends missed. Or maybe they just walked impervious in that simple Yoknapatawpha juvenile rural innocence where even an angel would have left his pocket book at the depot first. Anyway, they asked if she had an empty room and she rented them one; likely they had already unpacked those paper suitcases before she realised they didn't even know they were in a whorehouse.

Anyhow, there she was, having to pay the rent and pay off the cops and the man that supplied the beer and the laundry and pay Minnie, the maid, something on Saturday night, not to mention having to keep those big yellow diamonds shined and cleaned until they wouldn't look too much like big chunks of a broken beer-bottle; and that Yoknapatawpha innocence right in the middle of the girls running back and forth to the bathroom in nighties and negligees or maybe not even that, and the customers going and coming and Minnie running stacks of towels and slugs of gin up the stairs and the women screaming and fighting and pulling each other's hair over their boys and clients and money and Reba herself in the hall cursing a drunk while they tried to throw him out before the cops got there; until in less than a week she had that house as quiet and innocent as a girls' school until she could get Virgil and Fonzo upstairs into their room and in bed and, she hoped, asleep.

Naturally it couldn't last. To begin with, there was the barbers' college where they would have to listen to barbers all day long when you have to listen to enough laying just spending thirty minutes getting your hair cut. Then to come back there and get a flash of a leg or a chemise or maybe a whole naked female behind running through a door, would be bound to give them ideas after a time even though Virgil and Fonzo still thought they were all Reba's nieces or wards or something just in town maybe attending female equivalents of barbers' colleges themselves. Not to mention that pure instinct which Virgil and Fonzo (did I say he was Grover Winbush's nephew) had inherited from the pure fountain-heads themselves.

It didn't last past the second month. And since the Memphis red-light district is not all that big, it was only the course of time until they and Clarence turned up at the same time in the same place, especially as Virgil and Fonzo, still forced to devote most of their time to learning yet and not earning, had to hunt for bargains. Where right away Virgil showed himself the owner of a really exceptional talent—a capacity to take care of two girls in succession to their satisfaction or at least until they hollered quit, that was enough for two dollars, in his youthful enthusiasm and innocence not only doing it for pleasure but even paying for the chance until Clarence discovered him and put him into the money.

He—Clarence—would loaf around the pool rooms and the sort of hotel lobbies he patronised himself, until he would find a sucker who refused to believe his bragging about his—what's the word?—protégé's powers, and Clarence would bet him; the first time the victim would usually give odds. Of course Virgil would fail now and then—

"And pays half the bet," I said.

"What?" Clarence said. "Penalise the boy for doing his best? Besides, it dont happen once in ten times and he's going to get better and better as time goes on. What a future that little sod's got if the supply of two-dollar whores just holds out."

Anyway, that's what we were going to do tonight. "Much obliged," I said. "You go ahead. I'm going to make a quiet family call on an old friend and then coming back to bed. Let me have twenty-five—make it thirty of the money."

"Flem gave me a hundred."

"Thirty will do," I said.

"Be damned if that's so," he said. "You'll take half of it. I dont aim to take you back to Jefferson and have you tell Flem a god-damn lie about me. Here."

I took the money. "See you at the station tomorrow at train-time."

"What?" he said.

"I'm going home tomorrow. You dont have to."

"I promised Flem I'd stay with you and bring you back."

"Break it," I said. "Haven't you got fifty dollars of his money?"

"That's it," he said. "Damn a son of a bitch that'll break his word after he's been paid for it."

Wednesday evenings were nearly always quiet unless there was a convention in town, maybe because so many of the women (clients too) came from little Tennessee and Arkansas and Mississippi country towns and Baptist and Methodist families that they established among the joints and dives and cathouses themselves some analogous? analogous rhythm to the midweek prayer-meeting night. Minnie answered the bell. She had her hat on. I mean her whole head was in it like a football helmet.

"Evening, Minnie," I said. "You going out?"

"No sir," she said. "You been away? We aint seen you in a long time."

"Just busy," I answered. That was what Reba said too. The place was quiet: nobody in the diningroom but Reba and a new girl and one customer, drinking beer, Reba in all her big yellow diamonds but wearing a wrapper instead of the evening gown she would have had on if it had been Saturday night. It was a new wrapper but it was already fastened with safety pins. I answered the same thing too. "Just busy," I said.

"I wish I could return the compliment," she said. "I might as well be running a Sunday School. Meet Captain Strutter-buck," she said. He was tall, pretty big, with a kind of rousterbout's face; I mean, that tried to look tough but wasn't sure yet how you were going to take it, and hard pale eyes that looked at you hard enough, only he couldn't seem to look at you with both of them at the same time. He was about fifty. "Captain Strutterbuck was in both wars," Reba said. "That Spanish one about twenty-five years ago, and the last one too. He was just telling us about the last one. And this is Thelma. She just came in last week."

"Howdy," Strutterbuck said. "Were you a buddy too?"

"More or less," I said.

"What outfit?"

"Lafayette Escadrille," I said.

"Laughing what?" he said. "Oh, La-Fayette Esker-Drill. Flying boys. Dont know anything about flying, myself. I was cavalry, in Cuba in '98 and on the Border in '16, not com-missioned any longer, out of the army in fact: just sort of a private citizen aide to Black Jack because I knew the country. So when they decided to send him to France to run the show over there, he told me if I ever got across to look him up, he would try to find something for me. So when I heard that Rick—Eddie Rickenbacker, the Ace," he told Reba and the new girl, "the General's driver—that Rick had left him for the air corps, I decided that was my chance and I managed to get over all right but he already had another driver, a Sergeant Somebody, I forget his name. So there I was, with no status. But I still managed to see a little of it, from the back seat you might say—Argonne, Showmont, Vymy Ridge, Shatter Theory; you probably saw most of the hot places yourself. Where were you stationed?"

"Y.M.C.A.," I said.

"What?" he said. He got up, slow. He was tall, pretty big; this probably wasn't the first time both his eyes had failed to look at the same thing at the same time. Maybe he depended on it. By that time Reba was up too. "You wouldn't be trying to kid me, would you?" he said.

"Why?" I said. "Dont it work?"

"All right, all right," Reba said. "Are you going up stairs with Thelma, or aint you? If you aint, and you usually aint, tell her so."

"I dont know whether I am or not," he said. "What I think right now is——"

"Folks dont come in here to think," Reba said. "They come in here to do business and then get out. Do you aim to do any business or dont you?"

"Okay, okay," he said. "Let's go," he told Thelma. "Maybe I'll see you again," he told me.

"After the next war," I said. He and Thelma went out. "Are you going to let him?" I said.

"He gets a pension from that Spanish war," Reba said. "It came today. I saw it. I watched him sign his name on the back of it so I can cash it."

"How much?" I said.

"I didn't bother with the front of it. I just made damn sure he signed his name where the notice said sign. It was a United States Government postoffice money order. You dont fool around with the United States Government."

"A postoffice money order can be for one cent provided you can afford the carrying charges," I said. She looked at me. "He wrote his name on the back of a piece of blue paper and put it back in his pocket. I suppose he borrowed the pen from you. Was that it?"

"All right, all right," she said. "What do you want me to

do: lean over the foot of the bed and say, Just a second there, Buster?—" Minnie came in with another bottle of beer. It was for me.

"I didn't order it," I said. "Maybe I should have told you right off. I'm not going to spend any money tonight."

"It's on me then. Why did you come here then? Just to try to pick a fight with somebody?"

"Not with him," I said. "He even got his name out a book. I dont remember what book right now, but it was a better book than the one he got his war out of."

"All right, all right," she said. "Why in hell did you tell him where you were staying? Come to think of it, why are you staying there?"

"Staying where?" I said.

"At the Y.M.C.A. I have some little squirts in here now and then that ought to be at the Y.M.C.A. whether they are or not. But I never had one of them bragging about it before."

"I'm at the Teaberry," I said. "I belonged to the Y.M.C.A. in the war."

"The Y.M.C.A.? In the war? They dont fight. Are you trying to kid me too?"

"I know they dont," I said. "That's why I was in it. That's right. That's where I was. Gavin Stevens, a lawyer down in Jefferson, can tell you. The next time he's in here ask him."

Minnie appeared in the door with a tray with two glasses of gin on it. She didn't say anything: she just stood in the door there where Reba could see her. She still wore the hat.

"All right," Reba said. "But no more. He never paid for that beer yet. But Miss Thelma's new in Memphis and we want to make her feel at home." Minnie went on. "So you're not going to unbutton your pocket tonight."

"I came to ask you a favor," I said. But she wasn't even listening.

"You never did spend much. Oh, you were free enough buying beer and drinks around. But you never done any jazzing. Not with any of my girls, anyway." She was looking at me. "Me neither. I've done outgrowed that too. We could get along." She was looking at me. "I heard about that little business of yours down there in the country. A lot of folks in business here dont like it. They figure you are cutting into

trade un—un— What's that word? lawyers and doctors are always throwing it at you—"

"Unethical," I said. "It means dry."

"Dry?" she said.

"That's right. You might call my branch of your business
the arid or water-proof branch. The desert outpost branch."

"Yes, sure, I see what you mean. That's it exactly. That's
what I would tell them: that just looking at pictures might do
all right for a while down there in the country where there
wasn't no other available handy outlet but that sooner or later
somebody was going to run up enough temperature to where
he would have to run to the nearest well for a bucket of real
water, and maybe it would be mine." She was looking at me.
"Sell it out and come on up here."

"Is this a proposition?" I said.

"All right. Come on up here and be the landlord. The beer
and drinks is already on the house and you wouldn't need
much but cigarettes and clothes and a little jack to rattle in
your pocket and I can afford that and I wouldn't have to be
always watching you about the girls, just like Mr Binford because I could always trust him too, always—" She was looking at me. There was something in her eyes or somewhere I
never had seen before or expected either for that matter. "I
nee—a man can do what a woman cant. You know: paying off
protection, handling drunks, checking up on the son a bitching beer and whiskey peddlers that mark up prices and mis-
count bottles if you aint watching day and night like a
god-damn hawk." Sitting there looking at me, one fat hand
with that diamond the size of a piece of gravel holding the
beer glass. "I need . . . I . . . not jazzing; I done outgrowed
that too long a time ago. It's—it's . . . Three years ago he
died, yet even now I still cant quite believe it." It shouldn't
have been there: the fat raddled face and body that had worn
themselves out with the simple hard physical work of being a
whore and making a living at it like an old prize fighter or
football player or maybe an old horse until they didn't look
like a man's or a woman's either in spite of the cheap rouge
and too much of it and the big diamonds that were real
enough even if you just did not believe that color, and the
eyes with something in or behind them that shouldn't have

been there; that, as they say, shouldn't happen to a dog. Minnie passed the door going back down the hall. The tray was empty now. "For fourteen years we was like two doves." She looked at me. Yes, not even to a dog. "Like two doves," she roared and lifted the glass of beer then banged it down hard and shouted at the door: "Minnie!" Minnie came back to the door. "Bring the gin," Reba said.

"Now, Miss Reba, you dont want to start that," Minnie said. "Dont you remember, last time you started grieving about Mr Binford we had po-lice in here until four oclock in the morning. Drink your beer and forget about gin."

"Yes," Reba said. She even drank some of the beer. Then she set the glass down. "You said something about a favor. It cant be money—I aint talking about your nerve: I mean your good sense. So it might be interesting—"

"Except it is money," I said. I took out the fifty dollars and separated ten from it and pushed the ten across to her. "I'm going away for a couple of years. That's for you to remember me by." She didn't touch it. She wasn't even looking at it though Minnie was. She just looked at me. "Maybe Minnie can help too," I said. "I want to make a present of forty dollars to the poorest son of a bitch I can find. Who is the poorest son of a bitch anywhere at this second that you and Minnie know?"

They were both looking at me, Minnie too from under the hat. "How do you mean, poor?" Reba said.

"That's in trouble or jail or somewhere that maybe wasn't his fault."

"Minnie's husband is a son of a bitch and he's in jail all right," Reba said. "But I wouldn't call him poor. Would you, Minnie?"

"Nome," Minnie said.

"But at least he's out of woman trouble for a while," Reba told Minnie. "That ought to make you feel a little better."

"You dont know Ludus," Minnie said. "I like to see any place, chain gang or not, where Ludus cant find some fool woman to believe him."

"What did he do?" I said.

"He quit his job last winter and laid around here ever since, eating out of my kitchen and robbing Minnie's pocket book every night after she went to sleep, until she caught him actually giving the money to the other woman, and when she tried to ask him to stop he snatched the flatiron out of her hand and damn near tore her ear off with it. That's why she has to wear a hat all the time even in the house. So I'd say if any—if anybody deserved them forty dollars it would be Minnie——"

A woman began screaming at the top of the stairs in the upper hall. Minnie and Reba ran out. I picked up the money and followed. The woman screaming the curses was the new girl, Thelma, standing at the head of the stairs in a flimsy kimono, or more or less of it. Captain Strutterbuck was halfway down the stairs, wearing his hat and carrying his coat in one hand and trying to button his fly with the other. Minnie was at the foot of the stairs. She didn't outshout Thelma nor even shout her silent: Minnie just had more volume, maybe more practice:

"Course he never had no money. He aint never had more than two dollars at one time since he been coming here. Why you ever let him get on the bed without the money in your hand first, I dont know. I bet he never even took his britches off. A man wont take his britches off, dont never have no truck with him a-tall; he done already shook his foot, no matter what his mouth still saying."

"All right," Reba told Minnie. "That'll do." Minnie stepped back; even Thelma hushed; she saw me or something and even pulled the kimono back together in front. Strutterbuck came on down the stairs, still fumbling at the front of his pants; maybe the last thing he did want was for both his eyes to look at the same thing at the same time. But I dont know; according to Minnie he had no more reason to be alarmed and surprised now at where he was than a man walking a tight rope. Concerned of course and damned careful, but not really alarmed and last of all surprised. He reached the downstairs floor. But he was not done yet. There were still eight or ten feet to the front door.

But Reba was a lady. She just held her hand out until he quit fumbling at his fly and took the folded money order out of whatever pocket it was in and handed it to her. A lady. She never raised her hand at him. She never even cursed him. She just went to the front door and took hold of the knob and turned and said, "Button yourself up. Aint no man going to walk out of my house at just eleven oclock at night with his pants still hanging open." Then she closed the door after him and locked it. Then she unfolded the money order. Minnie was right. It was for two dollars, issued at Lonoke, Arkansas. The sender's name was spelled Q'Milla Strutterbuck. "His sister or his daughter?" Reba said. "What's your guess?"

Minnie was looking too. "It's his wife," she said. "His sister or mama or grandma would sent five. His woman would sent fifty—if she had it and felt like sending it. His daughter would sent fifty cents. Wouldn't nobody but his wife sent two dollars."

She brought two more bottles of beer to the diningroom table. "All right," Reba said. "You want a favor. What favor?"

I took out the money again and shoved the ten across to her again, still holding the other forty. "This is for you and Minnie, to remember me until I come back in two years. I want you to send the other to my great-uncle in the Mississippi penitentiary at Parchman."

"Will you come back in two years?"

"Yes," I said. "You can look for me. Two years. The man I'm going to be working for says I'll be back in one but I dont believe him."

"All right. Now what do I do with the forty?"

"Send it to my great-uncle Mink Snopes in Parchman."

"What's he in for?"

"He killed a man named Zack Houston back in 1908."

"Did Houston deserve killing?"

"I dont know. But from what I hear, he sure worked to earn it."

"The poor son of a bitch. How long is your uncle in for?"

"Life," I said.

"All right," she said. "I know about that too. When will he get out?"

"About 1948 if he lives and nothing else happens to him."

"All right. How do I do it?" I told her, the address and all.

"You could send it, From another prisoner."

"I doubt it," she said. "I aint never been in jail. I dont aim to be."

"Send it From a friend then."

"All right," she said. She took the money and folded it. "The poor son of a bitch," she said.

"Which one are you talking about now?"

"Both of them," she said. "All of us. Every one of us. The poor son of a bitches."

I hadn't expected to see Clarence at all until tomorrow morning. But there he was, a handful of crumpled bills scattered on the top of the dresser like the edge of a crap game and Clarence undressed down to his trousers standing looking at them and yawning and rooting in the pelt on his chest. This time they—Clarence—had found a big operator, a hot sport who, Virgil having taken on the customary two successfully, bet them he couldn't handle a third one without stopping, offering them the odds this time, which Clarence covered with Flem's other fifty since this really would be a risk; he said how he even gave Virgil a chance to quit and not hold it against him: "'We're ahead now, you know; you done already proved yourself.' And do you know, the little sod never even turned a hair. 'Sure,' he says. 'Send her in.' And now my conscience hurts me," he said, yawning again. "It was Flem's money. My conscience says dont tell him a durn thing about it: the money just got spent like he thinks it was. But shucks, a man dont want to be a hog."

So we went back home. "Why do you want to go back to the jail?" Flem said. "It'll be three weeks yet."

"Call it for practice," I said. "Call it a dry run against my conscience." So now I had a set of steel bars between; now I was safe from the free world, safe and secure for a little while yet from the free Snopes world where Flem was parlaying his wife into the presidency of a bank and Clarence even drawing perdiem as a state senator between Jackson and Gayoso Street to take the wraps off Virgil whenever he could find another Arkansas sport who refused to believe what he was looking at, and Byron in Mexico or wherever he was with whatever was still left of the bank's money, and mine and Clarence's father I.O. and all of our Uncle Wesley leading a hymn with one hand and fumbling the skirt of an eleven-year-old infant with the other; I dont count Wallstreet and Admiral Dewey and their father Eck, because they dont belong to us: they are only our shame.

Not to mention Uncle Murdering Mink six or seven weeks
later (I had to wait a little while you see not to spook him too
quick). "Flem?" he said. "I wouldn't a thought Flem wanted
me out. I'd a thought he'd been the one wanted to keep me
here longest."

"He must have changed," I said. He stood there in his
barred overalls, blinking a little—a damn little worn-out
dried-up shrimp of a man not as big as a fourteen-year-old
boy. Until you wondered how in hell anything as small and
frail could have held enough mad, let alone steadied and
aimed a ten-gauge shotgun, to kill anybody.

"I'm obliged to him," he said. "Only, if I got out tomorrow, maybe I wont done changed. I been here a long time
now. I aint had much to do for a right smart while now but
jest work in the field and think. I wonder if he knows to risk
that? A man wants to be fair, you know."

"He knows that," I said. "He dont expect you to change
inside here because he knows you cant. He expects you to
change when you get out. Because he knows that as soon as
the free air and sun shine on you again, you cant help but be
a changed man even if you dont want to."

"But jest suppose I wouldn't—" He didn't add *change in
time* because he stopped himself.

"He's going to take that risk," I said. "He's got to. I mean,
he's got to now. He couldn't have stopped them from sending you here. But he knows you think he didn't try. He's got
to help you get out not only to prove to you he never put you
here but so he can quit thinking and remembering that you
believe he did. You see?"

He was completely still, just blinking a little, his hands
hanging empty but even now shaped inside the palms like the
handles of a plow and even his neck braced a little as though
still braced against the loop of the plowlines. "I just got five
more years, then I'll get out by myself. Then wont nobody
have no right to hold expectations against me. I wont owe
nobody no help then."

"That's right," I said. "Just five more years. That's practically nothing to a man that has already put in fifteen years
with a man with a shotgun watching him plow cotton that
aint his whether he feels like plowing that day or not, and

another man with a shotgun standing over him while he eats grub that he either ate it or not whether he felt like eating or not, and another man with a shotgun to lock him up at night so he could either go to sleep or stay awake whether he felt like doing it or not. Just five years more, then you'll be out where the free sun and air can shine on you without any man with a shotgun's shadow to cut it off. Because you'll be free."

"Free," he said, not loud: just like that: "Free." That was all. It was that easy. Of course the guard I welshed to cursed me; I had expected that: it was a free country; every convict had a right to try to escape just as every guard and trusty had the right to shoot him in the back the first time he didn't halt. But no unprintable stool pigeon had the right to warn the guard in advance.

I had to watch it too. That was on the bill too: the promissory note of breathing in a world that had Snopeses in it. I wanted to turn my head or anyway shut my eyes. But refusing to not look was all I had left now: the last sorry lousy almost worthless penny—the damn little thing looking like a little girl playing mama in the calico dress and sunbonnet that he believed was Flem's idea (that had been difficult; he still wanted to believe that a man should be permitted to run at his fate, even if that fate was doom, in the decency and dignity of pants; it took a little doing to persuade him that a petticoat and a woman's sunbonnet was all Flem could get). Walking; I had impressed that on him: not to run, but walk, as forlorn and lonely and fragile and alien in that empty penitentiary compound as a paper doll blowing across a rolling mill; still walking even after he had passed the point where he couldn't come back and knew it; even still walking on past the moment when he knew that he had been sold and that he should have known all along he was being sold, not blaming anybody for selling him nor even needing to sell him because hadn't he signed—put his cross, his mark; he couldn't read and write—that same promissory note too to breathe a little while, since his name was Snopes?

So he even ran before he had to. He ran right at them before I even saw them, before they stepped out of the ambush. I was proud, not just to be kin to him but of belonging to what Reba called all of us poor son of a bitches. Because it took five of them striking and slashing at his head with pistol barrels and even then it finally took the blackjack to stop him, knock him out.

The Warden sent for me. "Dont tell me anything," he said. "I wish I didn't even know as much already as I suspect. In fact, if it was left to me, I'd like to lock you and him both in a cell and leave you, you for choice in handcuffs. But I'm under a bond too so I'm going to move you into solitary for a week or so, for your own protection. And not from him."

"Dont brag or grieve," I said. "You had to sign one of them too."

"What?" he said. "What did you say?"

"I said you dont need to worry. He hasn't got anything against me. If you dont believe me, send for him."

So he came in. The bruises and slashes from the butts and the blades of the sights were healing fine. The blackjack of course never had showed. "Hidy," he said. To me. "I reckon you'll see Flem before I will now."

"Yes," I said.

"Tell him he hadn't ought to used that dress. But it dont matter. If I had made it out then, maybe I would a changed. But I reckon I wont now. I reckon I'll jest wait."

So Flem should have taken that suggestion about the ten grand. He could still do it. I could write him a letter: *Sure you can raise ten thousand. All you need to do is swap Manfred de Spain a good jump at your wife. No: that wont do: trying to peddle Eula Varner to Manfred de Spain is like trying to sell a horse to a man that's already been feeding and riding it for ten or twelve years. But you got that girl, Linda. She aint but eleven or twelve but what the hell, put smoked glasses and high heels on her and rush her in quick and maybe De Spain wont notice it.*

Except that I wasn't going to. But it wasn't that that worried me. It was knowing that I wasn't, knowing I was going to throw it away—I mean my commission of the ten grand for contacting the Chi syndicate for him. I dont remember just when it was, I was probably pretty young, when I realised that I had come from what you might call a family, a clan, a race, maybe even a species, of pure sons of bitches. So I said, *Okay, okay, if that's the way it is, we'll just show them. They call the best of lawyers, lawyers' lawyers and the best of actors an*

actor's actor and the best of athletes a ball-player's ball-player.
All right, that's what we'll do: every Snopes will make it his pri-
vate and personal aim to have the whole world recognise him as
THE son of a bitch's son of a bitch.

But we never do it. We never make it. The best we ever do
is to be just another Snopes son of a bitch. All of us, every
one of us—Flem, and old Ab that I dont even know exactly
what kin he is, and Uncle Wes and mine and Clarence's father
I.O., then right on down the line: Clarence and me by what
you might call simultaneous bigamy, and Virgil and Vardaman
and Bilbo and Byron and Mink. I dont even mention Eck and
Wallstreet and Admiral Dewey because they dont belong to
us. I have always believed that Eck's mother took some extra-
curricular nightwork nine months before he was born. So the
one true bitch we had was not a bitch at all but a saint and
martyr, the one technically true pristine immaculate unchal-
lengeable son of a bitch we ever produced wasn't even a
Snopes.

Five

WHEN his nephew was gone, the Warden said, "Sit down." He did so. "You got in the paper," the Warden said. It was folded on the desk facing him; he couldn't have read it:

TRIES PRISON BREAK

DISGUISED IN WOMAN'S CLOTHES

Parchman, Miss. Sept 8, 1923 M.I. "Mink" Snopes, under life sentence for murder from Yoknapatawpha County . . .

"What does the 'I' in your name stand for?" the Warden said. His voice was almost gentle. "We all thought your name was just Mink. That's what you told us, wasn't it?"

"That's right," he said. "Mink Snopes."

"What does the 'I' stand for? They've got it M.I. Snopes here."

"Oh," he said. "Nothing. Just M.I. Snopes like I.C. Railroad. It was them young fellers from the paper in the hospital that day. They kept on asking me what my name was and I said Mink Snopes and they said Mink aint a name, it's jest a nickname. What's your real name? And so I said M.I. Snopes."

"Oh," the Warden said. "Is Mink all the name you've got?"

"That's right. Mink Snopes."

"What did your mother call you?"

"I dont know. She died. The first I knowed my name was just Mink." He got up. "I better go. They're likely waiting for me."

"Wait," the Warden said. "Didn't you know it wouldn't work? Didn't you know you couldn't get away with it?"

"They told me," he said. "I was warned." He stood, not moving, relaxed, small and frail, his face downbent a little, musing, peaceful, almost like faint smiling. "He hadn't ought to fooled me to get caught in that dress and sunbonnet," he said. "I wouldn't a done that to him."

"Who?" the Warden said. "Not your . . . is it nephew?"

"Montgomery Ward?" he said. "He was my brother's grandson. No. Not him." He waited a moment. Then he said again, "Well I better—"

"You would have got out in five more years," the Warden said. "You know they'll probably add on another twenty now, dont you?"

"I was warned of that too," he said.

"All right," the Warden said. "You can go."

This time it was he who paused, stopped. "I reckon you never did find out who sent me them forty dollars."

"How could I?" the Warden said. "I told you that at the time. All it said was From a Friend. From Memphis."

"It was Flem," he said.

"Who?" the Warden said. "The cousin you told me refused to help you after you killed that man? That you said could have saved you if he had wanted to? Why would he send you forty dollars now, after fifteen years?"

"It was Flem," he said. "He can afford it. Besides, he never had no money hurt against me. He was jest getting a holt with Will Varner then and maybe he figgered he couldn't resk getting mixed up with a killing, even if hit was his blood kin. Only I wish he hadn't used that dress and sunbonnet. He never had to do that."

They were picking the cotton now; already every cotton county in Mississippi would be grooming their best fastest champions to pick against the best of Arkansas and Missouri for the championship picker of the Mississippi Valley. But he wouldn't be here. No champion at anything would ever be here because only failures wound up here: the failures at killing and stealing and lying. He remembered how at first he had cursed his bad luck for letting them catch him but he knew better now: that there was no such thing as bad luck or good luck: you were either born a champion or not a champion and that if he had been born a champion Houston not only couldn't, he wouldn't have dared, misuse him about that cow to where he had to kill him; that some folks were born to be failures and get caught always, some folks were born to be lied to and believe it, and he was one of them.

It was a fine crop, one of the best he remembered, as

though everything had been exactly right: season: wind and sun and rain to sprout it, the fierce long heat of summer to grow and ripen it. As though back there in the spring the ground itself had said, *All right, for once let's confederate instead of fighting*—the ground, the dirt which any and every tenant-farmer and share-cropper knew to be his sworn foe and mortal enemy—the hard implacable land which wore out his youth and his tools and then his body itself. And not just his body but that soft mysterious one he had touched that first time with amazement and reverence and incredulous excitement the night of his marriage, now worn too to leather-toughness that half the time, it seemed to him most of the time, he would be too spent with physical exhaustion to remember it was even female. And not just their two, but those of their children, the two girls to watch growing up and be able to see what was ahead of that tender and elfin innocence; until was it any wonder that a man would look at that inimical irreconcilable square of dirt to which he was bound and chained for the rest of his life, and say to it: *You got me, you'll wear me out because you are stronger than me since I'm jest bone and flesh. I cant leave you because I cant afford to, and you know it. Me and what used to be the passion and excitement of my youth until you wore out the youth and I forgot the passion, will be here next year with the children of our passion for you to wear that much nearer the grave, and you know it; and the year after that, and the year after that, and you know that too. And not just me, but all my tenant and cropper kind that have immolated youth and hope on thirty or forty or fifty acres of dirt that wouldn't nobody but our kind work because you're all our kind have. But we can burn you. Every late February or March we can set fire to the surface of you until all of you in sight is scorched and black, and there aint one god damn thing you can do about it. You can wear out our bodies and dull our dreams and wreck our stomachs with the sowbelly and cornmeal and molasses which is all you afford us to eat but every spring we can set you afire again and you know that too.*

It was different now. He didn't own this land; he referred of course to the renter's or cropper's share of what it made. Now, what it produced or failed to produce—bumper or bust, flood or drouth, cotton at ten cents a pound or a dollar a pound—would make not one tittle of difference in his present life. Because now (years had passed; the one in which he would have been free again if he had not allowed his nephew to talk him into that folly which anybody should have known—even that young fool of a lawyer they had made him take back there at the trial when he, Mink, could have run his case much better, that didn't have any sense at all, at least knew this much and even told him so and even what the result to him would be—not only wouldn't work, it wasn't even intended to work, was now behind him) he had suddenly discovered something. People of his kind never had owned even temporarily the land which they believed they had rented between one New Year's and the next one. It was the land itself which owned them, and not just from a planting to its harvest but in perpetuity; not the owner, the landlord who evacuated them from one worthless rental in November, onto the public roads to seek desperately another similar worthless one two miles or ten miles or two counties or ten counties away before time to seed the next crop in March, but the land, the earth itself passing their doomed indigence and poverty from holding to holding of its thralldom as a family or a clan does a hopelessly bankrupt tenth cousin.

That was past now. He no longer belonged to the land even on those sterile terms. He belonged to the government, the State of Mississippi. He could drag dust up and down cotton middles from year in to year out and if nothing whatever sprang up behind him, it would make no difference to him. No more now to go to a commissary store every Saturday morning to battle with the landlord for every gram of the cheap bad meat and meal and molasses and the tumbler of snuff which was his and his wife's one spendthrift orgy. No more to battle with the landlord for every niggard sack of fertilizer, then gather the poor crop which suffered from that niggard lack and still have to battle the landlord for his niggard insufficient share of it. All he had to do now was just to keep moving; even the man with the shotgun standing over him neither knew nor cared whether anything came up behind him or not just so he kept moving, any more than he cared. At first he was ashamed, in shame and terror lest the others find that he felt this way; until one day he knew (he could not have said how) that all the others felt like this; that, given time enough, Parchman brought them all to this; he thought in a kind of musing amazement: *Yes sir, a man can get used to jest anything, even to being in Parchman if you jest give him time enough.*

But Parchman just changed the way a man looked at what he saw after he got in Parchman. It didn't change what he brought with him. It just made remembering easier because Parchman taught him how to wait. He remembered back there that day even while the Judge was still saying "life" down at him, when he still believed that Flem would come in and save him, until he finally realised that Flem wasn't, had never intended to, how he had pretty near actually said it out loud: *Just let me go long enough to get out to Frenchman's Bend or wherever he is and give me ten minutes and I'll come back here and you can go on and hang me if that's what you want to do.* And how even that time three or five or eight years or whenever it was back there when Flem had used that nephew —what was his name? Montgomery Ward—to trick him into trying to escape in a woman's dress and sunbonnet and they had given him twenty years more exactly like that young fool lawyer had warned him they would at the very beginning, how even while he was fighting with the five guards he was still saying the same thing: *Just let me go long enough to reach Jefferson and have ten minutes and I will come back myself and you can hang me.*

He didn't think things like that any more now because he had learned to wait. And, waiting, he found out that he was listening, hearing too; that he was keeping up with what went on by just listening and hearing even better than if he had been right there in Jefferson because like this all he had to do was just watch them without having to worry about them too. So his wife had gone back to her people they said and died and his daughters had moved away too, grown girls now, likely somebody around Frenchman's Bend would know where. And Flem was a rich man now, president of the bank and living in a house he rebuilt that they said was as big as the Union Depot in Memphis, with his daughter, old Will Varner's girl's bastard, that was grown now, that went away and married and her and her husband had been in another war they had in Spain and a shell or cannon ball or something blew up and killed the husband but just made her stone deaf. And she was back home now, a widow, living with Flem, just the two of them in the big house where they claimed she couldn't even hear it thunder, the rest of the folks in Jefferson not thinking much of it because she was already mixed up in a nigger Sunday school and they said she was mixed up in something called commonists, that her husband had belonged to and that in fact they were both fighting on the commonist side in that war.

Flem was getting along now. They both were. When he got out in 1948 he and Flem would both be old men. Flem might not even be alive for him to get out for in 1948 and he himself might not even be alive to get out in 1948 and he could remember how at one time that too had driven him mad: that Flem might die, either naturally or maybe this time the other man wouldn't be second class and doomed to fail and be caught, and it would seem to him that he couldn't bear it: who hadn't asked for justice since justice was only for the best, for champions, but at least a man might expect a chance, anybody had a right to a chance. But that was gone too now, into, beneath the simple waiting; in 1948 he and Flem both would be old men and he even said aloud: "What a shame we cant both of us jest come out two old men setting peaceful in the sun or the shade, waiting to die together, not even thinking no more of hurt or harm or getting even, not even remembering no more about hurt or harm or anguish or revenge,"—two old men not only incapable of further harm to anybody but even incapable of remembering hurt or harm, as if whatever necessary amount of the money which Flem no longer needed and soon now would not need at all ever again, could be used to blot, efface, obliterate those forty years which he, Mink, no longer needed now and soon also, himself too, would not even miss. *But I reckon not,* he thought. *Cant neither of us help nothing now. Cant neither one of us take nothing back.*

So again he had only five more years and he would be free. And this time he had learned the lesson which the fool young lawyer had tried to teach him thirty-five years ago. There were eleven of them. They worked and ate and slept as a gang, a unit, living in a detached wire-canvas-and-plank hut (it was summer); shackled to the same chain they went to the mess hall to eat, then to the field to work and, chained again, back to the hut to sleep again. So when the escape was planned, the other ten had to take him into their plot to prevent his giving it away by simple accident. They didn't want to take him in; two of them were never converted to the idea. Because ever since his own abortive attempt eighteen or twenty years ago he had been known as a sort of self-ordained priest of the doctrine of non-escape.

So when they finally told him simply because he would have to be in on the secret to protect it, whether he joined them or not, the moment he said, cried, "No! Here now, wait! Wait! Dont you see, if any of us tries to get out they'll come down on all of us and wont none of us ever get free even when our forty years is up," he knew he had already talked too much. So when he said to himself, "Now I got to get out of this chain and get away from them," he did not mean *Because if dark catches me alone in this room with them and no guard handy, I'll never see light again* but simply *I got to get to the Warden in time, before they try it maybe tonight even and wreck ever body.*

And even he would have to wait for the very darkness he feared, until the lights were out and they were all supposed to have settled down for sleep, so that his murderers would make their move, since only during or because of the uproar of the attack on him could he hope to get the warning, his message, to a guard and be believed. Which meant he would have to match guile with guile: to lie rigid on his cot until they set up the mock snoring which was to lull him offguard, himself tense and motionless and holding his own breath to distinguish in time through the snoring whatever sound would herald the plunging knife (or stick or whatever it would be) in time to roll, fling himself off the cot and in one more convulsive roll underneath it as the men—he could not tell how many since the spurious loud snoring had if anything increased—hurled themselves onto the vacancy where a split second before he had been lying.

"Grab him," one hissed, panted. "Who's got the knife?" Then another:

"I've got the knife. Where in hell is he?" Because he—
Mink—had not even paused; another convulsive roll and he
was out from under the cot, on all-fours among the thrashing
legs, scrabbling, scuttling to get as far away from the cot as he
could. The whole room was now in a sort of sotto-voce uproar. "We got to have a light," a voice muttered. "Just a second of light." Suddenly he was free, clear; he could stand up.
He screamed, shouted: no word, cry: just a loud human
sound; at once the voice muttered, panted: "There. Grab
him," but he had already sprung, leaped, to carom from invisible body to body, shouting, bellowing steadily even after
he realised he could see, the air beyond the canvas walls not
only full of searchlights but the siren too, himself surrounded,
enclosed by the furious silent faces which seemed to dart like
fish in then out of the shoulder-high light which came in over
the plank half-walls, through the wire mesh; he even saw the
knife gleam once above him as he plunged, hurling himself
among the surging legs, trying to get back under a cot, any
cot, anything to intervene before the knife. But it was too
late, they could also see him now. He vanished beneath them
all. But it was too late for them too: the glaring and probing
of all the searchlights, the noise of the siren itself, seemed to
concentrate downward upon, into the flimsy ramshackle cubicle filled with cursing men. Then the guards were among
them, clubbing at heads with pistols and shotgun barrels,
dragging them off until he lay exposed, once more battered
and bleeding but this time still conscious. He had even managed one last convulsive wrench and twist so that the knife
which should have pinned him to it merely quivered in the
floor beside his throat.

"Hit was close," he told the guard. "But looks like we
made hit."

But not quite. He was in the infirmary again and didn't
hear until afterward how on the very next night two of them
—Stillwell, a gambler who had cut the throat of a Vicksburg
prostitute (he had owned the knife) and another, who had
been the two who had held out against taking him into the
plot at all but advocated instead killing him at once—made
the attempt anyway though only Stillwell escaped, the other
having most of his head blown off by a guard's shotgun blast.

Then he was in the Warden's office again. This time he had needed little bandaging and no stitches at all; they had not had time enough, and no weapons save their feet and fists except Stillwell's knife. "It was Stillwell that had the knife, wasn't it?" the Warden said.

He couldn't have said why he didn't tell. "I never seen who had it," he answered. "I reckon hit all happened too quick."

"That's what Stillwell seems to think," the Warden said. He took from his desk a slitted envelope and a sheet of cheap ruled paper, folded once or twice. "This came this morning. But that's right: you cant read, can you?"

"No," he said. The Warden unfolded the sheet.

"It was mailed yesterday in Texarkana. It says 'He's going to have to explain Jake Barron' (he was the other convict, whom the guard had killed) 'to somebody someday so take good care of him. Maybe you better take good care of him anyway since there are some of us still inside'." The Warden folded the letter back into the envelope and put it back into the drawer and closed the drawer. "So there you are. I cant let you go around loose inside here, where any of them can get at you. You've only got five more years; even though you didn't stop all of them, probably on a recommendation from me, the Governor would let you out tomorrow. But I cant do that because Stillwell will kill you."

"If Cap'm Jabbo" (the guard who shot) "had jest killed Stillwell too, I could go home tomorrow?" he said. "Couldn't you trace out where he's at by the letter, and send Cap'm Jabbo wherever that is?"

"You want the same man to kill Stillwell that kept Stillwell from killing you two nights ago?"

"Send somebody else then. It dont seem fair for him to get away when I got to stay here five more years." Then he said, "But hit's all right. Maybe we did have at least one champion here, after all."

"Champion?" the Warden said. "One what here?" But he didn't answer that. And now for the first time he began to count off the days and months. He had never done this before, not with that original twenty years they had given him at the start back there in Jefferson, nor even with the second twenty years they had added onto it after he let Montgomery

Ward persuade him into that woman's mother hubbard and
sunbonnet. Because nobody was to blame for that but himself; when he thought of Flem in connection with it, it was
with a grudging admiration, almost pride that they were of
the same blood; he would think, say aloud, without envy
even: "That Flem Snopes. You cant beat him. There aint a
man in Missippi nor the U.S. and A. both put together that
can beat Flem Snopes."

But this was different. He had tried himself to escape and
had failed and had accepted the added twenty years of penalty
without protest; he had spent fifteen of them not only never
trying to escape again himself but had risked his life to foil ten
others who planned to: as his reward for which he would have
been freed the next day, only a trained guard with a shotgun
in his hands let one of the ten plotters get free. So these last
five years did not belong to him at all. He had discharged his
forty years in good faith; it was not his fault that they actually
added up to only thirty-five, and these five extra ones had
been compounded onto him by a vicious, even a horseplayish,
gratuitor.

That Christmas his (now: for the first time) slowly diminishing sentence began to be marked off for him. It was a
Christmas card, postmarked in Mexico, addressed to him in
care of the Warden, who read it to him; they both knew who
it was from: *Four years now Not as far as you think* On Valentine's Day it was home-made: the coarse ruled paper bearing,
drawn apparently with a carpenter's or a lumberman's red
crayon, a crude heart into which a revolver was firing. "You
see?" the Warden said. "Even if your five years were up . . ."

"It aint five now," he said. "Hit's four years and six months
and nineteen days. You mean, even then you wont let me
out?"

"And have you killed before you could even get home?"

"Send out and ketch him."

"Send where?" the Warden said. "Suppose you were outside and didn't want to come back and knew I wanted to get
you back. Where would I send to catch you?"

"Yes," he said. "So there jest aint nothing no human man
can do."

"Yes," the Warden said. "Give him time and he will do something else the police somewhere will catch him for."

"Time," he said. "Suppose a man aint got time jest to depend on time."

"At least you have got your four years and six months and nineteen days before you have to worry about it."

"Yes," he said. "He'll have that much time to work in."

Then Christmas again, another card with the Mexican postmark: *Three years now Not near as far as you think* He stood there, fragile and small and durable in the barred overalls, his face lowered a little, peaceful. "Still Mexico, I notice," he said. "Maybe He will kill him there."

"What?" the Warden said. "What did you say?"

He didn't answer. He just stood there, peaceful, musing, serene. Then he said: "Before I had that-ere cow trouble with Zack Houston, when I was still a boy, I used to go to church ever Sunday and Wednesday prayer meeting too with the lady that raised me until I——"

"Who were they?" the Warden said. "You said your mother died."

"He was a son of a bitch. She wasn't no kin a-tall. She was jest his wife.—ever Sunday until I——"

"Was his name Snopes?" the Warden said.

"Yes. Snopes.—until I got big enough to burn out on God like you do when you think you are already growed up and dont need nothing from nobody. Then when you told me how by keeping nine of them ten fellers from breaking out I didn't jest add five more years to my time, I fixed it so you wasn't going to let me out a-tall, I taken it back."

"Took what back?" the Warden said. "Back from who?"

"I taken it back from God."

"You mean you've rejoined the church since that night two years ago? No you haven't. You've never been inside the chapel since you came here back in 1908." Which was true. Though the present Warden and his predecessor had not really been surprised at that. What they had expected him to gravitate to was one of the small violent irreconcilable non-comformist non-everything and -everybody else which existed along with the regular prison religious establishment in probably all Southern rural penitentiaries—small fierce cliques and groups (this one called themselves Jehovah's Shareholders) headed by self-ordained leaders who had reached prison through a curiously consistent pattern: by the conviction of crimes peculiar to the middle class, to respectability, originating in domesticity or anyway uxoriousness: bigamy, rifling the sect's funds for a woman: his wife or someone else's or, in an occasional desperate case, a professional prostitute.

"I didn't need no church," he said. "I done it in confidence."

"In confidence?" the Warden said.

"Yes," he said, almost impatiently. "You dont need to write God a letter. He has done already seen inside you long before He would even need to bother to read it. Because a man will learn a little sense in time even outside. But he learns it quick in here. That when a Judgment powerful enough to help you, will help you if all you got to do is jest take back and accept it, you are a fool not to."

"So He will take care of Stillwell for you," the Warden said.

"Why not? What's He got against me?"

"Thou shalt not kill," the Warden said.

"Why didn't He tell Houston that? I never went all the way in to Jefferson to have to sleep on a bench in the depot jest to try to buy them shells, until Houston made me."

"Well I'll be damned," the Warden said. "I will be eternally damned. You'll be out of here in three more years anyway but if I had my way you'd be out of here now, today, before whatever the hell it is that makes you tick starts looking cross-eyed at me. I dont want to spend the rest of my life even thinking somebody is thinking the kind of hopes about me you wish about folks that get in your way. Go on now. Get back to work."

So when it was only October, no holiday Valentine or Christmas card month that he knew of, when the Warden sent for him, he was not even surprised. The Warden sat looking at him for maybe half a minute, with something not just aghast but almost respectful in the look, then said: "I will be damned." It was a telegram this time. "It's from the Chief of Police in San Diego, California. There was a church in the

Mexican quarter. They had stopped using it as a church, had a new one or something. Anyway it had been deconsecrated so what went on inside it since even the police haven't quite caught up with yet. Last week it fell down. They dont know why: it just fell down all of a sudden. They found a man in it—what was left of him. This is what the telegram says: 'Fingerprints FBI identification your man Number 08213 Shuford H. Stillwell'." The Warden folded the telegram back into the envelope and put it back into the drawer. "Tell me again about that church you said you used to go to before Houston made you kill him."

He didn't answer that at all. He just drew a long breath and exhaled it. "I can go now," he said. "I can be free."

"Not right this minute," the Warden said. "It will take a month or two. The petition will have to be got up and sent to the Governor. Then he will ask for my recommendation. Then he will sign the pardon."

"The petition?" he said.

"You got in here by law," the Warden said. "You'll have to get out by law."

"A petition," he said.

"That your family will have a lawyer draw up, asking the Governor to issue a pardon. Your wife—but that's right, she's dead. One of your daughters then."

"Likely they done married away too by now."

"All right," the Warden said. Then he said, "Hell, man, you're already good as out. Your cousin, whatever he is, right there in Jackson now in the legislature—Egglestone Snopes, that got beat for Congress two years ago?"

He didn't move, his head bent a little; he said, "Then I reckon I'll stay here after all." Because how could he tell a stranger: *Clarence, my own oldest brother's grandson, is in politics that depends on votes. When I leave here I wont have no vote. What will I have to buy Clarence Snopes's name on my paper?* Which just left Eck's boy, Wallstreet, whom nobody yet had ever told what to do. "I reckon I'll be with you them other three years too," he said.

"Write your sheriff yourself," the Warden said. "I'll write the letter for you."

"Hub Hampton that sent me here is dead."

"You've still got a sheriff, haven't you? What's the matter with you? Have forty years in here scared you for good of fresh air and sunshine?"

"Thirty-eight years this coming summer," he said.

"All right. Thirty-eight. How old are you?"

"I was born in eighty-three," he said.

"So you've been here ever since you were twenty-five years old."

"I dont know. I never counted."

"All right," the Warden said. "Beat it. When you say the word I'll write a letter to your sheriff."

"I reckon I'll stay," he said. But he was wrong. Five months later the petition lay on the Warden's desk.

"Who is Linda Snopes Kohl?" the Warden said.

He stood completely still for quite a long time. "Her paw's a rich banker in Jefferson. His and my grandpaw had two sets of chillen."

"She was the member of your family that signed the petition to the Governor to let you out."

"You mean the sheriff sent for her to come and sign it?"

"How could he? You wouldn't let me write the sheriff."

"Yes," he said. He looked down at the paper which he could not read. It was upside down to him, though that meant nothing either. "Show me where the ones signed to not let me out."

"What?" the Warden said.

"The ones that dont want me out."

"Oh, you mean Houston's family. No, the only other names on it are the District Attorney who sent you here and your sheriff, Hubert Hampton junior, and V. K. Ratliff. Is he a Houston?"

"No," he said. He drew the slow deep breath again. "So I'm free."

"With one thing more," the Warden said. "Your luck's not even holding: it's doubling." But he handled that too the next morning after they gave him a pair of shoes, a shirt, overalls and jumper and a hat, all brand new, and a ten-dollar bill and the three dollars and eighty-five cents which were still left from the forty dollars Flem had sent him eighteen years ago, and the Warden said, "There's a deputy here today with a prisoner from Greenville. He's going back tonight. For a dollar he'll drop you off right at the end of the bridge to Arkansas, if you want to go that way."

"Much obliged," he said. "I'm going by Memphis first. I got some business to attend to there."

It would probably take all of the thirteen dollars and eighty-five cents to buy a pistol even in a Memphis pawn shop. He had planned to beat his way to Memphis on a freight train, riding the rods underneath a boxcar or between two of them, as he had done once or twice as a boy and a youth. But as soon as he was outside the gate, he discovered that he was afraid to. He had been shut too long, he had forgotten how; his muscles might have lost the agility and co-ordination, the simple bold quick temerity for physical risk. Then he thought of watching his chance to scramble safely into an empty car and found that he dared not that either, that in thirty-eight years he might even have forgotten the unspoken rules of the freemasonry of petty lawbreaking without knowing it until too late.

So he stood beside the paved highway which, when his foot touched it last thirty-eight years ago, had not even been gravel but instead was dirt marked only by the prints of mules and the iron tires of wagons; now it looked and felt as smooth and hard as a floor, what time you could see it or risk feeling it either for the cars and trucks rushing past on it. In the old days any passing wagon would have stopped to no more than his raised hand. But these were not wagons so he didn't know what the new regulations for this might be either; in fact if he had known anything else to do but this he would already be doing it instead of standing, frail and harmless and not much larger than a child in the new overalls and jumper still showing their off-the-shelf creases and the new shoes and the hat, until the truck slowed in toward him and stopped and the driver said, "How far you going, dad?"

"Memphis," he said.

"I'm going to Clarksdale. You can hook another ride from there. As good as you can here, anyway."

It was fall, almost October, and he discovered that here was something else he had forgotten about during the thirty-eight years: seasons. They came and went in the penitentiary too but for thirty-eight years the only right he had to them was the privilege of suffering because of them: from the heat and sun of summer whether he wanted to work in the heat of the day or not, and the rain and icelike mud of winter whether he wanted to be out in it or not. But now they belonged to him again: October next week, not much to see in this flat Delta country which he had misdoubted the first time he laid eyes on it from the train window that day thirty-eight years ago: just cotton stalks and cypress needles. But back home in the hills, all the land would be gold and crimson with hickory and gum and oak and maple, and the old fields warm with sage and splattered with scarlet sumac; in thirty-eight years he had forgotten that.

When suddenly, somewhere deep in memory, there was a tree, a single tree. His mother was dead; he couldn't remember her nor even how old he was when his father married again. So the woman wasn't even kin to him and she never let him forget it: that she was raising him not from any tie or claim and not because he was weak and helpless and a human being, but because she was a Christian. Yet there was more than that behind it. He knew that at once—a gaunt harried slattern of a woman whom he remembered always either with a black eye or holding a dirty rag to her bleeding where her husband had struck her. Because he could always depend on her, not to do anything for him because she always failed there, but for constancy, to be always there and always aware of him, surrounding him always with that shield which actually protected, defended him from nothing but on the contrary seemed actually to invite more pain and grief. But simply to be there, lachrymose, harassed, yet constant.

She was still in bed, it was midmorning; she should have been hours since immolated into the ceaseless drudgery which composed her days. She was never ill, so it must have been the man had beat her this time even harder than he knew, lying there in the bed talking about food—the fatback, the coarse meal, the molasses which as far as he knew was the only food all people ate except when they could catch or kill something else; evidently this new blow had been somewhere about her stomach. "I cant eat hit," she whimpered. "I need to relish something else. Maybe a squirrel." He knew now;

that was the tree. He had to steal the shotgun: his father would have beat him within an inch of his life—to lug the clumsy weapon even taller than he was, into the woods, to the tree, the hickory, to ambush himself beneath it and crouch, waiting, in the drowsy splendor of the October afternoon, until the little creature appeared. Whereupon he began to tremble (he had but the one shell) and he remembered that too: the tremendous effort to raise the heavy gun long enough, panting against the stock *Please God please God* into the shock of the recoil and the reek of the black powder until he could drop the gun and run and pick up the still warm small furred body with hands that trembled and shook until he could barely hold it. And her hands trembling too as she fondled the carcass. "We'll dress hit and cook hit now," she said. "We'll relish hit together right now." The hickory itself was of course gone now, chopped into firewood or wagon spokes or single trees years ago; perhaps the very place where it had stood was eradicated now into plowed land—or so they thought who had felled and destroyed it probably. But he knew better: unaxed in memory and unaxeable, inviolable and immune, golden and splendid with October. *Why yes* he thought; *it aint a place a man wants to go back to; the place dont even need to be there no more. What aches a man to go back to is what he remembers.*

Suddenly he craned his neck to see out the window. "Hit looks like—" and stopped. But he was free; let all the earth know where he had been for thirty-eight years. "—Parchman," he said.

"Yep," the driver said. "P.O.W. camp."

"What?" he said.

"Prisoners from the war."

"From the war?"

"Where you been the last five years, dad?" the driver said. "Asleep?"

"I been away," he said. "I mind one war they fit with the Spaniards when I was a boy, and there was another with the Germans after that one. Who did they fight this time?"

"Everybody." The driver cursed. "Germans, Japanese, Congress too. Then they quit. If they had let us lick the Russians too, we might a been all right. But they just licked the Krauts and Japs and then decided to choke everybody else to death with money."

He thought *Money.* He said: "If you had twenty-five dollars and found thirty-eight more, how much would you have?"

"What?" the driver said. "I wouldn't even stop to pick up just thirty-eight dollars. What the hell you asking me? You mean you got sixty-three dollars and cant find nothing to do with it?"

Sixty-three, he thought. *So that's how old I am.* He thought quietly: *Not justice; I never asked that; jest fairness, that's all.* That was all; not to have anything for him: just not to have anything against him. That was all he wanted, and sure enough, here it was.

LINDA

Six

V. K. RATLIFF

"You aint even going to meet the train?" Chick says. Lawyer never even looked up, setting there at the desk with his attention (his nose anyway) buried in the papers in front of him like there wasn't nobody else in the room. "Not just a new girl coming to town," Chick says, "but a wounded female war veteran. Well, maybe not a new girl," he says. "Maybe that's the wrong word. In fact maybe 'new' is the wrong word all the way round. Not a new girl in Jefferson, because she was born and raised here. And even if she was a new girl in Jefferson or new anywhere else once, that would be just once because no matter how new you might have been anywhere once, you wouldn't be very new anywhere anymore after you went to Spain with a Greenwich Village poet to fight Hitler. That is, not after the kind of Greenwich Village poet that would get you both blown up by a shell anyhow. That is, provided you were a girl. So just say, not only an old girl that used to be new, coming back to Jefferson, but the first girl old or new either that Jefferson ever had to come home wounded from a war. Men soldiers yes, of course yes. But this is the first female girl soldier we ever had, not to mention one actually wounded by the enemy. Naturally we dont include rape for the main reason that we aint talking about rape." Still his uncle didn't move. "I'd think you'd have the whole town down there at the depot to meet her. Out of simple sympathetic interest, not to mention pity: a girl that went all the way to Spain to a war and the best she got out of it was to lose her husband and have both ear-drums busted by a shell. Mrs Cole," he says.

Nor did Lawyer look up even then. "Kohl," he says.

"That's what I said," Chick says. "Mrs Cole."

This time Lawyer spelled it. "K-o-h-l," he says. But even before he spelled it, it had a different sound from the way Chick said it. "He was a sculptor, not a poet. The shell didn't kill him. It was an aeroplane."

"Oh well, no wonder, if he was just a sculptor," Chick says. "Naturally a sculptor wouldn't have the footwork to dodge machine gun bullets like a poet. A sculptor would have to stay in one place too much of his time. Besides, maybe it wasn't Saturday so he didn't have his hat on."

"He was in the aeroplane," Lawyer says. "It was shot down. It crashed and burned."

"What?" Chick says. "A Greenwich Village sculptor named K-o-h-l actually in an aeroplane where it could get shot down by an enemy?" He was looking more or less at the top of his uncle's head. "Not Cole," he says: "K-o-h-l. I wonder why he didn't change it. Dont they, usually?"

Now Lawyer closed the papers without no haste a-tall and laid them on the desk and pushed the swivel chair back and set back in it and clasped his hands behind his head. His hair had done already started turning gray when he come back from the war in France in 1919. Now it was pretty near completely white, and him setting there relaxed and easy in the chair with that white mop of it and the little gold key he got when he was at Harvard on his watch chain and one of the cob pipes stuck upside down in his shirt pocket like it was a pencil or a toothpick, looking at Chick for about a half a minute. "You didn't find that at Harvard," he says. "I thought that maybe after two years in Cambridge, you might not even recognise it again when you came back to Mississippi."

"All right," Chick says. "I'm sorry." But Lawyer just sat there easy in the chair, looking at him. "Damn it," Chick says, "I said I'm sorry."

"Only you're not sorry yet," Lawyer says. "You're just ashamed."

"Aint it the same thing?" Chick says.

"No," Lawyer says. "When you are just ashamed of something, you dont hate it. You just hate getting caught."

"Well, you caught me," Chick says. "I am ashamed. What more do you want?" Only Lawyer didn't even need to answer that. "Maybe I cant help it yet, even after two years at Harvard," Chick says. "Maybe I just lived too long a time among what us Mississippi folks call white people before I went there. You cant be ashamed of me for what I didn't know in time, can you?"

"I'm not ashamed of you about anything," Lawyer says.

"All right," Chick says. "Sorry, then."

"I'm not sorry over you about anything either," Lawyer says.

"Then what the hell is all this about?" Chick says.

So a stranger that never happened to be living in Jefferson or Yoknapatawpha County ten or twelve years ago might have thought it was Chick that was the interested party. Not only interested enough to be jealous of his uncle, but interested enough to already be jealous even though the subject or bone of contention not only hadn't even got back home yet, he wouldn't even seen her since ten years ago. Which would make him jealous not only over a gal he hadn't even seen in ten years, but that he wasn't but twelve or thirteen years old and she was already nineteen, a growed woman, when he seen her that last time—a insurmountable barrier of difference in age that would still been a barrier even with three or four more years added onto both of them, providing of course it was the gal that still had the biggest number of them. In fact you would think how a boy jest twelve or thirteen years old couldn't be man-jealous yet; wouldn't have enough fuel yet to fire jealousy and keep it burning very long or even a-tall over a gal nineteen years old or any other age between eight and eighty for that matter, except that how young does he have to be before he can dare to risk not having that fuel capable of taking fire and combusting? jest how young must he be to be safe for a little while longer yet, as the feller says, from having his heart strangled as good as any other man by that one strand of Lilith's hair? or how old either, for the matter of that. Besides, this time when she come back, even though she would still be the same six or seven years older, this time they would be jest six or seven years older than twenty-two or twenty-three instead of six or seven years older than twelve or thirteen, and that aint no barrier a-tall. This time he wouldn't be no innocent infantile bystanding victim of that loop because this time he would be in there fighting for the right and privilege of being lassoed; fighting not jest for the right and privilege of being strangled too, but of being strangled first.

Which was exactly what he looked like he was trying to do: nudging and whetting at his uncle, reaching around for whatever stick or club or brickbat come to his hand like he was still jest twelve or thirteen years old or even less than that, grabbing up that one about Linda's husband being a Jew for instance, because even at jest twelve, if he had stopped long enough to think, he would a knowed that that wouldn't even be a good solid straw as far as his present opponent or rival was concerned.

Maybe that—swinging that straw at his uncle about how Lawyer had been the main one instrumental in getting Linda up there in New York where couldn't no homefolks look after her and so sho enough she had went and married a Jew— was what give Chick away. Because he aint even seen her again yet; he couldn't a knowed all that other yet. I mean, knowed that even at jest twelve he already had all the jealousy he would ever need at twenty-two or eighty-two either. He would need to actively see her again to find out he had jest as much right as any other man in it to be strangled to death by this-here new gal coming to town, and wasn't no man wearing hair going to interfere in the way and save him. When he thought about her now, he would have to remember jest what that twelve- or thirteen-year-old boy had seen: not a gal but a woman growed, the same general size and shape of his own maw, belonging to and moving around in the same alien human race the rest of the world except twelve-year-old boys belonged to. And, if it hadn't been for his uncle finally stopping long enough his-self to look at her and then you might say ketching Chick by the scruff of the neck and grinding his attention onto her by conscripting up half his out-of-school time toting notes back and forth to her for them after-school icecream-parlor dates her and Lawyer started to having, nowhere near as interesting.

So when Chick remembered her now, he would still have to see what twelve or thirteen years old had seen: *Hell fire, she's durn nigh old as maw.* He would have to actively look at her again to see what twenty-two or twenty-three would see: *Hell fire, suppose she is a year or two older than me, jest so it's me that's the man of the two of us.* So you and that stranger both would a thought how maybe it taken a boy of twelve or thirteen; maybe only a boy of twelve or thirteen is capable of pure and undefiled, what you might call virgin, jealousy toward a

man of thirty over a gal of nineteen—or of any other age between eight and eighty for that matter, jest as it takes a boy of
twelve or thirteen to know the true anguish and passion and
hope and despair of love; you and that stranger both thinking
that right up to that last final moment when Chick give his-
self away free-for-nothing by grabbing up that one about
Linda's husband being not only a poet but a Jew too to hit at
his uncle with. Then even that stranger would a realised Chick
wasn't throwing it at Linda a-tall: he was throwing it at his
uncle; that it wasn't his uncle he was jealous of over Linda
Snopes: he was jealous of Linda over his uncle. Then even
that stranger would a had to say to Chick in his mind: *Maybe
you couldn't persuade me onto your side at first, but we're sholy
in the same agreement now.*

Leastways if that stranger had talked to me a little. Because
I could remember, I was actively watching it, that time back
there when Lawyer first got involved into Linda's career as
the feller says. I dont mean when Lawyer thought her career
got mixed up into hisn, nor even when he first thought he actively noticed her. Because she was already twelve or thirteen
herself then and so Lawyer had already knowed her all her life
or anyway since she was them one or two years old or whenever it is when hit's folks begin to bring it out into the street
in a baby buggy or toting it and you first notice how it not
only is beginning to look like a human being, hit even begins
to look a little like some specific family of folks you are acquainted with. And in a little town like Jefferson where not
only ever body knows ever body else but ever body has got to
see ever body else in town at least once in the twenty-four
hours whether he wants to or not, except for the time Lawyer
was away at the war likely he had to see her at least once a
week. Not to mention having to know even before he could
recognise her to remember, that she was Eula Varner's daughter that all Jefferson and Yoknapatawpha County both that
had ever seen Eula Varner first, couldn't help but look at Eula
Varner's child with a kind of amazement, like at some minute-
sized monster, since anybody, any man anyhow, that ever
looked at Eula once couldn't help but believe that all that
much woman in jest one simple normal-sized chunk couldn't
a possibly been fertilised by anything as frail and puny in

comparison as jest one single man; that it would a taken that
whole generation of young concentrated men to seeded them
as the feller says, splendid—no: he would a said magnificent—
loins.

And I dont mean when Lawyer voluntarily went outen his
way and adopted Linda's career into a few spare extra years of
hisn like he thought he was doing. What I mean is, when Eula
Varner taken that first one look of hern at Lawyer—or let him
take that first one look of hisn at her, whichever way you want
to put it—and adopted the rest of his life into that one of
whatever first child she happened to have, providing of course
it's a gal. Like when you finally see the woman that had ought
to been yourn all the time, only it's already too late. The
woman that ought to been sixteen maybe at this moment and
you not more than nineteen (which at that moment when he
first seen Eula Lawyer actively was; it was Eula that was out of
focus, being as she was already a year older than Lawyer to
start with) and you look at her that first one time and in the
next moment says to her: "You're beautiful. I love you. Let's
dont never part again," and she says, "Yes, of course"—no
more concerned than that: "Of course I am. Of course you
do. Of course we wont." Only it's already too late. She is already married to somebody else. Except it wasn't too late. It
aint never too late and wont never be, providing, no matter
how old you are, you still are that-ere nineteen-year-old boy
that said that to that sixteen-year-old gal at that one particular moment outen all the moments you might ever call yourn.
Because how can it ever be too late to that nineteen-year-old
boy, because how can that sixteen-year-old gal you had to say
that to ever be violated, it dont matter how many husbands
she might a had in the meantime, providing she actively was
the one that had to say "Of course" right back at you? And
even when she is toting the active proof of that violation
around in her belly or even right out in plain sight on her arm
or dragging at the tail of her skirt, immolating hit and her
both back into virginity wouldn't be no trick a-tall to that
nineteen-year-old boy since naturally that sixteen-year-old gal
couldn't possibly be fertilised by no other seed except hisn, I
dont care who would like to brag his-self as being the active
instrument.

Except that Lawyer didn't know all that yet neither. Mainly because he was too busy. I mean, that day when Eula first walked through the Jefferson Square where not jest Lawyer but all Jefferson too would have to see her. That time back there when Flem had finally grazed up Uncle Billy Varner and Frenchman's Bend and so he would have to move on some-where, and Jefferson was as good a place as any since as the feller says any spoke leads sooner or later to the rim. Or in fact maybe Jefferson was for the moment unavoidable, being as Flem had done beat me outen my half of that café me and Grover Winbush owned, and since there wasn't no easy quick practical way to get Grover out to Frenchman's Bend, Flem would simply have to make a stop-over at least in Jefferson while he evicted Grover outen the rest of it.

Anyhow, Lawyer seen her at last. And there he was, enter-ing not jest bare-handed but practically nekkid too, that en-gagement that he couldn't afford to do anything but lose it —Lawyer, a town-raised bachelor that was going to need a Master of Arts from Harvard and a Doctor of Philosophy from Heidelberg jest to stiffen him up to where he could cope with the natural normal Yoknapatawpha County folks that never wanted nothing except jest to break a few aggra-vating laws that was in their way or get a little free money outen the county treasury; and Eula Varner that never needed to be educated nowhere because jest what the Lord had al-ready give her by letting her stand up and breathe and maybe walk around a little now and then was trouble and danger enough for ever male man in range. For Lawyer to win that match would be like them spiders that the end of the honey-moon is when she finally finishes eating up his last drumstick. Which likely enough Lawyer knowed too, being nineteen years old and already one year at Harvard. Though even with-out Harvard, a boy nineteen years old ought to know that much about women jest by instinct, like a child or a animal knows fire is hot without having to actively put his hand or his foot in it. Even when a nineteen-year-old boy says "You're beautiful and I love you," even he ought to know whether it's a sixteen-year-old gal or a tiger that says "Certainly" back at him.

Anyhow, there Lawyer was, rushing headlong into that

engagement that not only the best he could expect and hope for but the best he could want would be to lose it, since losing it wouldn't do nothing but jest knock off some of his hide here and there. Rushing in with nothing in his hand to fight with but that capacity to stay nineteen years old the rest of his life, to take on that McCarron boy that had not only cuckolded him before he ever seen Eula, but that was going to keep on cuckolding him in one or another different name and shape even after he would finally give up. Because maybe Flem never had no reason to pick out Jefferson to come to; maybe one spoke was jest the same as another to him since all he wanted was a rim. Or maybe he jest didn't know he had a reason for Jefferson. Or maybe married men dont even need reasons, being as they already got wives. Or maybe it's women that dont need reasons, for the simple reason that they never heard of a reason and wouldn't recognise it face to face, since they dont function from reasons but from necessities that couldn't nobody help nohow and that dont nobody but a fool man want to help in the second place, because he dont know no better; it aint women, it's men that takes ignorance seriously, getting into a skeer over something for no more reason than that they dont happen to know what it is.

So it wasn't Grover Winbush and what you might call that dangling other half of mine and his café that brought Miz Flem Snopes to Jefferson so she could walk across the Square whatever that afternoon was when Lawyer had to look at her. It wasn't even Eula herself. It was that McCarron boy. And I seen some of that too and heard about all the rest of it. Because that was about all folks within five miles of Varner's store talked about that spring. The full unchallenged cynosure you might say of the whole Frenchman's Bend section, from sometime in March to the concluding dee-neweyment or meelee which taken place jest beyond the creek bridge below Varner's house one night in the following July—that McCarron boy coming in to Frenchman's Bend that day without warning out of nowhere like a cattymount into a sheep-pen among them Bookwrights and Binfords and Quicks and Tulls that for about a year now had been hitching their buggies and saddle mules to Will Varner's fence. Like a wild buck from the woods jumping the patch fence and already trompling them tame domestic local carrots and squashes and eggplants that until that moment was thinking or leastways hoping that Eula's maiden citadel was actively being threatened and endangered, before they could even blench, let alone cover their heads. Likely—in fact, they had done a little local bragging to that effect—they called theirselves pretty unbitted too, until he come along that day, coming from nowhere jest exactly like a wild buck from the woods, like he had done located Eula from miles and even days away outen the hard unerring air itself and come as straight as a die to where she was waiting, not for him especially but maybe for jest any wild strong buck that was wild and strong enough to deserve and match her.

Yes sir. As the feller says, the big buck: the wild buck right off the mountain itself, with his tail already up and his eyes already flashing. Because them Bookwrights and Quicks and Tulls was pretty fair bucks theirselves, on that-ere home Frenchman's Bend range and reservation you might say, providing them outside boundary limits posted signs wasn't violated by these-here footloose rambling uninvited strangers. In fact, they was pretty good at kicking and gouging and no holts barred and no bad feelings afterward, in all innocent friendliness and companionship not jest among one another but with that same friendly willingness to give and take when it was necessary to confederate up and learn him a lesson on some foreigner from four or five or six miles away that ought to stayed at home, had no business there, neither needed nor wanted, that had happened to see Eula somewhere once or maybe jest heard about her from somebody else that had watched her walk ten or fifteen feet. So he had to come crowding his buggy or mule up to Varner's picket fence some Sunday night, then coming innocently back down the road toward the gum and cypress thicket where the road crossed the creek bridge, his head still filled with female Varner dreams until the unified corporation stepped outen the thicket and bushwhacked them outen it and throwed creek water on him and put him back in the buggy or on the mule and wrapped the lines around the whipstock or the horn and headed him on toward wherever it was he lived and if he'd a had any sense he wouldn't a left it in the first place or at least in this direction.

But this here new one was a different animal. Because they—including them occasional volunteers—was jest bucks in the general—or maybe it's the universal—Frenchman's Bend pattern, while McCarron wasn't in nobody's pattern; he was unbitted not because he was afraid of a bit but simply because so fur he didn't prefer to be. So there not only wasn't nere a one of them would stand up to him alone, the whole unified confederated passel of them, that never hesitated one second to hide in that thicket against any other interloper that come sniffing at Varner's fence, never nerved theirselves up to him until it was already too late. Oh sho, they had chances. They had plenty of chances. In fact, he give them so many chances that by the end of May they wouldn't even walk a Frenchman's Bend road after dark, even in sight of one of their own houses, without they was at least three of them. Because this here was a different kind of a buck, coming without warning right off the big mountain itself and doing what Lawyer would call arrogating to his-self what had been the gynecological cynosure of a whole section of north Missippi for going on a year or two now. Not ravishing Eula away: not riding up on his horse and snatching her up behind him and galloping off, but jest simply moving in and dispossessing them; not even evicting them but like he was keeping them on hand for a chorus you might say, or maybe jest for spice, like you keep five or six cellars of salt setting handy while you are eating the watermelon, until it was already too late, until likely as not, as fur as they or Frenchman's Bend either knowed, Eula was already pregnant with Linda.

Except I dont think that was exactly it. I dont think I prefer it happened that way. I think I prefer it to happened all at once. Or that aint quite right neither. I think what I prefer is, that them five timorous local stallions actively brought about the very exact thing they finally nerved their desperation up to try to prevent. There they all was, poised on the brink you might say of that-ere still intact maiden citadel, all seven of them: Eula and McCarron, and them five Tulls and Bookwrights and Turpins and Binfords and Quicks. Because what them Tulls and Quicks would a called the worst hadn't happened yet. I dont mean the worst in respects to Eula's chastity nor to the violated honor of Uncle Billy Varner's home, but

in respects to them two years' investment of buggies and
mules tied to the Varner fence when them and the five folks
keeping them hitched there half the night both had ought to
been home getting a little rest before going back to the field
to plow at sunup, instead of having to live in a constantly
shifting confederation of whatever four of them happened to
believe that the fifth one was out in front in that-ere steeple-
chase, not to mention the need for all five of them having to
gang up at a moment's notice maybe at almost any time on
some stray interloper that turned up without warning with his
head full of picket fence ideas too.

So I prefer to believe it hadn't happened yet. I dont know
what Eula and McCarron was waiting on. I mean, what
McCarron was waiting on. Eula never done no waiting.
Likely she never even knowed what the word meant, like the
ground, dirt, the earth, whatever it is in it that makes seed
sprout at the right time, dont know nor need to know what
waiting means. Since to know what waiting means, you got to
be skeered or weak or self-doubtful enough to know what impatience or hurry means, and Eula never needed them no
more than that dirt does. All she needed was jest to be, like
the ground of the field, until the right time come, the right
wind, the right sun, the right rain; until in fact that-ere single
unique big buck jumped that tame garden fence outen the
big woods or the high mountain or the tall sky, and finally got
through jest standing there among the sheep with his head
up, looking proud. So it was McCarron that put off what you
might call that-ere inevitable, that long. Maybe that was why:
having to jest stand there for a while looking proud among
the sheep. Maybe that was it: maybe he was jest simply having too much fun at first, playing with them Bookwright and
Quick sheep, tantalising them up maybe to see jest how much
they would have to stand to forget for a moment they was
sheep, or to remember that maybe they was sheep but at least
there was five of them, until at last they would risk him jest
like he actively wasn't nothing but jest one more of them natural occupational local hazards Eula had done already got
them accustomed to handling.

So maybe you can figger what they was waiting on. They
was church folks. I mean, they went to church a heap of

Sundays, and Wednesday night prayer meeting too, unless something else come up. Because church was as good a place as any to finish up one week and start another, especially as there wasn't no particular other place to go on Sunday morning; not to mention a crap game down back of the spring while the church was busy singing or praying or listening; and who knowed but how on almost any Wednesday night you might ketch some young gal and persuade her off into the bushes before her paw or maw noticed she was missing. Or maybe they never needed to ever heard it, since likely it wasn't even Samson and Delilah that was the first ones to invent that hair-cutting eupheemism neither. So the whole idea might be what you would call a kind of last desperate instinctive hereditary expedient waiting handy for ever young feller (or old one either) faced with some form of man-trouble over his gal. So at least you knowed what they was waiting for. Naturally they would preferred to preserve that-ere maiden Varner citadel until one of them could manage to shake loose from the other four by luck or expedient long enough to ravage it. But now that this uninvited ringer had come in and wrecked ever thing anyhow, at least they could use that violation and rapine not only for revenge but to evict him for good from meddling around Frenchman's Bend.

Naturally not jest laying cravenly back to ketch him at a moment when he was wore out and exhausted with pleasure and success; they wasn't that bad. But since they couldn't prevent the victory, at least ketch him at a moment when he wasn't watching, when his mind was still fondly distracted and divided between what you might call bemusements with the recent past, which would a been last night, and aspirations toward the immediate future, which would be in a few minutes now as soon as the buggy reached a convenient place to hitch the horse. Which is what they—the ambushment—done. They was wrong of course; hadn't nothing happened yet. I mean, I prefer that even that citadel was still maiden right up to this moment. No: what I mean is, I wont have nothing else for the simple dramatic verities except that ever thing happened right there that night and all at once; that even that McCarron boy, that compared to them other five was a wild stag surrounded by a gang of goats—that even he wasn't enough by his-self but that it taken all six of them even to ravage that citadel, let alone seed them loins with a child: that July night and the buggy coming down the hill until they heard the horse's feet come off the creek bridge and the five of them, finally nerved up to even this last desperate gambit, piling outen that familiar bushwhacking thicket that up to this time had handled them local trespassing rams so simple and easy you wouldn't hardly need to dust off your hands afterward.

Naturally they never brought no bystanders with them and after the first two or three minutes there wasn't no witness a-tall left, since he was already laying out cold in the ditch. So my conjecture is jest as good as yourn, maybe better since I'm a interested party, being as I got what the feller calls a theo-rem to prove. In fact, it may not took even three minutes, one of them jumping to ketch the horse's head and the other four rushing to snatch McCarron outen the buggy, providing of course he was still in the buggy by that time and not al-ready blazing bushes up the creek, having chosen quick be-tween discretion and valor, it dont matter a hoot who was looking, as had happened before with at least one of the in-vaders that had been quick enough.

Which, by the trompled evidence folks went to look at the next day, McCarron wasn't, though not for the already prece-dented reason. Nor did the evidence explain jest what the wagon-spoke was doing there neither that broke McCarron's arm: only that McCarron had the wagon-spoke now in his re-maining hand in the road while Eula was standing up in the buggy with that lead-loaded buggy whip of Will's reversed in both hands like a hoe or a axe, swinging the leaded butt of it at whatever head come up next.

Not over three minutes, at the outside. It wouldn't needed more than that. It wouldn't wanted more: it was all that sim-ple and natural—a pure and simple natural circumstance as simple and natural and ungreedy as a tide-wave or a cloud-burst, that didn't even want but one swipe—a considerable of trompling and panting and cussing and nothing much to see except a kind of moil of tangled shadows around the horse (It never moved. But then it spent a good part of its life ever summer right in the middle of Will's sawmill and it stood

right there in the yard all the time Will was evicting Ab
Snopes from a house he hadn't paid no rent on in two years,
which was the nearest thing to a cyclone Frenchman's Bend
ever seen; it was said that Will could drive up to a depot and
get outen the buggy and not even hitch it while a train
passed, and only next summer it was going to be tied to the
same lot gate that them wild Texas ponies Flem Snopes
brought back from Texas demolished right up to the hinges
when they run over Frenchman's Bend.) and buggy and the
occasional gleam of that hickory wagon-spoke interspersed
among the mush-melon thumps of that loaded buggy whip
handle on them Frenchman's Bend skulls.

And then jest the empty horse and buggy standing there in
the road like the tree or rock or barn or whatever it was the
tide-wave or cloud-burst has done took its one rightful ungreedy swipe at and went away, and that-ere one remaining
evidence—it was Theron Quick; for a week after it you could
still see the print of Will Varner's loaded buggy whip across the
back of his skull; not the first time naming him Quick turned
out to be what the feller calls jest a humorous allusion—laying
cold in the weeds beside the road. And that's when I believe it
happened. I dont even insist or argue that it happened that
way. I jest simply decline to have it any other way except that
one because there aint no acceptable degrees between what
has got to be right and what jest can possibly be.

So it never even stopped. I mean, the motion, movement.
It was one continuous natural rush from the moment five of
them busted outen that thicket and grabbed at the horse, on
through the cussing and trompling and hard breathing and
the final crashing through the bushes and the last rapid and
fading footfall since likely the other four thought Theron was
dead; then jest the peaceful quiet and the dark road and the
horse standing quiet in the buggy in the middle of it and
Theron Quick sleeping peacefully in the weeds. And that's
when I believe it happened: not no cessation at-tall, not even
no active pausing: not jest that maiden bastion capitulate and
over-run but them loins themselves seeded, that child, that
girl, Linda herself created into life right there in the road with
likely Eula having to help hold him up offen the broke arm
and the horse standing over them among the stars like one of

them mounted big-game trophy heads sticking outen the parlor or the liberry or (I believe they call them now) den wall.
In fact maybe that's what it was.

So in almost no time there was Will Varner with a pregnant
unmarried daughter. I mean, there Frenchman's Bend was
because even in them days when you said "Frenchman's
Bend" you smiled at Uncle Billy Varner, or vice versa. Because
if Eula Varner was a natural phenomenon like a cyclone or a
tide-wave, Uncle Billy was one too even if he wasn't no more
than forty yet: that had shaved notes and foreclosed liens and
padded furnish bills and evicted tenants until the way Will
Varner went Frenchman's Bend had done already left and the
folks that composed it had damn sho better hang on and go
too, unless they jest wanted to settle down in vacant space
twenty-two miles south-east of Jefferson.

Naturally the McCarron boy was the man to handle the
Varner family honor right there on the spot. After the first
shock, folks all thought that's what he had aimed to do. He
was the only child of a well-to-do widowed maw up in
Tennessee somewhere until he happened to be wherever it
was his fate arranged for him to have his look at Eula Varner
like theirn would do for Lawyer Stevens and Manfred de
Spain about a year later. And, being the only child of a well-
to-do maw only educated in one of them fancy gentleman's
schools, you would naturally expect him to lit out without
even stopping to have his broke arm splinted up, let alone
waiting for Will Varner to reach for his shotgun.

Except you would been wrong. Maybe you not only dont
run outen the middle of a natural catastrophe—you might be
flung outen it by centrifugal force or, if you had any sense,
you might tried to dodge it. But you dont change your mind
and plans in the middle of it.—or he might in his case even
wanted to stay in the middle of that particular one until it
taken the rest of his arms and legs too, as likely any number
of them other Quicks and Tulls and Bookwrights would
elected to do. Not to mention staying in that select prep
school that even in that short time some of them high acade-
mic standards of honor and chivalry rubbed off on him by jest
exposure. Anyhow it wasn't him that left that-ere now-fly-
specked Varner family honor high and dry. It was Eula herself

that done it. So now all you can do is try to figger. So maybe
it was the McCarron boy that done it, after all. Like maybe
that centrifugal force that hadn't touched him but that one
light time and he had already begun to crumple. That simple
natural phenomenon that maybe didn't expect to meet another phenomenon, even a natural one, but at least expected
or maybe jest hoped for something at least tough enough to
crash back without losing a arm or a leg the first time they
struck. Because next time it might be a head, which would
mean the life along with it, and then all that force and power
and unskeeredness and unskeerableness to give and to take
and suffer the consequences it taken to be a female natural
phenomenon in its phenomenal moment, would be wasted,
throwed away. Because I aint talking about love. Natural phenomenons aint got no more concept of love than they have of
the alarm and uncertainty and impotence you got to be capable of to know what waiting means. When she said to herself,
and likely she did: *The next one of them creek bridge episodes
might destroy him completely*, it wasn't that McCarron boy's
comfort she had in mind.

Anyhow, the next morning he was gone from Frenchman's
Bend. I presume it was Eula that put what was left of the
buggy whip back into the socket and druv the buggy back up
the hill. Leastways they waked Will, and Will in his nightshirt
(no shotgun: it would be anywhere up to twenty-eight days,
give or take a few, before he would find out he needed the
shotgun; it was jest his little grip of veterinary tools yet)
patched up the arm to where he could drive on home or
somewhere that more than a local cow-and-mule doctor
could get a-holt of him. But he was back in Jefferson at least
once about a month later, about the time when Eula likely
found out if she didn't change her condition pretty quick
now, it was going to change itself for her. And he even paid
the mail rider extra to carry a special wrote-out private message to Eula. But nothing come of that neither, and at last he
was gone. And sho enough, about sixty-five or seventy days
after that-ere hors-de-combat creek-bridge evening—and if
you had expected a roar of some kind to come up outen the
Varner residence and environment, you would been wrong
there too: it was jest a quick announcement that even then

barely beat the wedding itself—Herman Bookwright and
Theron Quick left Frenchman's Bend suddenly overnight too
though it's my belief they was both not even bragging but
jest wishing they had, and Eula and Flem was married; and
after the one more week it taken Will to do what he thought
was beating Flem down to accepting that abandoned Old
Frenchman place as full receipt for Eula's dowry, Eula and
Flem left for Texas, which was fur enough away so that when
they come back, that-ere new Snopes baby would look at least
reasonably legal or maybe what I mean is orthodox. Not to
mention as Texas would be where it had spent the presumable
most of its prenatal existence, wouldn't nobody be surprised
if it was cutting its teeth at three months old. And when they
was back in Frenchman's Bend in September exactly one year
later, anybody meddlesome enough to remark how it had got
to be a pretty good size gal in jest them three possible
months, all he had to do was remind his-self that them three
outside months had been laid in Texas likewise.

Jest exactly fourteen months since that McCarron boy
started to crumple at the seams at that first encounter. But it
wasn't waiting. I mean, Eula. Natural phenomenons aint got
no room for self-doubt and alarms and impatience to even
know what waiting means. She was jest being, breathing, setting with that baby in a rocking chair on Varner's front gallery
while Flem changed enough money into them sixty silver dollars and buried them in that Old Frenchman place rose garden jest exactly where me and Henry Armstid and Odum
Bookwright couldn't help but find them. And still jest being
and breathing, setting with the baby in the wagon that day
they moved in to Jefferson so Flem could get a active holt on
Grover Winbush to evict him outen the other half of that café
me and Grover owned. And still jest being and breathing but
not setting now because likely even the tide-wave dont need
to be informed when it's on the right spoke to whatever rim
it's due at next, her and Flem and the baby living in that canvas tent behind the café between when she would walk across
the Square until finally Manfred de Spain, the McCarron that
wouldn't start or break up when they collided together,
would look up and see her. Who hadn't had none of them
select advantages of being the only child of a well-to-do

widowed maw living in Florida hotels while he was temporarily away at them select eastern schools, but instead had had to
make out the best he could with jest being the son of a
Confederate cavalry officer, that graduated his-self from West
Point into what his paw would a called the Yankee army and
went to Cuba as a lieutenant and come back with a long
jagged scar down one cheek that the folks trying to beat him
for mayor rumored around wasn't made by no Spanish bayonet a-tall but instead by a Missouri sergeant with a axe in a
crap game: which whether it was so or not, never stood up
long between him and getting elected mayor of Jefferson, nor
between him and getting to be president of Colonel Sartoris's
bank when that come up, not to mention between him and
Eula Varner Snopes when that come up.

I aint even mentioning Lawyer. It wasn't even his bad luck
he was on that rim too because tide-waves aint concerned
with luck. It was his fate. He jest got run over by coincidence,
like a ant using the same spoke a elephant happened to find
necessary or convenient. It wasn't that he was born too soon
or too late or even in the wrong place. He was born at exactly
the right time, only in the wrong envelope. It was his fate and
doom not to been born into one of them McCarron separate
covers too instead of into that fragile and what you might call
gossamer-sinewed envelope of boundless and hopeless aspiration Old Moster give him.

So there he was, rushing headlong into that engagement
that the best he could possibly hope would be to lose it quick,
since any semblance or intimation of the most minorest victory would a destroyed him like a lightning-bolt, while Flem
Snopes grazed gently on up them new Jefferson pastures, him
and his wife and infant daughter still living in the tent behind
the café and Flem his-self frying the hamburgers now after
Grover Winbush found out suddenly one day that he never
owned one half of a café neither; then the Rouncewells that
thought they still owned what Miz Rouncewell called the
Commercial Hotel against all the rest of Yoknapatawpha
County calling it the Rouncewell boarding house, found they
was wrong too and the Flem Snopeses lived there now, during the month or so it taken him to eliminate the Rouncewells outen it, with the next Snopes from Frenchman's Bend

imported into the tent behind the café and frying the hamburgers because Flem his-self was now superintendent of the power plant; Manfred de Spain had not only seen Eula, he was already mayor of Jefferson when he done it.

And still Lawyer was trying, even while at least once ever day he would have to see his mortal victorious rival and conqueror going in and out of the mayor's office or riding back and forth across the Square in that red brass-trimmed EMF roadster that most of north Missippi, let alone jest Yoknapatawpha County, hadn't seen nothing like before; right on up and into that alley behind the Ladies' Cotillion Club Christmas ball where he tried to fight Manfred with his bare fists until his sister's husband drug him up outen the gutter and held him long enough for Manfred to get outen sight and then taken him home to the bathroom to wash him off and says to him: "What the hell do you mean? Dont you know you dont know how to fight?" And Lawyer leaning over the washbowl trying to stanch his nose with handfulls of tissue paper, saying, "Of course I know it. But can you suh-jest a better way than this for me to learn?"

And still trying, on up to that last desperate cast going all the way back to that power-house brass business. I mean, that pile of old wore-out faucets and valves and pieces of brass pipe and old bearings and such that had accumulated into the power plant until they all disappeared sometime during the second year of Flem's reign as superintendent, though there wasn't no direct evidence against nobody even after the brass safety-valves vanished from both the boilers and was found to been replaced with screwed-in steel plugs; it was jest that finally the city auditors had to go to the superintendent and advise him as delicate as possible that that brass was missing and Flem quit chewing long enough to say "How much?" and paid them and then the next year they done the books again and found they had miscounted last year and went to him again and suh-jested they had made a mistake before and Flem quit chewing again long enough to say "How much?" and paid them that too. Going (I mean Lawyer) all the way back to them old by-gones even though Flem was not only long since resigned from being superintendent, he had even bought two new safety-valves outen his own pocket as a free civic gift to the community; bringing all that up again, with evidence, in a suit to impeach Manfred outen the mayor's office until Judge Dukinfield recused his-self and appointed Judge Stevens, Lawyer's paw, to hear the case. Only we didn't know what happened then because Judge Stevens cleared the court and heard the argument in chambers as they calls it, jest Lawyer and Manfred and the judge his-self. And that was all; it never taken long; almost right away Manfred come out and went back to his mayor's office, and the tale, legend, report, whatever you want to call it, of Lawyer standing there with his head bent a little in front of his paw, saying, "What must I do now, Papa? Papa, what can I do now?"

But he was chipper enough the next morning when I seen him off on the train, that had done already graduated from Harvard and the University law school over at Oxford and was now on his way to a town in Germany to go to school some more. Yes sir, brisk and chipper as you could want. "Here you are," he says. "This is what I want with you before I leave: to pass the torch on into your personal hand. You'll have to hold the fort alone now. You'll have to tote the load by yourself."

"What fort?" I says. "What load?"

"Jefferson," he says. "Snopeses. Think you can handle them alone for two years?" That's what he thought then: that he was all right now; he had done been disenchanted for good at last of Helen, and so now all he had to worry about was what them Menelaus-Snopeses might be up to in the Yoknapatawpha-Argive community while he had his back turned. Which was all right; it would ease his mind. He would have plenty of time after he come back to find out that aint nobody yet ever lost Helen, since for the rest of not jest her life but hisn too she dont never get shut of him. Likely it's because she dont want to.

Except it wasn't two years. It was nearer five. That was in the early spring of 1914, and that summer the war come, and maybe that—a war—was what he was looking for. Not hoping for, let alone expecting to have one happen jest on his account, since like most other folks in this country he didn't believe no war was coming. But looking for something, anything, and certainly a war would do as well as another, since

no matter what his brains might a been telling him once he
had that much water between him and Eula Snopes, even his
instincts likely told him that jest two years wasn't nowhere
near enough for him or Helen either to have any confidence
in that disenchantment. So even if he couldn't anticipate no
war to save him, back in his mind somewhere he was still confident that Providence would furnish something, since like he
said, God was anyhow a gentleman and wouldn't bollix up
the same feller twice with the same trick, at least in the same
original package.

So he had his war. Only you would a wondered—at least I
did—why he never went into it on the German side. Not jest
because he was already in Germany and the German army
handy right there surrounding him, but because he had already told me how, although it was the culture of England
that had sent folks this fur across the water to establish
America, right now it was the German culture that had the
closest tie with the modern virile derivations of the northern
branch of the old Aryan stock. Because he said that tie was
mystical, not what you seen but what you heard, and that the
present-day Aryan, in America at least, never had no confidence a-tall in what he seen, but on the contrary would believe anything he jest heard and couldn't prove; and that the
modern German culture since the revolutions of 1848 never
had no concern with, and if anything a little contempt for,
anything that happened to man on the outside, or through the
eyes and touch, like sculpture and painting and civil laws for
his social benefit, but jest with what happened to him through
his ears, like music and philosophy and what was wrong inside
of his mind. Which he said was the reason why German was
such a ugly language, not musical like Italian and Spanish nor
what he called the epicene exactitude of French, but was harsh
and ugly, not to mention full of spit (like as the feller says, you
speak Italian to men, French to women, and German to
horses) so that there wouldn't be nothing to interfere and distract your mind from what your nerves and glands was hearing: the mystical ideas, the glorious music—Lawyer said, the
best of music, from the mathematical inevitability of Mozart
through the godlike passion of Beethoven and Bach to the
combination bawdy-house street-carnival uproar that Wagner

made—that come straight to the modern virile northern Aryan's heart without bothering his mind a-tall.

Except that he didn't join the German army. I dont know what lies he managed to tell the Germans to get out of Germany where he could join the enemy fighting them, nor what lies he thought up for the English and French to explain why a student out of a German university was a safe risk to have around where he might overhear somebody telling what surprise they was fixing up next. But he done it. And it wasn't the English army he joined neither. It was the French one: them folks that, according to him, spent all their time talking about epicene exactitudes to ladies. And I didn't know why even four years later when I finally asked him: "After all you said about that-ere kinship of German culture, and the German army right there in the middle of you, or leastways you in the middle of it, you still had to lie or trick your way out to join the French one." Because all he said was, "I was wrong." And not even another year after that when I said to him, "Even despite that splendid glorious music and them splendid mystical ideas?" he jest says:

"They are still glorious, still splendid. It's the word *mystical* that's wrong. The music and the ideas both come out of obscurity, darkness. Not out of shadow: out of obscurity, obfuscation, darkness. Man must have light. He must live in the fierce full constant glare of light, where all shadow will be defined and sharp and unique and personal: the shadow of his own singular rectitude or baseness. All human evils have to come out of obscurity and darkness where there is nothing to dog man constantly with the shape of his own deformity."

In fact not until two or three years more and he was back home now, settled now; and Eula, still without having to do no more than jest breathe as far as he was concerned, had already adopted the rest of his life as long as it would be needed, into the future of that eleven- or twelve-year-old girl, and I said to him:

"Helen walked in light." And he says,

"Helen was light. That's why we can still see her, not changed, not even dimmer, from five thousand years away." And I says,

"What about all them others you talk about? Semiramises

and Judiths and Liliths and Francescas and Isoldes?" And he says,

"But not like Helen. Not that bright, that luminous, that enduring. It's because the others all talked. They are fading steadily into the obscurity of their own vocality within which their passions and tragedies took place. But not Helen. Do you know there is not one recorded word of hers anywhere in existence, other than that one presumable Yes she must have said that time to Paris?"

So there they was. That gal of thirteen and fourteen and fifteen that wasn't trying to do nothing but jest get shut of having to go to school by getting there on time and knowing the lesson to make the rise next year, that likely wouldn't barely ever looked at him long enough to know him again except that she found out on a sudden that for some reason he was trying to adopt some of her daily life into hisn, or adopt a considerable chunk of his daily life into hern, whichever way you want to put it. And that bachelor lawyer twice her age, that was already more or less in the public eye from being county attorney, not to mention in a little town like Jefferson where ever time you had your hair cut your constituency knowed about it by suppertime. So that the best they knowed to do was to spend fifteen minutes after school one or two afternoons a week at a table in the window of Uncle Willy Christian's drugstore while she et a ice cream sody or a banana split and the ice melted into the unteched coca cola in front of him. Not jest the best but the only thing, not jest for the sake of her good name but also for them votes that two years from now might not consider buying ice cream for fourteen-year-old gals a fitting qualification for a county attorney.

About twice a week meeting her by that kind of purely coincidental accident that looked jest exactly as accidental as you would expect: Lawyer ambushed behind his upstairs office window across the street until the first of the let-out school would begin to pass, which would be the kindergarden and the first grade, then by that same accidental coincidence happening to be on the corner at the exact time to cut her outen the seventh or eighth or ninth grade, her looking a little startled and surprised the first time or two; not alarmed: jest startled a little, wondering jest a little at first maybe what he wanted. But not for long; that passed too and pretty soon Lawyer was even drinking maybe a inch of the coca cola before it got too lukewarm to swallow. Until one day I says to him: "I envy you," and he looked at me and I says, "Your luck," and he says,

"My which luck?" and I says,

"You are completely immersed twenty-four hours a day in being busy. Most folks aint. Almost nobody aint. But you are. Doing the one thing you not only got to do, but the one thing in the world you want most to do. And if that wasn't already enough, it's got as many or maybe even more interesting technical complications in it than if you had invented it yourself instead of jest being discovered by it. For the sake of her good name, you got to do it right out in that very same open public eye that would ruin her good if it ever found a chance, but maybe wouldn't never even suspect you and she knowed one another's name if you jest kept it hidden in secret. Dont you call that keeping busy?"

Because he was unenchanted now, you see, done freed at last of that fallen seraphim. It was Eula herself had give him a salve, a ointment, for that bitter thumb the poets say ever man once in his life has got to gnaw at: that gal thirteen then fourteen then fifteen setting opposite him in Christian's drugstore maybe two afternoons a week in the intervals of them coincidental two or three weeks ever year while Miz Flem Snopes and her daughter would be on a holiday somewhere at the same coincidental time Manfred de Spain would be absent on hisn—not Mayor de Spain now but Banker de Spain since Colonel Sartoris finally vacated the presidency of the bank him and De Spain's paw and Will Varner had established, by letting his grandson run the automobile off into a ditch on the way to town one morning, and now Manfred de Spain was president of the bank, moving outen the mayor's office into the president's office at about the same more or less coincidental moment that Flem Snopes moved outen being the ex-superintendent of the power plant, into being vice president of the bank, vacating simultaneously outen that little cloth cap he come to Jefferson in (jest vacated, not abandoned it, the legend being he sold it to a Negro boy for ten cents. Which wouldn't be a bad price, since who knows if

maybe some of that-ere financial acumen might not a sweated
off onto it.) into a black felt planter's hat suitable to his new
position and avocation.

Oh yes, Lawyer was unenchanted now, even setting alone
now and then in Christian's window while the ice melted into
the coca cola until they would get back home, maybe to be
ready and in practice when them two simultaneous coinci-
dences was over and school would open again on a whole
fresh year of two afternoons a week—providing of course that
sixteen- and seventeen-year-old gal never run into a Hoke
McCarron or a Manfred de Spain of her own between two of
them and Lawyer could say to you like the man in the book:
*What you see aint tears. You jest think that's what you're look-
ing at.*

Sixteen and seventeen and going on eighteen now and
Lawyer still lending her books to read and keeping her stall-
fed twice a week on ice cream sundays and banana splits so
anyhow Jefferson figgered it knowed what Lawyer was up to
whether he admitted it out or not. And naturally Eula had already knowed for five or six years what she was after. Like
there's a dog, maybe not no extra dog but leastways a good
sound what you might call a dog's dog, that dont seem to belong to nobody else, that seems to show a preference for your
vicinity, that even after the five or six years you aint completely convinced there wont never be no other dog available,
and that even them five or six years back and even with another five or six years added onto now, you never needed and
you aint going to need that dog personally, there aint any use
in simply throwing away and wasting its benefits and accom-
plishments, even if they aint nothing but fidelity and devotion, by letting somebody else get a holt of it. Or say you got
a gal child coming along, that the older and bigger she gets,
the more of a nuisance she's bound to be on your time and
private occupations: in which case not only wont that fidelity
and devotion maybe come into handy use, but even the dog
itself might that could still be capable of them long after even
hit had give up all expectation of even one bone.

Which is what Jefferson figgered. But not me. Maybe back
there that time when she got rid of Hoke McCarron, even after she knowed she was pregnant, because she figgered that

one more creek bridge would destroy his usefulness completely, even if it wasn't his comfort she had in mind at the
moment; there is still moments when even female physical
phenomenons is female first whether they want to be or not.
So I believe that woman aint so different from men: that if it
aint no trouble nor shock neither for a man to father onto
his-self the first child, no matter how many other men holp to
get it, of the woman he loved and lost and still cant rid outen
his mind, it aint no trouble neither for that woman to father
a dozen different men's chillen onto that man that lost her
and still never expected nothing of her except to accept his
devotion.

And since she was a female too, likely by the time Linda
was thirteen or fourteen or even maybe as soon as she got
over that first startle, which would a been at the second or
third ice cream sody, she taken for granted she knowed what
he was aiming at too. And she would a been wrong. That
wasn't Lawyer. Jest to train her up and marry her wasn't it.
She wouldn't a been necessary for that—I mean, the simple
natural normal following lifetime up to the divorce of steady
uxorious hymeneal conflict that any female he could a picked
outen that school crowd or from Christian's sody counter
would been fully competent for. Jest that wouldn't a been
worth his effort. He had to be the sole one masculine feller
within her entire possible circumambience, not jest to recognise she had a soul still capable of being saved from what he
called Snopesism: a force and power that stout and evil as to
jeopardise it jest from her believing for twelve or thirteen
years she was blood kin when she actively wasn't no kin a-tall,
but that couldn't nobody else in range and reach but him save
it—that-ere bubble-glass thing somewhere inside her like one
of them shimmer-colored balls balanced on the seal's nose,
fragile yet immune too jest that one constant fragile inch
above the smutch and dirt of Snopes as long as the seal dont
trip or stumble or let her attention wander.

So all he aimed to do was jest to get her outen Jefferson or,
better, safer still, completely outen Missippi, starting off with
the nine months of the school year until somebody would
find her and marry her and she would be gone for good—a
optimist pure and simple and undefiled if there ever was one

since ever body knowed that the reason Flem Snopes was vice president of De Spain's bank was the same reason he was ex-superintendent of the power plant: in the one case folks wanting to smile at Eula Varner had to at least be able to pronounce Flem Snopes, and in the other De Spain had to take Flem along with him to get the use of Will Varner's voting stock to get his-self president. And the only reason why Will Varner never used this chance to get back at Flem about that old Frenchman homesite that Will thought wasn't worth nothing until Flem sold it to me and Odum Bookwright and Henry Armstid for my half of mine and Grover Winbush's café and a two-hundred dollar mortgage on Odum's farm and them five or six dollars or whatever they was where Henry's wife tried to keep them buried from him behind the outhouse, was the same reason why Eula didn't quit Flem and marry De Spain: that staying married to Flem kept up a establishment and a name for that gal that otherwise wouldn't a had either. So once that gal was married herself or leastways settled for good away from Jefferson so she wouldn't need Flem's name and establishment no more, and in consequence Flem wouldn't have no holt over her anymore, Flem his-self would be on the outside trying to look back in and Flem knowed it.

Only Lawyer didn't know it. He believed right up to the last that Flem was going to let him get Linda away from Jefferson to where the first strange young man that happened by would marry her and then Eula could quit him and he would be finished. He—I mean Lawyer—had been giving her books to read ever since she was fourteen and then kind of holding examinations on them while the coca cola ice melted. Then she was going on seventeen, next spring she would graduate from the high school and now he was ordering off for the catalogues from the high select girls' schools up there close to Harvard.

Now the part comes that dont nobody know except Lawyer, who naturally never told it. So as he his-self would say, you got to surmise from the facts in evidence: not jest the mind-improving books and the school catalogues accumulating into a dusty stack in his office, but the ice cream sessions a thing of the past too. Because now she was going to and from school the back way, up alleys. Until finally in about a week maybe Lawyer realised that she was dodging him. And she was going to graduate from high school in less than two months now and there wasn't no time to waste. So that morning Lawyer went his-self to talk to her maw and he never told that neither so now we got to presume on a little more than jest evidence. Because my childhood too come out of that same similar Frenchman's Bend background and mill-yew that Flem Snopes had lifted his-self out of by his own un-aided bootstraps, if you dont count Hoke McCarron. So all I had to do was jest to imagine my name was Flem Snopes and that the only holt I had on Will Varner's money was through his daughter, and if I ever lost what light holt I had on the grand-daughter, the daughter would be gone. Yet here was a durn meddling outsider with a complete set of plans that would remove that grand-daughter to where I wouldn't never see her again, if she had any sense a-tall. And since the daugh-ter had evidently put up with me for going on eighteen years now for the sake of that grand-daughter, the answer was sim-ple: all I needed to do was go to my wife and say, "If you give that gal permission to go away to school, I'll blow up this-here entire Manfred de Spain business to where she wont have no home to have to get away from, let alone one to come back to for Christmas and holidays."

And for her first eighteen years Eula breathed that same Frenchman's Bend mill-yew atmosphere too so maybe all I got to do is imagine my name is Eula Varner to know what she said back to Lawyer: "No, she cant go off to school but you can marry her. That will solve ever thing." You see? Because the kind of fidelity and devotion that could keep faithful and devoted that long without even wanting no bone anymore, was not only too valuable to let get away, it even deserved to be rewarded. Because maybe the full rounded sat-isfaction and completeness of being Helen was bigger than a thousand Parises and McCarrons and De Spains could satisfy. I don't mean jest the inexhaustible capacity for passion, but of power: the power not jest to draw and enchant and consume, but the power and capacity to give away and reward; the power to draw to you, not more than you can handle because the words 'cant-handle' and 'Helen' aint even in the same language, but to draw to you so much more than you can possibly need that you could even afford to give the surplus away, be that prodigal—except that you are Helen and you cant give nothing away that was ever yourn: all you can do is share it and reward its fidelity and maybe even, for a moment, soothe and assuage its grief. And cruel too, prodigal in that too, because you are Helen and can afford it; you got to be Helen to be that cruel, that prodigal in cruelty, and still be yourself unscathed and immune, likely calling him by his first name for the first time too: "Marry her, Gavin."

And saw in his face not jest startlement and a little surprise like he seen in Linda's that time, but terror, fright, not at having to answer "No" that quick nor even at being asked it because he believed he had done already asked and decided that suh-jestion forever a long while back. It was at having it suh-jested to him by her. Like, since he hadn't been able to have no hope since that moment when he realised Manfred de Spain had already looked at her too, he had found out how to live at peace with hoping since he was the only one alive that knowed he never had none. But now, when she said that right out loud to his face, it was like she had said right out in public that he wouldn't a had no hope even if Manfred de Spain hadn't never laid eyes on her. And if he could jest get that "No" out quick enough, it would be like maybe she hadn't actively said what she said, and he would still not be destroyed.

At least wasn't nobody, no outsider, there to hear it so maybe even before next January he was able to believe hadn't none of it even been said, like miracle: what aint believed aint seen. Miracle, pure miracle anyhow, how little a man needs to outlast jest about anything. Which—miracle—is about what looked like had happened next January: Linda graduated that spring from high school and next fall she entered the Seminary where she would be home ever night and all day Saturday and Sunday the same as before so Flem could keep his hand on her. Then jest after Christmas we heard how she had withdrawed from the Seminary and was going over to Oxford and enter the University. Yes sir, over there fifty miles from Flem day and night both right in the middle of a nest of five or six hundred bachelors under twenty-five years old any one of which could marry her that had two dollars for a license. A pure miracle, especially after I run into Eula on the street and says,

"How did you manage it?" and she says,

"Manage what?" and I says,

"Persuade Flem to let her go to the University," and she says,

"I didn't. It was his idea. He gave the permission without even consulting me. I didn't know he was going to do it either." Only the Frenchman's Bend background should have been enough, without even needing the sixteen or seventeen years of Jefferson environment, to reveal even to blind folks that Flem Snopes didn't deal in miracles: that he preferred spot cash or at least a signed paper with a X on it. So when it was all over and finished, Eula dead and De Spain gone from Jefferson for good too and Flem was now president of the bank and even living in De Spain's rejuvenated ancestral home and Linda gone with her New York husband to fight in the Spanish war, when Lawyer finally told me what little he actively knowed, it was jest evidence I had already presumed on. Because of course all Helen's children would have to inherit something of generosity even if they couldn't inherit more than about one millionth of their maw's bounty to be generous with. Not to mention that McCarron boy, that even if he wasn't durable enough to stand more than that-ere first creek bridge, was at least brave enough or rash enough to try to. So likely Flem already knowed in advance that he wouldn't have to bargain, swap, with her. That all he needed was jest to do what he probably done: ketching her after she had give up and then had had them three months to settle down into having give up, then saying to her: "Let's compromise. If you will give up them eastern schools, maybe you can go to the University over at Oxford." You see? Offering to give something, that in all the fourteen or fifteen years she could remember knowing him in, she had never dreamed he would do.

Then that day in the next April; she had been at the University over at Oxford since right after New Year's. I was jest leaving for Rockyford to deliver Miz Ledbetter's new sewing machine when Flem stopped me on the Square and offered me four bits extra to carry him by Varner's store a minute. Urgent enough to pay me four bits when the mail carrier would have took him for nothing; secret enough that he couldn't risk either public conveyance: the mail carrier that would a took him out and back free but would a needed all day, and a hired automobile that would had him at Varner's front gate in not much over a hour.

Secret enough and urgent enough to have Will Varner storming into his daughter's and son-in-law's house in Jefferson at daylight the next morning loud enough to wake up the whole neighborhood until somebody (Eula naturally) stopped him. So we got to presume on a few known facts again: that old Frenchman place that Will deeded to Flem because he thought it was worthless until Flem sold it to me and Odum Bookwright and Henry Armstid for a half interest in my café and a mortgage on Odum's farm and them six or seven dollars that Henry Armstid's wife thought she had hid from him, less of course the active silver dollars Flem had had to invest into that old rose garden with a shovel where we— or any other Ratliffs and Bookwrights and Armstids that was handy—would find them. And that president's chair in the bank that we knowed now Flem had had his eye on ever since Manfred de Spain taken it over after Colonel Sartoris. And that gal that had done already inherited generosity from her maw and then was suddenly give another gob of it that she not only never in the world expected but that she probably never knowed how bad she wanted it until it was suddenly give to her free.

What Flem taken out to Frenchman's Bend that day was a will. Maybe when Linda finally got over the shock of getting permission to go away to school after she had long since give up any hope of it, even if no further away than Oxford, maybe when she looked around and realised who that per-mission had come from, she jest could not bear to be under obligations to him. Except I dont believe that neither. It wasn't even that little of bounty and generosity which would be all Helen's child could inherit from her, since half of even Helen's child would have to be corrupted by something less than Helen, being as even Helen couldn't get a child on her-self alone. What Linda wanted was not jest to give. It was to be needed: not jest to be loved and wanted, but to be needed too; and maybe this was the first time in her life she ever had anything that anybody not jest wanted but needed too.

It was a will; Eula of course told Lawyer. Flem his-self could a suh-jested the idea to Linda; it wouldn't a been difficult. Which I dont believe neither. He didn't need to; he knowed her well enough to presume on that, jest like she knowed him enough to presume too. It was Linda herself that evolved the idea when she realised that as long as he lived and drawed breath as Flem Snopes, he wasn't never going to give her permission to leave Jefferson for any reason. And her asking herself, impotent and desperate: *But why? why?* until finally she answered it—a answer that maybe wouldn't a helt much water but she was jest sixteen and seventeen then, during which sixteen and seventeen years she had found out that the only thing he loved was money. Because she must a knowed something anyway about Manfred de Spain. Jefferson wasn't that big, if in fact any place is. Not to mention them two or three weeks of summer holiday at the seashore or mountains or wherever, when here all of a sudden who should turn up but a old Jefferson neighbor happening by accident to take his vacation too from the bank at the same time and place. So what else would she say? *It's grandfather's money, that his one and only chance to keep any holt on it is through mama and me so he believes that once I get away from him his holt on both of us will be broken and mama will leave too and marry Manfred and any hope of grandfather's money will be gone forever.*

Yet here was this man that had had sixteen or seventeen years to learn her he didn't love nothing but money and would do anything you could suh-est to get another dollar of it, coming to her his-self, without no pressure from nobody and not asking for nothing back, saying, *You can go away to school if you still want to; only, this first time anyhow stay at least as close to home as Oxford;* saying in effect: *I was wrong. I wont no longer stand between you and your life, even though I am convinced I will be throwing away all hope of your grandpaw's money.*

So what else could she do but what she done, saying in effect back at him: *If you jest realised now that grandfather's money aint as important as my life, I could a told you that all the time; if you had jest told me two years ago that all you was was jest skeered, I would a eased you then*—going (Lawyer hisself told me this) to a Oxford lawyer as soon as she was settled in the University and drawing up a will leaving whatever share she might ever have in her grandpaw's or her maw's estate to her father Flem Snopes. Sho, that wouldn't a held no water neither but she was jest eighteen and that was all she had to give that she thought anybody wanted or needed from her; and besides, all the water it would need to hold would be what old Will Varner would sweat out when Flem showed it to him.

So jest after ten that morning I stopped not at the store where Will would be at this hour but at his front gate jest exactly long enough for Flem to get out and walk into the house until he coincided with Miz Varner I reckon it was and turn around and come back out and get back into the pickup and presumably at their four oclock a.m. morning family breakfast it occurred to Miz Varner or anyway she decided to or anyhow did hand Will the paper his son-in-law left yestiddy for him to look at. And by sun-up Will had that whole Snopes street woke up hollering inside Flem's house until Eula got him shut up. And by our normal ee-feet Jefferson breakfast time Manfred de Spain was there too. And that done it. Will Varner, that Flem had done already tricked outen that Old Frenchman place, then turned right around and used him again to get his-self and Manfred de Spain vice president and president respectively of Colonel Sartoris's bank, and now Flem had done turned back around the third time and somehow tricked his grand-daughter into giving him a quit-claim to half of his active cash money that so far even Flem hadn't found no way to touch. And Flem that all he wanted was for Manfred de Spain to resign from the bank so he could be president of it and would jest as lief done it quiet and discreet and all private in the family you might say by a simple friendly suh-jestion from Will Varner to Manfred to resign from the bank, as a even swap for that paper of Linda's which should a worked with anybody and would with anybody else except Manfred. He was the trouble; likely Eula could a handled them all except for him. Maybe he got that-ere scar on his face by actively toting a flag up a hill in Cuba and running over a cannon or a fort with it, and maybe it come from the axe in that crap game like that old mayor's race rumor claimed. But leastways it was on his front and not on his back and so maybe a feller could knock him out with a piece of lead pipe and pick his pocket while he was laying there, but couldn't no Snopes nor nobody else pick it jest by pointing at him what the other feller thought was a pistol.

And Eula in the middle of them, that likely could a handled it all except for Manfred, that had even made Will shut up but she couldn't make Manfred hush. That had done already spent lacking jest a week of nineteen years holding together a home for Linda to grow up and live in so she wouldn't never need to say *Other children have got what I never had;* there was Eula having to decide right there right now, *If I was a eighteen-year-old gal, which would I rather have: my mother publicly notarised as a suicide, or publicly condemned as a whore?* and by noon the next day all Jefferson knowed how the afternoon before she come to town and went to the beauty parlor that hadn't never been in one before because she never needed to, and had her hair waved and her fingernails shined and went back home and presumably et supper or anyhow was present at it since it wasn't until about eleven oclock that she seemed to taken up the pistol and throwed the safety off.

And the next morning Lawyer and his sister drove over to Oxford and brought Linda home; a pure misfortunate coincidence that all this had to happen jest a week before her nineteenth birthday. But as soon as Flem received that will from her, naturally he figgered Will Varner would want to see it as soon as possible, being a interested party; it was Will that never had no reason a-tall to pick out that special day to come bellering in to town two hours after he first seen it. He could a jest as well waited two weeks or even a month to come in, since wasn't nobody hurrying him; Flem would certainly a waited on his convenience.

And Lawyer that tended to the rest of it too: arranged for the funeral and sent out to Frenchman's Bend for Miz Varner and the old Methodist preacher that had baptised Eula, and then seen to the grave. Because naturally the bereaved husband couldn't be expected to break into his grief jest to do chores. Not to mention having to be ready to take over the bank after a decent interval, being as Manfred de Spain hisself had packed up and departed from Jefferson right after the burying. And then, after another decorious interval, a little longer this time being as a bank aint like jest a house because a bank deals with active cash money and cant wait, getting ready to move into De Spain's house too since De Spain had give ever evident intention of not aiming to return to Jefferson from this last what you might still call Varner trip and there wasn't no use in letting a good sound well-situated house stand vacant and empty. Which—De Spain's house—was likely a part of that same swapping and trading between Flem and Will Varner that included Varner's bank stock votes and that-ere financial Midsummer Night's Dream masque or rondeau that Linda and that Oxford lawyer composed betwixt them that had Linda's signature on it. Not to mention Lawyer being appointed by old man Will to be trustee of Linda's money since it was now finally safe from Flem until he thought up something that Lawyer would believe too this time, Will appointing Lawyer for the reason that likely he couldn't pass by Lawyer to get to no one else, Lawyer being not only in the middle of that entire monetary and sepulchrial crisis but all around ever part of it too, like one of them frantic water bugs skating and rushing immune and unwettable on top of a stagnant pond.

I mean, Lawyer was now busy over the headstone Flem had decided on. Because it would have to be made in Italy which would take time, and so would demand ever effort on Lawyer's part before Linda could pack up and leave Jefferson too, being as Flem felt that that same filial decorum demanded that Linda wait until her maw's headstone was up and finished before leaving. Only I dont mean jest headstone: I mean monument: Lawyer combing and currying not jest Jefferson and Frenchman's Bend but most of the rest of Yoknapatawpha County too, hunting out ever photograph of Eula he could locate to send to Italy so they could carve Eula's face in stone to put on it. Which is when I noticed again how there aint nobody quite as temerious as a otherwise timid feller that finds out that his moral standards and principles is now demanding him to do something that, if all

he had to depend on was jest his own satisfaction and curiosity, he wouldn't a had the brass to do, penetrating into ever
house that not only might a knowed Eula but that jest had a
Brownie kodak, thumbing through albums and intimate pho-
tographic family records, courteous and polite of course but
jest a man obviously not in no condition to be said No to, let
alone merely Please.

He could keep busy now. Because he was contented and
happy now, you see. He never had nothing to worry him
now. Eula was safely gone now and now he could be safe forever more from ever again having to chew his bitter poetic
thumbs over the constant anticipation of who would turn
up next named McCarron or De Spain. And now Linda was
not only safe for good from Flem, he, Lawyer, even had the
full charge and control of her money from her maw and
grandpaw, so that now she could go anywhere she wanted—
providing of course he could nag and harry them folks across
the water to finish carving that face before the millennium or
judgment day come, gathering up all the pictures of Eula he
could find and sending them to Italy and then waiting until a
drawing or a photograph of how the work was coming along
would get back for him to see jest how wrong it was, and he
would send me word to be at his office at a certain hour for
the conference, with the newest fresh Italian sketch or photograph laid out on the desk with a special light on it and him
saying, "It's the ear, or the line of the jaw, or the mouth—
right here: see what I mean?" and I would say,

"It looks all right to me. It looks beautiful to me." And he
would say,

"No. It's wrong right here. Hand me a pencil." Except he
would already have a pencil, and he couldn't draw neither so
he would have to rub that out and try again. Except that time
was passing so he would have to send it back; and Flem and
Linda living in De Spain's house now and now Flem had
done bought a automobile that he couldn't drive but anyhow
he had a daughter that could, leastways now and then; until
at last even that was over. It was October and Lawyer sent me
word the unveiling at the graveyard would be that afternoon.
Except I had done already got word to Chick, since from the
state of peace and contentment Lawyer had got his-self into

by this time, it might take both of us. So Chick stayed outen school that afternoon so all three of us went out to the cemetary together in Lawyer's car. And there was Linda and Flem too, in Flem's car with the Negro driver that was going to drive her on to Memphis to take the New York train with her packed grips already in the car, and Flem leaning back in the seat with that black hat on that even after five years still didn't look like it actively belonged to him, chewing, and Linda beside him in her dark going-away dress and hat with her head bent a little and them little white gloves shut into fists on her lap. And there it was: that-ere white monument with on the front of it that face that even if it was carved outen dead stone, was still the same face that ever young man no matter how old he got would still never give up hope and belief that some day before he died he would finally be worthy to be wrecked and ruined and maybe even destroyed by it, above the motto that Flem his-self had picked:

A virtuous wife is a crown to her husband
Her children rise and call her blessed

Until at last Flem leaned out the window and spit and then set back in the car and tells her: "All right. You can go now."

Yes sir, Lawyer was free now. He never had nothing to worry him now: him and Chick and me driving back to the office and him talking about how the game of football could be brought up to date in keeping with the progress of the times by giving ever body a football too so ever body would be in the game; or maybe better still, keep jest one football but abolish the boundaries so that a smart feller for instance could hide the ball under his shirt-tail and slip off into the bushes and circle around town and come in through a back alley and cross the goal before anybody even missed he was gone; right on into the office where he set down behind the desk and taken up one of the cob pipes and struck three matches to it until Chick taken it away from him and filled it from the tobacco jar and handed it back and Lawyer says, "Much obliged," and dropped the filled pipe into the waste basket and folded his hands on the desk, still talking, and I says to Chick:

"Watch him. I wont be long," and went around into the

alley; I never had much time so what was in the pint bottle was pretty bad but leastways it had something in it that for a moment anyhow would feel like alcohol. And I got the sugar bowl and glass and spoon from the cabinet and made the toddy and set it on the desk by him and he says,

"Much obliged," not even touching it, jest setting there with his hands folded in front of him, blinking quick and steady like he had sand in his eyes, saying: "All us civilised people date our civilisation from the discovery of the principle of distillation. And even though the rest of the world, at least that part of it in the United States, rates us folks in Mississippi at the lowest rung of culture, what man can deny that, even if this is as bad as I think it's going to be, we too grope toward the stars?" Then all of a sudden he begun to cry, still setting there, his hands still folded before him, not even hiding his face, saying, "Why did she do it, V.K.? That— all that—that she walked in, lived in, breathed in—it was only loaned to her; it wasn't hers to destroy and throw away. It belonged to too many. It belonged to all of us. Why, V.K.?" he says. "Why?"

"Maybe she was bored," I says, and he says:

"Bored. Yes, bored. She loved, had the capacity to love, to give and to take it. Only she tried twice and failed twice not jest to find somebody strong enough to deserve it but even brave enough to accept it. Yes," he says, setting there bolt upright with jest the tears running down his face, at peace now, with nothing nowhere in the world anymore to anguish or grieve him. "Of course she was bored."

Seven

V. K. RATLIFF

So he was free. He had not only got shut of his sireen, he had even got shut of the ward he found out she had heired to him. Because I says, "Grinnich Village?" and he says,

"Yes. A little place without physical boundaries located as far as she is concerned in New York city, where young people of all ages below ninety go in search of dreams." Except I says,

"Except she never had to leave Missippi to locate that place." And then I said it, what Eula herself must have, had to have, said to him that day: "Why didn't you marry her?"

"Because she wasn't but nineteen," he says.

"And you are all of thirty-five, aint you," I says. "When the papers are full of gals still carrying a doll in one hand marrying folks of sixty and seventy, providing of course they got a little extra money."

"I mean, she's got too much time left to run into something where she might need me. How many papers are full of people that got married because someday they might need the other one?"

"Oh," I says. "So all you got to do now is jest stay around close where you can hear the long distance telephone or the telegram boy can find you. Because naturally you wont be waiting for her to ever come back to Missippi. Or maybe you are?"

"Naturally not," he says. "Why should she?"

"Thank God?" I says. He didn't answer. "Because who knows," I says, "she may done already found that dream even in jest these . . . two days, aint it? three? Maybe he was already settled there when she arrived. That's possible in Grinnich Village, aint it?"

Then he said it too. "Yes," he says, "thank God." So he was free. And in fact, when you had time to look around a little, he never had nothing no more to do but jest rest in peace and quiet and contentment. Because not only him but all

Jefferson was free of Snopeses; for the first time in going on
twenty years, Jefferson and Yoknapatawpha County too was
in what you might call a kind of Snopes doldrum. Because at
last even Flem seemed to be satisfied: setting now at last in
the same chair the presidents of the Merchants and Farmers
Bank had been setting in ever since the first one, Colonel
Sartoris, started it twenty years ago, and actively living in the
very house the second one of it was born in, so that all he
needed to do too after he had done locked up the money and
went home was to live in solitary peace and quiet and contentment too, not only shut of the daughter that had kept
him on steady and constant tenterhooks for years whether she
might not escape at any moment to where he couldn't watch
her and the first male feller that come along would marry her
and he would lose her share of Will Varner's money, but shut
of the wife that at any time her and Manfred de Spain would
get publicly caught up with and cost him all the rest of
Varner's money and bank voting stock too.

In fact, for the moment Flem was the only true Snopes actively left in Jefferson. Old man Ab never had come no closer
than that hill two miles out where you could jest barely see
the water tank, where he taken the studs that day back about
1910 and hadn't moved since. And four years ago Flem had ci-
devanted I.O. back to Frenchman's Bend for good. And even
before that Flem had eliminated Montgomery Ward into the
penitentiary at Parchman where Mink already was (Mink
hadn't really resided in Jefferson nohow except jest them few
weeks in the jail waiting for his life sentence to be awarded).
And last month them four half-Snopes Indians that Byron
Snopes, Colonel Sartoris's bank clerk that resigned by the
simple practical expedient of picking up as much of the loose
money he could tote and striking for the nearest U.S. border,
sent back collect from Mexico until somebody could get close
enough to fasten the return prepaid tags on them before
whichever one had it at the moment could get out that
switch-blade knife. And as for Eck's boy, Wallstreet Panic and
his brother Admiral Dewey, they hadn't never been Snopes to
begin with since all Wallstreet evidently wanted to do was run
a wholesale grocery business by the outrageous unSnopesish
method of jest selling ever body exactly what they thought

they was buying, for exactly what they thought they was going to pay for it.

Or almost satisfied that is. I mean Flem and his new house.
It was jest a house: two storey, with a gallery for Major de
Spain, Manfred's paw, to set on when he wasn't fishing or
hunting or practising a little law, and it was all right for that-
ere second president of the Merchants and Farmers Bank to
live in, especially since he had been born in it. But this was
a different president. His road to that chair and that house
had been longer than them other two. Likely he knowed he had
had to come from too fur away to get where he was, and had
to come too hard to reach it by the time he did. Because
Colonel Sartoris had been born into money and respectability
too, and Manfred de Spain had been born into respectability
at least even if he had made a heap of the money since. But he,
Flem Snopes, had had to earn both of them, snatch and tear
and scrabble both of them outen the hard enduring resisting
rock you might say, not jest with his bare hands but with jest
one bare hand since he had to keep the other bare single hand
fending off while he tore and scrabbled with the first one. So
the house the folks owning the money would see Manfred de
Spain walk into ever evening after he locked the money up and
went home, wouldn't be enough for Flem Snopes. The house
they would see him walk into ever evening until time to unlock the money tomorrow morning, would have to be the
physical symbol of all them generations of respectability and
aristocracy that not only would a been too proud to mishan-
dle other folks' money, it couldn't possibly ever needed to.

So there was another Snopes in Jefferson after all. Not
transplanted in from Frenchman's Bend: jest imported in for
temporary use. This was Wat Snopes, the carpenter, Watkins
Products Snopes his full name was, like it was painted on both
sides and the back of Doc Meeks's patent medicine truck; evidently there was a Snopes somewhere now and then that
could read reading, whether he could read writing or not. So
during the next nine or ten months anybody that had or
could think up the occasion, could pass along the street and
watch Wat and his work gang of kinfolks and in-laws tearing
off Major de Spain's front gallery and squaring up the back of
the house and building and setting up them colyums to reach

all the way from the ground up to the second storey roof, until even when the painting was finished it still wouldn't be as big as Mount Vernon of course, but then Mount Vernon was a thousand miles away so there wasn't no chance of invidious or malicious eye-to-eye comparison.

So that when he locked up the bank and come home in the evening he could walk into a house and shut the door that the folks owning the money he was custodian of would some of them be jealous a little but all of them, even the jealous ones, would be proud and all of them would approve, laying down to rest undisturbed at night with their money that immaculate, that impeccable, that immune. He was completely complete, as the feller says, with a Negro cook and a yard boy that could even drive that-ere automobile now and then since he no longer had a only daughter to drive it maybe once a month to keep the battery up like the man told him he would have to do or buy a new one.

But it was jest the house that was altered and transmogrified and symbolised: not him. The house he disappeared into about four p.m. ever evening until about eight a.m. tomorrow, might a been the solid aristocratic ancestral symbol of Alexander Hamilton and Aaron Burr and Astor and Morgan and Harriman and Hill and ever other golden advocate of hard quick-thinking vested interest, but the feller the owners of that custodianed money seen going and coming out of it was the same one they had done got accustomed to for twenty years now: the same little snap-on bow tie he had got outen the Frenchman's Bend mule wagon in and only the hat was new and different; and even that old cloth cap, that maybe was plenty good enough to be Varner's clerk in but that wasn't to be seen going in and out of a Jefferson bank on the head of its vice president—even the cap not throwed away or even give away, but sold, even if it wasn't but jest a dime because ten cents is money too around a bank, so that all the owners of that money that he was already vice custodian of, could look at the hat and know that, no matter how little they might a paid for one similar to it, hisn had cost him ten cents less. It wasn't that he rebelled at changing Flem Snopes: he done it by deliberate calculation, since the feller you trust aint necessarily the one you never knowed to do nothing untrustable: it's the one you have seen from experience that he knows exactly when being untrustable will pay a net profit and when it will pay a loss.

And that was jest the house on the outside too, up to the moment when he passed in and closed the front door behind him until eight oclock tomorrow. And he hadn't never invited nobody in, and so far hadn't nobody been able to invent no way in, so the only folks that ever seen the inside of it was the cook and the yard man and so it was the yard man that told me: all them big rooms furnished like De Spain left them, plus them interior decorated sweets the Memphis expert learned Eula that being vice president of a bank he would have to have; that Flem never even went into them except to eat in the diningroom, except that one room at the back where when he wasn't in the bed sleeping he was setting in another swivel chair like the one in the bank, with his feet propped against the side of the fireplace: not reading, not doing nothing: jest setting with his hat on, chewing that same little mouth-sized chunk of air he had been chewing ever since he quit tobacco when he finally got to Jefferson and heard about chewing gum and then quit chewing gum too when he found out folks considered the vice president of a bank rich enough not to have to chew anything. And how Wat Snopes had found a picture in a magazine how to do over all the fireplaces with colonial molding and colyums and cornices too and at first Flem would jest set with his feet propped on the white paint, scratching it a little deeper ever day with the pegs in his heels. Until one day about a year after the house was finished over, Wat Snopes was there to eat dinner and after Wat finally left the yard man said how he went into the room and seen it: not a defiance, not a simple reminder of where he had come from but rather as the feller says a reaffirmation of his-self and maybe a warning to his-self too: a little wood ledge, not even painted, nailed to the front of that hand-carved hand-painted Mount Vernon mantelpiece at the exact height for Flem to prop his feet on it.

And time was when that first president, Colonel Sartoris, had come the four miles between his ancestral symbol and his bank in a surrey and matched pair drove by a Negro coachman in a linen duster and one of the Colonel's old plug hats;

and time aint so was when the second president still come and
went in that fire-engine colored EMF racer until he bought
that black Packard and a Negro too except in a white coat and
a showfer's cap to drive it. This here new third president had
a black automobile too even if it wasn't a Packard, and a
Negro that could drive it too even if he never had no white
coat and showfer's cap yet and even if the president didn't
ride back and forth to the bank at least not yet. Them two
previous presidents would ride around the county in the
evening after the bank closed and on Sunday, in that surrey
and pair or the black Packard, to look at the cotton farms
they represented the mortgages on while this new president
hadn't commenced that neither. Which wasn't because he jest
couldn't believe yet that he actively represented the mortgages. He never doubted that. He wasn't skeered to believe
it, and he wasn't too meek to nor doubtful to. It was because
he was watching yet and learning yet. It wasn't that he had
learned two lessons while he thought he was jest learning that
single one about how he would need respectability, because
he had done already brought that second lesson in from
Frenchman's Bend with him. That was humility, the only kind
of humility that's worth a hoot: the humility to know they's a
heap of things you dont know yet but if you jest got the patience to be humble and watchful long enough, especially
keeping one eye on your back trail, you will. So now on the
evenings and Sundays there was jest that house where you
wasn't invited in to see him setting in that swivel chair in that
one room he used, with his hat on and chewing steady on
nothing and his feet propped on that little wooden additional
ledge nailed in unpainted paradox to that hand-carved and
-painted mantel like one of them framed mottoes you keep
hanging on the wall where you work or think, saying *Remember Death* or *Keep Smiling* or *-Working* or *God is Love* to remind not jest you but the strangers that see it too, that you
got at least a speaking acquaintance with the fact that it might
be barely possible it taken a little something more than jest
you to get you where you're at.

But all that, foot-rest and all, would come later. Right now,
Lawyer was free. And then—it wasn't quite three days after
Linda reached New York, but it wasn't no three hundred

neither—he become, as the feller says, indeed free. He was leaning against the counter in the postoffice lobby with the letter already open in his hand when I come in; it wasn't his fault neither that the lobby happened to be empty at the moment.

"His name is Barton Kohl," he says.

"Sho now," I says. "Whose name is?"

"That dream's name," he says.

"Cole," I says.

"No," he says. "You're pronouncing it Cole. It's spelled K-o-h-l."

"Oh," I says. "Kohl. That dont sound very American to me."

"Does Vladimir Kyrilytch sound very American to you?"

But the lobby was empty. Which, as I said, wasn't his fault. "Confound it," I says, "with one Ratliff in ever generation for them whole hundred and fifty years since your durn Yankee Congress banished us into the Virginia mountains, has had to spend half his life trying to live down his front name before somebody spoke it out loud where folks could hear it. It was Eula told you."

"All right," he says. "I'll help you bury your family shame.—Yes," he says. "He's a Jew. A sculptor, probably a damned good one."

"Because of that?" I says.

"Probably, but not exclusively. Because of her."

"Linda'll make him into a good sculptor, no matter what he was before, because she married him?"

"No. He would have to be the best of whatever he was for her to pick him out."

"So she's married now," I says.

"What?" he says. "No. She just met him, I tell you."

"So you aint—" I almost said *safe yet* before I changed it: "—sure yet. I mean, she aint decided yet."

"What the hell else am I talking about? Dont you remember what I told you last fall? that she would love once and it would be for keeps?"

"Except that you said 'doomed to'."

"All right," he says.

"Doomed to fidelity and grief, you said. To love once quick and lose him quick and for the rest of her life to be faithful and to grieve. But leastways she aint lost him yet. In fact, she aint even got him yet. That's correct, aint it?"

"Didn't I say all right?" he says.

That was the first six months, about. Another year after that, that-ere little footrest ledge was up on that hand-painted Mount Vernon mantel—that-ere little raw wood step like out of a scrap-pile, nailed by a country carpenter onto that what you might call respectability's virgin Matterhorn for the al-pine climber to cling to panting, gathering his-self for that last do-or-die upsurge to deface the ultimate crowning pinnacle and peak with his own victorious initials. But not this one; and here was that humility again: not in public where it would be a insult to any and all that held Merchants and Farmers Bank al-pine climbing in veneration, but in private like a secret chapel or a shrine: not to cling panting to it, des-perate and indomitable, but to prop his feet on it while set-ting at his ease.

This time I was passing the office stairs when Lawyer come rushing around the corner as usual, with most of the law pa-pers flying along loose in his outside pockets but a few of them still in his hand too as usual. I mean, he had jest two gaits: one standing more or less still and the other like his coat-tail was on fire. "Run back home and get your grip," he says. "We're leaving Memphis tonight for New York."

So we went up the stairs and as soon as we was inside the office he changed to the other gait as usual. He throwed the loose papers onto the desk and taken one of the cob pipes outen the dish and set down, only when he fumbled in his coat for the matches or tobacco or whatever it was he discov-ered the rest of the papers and throwed them onto the desk and set back in the chair like he had done already had all the time in the world and couldn't possibly anticipate nothing else happening in the next hundred years neither. "For the house-warming," he says.

"You mean the reception, dont you? Aint that what they call it after the preacher has done collected his two dollars?" He didn't say anything, jest setting there working at lighting that pipe like a jeweler melting one exact drop of platinum maybe into a watch. "So they aint going to marry," I says. "They're jest going to confederate. I've heard that: that that's why they call them Grinnich Village samples dreams: you can wake up without having to jump outen the bed in a dead run for the nearest lawyer."

He didn't move. He jest bristled, that lively and quick he never had time to change his position. He set there and bristled like a hedgehog, not moving of course: jest saying cold and calm since even a hedgehog, once it has got itself arranged and prickled out, can afford a cold and calm collected voice too: "All right. I'll arrogate the term 'marriage' to it then. Do you protest or question it? Maybe you would even suggest a better one?—Because there's not enough time left," he says. "Enough left? There's none left. Young people today dont have any left because only fools under twenty-five can believe, let alone hope, that there's any left at all—for any of us, anybody alive today—"

"It dont take much time to say We both do in front of a preacher and then pay him whatever the three of you figger it's worth."

"Didn't I just say there's not even that much left if all you've had is just twenty-five or thirty years—"

"So that's how old he is," I says. "You stopped at jest twenty-five before."

He didn't stop at nowhere now: "Barely a decade since their fathers and uncles and brothers just finished the one which was to rid the phenomenon of government forever of the parasites—the hereditary proprietors, the farmers-general of the human dilemma who had just killed eight million human beings and ruined a forty-mile wide strip down the middle of western Europe. Yet less than a dozen years later and the same old cynical manipulators not even bothering to change their names and faces but merely assuming a set of new titles out of the shibboleth of the democratic lexicon and its mythology, not even breaking stride to coalesce again to wreck the one doomed desperate hope——" *Now he will resume the folks that broke President Wilson's heart and killed the League of Nations* I thought but he was the one that didn't even break stride: "That one already in Italy and one a damned sight more dangerous in Germany because all Mussolini has to work with are Italians while this other man has Germans. And the one in Spain that all he needs is to be let alone a little longer by the rest of us who still believe that if we just keep our eyes closed long enough it will all go away. Not to mention——"

"Not to mention the one in Russia," I said.

"——the ones right here at home: the organizations with the fine names confederated in unison in the name of God against the impure in morals and politics and with the wrong skin color and ethnology and religion: K.K.K. and Silver Shirts; not to mention the indigenous local champions like Long in Louisiana and our own Bilbo in Mississippi, not to mention our very own Senator Clarence Egglestone Snopes right here in Yoknapatawpha County——"

"Not to mention the one in Russia," I says.

"What?" he says.

"So that's why," I says. "He aint jest a sculptor. He's a Communist too."

"What?" Lawyer says.

"Barton Kohl. The reason they didn't marry first is that Barton Kohl is a Communist. He cant believe in churches and marriage. They wont let him."

"He wanted them to marry," Lawyer says. "It's Linda that wont." So now it was me that said What? and him setting there fierce and untouchable as a hedgehog. "You dont believe that?" he says.

"Yes," I says. "I believe it."

"Why should she want to marry? What could she have ever seen in the one she had to look at for nineteen years, to make her want any part of it?"

"All right," I says. "All right. Except that's the one I dont believe. I believe the first one, about there aint enough time left. That when you are young enough, you can believe. When you are young enough and brave enough at the same time, you can believe in intolerance and hope and, if you are sho enough brave, act on it." He still looked at me. "I wish it was me," I says.

"Not just to marry somebody, but to marry anybody just so it's marriage. Just so it's not adultery. Even you."

"Not that," I says. "I wish I was either one of them. To believe in intolerance and hope and act on it. At any price. Even at having to be jest twenty-one again like she is, to do it. Even to being a thirty-year-old Grinnich Village sculptor like he is."

"So you do refuse to believe that all she wants is to cuddle up together and be what she calls happy."

"Yes," I says. "So do I." So I didn't go that time, not even when he said:

"Nonsense. Come on. Afterward we will run up to Saratoga and look at that ditch or hill or whatever it was where your first immigrant Vladimir Kyrilytch Ratliff ancestor entered your native land."

"He wasn't no Ratliff then yet," I says. "We dont know what his last name was. Likely Nelly Ratliff couldn't even spell that one, let alone pronounce it. Maybe in fact neither could he. Besides, it wasn't even Ratliff then. It was Ratcliffe.— No," I says, "jest you will be enough. You can get cheaper corroboration than one that will not only need a round-trip ticket but three meals a day too."

"Corroboration for what?" he says.

"At this serious moment in her life when she is fixing to officially or leastways formally confederate or shack up with a gentleman friend of the opposite sex as the feller says, aint the reason for this trip to tell her and him at last who she is? or leastways who she aint?" Then I says, "Of course. She already knows," and he says,

"How could she help it? How could she have lived in the same house with Flem for nineteen years and still believe he could possibly be her father, even if she had incontrovertible proof of it?"

"And you aint never told her," I says. Then I says, "It's even worse than that. Whenever it occurs to her enough to maybe fret over it a little and she comes to you and says maybe, 'Tell me the truth now. He aint my father,' she can always depend on you saying, 'You're wrong, he is'. Is that the dependence and need you was speaking of?" Now he wasn't looking at me. "What would you do if she got it turned around backwards and said to you, 'Who is my father?'" No, he wasn't looking at me. "That's right," I says. "She wont never ask that. I reckon she has done watched Gavin Stevens too, enough to know there's some lies even he ought not to need to cope with." He wasn't looking at me a-tall. "So that-there dependence is on a round-trip ticket too," I says.

He was back after ten days. And I thought how maybe if that sculptor could jest ketch her unawares, still half asleep maybe, and seduce her outen the bed and up to a altar or even jest a j.p. before she noticed where she was at, maybe he—Lawyer—would be free. Then I knowed that wasn't even wishful thinking because there wasn't nothing in that idea that could been called thinking a-tall. Because once I got rid of them hopeful cobwebs I realised I must a knowed for years what likely Eula knowed the moment she laid eyes on him: that he wouldn't never be free because he wouldn't never want to be free because this was his life and if he ever lost it he wouldn't have nothing left. I mean, the right and privilege and opportunity to dedicate forever his capacity for responsibility to something that wouldn't have no end to its appetite and that wouldn't never threaten to give him even a bone back in recompense. And I remembered what he said back there about how she was doomed to fidelity and monogamy —to love once and lose him and then to grieve and I said I reckoned so, that being Helen of Troy's daughter was kind of like being say the ex-Pope of Rome or the ex-Emperor of Japan: there wasn't much future to it. And I knowed now he was almost right, he jest had that word 'doomed' in the wrong place: that it wasn't her that was doomed, she would likely do fine; it was the one that was recipient of the fidelity and the monogamy and the love, and the one that was the proprietor of the responsibility that never even wanted, let alone expected, a bone back, that was the doomed ones; and how even between them two the lucky one might be the one that had the roof fall on him while he was climbing into or out of the bed.

So naturally I would a got a fur piece quick trying to tell him that so naturally my good judgment told me not to try it. And so partly by jest staying away from him but mainly by fighting like a demon, like Jacob with his angel, I finally resisted actively saying it—a temptation about as strong as a human man ever has to face, which is to deliberately throw away the chance to say afterward, "I told you so." So time passed. That little additional mantel-piece foot-rest was up now that hadn't nobody ever seen except that Negro yard man—a Jefferson legend after he mentioned it to me and him (likely) and me both happened to mention it in turn to some of our close intimates: a part of the Snopes legend and another Flem Snopes monument in that series mounting on and up from that water tank that we never knowed yet if they had got out of it all that missing Flem Snopes regime powerhouse brass them two mad skeered Negro firemen put into it.

Then it was 1936 and there was less and less of that time left: Mussolini in Italy and Hitler in Germany and sho enough, like Lawyer said, that one in Spain too; Lawyer said, "Pack your grip. We will take the airplane from Memphis tomorrow morning.—No no," he says, "you dont need to fear contamination from association this time. They're going to be married. They're going to Spain to join the Loyalist army and apparently he nagged and worried at her until at last she probably said, 'Oh hell, have it your way then'."

"So he wasn't a liberal emancipated advanced-thinking artist after all," I says. "He was jest another ordinary man that believed if a gal was worth sleeping with she was worth deserving to have a roof over her head and something to eat and a little money in her pocket for the balance of her life."

"All right," he says. "All right."

"Except we'll go on the train," I says. "It aint that I'm jest simply skeered to go in a airplane: it's because when we go across Virginia I can see the rest of the place where that-ere first immigrant Vladimir Kyrilytch worked his way into the United States." So I was already on the corner with my grip when he drove up and stopped and opened the door and looked at me and then done what the moving pictures call a double take and says,

"Oh hell."

"It's mine," I says. "I bought it."

"You," he says, "in a necktie. That never even had one on before, let alone owned one, in your life."

"You told me why. It's a wedding."

"Take it off," he says.

"No," I says.

"I wont travel with you. I wont be seen with you."

"No," I says. "Maybe it aint jest the wedding. I'm going

back to let all them V. K. Ratliff beginnings look at me for the
first time. Maybe it's them I'm trying to suit. Or leastways
not to shame." So we taken the train in Memphis that night
and the next day we was in Virginia—Bristol then Roanoke
and Lynchburg and turned north-east along side the blue
mountains and somewhere ahead, we didn't know jest where,
was where that first Vladimir Kyrilytch finally found a place
where he could stop, that we didn't know his last name or
maybe he didn't even have none until Nelly Ratliff, spelled
Ratcliffe then, found him, any more than we knowed what he
was doing in one of them hired German regiments in General
Burgoyne's army that got licked at Saratoga except that
Congress refused to honor the terms of surrender and banished the whole kit-and-biling of them to straggle for six years
in Virginia without no grub nor money and the ones like that
first V.K. without no speech neither. But he never needed
none of the three of them to escape not only in the right
neighborhood but into the exact right hayloft where Nelly
Ratcliffe, maybe hunting eggs or such, would find him. And
never needed no language to eat the grub she toted him; and
maybe he never knowed nothing about farming before the
day when she finally brought him out where her folks could
see him; nor never needed no speech to speak of for the next
development, which was when somebody—her maw or paw
or brothers or whoever it was, maybe jest a neighbor—noticed the size of her belly; and so they was married and so that
V.K. actively did have a active legal name of Ratcliffe, and the
one after him come to Tennessee and the one after him
moved to Missippi, except that by that time it was spelled
Ratliff, where the oldest son is still named Vladimir Kyrilytch
and still spends half his life trying to keep anybody from finding it out.

The next morning we was in New York. It was early; not
even seven oclock yet. It was too early. "Likely they aint even
finished breakfast yet," I says.

"Breakfast hell," Lawyer says. "They haven't even gone to
bed yet. This is New York, not Yoknapatawpha County." So we
went to the hotel where Lawyer had already engaged a room.
Except it wasn't a room, it was three of them: a parlor and two
bedrooms. "We can have breakfast up here too," he says.

"Breakfast?" I says.

"They'll send it up here."

"This is New York," I says. "I can eat breakfast in the bed-room or kitchen or on the back gallery in Yoknapatawpha County." So we went downstairs to the diningroom. Then I says, "What time do they eat breakfast then? Sundown? Or is that jest when they get up?"

"No," he says. "We got a errand first.—No," he says, "we got two errands." He was looking at it again, though I will have to do him the justice to say he hadn't mentioned it again since that first time when I got in the car back in Jefferson. And I remember how he told me once how maybe New York wasn't made for no climate known to man but at least some weather was jest made for New York. In which case, this was sholy some of it: one of them soft blue drowsy days in the early fall when the sky itself seems like it was resting on the earth like a soft blue mist, with the tall buildings rushing up into it and then stopping, the sharp edges fading like the sunshine wasn't jest shining on them but kind of humming, like wires singing. Then I seen it: a store, with a show-window, a entire show-window with not nothing in it but one necktie.

"Wait," I says.

"No," he says. "It was all right as long as just railroad con-ductors looked at it but you cant face a preacher in it."

"No," I says, "wait." Because I had heard about these New York side-alley stores too. "If it takes that whole show-win-dow to deserve jest one necktie, likely they will want three or four dollars for it."

"We cant help it now," he says. "This is New York. Come on."

And nothing inside neither except some gold chairs and two ladies in black dresses and a man dressed like a congress-man or at least a preacher, that knowed Lawyer by active name. And then a office with a desk and a vase of flowers and a short dumpy dark woman in a dress that wouldn't a fitted nobody, with gray-streaked hair and the handsomest dark eyes I ever seen even if they was popped a little, that kissed Lawyer and then he said to her, "Myra Allanovna, this is Vladimir Kyrilytch," and she looked at me and said something; yes, I know it was Russian, and Lawyer saying: "Look at it. Just once if you can bear it," and I says,

"Sholy it aint quite as bad as that. Of course I had ruther it was yellow and red instead of pink and green. But all the same——" and she says,

"You like yellow and red?"

"Yessum," I says. Then I says, "In fact" before I could stop, and she says,

"Yes, tell me," and I says,

"Nothing. I was jest thinking that if you could jest imagine a necktie and then pick it right up and put it on, I would imagine one made outen red with a bunch or maybe jest one single sunflower in the middle of it," and she says,

"Sunflower?" and Lawyer says,

"Helianthe." Then he says, "No, that's wrong. Tournesol. Sonnenblume," and she says Wait and was already gone, and now I says Wait myself.

"Even a five-dollar necktie couldn't support all them gold chairs."

"It's too late now," Lawyer says. "Take it off." Except that when she come back, it not only never had no sunflower, it wasn't even red. It was jest dusty. No, that was wrong; you had looked at it by that time. It looked like the outside of a peach, that you know that in a minute, providing you can keep from blinking, you will see the first beginning of when it starts to turn peach. Except that it dont do that. It's still jest dusted over with gold, like the back of a sunburned gal. "Yes," Lawyer says, "send out and get him a white shirt. He never wore a white shirt before either."

"No, never," she says. "Always blue, not? And this blue, always? The same blue as your eyes?"

"That's right," I says.

"But how?" she says. "By fading them? By just washing them?"

"That's right," I says. "I jest washes them."

"You mean, you wash them? Yourself?"

"He makes them himself too," Lawyer says.

"That's right," I says. "I sells sewing machines. First thing I knowed I could run one too."

"Of course," she says. "This one for now. Tomorrow, the

other one, red with sonnenblume." Then we was outside again. I was still trying to say Wait.

"Now I got to buy two of them," I says. "I'm trying to be serious. I mean, please try to believe I am as serious right now as ere a man in your experience. Jest exactly how much you reckon was the price on that one in that window?"

And Lawyer not even stopping, saying over his shoulder in the middle of folks pushing past and around us in both directions: "I dont know. Her ties run up to a hundred and fifty. Say, seventy-five dollars—" It was exactly like somebody had hit me a quick light lick with the edge of his hand across the back of the neck until next I knowed I was leaning against the wall back out of the rush of folks in a fit of weak trembles with Lawyer more or less holding me up. "You all right now?" he says.

"No I aint," I says. "Seventy-five dollars for a necktie? I cant! I wont!"

"You're forty years old," he says. "You should a been buying at the minimum one tie a year ever since you fell in love the first time. When was it? eleven? twelve? thirteen? Or maybe it was eight or nine, when you first went to school—provided the first grade teacher was female of course. But even call it twenty. That's twenty years, at one dollar a tie a year. That's twenty dollars. Since you are not married and never will be and dont have any kin close enough to exhaust and wear you out by taking care of you or hoping to get anything out of you, you may live another forty-five. That's sixty-five dollars. That means you will have an Allanovna tie for only ten dollars. Nobody else in the world ever got an Allanovna tie for ten dollars."

"I wont!" I says. "I wont!"

"All right. I'll make you a present of it then."

"I cant do that," I says.

"All right. You want to go back there and tell her you dont want the tie?"

"Dont you see I cant do that?"

"All right," he says. "Come on. We're already a little late." So when we got to this hotel we went straight to the saloon.

"We're almost there," I says. "Cant you tell me yet who it's going to be?"

"No," he says. "This is New York. I want to have a little fun and pleasure too." And a moment later, when I realised that Lawyer hadn't never laid eyes on him before, I should a figgered why he had insisted so hard on me coming on this trip. Except that I remembered how in this case Lawyer wouldn't need no help since you are bound to have some kind of affinity of outragement anyhow for the man that for twenty-five years has been as much a part and as big a part of your simple natural normal anguish of jest having to wake up again tomorrow, as this one had. So I says,

"I'll be durned. Howdy, Hoke." Because there he was, a little gray at the temples, with not jest a sunburned outdoors look but a rich sunburned outdoors look that never needed that-ere dark expensive-looking city suit, let alone two waiters jumping around the table where he was at, to prove it, already setting there where Lawyer had drawed him from wherever it was out west he had located him, the same as he had drawed me for this special day. No, it wasn't Lawyer that had drawed McCarron and me from a thousand miles away and two thousand more miles apart, the three of us to meet at this moment in a New York saloon: it was that gal that done it—that gal that never had seen one of us and fur as I actively heard it to take a oath, never had said much more than good morning to the other two—that gal that likely not even knowed but didn't even care that she had inherited her maw's fatality to draw four men anyhow to that web, that one strangling hair; drawed all four of us without even lifting her hand—her husband, her father, the man that was still trying to lay down his life for her maw if he could jest find somebody that wanted it, and what you might call a by-standing family friend—to be the supporting cast while she said "I do" outen the middle of a matrimonial production line at the City Hall before getting on a ship to go to Europe to do whatever it was she figgered she was going to do in that war. So I was the one that said, "This is Lawyer Stevens, Hoke," with three waiters now (he was evidently that rich) bustling around helping us set down.

"What's yours?" he says to Lawyer. "I know what V.K. wants.—Bushmill's," he says to the waiter. "Bring the bottle.—You'll think you're back home," he says to me. "It tastes jest like that stuff Calvin Bookwright used to make—do you

remember?" Now he was looking at it too. "That's an
Allanovna, isn't it?" he says. "You've branched out a little
since Frenchman's Bend too, haven't you?" Now he was
looking at Lawyer. He taken his whole drink at one swallow
though the waiter was already there with the bottle before he
could a signalled. "Dont worry," he says. "You've got my
word. I'm going to keep it."

"You stop worrying too," I says. "Lawyer's already got
Linda. She's going to believe him first, no matter what anybody else might forget and try to tell her." And we could
have et dinner there too, but Lawyer says,

"This is New York. We can eat dinner in Uncle Cal Bookwright's springhouse back home." So we went to that diningroom. Then it was time. We went to the City Hall in a
taxicab. While we was getting out the other taxicab come up
and they got out. He was not big, he jest looked big, like a
football player. No: like a prize fighter. He didn't look jest
tough, and ruthless aint the word neither. He looked like he
would beat you or maybe you would beat him but you probably wouldn't, or he might kill you or you might kill him
though you probably wouldn't. But he wouldn't never dicker
with you, looking at you with eyes that was pale like Hub
Hampton's but they wasn't hard: jest looking at you without
no hurry and completely, missing nothing, and with already a
pretty good idea beforehand of what he was going to see.

We went inside. It was a long hall, a corridor, a line of folks
two and two that they would a been the last one in it except
it was a line that never had no last: jest a next to the last and
not that long: on to a door that said REGISTRAR and inside.
That wasn't long neither; the two taxicabs was still waiting.
"So this is Grinnich Village," I says. The door give right off
the street but with a little shirt-tail of ground behind it you
could a called a yard though maybe city folks called it a garden; it even had one tree in it, with three things on it that un-
doubtedly back in the spring or summer was leaves. But inside
it was nice: full of folks of course, with two waiters dodging
in and out with trays of glasses of champagne and three or
four of the company helping too, not to mention the folks
that was taking over the apartment while Linda and her new
husband was off at the war in Spain—a young couple about

the same age as them. "Is he a sculptor too?" I says to Lawyer.

"No," Lawyer says. "He's a newspaper man."

"Oh," I says. "Then likely they been married all the time."

It was nice: a room with plenty of window-lights. It had a heap of stuff in it too but it looked like it was used—a wall full of books and a piano and I knowed they was pictures because they was hanging on the wall and I knowed that some of the other things was sculpture but the rest of them I didn't know what they was, made outen pieces of wood or iron or strips of tin and wires. Except that I couldn't ask then because of the rest of the poets and painters and sculptors and musicians, since he would still have to be the host until we—him and Linda and Lawyer and Hoke and me—could slip out and go down to where the ship was; evidently a heap of folks found dreams in Grinnich Village but evidently it was a occasion when somebody married in it. And one of them wasn't even a poet or painter or sculptor or musician or even jest a ordinary moral newspaper man but evidently a haberdasher taking Saturday evening off. Because we was barely in the room before he was not only looking at it too but rubbing it between his thumb and finger. "Allanovna," he says.

"That's right," I says.

"Oklahoma?" he says. "Oil?"

"Sir?" I says.

"Oh," he says. "Texas. Cattle then. In Texas you can choose your million between oil and cattle, right?"

"No sir," I says, "Missipi. I sell sewing machines." So it was a while before he finally come to me to fill my glass again.

"I understand you grew up with Linda's mother," he says.

"That's right," I says. "Did you make these?"

"These what?" he says.

"In this room," I says.

"Oh," he says. "Do you want to see more of them? Why?"

"I dont know yet," I says. "Does that matter?" So we shoved on through the folks—it had begun to take shoving by now—into a hall and then up some stairs. And this was the best of all: a loft with one whole side of the roof jest window-lights—a room not jest where folks used but where somebody come off by his-self and worked. And him jest standing a little behind me, outen the way, giving me time and room both to look. Until at last he says,

"Shocked? Mad?" Until I says,

"Do I have to be shocked and mad at something jest because I never seen it before?"

"At your age, yes," he says. "Only children can stand surprise for the pleasure of surprise. Grown people cant bear surprise unless they are promised in advance they will want to own it."

"Maybe I aint had enough time yet," I says.

"Take it then," he says. So he leaned against the wall with his arms folded like a football player, with the noise of the party where he was still supposed to be host at coming up the stairs from below, while I taken my time to look: at some I did recognise and some I almost could recognise and maybe if I had time enough I would, and some I knowed I wouldn't never quite recognise, until all of a sudden I knowed that wouldn't matter neither, not jest to him but to me too. Because anybody can see and hear and smell and feel and taste what he expected to hear and see and feel and smell and taste, and wont nothing much notice your presence nor miss your lack. So maybe when you can see and feel and smell and hear and taste what you never expected to and hadn't never even imagined until that moment, maybe that's why Old Moster picked you out to be one of the ones to be alive.

So now it was time for that-ere date. I mean the one that Lawyer and Hoke had fixed up, with Hoke saying, "But what can I tell her—her husband—her friends?" and Lawyer says,

"Why do you need to tell anybody anything? I've attended to all that. As soon as enough of them have drunk her health, just take her by the arm and clear out. Just dont forget to be aboard the ship by eleven-thirty." Except Hoke still tried, the two of them standing in the door ready to leave, Hoke in that-ere dark expensive city suit and his derby hat in his hand, and Linda in a kind of a party dress inside her coat. And it wasn't that they looked alike, because they didn't. She was tall for a woman, so tall she didn't have much shape (I mean, the kind that folks whistle at), and he wasn't tall for a man and in fact kind of stocky. But their eyes was exactly alike. Anyhow, it seemed to me that anybody that seen them couldn't help but know they was kin. So he still had to try it: "A old friend of her mother's family. Her grand-father and my father may have been distantly related—" and Lawyer saying,

"All right, all right, beat it. Dont forget the time," and Hoke saying,

"Yes yes, we'll be at Twenty-One for dinner and afterward at the Stork Club if you need to telephone." Then they was gone and the rest of the company went too except three other men that I found out was newspaper men too, foreign corre-spondents; and Kohl his-self helped his new tenant's wife cook the spaghetti and we et it and drunk some more wine, red this time, and they talked about the war, about Spain and Ethiopia and how this was the beginning: the lights was going off all over Europe soon and maybe in this country too; until it was time to go to the ship. And more champagne in the bedroom there, except that Lawyer hadn't hardly got the first bottle open when Linda and Hoke come in.

"Already?" Lawyer says. "We didn't expect you for at least a hour yet."

"She—we decided to skip the Stork Club," Hoke says. "We took a fiacre through the Park instead. And now," he says, that hadn't even put the derby hat down.

"Stay and have some champagne," Lawyer says, and Kohl said something too. But Linda had done already held out her hand.

"Goodbye, Mr McCarron," she says. "Thank you for the evening and for coming to my wedding."

"Cant you say 'Hoke' yet?" he says.

"Goodbye, Hoke," she says.

"Wait in the cab then," Lawyer says. "We'll join you in a minute."

"No," Hoke says. "I'll take another cab and leave that one for you." Then he was gone. She shut the door behind him and came toward Lawyer, taking something outen her pocket.

"Here," she says. It was a gold cigarette lighter. "I know you wont ever use it, since you say you think you can taste the fluid when you light your pipe."

"No," Lawyer says. "What I said was, I know I can taste it."

"All right," she says. "Take it anyway." So Lawyer taken it. "It's engraved with your initials: see?"

"G.L.S.," Lawyer says. "They are not my initials. I just have two: G.S."

"I know. But the man said a monogram should have three so I loaned you one of mine." Then she stood there facing him, as tall as him almost, looking at him. "That was my father," she says.

"No," Lawyer says.

"Yes," she says.

"You dont mean to tell me he told you that," Lawyer says.

"You know he didn't. You made him swear not to."

"No," Lawyer says.

"You swear then."

"All right," Lawyer says. "I swear."

"I love you," she says. "Do you know why?"

"Tell me," Lawyer says.

"It's because every time you lie to me I can always know you will stick to it."

Then the second sentimental pilgrimage. No, something else come first. It was the next afternoon. "Now we'll go pick up the necktie," Lawyer says.

"No," I says.

"You mean you want to go alone?"

"That's right," I says. So I was alone, the same little office again and her still in the same dress that wouldn't fitted nobody, already looking at my empty collar even before I put the necktie and the hundred and fifty dollars on the desk by the new one that I hadn't even teched yet because I was afraid to. It was red jest a little under what you see in a black-gum leaf in the fall, with not no single sunflower nor even a bunch of them but little yellow sunflowers all over it in a kind of diamond pattern, each one with a little blue center almost the exact blue my shirts gets to after a while. I didn't dare touch it. "I'm sorry," I says. "But you see I jest cant. I sells sewing machines in Missippi. I cant have it knowed back there that I paid seventy-five dollars a piece for neckties. But if I'm in the Missippi sewing machine business and cant wear seventy-five dollar neckties, so are you in the New York necktie business and cant afford to have folks wear or order neckties and not pay for them. So here," I says. "And I ask your kindness to excuse me."

But she never even looked at the money. "Why did he call you Vladimir Kyrilytch?" she says. I told her.

"Except we live in Missippi now, and we got to live it down. Here," I says. "And I ask you again to ex——"

"Take that off my desk," she says. "I have given the ties to you. You cannot pay for them."

"Dont you see I cant do that neither?" I says. "No more than I could let anybody back in Missippi order a sewing machine from me and then say he had done changed his mind when I delivered it to him?"

"So," she says. "You cannot accept the ties, and I cannot accept the money. Good. We do this——" There was a thing on the desk that looked like a cream pitcher until she snapped it open and it was a cigarette lighter. "We burn it then, half for you, half for me——" until I says,

"Wait! Wait!" and she stopped. "No," I says, "no. Not burn money," and she says,

"Why not?" and us looking at each other, her hand holding the lit lighter and both our hands on the money.

"Because it's money," I says. "Somebody somewhere at some time went to—went through— I mean, money stands for too much hurt and grief somewhere to somebody that jest the money wasn't never worth—I mean, that aint what I mean . . . ." and she says,

"I know exactly what you mean. Only the gauche, the illiterate, the frightened and the pastless destroy money. You will keep it then. You will take it back to—how you say?"

"Missippi," I says.

"Missippi. Where is one who, not needs: who cares about so base as needs? Who wants something that costs one hundred fifty dollar—a hat, a picture, a book, a jewel for the ear; something never never never anyhow just to eat—but believes he—she—will never have it, has even long ago given up, not the dream but the hope— This time do you know what I mean?"

"I know exactly what you mean because you jest said it," I says.

"Then kiss me," she says. And that night me and Lawyer went up to Saratoga.

"Did you tell Hoke better than to try to give her a lot of money, or did he jest have that better sense his-self?" I says.

"Yes," Lawyer says.

"Yes which?" I says.

"Maybe both," Lawyer says. And in the afternoon we watched the horses, and the next morning we went out to Bemis's Heights and Freeman's Farm. Except that naturally there wasn't no monument to one mercenary Hessian soldier that maybe couldn't even speak German, let alone American, and naturally there wasn't no hill or ditch or stump or rock that spoke up and said aloud: On this spot your first ancestral V.K. progenitor foreswore Europe forever and entered the United States. And two days later we was back home, covering in two days the distance it taken that first V.K. four generations to do; and now we watched the lights go out in Spain and Ethiopia, the darkness that was going to creep eastward across all Europe and Asia too, until the shadow of it would fall across the Pacific islands until it reached even America. But that was a little while away yet when Lawyer says,

"Come up to the office," and then he says, "Barton Kohl is dead. The airplane—it was a worn-out civilian passenger-carrier, armed with 1918 infantry machine guns, with home-made bomb bays through which the amateur crew dumped by hand the home-made bombs; that's what they fought Hitler's Luftwaffe with—was shot down in flames so she probably couldn't have identified him even if she could have reached the crash. She doesn't say what she intends to do now."

"She'll come back here," I says.

"Here?" he says. "Back here?" then he says, "Why the hell shouldn't she? It's home."

"That's right," I says. "It's doom."

"What?" he says. "What did you say?"

"Nothing," I says. "I jest said I think so too."

Eight

C HARLES MALLISON
Linda Kohl (Snopes that was, as Thackeray would say. Kohl that was too since he was dead) wasn't the first wounded war hero to finally straggle back to Jefferson. She was just the first one my uncle bothered to meet at the station. I dont mean the railroad station; by 1937 it had been a year or so since a train had passed through Jefferson that a paid passenger could have got off of. And not even the bus depot because I dont even mean Jefferson. It was the Memphis airport we went to meet her at, my uncle apparently discovering at the last minute that morning that he was not able to make an eighty-mile trip and back alone in his car.

She was not even the first female hero. For two weeks back in 1919 we had had a nurse, an authentic female lieutenant— not a denizen, citizen of Jefferson to be sure but at least kin to (or maybe just interested in a member of) a Jefferson family, who had been on the staff of a base hospital in France and—so she said—had actually spent two days at a casualty clearing station within sound of the guns behind Montdidier.

In fact, by 1919 even the five-year-old Jeffersonians like I was then were even a little blasé about war heroes, not only unscratched ones but wounded too getting off trains from Memphis Junction or New Orleans. Not that I mean that even the unscratched ones actually called themselves heroes or thought they were or in fact thought one way or the other about it until they got home and found the epithet being dinned at them from all directions until finally some of them, a few of them, began to believe that perhaps they were. I mean, dinned at them by the ones who organised and correlated the dinning—the ones who hadn't gone to that war and so were already on hand in advance to organise the big debarkation-port parades and the smaller county-seat local ones, with inbuilt barbecue and beer; the ones that hadn't gone to that one and didn't intend to go to the next one nor the one after that either, as long as all they had to do to stay out was to buy the tax-free bonds and organise the hero-dinning parades so that the next crop of eight- and nine- and ten-year-old males could see the divisional shoulder patches and the wound- and service-stripes and the medal ribbons.

Until some of them anyway would begin to believe that that many voices dinning it at them must be right, and they were heroes. Because, according to Uncle Gavin, who had been a soldier too in his fashion: in the American Field Service with the French army in '16 and '17 until we got into it, then still in France as a Y.M.C.A. secretary or whatever they were called, they had nothing else left: young men or even boys most of whom had only the vaguest or completely erroneous idea of where and what Europe was, and none at all about armies, let alone about war, snatched up by lot overnight and regimented into an expeditionary force, to sur- vive (if they could) before they were twenty-five years old what they would not even recognise at the time to be the biggest experience of their lives. Then to be spewed, again willy nilly and again overnight, back into what they believed would be the familiar world they had been told they were en- during disruption and risking injury and death so that it would still be there when they came back, only to find that it wasn't there anymore. So that the bands and the parades and the barbecues and all the rest of the hero-dinning not only would happen only that once and was already fading even be- fore they could get adjusted to it, it was already on the way out before the belated last of them even got back home, al- ready saying to them above the cold congealing meat and the flat beer while the last impatient brazen chord died away: "All right, little boys; eat your beef and potato salad and drink your beer and get out of our way, who are already up to our necks in this new world whose single and principal industry is not just solvent but dizzily remunerative peace."

So, according to Gavin, they had to believe they were heroes even though they couldn't remember now exactly at what point or by what action they had reached, entered for a moment or a second, that heroic state. Because otherwise they had nothing left: with only a third of life over, to know now that they had already experienced their greatest experi- ence, and now to find that the world for which they had so endured and risked was in their absence so altered out of recognition by the ones who had stayed safe at home as to have no place for them in it anymore. So they had to believe that at least some little of it had been true. Which (according to Gavin) was the why of the Veterans' clubs and legions: the one sanctuary where at least once a week they could find refuge among the other betrayed and dispossessed reaffirming to each other that at least that one infinitesimal scrap had been so.

In fact (in Jefferson anyway) even the ones that came back with an arm or a leg gone came back just like what they were when they left: merely underlined, italicised. There was Tug Nightingale. His father was the cobbler, with a little cubby-hole of a shop around a corner off the Square—a little scrawny man who wouldn't have weighed a hundred pounds with his last and bench and all his tools in his lap, with a fierce moustache which hid most of his chin too, and fierce undefeated intolerant eyes—a Hardshell Baptist who didn't merely have to believe it, because he knew it was so: that the earth was flat and that Lee had betrayed the whole South when he surrendered at Appomattox. He was a widower. Tug was his only surviving child. Tug had got almost as far as the fourth grade when the principal himself told Mr Nightingale it would be better for Tug to quit. Which Tug did, and now he could spend all his time hanging around the auction lot behind Dilazuck's livery stable, where he had been spending all his spare time anyhow, and where he now came into his own: falling in first with Marvin Hait, our local horse- and mule-trader, then with Pat Stamper himself, who in the horse and mule circles not just in Yoknapatawpha County or north Mississippi but over most of Alabama and Tennessee and Arkansas too, was to Marvin Hait what Fritz Kreisler would be to the fiddle-player at a country picnic, and so recognised genius when he saw it. Because Tug didn't have any piddling mere affinity for and rapport with mules: he was an *homme fatal* to them, any mule, horse or mare either, being putty in his hands; he could do anything with them except buy and sell them for a profit. Which is why he never rose higher than a simple hostler and handy-man and so finally had to become a house-painter also to make a living: not a first rate one, but at least he could stir the paint and put it on a wall or fence after somebody had shown him where to stop.

Which was his condition up to about 1916, when he was about thirty years old, maybe more, when something began to happen to him. Or maybe it had already happened and we—Jefferson—only noticed it then. Up to now he had been what you might call a standard-type provincial county-seat house-painter: a bachelor, living with his father in a little house on the edge of town, having his weekly bath in the barbershop on Saturday night and then getting a little drunk afterward—not too much so: only once every two or three years waking up Sunday morning in the jail until they would release him on his own recognizance; this not for being too drunk but for fighting, though the fighting did stem from the whiskey, out of that mutual stage of it when the inevitable one (never the same one: it didn't need to be) challenged his old fixed father-bequeathed convictions that General Lee had been a coward and a traitor and that the earth was a flat plane with edges like the shed roofs he painted—then shooting a little dice in the big ditch behind the cemetery while he sobered up Sunday afternoon to go back to his turpentine Monday morning; with maybe four trips a year to the Memphis brothels.

Then it happened to him. He still had the Saturday night barbershop bath and he still drank a little, though as far as Jefferson knew, never enough anymore to need to go to combat over General Lee and Ptolemy and Isaac Newton, so that not only the jail but the harassed night marshal too who at the mildest would bang on the locked barbershop or poolroom door at two oclock Sunday morning, saying, "If you boys dont quiet down and go home," knew him no more. Nor did the dice game in the cemetery ditch; on Sunday morning now he would be seen walking with his scrawny fiercely-moustached miniature father toward the little backstreet Hardshell church, and that afternoon sitting on the minute gallery of their doll-sized house poring (whom the first three grades of school rotationally licked and the fourth one completely routed) over the newspapers and magazines which brought us all we knew about the war in Europe.

He had changed. Even we (Jefferson. I was only three then) didn't know how much until the next April, 1917, after the Lusitania and the President's declaration, and Captain (Mister then until he was elected captain of it) Mack Lendon organised the Jefferson company to be known as the Sartoris Rifles in honor of the original Colonel Sartoris (there would be no Sartoris in it since Bayard and his twin brother John were already in England training for the Royal Flying Corps) and then we heard the rest of it: how Tug Nightingale, past thirty now and so even when the draft came would probably escape it, was one of the first to apply, and we—they—found out what his dilemma was: which was simply that he did not dare let his father find out that he planned to join the Yankee army, since if his father ever learned it, he, Tug, would be disinherited and thrown out. So it was more than Captain Lendon who said, "What? What's that?" and Lendon and another—the one who would be elected his First Sergeant—went home with Tug and the sergeant-to-be told it:

"It was like being shut up in a closet with a buzz saw that had jumped off the axle at top speed, or say a bundle of dynamite with the fuse lit and snapping around the floor like a snake, that you not only cant get close enough to step on it, you dont want to: all you want is out, and Mack saying, 'Wait, Mr Nightingale, it aint the Yankee army: it's the army of the United States: your own country,' and that durn little maniac shaking and seething until his moustache looked like it was on fire too, hollering, 'Shoot the sons of bitches! Shoot em! Shoot em!' and then Tug himself trying it: 'Papa, papa, Captain Lendon and Crack here both belong to it,' and old man Nightingale yelling, 'Shoot them then. Shoot all the blue-bellied sons of bitches,' and Tug still trying, saying, 'Papa, papa, if I dont join now, when they pass that draft they will come and get me anyway,' and still that little maniac hollering, 'Shoot you all! Shoot all you sons of bitches!' Yes sir. Likely Tug could join the German army or maybe even the French or British, and had his blessing. But not the one that General Lee betrayed him to that day back in 1865. So he threw Tug out. The three of us got out of that house as fast as we could, but before we even reached the sidewalk he was already in the room that was evidently Tug's. He never even waited to open the door: just kicked the window out, screen and all, and started throwing Tug's clothes out into the yard."

So Tug had crossed his Rubicon, and should have been safe now. I mean, Captain Lendon took him in. He—Lendon—was one of a big family of brothers in a big house with a tremendous mother weighing close to two hundred pounds, who liked to cook and eat both so one more wouldn't matter; maybe she never even noticed Tug. So he should have been safe now while the company waited for orders to move. But the others wouldn't let him alone; his method of joining the colors was a little too unique, not to mention East Lynne; there was always one to say:

"Tug, is it really so that General Lee didn't need to give up when he did?" and Tug would say,

"That's what papa says. He was there and seen it, even if he wasn't but seventeen years old." And the other would say:

"So you had to go clean against him, clean against your own father, to join the Rifles?" And Tug sitting there quite still now, the hands that never would be able to paint more than the roughest outhouse walls and finesseless fences but which could do things to the intractable and unpredictable mule which few other hands dared, hanging quiet too between his knees, because by now he would know what was coming next. And the other—and all the rest of them within range—watching Tug with just half an eye since the other three halves would be watching Captain Lendon across the room; in fact they usually waited until Lendon had left, was actually out.

"That's right," Tug would say; then the other:

"Why did you do it, Tug? You're past thirty now, safe from the draft, and your father's an old man alone here with nobody to take care of him."

"We cant let them Germans keep on treating folks like they're doing. Somebody's got to make them quit."

"So you had to go clean against your father to join the army to make them quit. And now you'll have to go clean against him again to go round to the other side of the world where you can get at them."

"I'm going to France," Tug would say.

"That's what I said: halfway round. Which way are you going? east or west? You can pick either one and still get there.
Or better still, and I'll make you a bet. Pick out east, go on
east until you find the war, do whatever you aim to do to
them Germans and then keep right on going east, and I'll bet
you a hundred dollars to one that when you see Jefferson
next time, you'll be looking at it right square across Miss
Joanna Burden's mailbox one mile west of the courthouse."
But by that time Captain Lendon would be there; probably
somebody had gone to fetch him. He may have been such a
bad company commander that he was relieved of his command long before it ever saw the lines, and a few years after
this he was going to be the leader in something here in
Jefferson that I anyway am glad I dont have to lie down with
in the dark every time I try to go to sleep. But at least he held
his company together (and not by the bars on his shoulders
since if they had been all he had, he wouldn't have had a man
left by the first Saturday night, but by simple instinctive humanity, of which even he, even in the middle of that business
he was going to be mixed up in later, seemed to have had a
little, like now) until a better captain could get hold of it. He
was already in uniform. He was a cotton man, a buyer for one
of the Memphis export houses, and he spent most of his commissions gambling on cotton futures in the market, but he
never had looked like a farmer until he put on the uniform.

"What the hell's going on here?" he said. "What the hell
do you think Tug is? a damn ant running around a damn orange or something? He aint going *around* anything: he's going straight *across* it, across the water to France to fight for his
country, and when they dont need him in France any longer
he's coming back across the same water, back here to
Jefferson the same way he went out of it, like we'll all be
damn glad to get back to it. So dont let me hear any more of
this" (excrement: my word) "any more."

Whether or not Tug would continue to need Captain
Lendon, he didn't have him much longer. The company was
mustered that week and sent to Texas for training; whereupon, since Tug was competent to paint any flat surface provided it was simple enough, with edges and not theoretical
boundaries, and possessed that gift with horses and mules

which the expert Pat Stamper had recognised at once to par-
take of that inexplicable quality called genius, naturally the
army made him a cook and detached him the same day, so
that he was not only the first Yoknapatawpha County soldier
(the Sartoris boys didn't count since they were officially
British troops) to go overseas, he was among the last of all
American troops to get back home, which was in late 1919,
since obviously the same military which would decree him
into a cook, would mislay where it had sent him (not lose
him; my own experience between '42 and '45 taught me that
the military never loses anything: it merely buries it).

So now he was back home again, living alone now (old Mr
Nightingale had died in that same summer of 1917, killed,
Uncle Gavin said, by simple inflexibility, having set his intractable and contemptuous face against the juggernaut of
history and science both that April day in 1865 and never
flinched since), a barn and fence painter once more, with his
Saturday night bath in the barbershop and again drinking and
gambling again within his means, only with on his face now a
look, as V. K. Ratliff put it, as if he had been taught and believed all his life that the fourth dimension was invisible, then
suddenly had seen one. And he didn't have Captain Lendon
now. I mean, Lendon was back home too but they were no
longer commander and man. Or maybe it was that even that
natural humanity of Captain Lendon's, of which he should
have had a pretty good supply since none of it seemed to be
within his reach on his next humanitarian crises after that one
when he shielded Tug from the harsh facts of cosmology,
would not have sufficed here.

This happened in the barbershop too (no, I wasn't there; I
still wasn't old enough to be tolerated in the barbershop at
ten oclock on Saturday night even if I could have got away
from Mother; this was hearsay from Ratliff to Uncle Gavin to
me). This time the straight man was Skeets Magowan, Uncle
Willy Christian's soda-jerker—a young man with a swagger
and dash to him, who probably smelled more like toilet water
than just water, with a considerable following of fourteen-
and fifteen-year-old girls at Uncle Willy's fountain, who we
realised afterward had been just a little older than we always
thought and, as Ratliff said, even ten years later would never

know as much as he—Skeets—figured he had already forgotten ten years ago; he had just been barbered and scented, and Tug had finished his bath and was sitting quietly enough while the first drink or two began to take hold.

"So when you left Texas, you went north," Skeets said.

"That's right," Tug said.

"Come on," Skeets said. "Tell us about it. You left Texas going due north, to New York. Then you got on the boat, and it kept right on due north too."

"That's right," Tug said.

"But suppose they fooled you a little. Suppose they turned the boat, to the east or west or maybe right back south——"

"God damn it," Tug said. "Dont you think I know where north is? You can wake me up in the bed in the middle of the night and I can point my hand due north without even turning on the light."

"What'll you bet? Five dollars? Ten?"

"I'll bet you ten dollars to one dollar except that any dollar you ever had you already spent on that shampoo or that silk shirt."

"All right, all right," Skeets said. "So the boat went straight north, to France. And you stayed in France two years and then got on another boat and it went straight north too. Then you got off that boat and got on a train and it—"

"Shut up," Tug said.

"—went straight north too. And when you got off, you were back in Jefferson."

"Shut up, you goddam little bastard," Tug said.

"So dont you see what that means? Either one of two things: either they moved Jefferson—" Now Tug was on his feet though even now apparently Skeets knew no better: "—which all the folks that stayed around here and didn't go to that war can tell you they didn't. Or you left Jefferson going due north by way of Texas and come back to Jefferson still going due north without even passing Texas again——" It took all the barbers and customers and loafers too and finally the night marshal himself to immobilise Tug. Though by that time Skeets was already in the ambulance on his way to the hospital.

And there was Bayard Sartoris. He got back in the spring of

'19 and bought the fastest car he could find and spent his time ripping around the county or back and forth to Memphis until (so we all believed) his aunt, Mrs Du Pre, looked over Jefferson and picked out Narcissa Benbow and then caught Bayard between trips with the other hand long enough to get them married, hoping that would save Bayard's neck since he was now the last Sartoris Mohican (John had finally got himself shot down in July of '18) only it didn't seem to work. I mean, as soon as he got Narcissa pregnant, which must have been pretty quick, he was back in the car again until this time Colonel Sartoris himself stepped into the breach, who hated cars yet gave up his carriage and pair to let Bayard drive him back and forth to the bank, to at least slow the car down during that much of the elapsed mileage. Except that Colonel Sartoris had a heart condition, so when the wreck came it was him that died: Bayard just walked out of the crash and disappeared, abandoned pregnant wife and all, until the next spring when he was still trying to relieve his boredom by seeing how much faster he could make something travel than he could invent a destination for; this time another aeroplane: a new experimental type at the Dayton testing field: only this one fooled him by shedding all four of its wings in midair.

That's right: boredom, Uncle Gavin said—that war was the only civilised condition which offered any scope for the natural blackguardism inherent in men, that not just condoned and sanctioned it but rewarded it, and that Bayard was simply bored: he would never forgive the Germans not for starting the war but for stopping it, ending it. But Mother said that was wrong. She said that Bayard was frightened and ashamed: not ashamed because he was frightened but terrified when he discovered himself to be capable of, vulnerable to being ashamed. She said that Sartorises were different from other people. That most people, nearly all people, loved themselves first, only they knew it secretly and maybe even admitted it secretly; and so they didn't have to be ashamed of it—or if they were ashamed, they didn't need to be afraid of being ashamed. But that Sartorises didn't even know they loved themselves first, except Bayard. Which was all right with him and he wasn't ashamed of it until he and his twin brother reached England and got into flight training without parachutes in aeroplanes made out of glue and baling-wire; or maybe not even until they were at the front, where even for the ones that had lived that far the odds were near zero against scout pilots surviving the first three weeks of active service. When suddenly Bayard realised that, unique in the squadron and, for all he knew, unique in all the R.F.C. or maybe all military air forces, he was not one in-dividual creature at all but there were two of him since he had a twin engaged in the same risk and chance. And so in effect he alone out of all the people flying in that war had been vouchsafed a double indemnity against those odds (and vice versa of course since his twin would enjoy the identical obverse vouchsafement)—and in the next second, with a kind of terror, discovered that he was ashamed of the idea, knowledge, of being capable of having thought it even.

That was what Mother said his trouble was—why he appar-ently came back to Jefferson for the sole purpose of trying, in that sullen and pleasureless manner, to find out just how many different ways he could risk breaking his neck that would keep the most people anguished or upset or at least an-noyed: that completely un-Sartoris-like capacity for shame which he could neither live with nor quit; could neither live in toleration with it nor by his own act repudiate it. That was why the risking, the chancing, the fatalism. Obviously the same idea—twinship's double indemnity against being shot down—must have occurred to the other twin at the same moment, since they were twins. But it probably hadn't wor-ried John anymore than the things he had done in his war (Uncle Gavin said—and in about five years I was going to have a chance to test it myself—that no man ever went to a war, even in the Y.M.C.A., without bringing back something he wished he hadn't done or anyway would stop thinking about) worried that old original Colonel Sartoris who had been their great-grandfather; only he, Bayard, of all his line was that weak, that un-Sartoris.

So now (if Mother was right) he had a double burden. One was, anguish over what base depths of imagination and selfish hope he knew himself to be, not so much capable of as doomed to be ashamed of; the other, the fact that if that twinship double indemnity did work in his favor and John was shot down first, he—Bayard—would, no matter how much

longer he survived, have to face his twin some day in the omniscience of the mutual immortality, with the foul stain of his
weakness now beyond concealment. The foul stain being not
the idea, because the same idea must have occurred to his
twin at the same instant with himself although they were in
different squadrons now, but that of the two of them, John
would not have been ashamed of it. The idea being simply
this: John had managed to shoot down three huns before he
himself was killed (he was probably a better shot than Bayard
or maybe his flight commander liked him and set up targets)
and Bayard himself had racked up enough ninths and six-
teenths, after the British method of scoring—unless somebody was incredible enough to say "Not me; I was too damn
scared to remember to pull up the cocking handles"—to add
up to two and maybe an inch over; now that John was gone
and no longer needed his, suppose, just suppose he could
wangle, bribe, forge, corrupt the records and whoever kept
them, into transferring all the Sartoris bumf under one name,
so that one of them anyway could come back home an ace—
an idea not base in itself, because John had not only thought
of it too but if he had lived and Bayard had died, would have
managed somehow to accomplish it, but base only after he,
Bayard, had debased and befouled it by being ashamed of it.
And he could not quit it of his own volition, since when he
faced John's ghost some day in the course of simple fatality,
John would be just amused and contemptuous; where if he
did it by putting the pistol barrel in his mouth himself, that
ghost would be not just risible and contemptuous but forever
unreconciled, irreconcilable.

But Linda Snopes—excuse me: Snopes Kohl—would be our
first female one. So you would think the whole town would
turn out, or at least be represented by delegates: from the civic
clubs and churches, not to mention the American Legion and
the V.F.W., which would have happened if she had been
elected Miss America instead of merely blown up by a Franco
shell or landmine or whatever it was that went off in or under
the ambulance she was driving and left her stone deaf. So I
said, "What does she want to come back home for? There's
nothing for her to join. What would she want in a Ladies'
Auxiliary, raffling off home-made jam and lamp shades. Even

if she could make jam, since obviously cooking is the last thing
a sculptor would demand of his girl. Who was just passing
time anyway between Communist meetings until somebody
started a Fascist war he could get into. Not to mention the
un-kosher stuff she would have had to learn in Jefferson,
Mississippi. Especially if where she learned to cook was in that
Dirty Spoon her papa beat Ratliff out of back there when they
first came to town." But I was wrong. It wouldn't be municipal: only private: just three people only incidentally from
Jefferson because they were mainly out of her mother's past:
my uncle, her father, and Ratliff. Then I saw there would be
only two. Ratliff wouldn't even get in the car.

"Come on," Uncle Gavin said. "Go with us."

"I'll wait here," Ratliff said. "I'll be the local committee.
Until next time," he said at me.

"What?" Uncle Gavin said.

"Nothing," Ratliff said. "Jest a joke Chick told me that I'm
reminding him of."

Then I saw it wasn't going to be even two out of her
mother's past. We were not even going by the bank, let alone
stop at it. I said, "What the hell would Mr Snopes want,
throwing away at least six hours of good usury to make a trip
all the way to Memphis to meet his daughter, after all the expense he had to go to to get her out of Jefferson—not only
butchering up De Spain's house, but all that imported Italian
marble over her mother's grave to give her something worth
going away from or not coming back to if you like that
better."

I said: "So it's my fault I wasn't born soon enough either
to defend Das Democracy in your war or Das Kapital in hers.
Meaning there's still plenty of time for me yet. Or maybe
what you mean is that Hitler and Mussolini and Franco all
three working together cannot get an authentic unimpeachable paid-up member of the Harvard R.O.T.C. into really
serious military trouble. Because I probably wont make Por-
cellian either; F.D.R. didn't."

I said: "That's it. That's why you insisted on me coming
along this morning: although she hasn't got any eardrums
now and cant hear you say No or Please No or even For
God's sake No, at least she cant marry you before we get back

to Jefferson with me right here in the car too. But there's the rest of the afternoon when you can chase me out, not to mention the eight hours of the night when Mother likes to believe I am upstairs asleep. Not to mention I've got to go back to Cambridge next month—unless you believe your . . . is it virginity or just celibacy? is worth even that sacrifice? But then why not, since it was your idea to send me all the way to Cambridge, Mass for what we laughingly call an education. Being as Mother says she's been in love with you all her life, only she was too young to know it and you were too much of a gentleman to tell her. Or does Mother really always know best?"

By this time we had reached the airport; I mean Memphis. Uncle Gavin said, "Park the car and let's have some coffee. We've probably got at least a half-hour yet." We had the coffee in the restaurant; I dont know why they dont call it the Skyroom here too. Maybe Memphis is still off quota. Ratliff said she would have to marry somebody sooner or later, and every day that passed made it that much sooner. No, that wasn't the way he put it: that he—Uncle Gavin—couldn't escape forever, that almost any day now some woman would decide he was mature and dependable enough at last for steady work in place of merely an occasional chore; and that the sooner this happened the better, since only then would he be safe. I said, "How safe? He seems to me to be doing all right; I never knew anybody that scatheless."

"I dont mean him," Ratliff said. "I mean us, Yoknapatawpha County; that he would maybe be safe to live with then because he wouldn't have so much time for meddling."

In which case, saving us would take some doing. Because he—Gavin—had one defect in his own character which always saved him, no matter what jeopardy it left the rest of us in. I mean, the fact that people get older, especially young girls of fifteen or sixteen, who seem to get older all of a sudden in six months or one year than they or anybody else ever does in about ten years. I mean, he always picked out children, or maybe he was just vulnerable to female children and they chose him, whichever way you want it. That the selecting or victim-falling was done at an age when the oath of eternal fidelity would have ceased to exist almost before the breath

was dry on it. I'm thinking now of Melisandre Backus naturally, before my time and Linda Snopes's too. That is,
Melisandre was twelve and thirteen and fourteen several years
before she vacated for Linda to take her turn in the vacuum,
Gavin selecting and ordering the books of poetry to read to
Melisandre or anyway supervise and check on, which was
maybe how by actual test, trial and error, he knew which ones
to improve Linda's mind and character with when her turn
came, or anyway alter them.

Though pretty soon Melisandre committed the irrevocable
error of getting a year older and so quitting forever that fey
unworld of Spenser and the youth Milton, for the human race
where even the sort of girl that he picked out or that picked
out him, when a man talked about fidelity and devotion to
her, she was in a position to tell him either to put up or shut
up. Anyway, he was saved that time. Though I wasn't present
to remember exactly what the sequence was: whether Gavin
went off to Harvard first or maybe it was between Harvard
and Heidelberg, or whether she got married first. Anyway,
when he got back from his war, she was married. To a New
Orleans underworld bigshot named Harriss with two esses.
And how in the world or where on earth she ever managed to
meet him—a shy girl, motherless and an only child, who lived
on what used to be one of our biggest plantations two or
three miles from town but that for years had been gradually
going to decay, with her widowered father who spent all his
time on the front gallery in summer and in the library in winter with a bottle of whiskey and a volume of Horace. Who
(Melisandre) had as far as we knew never been away from it
in her life except to be driven daily in to town by a Negro
coachman in a victoria while she graduated from the grammar
school then the high school then the Female Academy. And a
man about whom all we knew was what he said: that his name
was Harriss with two esses, which maybe it was, and that he
was a New Orleans importer. Which we knew he was, since
(this was early 1919, before Uncle Gavin got back home) even
Jefferson recognised when it saw one a bullet-proof Cadillac
that needed two chauffeurs, both in double-breasted suits
that bulged a little at the left armpit.

Not to mention the money. Mr Backus died about then and

of course there were some to say it was with a broken heart over his only child marrying a bootleg czar. Though apparently he waited long enough to make sure his son-in-law was actually a czar or anyway the empire a going and solvent one, since the money had already begun to show a little before he died—the roofs and galleries patched and shored up even if Mr Backus evidently burked at paint on the house yet, and gravel in the drive so that when she came home to spend that first Christmas, she and the nurse and the czarevitch could go back and forth to town in an automobile instead of the old victoria drawn by a plow-team. Then Mr Backus died and the house and outbuildings too got painted. And now Harriss with both his esses began to appear in Jefferson, making friends even in time though most of Yoknapatawpha County was unsold still, just neutral, going out there in the Model T's and on horses and mules, to stand along the road and watch what had been just a simple familiar red-ink north Mississippi cotton plantation being changed into a Virginia or Long Island horse farm, with miles of white panel fence where the rest of us were not a bit too proud of what we called bobwire and any handy sapling post, and white stables with electric light and steam heat and running water and butlers and footmen for the horses where a lot of the rest of us still depended on coal oil lamps for light and our wives to tote firewood and water from the nearest woodlot and spring or well.

Then there were two children, an heir and a princess too, when Harriss died with his two esses in a New Orleans barber's chair of his ordinary thirty-eight calibre occupational disease. Whereupon the horses and their grooms and valets became sold and the house closed except for a caretaker, vacant now of Mrs Harriss with her two esses and the two children and the five maids and couriers and nannies and secretaries, and now Mother and the other ones who had been girls with her in the old Academy days would get the letters and postcards from the fashionable European cities telling how just the climate at first but presently, in time, the climate and the schools both were better for the children and (on Mother's naturally) she hoped Gavin was well and maybe even married. "So at least he's safe from that one," I told Ratliff, who said,

"Safe?"

"Why the hell not? She not only got too big for the fairy tale, she's got two children and all that money: what the hell does she want to marry anybody for? Or not Gavin anyway; he dont want money: all he wants is just to meddle and change. Why the hell isn't he safe now?"

"That's right," Ratliff said. "It looks like he would almost have to be, dont it? At least until next time." Joke. And still worth repeating two hours ago when he declined to come with us. And Gavin sitting there drinking a cup of what whoever ran the airport restaurant called coffee, looking smug and inscrutable and arrogant and immune as a louse on a queen's arse. Because maybe Linda Kohl (pardon me, Snopes Kohl) had plenty of money too, not only what her mother must have left her but what Uncle Gavin, as her guardian, had managed to chisel out of old Will Varner. Not chiseled out of her father too because maybe old Snopes was glad to stump up something just to have what Gavin or Ratliff would call that reproachless virgin rectitude stop looking at him. But she didn't have two children so all Ratliff and I had to trust, depend on this time was that old primary condition founded on simple evanescence, that every time a moment occurred they would be one moment older: that they had to be alive for him to notice them, and they had to be in motion to be alive, and the only moment of motion which caught his attention, his eye, was that one at which they entered puberty like the swirl of skirt or flow or turn of limb when entering, passing through a door, slowed down by the camera trick but still motion, still a moment, irrevocable.

That was really what saved him each time: that the moment had to be motion. They couldn't stop in the door, and once through it they didn't stop either; sometimes they didn't even pause long enough to close it behind them before going on to the next one and through it, which was into matrimony— from maturation to parturition in one easy lesson you might say. Which was all right. Uncle Gavin wouldn't be at that next door. He would still be watching the first one. And since life is not so much motion as an inventless repetition of motion, he would never be at that first door long before there would be another swirl, another unshaped vanishing adolescent leg.

So I should have thought to tell Ratliff that, while I was in Memphis helping Uncle Gavin say goodbye to this one, he might be looking around the Square to see who the next one was going to be, as Linda had already displaced Melisandre Backus probably before Melisandre even knew she had been dispossessed. Then in the next moment I knew that would not be necessary; obviously Uncle Gavin had already picked her out himself, which was why he could sit there placid and composed, drinking coffee while we waited for the plane to be announced.

Which it was at last. We went out to the ramp. I stopped at the rail. "I'll wait here," I said. "You'll want a little privacy while you can still get it even if it's only anonymity and not solitude. Have you got your slate ready? or maybe she'll already have one built-in on her cuff, or maybe strapped to her leg like aviators carry maps." But he had gone on. Then the plane taxi-ed up, one of the new D.C.3's, and in time there she was. I couldn't see her eyes from this distance but then it wasn't them, it was just her ears the bomb or shell or mine or whatever it was blew up—the same tall girl too tall to have a shape but then I dont know: women like that and once you get their clothes off they surprise you even if she was twenty-nine years old now. Then I could see her eyes, so dark blue that at first you thought they were black. And I for one never did know how or where she got them or the black hair either since old Snopes's eyes were the color of stagnant pond water and his hair didn't have any color at all, and her mother had had blue eyes too but pale blue to go with her hair. So that when I tried to remember her, she always looked like she had just been raided out of a brothel in the Scandinavian Valhalla and the cops had just managed to fling a few garments on her before they hustled her into the wagon. Fine eyes too, that probably if you were the one to finally get the clothes off you would have called them beautiful too. And she even had the little pad and pencil in her hand while she was kissing Gavin. I mean, kissing him. Though evidently he would need a little time to get used to using it or depending on it because he said aloud, just like she was anybody else:

"Here's Chick too," and she remembered me; she was as tall as Gavin and damn near as tall as me, as well as a nail-biter though maybe that had come after the shell or perhaps after the bereavement. And when she shook hands she really had driven that ambulance and apparently changed the tires on it too, speaking not loud but in that dry harsh quacking voice that deaf people learn to use, even asking about Mother and Father as if she really cared, like any ordinary Jefferson woman that never dreamed of going to wars and getting blown up. Though Uncle Gavin remembered now, or at least was learning fast, taking the pad and pencil and scrawling something on it, baggage I reckon, since she said "Oh yes," just like she could hear too and got the checks out of her handbag.

I brought the car up while they untangled the bags. So she had lived with the guy for years before they married but it didn't show on her. And she had gone to Spain to the war and got blown up at the front, and that didn't show on her either. I said, "Why dont you let her drive? Then maybe she wont be so nervous because she cant talk to you."

"Maybe you'd better drive then," he said. So we did, and brought the hero home, the two of them in the back. And somebody may have said, "Why dont we all ride in front? the seat's wide enough." Though I dont remember it. Or somebody may have said, "In the back seat my/your hair will blow." Which would have been Mother, who claimed to be unable to exist without a gale blowing except in a car on the hottest day, saying, "Roll up your window (Charley or Chick or Gavin or whoever's window hadn't been closed tight yet), my hair's blowing." So I dont remember that either: only Uncle Gavin: "You can relax now. You're quite safe. I'm holding her hand."

Which they were, she holding his hand in both hers on her lap and every mile or so the duck voice would say, "Gavin," and then after a mile or so, "Gavin." And evidently she hadn't had the pad and pencil long enough to get used to them either or maybe when you lose hearing and enter real silence you forget that everything does not take place in that privacy and solitude. Or maybe after he took the pencil from her to answer on the pad, she couldn't wait to get the pencil back so both should have had slates: "Yes it does. I can feel it, somewhere in my skull or the back of my mouth. It's an ugly sound. Isn't it?" But evidently Gavin was learning because it

was still the duck voice: "Yes it is. I can feel it, I tell you."
And still the duck voice: "How? If I try to practise, how can
I know when it's right?" Which I agree with myself: if you're
going to take time out from your law practice and being
county attorney to restore to your deaf girl-friend the lost
bridehead of her mellifluity, how would you go about it.
Though what a chance for a husband: to teach your stone-
deaf wife that all she needed to make her tone and pitch beautiful was merely to hold her breath while she spoke. Or maybe
what Uncle Gavin wrote next was simply Jonson (or some of
that old Donne or Herrick maybe or even just Suckling
maybe—any or all of them annotated to that one ear—eye
now—by that old Stevens) *Vale not these cherry lips with vacant speech But let me drink instead thy tender Yes.* Or maybe
what he wrote was simpler still: *Hold it till we get home. This
is no place to restore your voice. Besides, this infant will have to
go back to Cambridge next month and then we'll have plenty of
time, plenty of privacy.*

Thus we brought the hero home. Now we could see
Jefferson, the clock on the courthouse, not to mention her father's water tank, and now the duck voice was saying Ratliff.
"Bart liked him. He said he hadn't expected to like anybody
from Mississippi, but he was wrong." What Gavin wrote this
time was obvious, since the voice said: "Not even you. He
made me promise—I mean, whichever one of us it was,
would give Ratliff one of his things. You remember it—the
Italian boy that you didn't know what it was even though you
had seen sculpture before, but Ratliff that had never even
seen an Italian boy, nor anything else beyond the Confederate
monument in front of the courthouse, knew at once what it
was, and even what he was doing?" And I would have liked
the pad myself long enough to write *What was the Italian boy
doing?* only we were home now, the hero; Gavin said:

"Stop at the bank first. He should have some warning; simple decency commands it. Unless he has had his warning and
has simply left town for a little space in which to wrestle with
his soul and so bring it to the moment which it must face.
Assuming of course that even he has realised by now that he
simply cannot foreclose her out of existence like a mortgage
or a note."

"And have a public reception here in the street before she has had a chance to fix her makeup?" I said.

"Relax," he said again. "When you are a little older you will discover that people really are much more gentle and considerate and kind than you want right now to believe."

I pulled up at the bank. But if I had been her I wouldn't even have reached for the pencil, duck quack or not, to say, "What the hell? Take me on home." She didn't. She sat there, holding his hand in both hers, not just on her lap but right against her belly, looking around at the Square, the duck voice saying, "Gavin. Gavin." Then: "There goes Uncle Willy, coming back from dinner." Except it wasn't old man Christian: he was dead. But then it didn't really matter whether anybody wrote that on the pad or not. And Gavin was right. Nobody stopped. I watched two of them recognise her. No, I mean they recognised juxtaposition: Gavin Stevens' car at the curb before the bank at twenty-two minutes past one in the afternoon with me at the wheel and Gavin and a woman in the back seat. Who had all heard about Linda Kohl I mean Snopes Kohl, anyhow that she was female and from Jefferson and had gone near enough to a war for it to bust her eardrums. Because he is right: people are kind and gentle and considerate. It's not that you dont expect them to be, it's because you have already made up your mind they are not and so they upset you, throw you off. They didn't even stop, just one of them said Howdy Gavin and went on.

I got out and went into the bank. Because what would I do myself if I had a daughter, an only child, and her grandfather had plenty of money for it and I could have afforded myself to let her go away to school. Only I didn't and nobody knew why I wouldn't, until suddenly I let her go, but only as far as the University which was only fifty miles away; and nobody knew why for that either: only that I aimed to become president of the bank that the president of it now was the man everybody believed had been laying my wife ever since we moved to town. That is, nobody knew why until three months later, when my wife went to the beauty parlor for the first time in her life and that night shot herself carefully through the temple so as not to disarrange the new permanent, and when the dust finally settled sure enough that fornicating bank president had left town and now I was not only president of his bank but living in his house and you would have thought I wouldn't need the daughter anymore and she could go wherever the hell she wanted provided it wasn't ever Jefferson, Mississippi again. Except I wouldn't even let her do that until we could both sit in the car and see the monument over her mother's grave unveiled, sitting there defenseless before the carved face and the carved defenseless taunt:

A Virtuous Wife is a Crown to her Husband
Her Children Rise and Call her Blessed

and then I said, "All right. You can go now." And I came back out.

"Mr Snopes has taken the afternoon off," I said. "To go home and wait there for his daughter." So we went there, on to the colonial monstrosity which was the second taunt. He had three monuments in Jefferson now: the water tank, the gravestone, and the mansion. And who knows at which of the windows he lurked his wait or waited out his lurk, whichever way you prefer. "Maybe I should come in too," I said.

"Maybe we should each have a pad and pencil," Uncle Gavin said. "Then everybody could hear." We were expected. Almost at once the Negro yardman-chauffeur came out the front door. I got the luggage out onto the sidewalk while they still stood there, she as tall as him and Gavin in her arms just as much as she was in his, kissing right on the street in the broad daylight, the duck voice saying, "Gavin. Gavin" not so much as if she still couldn't believe it was him at last but as if she still hadn't got used to the new sound she was convinced she made. Then she turned him loose and he said, "Come on," and we got back in the car, and that was all. The hero was home. I turned in the middle of the block and looked not back, I would have liked to say if it had been true: the houseman still scuttling up the walk with the bags and she still standing there, looking at us, a little too tall for my taste, immured, inviolate in silence, invulnerable, serene.

That was it: silence. If there were no such thing as sound. If it only took place in silence, no evil man has invented could really harm him: explosion, treachery, the human voice.

That was it: deafness. Ratliff and I couldn't beat that.

Those others, the other times had flicked the skirt or flowed or turned the limb at and into mere puberty; beyond it and immediately, was the other door immediately beyond which was the altar and the long line of drying diapers: fulfillment, the end. But she had beat him. Not in motion continuous through a door, a moment, but immobilised by a thunderclap into silence, herself the immobile one while it was the door and the walls it opened which fled away and on, herself no mere moment's child but the inviolate bride of silence, inviolable in maidenhead, fixed, forever safe from change and alteration. Finally I ran Ratliff to ground; it took three days.

"Her husband is sending you a present," I said. "It's that sculpture you liked: the Italian boy doing whatever it was you liked that Gavin himself who has not only seen Italian boys before but maybe even one doing whatever this one is doing, didn't even know where first base was. But it's all right. You dont have a female wife nor any innocent female daughters either. So you can probably keep it right there in the house. —She's going to marry him," I said.

"Why not?" he said. "I reckon he can stand it. Besides, if somebody jest marries him, maybe the rest of us will be safe."

"The rest of them, you mean?" I said.

"I mean jest what I said," Ratliff answered. "I mean the rest of all of us."

Nine

CHARLES MALLISON
Gavin was right. That was late August. Three weeks later I was back in Cambridge again, hoping, I mean trying, or maybe what I mean is I belonged to the class that would or anyway should, graduate next June. But I had been in Jefferson three weeks, plenty long enough even if they had insisted on having banns read: something quite unnecessary for a widow who was not only a widow but a wounded war hero too. So then I thought maybe they were waiting until they would be free of me. You know: the old road-company drammer reversed in gender: the frantic child clinging this time to the prospective groom's coat-tail, crying "Papa papa papa" (in this case Uncle uncle uncle) "please dont make us marry Mrs Smith."

Then I thought (it was Thanksgiving now; pretty soon I would be going home for Christmas) *Naturally it wont occur to any of them to bother to notify me way up here in Massachusetts.* So I even thought of writing and asking, not Mother of course and certainly not Uncle Gavin, since if it had happened he would be too busy to answer, and if it hadn't he would still be too busy either dodging for his life if he was the one still saying No, or trying to learn her enough language to hear Please if he was the one saying Yes. But to Ratliff, who would be an interested bystander even if you couldn't call that much curiosity about other people's affairs which he possessed merely innocent—maybe even a wire: *Are they bedded formally yet or not? I mean is it rosa yet or still just sub, assuming you assume the same assumption they teach us up here at Harvard that once you get the clothes off those tall up-and-down women you find out they aint all that up-and-down at all.*

Then it was Christmas and I thought *Maybe I wronged them. Maybe they have been waiting for me all along, not to interrupt my education by an emergency call but for the season of peace and goodwill to produce me available to tote the ring or bouquet or whatever it is.* But I didn't even see her. Uncle Gavin and I even spent most of one whole day together. I was going out to Sartoris to shoot quail with Benbow (he wasn't but seventeen but he was considered one of the best bird shots in the county, second only to Luther Biglin, a half-farmer half-dog-trainer half-market-hunter who shot left-handed, not much older than Benbow, in fact about my age, who lived up near Old Wyliesport on the river) and Uncle Gavin invited himself along. He—Gavin—wouldn't be much of a gun even if he stopped talking long enough but now and then he would go with me. And all that day, nothing; it was me that finally said:

"How are the voice lessons coming?"

"Mrs Kohl? Fair. But your fresh ear would be the best judge," and I said:

"When will that be?" and he said:

"Any time you're close enough to hear it." And again on Christmas day, it was me. Ratliff usually had Christmas dinner with us, Uncle Gavin's guest though Mother liked him too, whether or not because she was Uncle Gavin's twin. Or sometimes Uncle Gavin ate with Ratliff and then he would take me because Ratliff was a damned good cook, living alone in the cleanest little house you ever saw, doing his own housework and he even made the blue shirts he always wore. And this time too it was me.

"What about Mrs Kohl for dinner too?" I asked Mother, and Uncle Gavin said:

"My God, did you come all the way down here from Cambridge to spend Christmas too looking at that old fish-blooded suh—" and caught himself in time and said, "Excuse me, Maggie," and Mother said:

"Certainly she will have to take her first Christmas dinner at home with her father." And the next day I left. Spoade—his father had been at Harvard back in 1909 with Uncle Gavin—had invited me to Charleston to see what a Saint Cecilia ball looked like from inside. Because we always broke up then anyway; the day after Christmas Father always went to Miami to spend a week looking at horses and Mother would go too, not that she was interested in running horses but on the contrary: because of her conviction that her presence or anyway adjacence or at least contiguity would keep him from buying one.

Then it was 1938 and I was back in Cambridge. Then it was

September 1938 and I was still or anyway again in Cambridge, in law school now. Munich had been observed or celebrated or consecrated, whichever it was, and Uncle Gavin said, "It wont be long now." But he had been saying that back last spring. So I said:

"Then what's the use in me wasting two or three more years becoming a lawyer when if you're right nobody will have time for civil cases anymore, even if I'm still around to prosecute or defend them?" and he said:

"Because when this one is over, all humanity and justice will have left will be the law:" and I said:

"What else is it using now?" and he said:

"These are good times, boom halcyon times when what do you want with justice when you've already got welfare? Now the law is the last resort, to get your hand into the pocket which so far has resisted or foiled you."

That was last spring, in June when he and Mother (they had lost Father at Saratoga though he had promised to reach Cambridge in time for the actual vows) came up to see me graduate in Ack. and I said, "What? No wedding bells yet?" and he said:

"Not mine anyway:" and I said:

"How are the voice lessons coming? Come on," I said, "I'm a big boy now; I'm a Harvard A.M. too even if I wont have Heidelberg. Tell me. Is that really all you do when you are all cosy together? practise talking?" and he said:

"Hush and let me talk a while now. You're going to Europe for the summer; that's my present to you. I have your tickets and your passport application; all you need do is go down to the official photographer and get mugged."

"Why Europe? and Why now? besides, what if I dont want to go?" and he said:

"Because it may not be there next summer. So it will have to be this one. Go and look at the place; you may have to die in it."

"Why not wait until then, then?" and he said:

"You will go as a host then. This summer you can still be a guest." There were three of us; by fast footwork and pulling all the strings we could reach, we even made the same boat. And that summer we—I: two of us at the last moment found themselves incapable of passing Paris—saw a little of Europe on a bicycle. I mean, that part still available: that presumable corridor of it where I might have to do Uncle Gavin's dying: Britain, France, Italy—the Europe which Uncle Gavin said would be no more since the ones who survived getting rid of Hitler and Mussolini and Franco would be too exhausted and the ones who merely survived them wouldn't care anyway.

So I did try to look at it, to see, since even at twenty-four I still seemed to believe what he said just as I believed him at fourteen and (I presume: I cant remember) at four. In fact, the Europe he remembered or thought he remembered was already gone. What I saw was a kind of composed and collected hysteria: a frenetic holiday in which everybody was a tourist, native and visitor alike. There were too many soldiers. I mean, too many people dressed as, and for the moment behaving like, troops, as if for simple police or temporary utility reasons they had to wear masquerade and add to the Maginot Line (so that they—the French ones anyway—seemed to be saying, "Have a heart; dont kid us. We dont believe it either.") right in the middle of the fight for the thirty-nine hour week; the loud parliamentary conclaves about which side of Piccadilly or the Champs Elysées the sandbags would look best on like which side of the room to hang the pictures; the splendid glittering figure of Gamelin still wiping the soup from his moustache and saying, "Be calm. I am here"—as though all Europe (oh yes, us too; the place was full of Americans too) were saying, "Since Evil is the thing, not only *de rigueur* but successful too, let us all join Evil and so make it the Good."

Then me too in Paris for the last two weeks, to see if the Paris of Hemingway and the Paris of Scott Fitzgerald (they were not the same ones; they merely used the same room) had vanished completely or not too; then Cambridge again, only a day late: all of which, none of which that is ties up with anything but only explains to me why it was almost a year and a half before I saw her again. And so we had Munich: that moment of respectful silence, then once more about our affairs; and Uncle Gavin's letter came saying "It wont be long now." Except that it was probably already too late for me. When I had to go—no, I dont mean that: when the time came for me to go—I wanted to be a fighter pilot. But I was already twenty-four now; in six years I would be thirty and even now it might be too late; Bayard and John Sartoris were twenty when they went to England in '16 and Uncle Gavin told me about one RFC (I mean RAF now) child who was a captain with such a record that the British government sent him back home and grounded him for good so that he might at least be present on the day of his civilian majority. So I would probably wind up as a navigator or engineer on bombers, or maybe at thirty they wouldn't let me go up at all.

But still no wedding bells. Maybe it was the voice. My spies —I only needed one of course: Mother—reported that the private lessons were still going on, so maybe she felt that the Yes would not be dulcet enough yet to be legal. Which— legality—she would of course insist on, having tried cohabitation the first time *au naturel* you might say, and it blew up in her face. No, that's wrong. The cohabitation didn't blow up until after it became legal, until whichever one it was finally said, "Oh hell then, get the license and the preacher but please for sweet please sake shut up." So now she should fear a minister or a j.p. like Satan or the hangman, since to appear before one in the company of someone of the opposite sex would be the same as a death warrant. Which she certainly would not wish for Uncle Gavin, since not only was the Yes to him going to be tender enough to have brought her all the way back to Jefferson to say it, he wouldn't leave enough money to make it worth being his widow in case that Yes wasn't so tender.

No, that's wrong too. If she had to shack up with a man for five years before he would consent to marry her, I mean, with a sculptor so advanced and liberal that even Gavin couldn't recognise what he sculpted, made, he must have been pretty advanced in liberalism. And if he had to quit anything as safe and pleasant as being a Greenwich Village sculptor living with a girl that could afford and wanted to pay the rent and buy the grub whether he married her or not—if he had to quit all this to go to Spain to fight on what anybody could have told him would be the losing side, he must have been advanced even beyond just liberalism. And if she loved him enough to wait five years for him to say All right, dammit, call the parson, and then went to Spain to get blown up herself just to be with him, she must be one of them too since apparently you cant even be moderate about Communism: you either violently are or violently not. (I asked him; I mean of course Uncle Gavin. "Suppose she is," he said. "All right," I said. "So what the hell?" he said. "All right, all right," I said. "What the hell's business is it of yours anyway?" he said. "All right, all right, all right," I said.) And just being blown up wouldn't cure it. So there would be no wedding bells; that other one had been a mere deviation due to her youth, not to happen again; she was only for a moment an enemy of the people, and paid quickly for it.

So there would be no preacher. They were just going to practise Peoples' Democracy, where everybody was equal no matter what you looked like when he finally got your clothes off, right here in Jefferson. So all you had to figure out was, how the bejesus they would manage it in a town no bigger and equal than Jefferson. Or not they: he, Gavin. I mean, it would be his trouble, problem, perhaps need. Not hers. She was free, absolved of mundaneity; who knows, who is not likewise castrate of sound, circumcised from having to hear, of need too. She had the silence: that thunderclap instant to fix her forever inviolate and private in solitude; let the rest of the world blunder in all the loud directions over its own feet trying to find first base at the edge of abyss like one of the old Chaplin films.

He would have to find the ways and means; all she would bring would be the capability for compliance, and what you might call a family precedence. Except that she wasn't her mother, not to mention Gavin not being Manfred de Spain. I mean—I was only thirteen when Mrs Snopes shot herself that night so I still dont know how much I saw and remembered and how much was compelled onto or into me from Uncle Gavin, being, as Ratliff put it, as I had spent the first eleven or twelve years of my existence in the middle of Uncle Gavin, thinking what he thought and seeing what he saw, not because he taught me to but maybe just because he let me, allowed me to. I mean, Linda and Uncle Gavin wouldn't have that one matchless natural advantage which her mother and Manfred de Spain had, which was that aura, nimbus, condi-

tion, whatever the word is, in which Mrs Snopes not just existed, lived, breathed in but created about herself by just existing, living, breathing. I dont know what word I want: an
aura not of license, unchastity, because (this may even be
Ratliff; I dont remember now) little petty moral conditions
like restraint and purity had no more connection with a
woman like Mrs Snopes—or rather, a woman like her had no
more concern with or even attention for them—than conven-
tions about what force you use or when or how or where have
to do with wars or cyclones. I mean, when a community suddenly discovered that it has the sole ownership of Venus for
however long it will last, she cannot, must not be a chaste
wife or even a faithful mistress whether she is or not or really
wants to be or not. That would be not only intolerable, but a
really criminal waste; and for the community so accoladed to
even condone, let alone abet, the chastity, continence, would
be an affront to the donors deserving their godlike vengeance. Like having all miraculous and matchless season—
wind, sun, rain, heat and frost—concentrated into one miraculous instant over the county, then us to try to arrogate to
ourselves the puny right to pick and choose and select instead of every man woman and child that could walk turning
out to cultivate to the utmost every seed the land would hold.
So we—I mean the men and the women both—would not
even ask to escape the anguish and uproar she would cause by
breathing and existing among us and the jealousy we knew
ourselves to be unworthy of, so long as we did have one who
could match and cope with her in fair combat and so be our
champion and pride like the county ownership of the fastest
horse in the country. We would all be on hers and De Spain's
side; we would even engineer and guard the trysts; only the
preachers would hate her because they would be afraid of her
since the god she represented without even trying to, for the
men to pant after and even the women to be proud that at
least one of their sex was its ambassador, was a stronger one
than the pale and desperate Galilean who was all they had to
challenge with.

Because Linda didn't have that quality; that one was not
transferable. So all that remained for her and Gavin was continence. To put it crudely, morality. Because where could they

go. Not to her house because between her and her father, the wrong one was deaf. And not to his because the house he lived in wasn't his but Mother's and one of the earliest (when the time came of course) principles he taught me was that a gentleman does not bring his paramour into the home of: in this order: His wife. His mother. His sister. His mistress. And they couldn't make the coincidental trips to the available places in Memphis or New Orleans or maybe as far away as St Louis and Chicago that (we assumed) her mother and Manfred de Spain used to make, since even police morality, not to mention that of that semi-underworld milieu to which they would have had to resort, would have revolted at the idea of seducing a stone deaf woman from the safety and innocence of her country home town, to such a purpose. So that left only his automobile, concealed desperately and frantically behind a bush—Gavin Stevens, aged fifty, M.A. Harvard, Ph.D. Heidelberg, Ll.B. Mississippi, American Field Service and Y.M.C.A., France, 1915–1918, County Attorney; and Linda Kohl, thirty, widow, wounded in action with the Communist forces in Spain, fumbling and panting in a parked automobile like they were seventeen years old.

Especially when the police found out (I mean if, of course, if somebody came and told them) that she was a communist. Or Jefferson either, for that matter. We had two Finns who had escaped by the skin of their teeth from Russia in 1917 and from Europe in 1919 and in the early twenties wound up in Jefferson; nobody knew why—one the cobbler who had taken over Mr Nightingale's little shop, the other a tinsmith—who were not professed communists nor confessed either since they still spoke too little English by the time Mr Roosevelt's N.R.A. and the labor unions had made 'communist' a dirty word referring mostly to John L. Lewis's C.I.O. In fact, there was no need as they saw it to confess or profess either. They simply took it for granted that there was a proletariat in Jefferson as specific and obvious and recognisable as the day's climate, and as soon as they learned English they would find it and, all being proletarians together, they would all be communists together too as was not only their right and duty but they couldn't help themselves. That was fifteen years ago now, though the big one, the cobbler, the one slower at learning

English, was still puzzled and bewildered, believing it was simply the barrier of language instead of a condition in which the Jefferson proletariat not only declined to know it was the proletariat but even to be content as the middle class, being convinced instead that it was merely in a temporary interim state toward owning in its turn Mr Snopes's bank or Wall-street Snopes's wholesale grocery chain or (who knows?) on the way to the Governor's mansion in Jackson or even the White House in Washington.

The little one, the tinsmith, was quicker than that. Maybe, as distinct from the cobbler's sedentary and more meditative trade, he got around more. Anyway he had learned some time ago that any proletariat he became a member of in Jefferson he would have to manufacture first. So he set about it. The only means he had was to recruit, convert communists, and the only material he had were Negroes. Because among us white male Jeffersons there was one concert of unanimity, no less strong and even louder at the bottom, extending from the operators of Saturday curb-side peanut- and popcorn-vending machines, through the side street and back alley gro-cers, up to the department store owners and automobile and gasoline agencies, against everybody they called communists now—Harry Hopkins, Hugh Johnson and everybody else as-sociated with N.R.A., Eugene Debs, the I.W.W., the C.I.O.— any and everybody who seemed even to question our native-born Jefferson right to buy or raise or dig or find any-thing as cheaply as cajolery or trickery or threat or force could do it, and then sell it as dear as the necessity or ignorance or timidity of the buyer would stand. And that was what Linda had, all she had in our alien capitalist waste this far from home if she really was a communist and Communism really is not just a political ideology but a religion which has to be practised in order to stay alive—two Arctic Circle immigrants: one practically without human language, a troglodyte, the other a little quick-tempered irreconcilable hornet because of whom both of them were already well advanced outside the Jefferson pale, not by being professed communists: nobody would have cared how much of a communist the little one merely professed himself to be so long as he didn't actually interfere with local wage scales, just as they could have been

Republicans so long as they didn't try to interfere with our Democratic town and county elections or Catholics as long as they didn't picket churches or break up prayer meetings, but Negro-lovers: consorters, political affiliators with Negroes. Not social consorters: we would not have put up with that from even them and the little one anyway knew enough Jefferson English to know it. But association of any sort was too much; the local police were already looking crosseyed at them even though we didn't really believe a foreigner could do any actual harm among our own loyal colored.

So, you see, all they—Gavin and Linda—had left now was marriage. Then it was Christmas 1938, the last one before the lights began to go out, and I came home for the holidays and she came to supper one night. Not Christmas dinner. I dont know what happened there: whether Mother and Gavin decided it would be more delicate to ask her and let her decline, or not ask her at all. No, that's wrong. I'll bet Mother invited them both—her and old Snopes too. Because women are marvellous. They stroll perfectly bland and serene through a fact that the men have been bloodying their heads against for years; whereupon you find that the fact not only wasn't important, it wasn't really there. She invited them both, exactly as if she had been doing it whenever she thought of it maybe at least once a month for the last hundred years, whenever she decided to give them a little pleasure by having them to a meal, or whenever she decided it would give her pleasure to have them whether they thought so or not; and Linda declined for both of them in exactly the same way.

So you can imagine that Christmas dinner in that house that nobody I knew had seen the inside of except Mother (oh yes, she would have by now, with Linda home again) and Uncle Gavin: the diningroom—table chairs sideboard cabinets chandeliers and all—looking exactly as it had looked in the Memphis interior decorator's warehouse when he—Snopes—traded in Major de Spain's mother's furniture for it, with him at one end of the table and Linda at the other and the yard man in a white coat serving them—the old fish-blooded son of a bitch who had a vocabulary of two words, one being No and the other Foreclose, and the bride of silence more immaculate in that chastity than ever Caesar's wife

because she was invulnerable too, forever safe, in that chastity
forever pure, that couldn't have heard him if he had had anything to say to her, anymore than he could have heard her
since he wouldn't even recognise the language she spoke in.
The two of them sitting there face to face through the long
excruciating ritual which the day out of all the days compelled; and nobody to know why they did it, suffered it, why
she suffered and endured it, what ritual she served or compulsion expiated—or who knows? what portent she postu-
lated to keep him reminded. Maybe that was why. I mean,
why she came back to Jefferson. Evidently it wasn't to marry
Gavin Stevens. Or at least not yet.

So it would be just an ordinary supper, though Mother
would have said (and unshakably believed) that it was in
honor of me being at home again. And didn't I just say that
women are wonderful? She—Linda: a present from Guess
Who—had a little pad of thin ivory leaves just about big
enough to hold three words at a time, with gold corners, on
little gold rings to turn the pages, with a little gold stylus
thing to match, that you could write on and then efface it
with a handkerchief or a piece of kleenex or, in a mere masculine emergency, a little spit on your thumb and then use it
again (sure, maybe he gave it to her in return for that gold
cigarette lighter engraved GLS when he didn't have L for his
middle initial or in fact any middle initial at all, that she gave
him about five years ago that he never had used because nobody could unconvince him he could taste the fluid through
his cob pipe). And though Mother used the pad like the rest
of us, it was just coincidental, like any other gesture of the
hands while talking. Because she was talking to Linda at the
same time, not even watching her hand but looking at Linda
instead, so that she couldn't have deciphered the marks she
was making even provided she was making marks, just talking
away at Linda exactly as she did to the rest of us. And be
damned if Linda wouldn't seem to understand her, the two of
them chattering and babbling away at one another like
women do, so that maybe no women ever listen to the other
one because they dont have to, they have already communicated before either one begins to speak.

Because at those times Linda would talk. Oh yes, Gavin's

voice lessons had done some good because they must have, there had been too many of them or anyway enough of them, assuming they did spend some of the time together trying to soften down her voice. But it was still the duck's voice: dry, lifeless, dead. That was it: dead. There was no passion, no heat in it; and, what was worse, no hope. I mean, in bed together in the dark and to have more of love and excitement and ecstasy than just one can bear and so you must share it, murmur it, and to have only that dry and lifeless quack to murmur, whisper with. This time (there were other suppers during the next summer but this was the first one when I was at table too) she began to talk about Spain. Not about the war. I mean, the lost war. It was queer. She mentioned it now and then, not as if it had never happened but as if their side hadn't been licked. Some of them like Kohl had been killed and a lot of the others had had the bejesus blown out of the eardrums and arms and legs like her, and the rest of them were scattered (and in no time now would begin to be proscribed and investigated by the F.B.I., not to mention harried and harassed by the amateurs, but we hadn't quite reached that yet) but they hadn't been whipped and hadn't lost anything at all. She was talking about the people in it, the people like Kohl. She told about Ernest Hemingway and Malraux, and about a Russian, a poet that was going to be better than Pushkin only he got himself killed; and Mother scribbling on the pad but not paying any more attention to what she thought she was writing than Linda was, saying,

"Oh, Linda, no!"—you know: how tragic, to be cut off so young, the work unfinished, and Gavin taking the pad away from Mother but already talking too:

"Nonsense. There's no such thing as a mute inglorious Milton. If he had died at the age of two, somebody would still write it for him."

Only I didn't bother with the pad; I doubt if I could have taken it away from them. "Named Bacon or Marlowe," I said.

"Or maybe a good sound synthetic professional name like Shakespeare," Uncle Gavin said.

But Linda hadn't even glanced at the pad. I tell you, she and Mother didn't need it.

"Why?" she said. "What line or paragraph or even page can

you compose and write to match giving your life to say No to people like Hitler and Mussolini?" and Gavin not bothering with the pad either now:

"She's right. She's absolutely right, and thank God for it. Nothing is ever lost. Nothing. Nothing." Except Linda of course. Gavin said how Kohl had been a big man, I dont mean just a hunk of beef, but virile, alive; a man who loved what the old Greeks meant by laughter, who would have been a match for, competent to fulfill, any woman's emotional and physical life too. And Linda was just thirty now and oh yes, the eyes were beautiful, and more than just the eyes; maybe it never mattered to Kohl what was inside her clothes, nor would to anyone else lucky enough to succeed him, including Uncle Gavin. So now I understood at last what I was looking at: neither Mother nor Linda either one needed to look at what Mother thought she was scribbling on that damned ivory slate since evidently from the second day after Linda got home Mother had been as busy and ruthless and undevious as one of the old Victorian head-hunting mamas during the open season at Bath or Tunbridge Wells in Fielding or Dickens or Smollett. Then I found out something else. I remembered how not much more than a year ago we were alone in the office and Ratliff said,

"Look-a-here, what you want to waste all this good weather being jealous of your uncle for? Somebody's bound to marry him sooner or later. Some day you're going to out-grow him and you'll be too busy yourself jest to hang around and protect him. So it might jest as well be Linda." You see what I mean? that evidently it was transferable. I mean, what-ever it was her mother had had. Gavin had seen her once when she was thirteen years old, and look what happened to him. Then Barton Kohl saw her once when she was nineteen years old, and look where he was now. And now I had seen her twice, I mean after I was old enough to know what I was looking at: once at the Memphis airport last summer, and here tonight at the supper table, and now I knew it would have to be me to take Uncle Gavin off to the library or den or wherever such interviews happen, and say:

"Look here, young man. I know how dishonorable your in-tentions are. What I want to know is, how serious they are."

Or if not him, at least somebody. Because it wouldn't be him. Ratliff had told me how Gavin said her doom would be to love once and lose him and then to mourn. Which could have been why she came back to Jefferson: since if all you want is to grieve, it doesn't matter where you are. So she was lost; she had even lost that remaining one who should have married her for no other reason than that he had done more than anybody else while she was a child, to make her into what she was now. But it wouldn't be him; he had his own prognosis to defend, make his own words good no matter who anguished and suffered.

Yes, lost. She had been driving that black country-banker-cum-Baptist-deacon's car ever since she got home; apparently she had assumed at first that she would drive it alone, until old Snopes himself objected because of the deafness. So each afternoon she would be waiting in the car when the bank closed and the two of them would drive around the adjacent country while he could listen for the approaching horns if any. Which—the country drives—was in his character since the county was his domain, his barony—the acres, the farms, the crops—since even where he didn't already hold the mortgage, perhaps already in process of foreclosure even, he could measure and calculate with his eye the ones which so far had escaped him.

That is, except one afternoon a week, usually Wednesday. Old Snopes neither smoked nor drank nor even chewed tobacco; what his jaws worked steadily on was, as Ratliff put it, the same little chunk of Frenchman's Bend air he had brought in his mouth when he moved to Jefferson thirty years ago. Yes, lost: it wasn't even to Uncle Gavin: it was Ratliff she went to that afternoon and said, "I cant find who sells the whiskey now." No, not lost so much, she had just been away too long, explaining to Ratliff why she hadn't gone to Uncle Gavin: "He's the County Attorney; I thought—" and Ratliff patting her on the back right there in the street, saying for anybody to hear it since obviously she couldn't:

"You been away from home too long. Come on. We'll go git him."

So the three of them in Gavin's car drove up to Jakeleg Wattman's so-called fishing camp at Wylie's Crossing so she would know where and how herself next time. Which was to drive up to Jakeleg's little unpainted store (Jakeleg kept it unpainted so that whenever a recurrent new reform-administration sheriff would notify him he had to be raided again, Jakeleg wouldn't have a lot of paint to scratch up in drawing the nails and dismantling the sections and carrying them another mile deeper into the bottom until the reform reached its ebb and he could move back convenient to the paved road and the automobiles) and get out of the car and step inside where the unpainted shelves were crowded with fish-hooks and sinkers and lines and tobacco and flashlight batteries and coffee and canned beans and shotgun shells and the neat row of United States Internal Revenue Department liquor licenses tacked on the wall and Jakeleg in the flopping rubber hip boots he wore winter and summer with a loaded pistol in one of them, behind the chicken-wire barricaded counter, and you would say, "Howdy, Jake. What you got today?" And he would tell you: the same one brand like he didn't care whether you liked that brand or not, and the same one price like he didn't give a damn whether that suited you either. And as soon as you said how many the Negro man (in the flopping hip boots Jakeleg had worn last year) would duck out or down or at least out of sight and reappear with the bottles and stand holding them until you had given Jakeleg the money and got your change (if any) back and Jakeleg would open the wicket in the wire and shove the bottles through and you would return to your car and that was all there was to it; taking (Uncle Gavin) Linda right on in with him, saying as likely as not: "Howdy, Jake. Meet Mrs Kohl. She cant hear but there's nothing wrong with her taste and swallowing." And maybe Linda said,

"What does he have?" and likely what Uncle Gavin wrote on the pad for that was *Thats fighting talk here This is a place where you take it or leave it Just give him eight dollars or sixteen if you want 2.* So next time maybe she came alone. Or maybe Uncle Gavin himself walked into the bank and on to that little room at the back and said, "Look here, you old fish-blooded son of a bitch, are you going to just sit here and let your only female daughter that wont even hear the trump of doom, drive alone up yonder to Jakeleg Wattman's bootleg

joint to buy whiskey?" Or maybe it was simple coincidence: a
Wednesday afternoon and he—Mr Snopes—cant say, "Here,
hold on; where the hell you going? This aint the right road."
Because she cant hear him and in fact I dont know how he
did talk to her since I cant imagine his hand writing anything
except adding a percent. symbol or an expiration date; maybe
they just had a county road map he could point to that
worked up until this time. So now he had not one dilemma
but three: not just the bank president's known recognisable
car driving up to a bootleg joint, but with him in it; then the
dilemma of whether to let every prospective mortgagee in
Yoknapatawpha County hear how he would sit there in the
car and let his only female child walk into a notorious river-
bottom joint to buy whiskey, or go in himself and with his
own Baptist deacon's hand pay out sixteen dollars' worth of
his own life's blood.

Lost. Gavin told me how over a year ago the two Finn
communists had begun to call on her at night (at her invitation of course) and you can imagine this one. It would be the
parlor. Uncle Gavin said she had fixed up a sitting room for
herself upstairs, but this would be in the parlor diagonally
across the hall from the room where old Snopes was supposed
to spend all his life that didn't take place in the bank. The
capitalist parlor and the three of them, the two Finnish immigrant laborers and the banker's daughter, one that couldn't
speak English and another that couldn't hear any language,
trying to communicate through the third one who hadn't yet
learned to spell, talking of hope, millennium, dream: of the
emancipation of man from his tragedy, the liberation at last
and forever from pain and hunger and injustice, of the human
condition. While two doors away in the room where he did
everything but eat and keep the bank's cash money, with his
feet propped on that little unpainted ledge nailed to his Adam
fireplace and chewing steadily at what Ratliff called his little
chunk of Frenchman's Bend air, the capitalist himself who
owned the parlor and the house, the very circumambience
they dreamed in, who had begun life as a nihilist and then
softened into a mere anarchist and now was not only a conservative but a tory too: a pillar, rock-fixed, of things as they
are.

Lost. Shortly after that she began what Jefferson called meddling with the Negroes. Apparently she went without invitation or warning, into the different classrooms of the Negro grammar and high school, who couldn't hear thunder mind you and so all she could do was watch—the faces, expressions, gestures of the pupils and teachers both who were already spooked, perhaps alarmed, anyway startled and alerted to cover, by the sudden presence of the unexplained white woman who was presently talking to the teacher in the quacking duck's-voice of the deaf and then holding out a tablet and pencil for the teacher to answer. Until presently, as quick as the alarmed messenger could find him I suppose, the Principal was there—a college-bred man Uncle Gavin said of intelligence and devotion too—and then she and the Principal and the senior woman teacher were in the Principal's office, where it probably was not so much that she, the white woman, was trying to explain, as that they, the two Negroes, had already divined and maybe understood even if they did not agree with her. Because they, Negroes, when the problems are not from the passions of want and ignorance and fear—gambling, drink—but are of simple humanity, are a gentle and tender people, a little more so than white people because they have had to be; a little wiser in their dealings with white people than white people are with them, because they have had to survive in a minority. As if they already knew that the ignorance and superstition she would have to combat—the ignorance and superstition which would counteract, cancel her dream and, if she remained bullheaded enough in perseverance, would destroy her—would not be in the black race she proposed to raise but in the white one she represented.

So finally the expected happened, anticipated by everyone except her apparently, maybe because of the deafness, the isolation, the solitude of living not enclosed with sound but merely surrounded by gestures. Or maybe she did anticipate it but, having been through a war, she just didn't give a damn. Anyway, she bulled right ahead with her idea. Which was to establish a kind of competitive weekly test, the winners, who would be the top students for that week in each class, to spend the following week in a kind of academy she would establish, with white teachers, details to be settled later

but for temporary they would use her sitting room in her father's house for a sort of general precept, the winners of each
week to be replaced by next week's winners; these to embrace
the whole school from kindergarten to seniors, her theory being that if you were old enough to be taught at eighteen you
were old enough at eight too when learning something new
would be even easier. Because she couldn't hear, you see, not
just the words but the tones, over- and under-tones of alarm,
fright, terror in which the black voice would have to say
Thank you. So it was the Principal himself who finally came to
see Uncle Gavin at the office—the intelligent dedicated man
with his composed and tragic face.

"I've been expecting you," Uncle Gavin said. "I know what
you want to say."

"Thank you," the Principal said. "Then you know yourself
it wont work. That you are not ready for it yet and neither are
we."

"Not many of your race will agree with you," Uncle Gavin
said.

"None of them will," the Principal said. "Just as none of
them agreed when Mr Washington said it."

"Mr Washington?"

"Booker T.," the Principal said. "Mr Carver too."

"Oh," Uncle Gavin said. "Yes?"

"That we have got to make the white people need us first.
In the old days your people did need us, in your economy if
not your culture, to make your cotton and tobacco and in-
digo. But that was the wrong need, bad and evil in itself. So
it couldn't last. It had to go. So now you dont need us. There
is no place for us now in your culture or economy either. We
both buy the same installment-plan automobiles to burn up
the same gasoline in, and the same radios to listen to the same
music and the same ice boxes to keep the same beer in, but
that's all. So we have got to make a place of our own in your
culture and economy too. Not you to make a place for us just
to get us out from under your feet, as in the South here, or
to get our votes for the aggrandisement of your political
perquisites, as in the North, but *us* to make a place for ourselves by compelling you to need us, you cannot do without
us because nobody else but us can fill that place in your econ-

omy and culture which only we can fill and so that place will have to be ours. So that you will not just say Please to us, you will need to say Please to us, you will want to say Please to us. Will you tell her that? Say we thank her and we wont forget this. But to leave us alone. Let us have your friendship all the time, and your help when we need it. But keep your patronage until we ask for it."

"This is not patronage," Uncle Gavin said. "You know that too."

"Yes," the Principal said. "I know that too. I'm sorry. I am ashamed that I . . . ." Then he said: "Just say we thank her and will remember her, but to let us alone."

"How can you say that to someone who will face that much risk, just for justice, just to abolish ignorance?"

"I know," the Principal said. "It's difficult. Maybe we cant get along without your help for a while yet, since I am already asking for it.—Goodday, sir," he said, and was gone. So how could Uncle Gavin tell her either. Or anybody else, everybody else, white and black both. Since it wasn't that she couldn't hear: she wouldn't listen, not even to the unified solidarity of No in the Negro school itself—that massive, not resistance but immobility, like the instinct of the animal to lie perfectly still, not even breathing, not even thinking. Or maybe she did hear that because she reversed without even stopping, from the school, to the board of education itself: if she could not abolish the ignorance by degrees of individual cases, she would attempt it wholesale by putting properly-educated white teachers in the Negro school, asking no help, not even from Gavin, hunting down the school board then, they retreating into simple evaporation, the County Board of Supervisors in their own sacred lair, armed with no petty ivory tablet and gold stylus this time but with a vast pad of yellow foolscap and enough pencils for everybody. Evidently they committed the initial error of letting her in. Then Gavin said it went something like this:

The president, writing: *Assuming for the moment just for argument you understand that we substitute white teachers in the negro school what will become of the negro teachers or perhaps you plan to retire them on pensions yourself*

The duck's voice: "Not exactly. I will send them North to

white schools where they will be accepted and trained as white teachers are."

The pencil: *Still assuming for the sake of argument we have got the negro teachers out where will you find white teachers to fill vacancies left by negroes In Mississippi and how long do you think they will be permitted to fill negro vacancies In Mississippi*

The duck's voice: "I will find them if you will protect them."

The pencil: *Protect them from who Mrs Kohl* Only she didn't need to answer that. Because it had already started: the words *Nigger Lover* scrawled huge in chalk on the sidewalk in front of the mansion the next morning for her father to walk steadily through them in his black banker's hat and his little snap-on bow tie, chewing his steady chunk of Frenchman's Bend air. Sure he saw it. Gavin said nobody could have helped seeing it, that by noon a good deal of the rest of Jefferson had managed to happen to pass by to look at it. But what else—a banker, THE banker—could he do? spit on his handkerchief and get down on his knees and rub it out? And later Linda came out on her way back to the courthouse to badger the rest of the county authorities back behind their locked doors. And maybe, very likely, she really didn't see it. Anyway, it wasn't either of them nor the cook nor the yard man either. It was a neighbor, a woman, who came with a broom and at least obscured it, viciously, angrily, neither to defend Linda's impossible dream nor even in instinctive female confederation with another female, but because she lived on this street. The words could have been the quick short primer-bald words of sex or excrement, as happened now and then even on sidewalks in this part of town, and she would have walked through them too since to pause would have been public admission that a lady knew what they meant. But nobody was going to write *Nigger Lover* nor *-Hater* either, delineate in visible taunting chalk that ancient subterrene atavistic ethnic fear on the sidewalk of the street she (and her husband of course) lived and owned property on.

Until at last the president of the Board of Supervisors crossed the Square to the bank and on to that back room where old Snopes sat with his feet propped on that mantelpiece between foreclosures, and I would have liked to hear that: the outsider coming in and saying, more or less: Cant you for God's sake keep your daughter at home or at least out of the courthouse. In desperation, because what change could he have hoped to get back, she was not only thirty years old and independent and a widow, she was a war veteran too who had actually—Ratliff would say, actively—stood gunfire. Because she didn't stop; it had got now to where the Board of Supervisors didn't dare unlock their door while they were in session even to go home at noon to eat, but instead had sandwiches from the Dixie Café passed in through the back window. Until suddenly you were thinking how suppose she were docile and amenable and would have obeyed him, but it was he, old Snopes, that didn't dare ask, let alone order, her to quit. You didn't know why of course. All you could do was speculate: on just what I.O.U. or mortgage bearing his signature she might have represented out of that past which had finally gained for him that back room in the bank where he could sit down and watch himself grow richer by lending and foreclosing other people's I.O.U.'s.

Because pretty soon he had something more than just that unsigned *Nigger Lover* to have to walk through practically any time he came out his front door. One night (this was while I was in Europe) a crude cross soaked in gasoline blazed suddenly on the lawn in front of the mansion until the cops came and put it out, outraged and seething of course, but helpless; who—the cops—would still have been helpless even if they hadn't been cops. You know: if she had only lived alone, or had been the daughter of a mere doctor or lawyer or even a minister, it would have been one thing, and served them both—her and her old man—right. Instead, she had to be the daughter not just of *a* banker but THE banker, so that what the cross really illuminated was the fact that the organisation which put it there were dopes and saps: if the sole defense and protection of its purity rested in hands which didn't—or what was worse, couldn't—distinguish a banker's front yard, the white race was in one hell of a fix.

Then the next month was Munich. Then Hitler's and Stalin's pact and now when he came out of his house in the morning in his black banker's hat and bow tie and his little cud of Ratliff's Frenchman's Bend air, what he walked through was no longer anonymous and unspecific, the big scrawled letters, the three words covering the sidewalk before the house in their various mutations and combinations:

> KOHL
> COMMUNIST
> JEW
>
> JEW
> KOHL
> COMMUNIST
>
> COMMUNIST
> KOHL
> JEW

and he, the banker, the conservative, the tory who had done more than any other man in Jefferson or Yoknapatawpha County either to repeal time back to 1900 at least, having to walk through them as if they were not there or were in another language and age which he could not be expected to understand, with all Jefferson watching him at least by proxy, to see if his guard would ever drop. Because what else could he do. Because now you knew you had figured right and it actually was *durst not*, with that record of success and victory behind him which already had two deaths in it: not only the suicide which left her motherless, but if he had been another man except the one whose wife would finally have to shoot herself, he might have raised the kind of daughter whose Barton Kohl wouldn't have been a Jewish sculptor with that Spanish war in his horoscope. Then in the very next second you would find you were thinking the exact opposite: that those words on his sidewalk he had to walk through every time he left home were no more portents and threats of wreckage and disaster to him than any other loan he had guessed wrong on would be an irremediable disaster, as long as money itself remained unabolished. That the last thing in the world he was thinking to himself was *This is my cross; I will bear it* because what he was thinking was *All I got to do now is keep folks thinking this is a cross and not a gambit.*

Then Poland. I said, "I'm going now," and Gavin said, "You're too old. They wouldn't possibly take you for flight

training yet," and I said, "Yet?" and he said, "Finish one more
year of law. You dont know what will be happening then, but
it wont be what you're looking at now." So I went back to
Cambridge and he wrote me how the F.B.I. was investigating
her now and he wrote me: *I'm frightened. Not about her. Not
at what they will find out because she would tell them all that
herself if it only occurred to them that the simple thing would be
to come and ask her.* And told me the rest of it: how she had
at last quit beating on the locked door behind which the
Board of Supervisors and the School Board crouched holding
their breath, and now she was merely meeting a class of small
children each Sunday at one of the Negro churches, where
she would read aloud in the dry inflectionless quacking, not
the orthodox biblical stories perhaps but at least the Mesopotamian folklore and the Nordic fairy tales which the
Christian religion has arrogated into its seasonal observances,
safe now since even the white ministers could not go on
record against this paradox. So now there was no more *Jew
Communist Kohl* on the sidewalk and no more *Nigger Lover*
either (you would like to think, from shame) to walk through
in order to be seen daily on the Square: the bride of quietude
and silence striding inviolate in the isolation of unhearing, immune, walking still like she used to walk when she was fourteen and fifteen and sixteen years old: exactly like a young
pointer bitch just about to locate and pin down a covey of
birds.

So that when I got home Christmas I said to Gavin: "Tell
her to tear up that goddamn party card, if she's got one. Go
on. Tell her. She cant help people. They are not worth it.
They dont want to be helped any more than they want advice
or work. They want cake and excitement, both free. Man
stinks. How the hell can she have spent a year in a war
that not only killed her husband and blew the bejesus out of
the inside of her skull, but even at that price the side she was
fighting for still lost, without finding that out? Oh sure, I
know, I know, you and Ratliff both have told me often
enough; if I've heard Ratliff one time I've heard him a hundred: 'Man aint really evil, he jest aint got any sense.' But so
much the more reason, because that leaves him completely
hopeless, completely worthless of anybody's anguish and

effort and trouble." Then I stopped, because he had put his hand on my head. He had to reach up to do it now but he did it exactly as he used to when I was half as tall and only a third as old, gentle and tender and stroking it a little, speaking quiet and gentle too:

"Why dont you tell her?" he said. Because he is a good man, wise too except for the occasions when he would aberrate, go momentarily haywire and take a wrong turn that even I could see was wrong, and then go hell-for-leather, with absolutely no deviation from logic and rationality from there on, until he wound us up in a mess or trouble or embarrassment that even I would have had sense enough to dodge. But he is a good man. Maybe I was wrong sometimes to trust and follow him but I never was wrong to love him.

"I'm sorry," I said.

"Dont be," he said. "Just remember it. Dont ever waste time regretting errors. Just dont forget them."

So I ran Ratliff to earth again. No: I just took advantage of him. It was the regular yearly Christmas-season supper that Ratliff cooked himself at his house and invited Uncle Gavin and me to eat it with him. But this time Gavin had to go to Jackson on some drainage district business so I went alone, to sit in Ratliff's immaculate little kitchen with a cold toddy of old Mr Calvin Bookwright's corn whiskey that Ratliff seemed to have no trouble getting from him, though now, in his old age, with anybody else Mr Cal might sell it to you or give it to you or order you off his place, you never knew which; sipping the cold toddy as Ratliff made them—first the sugar dissolved into a little water, then the whiskey added while the spoon still stirred gently, then rain water from the cistern to fill the glass—while Ratliff in a spotless white apron over one of the neat tieless faded blue shirts which Uncle Gavin said he made himself, cooked the meal, cooking it damned well, not just because he loved to eat it but because he loved the cooking, the blending up to perfection's ultimate moment. Then he removed the apron and we ate it at the kitchen table, with the bottle of claret Uncle Gavin and I always furnished. Then with the coffee and the decanter of whiskey we moved (as always) to the little immaculate room he called his parlor, with the spotlessly waxed melodeon in the corner and the waxed chairs and the fireplace filled with fluted green paper in the summer but with a phony gas-log in the winter, now that progress had reached, whelmed us, and the waxed table in the center of the room on which, on a rack under a glass bell, rested the Allanovna necktie—a rich not-quite-scarlet, not-quite-burgundy ground patterned with tiny yellow sunflowers each with a tiny blue center of almost the exact faded blue of his shirts, that he had brought home from New York that time three or four years ago when he and Gavin went to see Linda married and off to Spain, that I would have cut my tongue out before I would have told him it probably cost whoever (Gavin I suppose) paid for it around seventy-five dollars; until that day when I inadvertently said something to that effect and Ratliff said, "I know how much. I paid it. It was a hundred and fifty dollars." "What?" I said. "A hundred and fifty?" "There was two of them," he said. "I never saw but one," I said. "I doubt if you will," he said. "The other one is a private matter."—and beside it, the piece of sculpture that Barton Kohl had bequeathed him that, if Gavin was still looking for first base, I had already struck out because I didn't even know what it was, let alone what it was doing.

"All it needs is that gold cigarette lighter she gave him," I said. "The Linda Snopes room."

"No," he said. "The Eula Varner room. It ought to have more in it, but maybe this will do. Leastways it's something. When a community is lucky enough to be the community that every thousand years or so has a Eula Varner to pick it out to do her breathing in, the least we can do is for somebody to set up something; a . . . . monument aint quite the word I want."

"Shrine," I said.

"That's it," he said. "A shrine to mark and remember it, for the folks that wasn't that lucky, that was already doomed to be too young . . . ." He stopped. He stood there quite still. Except that you would think of him as being quizzical, maybe speculative, but not bemused. Then I said it:

"You were wrong. They aren't going to."

"What?" he said. "What's that?"

"She's not going to marry Gavin."

"That's right," he said. "It will be worse than that."

Now it was me that said, "What? What did you say?" But he was already himself again, bland, serene, inscrutable.

"But I reckon Lawyer can stand that too," he said.

Ten

G AVIN STEVENS
I could have suggested that, told her to do that, and she would have done it—torn the card up at once, quickly, immediately, with passion and exultation. She was like her mother in one thing at least: needing, fated to need, to find something competent enough, strong enough (in her case, this case, not tough enough because Kohl was tough enough: he happened to be mere flesh and bones and so wasn't durable enough) to take what she had to give; and at the same time doomed to fail, in this, her case, not because Barton failed her but because he also had doom in his horoscope. So if the Communist party, having already proved itself immune to bullets and therefore immortal, had replaced him, not again to bereave her, of course she would have torn her card up, with passion and exultation and joy too. Since what sacrifice can love demand more complete than abasement, abnegation, particularly at the price of what the unknowing materialist world would in its crass insensitive ignorance dub cowardice and shame? I have always had a sneaking notion that that old Christian martyr actually liked, perhaps even loved, his aurochs or his lion.

But I did suggest something else. It was 1940 now. The Nibelung maniac had destroyed Poland and turned back west where Paris, the civilised world's eternal and splendid courtesan, had been sold to him like any whore and only the English national character turned him east again; another year and Lenin's frankenstein would be our ally but too late for her; too late for us too, the western world's peace for the next hundred years, as a tubby little giant of a man in England was already saying in private, but needs must when the devil etcetera.

It began in my office. He was a quiet, neat, almost negative man of no particular age between twenty-five and fifty, as they all appear, who showed me briefly the federal badge (his name was Gihon) and accepted the chair and said Thank you and opened his business quietly and impersonally, as they do, as if they are simply delivering a not-too-important message. Oh yes, I was doubtless the last, the very last on his list since he would have checked thoroughly on or into me without my knowing it as he had days and maybe months ago penetrated and resolved and sifted all there was to be learned about her.

"We know that all she has done, tried to do, has been done quite openly, where everybody would have a chance to hear about it, know about it——"

"I think you can safely say that," I said.

"Yes," he said. "—quite openly. Quite harmless. With the best of intentions, only not very . . . practical. Nothing in fact that a lady wouldn't do, only a little . . . ."

"Screwy," I suggested.

"Thank you. But there you are. I can tell you in confidence that she holds a Communist party card. Naturally you are not aware of that."

Now I said, "Thank you."

"And, once a communist—— I grant you, that's like the old saying (no imputation of course, I'm sure you understand that), Once a prostitute. Which anyone after calm reflection knows to be false. But there you are. This is not a time of calmness and reflection; to ask or expect, let alone hope, for that from the Government and the people too, faced with what we are going to have to meet sooner probably than we realise——"

"Yes," I said. "What do you want me to do? What do you assume I can do?"

"She . . . I understand, have been informed, that you are her earliest and still are her closest friend—"

"No imputation of course," I said. But he didn't say Thank you in his turn. He didn't say anything, anything at all. He just sat there watching me through his glasses, gray, negative as a chameleon, terrifying as the footprint on Crusoe's beach, too negative and neuter in that one frail articulation to bear the terrible mantle he represented. "What you want then is for me to use my influence——"

"—as a patriotic citizen who is intelligent enough to know that we too will be in this war within five years—I set five years as an outside maximum since it took the Germans only three years before to go completely mad and defy us into that

one—with exactly who for our enemy we may not know until it is already too late——"

"—to persuade her to surrender that card quietly to you
and swear whatever binding oath you are authorised to give
her," I said. "Didn't you just say yourself that Once a whore
(with no imputations) always a whore?"

"I quite agree with you," he said. "In this case, not the one
with the imputations."

"Then what do you want of me—her?"

He produced a small notebook and opened it; he even had
the days of the week and the hours: "She and her husband
were in Spain, members of the Loyalist Communist army six
months and twenty-nine days until he was killed in action; she
herself remained, serving as an orderly in the hospital after her
own wound, until the Loyalists evacuated her across the border into France—"

"Which is on record even right here in Jefferson."

"Yes," he said. "Before that she lived for seven years in
New York city as the common law wife—"

"—which of course damns her not only in Jefferson,
Mississippi, but in Washington too." But he had not even
paused.

"—of a known registered member of the Communist party,
and the close associate of other known members of the
Communist party, which may not be in your Jefferson
records."

"Yes," I said. "And then?"

He closed the notebook and put it back inside his coat and
sat looking at me again, quite cold, quite impersonal, as if the
space between us were the lens of a microscope. "So she knew
people, not only in Spain but in the United States too,
people who so far are not even in our records—Communist
members and agents, important people, who are not as
noticeable as Jewish sculptors and Columbia professors and
other such intelligent amateurs——" Because that was when I
finally understood.

"I see," I said. "You offer a swap. You will trade her immunity for names. Your bureau will whitewash her from an
enemy into a simple stool-pigeon. Have you a warrant of any
sort?"

"No," he said. I got up.

"Then good-day, sir." But he didn't move yet.

"You wont suggest it to her?"

"I will not," I said.

"Your country is in danger, perhaps in jeopardy."

"Not from her," I said. Then he rose too and took his hat from the desk.

"I hope you wont regret this, Mr Stevens."

"Good-day, sir," I said.

Or that is, I wrote it. Because it was three years now and she had tried, really tried to learn lip-reading. But I dont know. Maybe to live outside human sound is to live outside human time too, and she didn't have time to learn, to bother to learn. But again I dont know. Maybe it didn't take even three years of freedom, immunity from it to learn that perhaps the entire dilemma of man's condition is because of the ceaseless gabble with which he has surrounded himself, enclosed himself, insulated himself from the penalties of his own folly, which otherwise—the penalties, the simple red ink— might have enabled him by now to have made his condition solvent, workable, successful. So I wrote it:

Leave here   Go away

"You mean, move?" she said. "Find a place of my own? an apartment or a house?"

I mean leave Jefferson I wrote. *Go completely away for good Give me that damn card & leave Jefferson*

"You said that to me before."

"No I didn't," I said. I even spoke it, already writing, already planning out the whole paragraph it would take: *We've never even mentioned that card or the Communist party either. Even back there three years ago when you first tried to tell me you had one and show it to me and I wouldn't let you, stopped you, refused to listen: dont you remember?* But she was already talking again:

"I mean back there when I was fifteen or sixteen and you said I must get away from Jefferson."

So I didn't even write the other; I wrote *But you couldnt then   Now you can   Give me the card & go* She stood quietly for a moment, a time. We didn't even try to use the ivory tablet on occasions of moment and crisis like this. It was a bijou, a gewgaw, a bangle, feminine; really almost useless: thin ivory sheets bound with gold and ringed together with more of it, each sheet about the size of a playing card so that it wouldn't really contain more than about three words at a time, like an anagram, an acrostic at the level of children—a puzzle say or maybe a continued story ravished from a primer. Instead, we were in her upstairs sitting room she had fitted up, standing at the mantel which she had designed at the exact right height and width to support a foolscap pad when we had something to discuss that there must be no mistake about or something which wasn't worth not being explicit about, like money, so that she could read the words as my hand formed them, like speech, almost like hearing.

"Go where?" she said. "Where could I go?"

Anywhere   New York   Back to Europe of course but in New York some of the people still you & Barton knew the friends your own age She looked at me. With the pupils expanded like this, her eyes looked almost black; blind too.

"I'm afraid," she said.

I spoke; she could read single words if they were slow: "You? Afraid?" She said:

"Yes. I dont want to be helpless. I wont be helpless. I wont have to depend."

I thought fast, like that second you have to raise or draw or throw in your hand, while each fraction of the second effaces another pip from your hole card. I wrote quite steadily while she watched: *Then why am I here* and drew my hand back so she could read it. Then she said, in that dry, lifeless, what Chick calls duck's quack:

"Gavin." I didn't move. She said it again: "Gavin." I didn't move. She said: "All right. I lied. Not the depend part. I wont depend. I just must be where you are." She didn't even add *Because you're all I have now.* She just stood, our eyes almost level, looking at me out of, across, something—abyss, darkness; not abject, not questioning, not even hoping; in a moment I would know it; saying again in the quacking voice: "Gavin."

I wrote rapidly, in three- or four-word bursts, gaggles, clumps, whatever you want to call them, so she could read as I wrote: *Its all right dont Be afraid I Refuse to marry you*

20 years too much Difference for it To work besides I Dont want to

"Gavin," she said.

I wrote again, ripping the yellow sheets off the pad and shoving them aside on the mantel: *I dont want to*

"I love you," she said. "Even when I have to tell a lie, you have already invented it for me."

I wrote: *No lie nobody Mentioned Barton Kohl*

"Yes," she said.

I wrote *No*

"But you can me," she said. That's right. She used the explicit word, speaking the hard brutal guttural in the quacking duck's voice. That had been our problem as soon as we undertook the voice lessons: the tone, to soften the voice which she herself couldn't hear. "It's exactly backward," she told me. "When you say I'm whispering, it feels like thunder inside my head. But when I say it this way, I cant even feel it." And this time it would be almost a shout. Which is the way it was now, since she probably believed she had lowered her voice, I standing there while what seemed to me like reverberations of thunder died away.

"You're blushing," she said.

I wrote: *that word*

"What word?"

that you just said

"Tell me another one to use. Write it down so I can see it and remember it."

I wrote: *There is no other thats the right one only one I am old fashioned it still shocks me a little No what shocks is when a woman uses it & is not shocked at all until she realises I am* Then I wrote: *thats wrong too what shocks is that all that magic passion excitement be summed up & dismissed in that one bald unlovely sound*

"All right," she said. "Dont use any word then."

I wrote: *Do you mean you want to*

"Of course you can," she said. "Always. You know that."

I wrote *Thats not what I asked you* She read it. Then she didn't move. I wrote *Look at me* She did so, looking at me from out or across what it was that I would recognise in a moment now.

"Yes," she said.

I wrote *Didnt I just tell you you dont ever have to be afraid* and this time I had to move the pad slightly to draw her attention to it, until she said, not looking up:

"I dont have to go away either?"

I wrote *No* under her eyes this time, then she looked up, at me, and I knew what it was she looked out of or across: the immeasurable loss, the appeaseless grief, the fidelity and the enduring, the dry quacking voice saying, "Gavin. Gavin. Gavin." while I wrote:

because were the 2 in all the world who can love each other without having to the end of it tailing off in a sort of violent rubric as she clasped me, clinging to me, quite hard, the dry clapping voice saying,

"Gavin. Gavin. I love you. I love you," so that I had to break free to reach the pad and write

Give me the card

She stared down at it, her hands arrested in the act of leaving my shoulders. "Card?" she said. Then she said, "I've lost it."

Then I knew: a flash, like lightning. I wrote *your father* even while I was saying out loud: "Oh the son of a bitch, the son of a bitch," saying to myself, *Wait. Wait! He had to. Put yourself in his place. What else could he do, what other weapon did he have to defend his very existence before she destroyed it— the position he had sacrificed everything for—wife home friends peace—to gain the only prize he knew since it was the only one he could understand since the world itself as he understood it as- sured him that was what he wanted because that was the only thing worth having.* Of course: his only possible weapon: gain possession of the card, hold the threat of turning it in to the F.B.I. over her and stop her before she destroyed him. Yet all this time I was telling myself *You know better. He will use it to destroy her. It was he himself probably who scrawled Jew Communist Kohl on his own sidewalk at midnight to bank a re- serve of Jefferson sympathy against the day when he would be compelled to commit his only child to the insane asylum.* I wrote:

Ransacked your room drawers desk

"Somebody did," she said. "It was last year. I thought—" I wrote:

It was your father

"Was it?" Yes, it was exactly that tone. I wrote:

Dont you know it was

"Does it matter? They will send me another one I suppose. But that doesn't matter either. I haven't changed. I dont have to have a little printed card to show it."

This time I wrote slowly and carefully: *You dont have to go I wont ask anymore but when I do ask you again to go will you just believe me & go at once I will make all plans will you do that*

"Yes," she said.

I wrote *Swear*

"Yes," she said. "Then you can marry." I couldn't have written anyway; she had caught up both my hands, holding them between hers against her chest. "You must. I want you to. You mustn't miss that. Nobody must never have had that once. Nobody. Nobody." She was looking at me. "That word you didn't like. My mother said that to you once too, didn't she." It wasn't even a question. "Did you?"

I freed my hands and wrote *You know we didnt*

"Why didn't you?"

I wrote *Because she felt sorry for me when you do things for people just because you feel sorry for them what you do is probably not very important to you*

"I dont feel sorry for you. You know that. Dont you know it will be important to me?"

I wrote *Then maybe was because I wasnt worthy of her & we both knew it but I thought if we didnt maybe she might always think maybe I might have been* and ripped the sheet off and crumpled it into my pocket and wrote *I must go now*

"Dont go," she said. Then she said, "Yes, go. You see, I'm all right now, I'm not even afraid anymore."

I wrote *why should you ever have been* then on the same sheet *My hat* and she went and got it while I gathered up the rest of the used sheets into my pocket and took the hat and went toward the door, the quacking voice saying "Gavin" until I turned. "How did we say it? the only two people in the world that love each other and dont have to? I love you, Gavin," in that voice, tone which to her was whispering, murmuring perhaps but to anyone tragic enough to still have ears was as penetrating and shocking almost as an old-time klaxon automobile horn.

And out, fast and quick out of his house, his mansion, his palace, on to his bank fast and quick too, right on back into that little room and bump, nudge, startle the propped feet off the fireplace, my hand already out: "I will now take that card, if you please." Except that would be wantonly throwing away an opportunity, a gift actually; why let him pick his moment to surrender, produce the evidence on his side, to the F.B.I.? Why not strike first, sic the F.B.I. on him before he could, as Ratliff would say, snatch back: that mild neutral gray man flashing that badge on him, saying, "We have it on authority, Mr Snopes, that you have a Communist party card in your possession. Do you care to make a statement?"

But I didn't know where Gihon would be now and, his declared enemy, he wouldn't believe me. So the F.B.I. as represented by him was out; I would have to go straight to that vast Omnipotence called Govment; the stool-pigeoning itself must be unimpeachable; it must stem from the milieu and hold rigidly to the vernacular. A postcard of course, a penny postcard. I thought first of addressing it to the President of the United States but with the similar nut mail Mr Roosevelt was probably already getting, mine would be drowned in that flood. Which left the simple military. But although the military never looses any piece of paper once it has been written on and signed (anything else yes, it will abandon or give away or destroy, but a piece of signed paper never, though it have to subsidise and uniform a thousand people to do nothing else but guard it), that it would inevitably reappear someday even if it took a hundred years, that would be too long also. Whereupon I suddenly overheard myself asking, What's wrong with your first idea of the F.B.I.? to which the only answer was, Nothing. So I could even see the completed card. The vernacular was an informed one, it knew there were two Hoovers: one a carpet sweeper and the other had been President, and that the head of the F.B.I. was said to be named Hoover. So I could see it:

Herbert Hoover
F.B.I. Department

then paused, because not Washington; this vernacular was not only knowledgeable but consistent too so I thought first of Parchman, Mississippi, the State Penitentiary, except that the mail clerk there would probably be a trusty possibly in for life so what would a span of time computable in mere days, especially in regard to a piece of mail, be to him? and again it would be lost. Then I had the answer: Jackson, the Capital. It would be perfect: not really a big city, so that the agents there would be just bored and idle enough to leap at this opportunity; besides not being far. So that's what it would be:

> *Herbert Hoover*
> *F B & I Depment*
> *Jackson Miss*
> *If you will come up to Jefferson Miss and serch*
> *warant the bank and home of Flem Snopes you will*
> *fined a commonist party Card*
>   *Patrotic Citizen*

whereupon you will object that 'search warrant' is a little outside this writer's vernacular and that the spelling of 'find' is really going a little too far. Whereupon I rebut you that this writer knows exactly what he is talking about; that 'search warrant' and 'fined' are the two words of them all which he would never make any mistake regarding, no matter how he might spell them: the one being constantly imminent in his (by his belief, in yours too) daily future and the other or its synonym 'jailed' being its constant coadjutant.

If I only dared. You see? even if I burgled his house or bank vault and found the card and erased her name and substituted his to pass their gimlet muster, she herself would be the first to leap, spring, deny, refute, claim and affirm it for her own; she would probably have gone to Gihon or any else available before this and declared her convictions if it had occurred to her they might be interested. Whereupon, from then until even the stronger alliance of cosmic madmen had finally exhausted themselves into peace and oblivion, she would be harried and harassed and spied upon day and night, waking and eating and sleeping too. So finally I had to fall back, not on her innocent notion that it wasn't important, really wouldn't matter anyway, but on my own more evil or—and/or—legal conviction that it was his only weapon of defense and he wouldn't use it until he was frightened into it.

Or hope perhaps. Anyway, that's how it stood until in fact the Battle of Britain saved her; otherwise all that remained was simply to go to him and say, "I want that card," which would be like walking up to a stranger and saying Did you steal my wallet. So the Battle of Britain saved her, him too for a time. I mean, the reports, stories now coming back to us of the handful of children fighting it. Because during the rest of that spring and summer and fall of 1940 she was getting more and more restless. Oh, she was still doing her Negro Sunday school classes, still "meddling" as the town called it, but after a fashion condoned now, perhaps by familiarity and also that no one had discovered yet any way to stop her.

This, until June when Chick came home from Cambridge. Whereupon I suddenly realised—discovered—two things: that it was apparently Chick now who was our family's representative in her social pattern; and that she knew more than even he of the R.A.F. names and the machines they flew: Malan and Aitken and Finucane and Spitfire and Beaufighter and Hurricane and Mosquito and Buerling and Deere and the foreigners too like the Americans who wouldn't wait and the Poles and Frenchmen who declined to be whipped: Daymond and Wzlewski and Clostermann; until that September, when we compromised: Chick agreed to take one more year of law and we agreed to let it be the University over at Oxford instead of Cambridge. Which was perhaps the reason: when he left, she no longer had anyone to swap the names with. So I should not have been surprised when she came to the office. Nor did she say I must do something to help, I've got to do something, I cant just sit here idle; she said:

"I'm going away. I've got a job, in a factory in California where they make aircraft to be sent to England and Russia," and I scribbling, scrawling *Wait.* "It's all right," she said. "It's all settled. I wrote them that I couldn't hear but that I was familiar enough with truck engines and gears to learn what they needed. And they said for me to come on out, just bring a few papers with me. You know: letters saying you have known me long enough to assure them she is moral and doesn't get too tight and nobody has caught her stealing yet. That's what you are to do because you can even sign them Chairman of the Yoknapatawpha County, Mississippi Draft Board," and I still scrawling Wait, or no, not writing it again because I already had: just gripping her with one hand and holding the pad up with the other until she read it and stopped or stopped long enough to read it or at least hushed and I could write:

at this factory all factories an individual of limitless power called Security whose job position is the 1 thing on earth between him & being drafted into the and ripped that sheet off, already writing again, her hand, her arm across my shoulder so I could feel her breathing and feel smell her hair against my cheek: *army which naturally he will defend with his life by producing not too far apart provable subversives so that sooner or later he will reach you & fire you you re* and ripped that one off, not stopping: *member the Mississippi coast Biloxi Ocean Springs you were there*

"Yes. With Mother and" and now I thought she would stop but she didn't even pause: "Manfred. I remember."

I wrote *Pascagoula a shipyard where they are building ships to carry airplanes guns tanks to help Russia if California will take you so will they will you go there*

"Yes," she said. She said, "Russia." She drew a long breath. "But the Security will be there too."

I wrote *yes but thats close I could come there quick & even if Security I could probably find you something else*

"Yes," she said, breathing quiet and slow at my shoulder. "Close. I could come home on week-ends."

I wrote *you might have to work weekends they need ships*

"Then you can come there. The draft board is closed on week-ends, isn't it?"

I wrote *well see*

"But together some times now and then. That's why I was afraid about California, because it's so far. But Pascagoula is close. At least occasionally now and then."

I wrote *Of course*

"All right," she said. "Of course I'll go."

Which she did, right after New Year's, 1941 now. I knew a lawyer there so she had a small apartment with its own entrance in a private home. And apparently her belief was that, once she was free of Jefferson, at least twelve hours away from interdiction by Snopes or me or either or both, nobody could challenge her intention to buy a small car and run it herself, until I threatened to tell the Pascagoula police myself that she was deaf the first time I heard about it. So she agreed to refrain and my lawyer friend arranged for her in a car pool and presently she was at work as a tool-checker, though almost at once she wrote that she had almost got them to agree to let her become a riveter, where the deafness would be an actual advantage. Anyway, she could wear overalls again, once more minuscule in that masculine or rather sexless world engaged, trying to cope with the lethal mechanical monstrosities which war has become now, and perhaps she was even at peace again, if peace is possible to anyone. Anyway, at first there were the letters saying *When you come we will* and then *If you come dont forget* and then several weeks and just a penny postcard saying *I miss you* and nothing more—that almost inarticulate paucity of the picture cards saying *Wish you were here* or *This is our room* which the semi-literate send back, until the last one, a letter again. I mean, in an envelope: *It's all right. I understand. I know how busy the draft board has to be. Just come when you can because I have something to ask you.* To which I answered at once, immediately (I was about to add, Because I dont know what I thought. Only I know exactly what I thought) *Ask me or tell me?* so that I already knew beforehand what her answer would be: *Yes. Ask you.*

So (it was summer again now) I telegraphed a date and she answered *Have booked room will meet what train love* and I answered that (who had refused to let her own one) *Coming by car will pick you up at shipyard Tuesday quitting time love* and I was there. She came out with the shift she belonged in, in the overall, already handing me the tablet and stylus before she kissed me, clinging to me, hard, saying, "Tell me everything," until I could free myself to write, restricted again to the three- or four-word bursts and gaggles before having to erase:

You tell me what It is

"Let's go to the beach." And I:

You dont want to Go home first & Change

"No. Let's go to the beach." We did. I parked the car and

it seemed to me I had already written *Now tell me* but she was already out of the car, already waiting for me, to take the tablet and stylus from me and thrust them into her pocket, then took my near arm in both her hands, we walking so, she clinging with both hands to my arm so that we would bump and stagger every few steps, the sun just setting and our one shadow long along the tide-edge before us and I thinking *No no, that cant be it,* when she said "Wait" and released me, digging into the other overall pocket from the tablet. "I've got something for you. I almost forgot it." It was a shell; we had probably trodden on a million of them since we left the car two hundred yards back, I still thinking *It cant be that. That cant be so.* "I found it the first day. I was afraid I might lose it before you got here, but I didn't. Do you like it?"

"It's beautiful," I said.

"What?" she said, already handing me the tablet and stylus. I wrote:

Damn fine now Tell me

"Yes," she said. She clung, gripping my arm hard and strong in both hands again, we walking again and I thinking *Why not why shouldn't it be so, why should there not be somewhere in the world at least one more Barton Kohl or at least a fair substitute, something to do, at least something a little better than grief,* when she said "Now" and stopped and turned us until we faced the moment's pause before the final plunge of the sun, the tall and ragged palms and pines fixed by that already fading explosion until the night breeze would toss and thresh them. Then it passed. Now it was just sunset. "There," she said. "It's all right now. We were here. We saved it. Used it. I mean, for the earth to have come all this long way from the beginning of the earth, and the sun to have come all this long way from the beginning of time, for this one day and minute and second out of all the days and minutes and seconds, and nobody to use it, no two people who are finally together at last after all the difficulties and waiting, and now they are together at last and are desperate because of all the long waiting, they are even running along the beach toward where the place is, not far now, where they will finally be alone together at last and nobody in the world to know or care or interfere so that it's like the world itself wasn't except you so now the world that wasn't even invented yet can begin." And I thinking *Maybe it's the fidelity and the enduring which must be so at least once in your lifetime, no matter who suffers. That you have heard of love and loss and grief and fidelity and enduring and you have seen love and loss and maybe you have even seen love and loss and grief but not all five of them—or four of them since the fidelity and enduring I am speaking of were inextricable: one*—this, even while she was saying, "I dont mean just—" and stopped herself before I could have raised the hand to clap to on her lips—if I had been going to, saying: "It's all right, I haven't forgotten; I'm not going to say that one anymore." She looked at me. "So maybe you already know what I'm going to ask you."

"Yes," I said; she could read that. I wrote *marriage*

"How did you know?"

What does it Matter I wrote. *Im glad*

"I love you," she said. "Let's go eat. Then we will go home and I can tell you."

I wrote *Not home first To change*

"No," she said. "I wont need to change where we're going."

She didn't. Among the other female customers, she could have worn anything beyond an ear trumpet and a G string, and even then probably the ear trumpet would have drawn the attention. It was a joint. By midnight on Saturday (possibly any other night in such boom ship-building times) it would be bedlam, jumping as they say; with the radio going full blast, it already was to me. But then, I was not deaf. But the food—the flounder and shrimp—was first rate and the waitress produced glasses and ice to match the flask I had brought; and with all the other uproar her voice was not so noticeable. Because she used it, as if by premeditation about things I would need only Yes and No for, babbling actually, about the shipyard, the work, the other people, sounding almost like a little girl home on her first holiday from school, eating rapidly too, not chewing it enough, until we had done and she said, "We can go now."

She hadn't told me yet where I was to stay, nor did I know where her place was either. So when we were in the car again I snapped on the dash light so she could see the tablet and

wrote *Where*. "That way," she said. It was back toward the
center of town and I drove on until she said, "Turn here" and
I did; presently she said, "There it is," so that I had to pull in
to the curb to use the tablet:

Which is

"The hotel," she said. "Right yonder." I wrote:

*We want to talk Havent you got a Sitting room your place
Quiet & private*

"We're going to both stay there tonight. It's all arranged.
Our rooms are next door with just the wall between and I
had both beds moved against it so after we talk and are in bed
any time during the night I can knock on the wall and you
can hear it and if I hold my hand against the wall I can feel
you answer.—I know, I wont knock loud enough to disturb
anybody, for anybody to hear it except you."

The hotel had its own parking lot. I took my bag and we
went in. The proprietor knew her, perhaps by this time everybody in the town knew or knew of the young deaf woman
working in the shipyard. Anyway, nobody stopped us, he
called her by name and she introduced me and he gave me
the two keys and still nobody stopped us, on to her door and
I unlocked it, her overnight bag was already in the room and
there were flowers in a vase too and she said, "Now I can
have a bath. Then I will knock on the wall," and I said,

"Yes," since she could read that and went to my room; yes,
why should there have to be fidelity and enduring too just because you imagined them? If mankind matched his dreams
too, where would his dreams be? Until presently she knocked
on the wall and I went out one door, five steps, into the other
one and closed it behind me. She was in bed, propped on
both pillows, in a loose jacket or robe, her hair (evidently she
had cut it short while she was driving the ambulance but now
it was long enough again to bind in a ribbon dark blue like
her eyes) brushed or dressed for the night, the tablet and stylus in one hand on her lap, the other hand patting the bed beside her for me to sit down.

"You wont really need this," she said, raising the tablet
slightly then lowering it again, "since all you'll need is just to
say Yes and I can hear that. Besides, since you already know
what it is, it will be easy to talk about. And maybe if I tell you

I want you to do it for me, it will be even easier for you to do. So I do say that. I want you to do it for me." I took the tablet:

Of course I will Do what

"Do you remember back there at the beach when the sun finally went down and there was nothing except the sunset and the pines and the sand and the ocean and you and me and I said how that shouldn't be wasted after all that waiting and distance, there should be two people out of all the world desperate and anguished for one another to deserve not to waste it any longer and suddenly they were hurrying, running toward the place at last not far now, almost here now and no more the desperation and the anguish no more, no more—" when suddenly, as I watched, right under the weight of my eyes you might say, her face sprang and ran with tears, though I had never seen her cry before and apparently she herself didn't even know it was happening. I wrote:

Stop it

"Stop what?" And I:

youre crying

"No I'm not." And I:

look at your Face

There was the customary, the standard, hand-glass and box of kleenex on the table but instead I took my handkerchief and held it out. But instead she simply set the heels of her palms to her face, smearing the moisture downward and outward like you do sweat, even snapping, flicking the moisture away at the end of the movement as you do sweat.

"Dont be afraid," she said. "I'm not going to say that word. Because I dont even mean that. That's not important, like breathing's not important as long as you dont even have to think about it but just do it when it's necessary. It's important only when it becomes a question or a problem or an issue, like breathing's important only when it becomes a question or a problem of whether or not you can draw another one. It's the rest of it, the little things: it's this pillow still holding the shape of the head, this necktie still holding the shape of the throat that took it off last night even just hanging empty on a bedpost, even the empty shoes on the floor still sit with the right one turned out a little like his feet were still in them and even still walking the way he walked, stepping a little higher with one foot than the other like the old-time Negroes say a proud man walks——" And I:

stop it stop It youre crying Again

"I cant feel it. I cant feel anything on my face since that day, not heat nor cold nor rain nor water nor wind nor anything." This time she took the handkerchief and used it but when I handed her the mirror and even started to write *wheres your compact* she didn't even take the mirror. "I'll be careful now.—So that's what I want you to have too. I love you. If it hadn't been for you, I probably wouldn't have got this far. But I'm all right now. So I want you to have that too. I want you to do it for me." And I:

But what for you You never have Told me yet

"Marry," she said. "I thought you knew. Didn't you tell me you knew what it was?" And I:

Me marry You mean me

"Who did you think I meant? Did you think I was—— Gavin."

"No," I said.

"I read that. You said No. You're lying. You thought I meant me."

"No," I said.

"Do you remember that time when I told you that any time you believed you had to lie for my sake, I could always count on you sticking to it, no matter how bad you were disproved?"

"Yes," I said.

"So that's settled, then," she said. "No, I mean you. That's what I want you to do for me. I want you to marry. I want you to have that too. Because then it will be all right. We can always be together no matter how far apart either one of us happens to be or has to be. How did you say it? the two people in all the earth out of all the world that can love each other not only without having to but we dont even have to not say that word you dont like to hear? Will you promise?"

"Yes," I said.

"I know you cant just step outdoors tomorrow and find her. It may take a year or two. But all you've got to do is just stop resisting the idea of being married. Once you do that it's all right because the rest of it will happen. Will you do that?"

"I swear," I said.

"Why, you said Swear, didn't you?"

"Yes," I said.

"Then kiss me." I did so, her arms quite hard, quite strong around my neck; a moment, then gone. "And early tomorrow morning, go back home." And I, writing:

I was going to Stay all day

"No. Tomorrow. Early. I'll put my hand on the wall and when you're in bed knock on it and if I wake up in the night I can knock and if you're awake or still there you can knock back and if I dont feel you knock you can write me from Jefferson tomorrow or the next day. Because I'm all right now. Good night, Gavin."

"Good night, Linda," I said.

"I read that too. I love you."

"I love you," I said.

"I read that too but write it on the tablet anyway and I can have that for a—what do you call it?—eye-opener in the morning."

"Yes," I said, extending my hand for the tablet.

Eleven

CHARLES MALLISON
This time, I was in uniform. So now all I need is to decide, find out, what this-time I mean or time for what I mean. It wasn't the next time I saw Linda, because she was still in Pascagoula building ships for Russia too now. And it wasn't the next time I was in Jefferson, because I passed through home en route to the brown suit. So maybe I mean the next time I ran Ratliff to earth. Though maybe what I really mean is that the next time I saw Uncle Gavin after his marriage, he was a husband.

Because it was 1942 and Gavin was married now, to Melisandre Harriss (Backus that was as Thackeray said); that pitcher had went to that well jest that one time too many, as Ratliff said, provided of course he had said it. One Sunday morning there was Pearl Harbor and I wired Gavin by return mail you might say from Oxford *This is it am gone now.* I wired Gavin because otherwise I would have had to talk to Mother on the telephone and on long distance Mother ran into money, so by wiring Gavin for forty-two cents the telephone call from Mother would be on Father's bill in Jefferson.

So I was at home in time to be actually present at the first innocent crumblings of what he had obviously assumed to be his impregnable bastions; to 'stand up' with him, be groomsman to his disaster. It happened like this. I was unable to get into the government flight-training program course at the University but they told me that anybody with a college degree and any number of hours from one up of flying time, especially solo, would have about as good a chance of going straight into military training for a commission. So there was a professional crop-duster operating from the same field and he took me on as a student, on even bigger aircraft, one of (he claimed) the actual type of army primary training, than the little fifty h.p. popguns the official course used.

So when I sent Uncle Gavin the wire I had around fifteen logged hours, three of which were solo, and when Mother rang my telephone I was already packed up and the car already pointed toward Jefferson. So I was there to see the beginning of it whether Gavin recognised it as banns or not. I mean the Long Island horse farm that Miss Melisandre Harriss Backus that was used to bring the two children (they were grown now; Gavin was marrying not step-children but in-laws) back home to now and then from Europe until the Germans began to blow up Americans in actual sight of the Irish coast. So after that it had to be South America, this last time bringing the Argentine steeple-chasing cavalry officer that that maniac boy of the two Harriss children (I dont mean that both Aunt Melisandre's children were maniacs but that only one of them was a boy) believed was trying to marry the money his mother was still trustee of instead of just his sister who just had an allowance like him. So he (the maniac of course) set out to murder the Argentine steeple-chaser with that wild stallion of Rafe McCallum's that he (the maniac) bought or tricked or anyway got inside that stall where the innocent Argentine would have walked up in the dark and opened the door on what he (the innocent Argentine) thought was going to be not only a gentle horse but a partly blind one too. Except that Gavin read his tea-leaves or used his second sight or divining rod or whatever it was he did in cases like this, and got hold of Rafe in time to reach the stall door first and stop him.

So the Argentine was saved, and that night the maniac took his choice between the army recruiting station in Memphis, and Uncle Gavin, and chose the army so he was safe, and that afternoon the Argentine and the maniac's sister were married and left Jefferson and they were safe. But Uncle Gavin remained, and the next day I had to go on to ground school, pre-flight, so when I got home next time I was in uniform and Gavin was not only a husband but father too of a step-son who would have been as neat a by-standing murderer as you could hope to see except for a stroke of arrant meddling which to a dog shouldn't happen, and a step-daughter married to an Argentine steeple-chasing son-in-law. (By which time I was married too, to a bomb-sight—I hadn't made pilot but at least I would be riding up front—allotted to me by a government which didn't trust me with it and so set spies to watch what I did with it, which before entrusting it to me had trained me not to trust my spies nor anybody else respecting it, in a locked black case which stayed locked by a chain to me even while I was asleep—a condition of constant discomfort of course but mainly of unflagging mutual suspicion and mutual distrust and in time mutual hatred which you even come to endure, which is probably the best of all training for successful matrimony.)

So when I saw Jefferson next I was in uniform, long enough to call on the squire and his dame among his new ancestral white fences and electric-lit stables and say Bless you my children and then run Ratliff once more to earth.

"He cant marry her now," I said. "He's already got a wife."

And you never thought of soberly in connection with Ratliff either. Anyway, not before now, not until this time. "That's right," he said. "She aint going to marry him. It's going to be worse than that."

FLEM

Twelve

WHEN the pickup truck giving him the ride onward from
Clarksdale turned off at a town called Lake Cormorant
and he had to get out, he had to walk. And he was apparently
still nowhere near Memphis. He was realising now that this
was the biggest, in a way terrifying, thing that had happened
to him in the thirty-eight years: he had forgotten distance. He
had forgot how far one place could be from another. And
now he was going to have to eat too. Because all he had was
the ten dollar bill they had given him along with the new
overalls and hat and shoes at the Parchman gate, plus the
three dollars and eighty-five cents still left out of the forty
dollars his cousin Flem—it must have been Flem; after he finally realised that Flem wasn't going to come or even send in
from Frenchman's Bend to help him and he quit calling down
from the jail window to anybody passing that would send
word out to Flem, nobody else but Flem and maybe the
judge knew or even bothered to care what became of him,
where he was—had sent him back there eighteen years ago
just before Flem sent Montgomery Ward to trick him into
trying to escape in that woman's wrapper and sunbonnet and
he got caught of course and they gave him the other twenty
years.

It was a small tight neatly-cluttered store plastered with
placards behind a gasoline pump beside the highway; a battered dust- and mud-stained car was parked beside it and inside were only the proprietor and a young Negro man in the
remnants of an army uniform. He asked for a loaf of bread and
suddenly he remembered sardines, the taste of them from almost forty years ago; he could afford another nickel one time,
when to his shock and for the moment unbelief, possibly in his
own hearing, he learned that the tin would now cost him
twenty-six cents—the small flat solid-feeling tin ubiquitous
for five cents through all his previous days until Parchman
—and even while he stood in that incredulous shock the

proprietor set another small tin before him, saying, "You can have this one for eleven."

"What is it?" he said.

"Lunch meat," the proprietor said.

"What is lunch meat?" he said.

"Dont ask," the proprietor said. "Just eat it. What else can you buy with eleven cents?"

Then he saw against the opposite wall a waist-high stack of soft drink cases and something terrible happened inside his mouth and throat—a leap, a spring of a thin liquid like fire or the myriad stinging of ants all the way down to his stomach; with a kind of incredulous terror, even while he was saying *No! No! That will cost at least a quarter too,* his voice was saying aloud: "I reckon I'll have one of them."

"A whole case?" the proprietor said.

"You cant jest buy one bottle?" he said, counting rapidly, thinking *At least twenty bottles. That would take all the ten dollars. Maybe that will save me.* Nor, when the proprietor set the uncapped coldly sweating bottle on the counter before him, did he even have time to tell himself *I'm going to pick it up and put my mouth on it before I ask the price because otherwise I might not be able to touch it,* because his hand had already picked up the bottle, already tilting it, almost ramming the neck into his mouth, the first swallow coldly afire and too fast to taste until he could curb, restrain the urgency and passion so he could taste and affirm that he had not forgot the taste at all in the thirty-eight years: only how good it was, draining that bottle in steady controlled swallows now and only then removing it and in horror hearing his voice saying, "I'll have another one," even while he was telling himself *Stop it! Stop it!* then stood perfectly calm and perfectly composed while the proprietor uncapped the second sweating bottle and took that one up and closed his eyes gently and drank it steadily empty and fingered one of the bills loose in the pocket where he carried the three dollar ones (the ten dollar note was folded carefully beneath a wad of newspaper and safety-pinned inside the fob pocket of the overall bib) and put it on the counter, not looking at it nor at anything while he waited for the proprietor to ask for a second bill or maybe two more;

until the proprietor laid sixty-eight cents in coins on the counter and picked up the bill.

Because the two empty bottles were still sitting on the counter in plain sight; he thought rapidly *If I could jest pick up the change and git outside before he notices them*—if not an impossibility, certainly a gamble he dared not take, had not time to risk: to gamble perhaps two dollars against a shout, a leap over the counter to bar the door until another sheriff came for him. So he said, not touching the change: "You never taken out for the sody."

"What's that?" the proprietor said. He scattered the coins on the counter. "Lunch meat, eleven; bread——" He stopped and as suddenly huddled the coins into a pile again. "Where did you say you come from?"

"I never said," Mink said. "Down the road."

"Been away a long time, have you?"

"That's right," he said.

"Much obliged," the proprietor said. "I sure forgot about them two cokes. Damn labor unions have even run coca cola up out of sight like everything else. You had two of them, didn't you?" taking the half dollar from the change and shoving the rest of it across to him. "I dont know what folks are going to do unless somebody stops them somewhere. Looks like we're going to have to get shut of these damn Democrats to keep out of the poorhouse. Where'd you say you were headed? Memphis?"

"I aint said," he started to say. But the other was already, or still, speaking to the Negro now, already extending toward the Negro another opened soda.

"This is on the house. Jump in your car and run him up to the crossroads; he'll have a double chance to catch a ride there, maybe someone from the other highway."

"I wasn't fixing to leave yet," the Negro said.

"Yes you are," the proprietor said. "Just a half a mile? You got plenty of time. Dont let me see you around here until you get back. All right," he said to Mink. "You'll sure catch a ride there."

So he rode again, in the battered mud-stained car; just for a moment the Negro slid his eyes toward him, then away.

"Where down the road did you come from?" the Negro said. He didn't answer. "It was Parchman, wasn't it?" Then the car stopped. "Here's the crossroads," the Negro said. "Maybe you can catch a ride."

He got out. "Much obliged," he said.

"You done already paid him," the Negro said. So now he walked again. But mainly it was to be out of the store; he must not stop at one again. If the bottles had been a dollar a piece, there was a definite limit beyond which temptation, or at least his lack of will power, could no longer harm him. But at only a quarter a piece, until he could reach Memphis and actually have the pistol in his hand, there was no foreseeable point within the twelve remaining dollars where he would have peace; already, before he was even outside the store, he was saying *Be a man, Be a man. You got to be a man, you got too much to do, too much to resk;* and, walking again, he was still sweating a little, not panting so much as simply breathing deeply like one who has just blundered unwarned into then out of the lair, the arms, of Semiramis or Messalina, still incredulous, still aghast at his own temerity and still amazed that he has escaped with his life.

And now he was discovering something else. For most of the twenty-odd years before he went to Parchman, and during all the thirty-eight since, he had walked only on soft dirt. Now he walked on concrete; not only were his feet troubling him but his bones and muscles ached all the way up to his skull, until presently he found a foul puddle of water among rank shadeless weeds at the end of a culvert and removed the new stiff brogans they had given him with the new overalls and sat with his feet in the water, eating the tinned meat and the bread, thinking *I got to watch myself. Maybe I dassent to even go inside where they sell hit,* thinking, not with despair really: still indomitable: *Likely hit will cost the whole ten dollar bill, maybe more. That jest leaves three dollars and eighty-five cents and I done already spent eighty-two of that* and stopped and took the handful of coins from his pocket and spread them carefully on the ground beside him; he had had three one-dollar bills and the eighty-five cents and he counted slowly the eighty-five cents, a half-dollar, a quarter, and two nickels, and set them aside. He had given the man at the store one of the dollar bills and the man had given him back change for bread, eleven cents, lunch meat eleven cents, which was twenty-two cents, then the man had taken up the half-dollar for the sodas, which was seventy-two cents, which should have left twenty-eight cents; counting what remained slowly over coin by coin again, then counting the coins he had already set aside to be sure they were right. And still it was only eighteen cents instead of twenty-eight. A dime was gone somewhere. And the lunch meat was just eleven cents, he remembered that because there had been a kind of argument about it. So it was the bread, it would have to be the bread. *It went up another dime right while I was standing there* he thought. *And if bread could jump up ten cents right while I was looking at it, maybe I cant buy a pistol even for the whole thirteen dollars. So I got to stop somewhere and find a job.*

The highway was dense with traffic, but going fast now, the automobiles big ones, brand new, and the trucks were big as railroad cars; no more the dusty pickups which would have offered him a lift, but vehicles now of the rich and hurried who would not even have seen a man walking by himself in overalls. Or probably worse: they probably would have hedged away with their own size and speed and shining paint any other one of them which might have stopped for him since they would not have wanted him under their feet in Memphis either. Not that it mattered now. He couldn't even see Memphis yet. And now he couldn't even say when he was going to see it, thinking *So I may need as much as ten dollars more before I even get to where I can buy one.* But at least he would have to reach Memphis before that became an actual problem, obstacle; at least when he did reach Memphis the thirteen dollars and three cents he still had must be intact, no matter how much more he might have to add to it to get there. So he would have to get more money some way, who knew he could not be trusted in another roadside store where they sold soda pop. *So I will have to stop somewhere and ask for work and I aint never asked no man for work in my life so maybe I dont even know how,* thinking: *And that will add at least one more day, maybe even more than one,* thinking quietly but still without despair: *I'm too old for this. A feller sixty-three years old ought not to have to handle such as this,* thinking, but without despair: quite indomitable still: *But a man that's done already had to wait thirty-eight years, one more day or two or even three aint going to hurt.*

The woman was thick but not fat and not old, a little hard-looking, in a shapeless not very clean dress, standing in a small untidy yard pulling dead clematis vines from a frame beside a small house. "Are you a man of God?" she said.

"Ma'am?" he said.

"You look like a preacher."

"Nome," he said. "I been away."

"What kind of work can you do?"

"I kin do that. I kin rake the yard."

"What else?"

"I been a farmer. I reckon I can do most anything."

"I reckon first you want something to eat," she said. "All right. We're all God's creatures. Finish pulling down these vines. Then you'll find a rake by the kitchen door. And remember. I'll be watching you."

Perhaps she was, from behind the curtains. He couldn't tell. He didn't try to. Though evidently she was, already standing on the minuscule front gallery when he put the last rake-full on the pile, and told him where the wheelbarrow was and gave him three kitchen matches and stood watching while he wheeled the trash into the adjoining vacant lot and set fire to it. "Put the wheelbarrow and rake back where you got them and come in the kitchen," she said. He did so—a stove, sink, refrigerator, a table and chair set and on the table a platter of badly-cooked greens with livid pork lumps in it and two slices of machine-made bread on a saucer and a glass of water; he standing for a time quite still, his hands hanging quietly at his sides, looking at it. "Are you too proud to eat it?" she said.

"It aint that," he said. "I aint hungry. I needed the money to get on. I got to get to Memphis and then back to Missippi."

"Do you want that dinner, or dont you?" she said.

"Yessum," he said. "Much obliged," and sat down, she watching him a moment, then she opened the refrigerator and took out an opened tin and set it on the table before him. It contained one half of a canned peach.

"Here," she said.

"Yessum," he said. "Much obliged." Perhaps she was still watching him. He ate what he could (it was cold) and had carried the plate and knife and fork to the sink to wash them when she came suddenly in again.

"I'll do that," she said. "You go on up the road four miles. You'll come to a mailbox with Brother Goodyhay on it. You can read, cant you?"

"I'll find it," he said.

"Tell him Beth Holcomb sent you."

He found it. He had to. He thought *I got to find it,* thinking how maybe he would be able to read the name on the mailbox simply because he would have to read it, would have to penetrate through the inscrutable hieroglyph; thinking while he stood looking at the metal hutch with the words *Bro J C Goodyhay* not stencilled but painted on it, not sloven nor careless but impatiently, with a sort of savage impatience: thinking, either before or at least simultaneous with his realisation that someone nearby was shouting at him, *Maybe I could read all the time and jest never knowed it until I had to.* Anyway, hearing the voice and looking up the tiny savagely untended yard, to another small frame house on that minuscule gallery of which a man stood waving one arm and shouting at him: "This is it. Come on."—a lean quick-moving man in the middle thirties with coldly seething eyes and the long upper lip of a lawyer or an orator and the long chin of the old-time comic strip Puritan, who said,

"Hell, you're a preacher."

"No," he said. "I been away. I'm trying to get to——"

"All right, all right," the other said. "I'll meet you round back," and went rapidly back into the house. He, Mink, went around it into the back yard which if anything was of an even more violent desolation than the front, since the back yard contained another house not dismantled so much as collapsed—a jumble of beams, joists, window- and door-frames and even still-intact sections of siding, among which moved or stood rather a man apparently as old as he, Mink, was, although he wore a battle jacket of the type which hadn't been copied from the British model until after Pearl Harbor, with the shoulder-patch of a division which hadn't existed before

then either, who when Mink came in sight began to chop
rapidly with the axe in his hand among the jumble of lumber
about him; barely in time as the back door of the house
crashed open and the first man came out, carrying a buck
saw; now Mink saw the saw-buck and a small heap of sawn
lengths. "All right, all right," the first man said, handing
Mink the saw. "Save all the sound pieces. Dont split the nails
out, pull them out. Saw up all the scraps, same length. Dad is
in charge. I'll be in the house," and went back into it; even
doors which he barely released seemed to clap to behind him
violently, as though his passage had sucked them shut.

"So they caught you too did they, mac?" the man in the
battle jacket (he would be Dad) said.

Mink didn't answer that. He said: "Is that the reverend?"

"That's Goodyhay," the other said. "I aint heard him
preach yet but even if he hadn't opened his mouth he would
be a better preacher than he is a cook. But then, somebody's
got to scorch the biscuits. They claim his wife ran off with a
sonabitching Four-F potato chip salesman before he even got
back from fighting in the Pacific. They were all doing it back
then and what I notice, they aint quit, even without any war
to blame it on. But what the hell, I always say there's still a
frog in the puddle for every one that jumps out. So they
caught you too, huh?"

This time he answered. "I got to get to Memphis and then
back down to Missippi. I'm already behind. I got to get on
tonight. How much does he pay here?"

"That's what you think," the other said. "That's what I
thought three days ago: pick up a dollar or so and move on.
Because you're building a church this time, bully boy. So
maybe we both better hope the bastard can preach since we
aint going to get our money until they take up the collection
Sunday."

"Sunday?" he said.

"That's right," the other said. "This is Thursday; count it."

"Sunday," he said. "That's three days."

"That's right," the other said. "Sunday's always three days
after Thursday around here. It's a law they got."

"How much will we get on Sunday?"

"It may be as much as a dollar cash; you're working for the

Lord now, not mammon, jack. But anyway you'll be fed and slept—"

"I cant work that long for jest a dollar," he said. "I aint got the time."

"It may be more than a dollar. What I hear around here, he seems to have something. Anyway, he gets them. It seems he was a Marine sergeant on one of them landing barges out in the Pacific one day when a Jap dive bomber dove right at them and everybody tried to jump off into the water before the bomb hit, except one mama's boy that got scared or tangled up in something so he couldn't jump and the reverend (except he hadn't turned reverend then, not for the next few minutes yet) went back to try and untangle him, when the whole barge blew up and took the reverend and the mama's boy both right on down to the bottom with it before the reverend could get them both loose and up to the top again. Which is just the official version when they gave him the medal, since according to the reverend or leastways his congregation— What I hear, the rest of them are mostly ex-soldiers too or their wives or the other broads they just knocked up without marrying, mostly young, except for a few old ones that seem to got dragged in by the passing suction you might say; maybe the moms and pops of soldiers that got killed, or the ones like that Sister Holcomb one that caught you down the road, that probably never thawed enough to have a child of any kind and God help the husband either if she ever had one, that wasn't even sucked in but flagged the bus herself because the ride looked like it was free———" He stopped. Then he said: "No, I know exactly why she come: to listen to some of the words he uses doing what he calls preaching. Where was I? Oh yes: that landing barge. According to the reverend, he was already safe and dead and peacefully out of it at last on the bottom of the Pacific ocean when all of a sudden Jesus Himself was standing over him saying Fall in and he did it and Jesus said TenSHUN about FACE and assigned him to this new permanent hitch right down here on the edge of Memphis, Tennessee. He's got something, enough of whatever it took to recruit this new-faith boot-camp to need a church to hold it. And I be damned if I dont believe he's even going to get a carpenter to nail it together. What did he say when he first saw you?"

"What?" Mink said.

"What were his first words when he looked at you?"

"He said, 'Hell, you're a preacher'."

"You see what I mean? He's mesmerised enough folks to scour the country for any edifice that somebody aint actually sitting on the front porch of, and knocking it down and hauling it over here to be broke up like we're doing. But he aint got a master carpenter yet to nail it together into a church. Because master carpenters belong to unions, and deal in cash money per diem on the barrel-head, where his assignment come direct from Jesus Christ Who aint interested in money or at least from the putting-out angle. So him and his outpost foxholes up and down the road like that Sister Holcomb that snagged you are sifting for one."

"Sifting?" he said.

"Sivving. Like flour. Straining folks through this back yard until somebody comes up that knows how to nail that church together when we get enough boards and planks and window-frames ripped aloose and stacked up. Which maybe we better get at it. I aint actually caught him spying behind a window-shade yet but likely even an ex-Marine sergeant reformed into the ministry is no man to monkey with too far."

"You mean I cant leave?"

"Sure you can. All the out-doors is yours around here. You aint going to get any money until they take up that collection Sunday though. Not to mention a place to sleep tonight and what he calls cooking if you aint particular."

In fact, this house had no shades nor curtains whatever to be spied from behind. Indeed, as he really looked about it for the first time, the whole place had an air of violent transience similar to the indiscriminate jumble of walls and windows and doors among which he and the other man worked: merely still nailed together and so standing upright; from time to time, as the stack of reclaimed planks and the pile of fire-lengths to which his saw was reducing the spoiled fragments slowly rose, Mink could hear the preacher moving about inside the intact one, so that he thought *If he jest went back inside to compose up his sermon, it sounds like getting ready to preach takes as much activity and quickness as harnessing up a mule.* Now it was almost sunset; he thought *This will have to be at least a half a dollar. I got to have it. I got to get on. I cant wait till Sunday,* when the back door jerked, burst open and the preacher said, "All right. Supper's ready. Come on."

He followed Dad inside. Nothing was said by anyone about washing. "I figgered—" he began. But it was already too late. This was a kitchen too but not spartan so much as desolate, like a public camp-site in a roadside park, with what he called another artermatic stove since he had never seen a gas or electric stove until he saw Mrs Holcomb's, Goodyhay standing facing it in violent immobility enclosed in a fierce sound of frying; Mink said again, "I figgered—" as Goodyhay turned from the stove with three platters bearing each a charred splat of something which on the enamel surfaces looked as alien and solitary and not for eating as the droppings of cows. "I done already et," Mink said. "I figgered I would jest get on."

"What?" Goodyhay said.

"Even after I get to Memphis, I still aint hardly begun," he said. "I got to get on tonight."

"So you want your money now," Goodyhay said, setting the platters on the table where there already sat a tremendous bottle of tomato ketchup and a plate of machine-sliced bread and a sugar bowl and a can of condensed milk with holes punched in the top. "Sit down," Goodyhay said, turning back to the stove, where Mink could smell the coffee overboiled too with that same violent impatience of the fried hamburger and the wood-piles in the yard and the lettering on the mailbox; until Goodyhay turned again with the three cups of coffee and said again, "Sit down." Dad was already seated. "I said, sit down," Goodyhay said. "You'll get your money Sunday after the collection."

"I cant wait that long."

"All right," Goodyhay said, dashing ketchup over his plate. "Eat your supper first. You've already paid for that." He sat down; the other two were already eating. In fact Goodyhay had already finished, rising in the same motion with which he put his fork down, still chewing, and went and swung inward an open door (on the back of which was hanging what Mink did not recognise to be a camouflaged battle helmet worn by Marine troops on the Pacific beach-heads and jungles because what he was looking at was the automatic pistol-butt projecting from its webbing belt beneath the helmet) and from the refrigerator behind it took a tin also of canned peach halves and brought it to the table and dealt, splashed the halves and the syrup with exact impartiality onto the three greasy plates and they ate that too, Goodyhay once more finishing first; and now, for the first time since Mink had known him, sitting perfectly motionless, almost as though asleep, until they had finished also. Then he said, "Police it," himself leading the way to the sink with his plate and utensils and cup and washed them beneath the tap then stood and watched while the other two followed suit and dried and racked them as he had done. Then he said to Mink: "All right. You going or staying?"

"I got to stay," Mink said. "I got to have the money."

"All right," Goodyhay said. "Kneel down," and did so first again, the other two following, on the kitchen floor beneath the hard dim glare of the single unshaded low-watt bulb on a ceiling cord, Goodyhay on his knees but no more, his head up, the coldly seething desert-hermit's eyes not even closed, and said, "Save us, Christ, the poor sons of bitches," and rose and said, "All right. Lights out. The truck'll be here at seven oclock."

The room was actually a lean-to, a little larger than a closet. It had one small window, a door connecting with the house, a single bulb on a drop cord, a thin mattress on the floor with a tarpaulin cover but no pillows nor sheets, and nothing else, Goodyhay holding the door for them to enter and then closing it. They were alone.

"Go ahead," Dad said. "Try it."

"Try what?" Mink said.

"The door. It's locked. Oh, you can get out any time you want; the window aint locked. But that door leads back into the house and he dont aim to have none of us master carpenter candidates maybe ramshagging the joint as a farewell gesture on the way out. You're working for the Lord now, buster, but there's still a Marine sergeant running the detail." He yawned. "But at least you will get your two dollars Sunday—three, if he counts today as a day too. Not to mention hearing him preach. Which may be worth even three dollars. You know: one of them special limited editions they can charge ten prices for because they never printed but two or three of." He blinked at Mink. "Because why. It aint going to last much longer." He blinked at Mink. "Because they aint going to let it."

"They wont even pay me two dollars?" Mink said.

"No no," the other said. "I mean the rest of the folks in the neighborhood he aint converted yet, aint going to put up with no such as this. The rest of the folks that already had to put up with that damn war for four-five years now and want to forget about it. That've already gone to all that five years of trouble and expense to get shut of it, only just when they are about to get settled back down again, be damned if here aint a passel of free-loading government-subsidised ex-drafted sons of bitches acting like whatever had caused the war not only actually happened but was still going on, and was going to keep on going on until somebody did something about it. A passel of mostly non-tax-paying folks that like as not would have voted for Norman Thomas even ahead of Roosevelt, let alone Truman, trying to bring Jesus Christ back alive in the middle of 1946. So it may be worth three dollars just to hear him in the free outside air. Because next time you might have to listen through a set of jail bars." He yawned again, prodigiously, beginning to remove the battle jacket. "Well, we aint got a book to curl up with in here even if we wanted to. So all that leaves is to go to bed."

Which they did. The light was off, he lay breathing quietly on his back, his hands folded on his breast. He thought *Sholy it will be three dollars. Sholy they will count today too,* thinking *And Sunday will make three days lost because even if I got to Memphis Sunday after we are paid off the stores where I can buy one will still be closed until Monday morning,* thinking *But I reckon I can wait three more days,* a little wryly now: *Likely because I cant figger out no way to help it,* and almost immediately was asleep, peacefully, sleeping well because it was daylight when he knew next, lying there peacefully for a little time yet before he realised he was alone. It seemed to him afterward that he still lay there peaceful and calm, his hand still playing idly with the safety pin it had found lying open on his chest, for the better part of a minute after he knew what had happened; then sitting, surging up, not even needing to see the open window and the dangling screen, his now frantic hand scrabbling from the bib pocket of the overalls the wad of newspaper beneath which the ten dollar bill had been pinned, his voice making a puny whimpering instead of the cursing he was trying for, beating his fists on the locked door until it jerked open and Goodyhay stood in it, also taking one look at the ravished window.

"So the son of a bitch robbed you," Goodyhay said.

"It was ten dollars," Mink said. "I got to ketch him. Let me out."

"Hold it," Goodyhay said, still barring the doorway. "You cant catch him now."

"I got to," he said. "I got to have that ten dollars."

"You mean you've got to have ten dollars to get home?"

"Yes!" he said, cursing again. "I cant do nothing without it. Let me out."

"How long since you been home?" Goodyhay said.

"Thirty-eight years. Tell me which way you figger he went."

"Hold it," Goodyhay said, still not moving. "All right," he said. "I'll see you get your ten dollars back Sunday. Can you cook?"

"I can fry eggs and meat," Mink said.

"All right. You cook breakfast and I'll load the truck. Come on." Goodyhay showed him how to light the stove and left him; he filled up last night's coffee pot with water as his tradition was until the grounds had lost all flavor and color too, and sliced the fatback and dusted it with meal into the skillet in his tradition also, and got eggs out to fry, standing for a while with the door in his hand while he looked, mused, at the heavy holstered pistol beneath the helmet, thinking quietly *If I jest had that for two days I wouldn't need no ten dollars,* thinking *I done been robbed in good faith without warning; why aint that enough to free me to rob in my turn. Not to mention my need being ten times, a hundred times, a thousand times more despaired than ara other man's need for jest ten dollars,* thinking quietly, peacefully indeed now *No. I aint never stole. I aint never come to that and I wont never.*

When he went to the door to call them, Goodyhay and another man had the truck loaded with intact sections of wall and disassembled planks; he rode on top of the load, once more on the highway toward Memphis; he thought *Maybe they'll even go through Memphis and if I jest had the ten dollars* and then quit, just riding, in motion, until the truck turned into a side road; now they were passing, perhaps entering, already on, a big place, domain, plantation—broad cotton fields still white for the pickers; presently they turned into a farm road across a field and came to a willow-grown bayou and another pickup truck and another stack of dismembered walls and a group of three or four men all curiously similar somehow to Goodyhay and the driver of his—their—truck; he, Mink, couldn't have said how nor why, and not even speculating: remarking without attention another battle jacket, remarking without much attention either a rectangle of taut string between driven stakes in the dimensions of whatever it was they were going to build, where they unloaded the truck and Goodyhay said, "All right. You and Albert go back for another load."

So he rode in the cab also this time, back to the parsonage or whatever it was, where he and Albert loaded the truck and they returned to the bayou, where by this time, with that many folks working—if any of the other four worked half as fast and as hard as Goodyhay did—they would probably have one wall already up. Instead, the other truck and Goodyhay and the stake-and-string rectangle were gone and only three men sat quietly beside the pile of lumber. "Well?" Albert said.

"Yep," one of the others said. "Somebody changed his mind."

"Who?" Mink said. "Changed what? I got to get on. I'm already late."

"Fellow that owns this place," Albert said. "That gave us permission to put the chapel here. Somebody changed his mind for him. Maybe the bank that holds his mortgage. Maybe the Legion."

"What Legion?" he said.

"The American Legion. That's still holding the line at 1918. You never heard of it?"

"Where's Reverend Goodyhay?" he said. "I got to get on."

"All right," Albert said. "So long." So he waited. Now it was early afternoon when the other truck returned, being driven fast, Goodyhay already getting out of it before it stopped.

"All right," he said. "Load up." Then they were on the Memphis highway again, going fast now to keep at least in sight of Goodyhay, as fast as any of the traffic they dashed among, he thinking *If I jest had the ten dollars, even if we aint going all the way to Memphis this time neither.* They didn't. Goodyhay turned off and they ran again, faster than they dared except that Goodyhay in the front truck would have lost them, into a region of desolation, the lush Delta having played out now into eroded barren clay hills; into a final, the uttermost of desolation, where Goodyhay stopped—a dump, a jumbled plain of rusted automobile bodies and boilers and gin machinery and brick and concrete rubble; already the stakes had been re-driven and the rectangular string tautened rigid between them, Goodyhay standing beside his halted truck beckoning his arm, shouting, "All right. Here we are. Let's go."

So there was actual work again at last. But it was already late; most of the day was gone and tomorrow was Saturday, only one more full day. But Goodyhay didn't even give him a chance to speak. "Didn't I tell you you'd get your ten dollars Sunday? All right then." Nor did Goodyhay say, "Can you cook supper?" He just jerked, flung open the refrigerator door and jerked out the bloodstained paper of hamburger meat and left the kitchen. And now Mink remembered from somewhere that he had cooked grits once and found grits and the proper vessel. And tonight Goodyhay didn't lock the door; he, Mink, tried it to see, then closed it and lay down, again peacefully on his back, his hands folded on his breast like a corpse, until Goodyhay waked him to fry the side meat and the eggs again. The pickup truck was already there and a dozen men were on hand this time and now you could begin to see what the chapel (they called it) was going to look like; until dark. He said: "It aint cold tonight and besides I can lay under that-ere roofing paper and get started at daylight until the rest of them—"

"We dont work on Sunday," Goodyhay said. "Come on. Come on." Then it was Sunday. It was raining: the thin steady drizzle of early fall. A man and his wife called for them, not a pickup this time but a car, hard-used and a little battered. They turned again into a crossroad, not into desolate country this time but simply empty, coming at last to an unpainted box of a building which something somewhere back before the thirty-eight years in the penitentiary recognised, remembered. *It's a nigger schoolhouse* he thought, getting out among five or six other stained and battered cars and pickup trucks and a group of people already waiting, a few older ones but usually men and women about the age of Goodyhay or a little younger; again he sensed that identity, similarity among them even beyond the garments they wore—more battle jackets, green army slickers, one barracks cap still showing where the officer's badge had been removed; someone said, "Howdy," at his elbow. It was Albert and now he, Mink, recognised the Miss or Mrs Holcomb whose yard he had raked, and then he saw a big Negro woman—a woman no longer young, who looked at the same time gaunt yet fat too. He stopped, not quite startled: just watchful.

"You all take niggers too?" he said.

"We do this one," Albert said. Goodyhay had already entered the house. The rest of them now moved slowly toward the door, clotting a little. "Her son had it too just like she was a white woman, even if they didn't put his name on the same side of the monument with the others. See that woman yonder with the yellow hat?" The hat was soiled now but still flash, the coat below it had been white once too, a little flash too; the face between could have been twenty-five and probably at one time looked it, thin now, not quite raddled. "That's right," Albert said. "She still looks a little like a whore yet but you should have seen her last spring when she came out of that Catalpa Street house. Her husband commanded an infantry platoon back there when the Japs were running us out of Malaya, when we were falling back all mixed up together—Aussies, British, French from Indo China—not trying to hold anything anymore except a line of foxholes after dark fell long enough to get the stragglers up and move again tomorrow, including the ones in the foxholes too if any of them were still there by daylight. His platoon was the picket that night, him in one foxhole and his section strung out, when the nigger crawled up with the ammunition. He was

new, you see. I mean, the nigger. This was as close as he had
been to a Jap yet.

"So you know how it is: crouched in the stinking pitch dark
in a stinking sweating hole in the ground with your eyes and
ears both strained until in another minute they will pop right
out of your head like marbles, and all around in front of
you the chirping voices like crickets in a hayfield until you realise they aint crickets because pretty soon what they are
chirping is English: 'Maline. Tonigh youdigh. Maline. Tonigh
youdigh.' So here comes the nigger with his sack of grenades
and Garand clips and the lieutenant tells him to get down
into the hole and puts the nigger's finger on the trigger of the
Garand and tells him to stay there while he crawls back to report to the p.c. or something.

"You know how it is. A man can stand just so much. He
dont even know when it will be but all of a sudden a moment
comes and he knows that's all, he's already had it; he hates it
as much as you do but he didn't ask for it and he cant help it.
That's the trouble; you dont know beforehand, there's nothing to warn you, to tell you to brace. Especially in war. It
makes you think that just something no tougher than men
aint got any business in war, dont it? that if they're going to
keep on having them, they ought to invent something a little
more efficient to fight them with. Anyway, it's the next morning, first light, when the first of the cut-off heads that maybe
last night you split a can of dog-ration with, comes tumbling
down among you like somebody throwing a basket ball. Only
this time it's that black head. Because why not? a nigger bred
up on a Arkansas plantation, that a white man, not just a lieutenant but talking Arkansas to boot, says, 'Take a holt of this-
here hoe or rifle and stay here till I get back.' So as soon as
we finished fighting the Japs far enough back to get organised
to spend another day dodging the strafing planes, the lieutenant goes around behind the dump of stuff we can tote
with us and are trying to set fire to it and make it burn—It's
funny about jungles. You're sweating all the time, even in the
dark, and you are always parched for water because there aint
any in a jungle no matter what you thought, and when you
step into a patch of sun you blister before you can even button your shirt. Until you believe that if you so much as drop

a canteen or a bayonet or even strike a boot-calk against a root a spark will jump out and set the whole country afire. But just try to start one. Just try to burn something up and you'll see different. Anyway, the lieutenant went around behind the dump where he would have a little privacy and put his pistol barrel in his mouth. Sure, she can get in here."

Now they were all inside, and he recognised this from thirty-eight years back too—how the smell of Negroes remained long after the rooms themselves were vacant of them —the smell of poverty and secret fear and patience and enduring without enough hope to deodorise it—they (he supposed they would call themselves a congregation) filing onto the backless benches, the woman in the yellow hat on the front one, the big Negress alone on the back one, Goodyhay himself facing them at the end of the room behind a plank laid across two saw-horses, his hands resting, not clenched: just closed into fists, on the plank until they were quiet.

"All right," Goodyhay said. "Anybody that thinks all he's got to do is sit on his stern and have salvation come down on him like a cloudburst or something, dont belong in here. You got to get up on your feet and hunt it down until you can get a hold of it and then hold it, even fighting off if you have to. And if you cant find it, then by God make it. Make a salvation He will pass and then earn the right to grab it and hold on and fight off too if you have to but anyway hold it, hell and high water be damned——" when a voice, a man, interrupted:

"Tell it again, Joe. Go on. Tell it again."

"What?" Goodyhay said.

"Tell it again," the man said. "Go on."

"I tried to," Goodyhay said. "You all heard me. I cant tell it."

"Yes you can," the man said; now there were women's voices too:

"Yes, Joe. Tell it," and he, Mink, still watching the hands not clenched but just closed on the plank, the coldly seething anchorite's eyes—the eyes of a fifth-century hermit looking at nothing from the entrance of his Mesopotamian cave—the body rigid in an immobility like a tremendous strain beneath a weight.

"All right," Goodyhay said. "I was laying there. I was all right, everything snafu so I was all right. You know how it is in water when you dont have any weight at all, just laying there with the light coming way down from up on top like them lattice blinds when they shake and shiver slow in a breeze without making any sound at all. Just laying there watching my hands floating along without me even having to hold them up, with the shadow of them lattice blinds winking and shaking across them, and my feet and legs too, no weight atall, nowhere to have to go or march, not even needing to breathe, not even needing to be asleep or nothing: just all right. When there He was standing over me, looking like any other shavetail just out of a foxhole, maybe a little older, except he didn't have a hat, bucket: just standing there bareheaded with the shadow of the lattice running up and down him, smoking a cigarette. 'Fall in, soldier,' He said.

" 'I cant,' I says. Because I knew that as long as I laid still, I would be all right. But that once I let myself start thinking about moving, or tried to, I would find out I couldn't. But what the hell, why should I? I was all right. I had had it. I had it made. I was sacked up. Let them do whatever they ....ing wanted to with their ....ing war up on top.

" 'That's once,' He said. 'You aint got but three times. You, the Top Soldier, saying cant. At Château Thierry and St Mihiel the company would have called you the Top Soldier. Do they still do that in the Corps on Guadalcanal?'

" 'Yes,' I says.

" 'All right, Top Soldier,' He said. 'Fall in.' So I got up. 'At ease,' He said. 'You see?' He said.

" 'I thought I couldn't,' I says. 'I didn't believe I could.'

" 'Sure,' He said. 'What else do we want with you. We're already full up with folks that know they can but dont, since because they already know they can, they dont have to do it. What we want are folks that believe they cant, and then do it. The other kind dont need us and we dont need them. I'll say more: we dont even want them in the outfit. They wont be accepted; we wont even have them under our feet. If it aint worth that much, it aint worth anything. Right?'

" 'Yes sir,' I says.

" 'You can say Sir up there too if you want,' He said. 'It's a free country. Nobody gives a damn. You all right now?'

" 'Yes sir,' I says.

" 'TenSHUN!' He said. And I made them pop, mud or no mud. 'About FACE!' He said. And He never saw one smarter than that one neither. 'Forward MARCH!' He said. And I had already stepped off when He said, 'Halt!' and I stopped. 'You're going to leave him laying there,' He said. And there he was, I had forgot about him, laying there as peaceful and out of it too as you please—the damned little bastard that had gone chicken at the exact wrong time, like they always do, turned the wheel aloose and tried to duck and caused the whole damn mess; lucky for all of us he never had a ....ing bar on his shoulder so he could have ....ed up the whole detail and done for all of us.

" 'I cant carry him too,' I says.

" 'That's two times,' He said. 'You've got one more. Why not go on and use it now and get shut of it for good?'

" 'I cant carry him too,' I says.

" 'Fine,' He said. 'That's three and finished. You wont ever have to say cant again. Because you're a special case; they gave you three times. But there's a general order coming down to-day that after this nobody has but one. Pick him up.' So I did. 'Dismiss,' He said. And that's all. I told you I cant tell it. I was just there. I cant tell it." He, Mink, watching them all, himself alien, not only unreconciled but irreconcilable: not contemptuous, because he was just waiting, not impatient because even if he were in Memphis right this minute, at ten or eleven or whatever oclock it was on Sunday morning, he would still have almost twenty-four hours to get through somehow before he could move on to the next step. He just watched them: the two oldish couples, man and wife of course, farmers obviously, without doubt tenant-farmers come up from the mortgaged bank- or syndicate-owned cotton plantation from which the son had been drafted three or four or five years ago to make that far from home that sacrifice, old, alien too, too old for this, unreconciled by the meagre and arid tears which were less of tears than blisters; none of the white people actually watching as the solitary Negro woman got up from her back bench and walked down the

aisle to where the young woman's soiled yellow hat was
crushed into the crook of her elbow like a child in a child's
misery and desolation, the white people on the bench making
way for the Negress to sit down beside the young white
woman and put her arm around her; Goodyhay still standing,
his arms propped on the closed fists on the plank, the cold
seething eyes not even closed, speaking exactly as he had spoken three nights ago while the three of them knelt on the
kitchen floor: "Save us, Christ. The poor sons of bitches."
Then Goodyhay was looking at him. "You, there," Goodyhay
said. "Stand up." Mink did so. "He's trying to get home. He
hasn't put in but one full day, but he needs ten dollars to get
home on. He hasn't been home in thirty-eight years. He
needs nine bucks more. How about it?"

"I'll take it," the man in the officer's cap said. "I won thirty-
four in a crap game last night. He can have ten of that."

"I said, nine," Goodyhay said. "He's got one dollar coming. Give him the ten and I'll give you one. He says he's got
to go to Memphis first. Anybody going in tonight?"

"I am," another said.

"All right," Goodyhay said. "Anybody want to sing?" That
was how he saw Memphis again under the best, the matchless condition for one who hadn't seen it in . . . . He could
figure that. He was twenty years old when he got married.
Three times before that he had wrenched, wrung enough
money from the otherwise unpaid labor he did on the tenant
farm of the kinsman who had raised him from orphanhood,
to visit the Memphis brothels. The last visit was in the same
year of his marriage. He was twenty-six years old when he
went to Parchman. Twenty dollars from twenty-six dollars
was six dollars. He was in Parchman thirty-eight years. Six
dollars and thirty-eight dollars was forty-four dollars to see
Memphis again not only after forty-four years but under the
matchless condition: at night, the dark earth on either hand
and ahead already random and spangled with the neon he had
never seen before, and in the distance the low portentous
glare of the city itself, he sitting on the edge of the seat as a
child sits, almost as small as a child, peering ahead as the car
rushed, merging into one mutual spangled race bearing toward, as though by the acceleration of gravity or suction, the

distant city; suddenly off to the right a train fled dragging a long string of lighted windows as rapid and ephemeral as dream; he became aware of a convergence like the spokes of a gigantic dark wheel lying on its hub, along which sped dense and undeviable as ants, automobiles and what they told him were called buses as if all the earth was hurrying, plunging, being sucked decked with diamond and ruby lights, into the low glare on the sky as into some monstrous, frightening, unimaginable joy or pleasure.

Now the converging roads themselves were decked with globular lights as big and high in the trees as roosting turkeys. "Tell me when we get close," he said.

"Close to what?" the driver said.

"Close to Memphis."

"We're already in Memphis," the driver said. "We crossed the city limits a mile back." So now he realised that if he had still been walking, alone, with none to ask or tell him, his troubles would have really begun only after he reached Memphis. Because the Memphis he remembered from forty-four years back no longer existed; he thought *I been away too long; when you got something to handle like I got to handle, and by yourself and not no more to handle it with than I got, not to mention eighty more miles to go yet, a man jest cant afford to been away as long as I had to be.* Back then you would catch a ride in somebody's wagon coming in from Frenchman's Bend or maybe two or three of you would ride plow-mules in to Jefferson, with a croker sack of corn behind the borrowed saddle, to leave the mules in the lot behind the Commercial Hotel and pay the nigger there a quarter to feed them until you got back, and get on the train at the depot and change at the Junction to one that went right into the middle of Memphis, the depot there almost in the center of town.

But all that was changed now. They had told him four days ago that most of the trains were gone, quit running, even if he had had that much extra money to spend just riding. They had told him how they were buses now but in all the four days he had yet to see anything that looked like a depot where he could buy a ticket and get on one. And as for the edge of Memphis that back there forty-four years ago a man could have walked in from in an hour, he, according to the driver, had already crossed it over a mile back yet still all he could see of it was just that glare on the sky. Even though he was actually in Memphis, he was apparently still as far from the goal he remembered and sought, as from Varner's store to Jefferson; except for the car giving him a ride and the driver of it who knew in general where he needed to go, he might have had to spend even the ten dollars for food wandering around inside Memphis before he ever reached the place where he could buy the pistol.

Now the car was wedged solid into a rushing mass of other vehicles all winking and glittering and flashing with colored lights; all circumambience in fact flashed and glared luminous and myriad with color and aloud with sound; suddenly a clutch of winking red green and white lights slid across the high night itself; he knew, sensed what they were but was much too canny to ask, telling, hissing to himself: *Remember. Remember. It wont hurt you long as dont nobody find out you dont know it.*

Now he was in what he knew was the city. For a moment it merely stood glittering and serried and taller than stars. Then it engulfed him; it stooped soaring down, bearing down upon him like breathing the vast concrete mass and weight until he himself was breathless, having to pant for air. Then he knew what it was. *It's un-sleeping,* he thought. *It aint slept in so long now it's done forgot how to sleep and now there aint no time to stop long enough to try to learn how again*; the car rigid in its rigid mass, creeping then stopping then creeping again to the ordered blink and change of colored lights like the railroads used to have, until at last it drew out and could stop.

"Here's the bus station," the driver said. "This was where you wanted, wasn't it?"

"It's fine," he said.

"Buses leave here for everywhere. You want me to come in with you and find out about yours?"

"Much obliged," he said. "It's jest fine."

"So long then," the driver said.

"I thank you kindly," he said. "So long." Sure enough, it was a bus depot at last. Only if he went inside, one of the new laws he had heard about in Parchman—laws that a man couldn't saw boards and hammer nails unless he paid money to an association that would let him, couldn't even raise cotton on his own land unless the government said he could— might be that he would have to get on the first bus that left, no matter where it was going. So there was the rest of the night, almost all of it since it wasn't even late yet. But it would only be twelve hours and for that time he could at least make one anonymous more among the wan anonymous faces thronging about him, hurrying and myriad beneath the colored glare, passionate and gay and unsleeping. Then something happened. Without warning the city spun, whirled, vertiginous, infinitesimal and dizzying, then as suddenly braked and immobilised again and he not only knew exactly where he was, but how to pass the twelve hours. He would have to cross the street, letting the throng itself enclot and engulf him as the light changed; once across he could free himself and go on. And there it was: the Confederate Park they called it—the path and flowerbed crisscrossed vacancy exactly as he remembered it, the line of benches along the stone parapet in the gaps of which the old iron cannon from the War squatted and beyond that the sense and smell of the River, where forty-four and -five and -six years ago, having spent half his money in the brothel last night and the other half saved for tonight, after which he would have nothing left but the return ticket to Jefferson, he would come to watch the steamboats.

The levee would be lined with them bearing names like Stacker Lee and Ozark Belle and Crescent Queen, come from as far apart as Cairo and New Orleans, to meet and pass while he watched them, the levee clattering with horse- and mule-drawn drays and chanting stevedores while the cotton bales and the crated machinery and the rest of the bags and boxes moved up and down the gang-planks, and the benches along the bluff would be crowded with other people watching them too. But now the benches were vacant and even when he reached the stone parapet among the old cannon there was nothing of the River but the vast and vacant expanse, only the wet dark cold blowing, breathing up from across the vast empty River so that already he was buttoning the cotton jumper over his cotton shirt; no sound here at all: only the constant unsleeping murmur of the city behind him, no movement save the minute crawl of the automobiles on the bridge far down the River, hurrying, drawn also toward and into that unceasing murmur of passion and excitement, into this backwash of which he seemed to have blundered, strayed, and then abandoned, betrayed by having had to be away so long. And cold too, even here behind one of the old cannon, smelling the cold aged iron too, huddled into the harsh cotton denim too new to have acquired his own body's shape and so warm him by contact; it was going to be too cold here before much longer even though he did have peace and quiet to pass the rest of the twelve hours in. But he had already remembered the other one, the one they called Court Square, where he would be sheltered from the River air by the tall buildings themselves provided he waited a little longer to give the people who might be sitting on the benches there time to get sleepy and go home.

So when he turned back toward the glare and the murmur, the resonant concrete hum though unsleeping still, now had a spent quality like rising fading smoke or steam, so that what remained of it was now high among the ledges and cornices; the random automobiles which passed now, though gleaming with colored lights still, seemed now as though fleeing in terror, in solitude from solitude. It was warmer here. And after while he was right: there was nobody here save himself; on a suitable bench he lay down, drawing and huddling his knees up into the buttoned jumper, looking no larger than a child and no less waif, abandoned, when something hard was striking the soles of his feet and time, a good deal of it, had passed and the night itself was now cold and vacant. It was a policeman; he recognised that even after the forty-four years of change and alteration.

"Damn Mississippi," the policeman said. "I mean, where are you staying in town here? You mean, you haven't got anywhere to sleep? You know where the railroad station is? Go on down there; you can find a bed for fifty cents. Go on now." He didn't move, waiflike and abandoned true enough but no more pitiable than a scorpion. "Hell, you're broke too. Here." It was a half-dollar. "Go on now. Beat it. I'm going to stand right here and watch you out of sight."

"Much obliged," he said. A half a dollar. So that was another part of the new laws they had been passing; come to remember, he had heard about that in Parchman too; they called it Relief or W P and A: the same government that wouldn't let you raise cotton on your own land would turn right around and give you a mattress or groceries or even cash money, only first you had to swear you didn't own any property of your own and even had to prove it by giving your house or land or even your wagon and team to your wife or children or any kinfolks you could count on, depend on, trust. And who knew: even if second-hand pistols had gone up too like everything else, maybe the one fifty cents more would be enough without another policeman.

Though he found another. Here was the depot. It at least hadn't changed: the same hollowly sonorous rotunda through which he had passed from the Jefferson train on the three other times he had seen Memphis—that first unforgettable time (he had figured it now: the last time had been forty-four years ago and the first time was three dollars onto that which was forty-seven years) with the niggard clutch of wrenched and bitter dollars and the mentor and guide who had told him about the houses in Memphis for no other purpose, filled with white women any one of which he could have if he had the money: whose experiences until now had been furious unplanned episodes as violent as vomiting, with no more preparation than the ripping of buttons before stooping downward into the dusty roadside weeds or cotton middle where the almost invisible unwashed Negro girl lay waiting. But different in Memphis: himself and his guide stepping out into the street where the whole city lay supine now to take him into itself like embrace, like arms, the very meagre wad of bills in his pocket on fire too which he had wrung, wrested from between-crops labor at itinerant sawmills, or from the implacable rented ground by months behind a plow, his pittance of which he would have to fight his father each time to get his hands on a nickel of it. It was warm here too and almost empty and this time the policeman had jerked him awake before he had even known he was going to sleep. Though this one was not in uniform. But he knew about that kind too.

"I said, what train are you waiting for?" the policeman said.

"I aint waiting for no train," he said.

"All right," the policeman said. "Then get out of here. Go on home." Then, exactly like the other one: "You aint got anywhere to sleep? Okay, but you damn sure got some place to leave from, whether you go to bed or not. Go on now. Beat it." And then, since he didn't move: "Go on, I said. What're you waiting for?"

"The half a dollar," he said.

"The what?" the policeman said. "The half a— Why, you——" so that this time he moved, turned quickly, already dodging, not much bigger than a small boy and therefore about as hard for a man the size of the policeman to catch in a place as big as this. He didn't run: he walked, just fast enough for the policeman to be not quite able to touch him, yet still not have cause to shout at him, through the rotunda and out into the street, not looking back at the policeman standing in the doorway shouting after him: "And dont let me catch you in here again neither."

He was becoming more and more oriented now. There was another depot just down a cross street but then the same thing would happen there; evidently the railroad policemen who just wore clothes like everybody else didn't belong to the W P and A free relief laws. Besides, the night was moving toward its end now; he could feel it. So he just walked, never getting very far away because he knew where he was now; and now and then in the vacant side streets and alleys he could stop and sit down, in a doorway or behind a cluster of garbage or trash cans and once more be waking up before he knew he had gone to sleep. Then he would walk again, the quiet and empty city—this part of it anyway—his impeachless own, thinking, with the old amazement no less fresh and amazed for being almost as old as he: *A man can get through anything if he can jest keep on walking.*

Then it was day, not waking the city; the city had never slept, not resuming but continuing back into visibility the faces pallid and wan and unsleeping, hurrying, passionate and gay, toward the tremendous, the unimaginable pleasures. He knew exactly where he was now; this pavement could have shown his print from forty-four years ago; for the first time since he came out the Parchman gate five mornings ago he was confident, invulnerable and immune. *I could even spend a whole dollar of it now and hit wouldn't stop me,* he thought, inside the small dingy store where a few Negroes were already trafficking. A Negro man seemed to be running it or anyway serving the customers. Maybe he even owned it; maybe the new laws even said a nigger could even own a store, remembering something else from thirty-eight years back.

"Animal crackers," he said. Because he was there now, safe, immune and invulnerable. "I reckon they done jumped them up ten or fifteen cents too, aint they?" looking at the small cardboard box colored like a circus wagon itself and blazoned with beasts like a heraldry.

"Ten cents," the Negro said.

"Ten cents more than what?" he said.

"It's ten cents," the Negro said. "Do you want it or dont you?"

"I'll take two of them," he said. He walked again, in actual sunlight now, himself one with the hurrying throng, eating his minute vanilla menagerie; there was plenty of time now since he was not only safe but he knew exactly where he was; by merely turning his head (which he did not) he could have seen the street, the actual housefront (he didn't know it of course and probably wouldn't have recognised her either, but his younger daughter was now the madam of it) which he had entered with his mentor that night forty-seven years ago, where waited the glittering arms of women not only shaped like Helen and Eve and Lilith, not only functional like Helen and Eve and Lilith, but colored white like them too, where he had said No not just to all the hard savage years of his hard and barren life, but to Death too in the bed of a public prostitute.

The window had not changed: the same unwashed glass behind the wire grillework containing the same tired banjos and ornate clocks and trays of glass jewelry. "I want to buy a pistol," he said to one of the two men blue-jowled as pirates behind the counter.

"You got a permit?" the man said.

"A permit?" he said. "I jest want to buy a pistol. They told me before you sold pistols here. I got the money."

"Who told you we sold pistols here?" the man said.

"Maybe he dont want to buy one but just reclaim one," the second man said.

"Oh," the first said. "That's different. What sort of pistol do you want to reclaim, dad?"

"What?" he said.

"How much money have you got?" the first said. He removed the wadded paper from the bib of his overalls and took out the ten-dollar bill and unfolded it. "That all you got?"

"Let me see the pistol," he said.

"You cant buy a pistol for ten dollars, grandpaw," the first said. "Come on. Try them other pockets."

"Hold it," the second said. "Maybe he can reclaim one out of my private stock." He stooped and reached under the counter.

"That's an idea," the first said. "Out of your private stock, he wouldn't need a permit." The second man rose and laid an object on the counter. Mink looked at it quietly.

"Hit looks like a cooter," he said. It did: snub-nosed, short-barrelled, swollen of cylinder and rusted over, with its curved butt and flat reptilian hammer it did resemble the fossil relic of some small antediluvian terrapin.

"What are you talking about?" the first said. "That's a genuine bulldog detective special forty-one, the best protection a man could have. That's what you want, aint it—protection? Because if it's more than that; if you aim to take it back to Arkansaw and start robbing and shooting folks with it, the Law aint going to like it. They'll put you in jail for that even in Arkansaw. Even right down in Missippi you cant do that."

"That's right," Mink said. "Protection." He put the bill on the counter and took up the pistol and broke it and held the barrel up to the light. "Hit's dirty inside," he said.

"You can see through it, cant you?" the first said. "Do you think a forty-one calibre bullet cant go through any hole you can see through?" Mink lowered the pistol and was in the act of closing it again when he saw that the bill was gone.

"Wait," he said.

"Sure, sure," the first said, putting the bill back on the counter. "Give me the pistol. We cant reclaim even that one to you for just ten dollars."

"How much will you have to have?"

"How much have you got?"

"I got jest three more. I got to get home to Jefferson."

"Sure he's got to get home," the second said. "Let him have it for eleven. We aint robbers."

"It aint loaded," he said.

"There's a store around the corner on Main where you can buy all the forty-ones you want at four dollars a box," the first said.

"I aint got four dollars," he said. "I wont have but two now. And I got to get——"

"What does he want with a whole box, just for protection?" the second said. "Tell you what. I'll let you have a couple out of my private stock for another dollar."

"I got to have at least one bullet to try it with," he said. "Unless you will guarantee it."

"Do we ask you to guarantee you aint going to rob or shoot anybody with it?" the first said.

"Okay, okay, he's got to try it out," the second said. "Give him another bullet for a — you could spare another quarter, couldn't you? Them forty-one bullets are hard to get, you know."

"Could it be a dime?" he said. "I got to get home yet."

"Okay, okay," the second said. "Give him the pistol and three bullets for twelve dollars and a dime. He's got to get home. To hell with a man that'll rob a man trying to get home."

So he was all right; he stepped out into the full drowsing sunlight of Indian summer, into the unsleeping and passionate city. He was all right now. All he had to do now was to get to Jefferson, and that wasn't but eighty miles.

Thirteen

WHEN Charles Mallison got home in September of 1945, there was a new Snopes in Jefferson. They had got shot down ("of course," Charles always added, telling it) though it wasn't a crash. It wasn't even a bail-out; Plex (Plexiglass, the pilot. His name was Harold Baddrington but he had an obsession on the subject of cellophane, which he called plexiglass, amounting to a phobia; the simple sight or even the mere idea of a new pack of cigarettes or a new shirt or handkerchief as you had to buy them now pre-encased in an invisible impenetrable cocoon, threw him into the sort of virulent almost hysterical frenzy which Charles had seen the idea of Germans or Japanese throw some civilians into, especially ones around fifty years old. He—Plex—had a scheme for winning the war with cellophane: instead of bombs, the seventeens and twenty-fours and the British Lancasters and Blenheims would drop factory-vulcanised packs of tobacco and new shirts and underclothes, and while the Germans were queued up waiting turns at the ice-pick, they could be strafed en masse or even captured without a shot by paratroop drops.) made a really magnificent one-engine landing. The trouble was, he picked out a farm that a German patrol had already selected that morning to practise a new occupation innovation or something whose directive had just come down, so in almost no time the whole crew of them were in the POW camp at Limbourg, which almost immediately turned out to be the most dangerous place any of them had been in during the war; it was next door to the same marshalling yard that the RAF bombed regularly every Wednesday night from an altitude of about thirty or forty feet. They would spend six days watching the calendar creep inexorably toward Wednesday, when as regular as clockwork the uproar of crashes and thuds and snarling engines would start up and the air full of searchlights and machine gun bullets and whizzing fragments of AA, the entire barracks crouching under bunks or anything else that would interpose another inch of thickness, no matter what, with that frantic desire, need, impulse to rush outdoors waving their arms and shouting up at the pandemonium overhead: "Hey, fellows! For Christ's sake have a heart! It's us! It's us!" If it had been a moving picture or a book instead of a war, Charles said they would have escaped. But he himself didn't know and never knew anyone who ever actually escaped from a genuine authentic stalag, so they had to wait for regular routine liberation before he came back home and found there was already another Snopes in Jefferson.

But at least they—Jefferson—were holding their own. Because in that same summer, 1945, when Jefferson gained the new Snopes, Ratliff eliminated Clarence. Not that Ratliff shot him or anything like that: he just simply eliminated Clarence as a factor in what his, Charles's, Uncle Gavin also called their constant Snopes-fear and -dread, or you might say, Snopes-dodging. It happened during the campaign which ended in the August primary election; Charles hadn't got back home yet by a month, nor was his Uncle Gavin actually present at the picnic where it actually happened, where Clarence Snopes was actually defeated in the race for Congress which, being a national election, wouldn't even take place until next year. That's what he, Charles, meant by Ratliff doing it. He was in the office when his Uncle Gavin this time ran Ratliff to earth and bayed him and said, "All right. Just exactly what did happen out there that day?"

Senator Clarence Egglestone Snopes, pronounced "Cla'nce" by every free white Yoknapatawpha American whose right and duty it was to go to the polls and mark his X each time old man Will Varner told him to; just Senator Clarence Snopes for the first few years after old Varner ordained or commanded—anyway, translated—him into the Upper House of the State legislature in Jackson; beginning presently to put on a little flesh (he had been a big, hulking youth and young man but reasonably hard and active in an awkward kind of way until the sedentary brain-work of being one of the elected fathers and guardians and mentors of the parliamentary interests of Yoknapatawpha County began to redden his nose and pouch his eyes and paunch his belt a little) until one hot July day in the middle twenties when no other man in Jefferson or Yoknapatawpha County either under sixty years of age had on a coat, Clarence appeared on the Square in a complete white linen suit with a black Windsor tie, and either just before or just after or maybe it was that same simultaneous start or shock brought it to their notice, they realised that he was now signing himself Senator C.E. Snopes, and his, Charles's, Uncle Gavin said, "Where did the E come from?" and Ratliff said,

"Maybe he picked it up along with that-ere white wedding suit going and coming through Memphis to get back and forth to Jackson to work. Because why not? Aint even a elected legislative senator got a few private rights like any free ordinary voter?"

What Charles meant was that Clarence already had them all a little off-balance like a prize fighter does his opponent without really hitting him yet. So their emotion was simple docility when they learned that their own private Cincinnatus was not even C. any longer but was Senator Egglestone Snopes; his Uncle Gavin merely said, "Egglestone? Why Egglestone?" and Ratliff merely said,

"Why not?" and even his Uncle Gavin merely said,

"Yes, why not?" So they didn't really mark it when one day the C. was back again—Senator C. Egglestone Snopes now, with a definite belly and the pouched eyes and a lower lip now full from talking, forensic. Because Clarence was making speeches, anywhere and everywhere, at bond rallies and women's clubs, any place or occasion where there was a captive audience, because Charles was still in the German prison camp when his Uncle Gavin and Ratliff realised that Clarence intended to run for Congress in Washington and that old Will Varner might quite possibly get him elected to it—the same Clarence Snopes who had moved steadily onward and upward from being old Varner's privately appointed constable in Varner's own private Beat Two, then Supervisor of the Beat and then elected out of the entire county by means of old Will's diffused usurious capacity for blackmail, to be the County representative in Jackson; and now, 1945, tapped by all the mutually compounding vote-swapping Varners of the whole Congressional district for the House of Representatives in Washington itself, where in the clutches not of a mere neighborhood or sectional Will Varner but of a Will Varner of really national or even international scope, there would be no limit to what he might be capable of unless somebody did something about it. This, until that day in July at the annual Varner's Mill picnic where by custom and tradition not only the local candidates for county and state offices but even the regional and sectional ones for national offices, like Clarence, even though the election itself would not happen until next year, started the ball rolling. Whereupon Clarence not only failed to appear on the speakers' platform to announce his candidacy, he disappeared from the picnic grounds before the dinner was even served. And the next day word went over the county that Clarence had not only decided not to run for Congress, he was even withdrawing from public life altogether when his present term in the State Senate was up.

So what Charles's Uncle Gavin really wanted to know was not so much what had happened to Clarence, as what had happened to old Will Varner. Because whatever eliminated Clarence from the congressional race would have to impact not on Clarence but on old Will; it wouldn't have needed to touch Clarence at all in fact. Because nobody really minded Clarence just as you dont mind a stick of dynamite until somebody fuses it; otherwise he was just so much sawdust and greasy paper that wouldn't even burn good set on fire. He was unprincipled and without morals of course but without a guiding and prompting and absolving hand or intelligence, Clarence himself was anybody's victim since all he had was his blind instinct for sadism and over-reaching, and was himself really dangerous only to someone he would have the moral and intellectual ascendency of, which out of the entire world's population couldn't possibly be anybody except another Snopes, and out of the entire Snopes population couldn't possibly be more than just one of them. In this case it was his youngest brother Doris—a hulking youth of seventeen who resembled Clarence not only in size and shape but the same mentality of a child and the moral principles of a wolverine, the only difference being that Doris hadn't been elected to the State legislature yet. Back in the late twenties Byron Snopes, who looted Colonel Sartoris's bank and fled to Texas, sent back C.O.D. four half-Snopes half-Apache Indian children which Clarence, spending the summer at home

between two legislative sessions, adopted into a kind of peonage of practical jokes. Only, being a state senator now,
Clarence had to be a little careful about his public dignity, not
for the sake of his constituency but because even he knew a
damn sight better than to take chances with old Will Varner's
standards of *amour propre*. So he would merely invent the
jokes and use his brother Doris to perpetrate them, until the
four Indian children finally caught Doris alone in no man's
land and captured him and tied him to a stake in the woods
and even had the fire burning when someone heard his
screams and got there in time to save him.

But Clarence himself was in his late twenties then, already
a state senator; his career had begun long before that, back
when he was eighteen or nineteen years old out at Varner's
store and became leader of a subjugated (he was big and
strong and Ratliff said really liked fighting, provided the
equality in size was enough in his favor) gang of cousins and
toadies who fought and drank and gambled and beat up
Negroes and terrified women and young girls around Frenchman's Bend until (Ratliff said) old Varner became irritated
and exasperated enough to take him out of the public domain
by ordering the local j.p. to appoint Clarence his constable.
That was where and when Clarence's whole life, existence,
destiny, seemed at last to find itself like a rocket does at the
first touch of fire.

Though that figure wasn't quite right. His career didn't go
quite that fast, not at first anyway. Or maybe it wasn't his
career so much as his exposure, revealment. At first it was
almost like he was just looking around, orienting himself,
learning just where he now actually was; and only then looking in a sort of amazed incredulity at the vista opening before
him. Merely amazed at first, before the exultation began, at
the limitless prospect which nobody had told him about.
Because at first he even behaved himself. At first everybody
thought that, having been as outrageous as he had been with
no other backing than the unanimity of his old lawless pack,
he would be outrageous indeed now with the challengeless
majesty of organised law according to Will Varner to back
him. But he fooled them. Instead, he became the champion
and defender of the civic mores and the public peace of

Frenchman's Bend. Of course the first few Negroes who ran afoul of his new official capacity suffered for it. But there was now something impersonal even to the savaging of Negroes. Previous to his new avatar, he and his gang had beaten up Negroes as a matter of principle. Not chastising them as individual Negroes nor even, Charles's Uncle Gavin said, warring against them as representatives of a race which was alien because it was of a different appearance and therefore enemy *per se*, but (and his Uncle Gavin said Clarence and his gang did not know this because they dared not know it was so) because they were afraid of that alien race. They were afraid of it not because it was black but because they—the white man—had taught the black one how to threaten the white economy of material waste, when the white man compelled the black man to learn how to do more with less and worse if the black man wanted to survive in the white economy—less and worse of tools to farm and work with, less of luxury to be content with, less of waste to keep alive with. But not anymore now. Now when Clarence manhandled a Negro with the blackjack he carried or with the butt of the pistol which he now officially wore, it was with a kind of detachment, as if he were using neither the man's black skin nor even his human flesh, but simply the man's present condition of legal vulnerability as testing-ground or sounding-board on which to prove again, perhaps even reassure himself from day to day, just how far his—Clarence's—official power and legal immunity actually went and just how physically strong even with the inevitable passage of time he—Clarence—actually remained.

Because they were not always Negroes. In fact, one of the first victims of Clarence's new condition was his lieutenant, his second-in-command, in the old gang; if anything, Clarence was even more savage this time because the man had tried to trade on the old relationship and the past; it was as if he, Clarence, had now personally invested a kind of incorruptibility and integrity into his old natural and normal instinct and capacity for violence and physical anguish; had had to borrow them—the incorruptibility and the integrity—at so high a rate that he had to defend them with his life. Anyway, he had changed. And, Charles's Uncle Gavin said, since previous to his elevation to grace, everybody had believed

Clarence incapable of change, now the same people believed immediately that the new condition was for perpetuity, for the rest of his life. They still believed this even after they found out—it was no rumor; Clarence himself bragged, boasted quietly of it—that he was a member of the Ku Klux Klan when it appeared in the county (it never got very far and didn't last very long; it was believed that it wouldn't have lasted at all except for Clarence), taken in because the Klan needed him or could use him, or, as Charles's Uncle Gavin said, probably because there was no way under heaven that they could have kept him out since it was his dish just as he was its. This was before he became constable of Frenchman's Bend; his virgin advent from private life you might say, his initial accolade of public recognition, comparatively harmless yet since even a Ku Klux Klan would have more sense than to depend on Clarence very far; he remained just one more obedient integer, muscle-man—what in a few more years people would mean by 'goon'—until the day came when old Will Varner's irritation or exasperation raised him to constable, whereupon within the year it was rumored that he was now an officer in the Klavern or whatever they called it; and in two more years was himself the local Dragon or Kleagle: who having been designated by old Varner custodian of the public peace, had now decreed himself arbiter of its morals too.

Which was probably when he really discerned at last the breadth and splendor of his rising destiny; with amazement and incredulity at that apparently limitless expanse and, who knows? maybe even humility too that he should have been chosen, found worthy—that limitless field for his capacity and talents: not merely to beat, hammer men into insensibility and submission, but to use them; not merely to expend their inexhaustible numbers like ammunition or consume them like hogs or sheep, but to use, employ them like mules or oxen, with one eye constant for the next furrow tomorrow or next year; using not just their competence to mark an X whenever and wherever old Will Varner ordered them to, but their capacity for passion and greed and alarm as well, as though he—Clarence—had been in the business of politics all his life instead of those few mere years as a hick constable. And, as Charles's uncle said, doing it all by simple infallible instinct,

without preceptor or example. Because this was even before
Huey Long had risen far enough to show their own Mississippi Bilbo just what a man with a little brass and courage and
no inhibitions could really accomplish.

So when Clarence announced for the State legislature,
they—the County—knew he would need no other platform
than Uncle Billy Varner's name. In fact they decided immediately that his candidacy was not even Clarence's own idea but
Uncle Billy's; that Uncle Billy's irritation had simply reached
a point where Clarence must be removed completely from his
sight. But they were wrong. Clarence had a platform. Which
was the moment when some of them, a few of them like
Charles's uncle and Ratliff and a few more of the young ones
like Charles (he was only eight or ten then) who would listen
(or anyway had to listen, like Charles) to them, discovered
that they had better fear him, tremble and beware. His platform was his own. It was one which only his amoral temerity
would have dared because it set him apostate to his own constituency; the thin deciding margin of his vote came from
sources not only beyond the range of Will Varner's autocracy,
it came from people who under any other conditions would
have voted for almost any other member of the human race
first: he came out publicly against the Ku Klux Klan. He had
been the local Kleagle, Dragon, whatever the title was, right
up to the day he announced his candidacy—or so the County
thought. But now he was its mortal enemy, stumping the
county apparently only coincidentally to win an office, since
his dedication was to destroy a dragon, winning the race by
that scant margin of votes coming mostly from Jefferson itself—school-teachers, young professional people, women—
the literate and liberal innocents who believed that decency
and right and personal liberty would prevail simply because
they were decent and right; who until Clarence offered them
one, had had no political unanimity and had not even bothered always to vote, until at last the thing they feared and
hated seemed to have produced for them a champion. So he
went to Jackson not as the successful candidate for a political
office but as the dedicated paladin of a cause, walking
(Charles's uncle said) into the legislative halls in an aura half
the White Knight's purity and half the shocked consternation

of his own kind whom he had apparently wrenched himself from and repudiated. Because he did indeed destroy the Ku Klux Klan in Yoknapatawpha County; as one veteran Klansman expressed it: "Durn it, if we cant beat a handful of school-teachers and editors and Sunday School superintendents, how in hell can we hope to beat a whole race of niggers and catholics and jews?"

So Clarence was in. Now he had it made, as Charles's generation would say. He was safe now for the next two years when there would be another election, to look around, find out where to go next like the alpinist on his ledge. That's what Charles's uncle said it was: like the mountain climber. Except that the climber climbs the mountain not just to get to the top. He would try to climb it even if he knew he would never get there. He climbs it simply because he can have the solitary peace and contentment of knowing constantly that only his solitary nerve, will and courage stand between him and destruction, while Clarence didn't even know it was a mountain because there wasn't anything to fall off, you could only be pushed off; and anybody that felt himself strong enough or quick enough to push Clarence Snopes off anything was welcome to try it.

So at first what the County thought Clarence was doing now was simply being quiet while he watched and listened to learn the rules of the new trade. They didn't know that what he was teaching himself was how to recognise opportunities when they occurred; that he was still doing that even after he began at last to talk, address the House, himself still the White Knight who had destroyed bigotry and intolerance in Yoknapatawpha County in the eyes of the innocent illusionees whose narrow edge of additional votes had elected him, long after the rest of the County realised that Clarence was preaching the same hatred of Negroes and Catholics and Jews that had been the tenet of the organization by wrecking which he had got where he now was; when the Silver Shirts appeared, Clarence was one of the first in Mississippi to join it, joining, his uncle said, not because of the principles the Silver Shirts advocated but simply because Clarence probably decided that it would be more durable than the merely county-autonomous Klan which he had wrecked. Because by this

time his course was obvious: to join things, anything, any organization to which human beings belonged, which he might
compel or control or coerce through the emotions of religion
or patriotism or just simple greed, political gravy-hunger; he
had been born into the Baptist church in Frenchman's Bend;
he was now affiliated in Jackson, where (he had been re-
elected twice now) he now taught a Sunday School class; in
that same summer the County heard that he was contemplat-
ing resigning his seat in the Legislature long enough to do a
hitch in the army or navy to be eligible for the American
Legion.

Clarence was in now. He had it made. He had—Charles
was about to say 'divided the county' except that 'divided'
implied balance or at least suspension even though the lighter
end of the beam was irrevocably in the air. Where with
Clarence and Yoknapatawpha County, the lesser end of that
beam was not in suspension at all but rather in a condition of
aerial banishment, making now only the soundless motions of
vociferation in vacuum; Clarence had engulfed the county
whole as whales and owls do and, as owls do, disgorged onto
that airy and harmless pinnacle the refuse of bones and hair
he didn't need—the doomed handful of literate liberal under-
paid white-collar illusionees who had elected him into the
State senate because they thought he had destroyed the Ku
Klux Klan, plus the other lesser handful of other illusionees
like Charles's Uncle Gavin and Ratliff who were even more
doomed since where the school- and music-teachers and the
other white-collar innocents who learned by heart President
Roosevelt's speeches, could believe anew each time that
honor and justice and decency would prevail just because they
were honorable and just and decent, his uncle and Ratliff
never had believed this and never would.

Clarence didn't destroy them. There were not enough of
them. There were so few of them in fact that he could continue to send them year after year the mass-produced
Christmas cards which it was said he obtained from the same
firm he was instrumental in awarding the yearly contract for
automobile license plates. As for the rest of the county voters,
they only waited for Clarence to indicate where he wanted the
X marked to elect him to any office he wanted, right up to the

ultimate one which the County (including for a time even
Charles's uncle's branch of the illusioneed) believed was his
goal: Governor of the State. Huey Long now dominated the
horizon of every Mississippi politician's ambition; it seemed
only natural to the County that their own should pattern on
him; even when Clarence took up Long's soak-the-rich battle-
cry as though he, Clarence, had invented it, even Charles's
Uncle Gavin and Ratliff still believed that Clarence's sights
were set no higher than the Governor's Mansion. Because,
though at that time—1930–'35—Mississippi had no specific
rich to soak—no industries, no oil, no gas to speak of—the
idea of taking from anybody that had it that which they deserved no more than he did, being no more intelligent or in-
dustrious but simply luckier, struck straight to the voting
competence of every share-cropper and tenant-farmer not
only in Yoknapatawpha County but in all the rest of Mississippi too; Clarence could have been elected Governor of
Mississippi on the simple platform of soaking the rich in
Lousiana or Alabama, or for that matter in Maine or Oregon.

So their (his uncle's and Ratliff's little forlorn cell of unre-
constructed purists) shock at the rumor that Clarence had
contemplated for a moment taking over the American Legion
in Mississippi was nothing to the one when they learned three
years ago (Charles himself was not present; he had already departed from Yoknapatawpha County to begin training for his
ten months in the German POW camp) that the most potent
political faction in the State, the faction which was sure to
bring their man in as Governor, had offered to run Clarence
for lieutenant governor, and Clarence had declined. He gave
no reason but then he didn't need to because now all the
County—not just Charles's uncle's little cell, but everybody—
knew what Clarence's aim, ambition was and had been all the
time: Washington, Congress. Which was horror only among
the catacombs behind the bestiarium; with everyone else it
was triumph and exultation: who had already ridden Clarence's coat-tails to the (comparatively) minor-league hog-
trough at Jackson and who saw now the clear path to that vast
and limitless one in Washington.

And not just shock and horror, but dread and fear too of
the man who had used the Ku Klux Klan while he needed it

and then used their innocence to wreck the Klan when he no longer did, who was using the Baptist church as long as he believed it would serve him; who had used WPA and NRA and AAA and CCC and all the other agencies created in the dream or hope that people should not suffer or, if they must, at least suffer equally alike in times of crisis and fear; either being for them or against them as the political breeze indicated, since in the late thirties he turned against the party which had fathered them, ringing the halls which at least occasionally had echoed the voices of statesmen and humanitarians, with his own voice full of racial and religious and economic intolerance (once the strongest plank in his political creed had been soaking the rich; now the loudest one was the menace of organised labor) with nothing to intervene between him and Congress but that handful of innocents still capable of believing that evil could be destroyed simply because it was evil, whom Clarence didn't even fear enough to stop sending them the cheap Christmas cards.

"Which wont be enough," Charles's uncle said, "as it never has been enough in the country, even if they could multiply themselves by the ten-thousand. Because he would only fool them again."

"Maybe," Ratliff said. (This was Charles's Uncle Gavin telling him what had happened when he got back home in September after it was all over and whatever it was had licked Clarence, caused him to withdraw from the race, at old Will Varner's annual picnic in July; this was back in April when his uncle and Ratliff were talking.) "What you need is to have the young folks back for at least a day or two between now and the seventeenth of next August. What a shame the folks that started this war and drafted all the young voters away never had sense enough to hold off at least long enough to keep Clarence Snopes outen Congress, aint it?"

"*You* need?" Charles's uncle said. "What do you mean, *you?*"

"I thought you jest said how the old folks like you and me cant do nothing about Clarence but jest fold our hands and feel sorry," Ratliff said.

"No more we can," his uncle said. "Oh, there are enough of us. It was the ones of your and my age and generation who

carried on the good work of getting things into the shape
they're in now. But it's too late for us now. We cant now;
maybe we're just afraid to stick our necks out again. Or if not
afraid, at least ashamed. No: not afraid: we are just too old.
Call it just tired, too tired to be afraid any longer of losing.
Just to hate evil is not enough. You—somebody—has got to
do something about it. Only now it will have to be somebody
else, and even if the Japs should quit too before the seventeenth of August, there still wont be enough somebody elses
here. Because it wont be us."

"Maybe," Ratliff said. And his uncle was right. And then,
maybe Ratliff was right too. One of the first to announce for
the race to challenge Clarence from the district was a member
of his uncle's somebody elses—a man from the opposite end
of the district, who was no older than Charles: only—as
Charles put it—braver. He announced for Congress even before Clarence did. The election for Congress wouldn't be
until next year, 1946, so there was plenty of time. But then,
Clarence always did it this way: waited until the other candidate or candidates had announced and committed or anyway
indicated what their platforms would be. And Clarence had
taught Yoknapatawpha County to know why: that by waiting
to be the last, he didn't even need to invent a platform because by that time his chief, most dangerous opponent had
supplied him with one. As happened now, Clarence using this
one in his turn, using his valor as an instrument to defeat him
with.

His name was Devries; Yoknapatawpha County had never
heard of him before 1941. But they had since. In 1940 he had
been Number One in his ROTC class at the University, had
graduated with a regular army commission and by New Year's
1942 was already overseas; in 1943 when he was assigned back
to the United States to be atmosphere in bond drives, he was
a major with (this is Charles telling it) enough ribbons to
make a four-in-hand tie which he had acquired while commanding Negro infantry in battle, having been posted to
Negro troops by some brass-hatted theorist in Personnel
doubtless on the premise that, being a Southerner he would
indubitably 'understand' Negroes; and (Charles supposed)
just as indubitably commanded them well for the same rea-

son: that, being a Southerner, he knew that no white man understood Negroes and never would so long as the white man compelled the black man to be first a Negro and only then a man, since this, the impenetrable dividing wall, was the black man's only defense and protection for survival. Maybe he couldn't sell bonds. Anyway apparently he didn't really put his back into it. Because the story was that almost before his folks knew he was home he was on his way back to the war and when he came out this time, in 1944, he was a full bird colonel with next to the last ribbon and a tin leg; and while he was on his way to Washington to be given the last one, the top one, the story came out how he had finished the second tour up front and was already posted stateside when the general pinned the next to the last medal on him. But instead he dropped the medal into his foot-locker and put back on the battle fatigues and worried them until they let him go back up the third time and one night he turned the rest of the regiment over to the second and with a Negro sergeant and a runner crawled out to where what was left of the other battalion had been trapped by a barrage and sent them back with the runner for guide, he and the sergeant holding off one attack single-handed until they were clear, then he, Devries, was carrying the sergeant back when he took one too and this time a hulking giant of an Arkansas Negro cotton-field hand crawled out and picked them both up and brought them in. And when he, Devries, came out of the ether with the remaining leg he worried enough people until they sent in the field hand and he, Devries, had the nurse dig the medal out of the foot-locker and said to the field hand, "Lift me up, you big bastard," and pinned the medal on him.

That was Clarence's opponent for Congress. That is, even if the army hadn't anyone else at all for the experts to assume he understood Negroes, Devries (this is Charles talking) couldn't have talked himself back up front with one leg missing. So all he had now to try to persuade to send him somewhere were civilians, and apparently the only place he could think of was Congress. So (this is still Charles) maybe it would take somebody with no more sense than to volunteer twice for the same war, to have the temerity to challenge a long-vested interest like Clarence Snopes. Because even if

they had arranged things better, more practical: either for
1944 to have happened in 1943 or have the election year itself
moved forward one, or in fact if the Japs quit in 1945 too and
all the ruptured ducks in the Congressional District were back
home in time, there still would not be enough of them and in
the last analysis all Devries would have would be the heirs of
the same unco-ordinated political illusionees innocent enough
to believe still that demagoguery and bigotry and intolerance
must not and cannot and will not endure simply because they
are bigotry and demagoguery and intolerance, that Clarence
himself had already used up and thrown away twenty-odd
years ago; Charles's uncle said to Ratliff:

"They'll always be wrong. They think they are fighting
Clarence Snopes. They're not. They're not faced with an individual nor even a situation: they are beating their brains out
against one of the foundation rocks of our national character
itself. Which is the premise that politics and political office are
not and never have been the method and means by which we
can govern ourselves in peace and dignity and honor and
security, but instead are our national refuge for our incompe-
tents who have failed at every other occupation by means of
which they might make a living for themselves and their families; and whom as a result we would have to feed and clothe
and shelter out of our own private purses and means. The
surest way to be elected to office in America is to have fathered
seven or eight children and then lost your arm or leg in a
sawmill accident: both of which—the reckless optimism which
begot seven or eight children with nothing to feed them by
but a sawmill, and the incredible ineptitude which would put
an arm or a leg in range of a moving saw—should already have
damned you from any form of public trust. They cant beat
him. He will be elected to Congress for the simple reason that
if he fails to be elected, there is nothing else he can do that
anybody on earth would pay him for on Saturday night; and
old Will Varner and the rest of the interlocked Snopes kin and
connections have no intention whatever of boarding and feeding Clarence for the rest of his life. You'll see."

It looked like he was going to be right. It was May now,
almost time for the political season to open; a good one again
after four years, now that the Germans had collapsed too.

And still Clarence hadn't announced his candidacy in actual words. Everybody knew why of course. What they couldn't figure out yet was just how Clarence planned to use Devries's military record for his, Clarence's, platform; exactly how Clarence intended to use Devries's military glory to beat him for Congress with it. And when the pattern did begin to appear at last, Yoknapatawpha County—some of it anyway— found out something else about Clarence they had lived in innocence with for twenty and more years. Which was just how dangerous Clarence really was in his capacity to unify normal—you might even say otherwise harmless—human baseness and get it to the polls. Because this time he compelled them whose champion he was going to be, to come to him and actually beg him to be their champion; not just beg him to be their knight, but themselves to invent or anyway establish the cause for which they would need him.

Charles's Uncle Gavin told him how suddenly one day in that May or early June, the whole county learned that Clarence was not only not going to run for Congress, he was going to retire from public life altogether; this not made as a formal public announcement but rather breathed quietly from sheep to sheep of old Will Varner's voting flock which had been following Clarence to the polls for twenty-five years now; gently, his Uncle Gavin said, even a little sadly, with a sort of mild astonishment that it was not self-evident:

"Why, I'm an old man now," Clarence (he was a little past forty) said. "It's time I stepped aside. Especially since we got a brave young man like this Captain Devries—"

"Colonel Devries," they told him.

"Colonel Devries.—to represent you, carry on the work which I tried to do to better our folks and our county—"

"You mean, you're going to endorse him? You going to support him?"

"Of course," Clarence said. "Us old fellows have done the best we could for you, but now the time has come for us to step down. What we need in Congress now is the young men, especially the ones that were brave in the war. Of course General Devries—"

"Colonel Devries," they told him.

"Colonel Devries.—is a little younger maybe than I would

have picked out myself. But time will cure that. Of course he's got some ideas that I myself could never agree with and that lots of other old fogies like me in Missippi and the South wont never agree with either. But maybe we are all too old now, out of date, and the things we believed in and stood up for and suffered when necessary, aint true anymore, aint what folks want anymore, and his new ideas are the right ones for Yoknapatawpha County and Missippi and the South—"

And then of course they asked it: "What new ideas?"

And that was all. He told them: this man, Colonel Devries (no trouble anymore about the exactness of his rank) who had become so attached to Negroes by commanding them in battle that he had volunteered twice, possibly even having to pull a few strings (since everyone would admit that he had more than done his share of fighting for his country and democracy and was entitled to—more: had earned the right to—be further excused) to get back into the front lines in order to consort with Negroes; who had there risked his life to save one Negro and then had his own life saved by another Negro. A brave man (had not his government and country recorded and affirmed that by the medals it gave him, including that highest one in its gift?) and an honorable one (that medal meant honor too; did not its very designation include the word?), what course would—could—dared he take, once he was a member of that Congress already passing legislation to break down forever the normal and natural (natural? God Himself had ordained and decreed them) barriers between the white man and the black one. And so on. And that was all; as his uncle said, Clarence was already elected, the County and the District would not even need to spend the money to have the ballots cast and counted; that Medal of Honor which the government had awarded Devries for risking death to defend the principles on which that government was founded and by which it existed, had destroyed forever his chance to serve in the Congress which had accoladed him.

"You see?" Charles's uncle said to Ratliff. "You cant beat him."

"You mean, even you cant think of nothing to do about it?" Ratliff said.

"Certainly," his uncle said. "Join him."

"Join him?" Ratliff said.

"The most efficacious, the oldest—oh yes, without doubt the first, the very first, back to the very dim moment when two cave men confederated against the third one—of all political maxims."

"Join—*him?*" Ratliff said.

"All right," his uncle said. "You tell me then. I'll join you."

His uncle told how Ratliff blinked at him a while. "They must be some simpler way than that. It's a pure and simple proposition; there must be a pure and simple answer to it. Clarence jest purely and simply wants to get elected to Congress, he dont keer how; there must be some pure and simple way for the folks that purely and simply dont want him in Congress to say No to him, they dont keer how neither."

His uncle said again, "All right. Find it. I'll join you." But evidently it wasn't that pure and simple to Ratliff either: only to Clarence. His uncle said that after that Clarence didn't even need to make a campaign, a race; that all he would need to do would be to get up on the speakers' platform at Varner's Mill picnic long enough to be sure that the people who had turned twenty-one since old Will Varner had last told them who to vote for, would know how to recognise the word Snopes on the ballot. In fact, Devries could have quit now, and his uncle said there were some who thought he ought to. Except how could he, with that medal—all five or six of them—for guts and valor in the trunk in the attic or wherever he kept them. Devries even came to Jefferson, into Clarence's own bailiwick, and made his speech as if nothing were happening. But there you were. There were not enough soldiers back yet who would know what the medal meant. And even though the election itself would not happen until next year, nobody could know now that the Japs would cave this year too. To the others, the parents and Four F cousins and such to whom they had sent their voting proxies, Devries was a nigger-lover who had actually been decorated by the Yankee government for it. In fact, the story now was that Devries had got his Congressional Medal by choosing between a Negro and a white boy to save, and had chosen the Negro and left the white boy to die. Though Charles's uncle said that Clarence himself did not start this one: they must do him that justice at least. Not that Clarence would have flinched from starting it: he simply didn't need that additional ammunition now, having been, not so much in politics but simply a Snopes long enough now to know that only a fool would pay two dollars for a vote when fifty cents would buy it.

It must have been even a little sad: the man who had already been beaten in advance by the very medal which wouldn't let him quit. It was more than just sad. Because his Uncle Gavin told him how presently even the ones who had never owned a mechanical leg and, if the odds held up, never would, began to realise what owning, having to live with one, let alone stand up and walk on it, must have meant. Devries didn't sit in the car on the Square or even halted on the road, letting the constituency, the votes, do the standing and walking out to the car to shake his hand and listen to him as was Clarence's immemorial and successful campaigning method. Instead, he walked himself, swinging that dead mechanical excrescence or bracing it to stand for an hour on a platform to speak, rationalising for the votes which he already knew he had lost, while trying to keep all rumor of the chafed and outraged stump out of his face while he did it. Until at last Charles's uncle said how the very ones who would still vote for him would dread having to look at him and keep the rumor of that stump out of their faces too; until they themselves began to wish the whole thing was over, the debacle accomplished, wondering (his uncle said) how they themselves might end it and set him free to go home and throw the tin leg away, chop it up, destroy it, and be just peacefully maimed.

Then the day approached for Uncle Billy Varner's election-year picnic, where by tradition all county aspirants for office, county state or national, delivered themselves and so Clarence too would have to announce formally his candidacy, his Uncle Gavin saying how they clutched even at that straw: that once Clarence had announced for Congress, Devries might feel he could withdraw his name and save his face.

Only he didn't have to. After the dinner was eaten and the speakers gathered on the platform, Clarence wasn't even among them; shortly afterward the word spread that he had

even left the grounds and by the next morning the whole
County knew that he had not only withdrawn from the race
for Congress, he had announced his retirement from public
life altogether. And that this time he meant it because it was
not Clarence but old man Will Varner himself who had sent
the word out that Clarence was through. That was July, 1945;
a year after that, when the election for Congress finally came
around, the Japs had quit too and Charles and most of the
rest of them who knew what Devries's medal meant, were
home in person with their votes. But they merely increased
Devries's majority; he didn't really need the medal because
Ratliff had already beat Clarence Snopes. Then it was
September, Charles was home again and the next day his
uncle ran Ratliff to earth on the Square and brought him up
to the office and said,

"All right. Tell us just exactly what happened out there that
day."

"Out where what day?" Ratliff said.

"You know what I mean. At Uncle Billy Varner's picnic
when Clarence Snopes withdrew from the race for Congress."

"Oh, that," Ratliff said. "Why, that was what you might
call a kind of a hand of God, holp a little of course by them
two twin boys of Colonel Devries's sister."

"Yes," his uncle said. "That too: why Devries brought his
sister and her family all the way over here from Cumberland
County just to hear him announce for a race everybody knew
he had already lost."

"That's that hand of God I jest mentioned," Ratliff said.
"Because naturally otherwise Colonel Devries couldn't a possibly heard away over there in Cumberland County about one
little old lonesome gum thicket behind Uncle Billy Varner's
water mill now, could he?"

"All right, all right," his uncle said. "Thicket. Twin boys.
Stop now and just tell us."

"The twin boys was twin boys and the thicket was a dog
thicket," Ratliff said. "You and Chick both naturally know
what twin boys is and I was about to say you and Chick both
of course know what a dog thicket is too. Except that on second thought I reckon you dont because I never heard of a
dog thicket neither until I seen this clump of gum and ash

and hickory and pinoak switches on the bank jest above Varner's mill-pond where it will be convenient for the customers like them city hotels that keeps a reservoy of fountain pen ink open to anybody that needs it right next to the writing room—"

"Hold it," his uncle said. "Dog thicket. Come on now. I'm supposed to be busy this morning even if you're not."

"That's what I'm trying to tell you," Ratliff said. "It was a dog way-station. A kind of a dog postoffice you might say. Every dog in Beat Two uses it at least once a day, and every dog in the Congressional District, let alone jest Yoknapatawpha County, has lifted his leg there at least once in his life and left his visiting card. You know: two dogs comes trotting up and takes a snuff and Number One says, 'I be dawg if here aint that old bob-tail Bluetick from up at Wylie's Crossing. What you reckon he's doing away down here?' 'No it aint,' Number Two says. 'This here is that-ere fyce that Eck Grier swapped Odum Bookwright for that half a day's work shingling the church that time, dont you remember?' and Number One says, 'No, that fyce come afterward. This here is that old Wylie's Crossing Bluetick. I thought he'd a been skeered to come back here after what that Littlejohn half Airedale done to him that day.' You know: that sort of thing."

"All right," his uncle said. "Go on."

"That's all," Ratliff said. "Jest that-ere what you might call select dee-butant Uncle Billy Varner politics coming-out picnic and every voter and candidate in forty miles that owned a pickup or could bum a ride in one or even a span of mules either if wasn't nothing else handy, the sovereign votes theirselves milling around the grove where Senator Clarence Egglestone Snopes could circulate among them until the time come when he would stand up on the platform and actively tell them where to mark the X. You know: ever thing quiet and peaceful and ordinary and law-abiding as usual until this-here anonymous underhanded son-of-a-gun—I wont say scoundrel because evidently it must a been Colonel Devries his-self since couldn't nobody else a knowed who them two twin boys was, let alone what they was doing that far from Cumberland County; leastways not them particular two twin boys and that-ere local dog thicket in the same breath you might say—until whoever this anonymous underhanded feller was, suh-jested to them two boys what might happen say if two folks about that size would shoo them dogs outen that thicket long enough to cut off a handful of them switches well down below the dog target level and kind of walk up behind where Senator C. Egglestone Snopes was getting out the vote, and draw them damp switches light and easy, not to disturb him, across the back of his britches-legs. Light and easy, not to disturb nobody, because apparently Clarence nor nobody else even noticed the first six or eight dogs until maybe Clarence felt his britches-legs getting damp or maybe jest cool, and looked over his shoulder to see the waiting line-up of his political fate with one eye while already breaking for the nearest automobile or pickup you could roll the windows up in with the other, with them augmenting standing-room-only customers strung out behind him like the knots in a kite's tail until he got inside the car with the door slammed and the glass rolled up, them frustrated dogs circling round and round the automobile like the spotted horses and swan-boats on a flying jenny, except the dogs was travelling on three legs, being already loaded and cocked and aimed you might say. Until somebody finally located the owner of the car and got the key and druv Clarence home, finally outdistancing the last dog in about two miles, stopping at last in the ex-Senator's yard where he was safe, the Snopes dogs evidently having went to the picnic too, while somebody went into the house and fetched out a pair of dry britches for the ex-Senator to change into in the automobile. That's right. Ex-Senator. Because even with dry britches he never went back to the picnic; likely he figgered that even then it would be too much risk and strain. I mean, the strain of trying to keep your mind on withdrawing from a political race and all the time having to watch over your shoulder in case some dog recollected your face even if your britches did smell fresh and uninteresting."

"Well I'll be damned," his uncle said. "It's too simple. I dont believe it."

"I reckon he figgered that to convince folks how to vote for him and all the time standing on one foot trying to kick dogs away from his other leg, was a little too much to expect of even Missippi voters," Ratliff said.

"I dont believe you, I tell you," his uncle said. "That wouldn't be enough to make him withdraw even if everybody at the picnic had known about it, seen it. Didn't you just tell me they got him into a car and away almost at once?" Then his uncle stopped. He looked at Ratliff, who stood blinking peacefully back at him. His uncle said: "Or at least—"

"That's right," Ratliff said. "That was the trade."

"What trade?" his uncle said.

"It was likely that same low-minded anonymous scoundrel again," Ratliff said. "Anyhow, somebody made the trade that if Senator Snopes would withdraw from this-here particular race for Congress, the folks that had seen them pro-Devries dogs would forget it, and the ones that hadn't wouldn't never need to know about it."

"But he would have beat that too," his uncle said. "Clarence Snopes stopped or even checked just because a few dogs raised their legs against him? Hell, he would have wound up having every rabies tag in Yoknapatawpha County counted as an absentee ballot."

"Oh, you mean Clarence," Ratliff said. "I thought you meant Uncle Billy Varner."

"Uncle Billy Varner?" his uncle said.

"That's right," Ratliff said. "It was Uncle Billy his-self that that low-minded rascal must a went to. Leastways Uncle Billy his-self sent word back that same afternoon that Senator Clarence Egglestone Snopes had withdrawed from the race for Congress; Uncle Billy never seemed to notified the ex-Senator a-tall. Oh yes, they told Uncle Billy the same thing you jest said: how it wouldn't hurt Clarence none in the long run; they even used your same words about the campaign tactics of the dogs, only a little stronger. But Uncle Billy said No, that Clarence Snopes wasn't going to run for nothing in Beat Two.

"'But he aint running in jest Beat Two,' they said. 'He aint even running in jest Yoknapatawpha County now. He's running in a whole one-eighth of the State of Missippi.' And Uncle Billy said:

"'Durn the whole hundred eighths of Missippi and Yoknapatawpha County too. I aint going to have Beat Two and Frenchman's Bend represented nowhere by nobody that ere a son a bitching dog that happens by cant tell from a fence-post.'"

His uncle was looking at Ratliff. He had been looking at Ratliff for some time. "So this anonymous meddler you speak of not only knew the twin nephews and that dog thicket, he knew old Will Varner too."

"It looks like it," Ratliff said.

"So it worked," his uncle said.

"It looks like it," Ratliff said.

Both he and his uncle looked at Ratliff sitting neat and easy, blinking, bland and inscrutable in one of the neat blue shirts he made himself, which he never wore a tie with though Charles knew he had two at home he had paid Allanovna seventy-five dollars apiece for that time his uncle and Ratliff went to New York ten years ago to see Linda Snopes married, which Ratliff had never had on. "O Cincinnatus," his uncle said.

"What?" Ratliff said.

"Nothing," his uncle said. "I was just wondering who it was that told those twin boys about that dog thicket."

"Why, Colonel Devries, I reckon," Ratliff said. "A soldier in the war with all them medals, after three years of practice on Germans and I-talians and Japanese, likely it wasn't nothing to him to think up a little political strategy too."

"They were mere death-worshippers and simple pre-absolved congenital sadists," his uncle said. "This was a born bred and trained American professional ward-level politician."

"Maybe aint neither of them so bad, providing a man jest keeps his eyes open and uses what he has, the best he knows," Ratliff said. Then he said, "Well," and rose, lean and easy, perfectly bland, perfectly inscrutable, saying to Charles now: "You mind that big oat field in the bend below Uncle Billy's pasture, Major? It stayed full of geese all last winter they say. Why dont you come out when the season opens and shoot a few of them? I reckon Uncle Billy will let us."

"Much obliged," Charles said.

"It's a trade then," Ratliff said. "Good day, gentlemen." Then Ratliff was gone. Now Charles was looking at his uncle, whereupon his uncle drew a sheet of paper to him and began to write on it, not fast: just extremely preoccupied, absorbed.

"So, quote," Charles said, "it will have to be you, the young people unquote. I believe that's about how it went, wasn't it?—that summer back in '37 when us moralists were even having to try to beat Roosevelt himself in order to get to Clarence Snopes?"

"Good day, Charles," his uncle said.

"Because quote it wont be us," Charles said. "We are too old, too tired, have lost the capacity to believe in ourselves—"

"Damn it," his uncle said, "I said good day."

"Yes sir," Charles said. "In just a moment. Because quote the United States, America: the greatest country in the world if we can just keep on affording it unquote. Only, let 'afford' read 'depend on God'. Because He saved you this time, using V.K. Ratliff of course as His instrument. Only next time Ratliff may be off somewhere selling somebody a sewing machine or a radio" (That's right, Ratliff now had a radio agency too, the radio riding inside the same little imitation house on the back of his pickup truck that the demonstrator sewing machine rode in; two years more and the miniature house would have a miniature TV stalk on top of it.) "and God may not be able to put His hand on him in time. So what you need is to learn how to trust in God without depending on Him. In fact, we need to fix things so He can depend on us for a while. Then He wont need to waste Himself being everywhere at once." Now his uncle looked up at him and suddenly Charles thought *Oh yes, I liked Father too all right but Father just talked to me while Uncle Gavin listened to me, no matter how foolish what I was saying finally began to sound even to me, listening to me until I had finished, then saying, "Well, I dont know whether it will hold together or not but I know a good way to find out. Let's try it." Not you try it but us try it.*

"Yes," his uncle said. "So do I."

Fourteen

Though by the time Ratliff eliminated Clarence back into private life in Frenchman's Bend, there had already been a new Snopes living in Jefferson for going on two years. So Jefferson was merely holding its own in what Charles's uncle would call the Snopes condition or dilemma.

This was a brand new one, a bachelor named Orestes, called Res. That's right, Orestes. Even Charles's Uncle Gavin didn't know how either. His uncle told him how back in 1943 the town suddenly learned that Flem Snopes now owned what was left of the Compson place. Which wasn't much. The tale was they had sold a good part of it off back in 1909 for the municipal golf course in order to send the oldest son, Quentin, to Harvard, where he committed suicide at the end of his freshman year; and about ten years ago the youngest son, Benjy, the idiot, had set himself and the house both on fire and burned up in it. That is, after Quentin drowned himself at Harvard and Candace's, the sister's, marriage blew up and she disappeared, nobody knew where, and her daughter, Quentin, that nobody knew who her father was, climbed down the rainpipe one night and ran off with a carnival, Jason, the middle one, finally got rid of Benjy too by finally persuading his mother to commit him to the asylum only it didn't stick, Jason's version being that his mother whined and wept until he, Jason, gave up and brought Benjy back home, where sure enough in less than two years Benjy not only burned himself up but completely destroyed the house too.

So Jason took the insurance and borrowed a little more on the now vacant lot and built himself and his mother a new brick bungalow up on the main street to the Square. But the lot was a valuable location; Jefferson had already begun to surround it; in fact the golf links had already moved out to the country club back in 1929, selling the old course back to Jason Compson. Which was not surprising. While he was still in high school Jason had started clerking after school and on Saturdays in Uncle Ike McCaslin's hardware store, which even then was run by a man named Earl Triplett that Uncle

Ike got from somewhere, everybody supposed off a deer-stand or a Delta fishing lake, since that was where Uncle Ike spent most of his time. For which reason it was not surprising for the town to assume presently that Triplett had long since gently eliminated Uncle Ike from the business even though Uncle Ike still loafed in the store when he wasn't hunting or fishing and without doubt Triplett still let him have his rifle and shotgun ammunition and fishing tackle at cost. Which without doubt the town assumed Jason did too when Jason had eliminated Triplett in his turn back to his deer-stand or trot-line or minnow-bucket.

Anyhow, for all practical purposes Jason Compson was now the McCaslin Hardware Company. So nobody was surprised when it was learned that Jason had bought back into the original family holding the portion which his father had sacrificed to send his older brother to Harvard—a school which Jason held in contempt for the reason that he held all schools beyond the tenth grade to be simply refuges for the inept and the timid. Charles's uncle said that what surprised him was when he went to the Courthouse and looked at the records and saw that, although Jason had apparently paid cash for the abandoned golf course, he had not paid off the mortgage on the other part of the property on which he had raised the money to build his new bungalow, the interest on which he had paid promptly in to Flem Snopes's bank ever since, and apparently planned to continue. This, right up to Pearl Harbor. So that you would almost believe Jason had a really efficient and faithful spy in the Japanese Diet. And then in the spring of 1942, another spy just as efficient and loyal in the U.S. Cabinet too; his uncle said that to listen to Jason, you would believe he not only had advance unimpeachable information that an air-training field was to be located in Jefferson, he had an unimpeachable promise that it would be located nowhere else save on that old golf links; his uncle said how back then nobody in Jefferson knew or had thought much about air-fields and they were willing to follow Jason in that anything open enough to hit golf balls in was open enough to land airplanes on.

Or anyway the right one believed him. The right one being Flem Snopes, the president of the bank which held the mortgage on the other half of Jason's property. His Uncle Gavin said it must have been like a two-handed stud game when both have turned up a hole-ace and by mutual consent decreed the other two aces dead cards. He—Gavin—said that of course nobody knew what really happened. All they knew was what they knew about Jason Compson and Flem Snopes; Gavin said there must have come a time when Flem, who knew all along that he didn't know as much about air-fields as Jason did, must have had a terrifying moment when he believed maybe he didn't know as much about money either. So Flem couldn't risk letting Jason draw another card and maybe raise him; he had to call.

Or (his uncle said) so Jason thought. That Jason was simply waving that imaginary air-field around the Square to spook Mr Snopes into making the first move. Which was evidently what Snopes did: he called in the note his bank held on Jason's mortgage. All amicable and peaceful of course, which was the way Jason expected it, inviting him (Jason) into that private back room in the bank and saying, "I'm just as sorry about this as you can ever be, Mr Compson. But you can see how it is. With our country fighting for its very life and existence on both sides of the world, it's every man's duty and privilege too to add his little mite to the battle. So my board of directors feel that every possible penny of the bank's resources should go into matters pertaining directly to the war effort."

Which was just what Jason wanted: "Why certainly, Mr Snopes. Any patriotic citizen will agree whole-heartedly with you. Especially when there is a direct war effort right here in Jefferson, like this air-field I understand they have practically let the contract for, just as soon as the title to the land is cleared": naming his price for the ex-golf course, out of which sum naturally the mortgage note would be paid. Or, if Mr Snopes and his directors preferred, he, Jason, would name a lump sum for the entire Compson property, including the mortgage, and so leave the bank's directors or some patriotic civic body representing the town itself to deal with the Government for the air-field; he, Jason, reserving only the right to hope that the finished flying field might be christened Compson Field as a monument not to him, Jason, but to the hope that his family had had a place in the history of Jefferson at least not to be ashamed of, including as it did one Governor and one brigadier general, whether it was worth commemorating or not. Because Charles's uncle said that Jason was shrewd too in his way, enough to speculate that the man who had spent as much as Snopes had to have his name on a marble monument over the grave of his unfaithful wife, might spend some more to have an air-field named for him too.

Or so Jason thought. Because in January '43 Jefferson learned that Mr Snopes—not the bank: Mr Private Individual Snopes—now owned the Compson place. And now his Uncle Gavin said how Jason exposed his hand a little from triumph. But then, who could really blame him since until now nobody but the Italian marble syndicate had ever managed to sell Flem Snopes anything as amorphous as prestige. And what the Italians had sold him was respectability, which was not a luxury but a necessity: referring (Jason did) to his old home property as Snopes Field, even (Charles's uncle said) waylaying, ambushing Mr Snopes himself now and then on the street when there was an audience, to ask about the progress of the project; this after even the ones who didn't know what an air-field really was, had realised there would not be one here since the Government had already designated the flatter prairie land to the east near Columbus, and the perfectly flat Delta land to the west near Greenville, as the only acceptable terrain for flight training. Because then Jason began to commiserate with Mr Snopes in reverse, by delivering long public tirades on the Government's stupidity; that Mr Snopes in fact was ahead of his time but that inevitably, in the course of time as the war continued and we all had to tighten our belts still further, the Snopes concept of a flying field composed of hills would be recognised as the only practical one and would become known throughout the world as the Snopes Airport Plan since under it runways that used to have to be a mile long could be condensed into half that distance since by simply bulldozing away the hill beneath it both sides of the runway could be used for each takeoff and landing, like a fly on a playing card wedged in a crack.

Or maybe Jason was whistling in the dark, his Uncle Gavin said, saying No in terror to terrified realisation, already too

late. Because Jason was shrewd in his way, having had to practise shrewdness pretty well to have got where he now was
without any outside help and not much of a stake either. That
maybe as soon as he signed the deed and before he even
cashed the check, it may have occurred to him that Flem
Snopes had practised shrewdness pretty well too, to be president of a bank now from even less of a stake than he, Jason,
who at least had had a house and some land where Flem's had
been only a wife. That Jason may have divined, as through
some prescience bequeathed him by their mutual master, the
Devil, that Flem Snopes didn't want and didn't intend to
have a flying field on that property. That it was only Jason
Compson who assumed that that by-product of war would go
on forever which condemned and compelled real estate to the
production and expension of airplanes and tanks and cannon,
but that Flem Snopes knew better. Flem Snopes knew that
the airplanes and tanks and guns were self-consuming in their
own nihilism and inherent obsolescence, and that the true by-
product of the war which was self-perpetuating and -com-
pounding and would prevail and continue to self-compound
into perpetuity, was the children, the birth-rate, the space on
which to build walls to house it from weather and temperature and contain its accumulating junk.

   Too late. Because now Snopes owned it and all he had to
do was just to sit still and wait while the war wore itself out.
Since whether America, Jefferson, won it or lost it wouldn't
matter; in either case population would compound and
Government or somebody would have to house it, and the
houses would have to stand on something somewhere—a plot
of land extending a quarter of a mile in both directions except
for a little holding in one corner owned by a crotchety old
man named Meadowfill, whom Flem Snopes would take care
of in ten or fifteen minutes as soon as he got around to needing it, which even before Pearl Harbor had already begun to
be by-passed and surrounded and enclosed by the town. So
what Jason did next didn't surprise anyone; Charles's uncle
said the only surprising thing was why Jason chose him, Gavin
Stevens, to try to bribe either to find a flaw in the title he had
conveyed to Mr Snopes; or if he, Stevens, couldn't find one,
to invent one into it. His uncle said Jason answered that one

himself: "Hell, aint you supposed to be the best-educated lawyer in this section? Not only Harvard but that German place too?"

"That is, if Harvard cant trick your property back from Flem Snopes, Heidelberg should," his uncle said. "Get out of here, Jason."

"That's right," Jason said. "You can afford virtue, now that you have married money, cant you?"

"I said get out of here, Jason," his uncle said.

"Okay, okay," Jason said. "I can probably find a lawyer somewhere that aint got enough money in Flem Snopes's bank to be afraid of him."

Except that Jason Compson shouldn't have needed anybody to tell him that Flem Snopes wasn't going to buy a title from anybody capable of having a flaw in it, or anything else in it to make it vulnerable. But Jason continued to try; his—Charles's—uncle told him about it: Jason going about the business of trying to find some way, any way to overturn or even just shake Snopes's title, with a kind of coldly seething indefatigable outrage like that of a revivalist who finds that another preacher has stepped in behind his back and converted the client or patient he had been working on all summer, or a liar or a thief who has been tricked or robbed by another liar or thief. But he failed each time, Snopes's title to the entire old Compson place stood so that even Jason gave up at last; and that same week the same Wat Snopes who had transformed the old De Spain house into Flem's ante bellum mansion twenty years ago, came in again and converted the Compson carriage house (it was detached from the main house so Benjy had failed to burn it) into a small two-storey residence, and a month later the new Jefferson Snopes, Orestes, was living in it. And not merely as Flem Snopes's agent in actual occupation against whatever machinations Jason might still discover or invent. Because by summer Res had fenced up the adjacent ground into lots and was now engaged in the business of buying and selling scrubby cattle and hogs. Also, by that time he was engaged in an active kind of guerrilla feud with old man Meadowfill, whose orchard boundary was Res Snopes's hog-lot fence.

Even before the war old Meadowfill had a reputation in

Jefferson: he was so mean as to be solvent and retired even from the savings on a sawmill. He had been active as a mill-owner and timber-dealer for a year or so after he bought his little corner of the Compson place and built his little un-wired un-plumbing-ed house, until he sold his mill and re-tired into the house with his gray drudge of a wife and their one child; where, since it was obvious to anyone that a man retiring still alive and with all his limbs from a sawmill could not possibly possess one extra dollar for anyone to borrow or sell him anything for, he could devote his full time to gaining and holding the top name for curmudgeonry in all Jefferson and probably all Yoknapatawpha County too.

Charles remembered the daughter—a quiet modest mousy girl nobody even looked at twice until suddenly in 1942 she graduated not only valedictorian of her high school class but with the highest grades ever made in it, plus a five-hundred-dollar scholarship offered by the president of the Bank of Jefferson (not Snopes's bank: the other one) as a memorial to his only son, a Navy pilot who had been killed in one of the first Pacific battles. She refused the scholarship. She went to Mr Holland and told him she had already taken a job with the telephone company and wouldn't need the scholarship but in-stead she wanted to borrow five hundred dollars from the bank against her future salary, and, pressed, finally divulged the reason for it: to put a bathroom in her home; how once a week, on Saturday night, winter and summer, the mother would heat water on the kitchen stove and fill a round gal-vanised wash-tub in the middle of the floor, in which single filling all three of them bathed in turn: the father, then the child, then last of all the mother: at which point Mr Holland himself took over, had the bathroom installed despite old Meadowfill's outraged fury (he didn't intend to have his house meddled with at all by outsiders and strangers but if it was he wanted the cash money instead) and gave Essie a job for life in his bank.

Whereupon, now that the only child was not only secure but was actually contributing to the family budget, old Meadowfill soared to heights of outrageousness of which even he hadn't dreamed. Up to this time he had done the grocery shopping himself, walking to town each morning with an empty jute feed-sack, to haggle in the small dingy back- and side-street stores which catered mostly to Negroes, for wilted and damaged left-overs of food which even Negroes would have scorned. The rest of the day he would spend, not lurking exactly but certainly in wait, ambushed, about his yard to shout and curse at the stray dogs which crossed his unfenced property, and the small boys who had a game of raiding the few sorry untended fruit trees which he called his orchard. Now he stopped that. He waited exactly one year, as though to be really sure Essie had her job for good. Then on the morning following her death he went and bought from the family of a paralytic old lady neighbor the wheel chair she had inhabited for years, not even waiting until the funeral had left the house, and pushed the chair home along the street for his last appearance on it, and retired into the chair. Not completely at first. Although Charles's uncle said that Essie now did the daily shopping, Meadowfill could still be seen in the yard, still snarling and cursing at the small boys or throwing rocks (he kept a small pile handy, like the cannon balls of a war memorial) at the stray dogs. But he never left his own premises anymore and presently he seemed to have retired permanently into the wheel chair, sitting in it like it was a rocking chair in a window which looked out over the vegetable patch he no longer worked at all now, and the scraggy fruit trees he had always been either too stingy or too perverse to spray and tend enough to produce even an edible crop, let alone a salable one.

Then Flem Snopes let Jason Compson over-reach himself out of his ancestral acres, and Res Snopes built a hog-lot along the boundary of old Meadowfill's orchard and made a new man of old Meadowfill. Because the trespassing of little boys merely broke a limb now and then, and stray dogs merely dug up flowerbeds if he had had flowerbeds. But one rooting hog could foul and sour and make sterile the very dirt itself. So now Meadowfill had a reason for staying alive. He even abandoned the wheel chair temporarily, it would have been in his way now, spending all day while Snopes and a hired Negro built the wire fence along his boundary, watching the digging of every post hole and the setting and tamping of the post, grasping the post in both hands to shake and test it, on the verge of apoplexy, a little mad by this time, shouting at Snopes and his helper as they stretched the wire: "Tighter! Tighter! Hell fire, what do you figger you're doing? hanging a hammock?" until Snopes—a lean gangling man with a cast in one sardonic eye—would say,

"Now, Mr Meadowfill, dont you worry a-tall. Before I would leave a old broke-down wheel-chair gentleman like you to have to climb this fence by hand, I aim to put slip bars in it that you could even get down and crawl under when you dont feel like opening them," with Meadowfill almost past speech now, saying,

"If ara one of them hogs—if jest ara durn one of them hogs—" and Snopes:

"Then all you got to do is jest ketch it and shut it up in your kitchen or bedroom or any other handy place and the pound law will make me pay you a dollar for it. In fact, that might even be good easy work for a retired wheel-chair old gentleman—" By which time Meadowfill would be in such a state that Snopes would call toward the kitchen, from the window or door of which by this time the gray wife would be watching or anyway hovering: "Maybe you better come and git him away from here."

Which she would do—until the next day. But at last the fence was finished. Or at least Snopes was no longer where Meadowfill could curse at him: only the hogs rooting and rubbing along the new fence which did hold them, or anyway so far. But only so far, only up to the moment it got too dark to see the orchard last night. So now he had something to stay alive for, to get up in the morning for, hurry out of bed and across to the window as soon as darkness thinned, to see if perhaps darkness itself hadn't betrayed him in which he couldn't have seen a hog in his orchard even if he had been able to stay awake twenty-four hours a day watching for it; to get into his chair and wheel himself across to the window and see his orchard for one more night anyway unravished, for one more night at least he had been spared. Then to be-grudge the very time he would have to spend at table eating, since this would leave the orchard unguarded, unwatched of course he meant. Because, as Charles's uncle said, Meadowfill wasn't worrying at all about what he would do next when he

did look out the window and actually see a hog on his property—an old bastard who, as Charles himself remembered,
had already alienated all his neighbors before he committed
himself to invalidism and the wheel chair, so that not one of
them would have raised a hand to eject the hog for him or do
anything else for him except maybe hide the body if and when
his gray drab of a wife did what she should have done years
ago: murdered him some night. Meadowfill hadn't thought
about what to do with the hog at all. He didn't need to. He
was happy, for the first time in his life probably, Charles's
Uncle Gavin said: that you are happy when your life is filled,
and any life is filled when it is so busy living from moment to
moment that it has no time over to remember yesterday or
dread tomorrow. Which of course couldn't last, his uncle said.
That in time Meadowfill would reach the point where if he
didn't look out that window some morning and see a hog in
his orchard, he would die of simple hope unbearably deferred;
and if he did some morning look out and see one, he would
surely die because he would have nothing else left.

The atom bomb saved him. Charles meant that at last the
Japs quit too and now the troops could come home from all
directions, back to the women they had begun to marry before the echo of the first Pearl Harbor bomb had died away,
and had been marrying ever since whenever they could get
two days' leave, coming back home now either to already going families or to marry the rest of the women they hadn't
got around to yet, the blood-money already in the hands of
the Government Housing Loan (as his Uncle Gavin put it:
"The hero who a year ago was rushing hand grenades and
Garand clips up to front-line foxholes, is now rushing baskets
of soiled didies out of side- and back-street Veterans Administration tenements.") and now Jason Compson was under-
going an anguish which he probably believed not only no
human should suffer, but no human could really bear.
Because when Charles reached home in September of '45,
Jason's old lost patrimony was already being chopped up into
a subdivision of standardised Veterans' Housing matchboxes;
within the week Ratliff came to the office and told him and
his uncle the official name of the subdivision: Eula Acres. Not
Jason's old triumphant jeering gibe of Snopes Field, Snopes's

Demolitional Jump-off, but Eula Acres, Eula's Uxorious Nest-place. And Charles didn't know whether old Flem Snopes had named it that himself or not but he would remember his uncle's face while Ratliff was telling them. But even without that he, Charles, would still prefer to believe it was not really Flem but his builder and (the town assumed) partner Wat Snopes who thought of it, maybe because Charles still wanted to believe that there are some things, at least one thing, that even Flem Snopes wouldn't do, even if the real reason was that Flem himself never thought of naming it anything because to him it couldn't matter whether it had a name or not. By Christmas it was already dotted over with small brightly-painted pristinely new hutches as identical (and about as permanent) as squares of gingerbread or tea-cakes, the ex-soldier or -sailor or -marine with his ruptured duck pushing the perambulator with one hand and carrying the second (or third) infant in the other arm, waiting to get inside almost before the last painter could gather up his drop-cloth. And by New Year's a new arterial highway had been decreed and surveyed which would run the whole length of Mr Snopes's subdivision, including the corner which old Meadow-fill owned; whereupon there opened before Meadowfill a prospect of excitement and entertainment beside which the mere depredations of a hog would have been as trivial as the trespass of a frog or a passing bird. Because now one of the big oil companies wanted to buy the corner where Meadowfill's lot and the old Compson place (now Snopes) joined—that is, a strip of Meadowfill's orchard, with a contiguous strip of Res Snopes's hog-lot—to build a filling station on.

Because old Meadowfill didn't even own thirteen feet of the strip of his land which the oil company wanted. In fact, as the town knew, the title to none of his land vested in him. During the early second Roosevelt days he had naturally been among the first to apply for relief, learning to his outraged and incredulous amazement that a finicking and bureaucratic federal government declined absolutely and categorically to let him be a pauper and a property-owner at the same time. So he came to Charles's Uncle Gavin, choosing Stevens from among the other Jefferson lawyers for the simple reason that he, Meadowfill, knew that in five minutes he would have Stevens so mad that very likely Stevens would refuse to accept any fee at all for drawing the deed transferring all his property to his nine-year-old (this was 1934) daughter. He was wrong only in his estimate of the time, since it required only two minutes for Charles's uncle to reach the boil which carried him into the Chancery Clerk's vault, where he discovered that the deed which Jason Compson's father had executed to Meadowfill read 'South to the road known as the Freedom Springs Road, thence East along said Road . . .' The Freedom Springs road being, by the time Meadowfill bought his corner, an eroded thicket-grown ditch ten feet deep with only a footpath in it: as ponderable and inescapable a geographical condition as the Grand Canyon, since this was before the era when the bull-dozer and the dragline would not only alter but efface geography. Which was thirteen feet short of the actual survey-line boundary which Mahataha, the Chickasaw matriarch, had granted to Quentin Compson in 1821, and Charles's uncle said his first impulse was the ethical one to tell old Meadowfill how he actually owned thirteen feet more of the surface of the earth than he thought he did, provided he did something about it before somebody else did. But if he, Stevens, did that, he would be ethically bound to accept Meadowfill's ten dollars for the title-search, so he decided to let one ethic cancel the other and allow simple justice to prevail.

   That was the situation when the survey line for the new highway was run to follow the old Chickasaw line, and Meadowfill discovered that his property only extended to the ditch which was thirteen feet short of it. But rage was a mild term for his condition when the oil company approached him to buy his part of the corner and he found that his mortal en-emy, the hog-raising Snopes, owned the thirteen feet without a clear title to which the oil company would buy none of his, Meadowfill's, ground. There was rage in it too of course, since rage had been Meadowfill's normal condition for a year now. But now it was triumph too. More: it was vindication, revenge. Revenge on the Compsons who had uttered a false deed to him, allowing him to buy in good faith. Revenge on the community which had badgered him for years with small boys and stray dogs, by holding up a new tax-paying industry (if he could, by stopping the new highway itself). Revenge on the man who for a year now had ruined his sleep and his digestion too by the constant threat of that hog-lot. Because he simply declined to sell any part of his property, under any conditions, to anyone: which, since his was in front of Snopes's, except for the thirteen-foot strip, would cut the oil company off from its proposed corner station as effectively as a toll-gate, as a result of which the oil company declined to buy any part of Snopes's.

Of course, as the town knew, Snopes (Charles meant of course Res Snopes) had already approached Essie Meadowfill, in whose name the deed lay, who answered, as the town knew too: "You'll have to see papa." Because Snopes was under a really impossible handicap: his hog-lot had forever interdict him from approaching old Meadowfill in person, of having any sort of even momentary civilised contact with him. In fact, Snopes was under two insurmountable handicaps: the second one being the idea, illusion, dream that mere money could move a man who for years now had become so accustomed to not having or wanting one extra dollar, that the notion of a thousand could not even tempt him. So Snopes misread his man. But he didn't quit trying. (That's right. A stranger might have wondered what Flem Snopes was doing all this time, who owned the land in the first place. But they in the town were not strangers.) He went to the oil company's purchasing agent and said, "Tell him if he'll sign his deed, I'll give him ten percent. of what you pay me for them thirteen feet." Then he said, "All right. Fifty percent. then. Half of it." Then he said, "All right. How much will he take?" Then he said—and according to the oil company man, bland and affable and accommodating was no description for his voice: "All right. A good citizen cant stand in the way of progress, even if it does cost him money. Tell him if he will sign he can have them thirteen feet."

This time apparently Meadowfill didn't even bother to say No, sitting in his wheel chair at the window where he could look out upon the land which he wouldn't sell and the adjoining land which its owner couldn't sell because of him. So in a way, Snopes had a certain amount of local sympathy in his next move, which he made shortly before something happened to Essie Meadowfill which revealed her to be, underneath anyway, anything but mousy; and although demure might still be one word for her, the other wasn't quietness but determination.

One morning when Meadowfill wheeled his chair from the breakfast table to the window and looked out, he saw what he had been waiting to see for over a year now: a loose hog rooting among the worthless peaches beneath his worthless and untended trees; and even as he sat bellowing for Mrs Meadowfill, Snopes himself crossed the yard with an ear of corn and a loop of rope and snared the hog by one foot and half-drove half-led it back across the yard and out of sight, old Meadowfill leaning from the chair into the open window, bellowing curses at both of them even after they had disappeared.

The next morning he was already seated at the window when he actually saw the hog come at a steady trot up the lane and into his orchard; he was still leaning in the open window bellowing and cursing when the drab wife emerged from the house, clutching a shawl about her head, and hurried up the lane to knock at Snopes's locked front door until Meadowfill's bellowing, which had never stopped, drew her back home. By that time most of the neighbors were there watching what followed: the old man still bellowing curses from the wheel chair in the window while his wife tried single-handed to drive the hog out of the unfenced yard, when Snopes himself appeared (from where everybody knew now he had been concealed watching), innocent, apologetic and amazed, with his ear of corn and his looped plow-line, and caught the hog and removed it.

Next, Meadowfill had the rifle—an aged, battered single-shot .22. That is, it looked second-hand simply by being in his possession, though nobody knew when he had left the wheel chair and the window (not to mention the hog) long enough to have hunted down the small boy owner and haggled or browbeat him out of it; the town simply could not imagine him ever having been a boy passionate and proud to own a single-shot .22 and to have kept it all these long years as a memento of that pure and innocent time. But he had it, cartridges too—not solid bullets but loaded with tiny shot such as naturalists use: incapable of killing the hog at all and even of hurting it much at this distance. In fact, Charles's uncle said Meadowfill didn't even really want to drive the hog away: he simply wanted to shoot it every day as other old people play croquet or bingo.

He would rush straight from the breakfast table, to crouch in his wheeled ambush at the window until the hog appeared. Then (he would have to rise from the chair to do this) he would stand up and slowly and quietly raise the window sash and the screen (he kept the grooves of both greased for speed and silence, and had equipped both of them with handles at the bottom so that he could raise either one with a single jerk) and deliver the shot, the hog giving its convulsive start and leap, until, forgetting, it would settle down again and receive the next shot, until at last its dim processes would connect the sting with the report and after the next shot it would go home, to return no more until tomorrow morning. Until finally it even connected the scattered peaches themselves with the general inimicality and for a whole week it didn't return at all; then the neighborhood legend rose that Meadowfill had contracted with the boy who delivered the Memphis and Jackson papers (he didn't take a paper himself, not being interested in any news which cost a dollar a month) to scavenge the neighborhood garbage cans and bait his orchard at night.

Now the town wondered more than ever just exactly what Snopes could be up to. That is, Snopes would naturally be expected to keep the hog at home after the first time old Meadowfill shot it. Or even sell it, which was Snopes's profession or trade, though probably no one would give the full market price per pound for a hog containing fourteen or fifteen months of Number Ten lead shot. Until finally Charles's uncle said they divined Snopes's intention: his hope that someday, either by error or mistake or maybe simple rage, swept beyond all check of morality or fear of consequences by his vice like a drunkard or gambler, Meadowfill would put a solid bullet in the gun; whereupon Snopes would not merely sue him for killing the hog, he would invoke the town ordinance against firing guns inside the city limit, and between the two of them somehow blackmail Meadowfill into making his, Snopes's, lot available to the oil company. Then the thing happened to Essie Meadowfill.

It was a Marine corporal. The town never did know how or where Essie managed to meet him. She had never been anywhere except occasionally for the day in Memphis, like everybody in north Mississippi went at least once a year. She had never missed a day from the bank except her summer vacations, which as far as anybody knew, she spent carrying her share of the load of the wheel chair's occupation. Yet she met him, maybe through a love-lorn correspondence agency. Anyway, still carrying the parcels of the day's marketing, she was waiting at the station when the Memphis bus came in and he got out of it, whom Jefferson had never seen before, he carrying the grocery bag now along the street where Essie was now an hour late (people used to set their watches by her passing). And the town realised that 'mousy' had been the wrong word for her for years evidently since obviously no girl deserving the word 'mousy' could have bloomed that much, got that round and tender and girl-looking just in the brief time since the bus came up. And 'quiet' was going to be the wrong word too; she was going to need the determination whether her Marine knew it yet or not, the two of them walking into the house and up to the wheel chair, into the point blank range of that rage compared to which the cursing of small boys and throwing rocks at dogs and even shooting live ammunition at Snopes's hog was mere reflex hysteria, since this trespasser threatened the very system of peonage by which Meadowfill lived, and saying, "Papa, this is McKinley Smith. We're going to be married." Then walking back out to the street with him five minutes later and there, in full view of whoever wanted to look, kissing him—maybe not the first time she ever kissed him but probably the first time she ever kissed anyone without bothering (more, caring) whether or not it was a sin. And evidently McKinley had some determination too: son of an east Texas tenant farmer, who probably had barely heard of Mississippi until he met Essie wherever and however that was; who, once he realised that, because of the wheel chair and the gray mother, Essie was not going to cut away from her family and marry him regardless, should have given up and gone back to Texas by the next bus.

Or maybe what they had was a single determination held in collaboration, like they seemed to own everything else in common. They were indeed doomed and fated, whether they were star-crossed too or not. Because they even acted alike. It was obvious at once that he had cast his lot for keeps in Jefferson and since for some time now (this was January, 1946, Charles was home now and saw the rest of it himself) the United States had been full of ex-G.I.'s going to school whether they were fitted for it or not or even really wanted to go, the obvious thing would be for him to enter the vocational school which had just been added to the Jefferson Academy, where at Government expense he could hold her hand at least once every day while they waited for simple meanness finally to kill off old Meadowfill. But Essie's Marine dismissed higher education as immediately and firmly as Essie had, and for the same reason. He explained it: "I was a soldier for two years. The only thing I learned in that time was, the only place you can be safe in is a private hole, preferably with a iron lid you can pull down on top of you. I aim to own me a hole. Only I aint a soldier now and so I can pick where I want it, and even make it comfortable. I'm going to build a house."

He bought a small lot. In Eula Acres of course. And Essie selected it of course. It was not even very far from where she had lived most of her life; in fact, after the house began to go up, Meadowfill (he had to unless he gave the hog up and went back to bed) could sit right there in his window and watch every plank of its daily advancement: a constant reminder and warning that he dared not make the mistake of dying. Which at least was a valid reason for sitting in the wheel chair at the window, since he no longer had the hog, it anyway had given up—or anyway for the time being. Or Snopes had given up—for the time being, the hog having made its last sortie about the same day that Essie brought her Marine to the house for that first interview, and had not appeared in the orchard since. Snopes still owned it, or plenty of others (by the wind from that direction) or—since that was his business—he could have replaced it whenever he decided the time was right again. But for now at least he had desisted, patched his fence or (as the neighbors believed) simply stopped leaving the gate unfastened on what he considered strategic days. So now all old Meadowfill had to watch was the house.

McKinley built it himself, doing all the rough heavy work, with one professional carpenter to mark off the planks for him to saw, with the seething old man ambushed in the wheel chair behind the window without even the hog anymore to vent his rage on. Obviously, as well as from habit, Meadowfill would have to keep the loaded rifle at hand. He could have no way whatever of knowing the hog would not come back; and now the town began to speculate on just how long it would be, how much he would be able to stand, before he fired the rifle at one of them—McKinley or the carpenter. Presently it would have to be the carpenter unless Meadowfill took to jacklighting, because one day (it was spring now) McKinley had a mule too and the town learned that he had rented a small piece of land two miles from town and was making a cotton crop on it. The house was about finished now, down to the millwork and trim which only the expert carpenter could do, so McKinley would depart on the mule each morning at sunrise, to be gone until nightfall. Which was when old Meadowfill probably touched the absolute of rage and impotence: McKinley might yet have been harried or frightened into selling his unfinished house and lot at any moment, possibly even for a profit. But no man in his senses would buy a cotton crop that hadn't even sprouted yet. Nothing could help him now but death—his own or McKinley's.

Then the hog came back. It simply reappeared; probably one morning Meadowfill wheeled himself from the breakfast table to the window, expecting to face nothing save one more day of static outrage, when there was the hog again, rooting for the ghosts of last year's peaches as though it had never been away. In fact, maybe that's what Meadowfill wanted to believe at that moment: that the hog had never been away at all and so all that had happened since to outrage him had been only a dream, and even the dream to be exorcised away by the next shot he would deliver. Which was immediately; evidently he had kept the loaded rifle at his hand all the time; some of the neighbors said they heard the vicious juvenile spat while they were still in bed.

The sound of it had spread over the rest of town by noon though Charles's Uncle Gavin was one of the few who actually felt the repercussion. He was just leaving the office to go

home to dinner when he heard the feet on the stairs. Then
Res Snopes entered, the five-dollar bill already in his hand.
He laid it on the desk and said, "Good morning, Lawyer. I
wont keep you long. I jest want a little advice—about five
dollars' worth." Then Snopes told it, Charles's uncle not even
touching the bill yet: just looking from it to its owner who
had never been known to pay five dollars for anything he
didn't already know he could sell for at least twenty-five cents
profit: "It's that hawg of mine that old gentleman—Mister
Meadowfill—likes to shoot with them little bird-shot."

"I heard about it," his uncle said. "Just what do you want
for your five dollars?" His uncle told it: Snopes standing beyond the desk, not secret: just polite and inscrutable. "For
telling you what you already know? that once you sue him for
injuring your hog, he will invoke the law against livestock
running loose inside the city limits? For telling you what you
already knew over a year ago when he fired the first shot at it?
Either fix the fence or get rid of the hog."

"It costs a right smart to feed a hawg," Snopes said. "As for
getting rid of it, that old gentleman has done shot it so much
now, I doubt wouldn't nobody buy it."

"Then eat it," his uncle said.

"A whole hawg, for jest one man? Let alone with going on
two years of bird-shot in it?"

"Then give it away," his uncle said, and tried to stop himself but it was too late.

"That's your legal lawyer's advice then," Snopes said. "Give
the hawg away. Much obliged," he said, already turning.

"Here," his uncle said, "wait"; holding out the bill.

"I come to you for legal lawyer's advice," Snopes said.
"You give it to me: give the hawg away. I owe the fee for
it. If five dollars aint enough, say so." Then he was gone.
Charles's uncle was thinking fast now, not *Why did he choose
me?* because that was obvious: his uncle had drawn Essie Meadowfill's deed to the property under dispute; his uncle was
the only person in Jefferson outside Meadowfill's family with
whom old Meadowfill had had anything resembling human
contact in almost twenty years. Nor even *Why did Snopes need
to notify any outsider, lawyer or not, that he intended to give
that hog away?* Nor even *Why did he lead me into saying the*

actual words first myself, technically constituting them paid-for legal advice? Instead, what his uncle thought was *How, by giving that hog away, is he going to compel old Meadowfill to sell that lot?*

His Uncle Gavin always said he was not really interested in truth nor even in justice: that all he wanted was just to know, to find out, whether the answer was any of his business or not; and that all means to that end were valid, provided he left neither hostile witnesses nor incriminating evidence. Charles didn't believe him; some of his methods were not only too hard, they took too long; and there are some things you simply do not do even to find out. But his uncle said that he, Charles, was wrong: that curiosity is another of the mistresses whose slaves decline no sacrifice.

The trouble in this case was, his uncle didn't know what he was looking for. He had two methods—inquiry and observation—and three leads—Snopes, the hog, and Meadowfill—to discover what he might not recognise in time even when he found it. He couldn't use inquiry, because the only one who might know the answer—Snopes—had already told all he intended for anyone to know. And he couldn't use observation on the hog because, like Snopes, it could move too. Which left only the one immobile: old Meadowfill. So he picked Charles up the next morning and at daylight they were ambushed also in his uncle's parked car where they could see the Meadowfill house and orchard and the lane leading to Snopes's house and, as the other point of the triangle, the little new house which McKinley Smith had almost finished. They sat there for two hours. They watched McKinley depart on his mule for his cotton patch. Then Snopes himself came out of his yard into the lane and went on toward town, the Square. Presently it was time for even Essie Meadowfill to go to work. Then there remained only old Meadowfill ambushed behind his window. Only the hog was missing.

"If that's what we're waiting for," Charles said.

"I agree," his uncle said.

"I mean, to distract the eyes that have probably been watching us for the last two hours long enough for us to get away."

"I didn't want to come either," his uncle said. "But I had to or give that five dollars back."

And the next morning was the same. By then it was too late to quit; they both had too much invested now, not even counting Snopes's five dollars: two days of getting up before dawn, to sit for two hours in the parked car without even a cup of coffee, waiting for what they were not even sure they would recognise when they saw it. It was the third morning; McKinley and his mule had departed on schedule: so regular and normal that he and his uncle didn't even realise they had not seen Snopes yet until Essie Meadowfill herself came out of the house on her way to work. To Charles it was like one of those shocks, starts such as when you find yourself waking up without knowing until then you were asleep; his uncle was already getting out of the car to begin to run when they saw the hog. That is, it was the hog and it was doing exactly what they expected it to do: moving toward Meadowfill's orchard at that twinkling purposeful porcine trot. Only it was not where it should have been when it first became visible. It was going where they expected it to be going, but it was not coming from where it should have been coming from. It was coming not from the direction of Snopes's house but from that of McKinley Smith's. His uncle was already running, possibly from what Ratliff called his uncle's simple instinct or affinity for being where something was going to happen, even if he wasn't always quite on time, hurrying—Charles too of course—across the street and the little yard and into the house before old Meadowfill would see the hog through the window and make the shot.

His uncle didn't knock; they entered running, his uncle choosing by simple orientation the door beyond which old Meadowfill would have to be to use that particular window and he was there, leaning forward in the wheel chair at the window, the glass sash of which was already raised though the screen was still down, the little rifle already half raised in one hand, the other hand grasping the handle to the screen to jerk it up. But he—Meadowfill—was just sitting there yet, looking at the hog. The town had got used to seeing meanness and vindictiveness and rage in his face; they were normal. But this time there was nothing in his face but gloating. He didn't even turn his head when Charles and his uncle entered: he just said, "Come right in; you got a grandstand seat." Now they could hear him cursing: not hard honest outdoors swearing but the quiet murmuring indoors obscenity which, Charles thought, if he ever had used it, his gray hairs should have forgot it now.

Then he began to stand up from the wheel chair and then Charles saw it too—a smallish lump a little longer than a brick, wrapped in a piece of gunny-sack, bound in a crotch of the nearest peach tree about twenty feet from the house so that it pointed at the window, his uncle saying, "Stop! Stop! Dont raise it!" and even reaching for the screen, but too late; old Meadowfill, standing now, leaned the rifle beside the window and put both hands on the handle and jerked the screen up. Then the light sharp vicious spat of the .22 cartridge from the peach tree; his uncle said he was actually looking at the rising screen when the wire frayed and vanished before the miniature blast; Charles himself seemed actually to hear the tiny pellets hiss across old Meadowfill's belly and chest as the old man half-leaped half-fell backward into the chair which rushed from under him, leaving him asprawl on the floor, where he lay for a moment with on his face an expression of incredulous outrage: not pain, not anguish, fright: just outrage, already reaching for the rifle as he sat up.

"Somebody shot me!" he said.

"Certainly," his uncle said, taking the rifle away from him. "That hog did. Can you blame it? Just lie still now until we can see."

"Hog, hell," old Meadowfill said. "It was that blank blank blank McKinley Smith!"

He wasn't hurt: just burned, blistered, the tiny shot which had had to penetrate not only his pants and shirt but his winter underwear too, barely under his skin. But mad as a hornet, raging, bellowing and cursing and still trying to take the rifle away from Charles's uncle (Mrs Meadowfill was in the room now, the shawl already clutched about her head as if some fatalistic hopeless telepathy communicated to her the instant the hog crossed their unfenced boundary, like the electric eye that opens doors) until at last he exhausted himself into what would pass with him for rationality. Then he told it: how Snopes had told Essie two days ago that he had given the hog to McKinley as a house-warming present or maybe even—Snopes hoped—a wedding gift some day soon, with Charles's uncle saying, "Hold on a minute. Did Essie say Mr Snopes gave the hog to McKinley, or did she say Mr Snopes told her he had?"

"What?" Meadowfill said. "What?" Then he just began to curse again.

"Lie still," Charles's uncle said. "You've been shooting that hog for over a year now without hurting it so I reckon you can stand one shot yourself. But we'll have a doctor on your wife's account."

His uncle had the gun too: a very neat home-made booby-trap: a cheap single-shot .22 also, sawed off barrel and stock and fastened to a board, the whole thing wrapped in the piece of feed sack and bound in the crotch of the tree, a black strong small-gauge length of reel-backing running from the trigger through a series of screw-eyes to the sash of the window screen, the muzzle trained at the center of the window about a foot above the sill.

"If he hadn't stood up before he raised that screen, the charge would have hit him square in the face," Charles said.

"So what?" his uncle said. "Do you think who put it there cared? Whether it merely frightened and enraged him into rushing at Smith with that rifle" (it had a solid bullet in it this time, the big one: the long rifle; this time old Meadowfill aimed to hurt what he shot) "and compelling Smith to kill him in self-defense, or whether the shot blinded him or killed him right there in his wheel chair and so solved the whole thing? Her father dead and her sweetheart in jail for murdering him, and only Essie to need to deal with?"

"It was pretty smart," Charles said.

"It was worse. It was bad. Nobody would ever have believed anyone except a Pacific veteran would have invented a booby-trap, no matter how much he denied it."

"It was still smart," Charles said. "Even Smith will agree."

"Yes," his uncle said. "That's why I wanted you along. You were a soldier too. I may need an interpreter to talk to him."

"I was just a major," Charles said. "I never had enough rank to tell anything to any sergeant, let alone a Marine one."

"He was just a corporal," his uncle said.

"He was still a Marine," Charles said.

Only they didn't go to Smith first; he would be in his cotton patch now anyway. And, Charles told himself, if Snopes had been him, there wouldn't be anybody in Snopes's house either. But there was. Snopes opened the door himself; he was wearing an apron and carrying a frying pan; there was even a fried egg in it. But there wasn't anything in his face at all. "Gentle-men," he said. "Come in."

"No thanks," Charles's uncle said. "It wont take that long. This is yours, I think." There was a table; his uncle laid the sack-wrapped bundle on it and flipped the edge of the sacking, the mutilated rifle sliding across the table. And still there was nothing whatever in Snopes's face or voice:

"That-ere is what you lawyers call debatable, aint it?"

"Oh yes," Charles's uncle said. "Everybody knows about finger-prints now, just as they do about booby-traps."

"Yes," Snopes said. "Likely you aint making me a present of it."

"That's right," his uncle said. "I'm selling it to you. For a deed to Essie Meadowfill for that strip of your lot the oil company wants to buy, plus that thirteen feet that Mr Meadowfill thought he owned." And now indeed Snopes didn't move, immobile with the cold egg in the frying pan. "That's right," his uncle said. "In that case, I'll see if McKinley Smith wants to buy it."

Snopes looked at his uncle a moment. He was smart; you would have to give him that, Charles thought. "I reckon you would," he said. "Likely that's what I would do myself."

"That's what I thought," his uncle said.

"I reckon I'll have to go and see Cousin Flem," Snopes said.

"I reckon not," his uncle said. "I just came from the bank."

"I reckon I would have done that myself too," Snopes said. "What time will you be in your office?"

And he and his uncle could have met Smith at his house at sundown too. Instead, it was not even noon when Charles and his uncle stood at the fence and watched McKinley and the mule come up the long black shear of turning earth like the immobilised wake of the plow's mold-board. Then he was standing across the fence from them, naked from the waist up in his overalls and combat boots. Charles's uncle handed him the deed. "Here," his uncle said.

Smith read it. "This is Essie's."

"Then marry her," his uncle said. "Then you can sell the lot and buy a farm. Aint that what you both want? Haven't you got a shirt or a jumper here with you? Get it and you can ride back with me; the major here will bring the mule."

"No," Smith said; he was already shoving, actually ramming the deed into his pocket as he turned back to the mule. "I'll bring him in. I'm going home first. I aint going to marry nobody without a necktie and a shave."

Then they had to wait for the Baptist minister to wash his hands and put on his coat and necktie; Mrs Meadowfill was already wearing the first hat anybody had ever seen on her; it looked a good deal like the first hat anybody ever made. "But papa," Essie said.

"Oh," Charles's uncle said. "You mean that wheel chair. It belongs to me now. It was a legal fee. I'm going to give it to you and McKinley for a christening present as soon as you earn it."

Then it was two days later, in the office.

"You see?" his uncle said. "It's hopeless. Even when you get rid of one Snopes, there's already another one behind you even before you can turn around."

"That's right," Ratliff said serenely. "As soon as you look, you see right away it aint nothing but jest another Snopes."

LINDA KOHL was already home too when Charles got back. From her war also: the Pascagoula shipyard where she had finally had her way and became a rivetter; his Uncle Gavin told him, a good one. At least her hands, fingernails, showed it: not bitten, gnawed down, but worn off. And now she had a fine, a really splendid dramatic white streak in her hair running along the top of her skull almost like a plume. A collapsed plume; in fact, maybe that was what it was, he thought: a collapsed plume lying flat athwart her skull instead of cresting upward first then back and over; it was the fall of 1945 now and the knight had run out of tourneys and dragons, the war itself had slain them, used them up, made them obsolete.

In fact Charles thought how all the domestic American knights-errant liberal reformers would be out of work now, with even the little here-to-fore lost places like Yoknapatawpha County, Mississippi fertilised to overflowing not only with ex-soldiers' blood money but with the two or three or four dollars per hour which had been forced on the other ex-rivetters and -bricklayers and -machinists like Linda Kohl Snopes, he meant Linda Snopes Kohl, so fast that they hadn't had time to spend it. Even the two Finn communists, even the one that still couldn't speak English, had got rich during the war and had had to become capitalists and bull-market investors simply because they had not yet acquired any private place large enough to put that much money down while they turned their backs on it. And as for the Negroes, by now they had a newer and better high school building in Jefferson than the white folks had. Plus an installment-plan automobile and radio and refrigerator full of canned beer down-paid with the blood money which at least drew no color-line in every unwired unscreened plumbing-less cabin: double-plus the new social-revolution laws which had abolished not merely hunger and inequality and injustice, but work too by substituting for it a new self-compounding vocation or profession for which you would need no schooling at all: the simple production of children. So there was nothing for Linda to tilt against now in Jefferson. Come to think of it, there was nothing for her to tilt against anywhere now, since the Russians had fixed the Germans and even they didn't need her anymore. In fact, come to think of it, there was really nothing for her in Jefferson at all anymore, now that his Uncle Gavin was married—if she had ever wanted him for herself. Because maybe Ratliff was right and whatever she had ever wanted of him, it wasn't a husband. So in fact you would almost have to wonder why she stayed in Jefferson at all now, with nothing to do all day long but wait, pass the time somehow until night and sleep came, in that Snopes-colonial mausoleum with that old son of a bitch that needed a daughter or anybody else about as much as he needed a spare necktie or another hat. So maybe everybody was right this time and she wasn't going to stay in Jefferson much longer, after all.

But she was here now, with her nails his uncle said not worn down from smithing but scraped down to get them clean (and whether his uncle added it or not: feminine) again with no more ships to rivet, and that really dramatic white plume collapsed in gallantry across her skull with all the dragons dead. Only, even blacksmithing hadn't been enough. What he meant was, she wasn't any older. No, that wasn't what he meant: not just older. Something had happened to him during the three-plus years between December '41 and April '45 or at least he hoped it had or at least what had seemed suffering and enduring to him at least met the standards of suffering and enduring enough to enrich his spiritual and moral development whether it did anything for the human race or not, and if it had purified his soul it must show on his outside too or at least he hoped it did. But she hadn't changed at all, least of all the white streak in her hair which it seemed that some women did deliberately to themselves. When he finally—He thought, All right, finally. So what if he did spend the better part of his first three days at home at least hoping he didn't look like he was hanging around the Square in case she did cross it or enter it. There were towns bigger than Jefferson that didn't have a girl—woman—in it that the second you saw her ten years ago getting out of an airplane you were already wondering what she would look like with

her clothes off except that she was too old for you, the wrong
type for you except that that was exactly backward, you were
too young for her, the wrong type for her and so only your
uncle that you had even spent some of the ten months in the
Nazi stalag wondering if he ever got them off before he got
married to Aunt Melisandre or maybe even after and if he
didn't, what happened, what was wrong. Because his uncle
would never tell him himself whether he ever did or not but
maybe after three years and a bit he could tell by looking at
her, that maybe a woman really couldn't hide that from another man who was call it why not *simpatico*. Except that
when he finally saw her on the street on the third day there
was nothing at all, she had not changed at all, except for the
white streak which didn't count anyway—the same one that
on that day ten years ago when he and his uncle had driven up
to the Memphis airport to get her, was at that first look a little too tall and a little too thin for his type so that in that same
second he was saying *Well that's one anyway that wont have to
take her clothes off on my account* and then almost before he
could get it out, something else was already saying *Okay,
Buster, who suggested she was going to?* and he had been right:
not her for him, but rather not him for her: a lot more might
still happen to him in his life yet (he hoped) but removing
that particular skirt wouldn't be one even if when you got the
clothes off the too tall too thin ones sometimes they surprised
you. And just as well; evidently his soul or whatever it was had
improved some in the three years and a bit; anyway he knew
now that if such had been his fate to get this particular one
off, what would happen to him might, probably would, have
several names but none of them would be surprise.

With no more ships to rivet now, and what was worse: no
need anymore for ships to rivet. So not just he, Charles, but
all the town in time sooner or later would see her—or be told
about it by the ones who had—walking, striding, most of the
time dressed in what they presumed was the same army-sur-
plus khaki she had probably rivetted the ships in, through the
back streets and alleys of the town or the highways and lanes
and farm roads and even the fields and woods themselves
within two or three miles of town, alone, walking not fast so
much as just hard, as if she were walking off insomnia or per-

haps even a hangover. "Maybe that's what it is," Charles said. Again his uncle looked up, a little impatiently, from the brief.

"What?" he said.

"You said maybe she has insomnia. Maybe it's hangover she's walking off."

"Oh," his uncle said. "All right." He went back to the brief. Charles watched him.

"Why dont you walk with her?" he said.

This time his uncle didn't look up. "Why dont you? Two ex-soldiers, you could talk about war."

"She couldn't hear me. I wouldn't have time to write on a pad while we were walking."

"That's what I mean," his uncle said. "My experience has been that the last thing two ex-soldiers under fifty years old want to talk about is war. You two even cant."

"Oh," he said. His uncle read the brief. "Maybe you're right," he said. His uncle read the brief. "Is it all right with you if I try to lay her?" His uncle didn't move. Then he closed the brief and sat back in the chair.

"Certainly," he said.

"So you think I cant," Charles said.

"I know you cant," his uncle said. He added quickly: "Dont grieve; it's not you. Just despair if you like. It's not anybody."

"So you know why," Charles said.

"Yes," his uncle said.

"But you're not going to tell me."

"I want you to see for yourself. You will probably never have the chance again. You read and hear and see about it in all the books and pictures and music, in Harvard and Heidelberg both. But you are afraid to believe it until you actually see it face to face, because you might be wrong and you couldn't bear that. I mean, you can never have, refused to have, believed it, and be happy. What you cant bear is to doubt it."

"I never got to Heidelberg," Charles said. "All I had was Harvard and *Stalag* umpty-nine."

"All right," his uncle said. "The high school and the Jefferson Academy then."

Anyway he, Charles, knew the answer now. He said so.

"Oh, that. Even little children know all that nowadays. She's frigid."

"Well, that's as good a Freudian term as another to cover chastity or discretion," his uncle said. "Beat it now. I'm busy. Your mother invited me to dinner so I'll see you at noon."

So it was more than that, and his uncle was not going to tell him. And his uncle had used the word 'discretion' also to cover something he had not said. Though he, Charles, at least knew what that was because he knew his uncle well enough to know that the discretion applied not to Linda but to him. If he had never been a soldier himself, he would not have bothered, let alone waited, to ask his uncle's leave: he would probably already have waylaid her at some suitably secluded spot in the woods on one of her walks, on the innocent assumption of those who have never been in a war that she, having come through one, had been wondering for days now what in hell was wrong with Jefferson, why he or any other personable male had wasted all this time. Because he knew now why young people rushed so eagerly to war was their belief that it was one endless pre-sanctioned opportunity for unlicensed rapine and pillage; that the tragedy of war was that you brought nothing away from it but only left something valuable there; that you carried into war things which, except for the war, you could have lived out your life in peace with without ever having to know they were inside you.

So it would not be him. He had been a soldier too even if he had brought back no wound to prove it. So if it would take physical assault on her to learn what his uncle said he didn't know existed, he would never know it; he would just have to make one more in the town who believed she was simply walking off one hangover to be ready for the next one, having evidence to go on, or at least a symptom. Which was that once a week, Wednesday or Thursday afternoon (the town could set its watches and calendars by this too) she would be waiting at the wheel of her father's car outside the bank when it closed and her father came out and they would drive up to what Jakeleg Wattman euphemeously called his fishing camp at Wylie's Crossing, and lay in her next week's supply of bootleg whiskey. Not her car: her father's car. She could have owned a covey of automobiles out of that fund his

uncle was trustee of from her grandfather, old Will Varner
rich out at Frenchman's Bend or maybe from Varner and her
father together as a part of or maybe a result of that old uproar and scandal twenty years ago when her mother had
committed suicide and the mother's presumed lover had
abandoned the bank and his ancestral home both to her father, not to mention the sculptor she married being a New
York Jew and hence (as the town was convinced) rich. And
driven it—them—too, even stone deaf, who could have afforded to hire somebody to sit beside her and do nothing else
but listen. Only she didn't. Evidently she preferred walking,
sweating out the hard way the insomnia or hangover or whatever the desperate price she paid for celibacy—unless of
course Lawyer Gavin Stevens had been a slicker and smoother
operator for the last ten years than anybody suspected;
though even he had a wife now.

And her supply: not her father's. Because the town, the
county, knew that too: Snopes himself never drank, never
touched it. Yet he would never let his daughter make the trip
alone. Some were satisfied with the simple explanation that
Wattman, like everybody else nowadays, was making so much
money that he would have to leave some of it somewhere,
and Snopes, a banker, figured it might as well be in his bank
and so he called on Jakeleg once a week exactly as he would
and did look in socially on any other merchant or farmer or
cotton-ginner of the bank's profitable customers or clients.
But there were others, among them his Uncle Gavin and his
uncle's special crony, the sewing machine agent and rural bucolic grass-roots philosopher and Cincinnatus, V. K. Ratliff,
who went a little further: it was for respectability, the look of
things: that on those afternoons Snopes was not just a banker,
he was a leading citizen and father; and even though his widowed only daughter was pushing forty and had spent the four
years of the war working like a man in a military shipyard
where unspinsterish things had a way of happening to women
who were not even widows, he still wasn't going to let her
drive alone fifteen miles to a bootlegger's joint and buy a bottle of whiskey.

Or a case of it; since it was hangover she walked off, she
would need, or anyway need to have handy, a fresh bottle

every day. So presently even the town would realise it wasn't
just hangover since people who can afford a hangover every
day dont want to get rid of it, walk it off, even if they had
time to. Which left only jealousy and rage; what she walked
four or five miles every day to conquer or anyway contain was
the sleepless frustrated rage at his Uncle Gavin for having
jilted her while she was away rivetting ships to save Democracy, to marry Melisandre Harriss Backus that was as Thackeray says, thinking (Charles) how he could be glad it wasn't
him that got the clothes off since if what was under them—
provided of course his uncle had got them off—had driven his
uncle to marry a widow with two grown children, one of
them already married too, so that his Uncle Gavin might already have been a grandfather before he even became a bride.

Then apparently jealousy and frustrated unforgiving rage
were wrong too. Christmas came and went and the rest of
that winter followed it, into spring. His uncle was not only
being but even acting the squire now. No boots and breeks
true enough and although a squire might have looked liked
one behind a Phi Beta Kappa key even in Mississippi, he never
could under a shock of premature white hair like a concert pianist or a Hollywood Cadillac agent. But at least he behaved
like one, once each month and sometimes oftener, sitting at
the head of the table out at Rose Hill with Charles's new
Aunt Melisandre opposite him and Linda and Charles across
from each other while his uncle interpreted for Linda from
the ivory tablet. Or rather, interpreted for himself into audi-
ble English to Charles and his new Aunt Em. Because Linda
didn't talk now any more than she ever had: just sitting there
with that white streak along the top of her head like a collapsed plume, eating like a man; Charles didn't mean eating
grossly: just soundly, heartily, and looking . . . yes, by God,
that was exactly the word: happy. Happy, satisfied, like when
you have accomplished something, produced, created, made
something: gone to some—maybe a lot—trouble and expense, stuck your neck out maybe against your own better
judgment; and sure enough, be damned if it didn't work, exactly as you thought it would, maybe even better than you
had dared hope it would. Something you had wanted for
yourself only you missed it so you began to think it wasn't so,

was impossible, until you made one yourself, maybe when it was too late for you to want it anymore but at least you had proved it could be.

And in the drawing room afterward also, with coffee and brandy for the ladies and port and a cigar for Charles though his uncle still stuck to the cob pipes which anyway used to cost only a nickel. Still happy, satisfied; and that other thing which Charles had sensed, recognised: proprietorial. As if Linda herself had actually invented the whole business: his Uncle Gavin, his Aunt Melisandre, Rose Hill—the old, once-small and -simple frame house which old Mr Backus with his Horace and Catullus and his weak whiskey-and-water would not recognise now save by its topographical location, trans-mogrified by the New Orleans gangster's money as old Snopes had tried to do to the De Spain house with his Yoknapatawpha County gangster's money and failed since here the rich and lavish cash had been spent with taste so that you didn't really see it at all but merely felt it, breathed it, like warmth or temperature; with, surrounding it, enclosing it, the sense of the miles of white panel fences marking the combed and curried acres and the electric-lighted and -heated stables and tack rooms and grooms' quarters and the manager's house all in one choral concord in the background darkness—and then invented him, Charles, to be present to at least look at her creation whether he approved of what she had made or not.

Then the hour to say Thank you and Goodnight and drive back to town through the April or May darkness and escort Linda home, back to her father's Frenchman's Bend-dreamed palace, to draw up at the curb, where she would say each time in the harsh duck voice (he, Charles, thinking each time too *Which maybe at least wouldn't sound quite so bad in the dark whispering after you finally got the clothes off,* thinking *If of course it had been you*): "Come in for a drink." Nor enough light in the car for her to have read the ivory tablet if she had offered it. Because he would do this each time too: grin, he would hope loud enough, and shake his head—sometimes there would be moonlight to help—Linda already opening the door on her side so that Charles would have to get out fast on his to get around the car in time. Though no matter how fast that was, she would be already out, already turning up the walk toward the portico: who perhaps had left the South too young too long ago to have formed the Southern female habit-rite of a cavalier's unflagging constancy, or maybe the simple rivetting of ships had cured the old muscles of the old expectation. Whichever it was, Charles would have to overtake, in effect outrun her already halfway to the house; whereupon she would check, almost pause in fact, to glance back at him, startled—not alarmed: just startled; merely what Hollywood called a double-take, still not so far dis-severed from her Southern heritage but to recall that he, Charles, dared not risk some casual passerby reporting to his uncle that his nephew permitted the female he was seeing home to walk at least forty feet unaccompanied to her front door.

So they would reach that side by side anyway—the vast dim home-made columned loom of her father's dream, night-mare, monstrous hope or terrified placatement, whichever it was, whatever it had been; the cold mausoleum in which old Snopes had immolated that much of his money at least without grace or warmth, Linda stopping again to say, "Come in and have a drink," exactly as though she hadn't said it forty feet back at the car, Charles still with nothing but the grin and the shake of the head as if he had only that moment discovered his ability to do that too. Then her hand, hard and firm like a man's since after all it was a ship-rivetter's or at least an ex-ship-rivetter's. Then he would open the door, she would stand for an instant in it in the midst of motion against a faint light in the hall's depth; the door would close again.

Oh yes, it could have had several names but surprise would not have been one of them, thinking about his uncle, the poor dope, if his uncle really had got the clothes off once maybe. Whereupon he thought how maybe his uncle actually had, that once, and couldn't stand it, bear it, and ran, fled back those eighteen or twenty years to Melisandre Backus (that used to be) where he would be safe. So if the word wouldn't be surprise, maybe it wouldn't really have to be grief either: just relief. A little of terror maybe at how close the escape had been, but mainly relief that it had been escape under any condition, on any terms. Because he, Charles, had been too young at the time. He didn't know whether he actually remembered Linda's mother as his uncle and Ratliff obviously did, or not. But he had had to listen to both of them often enough and long enough to know that he surely did know all that they remembered, Ratliff especially; he could almost hear Ratliff saying again: "We was lucky. We not only had Helen of Argos right here in Jefferson, which most towns dont, we even knowed who she was and then we even had our own Paris to save us Argoses by jest wrecking Troy instead. What you want to do is not to own Helen, but jest own the right and privilege of looking at her. The worst thing that can happen to you is for her to notice you enough to stop and look back."

So, assuming that whatever made Helen was transferable or anyway inheritable, the word would not be grief at all but simple and perhaps amazed relief; and maybe his uncle's luck and fate was simply to be cursed with less of fire and heat than Paris and Manfred de Spain; to simply have taken simple fear from that first one time (if his uncle really had got them off that first one time) and fled while he still had life. You know: the spider lover wise enough with age or cagy enough with experience or maybe just quick enough to spook from sheer timid instinct, to sense, anticipate, that initial tender caressing probe of the proboscis or suction tube or whatever it is his gal uses to empty him of his blood too while all he thinks he is risking is his semen; and leap, fling himself free, losing of course the semen and most of the rest of his insides too in the same what he thought at first was just peaceful orgasm, but at least keeping his husk, his sac, his life. Or the grape say, a mature grape, a little on the over-sunned and juiceless side, but at least still intact enough even if only in sapless hull after the spurting ejaculation of the nymphic kiss, to retain at least the flattened semblance of a grape. Except that about then you would have to remember what Ratliff said that time: "No, she aint going to marry him. It's going to be worse than that," and you would wonder what in the world Helen or her inheritrix could or would want with that emptied sac or flattened hull, and so what in the hell could Ratliff have meant. Or anyway thought he meant. Or at least was afraid he might have meant or mean?

Until it finally occurred to him to do the reasonable and

logical thing that anybody else would have thought about do-ing at first: ask Ratliff himself what he meant or thought he meant or was afraid he meant. So he did. It was summer now, June; McKinley Smith's cotton was not only up, Essie was pregnant. The whole town knew it; she had made a public an-nouncement in the bank one morning as soon as the doors opened and the first depositors had lined up at the windows; in less than two months she and McKinley had won old Meadowfill's wheel chair.

"Because this aint enough," Ratliff said.

"Enough what?" Charles said.

"Enough to keep her busy and satisfied. No ships to rivet, and now she's done run out of colored folks too for the time being. This-here is peace and plenty—the same peace and plenty us old folks like me and your uncle spent four whole years sacrificing sugar and beefsteak and cigarettes all three to keep the young folks like you happy while you was winning it. So much plenty that even the down-trod communist shoe-patchers and tinsmiths and Negro children can afford to not need her now. I mean, maybe if she had asked them first they never actively needed her before neither, only they couldn't afford in simple dollars and cents to say so. Now they can." He blinked at Charles. "She has done run out of injustice."

"I didn't know you could do that," Charles said.

"That's right," Ratliff said. "So she will have to think of something, even if she has to invent it."

"All right," Charles said. "Suppose she does. If she was tough enough to stand what we thought up around here, she can certainly stand anything she can invent herself."

"I aint worried about her," Ratliff said. "She's all right. She's jest dangerous. I'm thinking about your uncle."

"What about him?" Charles said.

"When she finally thinks of something and tells him, he will likely do it," Ratliff said.

THEY MET that morning in the postoffice, as they often did by complete uncalculation at morning mail-time, she dressed as usual in the clothes she seemed to spend most of her time walking about the adjacent countryside in—the expensive English brogues scuffed and scarred but always neatly polished each morning, with wool stockings or socks beneath worn flannel trousers or a skirt or sometimes what looked like a khaki boiler-suit under a man's stained burberry; this in the fall and winter and spring; in the summer it would be cotton—dress or skirt or trousers, her head with its single white plume bare even in the worst weather. Afterward they would go to the coffee shop in the Holston House and drink coffee but this time instead Stevens took the gold-cornered ivory tablet he had given her ten years ago and wrote:

An appointment At the office To see me

"Shouldn't you make an appointment to see lawyers?" she said.

His next speech of course would be, "So it's as a lawyer you need me now." And if they both could have used speech he would have said that, since at the age of fifty-plus talking is no effort. But writing is still an effort at any age, so even a lawyer pauses at the obvious if he has got to use a pen or pencil. So he wrote *Tonight after supper At your house*

"No," she said.

He wrote *Why*

"Your wife will be jealous. I dont want to hurt Milly."

His next of course would be: "Melisandre, jealous? Of you and me? After all this, all this time?" Which of course was too long to write on a two-by-three-inch ivory tablet. So he had already begun to write *Nonsense* when he stopped and erased it with his thumb. Because she was looking at him, and now he knew too. He wrote *You want her To be jealous*

"She's your wife," she said. "She loves you. She would have to be jealous." He hadn't erased the tablet yet; he needed only to hold it up before her face until she looked at it again. "Yes," she said. "Being jealous is part of love too. I want you to have all of it too. I want you to have everything. I want you to be happy."

"I am happy," he said. He took one of the unopened envelopes just out of his mailbox and wrote on the back of it *I am happy I was given the privilege of meddling with impunity in other peoples affairs without really doing any harm by belonging to that avocation whose acolytes have been absolved in advance for holding justice above truth I have been denied the chance to destroy what I loved by touching it Can you tell me now what it is here or shall I come to your house after supper tonight*

"All right," she said. "After supper then."

At first his wife's money was a problem. In fact, if it hadn't been for the greater hysteria of the war, the lesser hysteria of that much sudden money could have been a serious one. Even four years later Melisandre still tried to make it a problem: on these warm summer evenings the Negro houseman and one of the maids would serve the evening meal on a flagged terrace beneath a wistaria arbor in the back yard, whereupon each time there were guests, even the same guest or guests again, Melisandre would say, "It would be cooler in the diningroom" (in the rebuilt house the diningroom was not quite as large as a basketball court) "and no bugs either. But the diningroom makes Gavin nervous." Whereupon he would say, as he always did too, even before the same guest or guests again: "Dammit, Milly, nothing can make me nervous because I was already born that way."

They were sitting there now over the sandwiches and the iced tea. She said, "Why didn't you invite her out here." He merely chewed so she said, "But of course you did." So he merely chewed and she said, "So it must be something serious." Then she said, "But it cant be serious or she couldn't have waited, she would have told you right there in the postoffice." So then she said, "What do you suppose it is?" and he wiped his mouth and dropped the napkin, rising, and came around the table and leaned and kissed her.

"I love you," he said. "Yes. No. I dont know. Dont wait up."

Melisandre had given him a Cadillac roadster for her wedding present to him; this was during the first year of the war

and God only knew where she had got a new Cadillac convertible and what she had paid for it. "Unless you really dont
want it," she said.

"I do," he said. "I've always wanted a Cadillac convertible
—provided I can do exactly what I want to with it."

"Of course you can," she said. "It's yours." So he drove the
car back to town and arranged with a garage to store it for ten
dollars a month and removed the battery and radio and the
tires and the spare wheel and sold them and took the keys and
the bill of sale to Snopes's bank and mortgaged the car for the
biggest loan they would make on it. By that time progress, industrial renascence and rejuvenation had reached even rural
Mississippi banks, so Snopes's bank now had a professional
cashier or working vice president imported from Memphis six
months back to give it the New Look, that is, to bring rural
banks abreast of the mental condition which accepted, could
accept, the automobile as a definite ineradicable part not only
of the culture but the economy also; where, as Stevens knew,
Snopes alone would not lend God Himself one penny on an
automobile. So Stevens could have got the loan from the imported vice president on his simple recognisance, not only for
the above reason but because the vice president was a stranger
and Stevens represented one of the three oldest names in the
county and the vice president would not have dared to say No
to him. But Stevens didn't do it that way; this was to be, as
the saying had it, Snopes's baby. He waylaid, ambushed,
caught Snopes himself in public, in the lobby of his bank with
not only all the staff but the moment's complement of customers, to explain in detail how he didn't intend to sell his
wife's wedding gift but simply to convert it into war-bonds
for the duration of the war. So the loan was made, the keys
surrendered and the lien recorded, which Stevens naturally
had no intention whatever of ever redeeming, plus the ten
dollars a month storage accrued to whatever moment when
Snopes realised that his bank owned a brand-new though outdated Cadillac automobile complete except for battery and
tires.

Though even with the six-year-old coupé which (as it were)
he had got married from, the houseman still got there first to
hold the door for him to get in and depart, down the long

driveway lined immediately with climbing roses on the white-paneled fences where the costly pedigreed horses had once ranged in pampered idleness; gone now since there was no one on the place to ride them unless somebody paid him for it, Stevens himself hating horses even more than dogs, rating the horse an unassailable first in loathing since though both were parasites, the dog at least had the grace to be a syco-phant too; it at least fawned on you and so kept you healthily ashamed of the human race. But the real reason was, though neither the horse nor the dog ever forgot anything, the dog at least forgave you, which the horse did not; and his, Stevens', thought was that what the world needed was more forgiving: that if you had a good sensitive quick-acting capac-ity for forgiving, it didn't really matter whether you ever learned or even remembered anything or not.

Because he had no idea what Linda wanted either; he thought *Because women are wonderful: it doesn't really matter what they want or if they themselves even know what it is they think they want.* At least there was the silence. She would have to organise, correlate, tell him herself, rather than have what-ever it was she wanted him to know dug out of her by means of the infinitesimal legal mining which witnesses usually re-quired; he would need only write on the tablet *At least dont make me have to write out in writing whatever questions you want me to ask you so whenever you come to one of them just ask it yourself and go on from there.* Even as he stopped the car he could already see her, her white dress in the portico, between two of the columns which were too big for the house, for the street, for Jefferson itself; it would be dim and probably cooler and anyway pleasant to sit there. But there was the si-lence; he thought how there should be a law for everybody to carry a flashlight in his car or perhaps he could ask her with the tablet to get a flashlight from the house so she could read the first sentence; except that she couldn't read the request for the flashlight until she was inside the house.

She kissed him, as always unless they met on the street, al-most as tall as he; he thought *Of course it will have to be up-stairs, in her sitting room with the doors closed too probably; anything urgent enough to demand a private appointment,* fol-lowing her through the hall at the end of which was the door to the room where her father (he believed that out of all Jefferson only he and Ratliff knew better) sat, local legend had it not reading, not chewing tobacco: just sitting with his feet propped on the unpainted wooden ledge he had had his Frenchman's Bend carpenter-kinsman nail at the proper height across the Adam mantel; on up the stairs and, sure enough, into her sitting room whose own mantel had been designed to the exact height for them to stand before while he used the foolscap pad and pencil which was its fixture since she led him here only when there was more than the two-by-three ivory surface could hold. Though this time he hadn't even picked up the pencil when she spoke the eight or nine words which froze him for almost half that many seconds. He repeated one of them.

"Mink?" he said. "Mink?" He thought rapidly: *Oh hell, not this,* thinking rapidly: *Nineteen . . . eight. Twenty years then twenty more on top of that. He will be out in two more years anyway. We had forgotten that. Or had we.* He didn't need to write *Tell me* either; she was already doing that; except for the silence he could, would have asked her what in the world, what stroke of coincidence (he had not yet begun to think chance, fate, destiny) had caused her to think of the man whom she had never seen and whose name she could have heard only in connection with a cowardly and savage murder. But that didn't matter now: which was the instant when he began to think destiny and fate.

With the houseman to do the listening, she had taken her father's car yesterday and driven out to Frenchman's Bend and talked with her mother's brother Jody; she stood now facing him beside the mantel on which the empty pad lay, telling him: "He had just twenty years at first, which would have been nineteen twenty-eight; he would have got out then. Only in nineteen twenty-five he tried to escape. In a woman's what Uncle Jody called a mother hubbard and a sunbonnet. How did he get hold of a mother hubbard and a sunbonnet in the penitentiary."

Except for the silence he could have used gentleness. But all he had now was the yellow pad. Because he knew the answer himself now, writing *What did Jody tell you*

"That it was my . . . other cousin, Montgomery Ward,

that had the dirty magic lantern slides until they sent him to Parchman too, in nineteen twenty-five too, you remember?" Oh yes, he remembered: how he and the then sheriff, old Hub Hampton, dead now, both knew that it was Flem Snopes himself who planted the moonshine liquor in his kinsman's studio and got him sentenced to two years in Parchman, yet how it was Flem himself who not only had two private interviews with Montgomery Ward while he lay in jail waiting trial, but put up the money for his bond and surety which permitted Montgomery Ward a two-day absence from the jail and Jefferson too before returning to accept his sentence and be taken to Parchman to serve it, after which Jefferson saw him no more nor heard of him until eight or ten years ago the town learned that Montgomery Ward was now in Los Angeles, engaged in some quite lucrative adjunct or correlant to the motion picture industry or anyway colony. *So that's why Montgomery Ward had to go to Parchman and nowhere else,* he thought, *instead of merely Atlanta or Leavenworth where only the dirty postcards would have sent him.* Oh yes, he remembered that one, and the earlier one too: in the courtroom also with the little child-sized gaunt underfed maniacal murderer, when the Court itself leaned down to give him his constitutional right to elect his plea, saying, "Dont bother me now; cant you see I'm busy?" then turning to shout again into the packed room: "Flem! Flem Snopes! Wont anybody here get word to Flem Snopes——" Oh yes, he, Stevens, knew now why Montgomery Ward had had to go to Parchman: Flem Snopes had bought twenty more years of life with that five gallons of planted evidence.

He wrote *You want me to get him out now*

"Yes," she said. "How do you do it?"

He wrote *He will be out in 2 more years why not wait till then* He wrote *He has known nothing else but that cage for 38 years He wont live a month free like an old lion or tiger At least give him 2 more years*

"Two years of life are not important," she said. "Two years of jail are."

He had even moved the pencil again when he stopped and spoke aloud instead; later he told Ratliff why. "I know why," Ratliff said. "You jest wanted to keep your own skirts clean.

Maybe by this time she had done learned to read your lips and even if she couldn't you would at least been on your own record anyhow." "No," Stevens said. "It was because I not only believe in and am an advocate of fate and destiny, I admire them; I want to be one of the instruments too, no matter how modest." So he didn't write: he spoke:

"Dont you know what he's going to do the minute he gets back to Jefferson or anywhere else your father is?"

"Say it slow and let me try again," she said.

He wrote *I love you* thinking rapidly *If I say No she will find somebody else, anybody else, maybe some jackleg who will bleed her to get him out then continue to bleed her for what the little rattlesnake is going to do the moment he is free* and wrote *Yes we can get him out it will take a few weeks a petition I will draw them up for you his blood kin the judge sheriff at the time Judge Long and Old Hub Hampton are dead but Little Hub will do even if he wont be sheriff again until next election I will take them to the Governor myself*

Ratliff too, he thought. Tomorrow the petition lay on his desk, Ratliff standing over it pen in hand. "Go on," Stevens said. "Sign it. I'm going to take care of that too. What do you think I am—a murderer?"

"Not yet anyway," Ratliff said. "How take care of it?"

"Mrs Kohl is going to," Stevens said.

"I thought you told me you never mentioned out loud where she could hear it what Mink would do as soon as he got back inside the same town limits with Flem," Ratliff said.

"I didn't need to," Stevens said. "Linda and I both agreed that there was no need for him to come back here. After forty years, with his wife dead and his daughters scattered God knows where; that in fact he would be better off if he didn't. So she's putting up the money. She wanted to make it a thousand but I told her that much in a lump would destroy him sure. So I'm going to leave two-fifty with the Warden, to be handed to him the minute before they unlock the gate to let him through it, with the understanding that the moment he accepts the money, he has given his oath to cross the Mississippi state line before sundown, and that another two-fifty will be sent every three months to whatever address he selects, provided he never again crosses the Mississippi line as long as he lives."

"I see," Ratliff said. "He cant tech the money a-tall except on the condition that he dont never lay eyes on Flem Snopes again as long as he lives."

"That's right," Stevens said.

"Suppose jest money aint enough," Ratliff said. "Suppose he wont take jest two hundred and fifty dollars for Flem Snopes."

"Remember," Stevens said. "He's going to face having to measure thirty-eight years he has got rid of, put behind him, against two more years he has still got to spend inside a cage to get rid of. He's selling Flem Snopes for these next two years, with a thousand dollars a year bonus thrown in free for the rest of his life. Sign it."

"Dont rush me," Ratliff said. "Destiny and fate. They was what you told me about being proud to be a handmaid of, wasn't they?"

"So what?" Stevens said. "Sign it."

"Dont you reckon you ought to maybe included a little luck into them too?"

"Sign it," Stevens said.

"Have you told Flem yet?"

"He hasn't asked me yet," Stevens said.

"When he does ask you?" Ratliff said.

"Sign it," Stevens said.

"I already did," Ratliff said. He laid the pen back on the desk. "You're right. We never had no alternative not to. If you'd a said No, she would jest got another lawyer that wouldn't a said No nor even invented that two-hundred-and-fifty-dollar gamble neither. And then Flem Snopes wouldn't a had no chance a-tall."

None of the other requisite documents presented any difficulty either. The judge who had presided at the trial was dead of course, as was the incumbent sheriff, Old Hub Hampton. But his son, known as Little Hub, had inherited not only his father's four-yearly alternation as sheriff, but also his father's capacity to stay on the best of political terms with his alternating opposite number, Ephriam Bishop. So Stevens had those two names; also the foreman of the Grand Jury at the time was a hale (hence still quick) eighty-five, even running a small electric-driven corn-mill while he wasn't hunting and fishing with Uncle Ike McCaslin, another octogenarian: plus a few other select signatures which Stevens compelled onto his petition as simply and ruthlessly as he did Ratliff's. Though what he considered his strongest card was a Harvard classmate, an amateur in state politics who had never held any office, who for years had been a sort of friend-of-the-court adviser to Governors simply because all the state factions knew he was not only a loyal Mississippian but one already too wealthy to want anything.

So Stevens would have—indeed, intended to have—nothing but progress to report to his client after he sent the documents in to the State capital and the rest of the summer passed toward and into fall—September, when Mississippi (including Governors and Legislatures and Pardon Boards) would put their neckties and coats back on and assume work again. Indeed, he felt he could almost select the specific day and hour he preferred to have the prisoner freed, choosing late September and explaining why to his client on the pad of yellow office foolscap, specious, voluble, convincing since he himself was convinced. September, the mounting apex of the cotton-picking season when there would be not only work, familiar work, but work which of all the freed man had the strongest emotional ties with, which after thirty-eight years of being compelled to it by loaded shotguns, he would now be paid by the hundred-weight for performing it. This, weighed against being freed at once, back in June, with half a summer of idleness plus the gravitational pull back to where he was born; not explaining to Linda his reasons why the little child-size creature who must have been mad to begin with and whom thirty-eight years in a penitentiary could not have improved any, must not come back to Jefferson; hiding that too behind the rational garrulity of the pencil flying along the ruled lines—until suddenly he would look up (she of course had heard nothing) and Ratliff would be standing just inside the office door looking at them, courteous, bland, inscrutable, and only a little grave and thoughtful too now. So little in fact that Linda anyway never noticed it, at least not before Stevens, touching, jostling her arm or elbow as he rose (though this was never necessary; she had felt the new presence by now), saying, "Howdy, V.K. Come in. Is it that time already?"

"Looks like it," Ratliff would say. "Mawnin, Linda."

"Howdy, V.K.," she would answer in her deaf voice but almost exactly with Stevens' inflection: who could not have heard him greet Ratliff since, and even he could not remember when she could have heard him before. Then Stevens would produce the gold lighter monogrammed GLS though L was not his initial, and light her cigarette, then at the cabinet above the wash basin he and Ratliff would assemble the three thick tumblers and the sugar basin and the single spoon and a sliced lemon and Ratliff would produce from his clothing somewhere the flask of corn whiskey a little of which old Mr Calvin Bookwright still made and aged each year and shared now and then with the few people tactful enough to retain his precarious irascible friendship. Then, Linda with her cigarette and Stevens with his cob pipe, the three of them would sit and sip the toddies, Stevens still talking and scribbling now and then on the pad for her to answer, until she would set down her empty glass and rise and say goodbye and leave them. Then Ratliff said:

"So you aint told Flem yet." Stevens smoked. "But then of course you dont need to, being as it's pretty well over the county now that Mink Snopes's cousin Linda or niece Linda or whichever it is, is getting him out." Stevens smoked. Ratliff picked up one of the toddy glasses. "You want another one?"

"No much obliged," Stevens said.

"So you aint lost your voice," Ratliff said. "Except, maybe back there in that vault in the bank where he would have to be counting his money, he cant hear what's going on. Except maybe that one trip he would have to make outside." Stevens smoked. "To go across to the Sheriff's office." Stevens smoked. "You right sho you dont want another toddy?"

"All right," Stevens said. "Why?"

"That's what I'm asking you. You'd a thought the first thing Flem would a done would been to go to the Sheriff and remind him of them final words of Mink's before Judge Long invited him to Parchman. Only he aint done that. Maybe because at least Linda told him about them two hundred and fifty dollars and even Flem Snopes can grab a straw when there aint nothing else in sight? Because naturally Flem cant walk right up to her and write on that tablet The minute you let that durn little water moccasin out he's going to come straight back here and pay you up to date for your maw's grave and all the rest of it that these Jefferson meddlers has probably already persuaded you I was to blame for; naturally he dont dare risk putting no such idea as that in her head and have her grab a holt of you and go to Parchman and take him out tonight and have him back in Jefferson by breakfast to-morrow, when as it is he's still got three more weeks, during which anything might happen: Linda or Mink or the Governor or the Pardon Board might die or Parchman itself might blow up. When did you say it would be?"

"When what will be?" Stevens said.

"The day they will let him out."

"Oh. Some time after the twentieth. Probably the twenty-sixth."

"The twenty-sixth," Ratliff said. "And you're going down there before?"

"Next week," Stevens said. "To leave the money and talk with the Warden myself. That he is not to touch the money until he promises to leave Mississippi before sundown and never come back."

"In that case," Ratliff said, "everything's all right. Especially if I—" He stopped.

"If you what?" Stevens said.

"Nothing," Ratliff said. "Fate, and destiny, and luck, and hope, and all of us mixed up in it—us and Linda and Flem and that durn little half-starved wildcat down there in Parchman, all mixed up in the same luck and destiny and fate and hope until cant none of us tell where it stops and we be-gin. Especially the hope. I mind I used to think that hope was about all folks had, only now I'm beginning to believe that that's about all anybody needs—jest hope. The pore son of a bitch over yonder in that bank vault counting his money be-cause that's the one place on earth Mink Snopes cant reach him in, and long as he's got to stay in it he might as well count money to be doing something, have something to do. And I wonder if maybe he wouldn't give Linda back her two hundred and fifty dollars without even charging her no interest on it, for them two years of pardon. And I wonder jest how much of the rest of the money in that vault he would pay to have another twenty years added onto them. Or maybe jest ten more. Or maybe jest one more."

Ten days later Stevens was in the Warden's office at the State Penitentiary. He had the money with him—twenty-five ten-dollar notes, quite new. "You dont want to see him yourself?" the Warden said.

"No," Stevens said. "You can do it. Anybody can. Simply offer him his choice: take the pardon and the two hundred and fifty dollars and get out of Mississippi as fast as he can, plus another two hundred and fifty every three months for the rest of his life if he never crosses the state line again; or stay here in Parchman another two years and rot and be damned to him."

"Well, that ought to do it," the Warden said. "It certainly would with me. Why is it whoever owns the two hundred and fifty dollars dont want him to come back home so bad?"

Stevens said rapidly, "Nothing to come back to. Family gone and scattered, wife died twenty-five or thirty years ago and nobody knows what became of his two daughters. Even the tenant house he lived in either collapsed of itself or maybe somebody found it and chopped it up and hauled it away for firewood."

"That's funny," the Warden said. "Almost anybody in Mississippi has got at least one cousin. In fact, it's hard not to have one."

"Oh, distant connections, relations," Stevens said. "Yes, it seems to have been the usual big scattered country clan."

"So one of these big scattered connections dont want him back home enough to pay two hundred and fifty dollars for it."

"He's mad," Stevens said. "Somebody here during the last thirty-eight years must have had that idea occur to them and suggested it to you even if you hadn't noticed it yourself."

"We're all mad here," the Warden said. "Even the prisoners too. Maybe it's the climate. I wouldn't worry, if I were you. They all make these threats at the time—big threats, against the Judge or the prosecuting lawyer or a witness that stood right up in public and told something that any decent man would have kept to himself; big threats: I notice there's no place on earth where a man can be as loud and dangerous as handcuffed to a policeman. But even one year is a long time sometimes. And he's had thirty-eight of them. So he dont get the pardon until he agrees to accept the money. Why do you know he wont take the money and double-cross you?"

"I've noticed a few things about people too," Stevens said. "One of them is, how a bad man will work ten times as hard and make ten times the sacrifice to be credited with at least one virtue no matter how spartan, than the upright man will to avoid the most abject vice provided it's fun. He tried to kill his lawyer right there in the jail during the trial when the lawyer suggested pleading him crazy. He will know that the only sane thing to do is to accept the money and the pardon, since to refuse the pardon because of the money, in two more years he not only wouldn't have the two thousand dollars, he might even be dead. Or, what would be infinitely worse, he would be alive and free at last and poor, and Fle—" and stopped himself.

"Yes?" the Warden said. "Who is Fleh, that might be dead himself in two more years and so out of reach for good? The one that owns the two hundred and fifty dollars? Never mind," he said. "I'll agree with you. Once he accepts the money, everything is jake, as they say. That's what you want?"

"That's right," Stevens said. "If there should be any sort of hitch, you can call me at Jefferson collect."

"I'll call you anyway," the Warden said. "You're trying too hard not to sound serious."

"No," Stevens said. "Only if he refuses the money."

"You mean the pardon, dont you?"

"What's the difference?" Stevens said.

So when about mid-afternoon on the twenty-sixth he answered his telephone and Central said, "Parchman, Mississippi, calling Mr Gavin Stevens. Go ahead, Parchman," and the faint voice said, "Hello. Lawyer?" Stevens thought rapidly *So I am a coward, after all. When it happens two years from now, at least none of it will spatter on me. At least I can tell her now because this will prove it* and said into the mouthpiece:

"So he refused to take the money."

"Then you already know," Ratliff's voice said.

". . . What?" Stevens said after less than a second actually. "Hello?"

"It's me," Ratliff said. "V.K. At Parchman. So they already telephoned you."

"Telephoned me what?" Stevens said. "He's still there? He refused to leave?"

"No, he's gone. He left about eight this morning. A truck going north—"

"But you just said he didn't take the money."

"That's what I'm trying to tell you. We finally located the money about fifteen minutes ago. It's still here. He—"

"Hold it," Stevens said. "You said eight this morning. Which direction?"

"A Negro seen him standing by the highway until he caught a ride on a cattle truck going north, toward Tutwiler. At Tutwiler he could have went to Clarksdale and then on to Memphis. Or he could have went from Tutwiler to Batesville and on to Memphis that-a-way. Except that anybody wanting to go from Parchman to Jefferson could go by Batesville too lessen he jest wanted to go by way of Chicago or New Orleans for the trip. Otherwise he could be in Jefferson pretty close to now. I'm leaving right now myself but maybe you better—"

"All right," Stevens said.

"And maybe Flem too," Ratliff said.

"Damn it, I said all right," Stevens said.

"But not her yet," Ratliff said. "Aint no need to tell her yet that likely she's jest finished killing her maw's husband—"

But he didn't even hear that, the telephone was already down; he didn't even have his hat when he reached the Square, the street below, the bank where Snopes would be in one direction, the Courthouse where the Sheriff would be in the other: not that it really mattered which one he saw first, thinking *So I really am a coward after all the talk about destiny and fate that didn't even sell Ratliff.*

"You mean," the Sheriff said, "he had already spent thirty-eight years in Parchman, and the minute somebody gets him out he's going to try to do something that will send him straight back even if it dont hang him first this time? Dont be foolish. Even a fellow like they say he was would learn that much sense in thirty-eight years."

"Ha," Stevens said without mirth. "You expressed it exactly that time. You were probably not even a shirt-tail boy back in 1908. You were not in that courtroom that day and saw his face and heard him. I was."

"All right," the Sheriff said. "What do you want me to do?"

"Arrest him. What do you call them? roadblocks? Dont even let him get into Yoknapatawpha County."

"On what grounds?"

"You just catch him, I'll furnish you with grounds as fast as you need them. If necessary we will hold him for obtaining money under false pretences."

"I thought he didn't take the money."

"I dont know what happened yet about the money. But I'll figure out some way to use it, at least long enough to hold him on for a while."

"Yes," the Sheriff said. "I reckon you would. Let's step over to the bank and see Mr Snopes; maybe all three of us can figure out something. Or maybe Mrs Kohl. You'll have to tell her too, I reckon."

Whereupon Stevens repeated almost verbatim what Ratliff had said into the telephone after he had put it down: "Tell a woman that apparently she just finished murdering her father at eight oclock this morning?"

"All right, all right," the Sheriff said. "You want me to come to the bank with you?"

"No," Stevens said. "Not yet anyway."

"I still think you have found a booger where there wasn't one," the Sheriff said. "If he comes back here at all, it'll just be out at Frenchman's Bend. Then all we'll have to do is pick him up the first time we notice him in town and have a talk with him."

"Notice, hell," Stevens said. "Aint that what I'm trying to tell you? that you dont notice him. That was the mistake Zack Houston made thirty-eight years ago: he didn't notice him either until he stepped out from behind that bush that morning with that shotgun—if he even stepped out of the bushes before he shot, which I doubt."

He recrossed the Square rapidly, thinking *Yes, I really am a coward, after all,* when that quantity, entity with which he had spent a great deal of his life talking with or rather having to listen to (his skeleton perhaps, which would outlast the rest of him by a few months or years—and without doubt would spend that time moralising at him while he would be helpless to answer back) answered immediately *Did anyone ever say you were not?* Then he *But I am not a coward: I am a humanitarian.* Then the other *You are not even an original; that word is customarily used as a euphemism for it.*

The bank would be closed now. But when he crossed the Square to the Sheriff's office the car with Linda behind the wheel had not been waiting so this was not the day of the weekly whiskey-run. The shades were drawn but after some knob-rattling at the side door one of the book-keepers peered out and recognised him and let him in; he passed on through the machine-clatter of the day's recapitulation—the machines themselves sounding immune and even inattentive to the astronomical sums they reduced to staccato trivia—and knocked at the door on which Colonel Sartoris had had the word PRIVATE lettered by hand sixty years ago, and opened it.

Snopes was sitting not at the desk but with his back to it, facing the cold now empty fireplace, his feet raised and crossed against the same heel-scratches whose initial inscribing Colonel Sartoris had begun. He was not reading, he was not doing anything: just sitting there with his black planter's hat on, his lower jaw moving faintly and steadily as though he were chewing something, which as the town knew also he was not; he didn't even lower his feet when Stevens came to the desk (it was a broad flat table littered with papers in a sort of neat, almost orderly way) and said almost in one breath:

"Mink left Parchman at eight oclock this morning. I dont know whether you know it or not but we—I had some money waiting to be given to him at the gate, under condition that in accepting it he had passed his oath to leave Mississippi without returning to Jefferson and never cross the state line again. He didn't take the money; I dont know yet how since he was not to be given the pardon until he did. He caught a ride in a passing truck and has disappeared. The truck was headed north."

"How much was it?" Snopes said.

"What?" Stevens said.

"The money," Snopes said.

"Two hundred and fifty dollars," Stevens said.

"Much obliged," Snopes said.

"Good God, man," Stevens said. "I tell you a man left Parchman at eight oclock this morning on his way here to murder you and all you say is much obliged?"

The other didn't move save for the faint chewing motion; Stevens thought with a kind of composed and seething rage: *If he would only spit now and then.* "Then all he had was that ten dollars they give them when they turn them loose," Snopes said.

"Yes," Stevens said. "As far as we—I know. But yes." *Or even just go through the motions of spitting now and then* he thought.

"Say a man thought he had a grudge against you," Snopes said. "A man sixty-three years old now with thirty-eight of that spent in the penitentiary and even before that wasn't much, not much bigger than a twelve-year-old boy—"

That had to use a shotgun from behind a bush even then Stevens thought. *Oh yes, I know exactly what you mean: too small and frail even then, even without thirty-eight years in jail, to have risked a mere knife or bludgeon. And he cant go out to Frenchman's Bend, the only place on earth where someone might remember him enough to lend him one because even though nobody in Frenchman's Bend would knock up the muzzle aimed at you, they wouldn't lend him theirs to aim with. So he will either have to buy a gun for ten dollars, or steal one. In which cases you might even be safe: the ten-dollar one wont shoot and in the other some policeman might save you honestly.* He thought rapidly *Of course. North. He went to Memphis. He would have to. He wouldn't think of anywhere else to go to buy a gun with ten dollars.* And, since Mink had only the ten dollars, he would have to hitch-hike all the way, first to Memphis, provided he got there before the pawn shops closed, then back to Jefferson. Which could not be before tomorrow, since anything else would leave simple destiny and fate too topheavy with outrageous hope and coincidence for even Ratliff's sanguine nature to pass. "Yes," he said. "So do I. You have at least until tomorrow night." He thought rapidly *And now for it. How to persuade him not to tell her without letting him know that was what he agreed to, promised, and that it was me who put it into his mind.* So suddenly he heard himself say: "Are you going to tell Linda?"

"Why?" Snopes said.

"Yes," Stevens said. Then heard himself say in his turn: "Much obliged." Then, suddenly indeed this time: "I'm responsible for this, even if I probably couldn't have stopped it. I just talked to Eef Bishop. What else do you want me to do?" *If he would just spit once* he thought.

"Nothing," Snopes said.

"What?" Stevens said.

"Yes," Snopes said. "Much obliged."

At least he knew where to start. Only, he didn't know how. Even if—when—he called the Memphis police, what would—could—he tell them: a city police force a hundred miles away, who had never heard of Mink and Flem Snopes and Zack Houston, dead these forty years now, either. When he, Stevens, had already failed to move very much the local Sheriff who at least had inherited the old facts. How to explain what he himself was convinced Mink wanted in Memphis, let alone convince them that Mink was or would be in Memphis. And even if he managed to shake them that much, how to describe whom they were supposed to look for: whose victim forty years ago had got himself murdered mainly for the reason that the murderer was the sort of creature whom nobody, even his victim, noticed enough in time to pay any attention to what he was or might do.

Except Ratliff. Ratliff alone out of Yoknapatawpha County would know Mink on sight. To be unschooled, untravelled, and to an extent unread, Ratliff had a terrifying capacity for knowledge or local information or acquaintanceship to match the need of any local crisis. Stevens admitted to himself now what he was waiting, dallying, really wasting time for: for Ratliff to drive back in his pickup truck from Parchman, to be hurried on to Memphis without even stopping, cutting the engine, to reveal Mink to the Memphis police and so save Mink's cousin, kinsman, whatever Flem was, from that just fate; knowing—Stevens—better all the while: that what he

really wanted with Ratliff was to find out how Mink had not
only got past the Parchman gate without that absolutely con-
tingent money, but had managed it in such a way that apparently only the absolutely unpredicted and unwarranted
presence of Ratliff at a place and time that he had no business
whatever being, revealed the fact that he hadn't taken it.

It was not three oclock when Ratliff phoned; it would be
almost nine before he reached Jefferson. It was not that the
pickup truck wouldn't have covered the distance faster. It was
that no vehicle owned by Ratliff (provided he was in it and
conscious, let alone driving it) was going to cover it faster.
Besides, at some moment not too long after six oclock he was
going to stop to eat at the next dreary repetitive little cotton-
gin hamlet, or (nowadays) on the highway itself, drawing
neatly in and neatly parking before the repetitive Dixie Cafés
or Mac's or Lorraine's, to eat, solitary, neatly and without
haste the meat a little too stringy to chew properly and too
overcooked to taste at all, the stereotyped fried potatoes and
the bread you didn't chew but mumbled, like kleenex or one
of the paper napkins, the machine-chopped pre-frozen lettuce
and tomatoes like (except for the tense inviolate color) something exhumed by paleontologists from tundras, the machine-
made pre-frozen pie and what they would call coffee—the
food perfectly pure and perfectly tasteless except for the dous-
ing of machine-made tomato ketchup.

He (Stevens) could, perhaps should, have had plenty of
time to drive out to Rose Hill and eat his own decent evening
meal. Instead, he telephoned his wife.

"I'll come in and we can eat at the Holston House," she
said.

"No, Honey. I've got to see Ratliff as soon as he gets back
from Parchman."

"All right. I think I'll come in and have supper with
Maggie" (Maggie was his sister) "and maybe we'll go to the
picture show and I'll see you tomorrow. I can come in to
town cant I if I promise to stay off the streets?"

"You see, you dont help me. How can I resist togetherness
if you wont fight back?"

"I'll see you tomorrow then," she said. "Goodnight." So
they ate at the Holston House; he didn't feel quite up to his

sister and brother-in-law and his nephew Charles tonight. The
Holston House still clung to the old ways, not desperately
nor even gallantly: just with a cold and inflexible indomi-
tabilty, owned and run by two maiden sisters (that is, one of
them, the younger, had been married once but so long ago
and so briefly that it no longer counted) who were the last descendants of the Alexander Holston, one of Yoknapatawpha
County's three original settlers, who had built the log ordinary which the modern edifice had long since swallowed, who
had had his part—been in fact the catalyst—in the naming of
Jefferson a hundred and thirty years ago; they still called the
diningroom simply the diningroom and (nobody knew how)
they still kept Negro man waiters, some of whose seniority
still passed from father to son; the guests still ate the table-
d'hôte meals mainly at two long communal tables at the head
of each of which a sister presided; no man came there without
a coat and necktie and no woman with her head covered
(there was a dressing room with a maid for that purpose) not
even if she had a railroad ticket in her hand.

Though his sister did pick his wife up in time for the picture show. So he was back in the office when a little after
eight-thirty he heard Ratliff on the stairs and said, "All right.
What happened?" Then he said, "No. Wait. What were you
doing at Parchman?"

"I'm a—what do you call it? optimist," Ratliff said. "Like
any good optimist, I dont expect the worst to happen. Only,
like any optimist worth his salt, I like to go and look as soon
as possible afterward jest in case it did. Especially when the
difference between the best and the worst is liable to reach all
the way back up here to Jefferson. It taken a little doing, too.
This was about ten oclock this morning; he had been gone a
good two hours by then, and they was a little impatient with
me. They had done done their share, took him and had him
for thirty-eight years all fair and regular, like the man said for
them to, and they felt they had done earned the right to be
shut of him. You know: his new fresh pardon and them new
fresh two hundred and fifty dollars all buttoned up neat and
safe and secure in his new fresh over-halls and jumper and the
gate locked behind him again jest like the man said too and
the official Mink Snopes page removed outen the ledger and

officially marked Paid in Full and destroyed a good solid two hours back, when here comes this-here meddling out-of-town son-of-a-gun that aint even a lawyer saying Yes yes, that's jest fine, only let's make sho he actively had that money when he left.

"The Warden his-self had tended to the money in person: had Mink in alone, with the table all ready for him, the pardon in one pile and them two hundred and fifty dollars that Mink hadn't never seen that much at one time before in his life, in the other pile; and the Warden his-self explaining how there wasn't no choice about it: to take the pardon he would have to take the money too, and once he teched the money he had done give his sworn word and promise and bible oath to strike for the quickest place outside the State of Missippi and never cross the line again as long as he lived. 'Is that what I got to do to get out?' Mink says. 'Take the money?' 'That's it,' the Warden says and Mink reached and taken the money and the Warden his-self helped him button the money and the pardon both inside his jumper and the Warden shaken his hand and the trusty come to take him out to where the turnkey was waiting to unlock the gate into liberty and freedom—"

"Wait," Stevens said. "Trusty."

"Aint it?" Ratliff said with pleased, almost proud approval. "It was so simple. Likely that's why it never occurred to none of them, especially as even a Parchman deserving any name a-tall for being well-conducted, aint supposed to contain no-body eccentric and antisocial enough to behave like he considered anything like free-will choice to even belong in the same breath with two hundred and fifty active dollars give him free for nothing so he never even had to say Much obliged for them. That's what I said too: 'That trusty. He left here for the gate with them two hundred and fifty dollars. Let's jest see if he still had them when he went outen it.' So that's what I said too: 'That trusty.'

" 'A lifer too,' the Warden says. 'Killed his wife with a ball peen hammer, was converted and received salvation in the jail before he was even tried and has one of the best records here, is even a lay-preacher.'

" 'Than which, if Mink had had your whole guest list to

pick from and time to pick in, he couldn't a found a better feller for his purpose,' I says. 'So it looks like I'm already fixing to begin to have to feel sorry for this-here snatched brand even if he was too impatient to think of a better answer to the enigma of wedlock than a garage hammer. That is, I reckon you still got a few private interrogation methods for reluctant conversationalists around here, aint you?'

"That's why I was late calling you: it taken a little time too though I got to admit nothing showed on his outside. Because people are funny. No, they aint funny: they're jest sad. Here was this feller already in for life and even if they had found out that was a mistake or somebody even left the gate unlocked, he wouldn't a dast to walk outen it because the gal's paw had done already swore he would kill him the first time he crossed the Parchman fence. So what in the world could he a done with two hundred and fifty dollars even if he could ever a dreamed he could get away with this method of getting holt of it."

"But how, dammit?" Stevens said. "How?"

"Why, the only way Mink could a done it, which was likely why never nobody thought to anticipate it. On the way from the Warden's office to the gate he jest told the trusty he needed to step into the gentlemen's room a minute and when they was inside he give the trusty the two hundred and fifty dollars and asked the trusty to hand it back to the Warden the first time the trusty conveniently got around to it, the longer the better after he, Mink, was outside the gate and outen sight, and tell the Warden Much obliged but he had done changed his mind and wouldn't need it. So there the trusty was: give Mink another hour or two and he would be gone, likely forever, nobody would know where or care. Because I dont care where you are: the minute a man can really believe that never again in his life will he have any use for two hundred and fifty dollars, he's done already been dead and has jest this minute found it out. And that's all. I dont—"

"I do," Stevens said. "Flem told me. He's in Memphis. He's too little and frail and old to use a knife or a club so he will have to go to the nearest place he can hope to get a gun with ten dollars."

"So you told Flem. What did he say?"

"He said, Much obliged," Stevens said. After a moment he said, "I said, when I told Flem Mink had left Parchman at eight oclock this morning on his way up here to kill him, he said Much obliged."

"I heard you," Ratliff said. "What would you a said? You would sholy be as polite as Flem Snopes, wouldn't you? So maybe it's all right, after all. Of course you done already talked to Memphis."

"Tell them what?" Stevens said. "How describe to a Memphis policeman somebody I wouldn't recognise myself, let alone that he's actually in Memphis trying to do what I assume he is trying to do, for the simple reason that I dont know what to do next either?"

"What's wrong with Memphis?" Ratliff said.

"I'll bite," Stevens said. "What is?"

"I thought it would took a heap littler place than Memphis not to have nobody in it you used to go to Harvard with."

"Well I'll be damned," Stevens said. He put in the call at once and presently was talking with him: the classmate, the amateur Cincinnatus at his plantation not far from Jackson, who had already been instrumental in getting the pardon through, so that Stevens needed merely explain the crisis, not the situation.

"You dont actually know he went to Memphis, of course," the friend said.

"That's right," Stevens said. "But since we are forced by emergency to challenge where he might be, at least we should be permitted one assumption in good faith."

"All right," the friend said. "I know the Mayor and the Commissioner both. All you want—all they can do really—is check any places where anyone might have tried to buy a gun or pistol for ten dollars since say noon today. Right?"

"Right," Stevens said. "And ask them please to call me collect here when—if they do."

"I'll call you myself," the friend said. "You might say I also have a small equity in your friend's doom."

"When you call me that to Flem Snopes, smile," Stevens said.

That was Thursday; during Friday Central would run him to earth all right no matter where he happened to be about the Square. However there was plenty to do in the office if he composed himself to it. Which he managed to do in time and was so engaged when Ratliff came in carrying something neatly folded in a paper bag and said, "Good mawnin," Stevens not looking up, writing on the yellow foolscap pad, steadily, quite composed in fact even with Ratliff standing for a moment looking down at the top of his head. Then Ratliff moved and took one of the chairs beyond the desk, the one against the wall, then half rose and placed the little parcel neatly on the filing case beside him and sat down, Stevens still writing steadily between pauses now and then to read from the open book beneath his left hand; until presently Ratliff reached and took the morning Memphis paper from the desk and opened it and rattled faintly the turn of the page and after a while rattled that one faintly, until Stevens said,

"Dammit, either get out of here or think about something else. You make me nervous."

"I aint busy this mawnin," Ratliff said. "If you got anything to tend to outside, I can set here and listen for the phone."

"I have plenty I can do here if you'll just stop filling the damned air with—" He flung, slammed the pencil down. "Obviously he hasn't reached Memphis yet or anyway hasn't tried to buy the gun, or we would have heard. Which is all we want: to get the word there first. Do you think that any reputable pawnshop or sporting-goods store that cares a damn about its license will sell him a gun now after the police—"

"If my name was Mink Snopes, I dont believe I would go to no place that had a license to lose for selling guns or pistols."

"For instance?" Stevens said.

"Out at Frenchman's Bend they said Mink was a considerable hell-raiser when he was young, within his means of course, which wasn't much. But he made two or three of them country-boy Memphis trips with the young bloods of his time— Quicks and Tulls and Turpins and such: enough to probably know where to begin to look for the kind of places that dont keep the kind of licenses to have police worrying them ever time a gun or a pistol turns up in the wrong place or dont turn up in the right one."

"Dont you think the Memphis police know as much about

Memphis as any damned little murdering maniac, let alone one that's been locked up in a penitentiary for forty years? The Memphis police, that have a damned better record than a dozen, hell, a hundred cities I could name—"

"All right, all right," Ratliff said.

"By God, God Himself is not so busy but that a homicidal maniac with only ten dollars in the world can hitch-hike a hundred miles and buy a gun for ten dollars then hitch-hike another hundred and shoot another man with it."

"Dont that maybe depend on who God wants shot this time?" Ratliff said. "Have you been by the sheriff's this mawnin?"

"No," Stevens said.

"I have. Flem aint been to him either yet. And he aint left town neither. I checked on that too. So maybe that's the best sign we want: Flem aint worried. Do you reckon he told Linda?"

"No," Stevens said.

"How do you know?"

"He told me."

"Flem did? You mean he jest told you, or you asked him?"

"I asked him," Stevens said. "I said, 'Are you going to tell Linda?' "

"And what did he say?"

"He said, 'Why?' " Stevens said.

"Oh," Ratliff said.

Then it was noon. What Ratliff had in the neat parcel was a sandwich, as neatly made. "You go home and eat dinner," he said. "I'll set here and listen for it."

"Didn't you just say that if Flem himself dont seem to worry, why the hell should we?"

"I wont worry then," Ratliff said. "I'll jest set and listen."

Though Stevens was back in the office when the call came in midafternoon. "Nothing," the classmate's voice said. "None of the pawnshops nor any other place a man might go to buy a gun or pistol of any sort, let alone a ten-dollar one. Maybe he hasn't reached Memphis yet, though it's more than twenty-four hours now."

"That's possible," Stevens said.

"Maybe he never intended to reach Memphis."

"All right, all right," Stevens said. "Shall I write the Commissioner myself a letter of thanks or—"

"Sure. But let him earn it first. He agreed that it not only wont cost much more, it will even be a good idea to check his list every morning for the next two or three days, just in case. I thanked him for you. I even went further and said that if you ever found yourselves in the same voting district and he decided to run for an office instead of just sitting for it—" as Stevens put the telephone down and turned to Ratliff again without seeing him at all and said,

"Maybe he never will."

"What?" Ratliff said. "What did he say?" Stevens told, repeated, the gist. "I reckon that's all we can do," Ratliff said.

"Yes," Stevens said. He thought *Tomorrow will prove it. But I'll wait still another day. Maybe until Monday.*

But he didn't wait that long. On Saturday his office was always, not busy with the county business he was paid a salary to handle, so much as constant with the social coming and going of the country men who had elected him to his office. Ratliff, who knew them all too, as well or even better, was unobtrusive in his chair against the wall where he could reach the telephone without even getting up; he even had another neat home-made sandwich, until at noon Stevens said,

"Go on home and eat a decent meal, or come home with me. It wont ring today."

"You must know why," Ratliff said.

"Yes. I'll tell you Monday. No: tomorrow. Sunday will be appropriate. I'll tell you tomorrow."

"So you know it's all right now. All settled and finished now. Whether Flem knows it yet or not, he can sleep from now on."

"Dont ask me yet," Stevens said. "It's like a thread; it's true only until I—something breaks it."

"You was right all the time then. There wasn't no need to tell her."

"There never has been," Stevens said. "There never will be."

"That's jest what I said," Ratliff said. "There aint no need now."

"And what I just said was there never was any need to

tell her and there never would have been, no matter what happened."

"Not even as a moral question?" Ratliff said.

"Moral hell and question hell," Stevens said. "It aint any question at all: it's a fact: the fact that not you nor anybody else that wears hair is going to tell her that her act of pity and compassion and simple generosity murdered the man who passes as her father whether he is or not or a son of a bitch or not."

"All right, all right," Ratliff said. "This here thread you jest mentioned. Maybe another good way to keep it from getting broke before time is to keep somebody handy to hear that telephone when it dont ring at three oclock this afternoon."

So they were both in the office at three oclock. Then it was four. "I reckon we can go now," Ratliff said.

"Yes," Stevens said.

"But you still wont tell me now," Ratliff said.

"Tomorrow," Stevens said. "The call will have to come by then."

"So this-here thread has got a telephone wire inside of it after all."

"So-long," Stevens said. "See you tomorrow."

And Central would know where to find him at any time on Sunday too and in fact until almost half past two that afternoon he still believed he was going to spend the whole day at Rose Hill. His life had known other similar periods of unrest and trouble and uncertainty even if he had spent most of it as a bachelor; he could recall one or two of them when the anguish and unrest was due to the fact that he was a bachelor, that is, circumstances, conditions insisted on his continuing celibacy despite his own efforts to give it up. But back then he had had something to escape into: nepenthe, surcease: the project he had decreed for himself back in Harvard of translating the Old Testament back into the classic Greek of its first translating; after which he would teach himself Hebrew and really attain to purity; he had thought last night *Why yes, I have that for tomorrow; I had forgotten about that.* Then this morning he knew that that would not suffice anymore, not ever again now. He meant of course the effort: not just the capacity to concentrate but to believe in it; he was too old now and the real tragedy of age is that no anguish is any longer grievous enough to demand, justify, any sacrifice.

So it was not even two-thirty when with no surprise really he found himself getting into his car and still no surprise when, entering the empty Sunday-afternoon Square, he saw Ratliff waiting at the foot of the office stairs, the two of them, in the office now, making no pretence as the clock crawled on to three. "What happened that we set exactly three oclock as the magic deadline in this-here business?" Ratliff said.

"Does it matter?" Stevens said.

"That's right," Ratliff said. "The main thing is not to jar or otherwise startle that-ere thread." Then the courthouse clock struck its three heavy mellow blows into the sabbath somnolence and for the first time Stevens realised how absolutely he had not just expected, but known, that his telephone would not ring before that hour. Then in that same second, instant, he knew why it had not rung; the fact that it had not rung was more proof of what it would have conveyed than the message itself would have been.

"All right," he said. "Mink is dead."

"What?" Ratliff said.

"I dont know where, and it doesn't matter. Because we should have known from the first that three hours of being free would kill him, let alone three days of it." He was talking rapidly, not babbling: "Dont you see? a little kinless tieless frail alien animal that never really belonged to the human race to start with, let alone belonged in it, then locked up in a cage for thirty-eight years and now at sixty-three years old suddenly set free, shoved, flung out of safety and security into freedom like a krait or a fer-de-lance quick and deadly dangerous as long as it can stay inside the man-made man-tended tropic immunity of its glass box, but wouldn't live even through the first hour set free, flung, hoicked on a pitchfork or a pair of long-handled tongs into a city street?"

"Wait," Ratliff said, "wait."

But Stevens didn't even pause. "Of course we haven't heard yet where he was found or how or by whom identified because nobody cares; maybe nobody has even noticed him yet. Because he's free. He can even die wherever he wants to now. For thirty-eight years until last Thursday morning he couldn't have had a pimple or a hangnail without it being in a record five minutes later. But he's free now. Nobody cares when or where or how he dies provided his carrion doesn't get under somebody's feet. So we can go home now, until somebody does telephone and you and Flem can go and identify him."

"Yes," Ratliff said. "Well—"

"Give it up," Stevens said. "Come on out home with me and have a drink."

"We could go by first and kind of bring Flem up to date," Ratliff said. "Maybe even he might take a dram then."

"I'm not really an evil man," Stevens said. "I wouldn't have loaned Mink a gun to shoot Flem with; I might not even have just turned my head while Mink used his own. But neither am I going to lift my hand to interfere with Flem spending another day or two expecting any moment that Mink will."

He didn't even tell the Sheriff his conviction that Mink was dead. The fact was, the Sheriff told him; he found the Sheriff in his courthouse office and told him his and Ratliff's theory of Mink's first objective and the reason for it and that the Memphis police would still check daily the places where Mink might try to buy a weapon.

"So evidently he's not in Memphis," the Sheriff said. "That's how many days now?"

"Since Thursday."

"And he's not in Frenchman's Bend."

"How do you know?"

"I drove out yesterday and looked around a little."

"So you did believe me, after all," Stevens said.

"I get per diem on my car," the Sheriff said. "Yesterday was a nice day for a country drive. So he's had four days now, to come a hundred miles. And he dont seem to be in Memphis. And I know he aint in Frenchman's Bend. And according to you, Mr Snopes knows he aint in Jefferson here. Maybe he's dead." Whereupon, now that another had stated it, spoke it aloud, Stevens knew that he himself had never believed it, hearing without listening while the Sheriff went on: "A damned little rattlesnake that they say never had any friends to begin with and nobody out at the Bend knows what became of his wife and his two girls or even when they disappeared.

To be locked up for thirty-eight years and then suddenly turned out like you do a cat at night, with nowhere to go and nobody really wanting him out. Maybe he couldn't stand being free. Maybe just freedom killed him. I've known it to happen."

"Yes," Stevens said, "you're probably right," thinking qui-etly *We wont stop him. We cant stop him—not all of us together, Memphis police and all. Maybe even a rattlesnake with destiny on his side dont even need luck, let alone friends.* He said: "Only we dont know yet. We cant count on that."

"I know," the Sheriff said. "I deputised two boys at Varner's store yesterday that claim they remember him, would know him again. And I can have Mr Snopes followed, watched back and forth to the bank. But dammit, watch for who, what, when, where? I cant put a man inside his house until he asks for it, can I? His daughter. Mrs Kohl. Maybe she could do something. You still dont want her to know?"

"You must give me your word," Stevens said.

"All right," the Sheriff said. "I suppose your Jackson buddy will let you know the minute the Memphis police get any sort of a line, wont he?"

"Yes," Stevens said. Though the call didn't come until Wednesday. Ratliff had rung him up a little after ten Tuesday night and told him the news, and on his way to the office this morning he passed the bank whose drawn shades would not be raised today, and as he stood at his desk with the telephone in his hand he could see through his front window the som-bre black-and-white-and-violet convolutions of tulle and rib-bon and waxen asphodels fastened to the locked front door.

"He found a ten-dollar pistol," the classmate's voice said. "Early Monday morning. It wasn't really a properly-licensed pawnshop, so they almost missed it. But under a little . . . persuasion the proprietor recalled the sale. But he said not to worry, the pistol was only technically still a pistol and it would require a good deal more nourishment than the three rounds of ammunition they threw in with it to make it function."

"Ha," Stevens said without mirth. "Tell the proprietor from me he doesn't know his own strength. The pistol was here last night. It functioned."

Seventeen

WHEN he reached the Junction a little before eleven oclock Monday morning, he was in the cab of another cattle truck. The truck was going on east into Alabama but even if it had turned south here actually to pass through Jefferson, he would have left it at this point. If it had been a Yoknapatawpha County truck or driven by someone from the county or Jefferson, he would not have been in it at all.

Until he stepped out of the store this morning with the pistol actually in his pocket, it had all seemed simple; he had only one problem: to get the weapon; after that, only geography stood between him and the moment when he would walk up to the man who had seen him sent to the penitentiary without raising a finger, who had not even had the decency and courage to say No to his bloodcry for help from kin to kin, and say, "Look at me, Flem," and kill him.

But now he was going to have to do what he called 'figger' a little. It seemed to him that he was confronted by an almost insurmountable diffusion of obstacles. He was in thirty miles of Jefferson now, home, one same mutual north Mississippi hill-country people even if there was still a trivial county-line to cross; it seemed to him that from now on anyone, everyone he met or who saw him, without even needing to recognise or remember his specific face and name, would know at once who he was and where he was going and what he intended to do. On second thought—an immediate, flashing, almost simultaneous second thought—he knew this to be a physical impossibility, yet he dared not risk it; that the thirty-eight years of being locked up in Parchman had atrophied, destroyed some quality in him which in people who had not been locked up had very likely got even sharper, and they would recognise, know, divine who he was without his even knowing it had happened. *It's because I done had to been away so long* he thought. *Like now I'm fixing to have to learn to talk all over again.*

He meant not talk, but think. As he walked along the highway (blacktop now, following a graded survey line, on which automobiles sped, which he remembered as winding dirt along which slow mules and wagons, or at best a saddle horse, followed the arbitrary and random ridges) it would be impossible to disguise his appearance—change his face, his expression, alter his familiar regional clothes or the way he walked; he entertained for a desperate and bizarre moment then dismissed it the idea of perhaps walking backward, at least whenever he heard a car or truck approaching, to give the impression that he was going the other way. So he would have to change his thinking, as you change the color of the bulb inside the lantern even though you cant change the lantern itself; as he walked he would have to hold himself unflagging and undeviating to *thinking* like he was someone who had never heard the name Snopes and the town *Jefferson* in his life, wasn't even aware that if he kept on this road he would have to pass through it; to think instead like someone whose destination and goal was a hundred and more miles away and who in spirit was already there and only his carcass, his progressing legs, walked this particular stretch of road.

Also, he was going to have to find somebody he could talk with without rousing suspicion, not to get information so much as to validate it. Until he left Parchman, was free at last, the goal for which he had bided patiently for thirty-eight years now practically in his hand, he believed he had got all the knowledge he would need from the, not day to day of course and not always year to year, but at least decade to decade trickling which had penetrated even into Parchman— how and where his cousin lived, how he spent his days, his habits, what time he came and went and where to and from; even who lived in or about his house with him. But now that the moment was almost here, that might not be enough. It might even be completely false, wrong; he thought again *It's having to been away so long like I had to been; having to been in the place I had to been,* as though he had spent those thirty-eight years not merely out of the world but out of life, so that even facts when they finally reached him had already ceased to be truth in order to have penetrated there; and, being inside Parchman walls, were *per se* inimical and betraying and fatal to him if he attempted to use them, depend on them, trust them.

Third, there was the pistol. The road was empty now, running between walls of woods, no sound of traffic and no house or human in sight and he took the pistol out and looked at it again with something like despair. It had not looked very much like a pistol in the store this morning; here, in the afternoon's sunny rural solitude and silence, it looked like nothing recognisable at all; looking, if anything, more than ever like the fossilised terrapin of his first impression. Yet he would have to test it, spend one of his three cartridges simply to find out if it really would shoot and for a moment, a second something nudged at his memory. *It's got to shoot* he thought. *It's jest got to. There aint nothing else for hit to do. Old Moster jest punishes; He dont play jokes.*

He was hungry too. He had not eaten since the animal crackers at sunrise. He had a little money left and he had already passed two gasoline station-stores. But he was home now; he dared not stop in one and be seen buying the cheese and crackers which he could still afford. Which reminded him of night also. The sun was now less than three hours high; he could not possibly reach Jefferson until tomorrow so it would have to be tomorrow night so he turned from the highway into a dirt crossroad, by instinct almost since he could not remember when he had begun to notice the wisps of cotton lint snared into the roadside weeds and brambles from the passing gin-bound wagons, since this type of road was familiar out of his long-ago tenant-farmer freedom too: a Negro road, a road marked with many wheels and traced with cotton-wisps, yet dirt, not even gravel, since the people who lived on and used it had neither the voting-power to compel nor the money to persuade the Beat Supervisor to do more than scrape and grade it twice a year.

So what he found was not only what he was hunting for but what he had expected: a weathered paintless dogtrot cabin enclosed and backed by a ramshackle of also-paintless weathered fences and outhouses—barns, cribs, sheds—on a rise of ground above a creek-bottom cotton-patch where he could already see the whole Negro family and perhaps a neighbor or so too dragging the long stained sacks more or less abreast up the parallel rows—the father, the mother, five children between five or six and twelve, and four girls and young men who were probably the neighbors swapping the work, he, Mink, waiting at the end of the row until the father, who would be the boss, reached him.

"Hidy," Mink said. "Looks like you could use another hand in here."

"You want to pick?" the Negro said.

"What you paying?"

"Six bits."

"I'll help you a spell," Mink said. The Negro spoke to the twelve-year-old girl beside him.

"Hand him your sack. You go on to the house and start supper."

He took the sack. There was nothing unfamiliar about it. He had been picking cotton at this time of the year all his life. The only difference was that for the last thirty-eight years there had been a shotgun and a bullwhip at the end of the row behind him as a promise for lagging, where here again were the weighing scales and the money they designated as a reward for speed. And, as he had expected, his employer was presently in the row next him.

"You dont stay around here," the Negro said.

"That's right," he said. "I'm jest passing through. On my way down to the Delta where my daughter lives."

"Where?" the Negro said. "I made a Delta crop one year myself."

It wasn't that he should have expected this next question and would have avoided it if he knew how. It was rather that the question would not matter if he only didn't forget to think himself someone else except who he was. He didn't hesitate; he even volunteered: "Doddsville," he said. "Not fur from Parchman." And he knew what the next question would have been too, the one the Negro didn't ask and would not ask, answering that one too: "I been over a year in a hospital up in Memphis. The doctor said walking would be good for me. That's why I'm on the road instead of the train."

"The Vetruns Hospital?" the Negro said.

"What?" he said.

"The Govment Vetruns Hospital?"

"That's right," he said. "The Govment had me. Over a year."

Now it was sundown. The wife had gone to the house some time ago. "You want to weigh out now?" the Negro said.

"I aint in no rush," he said. "I can give you a half a day tomorrow; jest so I knock off at noon. If your wife can fix me a plate of supper and a pallet somewhere, you can take that out of the weighing."

"I dont charge nobody to eat at my house," the Negro said.

The diningroom was an oilcloth-covered table bearing a coal oil lamp in the same leanto room where the woodburning stove now died slowly. He ate alone, the family had vanished, the house itself might have been empty, the plate of fried side-meat and canned corn and tomatoes stewed together, the pale soft barely cooked biscuits, the cup of coffee already set and waiting for him when the man called him to come and eat. Then he returned to the front room where a few wood embers burned on the hearth against the first cool of autumn night; immediately the wife and the oldest girl rose and went back to the kitchen to set the meal for the family. He turned before the fire, spreading his legs; at his age he would feel the cool tonight. He spoke, casual, conversational, in the amenities, idly; at first, for a little while, you would have thought inattentively:

"I reckon you gin and trade in Jefferson. I used to know a few folks there. The banker. Dee Spain his name was, I remember. A long time back, of course."

"I dont remember him," the Negro said. "The main banker in Jefferson now is Mr Snopes."

"Oh yes, I heard tell about him. Big banker, big rich. Lives in the biggest house in town with a hired cook and a man to wait on the table for jest him and that daughter is it that makes out she's deaf."

"She is deaf. She was in the war. A cannon broke her eardrums."

"So she claims." The Negro didn't answer. He was sitting in the room's—possibly the house's—one rocking chair, not moving anyway. But now something beyond just stillness had come over him: an immobility, almost like held breath. Mink's back was to the fire, the light, so his face was invisible; his voice anyway had not altered. "A woman in a war. She must have ever body fooled good. I've knowed them like that myself. She jest makes claims and ever body around is too polite to call her a liar. Likely she can hear ever bit as good as you and me."

Now the Negro spoke, quite sternly. "Whoever it was told you she is fooling is the one that's lying. There are folks in more places than right there in Jefferson that know the truth about her whether the word has got up to that Vetrun Hospital where you claim you was at or not. If I was you, I dont believe I would dispute it. Or leastways I would be careful who I disputed it to."

"Sho, sho," Mink said. "You Jefferson folks ought to know. You mean, she can't hear nothing? You could walk right up behind her say, into the same room even, and she wouldn't know it?"

"Yes," the Negro said. The twelve-year-old girl now stood in the kitchen door. "She's deaf. You dont need to dispute it. The Lord touched her, like He touches a heap of folks better than you, better than me. Dont worry about that."

"Your supper's ready," Mink said. The Negro got up.

"What you going to do tonight?" he said. "I aint got room for you."

"I dont need none," Mink said. "That doctor said for me to get all the fresh air I can. If you got a extry quilt, I'll sleep in the cotton truck and be ready for a early start back in that patch tomorrow."

The cotton which half-filled the bed of the pickup truck had been covered for the night with a tarpaulin, so he didn't even need the quilt. He was quite comfortable. But mainly he was off the ground. That was the danger, what a man had to watch against: once you laid flat on the ground, right away the earth started in to draw you back down into it. The very moment you were born out of your mother's body, the power and drag of the earth was already at work on you; if there had not been other womenfolks in the family or neighbors or even a hired one to support you, hold you up, keep the earth from touching you, you would not live an hour. And you knew it too. As soon as you could move you would raise your head even though that was all, trying to break that pull, trying to pull erect on chairs and things even when you still couldn't stand, to get away from the earth, save yourself. Then you could stand alone and take a step or two but even then during those first few years you still spent half of them on the ground, the old patient biding ground saying to you, "It's all right, it was just a fall, it dont hurt, dont be afraid." Then you are a man grown, strong, at your peak; now and then you can deliberately risk laying down on it in the woods hunting at night; you are too far from home to get back so you can even risk sleeping the rest of the night on it. Of course you will try to find something, anything—a plank, boards, a log, even brush-tops—something, anything to intervene between your unconsciousness, helplessness, and the old patient ground that can afford to wait because it's going to get you someday, except that there aint any use in giving you a full mile just because you dared an inch. And you know it; being young and strong you will risk one night on it but even you wont risk two nights in a row. Because even, say you take out in the field for noon and set under a tree or a hedgerow and eat your lunch and then lay down and you take a short nap and wake up and for a minute you dont even know where you are, for the good reason that you aint all there; even in that short time while you wasn't watching, the old patient biding unhurried ground has already taken that first light holt on you, only you managed to wake up in time. So, if he had had to, he would have risked sleeping on the ground this last one night. But he had not had to chance it. It was as if Old Moster Himself had said, "I aint going to help you none but I aint going to downright hinder you neither."

Then it was dawn, daybreak. He ate again, in solitude; when the sun rose they were in the cotton again; during these benisoned harvest days between summer's dew and fall's first frost the cotton was moisture-free for picking as soon as you could see it; until noon. "There," he told the Negro. "That ought to holp you out a little. You got a good bale for that Jefferson gin now so I reckon I'll get on down the road while I can get a ride for a change."

At last he was that close, that near. It had taken thirty-eight years and he had made a long loop down into the Delta and out again, but he was close now. But this road was a new approach to Jefferson, not the old one from Varner's Store which he remembered. These new iron numbers along the roads were different too from the hand-lettered mile-boards of recollection and though he could read figures all right, some, most of these were not miles because they never got any smaller. But if they had, in this case too he would have had to make sure:

"I believe this road goes right through Jefferson, dont it?"

"Yes," the Negro said. "You can branch off there for the Delta."

"So I can. How far do you call it to town?"

"Eight miles," the Negro said. But he could figger a mile whether he saw mile-posts or not, seven then six then five, the sun only barely past one oclock; then four miles, a long hill with a branch bottom at the foot of it and he said,

"Durn it, let me out at that bridge. I aint been to the bushes this morning." The Negro slowed the truck toward the bridge. "It's all right," Mink said. "I'll walk on from here. In fact I'd pure hate for that-ere doctor to see me getting out of even a cotton truck or likely he'd try his durndest to collect another dollar from me."

"I'll wait for you," the Negro said.

"No no," Mink said. "You want to get ginned and back home before dark. You aint got time." He got out of the cab and said, in the immemorial country formula of thanks: "How much do I owe you?" And the Negro answered in it:

"It aint no charge. I was coming anyway."

"Much obliged," Mink said. "Jest dont mention to that doctor about it if you ever run across him. See you in the Delta someday."

Then the truck was gone. The road was empty when he left it. Out of sight from the road would be far enough. Only, if possible, nobody must even hear the sound of the trial shot. He didn't know why; he could not have said that, having had to do without privacy for thirty-eight years, he now wanted, intended to savor, every minuscule of it which freedom entitled him to; also he still had five or six hours until dark, and probably even less than that many miles, following the dense brier-cypress-willow jungle of the creek bottom for perhaps a quarter of a mile, maybe more, when suddenly he stopped dead with a kind of amazed excitement, even exhilaration. Before him, spanning the creek, was a railroad trestle. Now he not only knew how to reach Jefferson without the constant risk of passing the people who from that old Yoknapatawpha County affinity would know who he was and what he intended to do, he would have something to do to pass the time until dark when he could go on.

It was as though he had not seen a railroad in thirty-eight years. One ran along one entire flank of the Parchman wire and he could see trains on it as far as he recalled every day. Also, from time to time gangs of convicts under their shotgun guards did rough construction or repair public works jobs in sight of railroads through the Delta where he could see trains. But even without the intervening wire, he looked at them from prison; the trains themselves were looked at, seen, alien in freedom, fleeing, existing in liberty and hence unreal, chimerae, apparitions, without past or future, not even going anywhere since their destinations could not exist for him: just in motion a second, an instant, then nowhere; they had not been. But now it would be different. He could watch them, himself in freedom, as they fled past in freedom, the two of them mutual, in a way even interdependent: it to do the fleeing in smoke and noise and motion, he to do the watching; remembering how thirty-eight or forty years ago, just before he went to Parchman in fact—this occasion connected also with some crisis in his affairs which he had forgotten now; but then so were all his moments: connected, involved in some crisis of the constant outrage and injustice he was always having to drop everything to cope with, handle, with no proper tools and equipment for it, not even the time to spare from the unremitting work it took to feed himself and his family; this was one of those moments or maybe it had been simply the desire to see the train which had brought him the twenty-two miles in from Frenchman's Bend. Anyway, he had had to pass the night in town whatever the reason was and had gone down to the depot to see the New Orleans–bound passenger train come in—the hissing engine, the lighted cars each with an uppity impudent nigger porter, one car in which people were eating supper while more niggers waited on them, before going back to the sleeping cars that had actual beds in them; the train pausing for a moment then gone: a long airtight chunk of another world dragged along the dark earth for the poor folks in overalls like him to gape at free for a moment without the train itself, let alone the folks in it, even knowing he was there.

But as free to stand and watch it as any man even if he did wear overalls instead of diamonds; and as free now, until he remembered something else he had learned in Parchman during the long tedious years while he prepared for freedom— the information, the trivia he had had to accumulate since when the time, the freedom came, he might not know until too late what he lacked: there had not been a passenger train through Jefferson since 1935, that the railroad which old Colonel Sartoris (not the banker they called Colonel but his father, the real colonel, that had commanded all the local boys in the old slavery war) had built, which according to the old folks whom even he, Mink, knew and remembered, had been the biggest thing to happen in Yoknapatawpha County, that was to have linked Jefferson and the county all the way from the Gulf of Mexico in one direction to the Great Lakes in the other, was now a fading weed-grown branch line knowing no wheels anymore save two local freight trains more or less every day.

In which case, more than ever would the track, the right-of-way be his path into town where the privacy of freedom it had taken him thirty-eight years to earn, would not be violated so he turned and retraced his steps perhaps a hundred yards and stopped, there was nothing: only the dense jungle dappled with September afternoon silence. He took out the pistol. *Hit does look like a cooter* he thought, with what at the moment he believed was just amusement, humor, until he realised it was despair because he knew now that the thing would not, could not possibly fire, so that when he adjusted the cylinder to bring the first of the three cartridges under the hammer and cocked it and aimed at the base of a cypress four or five feet away and pulled the trigger and heard the faint vacant click, his only emotion was calm vindication, almost of superiority, at having been right, of being in an unassailable position to say I told you so, not even remembering cocking

the hammer again since this time he didn't know where the
thing was aimed when it jerked and roared, incredible with
muzzle-blast because of the short barrel; only now, almost
too late, springing in one frantic convulsion to catch his hand
back before it cocked and fired the pistol on the last remaining cartridge by simple reflex. But he caught himself in time,
freeing thumb and finger completely from the pistol until he
could reach across with his left hand and remove it from the
right one which in another second might have left him with
an empty and useless weapon after all this distance and care
and time. *Maybe the last one wont shoot neither* he thought, but
for only a moment, a second, less than a second, thinking *No
sir. It will have to. It will jest have to. There aint nothing else for
it to do. I dont need to worry. Old Moster jest punishes; He dont
play jokes.*

And now (it was barely two oclock by the sun, at least four
hours till sundown) he could even risk the ground once more,
this late, this last time, especially as he had last night in the
cotton truck on the credit side. So he moved on again, beneath and beyond the trestle this time, just in case somebody
had heard the shot and came to look, and found a smooth
place behind a log and lay down. At once he began to feel the
slow, secret, tentative palping start as the old biding unimpa-
tient unhurried ground said to itself, "Well, well, be dawg if
here aint one already laying right here on my doorstep so to
speak." But it was all right, he could risk it for this short time.

It was almost as though he had an alarm clock; he woke exactly in time to see through a leafed interstice overhead the
last of sun drain, fade from the zenith, just enough light left
to find his way back through the jungle to the railroad and
mount onto it. Though it was better here, enough of day left
to see him most of the last mile to town before it faded completely, displaced by darkness random with the sparse lights of
the town's purlieus, the beginning, the first quiet edge-of-
town back street beneath the rigid semaphore arms of the
crossing warning and a single lonely street light where the
Negro boy on the bicycle had ample time to see him standing
in the center of the crossing and brake to a stop. "Hidy, son,"
he said, using the old country-negroid idiom for 'live' too:
"Which-a-way from here does Mr Flem Snopes stay?"

By now, since the previous Thursday night in fact, from about nine-thirty or ten each night until daybreak the next morning, Flem Snopes had had a bodyguard, though no white person in Jefferson, including Snopes himself, except the guard's wife, knew it. His name was Luther Biglin, a country man, a professional dog-trainer and market-hunter and farmer until the last Sheriff's election. Not only was his wife the niece of the husband of the Sheriff, Ephriam Bishop's wife's sister, Biglin's mother was the sister of the rural political boss whose iron hand ruled one of the county divisions (as old Will Varner ruled his at Frenchman's Bend) which had elected Bishop Sheriff. So Biglin was now jailor under Bishop's tenure. Though with a definite difference from the standard nepotic run. Where as often as not, the holders of such lesser hierarchic offices gave nothing to the position they encumbered, having not really wanted it anyway but accepting it merely under family pressure to keep some member of the opposite political faction out of it, Biglin brought to his the sort of passionate enthusiastic devotion and fidelity to the power and immaculacy and integrity of his kinsman-by-marriage's position as say Murat's orderly corporal might have felt toward the symbology of his master's baton.

He was not only honorable (even in his market-hunting of venison and duck and quail, where he broke only the law: never his word), he was brave too. After Pearl Harbor, although his mother's brother might, probably could and would, have found or invented for him absolution from the draft, Biglin himself volunteered for the Marine Corps, finding to his amazement that by military standards he had next to no vision whatever in his right eye. He had not noticed this himself. He was a radio man, not a reading man, and in shooting (he was one of the best wing-shots in the county though in an exuberant spendthrift southpaw fashion—he was left-handed, shooting from his left shoulder; in the course of two of his three previous vocations he shot up more shells than anyone in the county; at the age of thirty he had already shot out two sets of shotgun barrels) the defect had been an actual service to him since he had never had to train himself to keep both eyes open and see the end of the gun and the target at the same instant, or half-close the right one to eliminate parallax. So when (not by curiosity but by simple bureaucratic consanguinity) he learned—even quicker than the Sheriff did because he, Biglin, immediately believed it—that with Mink Snopes free at last from the state penitentiary, his old threats against his cousin, even though forty years old, durst not be ignored, let alone dismissed as his patron and superior seemed inclined to do.

So his aim, intent, was still basically to defend and preserve the immaculacy of his kinsman-by-marriage's office, which was to preserve the peace and protect human life and well-being, in which he modestly shared. But there was something else too, though only his wife knew it. Even the Sheriff didn't know about his plan, campaign; he only told his wife: "There may be nothing to it, like Cousin Eef says: just another of Lawyer Stevens's nightmares. But suppose Cousin Eef is wrong and Lawyer is right; suppose—" He could visualise it: the last split second, Mr Snopes helpless in bed beneath his doom, one last hopeless cry for the help which he knew was not there, the knife (hatchet, hammer, stick of stovewood, whatever the vengeance-ridden murderer would use) already descending when he, Biglin, would step, crash in, flashlight in one hand and pistol in the other: one single shot, the assassin falling across his victim, the expression of demonic anticipation and triumph fading to astonishment on his face— "Why, Mr Snopes will make us rich! He'll have to! There wont be nothing else he can do!"

Since Mr Snopes mustn't know about it either (the Sheriff had explained to him that in America you cant wet-nurse a free man unless he requests it or at least knowingly accepts it) he could not be inside the bedroom itself, where he should be, but would have to take the best station he could find or contrive outside the nearest window he could enter fastest or at least see to aim through. Which meant of course he would have to sit up all night. He was a good jailor, conscientious, keeping his jail clean and his prisoners properly fed and tended; besides the errands he did for the Sheriff. Thus the only time he would have to sleep in during the twenty-four hours would be between supper and the latest imperative moment when he must be at his station outside Snopes's bedroom window. So each night he would go to bed immediately after he rose from the supper table, and his wife would go to the picture show, on her return from which, usually about nine-thirty, she would wake him. Then, with his flashlight and pistol and a sandwich and a folding chair and a sweater against the chill as the late September nights cooled toward midnight, he would stand motionless and silent against the hedge facing the window where, as all Jefferson knew, Snopes spent all his life outside the bank, until the light went out at last; by which time, the two Negro servants would have long since left. Then he would move quietly across the lawn and open the chair beneath the window and sit down, sitting so immobile that the stray dogs which roamed all Jefferson during the hours of darkness, would be almost upon him before they would sense, smell, however they did it, that he was not asleep, and crouch and whirl in one silent motion and flee; until first light, when he would fold up the chair and make sure the crumpled sandwich wrapping was in his pocket, and depart; though by Sunday night, if Snopes had not been asleep and his daughter not stone deaf, now and then they could have heard him snoring—until that is the nocturnal dog crossing the lawn this time would sense, smell—however they did it—that he was asleep and harmless until actually touched by the cold nose.

Mink didn't know this. But even if he had, it probably would have made little difference. He would simply have regarded the whole thing—Biglin, the fact that Snopes was now being guarded—as just one more symptom of the infinite capacity for petty invention of the inimical forces which had always dogged his life. So even if he had known that Biglin was already on station under the window of the room where his cousin now sat (He had not hurried. On the contrary: once the Negro boy on the bicycle had given him directions, he thought *I'm even a little ahead. Let them eat supper first and give them two niggers time to be outen the way.*) he would have behaved no differently: not hiding, not lurking: just unseen unheard and irrevocably alien like a coyote or a small wolf; not crouching, not concealed by the hedge as Biglin himself would do when he arrived, but simply squatting on his hams—as, a country man, he could do for hours without discomfort—against it while he examined the house whose shape and setting he already knew out of the slow infinitesimal Parchman trickle of facts and information which he had had to garner, assimilate, from strangers yet still conceal from them the import of what he asked; looking in fact at the vast white columned edifice with something like pride that some-one named Snopes owned it; a complete and absolute unjeal-ousy: at another time, tomorrow, though he himself would never dream nor really ever want to be received in it, he would have said proudly to a stranger: "My cousin lives there. He owns it."

It looked exactly as he had known it would. There were the lighted rear windows of the corner room where his cousin would be sitting (they would surely have finished supper by now; he had given them plenty of time) with his feet propped on the little special ledge he had heard in Parchman how an-other kinsman Mink had never seen, Wat Snopes having been born too late, had nailed onto the hearth for that purpose. There were lights also in the windows of the room in front of that one, which he had not expected, knowing also about the special room upstairs the deaf daughter had fixed up for her-self. But no light showed upstairs at all, so evidently the daughter was still downstairs too. And although the lights in the kitchen indicated that the two Negro servants had not left either, his impulse was so strong that he had already begun to rise without waiting longer, to cross to the window and see, if necessary begin now: who had had thirty-eight years to practise patience in and should have been perfect. Because if he waited too long, his cousin might be in bed, perhaps even asleep. Which would be intolerable and must not be: there must be that moment, even if it lasted only a second, for him to say, "Look at me, Flem," and his cousin would do so. But he restrained himself, who had had thirty-eight years to learn to wait in, and sank, squatted back again, easing the hard lump of the pistol which he now carried inside the bib-front of his overalls; her room would be on the other side of the house where he couldn't see the lighted windows from here, and the lights in the other room meant nothing since if he was big rich like his cousin Flem, with a fine big house like that, he would have all the lights on downstairs too.

Then the lights went off in the kitchen; presently he could

hear the Negro man and the woman still talking as they approached and (he didn't even hold his breath) passed within
ten feet of him and went through the gate in the hedge, the
voices moving slowly up the lane beyond it until they died
away. Then he rose, quietly, without haste, not furtive, not
slinking: just small, just colorless, perhaps simply too small to
be noticed, and crossed the lawn to the window and (he had
to stand on tiptoe) looked into it at his cousin sitting in the
swivel chair like in a bank or an office, with his feet propped
against the chimney and his hat on, as he, Mink, had known
he would be sitting, looking not too different even though
Mink hadn't seen him in forty years; a little changed of
course: the black planter's hat he had heard about in Parchman but the little bow tie might have been the same one he
had been wearing forty years ago behind the counter in
Varner's store, the shirt a white city shirt and the pants were
dark city pants too and the shoes were polished city shoes instead of farmer's brogans. But no different, really: not reading, just sitting there with his feet propped and his hat on, his
jaw moving faintly and steadily as if he were chewing.

Just to be sure, he would circle the house until he could see
the lighted upper windows on the other side and had already
started around the back when he thought how he might as
well look into the other lighted room also while he was this
close to it and moved, no less quiet than a shadow and with
not much more substance, along the wall until he could stand
on tiptoe again and look in the next window, the next room.
He saw her at once and knew her at once—a room walled almost to the ceiling with more books than he knew existed, a
woman sitting beneath a lamp in the middle of the room
reading one, in horn rim glasses and that single white streak
through the center of her black hair that he had heard about
in Parchman too. For a second the old helpless fury and outrage possessed him again and almost ruined, destroyed him
this time—the rage and fury when, during the first two or
three years after he learned that she was back home again apparently for good and living right there in the house with
Flem, he would think *Suppose she aint deaf a-tall; suppose she's
jest simply got ever body fooled for whatever devilment of her
own she's up to,* since this—the real truth of whether she was

deaf or just pretending—was one gambit which he would not only have to depend on somebody else for, but on something as frail and undependable as second- or third-hand hearsay. Finally he had lied, tricked his way in to the prison doctor but there he was again: daring not to ask what he wanted to know, had to know, find out, learn: only that even the stone-deaf would—could—feel the concussion of the air if the sound were loud enough or close enough. "Like a—" Mink said before he could stop himself. But too late; the doctor finished it for him: "That's right. A shot. But even if you could make us believe you are, how would that get you out of here?" "That's right," Mink said. "I wouldn't need to hear that bull-whup: jest feel it."

But that would be all right; there was that room she had fixed up for herself upstairs, while every word from home that trickled down to him in Parchman—you had to believe folks some times, you had to, you jest had to—told how his cousin spent all his time in the one downstairs cattycorner across that house that was bigger they said than even the jail. Then to look in the window and find her, not upstairs and across the house where she should have been, where in a way it had been promised to him she would be, but right there in the next room. In which case everything else he had believed in and depended on until now was probably trash and rubble too; there didn't even need to be an open door between the two rooms so she could be sure to feel what the prison doctor had called the concussion because she wasn't even deaf. Everything had lied to him; he thought quietly *And I aint even got but one bullet left even if I would have time to use two before somebody come busting in from the street. I got to find a stick of stovewood or a piece of ahrn somewhere*—that close, that near to ruination and destruction before he caught himself back right on the brink, murmuring, whispering, "Wait now, wait. Aint I told you and told you Old Moster dont play jokes; He jest punishes? Of course she's deaf: aint all up and down Missippi been telling you that for ten years now? I dont mean that durn Parchman doctor nor all the rest of them durn jailbird son of a bitches that was all I had to try to find out what I had to know from, but that nigger jest yestiddy evening that got almost impident, durn nigh called a white man a liar to his face the least suh-jestion I made that maybe she was fooling folks. Niggers that dont only know all the undercover about white folks, let alone one that they already claim is a nigger-lover and even one of them commonists to boot, until all the niggers in Yoknapatawpha County and likely Memphis and Chicago too know the truth about whether she is deaf or not or ever thing else about her or not. Of course she's deaf, setting there with her back already to the door where you got to pass and they's bound to be a back door too that all you got to do is jest find it and walk right on out," and moved on, without haste: not furtive, just small and light-footed and invisible, on around the house and up the steps and on between the soaring columns of the portico like any other guest, visitor, caller, opening the screen door quietly into the hall and through it, passing the open door beyond which the woman sat, not even glancing toward it, and went on to the next one and drew the pistol from his overall bib; and, thinking hurriedly, a little chaotically, almost like tiny panting: *I aint got but one bullet so it will have to be in the face, the head; I cant resk jest the body with jest one bullet,* entered the room where his cousin sat and ran a few more steps toward him.

He didn't need to say, "Look at me, Flem." His cousin was already doing that, his head turned over his shoulder. Otherwise he hadn't moved, only the jaws ceased chewing in midmotion. Then he moved, leaned slightly forward in the chair and he had just begun to lower his propped feet from the ledge, the chair beginning to swivel around, when Mink from about five feet away stopped and raised the toad-shaped iron-rust-colored weapon in both hands and cocked and steadied it, thinking *Hit's got to hit his face*: not *I've got to* but *It's got to* and pulled the trigger and rather felt than heard the dull foolish almost inattentive click. Now his cousin, his feet now flat on the floor and the chair almost swiveled to face him, appeared to sit immobile and even detached too, watching too Mink's grimed shaking child-sized hands like the hands of a pet coon as one of them lifted the hammer enough for the other to roll the cylinder back one notch so that the shell would come again under the hammer; again that faint something out of the past nudged, prodded: not a warning nor even really a repetition: just faint and familiar and unimportant still since, whatever it had been, even before it had not been strong enough to alter anything nor even remarkable enough to be remembered; in the same second he had dismissed it. *Hit's all right* he thought *Hit'll go this time; Old Moster dont play jokes* and cocked and steadied the pistol again in both hands, his cousin not moving at all now though he was chewing faintly again, as though he too were watching the dull point of light on the cock of the hammer when it flicked away.

It made a tremendous sound though in the same instant Mink no longer heard it. His cousin's body was now making a curious half-stifled convulsive surge which in another moment was going to carry the whole chair over; it seemed to him, Mink, that the report of the pistol was nothing but that when the chair finished falling and crashed to the floor, the sound would wake all Jefferson. He whirled; there was a moment yet when he tried to say, cry "Stop! Stop! You got to make sho he's dead or you will have throwed away ever thing!" but he could not, he didn't remember when he had noticed the other door in the wall beyond the chair but it was there; where it led to didn't matter just so it led on and not back. He ran to it, scrabbling at the knob, still shaking and scrabbling at it even after he realised it was locked, still shaking the knob, quite blind now, even after the voice spoke behind him and he whirled again and saw the woman standing in the hall door; for an instant he thought *So she could hear all the time* before he knew better: she didn't need to hear; it was the same power had brought her here to catch him that by merely pointing her finger at him could blast, annihilate, vaporise him where he stood. And no time to cock and aim the pistol again even if he had had another bullet so even as he whirled he flung, threw the pistol at her, nor even able to follow that because in the same second it seemed to him she already had the pistol in her hand, holding it toward him, saying in that quacking duck's voice that deaf people use:

"Here. Come and take it. That door is a closet. You'll have to come back this way to get out."

Eighteen

"STOP the car," Stevens said. Ratliff did so. He was driving though it was Stevens' car. They had left the highway at the crossroads—Varner's store and gin and blacksmith shop, and the church and the dozen or so dwellings and other edifices, all dark now though it was not yet ten oclock, which composed the hamlet—and had now traversed and left behind the rest of the broad flat rich valley land on which old Varner—in his eighties now, his hair definitely gray, twelve years a widower until two years ago when he married a young woman of twenty-five or so who at the time was supposed to be engaged to, anyway courted by, his grandson—held liens and mortgages where he didn't own it outright; and now they were approaching the hills: a section of small worn-out farms tilted and precarious among the eroded folds like scraps of paper. The road had ceased some time back to be even gravel and at any moment now it would cease to be passable to anything on wheels; already, in the fixed glare (Ratliff had stopped the car) of the headlights, it resembled just one more eroded ravine twisting up the broken rise crested with shabby and shaggy pine and worthless blackjack. The sun had crossed the Equator, in Libra now; and in the cessation of motion and the quiet of the idling engine, there was a sense of autumn after the slow drizzle of Sunday and the bright spurious cool which had lasted through Monday almost; the jagged rampart of pines and scrub oak was a thin dike against the winter and rain and cold, under which the worn-out fields overgrown with sumac and sassafras and persimmon had already turned scarlet, the persimmons heavy with fruit waiting only for frost and the baying of potlicker possum hounds. "What makes you think he will be there even if we can get there ourselves?" Stevens said.

"Where else would he be?" Ratliff said. "Where else has he got to go? Back to Parchman, after all this recent trouble and expense it taken him to get out? What else has he got but home?"

"He hasn't even got that home anymore," Stevens said.

"When was it—three years ago—that day we drove out here about that boy—what was his name?"

"Turpin," Ratliff said.

"—that didn't answer his draft call and we came out looking for him. There wasn't anything left of the house then but the shell. Part of the roof, and what was left of the walls above the height convenient to pull off for firewood. This road was better then too."

"Yes," Ratliff said. "Folks kept it kind of graded and scraped up dragging out that kindling."

"So there's not even the shell anymore."

"There's a cellar under it," Ratliff said.

"A hole in the ground?" Stevens said. "A den like an animal?"

"He's tired," Ratliff said. "Even if he wasn't sixty-three or -four years old. He's been under a strain for thirty-eight years, let alone the last—this hyer's Thursday, aint it?—seven days. And now he aint got no more strain to prop him up. Jest suppose you had spent thirty-eight years waiting to do something, and sho enough one day you finally done it. You wouldn't have much left neither. So what he wants now is jest to lay down in the dark and the quiet somewhere for a spell."

"He should have thought of that last Thursday," Stevens said. "It's too late to do that now."

"Aint that exactly why we're out here?" Ratliff said.

"All right," Stevens said. "Drive on." Instead, Ratliff switched off the engine. Now indeed they could sense, feel the change of the season and the year. Some of the birds remained but the night was no longer full of the dry loud cacophony of summer nocturnal insects. There were only the crickets in the dense hedgerows and stubble of mown hayfields, where at noon the dusty grasshoppers would spurt, frenetic and random, going nowhere. And now Stevens knew what was coming, what Ratliff was going to talk about.

"You reckon she really never knowed what that durn little rattlesnake was going to do the minute they turned him loose?" Ratliff said.

"Certainly not," Stevens said, quickly, too quickly, too late. "Drive on."

But Ratliff didn't move. Stevens noticed that he still held

his hand over the switch key so that Stevens himself couldn't have started the engine. "I reckon she'll stop over in Memphis tonight," Ratliff said. "With that-ere fancy brand new automobile and all."

He—Stevens—remembered all that. His trouble was, to forget it. She had told him herself—or so he believed then—this morning after she had given him the necessary information to draw the deed: how she wasn't going to accept her so-called father's automobile either but instead had ordered a new one from Memphis, which would be delivered in time for her to leave directly after the funeral; he could bring the deed to the house for her signature when they said goodbye, or what they—she and he—would have of goodbye.

It was a big funeral: a prominent banker and financier who had not only died in his prime (financial anyway) of a pistol wound but from the wrong pistol wound, since by ordinary a banker dying of a pistol in his own bedroom at nine oclock in the evening should have just said goodnight to a State or Federal (maybe both) bank inspector. He (the deceased) had no auspices either: fraternal, civic, nor military: only finance; not an economy—cotton or cattle or anything else which Yoknapatawpha County and Mississippi were established on and kept running by, but belonging simply to Money. He had been a member of a Jefferson church true enough, as the outward and augmented physical aspect of the edifice showed, but even that had been not a subservience nor even an aspiration nor even really a confederation nor even an amnesty, but simply an armistice temporary between two irreconcilable tongues.

Yet not just the town but the county too came to it. He (Stevens) sat, a member of the cast itself, by the (*sic*) daughter's request, on the front row in fact and next her by her insistence: himself and Linda and her Uncle Jody, a balding man who had added another hundred pounds of jowl and belly to his father's long skeleton; and yes, Wallstreet Snopes, Wallstreet Panic Snopes, who not only had never acted like a Snopes, he never had even looked like one: a tall dark man except for the eyes of an incredible tender youthful periwinkle blue, who had begun as the delivery boy in a side street grocery to carry himself and his younger brother, Admiral

Dewey, through school, and went from there to create a wholesale grocery supply house in Jefferson serving all the county; and now, removed with his family to Memphis, owned a chain of wholesale grocery establishments blanketing half of Mississippi and Tennessee and Arkansas too; all of them facing the discreetly camouflaged excavation beside the other grave over which not her husband (who had merely ordained and paid for it) but Stevens himself had erected the outrageous marble lie which had been the absolution for Linda's freedom nineteen years ago. As it would be he who would erect whatever lie this one would postulate; they—he and Linda—had discussed that too this morning.

"No. Nothing," she said.

Yes he wrote.

"No," she said. He merely raised the tablet and held the word facing her; he could not have written *Its for your sake* Then he didn't need to. "You're right," she said. "You will have to do another one too."

He wrote *We will*

"No," she said. "You will. You always have for me. You always will for me. I know now I've never really had anybody but you. I've never really even needed anybody else but you."

Sitting there while the Baptist minister did his glib and rapid office, he (Stevens) looked around at the faces, town faces and country faces, the citizens who represented the town because the town should be represented at this obsequy; the ones who represented simply themselves because some day they would be where Flem Snopes now lay, as friendless and dead and alone too; the diffident anonymous hopeful faces who had owed him or his bank money and, as people will and can, hoped, were capable of believing even that, now that he was dead, the debt might, barely might become lost or forgotten or even simply undemanded, uncollected. Then suddenly he saw something else. There were not many of them: he distinguished only three, country faces also, looking no different from the other country faces diffident, even effacing, in the rear of the crowd; until suddenly they leaped, sprang out, and he knew who they were. They were Snopeses; he had never seen them before but they were incontrovertible: not alien at all: simply identical, not so much in expression as in position, attitude; he thought rapidly, in something like that second of simple panic when you are violently wakened: *They're like wolves come to look at the trap where another bigger wolf, the boss wolf, the head wolf, what Ratliff would call the bull wolf, died; if maybe there was not a shred or scrap of hide still snared in it.*

Then that was gone. He could not keep on looking behind him and now the minister had finished and the undertaker signaled for the select, the publicly bereaved, to depart; and when he looked, could look again, the faces were gone. He left Linda there. That is, her uncle would drive her home, where by this time the new automobile she had told him she had telephoned to Memphis for after she decided yesterday afternoon to drive alone to New York as soon as the funeral was over, would be waiting; she would probably be ready to leave, the new car packed and all, by the time he got there with the deed for her to sign.

So he went to the office and picked it up—a deed of gift (with the usual consideration of one dollar) returning the house and its lot to the De Spains. She had done it all herself, she hadn't even informed him in the process, let alone beforehand. She had been unable to locate Manfred, whom Snopes had dispossessed of it along with the bank and the rest of his, Manfred's, name and dignity in Jefferson, but she had found at last what remained of his kin—the only sister of old Major de Spain, Manfred's father, and her only child: a bedridden old woman living in Los Angeles with her spinster daughter of sixty, the retired principal of a suburban Los Angeles grammar school; she, Linda, tracing, running them down herself without even consulting her lawyer: an outrage really, when the Samaritan, the philanthropist, the benefactor, begins not only to find but even to invent his own generosities, not only without recourse to but even ignoring the lawyers and secretaries and public relations counsellors; outrageous, antisocial in fact, taking the very cake out of that many mouths.

The papers wanted only her signature; it had not been fifteen minutes yet when he slowed his car in toward the curb before the house, not even noticing the small group—men, boys, a Negro or so—in front of him except to say, The local committee validating her new automobile, and parked his own and got out with the briefcase and had even turned, his glance simply passing across the group because it was there, when he said with a quick, faint, not really yet surprise, It's a British Jaguar. It's brand new, and was even walking on when suddenly it was as if a staircase you are mounting becomes abruptly a treadmill, you still walking, mounting, expending energy and motion but without progress; so abrupt and sudden in fact that you are only your aura, your very momentum having carried your corporeality one whole step in advance of you; he thought *No place on earth from which a brand new Jaguar could be delivered to Jefferson, Mississippi since even noon yesterday, let alone not even telephoned for until last night,* thinking, desperately now *No! No! It is possible! They could have had one, found one in Memphis last night or this morning—this ramshackle universe which has nothing to hold it together but coincidence—*and walked smartly up and paused beside it, thinking *So she knew she was going to leave after last Thursday; she just didn't know until Tuesday night exactly what day that would be.* It was spanking unblemished new, the youngish quite decent-looking agent or deliverer stood beside it and at that moment the Negro houseman came out the front door carrying some of her luggage.

"Afternoon," Stevens said. "Damned nice car. Brand new, isn't it?"

"That's right," the young man said. "Never even touched the ground until Mrs Kohl telephoned for it yesterday."

"Lucky you had one on hand for her," Stevens said.

"Oh, we've had it since the tenth of this month. When she ordered it last July she just told us to keep it when it came in, until she wanted it. I suppose her father's . . . death changed her plans some."

"Things like that do," Stevens said. "She ordered it in July."

"That's right. They haven't caught the fellow yet, I hear."

"Not yet," Stevens said. "Damned nice car. Would like to afford one myself," and went on, into the open door and up the stairs which knew his feet, into the sitting room which knew him too. She stood watching him while he approached, dressed for the drive in a freshly-laundered suit of the faded khaki coveralls, her face and mouth heavily made-up against the wind of motion; on a chair lay the stained burberry and her purse and heavy gloves and a scarf for her head; she said, At least I didn't lie to you. I could have hidden it in the garage until you had come and gone, but I didn't. Though not in words: she said,

"Kiss me, Gavin," taking the last step to him herself and taking him into her arms, firm and without haste and set her mouth to his, firmly and deliberately too, and opened it, he holding her, his hand moving down her back while the dividing incleft outswell of her buttocks rose under the harsh khaki, as had happened before now and then, the hand unchallenged—it had never been challenged, it would never be, the fidelity unthreatened and secure even if there had been nothing at all between the hand and the inswelling incleft woman flesh, he simply touching her, learning and knowing not with despair or grief but just sorrow a little, simply supporting her buttocks as you cup the innocent hipless bottom of a child. But not now, not this time. It was terror now; he thought with terror *How did it go? the man 'whose irresistible attraction to women was that simply by being in their presence he gave them to convince themselves that he was capable of any sacrifice for them.' Which is backward, completely backward; the poor dope not only didn't know where first base was, he didn't even know he was playing baseball. You dont need to tempt them because they have long since already selected you by that time, choosing you simply because they believe that in the simple act of being selected you have at once become not merely willing and ready but passionately desirous of making a sacrifice for them just as soon as the two of you can think of one good enough, worthy.* He thought *Now she will realise that she cannot trust me* but only hoped she could so now the thrust of hips, gripping both shoulders to draw me into the backward-falling even without a bed, and was completely wrong; he thought *Why should she waste her time trusting me when she has known all her life that all she has to do is just depend on me.* She just stood holding him and kissing him until he himself moved first to be free. Then she released him and stood looking at his face out of the dark blue eyes not secret, not tender, perhaps not even gentle.

"Your mouth is a mess," she said. "You'll have to go to the bathroom.—You are right," she said. "You always are right about you and me." They were not secret: intent enough yes, but not secret; someday perhaps he would remember that they had never been really tender even. "I love you," she said. "You haven't had very much, have you. No, that's wrong. You haven't had anything. You have had nothing."

He knew exactly what she meant: her mother first, then her; that he had offered the devotion twice and got back for it nothing but the privilege of being obsessed, bewitched, besotted if you like; Ratliff certainly would have said besotted. And she knew he knew it; that was (perhaps) their curse: they both knew any and every mutual thing immediately. It was not because of the honesty, nor because she believed she had been in love with him all her life, that she had let him discover the new Jaguar and what it implied in the circumstances of her so-called father's death. It was because she knew she could not have kept concealed from him the fact that she had ordered the car from New York or London or wherever it came from, the moment she knew for sure he could get Mink the pardon.

She had pockets in all her clothes into which the little ivory tablet with its clipped stylus exactly fitted. He knew all of them, the coveralls too, and reached his hand and took it out. He could have written *I have everything. You trusted me. You chose to let me find you murdered your so-called father rather than tell me a lie.* He could, perhaps should have written *I have everything. Haven't I just finished being accessory before a murder.* Instead, he wrote *We have had everything*

"No," she said.

He wrote *Yes*

"No," she said.

He printed *YES* this time in letters large enough to cover the rest of the face of the tablet and erased it clean with the heel of his palm and wrote *Take someone with You to hear you Will be killed*

She barely glanced at it, nowhere near long enough anyone would have thought, to have read it, then stood looking at him again, the dark blue eyes that whether they were gentle or not or tender or not or really candid or not, it didn't matter. Her mouth was smeared too behind the faint smiling, itself—the smiling—like a soft smear, a drowsing stain. "I love you," she said. "I have never loved anybody but you."

He wrote *No*

"Yes," she said.

He wrote *No* again and even while she said Yes again he wrote *No No No No* until he had completely filled the tablet and erased it and wrote *Deed* And, standing side by side at the mantel where they transacted all her business which required communication between them, he spread the document and uncapped his pen for her to sign it and folded the paper and was putting it back into the briefcase when she said, "This too." It was a plain long envelope, he had noticed it on the mantel. When he took it he could feel the thick sheaf of banknotes through the paper, too many of them; a thousand dollars would destroy him in a matter of weeks, perhaps days, as surely as that many bullets. He had been tempted last night to tell her so: "A thousand dollars will kill him too. Will you be satisfied then?" even though he was still ignorant last night how much truth that would be. But he refrained. He would take care of that himself when the time came. "Do you know where you can find him?"

Ratliff does he wrote and erased it and wrote *Go out 2 minutes Bathroom your Mouth too* and stood while she read it and then herself stood a moment longer, not moving, her head bent as if he had written perhaps in cryptogram. "Oh," she said. Then she said: "Yes. It's time," and turned and went to the door and stopped and half-turned and only then looked at him: no faint smile, no nothing: just the eyes which even at this distance were not quite black. Then she was gone.

He already had the briefcase in his hand. His hat was on the table. He put the envelope into his pocket and scrubbed at his mouth with his handkerchief, taking up the hat in passing, and went on, down the stairs, wetting the handkerchief with spittle to scrub his mouth. There would be a mirror in the hall but this would have to do until he reached the office; there would be, was a back door of course but there was the houseman somewhere and maybe even the cook too. Besides, there was no law against crossing the front lawn itself from the front entrance and so through the side gate into the lane, from which he could reach the street without even having to not look at the new car again. Until Ratliff, happening to be standing by chance or coincidence near the foot of the office stairs, said, "Where's your car? Never mind, I'll go pick it up. Meantime you better use some water when you get up stairs."

He did, and locked the stained handkerchief into a drawer and sat in the office. In time he heard Ratliff's feet on the stairs though Ratliff shook the locked door only; here was another time when he could have worked at his youthful dream of restoring the Old Testament to its virgin's pristinity. But he was too old now. Evidently it takes more than just anguish to be all that anguishing. In time the telephone rang. "She's gone," Ratliff said. "I've got your car. You want to come and eat supper with me?"

"No," he said.

"You want me to telephone your wife that's what you're doing?"

"Dammit, I told you No," he said. Then he said, "Much obliged."

"I'll pick you up at eight oclock say," Ratliff said.

He was at the curb waiting; the car—his—moved immediately he was in it. "I'm not safe," he said.

"I reckon so," Ratliff said. "It's all over now, soon that is as we get used to it."

"I mean, you're not safe. Nobody is, around me. I'm dangerous. Cant you understand I've just committed murder?"

"Oh, that," Ratliff said. "I decided some time back that maybe the only thing that would make you safe to have around would be for somebody to marry you. That never worked but at least you're all right now. As you jest said, you finally committed a murder. What else is there beyond that for anybody to think up for you to do?" Now they were on the highway, the town behind them and they could pick up a little speed to face the twenty miles out to Varner's store. "You know the one in this business I'm really sorry for? It's Luther Biglin. You aint heard about that and likely wouldn't nobody else if it hadn't kind of come out today in what you might call a private interview or absolvement between Luther and Eef Bishop. It seems that ever night between last Thursday and the following Tuesday, Luther has been standing or setting guard as close as he could get outside that window from as soon as he could get there after Miz Biglin would get back from the picture show and wake him up, to daylight. You know: having to spend all day long taking care of his jail and prisoners in addition to staying close to the Sheriff's office in case Eef might need him, he would have to get some rest and the only way he could work it in would be after he et supper until Miz Biglin, who acted as his alarm clock, got back from the picture show, which would be from roughly seven oclock to roughly more or less half-past nine or ten oclock, depending on how long the picture show was, the balance of the night standing or setting in a folding chair jest outside Flem's window, not for a reward or even glory, since nobody but Miz Biglin knowed it, but simply outen fidelity to Eef Bishop's sworn oath to defend and protect human life in Jefferson even when the human life was Flem Snopes's. Yet outen the whole twenty-four hours Mink could a picked, he had to pick one between roughly seven oclock and roughly nine-thirty to walk in on Flem with that thing whoever sold it to him told him was a pistol, almost like Mink done it outen pure and simple spite—a thing which, as the feller says, to a dog shouldn't happen."

"Drive on," Stevens said. "Pick it up."

"Yes," Ratliff said. "So this is what it all come down to. All the ramshacking and foreclosing and grabbling and snatching, doing it by gentle underhand when he could but by honest hard trompling when he had to, with a few of us trying to trip him and still dodge outen the way when we could but getting over-trompled too when we couldn't. And now all that's left of it is a bed-rode old lady and her retired old maid school-teacher daughter that would a lived happily ever after in sunny golden California. But now they got to come all the way back to Missippi and live in that-ere big white elephant of a house where likely Miss Allison will have to go back to work again, maybe might even have to hump and hustle some to keep it up since how can they have mere friends and acquaintances, let alone strangers, saying how a Missippi-born and -bred lady refused to accept a whole house not only gift-free-for-nothing but that was actively theirn anyhow to begin with, without owing even much obliged to nobody for getting it back. So maybe there's even a moral in it somewhere, if you jest knowed where to look."

"There aren't any morals," Stevens said. "People just do the best they can."

"The pore sons of bitches," Ratliff said.

"The poor sons of bitches," Stevens said. "Drive on. Pick it up."

So somewhere about ten oclock he sat beside Ratliff in the dark car on a hill road that had already ceased to be a road and soon would cease to be even passable, while Ratliff said, "So you think she really didn't know what he was going to do when he got out?"

"Yes I tell you," Stevens said. "Drive on."

"We got time," Ratliff said. "He aint going nowhere. Talking about that thing he used for a pistol, that he dropped or throwed it away while he was running through that back yard. Eef Bishop let me look at it. That Memphis feller was right. It didn't even look like a pistol. It looked like a old old mud-crusted cooter. It had two shells in it, the hull and another live one. The cap of the hull was punched all right, only it and the live one both had a little nick jest outside the cap, both of the nicks jest alike and even in the same place, so that when Eef taken the live one out and turned the hull a little and set it back under the hammer and cocked it and snapped it and we opened the cylinder, there was another of them little nicks in the case jest outside the cap, like sometimes that moss-back firing-pin would hit the cap and sometimes it wouldn't. So it looks like Mink either tried out both of them shells before hand for practice test and both of them snapped once, yet he still walked in there to kill Flem jest hoping one of them would go off this time, which dont sound reasonable; or that he stood there in front of Flem and snapped maybe both of them at him and then turned the cylinder back to try again since that was all he had left he could do at that moment, and this time one of them went off. In that case, what do you reckon Flem's reason was for setting there in that chair letting Mink snap them two shells at him until one of them went off and killed him?"

"I dont know," Stevens said harshly. "Drive on!"

"Maybe he was jest bored too," Ratliff said. "Like Eula. Maybe there was two of them. The pore son of a bitch."

"He was impotent," Stevens said.

"What?" Ratliff said.

"Impotent. When he got in bed with a woman all he could do was go to sleep.—Yes!" Stevens said, "the poor sons of bitches that have to cause all the grief and anguish they have to cause! Drive on!"

"But suppose it was more than that," Ratliff said. "You was town-raised when you was a boy; likely you never heard of Give-me-lief. It was a game we played. You would pick out another boy about your own size and you would walk up to him with a switch or maybe a light stick or a hard green apple or maybe even a rock, depending on how hard a risk you wanted to take, and say to him, 'Gimme lief,' and if he agreed, he would stand still and you would take one cut or one lick at him with the switch or stick, as hard as you picked out, or back off and throw at him once with the green apple or the rock. Then you would stand still and he would take the same switch or stick or apple or rock or anyways another one jest like it, and take one cut or throw at you. That was the rule. So jest suppose—"

"Drive on!" Stevens said.

"—Flem had had his lief fair and square like the rule said, so there wasn't nothing for him to do but jest set there, since he had likely found out years back when she finally turned up here again even outen a communist war, that he had already lost—"

"Stop it!" Stevens said. "Dont say it!"

"—and now it was her lief and so suppose—"

"No!" Stevens said. "No!" But Ratliff was not only nearer the switch, his hand was already on it, covering it.

"—she knowed all the time what was going to happen when he got out, that not only she knowed but Flem did too—"

"I wont believe it!" Stevens said. "I wont! I cant believe it," he said. "Dont you see I cannot?"

"Which brings up something else," Ratliff said. "So she had a decision to make too that once she made it, it would be for

good and all and too late to change it. She could a waited two
more years and God His-self couldn't a kept Mink in Parchman without He killed him, and saved herself not jest the
bother and worry but the moral responsibility too, even if you
do say they aint no morals. Only she didn't. And so you wonder why. If maybe if there wasn't no folks in heaven it
wouldn't be heaven, and if you couldn't recognise them as
folks you knowed, wouldn't nobody want to go there. And
that some day her maw would be saying to her, 'Why didn't
you revenge me and my love that I finally found it, instead of
jest standing back and blind hoping for happen-so? Didn't
you never have no love of your own to learn you what it is?'
—Here," he said. He took out the immaculately clean, im-
peccably laundered and ironed handkerchief which the town
said he not only laundered himself but hemstitched himself
too, and put it into Stevens' blind hand and turned the switch
and flicked on the headlights. "I reckon we'll be about right
now," he said.

Now the road even ceased to be two ruts. It was a gash
now, choked with brier, still mounting. "I'll go in front,"
Ratliff said. "You growed up in town. I never even seen a
light bulb until after I could handle a straight razor." Then he
said, "There it is,"—a canted roofline where one end of the
gable had collapsed completely (Stevens did not recognise, he
simply agreed it could once have been a house) above which
stood one worn gnarled cedar. He almost stumbled through,
across what had been a fence, a yard fence, fallen too, choked
fiercely with rose vines long since gone wild again. "Walk behind me," Ratliff said. "They's a old cistern. I think I know
where it is. I ought to brought a flashlight."

And now, in a crumbling slant downward into, through,
what had been the wall's old foundation, an orifice, a black
and crumbled aperture yawned at their feet as if the ruined
house itself had gaped at them. Ratliff had stopped. He said
quietly: "You never seen that pistol. I did. It didn't look like
no one-for-ten-dollars pistol. It looked like one of a two-for-
nine-and-a-half pistols. Maybe he's still got the other one
with him," when Stevens, without stopping, pushed past him
and, fumbling one foot downward, found what had been a
step; and, taking the gold initialled lighter from his pocket

snapped it on and by the faint wavered gleam continued to descend, Ratliff, behind now, saying, "Of course. He's free now. He wont never have to kill nobody else in all his life," and followed, into the old cellar—the cave, the den where on a crude platform he had heaped together, the man they sought half-squatted half-knelt blinking up at them like a child interrupted at its bedside prayers: not surprised in prayer: interrupted, kneeling in the new overalls which were stained and foul now, his hands lying half-curled on the front of his lap, blinking at the tiny light which Stevens held.

"Hidy," he said.

"You cant stay here," Stevens said. "If we knew where you were, dont you know the Sheriff will think of this place too by tomorrow morning?"

"I aint going to stay," he said. "I jest stopped to rest. I'm fixing to go on pretty soon. Who are you fellers?"

"Never mind that," Stevens said. He took out the envelope containing the money. "Here," he said. It was two hundred and fifty dollars again. The amount was obvious out of the whole thousand it had contained. Stevens had not even troubled to rationalise his decision of the amount. The kneeling man looked at it quietly.

"I left that money in Parchman. I had done already got shut of it before I went out the gate. You mean a son of a bitch stole that too?"

"This is not that money," Stevens said. "They got that back. This is new money she sent you this morning. This is different."

"You mean when I take it I aint promised nobody nothing?"

"Yes," Stevens said. "Take it."

He did so. "Much obliged," he said. "That other time they said I would get another two hundred and fifty again in three months if I went straight across Missisip without stopping and never come back again. I reckon that's done stopped this time."

"No," Stevens said. "That too. In three months tell me where you are and I'll send it."

"Much obliged," Mink said. "Send it to M.I. Snopes."

"What?" Stevens said.

"To M.I. Snopes. That's my name: M.I."

"Come on," Ratliff said, almost roughly, "let's get out of here," taking him by the arm even as Stevens turned, Ratliff taking the burning lighter from him and holding it up while Stevens found the fading earthen steps again, once more up and out into the air, the night, the moonless dark, the worn-out eroded fields supine beneath the first faint breath of fall, waiting for winter. Overhead, celestial and hierarchate, the constellations wheeled through the zodiacal pastures: Scorpion and Bear and Scales; beyond cold Orion and the Sisters the fallen and homeless angels choired, lamenting. Gentle and tender as a woman, Ratliff opened the car door for Stevens to get in. "You all right now?" he said.

"Yes I tell you, goddammit," Stevens said.

Ratliff closed the door and went around the car and opened his and got in and closed it and turned the switch and snapped on the lights and put the car in gear—two old men themselves, approaching their sixties. "I dont know if she's already got a daughter stashed out somewhere, or if she jest aint got around to one yet. But when she does I jest hope for Old Lang Zyne's sake she dont never bring it back to Jefferson. You done already been through two Eula Varners and I dont think you can stand another one."

When the two strangers took the light away and were gone, he didn't lie down again. He was rested now, and any moment now the time to go on again would come. So he just continued to kneel on the crude platform of old boards he had gathered together to defend himself from the ground in case he dropped off to sleep. Luckily the man who robbed him of his ten dollars last Thursday night hadn't taken the safety-pin too, so he folded the money as small as it would fold into the bib pocket and pinned it. It would be all right this time; it made such a lump that even asleep he couldn't help but feel anybody fooling with it.

Then the time came to go on. He was glad of it in a way; a man can get tired, burnt out on resting like on anything else. Outside it was dark, cool and pleasant for walking, empty except for the old ground. But then a man didn't need to have to keep his mind steadily on the ground after sixty-three years. In fact, the ground itself never let a man forget it was there waiting, pulling gently and without no hurry at him be-

tween every step, saying, Come on, lay down; I aint going to
hurt you. Jest lay down. He thought *I'm free now. I can walk
any way I want to.* So he would walk West now, since that was
the direction people always went: west. Whenever they picked
up and moved to a new country, it was always west, like Old
Moster Himself had put it into a man's very blood and nature
his paw had give him at the very moment he squirted him
into his maw's belly.

Because he was free now. A little further along toward
dawn, anytime the notion struck him to, he could lay down.
So when the notion struck him he did so, arranging himself,
arms and legs and back, already feeling the first faint gentle
tug like the durned old ground itself was trying to make you
believe it wasn't really noticing itself doing it. Only he located
the right stars at that moment, he was not laying exactly right
since a man must face the East to lay down; walk West but
when you lay down, face the exact East. So he moved, shifted
a little, and now he was exactly right and he was free now, he
could afford to risk it; to show how much he dared risk it, he
even would close his eyes, give it all the chance it wanted;
whereupon, as if believing he really was asleep, it gradually
went to work a little harder, easy of course, not to really disturb him: just harder, increasing. Because a man had to spend
not just all his life but all the time of Man too guarding
against it, even back when they said man lived in caves, he
would raise up a bank of dirt to at least keep him that far off
the ground while he slept, until he invented wood floors to
protect him and at last beds too, raising the floors storey by
storey until they would be laying a hundred and even a thousand feet up in the air to be safe from the earth.

But he could risk it, he even felt like giving it a fair active
chance just to show him, prove what it could do if it wanted
to try. And in fact, as soon as he thought that, it seemed to
him he could feel the Mink Snopes that had had to spend so
much of his life just having unnecessary bother and trouble,
beginning to creep, seep, flow easy as sleeping; he could almost watch it, following all the little grass blades and tiny
roots, the little holes the worms made, down and down into
the ground already full of the folks that had the trouble but
were free now, so that it was just the ground and the dirt that

had to bother and worry and anguish with the passions and hopes and skeers, the justice and the injustice and the griefs, leaving the folks themselves easy now, all mixed and jumbled up comfortable and easy so wouldn't nobody even know or even care who was which anymore, himself among them, equal to any, good as any, brave as any, being inextricable from, anonymous with all of them: the beautiful, the splendid, the proud and the brave, right on up to the very top itself among the shining phantoms and dreams which are the milestones of the long human recording—Helen and the bishops, the kings and the unhomed angels, the scornful and graceless seraphim.

Charlottesville, Virginia
9 March, 1959

and to comfort and work, and to guard against passions and
thorny and stony, for conduct and influence, and the greats.

Beyond the other violences... but the full... and number
and conductive, and to say so well... nobody even show an
even the... to read... or expose children... among them,
right... among... parties... the... being... right...
man, among us... with all of them, the landlord, the spine,
had the hard middle... their... not as in the very top to
advance... the... ghastly ghastliness and people which are the
engines of... medicine... about... recurring sudden, and the
landlord, and... of the... through... it gets... the world and
against... at stake...

THE REIVERS

A Reminiscence

TO

Victoria, Mark, Paul, William, Burks

One

GRANDFATHER SAID:
This is the kind of a man Boon Hogganbeck was. Hung
on the wall, it could have been his epitaph, like a Bertillon
chart or a police poster; any cop in north Mississippi would
have arrested him out of any crowd after merely reading the
date.

It was Saturday morning, about ten oclock. We—your
great-grandfather and I—were in the office, Father sitting at
the desk totting up the money from the canvas sack and
matching it against the list of freight bills which I had just
collected around the Square; and I sitting in the chair against
the wall waiting for noon when I would be paid my
Saturday's (week's) wage of ten cents and we would go home
and eat dinner and I would be free at last to overtake (it was
May) the baseball game which had been running since breakfast without me: the idea (not mine: your great-grandfather's)
being that even at eleven a man should already have behind
him one year of paying for, assuming responsibility for, the
space he occupied, the room he took up, in the world's
(Jefferson, Mississippi's anyway) economy. I would leave
home with Father immediately after breakfast each Saturday
morning, when all the other boys on the street were merely
arming themselves with balls and bats and gloves—not to
mention my three brothers, who being younger and therefore
smaller than I, were more fortunate, assuming this was
Father's logic or premise: that since any adult man worth his
salt could balance or stand off four children in economic oc-
cupancy, any one of the children, the largest certainly, would
suffice to carry the burden of the requisite economic motions:
in this case, making the rounds each Saturday morning with
the bills for the boxes and cases of freight which our Negro
drivers had picked up at the depot during the week and delivered to the back doors of the grocery and hardware and
farmers' supply stores, and bring the canvas sack back to the
livery stable for Father to count and balance it, then sit in
the office for the rest of the morning ostensibly to answer the

725

telephone—this for the sum of ten cents a week, which it was assumed I would live inside of.

That's what we were doing when Boon came jumping through the door. That's right. Jumping. It was not really a high step up from the hallway, even for a boy of eleven (though John Powell, the head hostler, had had Son Thomas, the youngest driver, find, borrow, take—anyway, snaffle— from somewhere a wooden block as an intermediate step for me) and Boon could have taken it as he always did in his own six-foot-four stride. But not this time: jumping into the room. In its normal state his face never looked especially gentle or composed; at this moment it looked like it was about to explode right out from between his shoulders with excitement, urgency, whatever it was, jumping on across the office toward the desk and already hollering at Father: "Look out, Mr Maury, get out of the way," reaching, lunging across Father toward the lower drawer where the livery stable pistol lived; I couldn't tell whether it was Boon lunging for the drawer who knocked the chair (it was a swivel chair on casters) back or whether it was Father who flung the chair back to make himself room to kick at Boon's reaching hand, the neat stacks of coins scattering in all directions across the desk and Father hollering too now, still stomping either at the drawer or Boon's hand or maybe both:

"God damn it, stop it!"

"I'm going to shoot Ludus!" Boon hollered. "He's probably clean across the Square by now! Look out, Mr Maury!"

"No!" Father said. "Get away!"

"You wont let me have it?" Boon said.

"No, God damn it," Father said.

"All right," Boon said, already jumping again, back toward the door and out of it. But Father just sat there. I'm sure you have often noticed how ignorant people beyond thirty or forty are. I dont mean forgetful. That's specious and easy, too easy to say *Oh papa* (or grandpa) *or mama* (or grandma), *they're just old; they have forgotten*. Because there are some things, some of the hard facts of life, that you dont forget, no matter how old you are. There is a ditch, a chasm; as a boy you crossed it on a footlog. You come creeping and doddering back at thirty-five or forty and the footlog is gone; you may not even remember the footlog but at least you dont step out onto that empty gravity that footlog once spanned. That was Father then. Boon came jumping without warning into the office and almost knocked Father chair and all over grabbing at the drawer where the pistol was, until Father managed to kick or stomp or whatever it was his hand away, then Boon turned and went jumping back out of the office and apparently, obviously, Father thought that was all of it, that it was finished. He even finished cursing, just on principle, as though there were no urgency anywhere, heeling the chair back to the desk and seeing the scattered money which would have to be counted all over now and then he started to curse at Boon again, not even about the pistol but simply at Boon for being Boon Hogganbeck, until I told him.

"He's gone to try to borrow John Powell's," I said.

"What?" Father said. Then he jumped too, both of us, across the office and down into the hallway and down the hallway toward the lot behind the stable where John Powell and Luster were helping Gabe, the blacksmith, shoe three of the mules and one of the harness horses, Father not even taking time to curse now, just hollering "John! Boon! John! Boon!" every three steps.

But he was too late this time too. Because Boon fooled him—us. Because John Powell's pistol was not just a moral problem in the stable, it was an emotional one too. It was a .41 calibre snub-nosed revolver, quite old but in excellent condition because John had kept it that way ever since he bought it from his father the day he was twenty-one years old. Only, he was not supposed to have it. I mean, officially it did not exist. The decree, as old as the stable itself, was that the only pistol connected with it would be the one which stayed in the bottom right hand drawer of the desk in the office, and the mutual gentlemen's assumption was that no one on the staff of the establishment even owned a firearm from the time he came on duty until he went back home, let alone brought one to work with him. Yet—and John had explained it to all of us and had our confederated sympathy and understanding, a unified and impregnable front to the world and even to Father himself if that unimaginable crisis had ever arisen, which it would not have except for Boon Hogganbeck—

telling us (John) how he had earned the price of the pistol by doing outside work on his own time, on time apart from helping his father on the farm, time which was his own to spend eating or sleeping, until on his twenty-first birthday he had paid the final coin into his father's hand and received the pistol; telling us how the pistol was the living badge of his manhood, the ineffaceable proof that he was now twenty-one and a man; that he never intended, declined even to imagine the circumstance in which he would ever pull its trigger against a human being, yet he must have it with him; he would no more have left the pistol at home when he came away than he would have left his manhood in a distant closet or drawer when he came to work; he told us (and we believed him) that if the moment ever came when he would have to choose between leaving the pistol at home or not coming to work himself, there would have been but one possible choice for him.

So at first his wife had stitched a neat strong pocket exactly fitting the pistol on the inside of the bib of his overalls. But John himself realised at once that this wouldn't do. Not that the pistol might fall out at some irretrievable moment, but that the shape of it was obvious through the cloth; it couldn't have been anything else but a pistol. Obvious not to us: we all knew it was there, from Mr Ballott, the white stable foreman, and Boon, his assistant (whose duty was night duty and so he should have been at home in bed at this moment), on down through all the Negro drivers and hostlers, down to the last lowly stall-cleaner and even to me, who only collected the Saturday accumulation of freight bills and answered the telephone. On even to old Dan Grinnup, a dirty man with a tobacco-stained beard, who was never quite completely drunk, who had no official position in the stable, partly because of the whiskey maybe but mostly because of his name which was not Grinnup at all but Grenier: one of the three oldest names in the county until the family went to seed—old Doctor Habersham and his servant, Alexander Holston, and the Huguenot Louis Grenier who crossed the mountains from Virginia and Carolina after the Revolution and came down into Mississippi in the seventeen-nineties and established Jefferson and named it—who (old Dan) lived nowhere

(and had no family save an idiot nephew or cousin or
something still living in a tent in the river jungle beyond
Frenchman's Bend which had once been a part of the Grenier
plantation) until he (old Dan) would appear, never too drunk
to drive it, at the stable in time to take the hack to the depot
and meet the 9:30 pm and the 4:12 am trains and deliver the
drummers to the hotel, or on duty all night sometimes when
there were balls or minstrel or drama shows at the opera
house (at times, at some cold and scornful pitch of drink, he
would say that once Greniers led Yoknapatawpha society; now
Grinnups drove it) holding his job some said because Mr
Ballott's first wife had been his daughter, though we in the
stable all believed it was because when Father was a boy he
used to fox-hunt with old Dan's father out at Frenchman's
Bend.

Obvious (the pistol) not only to us but to Father himself.
Because Father knew about it too. He had to know about it;
our establishment was too small, too intricate, too closely-
knit. So Father's moral problem was exactly the same as John
Powell's, and both of them knew it and handled it as mutual
gentlemen must and should: if Father were ever compelled to
acknowledge the pistol was there, he would have to tell John
either to leave it at home tomorrow or not come back himself. And John knew this and, a gentleman too, he himself
would never be the one to compel Father to acknowledge the
pistol existed. So, instead of in the overall bib, John's wife
stitched the pocket just under the left armpit of the jumper itself, invisible (anyway unobtrusive) both when John was
wearing the jumper or when in warm weather (like now) the
jumper hung on John's private nail in the harness room. That
was the situation of the pistol when Boon, who was being
paid to be and who in a sense had given his word that he
would be at home in bed at this hour instead of hanging
around the Square where he would be vulnerable to what had
sent him rushing back to the stable, came jumping through
the office door a minute ago and made Father and John
Powell both liars.

Only Father was too late again. Boon fooled him—us.
Because Boon knew about that nail in the harness room too.
And smart too, too smart to come back up the hallway where

he would have to pass the office; when we reached the lot John and Luster and Gabe (the three mules and the horse too) were still watching the still-swinging side gate through which Boon had just vanished, carrying the pistol in his hand. John and Father looked at each other for about ten seconds while the whole edifice of *entendre-de-noblesse* collapsed into dust. Though the *noblesse*, the *oblige*, still remained.

"It was mine," John said.

"Yes," Father said. "He saw Ludus on the Square."

"I'll catch him," John said. "Take it away from him too. Say the word."

"Catch Ludus, somebody," Gabe said. Though short, he was a tremendously big man, bigger than Boon, with a terrifically twisted leg from an old injury in his trade; he would pick up the hind foot of a horse or mule and lock it behind the warped knee and (if there was something—a post—anything—for him to hold to) the horse or mule might throw itself but no more: neither snatch that foot free nor get enough balance to kick him with the other one. "Here, Luster, you jump and catch—"

"Aint nobody studying Ludus," John said. "Ludus the safest man there. I seen Boon Hogganbeck"—he didn't say Mister and he knew Father heard him: something he would never have failed to do in the hearing of any white man he considered his equal, because John was a gentleman. But Father was competent for *noblesse* too: it was that pistol which was unforgivable, and Father knew it,—"shoot before. Say the word, Mr Maury."

"No," Father said. "You run to the office and telephone Mr Hampton." (That's right. A Hampton was sheriff then too: this one's grandfather.) "Tell him I said to grab Mr Boon as quick as he can." Father went toward the gate.

"Go with him," Gabe told Luster. "He might need somebody to run for him. And latch that gate."

So the three of us went up the alley toward the Square, me trotting now to keep up, not really trying to overtake Boon so much as to stay between Boon and the pistol and John Powell. Because, as John himself had said, nobody needed to study Ludus. Because we all knew Boon's marksmanship, and with Boon shooting at Ludus, Ludus himself was safe. He

(Ludus) had been one of our drivers too until last Tuesday morning. This is what happened, as reconstructed from Boon and Mr Ballott and John Powell and a little from Ludus himself. A week or two before, Ludus had found a new girl, daughter (or wife: we didn't know which) of a tenant on a farm six miles from town. On Monday evening, when Boon came in to relieve Mr Ballott for the night shift, all the teams and wagons and drivers were in except Ludus. Mr Ballott told Boon to telephone him when Ludus came in, and went home. That was Mr Ballott's testimony. This was Boon's, corroborated in part by John Powell (Father himself had gone home some time before): Mr Ballott was barely out the front door when Ludus came in the back way, on foot. Ludus told Boon that the tire on one of his wheels had loosened and he had stopped at our house and seen Father, who had told him to drive the wagon into the pond in the pasture where the wood of the wheel would swell back to the tire, and stable and feed the mules in our lot and come and get them in the morning. Which you could have expected even Boon to believe, as John Powell immediately did not, since anyone who knew either would have known that, whatever disposition he made of the wagon for the night, Father would have sent Ludus to lead the team back to their stalls in the livery stable where they could be cleaned and fed properly. But that's what Boon said he was told, which he said was why he didn't interrupt Mr Ballott's evening meal to notify him, since Father knew where the mules and wagon were, and it was Father, not Mr Ballott, who owned them.

Now John Powell: but reluctantly; he would likely never have told it at all if Boon had not made his (John's) silence about the truth a larger moral issue than his loyalty to his race. Once he saw Ludus walk empty-handed into the back door of the stable at the next coincident moment to Mr Ballott's departure by the front one, leaving only Boon in charge, John didn't even bother to listen to what tale Ludus would tell. He simply went back through the hallway and across the lot into the alley and on to the end of the alley and was actually standing beside the wagon when Ludus returned to it. It now contained a sack of flour, a gallon jug of coal oil and (John said) a nickel sack of peppermint candy. This is

about what happened, because although John's word about
any horse or mule while inside the stable was law, inviolable,
even beyond Boon, right up to Mr Ballott or Father himself,
out here in no man's land he was just another wage hand in
Maury Priest's livery stable and he and Ludus both knew it.
Maybe Ludus even reminded him of this, but I doubt it.
Because all Ludus needed to say was something like: "If word
gets back to Maury Priest about how I borried this wagon
and team tonight, maybe the same word gonter get back to
him about what's sewed up in that jumper you wears."

And I dont think he said that either because he and John
both knew that too, just as they both knew that if Ludus
waited for John to report to Father what Ludus called the
"borrying" of the wagon and team, Father would never know
it, and if John waited for Ludus (or any other Negro in the
stable or Jefferson either) to tell Father about that pistol,
Father would never know that either. So Ludus probably said
nothing at all, and John only said, "All right. But if them
mules aint back in their stalls, without one sweat or whip
mark on them and not even looking sleepy, a good solid hour
before Mr Ballott gets here tomorrow morning" (You will
have already noticed how both of them had completely dismissed Boon from the affair: neither Ludus to say, "Mister
Boon knows these mules wont be in tonight; aint he the boss
until Mr Ballott comes back in the morning?" nor John to
say, "Anybody that would believe the tale you brought in
here tonight in place of them mules, aint competent to be the
boss of nothing. And I aint even good convinced yet that his
name is Boon Hogganbeck.") "Mr Maury aint just gonter
know where that team and wagon wasn't last night, he's
gonter know where they was."

But John didn't say it. And sure enough, although Ludus's
mules had been back in their stalls a good hour before daylight, fifteen minutes after Mr Ballott reached the stable at six
the next morning, he sent for Ludus and told him he was
fired. "Mr Boon knowed my team was out," Ludus said. "He
sent me himself to get him a jug of whiskey. I brung it back
to him about four this morning."

"I didn't send you anywhere," Boon said. "When he come
in here last night with that cock-and-bull story about them

mules being in Mr Maury's lot, I never even listened. I didn't even bother to ask him where that wagon actually was, let alone why he was in such a sweating need of a wagon and team last night. What I told him was, before he brought that wagon back this morning I would expect him to go by Mack Winbush's and bring me back a gallon of Uncle Cal Bookwright's whiskey. I give him the money for it—two dollars."

"And I brung you the whiskey," Ludus said. "I dont know what you done with it."

"You brought me a half a jug of rotgut, mainly lye and red pepper," Boon said. "I dont know what Mr Maury's going to do to you about keeping them mules out all night but it aint a circumstance to what Calvin Bookwright will do to you when I show him that whiskey and tell him you claim he made it."

"Mr Winbush stays a solid eight miles from town," Ludus said. "It would a been midnight before I could get back to—" and stopped.

"So that's why you needed a wagon," Boon said. "You finally tomcatted yourself clean out of Jefferson and now you got to ramshack the country to locate another back window you can crawl in. Well, you'll have plenty of time now; the only trouble is, you'll have to walk—"

"You tole me a jug of whiskey," Ludus said sullenly. "I brung you a jug—"

"It wasn't even half full," Boon said. Then to Mr Ballott: "Hell fire, you wont even have to give him a week's pay now." (The weekly pay of drivers was two dollars; this was 1905 remember.) "He already owes me that for that whiskey. What you waiting for? for Mr Maury to come in his-self and fire him?"

Though if Mr Ballott (and Father) had really intended to fire Ludus for good, they would have given him his week's pay. The very fact that they didn't indicated (and Ludus knew it) that he was merely being docked a week's pay (with vacation) for keeping a team out all night without proper authority; next Monday morning Ludus would appear with the other drivers at the regular time and John Powell would have his team ready for him as if nothing had happened. Only, Fate—Rumor—gossip, had to intervene.

So Father, Luster and I hurried up the alley toward the Square, me trotting now, and still too late. We hadn't even reached the end of the alley when we heard the shots, all five of them: WHOW WHOW WHOW WHOW WHOW like that, then we were in the Square and (it wasn't far: right at the corner in front of Cousin Isaac McCaslin's hardware store) we could see it. There were plenty of them; Boon sure picked his day for witnesses; First Saturdays were trade days even then, even in May when you would think people would be too busy getting land planted. But not in Yoknapatawpha County. They were all there, black and white: one crowd where Mr Hampton (the grandfather of this same Little Hub who is sheriff now, or will be again next year) and two or three bystanders wrestling with Boon, and another crowd where another deputy was holding Ludus about twenty feet away and still in the frozen attitude of running or frozen in the attitude of running or in the attitude of frozen running, whichever is right, and another crowd around the window of Cousin Ike's store which one of Boon's bullets (they never did find where the other four went) had shattered after creasing the buttock of a Negro girl who was now lying on the pavement screaming until Cousin Ike himself came jumping out of the store and drowned her voice with his, roaring with rage at Boon not for ruining his window but (Cousin Ike was young then but already the best woodsman and hunter this county ever had) for being unable to hit with five shots an object only twenty feet away.

It continued to go fast. Doctor Peabody's office was just across the street, above Christian's drug store; with Mr Hampton carrying John Powell's pistol and leading, Luster and another Negro man carried the girl, still screaming and bleeding like a stuck pig, up the stairs, Father following with Boon, then me and the deputy with Ludus, and as many more as could crowd onto the stairs until Mr Hampton stopped and turned and bellowed at them. Judge Stevens's office was just down the gallery from Doctor Peabody's; he was standing at the top of the steps as we came up. So we—I mean Father and me and Boon and Ludus and the deputy— went in there to wait for Mr Hampton to come back from Doctor Peabody's office. It wasn't long.

"All right," Mr Hampton said. "It barely creased her. Buy her a new dress" (there wasn't anything under it) "and a bag of candy and give her father ten dollars, and that'll settle Boon with her. I aint quite decided yet what'll settle him with me." He breathed hard at Boon a moment: a big man with hard little gray eyes, as big as Boon in fact though not as tall. "All right," he told Boon.

"He insulted me," Boon said. "He told Son Thomas I was a narrow-asted son of a bitch."

Now Mr Hampton looked at Ludus. "All right," he said.

"I never said he was norrer-asted," Ludus said. "I said he was norrer-headed."

"What?" Boon said.

"That's worse," Judge Stevens said.

"Of course it's worse," Boon said, cried. "Cant you see? And I aint even got any choice. Me, a white man, have got to stand here and let a damn mule-wrastling nigger either criticise my private tail, or state before five public witnesses that I aint got any sense. Cant you see? Because you cant take nothing back, not nothing. You cant even correct it because there aint nothing to correct neither one of them to." He was almost crying now, his big ugly florid walnut-tough walnut-hard face wrung and twisted like a child's. "Even if I managed to get another pistol somewhere to shoot Son Thomas with, I'd likely miss him too."

Father got up, quickly and briskly. He was the only one sitting down; even Judge Stevens was standing spraddled on the hearth before the cold fireplace with his hands under his coat-tails exactly like it was winter and there was a fire burning. "I must get back to work," Father said. "What does the old saw say about idle hands?" He said, not to anybody: "I want both of them, Boon and this boy, put under bond to keep the peace: say, a hundred dollars each; I will make the bond. Only, I want two mutual double-action bonds. I want two bonds, both of which will be abrogated, fall due, at the same moment that either one of them does anything that—that I—"

"That dont suit you," Judge Stevens said.

"Much obliged," Father said. "—the same second that either one of them breaks the peace. I dont know if that is legal or not."

"I dont either," Judge Stevens said. "We can try. If such a bond is not legal, it ought to be."

"Much obliged," Father said. We—Father and I and Boon—went toward the door.

"I could come back now, without waiting to Monday," Ludus said. "Iffen you needs me."

"No," Father said. We—Father and I and Boon—went on down the stairs, to the street. It was still First Saturday and trade day, but that's all it was now—that is, until somebody else named Boon Hogganbeck got hold of another pistol. We went on back along the street toward the stable, Father and I and Boon; he spoke now across the top of my head toward the back of Father's:

"A dollar a week for two hundred dollars is a year and forty-eight weeks. That window of Ike's will be another ten or fifteen I reckon, besides that girl that got in the way. Say two years and three months. I've got about forty dollars in money. If I gave you that as a cash down payment, I still dont reckon you'd put me and Ludus and Son Thomas in one of the empty stalls and lock the door for ten minutes. Would you?"

"No," Father said.

Two

T HAT was Saturday. Ludus was back at work Monday morning. On the next Friday my grandfather—the other one, Mother's father, your great-grandmother's father—died in Bay St Louis.

Boon didn't actually belong to us. I mean, not solely to us, the Priests. Or rather I mean the McCaslins and Edmondses, of whom we Priests are what might be called the cadet branch. Boon had three proprietors: not only us, as represented by Grandfather and Father and Cousin Ike McCaslin and our other cousin, Zachary Edmonds, to whose father, McCaslin Edmonds, Cousin Ike on his twenty-first birthday had abdicated the McCaslin plantation;—he belonged not just to us but to Major de Spain and General Compson too until he died. Boon was a corporation, a holding company in which the three of us—McCaslins, De Spain, and General Compson—had mutually equal but completely undefined shares of responsibility, the one and only corporation rule being that whoever was nearest at the crises would leap immediately into whatever breach Boon had this time created or committed or simply fallen heir to; he (Boon) was a mutual benevolent protective benefit association, of which the benefits were all Boon's and the mutuality and the benevolence and the protecting all ours.

His grandmother had been the daughter of one of old Issetibbeha's Chickasaws who married a white whiskey-trader; at times, depending on the depth of his cups, Boon would declare himself to be a least ninety-nine one-hundredths Chickasaw and in fact a lineal royal descendant of old Issetibbeha himself; the next time he would offer to fight any man who dared even intimate that he had one drop of Indian blood in his veins.

He was tough, faithful, brave and completely unreliable; he was six feet four inches tall and weighed two hundred and forty pounds and had the mentality of a child; over a year ago Father had already begun to say that at any moment now I would outgrow him.

In fact, although he was obviously a perfectly normal flesh-and-blood biological result (vide the moments in his cups when he was not merely ready and willing but even eager to fight any man or men either pro or con, depending on how the drink had taken him, for the right to ancestry) and hence he had to have been somewhere during those first nine or ten or eleven years, it was as if Boon had been created whole and already nine or ten or eleven years old, by the three of us, McCaslin-De Spain-Compson, as a solution to a dilemma one day at Major de Spain's hunting camp.

That's right, the same camp which you will probably continue to call McCaslin's camp for a few years after your Cousin Ike is gone, just as we—your fathers—continued to call it De Spain's camp for years after Major de Spain was gone. But in the time of my fathers, when Major de Spain bought or borrowed or leased the land (however men managed to acquire valid titles in Mississippi between 1865 and '70) and built the lodge and stables and kennels, it was his camp: who culled and selected the men he considered worthy to hunt the game he decreed to be hunted, and so in that sense not only owned who hunted it but where they hunted and even what: the bear and deer, and wolves and panthers also ranged it then, less than twenty miles from Jefferson— the four or five sections of river-bottom jungle which had been a portion of old Thomas Sutpen's vast kingly dream which in the end had destroyed not only itself but Sutpen too, which in those days was a sort of eastern gateway to the still almost virgin wilderness of swamp and jungle which stretched westward from the hills to the towns and plantations along the Mississippi.

It was only twenty miles then; our fathers could leave Jefferson at midnight in buggies and wagons (a man on a horse did it even quicker) on the fifteenth of November and be on a deer- or bear-stand by daybreak. Even in 1905 the wilderness had retreated only twenty more miles; the wagons bearing the guns and food and bedding had merely to start at sundown; and now a northern lumber company had built a narrow-gauge railroad for hauling logs, which connected with the main line, passing within a mile of Major de Spain's new camp, with a courtesy stop to let Major de Spain and his guests off, to be met by the wagons which had gone in the day before. Though by 1925 we could already see the doom. Major de Spain and the rest of that old group save your Cousin Ike and Boon, were gone now and (there was gravel now all the way from Jefferson to De Spain's flagstop) their inheritors switched off their automobile engines to the sound of axes and saws where a year ago there had been only the voices of the running hounds. Because Manfred de Spain was a banker, not a hunter like his father; he sold lease, land and timber and by 1940 (it was McCaslin's camp now) they—we—would load everything into pickup trucks and drive a hundred miles over paved highways to find enough wilderness to pitch tents in; then two hundred miles by 1960; though by 1980 the automobile will be as obsolete to reach wilderness with as the automobile will have made the wilderness it seeks. But perhaps they—you—will find wilderness on the backside of Mars or the moon, with maybe even bear and deer to run it.

But then, when Boon transmogrified at the camp one day, full panoplied and already ten or eleven or twelve years old, there were only twenty miles for Major de Spain and General Compson and McCaslin Edmonds and Walter Ewell and old Bob Legate and the half-dozen others who would come and go, to travel. But General Compson, although he had commanded troops not too unsuccessfully as a colonel at Shiloh, and again not too unsuccessfully as a brigadier during Johnston's retreat on and then from Atlanta, was a little short in terrain, topography, and would promptly get lost ten minutes after he left camp (the mule he preferred to ride would have brought him back at any time but, not only a paroled Confederate general but a Compson too, he declined to accept counsel or advice from a mule) so as soon as the last hunter was in from the morning's drive, everyone would take turns blowing a horn until General Compson at last got in. Which was satisfactory, anyway served, until General Compson's hearing began to fail too. Until finally one afternoon Walter Ewell and Sam Fathers, who was half Negro and half Chickasaw Indian, had to track him down and camp in the woods with him all night, facing Major de Spain with the alternative of either forbidding him to leave the tent or expelling him from the club, when lo, there was Boon Hogganbeck, already a giant, even

at ten or eleven already bigger than General Compson whose
nurse he became—a waif, who seemed to have had nothing
and known nothing but his name; even Cousin Ike is not sure
whether it was McCaslin Edmonds or Major de Spain who
found Boon first where whoever bore him had abandoned
him. All Ike knows—remembers—is that Boon was already
there, about twelve years old, out at old Carothers McCaslin's
place, where McCaslin Edmonds was already raising Ike as if
he was his father and now and without breaking stride took
over Boon too as though he had been Boon's father also,
though at that time McCaslin Edmonds himself was only
thirty.

Anyway, as soon as Major de Spain realised that he must
either expel General Compson from the club, which would
be difficult, or forbid him to leave the camp, which would be
impossible, and hence he must equip General Compson with
something resembling a Boon Hogganbeck, there was the
Boon Hogganbeck, produced either by McCaslin Edmonds
or perhaps by both of them—Edmonds and De Spain himself—in simultaneous crisis. Ike could remember that: the
loading of the bedding and guns and food into the wagon on
the fourteenth of November, with Tennie's Jim (grandfather
of this Bobo Beauchamp of whom you will hear presently)
and Sam Fathers and Boon (he, Ike, was only five or six then;
another four or five years before he would be ten and could
make one also) and McCaslin himself riding ahead on the
horse, to the camp where each morning Boon would follow
General Compson on a second mule until by simple force
probably, since at twelve Boon was already bigger than his
charge, Boon would compel him to the right direction in
time to reach camp before dark.

Thus General Compson made a woodsman of Boon despite
himself, you might say, in simple self-defense. But even eating
at the same table and ranging the same woods and sleeping in
the same rain even with Walter Ewell never made a marksman
of him; two of the camp's favorite stories were about Boon's
shooting, one told by Walter Ewell: of being on a stand where
he had left Boon (old General Compson had gone to his fathers at last—or to whatever bivouac old soldiers of that war,
blue or gray either, probably insisted on going to since prob-

ably no other place would suit them for anything resembling
a permanent stay—and now Boon was a regular hunter like
anybody else) and of hearing the hounds and realising that
the deer was going to cross at Boon's stand, then of hearing
the five shots from Boon's ramshackle pump gun (General
Compson had bequeathed it to him; it had never been in the
best condition while Compson owned it and Walter said his
real surprise was that the gun had fired even twice without
jamming, let alone five times) and then Boon's voice across
the woods between them: "God damn! Yonder he goes!
Head him! Head him!" And how he—Walter—hurried across
to Boon's stand and found the five exploded shells on the
ground and not ten paces away, the prints of the running
buck which Boon had not even touched.

The other story was Ike's. It was in summer this time; he
was no longer the child his uncle McCaslin had taken into the
camp where he had found at last the actual shape and substance of his dream. In a few more years he would be the best
hunter and woodsman among them, though the youngest;
not long now until, although with Major de Spain and his uncle McCaslin and General Compson and old Bob Legate
gone and Walter Ewell was now the senior by elimination, the
camp would be known as McCaslin's camp. But so far Ike had
merely found at last the shape of his dream, his heart's desire—the pathless wilderness marked only by the print of bear
and deer and panther and wolf, his the only human print to
mark it if he had his way—just as Boon finally found the
shape of his dream in the automobile your great-great grandfather bought in 1904, finding it not with humility and passion and joy as Ike found his, but with a kind of outrage that
nobody had even told him it existed until he was already past
thirty years old.

It was that summer. The one specific location Boon had in
concorded time-space was those two November weeks in De
Spain's hunting camp. During the other fifty, he had no location; there was no niche in space where police or post office
department knew they could find him tomorrow; homeless,
he was at home wherever the shadow of McCaslin or De
Spain or Compson fell; when General Compson died, Boon
lost nothing: only McCaslins and De Spains gained; as when

Major de Spain's time would finally come, Boon himself
would not even lose what McCaslin-Edmonds-Priest gained.
During the winter he lived in town, where he could go to
school (not his idea but McCaslin Edmonds's, abetted by
Major de Spain and, now and then, by your great-great
grandfather, though by the time he had spent five years trying
to get through the third grade—by which time he could read
and even do what he called "figger" in simple addition and
subtraction—his very size, which was now that of a grown
man, came to his aid and for very shame McCaslin had pity
on him), living—sleeping and eating—sometimes at De
Spain's and sometimes with us, being swapped about mainly
when the menfolks of either family had to be away from home
at night.

But in the spring, when planting time came, he always went
back to McCaslin at the farm. During the fall and winter in
town he did never-too-onerous odd jobs, particularly on
Saturdays at the livery stable, where he already had a certain
way (though never to match Ned's, of whom you will hear
later too) with horses and mules; your great-great grandfather
always said, not so much because of his size as because of his
innocence since the only other domestic animal that big and
that uninformed was a horse. But when he went back to
McCaslin at plowing time, he really went to work. Which was
why Ike said he was never sure whether it was he or Boon
that summer who first thought of the trip to the hunting
lodge to spend two or three days shooting squirrels. Anyway
McCaslin said he could go if he would take Boon with him,
and Major de Spain gave them the permission, and the next
morning Ash Jones, De Spain's Negro care-taker, met the
log-train with the wagon and he and Boon put their gear into
it and took their guns (Ike with the new twelve double
McCaslin had given him Christmas, Boon with the decrepit
heirloom General Compson had left him) and separated into
the woods, to meet at the lodge at noon.

This is how Ike told it: about two hours later, walking
slowly through the woods in the bright June morning, having
shot in the first thirty minutes from the mast-laden pin oaks
enough squirrels for himself and Ash and Boon all three for
supper tonight, when he began to hear a distant sound of

metal heavily and rapidly striking metal: of moving on toward it, the sound becoming louder and more violent now, with a hysterical note in it, himself definitely curious now: to the edge of the woods where Major de Spain had cleared off three or four acres of land for Ash in case Ash (which he hadn't yet) ever got around to wanting to make a crop: a single big pin oak standing alone thirty or forty yards inside the clearing, which (the tree) seemed to be alive with frantic squirrels darting and leaping among the branches; this, between frenzied abortive rushes half way down the trunk to reach the ground and escape before losing courage and rushing back up the trunk again, the sound of the hammering coming from the foot of the tree, and now he saw what was holding the squirrels prisoner among the branches. It was Boon, sitting on the ground at the foot of the tree, the dismembered pump gun scattered about him while he hammered the jammed receiver with the disjointed barrrel, not even ceasing to hammer as he turned his head, his furious sweating brick-colored face and his glaring and maddened eyes, shouting at Ike: "Dont shoot! Dont touch a one of them! They're mine!"

Then Grandfather bought that automobile and Boon found his soul's mate. By this time he was officially (by mutual McCaslin-Edmonds-Priest consent, even McCaslin Edmonds having given up or seen the light at last when Boon failed the third grade for the second time too—or maybe the real light McCaslin saw was that Boon would never stay on any farm long enough to learn to be a farmer) a member of the livery stable staff. At first the jobs were mostly still the odd ones—feeding, cleaning harness and buggies. But I told you he had a way with horses and mules, and soon he was a regular driver of hired vehicles—hacks and cabs which met the day-time trains, and the buggies and surreys and light wagons in which the drummers made the rounds of the country stores. He lived in town now, except when McCaslin and Zachary both were away at night and Boon would sleep in the house to protect the women and children. I mean, he lived in Jefferson. I mean, he actually had a home—a single rented room in what in my grandfather's time was the Commercial Hotel, established in hopeful rivalry of the Holston

House but never made the grade in that rivalry. But solid enough: where juries were lodged and fed during court terms and where country litigants and horse- and mule-traders felt more at ease than among the carpets and brass cuspidors and leather chairs and linen table-cloths across town; then in my time the Snopes Hotel with both hand-painted esses upside down when Mr Flem Snopes (the banker, murdered ten or twelve years ago by the mad kinsman who perhaps didn't believe his cousin had actually sent him to the penitentiary but at least could have kept him out or anyway tried to) began to lead his tribe out of the wilderness behind Frenchman's Bend, into town; then for a brief time in the mid-thirties leased by a brassy-haired gentlewoman who came briefly from nowhere and went briefly back, known to your father and the police as Little Chicago; and which you know, those glories but memories now, as Mrs Rouncewell's boarding house. But in Boon's time it was still the Commercial Hotel; in the intervals between sleeping on the floor of some Compson or Edmonds or Priest kitchen, when the menfolks had to be away over night, he was living there when my grandfather bought the automobile.

My grandfather didn't want an automobile at all; he was forced to buy one. A banker, president of the older Bank of Jefferson, the first bank in Yoknapatawpha County, he believed then and right on to his death many years afterward, by which time everybody else even in Yoknapatawpha County had realised that the automobile had come to stay, that the motor vehicle was an insolvent phenomenon like last night's toadstool and, like the fungus, would vanish with tomorrow's sun. But Colonel Sartoris, president of the newer, the mushroom Merchants and Farmers Bank, forced him to buy one. Or rather, another insolvent, a dreamy myopic gentian-eyed mechanical wizard named Bullock, compelled him to. Because my grandfather's car wasn't even the first one in Jefferson. (I dont count Manfred de Spain's red EMF racer. Although De Spain owned it and drove it daily through Jefferson streets for several years, it had no more place in the decorous uxorious pattern of a community than Manfred himself did, both of them being incorrigible and bachelor, not in the town but on it and up to no good like one pro-

longed unbroken Saturday night even while Manfred was actually mayor, its very scarlet color being not even a scornful
defiance of the town but rather a kind of almost inattentive
disavowal.)

Grandfather's was not even the first automobile to see
Jefferson or vice versa. It was not even the first one to inhabit
Jefferson. Two years before, one had driven all the way down
from Memphis, making the eighty-mile trip in less than three
days. Then it rained, and the car stayed in Jefferson two
weeks, during which time we almost had no electric lights at
all; nor, if the livery stable had depended solely on Boon, no
public transportation either. Because Mr Bullock was the man
—the one man, the sole human being nearer than Memphis
who knew how to—who kept the steam-driven electric plant
running; and from the moment the automobile indicated that
it was not going any further, at least today, Mr Bullock and
Boon were inseparable from it like two shadows, a big one
and a little one—the hulking giant smelling of ammonia and
harness oil, and the little grease-covered soot-colored man
with eyes like two bluebird feathers moulted onto a small
lump of coal, who would barely have tipped a hundred
pounds with all his (the city's too) tools in his pockets—the
one motionless, staring at the car with a kind of incredulous
yearning, like a fixed bull; the other dreaming at it, gentle,
tender, his grimed hand gentle as a woman's as he touched it,
stroked it, caressed it, then the next moment plunged to the
hips under the raised bonnet.

Then it rained all that night and was still raining the next
morning. The owner of the car was told, assured—by Mr
Bullock, it appeared; a little strange since nobody had ever
known him to be far enough away from the light plant or the
little shop in his back yard, to have ever used roads enough to
prophesy their condition—that the roads would be impassable
for at least a week, maybe ten days. So the owner went back
to Memphis by train, leaving the automobile to be stored in
what, in anybody else's back yard but Mr Bullock's, would
have been a horse- or cow-barn. Nor could we figure this:
how Mr. Bullock, a meek mild almost inarticulate little man in
a constant condition of unworldly grease-coated dream like
somnambulism—how, by what means, what mesmeric and

hypnotic gifts which until now even he could not have known he possessed, he had persuaded the complete stranger to abandon his expensive toy into Mr Bullock's charge.

But he did, and went back to Memphis; and now when electric trouble occurred in Jefferson, someone had to go by foot or horse or bicycle out to Mr Bullock's home on the edge of town, whereupon Mr Bullock would appear, vague and dreaming and without haste and still wiping his hands, around the corner of his house from his back yard; and by the third day Father finally found out where Boon would be (had been) during the time when he—Boon—should have been in the livery stable. Because on that day Boon himself revealed the secret, spilled the beans, with frantic and raging urgency. He and Mr Bullock had come to what would have been physical battle, had not Mr Bullock—that apparently inexhaustible reservoir of surprises and capabilities—drawn a greasy and soot-grimed but perfectly efficient pistol on Boon.

That was how Boon told it. He and Mr Bullock had been not merely in complete, but instantaneous, accord and understanding in the whole process of getting the automobile into Mr Bullock's hands and the owner of it out of town; so that, Boon naturally thought, Mr Bullock would quickly solve the mystery of how to operate it and they would slip it out after dark and ride in it. But to Boon's shocked and outraged amazement, all Mr Bullock wanted was to find out why it ran. "He's ruined it!" Boon said. "He's done took it all to pieces just to see what was inside! He wont never get it all back together again!"

But he—Bullock—did. He stood, mild and grease-stained and gently dreaming, when two weeks later the owner returned and cranked it up and drove away; and a year later he—Bullock—had made one of his own, engine gears and all, into a rubber-tired buggy; that afternoon, stinking noisily and sedately and not at all fast across the Square, he frightened Colonel Sartoris's matched carriage horses into bolting with the luckily empty surrey and more or less destroying it; by the next night there was formally recorded into the archives of Jefferson a city ordinance against the operation of any mechanically-propelled vehicle inside the corporate limits. So, as president of the older, the senior bank in Yoknapatawpha

County, my grandfather was forced to buy one or else be dictated to by the president of the junior one. You see what I mean? not senior and junior in the social hierarchy of the town, least of all rivals in it, but bankers, dedicated priests in the impenetrable and ineluctable mysteries of Finance; it was as though, despite his lifelong ramrod-stiff and unyielding opposition to, refusal even to acknowledge, the machine age, Grandfather had been vouchsafed somewhere in the beginning a sort of—to him—nightmare vision of our nation's vast and boundless future in which the basic unit of its economy and prosperity would be a small mass-produced cubicle containing four wheels and an engine.

So he bought the automobile, and Boon found his soul's lily maid, the virgin's love of his rough and innocent heart. It was a Winton Flyer. (This was the first one he—we—owned, before the White Steamer which Grandfather traded it for when Grandmother suddenly decided two years later that she couldn't bear the smell of gasoline.) You cranked it by hand while standing in front of it, with no more risk (provided you had remembered to take it out of gear) than a bone or two in your forearm; it had kerosene lamps for night driving and when rain threatened five or six people could readily put up the top and curtains in ten or fifteen minutes, and Grandfather himself equipped it with a kerosene lantern, a new axe and a small coil of barbed wire attached to a light block-and-tackle for driving beyond the town limits. With which equipment it could—and did once, of which I shall speak presently —go as far as Memphis. Also, all of us, grandparents, parents, aunts cousins and children, had special costumes for riding in it, consisting of veils, caps, goggles, gauntlet gloves and long shapeless throat-close neutral-colored garments called dusters, of which I shall also speak later.

By this time Mr Bullock had long since taught Boon to operate his home-made one. They couldn't use the streets of Jefferson of course—in fact never again did it cross the line of Mr Bullock's front fence—but there was an area of open land behind his house which in time Mr Bullock and Boon had beaten down and (relatively) smoothed into a fair motor drome. So by the time Boon and Mr Wordwin, the cashier in Grandfather's bank (he was a bachelor, one of our most prominent clubmen or men-about-town; in ten years he had been a groomsman in thirteen weddings) went to Memphis by train and brought the automobile back (in less than two days this time; a record) Boon was already destined to be the dean of Jefferson motorcar drivers.

Then, as far as Boon's dream was concerned, my grandfather abolished that automobile. He merely bought it, paid what Boon called a sizeable chunk of hard valuable cash for it, looked at it thoroughly and inscrutably once and then eliminated it from circulation. He—Grandfather—couldn't do that completely of course; there was that arrogant decree of Colonel Sartoris's which he—Grandfather—being the senior, could not permit himself to allow to stand, no matter what his own opinion of motor vehicles was. In fact, in this opinion he and Colonel Sartoris were absolutely eye-to-eye; until their deaths (by which time all Yoknapatawpha County's daytime air was odorous with gasoline fumes and its nights, Saturdays especially, filled with the clash of colliding fenders and the squeal of brakes) neither of them would lend a penny to any man they merely suspected was going to buy an automobile with it. Colonel Sartoris's crime was simply in having taken the *pas* of his senior in a move which they both approved—officially banning automobiles from Jefferson even before they got there. You see? Grandfather bought the automobile not as a defiance of Colonel Sartoris's decree. It was simply a calm and deliberately considered abrogation of it, even if only by weekly token.

Even before Colonel Sartoris's decree, Grandfather had had his carriage and horses moved from his back yard to the livery stable, where they were actually more accessible to Grandmother's telephone call than to her shout from an upstairs back window, because somebody always answered the telephone at the livery stable. Which Ned, in the kitchen or stable or wherever he happened to be (or was supposed to happen to be when Grandmother wanted him) didn't always. In fact, he was more often nowhere in range of any voice from Grandmother's house since one of them was his wife's. So now we come to Ned. He was Grandfather's coachman. His wife (the one he had then; he had four) was Delphine, Grandmother's cook. At that time he was "Uncle" Ned only to Mother. I mean, she was the one who insisted that all us children—three of us that is because Alexander couldn't call anybody anything yet—call him Uncle Ned. Nobody else cared whether we did or not, not even Grandmother who was a McCaslin too, and certainly not Ned himself who hadn't earned it even by just living long enough for the fringe of hair embracing his bald skull to begin to turn gray, let alone white (It never did. I mean, his hair: turn white nor even gray. When he died at seventy-four, except for having run through four wives he hadn't changed at all.) and who indeed may not have wanted to be called Uncle; none of these but only Mother, who in the McCaslin sense was not even kin to us, insisted on it. Because he—Ned—was a McCaslin, born in the McCaslin back yard in 1860. He was our family skeleton; we inherited him in turn, with his legend (which had no firmer supporter than Ned himself) that his mother had been the natural daughter of old Lucius Quintus Carothers himself and a Negro slave; never did Ned let any of us forget that he, along with Cousin Isaac, was an actual grandson to old time-honored Lancaster where we moiling Edmondses and Priests, even though three of us—you, me, and my Grandfather— were named for him, were mere diminishing connections and hangers-on.

So when Boon and Mr Wordwin arrived with the car, the carriage house was all ready for it: new-floored and -doored, with a brand new padlock already in Grandfather's hand while he walked slowly around the car, looking at it exactly as he would have examined the plow or reaper or wagon (the client too for that matter) on which a would-be patron of the bank was offering to borrow money. Then he motioned Boon to drive it on into the garage (oh yes, we already knew that was the name of an automobile shed, even in 1904, even in Mississippi).

"What?" Boon said.

"Drive it in," Grandfather said.

"You aint even going to try it?" Boon said.

"No," Grandfather said. Boon drove it into the garage and (just Boon) came out again. There had been astonishment in his face; now there was shock, divination, something like ter- ror. "Has it got a key?" Grandfather said.

"What?" Boon said.

"A catch. A pin. A hook. Something you start it with." Slowly Boon took something from his pocket and put it into Grandfather's hand. "Shut the doors," Grandfather said, and himself walked up and snapped the new padlock through the hasp and put that key into his pocket also. Now Boon was fighting a battle with himself. He was in crisis; the matter was desperate. I—we, Mr Wordwin, Grandmother, Ned, Delphine and everybody else white and black who had happened along the street when the automobile came up—watched him win it, or that initial engagement of pickets anyway.

"I'll come back after dinner, so Miss Sarah" (that was Grandmother) "can try it. About one oclock. I can come sooner if that'll be too late."

"I'll send word to the stable," Grandfather said. Because it was a full-scale action: no mere squabbling of outposts. It was all out, win or lose; logistics came into it, and terrain; feint thrust and parry, deception; but most of all, patience, the long view. It lasted the remaining three days until Saturday. Boon returned to the livery stable; all that afternoon he was never very far from the telephone, though not ostensibly, obviously so, revealing nothing; he even did his work—or so they thought, until Father discovered that Boon on his own authority had deputised Luster to meet with the hack the afternoon train whose arrival (unless it was late) always coincided with the time, moment Grandfather left the bank for the day. But although the battle was still a holding action requiring—nay, demanding—constant alertness and vigilance instead of a drive capable of carrying itself with its own momentum, Boon was still confident, still on top: "Sure. I sent Luster. The way this town is growing, we will need two hacks at them trains any day now, and I been had my eye on Luster for the second driver a good while now. Dont worry; I'm going to watch him."

But no telephone. By six oclock, even Boon admitted that today there would be none. But it was a holding action; nothing was lost yet, and in the dark he could even shift his forces a little. The next morning about ten he—we—entered the bank as though by passing after-thought. "Lemme have the keys," he told Grandfather. "All that Missippi dust and mud, let alone the Tennessee mud and dust already under it. I'll take the hose with me from the stable in case Ned has mislaid yours out of sight somewhere."

Grandfather was looking at Boon, just looking at him with no hurry, like Boon really was the one with the wagon or hay-baler offering to borrow fifteen dollars. "I dont want the inside of the carriage house wet," Grandfather said. But Boon matched him, as detached and even more indifferent, with even more time to spare, use.

"Sure, sure. Remember, the man said the engine ought to be run every day. Not to go nowhere: just to keep the spark plugs and magneto from rusting and costing you twenty, twenty-five dollars for a new one all the way from Memphis or somewhere, maybe all the way up to Detroit at the factory. I dont blame you; all I know is what he told you; I'd just have to take his word too. But then you can afford it. You own the automobile; if you want to rust it up, it aint nobody else's business. A horse would a been different. Even if you hadn't even paid a hundred dollars for a horse you'd a had me out there at daylight lunging him on a rope just to keep his guts working." Because Grandfather was a good banker and Boon knew it: that Grandfather not only knew when to foreclose, but when to compound and cancel too. He reached into his pocket and handed Boon the two keys—the one to the padlock and the thing that turned the automobile on. "Come on," Boon told me, already turning.

While we were still up the street we could already hear Grandmother hollering for Ned from the upstairs back window, though by the time we reached the gate she had quit. As we crossed the back yard to get the hose, Delphine came out the kitchen door. "Where is Ned?" she said. "We been hollering for him all morning. Is he up there at the livery stable?"

"Sure," Boon said. "I'll tell him too. Just dont expect him neither." Ned was there. He and two of my brothers were like a row of stairsteps trying to see through the cracks in the garage door. I reckon Alexander would have been there too except he couldn't walk yet; I dont know why Aunt Callie hadn't thought of it yet. Then Alexander was there; Mother came across the street from our house carrying him. So maybe Aunt Callie was still washing diapers. "Morning, Miss Alison," Boon said. "Morning, Miss Sarah," he said, because now Grandmother was there too, with Delphine behind her. And now there were two more ladies, neighbors, still in their boudoir caps. Because maybe Boon wasn't a banker nor even a very good trader either. But he was proving to be a pretty damned good guerrilla fighter. He went and unlocked the garage door and opened it. Ned was the first one inside.

"Well," Boon said to him, "you been here ever since daylight to peep at it through that crack. What do you think about it?"

"I dont think nothing about it," Ned said. "Boss Priest could a bought the best two-hundred-dollar horse in Yoknapatawpha County for this money."

"There aint any two-hundred-dollar horse in Yoknapatawpha County," Boon said. "If there was, this automobile would buy ten of them. Go be hooking up that hose."

"Go be hooking up that hose, Lucius," Ned said to me; he didn't even look around. He went to the automobile door and opened it. It was the back seat. Front seats didn't have doors in those days; you just walked up and got in. "Come on, Miss Sarah, you and Miss Alison," Ned said. "Delphine can wait with the chillen for the next trip."

"You go hook up that hose like I told you," Boon said. "I got to get it out of here before I can do anything to it."

"You aint gonter tote it out in your hand, is you?" Ned said. "I reckon we can ride that far. I reckon I'm gonter have to drive it so the sooner I starts, the quicker it will be." He said: "Hee hee hee." He said: "Come on, Miss Sarah."

"Will it be all right, Boon?" Grandmother said.

"Yessum, Miss Sarah," Boon said. Grandmother and Mother got in. Before Boon could close the door, Ned was already in the front seat.

"Get out of there," Boon said.

"Go ahead and tend to your business, if you knows how to," Ned said. "I aint gonter touch nothing until I learns how, and just setting here aint gonter learn me. Go on and hook up, or whatever you does to it."

Boon went around to the driver's side and set the switches

and levers, and went to the front and jerked the crank. On the third pull, the engine roared.

"Boon!" Grandmother cried.

"It's all right, Miss Sarah!" Boon hollered above the noise, running back to the guiding wheel.

"I don't care!" Grandmother said. "Get in quick! I'm nervous!" Boon got in and quieted the engine and shifted the levers; a moment, then the automobile moved quietly and slowly backward out of the shed, into the lot, the sunshine, and stopped.

"Hee hee hee," Ned said.

"Be careful, Boon," Grandmother said. I could see her hand gripping the stanchion of the top.

"Yessum," Boon said. The automobile moved again, backward, beginning to turn. Then it moved forward, still turning; Grandmother's hand still gripped the stanchion. Mother's face looked like a girl's. The car went slowly and quietly across the lot until it was facing the gate to the lane, to the outside, to the world, and stopped. And Boon didn't say anything: he just sat there behind the wheel, the engine running smooth and quiet, his head turned just enough for Grandmother to see his face. Oh yes, maybe he wasn't a negotiable paper wizard like Grandfather, and there were folks in Jefferson that would say he wasn't much of anything else either, but for this skirmish anyway he was a skirmish fighter of consummate skill and grace. Grandmother sat for maybe a half a minute. Then she drew a long breath and expelled it.

"No," she said. "We must wait for Mister Priest." Maybe it wasn't a victory, but anyway our side—Boon—had not only discovered the weak point in the enemy's (Grandfather's) front, by supper time that night the enemy himself would discover it too.

Discover in fact that his flank had been turned. The next afternoon (Saturday) after the bank closed, and each succeeding Saturday afternoon, and then when summer came, every afternoon except when rain was actually falling, Grandfather in front beside Boon and the rest of us in rotation—Grandmother, Mother, me and my three brothers and Aunt Callie that nursed us in turn, including Father, and Delphine and our various connections and neighbors and Grandmother's close friends in their ordered rote—in the linen dusters and goggles, would drive through Jefferson and the adjacent countryside; Aunt Callie and Delphine in their turns, but not Ned. He rode in it once: that one minute while it backed slowly out of the garage, and the two minutes while it turned and moved slowly forward across the lot until Grandmother lost her nerve and said No to the open gate and the public world, but not again. By the second Saturday he had realised, accepted—anyway became convinced—that even if Grandfather had ever intended to make him the official operator and custodian of the automobile, he could have approached it only over Boon's dead body. But although he declined to recognise that the automobile existed on the place, he and Grandfather had met on some unspoken gentlemen's ground regarding it: Ned never to speak in scorn or derogation of its ownership and presence, Grandfather never to order Ned to wash and polish it as he used to do the carriage—which Grandfather and Ned both knew Ned would have refused to do, even if Boon had let him: by which Grandfather visited on Ned his only punishment for his apostasy: he refused to give Ned the public chance to refuse to wash the automobile before Boon might have had a public chance to refuse to let him do it.

Because that was when Boon transferred—was transferred by mutual and instantaneous consent—from the day shift at the stable to the night shift. Otherwise, the livery business would have known him no more. That part of our Jefferson leisure class, friends or acquaintances of Father's or maybe just friends of horses, who could have used the stable as a permanent business address—if they had had any business or expected any mail—were less strangers there than Boon. If—when—you, meaning Father, wanted Boon now, you sent me to Grandfather's lot, where he would be washing and polishing the automobile—this, even during those first weeks when it had not left the lot since last Saturday and would not leave it again until the next one, backing it out of the shed and washing it again each morning, with tender absorption, right down to the last spoke and nut, then sitting guard over it while it dried.

"He's going to soak all the paint off of it," Mr Ballott said. "Does Boss know he's running the hose on that automobile four or five hours every day?"

"What if he did?" Father said. "Boon would still sit there in the lot all day looking at it."

"Put him on the night shift," Mr Ballott said. "Then he could do whatever he wants to with his daylight and John Powell could go home and sleep in a bed every night for a change."

"I already have," Father said. "As soon as I can find somebody to go to that lot and tell him."

There was a shuck mattress in the harness room on which until now John Powell or one of the other drivers or hostlers under his command always spent the night, mainly as night-watchmen against fire. Now Father installed a cot and mattress in the office itself, where Boon could get some sleep, which he needed, since now he could spend all day with complete immunity in Grandfather's lot either washing the automobile or just looking at it. Then it was summer, and now every afternoon, as many of us as the back seat would hold in our ordered turns would drive through the Square and into the country; Grandfather had already installed the extraneous emergency gear to be as much and inseparable a part of the automobile's equipment as the engine which moved it.

But always through the Square first. You would have thought that as soon as he bought the automobile, Grandfather would have done what you would have done, having bought the automobile for that end: laid in wait for Colonel Sartoris and his carriage and ambushed, bushwhacked him and really taught him how to pass ordinances restricting others' rights and privileges without consulting his betters first. But Grandfather didn't do this. We finally realised that he wasn't interested in Colonel Sartoris: he was interested in teams, vehicles. Because I told you he was a far-sighted man, a man capable of vision: Grandmother sitting tense and rigid and gripping the top stanchion and not even calling Grandfather Mister Priest now, as she had done as long as we had known her, but calling him by his given name as though she were no kin to him, the horse or team we were approaching reined-back and braced to shy and sometimes even rearing and Grandmother saying, "Lucius! Lucius!" and Grandfather (if a man was driving and there were no women or children in the buggy or wagon) saying quietly to Boon:

"Dont stop. Keep going. But slow now." Or, when a woman had the lines, telling Boon to stop and himself getting out, talking quietly and steadily to the spooked horse until he could get hold of the bit and lead the vehicle past and remove his hat to the ladies in the buggy and come back and get back into the front seat and only then answer Grandmother: "We must get them used to it. Who knows? there may be another automobile in Jefferson in the next ten or fifteen years."

In fact, that home-made dream which Mr Bullock had created single-handed in his back yard two years ago came within an ace of curing Grandfather of a habit which he had had since he was nineteen years old. He chewed tobacco. The first time he turned his head to spit out of the moving automobile, we in the back seat didn't know what was going to happen until it was already too late. Because how could we? None of us had ever ridden in an automobile before farther than (this was the first trip) from the carriage house to the lot gate, let alone one going fifteen miles an hour (And this was something else: when we were going ten miles an hour Boon always said we were doing twenty; at twenty, he always said forty; we discovered a straight stretch about half a mile long a few miles out of town where the automobile would get up to twenty-five, where I heard him tell a group of men on the Square that the automobile made sixty miles an hour; this was before he knew that we knew that the thing on the dashboard which looked like a steam gauge was a speedometer.) so how could we be expected to? Besides, it didn't make any difference to the rest of us; we all had our goggles and dusters and veils and even if the dusters were new, the spots and splashes were just brown spots and splashes and just because they were called dusters was no reason why they should not be called on to face anything else but dust. Maybe it was because Grandmother was sitting on the left side (in those days automobiles operated from the right side, like buggies; only Henry Ford, a man of even longer vision than Grandfather, had divined that the steering wheel would be on the left) directly behind

Grandfather. She said at once to Boon: "Stop the automobile," and sat there, not mad so much as coldly and implaca-
bly outraged and shocked. She was just past fifty then (she
was fifteen when she and Grandfather married) and in all
those fifty years she had no more believed that a man, let
alone her husband, would spit in her face than she could have
believed that Boon for instance would approach a curve in
the road without tooting the horn. She said, to nobody; she
didn't even raise her hand to wipe the spit away:

"Take me home."

"Now, Sarah," Grandfather said. "Now, Sarah." He threw
the chew away and took out the clean handkerchief from his
other pocket, but Grandmother wouldn't even take it. Boon
had already started to get out and go to a house we could see
and get a pan of water and soap and a towel, but Grandmother wouldn't have that either.

"Dont touch me," she said. "Drive on." So we went on,
Grandmother with the long drying brown splash across one
of her goggles and down her cheek even though Mother kept
on offering to spit on her handkerchief and wipe it off. "Let
me alone, Alison," Grandmother said.

But not Mother. She didn't mind tobacco, not in the car.
Maybe that was why. But more and more that summer it
would be just Mother and us and Aunt Callie and one or two
neighbor children in the back seat, Mother's face flushed and
bright and eager, like a girl's. Because she had invented a kind
of shield on a handle like a big fan, light enough for her to
raise in front of us almost as fast as Grandfather could turn his
head. So he could chew now, Mother always alert and ready
with the screen; all of us were quick now in fact, so that almost before the instant when Grandfather knew he was going
to turn his head to the left to spit, the screen had already
come up and all of us in the back seat had leaned to the right
like we were on the same wire, actually doing twenty and
twenty-five miles an hour now because there were already two
more automobiles in Jefferson that summer; it was as though
the automobiles themselves were beating the roads smooth
long before the money they represented would begin to compel smoother roads.

"Twenty-five years from now there wont be a road in the

county you cant drive an automobile on in any weather," Grandfather said.

"Wont that cost a lot of money, Papa?" Mother said.

"It will cost a great deal of money," Grandfather said. "The road-builders will issue bonds. The bank will buy them."

"Our bank?" Mother said. "Buy bonds for automobiles?"

"Yes," Grandfather said. "We will buy them."

"But what about us?—I mean, Maury."

"He will still be in the livery business," Grandfather said. "He will just have a new name for it. Priest's Garage maybe, or the Priest Motor Company. People will pay any price for motion. They will even work for it. Look at bicycles. Look at Boon. We dont know why."

Then the next May came and my other grandfather, Mother's father, died in Bay St Louis.

Three

I T WAS Saturday again. The next one in fact; Ludus was going to start getting paid again every Saturday night; maybe
he had even stopped borrowing mules. It was barely eight
oclock; I wasn't even half way around the Square with the
freight bills and my canvas sack to carry the money in, just
finishing in the Farmers Supply when Boon came in, fast, too
quick for him. I should have suspected at once. No, I should
have known at once, having known Boon all my life, let alone
having watched him for a year now with that automobile. He
was already reaching for the money-sack, taking it right out of
my hand before I could even close my fist. "Leave it," he said.
"Come on."

"Here," I said. "I've barely started."

"I said leave it. Shake it up. Hurry. They've got to make
Twenty-three," he said, already turning. He had completely
ignored the unpaid freight bills themselves. They were just
paper; the railroad company had plenty more of them. But
the sack contained money.

"Who's got to make Twenty-three?" I said. Number
Twenty-three was the southbound morning train. Oh yes,
Jefferson had passenger trains then, enough of them so they
had to number them to keep them separate.

"Goddammit," Boon said, "how can I break it gentle to
you when you wont even listen? Your grandpa died last night.
We got to hurry."

"He didn't!" I said, cried. "He was on the front gallery this
morning when we passed." He was. Father and I both saw
him, either reading the paper or just standing or sitting there
like he was every morning, waiting for time to go to the bank.

"Who the hell's talking about Boss?" Boon said. "I said
your other grandpa, your ma's papa down there at Jackson or
Mobile or wherever it is."

"Oh," I said. "Dont you even know the difference between
Bay St Louis and Mobile?" Because it was all right now. This
was different. Bay St Louis was three hundred miles; I hardly
knew Grandfather Lessep except twice at Christmas in Jefferson

759

and three times we went down there in the summer. Also, he had been sick a long time; we—Mother and us—had been there last summer actually to see him enter what was to be his last bed even if we didn't know it then (Mother and Aunt Callie, because your great-uncle Alexander had arrived a month before, had been down last winter when they thought he was going to die). I say "if", meaning Mother; to a child, when an old person becomes sick he or she has already quitted living; the actual death merely clears the atmosphere so to speak, incapable of removing anything which was already gone.

"All right, all right," Boon said. "Just come on. Jackson, Mobile, New Orleans—all I know is, it's down that way somewhere, and wherever it is, they still got to catch that train." And that—the name *New Orleans*, not dropped so much as escaped into that context—should have told me all, revealed the whole of Boon's outrageous dream, intent, determination; his later elaborate machinations to seduce me to it should merely have corroborated. But maybe I was still recovering from shock; also, at that moment I didn't have as many facts as Boon did. So we just went on, fast, I trotting to keep up, the shortest way across the Square, until we reached home.

Where was much commotion. It was barely two hours until the train and Mother was far too busy to take time to mourn or grieve: merely pale-faced, intent, efficient. Because I now learned what Boon had already told me twice: that Grandfather and Grandmother were going to bury Grandfather Lessep also. He and Grandfather had been roommates, in the same class at the University; they had been groomsmen in each other's wedding, which possibly had a little something to do with why Mother and Father chose one another out of all the earth to look into her eyes forever more (I understand you call it going steady), and Grandmother and Grandmother Lessep lived far enough apart to continue to be civil and even pleasant to the other mother of an only child. Besides that, people took funerals seriously in those days. Not death: death was our constant familiar: no family but whose annals were dotted with headstones whose memorialees had been too brief in tenure to bear a name even—unless of course the mother slept there too in that one grave, which

happened more often than you would like to think. Not to
mention the husbands and uncles and aunts in the twenties
and thirties and forties, and the grandparents and childless
great-uncles and -aunts who died at home then, in the same
rooms and beds they were born in, instead of in cubicled eu-
phonisms with names pertaining to sunset. But the funerals,
the ritual ceremonial of interment, with tenuous yet steel-
strong threads capable of extending even further and bearing
even more weight than the distance between Jefferson and
the Gulf of Mexico.

So Grandfather and Grandmother were also going to the
funeral. Which meant only incidentally that, lacking any other
close kinfolks in town, we—me and my three brothers and
Aunt Callie—would have to be sent out to Cousin Zachary
Edmonds' farm seventeen miles away to stay until Father and
Mother got back; it meant only incidentally that Father and
Mother would be gone four days. What it actually meant was
that Grandfather and Grandmother would not even come
back after four days. Because Grandfather never left Jefferson
at all, even to go only to Memphis, without spending two or
three days in New Orleans, which he loved, either going or
coming; and this time they might quite possibly take Mother
and Father with them. It meant in fact what Boon had already
told me twice by exuberant and still unbelieving inadvertence:
that the owner of that automobile, and everyone else having
or even assuming authority over it, would be three hundred
miles from it for anywhere from four days to a week. So all his
clumsy machinations to seduce and corrupt me were only corroboration. They were not even cumshaw, lagniappe. He
could have taken the car alone, and doubtless would if I had
been incorruptible, even knowing that someday he must
bring it back or come back himself in order to face lesser music than he would if—when—Grandfather's police caught up
with him. Because come back he must. Where else could he
go, who knew nowhere else, to whom the words, names—
Jefferson, McCaslin, De Spain, Compson—were not just
home but father and mother both? But some frayed ragtag of
judgment, some embryo gleam of simple yet-virgin discretion
and common sense, persuaded him at least to try me first, to
have me by as a kind of hostage. And he didn't need to try,

test me first. When grown people speak of the innocence of children, they dont really know what they mean. Pressed, they will go a step further and say, Well, ignorance then. The child is neither. There is no crime which a boy of eleven had not envisaged long ago. His only innocence is, he may not yet be old enough to desire the fruits of it, which is not innocence but appetite; his ignorance is, he does not know how to commit it, which is not ignorance but size.

But Boon didn't know this. He must seduce me. And he had so little time: only from the time the train left until dark. He could have started cold, from scratch, tomorrow or next day or any day up to and including Wednesday. But today, now, was his best, with the car visible to all Jefferson, already in motion, already involved in the condition of departure; it was as if the gods themselves had offered him these scot-free hours between eleven-two and sunset, he to scorn, ignore them at his peril. The car came up, Grandfather and Grandmother already in it, with the shoebox of fried chicken and devilled eggs and cake for dinner since there wouldn't be a dining car until they changed to the Limited at the junction at one oclock and Grandmother and Mother both knew Grandfather and Father well enough by this time to know they were not going to wait until one oclock to eat dinner, no matter who was dead. No: Grandmother too, if the bereaved had been anybody but Mother. No, that's wrong too; Grandmother had a wider range than her son's wife; maybe all Mother would have needed was to be a female. It's not men who cope with death; they resist, try to fight back and get their brains trampled out in consequence, where women just flank it, envelop it in one soft and instantaneous confederation of unresistance like cotton batting or cobwebs, already de-stingered and harmless, not merely reduced to size and usable but even useful like a penniless bachelor or spinster connection always available to fill an empty space or conduct an extra guest down to dinner. Their grips were already tied onto the fenders and Son Thomas had already brought Mother's and Father's out to the street and now we all followed, Mother in her black veil and Father with his black armband, us following with Aunt Callie carrying Alexander. "Goodbye," Mother said, "goodbye," kissing us veil and all, smelling like she always did but with something black in the smell too, like the thin black veil which really hid nothing, as if more than just a mechanical electric message over the copper wire had come that three hundred miles up from Bay St Louis; oh yes, I could smell it when she kissed me, saying, "You're the big boy, the man now. You must help Aunt Callie with the others, so they wont worry Cousin Louisa," already getting quick into the automobile beside Grandmother, when Boon said,

"I'll have to fill the tank for the trip out to McCaslin after dinner. I thought Lucius could come along now and help me on the way back from the depot." You see, how easy it was going to be. It was too easy, making you a little ashamed. It was as if the very cards of virtue and rectitude were stacked against Grandfather and Grandmother and Mother and Father. All right then: against me too. Even the fact that automobiles were only two or three years old in Jefferson abetted Boon—all right, us. Mr Rouncewell, the oil company agent who supplied all the stores in Yoknapatawpha County from his tanks on the side track at the depot, for the last two years had also had a special tank of gasoline, with a pump and a Negro to pump it; all Boon or anyone else who wanted gasoline had to do was, simply drive up and stop and get out and the Negro would lift off the front seat and measure the tank with his special notched stick and fill the tank and collect the money or (if Mr Rouncewell himself wasn't there) let you yourself write down your name and how many gallons in a greasy ledger. But, although Grandfather had owned the car almost a year now, not one of them—Grandfather or Grandmother or Father or Mother—had either the knowledge about how cars operated or the temerity (or maybe it was just the curiosity) to question or challenge Boon.

So he and I stood on the platform; Mother waved to us through the window as the train drew away. Now it was his move. He would have to say something, have to begin. He had managed to get the decks cleared and me in his power, at least until Aunt Callie began to wonder where I was to eat my dinner. I mean, Boon didn't know he didn't have to say anything, other than perhaps to tell me where we were going, and even that—the destination—didn't matter. He had learned nothing since about human beings, and apparently had even forgot what he once must have known about boys.

And now Boon himself didn't know how to begin. He had prayed for luck, and immediately, by return post you might say, had been vouchsafed more than he knew what to do with. They have told you before this probably that Fortune is a fickle jade, who never withholds but gives, either good or bad: more of the former than you ever believe (perhaps with justice) that you deserve; more of the latter than you can handle. So with Boon. So all he said was, "Well."

Nor did I help him; I took that revenge. All right, revenge on whom? Not on Boon of course: on me, my shame; perhaps on Father and Mother who had abandoned me to the shame; perhaps on Grandfather whose automobile had made the shame available—who knows? perhaps on Mr Bullock himself—that rapt and divinely-stricken somnambulist who had started the whole thing two innocent years ago. But I did feel sorry for Boon because he had so little time. It was after eleven now; Aunt Callie would be expecting me back in a matter of minutes, not because she knew it couldn't take more than ten minutes to drive back home after she heard Twenty-three whistle for the lower crossing, but because she would already be in a driving impatience to get us all fed and on the way to McCaslin; she had been born in the country and still preferred it. Boon wasn't looking at me. He very carefully wasn't looking at me. "Three hundred miles," he said. "Good thing somebody invented trains. If they'd a had to go by mule wagon like folks used to, they couldn't even get there in ten days, let alone back in ten days too."

"Father said four days," I said.

"That's right," Boon said. "So he did. Maybe we got four days to get back to the house in, but that still dont give us forever." We went back to the car and got in it. But he didn't start it. "Maybe when Boss gets back in te—four days he'll let me learn you to run this thing. You're big enough. Besides, you already know how. Have you ever thought about that?"

"No," I said. "Because he aint going to let me."

"Well, you dont need to rush at it. You got four days for him to change his mind in. Though my guess is nearer ten." Still he didn't move to start the car. "Ten days," he said.

"How far do you reckon this automobile could travel in ten days?"

"Father said four," I said.

"All right," he said. "How far in four days?"

"I aint going to know that either," I said. "Because aint any body around here going to find out to tell me."

"All right," he said. He started the car suddenly and backed and turned it, already going fast, neither toward the Square nor toward Mr Rouncewell's gasoline pump.

"I thought we had to get gasoline," I said.

We were going fast. "I changed my mind," Boon said. "I'll tend to that just before we leave for McCaslin after dinner. Then so much of it wont evaporate away just standing around." We were in a lane now, going fast between Negro cabins and vegetable patches and chicken yards, with chickens and mongrel dogs leaping frantically from the dust just in time, out of the lane and into a vacant field, a waste place marked faintly with tire tracks but no hooves; and now I recognised it: Mr Bullock's home-made motor drome where Colonel Sartoris's law had driven him two years ago and where he had taught Boon to operate an automobile. And still I didn't understand until Boon wrenched the car to a stop and said, "Move over here."

So I was late for dinner after all; Aunt Callie was already standing on the front gallery, carrying Alexander and already yelling at Boon and me even before he stopped the car to let me out. Because Boon licked me in fair battle after all; evidently he hadn't quite forgot all he remembered from his own youth about boys. I know better now of course, and I even knew better then: that Boon's and my fall were not only instantaneous but simultaneous too: back at the identical instant when Mother got the message that Grandfather Lessep was dead. But that's what I would have liked to believe: that Boon simply licked me. Anyway, that's what I told myself at the time: that, secure behind that inviolable and inescapable rectitude concomitant with the name I bore, patterned on the knightly shapes of my male ancestors as bequeathed—nay, compelled—to me by my father's word-of-mouth, further bolstered and made vulnerable to shame by my mother's doting conviction, I had been merely testing Boon; not trying

my own virtue but simply testing Boon's capacity to undermine it; and, in my innocence trusting too much in the armor
and shield of innocence; expected, demanded, assumed more
than that frail Milanese was capable of withstanding. I say
"frail Milanese" not advisedly but explicitly: having noticed in
my time how quite often the advocates and even the practitioners of virtue evidently have grave doubts of their own
regarding the impregnability of virtue as a shield, putting
their faith and trust not in virtue but rather in the god or
goddess whose charge virtue is; by-passing virtue as it were in
allegiance to the Over-goddess herself, in return for which
the goddess will either divert temptation away or anyhow
intercede between them. Which explains a lot, having likewise noticed in my time that the goddess in charge of virtue
seems to be the same one in charge of luck, if not of folly
also.

So Boon beat me in fair battle, using, as a gentleman
should and would, gloves. When he stopped the car and said,
"Move over," I thought I knew what he intended. We had
done this before at four or five convenient and discreet times
in Grandfather's lot, me sitting on Boon's lap holding the
wheel and steering while he let the automobile move slowly
in low gear across the lot. So I was ready for him. I was already *en garde* and had even begun the counter thrust, opening my mouth to say *It's too hot to sit on anybody today. Besides
we better get on back home* when I saw that he was already out
of the car on his side while he was still speaking, standing
there with one hand on the wheel and the engine still running. For another second or two I still couldn't believe it.
"Hurry up," he said. "Any minute now Callie will come running out of that lane toting that baby under one arm and already yelling."

So I moved under the wheel, and with Boon beside me,
over me, across me, one hand on mine to shift the gears, one
hand on mine to regulate the throttle, we moved back and
forth across that vacant sun-glared waste, forward a while,
backward a while, intent, timeless, Boon as much as I, immersed, rapt, steadying me (he was playing for such stakes,
you see), out of time, beyond it, invulnerable to time until
the courthouse clock striking noon a half mile away restored

us, hurled us back into the impending hard world of finagle
and deception.

"All right," Boon said, "quick," not even waiting but lifting me bodily across him as he slid under the wheel, the car
already rushing back across the field toward home, we talking
man-to-man now, mutual in crime, confederate of course but
not coeval yet because of my innocence; I already beginning
to say *What do I do now? You'll have to tell me,* when once
again Boon spoke first and made us equal too: "Have you figgered how to do it? We aint got much time."

"All right," I said. "Go on. Get on back to the house before Aunt Callie starts hollering." So you see what I mean
about Virtue? You have heard—or anyway you will—people
talk about evil times or an evil generation. There are no such
things. No epoch of history nor generation of human beings
either ever was or is or will be big enough to hold the un-
virtue of any given moment, anymore than they could contain
all the air of any given moment; all they can do is hope to be
as little soiled as possible during their passage through it.
Because what pity that Virtue does not—possibly cannot—
take care of its own as Non-virtue does. Probably it cannot:
Who to the dedicated to and the practitioners of Virtue, offer
in reward only cold and odorless and tasteless virtue: as compared not only to the bright rewards of sin and pleasure but
to the ever-watchful unflagging omniprescient skill—that incredible matchless capacity for invention and imagination—
with which even the tottering footsteps of infancy are steadily
and firmly guided into the primrose path. Because oh yes, I
had matured terrifyingly since that clock struck two minutes
ago. It has been my observation that, except in a few scattered cases of what might be called malevolent hyper-prema-
turity, children, like poets, lie rather for pleasure than profit.
Or so I thought I had until then, with a few negligible ex-
ceptions involving simple self-defense against creatures (my
parents) bigger and stronger than me. But not anymore. Or
anyway, not now. I was as bent as Boon, and—during the
next step anyway—even more culpable. Because (I realised;
no: knew; it was obvious; Boon himself admitted it in so
many words) I was smarter than Boon. I realised, felt suddenly that same exultant fever-flash which Faustus himself

must have experienced: that of we two doomed and irrevocable, I was the leader, I was the boss, the master.

Aunt Callie was already standing on the front gallery, carrying Alexander and yelling.

"Dry up," I said. "Aint dinner ready? The automobile broke down. Boon fixed it. We never had time to get the gasoline and now I have to eat in a hurry and go back and help him fill the tank." I went back to the dining room. Dinner was already on the table. Lessep and Maury were already eating. Aunt Callie had already dressed them (she had dressed them to go seventeen miles out to Cousin Zack's to spend four days as if they were going to Memphis; I dont know why, unless it was because she didn't have anything else to do between the time Mother and Father left and dinner. Because Maury and Alexander would both have to take a nap before we could leave) but by the front of his blouse, she would have to wash Maury off and dress him again.

Even then, I finished before they did and went back (Aunt Callie was still yelling, not loud in the house of course. But what could she do, single-handed—and a Negro—against Non-virtue?) across the street to Grandfather's. Ned probably left for town as soon as the automobile drove off. But he would probably come back for his dinner. He had. We stood in the back yard. He blinked at me. Quite often, most of the time in fact, his eyes had a reddish look, like a fox's. "Why dont you aim to stay out there?" he said.

"I promised some fellows we would slip off tomorrow and try a new fishing hole one of them knows about."

Ned blinked at me. "So you aims to ride out to McCaslin with Boon Hogganbeck and then turn right around and come back with him. Only you got to have something to tell Miss Louisa so she'll let you come back and so you needs me to front for you."

"No," I said. "I dont need anything from you. I'm just telling you so you'll know where I am and they wont blame you. I aint even going to bother you. I'm going to stay with Cousin Ike." Before the rest of them came, I mean my brothers, when Mother and Father were out late at night and Grandfather and Grandmother were gone too, I used to stay with Ned and Delphine. Sometimes I would sleep in their house all night, just for fun. I could have done that now, if it would have worked. But Cousin Ike lived alone in a single room over his hardware store. Even if Ned (or somebody else concerned) asked him point blank if I was with him Saturday night, it would be at least Monday by then, and I had already decided quick and hard not to think about Monday. You see, if only people didn't refuse quick and hard to think about next Monday, Virtue wouldn't have such a hard and thankless time of it.

"I see," Ned said. "You aint needing nothing from me. You just being big-hearted to save me bother and worry over you. Save everybody bother and worry that comes around wanting to know why you aint out at McCaslin where your paw told you to be." He blinked at me. "Hee hee hee," he said.

"All right," I said. "Tell Father I went fishing on Sunday while they were gone. See if I care."

"I aint fixing to tell nobody nothing about you," he said. "You aint none of my business. You's Callie's business unto your maw gets back. Unlessen you gonter transfer to Mr Ike's business for tonight, like you said." He blinked at me. "When is Boon Hogganbeck coming for yawl?"

"Pretty soon now," I said. "And you better not let Father or Boss hear you calling him Boon Hogganbeck."

"I calls him Mister in plenty of time for him to earn it," Ned said. "Let alone deserve it." He said, "Hee hee hee."

You see? I was doing the best I could. My trouble was, the tools I had to use. The innocence and the ignorance: I not only didn't have strength and knowledge, I didn't even have time enough. When the fates, gods—all right, Non-virtue— give you opportunities, the least they can do is give you room. But at least Cousin Ike was easy to find on Saturday. "You bet," he said. "Come and stay with me tonight. Maybe we'll go fishing tomorrow—just dont tell your father."

"No sir," I said. "Not stay with you tonight. I'm going to stay with Ned and Delphine, like I always do. I just wanted you to know, since Mother's not here where I can tell her. I mean, ask her." You see: doing the best I could with what I had, knew. Not that I was losing faith in ultimate success: it simply seemed to me that Non-virtue was wasting in merely testing me time which was urgent and even desperate for greater ends. I went back home, not running; Jefferson must not see me running: but as fast as I could without it. You see, I did not dare trust Boon unbacked in Aunt Callie's hands.

I was in time. In fact, it was Boon and the automobile who were late. Aunt Callie even had Maury and Alexander re-dressed again; if they had had naps since dinner, it was the shortest fastest sleep on record in our house. Also, Ned was there, where he had no business being. No, that's not right. I mean, his being there was completely wrong: not being at our house, he was often there, but being anywhere where he could be doing something useful with Grandfather and Grandmother out of town. Because he was carrying the bag-gage out—the wicker basket of Alexander's diapers and other personal odds and ends, the grips containing mine and Lessep's and Maury's clothes for four days, and Aunt Callie's cloth-wrapped bundle, lumping them without order at the gate and telling Aunt Callie: "You might just as well set down and rest your feet. Boon Hogganbeck's done broke that thing and is somewhere trying to fix it. If you really wants to get out to McCaslin before supper time, telefoam Mr Ballott at the stable to send Son Thomas with the carriage and I'll drive you out there like folks ought to travel."

And after a while it began to look like Ned was right. Half past one came (which time Alexander and Maury could have spent sleeping) and no Boon; then Maury and Alexander could have slept another half an hour on top of that; Ned had said "I tole you so" so many times by now that Aunt Callie had quit yelling about Boon and yelled at Ned himself until he went and sat in the scuppernong arbor; she was just about to send me to look for Boon and the automobile when he drove up. When I saw him, I was terrified. He had changed his clothes. I mean, he had shaved and he had on not merely a white shirt but a clean one, with a collar and necktie; with-out doubt when he got out of the car to load us in he would have a coat over his arm and the first thing Aunt Callie would see when she reached the car would be his grip on the floor. Horror, but rage too (not at Boon: I discovered, realised that at once) at myself, who should have known, anticipated this, having known (I realised this too now) all my life that who dealt with Boon dealt with a child and had not merely to cope with but even anticipate its unpredictable vagaries; not the folly of Boon's lack of the simplest rudiments of common sense, but the shame of my failure to anticipate, assume he would lack them, saying, crying to Whoever it is you indict in such crises: *Dont You realise I aint but eleven years old? How do You expect me to do all this at just eleven years old? Dont You see You are putting on me more than I can handle?* But in the next second, rage at Boon too: not that his stupidity had now wrecked for good our motor trip to Memphis (that's right, Memphis as our destination has never been mentioned, either to you or between Boon and me. Why should it have been? Where else did we have to go? Indeed, where else could any-one in north Mississippi want to go? Some aged and finished creature on his or her deathbed might contemplate or fear a more distant destination, but they were not Boon and me). In fact, at this moment I wished I had never heard of Memphis or Boon or automobiles either; I was on Colonel Sartoris's side now, to have abolished Mr Bullock and his dream both from the face of the earth at the instant of its inception. My rage at Boon was for having destroyed, cast down with that one childish blow like the blind kick of an infant's foot, the precarious and frantic ramshackle of my lies and false promises and false swearing; revealing the clay-footed sham for which I had bartered—nay, damned—my soul; that, or maybe the ex-posing of the true shoddy worthlessness of the soul I had been vain enough to assume the devil would pay anything for: like losing your maidenhead through some shabby inattentive mischance, such as not watching where you were going, in-nocent even of pleasure, let alone of sin. Then even the rage was gone. Nothing remained, nothing. I didn't want to go anywhere, be anywhere. I mean, I didn't want to be *is* any-where. If I had to be something, I wanted it to be *was.* I said, and I believed it (I know I believed it because I have said it a thousand times since and I still believe it and I hope to say it a thousand times more in my life and I defy anyone to say I will not believe it) *I will never lie again. It's too much trouble. It's too much like trying to prop a feather upright in a saucer of sand. There's never any end to it. You never get any rest. You're never finished. You never even use up the sand so that you can quit trying.*

Only, nothing happened. Boon got out, without any coat.
Ned was already loading our grips and baskets and bundles
into the car. He said grimly: "Hee hee hee." He said, "Come
on, get started so you can break down and still have time to
fix it and get back to town before dark." So he was talking to
Boon now. He said, "Are you coming back to town before
you leaves?"

Then Boon said: "Leave for where?"

"Leave to eat supper," Ned said. "Where does anybody
with good sense leave to do at sundown?"

"Oh," Boon said. "You worry about your supper. That's
the only supper you got to worry about eating."

We got in and started, me in front with Boon and the rest
of them in the back. We crossed the Square crowded with
Saturday afternoon, and then we were out of town. But there
we were. I mean, we were no forrader. We would come
presently to the fork of the road which led to Cousin Zack's
and we would even be going in the wrong direction. And
even if it had been the right direction, we still would not be
free; as long as we still had Aunt Callie and Lessep and Maury
and Alexander in the back seat, we were only free of Ned being where nobody in the world had expected him to be, saying Hee hee hee and Are you coming back to town before.
Boon had never once looked at me, nor I at him. Nor had he
spoken to me either; possibly he sensed that he had frightened me with his clean shirt and collar and necktie and the
shave in the middle of the day and all the rest of the give-
away aura of travel, departure, separation, severance; sensed
that I was not only frightened but angry that I had been vulnerable to fright; going on, the sunny early afternoon road
stretching on ahead for the seventeen miles during which
something would have to be decided, agreed upon; on across
the bright May land, our dust spurting and coiling behind us
unless we had to slow down for a bridge or a sandy stretch
which required the low gears; the seventeen miles which
would not last forever even though there were seventeen of
them, the mileposts diminishing much too rapidly while
something had to be done, decided sooner and sooner and
nearer and nearer and I didn't know what yet; or maybe just
something said, a voice, noise, a human sound, since no

matter what bitter forfeit Non-virtue may afterward wrench
and wring from you, loneliness, solitude, silence should not
be part of it. But at least Boon tried. Or maybe with him it
was just the silence too and any un-silence were better, no
matter how foolish nor long-ago pre-doomed. No, it was
more than that; we had less than half the distance left now
and something had to be done, started, fused-off:

"The roads are sure fine now, everywhere, even further
than Yoknapatawpha County. A man couldn't want better
roads for a long trip like a automobile funeral or something
like they are now. How far do you reckon this car could go
between now and sundown?" You see? addressed to nobody,
like the drowning man thrusting one desperate hand above
the surface hoping there might be a straw there. He found
none:

"I dont know," Aunt Callie said from the back seat, holding Alexander who had been asleep since we left town and
didn't deserve a car ride of one mile, let alone seventeen.
"And you aint gonter know neither, unlessen you studies it
out setting in that front seat locked up in that shed in Boss's
back yard tonight."

Now we were almost there. "So you want," Boon said, out
of the side of his mouth, just exactly loud enough for me to
hear, aimed exactly at my right ear like a gun or an arrow or
maybe a handful of sand at a closed window.

"Shut up," I said, exactly like him. The simple and cowardly thing would be to tell him suddenly to stop and as he
did so, leap from the car, already running, presenting to Aunt
Callie the split-second alternative either to abandon Alexander to Boon and try to run me down in the bushes, or stick
with Alexander and pursue me with simple yelling. I mean,
have Boon drive on and leave them at the house and I to
spring out from the roadside and leap back aboard as he
passed going back to town or any direction opposite from all
who would miss me and have authority over me; the cowardly
way, so why didn't I take it, who was already a lost liar, already damned by deceit, so why didn't I go the whole hog
and be a coward too? be irrevocable and irremediable like
Faustus became? glory in baseness, make, compel my new
Master to respect me for my completeness even if he did

scorn my size? Only I didn't. It wouldn't have worked, one of us anyway had to be practical; granted that Boon and I would be well on our way before Cousin Louisa could send someone to the field where Cousin Zack would be at three oclock in the afternoon during planting time, and granted that Cousin Zack couldn't possibly have overtaken us on his saddle horse: he wouldn't have tried to: he would have ridden straight to town and after one minute each with Ned and Cousin Ike, he would have known exactly what to do and would have done it, using the telephone and the police.

We were there. I got out and opened the gate (the same posts of old Lucius Quintus Carothers's time; your present Cousin Carothers has a cattle-guard in it now so automobiles can cross, not owning hooves) and we went on up the locust drive toward the house (it is still there: the two-room mud-chinked log half domicile and half fort which old Lucius came with his slaves and foxhounds across the mountains from Carolina in 1813 and built; it is still there somewhere, hidden beneath the clapboards and Greek revival and steamboat scrollwork which the women the successive Edmondses marry have added to it).

Cousin Louisa and everybody else on the place had already heard us approaching and (except probably the ones Cousin Zack could actually see from his horse) were all on the front gallery and steps and the yard when we drove up and stopped.

"All right," Boon said, again out of the side of his mouth, "do you want." Because, as you say nowadays, this was it; no time anymore, let alone privacy, to get some—any—inkling of what he now must desperately know. Because we—he and I—were so new at this, you see. We were worse than amateurs: innocents, complete innocents at stealing automobiles even though neither of us would have called it stealing since we intended to return it unharmed; and even, if people, the world (Jefferson anyway) had just let us alone, unmissed. Even if I could have answered him if he had asked. Because it was even worse for me than for him; both of us were desperate but mine was the more urgent desperation since I had to do something, and quick, in a matter of seconds now, while all he had to do was sit in the car with at most his fingers crossed. I didn't know what to do now; I had already told more lies than I had believed myself capable of inventing, and had had them believed or at least accepted with a consistency which had left me spellbound if not already appalled; I was in the position of the old Darkey who said, "Here I is, Lord. If You wants me saved, You got the best chance You ever seen standing right here looking at You." I had shot my bow, Boon's too. If Non-virtue still wanted either of us, it was now her move.

Which she did. She was dressed as Cousin Zachary Edmonds. He came out the front door at that moment and at the same moment I saw that a Negro boy in the yard was holding the reins of his saddle horse. You see what I mean? Zachary Edmonds, whom Jefferson never saw on a week-day between the first ground-breaking in March and laying-by in July, had been in town this morning (something urgent about the grist mill) and had stopped in Cousin Ike's store barely minutes after I had done so myself; which, dove-tailed neatly and exactly with the hour and more Non-virtue had required to shave Boon and change his shirt, had given Cousin Zack the exact time necessary to ride home and be getting off his horse at his doorstep when they heard us coming. He said— to me: "What are you doing out here? Ike told me you were going to stay in town tonight and he is going to take you fishing tomorrow."

So of course Aunt Callie began yelling then so I didn't need to say anything at all even if I had known anything to say. "Fishing?" she hollered. "On Sunday? If his paw could hear that, he would jump off that train this minute without even waiting to telegraph! His maw too! Miss Alison aint told him to stay in town with no Mister Ike nor nobody else! She told him to come on out here with me and these other chillen and if he dont behave his-self, Mister Zack would make him!"

"All right, all right," Cousin Zack said. "Stop yelling a minute; I cant hear him. Maybe he's changed his mind. Have you?"

"Sir?" I said. "Yes sir. I mean, no sir."

"Well, which? Are you going to stay out here, or are you going back with Boon?"

"Yes sir," I said. "I'm going back. Cousin Ike told me to

ask you if I could." And Aunt Callie yelled again (she had never really stopped except for maybe that one long breath when Cousin Zack told her to) but that was all: she still yelling and Cousin Zack saying,

"Stop it, stop it, stop it. I cant hear my ears. If Ike dont bring him out tomorrow, I'll send in for him Monday." I went back to the car; Boon had the engine already running.

"Well I'll be damned," he said, not loud but with complete respect, even awe a little.

"Come on," I said. "Get away from here." We went on, smoothly but quick, faster, back down the drive toward the gate.

"Maybe we're wasting something, just spending it on a automobile trip," he said. "Maybe I ought to use you for something that's got money in it."

"Just get on," I said. Because how could I tell him, how say it to him? *I'm sick and tired of lying, of having to lie.* Because I knew, realised now that it had only begun; there would be no end to it, not only no end to the lies I would continue to have to tell merely to protect the ones I had already told, but that I would never be free of the old worn-out ones I had already used and exhausted.

We went back to town. We went fast this time; if there was scenery now, nobody in that automobile used any of it. It was going on five oclock now. Boon spoke, tense and urgent but quite composed: "We got to let it cool a while. They saw me drive out of town taking you folks out to McCaslin; they'll see me come back with just you and me alone; they'll expect to see me put the car back in Boss's carriage house. Then they got to see me and you, but separate, just walking around like wasn't nothing going on." But how could I say that either? *No. Let's go now. If I've got to tell more lies, at least let it be to strangers.* He was still talking: "—car. What was that he said about were we coming back through town before we left?"

"What? Who said?"

"Ned. Back there just before we left town."

"I dont remember," I said. "What about the car?"

"Where to leave it. While I take a santer around the Square and you go home and get a clean shirt or whatever you'll need. I had to unload all the stuff out at McCaslin, remember.

Yours too. I mean, just in case some meddling busybody is hanging around just on the happen chance." We both knew who he meant.

"Why cant you lock it in the carriage house?"

"I aint got the key," he said. "All I got is the lock. Boss took the key away from me this morning and unlocked the lock and give the key to Mr Ballott to keep until he gets back. I'm supposed to run the car in as soon as I get back from McCaslin and lock the lock shut and Boss will telegraph Mr Ballott what train to unlock the door so I can meet them."

"Then we'll just have to risk it," I said.

"Yes, we'll have to risk it. Maybe with Boss and Miss Sarah gone, even Delphine aint going to see him again until Monday morning." So we risked it. Boon drove into the carriage house and got his grip and coat down from where he had hidden them in the loft and reached up again and dragged down a folded tarpaulin and put his grip and coat in on the floor of the back seat. The gasoline can was all ready: a brand new five-gallon can which Grandfather had had the tinsmith who made the tool-box more or less rebuild until it was smell-tight, since Grandmother didn't like the smell of gasoline, which we had never used yet because the automobile had never been this far before; the funnel and the chamois strainer were already in the tool-box with the tire tools and jack and wrenches that came with the car, and the lantern and axe and shovel and coil of barbed wire and the block-and-tackle which Grandfather had added, along with the tin bucket to fill the radiator when we passed creeks or barrow-pits. He put the can (it was full; maybe that was what took him the extra time before he came for us) in the back and opened the tarpaulin, not spreading it but tumbling it into the back until everything was concealed to just look like a jumbled mass of tarpaulin. "We'll shove yours under the same way," he said. "Then it wont look like nothing but a wad of tarpollyon somebody was too lazy to fold up. What you better do is go home and get your clean shirt and come straight back here and wait. I wont be long: just santer around the Square in case Ike wants to start asking questions too. Then we'll be gone."

We closed the door. Boon started to hang the open padlock

back in the staple. "No," I said; I couldn't even have said why, so fast I had progressed in evil. "Put it in your pocket."

But he knew why; he told me. "You damn right," he said. "We done gone through too much to have somebody happen-chance by and snap it shut because they thought I forgot to."

I went home. It was just across the street. A filling station is there now, and what was Grandfather's house is now chopped into apartments, precarious of tenure. The house was empty, unlocked of course since nobody in Jefferson locked mere homes in those innocent days. It was only a little after five, nowhere near sundown, yet the day was finished, done for; the empty silent house was not vacant at all but filled with presences like held breath; and suddenly I wanted my mother; I wanted no more of this, no more of free will; I wanted to return, relinquish, be secure, safe from the sort of decisions and deciding whose foster-twin was this having to steal an automobile. But it was too late now; I had already chosen, elected; if I had sold my soul to Satan for a mess of pottage, at least I would damn well collect the pottage and eat it too: hadn't Boon himself just reminded me, almost as if he had foreseen this moment of weakness and vacillation in the empty house, and forewarned me: "We done gone through too much to let nothing stop us now."

My clothes—fresh blouses, pants, stockings, my toothbrush —were out at McCaslin now. I had more in my drawer of course, except the toothbrush, which in Mother's absence it was a fair gamble that neither Aunt Callie nor Cousin Louisa would remember about. But I took no clothes, nothing; not that I forgot to but probably because I had never intended to. I just entered the house and stood inside the door long enough to prove to myself that of Boon and me it wouldn't be me who failed us, and went back across the street and across Grandfather's back yard to the lot. Nor was Boon the one who would fail us; I heard the engine running quietly before I reached the carriage house. Boon was already behind the wheel; I think the automobile was even already in gear. "Where's your clean shirt?" he said. "Never mind. I'll buy you one in Memphis. Come on. We can move now." He backed the car out. The open lock was once more hanging in the staple. "Come on," he said. "Dont stop to lock it. It's too late now."

"No," I said. I couldn't have said then why either: with the padlock snapped through the staple and hasp of the closed door, it would look like the automobile was safely inside. And so it would be: the whole thing no more than a dream from which I could wake tomorrow, perhaps now, the next moment, and be safe, saved. So I closed the door and locked the padlock and opened the lot gate for Boon to drive out and closed that too and got in, the car already in motion—if in fact it had ever completely stopped. "If we go the back way, we can dodge the Square," I said. And again he said:

"It's too late now. All they can do now is holler." But none hollered. But even with the Square behind, it still was not too late. That irrevocable decision was still a mile ahead, where the road to McCaslin forked away from the Memphis road, where I could say *Stop. Let me out* and he would do it. More: I could say *I've changed my mind. Take me back to McCaslin* and I knew he would do that too. Then suddenly I knew that if I said *Turn around. I will get that key from Mr Ballott and we will lock this automobile up in the carriage house where Boss believes it already is at this moment* and he would do that. And more: that he wanted me to do that, was silently begging me to do that; he and I both aghast not at his individual temerity but at our mutual, our confederated recklessness, and that Boon knew he had not the strength to resist his and so must cast himself on my strength and rectitude. You see? what I told you about Non-virtue? If things had been reversed and I had silently pled with Boon to turn back, I could have depended on his virtue and pity, where he to whom Boon pled had neither.

So I said nothing; the fork, the last frail impotent hand reached down to save me, flew up and passed and fled, was gone, irrevocable; I said *All right then. Here I come.* Maybe Boon heard it, since I was still boss. Anyway, he put Jefferson behind us; Satan would at least defend his faithful from the first one or two tomorrows; he said: "We aint really got anything to worry about but Hell Creek bottom tomorrow. Harrykin Creek aint anything."

"Who said it was?" I said. Hurricane Creek is four miles

from town; you have passed over it so fast all your life you probably dont even know its name. But people who crossed it then knew it. There was a wooden bridge over the creek itself, but even in the top of summer the approaches to it were a series of mudholes.

"That's what I'm telling you," Boon said. "It aint anything. Me and Mr Wordwin got through it that day last year without even using the block-and-tackle: just a shovel and axe Mr Wordwin borrowed from a house about a half a mile away, that now you mention it I dont believe he took back. Likely though the fellow come and got them the next day."

He was almost right. We got through the first mudhole and even across the bridge. But the other mudhole stopped us. The automobile lurched once, twice, tilted and hung spinning. Boon didn't waste any time, already removing his shoes (I forgot to say he had had them shined too) and rolled up his pants legs and stepped out into the mud. "Move over," he said. "Put it in low gear and start when I tell you. Come on. You know how to do it; you learned how this morning." I got under the wheel. He didn't even stop for the block-and-tackle. "I dont need it. It'll take too much time getting it out and putting it back and we aint got time." He didn't need it. There was a snake fence beside the road; he had already wrenched the top rail off and, himself knee-deep in mud and water, wedged the end under the back axle and said, "Now. Pour the coal to her," and lifted the automobile bodily and shot it forward lurching and heaving, by main strength up onto dry ground again, shouting at me: "Shut if off! Shut it off!" which I did, managed to, and he came and shoved me over and got in under the wheel; he didn't even stop to roll his muddy pants down.

Because the sun was almost down now; it would be nearly dark by the time we reached Ballenbaugh's, where we would spend the night; we went as fast as we dared now and soon we were passing Mr Wylie's—a family friend of ours; Father took me bird-hunting there that Christmas—which was eight miles from Jefferson and still four miles from the river, with the sun just setting behind the house. We went on; there would be a moon after a while, because our oil headlights were better to show someone else you were coming rather than to light you where you were going; when suddenly Boon said, "What's that smell? Was it you?" But before I could deny it he had jerked the automobile to a stop, sat for an instant, then turned and reached back and flung back the lumped and jumbled mass of the tarpaulin which had filled the back of the car. Ned sat up from the floor. He had on the black suit and hat and the white shirt with the gold collar stud without either collar or tie, which he wore on Sunday; he even had the small battered hand-grip (you would call it a brief- or attaché-case now) which had belonged to old Lucius McCaslin before even Father was born; I dont know what else he might have carried in it at other times. All I ever saw in it was the Bible (likewise from Great-great grandmother McCaslin) which he couldn't read, and a pint flask containing maybe a good double tablespoonful of whiskey. "I'll be a son of a bitch," Boon said.

"I wants a trip too," Ned said. "Hee hee hee."

Four

I GOT just as much right to a trip as you and Lucius," Ned said. "I got more. This automobile belongs to Boss and Lucius aint nothing but his grandboy and you aint no kin to him a-tall."

"All right, all right," Boon said. "What I'm talking about, you laid there under that tarpollyon all the time and let me get out in the mud and lift this whole car out single-handed by main strength."

"And hot under there too, mon," Ned said. "I dont see how I stood it. Not to mention having to hold off this-here sheet-iron churn from knocking my brains out every time you bounced, let alone waiting for that gasoline or whatever you calls it to get all joogled up to where it would decide to blow up too. What did you aim for me to do? That was just four miles from town. You'd a made me walk back home."

"This is ten miles now," Boon said. "What makes you think you aint going to walk them back home?"

I said, rapidly, quickly: "Have you forgot? That was Wylie's about two miles back. We might just as well be two miles from Bay St Louis."

"That's right," Ned said pleasantly. "The walking aint near so fur from here." Boon didn't look at him long.

"Get out and fold up that tarpollyon where it wont take up no more room than it has to," he told Ned. "And air it off some too if we got to ride with it."

"It was all that bumping and jolting you done," Ned said. "You talk like I broke my manners just on purpose to get caught."

Also, Boon lit the headlights while we were already stopped, and now he wiped his feet and legs off on a corner of the tarpaulin and put his socks and shoes on and rolled his pants back down; they were already drying. The sun was gone now; already you could see the moonlight. It would be full night when we reached Ballenbaugh's.

I understand that Ballenbaugh's is now a fishing camp run by an off-and-on Italian bootlegger—off I mean during the

one or two weeks it takes each new sheriff every four years to
discover the true will of the people he thought voted for him;
all that stretch of river-bottom which was a part of Thomas
Sutpen's doomed baronial dream and the site of Major de
Spain's hunting camp, is now a drainage district; the wilderness where Boon himself in his youth hunted (or anyway was
present while his betters did) bear and deer and panther, is
tame with cotton and corn now and even Wylie's Crossing
is only a name.

Even in 1905 there was still vestigial wilderness though
most of the deer and all the bears and panthers (also Major
de Spain and his hunters) were gone; the ferry also; and
now we called Wylie's Crossing the Iron Bridge, THE Iron
Bridge since it was the first iron bridge and for several years
yet the only one we in Yoknapatawpha County had or knew
of. But back in the old days, in the time of our own petty
Chickasaw kings, Issetibbeha and Moketubbe and the regi-
cide-usurper who called himself Doom and the first Wylie
came along and the Indians showed him the crossing and he
built his store and ferry boat and named it after himself, this
was not only the only crossing within miles but the head of
navigation too; boats (in the high water of winter, even a
small steamboat) came as it were right to Wylie's front door,
bringing the whiskey and plows and coal oil and peppermint
candy up from Vicksburg and carrying the cotton and furs
back.

But Memphis was nearer than Vicksburg even by mule-
team, so they built a road as straight from Jefferson to the
south end of Wylie's ferry boat as they could run it, and as
straight from the north end of the ferry boat to Memphis as
they could run that. So the cotton and freight began to come
and go that way, mule- or ox-drawn; whereupon there appeared immediately from nowhere an ancestryless giant calling himself Ballenbaugh; some said he actually bought from
Wylie the small dim heretofore peaceful one-room combined
residence and store, including whatever claim he (Wylie) considered he had in the old Chickasaw crossing; others said that
Ballenbaugh simply suggested to Wylie that he (Wylie) had
been there long enough now and the time had come for him
to move four miles back from the river and become a farmer.

Anyway, that's what Wylie did. And then his little wilder-
ness-cradled hermitage became a roaring place indeed: it
became dormitory, grubbing-station and saloon for the tran-
sient freighters and the fixed crews of hard-mouthed hard-
souled mule-skinners who met the wagons at both edges of
the bottom, with two and three and (when necessary) four
span of already geared-up mules, to curse the heavy wagons in
to the ferry on one side of the river, and from the ferry to
high ground once more on the other. A roaring place; who
faced it were anyway men. But just tough men then, no more,
until Colonel Sartoris (I dont mean the banker with his courtesy title acquired partly by inheritance and partly by propin-
quity, who was responsible for Boon and me being where we
at this moment were; I mean his father, the actual colonel,
C.S.A.—soldier, statesman, politician, duelist—the collateral
descending nephews and cousins of one twenty-year-old Yoknapatawpha County youth say, murderer) built his railroad in
the mid-seventies and destroyed it.

But not Ballenbaugh's, let alone Ballenbaugh. The wagon
trains came and drove the boats from the river and changed
the name of Wylie's Crossing to Ballenbaugh's Ferry; the railroads came and removed the cotton bales from the wagons
and therefore the ferry from Ballenbaugh's, but that was all;
forty years before, in the modest case of the trader, Wylie,
Ballenbaugh showed himself perfectly capable of anticipating
the wave of the future and riding it; now, in the person of his
son, another giant who in 1865 returned with (it was said) his
coat lined with uncut United States banknotes, from (he said)
Arkansas, where (he said) he had served and been honorably
discharged from a troop of partisan rangers, the name of
whose commander he was never subsequently able to recall, he
showed that he had lost none of his old deftness and skill and
omniscience. Formerly, people passed through Ballenbaugh's,
pausing for the night; now they travelled to Ballenbaugh's, always at night and often rapidly, to give Ballenbaugh as much
time as possible to get the horse or cow concealed in the
swamp before the law or the owner arrived. Because, in addition to gangs of angry farmers following the non-returning
prints of horses and cattle, and sheriffs following those of actual murderers into Ballenbaugh's, at least one federal revenue

agent left a set of non-returning footprints. Because where Ballenbaugh senior merely sold whiskey, this one made it too; he was now the patron of what is covered by the euphemious blanket-term of dance-hall, and by the mid-eighties Ballenbaugh's was a by-word miles around for horror and indignation; ministers and old ladies tried to nominate sheriffs whose entire platform would be running Ballenbaugh and his drunks and fiddlers and gamblers and girls out of Yoknapatawpha County and Mississippi too if possible. But Ballenbaugh and his entourage—stable, pleasure-dome, whatever you want to call it—never bothered us outsiders: they never came out of their fastness and there was no law compelling anyone to go there; also, seemingly his new avocation (avatar) was so rewarding that word went round that anyone with sights and ambition no higher than one spavined horse or dry heifer was no longer welcome there. So sensible people simply let Ballenbaugh's alone. Which certainly included sheriffs, who were not only sensible but family men too, and who had the example of the federal revenuer who had vanished in that direction not so long ago.

That is, until the summer of 1886, when a Baptist minister named Hiram Hightower—also a giant of a man, as tall and almost as big as Ballenbaugh himself, who on Sunday from 1861 to 1865 had been one of Forrest's company chaplains and on the other six days one of his hardest and most outrageous troopers—rode into Ballenbaugh's armed with a Bible and his bare hands and converted the entire settlement with his fists, one at a time when he could, two or three at a time when he had to. So when Boon and Ned and I approached it in this May dusk of 1905, Ballenbaugh was accomplishing his third avatar in the person of a fifty-year-old maiden: his only child: a prim fleshless severe iron-gray woman who farmed a quarter section of good bottom cotton- and corn-land and conducted a small store with a loft above it containing a row of shuck mattresses each with its neat perfectly clean sheets and pillow cases and blankets for the accommodation of fox- and coon-hunters and fishermen, who (it was said) returned the second time not for the hunting and fishing but for the table Miss Ballenbaugh set.

She heard us too. Nor were we the first; she told us that

thirteen automobiles had passed there in the last two years, five of them in the last forty days; she had already lost two hens and would probably have to begin keeping everything penned up, even the hounds. She and the cook and a Negro man were already on the front gallery, shading their eyes against the ghostly flicker of our headlights as we drove up. She not only knew Boon of old, she recognised the automobile first; already, even after only thirteen of them, her eye for individual cars was that good.

"So you really did make it to Jefferson, after all," she said.

"In a year?" Boon said. "Lord, Miss Ballenbaugh, this automobile has been a hundred times farther than Jefferson since then. A thousand times. You might as well give up: you got to get used to automobiles like everybody else." That was when she told us about the thirteen cars in two years, and the two hens.

"At least they got a ride on an automobile for a little piece anyway," she said. "Which is more than I can say."

"You mean to say you aint never rode in one?" Boon said. "Here, Ned," he said, "jump out of there and get them grips out too. Loosh, let Miss Ballenbaugh set up in front where she can see out."

"Wait," Miss Ballenbaugh said. "I must tell Alice about supper."

"Supper can wait," Boon said. "I bet Alice aint never had a car-ride neither. Come on, Alice. Who's that with you? Your husband?"

"I aint studying no husband," the cook said. "And I wouldn't be studying Ephum even if I was."

"Bring him on anyway," Boon said. The cook and the man came and got in too, into the back seat with the gasoline can and the folded tarpaulin. Ned and I stood in the lamplight from the open door and watched the automobile, the red tail-lamp, move on up the road, then stop and back and turn and come back past us, Boon blowing the horn now, Miss Ballenbaugh sitting erect and a little tense in the front seat, Alice and Ephum in the back seat waving to us as they passed.

"Whooee, boy," Ephum shouted at Ned. "Git a horse!"

"Showing off," Ned said; he meant Boon. "He better be sho proud Boss Priest aint standing here too. He'd show him off." The car stopped and backed and turned again and came back to us and stopped. After a moment Miss Ballenbaugh said,

"Well." Then she moved; she said briskly: "All right, Alice." So we had supper. And I knew why the hunters and fishermen came back. Then Ned went off with Ephum and I made my manners to Miss Ballenbaugh and, Boon carrying the lamp, we went upstairs to the loft above the store.

"Didn't you bring nothing?" Boon said. "Not even a clean handkerchief?"

"I wont need anything," I said.

"Well, you cant sleep like that. Look at them sheets. At least take off your shoes and pants. And your maw would make you brush your teeth too."

"No she wouldn't," I said. "She couldn't. I aint got anything to brush them with."

"That wouldn't stop her, and you know it. If you couldn't find something, you'd make something to do it with or know the reason why."

"All right," I said. I was already on my mattress. "Good night." He stood with his hand up to blow out the lamp.

"You all right?" he said.

"Shut up," I said.

"Say the word. We'll go back home. Not now but in the morning."

"Did you wait this long to get scared?" I said.

"Good night," he said. He blew out the lamp and got on his mattress. Then there was all the spring darkness: the big bass-talking frogs from the sloughs, the sound that the woods makes, the big woods, the wilderness with the wild things: coons and rabbits and mink and mushrats and the big owls and the big snakes—moccasins and rattlers—and maybe even the trees breathing and the river itself breathing, not to mention the ghosts—the old Chickasaws who named the land before the white men ever saw it, and the white men afterward —Wylie and old Sutpen and Major de Spain's hunters and the flatboats full of cotton and then the wagon trains and the brawling teamsters and the line of brigands and murderers which produced Miss Ballenbaugh; suddenly I realised what the noise was that Boon was making.

"What are you laughing at?" I said.

"I'm thinking about Hell Creek bottom. We'll hit it about eleven oclock tomorrow morning."

"I thought you said we'll have trouble there."

"You damn right we will," Boon said. "It'll take that axe and shovel and bob wire and block-and-tackle and all the fence rails and me and you and Ned all three. That's who I'm laughing at: Ned. By the time we are through Hell Creek to-morrow, he's going to wish he hadn't busted what he calls his manners nor et nor done nothing else under that tarpollyon until he felt Memphis itself under them wheels."

Then he waked me early. And everybody else within a half mile, though it still took some time to get Ned up from where he had slept in Ephum's house, to the kitchen to eat his breakfast (and even longer than that to get him out of the kitchen again with a woman in it). We ate breakfast—and af-ter that breakfast if I had been a hunter or a fisherman I wouldn't have felt like walking anywhere for a while—and Boon gave Miss Ballenbaugh another ride in the automobile, but without Alice and Ephum this time, though Ephum was there. Then we—Boon—filled the gasoline tank and the radi-ator, not because they needed it but I think because Miss Ballenbaugh and Ephum were there watching, and started. The sun was just rising as we crossed the Iron Bridge over the river (and the ghost of that steamboat too; I had forgot that last night) into foreign country, another county; by night it would even be another State, and Memphis.

"Providing we get through Hell Creek," Boon said.

"Maybe if you'd just stop talking about it," I said.

"Sure," Boon said. "Hell Creek bottom dont care whether you talk about it or not. It dont have to give a durn. You'll see." Then he said, "Well, there it is." It was only a little af-ter ten; we had made excellent time following the ridges, the roads dry and dusty between the sprouting fields, the land va-cant and peaceful with Sunday, the people already in their Sunday clothes idle on the front galleries, the children and dogs already running toward the fence or road to watch us pass; then in the surreys and buggies and wagons and horse-and mule-back, anywhere from one to three on the horse but not on the mule (A little after nine we passed another auto-

mobile, Boon said it was a Ford; he had an eye for automobiles like Miss Ballenbaugh's.) on the way to the small white
churches in the spring groves.

A wide valley lay before us, the road descending from the
plateau toward a band of willow and cypress which marked
the creek. It didn't look very bad to me, nowhere near as
wide as the river bottom we had already crossed, and we
could even see the dusty gash of the road mounting to the
opposite plateau beyond it. But Boon had already started to
curse, driving even faster down the hill almost as if he were
eager, anxious to reach and join battle with it, as if it were
something sentient, not merely inimical but unredeemable,
like a human enemy, another man. "Look at it," he said. "Innocent as a new-laid egg. You can even see the road beyond
it like it was laughing at us, like it was saying If you could just
get here you could durn near see Memphis; except just see if
you can get here."

"If it's all that bad, why dont we go around it?" Ned said.
"That's what I would do if it was me setting there where you
is."

"Because Hell Creek bottom aint got no around," Boon
said violently. "Go one way and you'd wind up in Alabama;
go the other way and you'll fall off in the Missippi River."

"I seen the Missippi River at Memphis once," Ned said.
"Now you mention it, I done already seen Memphis too. But
I aint never seen Alabama. Maybe I'd like a trip there."

"You aint never visited Hell Creek bottom before neither,"
Boon said. "Providing what you hid under that tarpollyon for
yesterday is education. Why do you reckon the only two automobiles we have seen between now and Jefferson was this
one and that Ford? Because there aint no other automobiles
in Missippi below Hell Creek, that's why."

"Miss Ballenbaugh counted thirteen passed her house in
the last two years," I said.

"Two of them was this one," Boon said. "And even them
other eleven she never counted crossing Hell Creek, did
she?"

"Maybe it depends on who's doing the driving," Ned said.
"Hee hee hee."

Boon stopped the car, quickly. He turned his head. "All

right. Jump out. You want to visit Alabama. You done already made yourself fifteen minutes late running your mouth."

"Why you got to snatch a man up just for passing the day with you?" Ned said. But Boon wasn't listening to him. I dont think he was really speaking to Ned. He was already out of the car; he opened the toolbox Grandfather had had made on the running board to hold the block-and-tackle and axe and spade and the lantern, taking everything out but the lantern and tumbling them into the back seat with Ned.

"So we wont waste any time," he said, speaking rapidly, but quite composed, calm, without hysteria or even urgency, closing the box and getting back under the wheel. "Let's hit it. What're we waiting for?"

Still it didn't look bad to me—just another country road crossing another swampy creek, the road no longer dry but not really wet yet, the holes and boggy places already filled for our convenience by previous pioneers with brush-tops and limbs, and sections of it even corduroyed with poles laid crossways in the mud (oh yes, I realised suddenly that the road—for lack of any closer term—had stopped being not really wet yet too) so perhaps Boon himself was responsible; he himself had populated the stagnant cypress- and willow-arched mosquito-whined gloom with the wraiths of stuck automobiles and sweating and cursing people. Then I thought we had struck it, except for that fact that I not only couldn't see any rise of drier ground which would indicate we were reaching, approaching the other side of the swamp, I couldn't even see the creek itself ahead yet, let alone a bridge. Again the automobile lurched, canted, and hung as it did yesterday at Hurricane Creek; again Boon was already removing his shoes and socks and rolling up his pants. "All right," he said to Ned over his shoulder, "get out."

"I dont know how," Ned said, not moving. "I aint learned about automobiles yet. I'll just be in your way. I'll set here with Lucius so you can have plenty of room."

"Hee hee hee," Boon said in savage and vicious mimicry. "You wanted a trip. Now you got one. Get out."

"I got my Sunday clothes on," Ned said.

"So have I," Boon said. "If I aint scared of a pair of britches, you needn't be."

"You can talk," Ned said. "You got Mr Maury. I has to work for my money. When my clothes gets ruint or wore out, I has to buy new ones myself."

"You never bought a garment of clothes or shoes or a hat neither in your life," Boon said. "You got one pigeon-tailed coat I know of that old Lucius McCaslin himself wore, let alone General Compson's and Major de Spain's and Boss's too. You can roll your britches up and take off your shoes or not, that's your business. But you're going to get out of this automobile."

"Let Lucius get out," Ned said. "He's younger than me and stouter too for his size."

"He's got to steer it," Boon said.

"I'll steer it, if that's all you needs," Ned said. "I been what you calls steering horses and mules and oxen all my life and I reckon gee and haw with that steering wheel aint no different from gee and haw with a pair of lines or a goad." Then to me: "Jump out, boy, and help Mr Boon. Better take your shoes and stockings—"

"Are you going to get out, or do I pick you up with one hand and snatch this automobile out from under you with the other?" Boon said. Ned moved then, fast enough when he finally accepted the fact that he had to, only grunting a little as he took off his shoes and rolled up his pants and removed his coat. When I looked back at Boon, he was already dragging two poles, sapling-sized tree trunks, out of the weeds and briers.

"Aint you going to use the block-and-tackle yet?" I said.

"Hell no," Boon said. "When the time comes for that, you wont need to ask nobody's permission about it. You'll already know it." *So it's the bridge* I thought. *Maybe there's not even a bridge at all and that's what's wrong.* And Boon read my mind there too. "Dont worry about the bridge. We aint even come to the bridge yet."

I would learn what he meant by that too, but not now. Ned stepped gingerly into the water, one foot at a time. "This water got dirt in it," he said. "If there's one thing I hates, it's dirt betwixt my nekkid toes."

"That's because your circulation aint warmed up yet," Boon said. "Take a holt of this pole. You said you aint acquainted with automobiles yet. That's one complaint you wont never have to make again for the rest of your life. All right"—to me—"ease her ahead now and whenever she bites, keep her going." Which we did, Boon and Ned levering their poles forward under the back axle, pinching us forward for another lurch of two or three or sometimes five feet, until the car hung spinning again, the whirling back wheels coating them both from knee to crown as if they had been swung at with one of the spray nozzles which house painters use now. "See what I mean?" Boon said, spitting, giving another terrific wrench and heave which sent us lurching forward, "about getting acquainted with automobiles? Exactly like horses and mules: dont never stand directly behind one that's got one hind foot already lifted."

Then I saw the bridge. We had come up onto a patch of earth so (comparatively) dry that Boon and Ned, almost in-distinguishable now with mud, had to trot with their poles and even then couldn't keep up, Boon hollering, panting, "Go on! Keep going!" until I saw the bridge a hundred yards ahead and then saw what was still between us and the bridge and I knew what he meant. I stopped the car. The road (the passage, whatever you would call it now) in front of us had not altered so much as it had transmogrified, exchanged mediums, elements. It now resembled a big receptacle of milk-infused coffee from which protruded here and there a few forlorn impotent hopeless odds and ends of sticks and brush and logs and an occasional hump of actual earth which looked startlingly like it had been deliberately thrown up by a plow. Then I saw something else, and understood what Boon had been telling me by indirection about Hell Creek bottom for over a year now, and what he had been reiterating with a kind of haunted bemused obsession ever since we left Jefferson yesterday. Standing hitched to a tree just off the road (canal) were two mules in plow-gear—that is, in bridles and collars and hames, the trace-chains looped over the hames and the plow-lines coiled into neat hanks and hanging from the hames also; leaning against another tree nearby was a heavy double-winged plow—a middle-buster—caked, wings shank and the beam itself, with more of the same mud which was rapidly encasing Boon and Ned, a double-tree, likewise mudcaked, leaning against the plow; and in the immediate background a new two-room paintless shotgun cabin on the gallery of which a man sat tilted in a splint chair, barefoot, his galluses down about his waist and his (likewise muddy) brogan shoes against the wall beside the chair. And I knew that this, and not Hurricane Creek, was where (Boon said) he and Mr Wordwin had had to borrow the shovel last year, which (Boon said) Mr Wordwin had forgot to return, and which (the shovel) Mr Wordwin might as well have forgot to borrow also for all the good it did them.

Ned had seen it too. He had already had one hard look at the mudhole. Now he looked at the already geared-up mules standing there swishing and slapping at mosquitoes while they waited for us. "Now, that's what I calls convenient—" he said.

"Shut up," Boon said in a fierce murmur. "Not a word. Dont make a sound." He spoke in a tense controlled fury, propping his muddy pole against the car and hauling out the block-and-tackle and the barbed wire and the axe and spade. He said Son of a bitch three times. Then he said to me: "You too."

"Me?" I said.

"But look at them mules," Ned said. "He even got a log-chain already hooked to that double-tree—"

"Didn't you hear me say shut up?" Boon said in that fierce, quite courteous murmur. "If I didn't speak plain enough, excuse me. What I'm trying to say is, shut up."

"Only, what in the world do he want with the middle-buster?" Ned said. "And it muddy clean up to the handles too. Like he been—You mean to say he gets in here with that team and works this place like a patch just to keep it boggy?" Boon had the spade, axe and block-and-tackle all three in his hands. For a second I thought he would strike Ned with any one or maybe all three of them. I said quickly:

"What do you want me—"

"Yes," Boon said. "It will take all of us. I—me and Mr Wordwin had a little trouble with him here last year; we got to get through this time—"

"How much did you have to pay him last year to get drug out?" Ned said.

"Two dollars," Boon said. "—so you better take off your whole pants, take off your shirt too; it'll be all right here—"

"Two dollars?" Ned said. "This sho beats cotton. He can farm right here setting in the shade without even moving. What I wants Boss to get me is a well-traveled mudhole."

"Fine," Boon said. "You can learn how on this one." He gave Ned the block-and-tackle and the piece of barbed wire. "Take it yonder to that willow, the big one, and get a good holt with it." Ned payed out the rope and carried the head block to the tree. I took off my pants and shoes and stepped down into the mud. It felt good, cool. Maybe it felt that way to Boon too. Or maybe his—Ned's too—was just release, freedom from having to waste any time now trying not to get muddy. Anyway, from now on he simply ignored the mud, squatting in it, saying Son of a bitch quietly and steadily while he fumbled the other piece of barbed wire into a loop on the front of the car to hook the block in. "Here," he told me, "you be dragging up some of that brush over yonder," reading my mind again too: "I dont know where it came from neither. Maybe he stacks it up there himself to keep handy for folks so they can find out good how bad they owe him two dollars."

So I dragged up the brush—branches, tops—into the mud in front of the car, while Boon and Ned took up the slack in the tackle and got ready, Ned and I on the take-up rope of the tackle, Boon at the back of the car with his prize pole again. "You got the easy job," he told us. "All you got to do is grab and hold when I heave. All right," he said. "Let's go."

There was something dreamlike about it. Not nightmarish: just dreamlike—the peaceful, quiet, remote, sylvan, almost primeval setting of ooze and slime and jungle-growth and heat in which the very mules themselves, peacefully swishing and stamping at the teeming infinitesimal invisible myriad life which was the actual air we moved and breathed in, were not only unalien but in fact curiously appropriate, being themselves biological dead-ends and hence already obsolete before they were born; the automobile: the expensive useless mechanical toy rated in power and strength by the dozens of horses, yet held helpless and impotent in the almost infantile clutch of a few inches of the temporary confederation of two mild and pacific elements—earth and water—which the frailest integers and units of motion as produced by the ancient unmechanical methods, had coped with for billions of generations without really having noticed it; the three of us, three forked identical and now unrecognisable mud-colored creatures engaged in a life-and-death struggle with it, the progress—if any—of which had to be computed in dreadful and glacier-like inches. And all the while, the man sat in his tilted chair on the gallery watching us while Ned and I strained for every inch we could get on the rope which by now was too slippery with mud to grip with the hands, and at the rear of the car Boon strove like a demon, titanic, ramming his pole beneath the automobile and lifting and heaving it forward; at one time he dropped, flung away the pole and, stooping, he grasped the car with his hands and actually ran it forward for a foot or two as though it were a wheel barrow. No man could stand it. No man should ever have to. I said so at last. I stopped pulling, I said, panted: "No. We cant do it. We just cant." And Boon, in an expiring voice as faint and gentle as the whisper of love:

"Then get out of the way or I'll run it over you."

"No," I said. I stumbled, slipping and plunging, back to him. "No," I said. "You'll kill yourself."

"I aint tired," Boon said in that light dry voice. "I'm just getting started good. But you and Ned can take a rest. While you're getting your breath, suppose you drag up some more of that brush—"

"No," I said, "no! Here he comes! Do you want him to see it?" Because we could see him as well as hear—the suck and plop of the mules' feet as they picked their delicate way along the edge of the mudhole, the almost musical jangle of the looped chains, the man riding one and leading the other, his shoes tied together by the laces looped over one of the hames, the double-tree balanced in front of him as the old buffalo hunters in the pictures carried their guns—a gaunt man, older than we—I anyway—had assumed.

"Morning, boys," he said. "Looks like you're about ready for me now. Howdy, Jefferson," he said to Boon. "Looks like you did get through last summer, after all."

"Looks like it," Boon said. He had changed, instantaneous

and complete, like a turned page: the poker player who has just seen the second deuce fall to a hand across the table. "We might a got through this time too if you folks didn't raise such heavy mud up here."

"Dont hold that against us," the man said. "Mud's one of our best crops up thisaway."

"At two dollars a mudhole, it ought to be your best," Ned said. The man blinked at Ned a moment.

"I dont know but what you're right," he said. "Here. You take this double-tree; you look like a boy that knows which end of a mule to hook to."

"Get down and do it yourself," Boon said. "Why else are we paying you two dollars to be the hired expert? You done it last year."

"That was last year," the man said. "Dabbling around in this water hooking log-chains to them things undermined my system to where I come down with rheumatism if I so much as spit on myself." So he didn't stir. He just brought the mules up and turned them side by side while Boon and Ned hooked the trace chains to the single trees and then Boon squatted in the mud to make the log-chain fast to the car.

"What do you want me to hook it to?" he said.

"I dont care myself," the man said. "Hook up to any part of it you want out of this mudhole. If you want all of it to come out at the same time, I'd say hook to the axle. But first I'd put all them spades and ropes back in the automobile. You wont need them no more, at least here." So Ned and I did that, and Boon hooked up and we all three stood clear and watched. He was an expert of course, but by now the mules were experts too, breaking the automobile free of the mud, keeping the strain balanced on the double-tree as delicately as wire walkers, getting the automobile into motion and keeping it there with no more guidance than a word now and then from the man who rode the near mule, and an occasional touch from the peeled switch he carried; on to where the ground was more earth than water.

"All right, Ned," Boon said. "Unhook him."

"Not yet," the man said. "There's another hole just this side of the bridge that I'm throwing in free. You aint been acquainted here for a year now." He said to Ned: "What we call the reserve patch up thisaway."

"You means the Christmas middle," Ned said.

"Maybe I do," the man said. "What is it?"

Ned told him. "It's how we done at McCaslin back before the Surrender when old L.Q.C. was alive, and how the Edmonds boys still does. Every spring a middle is streaked off in the best ground on the place, and every stalk of cotton betwixt that middle and the edge of the field belongs to the Christmas fund, not for the boss but for every McCaslin nigger to have a Christmas share of it. That's what a Christmas middle is. Likely you mud-farming folks up here never heard of it." The man looked at Ned a while. After a while Ned said, "Hee hee hee."

"That's better," the man said. "I thought for a minute me and you was about to misunderstand one another." He said to Boon: "Maybe somebody better guide it."

"Yes," Boon said. "All right," he told me. So I got under the wheel, mud and all. But we didn't move yet. The man said, "I forgot to mention it, so maybe I better. Prices have doubled around here since last year."

"Why?" Boon said. "It's the same car, the same mudhole; be damned if I dont believe it's even the same mud."

"That was last year. There's more business now. So much more that I cant afford not to go up."

"All right, goddammit," Boon said. "Go on." So we moved, ignominious, at the pace of the mules, on, into the next mudhole without stopping, on and out again. The bridge was just ahead now; beyond it, we could see the road all the way to the edge of the bottom and safety.

"You're all right now," the man said. "Until you come back." Boon was unhooking the log-chain while Ned freed the traces and handed the double-tree back up to the man on the mule.

"We aint coming back this way," Boon said.

"I wouldn't neither," the man said. Boon went back to the last puddle and washed some of the mud from his hands and came back and took four dollars from his wallet. The man didn't move.

"It's six dollars," he said.

"Last year it was two dollars," Boon said. "You said it's double now. Double two is four. All right. Here's four dollars."

"I charge a dollar a passenger," the man said. "There was two of you last year. That was two dollars. The price is doubled now. There's three of you. That's six dollars. Maybe you'd rather walk back to Jefferson than pay two dollars, but maybe that boy and that nigger wouldn't."

"And maybe I aint gone up neither," Boon said. "Suppose I dont pay you six dollars. Suppose in fact I dont pay you nothing."

"You can do that too," the man said. "These mules has had a hard day, but I reckon there's still enough git in them to drag that thing back where they got it from."

But Boon had already quit, given up, surrendered. "God damn it," he said, "this boy aint nothing but a child! Sholy for just a little child—"

"Walking back to Jefferson might be lighter for him," the man said, "but it wont be no shorter."

"All right," Boon said, "but look at the other one! When he gets that mud washed off, he aint even white!"

The man looked at distance a while. Then he looked at Boon. "Son," he said, "both these mules is color blind."

Five

B OON had told Ned and me that, once we had conquered
Hell Creek bottom, we would be in civilization; he drew
a picture of all the roads from there on cluttered thick as fleas
with automobiles. Though maybe it was necessary first to put
Hell Creek as far behind us as limbo, or forgetfulness, or at
least out of sight; maybe we would not be worthy of civilization until we had got the Hell Creek mud off. Anyway, nothing happened yet. The man took his six dollars and went away
with his mules and double-tree; I noticed in fact that he
didn't return to his little house but went on back through the
swamp and vanished, as if the day were over; so did Ned notice it. "He aint a hog," Ned said. "He dont need to be. He's
done already made six dollars and it aint even dinner time
yet."

"It is as far as I'm concerned," Boon said. "Bring the lunch
too." So we took the lunch box Miss Ballenbaugh had packed
for us and the block-and-tackle and axe and shovel and our
shoes and stockings and my pants (we couldn't do anything
about the automobile, besides being a waste of work until we
could reach Memphis, where surely—at least we hoped—
there wouldn't be any more mudholes) and went back down
to the creek and washed the tools off and coiled down the
block-and-tackle. And there wasn't much to be done about
Boon's and Ned's clothes either though Boon got bodily into
the water, clothes and all, and washed himself off and tried to
persuade Ned to follow suit since he—Boon—had a change
of clothes in his grip. But all Ned would do was to remove his
shirt and put his coat back on. I think I told you about his at-
taché case, which—the case—he didn't so much carry when
abroad as he wore it, as diplomats wear theirs, carrying (I
mean Ned's Bible and the two table spoonsful of—probably
—Grandfather's best whiskey) I suspect at times even less in
them.

Then we ate lunch—the ham and fried chicken and biscuits
and home-made pear preserves and cake and the jug of
buttermilk—and put back the emergency mud-defying gear

(which in the end had been not a defiance but an inglorious brag) and measured the gasoline tank—a gesture not to distance but to time—and went on. Because the die was indeed cast now; we looked not back to remorse or regret or might-have-been; if we crossed Rubicon when we crossed the Iron Bridge into another county, when we conquered Hell Creek we locked the portcullis and set the bridge on fire. And it did seem as though we had won to reprieve as a reward for invincible determination, or refusal to recognise defeat when we faced it or it faced us. Or maybe it was just Virtue who had given up, relinquished us to Non-virtue to cherish and nurture and coddle in the style whose right we had won with the now irrevocable barter of our souls.

The very land itself seemed to have changed. The farms were bigger, more prosperous, with tighter fences and painted houses and even barns; the very air was urban. We came at last to a broad highway running string-straight into distance and heavily marked with wheel-prints; Boon said, with a kind of triumph, as if we had doubted him or as if he had invented it to disprove us, created it, cleared and graded and smoothed it with his own hands (and perhaps even added the wheel-marks): "What did I tell you? The highway to Memphis." We could see for miles; much closer than that was a rapid and mounting cloud of dust like a portent, a promise. It was indubitable, travelling that fast and that much of it; we were not even surprised when it contained an automobile; we passed each other, commingling our dust into one giant cloud like a pillar, a signpost raised and set to cover the land with the adumbration of the future: the antlike to and fro, the incurable down-payment itch-foot; the mechanised, the mobilised, the inescapable destiny of America.

And now, gray with dust from toes to eyelids (particularly Boon's still-damp clothes) we could make time, even if, for a while, not speed; without switching off the engine Boon got out and walked briskly around the car to my side, saying briskly to me: "All right. Slide over. You know how. Just dont get the idea you're a forty-mile-a-hour railroad engine." So I drove, on across the sunny May afternoon. I couldn't look at it though, I was too busy, too concentrated (all right, too nervous and proud): the sabbath afternoon, workless, the cotton

and corn growing unvexed now, the mules themselves sabbatical and idle in the pastures, the people still in their Sunday
clothes on galleries and in shady yards with glasses of lemonade or saucers of the ice cream left from dinner. Then we
made speed too; Boon said, "We're coming to some towns
now. I better take it." We went on. Civilization was now constant: single country stores and crossroads hamlets; we were
barely free of one before here was another; commerce was rife
about us, the air was indeed urban, the very dust itself which
we raised and moved in had a metropolitan taste to tongue
and nostrils; even the little children and the dogs no longer
ran to the gates and fences to watch us and the three other
automobiles we had passed in the last thirteen miles.

Then the country itself was gone. There were no longer intervals between the houses and shops and stores; suddenly before us was a wide tree-bordered and ordered boulevard with
car-tracks in the middle; and sure enough, there was the street
car itself, the conductor and motorman just lowering the
back trolley and raising the front one to turn it around and
go back to Main street. "Two minutes to five oclock," Boon
said. "Twenty-three and a half hours ago we were in Jefferson, Missippi, eighty miles away. A record." I had been in
Memphis before (So had Ned. This morning he told us so;
thirty minutes from now he would prove it.) but always by
train, never like this: to watch Memphis grow, increase; to assimilate it deliberately like a spoonful of ice cream in the
mouth. I had never thought about it other than to assume we
would go to the Gayoso Hotel as we—I anyway—always had.
So I dont know what mind Boon read this time. "We're going to a kind a boarding house I know," he said. "You'll like
it. I had a letter last week from one of the g—ladies staying
there that she's got her nephew visiting her so you'll even
have somebody to play with. The cook can locate a place for
Ned to sleep too."

"Hee hee hee," Ned said. Besides the street cars there were
buggies and surreys—phaetons, traps, stanhopes, at least one
victoria, the horses a little white-eyed at us but still collected;
evidently Memphis horses were already used to automobiles
—so Boon couldn't turn his head to look at Ned. But he
could turn one eye.

"Just what do you mean by that?" he said.

"Nothing," Ned said. "Mind where you're going and nemmine me. Nemmine me nohow. I got friends here too. You just show me where this automobile gonter be at tomorrow morning and I'll be there too."

"And you damn well better be," Boon said. "If you aim to go back to Jefferson in it. Me and Lucius never invited you on this trip so you aint none of mine and his responsibility. As far as me and Jefferson are concerned, I dont give a damn whether you come back or not."

"When we gets this automobile back in Jefferson and has to try to look Boss Priest and Mr Maury in the eye, aint none of us gonter have time to give a damn who is back and who aint," Ned said. But it was too late now, far too late to keep on bringing that up. So Boon just said,

"All right, all right. All I said was, if you want to be back in Jefferson when you start doing your not having time to give a damn, you better be where I can see you when I start back." We were getting close to Main street now—the tall buildings, the stores, the hotels: the Gaston (gone now) and the Peabody (they have moved it since) and the Gayoso to which all us McCaslins-Edmonds-Priests devoted our allegiance as to a family shrine because our remote uncle and cousin, Theophilus McCaslin, Cousin Ike's father, had been a member of the party of horsemen which legend said (That is, legend to some people maybe. To us it was historical fact.) General Forrest's brother led at a gallop into the lobby itself and almost captured a Yankee general. We didn't go that far though. Boon turned into a side street, almost a back alley, with two saloons at the corner and lined with houses that didn't look old or new either, all very quiet, as quiet as Jefferson itself on Sunday afternoon. Boon in fact said so. "You ought to seen it last night, I bet. On any Saturday night. Or even on a week night when there's a fireman's or policeman's or a Elks or something convention in town."

"Maybe they've all gone to early prayer meeting," I said.

"No," Boon said. "I dont think so. Likely they're just resting."

"From what?" I said.

"Hee hee hee," Ned said in the back seat. Obviously, we

were learning, Ned had been in Memphis before. Though probably even Grandfather, though he might have known when, didn't know how often. And you see, I was only eleven. This time, the street being empty, Boon did turn his head.

"Just one more out of you," he told Ned.

"One more which?" Ned said. "All I says is, point out where this thing gonter be at tomorrow morning, and I'll already be setting in it when it leaves." So Boon did. We were almost there: a house needing about the same amount of paint the others did, in a small grassless yard but with a sort of lattice vestibule like a well-house at the front door. Boon stopped the car at the curb. Now he could turn and look at Ned.

"All right," he said. "I'm taking you at your word. And you better take me at mine. On the stroke of eight oclock tomorrow morning. And I mean the first stroke, not the last one. Because I aint even going to be here to hear it."

Ned was already getting out, carrying his little grip and his muddy shirt. "Aint you got enough troubles of your own on your mind, without trying to tote mine too?" he said. "If you can finish your business here by eight oclock tomorrow morning, how come you think I cant neither?" He walked on. Then he said, still walking on and not looking back: "Hee hee hee."

"Come on," Boon said. "Miss Reba'll let us wash up." We got out. Boon reached into the back and started to pick up his grip and said, "Oh yes," and reached to the dashboard and took the switch key out of the slot and put it in his pocket and started to pick up the grip and stopped and took the switch key out of his pocket and said, "Here. You keep it. I might lay it down somewhere and mislay it. Put it in your pocket good so it wont fall out. You can wad your handkerchief on top of it." I took the key and he started to reach for the grip again and stopped again and looked quick over his shoulder at the boarding house and turned sideways a little and took his wallet out of his hind pocket and opened it close to him and took out a five-dollar bill and stopped and then took out a one-dollar bill also and closed the wallet and slid it toward me behind his body, saying, not quick so much as quiet: "Keep this too. I might forget it somewhere too. Whenever we need money out of it I'll tell you how much to give me." Because I had never been inside a boarding house either; and remember, I was just eleven. So I put the wallet into my pocket too and Boon took the grip and we went through the gate and up the walk and into the lattice vestibule, and there was the front door. Boon had barely touched the bell when we heard feet inside. "What did I tell you?" Boon said rapidly. "They are probably all peeping from behind the window curtains at that automobile." The door opened. It was a young Negro woman but before she could open her mouth a white woman pushed her aside—a young woman too, with a kind hard handsome face and hair that was too red, with two of the biggest yellowish-colored diamonds I ever saw in her ears.

"Dammit, Boon," she said. "The minute Corrie got that dispatch yesterday I told her to telegraph you right back not to bring that child here. I've already had one in the house for a week now, and one hell-on-wheels is enough for any house or street either for that matter. Or even all Memphis, providing it's that one we already got. And dont lie that you never got the message neither."

"I didn't," Boon said. "We must have already left Jefferson before it got there. What do you want me to do with him then? tie him out in the yard?"

"Come on in," she said. She moved out of the door so we could enter; as soon as we did so, the maid locked the door again. I didn't know why then; maybe that was the way all people in Memphis did, even while they were at home. It was like any other hall, with a stairway going up, only at once I smelled something; the whole house smelled that way. I had never smelled it before. I didn't dislike it; I was just surprised. I mean, as soon as I smelled it, it was like a smell I had been waiting all my life to smell. I think you should be tumbled pellmell, without warning, only into experience which you might well have spent the rest of your life not having to meet. But with an inevitable (ay, necessary) one, it's not really decent of Circumstance, Fate, not to prepare you first, especially when the preparation is as simple as just being fifteen years old. That was the kind of smell it was. The woman was still talking. "You know as well as I do that Mr Binford disapproves like hell of kids using houses for holiday vacations; you heard him last summer when Corrie brought that little s.o.b. in here the first time because she claims he dont get enough refinement on that Arkansas tenant farm. Like Mr Binford says, they'll be in here soon enough anyhow, so why rush them until at least they have some jack and are capable of spending it. Not to mention the customers, coming in here for business and finding instead we're running a damn kindergarden." We were in the dining room now. It had a pianola in it. The woman was still talking. "What's his name?"

"Lucius," Boon said. "Make your manners to Miss Reba," he told me. I did so, the way I always did: that I reckon Grandfather's mother taught him and Grandmother taught Father and Mother taught us: what Ned calls "drug my foot." When I straightened up, Miss Reba was watching me. She had a curious look on her face.

"I'll be damned," she said. "Minnie, did you see that? Is Miss Corrie—"

"She dressing as fast as she can," the maid said. And that was when I saw it. I mean, Minnie's tooth. I mean, that was how—yes, why—I, you, people, everybody, remembered Minnie. She had beautiful teeth anyhow, like small richly alabaster matched and evenly serrated headstones against the rich chocolate of her face when she smiled or spoke. But she had more. The middle right hand upper one was gold; in her dark face it reigned like a queen among the white dazzle of the others, seeming actually to glow, gleam as with a slow inner fire or lambence of more than gold, until that single tooth appeared even bigger than both of Miss Reba's yellowish diamonds put together. (Later I learned—no matter how—that she had had the gold one taken out and an ordinary white one, like anybody else's, put in; and I grieved. I thought that, had I been of her race and age-group, it would have been worth being her husband just to watch that tooth in action across the table every day; a child of eleven, it seemed to me that the very food it masticated must taste different, better.)

Miss Reba turned to Boon again. "What you been doing? wrassling with hogs?"

"We got in a mudhole back down the road. We drove up. The automobile's outside now."

"I saw it," Miss Reba said. "We all did. Dont tell me it's yours. Just tell me if the police are after it. If they are, get it away from my door. Mr Binford's strict about having police around here too. So am I."

"The automobile's all right," Boon said.

"It better be," Miss Reba said. She was looking at me again. She said, "Lucius," not to anybody. "Too bad you didn't get here sooner. Mr Binford likes kids. He still likes them even after he begins to have doubts, and this last week would have raised doubts in anybody that aint a ossified corpse. I mean, he was still willing to give Otis the benefit of the doubt to take him to the zoo right after dinner. Lucius could have gone too. But then on the other hand, maybe not. If Otis is still using up doubts at the same rate he was before they left here, he aint coming back—providing there's some way to get him up close enough to the cage for one of them lions or tigers to reach him—providing a lion or tiger would want him which they wouldn't if they'd ever spent a week in the same house with him." She was still looking at me. She said, "Lucius," again, not at anybody. Then she said to Minnie: "Go up and tell everybody to stay out of the bathroom for the next half an hour." She said to Boon: "You got a change of clothes with you?"

"Yes," Boon said.

"Then wash yourself off and put them on; this is a decent place: not a joint. Let them use Vera's room, Minnie. Vera's visiting her folks up in Paducah." She said to Boon or maybe to both of us: "Minnie fixed a bed for Otis up in the attic. Lucius can sleep with him tonight—"

There were feet on the stairs, then in the hall and in the door. This time it was a big girl. I dont mean fat: just big, like Boon was big, but still a girl, young too, with dark hair and blue eyes and at first I thought her face was plain. But she came into the room already looking at me, and I knew it didn't matter what her face was. "Hi, kiddo," Boon said. But she didn't pay any attention to him at all yet; she and Miss Reba were both looking at me.

"Watch now," Miss Reba said. "Lucius, this is Miss

Corrie." I made my manners again. "See what I mean?" Miss Reba said. "You brought that nephew of yours over here hunting refinement. Here it is, waiting for him. He wont know what it means, let alone why he's doing it. But maybe Lucius could learn him to at least ape it. All right," she said to Boon. "Go get cleaned up."

"Maybe Corrie'll come help us," Boon said. He was holding Miss Corrie's hand. "Hi, kiddo," he said again.

"Not looking like a shanty-boat swamp-rat," Miss Reba said. "I'll keep this damned place respectable on Sunday anyhow."

Minnie showed us where the room and the bathroom were upstairs and gave us soap and a towel apiece and went out. Boon put his grip on the bed and opened it and took out a clean shirt and his other pants. They were his everyday pants but the Sunday ones he had on wouldn't be fit to wear anywhere until they were cleaned with naphtha probably. "You see?" he said. "I told you so. I done the best I could to make you bring at least a clean shirt."

"My blouse aint muddy," I said.

"But you ought to have a fresh one just on principle to put on after you bathe."

"I aint going to bathe," I said. "I had a bath yesterday."

"So did I," he said. "But you heard what Miss Reba said, didn't you?"

"I heard her," I said. "I never knew any ladies anywhere that wasn't trying to make somebody take a bath."

"By the time you've known Miss Reba a few hours longer, you'll find out you done learned something else about ladies too: that when she suggests you to do something, it's a good idea to do it while you're still deciding whether you're going to or not." He had already unpacked his other pants and shirt. It dont take long to unpack one pair of pants and one shirt from one grip, but he seemed to be having trouble, mainly about putting them down after he took them out, not looking at me, bending over the open grip, busy, holding the shirt in his hand while he decided where to put the pants, then putting the shirt on the bed and picking up the pants again and moving them about a foot further along the bed, then picking up the shirt again and putting it where the pants were;

then he cleared his throat loud and hard and went to the window and opened it and leaned out and spit and closed the window and came back to the bed, not looking at me, talking loud, like somebody that comes upstairs first on Christmas morning and tells you what you're going to get on the Christmas tree that aint the thing you wrote Santa Claus for:

"Dont it beat all how much a fellow can learn and in what a short time, about something he not only never knowed before, he never even had no idea he would ever want to know it, let alone would find it useful to him for the rest of his life—providing he kept it, never let it get away from him. Take you, for instance. Just think. Here it aint but yesterday morning, not even two days back yet, and think how much you have learned: how to drive a automobile, how to go to Memphis across the country without depending on the railroad, even how to get a automobile out of a mudhole. So that when you get big and own a automobile of your own, you will not only already know how to drive it but the road to Memphis too and even how to get it out of a mudhole."

"Boss says that when I get old enough to own an automobile, there wont be any more mudholes to get into. That all the roads everywhere will be so smooth and hard that automobiles will be foreclosed and reclaimed by the bank or even wear out without ever seeing a mudhole."

"Sure, sure," Boon said, "all right, all right. Say there aint no more need to know how to get out of a mudhole, at least you'll still know how to. Because why? Because you aint give the knowing how away to nobody."

"Who could I give it to?" I said. "Who would want to know how, if there aint any more mudholes?"

"All right, all right," Boon said. "Just listen to me a minute, will you? I aint talking about mudholes. I'm talking about the things a fellow—boy can learn that he never even thought about before, that forever afterward, when he needs them he will already have them. Because there aint nothing you ever learn that the day wont come when you'll need it or find use for it—providing you've still got it, aint let it get away from you by chance or, worse than that, give it away from carelessness or pure and simple bad judgment. Do you see what I mean now? Is that clear?"

"I dont know," I said. "It must be, or you couldn't keep on talking about it."

"All right," he said. "That's point number one. Now for point number two. Me and you have been good friends as long as we have known each other, we're having a nice trip together; you done already learned a few things you never seen nor heard of before, and I'm proud to be the one to be along and help you learn them. And tonight you're fixing to learn some more things I dont think you have thought about before neither—things and information and doings that a lot of folks in Jefferson and other places too will try to claim you aint old enough yet to be bothered with knowing about them. But shucks, a boy that not only learned to run a automobile but how to drive it to Memphis and get it out of that son of a bitch's private mudhole too, all in one day, is plenty old enough to handle anything he'll meet. Only—" He had to cough again, hard, and clear his throat and then go to the window and open it and spit again and close it again. Then he came back.

"And that's point number three. That's what I'm trying to impress on you. Everything a m—fel—boy sees and learns and hears about, even if he dont understand it at the time and cant even imagine he will ever have any use to know it, some day he will have a use for it and will need it, providing he has still got it and aint give it away to nobody. And then he will thank his stars for the good friend that has been his friend since he had to be toted around that livery stable on his back like a baby and held him on the first horse he ever rode, that warned him in time not to throw it away and lose it for good by forgetfulness or accident or mischance or maybe even just friendly blabbing about what aint nobody else's business but theirs—"

"What you mean is, whatever I see on this trip up here, not to tell Boss or Father or Mother or Grandmother when we get back home. Is that it?"

"Dont you agree?" Boon said. "Aint that not a bit more than just pure and sensible good sense and nobody's business but yours and mine? Dont you agree?"

"Then why didn't you just come right out and say so?" I said. Only he still remembered to make me take another bath;

the bathroom smelled even more. I dont mean stronger: I just mean more. I didn't know much about boarding houses, so maybe they could have one with just ladies in it. I asked Boon; we were on the way back down stairs then; it was beginning to get dark and I was hungry.

"You damn right they're ladies," he said. "If I so much as catch you trying to show any sass to any of them—"

"I mean, dont any men board here? live here?"

"No. Dont no men actively live here except Mr Binford, and there aint no boarding to speak of neither. But they have plenty of company here, in and out after supper and later on; you'll see. Of course this is Sunday night, and Mr Binford is pretty strict about Sunday: no dancing and frolicking: just visiting their particular friends quiet and polite and not wasting too much time, and Mr Binford sees to it they damn sure better keep on being quiet and polite while they are here. In fact, he's a good deal that way even on week nights. Which reminds me. All you need to do is be quiet and polite yourself and enjoy yourself and listen good in case he happens to say anything to you in particular, because he dont talk very loud the first time and he dont never like it when somebody makes him have to talk twice. This way. They're likely in Miss Reba's room."

They were: Miss Reba, Miss Corrie, Mr Binford and Otis. Miss Reba had on a black dress now, and three more diamonds, yellowing too. Mr Binford was little, the littlest one in the room above Otis and me. He had on a black Sunday suit and gold studs and a big gold watch chain and a heavy moustache, and a gold-headed cane and his derby hat and a glass of whiskey on the table at his elbow. But the first thing you noticed about him was his eyes because the first thing you found out was that he was already looking at you. Otis had his Sunday clothes on too. He was not even as big as me but there was something wrong about him.

"Evening, Boon," Mr Binford said.

"Evening, Mr Binford," Boon said. "This is a friend of mine. Lucius Priest." But when I made my manners to him, he didn't say anything at all. He just quit looking at me. "Reba," he said, "buy Boon and Corrie a drink. Tell Minnie to make these boys some lemonade."

"Minnie's putting supper on," Miss Reba said. She unlocked a closet door. It had a kind of bar in it—one shelf with glasses, another with bottles. "Besides, that one of Corrie's dont want lemonade no more than Boon does. He wants beer."

"I know it," Mr Binford said. "He slipped away from me out at the park. He would have made it only he couldn't find anybody to go into the saloon for him. Is yours a beer-head too, Boon?"

"No sir," I said. "I dont drink beer."

"Why?" Mr Binford said. "You dont like it or you cant get it?"

"No sir," I said. "I'm not old enough yet."

"Whiskey, then?" Mr Binford said.

"No sir," I said. "I dont drink anything. I promised my mother I wouldn't unless Father or Boss invited me."

"Who's his boss?" Mr Binford said to Boon.

"He means his grandfather," Boon said.

"Oh," Mr Binford said. "The one that owns the automobile. So evidently nobody promised him anything."

"You dont need to," Boon said. "He tells you what to do and you do it."

"You sound like you call him boss too," Mr Binford said. "Some times."

"That's right," Boon said. That's what I meant about Mr Binford: he was already looking at me before I even knew it.

"But your mother's not here now," he said. "You're on a tear with Boon now. Eighty—is it?—miles away."

"No sir," I said. "I promised her."

"I see," Mr Binford said. "You just promised her you wouldn't drink with Boon. You didn't promise not to go whore-hopping with him."

"You son of a bitch," Miss Reba said. I dont know how to say it. Without moving, she and Miss Corrie jumped, sprang, confederated, Miss Reba with the whiskey bottle in one hand and three glasses in the other.

"That'll do," Mr Binford said.

"Like hell," Miss Reba said. "I can throw you out too. Dont think I wont. What the hell kind of language is that?"

"And you too!" Miss Corrie said; she was talking at Miss Reba. "You're just as bad! Right in front of them—"

"I said, that'll do," Mr Binford said. "One of them cant get beer and the other dont drink it so maybe they both just come here for refinement and education. Call it they just got some. They just learned that whore and son of a bitch are both words to think twice before pulling the trigger on because both of them can backfire."

"Aw, come on, Mr Binford," Boon said.

"Why, be damned if here aint still another hog in this wallow," Mr Binford said. "A big one, too. Wake up, Miss Reba, before these folks suffocate for moisture." Miss Reba poured the whiskey, her hand shaking, enough to clink the bottle against the glass, saying son of a bitch. son of a bitch. son of a bitch. in a thick fierce whisper. "That's better," Mr Binford said. "Let's have peace around here. Let's drink to it." He raised his glass and was saying, "Ladies and gents all," when somebody—Minnie I suppose—began to ring a handbell somewhere in the back. Mr Binford got up. "That's better still," he said. "Hash-time. Learn us all the refinement and education that there's a better use for the mouth than running private opinions through it."

We went back toward the dining room, not fast, Mr Binford leading the way. There were feet again, going fast; two more ladies, girls—that is, one of them was still a girl—hurried down the stairs, still buttoning their clothes, one in a red dress and the other in pink, panting a little. "We hurried as fast as we could," one of them said quickly to Mr Binford. "We're not late."

"I'm glad of that," Mr Binford said. "I dont feel like lateness tonight." We went in. There were more than enough places at the table, even with Otis and me. Minnie was still bringing things, all cold—fried chicken and biscuits and vegetables left over from dinner, except Mr Binford's. His supper was hot: not a plate, a dish of steak smothered in onions at his place. (You see? how much ahead of his time Mr Binford was? Already a Republican. I dont mean a 1905 Republican—I dont know what his Tennessee politics were, or if he had any—I mean a 1961 Republican. He was more: he was a Conservative. Like this: a Republican is a man who made his money; a Liberal is a man who inherited his; a Democrat is a barefooted Liberal in a cross-country race; a Conservative is a Republican

who has learned to read and write.) We all sat down, the two
new ladies too; I had met so many people by now that I
couldn't get names anymore and had stopped trying; besides,
I never saw these two again. We began to eat. Maybe the reason Mr Binford's steak smelled so extra was that the rest of
the food had smelled itself out at noon. Then one of the new
ladies—the one who was no longer a girl—said,

"Were we, Mr Binford?" Now the other one, the girl, had
stopped eating too.

"Were you what?" Mr Binford said.

"You know what," the girl said, cried. "Miss Reba," she
said, "you know we do the best we can—dont dare make no
extra noise—no music on Sunday when all the other places
do—always shushing our customers up every time they just
want to have a little extra fun—but if we aint already setting
down at our places in this dining room when he sticks his
nose in the door, next Saturday we got to drop twenty-five
cents into that God damned box—"

"They are house rules," Mr Binford said. "A house without
rules is not a house. The trouble with you bitches is, you have
to act like ladies some of the time but you dont know how.
I'm learning you how."

"You cant talk to me that way," the older one said.

"All right," Mr Binford said. "We'll turn it around. The
trouble with you ladies is, you dont know how to quit acting
like bitches."

The older one was standing now. There was something
wrong about her too. It wasn't that she was old, like Grandmother is old, because she wasn't. She was alone. It was just
that she shouldn't have had to be here, alone, to have to go
through this. No, that's wrong too. It's that nobody should
ever have to be that alone, nobody, not ever. She said, "I'm
sorry, Miss Reba. I'm going to move out. Tonight."

"Where?" Mr Binford said. "Across the street to Birdie
Watts's? Maybe she'll let you bring your trunk back with you
this time—unless she's already sold it."

"Miss Reba," the woman said quietly. "Miss Reba."

"All right," Miss Reba said briskly. "Sit down and eat your
supper; you aint going nowhere. Yes," she said, "I like peace
too. So I'm going to mention just one more thing, then we'll

close this subject for good." She was talking up the table at Mr Binford now. "What the hell's wrong with you? What the hell happened this afternoon to get you into this God damned humor?"

"Nothing that I noticed," Mr Binford said.

"That's right," Otis said suddenly. "Nothing sure didn't happen. He wouldn't even run." There was something, like a quick touch of electricity; Miss Reba was sitting with her mouth open and her fork halfway in it. I didn't understand yet but everybody else, even Boon, did. And in the next minute I did too.

"Who wouldn't run?" Miss Reba said.

"The horse," Otis said. "The horse and buggy we bet on in the race. Did they, Mr Binford?" Now the silence was no longer merely electric: it was shocked, electrocuted. Remember I told you there was something wrong somewhere about Otis. Though I still didn't think this was quite it, or at least all of it. But Miss Reba was still fighting. Because women are wonderful. They can bear anything because they are wise enough to know that all you have to do with grief and trouble is just go on through them and come out on the other side. I think they can do this because they not only decline to dignify physical pain by taking it seriously, they have no sense of shame at the idea of being knocked out. She didn't quit, even then.

"A horse race," she said. "At the zoo? in Overton Park?"

"Not Overton Park," Otis said. "The driving park. We met a man on the street car that knowed which horse and buggy was going to win, and changed our mind about Overton Park. Only, they didn't win, did they, Mr Binford? But even then, we never lost as much as the man did, we didn't even lose forty dollars because Mr Binford give me twenty-five cents of it not to tell, so all we lost was just thirty-nine dollars and seventy-five cents. Only, on top of that, my twenty-five cents got away from me in that beer mix up Mr Binford was telling about. Didn't it, Mr Binford?" And then some more silence. It was quite peaceful. Then Miss Reba said,

"You son of a bitch." Then she said, "Go on. Finish your steak first if you want." And Mr Binford wasn't a quitter either. He was proud too: that gave no quarter and accepted none, like a game cock. He crossed his knife and fork neatly and without haste on the steak he had barely cut into yet; he even folded his napkin and pushed it back through the ring and got up and said,

"Excuse me, all," and went out, looking at nobody, not even Otis.

"Well, Jesus," the younger of the two late ones, the girl, said; it was then I noticed Minnie standing in the half-open kitchen door. "What do you know?"

"Get to hell out of here," Miss Reba said to the girl. "Both of you." The girl and the woman rose quickly.

"You mean . . . . leave?" the girl said.

"No," Miss Corrie said. "Just get out of here. If you're not expecting anybody in the next few minutes, why dont you take a walk around the block or something?" They didn't waste any time either. Miss Corrie got up. "You too," she told Otis. "Go upstairs to your room and stay there."

"He'll have to pass Miss Reba's door to do that," Boon said. "Have you forgot about that quarter?"

"It was more than a quarter," Otis said. "There was them eighty-five cents I made pumping the pee a noler for them to dance Saturday night. When he found out about the beer, he taken that away from me too." But Miss Reba looked at him.

"So you sold him out for eighty-five cents," she said.

"Go to the kitchen," Miss Corrie told Otis. "Let him come back there, Minnie."

"All right," Minnie said. "I'll try to keep him out of the ice-box. But he's too fast for me."

"Hell, let him stay here," Miss Reba said. "It's too late now. He should have been sent somewhere else before he ever got off that Arkansas train last week." Miss Corrie went to the chair next to Miss Reba.

"Why dont you go and help him pack?" she said, quite gently.

"Who the hell are you accusing?" Miss Reba said. "I will trust him with every penny I've got. Except for those God damn horses." She stood up suddenly, with her trim rich body and the hard handsome face and the hair that was too richly red. "Why the hell cant I do without him?" she said. "Why the hell cant I?"

"Now, now," Miss Corrie said. "You need a drink. Give Minnie the keys—No, she cant go to your room yet—"

"He gone," Minnie said. "I heard the front door. It dont take him long. It never do."

"That's right," Miss Reba said. "Me and Minnie have been here before, haven't we, Minnie?" She gave Minnie the keys and sat down and Minnie went out and came back with a bottle of gin this time and they all had a glass of gin, Minnie too (though she declined to drink with this many white people at once, each time carrying her full glass back to the kitchen then reappearing a moment later with the glass empty) except Otis and me. And so I found out about Mr Binford.

He was the landlord. That was his official even if unwritten title and designation. All places, houses like this, had one, had to have one. In the alien outside world fortunate enough not to have to make a living in this hard and doomed and self-destroying way, he had a harder and more contemptuous name. But here, the lone male not even in a simple household of women but in an hysteria of them, he was not just lord but the unthanked and thankless catalyst, the single frail power wearing the shape of respectability sufficient to compel enough of order on the hysteria to keep the unit solvent or anyway eating—he was the agent who counted down the money and took the receipt for the taxes and utilities, who dealt with the tradesmen from the liquor-dealers through the grocers and coal-merchants, down through the plumbers who thawed the frozen pipes in winter and the casual labor which cleaned the chimneys and gutters and cut the weeds out of the yard; his was the hand which paid the blackmail to the law; it was his voice which fought the losing battles with the street- and assessment-commissioners and cursed the newspaper boy the day after the paper wasn't delivered. And of these (I mean, landlords) in this society, Mr Binford was the prince and paragon: a man of style and presence and manner and ideas; incorruptible in principles, impeccable in morals, more faithful than many husbands during the whole five years he had been Miss Reba's lover: whose sole and only vice was horses running in competition on which bets could be placed. This he could not resist; he knew it was his weakness and he fought against it. But each time, at the cry of "They're off!" he was putty in the hands of any stranger with a dollar to bet.

"He knowed it his-self," Minnie said. "He was ashamed of his-self and for his-self both, for being so weak, of there being anything bigger than him; to find out he aint bigger than anything he could meet up with, he dont care where nor what, even if on the outside, to folks that didn't know him, he just looked like a banty rooster. So he would promise us and mean it, like he done that time two years ago when we finally had to throw him out. You remember how much work it taken to get him back that time," she told Miss Reba.

"I remember," Miss Reba said. "Pour another round."

"I dont know how he'll manage it," Minnie said. "Because when he leaves, he dont take nothing but his clothes, I mean, just the ones he's got on since it was Miss Reba's money that paid for them. But wont two days pass before a messenger will be knocking on the door with every cent of them forty dollars—"

"You mean thirty-nine, six-bits," Boon said.

"No," Minnie said. "Every one of them forty dollars, even that quarter, was Miss Reba's. He wont be satisfied less. Then Miss Reba will send for him and he wont come; last year when we finally found him he was working in a gang laying a sewer line way down past the Frisco depot until she had to beg him right down on her bended knee—"

"Come on," Miss Reba said. "Stop running your mouth long enough to pour the gin, anyway." Minnie began to pour. Then she stopped, the bottle suspended.

"What's that hollering?" she said. Now we all heard it—a faint bawling from somewhere toward the back.

"Go and see," Miss Reba said. "Here, give me the bottle." Minnie gave her the bottle and went back to the kitchen. Miss Reba poured and passed the bottle.

"He's two years older now," Miss Corrie said. "He'll have more sense—"

"What's he saving it for?" Miss Reba said. "Go on. Pass it." Minnie came back. She said:

"Man standing in the back yard hollering Mr Boon Hogganbeck at the back wall of the house. He got something big with him."

We ran, following Boon, through the kitchen and out onto the back gallery. It was quite dark now; the moon was not high enough yet to do any good. Two dim things, a little one and a big one, were standing in the middle of the back yard, the little one bawling "Boon Hogganbeck! Mister Boon Hogganbeck! Hellaw. Hellaw" toward the upstairs windows until Boon over-rode him by simple volume:

"Shut up! Shut up! Shut up!"

It was Ned. What he had with him was a horse.

Six

WE WERE all in the kitchen. "Good Godalmighty," Boon said. "You swapped Boss's automobile for a *horse?*" He had to say it twice even. Because Ned was still looking at Minnie's tooth. I mean, he was waiting for it again. Maybe Miss Reba had said something to her or maybe Minnie had spoken herself. What I do remember is the rich instantaneous glint of gold out of the middle of whatever Minnie said, in the electric light of the kitchen, as if the tooth itself had gained a new lustre, lambence from the softer light of the lamp in the outside darkness, like the horse's eyes had—this, and its effect on Ned.

It had stopped him cold for that moment, instant, like basilisk. So had it stopped me when I first saw it, so I knew what Ned was experiencing. Only his was more so. Because I realised this dimly too, even at only eleven: that I was too far asunder, not merely in race but in age, to feel what Ned felt; I could only be awed, astonished and pleased by it; I could not, like Ned, participate in that tooth. Here, in the ancient battle of the sexes, was a foeman worthy of his steel; in the ancient mystic solidarity of race, here was a high priestess worth dying for—if such was your capacity for devotion: which, it was soon obvious, was not what Ned intended (anyway hoped) to do with Minnie. So Boon had to repeat before Ned heard—or anyway, noticed—him.

"You know good as me," Ned said, "that Boss dont want no automobile. He bought that thing because he had to, because Colonel Sartoris made him. He had to buy that automobile to put Colonel Sartoris back in his place he had done up-started from. What Boss likes is a *horse*—and I dont mean none of these high-named harness plugs you and Mr Maury has in that livery stable: but a *horse*. And I got him one. The minute he sees this horse, he's gonter say right down much obliged to me just for being where I could get a holt of it before somebody else done it—" It was like a dream, a nightmare; you know it is, and if you can only touch something hard, real, actual, unaltered, you can wake yourself; Boon and

819

I had the same idea, instantaneous; I moved quicker only because there was less of me to put in motion. Ned stopped us; he read two minds: "No need to go look," he said. "He done already come and got it." Boon, frozen in midstride, glared at me, the two of us mutual in one horrified unbelief while I fumbled in my pocket. But the switch key was there. "Sho," Ned said, "he never needed that thing. He was a expert. He claimed he knowed how to reach his hand in behind the lock and turn it on from the back. He done it, too. I didn't believe it neither, until I seen it. It never give him no trouble a-tall. He even throwed in the halter with the horse—"

We—Boon and I—were not running, but fast enough, Miss Reba and Miss Corrie too, to the front door. The automobile was gone. That was when I realised that Miss Reba and Miss Corrie were there too, and that they had said nothing whatever themselves—no surprise, shock; watching and listening, not missing any part of it but not saying anything at all, as if they belonged to a different and separate society, kind, from Boon and me and Ned and Grandfather's automobile and the horse (whoever it belonged to) and had no concern with us and our doings but entertainment; and I remembered how that was exactly the way Mother would watch me and my brothers and whatever neighborhood boys were involved, not missing anything, quite constant and quite dependable, even warmly so, bright and kind but insulate until the moment, the need arrived to abolish the bone and (when necessary) staunch the consequent blood.

We went back to the kitchen, where we had left Ned and Minnie. We could already hear Ned: "—money you talking about, Good-looking, I got it or I can get it. Lemme get this horse put up and fed and me and you gonter step out and let that tooth do its shining amongst something good enough to match it, like a dish of catfish or maybe hog-meat if it likes hog-meat better—"

"All right," Boon said. "Go get that horse. Where does the man live?"

"Which man?" Ned said. "What you want with him?"

"To get Boss's automobile back. I'll decide then whether to send you to jail here or take you back to Jefferson and let Boss have the fun."

"Whyn't you stop talking a minute and listen to me?" Ned said. "In course I knows where the man lives: didn't I just trade a horse from him this evening? Let him alone. We dont want him yet. We wont need him until after the race. Because we aint just got the horse: he throwed in the horse race too. A man at Possum got a horse waiting right this minute to run against him as soon as we get there. In case you ladies dont know where Possum's at, it's where the railroad comes up from Jefferson and crosses the Memphis one where you changes cars unlessen you comes by automobile like we done—"

"All right," Boon said. "A man at Possum—"

"Oh," Miss Reba said. "Parsham."

"That's right," Ned said. "Where they has the bird dog trials. It aint no piece.—got a horse done already challenged this un to a three-heat race, fifty dollars a heat, winner take all. But that aint nothing: just a hundred and fifty dollars. What we gonter do is win back that automobile."

"How?" Boon said. "How the hell are you going to use the horse to win the automobile back from the man that has already give you the horse for it?"

"Because the man dont believe the horse can run. Why you think he swapped with me as cheap as a automobile? Why didn't he just keep the horse and win him a automobile of his own, if he wanted one, and have both of them—a horse and a automobile too?"

"I'll bite," Boon said. "Why?"

"I just told you. This horse done already been beat twice by that Possum horse because never nobody knowed him to make him run. So naturally the man will believe that if the horse wouldn't run them other two times, he aint gonter run this time neither. So all we got to do is, bet him the horse against Boss's automobile. Which he will be glad to bet because naturally he wouldn't mind owning the horse back too, long as he's already got the automobile, especially when it aint no more risk than just having to wait at the finish line until the horse finally comes up to where he can catch him and tie him behind the automobile and come on back to Memphis—"

This was the first time Miss Reba spoke. She said, "Jesus."

"—because he dont believe I can make that horse run

neither. But unlessen I done got rusty on my trading and made a mistake I dont know about, he dont disbelieve it enough not to be at Possum day after tomorrow to find out. And if you cant scrap up enough extra boot amongst these ladies here to make him good interested in betting that automobile against it, you better hadn't never laid eyes on Boss Priest in your born life. It would have tooken a braver man than me to just took his automobile back to him. But maybe this horse will save you. Because the minute I laid my eyes on that horse, it put me in mind of—"

"Hee hee hee," Boon said, in that harsh and savage parody. "You give away Boss's automobile for a horse that cant run, and now you're fixing to give the horse back providing I can scrape up enough boot to interest him—"

"Let me finish," Ned said. Boon stopped. "You gonter let me finish?" Ned said.

"Finish then," Boon said. "And make it—"

"—put me in mind of a mule I use to own," Ned said. Now they both stopped, looking at each other; we all watched them. After a moment Ned said, gently, almost dreamily: "These ladies wasn't acquainted with that mule. Naturally, being young ladies like they is, not to mention so fur away as Yoknapatawpha County. It's too bad Boss or Mr Maury aint here now to tell them about him."

I could have done that. Because the mule was one of our family legends. It was back when Father and Ned were young men, before Grandfather moved in from McCaslin to become a Jefferson banker. One day, during Cousin McCaslin's (Cousin Zack's uncle's) absence, Ned bred the mare of his matched standard-bred carriage team to the farm jack. When the consequent uproar exhausted itself and the mule colt was foaled, Cousin McCaslin made Ned buy it from him at ten cents a week subtracted from Ned's wages. It took Ned three years, by which time the mule had consistently beaten every mule matched against him for fifteen or twenty miles around, and was now being challenged by mules from forty and fifty, and beating them.

You were born too late to be acquainted with mules and so comprehend the startling, the even shocking, import of this statement. A mule which will gallop for a half-mile in the single direction elected by its rider even one time, becomes a neighborhood legend; one that will do it consistently time after time, is an incredible phenomenon. Because, unlike a horse, a mule is far too intelligent to break its heart for glory running around the rim of a mile-long saucer. In fact, I rate mules second only to rats in intelligence, the mule followed in order by cats, dogs, and horses last—assuming of course that you accept my definition of intelligence: which is the ability to cope with environment: which means to accept environment yet still retain at least something of personal liberty.

The rat of course I rate first. He lives in your house without helping you to buy it or build it or repair it or keep the taxes paid; he eats what you eat without helping you raise it or buy it or even haul it into the house; you cannot get rid of him; were he not a cannibal, he would long since have inherited the earth. The cat is third, with some of the same qualities but a weaker, punier creature; he neither toils nor spins, he is a parasite on you but he does not love you; he would die, cease to exist, vanish from the earth (I mean, in his so-called domestic form) but so far he has not had to (there is the fable, Chinese I think, literary I am sure: of a period on earth when the dominant creatures were cats: who after ages of trying to cope with the anguishes of mortality—famine, plague, war, injustice, folly, greed—in a word, civilised government—convened a congress of the wisest cat philosophers to see if anything could be done: who after long deliberation agreed that the dilemma, the problems themselves were insoluble and the only practical solution was to give it up, relinquish, abdicate, by selecting from among the lesser creatures a species, race optimistic enough to believe that the mortal predicament could be solved and ignorant enough never to learn better. Which is why the cat lives with you, is completely dependent on you for food and shelter but lifts no paw for you and loves you not; in a word, why your cat looks at you the way it does).

The dog I rate fourth. He is courageous, faithful, monogamous in his devotion; he is your parasite too: his failure (as compared to the cat) is that he will work for you—I mean, willingly, gladly, ape any trick, no matter how silly, just to please you, for a pat on the head; as sound and first-rate a parasite as any, his failure is that he is a sycophant, believing that he has to show gratitude also; he will debase and violate his own dignity for your amusement; he fawns in return for a kick, he will give his life for you in battle and grieve himself to starvation over your bones. The horse I rate last. A creature capable of but one idea at a time, his strongest quality is timidity and fear. He can be tricked and cajoled by a child into breaking his limbs or his heart too in running too far too fast or jumping things too wide or hard or high; he will eat himself to death if not guarded like a baby; if he had only one gram of the intelligence of the most backward rat, he would be the rider.

The mule I rate second. But second only because you can make him work for you. But that too only within his own rigid self-set regulations. He will not permit himself to eat too much. He will draw a wagon or a plow, but he will not run a race. He will not try to jump anything he does not indubitably know beforehand he can jump; he will not enter any place unless he knows of his own knowledge what is on the other side; he will work for you patiently for ten years for the chance to kick you once. In a word, free of the obligations of ancestry and the responsibilities of posterity, he has conquered not only life but death too and hence is immortal; were he to vanish from the earth today, the same chanceful biological combination which produced him yesterday would produce him a thousand years hence, unaltered, unchanged, incorrigible still within the limitations which he himself had proved and tested; still free, still coping. Which is why Ned's mule was unique, a phenomenon. Put a dozen mules on a track and when the word Go is given, a dozen different directions will be taken, like a scattering of disturbed bugs on the surface of a pond; the one of the twelve whose direction happens to coincide with the track, will inevitably win.

But not Ned's mule. Father said it ran like a horse, but without the horse's frantic frenzy, the starts and falterings and the frightened heart-breaking bursts of speed. It ran a race like a job: it sprang into what it had already calculated would be the exact necessary speed at Ned's touch (or voice or whatever his signal was) and that speed never altered until it crossed the finish line and Ned stopped it. And nobody, not even Father—who was Ned's, well, not groom exactly but rather his second and betting-agent—knew just what Ned did to it. Naturally the legend of that grew and mounted (doing no harm to their stable either) also. I mean, of just what magic Ned had found or invented to make that mule run completely unlike any known mule. But they—we—never learned what it was, nor did anybody else ever ride as its jockey, even after Ned began to put on years and weight, until the mule died, unbeaten at twenty-two years of age; its grave (any number of Edmondses have certainly already shown it to you) is out there at McCaslin now.

That's what Ned meant and Boon knew it, and Ned knew he knew it. They stared at each other. "This aint that mule," Boon said. "This is a horse."

"This horse got the same kind of sense that mule had," Ned said. "He aint got as much of it but it's the same kind." They stared at each other. Then Boon said,

"Let's go look at him." Minnie lighted a lamp. With Boon carrying it, we all went out the back porch and into the yard, Minnie and Miss Corrie and Miss Reba too. The moon was just getting up now and we could see a little. The horse was tied beneath a locust tree in the corner. Its eyes glowed, then flashed away; it snorted and we could hear one nervous foot.

"You ladies kindly stand back a minute, please," Ned said. "He aint used to much society yet." We stopped, Boon holding the lamp high; the eyes glowed coldly and nervously again as Ned walked toward it, talking to it until he could touch its shoulder, stroking it, still talking to it until he had the halter in his hand. "Now, dont run that lamp at him," he told Boon. "Just walk up and hold the light where the ladies can see a *horse* if they wants to. And when I says horse, I means *horse*. Not them plugs they calls horses back yonder in Jefferson."

"Stop talking and bring him out where we can see him," Boon said.

"You're looking at him now," Ned said. "Hold the lamp up." Nevertheless he brought the horse out and moved him a little. Oh yes, I remember him: a three-year-old three-quarters-bred (at least, maybe more: I wasn't expert enough to tell) chestnut gelding, not large, not even sixteen hands, but with the long neck for balance and the laid-back shoulders for speed and the big hocks for drive (and, according to Ned, Ned McCaslin for heart and will). So that even at only eleven, I believe I was thinking exactly what Boon proved a moment later that he was. He looked at the horse. Then he looked at Ned. But when he spoke his voice was no more than a murmur:

"This horse is—"

"Wait," Miss Corrie said. That's right. I hadn't even noticed Otis. That was something else about him: when you noticed him, it was just a second before it would have been too late. But that was still not what was wrong about him.

"God, yes," Miss Reba said. I tell you, women are wonderful. "Get out of here," she told Otis.

"Go in the house, Otis," Miss Corrie said.

"You bet," Otis said. "Come on, Lucius."

"No," Miss Corrie said. "Just you. Go on now. You can go up to your room now."

"It's early yet," Otis said. "I aint sleepy neither."

"I aint going to tell you twice," Miss Reba said. Boon waited until Otis was in the house. We all did, Boon holding the lamp high so its light fell mostly on his and Ned's faces, speaking again in that heatless monotone, he and Ned both:

"This horse is stolen," Boon murmured.

"What would you call that automobile?" Ned murmured.

Yes, wonderful; Miss Reba's tone was no more than Boon's and Ned's: only brisker: "You got to get it out of town."

"That's just exactly the idea I brought him here with," Ned said. "Soon as I eats my supper, me and him gonter start for Possum."

"Have you got any idea how far it is to Possum, let alone in what direction?" Boon said.

"Does it matter?" Ned said. "When Boss left town without taking that automobile with him right in his hand, did your mind worry you about how far Memphis was?"

Miss Reba moved. "Come in the house," she said. "Can anybody see him here?" she said to Ned.

"Nome," Ned said. "I got that much sense. I done already seen to that." He tied the horse again to the tree and we followed Miss Reba up the back steps.

"The kitchen," she said. "It's getting time for company to

start coming in." In the kitchen she said to Minnie: "Sit in my room where you can answer the door. Did you give me the keys back or have you—All right. Dont give no credit to anybody unless you know them; make the change before you even pull the cork if you can. See who's in the house now too. If anybody asks for Miss Corrie, just say her friend from Chicago's in town."

"In case any of them dont believe you, tell them to come around the alley and knock on the back door," Boon said.

"For Christ's sake," Miss Reba said. "Haven't you got troubles enough already to keep you busy? If you dont want Corrie having company, why the hell dont you buy her outright instead of just renting her once every six months?"

"All right, all right," Boon said.

"And see where everybody in the house is, too," Miss Reba told Minnie.

"I'll see about him, myself," Miss Corrie said.

"Make him stay there," Miss Reba said. "He's already played all the hell with horses I'm going to put up with in one day." Miss Corrie went out. Miss Reba went herself and closed the door and stood looking at Ned. "You mean, you were going to walk to Parsham and lead that horse?"

"That's right," Ned said.

"Do you know how far it is to Parsham?"

"Do it matter?" Ned said again. "I dont need to know how far it is to Possum. All I needs is Possum. That's why I changed my mind about leading him: it might be far. At first I thought, being as you're in the connection business—"

"What the hell do you mean?" Miss Reba said. "I run a house. Anybody that's too polite to call it that, I dont want in my front door or back door neither."

"I mean, one of your ladies' connections," Ned said. "That might have a saddle horse or even a plow horse or even a mule I could ride whilst Lucius rides the colt, and go to Possum that way. But we aint only got to run a solid mile the day after tomorrow, we got to do it three times and at least two of them gonter have to be before the next horse can. So I'm gonter walk him to Possum."

"All right," Miss Reba said. "You and the horse are in Parsham. All you need now is a horse race."

"Any man with a horse can find a horse race anywhere," Ned said. "All he needs is for both of them to be able to stand up long enough to start."

"Can you make this one stand up that long?"

"That's right," Ned said.

"Can you make him run while he's standing up?"

"That's right," Ned said.

"How do you know you can?"

"I made that mule run," Ned said.

"What mule?" Miss Reba said. Miss Corrie came in, shutting the door behind her. "Shut it good," Miss Reba said. She said to Ned: "All right. Tell me about that race." Now Ned looked at her, for a full quarter of a minute; the spoiled immune privileged-retainer impudence of his relations with Boon and the avuncular bossiness of those with me, were completely gone.

"You sounds like you want to talk sense for a while," he said.

"Try me," Miss Reba said.

"All right," Ned said. "A man, another rich white man, I dont call his name but I can find him; aint but one horse like that in twenty miles of Possum, let alone ten—owns a blood horse too that has already run twice against this horse last winter and beat him twice. That Possum horse beat this horse just enough bad the first time, for the other rich white man that owned this horse to bet twice as much the second time. And got beat just enough more bad that second time, that when this horse turns up in Possum day after tomorrow, wanting to run him another race, that Possum rich white man wont be just willing to run his horse again, he'll likely be proud and ashamed both to take the money."

"All right," Miss Reba said. "Go on."

"That's all," Ned said. "I can make this horse run. Only dont nobody but me know it yet. So just in case you ladies would like to make up a little jackpot, me and Lucius and Mr Hogganbeck can take that along with us too."

"That includes the one that's got that automobile now too?" Miss Reba said. "I mean, among the ones that dont know you can make it run?"

"That's right," Ned said.

"Then why didn't he save everybody trouble and send you

and the horse both to Parsham, since he believes all he's got
to do to have the horse and the automobile both, is to run
that race?" Now there was no sound; they just looked at each
other. "Come on," Miss Reba said. "You got to say something. What's your name?"

"Ned William McCaslin Jefferson Missippi," Ned said.

"Well?" Miss Reba said.

"Maybe he couldn't afford it," Ned said.

"Hell," Boon said. "Neither have we—"

"Shut up," Miss Reba said to Boon. She said to Ned: "I
thought you said he was rich."

"I'm talking about the one I swapped with," Ned said.

"Did he buy the horse from the rich one?"

"He had the horse," Ned said.

"Did he give you a paper of any kind when you swapped?"

"I got the horse," Ned said.

"You cant read," Miss Reba said. "Can you?"

"I got the horse," Ned said. Miss Reba stared at him.

"You've got the horse. You've got him to Parsham. You say
you got a system that will make him run. Will the same system get that automobile to Parsham too?"

"Use your sense," Ned said. "You got plenty of it. You
done already seen more and seen it quicker than anybody else
here. Just look a little harder and see that them folks I
swapped that horse from—"

"Them?" Miss Reba said. "You said a man." But Ned
hadn't even stopped:

"—is in exactly the same fix we is: they got to go back
home some time too sooner or later."

"Whether his name is Ned William McCaslin or Boon
Hogganbeck or whether it's them folks I swapped the horse
from, to go back home with just the horse or just the automobile aint going to be enough: he's got to have both of
them. Is that it?" Miss Reba said.

"Not near enough," Ned said. "Aint that what I been trying to tell you for two hours now?" Miss Reba stared at Ned.
She breathed quietly, once.

"So now you're going to walk him to Parsham, with every
cop in west Tennessee snuffing every road out of Memphis
for horse—"

"Reba!" Miss Corrie said.

"—by daylight tomorrow morning."

"That's right," Ned said. "It's long past too late for nobody to get caught now. But you doing all right. You doing fine. You tell me." She was looking at him; she breathed twice this time; she didn't even move her eyes when she spoke to Miss Corrie:

"That brakeman—"

"What brakeman?" Miss Corrie said.

"You know the one I mean. That his mother's uncle or cousin or something—"

"He's not a brakeman," Miss Corrie said. "He's a flagman. On the Memphis Special, to New York. He wears a uniform too, just like the conductor—"

"All right," Miss Reba said. "Flagman." Now she was talking to Boon: "One of Corrie's . . ." She looked at Ned a moment. "Connections. Maybe I like that word of yours, after all.—His mother's uncle or something is vice president or something of the railroad that goes through Parsham—"

"His uncle is division superintendent," Miss Corrie said.

"Division superintendent," Miss Reba said. "That is, between the times when he's out at the driving park here or in any of the other towns his trains go through where he can watch horse races while his nephew is working his way up from the bottom with the silver spoon already in his mouth as long as he dont bite down on it hard enough to draw too much notice. See what I mean?"

"The baggage car," Boon said.

"Right," Miss Reba said. "Then they'll be in Parsham and already out of sight by daylight tomorrow."

"Even with the baggage car, it will still cost money," Boon said. "Then to stay hid until the race, and then we got to put up a hundred and fifty for the race itself and all I got is fifteen or twenty dollars." He rose. "Go get that horse," he told Ned. "Where did you say the man you gave that automobile lives?"

"Sit down," Miss Reba said. "Jesus, the trouble you're already in when you get back to Jefferson, and you still got time to count pennies." She looked at Ned. "What did you say your name was?"

Ned told her again. "You wants to know about that mule. Ask Boon Hogganbeck about him."

"Dont you ever make him call you mister?" she said to Boon.

"I always does," Ned said. "Mister Boon Hogganbeck. Ask him about that mule."

She turned to Miss Corrie. "Is Sam in town tonight?"

"Yes," Miss Corrie said.

"Can you get hold of him now?"

"Yes," Miss Corrie said.

Miss Reba turned to Boon. "You get out of here. Take a walk for a couple of hours. Or go over to Birdie Watts's if you want. Only, for Christ's sake dont get drunk. What the hell do you think Corrie eats and pays her rent with while you're down there in that Missippi swamp stealing automobiles and kidnapping children? air?"

"I aint going nowhere," Boon said. "God damn it," he said to Ned, "go get that horse."

"I dont need to entertain him," Miss Corrie said. "I can use the telephone." It was not smug nor coy: it was just serene. She was much too big a girl, there was much too much of her, for smugness or coyness. But she was exactly right for serenity.

"You sure?" Miss Reba said.

"Yes," Miss Corrie said.

"Then get at it," Miss Reba said.

"Come here," Boon said. Miss Corrie stopped. "Come here, I said," Boon said. She approached then, just outside Boon's reach; I noticed suddenly that she wasn't looking at Boon at all: she was looking at me. Which was perhaps why Boon, still sitting, was able to reach suddenly and catch her arm before she could evade him, drawing her toward him, she struggling belatedly, as a girl that big would have to, still watching me.

"Turn loose," she said. "I've got to telephone."

"Sure, sure," Boon said, "plenty of time for that," drawing her on; until, with that counterfeit composure, that desperate willing to look at once forceful and harmless, with which you toss the apple in your hand (or any other piece of momentary distraction) toward the bull you suddenly find is also on your side of the fence, she leaned briskly down and kissed him, pecked him quickly on the top of the head, already drawing back. But again too late, his hand dropping and already gripping one cheek of her bottom, in sight of us all, she straining back and looking at me again with something dark and beseeching in her eyes—shame, grief, I dont know what—while the blood rushed slowly into her big girl's face that was not really plain at all except at first. But only a moment; she was still going to be a lady. She even struggled like a lady. But she was simply too big, too strong for even anyone as big and strong as Boon to hold with just one hand, with no more grip than that; she was free.

"Aint you ashamed of yourself," she said.

"Cant you save that long enough for her to make one telephone call even?" Miss Reba said to Boon. "If you're going to run fevers over her purity, why the hell dont you set her up in a place of her own where she can keep pure and still eat?" Then to Miss Corrie: "Go on and telephone. It's already nine oclock."

Already late for all we had to do. The place had begun to wake up—"jumping", as you say nowadays. But decorously: no uproar either musical or simply convivial; Mr Binford's ghost still reigned, still adumbrated his callipygian grottoes since only two of the ladies actually knew he was gone and the customers had not missed him yet; we had heard the bell and Minnie's voice faintly at the front door and the footsteps of the descending nymphs themselves had penetrated from the stairs; and even as Miss Corrie stood with the knob in her hand, the chink of glasses interspersed in orderly frequence the bass rumble of the entertained and the shriller pipes of their entertainers beyond the door she opened and went through and then closed again. Then Minnie came back too; it seems that the unoccupied ladies would take turnabout as receptionists during the emergency.

You see how indeed the child is father to the man, and mother to the woman also. Back there in Jefferson I had thought that the reason corruption, Non-virtue, had met so puny a foeman in me as to be not even worthy of the name, was because of my tenderness and youth's concomitant innocence. But that victory at least required the three hours between the moment I learned of Grandfather Lessep's death and that one when the train began to move and I realised that Boon would be in unchallenged possession of the key to Grandfather's automobile for at least four days. While here were Miss Reba and Miss Corrie: foemen you would say already toughened, even if not wizened, by constant daily experience to any wile or assault Non-virtue (or Virtue) might invent against them, already sacked and pillaged: who thirty minutes before didn't even know that Ned existed, let alone the horse. Not to mention the complete stranger whom Miss Corrie had just left the room tranquilly confident to conquer with no other weapon than the telephone.

She had been gone nearly two minutes now. Minnie had taken the lamp and gone back to the back porch; I noticed that Ned was not in the room either. "Minnie," Miss Reba said toward the back door, "was any of that chicken—"

"Yessum," Minnie said. "I already fixed him a plate. He setting down to it now." Ned said something. We couldn't hear it. But we could hear Minnie: "If all you got to depend on for appetite is me, you gonter starve twice between here and morning." We couldn't hear Ned. Now Miss Corrie had been gone almost four minutes. Boon stood up, quick.

"God damn it—" he said.

"Are you even jealous of a telephone?" Miss Reba said. "What the hell can he do to her through that damn gutta percha earpiece?" But we could hear Minnie: a quick sharp flat sound, then her feet. She came in. She was breathing a little quick, but not much. "What's wrong?" Miss Reba said.

"Aint nothing wrong," Minnie said. "He like most of them. He got plenty of appetite but he cant seem to locate where it is."

"Give him a bottle of beer. Unless you're afraid to go back out there."

"I aint afraid," Minnie said. "He just nature-minded. Maybe a little extra. I'm used to it. A heap of them are that way: so nature-minded dont nobody get no rest until they goes to sleep."

"I bet you are," Boon said. "It's that tooth. That's the hell of women: you wont let well enough alone."

"What do you mean?" Miss Reba said.

"You know damn well what I mean," Boon said. "You dont never quit. You aint never satisfied. You dont never have no mercy on a damn man. Look at her: aint satisfied until she has saved and scraped to put a gold tooth, a *gold tooth* in the middle of her face just to drive crazy a poor ignorant country nigger—"

"—or spending five minutes talking into a wooden box just to drive crazy another poor ignorant country bastard that aint done nothing in the world but steal an automobile and now a horse. I never knew anybody that needed to get married as bad as you do."

"He sure do," Minnie said from the door. "That would cure him. I tried it twice and I sho learned my lesson—" Miss Corrie came in.

"All right," she said: serene, no more plain than a big porcelain lamp with the wick burning inside is plain. "He's coming too. He's going to help us. He—"

"Not me," Boon said. "The son of a bitch aint going to help me."

"Then beat it," Miss Reba said. "Get out of here. How you going to do it? walk back to Missippi or ride the horse? Go on. Sit down. You might as well while we wait for him. Tell us," she said to Miss Corrie.

You see? "He's *not* a brakeman! He's a *flagman*! He wears a uniform just the same as the conductor's. He's going to help us." All the world loves a lover, quoth (I think) the Swan: who saw deeper than any into the human heart. What pity he had no acquaintance with horses, to have added All the world apparently loves a stolen race horse also. Miss Corrie told us; and Otis was in the room now though I hadn't seen him come in, with something still wrong about him though not noticing him until it was almost too late still wasn't it:

"We'll have to buy at least one ticket to Possum to have—"

"It's Parsham," Miss Reba said.

"All right," Miss Corrie said. "—something to check him as baggage on, like you do a trunk; Sam will bring the ticket and the baggage check with him. But it will be all right; an empty box car will be on a side track—Sam will know where—and all we have to do is get the horse in it and Sam said wall him up in one corner with planks so he cant slip down; Sam will have some planks and nails ready too; he said this was the best he could do at short notice because he didn't dare tell his uncle any more than he had to or his uncle would want to come too. So Sam says the only risk will be getting the horse from here to where the box car is waiting. He says it wont do for . . ." She stopped, looking at Ned.

"Ned William McCaslin Jefferson Missipi," Ned said.

". . . Ned to be walking along even a back street this late at night leading a horse; the first policeman they pass will stop him. So he—Sam—is bringing a blanket and he's going to wear his uniform and him and Boon and me will lead the horse to the depot and nobody will notice anything. Oh yes; and the passenger train will—"

"Jesus," Miss Reba said. "A whore, a pullman conductor and a Missipi swamp rat the size of a water tank leading a race horse through Memphis at midnight Sunday night, and nobody will notice it?"

"You stop!" Miss Corrie said.

"Stop what?" Miss Reba said.

"You know. Talking like that in front of—"

"Oh," Miss Reba said. "If he just dropped up here from Missippi with Boon on a friendly visit you might say, we might of could protected his ears. But using this place as headquarters while they steal automobiles and horses, he's got to take his chances like anybody else. What were you saying about the train?"

"Yes. The passenger train that leaves for Washington at four a.m. will pick the box car up and we'll all be in Possum before daylight."

"Parsham, God damn it," Miss Reba said. "We?"

"Aint you coming too?" Miss Corrie said.

Seven

THAT'S what we did. Though first Sam had to see the horse. He came in the back way, through the kitchen, carrying the horse blanket. He was in his uniform. He was almost as big as Boon.

So we—all of us again—stood once more in the back yard, Ned holding the lamp this time, to shine its light not on the horse but on Sam's brass-buttoned coat and vest and the flat cap with the gold lettering across the front. In fact, I had expected trouble with Ned over Sam and the horse, but I was wrong. "Who, me?" Ned said. "What for? We couldn't be no better off with a policeman himself leading that horse to Possum." On the contrary, the trouble we were going to have about Sam would be with Boon. Sam looked at the horse.

"That's a good horse," Sam said. "He looks like a damn good horse to me."

"Sure," Boon said. "He aint got no whistle nor bell neither on him. He aint even got a headlight. I'm surprised you can see him a-tall."

"What do you mean by that?" Sam said.

"I dont mean nothing," Boon said. "Just what I said. You're a iron horse man. Maybe you better go on to the depot without waiting for us."

"You bas—" Miss Reba said. Then she started over: "Cant you see, the man's just trying to help you? going out of his way so that the minute you get back home, the first live animal you'll see wont be the sheriff? He's the one to be inviting you to get to hell back where you came from and take your goddamn horse along with you. Apologise."

"All right," Boon said. "Forget it."

"You call that an apology?" Miss Reba said.

"What do you want?" Boon said. "Me to bend over and invite him to—"

"You hush! Right this minute!" Miss Corrie said.

"And you dont help none neither," Boon said. "You already got me and Miss Reba both to where we'll have to try to forget the whole English language before we can even pass the time of day."

"That's no lie," Miss Reba said. "That one you brought here from Arkansas was bad enough, with one hand in the ice box after beer and the other one reaching for whatever was little and not nailed down whenever anybody wasn't looking. And now Boon Hogganbeck's got to bring another one that's got me scared to even open my mouth."

"He didn't!" Miss Corrie said. "Otis dont take anything without asking first! Do you, Otis?"

"That's right," Miss Reba said. "Ask him. He certainly ought to know."

"Ladies, ladies, ladies," Sam said. "Does this horse want to go to Parsham tonight, or dont he?"

So we started. But at first Miss Corrie was still looking at Otis and me. "They ought to be in bed," she said.

"Sure," Miss Reba said. "Over in Arkansas or back down there in Missippi or even further than that, if I had my way. But it's too late now. You cant send one to bed without the other, and that one of Boon's owns part of the horse." Only at the last, Miss Reba couldn't go either. She and Minnie couldn't be spared. The place was jumping indeed now, but still discreetly, with sabbath decorum: Saturday night's fading tide-rip in one last spumy up-fling against the arduous hum-drum of day-by-day for mere bread and shelter.

So Ned and Boon put the blanket on the horse. Then from the sidewalk we—Ned and Otis and me—watched Boon and Sam in polyandrous . . . maybe not amity but at least armistice, Miss Corrie between them, leading the horse down the middle of the street from arc light to arc light through the Sunday evening quiet of Second and Third streets, toward the Union depot. It was after ten now; there were few lights, these only in the other boarding houses (I was experienced now; I was a sophisticate—not a connoisseur of course but at least cognizant; I recognised a place similar to Miss Reba's when I saw one). The saloons though were all dark. That is, I didn't know a saloon just by passing it: there were still a few degrees yet veiled to me; it was Ned who told us—Otis and me—they were saloons, and that they were closed. I had expected them to be neither one: neither closed nor open;

remember, I had been in Memphis (or in Catalpa Street) less than six hours, without my mother or father either to instruct me; I was doing pretty well.

"They calls it the blue law," Ned said.

"What's a blue law?" I said.

"I dont know neither," Ned said. "Lessen it means they blewed in all the money Saturday night and aint none of them got enough left now to make it worth burning the coal oil."

"That's just the saloons," Otis said. "It dont hurt nobody that way. What they dont sell Sunday night they can just save it and sell it to somebody, maybe the same folks, Monday. But pugnuckling's different. You can sell it tonight and turn right around and sell the same pugnuckling again tomorrow. You aint lost nothing. Likely if they tried to put that blue law onto pugnuckling, the police would come in and stop them."

"What's pugnuckling?" I said.

"You knows a heap, dont you?" Ned said to Otis. "No wonder Arkansaw cant hold you. If the rest of the folks there knows as much as you do at your age, time they's twenty-one even Texas wont be big enough."

"—t," Otis said.

"What's pugnuckling?" I said.

"Try can you put your mind on knuckling up some feed for that horse," Ned said to me, still louder. "To try to keep him quiet long enough to get him to Possum, let alone into that train in the first place. That-there railroad-owning conductor, flinging box cars around without even taking his hand out of his pocket, is somebody reminded him of that? Maybe even a bucket of soap and water too, so your aunt"—he was talking to Otis now—"can take you around behind something and wash your mouth out."

"—t," Otis said.

"Or maybe even the nearest handy stick," Ned said.

"—t," Otis said. And sure enough, we met a policeman. I mean, Otis saw the policeman even before the policeman saw the horse. "Twenty-three skiddoo," Otis said. The policeman knew Miss Corrie. Then apparently he knew Sam too.

"Where you taking him?" he said. "Did you steal him?"

"Borrowed him," Sam said. They didn't stop. "We rode him to prayer meeting tonight and now we're taking him back home." We went on. Otis said Twenty-three skiddoo again.

"I never seen that before," he said. "Every policeman I ever seen before speaking to anybody, they give him something. Like Minnie and Miss Reba already having a bottle of beer waiting for him before he could even get his foot inside, even if Miss Reba cussed him before he come and cussed him again after he left. And ever since I got here last summer and found out about it, every day I go up to Court Square where that I-talian wop has got that fruit and peanut stand and, sho enough, here the policeman comes and without even noticing it, takes a apple or a handful of peanuts." He was almost trotting to keep up with us; he was that much smaller than me. I mean, he didn't seem so much smaller until you saw him trotting to keep up. There was something wrong about him. When it's you, you say to yourself *Next year I'm going to be bigger than I am now,* simply because being bigger is not only natural, it's inevitable; it doesn't even matter that you cant imagine to yourself how or what you will look like then. And the same with other children; they cant help it either. But Otis looked like two or three years ago he had already reached where you wont be until next year, and since then he had been going backward. He was still talking. "So what I thought back then was that the only thing to be was a policeman. But I never taken long to get over that. It's too limited."

"Limited to what?" Ned said.

"To beer and apples and peanuts," Otis said. "Who's going to waste his time on beer and apples and peanuts?" He said Twenty-three skiddoo three times now. "This town is where the jack's at."

"Jacks?" Ned said. "In course they has jacks here. Dont Memphis need mules the same as anybody else?"

"Jack," Otis said. "Spondulicks. Cash. When I think about all that time I wasted in Arkansas before anybody ever told me about Memphis. That tooth. How much do you reckon that tooth by itself is worth? if she just walked into the bank and taken it out and laid it on the counter and said, Gimme change for it?"

"Yes," Ned said. "I mind a boy like you back there in

Jefferson used to keep his mind on money all the time too. You know where he's at now?"

"Here in Memphis, if he's got any sense," Otis said.

"He never got that far," Ned said. "The most he could get was into the state penitentiary at Parchman. And at the rate you sounds like you going, that's where you'll wind up too."

"But not tomorrow," Otis said. "Maybe not the next day neither. Twenty-three skiddoo, where even a durn policeman cant even pass by without a bottle of beer or a apple or a handful of peanuts put right in his hand before he can even ask for it. Them eighty-five cents them folks give me last night just for pumping the pee a noler that that son of a bitch taken away from me this evening. That I might a even pumped that pee a noler free for nothing if I hadn't found out by pure accident that they was aiming to pay me for it; if I had just happened to step out the door a minute, I might a missed it. And if I hadn't even been there, they would still a give it to somebody, anybody that just happened to pass by. See what I mean? Sometime just thinking about it, I feel like just giving up, just quitting."

"Quitting what?" Ned said. "Quitting for what?"

"Just quitting," Otis said. "When I think of all them years I spent over there on a durn farm in Arkansas with Memphis right here across the river and I never even knowed it. How if I had just knowed when I was four or five years old, what I had to wait until just last year to find out about, sometimes I just want to give up and quit. But I reckon I wont. I reckon maybe I can make it up. How much you folks figger on making out of that horse?"

"Never you mind about that horse," Ned said. "And the making up you needs to do is to make back up that street to wherever it is you gonter sleep tonight, and go to bed." He even paused, half turning. "Do you know the way back?"

"There aint nothing there," Otis said. "I already tried it. They watch too close. It aint like over in Arkansas, when Bee was still at Aunt Fittie's and I had that peep-hole. If you swapped that automobile for him, you must be figgering on at least two hundred—" This time Ned turned completely around. Otis sprang, leaped away, cursing Ned, calling him nigger—something Father and Grandfather must have been teaching me before I could remember because I dont know when it began, I just knew it was so: that no gentleman ever referred to anyone by his race or religion.

"Go on," I said. "They're leaving us." They were: almost two blocks ahead now and already turning a corner; we ran, trotted, Ned too, to catch up and barely did so: the depot was in front of us and Sam was talking to another man, in greasy overalls, with a lantern—a switchman, a railroad man anyway.

"See what I mean?" Ned said. "Can you imagine police sending out a man with a lantern to show us the way?" And you see what I mean too: all the world (I mean about a stolen race horse); who serves Virtue works alone, unaided, in a chilly vacuum of reserved judgment; where, pledge yourself to Non-virtue and the whole countryside boils with volunteers to help you. It seems that Sam was trying to persuade Miss Corrie to wait in the depot with Otis and me while they located the box car and loaded the horse into it, even voluntarily suggesting that Boon attend us with the protection of his size and age and sex: proving that Sam's half anyway of the polyandrous stalemate was amicable and trusting. But Miss Corrie would have no part of it, speaking for all of us. So we turned aside, following the lantern, through a gate into a maze of loading platforms and tracks; now Ned himself had to come forward and take the halter and quiet the horse to where we could move again in the aura now of the horse's hot ammoniac reek (you never smelled a frightened horse, did you?) and the steady murmur of Ned's voice talking to it, both of them—murmur and smell—thickened, dense, concentrated now between the loom of lightless baggage cars and passenger coaches among the green-and-ruby gleams of switch-points; on until we were clear of the passenger yard and were now following a cinder path beside a spur track leading to a big dark warehouse with a loading platform in front of it. And there was the box car too, but with a good twenty-five feet of moonlit (that's right. We were in moonlight now. Free of the street- and depot-lights, we—I—could see it now) vacancy between it and the nearest point of the platform—a good big jump for even a jumping horse, let alone a three-year-old flat racer that (according to Ned) had a little trouble running anyway. Sam cursed quietly the entire depot establishment: switchmen, yard crews, ticket sellers and all.

"I'll go get the goat," the man with the lantern said.

"We dont need no goat," Ned said. "No matter how far he can jump. What we needs is to either move that flatform or that box car."

"He means the switch engine," Sam told Ned. "No," he told the man with the lantern. "I expected this. For a switching crew to miss just twenty-five feet is practically zero. That's why I told you to bring the key to the section house. Get the crow-bars. Maybe Mr Boon wont mind helping you."

"Why dont you go yourself?" Boon said. "It's your railroad. I'm a stranger here."

"Why dont you take these boys on back home to bed, if you're all that timid around strangers?" Miss Corrie said.

"Why dont you take them back home yourself?" Boon said. "Your old buddy-buddy there has already told you once you aint got no business here."

"I'll go with him to get the crow-bars," Miss Corrie told Sam. "Will you keep your eye on the boys?"

"All right, all right," Boon said. "Let's do something, for Christ's sake. That train will be along in four or five hours while we're still debating who's first at the lick-log. Where's that tool shed, Jack?" So he and the man with the lantern went on; we had only moonlight now. The horse hardly smelled at all now and I could see it nuzzling at Ned's coat like a pet. And Sam was thinking what I had been thinking ever since I saw the platform.

"There's a ramp around at the back," he said. "Did he ever walk a ramp before? Why dont you take him on now and let him look at it. When we get the car placed, we can all help you carry him up if we have to—"

"Dont you waste your time worrying about us," Ned said. "You just get that box car to where we wont have to jump no ten-foot gash into it. This horse wants to get out of Memphis as bad as you does." Only I was afraid Sam would say, Dont you want this boy to go with you? Because I wanted to see that box car moved. I didn't believe it. So we waited. It wasn't long; Boon and the man with the lantern came back with two crow-bars that looked at least eight feet long and I watched (Miss Corrie and Otis too) while they did it. The man set his lantern down and climbed the ladder onto the roof and released the brake-wheel and Sam and Boon jammed the ends of the bars between the back wheels and the rails, pinching and nudging in short strokes like pumping and I still didn't believe it: the car looming black and square and high in the moon, solid and rectangular as a black wall inside the narrow silver frame of the moonlight, one high puny figure wrenching at the brake-wheel on top and two more puny figures crouching, creeping, nudging the silver-lanced iron bars behind the back wheels; so huge and so immobile that at first it looked, not like the car was moving forward, but rather Boon and Sam in terrific pantomimic obeisance were pinching infinitesimally rearward past the car's fixed and foundationed mass, the moon-mazed panoramic earth: so delicately balanced now in the massive midst of Motion that Sam and Boon dropped the bars and Boon alone pressed the car gently on with his hands as though it were a child's perambulator, up alongside the platform and into position and Sam said, "All right," and the man on top set the brake-wheel again. So all we had to do now was get the horse into it. Which was like saying, Here we are in Alaska; all we have to do now is find the goldmine. We went around to the back of the warehouse. There was a cleated ramp. But the platform had been built at the right height for the drays to load and unload from it, and the ramp was little more than a track for hand trucks and wheel barrows, stout enough but only about five feet wide, rail-less. Ned was standing there talking to the horse. "He done seen it," he said. "He know we want him to walk up it but he aint decided yet do he want to. I wish now Mr Boxcar man had went a little further and borried a whup too."

"You got one," Boon said. He meant me—one of my tricks, graces. I made it with my tongue, against the sounding-board of my mouth, throat, gorge—a sound quite sharp and loud, as sharp and loud when done right as the crack of a whip; Mother finally forbade me to do it anywhere inside our yard, let alone in the house. Then it made Grandmother jump once and use a swear word. But just once. That was almost a year ago so I might have forgotten how by this time.

"That's right," Ned said. "So we has." He said to me: "Get
you a long switch. They ought to be one in that hedge bush
yonder." There was: a privet bush; all this was probably somebody's lawn or garden before progress, industry, commerce,
railroads, came. I cut the switch and came back. Ned led the
horse up, facing the ramp. "Now you big folks, Mr Boon and
Mr Boxcar, come up one on either side like you was the gate
posts." They did so, Ned halfway up the ramp now, with the
lead rope, facing the horse and talking to it. "There you is," he
said. "Right straight up this here chicken-walk to glory and
Possum, Tennessee by sunup tomorrow." He came back
down, already turning the horse, moving fairly rapidly, speaking to me now: "He done seen the switch. Fall right in behind
him. Dont touch him nor pop till I tell you to." I did that, the
three of us—Ned, the horse, then me—moving directly away
from the ramp for perhaps twenty yards, when without stopping Ned turned and wheeled the horse, I still following, until it faced the rise of the ramp between Boon and Sam twenty
yards away. When it saw the ramp, it checked. "Pop," Ned
said. I made the sound, a good one; the horse sprang a little,
Ned already moving on, a little faster now, back toward the
ramp. "When I tells you to pop this time, touch him with the
switch. Dont hit: just tap him at the root of his tail a second
after you pops." He had already passed between Boon and
Sam and was on the ramp. The horse was now trying to decide
which to do: refuse, or run out (with the additional confusion
of having to decide which of Boon and Sam would run over
the easiest) or simply bolt over and through us all. You could
almost see it happening: which was maybe what Ned was
counting on: an intelligence panicky and timorous and capable
of only one idea at a time, the intrusion of a second one re-
duces all to chaos. "Pop," Ned said. This time I tapped the
horse too as Ned had told me. It surged, leaped, its fore feet
halfway up the ramp, the near hind foot (Boon's side) striking
the edge of the ramp and sliding off until Boon, before Ned
could speak, grasped the leg in both hands and set it back on
the ramp, leaning his weight against the flank, the horse motionless now, trembling, all four feet on the ramp now. "Now,"
Ned said, "lay your switch right light across his hocks so he'll
know he got something behind him to not let him fall."

"To not let him back off the ramp, you mean," Sam said. "We need one of the crow-bars. Go get it, Charley."

"That's right," Ned said. "We gonter need that crow-bar in a minute. But all we needs right now is that switch. You's too little," he told me. "Let Mr Boon and Mr Boxcar have it. Loop it behind his hocks like britching." They did so, one at each end of the limber switch. "Now, walk him right on up. When I say pop this time, pop loud, so he will think the lick gonter be loud too." But I didn't need to pop at all again. Ned said to the horse: "Come on, son. Let's go to Possum," and the horse moved, Boon and Sam moving with it, the switch like a loop of string pressing it on, its fore feet on the solid platform now, then one final scuffling scrabbling surge, the platform resounding once as if it had leaped onto a wooden bridge.

"It's going to take more than this switch or that boy popping his tongue either, to get him into that car," Sam said.

"What gonter get him into that box car is that crow-bar," Ned said. "Aint it come yet?" It was here now. "Prize that-ere chicken-walk loose," Ned said.

"Wait," Sam said. "What for?"

"So he can walk on it into that box car," Ned said. "He's used to it now. He's done already found out aint nothing at the other end gonter hurt or skeer him."

"He aint smelled the inside of an empty box car yet though," Sam said. "That's what I'm thinking about." But Ned's idea did make sense. Besides, we had gone much too far now to boggle even if Ned had commanded us to throw down both walls of the warehouse so the horse wouldn't have to turn corners. So Boon and the railroad man prized the ramp away from the platform.

"God damn it," Sam said. "Do it quiet, cant you?"

"Aint you right here with us?" Ned said. "Sholy you can get a little more benefit outen them brass buttons than just walking around in them." Though it took all of us, including Miss Corrie, to lift the ramp onto the platform and carry it across and lay it like a bridge from the platform into the black yawn of the open car door. Then Ned led the horse up and at once I understood what Sam had meant. The horse had not only never smelled an empty box car before, but unlike mere humans it could see inside too; I remember thinking *Now that we've torn up the ramp, we cant even get it down off the platform again before daylight catches us.* But nothing like that happened. I mean, nothing happened. I mean, I dont know what happened; none of us did. Ned led the horse, its hooves ringing loud and hollow on the planks, up to the end of the ramp which was now a bridge, Ned standing on the bridge just inside the door, talking to the horse, pulling lightly on the halter until the horse put one foot forward onto the bridge and I dont know what I was thinking; a moment ago I had believed that not in all Memphis were there enough people to get that horse into that black orifice, then the next instant I was expecting that same surge and leap which would have taken the horse inside the box car as it had up the ramp; when the horse lifted the foot and drew it back to the platform, it and Ned facing each other like a tableau. I heard Ned breathe once. "You folks just step back to the wall," he said. We did so. I didn't know then what he did. I just saw him, one hand holding the lead rope, the other stroking, touching the horse's muzzle. Then he stepped back into the car and vanished, the lead rope tightened but only his voice came out: "Come on, son. I got it."

"I'll be God damned," Sam said. Because that was all. The loose bridge clattered a little, the cavernous blackness inside the car boomed to the hooves, but no more. We carried the lantern in; the horse's eyes glowed coldly and vanished where Ned stood with it in the corner.

"Where's them planks and nails you talked about?" he asked Sam. "Bring that chicken-walk on in; that's already one whole wall."

"Hell," Sam said. "Hold on now."

"Folks coming in here tomorrow morning already missing a whole box car," Ned said, "aint gonter have time to be little-minded over a home-made ladder outen somebody's henhouse." So all of us again except Ned—including Miss Corrie—carried the ravished ramp into the car and set it up and held it in place while Boon and Sam and the railroad man (Sam had the planks and nails ready too) built a stall around the horse in the corner of the car; before Ned could even complain, Sam had a bucket for water and a box for grain and even a bundle of hay too; we all stood back now in the aura of the horse's contented munching. "He just the same as in Possum right this minute," Ned said.

"What you folks better wish is that he has already crossed that finish line first day after tomorrow," Sam said. "What time is it?" Then he told us himself: "Just past midnight. Time for a little sleep before the train leaves at four." He was talking to Boon now. "You and Ned will want to stay here with your horse of course; that's why I brought all that extra hay. So you bed down here and I'll take Corrie and the boys on back home and we'll all meet here at—"

"You says," Boon said, not harshly so much as with a kind of cold grimness. "You do the meeting here at four oclock. If you dont oversleep, maybe we'll see you." He was already turning. "Come on, Corrie."

"You're going to leave your boss's automobile—I mean your boss's horse—I mean this horse, whoever it really belongs to—here with nobody to watch it but this colored boy?" Sam said.

"Naw," Boon said. "That horse belongs to the railroad now. I got a baggage check to prove it. Maybe you just borrowed that railroad suit to impress women and little boys in but as long as you're in it you better use it to impress that baggage check or the railroad might not like it."

"Boon!" Miss Corrie said. "I'm not going home with anybody! Come on, Lucius, you and Otis."

"It's all right," Sam said. "We keep on forgetting how Boon has to slave for five or six months in that cotton patch or whatever it is, to make one night on Catalpa Street. You all go on. I'll see you at the train."

"Cant you even say much obliged?" Miss Corrie said to Boon.

"Sure," Boon said. "Who do I owe one to? the horse?"

"Try one on Ned," Sam said. He said to Ned: "You want me to stay here with you?"

"We'll be all right," Ned said. "Maybe if you go too it might get quiet enough around here to where somebody can get some sleep. I just wish now I had thought in time to—"

"I did," Sam said. "Where's that other bucket, Charley?" The railroad man—switchman, whatever he was—had it too;

it was in the same corner of the car with the planks and nails and tools and the feed; it contained a thick crude ham sandwich and a quart bottle of water and a pint bottle of whiskey. "There you are," Sam said. "Breakfast too."

"I see it," Ned said. "What's your name, Whitefolks?"

"Sam Caldwell," Sam said.

"Sam Caldwell," Ned said. "It strikes me that Sam Caldwell is a better name for this kind of horse business than twice some others a man could mention around here. A little more, and I could be wishing me and you was frequent enough to be permanent. Kindly much obliged."

"You're kindly welcome," Sam said. So we said goodnight to Sam and Ned and Charley (all of us except Boon and Otis, that is) and went back to Miss Reba's. The streets were empty and quiet now; Memphis was using the frazzled worn-out end of the week to get at least a little sleep and rest to face Monday morning with; we walked quietly too from vacant light to light between the dark windows and the walls: but one faint single light dimly visible in what my new infallible roué's instinct recognised immediately as a competitor of Miss Reba; a single light similar in wan-ness behind Miss Reba's curtains because even here throe must by this time have spent itself; even Minnie herself gone to bed or home or wherever she retired to at hers and Miss Reba's trade's evensong. Because Miss Reba herself unlocked the front door to us, smelling strongly of gin and, in her hard handsome competent way, even beginning to look like it. She had changed her dress too. This one didn't have hardly any top to it at all, and in those days ladies—women—didn't really paint their faces, so that was the first time I ever saw that too. And she had on still more diamonds, as big and yellowish as the first two. No: five. But Minnie hadn't gone to bed either. She was standing in the door to Miss Reba's room, looking just about worn out.

"All fixed?" Miss Reba said, locking the door behind us.

"Yes," Miss Corrie said. "Why dont you go to bed? Minnie, make her go to bed."

"You could a asked me that a hour back from now," Minnie said. "I just wish wouldn't nobody still be asking it two hours ahead from now. But you wasn't here that other time two years ago."

"Come on to bed," Miss Corrie said. "When we get back from Possum Wednesday—"

"God damn it, Parsham," Miss Reba said.

"All right," Miss Corrie said. "—Wednesday, Minnie will have found out where he is and we can go and get him."

"Sure," Miss Reba said. "And bury him right there in the same ditch this time, pick and shovel and all, if I had any sense. You want a drink?" she said to Boon. "Minnie's a damn christian scientist or republican or something and wont take one."

"Somebody around here has got to not take one," Minnie said. "It dont need no republican for that. All it needs is just to be wore out and want to go to bed."

"That's what we all need," Miss Corrie said. "That train leaves at four, and it's already after one. Come on, now."

"Go to bed then," Miss Reba said. "Who the hell's stopping you?" So we went up stairs. Then Otis and I went up stairs again; he knew the way: an attic, with nothing in it but some trunks and boxes and a mattress made up into a bed on the floor. Otis had a nightshirt but (the nightshirt still had the creases in it where Miss Corrie I suppose had bought it off the shelf in the store) he went to bed just like I had to: took off his pants and shoes and he turned off the light and lay down too. There was one little window and now we could see the moon and then I could even see inside the room because of the moonlight; there was something wrong with him; I was tired and coming up the stairs I had thought I would be asleep almost before I finished lying down. But I could feel him lying there beside me, not just wide awake, but rather like something that never slept in its life and didn't even know it never had. And suddenly there was something wrong with me too. It was like I didn't know what it was yet: only that there was something wrong and in a minute now I would know what and I would hate it; and suddenly I didn't want to be there at all, I didn't want to be in Memphis or ever to have heard of Memphis: I wanted to be at home. Otis said Twenty-three skiddoo again.

"The jack that's here," he said. "You can even smell it. It aint fair that it's just women can make money pugnuckling while all a man can do is just try to snatch onto a little of it while it's passing by—" There was that word again, that I had asked twice what it meant. But not anymore, not again: lying there tense and rigid with the moon-shaped window lying across mine and Otis's legs, trying not to hear him but having to: "—one of the rooms is right under here; on a busy night like Sad-dy was you can hear them right up through the floor. But there aint no chance here. Even if I could get a auger and bore a peep-hole through it, that nigger and Miss Reba wouldn't let me bring nobody up here to make no money off of and even if I did they would probably take the money away from me like that son of a bitch done that pee a noler money today. But it was different back home at Aunt Fittie's, when Bee—" He stopped. He lay perfectly still. He said Twenty-three skiddoo again.

"Bee?" I said. But it was too late. No, it wasn't too late. Because I already knew now.

"How old are you?" he said.

"Eleven," I said.

"You got a year on me then," he said. "Too bad you aint going to be here after tonight. If you just stayed around here next week, we might figger that peep-hole out someway."

"What for?" I said. You see, I had to ask it. Because what I wanted was to be back home. I wanted my mother. Because you should be prepared for experience, knowledge, knowing: not bludgeoned unaware in the dark as by a highwayman or footpad. I was just eleven, remember. There are things, circumstances, conditions in the world which should not be there but are, and you cant escape them and indeed, you would not escape them even if you had the choice, since they too are a part of Motion, of participating in life, being alive. But they should arrive with grace, decency. I was having to learn too much too fast, unassisted; I had nowhere to put it, no receptacle, pigeon-hole prepared yet to accept it without pain and lacerations. He was lying face-up, as I was. He hadn't moved, not even his eyes. But I could feel him watching me.

"You dont know much, do you?" he said. "Where did you say you was from?"

"Missippi," I said.

"—t," he said. "No wonder you dont know nothing."

"All right," I said. "Bee is Miss Corrie."

"Here I am, throwing money away like it wasn't nothing," he said. "But maybe me and you both can make something out of it. Sure. Her name is Everbe Corinthia, named for Grandmaw. And what a hell of a name that is to have to work under. Bad enough even over there around Kiblett where some of them already knowed it and was used to it and the others was usually in too much of a hurry to give a hoot whether she called herself nothing or not. But here in Memphis, in a house like this that they tell me every girl in Memphis is trying to get into it as soon as a room is vacant. So it never made much difference over there around Kiblett after her maw died and Aunt Fittie taken her to raise and started her out soon as she got big enough. Then when she found out how much more money there was in Memphis and come over here, never nobody knowed about the Everbe and so she could call herself Corrie. So whenever I'm over here visiting her, like last summer and now, since I know about the Everbe, she gives me five cents a day not to tell nobody. You see? Instead of telling you like I slipped up and done, if I had just went to her instead and said, At five cents a day I can try not to forget, but ten cents a day would make it twice as hard to. But never mind; I can tell her tomorrow that you know it too, and maybe we both can—"

"Who was Aunt Fittie?" I said.

"I dont know," he said. "Folks just called her Aunt Fittie. She might have been kin to some of us, but I dont know. Lived by herself in a house on the edge of town until she taken Bee in after Bee's maw died and soon as Bee got big enough, which never taken long because Bee was already a big girl even before she got to be ten or eleven or twelve or whenever it was and got started—"

"Started at what?" I said. You see? I had to. I had gone too far to stop now, like in Jefferson yesterday—or was it yesterday? last year: another time: another life: another Lucius Priest. "What is pugnuckling?"

He told me, with some of contempt but mostly a sort of incredulous, almost awed, almost respectful amazement. "That's where I had the peep-hole—a knot hole in the back wall with a tin slide over it that never nobody but me knowed how to work, while Aunt Fittie was out in front collecting the money and watching out. Folks your size would have to stand on a box and I would charge a nickel until Aunt Fittie found out I was letting grown men watch for a dime that otherwise might have went inside for fifty cents, and started hollering like a wildcat—"

Standing now, I was hitting him, so much to his surprise (mine too) that I had had to stoop and take hold of him and jerk him up within reach. I knew nothing about boxing and not too much about fighting. But I knew exactly what I wanted to do: not just hurt him but destroy him; I remember a second perhaps during which I regretted (from what ancient playing-fields-of-Eton avatar) that he was not nearer my size. But not longer than a second; I was hitting, clawing, kicking not at one wizened ten-year-old boy, but at Otis and the procuress both: the demon child who debased her privacy and the witch who debauched her innocence—one flesh to bruise and burst, one set of nerves to wrench and anguish; more: not just those two, but all who had participated in her debasement: not only the two panders, but the insensitive blackguard children and the brutal and shameless men who paid their pennies to watch her defenseless and undefended and unavenged degradation. He had plunged sprawling across the mattress, on his hands and knees now, scrabbling at his discarded trousers; I didn't know why (nor care), not even when his hand came out and up. Only then did I see the blade of the pocket knife in his fist, nor did I care about that either; that made us in a way the same size; that was my *carte blanche*. I took the knife away from him. I dont know how; I never felt the blade at all; when I flung the knife away and hit him again, the blood I saw on his face I thought was his.

Then Boon was holding me clear of the floor, struggling and crying now. He was barefoot, wearing only his pants. Miss Corrie was there too, in a kimono, with her hair down; it reached further than her waist. Otis was scrunched back against the wall, not crying but cursing like he had cursed at Ned. "What the damned hell," Boon said.

"His hand," Miss Corrie said. She paused long enough to look back at Otis. "Go to my room," she said. "Go on." He went out. Boon put me down. "Let me see it," she said. That was the first I knew where the blood came from—a neat cut across the cushions of all four fingers; I must have grasped the blade just as Otis tried to snatch it away. It was still bleeding. That is, it bled again when Miss Corrie opened my hand.

"What the hell were you fighting about?" Boon said.

"Nothing," I said. I drew my hand back.

"Keep it closed till I get back," Miss Corrie said. She went out and came back with a basin of water and a towel and a bottle of something and what looked like a scrap of a man's shirt. She washed the blood off and uncorked the bottle. "It's going to sting," she said. It did. She tore a strip from the shirt and bound my hand.

"He still wont tell what they were fighting about," Boon said. "At least I hope he started it: not half your size even if he is a year older. No wonder he pulled a knife—"

"He aint even as old," I said. "He's ten."

"He told me he was twelve," Boon said. Then I found out what was wrong about Otis.

"Twelve?" Miss Corrie said. "He'll be fifteen years old next Monday." She was looking at me. "Do you want—"

"Just keep him out of here," I said. "I'm tired. I want to go to sleep."

"Dont worry about Otis," she said. "He's going back home this morning. There's a train that leaves at nine oclock. I'm going to send Minnie to the depot with him and tell her to watch him get on it and stand where she can see his face through the window until the train moves."

"Sure," Boon said. "And he can have my grip to carry the refinement and culture back in. Bringing him over here to spend a week in a Memphis—"

"You hush," Miss Corrie said.

"—house hunting refinement and culture. Maybe he found it; he might a hunted for years through Arkansas cat-cribs and still not found nobody near enough his size to draw that pocket knife on—"

"Stop it! Stop it!" Miss Corrie said.

"Sure sure," Boon said. "But after all, Lucius has got to know the name of where he's at in order to brag about where he's been." Then they turned the light out and were gone.

Or so I thought. It was Boon this time, turning the light on again. "Maybe you better tell me what it was," he said.

"Nothing," I said. He looked down at me, huge, naked to the waist, his hand on the light to turn it out again.

"Eleven years old," he said, "and already knife-cut in a whore house brawl." He looked at me. "I wish I had knowed you thirty years ago. With you to learn me when I was eleven years old, maybe by this time I'd a had some sense too. Good night."

"Good night," I said. He turned off the light. Then I had been asleep, it was Miss Corrie this time, kneeling beside the mattress; I could see the shape of her face and the moon through her hair. She was the one crying this time—a big girl, too big to know how to cry daintily: only quietly.

"I made him tell me," she said. "You fought because of me. I've had people—drunks—fighting over me, but you're the first one ever fought for me. I aint used to it, you see. That's why I dont know what to do about it. Except one thing. I can do that. I want to make you a promise. Back there in Arkansas it was my fault. But it wont be my fault anymore." You see? You have to learn too fast; you have to leap in the dark and hope that Something—It—They—will place your foot right. So maybe there is after all something besides just Poverty and Non-virtue who look after their own.

"It wasn't your fault then," I said.

"Yes it was. You can choose. You can decide. You can say No. You can find a job and work. But it wont be my fault anymore. That's the promise I want to make you. For me to keep like you kept that one you told Mr Binford about before supper tonight. You'll have to take it. Will you take it?"

"All right," I said.

"But you'll have to say you'll take it. You'll have to say it out loud."

"Yes," I said. "I'll take it."

"Now try to go back to sleep," she said. "I've brought a chair and I'm going to sit here where I'll be ready to wake you in time to go to the depot."

"You go back to bed too," I said.

"I aint sleepy," she said. "I'll just sit here. You go on back to sleep." And this time, Boon again. The moon-shaped

square of window had shifted, so I had slept this time, his
voice trying at least for whisper or anyway monotone, looming still naked from the waist up over the kitchen chair where
Everbe (I mean Miss Corrie) sat, his hand grasping the back-
ward-straining of her arm:

"Come on now. We aint got but a hour left."

"Let me go." She whispered too. "It's too late now. Let me
go, Boon." Then his rasping murmur, still trying for, calling
itself whisper:

"What the hell do you think I came all the way for, waited
all this long for, all this working and saving up and waiting
for—" Then the shape of the mooned window had moved
still more and I could hear a rooster somewhere and my cut
hand was partly under me and hurting, which was maybe
what waked me. So I couldn't tell if this was the same time or
he had gone and then come back: only the voices, still trying
for whisper and if a rooster was crowing, it was time to get
up. And oh yes, she was crying again:

"I wont! I wont! Let me alone!"

"All right, all right. But tonight is just tonight; tomorrow
night, when we're settled down in Possum—"

"No! Not tomorrow either! I cant! I cant! Let me alone!
Please, Boon. Please!"

Eight

W E—Everbe and Boon and I—were at the depot in plenty of time—or so we thought. The first person we saw was Ned, waiting for us in front of it. He had on a clean white shirt—either a new one, or he had managed somehow to get the other one washed. But almost at once things began to go too fast for anyone to learn yet that the new shirt was one of Sam's. Ned didn't even give Boon time to open his mouth. "Calm yourself," he said. "Mr Sam is keeping Lightning whilst I finishes the outside arrangements. The box car has done already been picked up and switched onto the train waiting behind the depot right now for you all to get on. When Mr Sam Caldwell runs a railroad, it's run, mon. We done already named him too—Forkid Lightning." Then he saw my bandage. He almost pounced. "What you done to it?"

"I cut it," I said. "It's all right."

"How bad?" he said.

"Yes," Everbe said. "It's cut across all four fingers. He ought not to move it even." Nor did Ned waste any more time there either. He looked quickly about us.

"Where's that other one?" he said.

"That other what?" Boon said.

"Whistle-britches," Ned said. "That money-mouthed runt boy that was with us last night. I may need two hands on that horse. Who you think is gonter ride that race? me and you that's even twice as heavy as me? Lucius was going to, but being as we already got that other one, we dont need to risk it. He's even less weight than Lucius and even if he aint got as much sense as Lucius, he's at least old enough in meanness to ride a horse race, and wropped-up enough in money to want to win it, and likely too much of a coward to turn loose and fall off. Which is all we needs. Where is he?"

"Gone back to Arkansas," Boon said. "How old do you think he is?"

"What he looks like," Ned said. "About fifteen, aint he? Gone to Arkansas? Then somebody better go get him quick."

"Yes," Everbe said. "I'll bring him. There wont be time to

856

go back and get him now. So I'll stay and bring him on the next train this afternoon."

"Now you talking," Ned said. "That's Mr Sam's train. Just turn Whistle-britches over to Mr Sam; he'll handle him."

"Sure," Boon said to Everbe. "That'll give you a whole hour free to practise that No on Sam. Maybe he's a better man than me and wont take it." But she just looked at him.

"Then why dont you wait and bring Otis on and we'll meet you in Parsham tonight," I said. Now Boon looked at me.

"Well well," he said. "What's that Mr Binford said last night? If there still aint another fresh hog in this wallow. Except that this one's still just a shoat yet. That is, I thought it was."

"Please, Boon," Everbe said. Like that: "Please, Boon."

"Take him too and the both of you get to hell back to that slaughter house that maybe you ought not to left in the first place," Boon said. She didn't say anything this time. She just stood there, looking down a little: a big girl that stillness suited too. Then she turned, already walking.

"Maybe I will," I said. "Right on back home. Ned's got somebody else to ride the horse and you dont seem to know what to do with none of the folks trying to help us."

He looked, glared at me: a second maybe. "All right," he said. He strode past me until he overtook her. "I said, all right," he said. "Is it all right?"

"All right," she said.

"I'll meet the first train today. If you aint on it, I'll keep on meeting them. All right?"

"All right," she said. She went on.

"I bet aint none of you thought to bring my grip," Ned said.

"What?" Boon said.

"Where is it?" I said.

"Right there in the kitchen where I set it," Ned said. "That gold-tooth high-brown seen it."

"Miss Corrie'll bring it tonight," I said. "Come on." We went into the depot. Boon bought our tickets and we went out to where the train was waiting, with people already getting on it. Up ahead we could see the box car. Sam and the conductor and two other men were standing by the open door; one of them must have been the engineer. You see? not just one casual off-duty flagman, but a functioning train crew.

"You going to run him today?" the conductor said.

"Tomorrow," Boon said.

"Well, we got to get him there first," the conductor said, looking at his watch. "Who's going to ride with him?"

"Me," Ned said. "Soon as I can find a box or something to climb up on."

"Gimme your foot," Sam said. Ned cocked his knee and Sam threw him up into the car. "See you in Parsham tomorrow," he said.

"I thought you went all the way to Washington," Boon said.

"Who, me?" Sam said. "That's just the train. I'm going to double back from Chattanooga tonight on Two-O-Nine. I'll be back in Parsham at seven oclock tomorrow morning. I'd go with you now and pick up Two-O-Eight in Parsham tonight, only I got to get some sleep. Besides, you wont need me anyhow. You can depend on Ned until then."

So did Boon and I. I mean, need sleep. We got some, until the conductor waked us and we stood on the cinders at Parsham in the first light and watched the engine (there was a cattle-loading chute here) spot the box car, properly this time, and take its train again and go on, clicking car by car across the other tracks which went south to Jefferson. Then the three of us dismantled the stall and Ned led the horse out; and of course, naturally, materialised from nowhere, a pleasant-looking Negro youth of about nineteen, standing at the bottom of the chute, said, "Howdy, Mr McCaslin."

"That you, son?" Ned said. "Which a way?" So we left Boon for that time; his was the Motion role now, the doing: to find a place for all of us to live, not just him and me, but Otis and Everbe when they came tonight: to locate a man whose name Ned didn't even know, whom nobody but Ned said owned a horse, and then persuade him to run it, race it—one figment of Ned's imagination to race another figment—in a hypothetical race which was in the future and therefore didn't exist, against a horse it had already beaten twice (this likewise according only to Ned, or Figment Three), as a result of which Ned intended to recover Grandfather's automobile;

all this Boon must do while still keeping clear of being challenged about who really did own the horse. We—Ned and the
youth and me—were walking now, already out of town,
which didn't take long in those days—a hamlet, two or three
stores where the two railroads crossed, the depot and loading
chute and freight shed and a platform for cotton bales.
Though some of it has not changed: the big rambling multi-
galleried multi-storey-ed steamboat-gothic hotel where the
overalled aficionados and the professionals who trained the
fine bird dogs and the northern millionaires who owned them
(one night in the lounge in 1933, his Ohio business hanging
with everybody else's under the Damocles sword of the fed-
erally-closed banks, I myself heard Horace Lytle refuse five
thousand dollars for Mary Montrose) gathered for two weeks
each February (Paul Rainey also, who liked our country
enough—or anyway our bear and deer and panther enough—
to use some of the Wall Street money to own enough
Mississippi land for him and his friends to hunt them in: a
hound man primarily, who took his pack of bear hounds to
Africa to see what they would do on lion or vice versa)—when
the youth said,

"This white boy's going to sleep walking. Aint you got no
saddle?" But I wasn't going to sleep yet. I had to find out, to
ask:

"I didn't even know you knew anybody here, let alone getting word ahead to them."

Ned walked on as if I had not even spoken. After a while he
said over his shoulder: "So you wants to know how, do you?"
He walked on. He said: "Me and that boy's grandpappy are
Masons."

"Why are you whispering?" I said. "Boss is a Mason too
but I never heard him whisper about it."

"I didn't know I was," Ned said. "But suppose I was. What
do you want to belong to a lodge for, unless it's so secret cant
hardly nobody else get in it? And how are you gonter keep it
secret unless you treat it like one?"

"But how did you get word to him?" I said.

"Let me tell you something," Ned said. "If you ever need
to get something done, not just done but done quick and
quiet and so you can depend on it and not no blabbing and

gabbling around about it neither, you hunt around until you finds somebody like Mr Sam Caldwell, and turn it over to him. You member that. Folks around Jefferson could use some of him. They could use a heap of Sam Caldwells."

Then we were there. The sun was well up now. It was a dog-trot house, paintless but quite sound and quite neat among locust and chinaberry trees, in a swept yard inside a fence which had all its palings too and a hinged gate that worked, with chickens in the dust and a cow and a pair of mules in the stable lot behind it, and two pretty good hounds which had already recognised the youth with us, and an old man at the top of the gallery steps above them—an old man very dark in a white shirt and galluses and a planter's hat, with perfectly white moustaches and an imperial, coming down the steps now and across the yard to look at the horse. Because he knew, remembered the horse, and so one at least of Ned's figments vanished.

"You all buy him?" he said.

"We got him," Ned said.

"Long enough to run him?"

"Once, anyway," Ned said. He said to me: "Make your manners to Uncle Possum Hood." I did so.

"Rest yourself," Uncle Parsham said. "You all about ready for breakfast, aint you?" I could already smell it—the ham.

"All I want is to go to sleep," I said.

"He's been up all night," Ned said. "Both of us. Only he had to spend his in a house full of women hollering why and how much whilst all I had was just a quiet empty box car with a horse." But I was still going to help stable and feed Lightning. They wouldn't let me. "You go with Lycurgus and get some sleep," Ned said. "I'm gonter need you soon, be-fore it gets too hot. We got to find out about this horse, and the sooner we starts, the sooner it will be." I followed Lycurgus. It was a lean-to room, a bed with a bright perfectly clean harlequin-patched quilt; it seemed to me I was asleep before I even lay down, and that Ned was shaking me before I had ever slept. He had a clean heavy wool sock and a piece of string. I was hungry now. "You can eat your breakfast af-terwards," Ned said. "You can learn a horse better on a empty stomach. Here—" holding the sock open. "Whistle-britches

aint showed up yet. It might be better if he dont a-tall. He
the sort that no matter how bad you think you need him, you
find out afterward you was better off. Hold out your hand."
He meant the bandaged one. He slipped the sock over it,
bandage and all, and tied it around my wrist with the string.
"You can still use your thumb, but this'll keep you from forgetting and trying to open your hand and bust them cuts
again."

Uncle Parsham and Lycurgus were waiting with the horse.
He was bridled now, under an old, used, but perfectly cared-
for McClellan saddle. Ned looked at it. "We might run him
bareback, unless they makes us. But leave it on. We can try
him both ways and let him learn us which he likes best."

It was a small pasture beside the creek, flat and smooth,
with good footing. Ned shortened the leathers, to suit not me
so much as him, and threw me up. "You know what to do:
the same as with them colts out at McCaslin. Let him worry
about which hand he's on; likely all anybody ever tried to
learn him is just to run as fast as the bit will let him,
whichever way somebody points his head. Which is all we
wants too. You dont need no switch yet. Besides, we dont
want to learn a switch: we wants to learn him. Go on."

I moved him out, into the pasture, into a trot. He was
nothing on the bit; a cobweb would have checked him. I said
so. "I bet," Ned said. "I bet he got a heap more whip-calluses
on his behind than bit-chafes in his jaw. Go on. Move him."
But he wouldn't. I kicked, pounded my heels, but he just
trotted, a little faster in the back stretch (I was riding a circu-
lar course like the one we had beaten out in Cousin Zack's
paddock) until I realised suddenly that he was simply hurrying back to Ned. But still behind the bit; he had never once
come into the bridle, his whole head bent around and tucked
but with no weight whatever on the hand, as if the bit were a
pork-rind and he a Mohammedan (or a fish-spine and he a
Mississippi candidate for constable whose Baptist opposition
had accused him of seeking the Catholic vote or one of Mrs
Roosevelt's autographed letters and a secretary of the Citizens
Council or Senator Goldwater's cigar-butt and the youngest
pledge to the A.D.A.) on until he reached Ned, and with a
jerk I felt clean up to my shoulder, snatched his head free and

began to nuzzle at Ned's shirt. "U-huh," Ned said. He had one hand behind him; I could see a peeled switch in it now. "Head him back." He said to the horse: "You got to learn, son, not to run back to me until I sends for you." Then to me: "He aint gonter stop this time. But you make like he is: just one stride ahead of where, if you was him, you would think about turning to come to me, reach back with your hand and whop him hard as you can. Now set tight," and stepped back and cut the horse quick and hard across the buttocks.

It leapt, sprang into full run: the motion (not our speed nor even our progress: just the horse's motion) seemed terrific: graceless of course but still terrific. Because it was simple reflex from fright, and fright does not become horses. They are built wrong for it, being merely mass and symmetry, while fright demands fluidity and grace and bizarreness and the capacity to enchant and enthrall and even appall and aghast, like an impala or a giraffe or a snake; even as the fright faded I could feel, sense the motion become simply obedience, no more than an obedient hand gallop, on around the back turn and stretch and into what would be the home stretch, when I did as Ned ordered: one stride before the point at which he had turned to Ned before, I reached back and hit him as hard as I could with the flat of my sound hand; and again the leap, the spring, but only into willingness, obedience, alarm: not anger nor even eagerness. "That'll do," Ned said. "Bring him in." We came up and stopped. He was sweated a little, but that was all. "How do he feel?" Ned said.

I tried to tell him. "The front half of him dont want to run."

"He reached out all right when I touched him," Ned said.

I tried again. "I dont mean his front end. His legs feel all right. His head just dont want to go anywhere."

"U-huh," Ned said. He said to Uncle Parsham: "You seen one of them races. What happened?"

"I saw both of them," Uncle Parsham said. "Nothing happened. He was running good until all of a sudden he must have looked up and seen there wasn't nothing in front of him but empty track."

"U-huh," Ned said. "Jump down." I got down. He stripped off the saddle. "Hand me your foot."

"How do you know that horse has been ridden bareback before?" Uncle Parsham said.

"I aint," Ned said. "We gonter find out."

"This boy aint got but one hand," Uncle Parsham said. "Here, Lycurgus—"

But Ned already had my foot. "This boy learnt holding on riding Zack Edmonds's colts back in Missippi. I watched him at least one time when I didn't know what he was holding on with lessen it was his teeth." He threw me up. The horse did nothing: it squatted, flinched a moment, trembling a little; that was all. "U-huh," Ned said. "Let's go eat your breakfast. Whistle-britches will be here to work him this evening, then maybe Lightning will start having some fun outen this too."

Lycurgus's mother, Uncle Parsham's daughter, was cooking dinner now; the kitchen smelled of the boiling vegetables. But she had kept my breakfast warm—fried side meat, grits, hot biscuits and buttermilk or sweet milk or coffee; she untied my riding glove from my hand so I could eat, a little surprised that I had never tasted coffee since Lycurgus had been having it on Sunday morning since he was two years old. And I thought I was just hungry until I went to sleep right there in the plate until Lycurgus half dragged, half carried me to his bed in the lean-to. And, as Ned said, Mr Sam Caldwell was some Sam Caldwell; Everbe and Otis got down from the caboose of a freight train which stopped that long at Parsham a few minutes before noon. It was a through freight, not intended to stop until it reached Florence, Alabama or some place like that. I dont know how much extra coal it took to pump up the air brakes to stop it dead still at Parsham and then fire the boiler enough to regain speed and make up the lost time. Some Sam Caldwell. Twenty-three skiddoo, as Otis said.

So when the loud unfamiliar voice waked me and Lycurgus's mother tied the riding sock back on from where she had put it away when I went to sleep in my plate, and I went outside, there they all were: a surrey tied outside the gate and Uncle Parsham standing again at the top of his front steps, still wearing his hat, and Ned sitting on the next-to-bottom step and Lycurgus standing in the angle between steps and gallery as if the three of them were barricading the house; and in the yard facing them Everbe (yes, she brought it. I mean, Ned's grip) and Otis and Boon and the one who was doing the loud talking—a man almost as big as Boon and almost as ugly, with a red face and a badge and a holstered pistol stuck in his hind pocket, standing between Boon and Everbe who was still trying to pull away from the hand which was holding her arm.

"Yep," he was saying, "I know old Possum Hood. And more than that, old Possum Hood knows me, dont you, boy?"

"We all knows you here, Mr Butch," Uncle Parsham said with no inflection whatever.

"If any dont, it's just a oversight and soon corrected," Butch said. "If your womenfolks are too busy dusting and sweeping to invite us in the house, tell them to bring some chairs out here so this young lady can set down. You, boy," he told Lycurgus, "hand down two of them chairs on the gallery there where me and you"—he was talking at Everbe now—"can set in the cool and get acquainted while Sugar Boy"—he meant Boon. I dont know how I knew it—"takes these boys down to look at that horse. Huh?" Still holding Everbe's elbow, he would tilt her gently away from him until she was almost off-balance; then, a little faster though still not a real jerk, pull her back again, she still trying to get loose; now she used her other hand, pushing at his wrist. And now I was watching Boon. "You sure I aint seen you somewhere? at Birdie Watts's maybe? Where you been hiding, anyway? a good-looking gal like you?" Now Ned got up, not fast.

"Morning, Mr Boon," he said. "You and Mr Shurf want Lucius to bring the horse out?" Butch stopped tilting Everbe. He still held her though.

"Who's he?" he said. "As a general rule, we dont take to strange niggers around here. We dont object though, providing they notify themselves and then keep their mouths shut."

"Ned William McCaslin Jefferson Missippi," Ned said.

"You got too much name," Butch said. "You want something quick and simple to answer to around here until you

can raise a white mush-tash and goat-whisker like old Possum
there, and earn it. We dont care where you come from neither; all you'll need here is just somewhere to go back to. But
you'll likely do all right; at least you got sense enough to
recognise Law when you see it."

"Yes sir," Ned said. "I'm acquainted with Law. We got it
back in Jefferson too." He said to Boon: "You want the
horse?"

"No," Everbe said; she had managed to free her arm; she
moved quickly away; she could have done it sooner by just
saying Boon: which was what Butch—deputy, whatever he
was—wanted her to do, and we all knew that too. She moved,
quickly for a big girl, on until she had me between her and
Butch, holding my arm now; I could feel her hand trembling
a little as she gripped me. "Come on, Lucius. Show us the
way." She said, her voice tense: a murmur, almost passionate:
"How's your hand? Does it hurt?"

"It's all right," I said.

"You sure? You'd tell me? Does wearing that sock on it
help?"

"It's all right," I said. "I'd tell you." We went back to the
stable that way, Everbe almost dragging me to keep me between her and Butch. But it was no good; he simply walked
me off; I could smell him now—sweat and whiskey—and now
I saw the top of the pint bottle in his other hind pocket; he
(Butch) holding her elbow again and suddenly I was afraid,
because I knew I didn't—and I wasn't sure Boon did—know
Everbe that well yet. No: not afraid, that wasn't the word; not
afraid, because we—Boon alone—would have taken the pistol
away from him and then whipped him, but afraid for Everbe
and Uncle Parsham and Uncle Parsham's home and family
when it happened. But I was more than afraid. I was ashamed
that such reason for fearing for Uncle Parsham, who had to
live here, existed; hating (not Uncle Parsham doing the hating, but me doing it) it all, hating all of us for being the poor
frail victims of being alive, having to be alive—hating Everbe
for being the vulnerable helpless lodestar victim; and Boon for
being the vulnerable and helpless victimised; and Uncle
Parsham and Lycurgus for being where they had to, couldn't
help but, watch white people behaving exactly as white people

bragged that only Negroes behaved—just as I had hated Otis for telling me about Everbe in Arkansas and hated Everbe for being that helpless lodestar for human debasement which he had told me about and hated myself for listening, having to hear about it, learn about it, know about it; hating that such not only was, but must be, had to be if living was to continue and mankind be a part of it.

And suddenly I was anguished with homesickness, wrenched and wrung and agonised with it: to be home, not just to re-trace but to retract, obliterate: make Ned take the horse back to wherever and whoever and however he had got it and get Grandfather's automobile and take it back to Jefferson, in re-verse if necessary, travelling backward to unwind, ravel back into No-being, Never-being, that whole course of dirt roads, mudholes, the man and the color-blind mules, Miss Ballen-baugh and Alice and Ephum, so that, as far as I was concerned, they had never been; when sudden and quiet and plain inside me something said *Why dont you?* Because I could; I needed only say to Boon, "We're going home," and Ned would have returned the horse and my own abject confession would have the automobile located and recovered by the police at the price of merely my shame. Because I couldn't now. It was too late. Maybe yesterday, while I was still a child, but not now. I knew too much, had seen too much. I was a child no longer now; innocence and childhood were forever lost, forever gone from me. And Everbe was loose again. I had missed seeing how she did it this time: only that she was free, facing him; she said something inaudible, quick; anyway he was not even touching her now, just looking down at her, grinning.

"Sure, sure," he said. "Thrash around a little; maybe I like that too; makes it look a little better to old Sugar Boy too. All right, boy," he said to Ned. "Let's see that horse."

"You stay here," Ned told me. "Me and Lycurgus will get him." So I stood, next to Everbe at the fence; she was hold-ing my arm again, her hand still shaking a little. Ned and Lycurgus led the horse out. Ned was already looking toward us; he said quickly: "Where's that other one?"

"Dont tell me you got two of them," Butch said. But I knew what Ned meant. So did Everbe. She turned quickly.

"Otis!" she said. But he was nowhere in sight.

"Run," Ned told Lycurgus. "If he aint got into the house yet, maybe you can cut him off. Tell him his aunt wants him. And you stay right with him." Lycurgus didn't even wait to say Yes sir: he just gave the lead rope to Ned and departed running. The rest of us stood along the fence—Everbe trying for immobility since that was all she had to find effacement in, but too big for it like the doe is too big for the plum thicket which is all she has available for safety; Boon furious and seething, restraining himself who never before had restrained himself from anything. Not from fear; I tell you, he was not afraid of that gun and badge: he could and would have taken them both away from Butch and then, in a kind of glory, tossed the pistol on the ground halfway between them and then given Butch the first step toward it; and only half from the loyalty which would shield me—and my family (his family)—from the result of such a battle, no matter who won it. Because the other half was chivalry: to shield a woman, even a whore from one of the predators who debase police badges by using them as immunity to prey on her helpless kind. And a little further along, dissociated though present, Uncle Parsham, the patrician (he bore in his Christian name the patronymic of the very land we stood on) the aristocrat of us all and judge of us all.

"Hell," Butch said. "He cant win races standing still in a halter. Go on. Trot him across the lot."

"We just sent for his jockey," Ned said. "Then you can see him work. Then he said, "Unlessen you in a hurry to get back to yourn."

"My what?" Butch said.

"Your law work," Ned said. "Back in Possum or wherever it is."

"After coming all the way out here to see a race horse?" Butch said. "All I see so far is a plug standing half asleep in a lot."

"I'm sho glad you told me that," Ned said. "I thought maybe you wasn't interested." He turned to Boon. "So maybe what you and Miss Corrie better do is go on back to town now and be ready to meet the others when the train comes. You can send the surrey back for Mr Butch and Lucius and that other boy after we breezes Lightning."

"Ha ha ha," Butch said, without mirth, without anything. "How's that for a idea? Huh, Sugar Boy? You and Sweet Thing bobbasheely on back to the hotel now, and me and Uncle Remus and Lord Fauntleroy will mosey along any time up to midnight, providing of course we are through here." He moved easily along the fence to where Boon stood, watching Boon though addressing Ned: "I cant let Sugar Boy leave without me. I got to stay right with him, or he might get everybody in trouble. They got a law now, about taking good-looking gals across state lines for what they call immortal purposes. Sugar Boy's a stranger here; he dont know exactly where that state line's at, and his foot might slip across it while his mind's on something else—something that aint a foot. At least we dont call it foot around here. Huh, Sugar Boy?" He slapped Boon on the back, still grinning, watching Boon—one of those slaps which jovial men give one another, but harder, a little too hard but not quite too hard. Boon didn't move, his hands on the top rail of the gate. They were too sunburned or maybe too ingrained with dirt to turn white. But I could see the muscles. "Yes sir," Butch said, watching Boon, grinning, "all friends together for a while yet anyhow. Come one, come all, or come none—for a while longer anyhow. At least until something happens that might put a man not watching what he was doing out of circulation—a stranger say that wouldn't be missed nohow. Huh, Sugar Boy?" and slapped Boon again on the back, still harder this time, watching him, grinning. And Everbe saw Boon's hand this time too; she said, quick, not loud:

"Boon." Like that: "Boon." So had Uncle Parsham.

"Here come the other boy," he said. Otis was just coming around the corner of the house, Lycurgus looming almost twice as tall right behind him. Even knowing what was wrong about him didn't help Otis much. But Ned was the one who was looking at him hard. He came up gently; strolling, in fact.

"Somebody want me?" he said.

"It was me," Ned said. "But I aint seed you in daylight before and maybe my mind gonter change." He said to Lycurgus: "Get the tack." So we—they—tacked up and Lycurgus and Ned led the way back along the lane to the creek pasture, we following, even Butch giving his attention to the matter in hand now; unless, as the angler does, he was deliberately giving Everbe a little rest to build up her strength to rush and thrash once more against the hook of that tin star on his sweaty shirt. When we reached the pasture, Ned and Otis were already facing each other about eight feet apart; behind them, Lycurgus stood with the horse. Ned looked strained and tired. As far as I knew, he had had no sleep at all unless he actually had slept for an hour or so on the hay in the box car. But that's all he was: not exhausted by sleeplessness, just annoyed by it. Otis was picking his nose, still gently. "A know-boy," Ned was saying. "As knowing a boy as I ever seed. I just hopes that when you're twice your age, you will still know half as much."

"Much obliged," Otis said.

"Can you ride a horse?" Ned said.

"I been living on a Arkansas farm for a right smart number of years," Otis said.

"Can you ride a horse?" Ned said. "Nemmine where you used to live or still does."

"Now, that depends, as the fellow says," Otis said. "I figgered I was going back home this morning. That I would a long been in Kiblett, Arkansas, right this minute. But since my plans got changed without nobody asking me, I aint decided quite yet just what I'm going to do next. How much you paying to get that horse rode?"

"Otis!" Everbe said.

"We aint come to that yet," Ned said, as gentle as Otis. "The first thing is to get them three heats run and to be in front when at least two of them is finished. Then we'll git around to how much."

"Heh heh heh," Otis said, not laughing either. "That is, there aint going to be nothing to pay nobody with until you win it—that's you. And you cant even run at it without somebody setting on the horse—that's me. Is that right?"

"Otis!" Everbe said.

"That's right," Ned said. "We all of us working on shares so we'll have something to divide afterward. Your share will have to wait too, like ourn."

"Yeah," Otis said. "I seen that kind of share dividing in the Arkansas cotton business. The trouble is, the share of the fellow that does the sharing is always a little different from the share of the fellow that done the dividing. The fellow that done the sharing is still waiting for his share because he aint yet located where it's at. So from now on, I'll just take the cash-in-advance share and let you folks keep all the dividing."

"How much do that come to?" Ned said.

"You cant be interested, because you aint even run the first heat yet, let alone won it. But I dont mind telling you, in confidence, you might say. It'll be ten dollars."

"Otis!" Everbe said. She moved now; she cried, "Aint you ashamed?"

"Hold up, Miss," Ned said. "I'll handle it." He looked tired, but that was all. Without haste he drew a folded flour sack from his hip pocket and unfolded it and took out his worn snap-purse and opened it. "Hold out your hand," he told Lycurgus, who did so while Ned counted slowly onto the palm six frayed dollar bills and then about a cupful of coins of various denominations. "It's gonter be fifteen cents short, but Mr Hogganbeck will make it up."

"Make it up to what?" Otis said.

"To what you said. Ten dollars," Ned said.

"You cant seem to hear neither," Otis said. "What I said was twenty dollars." Now Boon moved.

"God damn it," he said.

"Just hold up," Ned told him. His hand didn't even stop, now returning the coins one by one from Lycurgus's hand, and then the frayed bills, back into the purse and closed it and folded it back into the flour sack and put the sack back into his pocket. "So you aint gonter ride the horse," he said to Otis.

"I aint seen my price—" Otis said.

"Mr Boon Hogganbeck there is fixing to hand it to you right now," Ned said. "Whyn't you just come right out like a man and say you aint gonter ride that horse? It dont matter why you aint." They looked at each other. "Come on. Say it out."

"Naw," Otis said. "I aint going to ride it." He said something else, foul, which was his nature; vicious, which was his nature; completely unnecessary, which was his nature too. Yes, even finally knowing what it was didn't help with him. By this time Everbe had him. She snatched him, hard. And this time he snarled. He cursed her. "Watch out. I aint near done talking yet—if I'm a mind."

"Say the word," Butch said. "I'll beat the hell out of him just on principle; I wont even bother with pleasure. How the hell did Sugar Boy ever let him get this far without at least one whelp on him?"

"No!" Everbe said to Butch. She still held Otis by the arm. "You're going back home on the next train!"

"Now you're tooting," Otis said. "I'd a been there right now except for you." She released him.

"Go on back to the surrey," she said.

"You cant risk it," Boon said rapidly to her. "You'll have to go with him." He said: "All right. You all go back to town. You can send for me and Lucius about sundown."

And I knew what that meant, what decision he had wrestled with and licked. But Butch fooled us; the confident angler was letting his fish have the backing too. "Sure," he said. "Send back for us." Everbe and Otis went on. "Now that that's settled, who is going to ride the horse?"

"This boy here," Ned said. "He a one-handed horse."

"Heh heh heh," Butch said; he was laughing this time. "I seen this horse run here last winter. If one hand can even wake him up, it will take more hands than a spider or a daddy-longlegs to get him out in front of that horse of Colonel Linscomb's."

"Maybe you right," Ned said. "That's what we gonter find out now. Son," he said to Lycurgus, "hand me my coat." I had not even noticed the coat yet, but now Lycurgus had it; also the peeled switch. Ned took both and put the coat on. He said to Boon and Butch: "Yawl stand over yonder under them trees with Uncle Possum where you'll be in the shade and wont distract his mind. Hand me your foot," he told me. We did so. I mean, Ned threw me up and Boon and Butch and Lycurgus went back to the tree where Uncle Parsham was already standing. Even though we had made only three trips around the pasture this morning, we had a vestigial path which Lightning would remember whether I could see it or not. Ned led him out to what had been our old starting-point this morning. He spoke, quiet and succinct. He was not

Uncle Remus now. But then, he never was when it was just me and members of his own race around:

"That track tomorrow aint but a half a mile, so you gonter go around it twice. Make like this is it, so when he sees that real track tomorrow, he'll already know beforehand what to expect and to do. You understand?"

"Yes," I said. "Ride him around it twice—"

He handed me the switch. "Get him going quick and hard. Cut him once with this before he even knows it. Then dont touch him again with it until I tells you to. Keep him going as fast as you can with your heels and talking to him but dont bother him: just set there. Keep your mind on it that you're going around twice, and try to think his mind onto that too, like you done with them colts out at McCaslin. You cant do it, but you got the switch this time. But dont touch him with it until I tells you to." He turned his back; he was doing something now inside the shelter of his coat—something infinitesimal with his hidden hands; suddenly I smelled something, faint yet sharp; I realise now that I should have recognised it at once but I didn't have time then. He turned back; as when he had coaxed the horse into the box car this morning, his hand touched, caressed Lightning's muzzle for maybe a second, then he stepped back, Lightning already trying to follow him had I not reined him back. "Go!" Ned said. "Cut him!"

I did. He leapt, sprang, out of simple fright: nothing else; it took a half stride to get his head back and another stride before he realised we wanted to follow the track, path again, at full gallop now, on just enough outside rein to hold him on the course, I already heeling him as hard as I could even before the fright began to fade. Only, there we were again, just like this morning: going good, obedient enough, plenty of power, but once more with that sense that his head didn't really want to go anywhere; until we entered the back stretch and he saw Ned again on the opposite side of the ring. It was the explosion again; he had taken the bit away from me; he had already left the path and was cutting straight across to Ned before I got balance enough to reach my good hand down and take the rein short and haul, wrench him angling back into the track, going hard now; I had to hold him on the outside to make the back turn and into the stretch where he could see Ned again and once more reached for the bit to go straight to him; I was using the cut hand too now to hold him onto the track; it seemed forever until Ned spoke. "Cut him," he said. "Then throw the switch away."

I did so and flung the switch backward; the leap again but I had him now since it only took one rein, the outside one to keep him on the course, going good now, around the first turn and I was ready for him this time when he would see Ned, on through the back stretch still going, into and around the last turn, still going, Ned standing now about twenty yards beyond where our finish line would be, speaking just exactly loud enough for Lightning to hear him and just exactly as he had spoken to him in the box car door last night—and I didn't need the switch now; I wouldn't have had time to use it if I had had it and I thought until then that I had ridden at least one horse that I called hot anyway: a half-bred colt of Cousin Zack's with Morgan on the bottom: but nothing like this, this burst, surge, as if until now we had been dragging a rope with a chunk of wood at the end of it behind us and Ned's voice had cut the rope: "Come on, son. I got it."

So we were standing there, Lightning's muzzle buried to the nostrils in Ned's hand, though all I could smell now was horse-reek and all I could see was the handful of grass which Lightning was eating; Ned himself saying "Hee hee hee" so gentle and quiet that I whispered too:

"What?" I said. "What?" But Boon didn't whisper, coming up.

"I'll be God damned. What the hell did you tell him?"

"Nothing," Ned said. "Just if he want his supper, to come on and get it." And not Butch either: bold, confident, unconvinceable, without scruple or pity.

"Well, well," he said. He didn't draw Lighting's head up out of Ned's hand: he jerked it up, then rammed the bit home when Lightning started back.

"Lemme do it," Ned said quickly. "What you want to find out?"

"Any time I need help handling horses around here, I'll holler," Butch said. "And not for you. I'll save you to holler for down in Missippi." He lifted Lightning's lip and looked at his gums, then at his eyes. "Dont you know it's against the law to dope a horse for a race? Maybe you folks down there in them swamps aint heard about it, but it's so."

"We got horse doctors in Missippi though," Ned said. "Send for one of them to come and see if he been doped."

"Sure, sure," Butch said. "Only, why did you give it to him a day ahead of the race? to see if it would work?"

"That's right," Ned said. "If I give him nothing. Which I aint. Which if you knows horses, you already knows."

"Sure, sure," Butch said again. "I dont interfere with no man's business secrets—providing they work. Is this horse going to run like that again tomorrow? I dont mean once: I mean three times."

"He dont need to do it but twice," Ned said.

"All right," Butch said. "Twice. Is he?"

"Ask Mr Hogganbeck there if he hadn't better do it twice," Ned said.

"I aint asking Mr Sugar Boy," Butch said. "I'm asking you."

"I can make him do it twice," Ned said.

"Fair enough," Butch said. "In fact, if all you got is three more doses, I wouldn't even risk but twice. Then if he misses the second one, you can use the last one to get back to Missippi on."

"I done thought of that too," Ned said. "Walk him back to the barn," he said to me. "Cool him out. Then we'll bath him."

Butch watched that too, some of it. We went back to the barn and untacked and Lycurgus brought a bucket and a rag and Lycurgus washed him down and dried him with croker sacks before stalling and feeding him—or had started to. Because Butch said, "Here, boy, run to the house and set the water bucket and some sugar on the front gallery. Me and Mr Sugar Boy are going to have a toddy." Though Lycurgus didn't move until Uncle Parsham said,

"Go." He went then, Boon and Butch following. Uncle Parsham stood at the door of the stable, watching them (Butch, that is)—a lean dramatic old man all black-and-white: black pants, white shirt, black face and hat behind the white hair and moustache and imperial. "Law," he said. He said it calmly, with cold and detached contempt.

"A man that never had nothing in it nohow, one of them little badges goes to his head so fast it makes yourn swim too," Ned said. "Except it aint the badge so much as that pistol, that likely all the time he was a little boy, he wanted to tote, only he knowed all the time that soon as he got big enough to own one, the law wouldn't let him tote it. Now with that badge too, he dont run no risk of being throwed in jail and having it took away from him; he can still be a little boy in spite of he had to grow up. The risk is, that pistol gonter stay on that little boy mind just so long before some day it gonter shoot at something alive before he even knowed he aimed to." Then Lycurgus came back.

"They waiting for you," he told me. "The surrey."

"It's back from town already?" I said.

"It never went to town," Lycurgus said. "It never left. She been setting in it out there with that-ere boy all the time, waiting for you all. She say to come on."

"Wait," Ned said. I stopped; I still had the riding sock on and I thought he meant that. But he was looking at me. "You gonter start running into folks now."

"What folks?" I said.

"That word has done got around to. About this race."

"How got around?" I said.

"How do word ever get around?" he said. "It dont need no messenger; all it needs is two horses that can run to be inside the same ten miles of each other. How you reckon that Law got here? maybe smelled that white girl four or five miles away like a dog? I know; maybe I hoped like Boon Hogganbeck still believes: that we could get these two horses together here all nice and private and run that race, win or lose, and me and you and him could either go back home or go any other place we wants providing it's longer away than Boss Priest's arm. But not now. You gonter start meeting them from now on. And tomorrow they gonter be thicker still."

"You mean we can run the race?"

"We got to now. Maybe we been had to ever since me and Boon realised that Boss had done took his hand off of that automobile for as long as twenty-four hours. But now we sho got to run it."

"What do you want me to do?" I said.

"Nothing. I'm just telling you so you wont be surprised in advance. All we got to do is get them two horses on the same track and pointed the same way and you just set there on Lightning and do like I tell you. Go on, now, before they start hollering for you."

Nine

Ned was right. I mean, about word already being around. There was nothing wrong with my hand when Everbe took the riding sock off. I mean, it felt like anybody's hand would that had been cut across the inside of the fingers yesterday. I dont believe it had bled any more even when I used it against Lightning's pulling this afternoon. But not Everbe. So we stopped at the doctor's first, about a mile this side of town. Butch knew him, knew where but I dont know how Everbe persuaded him to take us there—nagged him or threatened or promised or maybe just did it like a big girl trout so busy fussing around a child trout that she quit behaving like there was any such thing in existence as a barbed hook with a line fastened to it and so the fisherman had to do something even if only getting rid of the child trout. Or maybe it was not Everbe but rather the empty flask, since the next drink would have to be at the hotel in Parsham. Because as I came around the house, Lycurgus's mother was standing at the edge of the gallery holding a sugar bowl and a water bucket with a gourd dipper and Butch and Boon were just draining the two tumblers and Lycurgus was just picking up the empty flask where Butch had flung it into a rose bush.

So Butch took us to the doctor's—a little once-white house in a little yard filled with the kind of rank-growing rank-smelling dusty flowers that bloom in the late summer and fall, a fat iron-gray woman in pince-nez like a retired school teacher who even fifteen years later still hated eight-year-old children, who came to the door and looked at us once (Ned was right) and said back into the house, "It's them race-horse folks," and turned and vanished toward the back, Butch moving right on in before she could turn, jovial, already welcome—or somebody damn well better see that he was (the badge again, you see; wearing it or simply being known to possess one, to enter any house in any other manner would be not a mere individual betrayal but a caste betrayal and debasement)—saying,

"Howdy, Doc; got a patient for you," to an iron-gray man

too if the tobacco juice were bleached out of his unshaven whiskers, in a white shirt like Ned's but not as clean, and a black coat too with a long streak of day before yesterday's egg on it, who looked and smelled like something also, except it wasn't just alcohol, or anyway all alcohol. "Me and Brother Hogganbeck will wait in the parlor," Butch said. "Dont bother; I know where the bottle's at. Dont worry about Doc," he said to Boon. "He dont hardly ever touch whiskey unless he just has to. The law allows him one shot of ether as a part of the cure for every patient that can show blood or a broken bone. If it's just a little old cut or broke finger or ripped hide like this, Doc divides the treatment with the patient: he drinks all the ether and lets the patient have all the cure. Haw haw haw. This way."

So Butch and Boon went that way, and Everbe and I (you have doubtless noticed that nobody had missed Otis yet. We got out of the surrey; it appeared to be Butch's; anyway he was driving it; there had been some delay at Uncle Parsham's while Butch tried to persuade, then cajole, then force Everbe to get in the front seat with him, which she foiled by getting into the back seat and holding me by one arm and holding Otis in the surrey with her other hand, until Boon got in front with Butch—and first Butch, then the rest of us were somehow inside the doctor's hall but nobody remembered Otis at that moment) followed the doctor into another room containing a horse hair sofa with a dirty pillow and a wadded quilt on it, and a roll-top desk cluttered with medicine bottles and more of them on the mantel beneath which the ashes of last winter's final fire had not yet been disturbed, and a washstand with a bowl and pitcher and a chamber pot that somebody hadn't emptied yet either in one corner and a shotgun in the other; and if Mother had been there his finger nails would have touched no scratch belonging to her, let alone four cut fingers, and evidently Everbe agreed with her; she—Everbe—said, "I'll unwrap it," and did so. I said the hand was all right. The doctor looked at it through his steel-rimmed spectacles.

"What did you put on it?" he said. Everbe told him. I know what it is now. The doctor looked at her. "How'd you happen to have that handy?" he said. Then he lifted the spectacles by one corner and looked at her again and said, "Oh." Then he said, "Well, well," and lowered the spectacles again and—yes he did: it was a sigh—and said, "I aint been to Memphis in thirty-five years," and stood there a minute and—I tell you, it was a sigh—said, "Yes. Thirty-five years," and said, "If I was you I wouldn't do anything to it. Just bandage it again." Yes, exactly like Mother: he got the bandage out but she put it on. "You the boy going to ride that horse tomorrow?" he said.

"Yes," Everbe said.

"Beat that Linscomb horse this time, durn him."

"We'll try," Everbe said. "How much do we owe you?"

"Nothing," he said. "You already cured it. Just beat that durn Linscomb horse tomorrow."

"I want to pay you something for looking at it," Everbe said. "For telling us it's all right."

"No," he said. He looked at her: the old man's eyes behind the spectacles magnified yet unfocus-able, as irreparable as eggs, until you would think they couldn't possibly grasp and hold anything as recent as me and Everbe.

"Yes," Everbe said. "What is it?"

"Maybe if you had a extra handkerchief or something . . ." He said: "Yes, thirty-five years. I had one once, when I was a young man, thirty, thirty-five years ago. Then I got married, and it. . . ." He said, "Yes. Thirty-five years."

"Oh," Everbe said. She turned her back to us and bent over, her skirts rustled; it was not long; they rustled again and she turned back. "Here," she said. It was a garter.

"Beat that durn horse!" he said. "Beat him! You can do it!" Now we heard the voices—voice, that is, Butch's—loud in the little hall before we got there:

"What do you know? Sugar Boy wont take a drink no more. All boys together, give and take, never snatch without whistling first, and now he insults me." He stood grinning at Boon, triumphant, daring. Boon looked really dangerous now. Like Ned (all of us) he was worn out for sleep too. But all the load Ned had to carry was the horse; Everbe and Butch's badge were not his burden. "Huh, boy?" Butch said; now he was going to slap Boon on the back again with that jovial force which was just a little too hard but not quite.

"Dont do it again," Boon said. Butch stopped. He didn't retract the motion: he just stopped it, grinning at Boon.

"My name's Mister Lovemaiden," he said. "But call me Butch."

After a while Boon said, "Lovemaiden."

"Butch," Butch said.

After a while Boon said, "Butch."

"That's a boy," Butch said. He said to Everbe: "Doc fix you up all right? Maybe I ought to warned you about Doc. They claim when he was a young squirt fifty-sixty years ago, he would a had one snatch at your drawers before he even tipped his hat."

"Come on," Boon said. "You paid him?"

"Yes," Everbe said. We went outside. And that was when somebody said Where is Otis? No, it was Everbe of course; she just looked once and said, "Otis!" quite loud, strong, not to say urgent, not to say alarmed and desperate.

"Dont tell me he's scared of horses even tied to a gate post," Butch said.

"Come on," Boon said. "He's just gone on ahead; he aint got nowhere else to go. We'll pick him up."

"But why?" Everbe said. "Why didn't he—"

"How do I know?" Boon said. "Maybe he's right." He meant Butch. Then he meant Otis: "For all he's as knowing a little son of a bitch as ever come out of Arkansas or Missippi either for that matter, he's still a arrant coward. Come on." So we got in the surrey and went on to town. Except that I was on Everbe's side about Otis; when you couldn't see him was a good time to be already wondering where he was and why. I never saw anybody lose public confidence as fast as he could; he would have had a hard time now finding anybody in this surrey to take him to another zoo or anywhere else. And it wasn't going to be much longer before he couldn't have found anybody in Parsham either.

Only we didn't overtake him. He wasn't on the road all the way to the hotel. And Ned was wrong. I mean about the increasing swarm of horse-race devotees we would be running into from now on. Maybe I had expected to find the entire hotel veranda lined with them, waiting for us and watching us arrive. If so, I was wrong; there was nobody there at all. In the winter of course, during the quail season and especially during the two weeks of the National Trials, it would be different. But in those days, unlike London, Parsham had no summer season; people went elsewhere: to water or mountains: Raleigh, near Memphis, or Iuka not far away in Mississippi, or to the Ozarks or Cumberlands. (Nor, for that matter, does it have one now, nor indeed does any place else, either winter or summer season; there are no seasons at all anymore, with interiors artificially contrived at sixty degrees in summer and ninety degrees in winter, so that moss-backed recidivists like me must go outside in summer to escape cold and in winter to escape heat; including the automobiles also which once were mere economic necessities but are now social ones, the moment already here when, if all the human race ever stops moving at the same instant, the surface of the earth will seize, solidify: there are too many of us; humanity will destroy itself not by fission but by another beginning with f which is a verb-active also as well as a conditional state; I wont see it but you may: a law compelled and enforced by dire and frantic social—not economic: social—desperation permitting a woman but one child as she is now permitted but one husband.)

But in winter of course (as now) it was different, with the quail season and the Grand National trials, with the rich money of oil and wheat barons from Wall Street and Chicago and Saskatchewan, and the fine dogs with pedigrees more jealous than princes, and the fine breeding- and training-kennels only minutes away now by automobile—Red Banks and Michigan City and La Grange and Germantown, and the names—Colonel Linscomb whose horse (we assumed) we were going to race against tomorrow, and Horace Lytle and George Peyton as magical among bird dog people as Babe Ruth and Ty Cobb among baseball aficionados, and Mr Jim Avant from Hickory Flat and Mr Paul Rainey just a few miles down Colonel Sartoris's railroad toward Jefferson—hound men both, who (I suppose) among these mere pedigreed pointers and setters, called themselves slumming; the vast rambling hotel booming then, staffed and elegant, the very air itself suave and murmurous with money, littered with colored ribbons and cluttered with silver cups.

But there was nobody there now, the quiet street empty

with May dust (it was after six now; Parsham would be at home eating—or preparing to eat—supper) vacant even of Otis, though he could be, probably was, inside. And what was even more surprising, to me anyway, vacant also of Butch. He simply drove us up to the door and put us out and drove away, pausing only long enough to give Everbe one hard jeering leer and Boon one hard leering jeer, if anything a little harder than Everbe's, saying, "Dont worry, boy, I'll be back. If you got any business still hanging, better get it unhung before I get back or something might get tore," and drove away. So apparently he also had somewhere he had to be occasionally: a home; I was still ignorant and innocent (not as much as I was twenty-four hours ago, but still tainted) but I was on Boon's side, my loyalty was his, not to mention Everbe's, and I had assimilated enough (whether I had digested all of it yet or not) since yesterday, to know exactly what I meant when I hoped that maybe he had a wife in it— some innocent ravished out of a convent whose friendless avengeless betrayal would add another charge to the final accounting of his natural ruthless baseness; or better: an ambidextrous harridan who could cope with him at least by recording into his face each one of his counter-marital victories. Because probably half the pleasure he got out of fornication was having it known who the victim was. But I wronged him. He was a bachelor.

But Otis was not inside either: only the single temporary clerk in the half-shrouded lobby and the single temporary waiter flapping his napkin in the door of the completely shrouded dining room save for a single table set out for such anonymous passers-by as we were—so far were, that is. But Otis had not been seen. "I aint wondering so much where he's at," Boon said, "as I am about what the hell he has done this time that we aint found out about yet."

"Nothing!" Everbe said. "He's just a child!"

"Sure," Boon said. "Just a little armed child. When he gets big enough to steal—"

"Stop!" Everbe said. "I wont—"

"All right, all right," Boon said. "Find, then. Find enough money to buy a knife with a six-inch blade in place of that two-inch pocket knife, anybody that turns his back on him

had sho enough better be wearing one of them old-time iron
union suits like you see in museums. I got to talk to you," he
told her. "Supper'll be soon, and then we got to meet the
train. And that tin-badge stallion will be neighing and pranc-
ing back here any time now." He took her arm. "Come on."

That was when I had to begin to listen to Boon. I mean, I
had to. Everbe compelled it. She wouldn't even go with him
unless I came too. We—they—went to the ladies' parlor;
there wasn't much time now; we would have to eat supper
and then go to the depot to meet Miss Reba. In those days
females didn't run in and out of gentlemen's rooms in hotels
as, I am told, they do now, even wearing, I am told, what the
advertisements call the shorts or scanties capable of giving
women the freedom they need in their fight for freedom; in
fact, I had never seen a woman alone in a hotel before
(Mother would not have been here without Father) and I remember how I wondered how Everbe without a wedding
ring even could have got in. They—the hotels—had what
were known as ladies' parlors, like this one where we now
were—a smaller though still more elegant room, most of it
likewise shrouded in holland bags. But I was still on Boon's
side; I didn't pass the doorway but stopped outside, where
Everbe could know where I was, within call, even if she
couldn't actually see me. So I heard. Oh yes, listened. I would
have listened anyway; I had gone too far by now in sophisti-
cation and the facts of life to stop now, just as I had gone too
far in stealing automobiles and race horses to quit now. So I
could hear them: Everbe; and almost at once she was crying
again:

"No! I wont! Let me alone!" Then Boon:

"But why? You said you loved me. Was that just lying too?"
Then Everbe:

"I do love you. That's why. Let me alone! Turn me loose!
Lucius! Lucius!" Then Boon:

"Shut up. Stop now." Then nothing for a minute. I didn't
look, peep, I just listened. No: just heard: "If I thought you
were just two-timing me with that God damned tin-badged—"
Then Everbe:

"No! No! I'm not!" Then something I couldn't hear, until
Boon said:

"What? Quit? What do you mean, quit?" Then Everbe:

"Yes! I've quit! Not any more. Never!" Then Boon:

"How're you going to live? What will you eat? Where you going to sleep?" And Everbe:

"I'm going to get a job. I can work."

"What can you do? You aint got no more education than me. What can you do to make a living?"

"I can wash dishes. I can wash and iron. I can learn to cook. I can do something, I can even hoe and pick cotton. Let me go, Boon. Please. Please. I've got to. Cant you see I've got to?" Then her feet running, even on the thick carpet; she was gone. So Boon caught me this time. His face was pretty bad now. Ned was lucky; all he had to frazzle over was just a horse race.

"Look at me," Boon said. "Look at me good. What's wrong with me? What the hell's wrong with me? It used to be that I . . ." His face looked like it was going to burst. He started again: "And why me? Why the hell me? Why the hell has she got to pick out me to reform on? God damn it, she's a whore, cant she understand that? She's in the paid business of belonging to me exclusive the minute she sets her foot where I'm at like I'm in the paid business of belonging to Boss and Mr Maury exclusive the minute I set my foot where they're at. But now she's done quit. For private reasons. She cant no more. She aint got no more private rights to quit without my say-so too than I got to quit without Boss's and Mr Maury's say-so too—" He stopped, furious and baffled, raging and helpless; and more: terrified. It was the Negro waiter, flapping his napkin in this doorway now. Boon made a tremendous effort; Ned with nothing but a horse race to win didn't even know what trouble was. "Go tell her to come on to supper. We got to meet that train. Her room is Number Five."

But she wouldn't come out. So Boon and I ate alone. His face still didn't look much better. He ate like you put meat into a grinder: not like he either wanted it or didn't want it, but it was just time to eat. After a while I said, "Maybe he started walking back to Arkansas. He said two or three times this afternoon that that's where he would have been by now if folks hadn't kept on interfering with him."

"Sure," Boon said. "Maybe he just went on ahead to locate that dish-washing job for her. Or maybe he reformed too and they're both going right straight to heaven without stopping off at Arkansas or nowhere else, and he just went ahead to find out how to pass Memphis without nobody seeing them." Then it was time to go. I had been watching the edge of her dress beyond the dining room door for about two minutes, but now the waiter himself came.

"Two-O-Eight, sir," he said. "Just blowed for One Mile crossing." So we went across to the depot, not far, the three of us walking together, mutual overnight hotel guests. I mean we—they—were not fighting now; we—they—could even have talked, conversed, equable and inconsequential. Everbe would have, only Boon would need to speak first. Not far: merely to cross the tracks to reach the platform, the train already in sight now, the two of them (Boon and Everbe) shackled yet estranged, alien yet indissoluble, confounded yet untwainable by no more than what Boon thought was a whim: who (Boon) for all his years was barely older than me and didn't even know that women no more have whims than they have doubts or illusions or prostate troubles; the train, the engine passing us in hissing thunder, sparks flying from the brake shoes; it was the long one, the big one, the cannonball, the Special: the baggage cars, the half Jimcrow smoker, then the day coaches and the endless pullmans, the dining car at the end, slowing; it was Sam Caldwell's train and if Everbe and Otis had traveled to Parsham in the caboose of a scheduled through freight, Miss Reba would be in a drawing room, if indeed she was not in the president's private car; the train stopping at last though still no vestibule opened, no white-jacketed porter nor conductor, though certainly Sam would have been watching for us; until Boon said, "Hell. The smoker," and began to run. Then we all saw them, far ahead: Sam Caldwell in his uniform on the cinders helping Miss Reba down, someone—another woman—following her, and not from the smoking car at all but from the Jimcrow half of it where Negroes traveled; the train—it was the Special for Washington and New York, the cannonball wafting the rich women in diamonds and the men with dollar cigars in suave and insulate transmogrification across the earth—already moving again so that Sam had only time to wave back at us from the step, diminishing eastward behind the short staccato puffs and the long whistle blasts and at last the red diminishing twin lamps, and the two women standing among the grips and bags on the vacant cinders, Miss Reba bold and handsome and chic and Minnie beside her looking like death.

"We've had trouble," Miss Reba said. "Where's the hotel?" We went there. Now, in the lighted lobby, we could see Minnie. Her face was not like death. Death is peaceful. What Minnie's fixed close-lipped brooding face boded was not peaceful and it wasn't boded at her either. The clerk came. "I'm Mrs Binford," Miss Reba said. "You got my wire about a cot in my room for my maid?"

"Yes, Mrs Binford," the clerk said. "We have special quarters for servants, with their own dining room—"

"Keep them," Miss Reba said. "I said a cot in my room. I want her with me. We'll wait in the parlor while you make it up. Where is it?" But she had already located the ladies' parlor, we following. "Where is he?" she said.

"Where is who?" Everbe said.

"You know who," Miss Reba said. And suddenly I knew who, and that in another moment I would know why. But I didn't have time. Miss Reba sat down. "Sit down," she told Minnie. But Minnie didn't move. "All right," Miss Reba said. "Tell them." Minnie smiled at us. It was ghastly: a frantic predatory rictus, an anguished ravening gash out of which the beautiful and matchless teeth arched outward to the black orifice where the gold one had been; I knew now why Otis had fled Parsham even though he had had to do it on foot; oh yes, at that moment fifty-six years ago I was one with you now in your shocked and horrified unbelief, until Minnie and Miss Reba told us.

"It was him!" Minnie said. "I know it was him! He taken it while I was asleep!"

"Hell fire," Boon said. "Somebody stole a tooth out of your mouth and you didn't even know it?"

"God damn it, listen," Miss Reba said. "Minnie had that tooth made that way, so she could put it in and take it out—worked extra and scrimped and saved for—How many years was it, Minnie? three, wasn't it?—until she had enough money to have her own tooth took out and that God damned gold one put in. Oh sure, I tried my best to talk her out of it—ruin that set of natural teeth that anybody else would give a thousand dollars apiece, and anything else she had too; not to mention all the extra it cost her to have it made so she could take it out when she ate—"

"Took it out when she ate?" Boon said. "What the hell is she saving her teeth for?"

"I wanted that tooth a long time," Minnie said, "and I worked and saved to get it, extra work. I aint going to have it all messed up with no spit-mixed something to eat."

"So she would take it out when she ate," Miss Reba said, "and put it right there in front of her plate where she could see it, not only watch it but enjoy it too while she was eating. But that wasn't the way he got it; she says she put it back in when she finished breakfast, and I believe her; she aint never forgot it before because she was proud of it, it was valuable, it had cost her too much; no more than you would put that God damned horse down somewhere that's probably cost you a damned sight more than a gold tooth, and forget it—"

"I know I never," Minnie said. "I put it back as soon as I ate. I remember. Only I was plumb wore out and tired—"

"That's right," Miss Reba said. She was talking to Everbe now: "I reckon I was going good when you all come in last night. It was daybreak before I come to my senses enough to quit, and the sun was up when I finally persuaded Minnie to take a good slug of gin and see the front door was bolted and go on back to bed, and I went up myself and woke Jackie and told her to keep the place shut, I didn't care if every horny bastard south of St Louis come knocking, not to let nobody in before six oclock this evening. So Minnie went back and laid down on her cot in the store room off the back gallery and I thought at first maybe she forgot to lock that door—"

"Course I locks it," Minnie said. "That's where the beer's at. I been keeping that door locked ever since that boy got here because I remembered him from last summer when he come to visit."

"So there she was," Miss Reba said, "wore out and dead asleep on that cot with the door locked and never knowed nothing until—"

"I woke up," Minnie said. "I was still so tired and wore out that I slept too hard, like you do; I just laid there and I knowed something felt a little funny in my mouth. But I just thought maybe it was a scrap of something had done got caught in it no matter how careful I was, until I got up and went to the looking glass and looked—"

"I wonder they never heard her in Chattanooga, let alone just in Parsham," Miss Reba said. "And the door still locked—"

"It was him!" Minnie said, cried. "I know it was! He been worrying me at least once every day how much it cost and why didn't I sell it and how much could I get for it and where would I go to sell it at—"

"Sure," Miss Reba said. "That's why he squalled like a wildcat this morning when you told him he wasn't going back home but would have to come on to Parsham with you," she told Everbe. "So when he heard the train whistle, he run, huh? Where do you figger he is? Because I'm going to have Minnie's tooth back."

"We dont know," Everbe said. "He just disappeared out of the surrey about half past five oclock. We thought he would have to be here, because he aint got anywhere else to go. But we haven't found him yet."

"Maybe you aint looked right," Miss Reba said. "He aint the kind you can whistle out. You got to smoke him out like a rat or a snake." The clerk came back. "All right now?" Miss Reba said.

"Yes, Mrs Binford," the clerk said. Miss Reba got up.

"I'll get Minnie settled down and stay with her until she goes to sleep. Then I'd like some supper," she told the clerk. "It dont matter what it is."

"It's a little late," the clerk said. "The dining room—"

"And it's going to be still later after a while," Miss Reba said. "It dont matter what it is. Come on, Minnie." She and Minnie went out. Then the clerk was gone too. We stood there; none of us had sat down; she—Everbe—just stood there: a big girl that stillness looked well on; grief too, as long as it was still, like this. Or maybe not grief so much as shame.

"He never had no chance back there," she said. "That's why I thought . . . . To get him away even for just a week last summer. And then this year, especially after you all came too and as soon as I saw Lucius I knew that that was the way I had been wanting him to be all the time, only I didn't know neither how to tell him, learn him. And so I thought maybe just being around Lucius, even for just two or three days—"

"Sure," Boon said. "Refinement." Now he went to her, awkward. He didn't offer to put his arms around her again. He didn't even touch her, really. He just patted her back; it looked almost as hard, his hand did, as insensitive and heavy, as when Butch had slapped his this afternoon. But it wasn't at all. "It's all right," he said. "It aint nothing, see. You were doing the best you knowed. You done good. Come on, now."

It was the waiter again.

"Your coachman's in the kitchen, sir," he said. "He says it's important."

"My coachman?" Boon said. "I aint got no coachman."

"It's Ned," I said, already moving. Then Everbe was too, ahead of Boon. We followed the waiter back to the kitchen. Ned was standing quite close to the cook, a tremendous Negress who was drying dishes at the sink. He was saying,

"If it's money worrying your mind, Good-looking, I'm the man what—" and saw us and read Boon's mind like a flash: "Ease your worry. He's out at Possum's. What's he done this time?"

"What?" Boon said.

"It's Otis," I said. "Ned found him."

"I didn't," Ned said. "I hadn't never lost him. Uncle Possum's hounds did. Put him up a gum sapling behind the hen house about a hour ago, until Lycurgus went and got him. He wouldn't come in with me. In fact, he acted like he didn't aim to go nowhere right away. What's he done this time?" We told him. "So she's here too," he said. He said quietly: "Hee hee hee." He said: "Then he wont be there when I get back."

"What do you mean?" Boon said.

"Would you still be there, if you was him?" Ned said. "He knows that by this time that gal's done woke up and found that tooth missing. He must a been knowing that Miss Reba long enough by now to know she aint gonter stop until she gets her hand on him and turns him upside down and shake

until that tooth falls out of wherever he's got it. I told him
myself where I was going on that mule, and anybody there
can tell him what time that train got in and how long it will
take somebody to get back out there. Would you still be there
if you had that tooth?"

"All right," Boon said. "What's he going to do with it?"

"If it was anybody else but him," Ned said, "I'd say he had
three chances with it: sell it or hide it or give it away. But
since it's him, he aint got but two: sell it or hide it, and if it's
got to just stay hid somewhere, it might just as well be back
in that gal's mouth as fur as he's concerned. So the best place
to sell a gold tooth quick would be back in Memphis. Only
Memphis is too fur to walk, and to get on the train (which
would cost money, which he likely is got providing he is desperate enough to spend some of hisn) he would have to come
back to Possum, where somebody might see him. So the next
best quick place to sell that gold tooth will be at that race
track tomorrow. If it was you or me, we might likely bet that
tooth on one of them horses tomorrow. But he aint no betting man. Betting's too slow for him, not to mention uncer-
tain. But that race track will be a good place to start looking
for him. It's too bad I didn't know about that tooth whilst I
had my hand on him tonight. Maybe I could a reasoned it
out of him. Then, if he belonged to me, Mr Sam Caldwell
gonter be through here on that west-bound train at six-fawty
tomorrow morning and I'd a had him at the depot and
turned him over to Mr Sam and told Mr Sam not to lift his
hand offen him until the door shut on the first train leaving
for Arkansas tomorrow."

"Can you find him tomorrow?" Everbe said. "I've got to
find him. He's just a child. I'll pay for the tooth, I'll buy
Minnie another one. But I've got to find him. He'll say he
hasn't got it, he never saw it, but I've got—"

"Sho," Ned said. "That's what I'd say too if it was me. I'll
try. I'll be in early tomorrow morning to get Lucius, but the
best chance gonter be at that track tomorrow just before the
race." He said to me: "Folks is already kind of dropping by
Possum's lot like they wasn't noticing themselves doing it,
likely trying to find out who it is this time that still believes
that horse can run a race. So likely we gonter have a nice

crowd tomorrow. It's late now, so you go get some sleep whilst I takes that mule of Possum's back home to bed too. Where's your sock? You aint lost it?"

"It's in my pocket," I said.

"Be sho you dont," he said. "The mate to it is the left-footed one and a left-footed sock is unlucky unlessen you wears both of them." He turned, but no further than the fat cook; he said to her now: "Unlessen my mind changes to staying in town tonight. What time you setting breakfast, Good-looking?"

"The soonest time after your jaws is too far away to chomp it," the cook said.

"Good night, all," Ned said. Then he was gone. We went back to the dining room, where the waiter, in his shirt sleeves now and without his collar and tie, brought Miss Reba a plate of the pork chops and grits and biscuits and blackberry jam we had had for supper, neither hot nor cold now but luke-warm, en deshabille like the waiter, you might say.

"Did you get her to sleep?" Everbe said.

"Yes," Miss Reba said. "That little son of a—" and cut it off and said, "Excuse me. I thought I had seen everything in my business, but I never thought I'd have a tooth stolen in one of my houses. I hate little bastards. They're like little snakes. You can handle a big snake because you been already warned to watch out. But a little one has already bit you be-hind before you even knew it had teeth. Where's my coffee?" The waiter brought it and went away. And then even that big shrouded dining room was crowded; it was like every time Boon and Butch got inside the same four walls everything compounded, multiplied, leaving not really room for any-thing else. He—Butch—had been back to the doctor's, or maybe in the tin badge business you knew everybody who didn't dare refuse you a free drink. And it was getting late, and I was tired, but here he was again; and suddenly I knew that up to now he hadn't really been anything and that we were only just starting with him now, standing in the door, bulging, bright-eyed, confident, breezy and a little redder, the badge itself seeming to bulge at us as with a life of its own on his sweaty shirt, he—Butch—wearing it not as the official authorisation of his unique dedication, but as a boy scout

wears his merit badge: as both the unique and hard-won reward and emblem of a specialisation and the pre-absolution
for any other activities covered or embraced by its mystic
range; at that moment Everbe rose quickly across the table
and almost scuttled around it and into the chair next Miss
Reba, whom Butch was looking at, bulging at now. And that
was when I rated Boon down a notch and left Everbe first for
trouble. All Boon had was Butch; she had Boon and Butch
both.

"Well well," Butch said, "is all Catalpa Street moving east
to Possum?" So that at first I thought he might be a friend or
at least a business acquaintance of Miss Reba's. But if he was,
he didn't remember her name. But then even at eleven I was
learning that there are people like Butch who dont remember
anybody except in the terms of his immediate need of them,
and what he needed now (or anyway could use) was another
woman, he didn't care who provided she was more or less
young and pleasing. No: he didn't really need one: he just
happened to find one already in the path, like one lion on his
way to fight another lion over an antelope that he never had
any doubts about licking (I mean licking the lion, not the antelope) would still be a fool not to try throwing in, just for
luck you might say, another antelope if he happened to find
one straying in the path. Except that Miss Reba turned out
not to be an antelope. What Butch found was another lion.
He said: "This is what I call Sugar Boy using his head; what's
the use of him and me being all racked up over one hunk of
meat when here's another exactly like it in all important details except maybe a little difference in the pelt."

"Who's that?" Miss Reba said to Everbe. "Friend of yours?"

"No," Everbe said; she was actually crouching: a big girl,
too big to crouch. "Please—"

"She's telling you," Boon said. "She aint got no friends no
more. She dont want none. She's quit, gone out of business.
Soon as we finish losing this horse race, she's going away
somewhere and get a job washing dishes. Ask her."

Miss Reba was looking at Everbe. "Please," Everbe said.

"What do you want?" Miss Reba asked Butch.

"Nothing," Butch said. "Nothing a-tall. Me and Sugar Boy
was kind of bollixed up at one another for a while. But now

you showed up, everything is hunky dory. Twenty-three skid-doo." He came and took hold of Everbe's arm. "Come on. The surrey's outside. Let's give them a little room."

"Call the manager," Miss Reba said, quite loud, to me. I didn't even have to move; likely, if I had been looking, I could have seen the edge of him too beyond the door. He came in. "Is this man the law here?" Miss Reba said.

"Why, we all know Butch around here, Mrs Binford," the clerk said. "He's got as many friends in Parsham as anybody I know. Of course he's from up at Hardwick; properly speaking, we dont have a law officer right here in Parsham; we aint quite that big yet." Butch's rich and bulging warmth had embraced, invited the clerk almost before he could enter the door, as though he—the clerk—had fallen headlong into it and vanished like a mouse into a lump of still-soft ambergris. But now Butch's eyes were quite cold, hard.

"Maybe that's what's wrong around here," he told the clerk. "Maybe that's why you dont have no progress and advancement: what you need is a little more law."

"Aw, Butch," the clerk said.

"You mean, anybody that wants to can walk in off the street and drag whichever one of your women guests he likes the looks of best, off to the nearest bed like you were running a cat-house?" Miss Reba said.

"Drag who where?" Butch said. "Drag with what? a two-dollar bill?" Miss Reba rose.

"Come on," she said to Everbe. "There's a train back to Memphis tonight. I know the owner of this dump. I think I'll go see him tomorrow—"

"Aw, Butch," the clerk said. "Wait, Mrs Binford—"

"You go back out front, Virgil," Butch told the clerk. "It aint only four months to November; some millionaire with two registered bird dogs might walk in any minute, and there wont be nobody out there to show him where to sign his name at. Go on. We're all friends here." The clerk went. "Now that that's all out of the way," Butch said, reaching for Everbe's arm again.

"Then you'll do," Miss Reba said to Butch. "Let's me and you go out front, or anywhere else that's private, too. I got a word for you."

"About what?" Butch said. She didn't answer, already walking toward the door. "Private, you say?" Butch said. "Why, sure; any time I cant accommodate a good-looking gal private, I'll give Sugar Boy full lief to step in." They went out. And now, from the lobby, we couldn't see them beyond the door of the ladies' parlor, for almost a minute in fact, maybe even a little more, before Miss Reba came back out, still walking steadily, hard and handsome and composed; then Butch a second later, saying, "Is that so, huh? We'll just see about that," Miss Reba coming steadily on to where we waited, watching Butch go on across the lobby without even looking at us.

"All right?" Everbe said.

"Yes," Miss Reba said. "And that goes for you too," she told Boon. She looked at me. "Jesus," she said.

"What the hell did you do to him?" Boon said.

"Nothing," she said over her shoulder, because she was looking at me. "—thought I had seen all the cat-house problems possible. Until I had one with children in it. You brought one in"—she was talking to Everbe now—"that run the landlord off and robbed all the loose teeth and fourteen dollars' worth of beer; and if that wasn't enough, Boon Hogganbeck brings one that's driving my damned girls into poverty and respectability. I'm going to bed and you—"

"Come on," Boon said. "What did you tell him?"

"What's that town of yours?" Miss Reba said.

"Jefferson," Boon said.

"You big-town folks from places like Jefferson and Memphis, with your big city ideas, you dont know much about Law. You got to come to little places, like this. I know, because I was raised in one. He's the constable. He could spend a week in Jefferson or Memphis, and you wouldn't even see him. But here among the folks that elected him (the majority of twelve or thirteen that voted for him, and the minority of nine or ten or eleven that didn't and are already sorry for it or damned soon will be) he dont give a damn about the sheriff of the county nor the governor of the state nor the president of the United States all three rolled into one. Because he's a Baptist. I mean, he's a Baptist first, and then he's the Law. When he can be a Baptist and the Law both at the same time, he will. But any time the law comes conflicting up where nobody invited it, the law knows what it can do and where to do it. They tell how that old Pharaoh was pretty good at kinging, and another old one back in the Bible times named Caesar, that did the best he knew how. They should have visited down here and watched a Arkansas or Missippi or Tennessee constable once."

"But how do you know who he is?" Everbe said. "How do you even know there's one here?"

"There's one everywhere," Miss Reba said. "Didn't I just tell you I grew up in a place like this—as long as I could stand it? I dont need to know who he is. All I needed was to let that bastard know I knew there was one here too. I'm going—"

"But what did you tell him?" Boon said. "Come on. I may want to remember it."

"Nothing, I told you," Miss Reba said. "If I hadn't learned by now how to handle these damned stud horses with his badge in one hand and his fly in the other, I'd been in the poor house years ago. I told him if I saw his mug around here again tonight, I would send that sheep-faced clerk to wake the constable up and tell him a deputy sheriff from Hardwick has just registered a couple of Memphis whores at the Parsham Hotel. I'm going to bed, and you better too. Come on, Corrie. I put your outraged virtue on record with that clerk and now you got to back it up, at least where he can see you."

They went on. Then Boon was gone too; possibly he had followed Butch to the front door just to make sure the surrey was gone. Then suddenly Everbe swooped down at me, that big: a big girl, muttering rapidly:

"You didn't bring anything at all, did you? I mean, clothes. You been wearing the same ones ever since you left home."

"What's wrong with them?" I said.

"I'm going to wash them," she said. "Your underthings and stockings, your blouse. And the sock you ride with too. Come on and take them off."

"But I aint got any more," I said.

"That's all right. You can go to bed. I'll have these all ready again when you get up. Come on." So she stood outside the door while I undressed and shoved my blouse and underwear and stockings and the riding sock through the crack in the door to her and she said Goodnight and I closed the door and got into bed; and still there was something unfinished, that we hadn't done, attended to yet: the secret pre-race conference; the close, grim, fierce murmurous plotting of tomorrow's strategy. Until I realised that, strictly speaking, we had no strategy; we had nothing to plan for nor even with: a horse whose very ownership was dubious and even (unless Ned himself really knew) unknown, of whose past we knew only that he had consistently run just exactly fast enough to finish second to the other horse in the race; to be raced tomorrow, exactly where I anyway didn't know, against a horse none of us had ever seen and whose very existence (as far as we were concerned) had to be taken on trust. Until I realised that, of all human occupations, the racing of horses, and all concerned or involved in it, were the most certainly in God's hands. Then Boon came in; I was already in bed, already half asleep.

"What've you done with your clothes?" he said.

"Everbe's washing them," I said. He had taken off his pants and shoes and was already reaching to turn out the light. He stopped, dead still.

"Who did you say?" I was awake now but it was already too late. I lay there with my eyes closed, not moving. "What name did you say?"

"Miss Corrie is," I said.

"You said something else." I could feel him looking at me. "You called her Everbe." I could feel him looking at me. "Is that her name?" I could feel him looking at me. "So she told you her real name." Then he said, quite gently: "God damn," and I saw through my eyelids the room go dark, then the bed creaked as he lay down on it, as beds always do since there is so much of him, as I have heard them ever since I can remember when I would sleep with him: once or twice at home when Father would be away and he would stay in the house so Mother wouldn't be afraid, and at Miss Ballenbaugh's two nights ago, and in Memphis last night, until I remembered that I hadn't slept with him in Memphis: it was Otis. "Good night," he said.

"Good night," I said.

Ten

THEN it was morning, it was tomorrow: THE day on which I would ride my first actual horse-race (and by winning it, set Boon and Ned—me too of course, but then I was safe, immune; I was not only just a child, I was kin to them—free to go home again, not with honor perhaps, not even unscathed, but at least they could go back) toward which all the finagling and dodging and manipulating and scrabbling around (what other crimes subsequent to—all right, consequent to—the simple and really spontaneous and in a way innocent stealing of Grandfather's automobile, I didn't even know) had been leading up to; now it was here. "So she told you what her real name is," Boon said. Because you see, it was too late now; I had been half asleep last night and off my guard.

"Yes," I said; whereupon I realised that that was completely false: she hadn't told me; she didn't even know I knew it, that I had been calling her Everbe ever since Sunday night. But it was too late now. "But you've got to promise," I said. "Not promise her: promise me. Never to say it out loud until she tells it first."

"I promise," he said. "I aint never lied to you yet. I mean, lied bad. I mean . . . I aint . . . . All right," he said. "I done promised." Then he said again, like last night, gentle and almost amazed: "God damn." And my clothes—blouse, stockings and underwear and the riding sock—were neatly folded, laundered and ironed, on a chair just outside our door. Boon handed them in to me. "With all them clean clothes, you got to bathe again," he said.

"You just made me bathe Saturday," I said.

"We was on the road Saturday night," he said. "We never even got to Memphis until Sunday."

"All right. Sunday," I said.

"This is Tuesday," he said. "Two days."

"Just one day," I said. "Two nights, but just one day."

"You been travelling since," Boon said. "You got two sets of dirt now."

"It's almost seven oclock," I said. "We're already late for breakfast."

"You can bathe first," he said.

"I got to get dressed so I can thank Everbe for washing my clothes."

"Bathe first," Boon said.

"I'll get my bandage wet."

"Hold your hand on your neck," Boon said. "You aint going to wash that nohow."

"Why dont you bathe then?" I said.

"We aint talking about me. We're talking about you." So I went to the bathroom and bathed and put my clothes back on and went to the dining room. And Ned was right. Last night there had been just the one table, the end of it cleared and set up for us. Now there were seven or eight people, all men (but not aliens, foreigners mind you; in fact they were strangers only to us who didn't live in Parsham. None of them had got down from pullmans in silk underclothes and smoking Upmann cigars; we had not opened the cosmopolitan Parsham winter sporting season here in the middle of May. Some were in overalls, all but one was tieless: people like us except that they lived here, with the same passions and hopes and dialect, enjoying—Butch too—our inalienable constitutional right of free will and private enterprise which has made our country what it is, by holding a private horse-race between two local horses; if anyone, committee or individual, from no further away than the next county, had come to interfere or alter or stop it or even participate beyond betting on the horse of his choice, all of us, partisans of either horse, would have risen as one man and repulsed him). And besides the waiter, I saw the back of a maid in uniform just going through the swing door to the pantry or kitchen, and there were two men (one of them had the necktie) at our table talking to Boon and Miss Reba. But Everbe wasn't there, and for an instant, second, I had a horrified vision of Butch finally waylaying and capturing her by force, ambushing her in the corridor perhaps while she was carrying the chair to mine and Boon's door with my laundered clothes on it. But only for a second, and too fantastical; if she had washed for me last night, she had probably, doubtless been up quite late washing for herself and maybe Miss

Reba too, and was still asleep. So I went on to the table, where one of the men said,

"This the boy going to ride him? Looks more like you got him taped up for a fist-fight."

"Yes," Boon said, shoving the dish of ham toward me as I sat down; Miss Reba passed the eggs and grits across. "He cut himself eating peas last night."

"Haw haw," the man said. "Anyway, he'll be carrying less weight this time."

"Sure," Boon said. "Unless he eats the knives and forks and spoons while we aint watching him and maybe takes along one of the fire dogs for a snack."

"Haw haw," the man said. "From the way he run here last winter, he's going to need a good deal more than just less weight. But then, that's the secret, huh?"

"Sure," Boon said; he was eating again now. "Even if we never had no secret, we would have to act like we did."

"Haw haw," the man said again; they got up. "Well, good luck, anyway. That might be as good for that horse as less weight." The maid came, bringing me a glass of milk and carrying a plate of hot biscuits. It was Minnie, in a fresh apron and cap where Miss Reba had either loaned or hired her to the hotel to help out, with her ravished and unforgiving face, but calm and quiet now; evidently she had rested, even slept some even if she hadn't forgiven anybody yet. The two strangers went away.

"You see?" Miss Reba said to nobody. "All we need is the right horse and a million dollars to bet."

"You heard Ned Sunday night," Boon said. "You were the one that believed him. I mean, decided to believe him. I was different. After that God damned automobile vanished and all we had was the horse, I had to believe him."

"All right," Miss Reba said. "Keep your shirt on."

"And you can stop worrying too," Boon said to me. "She just went to the depot in case them dogs caught him again last night and Ned brought him in to the train. Or so she said—"

"Did Ned find him?" I said.

"Naw," Boon said. "Ned's in the kitchen now. You can ask him—or so she said. Yes. So maybe you had better worry some, after all. Miss Reba got shut of that tin badge for you, but that other one—what's his name: Caldwell—was on that train this morning."

"What are you talking about now?" Miss Reba said.

"Nothing," Boon said. "I aint got nothing to talk about now. I've quit. Lucius is the one that's got tin badge and pullman cap rivals now." But I was already getting up because I knew now where she was.

"Is that all the breakfast you want?" Miss Reba said.

"Let him alone," Boon said. "He's in love." I crossed the lobby. Maybe Ned was right, and all it took for a horse-race was two horses with the time to run a race, within ten miles of each other, and the air itself spread the news of it. Though not as far as the ladies' parlor yet. So maybe what I meant by crying looking well on Everbe was that she was big enough to cry as much as she seemed to have to do, and still have room for that many tears to dry off without streaking. She was sitting by herself in the ladies' parlor and crying again, the third time—no: four, counting two Sunday night. Until you wondered why. I mean, nobody made her come with us and she could have gone back to Memphis on any train that passed. Yet here she was, so she must be where she wanted to be. Yet this was the second time she had cried since we reached Parsham. I mean, anybody with as many extra tears as she had, still didn't have enough to waste that many on Otis. So I said,

"He's all right. Ned will find him today. Much obliged for washing my clothes. Where's Mr Sam? I thought he was going to be on that train."

"He had to take the train on to Memphis and take his uniform off," she said. "He cant go to a horse-race in it. He'll be back on the noon freight. I cant find my handkerchief."

I found it for her. "Maybe you ought to wash your face," I said. "When Ned finds him, he will get the tooth back."

"It aint the tooth," she said. "I'm going to buy Minnie another tooth. It's that . . . He never had no chance. He . . . Did you promise your mother you wouldn't never take things too?"

"You dont have to promise anybody that," I said. "You dont take things."

"But you would have promised, if she had asked you?"

"She wouldn't ask me," I said. "You dont take things."

"Yes," she said. She said: "I aint going to stay in Memphis. I talked to Sam at the depot this morning and he says that's a good idea too. He can find me a job in Chattanooga or somewhere. But you'll still be in Jefferson, so maybe I could write you a postcard where I'm at and then if you took a notion—"

"Yes," I said. "I'll write to you. Come on. They're still eating breakfast."

"There's something about me you dont know. You couldn't even guess it."

"I know it," I said. "It's Everbe Corinthia. I been calling you that two or three days now. That's right. It was Otis. But I wont tell anybody. But I dont see why."

"Why? A old-timey countrified name like that? Can you imagine anybody in Reba's saying, Send up Everbe Corinthia? They would be ashamed. They would die laughing. So I thought of changing it to Yvonne or Billie or Ken. But Reba said Corrie would do."

"Shucks," I said.

"You mean, it's all right? You say it." I said it. She listened. Then she kept on listening, exactly as you wait for an echo. "Yes," she said. "That's what it can be now."

"Then come on and eat breakfast," I said. "Ned's waiting for me and I got to go." But Boon came in first.

"There are too many people out there," he said. "Maybe I shouldn't a told that damn fellow you were going to ride him today." He looked at me. "Maybe I shouldn't a never let you leave Jefferson." There was a small door behind a curtain at the back of the room. "Come on," he said. It was another corridor. Then we were in the kitchen. The vast cook was at the sink again. Ned was sitting at a table finishing his breakfast, but mainly saying,

"When I sugars up a woman, it aint just empty talk. They can buy something with it too—" and stopped and rose at once; he said to me: "You ready? Time you and me was getting back to the country. They's too many folks around here. If they all had money and would bet it, and the horse they bet on would just be the wrong horse, and we just had the money to cover it and knowed the right horse to cover it with, we wouldn't just take no automobile back to Jefferson tonight: we'd take all Possum too, to maybe sugar back Boss Priest's nature. He aint never owned a town before, and he might like it."

"Wait," Boon said. "Aint we got to make some plans?"

"The onliest one that needs any plan is Lightning," Ned said. "And the only plan he needs is to plan to get out in front and stay there until somebody tells him to stop. But I know what you mean. We gonter run on Colonel Linscomb's track. The first heat is at two oclock. That's four miles from here. Me and Lightning and Lucius gonter show up there about two minutes beforehand. You better get out there earlier. You better leave here soon as Mr Sam gets off that freight train. Because that's yourn and his plan: to get to that track in time to bet the money, and to have some money to bet when you get there."

"Wait," Boon said. "What about that automobile? What the hell good will money do us if we go back home without—"

"Stop fretting about that automobile," Ned said. "Aint I told you them boys got to go back home not much longer than tonight too?"

"What boys?" Boon said.

"Yes sir," Ned said. "The trouble with Christmas is the first of January; that's what's wrong with it." Minnie came in with a tray of soiled dishes—the brown calm tragic hungry and inconsolable mask. "Come on," Ned told her, "gimme that smile again so I'll have the right measure to fit that tooth when I brings it back tonight."

"Dont do it, girl," the fat cook said. "Maybe that Missippi sugar will spend where it come from, but it wont buy nothing up here in Tennessee. Not in this kitchen, nohow."

"But wait," Boon said.

"You wait for Mr Sam," Ned said. "He can tell you. In fact, whilst me and Lucius are winning this race, maybe you and Mr Sam can locate around amongst the folks for Whistlebritches and that tooth." He had Uncle Parsham's buggy this time, with one of the mules. And he was right: the little hamlet had changed overnight. It was not that there were so many people in sight, any more than yesterday. It was the air

itself—an exhilaration, almost; for the first time I really realised that I was going to ride in a horse race before many
more hours, and I could taste my spit sudden and sharp
around my tongue.

"I thought you said last night that Otis would be gone
when you got back from town," I said.

"He was," Ned said. "But not far. He aint got nowhere to
go neither. The hounds give mouth twice during the night
back toward the barn; them hounds taken the same quick
mislike to him that human folks does. Likely soon as I left this
morning, he come up for his breakfast."

"But suppose he sells the tooth before we can catch him."

"I done fixed that," Ned said. "He aint gonter sell it. He
aint gonter find nobody to buy it. If he aint come up for
breakfast, Lycurgus gonter take the hounds and tree him
again, and tell him that when I come back from Parsham last
night, I said a man in Memphis offered that gal twenty-eight
dollars for that tooth, cash. He'll believe that. If it had been
a hundred dollars or even fifty, he wouldn't believe it. But
he'll believe a extra number like twenty-eight dollars, mainly
because he'll think it aint enough: that that Memphis man
was beating Minnie down. And when he tries to sell it at that
race track this evening, wont nobody give him even that
much, so wont be nothing left for him to do but wait until he
can get back to Memphis with it. So you get your mind off
that tooth and put it on this horse-race. On them last two
heats, I mean. We gonter lose the first one, so you dont need
to worry about that—"

"What?" I said. "Why?"

"Why not?" Ned said. "All we needs to win is two of
them."

"But why lose the first one? Why dont we win that one, get
that much ahead as soon as we can—" He drove on, maybe a
half a minute.

"The trouble with this race, it's got too many different
things mixed up in it."

"Too many what?" I said.

"Too many of everything," he said. "Too many folks. But
mainly, too many heats. If it was just one heat, one run, off in
the bushes somewhere and not nobody around but me and

you and Lightning and that other horse and whoever gonter ride him, we would be all right. Because we found out yestiddy we can make Lightning run one time. Only, now he got to run three of them."

"But you made that mule run every time," I said.

"This horse aint that mule," Ned said. "Aint no horse ever foaled was that mule. Or any other mule. And this horse we got to depend on now aint even got as much sense as some horses. So you can see what our fix is. We knows I can make him run once, and we hopes I can make him run twice. But that's all. We just hopes. So we cant risk that one time we *knows* I can make him run, until we got to have it. So the most we got at the best, is two times. And since we got to lose one of them, no matter what, we gonter lose the one we can maybe learn something from to use next time. And that's gonter be the first one."

"Have you told Boon that? so he wont—"

"Let him lose on the first heat, providing he dont put up all the money them ladies scraps up for him to bet. Which, from what I seen of that Miss Reba, he aint gonter do. That will make the odds that much better for them next two. Besides, we can tell him all he needs to know when the time comes. So you just—"

"I didn't mean that," I said. "I meant Boss's—"

"Didn't I tell you I was tending to that?" he said. "Now you quit worrying. I dont mean quit thinking about the race, because you cant do that. But quit worrying about winning it. Just think about what Lightning taught you yesterday about riding him. That's all you got to do. I'll tend to all the rest of it. You got your sock, aint you?"

"Yes," I said. Only we were not going back to Uncle Parsham's; we were not even going in that direction now.

"We got our own private stable for this race," Ned said. "A spring branch in a hollow that belongs to one of Possum's church members, where we can be right there not half a quarter from the track without nobody knowing to bother us until we wants them. Lycurgus and Uncle Possum went on with Lightning right after breakfast."

"The track," I said. Of course, there would have to be a track. I had never thought of that. If I thought at all, I reckon

I simply assumed that somebody would ride or lead the other horse up, and we would run the race right there in Uncle Parsham's pasture.

"That's right," Ned said. "A regular track, just like a big one except it's just a half a mile and aint got no grandstands and beer-and-whiskey counters like anybody that wants to run horse-racing right ought to have. It's right there in Colonel Linscomb's pasture, that owns the other horse. Me and Lycurgus went and looked at it last night. I mean the track, not the horse. I aint seen the horse yet. But we gonter have a chance to look at him today, leastways, one end of him. Only what we want is to plan for that horse to spend the last half of two of these heats looking at that end of Lightning. So I need to talk to the boy that's gonter ride him. A colored boy; Lycurgus knows him. I want to talk to him in a way that he wont find out until afterward that I talked to him."

"Yes," I said. "How?"

"Let's get there first," Ned said. We went on; it was new country to me, of course. Obviously we were now crossing Colonel Linscomb's plantation, or anyway somebody's—big neat fields of sprouting cotton and corn, and pastures with good fences and tenant cabins and cotton houses at the turn-row ends; and now I could see the barns and stables and sure enough, there was the neat white oval of the small track; we—Ned—turning now, following a faint road, on into a grove; and there it was, isolate and secure, even secret if we wished: a grove of beeches about a spring, Lightning standing with Lycurgus at his head, groomed and polished and even glowing faintly in the dappled light, the other mule tied in the background and Uncle Parsham, dramatic in black and white, even regal, prince and martinet in the dignity of solvent and workless age, sitting on the saddle which Lycurgus had propped against a tree into a sort of chair for him, all waiting for us. And then in the next instant I knew that was wrong: they were all waiting for me. And that was the real moment when—Lightning and me standing in (not to mention breathing it) the same air not a thousand feet from the race track and not much more than a tenth of that in minutes from the race itself—when I actually realised not only how Lightning's and my fate were now one, but that the two of us together carried that of the rest of us too, certainly Boon's and Ned's, since on us depended under what conditions they could go back home, or indeed if they could go back home— a mystical condition which a boy of only eleven should not really be called to shoulder. Which is perhaps why I noticed nothing, or anyway missed what I did see: only that Lycurgus handed Lightning's lead rope to Uncle Parsham and came and took our bridle and Ned said, "You get that message to him all right?" and Lycurgus said Yes sir, and Ned said to me, "Whyn't you go and take Lightning offen Uncle Possum so he wont have to get up?" and I did so, leaving Ned and Lycurgus standing quite close together at the buggy, and that not long before Ned came on to us, leaving Lycurgus to take the mule out of the buggy and loop the lines and traces up and tie the mule beside its mate and come on to us, where Ned was now squatting beside Uncle Parsham. He said: "Tell again about them two races last winter. You said nothing happened. What kind of nothing?"

"Ah," Uncle Parsham said. "It was a three-heat race just like this one, only they never run but two of them. By that time there wasn't no need to run the third one. Or maybe somebody got tired."

"Tired reaching into his hind pocket, maybe," Ned said.

"Maybe," Uncle Parsham said. "The first time, your horse run too soon, and the second time he run too late. Or maybe it was the whip whipped too soon the first time and not soon enough the second. Anyhow, at the first lick your horse jumped out in front, a good length, and stayed there all the way around the first lap, even after the whipping had done run out, like it does with a horse or a man either: he can take just so much whipping and after that it aint no more than spitting on him. Then they come into the home stretch and it was like your horse saw that empty track in front of him and said to himself, This aint polite; I'm a stranger here, and dropped back just enough to lay his head more or less on Colonel Linscomb's boy's knee, and kept it there until somebody told him he could stop. And the next time your horse started out like he still thought he hadn't finished that first heat, his head all courteous and polite about opposite Colonel Linscomb's boy's knee, on into the back turn of the last lap,

where that Memphis boy hit him the first lick, not late
enough this time, because all that full-length jump done this
time was to show him that empty track again."

"Not too late to scare McWillie," Lycurgus said.

"Skeer him how much?" Ned said.

"Enough," Lycurgus said. Ned squatted there. He must
have got a little sleep last night, even with the hounds treeing
Otis every now and then. He didn't look it too much though.

"All right," he said to me. "You and Lycurgus just stroll up
yonder to that stable a while. All you're doing is taking your
natural look at the horse you gonter ride against this evening.
For the rest of it, let Lycurgus do the talking, and dont look
behind you on the way back." I didn't even ask him why. He
wouldn't have told me. It was not far: past the neat half-mile
track with its white-painted rails that it would be nice to be
rich too, on to the barns, the stable that if Cousin Zack had
one like it out at McCaslin, Cousin Louisa would probably
have them living in it. There was nobody in sight. I dont
know what I had expected: maybe still more of the overalled
and tieless aficionados squatting and chewing tobacco along
the wall as we had seen them in the dining room at breakfast.
Maybe it was too early yet: which, I now realised, was probably exactly why Ned had sent us; we—Lycurgus—lounging
into the hallway which—the stable—was as big as our dedi-
cated-to-a-little-profit livery one in Jefferson and a good deal
cleaner—a tack room on one side and what must have been
an office on the other, just like ours; a Negro stableman
cleaning a stall at the rear and a youth who for size and age
and color might have been Lycurgus's twin, lounging on a
bale of hay against the wall, who said to Lycurgus: "Hidy,
son. Looking for a horse?"

"Hidy, son," Lycurgus said. "Looking for two. We thought
maybe the other one might be here too."

"You mean Mr van Tosch aint even come yet?"

"He aint coming a-tall," Lycurgus said. "Some other
folks running Coppermine this time. White folks named Mr
Boon Hogganbeck. This white boy gonter ride him. This is
McWillie," he told me. McWillie looked at me a minute.
Then he went back to the office door and opened it and
said something inside and stood back while a white man

("Trainer," Lycurgus murmured. "Name Mr Walter.") came and said,

"Morning, Lycurgus. Where you folks keeping that horse hid, anyway? You aint ringing in a sleeper on us, are you?"

"No sir," Lycurgus said. "I reckon he aint come out from town yet. We thought they might have sent him out here. So we come to look."

"You walked all the way here from Possum's?"

"No sir," Lycurgus said. "We rid the mules."

"Where'd you tie them? I cant even see them. Maybe you painted them with some of that invisible paint you put on that horse when you took him out of that box car yesterday morning."

"No sir," Lycurgus said. "We just rid as far as the pasture and turned them loose. We walked the balance of the way."

"Well, anyway you come to see a horse, so we wont disappoint you. Bring him out, McWillie, where they can look at him."

"Look at his face for a change," McWillie said. "Folks on that Coppermine been looking at Akron's hind end all winter, but aint none of them seen his face yet."

"Then at least this boy can start out knowing what he looks like in front. What's your name, son?" I told him. "You aint from around here."

"No sir. Jefferson, Mississippi."

"He travelling with Mr Hogganbeck that's running Coppermine now," Lycurgus said.

"Oh," Mr Walter said. "Mr Hogganbeck buy him?"

"I dont know, sir," Lycurgus said. "Mr Hogganbeck's running him." McWillie brought the horse out; he and Mr Walter stripped off the blanket. He was black, bigger than Lightning but very nervous; he came out showing eye-white; every time anybody moved or spoke near him his ears went back and he stood on the point of one hind foot as though ready to lash out with it, Mr Walter and McWillie both talking, murmuring at him but both of them always watching him.

"All right," Mr Walter said. "Give him a drink and put him back up." We followed him toward the front. "Dont let him discourage you," he said. "After all, it's just a horse-race."

"Yes sir," Lycurgus said. "That's what they says. Much oblige for letting us look at him."

"Thank you, sir," I said.

"Goodbye," Mr Walter said. "Dont keep them mules waiting. See you at post time this afternoon."

"No sir," Lycurgus said.

"Yes sir," I said. We went on, past the stables and the track once more.

"Mind what Mr McCaslin told us," Lycurgus said.

"Mr McCaslin?" I said. "Oh yes," I said. I didn't ask What? this time either. I think I knew now. Or maybe I didn't want to believe I knew; didn't want to believe even yet that at a mere eleven you could progress that fast in weary unillusion; maybe if I had asked What? it would be an admission that I had. "That horse is bad," I said.

"He's scared," Lycurgus said. "That's what Mr McCaslin said last night."

"Last night?" I said. "I thought you all came to look at the track."

"What do he want to look at that track for?" Lycurgus said. "That track dont move. He come to see that horse."

"In the dark?" I said. "Didn't they have a watchman or wasn't the stable locked or anything?"

"When Mr McCaslin make up his mind to do something, he do it," Lycurgus said. "Aint you found out that about him yet?" So we—I—didn't look back. We went on to our sanctuary, where Lightning—I mean Coppermine—and the two mules stamped and swished in the dappled shade and Ned squatted beside Uncle Parsham's saddle and another man sat on his heels across the spring from them—another Negro; I almost knew him, had known him, seen him, something—before Ned spoke:

"It's Bobo," he said. And then it was all right. He was a McCaslin too, Bobo Beauchamp, Lucas's cousin—Lucas Quintus Carothers McCaslin Beauchamp, that Grandmother, whose mother had described old Lucius to her, said looked (and behaved: just as arrogant, just as iron-headed, just as intolerant) exactly like him except for color. Bobo was another motherless Beauchamp child whom Aunt Tennie raised until the call of the out-world became too much for him and he went to Memphis three years ago. "Bobo used to work for the man that used to own Lightning," Ned said. "He come to watch him run." Because it was all right now: the one remaining thing which had troubled us—me: Bobo would know where the automobile was. In fact, he might even have it. But that was wrong, because in that case Boon and Ned would simply have taken it away from him—until suddenly I realised that the reason it was wrong was, I didn't want it to be; if we could get the automobile back for no more than just telling Bobo to go get it and be quick about it, what were we doing here? what had we gone to all this trouble and anxiety for? camouflaging and masquerading Lightning at midnight through the Memphis tenderloin to get him to the depot; ruthlessly using a combination of uxoriousness and nepotism to disrupt a whole box car from the railroad system to get him to Parsham; not to mention the rest of it: having to cope with Butch, Minnie's tooth, invading and outraging Uncle Parsham's home, and sleeplessness and (yes) homesickness and (me again) not even a change of underclothes; all that striving and struggling and finagling to run a horse-race with a horse which was not ours, to recover an automobile we had never had any business with in the first place, when all we had to do to get the automobile was to send one of the family colored boys to fetch it. You see what I mean? if the successful outcome of the race this afternoon wasn't really the pivot; if Lightning and I were not the last desperate barrier between Boon and Ned and Grandfather's anger, even if not his police; if without winning the race or even having to run it, Ned and Boon could go back to Jefferson (which was the only home Ned knew, and the only milieu in which Boon could have survived) as if nothing had happened, and take up again as though they had never been away, then all of us were engaged in a make-believe not too different from a boys' game of cops and robbers. But Bobo could know where the automobile was; that would be allowable, that would be fair; and Bobo was one of us. I said so to Ned. "I thought I told you to stop worrying about that automobile," he said. "Aint I promised you I'd tend to it when the right time come? You got plenty other things to fret your mind over: you got a horse-race. Aint that enough to keep it busy?" He said to Lycurgus: "All right?"

"I think so," Lycurgus said. "We never looked back to see."

"Then maybe," Ned said. But Bobo had already gone. I neither saw nor heard him; he was just gone. "Get the bucket," Ned told Lycurgus. "Now is a good time to eat our snack whilst we still got a little peace and quiet around here." Lycurgus brought it—a tin lard bucket with a clean dishcloth over it, containing pieces of corn bread with fried sidemeat between; there was another bucket of buttermilk sitting in the spring.

"You et breakfast?" Uncle Parsham said to me.

"Yes sir," I said.

"Then dont eat no more," he said. "Just nibble a piece of bread and a little water."

"That's right," Ned said. "You can ride better empty." So he gave me a single piece of corn bread and we all squatted now around Uncle Parsham's saddle, the two buckets on the ground in the center; we heard one step or maybe two up the bank behind us, then McWillie said,

"Hidy, Uncle Possum, morning, reverend"—that was Ned; and came down the bank, already—or still—looking at Lightning. "Yep, that's Coppermine, all right. These boys had Mr Walter skeered this morning that maybe yawl had rung in another horse on him. You running him, reverend?"

"Call him Mr McCaslin," Uncle Parsham said.

"Yes sir," McWillie said. "Mr McCaslin. You running him?"

"White man named Mr Hogganbeck is," Ned said. "We waiting on him now."

"Too bad you aint got something else besides Coppermine to wait with, that would maybe give Akron a race," McWillie said.

"I already told Mr Hogganbeck that, myself," Ned said. He swallowed. Without haste he lifted the bucket of buttermilk and drank, still without haste. McWillie watched him. He set the bucket down. "Set down and eat something," he said.

"Much obliged," McWillie said. "I done et. Maybe that's why Mr Hogganbeck's late, waiting to bring out that other horse."

"There aint time now," Ned said. "He'll have to run this

one now. The trouble is, the only one around here that knows
how to rate this horse, is the very one that knows better than
to let him run behind. This horse dont like to be in front. He
wants to run right behind up until he can see the finish line,
and have something to run at. I aint seen him race yet, but
I'd be willing to bet that the slower the horse in front of him
goes, the more carefuller he is not to get out in front where
he aint got no company—until he can see that finish line and
find out it's a race he's in and run at it. All anybody got to do
to beat him is to keep his mind so peaceful that when he does
notice he's in a race, it's too late. Some day somebody gonter
let him get far enough behind to scare him, then look out.
But it wont be this race. The trouble is, the onliest one
around here that knows that too, is the wrong one."

"Who's that?" McWillie said.

Ned took another bite. "Whoever's gonter ride that other
horse today."

"That's me," McWillie said. "Dont tell me Uncle Possum
and Lycurgus both aint already told you that."

"Then you oughter be talking to me instead," Ned said.
"Set down and eat; Uncle Possum got plenty here."

"Much obliged," McWillie said again. "Well," he said. "Mr
Walter'll be glad to know it aint nobody but Coppermine. We
was afraid we would have to break in a new one. See yawl at
the track." Then he was gone. But I waited another minute.

"But why?" I said.

"I dont know," Ned said. "We may not even need it. But if
we does, we already got it there. You mind I told you this
morning how the trouble with this race was, it had too many
different things all mixed up in it? Well, this aint our track and
country, and it aint even our horse except just in a borried
manner of speaking, so we cant take none of them extra
things out. So the next best we can do is, to put a few extry
ones into it on our own account. That's what we just done.
That horse up yonder is a Thoroughbred paper horse; why
aint he in Memphis or Louisville or Chicago running races,
instead of back here in a home-made country pasture running
races against whoever can slip in the back way, like us?
Because why, because I felt him last night and he's weedy, like
a horse that cant nothing catch for six furlongs, but fifty foot

more and he's done folded up right under you before you
knowed it. And so far, all that boy—"

"McWillie," I said.

"—McWillie has had to worry about is just staying on top
of him and keeping him headed in the right direction; he's
won twice now and likely he thinks if he just had the chance,
he would run Earl Sande and Dan Patch both clean outen the
horse business. Now we've put something else in his mind;
he's got two things in it now that dont quite fit one another.
So we'll just wait and see. And whilst we're waiting, you go
over behind them bushes yonder and lay down and rest.
Word's out now, and folks gonter start easing in and out of
here to see what they can find out, and over there they wont
worry you."

Which I did. Though not always asleep; I heard the voices;
I wouldn't have needed to see them even if I had raised onto
one elbow and opened one eye past a bush: the same overalls,
tieless, the sweated hats, the chewing tobacco, squatting, unhurried, not talking very much, looking inscrutably at the
horse. Nor always awake, because Lycurgus was standing over
me and time had passed; the very light looked post meridian.
"Time to go," he said. There was nobody with Lightning
now but Ned and Uncle Parsham; if they were all up at the
track already, it must be even later still. I had expected Boon
and Sam and probably Everbe and Miss Reba too. (But not
Butch. I hadn't even thought of him; maybe Miss Reba had
really got rid of him for good, back up to Hardwick or wherever it was the clerk said last night he really belonged. I had
forgotten him; I realised now what the morning's peace actually was.) I said so.

"Haven't they come yet?"

"Aint nobody told them where to come yet," Ned said.
"We dont need Boon Hogganbeck now. Come on. You can
walk him up and limber him on the way." I got up: the worn
perfectly cared-for McClellan saddle and the worn perfectly
cared-for cavalry bridle which was the other half of Uncle
Parsham's (somebody's) military loot from that Cause which,
the longer I live the more convinced I am, your spinster aunts
to the contrary, that whoever lost it, it wasn't us.

"Maybe they're looking for Otis," I said.

"Maybe they are," Ned said. "It's a good place to hunt for him, whether they finds him or not." We went on, Uncle Parsham and Ned walking at Lightning's head; Lycurgus would bring the buggy and the other mule around by the road, provided he could find enough clear space to hitch them in. Because already the pasture next to the track was filled up—wagons, the teams unhitched and reversed and tied to the stanchions and tail-gates; buggies, saddle-horses and -mules hitched to the fence itself; and now we—I—could see the people, black and white, the tieless shirts and the overalls, already dense along the rail and around the paddock. Because this race was home-made, remember; this was democracy, not triumphant because anything can be triumphant provided it is tenderly and firmly enough protected and guarded and shielded in its innocent fragility, but democracy working: Colonel Linscomb, the aristocrat, the baron, the suzerain, was not even present. As far as I knew, nobody knew where he was. As far as I knew, nobody cared. He owned one of the horses (I still didn't know for certain just who owned the one I was sitting on) and the dirt we were going to race on and the nice white rail enclosing it and the adjacent pasture which the tethered wagons and buggies were cutting up and the fence one entire panel of which a fractious or frightened saddle horse had just wrenched into kindling, but nobody knew where he was nor seemed to bother or care.

We went to the paddock. Oh yes, we had one; we had everything a race track should have except, as Ned said, grandstands and stalls for beer and whiskey; we had everything else that any track had, but we had democracy too: the judges were the night telegraph operator at the depot and Mr McDiarmid who ran the depot eating-room, who, the legend went, could slice a ham so thin that his entire family had made a summer trip to Chicago on the profits from one of them; our steward and marshal was a dog-trainer who shot quail for the black market and was now out on bond for his part in (participation in or maybe just his presence at) a homicide which had occurred last winter at a neighboring whiskey-still; did I not tell you this was free and elective will and choice and private enterprise at its purest? And there were Boon and Sam waiting for us. "I cant find him," Boon said. "Aint you seen him?"

"Seen who?" Ned said. "Jump down," he told me. The other horse was there too, still nervous, still looking what I would have called bad but that Lycurgus said Ned said was afraid. "Now, what did this horse—"

"That damn boy!" Boon said. "You said this morning he would be out here."

"Maybe he's behind something," Ned said. He came back to me. "What did this horse learn you yesterday? You was on a twice-around track that time too. What did he learn you? Think." I thought hard. But there still wasn't anything.

"Nothing," I said. "All I did was to keep him from going straight to you whenever he saw you."

"And that's exactly what you want to do this first heat: just keep him in the middle of the track and keep him going and then dont bother him. Dont bother nohow; we gonter lose this first heat anyway and get shut of it—"

"Lose it?" Boon said. "What the hell—"

"Do you want to run this horse-race, or do you want me to?" Ned asked him.

"All right," Boon said. "But, God damn it—" Then he said: "You said that damn boy—"

"Lemme ask you another way then," Ned said. "Do you want to run this horse race and lemme go hunt for that tooth?"

"Here they come," Sam said. "We aint got time now. Gimme your foot." He threw me up. So we didn't have time, for Ned to instruct me further, nor for anything else. But we didn't need it; our victory in the first heat (we didn't win it; it was only a dividend which paid off later) was not due to me nor even to Lightning, but to Ned and McWillie; I didn't even really know what was happening until afterward. Because of my (indubitable) size and (more than indubitable) inexperience, not to mention the unmanageable state toward which the other horse was now well on his way, it was stipulated and agreed that we should be led up to the wire by grooms, and there released at the word Go. Which we did (or were), Lightning behaving as he always did when Ned was near enough to nuzzle at his coat or hand, Acheron behaving as (I assumed, having seen him but that once) he always did when anyone was near his head, skittering, bouncing, snatching the

groom this way and that but gradually working up to the
wire; it would be any moment now; it seemed to me that I actually saw the marshal-murderer fill his lungs to holler Go,
when I dont know what happened, I mean the sequence: Ned
said suddenly:

"Set tight," and my head, arms, shoulders and all, snapped;
I dont know what it was he used—awl, ice-pick, or maybe just
a nail in his palm, the spring, the leap; the voice not hollering
Go! because it never had: only,

"Stop! Stop! Whoa! Whoa!" which we—Lightning and
me—did, to see Acheron's groom still on his knees where
Acheron had flung him, and Acheron and McWillie already at
top speed going into the first turn, McWillie sawing back on
him, wrenching Acheron's whole neck sideways. But he already had the bit, the marshal and three or four spectators
cutting across the ring to try to stop him in the back stretch,
though they might as well have been hollering at Sam's cannonball limited between two flag-stops. But McWillie had
slowed him now, though it was now a matter of mere choice:
whether to come on around the track or turn and go back,
the distance being equal, McWillie (or maybe it was Acheron)
choosing the former, Ned murmuring rapidly at my knee
now:

"Anyhow, we got one extra half a mile on him. This time
you'll have to do it yourself because them judges gonter—"
They were; they were already approaching. Ned said: "Just
remember. This un dont matter nohow—" Then they did: dis-
qualified him. Though they had seen nothing: only that he
had released Lightning's head before the word Go. So this
time I had a volunteer from the crowd to hold Lightning's
head, McWillie glaring at me while Acheron skittered and
plunged under him while the groom gradually worked him
back toward position. And this time the palm went to
McWillie. You see what I mean? Even if Non-virtue knew
nothing about back-country horse-racing, she didn't need to:
all necessary was to supply me with Sam, to gain that extra furtherance in evil by some primeval and insentient process like
osmosis or maybe simple juxtaposition. I didn't even wait for
Lightning to come in to the bridle, I didn't know why: I
brought the bit back to him and (with no little, in fact consid-

erable, help from the volunteer who was mine and Lightning's individual starter) held so, fixed; and sure enough, I saw the soles of Acheron's groom's feet and Acheron himself already two leaps on his next circuit of the track, Lightning and me still motionless. But McWillie was on him this time, before he reached the turn, so that the emergency squad not only reached the back stretch first but even stopped and caught Acheron and led him back. So our—mine and Ned's—net was only six furlongs, and the last one of them debatable. Though our main gain was McWillie; he was not just mad now, he was scared too, glaring at me again but with more than just anger in it, two grooms holding Acheron now long enough for us to be more or less in position, Lightning and me well to the outside to give them room, when the word Go came.

And that's all. We were off, Lightning strong and willing, every quality you could want in fact except eagerness, his brain not having found out yet that this was a race, McWillie holding Acheron back now so that we were setting the pace, on around the first lap, Lightning moving slower and slower, confronted with all that solitude, until Acheron drew up and passed us despite all McWillie could do; whereupon Lightning also moved out again, with companionship now, around the second lap and really going now, Acheron a neck ahead and our crowd even beginning to yell now as though they were getting their money's worth; the wire ahead now and McWillie, giving Acheron a terrific cut with his whip, might as well have hit Lightning too; twenty more feet, and we would have passed McWillie on simple momentum. But the twenty more feet were not there, McWillie giving me one last glare over his shoulder of rage and fright, but triumph too now as I slowed Lightning and turned him and saw it: not a fight but rather a turmoil, a seething of heads and shoulders and backs out of the middle of the crowd around the judges' stand, out of the middle of which Boon stood suddenly up like a pine sapling out of a plum thicket, his shirt torn half off and one flailing arm with two or three men clinging to it; I could see him bellowing. Then he vanished and I saw Ned running toward me up the track. Then Butch and another man came out of the crowd toward us. "What?" I said to Ned.

"Nemmine that," he said. He took the bridle with one hand, his other hand already digging into his hip pocket. "It's that Butch again; it dont matter why. Here." He held his hand up to me. He was not rushed, hurried: he was just rapid. "Take it. They aint gonter bother you." It was a cloth tobacco sack containing a hardish lump about the size of a pecan. "Hide it and keep it. Dont lose it. Just remember who it come from: Ned William McCaslin. Will you remember that? Ned William McCaslin Jefferson Missippi."

"Yes," I said. I put it in my hip pocket. "But what—" He didn't even let me finish.

"Soon as you can, find Uncle Possum and stay with him. Nemmine about Boon and the rest of them. If they got him, they got all the others too. Go straight to Uncle Possum and stay with him. He will know what to do."

"Yes," I said. Butch and the other man had reached the gate onto the track; part of Butch's shirt was gone too. They were looking at us.

"That it?" the man with him said.

"Yep," Butch said.

"Bring that horse here, boy," the man said to Ned. "I want it."

"Set still," Ned told me. He led the horse up to where they waited.

"Jump down, son," the man told me, quite kindly. "I dont want you." I did so. "Hand me the reins," he told Ned. Ned did so. "I'll take you bareback," the man told Ned. "You're under arrest."

Eleven

W E WERE going to have all the crowd too presently. We just stood there, facing Butch and the other man, who now held Lightning. "What's it for, Whitefolks?" Ned said.

"It's for jail, son," the other man said. "That's what we call it here. I dont know what you call it where you come from."

"Yes sir," Ned said. "We has that back home too. Only they mentions why, even to niggers."

"Oh, a lawyer," Butch said. "He wants to see a paper. Show him one.—Never mind, I'll do it." He took something from his hip pocket: a letter in a soiled envelope. Ned took it. He stood there quietly, holding it in his hand. "What do you think of that," Butch said. "A man that cant even read, wanting to see a paper. Smell it then. Maybe it smells all right."

"Yes sir," Ned said. "It's all right."

"Dont say you are satisfied if you aint," Butch said.

"Yes sir," Ned said. "It's all right." We had the crowd now. Butch took the envelope back from Ned and put it back in his pocket and spoke to them: "It's all right, boys; just a little legal difficulty about who owns this horse. The race aint cancelled. The first heat will still stand; the next ones are just put off until tomorrow. Can you hear me back there?"

"We likely cant, if the bets is cancelled too," a voice said. There was a guffaw, then two or three.

"I dont know," Butch said. "Anybody that seen this Memphis horse run against Akron them two heats last winter and still bet on him, has done already cancelled his money out before he even got it put up." He waited, but there was no laughter this time; then the voice—or another—said:

"Does Walter Clapp think that too? Ten foot more, and that chestnut would a beat him today."

"All right, all right," Butch said. "Settle it tomorrow. Aint nothing changed; the next two heats is just put off until tomorrow. The fifty-dollar heat bets is still up and Colonel Linscomb aint won but one of them. Come on, now; we got to get this horse and these witnesses in to town where we can get everything cleared up and be ready to run again tomorrow.

Somebody holler back there to send my surrey." Then I saw
Boon, a head above them. His face was quite calm now, still
blood-streaked, and somebody (I had expected him to be
handcuffed, but he wasn't; we were still democracy; he was
still only a minority and not a heresy) had tied the sleeves of his
torn shirt around his neck so that he was covered. Then I saw
Sam too; he was barely marked; he was the one who pushed
through first. "Now, Sam," Butch said. "We been trying for
thirty minutes to step around you, but you wont let us."

"You damn right I wont," Sam said. "I'll ask you again,
and let this be the last one. Are we under arrest?"

"Are who under arrest?" Butch said.

"Hogganbeck. Me. That Negro there."

"Here's another lawyer," Butch said to the other man. I
learned quite quick now that he was the Law in Parsham; he
was who Miss Reba had told us about last night: the elected
constable of the Beat, where Butch for all his badge and pistol was just another guest like we were, being (Butch) just
one more tenureless appointee from the nepotic files of the
County Sheriff's office in the county seat at Hardwick thirteen miles away. "Maybe he wants to see a paper too."

"No," the other man, the constable, told Sam. "You can go
whenever you want to."

"Then I'm going back to Memphis to find some law," Sam
said. "I mean the kind of law a man like me can approach
without having his britches and underwear both ripped off. If
I aint back tonight, I'll be here early tomorrow morning." He
had already seen me. He said, "Come on. You come with
me."

"No," I said. "I'm going to stay here." The constable was
looking at me.

"You can go with him, if you want," he said.

"No sir," I said. "I'm going to stay here."

"Who does he belong to?" the constable said.

"He's with me," Ned said. The constable said, as though
Ned had not spoken, there had been no sound:

"Who brought him here?"

"Me," Boon said. "I work for his father."

"I work for his grandfather," Ned said. "We done already
fixed to take care of him."

"Just hold on," Sam said. "I'll try to get back tonight. Then we can attend to everything."

"And when you come back," the constable said, "remember that you aint in Memphis or Nashville either. That you aint even in Hardwick County except primarily. What you're in right now, and what you'll be in every time you get off of a train at that depot yonder, is Beat Four."

"That's telling them, judge," Butch said. "The free state of Possum, Tennessee."

"I was talking to you too," the constable told Butch. "You may be the one that better try hardest to remember it." The surrey came up to where they were holding Boon. The constable gestured Ned toward it. Suddenly Boon was struggling; Ned was saying something to him. Then the constable turned back to me. "That Negro says you are going home with old Possum Hood."

"Yes sir," I said.

"I dont think I like that—a white boy staying with a family of niggers. You come home with me."

"No sir," I said.

"Yes," he said, but still really kind. "Come on. I'm busy."

"There's somewhere you stops," Ned said. The constable became completely motionless, half turned.

"What did you say?" he said.

"There's somewhere the Law stops and just people starts," Ned said. And still for another moment the constable didn't move—an older man than you thought at first, spare, quite hale, but older, who wore no pistol, in his pocket or anywhere else, and if he had a badge, it wasn't in sight either.

"You're right," he said. He said to me: "That's where you want to stay? with old Possum?"

"Yes sir," I said.

"All right," he said. He turned. "Get in, boys," he said.

"What you going to do with the nigger?" Butch said. He had taken the lines from the man who brought the surrey up; his foot was already on the stirrup to get into the driver's seat; Boon and Sam were already in the back. "Let him ride your horse?"

"You're going to ride my horse," the constable said. "Jump up, son," he told Ned. "You're the horse expert around here." Ned took the lines from Butch and got up and cramped the wheel for the constable to get up beside him. Boon was still looking down at me, his face battered and bruised but quiet now under the drying blood.

"Come on with Sam," he said.

"I'm all right," I said.

"No," Boon said. "I cant—"

"I know Possum Hood," the constable said. "If I get worried about him, I'll come back tonight and get him. Drive on, son." They went on. They were gone. I was alone. I mean, if I had been left by myself like when two hunters separate in the woods or fields, to meet again later, even as late as camp that night, I would not have been so alone. As it was, I was anything but solitary. I was an island in that ring of sweated hats and tieless shirts and overalls, the alien nameless faces already turning away from me as I looked about at them, and not one word to me of Yes or No or Go or Stay: who—me— was being re-abandoned who had already been abandoned once: and at only eleven you are not really big enough in size to be worth that much abandonment; you would be obliterated, effaced, dissolved, vaporised beneath it Until one of them said:

"You looking for Possum Hood? I think he's over yonder by his buggy, waiting for you." He was. The other wagons and buggies were pulling out now; most of them and all the saddled horses and mules were already gone. I went up to the buggy and stopped. I dont know why: I just stopped. Maybe there was nowhere else to go. I mean, there was no room for the next step forward until somebody moved the buggy.

"Get in," Uncle Parsham said. "We'll go home and wait for Lycurgus."

"Lycurgus," I said as though I had never heard the name before even.

"He rode on to town on the mule. He will find out what all this is about and come back and tell us. He's going to find out what time a train goes to Jefferson tonight."

"To Jefferson?" I said.

"So you can go home." He didn't quite look at me. "If you want to."

"I cant go home yet," I said. "I got to wait for Boon."

"I said if you want to," Uncle Parsham said. "Get in." I got in. He drove across the pasture, into the road. "Close the gate," Uncle Parsham said. "It's about time somebody remembered to." I closed the gate and got back in the buggy. "You ever drive a mule to a buggy?"

"No sir," I said. He handed me the lines. "I dont know how," I said.

"Then you can learn now. A mule aint like a horse. When a horse gets a wrong notion in his head, all you got to do is swap him another one for it. Most anything will do—a whip or spur or just scare him by hollering at him. A mule is different. He can hold two notions at the same time and the way to change one of them is to act like you believe he thought of changing it first. He'll know different, because mules have got sense. But a mule is a gentleman too, and when you act courteous and respectful at him without trying to buy him or scare him, he'll act courteous and respectful back at you—as long as you dont overstep him. That's why you dont pet a mule like you do a horse: he knows you dont love him: you're just trying to fool him into doing something he already dont aim to do, and it insults him. Handle him like that. He knows the way home, and he will know it aint me holding the lines. So all you need to do is tell him with the lines that you know the way too but he lives here and you're just a boy so you want him to go in front."

We went on, at a fair clip now, the mule neat and nimble, raising barely half as much dust as a horse would; already I could feel what Uncle Parsham meant; there came back to me through the lines not just power, but intelligence, sagacity; not just the capacity but the willingness to choose when necessary between two alternatives and to make the right decision without hesitation. "What do you do at home?" Uncle Parsham said.

"I work on Saturdays," I said.

"Then you going to save some of the money. What are you going to buy with it?" And so suddenly I was talking, telling him: about the beagles: how I wanted to be a fox-hunter like Cousin Zack and how Cousin Zack said the way to learn was with a pack of beagles on rabbits; and how Father paid me ten cents each Saturday at the livery stable and Father would

match whatever I saved of it until I could buy the first couple
to start my pack, which would cost twelve dollars and I already had eight dollars and ten cents; and then, all of a sudden too, I was crying, bawling; I was tired, not from riding a
mile race because I had ridden more than that at one time before, even though it wasn't real racing; but maybe from being
up early and chasing back and forth across the country without any dinner but a piece of cornbread. Maybe that was it:
I was just hungry. But anyway, there I sat, bawling like a
baby, worse than Alexander and even Maury, against Uncle
Parsham's shirt while he held me with one arm and took the
lines from me with his other hand, not saying anything at all,
until he said, "Now you can quit. We're almost home; you'll
have just time to wash your face at the trough before we go
in the house. You dont want womenfolks to see it like that."

Which I did. That is, we unhitched the mule first and wa-
tered him and hung the harness up and wiped him down and
stalled and fed him and pushed the buggy back under its shed
and then I smeared my face with water at the trough and
dried it (after a fashion) with the riding-sock and we went
into the house. And the evening meal—supper—was ready although it was barely five oclock, as country people, farmers,
ate; and we sat down: Uncle Parsham and his daughter and
me since Lycurgus was not yet back from town, and Uncle
Parsham said, "You gives thanks at your house too," and I
said,

"Yes sir," and he said,

"Bow your head," and we did so and he said grace, briefly,
courteously but with dignity, without abasement or cringing:
one man of decency and intelligence to another: notifying
Heaven that we were about to eat and thanking It for the
privilege, but at the same time reminding It that It had had
some help too; that if someone named Hood or Briggins (so
that was Lycurgus and his mother's name) hadn't sweated
some, the acknowledgment would have graced mainly empty
dishes, and said Amen and unfolded his napkin and stuck the
corner in his collar exactly as Grandfather did, and we ate: the
dishes of cold vegetables which should have been eaten hot at
the country hour of eleven oclock, but there were hot biscuits
and three kinds of preserves, and buttermilk. And still it

wasn't even sundown: the long twilight and even after that, still the long evening, the long night and I didn't even know where I was going to sleep nor even on what, Uncle Parsham sitting there picking his teeth with a gold tooth-pick just like Grandfather's and reading my mind like it was a magic lantern slide: "Do you like to go fishing?" I didn't really like it. I couldn't seem to learn to want—or maybe want to learn—to be still that long. I said quickly:

"Yes sir."

"Come on then. By that time Lycurgus will be back." There were three cane poles, with lines floats sinkers hooks and all, on two nails in the wall of the back gallery. He took down two of them. "Come on," he said. In the tool shed there was a tin bucket with nail holes punched through the lid. "Lycurgus's cricket bucket," he said. "I like worms my-self." They were in a shallow earth-filled wooden tray; he—no: I; I said,

"Lemme do it," and took the broken fork from him and dug the long frantic worms out of the dirt, into a tin can.

"Come on," he said, shouldering his pole, passing the sta-ble but turning sharp away and down toward the creek bot-tom, not far; there was a good worn path among the blackberry thickets and then the willows, then the creek, the water seeming to gather gently the fading light and then as gently return it; there was even a log to sit on. "This is where my daughter fishes," he said. "We call it Mary's hole. But you can use it now. I'll be on down the bank." Then he was gone. The light was going fast now; it would be night before long. I sat on the log, in a gentle whine of mosquitoes. It wouldn't be too difficult; all I would have to do would just be to say *I wont think* whenever it was necessary. After a while I thought about putting the hook into the water, then I could watch how long it would take the float to disappear into darkness when night finally came. Then I even thought about putting one of Lycurgus's crickets on the hook, but crickets were not always easy to catch and Lycurgus lived by a creek and would have more time to fish and would need them. So I just thought *I wont think*; I could see the float plainer than ever, now that it was on the water; it would probably be the last of all to vanish into the darkness, since the water itself would be

next to last; I couldn't see or hear Uncle Parsham at all, I
didn't know how much further he called on down the bank
and now was the perfect time, chance to act like a baby, only
what's the good of acting like a baby, of wasting it with nobody there to know it or offer sympathy—if anybody ever
wants sympathy or even in fact really to be back home because what you really want is just a familiar soft bed to sleep
in for a change again, to go to sleep in; there were whipporwills now and back somewhere beyond the creek an owl too,
a big one by his voice; maybe there were big woods there and
if Lycurgus's (or maybe they were Uncle Parsham's) hounds
were all that good on Otis last night, they sure ought to be
able to handle rabbits or coons or possums. So I asked him—
it was full night now for some time—he said quietly behind
me; I hadn't even heard him until then:

"Had a bite yet?"

"I aint much of a fisherman," I said. "How do your hounds
hunt?"

"Good," he said. He didn't even raise his voice: "Pappy."
Uncle Parsham's white shirt held light too, up to us where
Lycurgus took the two poles and we followed, up the path
again where the two hounds met us, on into the house again,
into the lamplight, a plate of supper with a cloth over it ready
for Lycurgus.

"Sit down," Uncle Parsham said. "You can talk while you
eat." Lycurgus sat down.

"They're still there," he said.

"They aint took them to Hardwick yet?" Uncle Parsham
said. "Possum hasn't got a jail," he told me. "They lock them
in the wood shed behind the school house until they can take
them to the jail at Hardwick. Men, that is. They aint had
women before."

"No sir," Lycurgus said. "The ladies is still in the hotel,
with a guard at the door. Just Mr Hogganbeck is in the wood
shed. Mr Caldwell went back to Memphis on Number Thirty-
one. He taken that boy with him."

"Otis?" I said. "Did they get the tooth back?"

"They never said," Lycurgus said, eating; he glanced briefly
at me. "And the horse is all right too. I went and seen him.
He's in the hotel stable. Before he left, Mr Caldwell made a

bond for Mr McCaslin so he can watch the horse." He ate. "A train leaves for Jefferson at nine-forty. We could make it all right if we hurry." Uncle Parsham took a vast silver watch from his pocket and looked at it. "We could make it," Lycurgus said.

"I cant," I said. "I got to wait." Uncle Parsham put the watch back. He rose. He said, not loud:

"Mary." She was in the front room; I hadn't heard a sound. She came to the door.

"I already did it," she said. She said to Lycurgus: "Your pallet's ready in the hall." Then to me: "You sleep in Lycurgus's bed where you was yestiddy."

"I dont need to take Lycurgus's bed," I said. "I can sleep with Uncle Parsham. I wont mind." They looked at me, quite still, quite identical. "I sleep with Boss a lot of times," I said. "He snores too. I dont mind."

"Boss?" Uncle Parsham said.

"That's what we call Grandfather," I said. "He snores too. I wont mind."

"Let him," Uncle Parsham said. We went to his room. His lamp had flowers painted on the china shade and there was a big gold-framed portrait on a gold easel in one corner: a woman, not very old but in old-timey clothes; the bed had a bright piece-work quilt on it like Lycurgus's and even in May there was a smolder of fire on the hearth. There was a chair, a rocking chair too, but I didn't sit down. I just stood there. Then he came in again. He wore a night-shirt now and was winding the silver watch. "Undress," he said. I did so. "Does your mother let you sleep like that at home?"

"No sir," I said.

"You aint got anything with you, have you?"

"No sir," I said. He put the watch on the mantel and went to the door and said,

"Mary." She answered. "Bring one of Lycurgus's clean shirts." After a while her hand held the shirt through the door-crack. He took it. "Here," he said. I came and put it on. "Do you say your Now I lay me in bed or kneeling down?"

"Kneeling down," I said.

"Say them," he said. I knelt beside the bed and said my prayers. The bed was already turned back. I got into it and he blew out the lamp and I heard the bed again and then—the moon would be late before it was very high tonight but there was already enough light—I could see him, all black and white against the white pillow and the white moustache and imperial, lying on his back, his hands folded on his breast. "Tomorrow morning I'll take you to town and we'll see Mr Hogganbeck. If he says you have done all you can do here and for you to go home, will you go then?"

"Yes sir," I said.

"Now go to sleep," he said. Because even before he said it, I knew that that was exactly what I wanted, what I had been wanting probably ever since yesterday: to go home. I mean, nobody likes to be licked, but maybe there are times when nobody can help being; that all you can do about it is not quit. And Boon and Ned hadn't quit, or they wouldn't be where they were right now. And maybe they wouldn't say that I had quit either, when it was them who told me to go home. Maybe I was just too little, too young; maybe I just wasn't able to tote whatever my share was, and if they had had somebody else bigger or older or maybe just smarter, we wouldn't have been licked. You see? like that: all specious and rational; unimpugnable even, when the simple truth was, I wanted to go home and just wasn't brave enough to say so, let alone do it. So now, having admitted at last that I was not only a failure but a coward too, my mind should be peaceful and easy and I should go on to sleep like a baby: where Uncle Parsham already was, just barely snoring (who should hear Grandfather once). Not that that mattered either, since I would be home tomorrow with nothing—no stolen horses nor chastity-stricken prostitutes and errant pullman conductors and Ned and Boon Hogganbeck in his normal condition once he had slipped Father's leash—to interfere with sleep, hearing the voice, the bawling two or three times before I struggled up and out, into daylight, sunlight; Uncle Parsham's side of the bed was empty and now I could hear the bawling from outside the house:

"Hellaw. Hellaw. Lycurgus. Lycurgus," and leapt, sprang from the bed, already running, across to the window where I could look out into the front yard. It was Ned. He had the horse.

Twelve

So once again, at two oclock in the afternoon, McWillie and I sat our (his was anyway) skittering mounts—we had scared Mr Clapp enough yesterday to where we had drawn for pole position this time and McWillie won it—poised for the steward-starter's (the bird dog trainer-market hunter-homicidist) Go.

A few things came before that though. One of them was Ned. He looked bad. He looked terrible. It wasn't just lack of sleep; we all had that lack. But Boon and I had at least spent the four nights in bed since we left Jefferson, where Ned had spent maybe two, one of the others in a box car with a horse and the other in a stable with him, both on hay if on anything. It was his clothes too. His shirt was filthy and his black pants were not much better. At least Everbe had washed some of mine night before last, but Ned hadn't even had his off until now: sitting now in a clean faded suit of Uncle Parsham's overalls and jumper while Mary was washing his shirt and doing what she could with his pants, at the kitchen table now, he and I eating our breakfast while Uncle Parsham sat and listened.

He said that a little before daylight one of the white men—it wasn't Mr Poleymus, the constable—woke him where he was asleep on some bales of hay and told him to take the horse and get out of town with it—

"Just you and Lightning, and not Boon and the others?" I said. "Where are they?"

"Where them white folks put um," Ned said. "So I said, Much oblige, Whitefolks, and took Lightning in my hand and—"

"Why?" I said.

"What do you care why? all we need to do now is be up behind that starting wire at two oclock this afternoon and win them two heats and get a holt of Boss's automobile and get on back to Jefferson that we hadn't ought to never left nohow—"

"We cant go back without Boon," I said. "If they let you and Lightning go, why didn't they let him go?"

"Look," Ned said. "Me and you got enough to do just running that horse-race. Why dont you finish your breakfast and then go back and lay down and rest until I calls you in time—"

"Stop lying to him," Uncle Parsham said. Ned ate, his head bent over his plate, eating fast. He was tired; his eyewhites were not even just pink anymore: they were red.

"Mr Boon Hogganbeck aint going anywhere for a while. He's in jail good this time. They gonter take him to Hardwick this morning where they can lock him up sho enough. But forget that. What you and me have got to do is—"

"Tell him," Uncle Parsham said. "He's stood everything else you folks got him into since you brought him here; what makes you think he cant stand the rest of it too, until you manage somehow to come out on the other side and can take him back home? Didn't he have to watch it too, right here in my yard and my house, and down yonder in my pasture both, not to mention what he might have seen in town since—that man horsing and studding at that gal, and her trying to get away from him, and not nobody but this eleven-year-old boy to run to? not Boon Hogganbeck and not the Law and not the grown white folks to count on and hope for, but just him? Tell him." And already the thing inside me saying *No No Dont ask Leave it Leave it.* I said,

"What did Boon do?" Ned chewed over his plate, blinking his reddened eyes like when you have sand in them.

"He whupped that Law. That Butch. He nigh ruint him. They let him out before they done me and Lightning. He never even stopped. He went straight to that gal—"

"It was Miss Reba," I said. "It was Miss Reba."

"No," Ned said. "It was that other one. That big one. They never called her name to me.—and whupped her and turned around—"

"He hit her?" I said. "Boon hit Ever—Miss Corrie?"

"Is that her name? Yes.—and turned around and went straight back until he found that Law and whupped him, pistol and all, before they could pull him off—"

"Boon hit her," I said. "He hit her."

"That's right," Ned said. "She is the reason me and Lightning are free right now. That Butch found out he couldn't get to her no other way, and when he found out that me and you and Boon had to win that race today before we could dare to go back home, and all we had to win it with was Lightning, he took Lightning and locked him up. That's what happened. That's all it was; Uncle Possum just told you how he watched it coming Monday, and maybe I ought to seen it too and maybe I would if I hadn't been so busy with Lightning, or maybe if I had been a little better acquainted with that Butch—"

"I dont believe it," I said.

"Yes," he said. "That's what it was. It was just bad luck, the kind of bad luck you cant count against beforehand. He likely just happened to be wherever he was just by chance when he seen her Monday and figgered right off that that badge and pistol would be all he would need, being likely used to having them be enough around here. Only this time they wasn't and so he had to look again, and sho enough, there was Lightning that we had to depend on to win that race so we could get back Boss's automobile and maybe go back home—"

"No!" I said. "No! It wasn't her! She's not even here! She went back to Memphis with Sam yesterday evening! They just didn't tell you! It was somebody else! It was another one!"

"No," Ned said. "It was her. You seen it Monday out here." Oh yes; and on the way back in the surrey that afternoon, and at the doctor's, and at the hotel that night until Miss Reba frightened him away, we—I anyway—thought for good. Because Miss Reba was only a woman too. I said:

"Why didn't somebody else help her? a man to help her— that man, that man that took you and Lightning, that told Sam and Butch both they could be whatever they wanted in Memphis or Nashville or Hardwick either, but that here in Possum he was the one—" I said, cried: "I dont believe it!"

"Yes," Ned said. "It was her that bought Lightning loose to run again today. I aint talking about me and Boon and them others; Butch never cared nothing about us, except to maybe keep Boon outen the way until this morning. All he needed was Lightning, only he had to throw in me and Boon and the rest to make Mr Poleymus believe him. Because Butch tricked him too, used him too, until whatever it was that happened this morning—whether that Butch, having done been paid off now, said it was all a mistake or it was the wrong horse, or maybe by that time Mr Poleymus his-self had added one to one and smelled a mouse and turned everybody loose and before he could turn around, Boon went and whupped that gal and then come straight back without even stopping and tried to tear that Butch's head off, pistol and all, with his bare hands, and Mr Poleymus smelled a whole rat. And Mr Poleymus may be little, and he may be old; but he's a man, mon. They told me how last year his wife had one of them strokes and cant even move her hand now, and all the chillen are married and gone, so he has to wash her and feed her and lift her in and outen the bed day and night both, besides cooking and keeping house too unlessen some neighbor woman comes in to help. But you dont know it to look at him and watch him act. He come in there—I never seen none of it; they just told me: two or three holding Boon and another one trying to keep that Butch from whupping him with the pistol whilst they was holding him—and walked up to Butch and snatched that pistol outen his hand and reached up and ripped that badge and half his shirt off too and telefoamed to Hardwick to send a automobile to bring them all back to jail, the women too. When it's women, they calls it fragrancy."

"Vagrancy," Uncle Parsham said.

"That's what I said," Ned said. "You call it whatever you want. I calls it jail."

"I dont believe it," I said. "She quit."

"Then we sho better say much obliged that she started again," Ned said. "Else me and you and Lightning—"

"She's quit," I said. "She promised me."

"Aint we got Lightning back?" Ned said. "Aint all we got to do now is just run him? Didn't Mr Sam say he will be back today and will know what to do, and then me and you and Boon will be just the same as already back home?"

I sat there. It was still early. I mean, even now it was still only eight oclock. It was going to be hot today, the first hot day, precursor of summer. You see, just to keep on saying *I dont believe it* served only for the moment; as soon as the words, the noise, died, there it still was—anguish, rage, outrage, grief, whatever it was—unchanged. "I have to go to

town right away," I said to Uncle Parsham. "If I can use one of the mules, I'll send you the money as soon as I get home."
He rose at once.

"Come on," he said.

"Hold on," Ned said. "It's too late now. Mr Poleymus sent for a automobile. They've already left before now."

"He can cut them off," Uncle Parsham said. "It aint a half a mile from here to the road they'll be on."

"I got to get some sleep," Ned said.

"I know it," Uncle Parsham said. "I'm going with him. I told him last night I would."

"I'm not going home yet," I said. "I'm just going to town for a minute. Then I'll come back here."

"All right," Ned said. "At least lemme finish my coffee." We didn't wait for him. One of the mules was gone, probably to the field with Lycurgus. But the other was there. Ned came out before we had the gear on. Uncle Parsham showed us the short cut to the Hardwick road, but I didn't care. I mean, it didn't matter to me now where I met him. If I hadn't been just about worn out with race horses and women and deputy sheriffs and everybody else that wasn't back home where they belonged, I might have preferred to hold my interview with Boon in some quick private place for both our sakes. But it didn't matter now; it could be in the middle of the big road or in the middle of the Square either, as far as I was concerned; there could be a whole automobile full of them. But we didn't meet the automobile; obviously I was being protected; to have had to do it in public would have been intolerable, gratuitously intolerable for one who had served Non-virtue this faithfully for four days and asked so little in return. I mean, not to have to see any more of them than I had to. Which was granted; the still-empty automobile had barely reached the hotel itself when we got there: a seven passenger Stanley Steamer: enough room even for the baggage of two—no, three: Minnie too—women on a two-day trip from Memphis to Parsham, which they would all be upstairs packing now, so even horse-stealing took care of its own. Ned cramped the wheel for me to get down. "You still dont want to tell me what you come for?" he said.

"No," I said. None of the long row of chairs on the gallery

were empty, Caesar could have held his triumph there and
had all the isolation Boon's and Butch's new status required;
the lobby was empty, and Mr Poleymus could have used that.
But he was a man, mon; they were in the ladies' parlor—Mr
Poleymus, the driver of the car (another deputy; anyway, in a
badge), Butch and Boon fresh and marked from battle.
Though only Boon for me, who read my face (he had known
it long enough) or maybe it was his own heart or anyway conscience; he said quickly:

"Look out, now, Lucius; look out!" already flinging up one
arm as he rose quickly, already stepping back, retreating, I
walking at him, up to him, not tall enough by more than half
and nothing to stand on either (that ludicrous anti-climax of
shame), having to reach, to jump even, stretch the best I
could to strike at his face; oh yes, I was crying, bawling again;
I couldn't even see him now: just hitting as high as I could,
having to jump at him to do so, against his Alp-hard Alp-tall
crags and cliffs and scafells, Mr Poleymus saying behind me:

"Hit him again. He struck a woman, I dont care who she
is," and (or somebody) holding me until I wrenched, jerked
free, turning, blind for the door or where I thought I remembered it, the hand guiding me now.

"Wait," Boon said. "Dont you want to see her?" You see, I
was tired and my feet hurt. I was about worn out, and I
needed sleep too. But more: I was dirty. I wanted fresh
clothes. She had washed for me Monday night but I didn't
want just re-washed clothes: I wanted a change of clothes that
had had time to rest for a while, like at home, smelling of rest
and quiet drawers and starch and bluing; but mainly my feet;
I wanted fresh stockings and my other shoes.

"I dont want to see nobody!" I said. "I want to go home!"

"All right," Boon said. "Here—anybody—will somebody
put him on that train this morning? I got money—can get
it—"

"Shut up," I said. "I aint going nowhere now." I went on,
still blind; or that is, the hand carried me.

"Wait," Boon said. "Wait, Lucius."

"Shut up," I said. The hand curved me around; there was
a wall now.

"Wipe your face," Mr Poleymus said. He held out a bandanna handkerchief but I didn't take it; my bandage would sop it up all right. Anyway, the riding-sock did. It was used to being cried into. Who knew? if it stayed with me long enough, it might even win a horse-race. I could see now; we were in the lobby. I started to turn but he held me. "Hold up a minute," he said. "If you still dont want to see anybody." It was Miss Reba and Everbe coming down the stairs carrying their grips but Minnie wasn't with them. The car-driving deputy was waiting. He took the grips and they went on; they didn't look toward us, Miss Reba with her head mad and hard and high; if the deputy hadn't moved quick she would have tromped right over him, grips and all. They went out. "I'll buy you a ticket home," Mr Poleymus said. "Get on that train." I didn't say Shut up to him. "You've run out of folks sure enough now. I'll stay with you and tell the conductor—"

"I'm going to wait for Ned," I said. "I cant go without him. If you hadn't ruined everything yesterday, we'd all been gone by now."

"Who's Ned?" he said. I told him. "You mean you're going to run that horse today anyhow? you and Ned by yourself?" I told him. "Where's Ned now?" I told him. "Come on," he said. "We can go out the side door." Ned was standing at the mule's head. The back of the automobile was toward us, so I couldn't see Miss Reba and Everbe. And Minnie still wasn't with them. Maybe she went back to Memphis yesterday with Sam and Otis; maybe now that she had Otis again she wasn't going to lift her hand off of him until it had that tooth in it. That's what I would have done, anyway.

"So Mr Poleymus finally caught you too, did he?" Ned said. "What's the matter? aint he got no handcuffs your size?"

"Shut up," I said.

"When you going to get him back home, son?" Mr Poleymus said to Ned.

"I hope tonight," Ned said; he wasn't being Uncle Remus or smart or cute or anything now. "Soon as I get rid of this horse-race and can do something about it."

"Have you got enough money?"

"Yes sir," Ned said. "Much oblige. We'll be all right after this race." He cramped the wheel and we got in. Mr Poleymus stood with his hand on the top stanchion. He said:

"So you really are going to race that Linscomb horse this afternoon."

"We gonter beat that Linscomb horse this afternoon," Ned said.

"You hope so," Mr Poleymus said.

"I know so," Ned said.

"How much do you know so?" Mr Poleymus said.

"I wish I had a hundred dollars of my own to bet on it," Ned said. They looked at each other; it was a good while. Then Mr Poleymus turned loose the stanchion and took from his pocket a worn snap-purse that when I saw it I thought I was seeing double because it was exactly like Ned's, scuffed and worn and even longer than the riding-sock, that you didn't even know who was paying who for what, and unsnapped it and took out two one-dollar bills and snapped the purse shut and handed the bills to Ned.

"Bet this for me," he said. "If you're right, you can keep half of it." Ned took the money.

"I'll bet it for you," he said. "But much oblige. By sundown tonight I can lend you half of three or four times this much." We drove on then—I mean, Ned drove on—turning; we didn't pass the automobile at all. "Been crying again," he said. "A race-horse jockey and still aint growed out of crying."

"Shut up," I said. But he was turning the buggy again, on across the tracks and on along what would have been the other side of the Square if Parsham ever got big enough to have a Square, and stopped; we were in front of a store.

"Hold him," Ned said and got out and went in the store, not long, and came back with a paper sack and got in and took the lines, back toward home—I mean Uncle Parsham's —now and with his free hand took from the big bag a small one; it was peppermint drops. "Here," he said. "I got some bananas too and soon as we get Lightning back to that private spring-branch paddock we uses, we can set down and eat um and then maybe I can get some sleep before I forget how to. And meanwhiles, stop fretting about that gal, now you done said your say to Boon Hogganbeck. Hitting a woman dont hurt her because a woman dont shove back at a lick like a man do; she just gives to it and then when your back is

turned, reaches for the flat-iron or the butcher knife. That's
why hitting them dont break nothing; all it does is just black
her eye or cut her mouf a little. And that aint nothing to a
woman. Because why? Because what better sign than a black
eye or a cut mouf can a woman want from a man that he got
her on his mind?"

So once more, in the clutch of our respective starting
grooms, McWillie and I sat our skittering and jockeying
mounts behind that wire. (That's right, skittering and jockeying, Lightning too; at least he had learned—anyway remembered—from yesterday—that he was supposed to be at least
up with Acheron when the running started, even if he hadn't
discovered yet that he was supposed—hoped—to be in front
when it stopped.)

This time Ned's final instructions were simple, explicit, and
succinct: "Just remember, I knows I can make him run once,
and I believes I can make him run twice. Only, we wants to
save that once I *knows*, until we knows we needs it. So here's
what I want you to do for this first heat: Just before them
judges and such hollers Go! you say to yourself *My name is
Ned William McCaslin* and then do it."

"Do what?" I said.

"I dont know yet neither," he said. "But Akrum is a horse,
and with a horse anything can happen. And with a nigger boy
on him, it's twice as likely to. You just got to watch and be
ready, so that when it do happen, you done already said *My
name is Ned William McCaslin* and then do it and do it
quick. And dont worry. If it dont work and dont nothing
happen, I'll be waiting right there at the finish, where I come
in. Because we knows I can make him run once."

Then the voice hollered Go! and our grooms sprang for
their lives and we were off (as I said, we had drawn this time
and McWillie had the pole). Or McWillie was off that is.
Because I dont remember, whether I had planned it or just
did it by instinct, so that when McWillie broke, I was already
braced and Lightning's first spring rammed him into the bridle all the way up to my shoulders, bad hand and all, Acheron
already in full run and three lengths ahead when I let
Lightning go, but still kept the three-length gap, both of us
going now but three horses apart, when I saw McWillie do

what you call nowadays a double-take: a single quick glance aside, using only his eyeballs, expecting to see me of course more or less at his knee, then seeming to drive on at full speed for another stride or so before his vision told his intelligence that Lightning and I were not there. Then he turned, jerked his whole head around to look back and I remember still the whites of his eyes and his open mouth; I could see him sawing frantically at Acheron to slow him; I sincerely believe I even heard him yell back at me: "Goddammit, white boy, if you gonter race, race!" the gap between us closing fast now because he now had Acheron wrenched back and crossways until he was now at right angles to the course, more or less filling the track sideways from rail to rail it looked like and facing the outside rail and for that moment, instant, second, motionless; I am convinced that McWillie's now frantic mind actually toyed with the idea of turning and running back until he could turn again with Lightning in front. Nor no premeditation, nothing: I just said in my mind *My name is Ned William McCaslin* and cut Lightning as hard as I could with the switch, pulling his head over so that when he sprang for the gap between Acheron's stern and the inside rail, we would scrape Acheron; I remember I thought *My leg will be crushed* and I sat there, the switch poised again, in complete detachment, waiting in nothing but curiosity for the blow, shock, crack, spurt of blood and bones or whatever it would be. But we had just exactly room enough or speed enough or maybe it was luck enough: not my leg but Lightning's hip which scraped across Acheron's buttocks: at which second I cut again with the switch as hard as I could. Nor any judge or steward, dog-trainer, market-hunter, or murderer, nor purist or stickler of the most finicking and irreproachable, to affirm it was not my own mount I struck; in fact, we were so inextricable at that second that, of the four of us, only Acheron actually knew who had been hit.

Then on. I mean, Lightning and me. I didn't—couldn't—look back yet, so I had to wait to learn what happened. They said that Acheron didn't try to jump the rail at all: he just reared and fell through it in a kind of whirling dust of white planks, but still on his feet, frantic now, running more or less straight out into the pasture, spectators scattering before him,

until McWillie wrenched him around; and they said that this
time McWillie actually set him quartering at the fence (it was
too late now to go back to the gap in it he had already made;
we—Lightning—were too far ahead by this time) as though
he were a hunter. But he refused it, running instead at full
speed along the rail, but still on the outside of it, the spectators hollering and leaping like frogs from in front of him as he
cleared his new path or precedent. That was when I began
to hear him again. He—they: McWillie and Acheron—was
closing fast now, though with the outside rail between us:
Lightning with the whole track to himself now and going
with that same fine strong rhythm and reach and power to
which it had simply not occurred yet that there was any hurry
about it; in the back stretch now and Acheron, who had already run at least one extra fifty yards and would have to run
another one before he finished, already abreast of us beyond
the rail; around the far turn of the first lap now and now I
could actually see McWillie's desperate mind grappling frantically with the rapidly diminishing choice of whether to swing
Acheron wide enough to bring him back through his self-
made gap and onto the track again and have him refuse its
jumbled wreckage, or play safe and stay where they were in
the new track which they had already cleared of obstacles.

Conservatism won (as it should and does); again the back
stretch (second lap now); now the far turn (second one also)
and even on the outside longer curve, they were drawing
ahead; there was the wire and Acheron a length at least ahead
and I believe I thought for an instant of going to the whip
just for the looks of the thing; on; our crowd was yelling now
and who could blame them? few if any had seen a heat like
this before between two horses running on opposite sides of
the rail; on, Acheron still at top speed along his path as empty
and open for him as the path to heaven; two lengths ahead
when we—Lightning—passed under the wire, and (Acheron:
evidently he liked running outside) already into his third lap
when McWillie dragged him by main strength away and into
the pasture and into a tightening circle which even he could
no longer negotiate. And much uproar behind us now:
shouts: "Foul! Foul! No! No! Yes! No heat! No heat! Yes it
was! No it wasn't! Ask the judge! Ask Ed! What was it,

Ed?"—that part of the crowd which Acheron had scattered from the outside rail now pouring across the track through the shattered gap to join the others in the infield; I was looking for Ned; I thought I saw him but it was Lycurgus, trotting up the track toward me until he could take Lightning's bit, already turning him back.

"Come on," he said. "You cant stop. You got to cool him out. Mr McCaslin said to get him away from the track, take him over yonder to them locust trees where the buggy's at, where he can be quiet and we can rub him down." But I tried to hold back.

"What happened?" I said. "Is it going to count? We won, didn't we? We went under the wire. They just went around it. Here," I said, "you take him while I go back and see."

"No, I tell you," Lycurgus said. He had Lightning trotting now. "Mr McCaslin dont want you there neither. He said for me and you to stay right with Lightning and have him ready to run again; that next heat's in less than a hour now and we got to win that one now, because if this throws this one out, we got to win the next one no matter what happens." So we went on. He lifted down a rail at the end of the track and we went through, on to the clump of locust trees about two hundreds yards away; now I could see Uncle Parsham's buggy hitched to one of them. And I could still hear the voices from the judges' stand in the infield and I still wanted to go back and find out. But Lycurgus had forestalled that too: he had the pails and sponges and cloths and even a churn of water in the buggy for us to strip Lightning and go to work on him.

So I had to get my first information about what had happened (and was still happening too) from hearsay—what little Lycurgus had seen before Ned sent him to meet me, and from others later—before Ned came up: the uproar, vociferation of protest and affirmation (oh yes, even after losing two races (or heats: whatever they were) last winter, and the first heat of this one yesterday, there were still people who had bet on Lightning. Because I was only eleven; I had not learned yet that no horse ever walked to post, provided he was still on his feet when he got there, that somebody didn't bet on) coming once or twice almost to blows, with Ned in the center of it, in effect the crux of it, polite and calm but dogged and insistent too, rebutting each attack: "It wasn't a race. It takes at least two horses to make a race, and one of these wasn't even on the track." And Ned:

"No sir. The rule book dont mention how many horses. It just talks about one horse at a time: that if it dont commit fouls and dont stop forward motion and the jockey dont fall off and it cross the finish line first, it wins." Then another:

"Then you just proved yourself that black won: it never fouled nothing but about twenty foot of that fence and it sho never stopped forward motion because I myself seen at least a hundred folks barely get out from under it in time and you yourself seen it pass that finish line a good two lengths ahead of that chestnut." And Ned:

"No sir. That finish line wire just runs across that track from one rail to the other. It dont run on down into Missippi too. If it done that, there are horses down there been crossing it ever since sunup this morning that we aint even heard about yet. No sir. It's too bad about that little flimsy railing, but we was too busy running our horse to have time to stop and wait for that other one to come back." When suddenly three newcomers were on the scene, or anyway in the telling of it: not three strangers, because one of them was Colonel Linscomb himself and they all knew him since they were his neighbors. So probably what they meant was that the other two were simply his guests, city men too or very likely simply of Colonel Linscomb's age and obvious solvency and likewise wearing coats and neckties, who—one of them—seemed to take charge of the matter, coming into the crowd clamoring around Ned and the harassed officials and saying,

"Gentlemen, let me offer a solution. As this man"—meaning Ned—"says, his horse ran according to the rules and went under the wire first. Yet we all saw the other horse run the fastest race and was in the lead at the finish. The owners of the horses are these gentlemen right here behind me: Colonel Linscomb, your neighbor, and Mr van Tosch from Memphis, near enough to be your neighbor too when you get to know him better. They have agreed, and your judges will approve it, to put this heat that was just run, into what the bankers call escrow. You all have done business with bankers whether you wanted to or not"—they said he even paused for the guffaw,

and got it—"and you know how they have a name for everything—"

"Interest on it too," a voice said and so he got that guffaw
free and joined it.

"What escrow means this time is, suspended. Not abolished
or cancelled: just suspended. The bets still stand just as you
made them; nobody won and nobody lost; you can increase
them or hedge them or whatever you want to; the stake
money for the last heat still stands and the owners are already
adding another fifty a side for the next heat, the winner of this
next heat to be the winner of the one that was just run: the
winner of the last heat to win both of them. Win this next
heat, and win all. What do you say?"

That's what I—we—Lycurgus and me—heard later. Right
now we knew nothing: just waiting for Ned or somebody to
come for us or send for us, Lightning cleaned and blanketed
now and Lycurgus leading him up and down, keeping him
moving, and I sitting against a tree with my riding-sock off to
dry out my bandage; it seemed hours, forever, then in the
next thinking it seemed no time, collapsed, condensed. Then
Ned came up, walking fast. I told you how he had looked terrible this morning, but that was partly because of his clothes.
His shirt was white (or almost) again now, and his pants were
clean too. But it would not have been his clothes this time,
even if they were still filthy. It was his face. He didn't look like
he had seen a simple and innocent hant: he looked like he had
without warning confronted Doom itself, except that Doom
had said to him: *Calm down. It will be thirty or forty minutes
yet before I will want you. Be ready then but in the meantime
stop worrying and tend to your business.* But he gave me—us—
no time. He went to the buggy and took his black coat out
and put it on, already talking:

"They put it in what they calls escrow. That means whoever
loses this next one has done lost everything. Tack up." But
Lycurgus already had the blanket off; it didn't take us long.
Then I was up, Ned standing at Lightning's head, holding
the bridle with one hand, his other hand in the pocket of the
coat, fumbling at something. "This one is gonter be easy for
you. We nudged him a little yestiddy, then you fooled him
bad today. So you aint gonter trick him again. But it wont

matter. We wont need to trick him now; I'll tend to this one myself. All you got to do is, still be on him at the finish. Dont fall off: that's all you got to do until right at the last. Just keep him between them two rails, and dont fall off of him. Remember what he taught you Monday. When you comes around the first lap, and just before he will think about where I was standing Monday, hit him. Keep him going; dont worry about that other horse, no matter where he is or what he's doing: just tend to yourn. You mind that?"

"Yes," I said.

"All right. Then here's the onliest other thing you got to do. When you comes around the last lap and around the back turn into the home stretch toward that wire, dont just believe, *know* that Lightning is where he can see the whole track in front of him. When you get there, you will know why. But before that, dont just think maybe he can, or that by now he sholy ought to, but *know* he can see that whole track right up to the wire and beyond it. If that other horse is in front of you, pull Lightning all the way across the track to the outside rail if you needs to where there wont be nothing in the way to keep him from seeing that wire and on beyond it too. Dont worry about losing distance; just have Lightning where he can see everything in front of him." His other hand was out now; Lightning was nuzzling his nose into it again and again I smelled that faint thin odor which I had smelled in Uncle Parsham's pasture Monday, that I or anybody else should recognise at once, and that I would recognise it if it would only happen when I had time. "Can you remember that?"

"Yes," I said.

"Then go on," he said. "Lead him on, Lycurgus."

"Aint you coming?" I said. Lycurgus pulled at the bridle; he had to get Lightning's muzzle out of Ned's hand by force; finally Ned had to put his hand back in his pocket.

"Go on," he said. "You knows what to do." Lycurgus led on; he had to for a while; Lightning even tried once to whirl back until Lycurgus snatched him.

"Hit him a little," Lycurgus said. "Get his mind back on what he's doing." So I did and we went on and so for the third time McWillie and I crouched our poised thunderbolts behind that wire. McWillie's starting groom having declined to be hurled to earth three times, and nobody else either volunteering or even accepting conscription, they used a piece of cotton-bagging jute stretched from rail to rail in the hands of two more democrats facing each other across the track. It was probably the best start we had had yet. Acheron, who had thought nothing of diving through a six-inch plank, naturally wouldn't go within six feet of it, and Lightning, though with his nose almost touching it, was standing as still as a cow now, I suppose scanning the crowd for Ned, when the starter hollered Go! and the string dropped and in the same second Acheron and McWillie shot past us, McWillie shouting almost in my ear:

"I'll learn you this time, white boy!" and already gone, though barely a length before Lightning pulled obediently up to McWillie's knee—the power, the rhythm, everything in fact except that still nobody had told his head yet this was a race. And, in fact, for the first time, at least since I had participated, been a factor, we even looked like a race, the two horses as though bolted together and staggered a little, on into the back stretch of the first lap, our relative positions, in relation to our forward motion, changing and altering with almost dreamlike indolence, Acheron drawing ahead until it would look like he really was about to leave us, then Lightning would seem to notice the gap and close it, it would even look like a challenge; I could hear them along the rail, who didn't really know Lightning yet: that he just didn't want to be that far back by himself; on around the back turn and into the home stretch of the first lap and I give you my word Lightning came into it already looking for Ned; I give you my word he whinnied; going at a dead run, he whinnied: the first time I ever heard a horse nicker while running. I didn't even know they could.

I cut him as hard as I could. He broke, faltered, sprang again; we had already made McWillie a present of two lengths so I cut him again; we went into the second lap two lengths back and travelling now on the peeled switch until the gap between him and Acheron replaced Ned in what Lightning called his mind, and he closed it again until his head was once more at McWillie's knee, completely obedient but not one

inch more—this magnificently equipped and organised organisation whose muscles had never been informed by their brain,
or whose brain had never been informed by its outposts of
observation and experience, that the sole aim and purpose of
this entire frantic effort was to get somewhere first. McWillie
was whipping now, so I didn't need to; he could no more
have drawn away from Lightning than he could have dropped
behind him, through the back stretch again and around the
back turn again, me still on Lightning and Lightning still between the rails, so all that remained from here out were Ned's
final instructions: to pull, ease him out, presenting McWillie
again with almost another length, until nothing impeded
his view of the track, the wire, and beyond it. He—Lightning—even saw Ned first. The first I knew was that neck-
snapping surge and lunge as though he—Lightning—had
burst through some kind of invisible band or yoke. Then I
saw Ned myself, maybe forty yards beyond the wire, small and
puny and lonely in the track's vacancy while Acheron and
McWillie's flailing arm fled rapidly back to us; then McWillie's
wrung face for an instant too, then gone too; the wire flashed
overhead. "Come on, son," Ned said. "I got it."

He—Lightning—almost unloaded me stopping, cutting
back across the track (Acheron was somewhere close behind
us, trying—I hoped—to stop too) and went to Ned at that
same dead run, bit bridle and all notwithstanding, and simply
stopped running, his nose already buried in Ned's hand, and
me up around his ears grabbing at whatever was in reach, sore
hand too. "We did it!" I said, cried. "We did it! We beat him!"

"We done this part of it," Ned said. "Just hope to your
stars it's gonter be enough." Because I had just ridden and
won my first race, you see. I mean, a man-size race, with people, grown people, more people than I could remember at
one time before, watching me win it and (some of them anyway) betting their money that I would. Also, I didn't have
time to notice, remark anything in his face or voice or what
he said, because they were already through the rail and on the
track, coming toward us: the whole moil and teem of sweated
hats and tieless shirts and faces still gaped with yelling. "Look
out now," Ned said; and still to me, nothing: only the faces
and the voices like a sea:

"That's riding him, boy! That's bringing him in!" but we not stopping, Ned leading Lightning on, saying,

"Let us through, Whitefolks; let us through, Whitefolks," until they gave back enough to let us go on, but still moving along with us, like the wave, until we reached the gate to the infield where the judges were waiting, and Ned said again: "Look out, now;" and now I dont remember: only the stopped horse with Ned at the bit like a tableau, and me looking past Lightning's ears at Grandfather leaning a little on his cane (the gold-headed one) and two other people whom I had known somewhere a long time ago just behind him.

"Boss," I said.

"What did you do to your hand?" he said.

"Yes sir," I said. "Boss."

"You're busy now," he said. "So am I." It was quite kind, quite cold. No: it wasn't anything. "We'll wait until we get home," he said. Then he was gone. Now the two people were Sam and Minnie looking up at me with her calm grim inconsolable face for it seemed to me a long time while Ned was still pawing at my leg.

"Where's that tobacco sack I give you to keep yestiddy?" he said. "You sholy aint lost it?"

"Oh yes," I said, reaching it from my pocket.

Thirteen

"SHOW THEM," Miss Reba told Minnie. They were in our—
I mean Boon's—no, I mean Grandfather's—automobile:
Everbe and Miss Reba and Minnie and Sam and Colonel
Linscomb's chauffeur; he was McWillie's father; Colonel
Linscomb had an automobile too. They—the chauffeur and
Sam and Minnie—had gone up to Hardwick to get Miss Reba
and Everbe and Boon and take them all on to Parsham, where
Miss Reba and Minnie and Sam could take the train for
Memphis. Except that Boon didn't come back with them. He
was in jail again, the third time now, and they had stopped at
Colonel Linscomb's to tell Grandfather. Miss Reba told it, sit-
ting in the car, with Grandfather and Colonel Linscomb and
me standing around it because she wouldn't come in; she told
about Boon and Butch.

"It was bad enough in the automobile going up there. But
at least we had that deputy, let alone that little old constable
you folks got that dont look like much but I'd say people
dont fool around with him much either. When we got to
Hardwick, they at least had sense enough to lock them in separate cells. The trouble was, they never had no way to lock up
Corrie's new friend's mouth—" and stopped; and I didn't
want to have to look at Everbe either: a big girl, too big for
little things to have to happen to like the black eye or the cut
mouth, whichever one she would have, unless maybe she
wouldn't—couldn't be content with less than both; sitting
there, having to, without anywhere to go or room to do it
even, with the slow painful blood staining up the cheek I
could see from here. "I'm sorry, kid; forget it," Miss Reba
said. "Where was I?"

"You were telling what Boon did this time," Grandfather
said.

"Oh yes," Miss Reba said. "—locked them up in separate
cells across the corridor and they were taking Corrie and me—
sure; they treated us fine: just like ladies—down to the jailor's
wife's room where we were going to stay, when What's-his-
name—Butch—pipes up and says, 'Well, there's one thing

about it: me and Sugar Boy lost some blood and skin and a couple of shirts too, but at least we got these' excuse my French," Miss Reba said. "—'Memphis whores off the street.' So Boon started in right away to tear that steel door down but they had remembered to already lock it, so you would think that would have calmed him: you know: having to sit there and look at it for a while. Anyhow, we thought so. Then when Sam came with the right papers or whatever they were—and much obliged to you," she told Grandfather. "I dont know how much you had to put up, but if you'll send the bill to me when I get home, I'll attend to it. Boon knows the address and knows me."

"Thank you," Grandfather said. "If there's any charge, I'll let you know. What happened to Boon? You haven't told me yet."

"Oh yes. They unlocked What's-his-name first; that was the mistake, because they hadn't even got the key back out of Boon's lock before he was out of the cell and on—"

"Butch," I said.

"Butch," Miss Reba said. "—one good lick anyhow, knocked him down and was right on top of him before anybody woke up. So they never even let Boon stop; all the out he got was that trip across the corridor and back, into the cell and locked up again before they even had time to take the key out of the lock. But at least you got to admire him for it." But she stopped.

"For what?" I said.

"What did you say?" she said.

"What he did that we're going to admire him for. You didn't tell us that. What did he do?"

"You think that still trying to tear that—"

"Butch," I said.

"—Butch's head off before they even let him out of jail, aint nothing?" Miss Reba said.

"He had to do that," I said.

"I'll be damned," Miss Reba said. "Let's get started; we got to catch that train. You wont forget to send that bill," she told Grandfather.

"Get out and come in," Colonel Linscomb said. "Supper's about ready. You can catch the midnight train."

"No much obliged," Miss Reba said. "No matter how long your wife stays at Monteagle, she'll come back home some day and you'll have to explain it."

"Nonsense," Colonel Linscomb said. "I'm boss in my house."

"I hope you'll keep on being," Miss Reba said. "Oh yes," she said to Minnie. "Show them." She—Minnie—didn't smile at us: she smiled at me. It was beautiful: the even matched and matchless unblemished porcelain march, curving outward to embrace, almost with a passion, the restored gold tooth which looked bigger than any three of the natural merely white ones possibly could. Then she closed her lips again, serene, composed, once more immune, once more invulnerable to that extent which our frail webs of bone and flesh and coincidence ever hold or claim on Invulnerability. "Well," Miss Reba said. McWillie's father cranked the engine and got back in; the automobile moved on. Grandfather and Colonel Linscomb turned and went back toward the house and I had begun to move too when the automobile horn tooted, not loud, once, and I turned back. It had stopped and Sam was standing beside it, beckoning to me.

"Come here," he said. "Miss Reba wants to see you a minute." He watched me while I came up. "Why didn't you and Ned tell me that horse was really going to run?" he said.

"I thought you knew," I said. "I thought that was why we came here."

"Sure, sure," he said. "Ned told me. You told me. Everybody told me. Only, why didn't somebody make me believe it? Oh sure, I never broke a leg. But if I'd just had Miss Reba's nerve, maybe I could have got that box car covered too. Here," he said. It was a tight roll of money, bills. "This is Ned's. Tell him the next time he finds a horse that wont run, not to wait to come and get me: just telegraph me." Miss Reba was leaning out, hard and handsome. Everbe was on the other side of her, not moving but still too big not to notice. She—Miss Reba—said:

"I didn't expect to wind up in jail here too. But then, maybe I didn't expect not to, neither. Anyway, Sam bet for me too. I put up fifty for Mr Binford and five for Minnie. Sam got three for two. I—I mean we—want to split fifty-fifty with

you. I aint got that much cash now, what with this unex-
pected side trip I took this morning—"

"I dont want it," I said.

"I thought you'd say that," she said. "So I had Sam put up
another five for you. You got seven-fifty coming. Here." She
held out her hand.

"I dont want it," I said.

"What did I tell you?" Sam said.

"Is it because it was gambling?" she said. "Did you promise
that too?" I hadn't. Maybe Mother hadn't thought about
gambling yet. But I wouldn't have needed to have promised
anybody anyway. Only, I didn't know how to tell her when I
didn't know myself why: only that I wasn't doing it for
money: that money would have been the last thing of all; that
once we were in it, I had to go on, finish it, Ned and me both
even if everybody else had quit; it was as though only by making Lightning run and run first, could we justify (not escape
consequences: simply justify) any of it. Not to hope to make
the beginning of it any less wrong—I mean, what Boon and
I had deliberately, of our own free will, to do back there in
Jefferson four days ago; but at least not to shirk, dodge—at
least to finish—what we ourselves had started. But I didn't
know how to say it. So I said,

"Nome. I dont want it."

"Go on," Sam said. "Take it so we can go. We got to catch
that train. Give it to Ned, or maybe to that old boy who took
care of you last night. They'll know what to do with it." So I
took the money; I had two rolls of it now, the big one and
this little one. And still Everbe hadn't moved, motionless, her
hands in her lap, big, too big for little things to happen to.
"At least pat her on the head," Sam said. "Ned never taught
you to kick dogs too, did he?"

"He wont though," Miss Reba said. "Watch him. Jesus,
you men. And here's another one that aint but eleven years
old. What the hell does one more matter? aint she been proving ever since Sunday she's quit? If you'd been sawing logs as
long as she has, what the hell does one more log matter when
you've already cancelled the lease and even took down the
sign?" So I went around the car to the other side. Still she
didn't move, too big for little things to happen to, too much

of her to have to be the recipient of things petty and picayune, like bird-splashes on a billboard or a bass drum; just sitting there, too big to shrink even, shamed (because Ned was right), her mouth puffed a little but mostly the black eye; with her, even a simple shiner was not content but must look bigger, more noticeable, more unhideable, than on anyone else.

"It's all right," I said.

"I thought I had to," she said. "I didn't know no other way."

"You see?" Miss Reba said. "How easy it is? That's all you need to tell us; we'll believe you. There aint the lousiest puniest bastard one of you, providing he's less than seventy years old, that cant make any woman believe there wasn't no other way."

"You did have to," I said. "We got Lightning back in time to run the race. It dont matter now any more. You better go on or you'll miss that train."

"Sure," Miss Reba said. "Besides, she's got supper to cook too. You aint heard that yet; that's the surprise. She aint going back to Memphis. She aint just reformed from the temptation business: she's reformed from temptation too, providing what they claim, is right: that there aint no temptation in a place like Parsham except a man's own natural hopes and appetites. She's got a job in Parsham washing and cooking and lifting his wife in and out of bed and washing her off, for that constable. So she's even reformed from having to divide half she makes and half she has with the first tin badge that passes, because all she'll have to do now is shove a coffee pot or a greasy skillet in the way. Come on," she told Sam. "Even you cant make that train wait from here."

Then they were gone. I turned and went back toward the house. It was big, with columns and porticoes and formal gardens and stables (with Lightning in one of them) and carriage houses and what used to be slave quarters—the (still is) old Parsham place, what remains of the plantation of the man, family, which gave its name to the town and the countryside and to some of the people too, like Uncle Parsham Hood. The sun was gone now, and soon the day would follow. And then, for the first time, I realised that it was all over, finished—all the four days of scuffling and scrabbling and dodging and lying and anxiety; all over except the paying-for. Grandfather and Colonel Linscomb and Mr van Tosch would be somewhere in the house now, drinking pre-supper toddies; it might be half an hour yet before the supper bell rang, so I turned aside and went through the rose garden and on to the back. And, sure enough, there was Ned sitting on the back steps.

"Here," I said, holding out the big roll of money. "Sam said this is yours." He took it. "Aint you going to count it?" I said.

"I reckon he counted it," Ned said. I took the little one from my pocket. Ned looked at it. "Did he give you that too?"

"Miss Reba did. She bet for me."

"It's gambling money," Ned said. "You're too young to have anything to do with gambling money. Aint nobody ever old enough to have gambling money, but you sho aint." And I couldn't tell him either. Then I realised that I had expected him, Ned anyway, to already know without having to be told. And in the very next breath he did know. "Because we never done it for money," he said.

"You aint going to keep yours either?"

"Yes," he said. "It's too late for me. But it aint too late for you. I'm gonter give you a chance, even if it aint nothing but taking a chance away from you."

"Sam said I could give it to Uncle Possum. But he wouldn't take gambling money either, would he?"

"Is that what you want to do with it?"

"Yes," I said.

"All right," he said. He took the little roll too and took out his snap purse and put both the rolls into it and now it was almost dark but I could certainly hear the supper bell here.

"How did you get the tooth back?" I said.

"It wasn't me," he said. "Lycurgus done it. That first morning, when I come back to the hotel to get you. It wasn't no trouble. The hounds had already treed him once, and Lycurgus said he thought at first he would just use them, put him up that gum sapling again and not call off the hounds until Whistle-britches wropped the tooth up in his cap or something, and dropped it. But Lycurgus said he was still a little rankled up over the up-start-y notions Whistle-britches had about horses, mainly about Lightning. So, since Lightning was gonter have to run a race that afternoon and would need his rest, Lycurgus said he decided to use one of the mules. He said how Whistle-britches drawed a little old bitty pocket knife on him, but Lycurgus is gonter take good care of it until he can give it to some of them." He stopped. He still looked bad. He still hadn't had any sleep. But maybe it is a relief to finally meet doom and have it set a definite moment to start worrying at.

"Well?" I said. "What?"

"I just told you. The mule done it."

"How?" I said.

"Lycurgus put Whistle-britches on the mule without no bridle or saddle and tied his feet underneath and told him any time he decided to wrop that tooth up in his cap and drop it off, he would stop the mule. And Lycurgus give the mule a light cut, and about half way round the first circle of the lot Whistle-britches dropped the cap, only there wasn't nothing in it that time. So Lycurgus handed the cap back up to him and give the mule another cut and Lycurgus said he had disremembered that this was the mule that jumped fences until it had already jumped that four-foot bob-wire and Lycurgus said it looked like it was fixing to take Whistle-britches right on back to Possum. But it never went far until it turned around and come back and jumped back into the lot again so next time Whistle-britches dropped the cap the tooth was in it. Only he might as well kept it, for all the good it done me. She went back to Memphis too, huh?"

"Yes," I said.

"That's what I figgered. Likely she knows as good as I do it's gonter be a long time before Memphis sees me or Boon Hogganbeck either again. And if Boon's back in jail again, I dont reckon Jefferson, Missippi's gonter see us tonight neither."

I didn't know either; and suddenly I knew that I didn't want to know; I not only didn't want to have to make any more choices, decisions, I didn't even want to know the ones being made for me until I had to face the results. Then

McWillie's father came to the door behind us, in a white coat; he was the houseman too. Though I hadn't heard any bell. I had already washed (changed my clothes too; Grandfather had brought a grip for me, and even my other shoes) so the houseman showed me the way to the dining room and I stood there; Grandfather and Mr van Tosch and Colonel Linscomb came in, the old fat Llewellyn setter walking at Colonel Linscomb's hand, and we all stood while Colonel Linscomb said grace. Then we sat down, the old setter beside Colonel Linscomb's chair, and ate, with not just McWillie's father but a uniformed maid too to change the plates. Because I had quit; I wasn't making choices and decisions anymore. I almost went to sleep in my plate, into the dessert, when Grandfather said:

"Well, gentlemen, shall the guard fire first?"

"We'll go to the office," Colonel Linscomb said. It was the best room I ever saw. I wished Grandfather had one like it. Colonel Linscomb was a lawyer too, so there were cases of law books, but there were farm- and horse-papers too and a glass case of jointed fishing rods and guns, and chairs and a sofa and a special rug for the old setter to lie on in front of the fireplace, and pictures of horses and jockeys on the walls, with the rose wreaths and the dates they won, and a bronze figure of Manassas (I didn't know until then that Colonel Linscomb was the one who had owned Manassas) on the mantel, and a special table for the big book which was his stud book, and another table with a box of cigars and a decanter and water pitcher and sugar bowl and glasses already on it, and a french window that opened onto the gallery above the rose garden so that you could smell the roses even in the house, and honeysuckle too and a mocking bird somewhere outside.

Then the houseman came back with Ned and set a chair at the corner of the hearth for him, and they—we—sat down— Colonel Linscomb in a white linen suit and Mr van Tosch in the sort of clothes they wore in Chicago (which was where he came from until he visited Memphis and liked it and bought a place to breed and raise and train race-horses too, and gave Bobo Beauchamp a job on it five or six years ago) and Grandfather in the Confederate-gray pigeon-tailed suit that he inherited (I mean, inherited not the suit but the Confederate gray because he hadn't been a soldier himself; he was only fourteen in Carolina, the only child, so he had to stay with his mother while his father was a color-sergeant of Wade Hampton's until a picket of Fitz-John Porter's shot him out of his saddle at one of the Chickahominy crossings the morning after Gaines's Mill and Grandfather stayed with his mother until she died in 1864, and still stayed until General Sherman finally eliminated him completely from Carolina in 1865 and he came to Mississippi hunting for the descendants of a distant kinsman named McCaslin—he and the kinsman even had the same baptismal names: Lucius Quintus Carothers—and found one in the person of a grand-daughter named Sarah Edmonds and in 1869 married her).

"Now," Grandfather told Ned, "begin at the beginning."

"Wait," Colonel Linscomb said. He leaned and poured whiskey into a glass and held it out toward Ned. "Here," he said.

"Thank you kindly," Ned said. But he didn't drink it. He set the glass on the mantel and sat down again. He had never looked at Grandfather and he didn't now: he just waited.

"Now," Grandfather said.

"Drink it," Colonel Linscomb said. "You may need it." So Ned took the drink and swallowed it at one gulp and sat holding the empty glass, still not looking at Grandfather.

"Now," Grandfather said. "Begin—"

"Wait," Mr van Tosch said. "How did you make that horse run?"

Ned sat perfectly still, the empty glass motionless in his hand while we watched him, waiting. Then he said, addressing Grandfather for the first time: "Will these white gentlemen excuse me to speak to you private?"

"What about?" Grandfather said.

"You will know," Ned said. "If you thinks they ought to know too, you can tell them."

Grandfather rose. "Will you excuse us?" he said. He started toward the door to the hall.

"Why not the gallery?" Colonel Linscomb said. "It's dark there; better for conspiracy or confession either." So we went that way. I mean, I was already up too. Grandfather paused again. He said to Ned:

"What about Lucius?"

"He used it too," Ned said. "Anybody got a right to know what his benefits is." We went out onto the gallery, into the darkness and the smell of the roses and the honeysuckle too, and besides the mocking bird which was in a tree not far away, we could hear two whipporwills and, as always at night in Mississippi and so Tennessee wasn't too different, a dog barking. "It was a sour dean," Ned said quietly.

"Dont lie to me," Grandfather said. "Horses dont eat sardines."

"This one do," Ned said. "You was there and saw it. Me and Lucius tried him out beforehand. But I didn't even need to try him first. As soon as I laid eyes on him last Sunday, I knowed he had the same kind of sense my mule had."

"Ah," Grandfather said. "So that's what you and Maury used to do to that mule."

"No sir," Ned said. "Mr Maury never knowed it neither. Nobody knowed it but me and that mule. This horse was just the same. When he run that last lap this evening, I had that sour dean waiting for him and he knowed it."

We went back inside. They were already looking at us. "Yes," Grandfather said. "But it's a family secret. I wont withhold it if it becomes necessary. But will you let me be the judge, under that stipulation? Of course, Van Tosch has the first claim on it."

"In that case, I'll either have to buy Ned or sell you Coppermine," Mr van Tosch said. "But shouldn't all this wait until your man Hogganbeck is here too?"

"You dont know my man Hogganbeck," Grandfather said. "He drove my automobile to Memphis. When I take him out of jail tomorrow, he will drive it back to Jefferson. Between those two points in time, his presence would have been missed no more than his absence is." Only this time he didn't have to even start to tell Ned to begin.

"Bobo got mixed up with a white man," Ned said. And this time it was Mr van Tosch who said Ah. And that was how we began to learn it: from Ned and Mr van Tosch both. Because Mr van Tosch was an alien, a foreigner, who hadn't lived in our country long enough yet to know the kind of white blackguard a young country-bred Negro who had never been away from home before, come to a big city to get more money and fun for the work he intended to do, would get involved with. It was probably gambling, or it began with gambling; that would be their simplest mutual meeting-ground. But by this time, it was more than just gambling; even Ned didn't seem to know exactly what it was—unless maybe Ned did know exactly what it was, but it was in a white man's world. Anyway, according to Ned, it was by now so bad—the money sum involved was a hundred and twenty-eight dollars—that the white man had convinced Bobo that, if the law found out about it, merely being fired from his job with Mr van Tosch would be the least of Bobo's troubles; in fact, he had Bobo believing that his real trouble wouldn't even start until after he no longer had a white man to front for him. Until at last, the situation, crisis, so desperate and the threat so great, Bobo went to Mr van Tosch and asked for a hundred and twenty-eight dollars, getting the answer which he had probably expected from the man who was not only a white man and a foreigner, but settled too, past the age when he could remember a young man's passions and predicaments, which was No. That was last fall—

"I remember that," Mr van Tosch said. "I ordered the man never to come on my place again. I thought he was gone." You see what I mean. He—Mr van Tosch—was a good man. But he was a foreigner.—Then Bobo, abandoned by that last hope, which he had never really believed in anyway, 'got up' as he put it (Ned didn't know how either or perhaps he did know or perhaps the way in which Bobo 'got it up' was such that he wouldn't even tell a member of his own race who was his kinsman too) fifteen dollars and gave it to the man, and bought with it just what you might expect and what Bobo himself probably expected. But what else could he do, where else turn? only more threat and pressure, having just proved that he could get money when driven hard enough— "But why didn't he come to me?" Mr van Tosch said.

"He did," Ned said. "You told him No." They sat quite still. "You're a white man," Ned said gently. "Bobo was a nigger boy."

"Then why didn't he come to me," Grandfather said. "Back where he should never have left in the first place, instead of stealing a horse?"

"What would you a done?" Ned said. "If he had come in already out of breath from Memphis and told you, Dont ask me no questions: just hand me a hundred and a few extra dollars and I'll go back to Memphis and start paying you back the first Saturday I gets around to it?"

"He could have told me why," Grandfather said. "I'm a McCaslin too."

"You're a white man too," Ned said.

"Go on," Grandfather said. —So Bobo discovered that the fifteen dollars which he had thought might save him, had actually ruined him. Now, according to Ned, Bobo's demon gave him no rest at all. Or perhaps the white man began to fear Bobo—that a mere dribble, a few dollars at a time, would take too long; or perhaps that Bobo, because of his own alarm and desperation, plus what the white man doubtless considered the natural ineptitude of Bobo's race, would commit some error or even crime which would blow everything up. Anyway, this was when he—the white man—began to work on Bobo to try for a one-stroke killing which would rid him of the debt, creditor, worry and all. His first idea was to have Bobo rifle Mr van Tosch's tack-room, load into the buggy or wagon or whatever it would be, as many saddles and bridles and driving harnesses as it would carry, and clear out; Bobo of course would be suspected at once, but the white man would be safely away by then; and if Bobo moved fast enough, which even he should have the sense to do, he had all the United States to flee into and find another job. But (Ned said) even the white man abandoned this one; he would not only have a buggy- or wagon-load of horseless horse-gear and daylight coming, it would have taken days to dispose of it piecemeal, even if he had had days to do it in.

So that was when they thought of a horse: to condense the wagon- or buggy-load of uncohered fragments of leather into one entity which could be sold in a lump, and—if the white man worked fast enough and didn't haggle over base dollars—without too much delay. That is, the white man, not Bobo, believed that Bobo was going to steal a horse for him.

Only, Bobo knew, if he didn't steal the horse, he could see the
end of everything—job, liberty, all—when next Monday
morning (the crisis reached its crux last Saturday, the same
day Boon and I—and Ned—left Jefferson in the automobile)
came. And the reason for the crisis at this particular moment,
what made it so desperate, was that there was a horse of Mr
van Tosch's so available for safe stealing, that it might almost
have been planted for that purpose. This of course was
Lightning (I mean, Coppermine) himself, who at the moment was in a sales stable less than half a mile away, where, as
Mr van Tosch's known groom (it was Bobo who delivered the
horse to the sales stable in the first place) Bobo could go and
get him at any time for no more trouble than putting a halter
on him and leading him away. Which by itself might have
been tolerable. The trouble was, the white man knew it—a
horse bred and trained for running, but which would not run,
and which in consequence was in such bad repute with Mr
van Tosch and Mr Clapp, the trainer, that it was at the sales
stable waiting for the first to come along who would make an
offer for it; in further consequence of which, Bobo could go
and remove it and it would very likely not even be reported
to Mr van Tosch unless he happened to inquire; in still further consequence of which, Bobo had until tomorrow morning (Monday) to do something about it, or else.

That was the situation when Ned left us in front of Miss
Reba's Sunday afternoon and walked around the corner to
Beale Street and entered the first blind tiger he came to and
found Bobo trying to outface his doom through the bottom
of a whiskey bottle. Grandfather said:

"So that's what it was. Now I'm beginning to understand.
A nigger Saturday night. Bobo already drunk, and your
tongue hanging out all the way from Jefferson to get to the
first saloon you could reach—" and stopped and said,
pounced almost: "Wait. That's wrong. It wasn't even Saturday. You got to Memphis Sunday evening," and Ned sitting
there, quite still, the empty glass in his hand. He said,

"With my people, Saturday night runs over into Sunday."

"And into Monday morning too," Colonel Linscomb said.
"You wake up Monday morning, sick, with a hangover, filthy
in a filthy jail, and lie there until some white man comes and

pays your fine and takes you straight back to the cotton field
or wherever it is and puts you back to work without even giving you time to eat breakfast. And you sweat it out there, and
maybe by sundown you feel you are not really going to die;
and the next day, and the day after that, and after that, until
it's Saturday again and you can put down the plow or the hoe
and go back as fast as you can to that stinking jail cell on
Monday morning. Why do you do it? I dont know."

"You cant know," Ned said. "You're the wrong color. If
you could just be a nigger one Saturday night, you wouldn't
never want to be a white man again as long as you live."

"All right," Grandfather said. "Go on."—So Bobo told
Ned of his predicament: the horse less than half a mile away,
practically asking to be stolen; and the white man who knew
it and who had given Bobo an ultimatum measurable now in
mere hours— "All right," Grandfather said. "Now get to my
automobile."

"We're already to it," Ned said. They—he and Bobo—went
to the stable to look at the horse. "And soon as I laid eyes on
him, I minded that mule I use to own." And Bobo, like me,
was too young actually to remember the mule; but, also like
me, he had grown up with its legend. "So we decided to go
to that white man and tell him something had happened and
Bobo couldn't get that horse outen that stable for him like
Bobo thought he could, but we could get him a automobile
in place of it.—Now, wait," he told Grandfather quickly. "We
knowed as good as you that that automobile would be safe at
least long enough for us to finish. Maybe in thirty or forty
years you can stand on a Jefferson street corner and count a
dozen automobiles before sundown, but you cant yet. Maybe
then you can steal a automobile and find somebody to buy it
that wont worry you with a lot of how-come and who and
why. But you cant now. So for a man that looked like I imagined he looked (I hadn't never seen him yet) to travel around
trying to sell a automobile quick and private, would be about
as hard as selling a elephant quick and private. You never had
no trouble locating where it was at and getting your hand on
it, once you and Mr van Tosch got started, did you?"

"Go on," Grandfather said. Ned did.

"Then the white man would say, What automobile? and

Bobo would let me tend to that; and then the white man would maybe say, What I'm doing in it nohow, and then Bobo would tell him I want that horse because I know how to make it run; that we already got a match race waiting Tuesday, and if the white man wanted, he could come along too and win enough on the horse to pay back three or four times them hundred and thirteen dollars, and then he wouldn't even have to worry with the automobile if he didn't want to. Because he would be the kind of a white man that done already had enough experience to know what would sell easy and what would be a embarrassment to get caught with. So that's what we were gonter do until yawl come and ruint it: let that white man just watch the first heat without betting yes or no, which he would likely do, and see Lightning lose it like he always done, which the white man would a heard all about too, by now; then we would say Nemmine, just wait to the next heat, and then bet him the horse against the automobile on that one without needing to remind him that when Lightning got beat this time, he would own him too." They —Grandfather and Colonel Linscomb and Mr van Tosch— looked at Ned. I wont try to describe their expressions. I cant. "Then yawl come and ruint it," Ned said.

"I see," Mr van Tosch said. "It was all just to save Bobo. Suppose you had failed to make Coppermine run, and lost him too. What about Bobo then?"

"I made him run," Ned said. "You seen it."

"But just suppose, for the sake of the argument," Mr van Tosch said.

"That would a been Bobo's look-out," Ned said. "It wasn't me advised him to give up Missippi cotton farming and take up Memphis frolicking and gambling for a living in place of it."

"But I thought Mr Priest said he's your cousin," Mr van Tosch said.

"Everybody got kinfolks that aint got no more sense than Bobo," Ned said.

"Well," Mr van Tosch said.

"Let's all have a toddy," Colonel Linscomb said briskly. He got up and mixed and passed them. "You too," he told Ned. Ned brought his glass and Colonel Linscomb poured. This time when Ned set the untasted glass on the mantel, nobody said anything.

"Yes," Mr van Tosch said. Then he said: "Well, Priest, you've got your automobile. And I've got my horse. And maybe I frightened that damn scoundrel enough to stay clear of my stable hands anyway." They sat there. "What shall I do about Bobo?" They sat there. "I'm asking you," Mr van Tosch said to Ned.

"Keep him," Ned said. "Folks—boys and young men any-how—in my people dont convince easy—"

"Why just Negroes?" Mr van Tosch said.

"Maybe he means McCaslins," Colonel Linscomb said.

"That's right," Ned said. "McCaslins and niggers both act like the mixtry of the other just makes it worse. Right now I'm talking about young folks, even if this one is a nigger McCaslin. Maybe they dont hear good. Anyhow, they got to learn for themselves that roguishness dont pay. Maybe Bobo learnt it this time. Aint that easier for you than having to break in a new one?"

"Yes," Mr van Tosch said. They sat there. "Yes," Mr van Tosch said again. "So I'll either have to buy Ned, or sell you Coppermine." They sat there. "Can you make him run again, Ned?"

"I made him run that time," Ned said.

"I said, again," Mr van Tosch said. They sat there. "Priest," Mr van Tosch said, "do you believe he can do it again?"

"Yes," Grandfather said.

"How much do you believe it?" They sat there.

"Are you addressing me as a banker or a what?" Grand-father said.

"Call it a perfectly normal and natural north-west Missis-sippi countryman taking his perfectly normal and natural God-given and bill-of-rights-defended sabbatical among the fleshpots of south-western Tennessee," Colonel Linscomb said.

"All right," Mr van Tosch said. "I'll bet you Coppermine against Ned's secret, one heat of one mile. If Ned can make Coppermine beat that black of Linscomb's again, I get the se-cret and Coppermine is yours. If Coppermine loses, I dont

want your secret and you take or leave Coppermine for five
hundred dollars—"

"That is, if he loses, I can have Coppermine for five hundred dollars, or if I pay you five hundred dollars, I dont have
to take him," Grandfather said.

"Right," Mr van Tosch said. "And to give you a chance to
hedge, I will bet you two dollars to one that Ned cant make
him run again." They sat there.

"So I've either got to win that horse or buy him in spite of
anything I can do," Grandfather said.

"Or maybe you didn't have a youth," Mr van Tosch said.
"But try to remember one. You're among friends here; try for
a little while not to be a banker. Try." They sat there.

"Two-fifty," Grandfather said.

"Five," Mr van Tosch said.

"Three-fifty," Grandfather said.

"Five," Mr van Tosch said.

"Four-and-a-quarter," Grandfather said.

"Five," Mr van Tosch said.

"Four-fifty," Grandfather said.

"Four-ninety-five," Mr van Tosch said.

"Done," Grandfather said.

"Done," Mr van Tosch said.

So for the fourth time McWillie on Acheron and I on
Lightning (I mean Coppermine) skittered and jockeyed behind that taut little frail jute string. McWillie wasn't speaking
to me at all now; he was frightened and outraged, baffled and
determined; he knew that something had happened yesterday
which should not have happened; which in a sense should not
have happened to anyone, certainly not to a nineteen-year-old
boy who was simply trying to win what he had thought was a
simple horse-race: no holds barred, of course, but at least a
mutual agreement that nobody would resort to necromancy.
We had not drawn for position this time. We—McWillie and
I—had been offered the privilege, but Ned said at once:
"Nemmine this time. McWillie needs to feel better after yesterday, so let him have the pole where he can start feeling
better now." Which, from rage or chivalry, I didn't know
which, McWillie refused, bringing us to what appeared in-

soluble impasse, until the official—the pending homicide one
—solved it quick by saying,

"Here, you boys, if you aim to run this race, get on up behind that-ere bagging twine where you belong." Nor had
Ned gone through his preliminary incantation or ritual of
rubbing Lightning's muzzle. I dont say, forgot to; Ned didn't
forget things. So obviously I hadn't been watching, noticing
closely enough; anyway, it was too late now. Nor had he given
me any last-minute instructions this time either; but then,
what was there for him to say? And last night Mr van Tosch
and Colonel Linscomb and Grandfather had agreed that,
since this was a private running, almost you might say a
grudge match, effort should be made and all concerned cau-
tioned to keep it private. Which would have been as easy to
do in Parsham as to keep tomorrow's weather private and restricted to Colonel Linscomb's pasture, since—a community
composed of one winter-resort hotel and two stores and a cat-
tle-chute and depot at a railroad intersection and the churches
and schools and scattered farm-houses of a remote countryside—any news, let alone word of any horse-race, not to mention a repeat between these two horses, spread across Parsham
as instantaneously as weather does. So they were here today
too, including the night-telegraphist judge who really should
sleep sometimes: not as many as yesterday, but a considerable
more than Grandfather and Mr van Tosch had given the impression of wanting—the stained hats, the tobacco, the tieless
shirts and overalls—when somebody hollered Go! and the
string snatched away and we were off.

We were off, McWillie as usual two strides out before
Lightning seemed to notice we had started, and pulled
quickly and obediently up until he could more or less lay his
cheek against McWillie's knee (in case he wanted to), near
turn, back stretch, mine and McWillie's juxtaposition altering,
closing and opening with that dreamlike and unhurried quality probably quite familiar to people who fly aeroplanes in
close formation; far turn and into the stretch for the first lap,
I by simple rote whipping Lightning onward about one stride
before he would remember to begin to look for Ned; I took
one quick raking glance at the faces along the rail looking for
Ned's and Lightning ran that whole stretch not watching

where he was going at all but scanning the rush of faces for
Ned's, likewise in vain; near turn again the back stretch again
and into the far turn, the home stretch; I was already swinging Lightning out toward the outside rail where (Acheron
might be beating us but at least he wouldn't obstruct our
view) he could see. But if he had seen Ned this time, he
didn't tell me. Nor could I tell him, Look! Look yonder!
There he is! because Ned wasn't there: only the vacant track
beyond the taut line of the wire as fragile-looking as a filtered
or maybe attenuated moonbeam, McWillie whipping furi-
ously now and Lightning responding like a charm, exactly
one neck back; if Acheron had known any way to run sixty
miles an hour, we would too—one neck back; if Acheron had
decided to stop ten feet before the wire, so would we—one
neck back. But he didn't. We went on, still paired but staggered a little, as though bolted together; the wire flicked
overhead, McWillie and I speaking again now—that is, he
was, yelling back at me in a kind of cannibal glee: "Yah-yah-
yah, yah-yah-yah," slowing also but not stopping, going
straight on (I suppose) to the stable; he and Acheron certainly
deserved to. I turned Lightning and walked back. Ned was
trotting toward us, Grandfather behind him though not trotting; our sycophants and adulators of yesterday had abandoned us; Caesar was not Caesar now.

"Come on," Ned said, taking the bit, rapid but calm: only
impatient, almost inattentive. "Hand—"

"What happened?" Grandfather said. "What the devil
happened?"

"Nothing," Ned said. "I never had no sour dean for him
this time, and he knowed it. Didn't I tell you this horse got
sense?" Then to me: "There's Bobo over yonder waiting.
Hand this plug back to him so he can take it on to Memphis.
We're going home tonight."

"But wait," I said. "Wait."

"Forget this horse," Ned said. "We dont want him. Boss
has got his automobile back and all he lost was four hundred
and ninety-six dollars and it's worth four hundred and ninety-
six dollars not to own this horse. Because what in the world
would we do with him, supposing they was to quit making
them stinking little fishes? Let Mr van Man have him back;

maybe some day Coppermine will tell him and Bobo what happened here yesterday."

We didn't go home tonight though. We were still at Colonel Linscomb's, in the office again, after supper again. Boon looked battered and patched up and a considerable subdued, but he was calm and peaceful enough. And clean too: he had shaved and had on a fresh shirt. I mean, a new shirt that he must have bought in Hardwick, sitting on the same straight hard chair Ned had sat on last night.

"Naw," he said. "I wasn't fighting him about that. I wasn't even mad about that no more. That was her business. Besides, you cant just cut right off: you got to—got—"

"Taper off?" Grandfather said.

"No sir," Boon said. "Not taper off. You quit, only you still got to clean up the trash, litter, no matter how good you finished. It wasn't that. What I aimed to break his neck for was for calling my wife a whore."

"You mean you're going to marry her?" Grandfather said. But it was not Grandfather: it was me that Boon pounced, almost jumped at.

"God damn it," he said, "if you can go bare-handed against a knife defending her, why the hell cant I marry her? Aint I as good as you are, even if I aint eleven years old?"

And that's about all. About six the next afternoon we came over the last hill, and there was the clock on the courthouse above the trees around the Square. Ned said, "Hee hee hee." He was in front with Boon. He said: "Seems like I been gone two years."

"When Delphine gets through with you tonight, maybe you'll wish you had," Grandfather said.

"Or maybe not come back a-tall," Ned said. "But a woman, got to keep sweeping and cooking and washing and dusting on her mind all day long, I reckon she needs a little excitement once in a while."

Then we were there. The automobile stopped. I didn't move. Grandfather got out, so I did too. "Mr Ballott's got the key," Boon said.

"No he hasn't," Grandfather said. He took the key from his pocket and gave it to Boon. "Come on," he said. We crossed the street toward home. And do you know what I

thought? I thought *It hasn't even changed*. Because it should
have. It should have been altered, even if only a little. I dont
mean it should have changed of itself, but that I, bringing
back to it what the last four days must have changed in me,
should have altered it. I mean, if those four days—the lying
and deceiving and tricking and decisions and undecisions, and
the things I had done and seen and heard and learned that
Mother and Father wouldn't have let me do and see and hear
and learn—the things I had had to learn that I wasn't even
ready for yet, had nowhere to store them nor even anywhere
to lay them down; if all that had changed nothing, was the
same as if it had never been—nothing smaller or larger or
older or wiser or more pitying—then something had been
wasted, thrown away, spent for nothing; either it was wrong
and false to begin with and should never have existed, or I
was wrong or false or weak or anyway not worthy of it.

"Come on," Grandfather said—not kind, not unkind, not
anything; I thought *If Aunt Callie would just come out
whether she's carrying Alexander or not and start hollering at
me*. But nothing: just a house I had known since before I
could have known another, at a little after six oclock on a May
evening, when people were already thinking about supper;
and Mother should have had a few gray hairs at least, kissing
me for a minute, then looking at me; then Father whom I had
always been a little . . . afraid is not the word but I cant think
of another—afraid of because if I hadn't been, I think I would
have been ashamed of us both. Then Grandfather said,
"Maury."

"Not this time, Boss," Father said. Then to me: "Let's get
it over with."

"Yes sir," I said, and followed him, on down the hall to the
bathroom and stopped at the door while he took the razor
strop from the hook and I stepped back so he could come out
and we went on; Mother was at the top of the cellar stairs; I
could see the tears, but no more; all she had to do would be
to say Stop or Please or Maury or maybe if she had just said
Lucius. But nothing, and I followed Father on down and
stopped again while he opened the cellar door and we went
in, where we kept the kindling in winter and the zinc-lined
box for ice in summer, and Mother and Aunt Callie had

shelves for preserves and jelly and jam, and even an old rocking chair for Mother and Aunt Callie while they were putting up the jars, and for Aunt Callie to sleep in sometimes after dinner, though she always said she hadn't been asleep. So here we were at last, where it had taken me four days of dodging and scrabbling and scurrying to get to; and it was wrong, and Father and I both knew it. I mean, if after all the lying and deceiving and disobeying and conniving I had done, all he could do about it was to whip me, then Father was not good enough for me. And if all that I had done was balanced by no more than that shaving strop, then both of us were debased. You see? it was impasse, until Grandfather knocked. The door was not locked, but Grandfather's father had taught him, and he had taught Father, and Father had taught me that no door required a lock: the closed door itself was sufficient until you were invited to enter it. But Grandfather didn't wait, not this time.

"No," Father said. "This is what you would have done to me twenty years ago."

"Maybe I have more sense now," Grandfather said. "Persuade Alison to go on back upstairs and stop snivelling." Then Father was gone, the door closed again. Grandfather sat in the rocking chair: not fat, but with just the right amount of paunch to fill the white waistcoat and make the heavy gold watch chain hang right.

"I lied," I said.

"Come here," he said.

"I cant," I said. "I lied, I tell you."

"I know it," he said.

"Then do something about it. Do anything, just so it's something."

"I cant," he said.

"There aint anything to do? Not anything?"

"I didn't say that," Grandfather said. "I said I couldn't. You can."

"What?" I said. "How can I forget it? Tell me how to."

"You cant," he said. "Nothing is ever forgotten. Nothing is ever lost. It's too valuable."

"Then what can I do?"

"Live with it," Grandfather said.

"Live with it? You mean, forever? For the rest of my life? Not ever to get rid of it? Never? I cant. Dont you see I cant?"

"Yes you can," he said. "You will. A gentleman always does. A gentleman can live through anything. He faces anything. A gentleman accepts the responsibility of his actions and bears the burden of their consequences, even when he did not himself instigate them but only acquiesced to them, didn't say No though he knew he should. Come here." Then I was crying hard, bawling, standing (no: kneeling; I was that tall now) between his knees, one of his hands at the small of my back, the other at the back of my head holding my face down against his stiff collar and shirt and I could smell him—the starch and shaving lotion and chewing tobacco and benzine where Grandmother or Delphine had cleaned a spot from his coat, and always a faint smell of whiskey which I always believed was from the first toddy which he took in bed in the morning before he got up. When I slept with him, the first thing in the morning would be Ned (he had no white coat; sometimes he didn't have on any coat or even a shirt, and even after Grandfather sent the horses to stay at the livery stable, Ned still managed to smell like them) with the tray bearing the decanter and water jug and sugar bowl and spoon and tumbler, and Grandfather would sit up in bed and make the toddy and drink it, then put a little sugar into the heel-tap and stir it and add a little water and give it to me until Grandmother came suddenly in one morning and put a stop to it. "There," he said at last. "That should have emptied the cistern. Now go wash your face. A gentleman cries too, but he always washes his face."

And this is all. It was Monday afternoon, after school (Father wouldn't let Mother write me an excuse, so I had to take the absent marks. But Miss Rhodes was going to let me make up the work) and Ned was sitting on the back steps again, Grandmother's steps this time, but in the shade this time too. I said:

"If we'd just thought to bet that money Sam gave us on Lightning that last time, we could have settled what to do about it good."

"I did settle it good," Ned said. "I got five for three this time. Old Possum Hood's got twenty dollars for his church now."

"But we lost," I said.

"You and Lightning lost," Ned said. "Me and that money was on Akrum."

"Oh," I said. Then I said, "How much was it?" He didn't move. I mean, he didn't do anything. I mean, he looked no different at all; it might have been last Friday instead of this one; all the four days of dodging and finagling and having to guess right and guess fast and not having but one guess to do it with, had left no mark on him, even though I had seen him once when he not only had had no sleep, he didn't even have any clothes to wear. (You see, how I keep on calling it four days? It was Saturday afternoon when Boon and I—we thought—left Jefferson, and it was Friday afternoon when Boon and Ned and I saw Jefferson again. But to me, it was the four days between that Saturday night at Miss Ballenbaugh's when Boon would have gone back home tomorrow if I had said so, and the moment when I looked down from Lightning Wednesday and saw Grandfather and passed to him, during which Ned had carried the load alone, held back the flood, shored up the crumbling levee with whatever tools he could reach—including me—until they broke in his hand. I mean, granted we had no business being behind that levee: a gentleman always sticks to his lie whether he told it or not.) And I was only eleven; I didn't know how I knew that too, but I did: that you never ask anyone how much he won or lost gambling. So I said: "I mean, would there be enough to pay back Boss his four hundred and ninety-six dollars?" And he still sat there, unchanged; so why should Mother have a gray hair since I saw her last? since I would have to be unchanged too? Because now I knew what Grandfather meant: that your outside is just what you live in, sleep in, and has little connection with who you are and even less with what you do. Then he said:

"You learned a considerable about folks on that trip; I'm just surprised you aint learnt more about money too. Do you want Boss to insult me, or do you want me to insult Boss, or do you want both?"

"How do you mean?" I said.

"When I offers to pay his gambling debt, aint I telling him to his face he aint got enough sense to bet on horses? And when I tells him where the money come from I'm gonter pay it with, aint I proving it?"

"I still dont see where the insult to you comes in," I said.

"He might take it," Ned said.

Then the day came at last. Everbe sent for me and I walked across town to the little back-street almost doll-size house that Boon was buying by paying Grandfather fifty cents every Saturday. She had a nurse and she should have been in bed. But she was sitting up, waiting for me, in a wrapper; she even walked across to the cradle and stood with her hand on my shoulder while we looked at it.

"Well?" she said. "What do you think?"

I didn't think anything. It was just another baby, already as ugly as Boon even if it would have to wait twenty years to be as big. I said so. "What are you going to call it?"

"Not it," she said. "Him. Cant you guess?"

"What?" I said.

"His name is Lucius Priest Hogganbeck," she said.

CHRONOLOGY

NOTE ON THE TEXTS

NOTES

Chronology

recognize different birds. The Falkner brothers become close to cousin Sallie Murry Wilkins (b. 1899), daughter of aunt Mary Holland Falkner Wilkins.

1903   Meets and occasionally plays with Lida Estelle Oldham (b. 1896), daughter of Republican attorney Lemuel Oldham, when her family moves to Oxford in fall.

1905   Enters first grade. Enjoys drawing and painting with watercolors.

1906   Skips to third grade. Grandmother Sallie Murry Falkner dies December 21.

1907   Grandmother Lelia Butler dies June 1. Third brother, Dean Swift Falkner, born August 15.

1909–13   Begins working in father's livery stable in June. Athletic activities are curtailed in late 1910 when he is put in a tight canvas brace to correct shoulder stoop. Draws, writes stories and poems, and starts to play hooky. Becomes increasingly attracted to Estelle Oldham and shows her his poems. Reads comic magazine *The Arkansas Traveller*, *Pilgrim's Progress*, *Moby-Dick* (telling his brother Murry, "It's one of the best books ever written"), Mark Twain, Joel Chandler Harris, Shakespeare, Fielding, Conrad, Balzac, and Hugo, among others. Shoots his dog accidentally while hunting rabbits in the fall of 1911 and does not hunt again for several years. Becomes active Boy Scout and begins to play high school football in fall 1913.

1914–15   Shows his poetry to law student Phil Stone, four years his senior. Stone becomes close friend, gives him books to read, including works by Swinburne, Keats, Conrad Aiken, Sherwood Anderson, and introduces him to writer and fellow townsman Stark Young. Helps plan yearbook and does sketches for it. Pitches and plays shortstop on baseball team. Returns to school briefly in fall 1915 to play football, then drops out. Hunts deer and bear at camp of "General" James Stone, Phil's father, near Batesville, in the Mississippi Delta thirty miles west of Oxford.

1916–17   Begins working early in 1916 as clerk at grandfather's bank, the First National, and hates it. Drinks his grandfather's liquor. By end of 1916 spends most of his time on campus of University of Mississippi, where he becomes friends with freshman Ben Wasson. Contributes drawings to university yearbook, *Ole Miss*. Continues to write verse influenced by Swinburne and A. E. Housman.

1918   Estelle Oldham tells Falkner she is "ready to elope" with him, despite her engagement to Cornell Franklin, a University of Mississippi graduate now successfully practicing law in Hawaii who is preferred by her family. Falkner insists on getting the Oldhams' consent, but both families oppose marriage, and Estelle's wedding to Franklin is set for April 18. Joins Phil Stone, then studying law at Yale, in New Haven early in April. Meets poets Stephen Vincent Benét and Robert Hillyer. Reads Yeats. Works as ledger clerk at Winchester Repeating Arms Co., where his name is recorded "Faulkner." Determined to join British forces, he and Stone practice English accents and mannerisms. Accepted by Royal Air Force in mid-June. Visits Oxford before reporting to Toronto Recruits' Depot on July 9, where he lists birthplace as Finchley, Middlesex, England, birthdate as May 25, 1898, and spells his name "Faulkner." Brother Murry, serving in the Marines, is wounded in the Argonne on November 1. Faulkner's service is limited to attending ground school. Discharged in December, returns to Oxford wearing newly-purchased officer's uniform and Royal Flying Corps wings and suffering, he claims, from effects of crashing a plane.

1919   Continues to work on poetry. Drinks with friends in gambling houses and brothels in Clarksdale and Charleston, Mississippi, Memphis, and New Orleans. Composes long cycle of poems influenced by classic pastoral tradition and modern poetry, especially T. S. Eliot. Sees Estelle frequently during her four-month visit home from Hawaii with her daughter, Victoria. "L'Après-Midi d'un Faune," 40-line poem, appears in *The New Republic* August 6. Other poems are not accepted. Registers in September as a special student at University of Mississippi, where father is now assistant secretary of university. Studies French, Spanish, and Shakespeare; publishes poems in campus paper, *The Mississippian*, and Oxford *Eagle*. First published story, "Landing in Luck," appears in *The Mississippian* in November. In December, agrees to be initiated into

Sigma Alpha Epsilon fraternity because of family tradition. Given nicknames "Count" and "Count No 'Count"
by fellow students, who consider him aloof and affected.

1920   Inscribes *The Lilacs*, 36-page hand-lettered giftbook of
poems, to Phil Stone on New Year's Day. Translates four
poems by Paul Verlaine that are published in *The Mississippian* in February and March. Awarded $10 poetry prize
by Professor Calvin S. Brown in June. Does odd jobs and
assists with Boy Scout troop. Helps build clay tennis
court beside Falkners' university-owned home; becomes a
good player. Joins The Marionettes, a new university
drama group; finishes one-act play (not produced) and
works on stage props and set design. Withdraws from
university in November during crackdown on fraternities.
Receives commission as honorary second lieutenant in
RAF; wears uniform with pips on various occasions.
Writes *Marionettes*, an experimental verse play; hand-let-
ters several copies of its 55 pages, adding illustrations influenced by Aubrey Beardsley. Wasson sells five at $5
apiece. The Marionettes decline to produce it.

1921   Favorably reviews *Turns and Movies*, volume of verse by
Conrad Aiken, in *The Mississippian*. Paints buildings on
campus. Presents Estelle Franklin with 88-page bound
typescript volume of poems entitled *Vision in Spring* during her visit home in the summer. Accepts invitation of
Stark Young to visit him in New York City in the fall.
Revisits New Haven, October–November, then rents
rooms in New York City and works as clerk in Lord &
Taylor bookstore managed by Stark Young's friend Elizabeth Prall. Returns home in December after Phil Stone
and Lemuel Oldham secure him position as postmaster at
university post office at salary of $1,500 a year.

1922   Writes while on duty at the post office, neglects customers, is reluctant to sort mail, does not always forward it,
and keeps patrons' magazines and periodicals in the office
until he and his friends have read them. Praises Edna St.
Vincent Millay and Eugene O'Neill in articles published in
The Mississippian. Grandfather John Wesley Thompson
Falkner dies March 13. Faulkner does last drawing for
yearbook *Ole Miss*. Plays golf. Writes poems, stories, and
criticism. *The Double Dealer*, a New Orleans magazine,

publishes his short poem "Portrait." Continues to read widely, including works by Conrad Aiken, Eugene O'Neill, and Elinor Wylie.

1923   Begins driving his own car. Becomes scoutmaster during summer. Submits collection *Orpheus, and Other Poems* to The Four Seas Company of Boston in June. They agree to publish it if Faulkner will pay manufacturing costs; Faulkner declines.

1924   Receives gift of James Joyce's *Ulysses* from Phil Stone. Reads Voltaire and stories by Thomas Beer, a popular magazine writer of the time. In May, Four Seas agrees to publish cycle of pastoral poems, *The Marble Faun*, and Faulkner sends $400 to cover publication costs. Phil Stone writes preface and takes active role in negotiations. Continues to write stories and verse, compiling gift volumes for friends. Removed as scoutmaster after local minister denounces his drinking. Faulkner resigns as postmaster October 31. ("I reckon I'll be at the beck and call of folks with money all my life, but thank God I won't ever again have to be at the beck and call of every son of a bitch who's got two cents to buy a stamp.") Visits Elizabeth Prall in New Orleans and meets her husband, Sherwood Anderson, whose work he admires. *The Marble Faun* published in December.

1925   Leaves for New Orleans in January, intending to earn his passage to Europe. Accepts Elizabeth Prall Anderson's invitation to stay in spare room while Sherwood Anderson is away on a lecture tour, then moves into quarters rented from artist William Spratling. Contributes essays, poems, stories, and sketches to the New Orleans *Times-Picayune* and *The Double Dealer*. Meets Anita Loos. Begins work on novel *Mayday*, which Sherwood Anderson, now a close friend, praises. Anderson recommends Faulkner's novel to publisher Boni & Liveright. Visits Stone's brother and his family at Pascagoula on Gulf Coast in June; falls in love with Helen Baird (b. 1904), a sculptor he had met in New Orleans. Sails as passenger on a freighter from New Orleans to Genoa with William Spratling July 7; throws mass of manuscript overboard en route. Travels through Italy and Switzerland to Paris, settling on Left Bank. Grows beard. Goes to Louvre and various galleries; sees paintings by Cezanne, Matisse, Picasso, and other modernists. Years later, says of James Joyce in Paris: "I would go to some effort to go to the café that he inhabited to look at him. But that was the only literary man that I remember seeing in Europe in those days." Works on articles, poems, and fiction, including two novels, *Mosquito* and *Elmer* (about a young American painter, never finished). Tours France on foot and by train; visits World War I battlefields which still show scars of fighting. Visits England briefly in October, but finds it too expensive and returns to France. Learns in Paris that novel *Mayday* has been accepted for publication by Boni & Liveright and retitled *Soldiers' Pay*; Faulkner likes new title. Sails to the United States in December. Visits his publishers in New York before returning to Oxford.

1926   Inscribes a hand-lettered, illustrated allegorical tale *Mayday* (the same title originally given novel) to Helen Baird in January. Moves in with Spratling at 632 St. Peter Street, New Orleans, in February, going back to Oxford for brief visits. *Soldiers' Pay* published by Boni & Liveright February 25 in printing of 2,500 copies (sells 2,084 by May). Mother, shocked by sexual material in the novel, says that the best thing he could do is leave the country; father refuses to read it. Reviews are generally favorable. Handletters a sequence of poems called *Helen: A Courtship* for Helen Baird in June. Vacations in Pascagoula, where he finishes typescript of novel *Mosquitoes* in early September. Returns to New Orleans in fall. Begins novels *Father Abraham*, about an avaricious Mississippi family named Snopes, and *Flags in the Dust*, depicting four generations of Sartoris family, based on Southern and family lore. Parodies Anderson's style in foreword to *Sherwood Anderson & Other Famous Creoles*, a collection of Spratling's sketches, which they publish themselves in an edition of 400 copies that sells out in a week at $1.50 a copy. Book offends Anderson and causes breach between him and Faulkner. Returns to Oxford at Christmas.

1927   Sees Estelle, who has returned to Oxford after beginning divorce proceedings against Cornell Franklin. Gives her daughter, Victoria, a 47-page tale, *The Wishing Tree*, typed and bound in varicolored paper, in February as a present for her eighth birthday. Helen Baird marries Guy C. Lyman in March. *Mosquitoes* published April 30. Puts *Father Abraham* aside to concentrate on *Flags in the Dust*. Works on it at Pascagoula during summer, and finishes revised typescript in late September. Horace Liveright rejects *Flags in the Dust* in late November and advises Faulkner not to offer it elsewhere.

1928   Begins "Twilight," story about the Compson family, early in the year. ("One day I seemed to shut a door, between me and all publishers' addresses and book lists. I said to myself, Now I can write.") Centered on Caddie Compson, it becomes *The Sound and the Fury*. ("I loved her so much I couldn't decide to give her life just for the duration of a short story. She deserved more than that. So my novel was created, almost in spite of myself.") Sends *Flags in the Dust*, extensively revised, and group of short stories to Ben Wasson, now New York literary agent. Wasson submits *Flags in the Dust* to eleven publishers, all of whom reject it. Faulkner continues to work on new novel. In September, Wasson shows *Flags in the Dust* to Harrison (Hal) Smith, editor at Harcourt, Brace and Company, who writes favorable report. Alfred Harcourt agrees to publish book on condition that it be cut. Faulkner uses $300 advance to go to New York. Dismayed at the cuts Wasson says are necessary, allows him to do most of the cutting. (" 'The trouble is,' he said, 'is that you had about 6 books in here. You were trying to write them all at once.' ") Tries unsuccessfully to sell short stories. Rents a small furnished flat in Greenwich Village and revises and types manuscript of *The Sound and the Fury*. Finishes in October, drinks heavily, and is found unconscious by friends Eric J. (Jim) Devine and Leon Scales, who take care of him in their apartment. Moves in with painter Owen Crump after recovering. Returns to Oxford in December.

1929   *Sartoris* (the cut and retitled *Flags in the Dust*) published by Harcourt, Brace and Company January 31 in first printing of 1,998. Starts writing *Sanctuary. The Sound and the Fury* accepted by new firm of Jonathan Cape and Harrison Smith in February; Faulkner receives $200 advance. Estelle's divorce becomes final on April 29. Faulkner receives $200 advance for new novel from Cape & Smith in early

May. Completes *Sanctuary* in late May; Smith writes him that it is too shocking to publish. Asks Smith for an additional $500 advance so that he can get married. Marries Estelle in Presbyterian Church in nearby College Hill, June 20. Borrows money from cousin Sallie Murry (Wilkins) Williams and her husband to go to Pascagoula, where he and Estelle have troubled honeymoon. Reads proofs of *The Sound and the Fury*, restoring italicized passages changed by Wasson. Returns to Oxford and takes job on night shift at the university power plant. Visits mother daily. *The Sound and the Fury* published October 7 in printing of 1,789. Reviews are enthusiastic, sales disappointing. Writes *As I Lay Dying* while at work, beginning October 25 and finishing December 11. ("I am going to write a book by which, at a pinch, I can stand or fall if I never touch ink again.")

1930   Finishes typescript of *As I Lay Dying* on January 12. Begins publishing stories in national magazines when *Forum* accepts "A Rose for Emily" for its April issue. Achieves mass-market success when *The Saturday Evening Post* accepts "Thrift" (appears September) and *Scribner's* accepts "Dry September" (published January 1931). April, purchases rundown antebellum house (lacks electricity and plumbing) and four acres of land in Oxford for $6,000 at 6% interest, with no money down. Names it Rowanoak (or Rowan Oak), and begins renovation, doing much of the work himself. Moves into it in June with Estelle and her children, Victoria (born 1919) and Malcolm (born 1923). Household staff includes Caroline Barr and Ned ("Uncle Ned") Barnett, former slave who had been servant of great-grandfather William Clark Falkner. Chatto & Windus publishes *Soldiers' Pay*, with introduction by Richard Hughes, June 20, first of Faulkner's works to appear in England. Sells "Red Leaves" and "Lizards in Jamshyd's Courtyard" to *The Saturday Evening Post* for $750 each (more than he had received for any novel). *As I Lay Dying*, where for the first time in print the Mississippi locale is identified as Yoknapatawpha County, published October 6 by Cape & Smith in printing of 2,522 copies. Harrison Smith now thinks *Sanctuary* may make money for ailing publishing firm, and sends galley proofs in November. Though the resetting costs Faulkner $270, he revises extensively. Finishes revision in December.

1931   Daughter Alabama, named for Faulkner's great-aunt Alabama, is born prematurely on January 11 and dies after nine days. *Sanctuary*, published February 9 by Cape & Smith, sells 3,519 copies by March 4—more than combined sales of *The Sound and the Fury* and *As I Lay Dying*; elicits high praise and increasing attention for Faulkner abroad. Gallimard acquires the rights to publish *As I Lay Dying* and *Sanctuary* in French. Many in Oxford are shocked by *Sanctuary*; Faulkner's father tells a coed carrying the book that it isn't fit for a nice girl to read, but his mother defends him. Chatto & Windus publishes *The Sound and the Fury* in April. "Spotted Horses" appears in *Scribner's* in June. Begins work on novel tentatively titled *Dark House* in August, developing theme used in rejected short story "Rose of Lebanon." *These 13*, a collection of stories, published by Cape & Smith September 21; sells better than any of his works except *Sanctuary*. Attends Southern Writers' Conference at University of Virginia in Charlottesville on his way to New York in October. Drinks heavily. Wooed by publishers Bennett Cerf and Donald Klopfer of Random House, Harold Guinzberg and George Oppenheimer of Viking, and Alfred A. Knopf. To keep him away from other publishers, Harrison Smith has Milton Abernethy take Faulkner on ship cruise to Jacksonville, Florida, and back to New York. Firm of Cape & Smith is dissolved by Jonathan Cape; Faulkner signs with new firm, Harrison Smith, Inc. Meets his French translator, Princeton professor Maurice Coindreau, banker and future secretary of defense Robert Lovett, Dorothy Parker, H. L. Mencken, Robert Benchley, John O'Hara, John Dos Passos, Frank Sullivan, and Corey Ford (will continue to see some of them on later trips). Spends hours talking and drinking with Dashiell Hammett and Lillian Hellman. Meets Nathanael West. Works on new novel (now called *Light in August*) and stories, one of them—"Turn About"—inspired by war stories told by Lovett (finished in Oxford, and published in *The Saturday Evening Post*, March 1932). Finishes self-deprecatory introduction to Random House's Modern Library edition of *Sanctuary* (published 1932). Makes contacts with film studios and writes film treatments. Earns enough money during stay in New York to pay bills at home. Drinks heavily; friends contact Estelle. She arrives early in December, and they return to Oxford before the middle of the month. Random House publishes story "Idyll in the Desert" in limited edition of 400 copies.

1932   Finishes manuscript of *Light in August* in February and revised typescript in March. Cape's new partnership, Cape & Ballou, goes into receivership in March, owing Faulkner $4,000 in royalties. Goes to work May 7 at Metro-Goldwyn-Mayer studio in Culver City, California, on six-week, $500-per-week contract. Leaves the studio almost immediately, not returning for a week. Takes a $30-a-month cottage on Jackson Street near studio and works unsuccessfully on series of treatments and scripts. At the end of contract makes plans to return home, but director-producer Howard Hawks hires him as scriptwriter for film *Today We Live*, based on "Turn About," beginning his longest Hollywood association. Father dies of heart attack August 7, and Faulkner returns home as head of family. "Dad left mother solvent for only about 1 year," he writes Ben Wasson. "Then it is me." Agreement with Hawks allows him to work in Oxford. Takes stepson Malcolm on walks through woods and bottoms, teaching him to distinguish dangerous from harmless snakes. Returns to Hollywood in October for three weeks, taking mother and brother Dean with him. *Light in August* published October 6 by new firm of Harrison Smith and Robert Haas. Paramount buys film rights to *Sanctuary* (released as *The Story of Temple Drake*, May 12, 1933). Faulkner receives $6,000 from sale. Continues working for MGM in Oxford. Spends part of Hollywood earnings on renovation of Rowan Oak.

1933   Begins flying lessons with Captain Vernon Omlie in February, and makes first solo flight April 20 after seventeen hours of dual instruction. *Today We Live* premieres in Oxford, April 12. *A Green Bough*, poems, published April 20 by Smith & Haas. Travels to New Orleans in May to work on film *Louisiana Lou* with director Tod Browning, but refuses to return to Hollywood for revisions; studio terminates contract May 13. Buys more land adjoining Rowan Oak. Works on stories and novel, *The Peasants*, which uses Snopes characters. Daughter Jill born June 24. Prepares a marked copy (apparently now lost) for a projected Random House limited edition of *The Sound and the Fury* (never published) that would print the Benjy section in three colors, and writes an introduction. ("I wrote this book and learned to read. . . . I discovered that there is actually something to which the shabby term Art not only can, but must, be applied.") Receives $500 for his work on it. Plans novel *Requiem for a Nun*. Buys Omlie's Waco C cabin biplane in fall. Concerned about brother Dean's future, arranges to have Omlie train Dean as a pilot. Flies with Omlie and Dean to New York to meet with publishers early in November, returning in time to go hunting. Earns pilot's license December 14.

1934   Begins new novel *A Dark House* in February, using material from stories "Evangeline" (written 1931) and "Wash" (written 1933). Flies with Omlie to New Orleans for dedication of Shushan Airport February 15. Participates in Mississippi air shows with Omlie, Dean, and others in spring, billed as "William Faulkner's (Famous Author) Air Circus" on one occasion; Faulkner avoids flying aerobatics. *Doctor Martino and Other Stories* published April 16 by Smith & Haas. Pressed for money, writes "Ambuscade," "Retreat," and "Raid," series of Civil War stories centering on Bayard Sartoris and black companion Ringo, hoping to sell them to *The Saturday Evening Post* (they appear in fall). Goes back to work with Hawks in Hollywood for $1,000 a week, from the end of June to late July. Finishes script *Sutter's Gold* in Oxford. Brother Murry is member of FBI team that kills John Dillinger in Chicago, July 22. Writes Smith in August that new novel, now titled *Absalom, Absalom!*, "is not quite ripe yet." Puts it aside and converts unpublished story "This Kind of Courage" into novel, *Pylon*. Sends first chapter to Harrison Smith in November and finishes it by end of December.

1935   Forms Okatoba Fishing and Hunting Club with R. L. Sullivan and Whitson Cook, receiving hunting and fishing rights to several thousand acres of General Stone's Delta land near Batesville, Mississippi. *Pylon* published by Smith & Haas, March 25. Pressed for money, works intensively at writing stories meant to sell. Returns to *Absalom, Absalom!* Resumes occasional flying, though the Waco now belongs to Dean. Goes to New York September 23 to negotiate a better contract with Smith & Haas and to sell stories to magazines. Returns home October 15, without gaining much from the trip. Brother Dean and his three

passengers are killed when the Waco crashes November
10. Faulkner assists undertaker in futile attempt to prepare
Dean's body for open-casket funeral. Distraught and
guilt-ridden, assumes responsibility for Dean's pregnant
wife, Louise, and stays for several weeks with her and his
grieving mother, who feels suicidal. On December 10,
goes to Hollywood for five-week, $1,000-per-week as-
signment with Hawks for Twentieth Century–Fox, taking
Absalom, Absalom! with him. Works on novel early in the
morning before going to the studio. Begins intermittent
and sometimes intense fifteen-year affair with Hawks's 28-
year-old secretary (later his script supervisor), Mississippi
divorcée Meta Doherty Carpenter.

1936   After successful completion of draft of script (*The Road to
Glory*), begins to drink heavily. Returns to Oxford on sick
leave January 13. Finishes manuscript of *Absalom, Absalom!*
January 31. Drinks heavily and is hospitalized in Wright's
Sanitarium, small private hospital in Byhalia, Mississippi,
fifty miles north of Oxford. Reluctant to delay revision of
novel by writing stories to make money, signs new contract with Twentieth Century–Fox, again for $1,000 a
week. Returns to Hollywood February 26, moving into
the Beverly Hills Hotel. Works on several scripts, sees old
friends. Dean, daughter of brother Dean Faulkner, born
March 22; Faulkner assumes role of surrogate father. Goes
boar hunting on Santa Cruz Island with Nathanael West
in April. Returns to Oxford early in June and writes to
agent when his stories don't sell: "Since last summer I
seem to have got out of the habit of writing trash . . ."
Draws map of Yoknapatawpha County for *Absalom, Absalom!* Goes back to Hollywood in mid-July for six-
month, $750-per-week contract, taking Estelle, Jill, and
two servants with him, and moves into a large house just
north of Santa Monica. Captain Omlie dies in crash as
passenger on commercial flight August 6. Sees Meta Carpenter, who has decided to marry pianist Wolfgang Rebner. Estelle and Faulkner both drink heavily. *Absalom,
Absalom!*, published October 26 by Random House
(which has absorbed the firm of Smith & Haas), receives
some critical praise, though sales are not enough to allow
freedom from scriptwriting, and Faulkner is unable to
sell film rights (had hoped to receive $50,000 for them).
Becomes increasingly unproductive at Twentieth Cen-

tury–Fox and is laid off in December after earning almost $20,000 for the year. Proposes to convert Bayard Sartoris–Ringo stories, now six in number, into novel and is encouraged by Bennett Cerf and Robert Haas. Harrison Smith leaves Random House. Makes final payment on Rowan Oak.

1937   Returns to studio from layoff February 26 at salary of $1,000 a week. Family moves closer to studio. Unhappiness at work and home exacerbates Faulkner's drinking. March to June, works on film script for *Drums Along the Mohawk*, directed by John Ford. Estelle and Jill return to Oxford in late May. Maurice Coindreau stays with Faulkner for week in June to discuss French translation of *The Sound and the Fury*. Writes "An Odor of Verbena," concluding episode in Bayard-Ringo series. Returns to Rowan Oak in late August, having earned over $21,000 for the year working for Twentieth Century–Fox. Begins story "The Wild Palms," then starts to expand it into a novel. Goes to New York in mid-October to prepare the Bayard-Ringo stories for publication with new Random House editor, Saxe Commins. Stays at Algonquin Hotel; sees old friends, including Harrison Smith, Joel Sayre, Eric J. Devine, and Meta Rebner. Renews friendship with Sherwood Anderson. Drinks heavily, collapses against steam pipe in hotel room, and suffers palm-sized third-degree burn on his back. Treated by doctor, then cared for by Eric J. Devine, who accompanies him back to Oxford. Resumes work on novel, *If I Forget Thee, Jerusalem* (to be published as *The Wild Palms* at publisher's insistence); says the theme of the book is: "Between grief and nothing I will take grief." Reads Keats and Housman aloud and does crossword puzzles with stepdaughter Victoria after breakup of her first marriage ("He kept me alive," she later says). Intense pain from burn makes sleeping difficult.

1938   *The Unvanquished*, Bayard-Ringo stories reworked with new material into novel, published February 15 by Random House. MGM buys screen rights for $25,000, of which Faulkner receives $19,000 after payment of commissions. Buys 320-acre farm seventeen miles northeast of Oxford and names it Greenfield Farm; insists on raising mules despite brother John's (who is tenant manager) preference for more profitable cattle (later acquires cattle for farm). Despite infection from skin graft performed at the end of February, continues work on *If I Forget Thee, Jerusalem*. Writes to Haas in July: "To me, it was written just as if I had sat on the one side of a wall and the paper was on the other and my hand with the pen thrust through the wall and writing not only on invisible paper but in pitch darkness too . . ." Goes to New York to read proofs of novel, now titled *The Wild Palms*, in late September. Returns to work on Snopes book *The Peasants* and plots out two more volumes, *Rus in Urbe* and *Ilium Falling*, to form trilogy. Takes Harold Ober as new literary agent.

1939   Elected to National Institute of Arts and Letters in January. *The Wild Palms*, published January 19, reviewed in *Time* cover story, sells more than 1,000 copies a week and tops sales of *Sanctuary* by late March. Raises $6,000 by cashing in life insurance policy and obtaining advance from Random House to save Phil Stone from financial disaster. Writes stories, hoping to earn money, and works on Snopes trilogy, retitling volumes *The Hamlet*, *The Town*, and *The Mansion*. Helps brother John at Greenfield Farm, sometimes serving tenants in commissary. Influential favorable essays on Faulkner published by George Marion O'Donnell and Conrad Aiken. Takes short holidays in New York City in October and December after testifying in Washington, D.C., in plagiarism suit brought against Twentieth Century–Fox by writer who claims (wrongly) to have written *The Road to Glory*. Donates manuscript of *Absalom, Absalom!* to relief fund for Spanish Loyalists. "Barn Burning" wins first O. Henry Memorial Award ($300 prize) for best short story published in an American magazine.

1940   Works on proofs of *The Hamlet*. Caroline Barr, in her mid-nineties, suffers stroke and dies January 31. Faulkner gives eulogy in parlor of Rowan Oak. ("She was born in bondage and with a dark skin and most of her early maturity was passed in a dark and tragic time for the land of her birth. She went through vicissitudes which she had not caused; she assumed cares and griefs which were not even her cares and griefs. She was paid wages for this, but pay is still just money. And she never received very much of that . . .") Writes stories about black families. *The Hamlet*, published by Random House April 1, is reviewed favorably, but sales fall below those of *The Wild Palms*. Faces mounting financial pressure from debts, family obligations, and back taxes, but is reluctant to raise funds by selling property. Appeals to Random House for higher advances against royalties, and proposes to make a novel out of series of stories about related black and white families. Tries to get a job in Hollywood. After unsatisfactory negotiations with Random House, goes to New York late in June to negotiate with Harold Guinzburg of The Viking Press, but Viking cannot substantially improve on the Random House offer. Resumes writing stories (five published in the year).

1941   Wires literary agent Harold Ober on January 16 asking for $100; uses part of it to pay electric bill. Organizes Lafayette County aircraft warning system in late June. Wishing to do more in anticipation of U.S. entry into World War II, thinks about securing military commission and hopes to teach air navigation. "The Bear" accepted by *The Saturday Evening Post* for $1,000 in November. Finishes work on series of stories forming novel *Go Down, Moses* in December.

1942   Goes to Washington, D.C., in unsuccessful attempt to secure military or naval commission. *Go Down, Moses, and Other Stories*, dedicated to Caroline Barr, published by Random House May 11. (Faulkner considers it a novel; "and Other Stories" added by publisher.) Deeply in debt and unable to sell stories, seeks Hollywood work through publishers, agents, and friends. Reports for five-month segment of low-paying ($300 a week), long-term Warner Bros. contract on July 27. Moves into Highland Hotel. Works on film about Charles de Gaulle until project is dropped. Resumes affair with Meta Carpenter (now divorced from Rebner). Sees other old friends, including Ruth Ford (University of Mississippi alumna who had once dated brother Dean), and Clark Gable and Howard Hawks, with whom he goes fishing and hunting. Becomes friends with writers A. I. ("Buzz") Bezzerides and Jo Pagano. Writes two scenes for *Air Force*, directed by Hawks. Gets month's leave to return to Oxford for Christmas while remaining on payroll.

1943   Returns to Warner Bros. January 16 on a 26-week, $350-per-week contract. Begins working with Hawks in March on *Battle Cry*, film depicting various Allied nations' roles in the war. Sends one of his RAF pips to nephew James Faulkner, who is training to become Marine Corps fighter pilot (pip is lost when nephew is forced to ditch his Corsair off Okinawa in 1945). Warner Bros. picks up 52-week option at $400 a week in late June; Faulkner drinks and collapses. Writes and revises lengthy and complex script for *Battle Cry*. When the film is canceled in August due to its high cost, takes leave of absence without pay to return to Oxford. Receives $1,000 advance from producer William Bacher to work at home on film treatment about the Unknown Soldier of World War I. Describes it in letter to Ober as "a fable, an indictment of war perhaps" and writes 51-page synopsis in fall.

1944   Reports back to Warner Bros. February 14, and moves in with Bezzerides family on Saltair Street, just north of Santa Monica. Begins work for Hawks on film version of Ernest Hemingway's *To Have and Have Not*. Estelle and Jill join him in June, and they move to an apartment in East Hollywood. Works with Hawks and screenwriter Leigh Brackett on film of Raymond Chandler's *The Big Sleep*. Depression, drinking, and periods of hospitalization follow departure of Jill and Estelle in September. Critic Malcolm Cowley writes the first of several essays on Faulkner, comparing him to Balzac and noting that all his works except *Sanctuary* are out of print. Works on script for *Mildred Pierce*, directed by Michael Curtiz. Requests leave without pay and returns home December 15, taking with him the script for *The Big Sleep*, which he finishes in Oxford.

1945   Works on the "fable" about the Unknown Soldier, hoping to make it into a novel. Returns to Hollywood and Warner Bros. in June, now at $500 a week. Cowley obtains publishers' approval in August to edit a collection of Faulkner's works for the Viking Portable Library series; Faulkner advises him on selections. Works on scripts for *Stallion Road* and briefly with Jean Renoir on *The Southerner*. Continues work on the "fable," rising at 4:00 A.M. and working until 8:00 A.M. before going to the studio. Hollywood agent William Herndon refuses to release him from agent-client agreement and Warner Bros. refuses to release him from exclusive contract. Writes: "I dont like this damn place any better than I ever did. That is one comfort: at least I cant be any sicker tomorrow for Mississippi than I was yesterday." Refusing to assign Warner Bros. film rights to his own writings (including the "fable"), leaves studio without permission September 18. Returns to Rowan Oak, bringing Lady Go-lightly, the mare Jill rode during her stay in California. Redraws map of Yoknapatawpha County and writes "1699–1945 The Compsons" to go with excerpt from *The Sound and the Fury* in Cowley's *Portable Faulkner*, says, "I should have done this when I wrote the book. Then the whole thing would have fallen into pattern like a jigsaw puzzle when the magician's wand touched it." Takes part in annual hunt in November. Short story, "An Error in Chemistry," wins second prize ($250) in *Ellery Queen's Mystery Magazine* contest in December.

1946   Feels trapped and depressed, drinks heavily. Cerf, Haas, and Ober persuade Jack Warner to give Faulkner leave of absence and release from rights assignment so he can finish his novel. Random House pays immediate advance of $1,000 and $500 a month after that. Faulkner worries that novel will take longer to complete than advances can cover. *The Portable Faulkner* published by Viking April 29. Tells class at University of Mississippi in May that the four greatest influences on his work were the Old Testament, Melville, Dostoevski, and Conrad. European reputation, especially in France, grows as works are translated. Jean-Paul Sartre writes of Faulkner's significance in "American Novelists in French Eyes," in September *Atlantic Monthly*. Sells film rights for stories "Death Drag" and "Honor" to RKO for combined net of $6,600, and "Two Soldiers" to Cagney Productions for $3,750. Random House issues *The Sound and the Fury* (with "1699–1945 The Compsons" re-titled "Appendix/Compson: 1699–1945" added as first part) and *As I Lay Dying* together in Modern Library edition in October. Nearly hits trees while landing airplane and does not fly as pilot again. Continues work on "fable." Works secretly, because of exclusive Warner Bros. contract, on film script (unidentified) at home.

1947   Meets in April with six literature classes at University of Mississippi on condition no notes be taken. Ranks Hemingway among top contemporaries, along with Thomas Wolfe, John Dos Passos, and John Steinbeck, but is quoted in wire-service account as saying that Hemingway "has no courage, has never gone out on a limb. He has never used a word where the reader might check his usage in a dictionary." Hemingway is deeply offended, and Faulkner writes apology. Long-time family servant Ned Barnett dies. In November *Partisan Review* refuses excerpt about a horse race from the "fable."

1948   Begins mystery novel in January, based on idea mentioned to Haas in 1940; calls it *Intruder in the Dust*, and finishes it in April. MGM buys film rights for $50,000 before publication. Published by Random House September 27, it is his most commercially successful book, selling over 15,000 copies. Feels free of financial pressure for the first time. Turns down Hamilton Basso's proposal of *New Yorker* profile: "I am working tooth and nail at my lifetime ambition to be the last private individual on earth . . ." Works on short-story collection proposed earlier in the year by Random House. Eager to visit friends, goes to New York for holiday in October and meets Malcolm Cowley for the first time. Collapses after few days and recuperates at Cowley's home in Sherman, Connecticut. Decides to arrange stories in collection by cycles, an idea suggested by Cowley three years earlier. Elected to the American Academy of Arts and Letters November 23.

1949   Director Clarence Brown brings MGM company to Oxford to film *Intruder in the Dust*. Faulkner revises screenplay and helps scout locations, but is not given credit because of legal complications with Warner Bros. Rewrites unpublished 1942 mystery story "Knight's Gambit," expanding it into novella. Buys sloop, which he names *The Ring Dove*, and sails it on Sardis Reservoir, 25 miles northwest of Oxford, during spring and summer. Eudora Welty visits and Faulkner takes her sailing. In August is sought out by 20-year-old Joan Williams, Bard College student and aspiring writer from Memphis, who admires his work. Reluctantly attends world premiere of *Intruder in the Dust* on October 9 at refurbished Lyric Theatre, owned by cousin Sallie Murry Williams and her husband. Event is considered to have caused the most excitement since Union General A. J. Smith burned Oxford in Civil

War. "A Courtship" wins O. Henry Award for 1949. Random House publishes *Knight's Gambit*, volume of mystery stories, November 27.

1950   Writes to Joan Williams in January, offering help as a mentor. Goes to New York for ten days in February, staying at Algonquin; sees publishers, old friends (actress Ruth Ford, Joel Sayre, and others), and Joan Williams. Begins sending her notes for a play he hopes they will write together. Writes letter to Memphis *Commercial Appeal* in March protesting failure of Mississippi jury to give death penalty to a white man convicted of murdering three black children. Receives American Academy's William Dean Howells Medal for Fiction in May; does not attend ceremony. Personal involvement with Joan Williams deepens when she returns to Memphis for summer. Gives her manuscript of *The Sound and the Fury*. She is reluctant to rewrite his material for play *Requiem for a Nun*, and their collaboration becomes increasingly difficult. *Collected Stories of William Faulkner* published August 2 by Random House and adopted by Book-of-the-Month Club as alternate fiction selection, receiving generally good reviews. Informed November 10 he will receive 1949 (delayed until 1950) Nobel Prize for Literature. Reluctant to attend, drinks heavily at annual hunt, contracts bad cold, but finally agrees to go to Stockholm with Jill to receive award on December 10. Meets Else Jonsson, widow of Thorsten Jonsson, one of Faulkner's earliest Swedish translators. Gives widely quoted address ("I believe that man will not merely endure: he will prevail"). Afterwards, writes to friend, "I fear that some of my fellow Mississippians will never forgive that 30,000$ that durn foreign country gave me for just sitting on my ass writing stuff that makes my own state ashamed to own me." *The New York Times* reports that 100,000 copies of his books have been sold in Modern Library editions, and that 2.5 million paperback copies are in print.

1951   Takes $5,000 of Nobel Prize money for his own use, establishes "Faulkner Memorial" trust fund with remainder for scholarships and other educational purposes. Goes to Hollywood in February for five weeks scriptwriting on *The Left Hand of God* for Hawks. Earns $14,000, including bonus, for finishing script ahead of schedule (Hawks does not direct film, and Faulkner does not receive writing credit when it is released in 1955). Sees Meta Carpenter for last time. The Levee Press of Greenville, Mississippi, publishes horse-race piece as *Notes on a Horsethief* February 10. *Collected Stories* receives National Book Award for Fiction March 6. Releases statement to Memphis *Commercial Appeal* doubting guilt and opposing execution of Willie McGee, a black man convicted of raping a white woman (McGee is later executed). Takes three-week trip in April to New York, England, and France, visiting Verdun battlefield, which figures in his "fable." Finishes manuscript of *Requiem for a Nun* in early June. (Writes in letter to Else Jonsson: "I am really tired of writing, the agony and sweat of it. I'll probably never quit though, until I die. But now I feel like nothing would be as peaceful as to break the pencil, throw it away, admit I dont know why, the answers either.") Hears from Ruth Ford that Lemuel Ayers would like to produce *Requiem for a Nun* on stage, and goes to New York for week in July to work on it. Drives Jill to school at Pine Manor Junior College in Wellesley, Massachusetts, with Estelle. *Requiem for a Nun*, with long prose introductions to its three acts, published by Random House October 2. Works on stage version in Cambridge, Massachusetts, in October and November. Becomes officer in the Legion of Honor of the Republic of France at ceremony at French Consulate in New Orleans October 26.

1952   Works on "fable" and trains horse; has two falls in February and March, injuring his back. Attends ceremony commemorating ninetieth anniversary of battle of Shiloh with novelist Shelby Foote, and walks over battlefield with him. Turns down honorary degree of Doctor of Letters from Tulane University (later declines all other attempts to award him honorary degree). Attacks "welfare and other bureaus of economic or industrial regimentation" in address delivered May 15 to Delta Council in Cleveland, Mississippi. Takes one-month trip to Europe, though plans to produce his play during Paris cultural festival had fallen through. Collapses in severe pain in Paris; doctors discover two old spinal compression fractures, possibly riding injuries, and advise surgical fusion. Faulkner refuses and visits Harold Raymond of Chatto & Windus in England, still suffering severe pain. Treated near Oslo, Norway, by masseur on advice of Else Jonsson. Returns home feeling better than he has in years, but is not allowed to ride. Helps Joan Williams with her writing, but relationship is increasingly troubled. Injures back in boating accident in August. Hospitalized in Memphis in September for convulsive seizure brought on by drinking and back pain, and again in October, after fall down stairs. X-rays reveal three additional old spinal compression fractures. Wears back brace. Helps Ford Foundation prepare *Omnibus* production of "The Faulkner Story" for television in November. Accepts editor and friend Saxe Commins' invitation to write at his Princeton home. Depression and drinking precipitate collapse and is admitted to private hospital in New York. After discharge stays in New York, working on "fable"; sees Joan Williams. Returns home for Christmas.

1953   Stays in Oxford until Estelle recovers from cataract operation. Returns to New York January 31 for indefinite stay, hoping to finish the "fable." Medical problems continue; has extensive physiological and neurological examinations to determine cause of memory lapses, but nothing new is discovered. Writes semi-autobiographical essay "Mississippi" for *Holiday* (appears April 1954). Returns to Oxford with Jill in late April when Estelle is hospitalized for severe hemorrhage. Goes back to New York May 9, when danger is over. Estelle accompanies him when he gives commencement address at Jill's graduation from Pine Manor. Jill attends University of Mexico in fall, and Estelle goes with her when she leaves in late August. Faulkner stays at Rowan Oak, working on "fable." Hospitalized in September in Memphis and in Wright's Sanitarium in Byhalia. Angered when *Life* magazine publishes two-part article on him, September 28–October 5. Drives to New York with Joan Williams in October; they see Dylan Thomas (whose earlier poetry reading Faulkner had found moving) shortly before Thomas's death in November, and attend subsequent memorial service. Finishes *A Fable* at Commins' house in early November. Leaves for Paris to work with Hawks and screenwriter Harry Kurnitz on film, *Land of the Pharaohs*. Meets 19-year-old admirer, Jean Stein, in St. Moritz on Christmas Eve. Spends Christmas holidays in Stockholm and sees Else Jonsson.

1954   Stays with Harold Raymond in Biddenden, Kent, En-
            gland, in early January, and then goes to Switzerland,
            Paris, and Rome, visiting friends, seeing Jean Stein, and
            working on film. Arrives in Cairo in mid-February suf-
            fering from alcoholic collapse and is taken to Anglo-
            American Hospital. Continues working on film, but
            Hawks and Kurnitz do not use most of what he writes.
            Joan Williams marries Ezra Bowen on March 6. Leaves
            Egypt March 29. Stays three weeks in Paris, spending one
            night in hospital. Returns home in late April, after short
            stay in New York. Writes preface for *A Fable*, but decides
            not to use it. Works on farm most of May; sells livestock
            and then rents it out for a year. *A Fable* published by Ran-
            dom House, August 2. At request of U.S. State Depart-
            ment, attends International Writers' Conference in São
            Paulo, Brazil, stopping off on the way at Lima, Peru. En-
            joys trip and offers his services again on return home. Jill
            marries Paul D. Summers, Jr., August 21, and moves to
            Charlottesville, Virginia, where Paul attends law school.
            Faulkner checks into Algonquin Hotel, New York, Sep-
            tember 10; divides time between New York and Oxford
            for next six months. Makes spoken record for Caedmon
            Records, works on stories and magazine pieces, and feels
            reassured of ability to earn money. Sees Jean Stein often.

1955   Writes article on hockey game at Madison Square Garden,
            "An Innocent at Rinkside," for *Sports Illustrated* (appears
            January 24). Accepts National Book Award for Fiction for
            A Fable, January 25. Works on script for *The Era of Fear*,
            ABC television program about McCarthyism, but in
            March angrily rejects contract which includes morals
            clause and requires membership in unions ABC deals
            with. Becomes increasingly involved in civil rights issues;
            writes letters to editors advocating school integration;
            receives abusive letters and phone calls, and his position
            angers his brothers. Gives lecture "On Privacy. The
            American Dream: What Happened to It" at the Univer-
            sity of Oregon and University of Montana in April (pub-
            lished in *Harper's*, May). *A Fable* wins Pulitzer Prize in
            May. Writes article on eighty-first running of Kentucky
            Derby for *Sports Illustrated*. Helps publicize *Land of the
            Pharaohs*. Leaves on State Department trip July 29. Spends
            three weeks in Japan, visiting Tokyo, Nagano, and Kyoto,
            and delighting Japanese hosts (remarks from colloquia

published as *Faulkner at Nagano*, 1956). Returns to New York by way of Philippines (to visit stepdaughter and family), Italy, France, England, and Iceland, combining State Department appearances and vacation. *Big Woods*, collection of hunting stories with new linking material, illustrated by Edward Shenton, published by Random House, October 14. Rushes to Oxford October 23 when mother, almost eighty-five, suffers cerebral hemorrhage; remains while she recuperates. Speaks against discrimination to integrated audience at Memphis meeting of Southern Historical Association, November 10; receives more threatening letters and phone calls. When Jean Stein visits the South, shows her New Orleans and Gulf Coast; they encounter Helen Baird Lyman on a Pascagoula beach. Begins *The Town*, second Snopes volume, in November.

1956   Columbia Pictures takes option on *The Sound and the Fury* for $3,500 (film is released by Twentieth Century–Fox in 1959), and Universal buys *Pylon* for $50,000 (released in 1958 as *The Tarnished Angels*, directed by Douglas Sirk). Goes to New York February 8 to discuss finances with Ober. Worried about imminent violence, writes two articles urging voluntary integration in South to prevent Northern intervention: "On Fear: The South in Labor" (*Harper's*, June), and "A Letter to the North" (*Life*, March). Increasingly alarmed by rising tensions over court-ordered integration of University of Alabama, agrees to interview with *The Reporter* magazine; desperate and drinking, says if South were pushed too hard there would be civil war. Interviewer quotes him as saying that "if it came to fighting I'd fight for Mississippi against the United States even if it meant . . . shooting Negroes." (Later repudiates the interview: "They are statements which no sober man would make, nor it seems to me, any sane man believe.") Does extensive interview with Jean Stein for *The Paris Review*. On return to Oxford, injures back again when he is thrown by horse. Begins vomiting blood March 18; hospitalized in Memphis. By early April feels well enough to go with Estelle to Charlottesville, Virginia, where first grandson, Paul D. Summers III, is born April 15. Works on *The Town* in Oxford during summer. With P. D. East, starts semi-annual satirical paper for Southern moderates, entitled *The South-*

ern Reposure. First and only issue appears in mid-summer. Writes essay for *Ebony*, appealing for moderation. Albert Camus' adaptation of *Requiem for a Nun* successfully staged in Paris. Goes to Washington, D.C., for four days in September as chairman of writers' group in Eisenhower Administration's People-to-People Program. Chooses Harvey Breit of *The New York Times* as co-chairman; attends meeting at Breit's home November 29.

1957   Continues chairman's work into early February. Refuses Estelle's offer of a divorce. Depressed by changing relationship with Jean Stein, suffers collapse. Goes to Charlottesville as University of Virginia's first writer-in-residence February 9; moves into house on Rugby Road. Meets professors Frederick L. Gwynn and Joseph Blotner, who assist him in setting schedules. Arrives in Athens March 17 for two-week visit at invitation of State Department; sees Greek adaptation of *Requiem for a Nun.* Cruises four days on private yacht in the Aegean. Accepts Silver Medal from Greek Academy. *The Town*, published May 1 by Random House, receives mixed reviews. Presents National Institute of Arts and Letters' Gold Medal for Fiction to John Dos Passos May 22. Concludes successful university semester of classroom and public appearances. Rides with friends and in the Farmington Hunt, and tours Civil War battlefields near Richmond. Returns to Rowan Oak for summer, tends to farm and boat, visits mother. Ignores telegrams from producer Jerry Wald reporting on production of film *The Long Hot Summer*, based on *The Hamlet* (released 1958). Goes to Charlottesville in November, intending to ride and fox-hunt, but falls ill with strep throat. Hunts quail near Oxford in December.

1958   Begins to type first draft of *The Mansion*, third and last of the Snopes trilogy, at Rowan Oak in early January. Returns to Charlottesville for second term as writer-in-residence, January 30, meeting classes and public groups. (Remarks are published in *Faulkner in the University: Class Conferences at the University of Virginia, 1957–58* in 1959.) At one session presents "A Word to Virginians," an appeal to state to take the lead in teaching blacks "the responsibilities of equality." Goes to Princeton for two weeks, March 1, meeting with students individually and in groups. Returns to Oxford in May. Declines, for political reasons, invitation to visit Soviet Union with group of writers. Saxe Commins dies July 17. Gives away niece Dean Faulkner, daughter of brother Dean, at her wedding November 9. Goes to Princeton for another week of student sessions, and then to New York to work on *The Mansion* with Random House editor Albert Erskine. Returns to Charlottesville and rides in the Keswick and Farmington hunts; is described by a fellow rider as "all nerve." Second grandchild, William Cuthbert Faulkner Summers, born December 2.

1959   Works on *The Mansion* and hunts quail in Oxford. *Requiem for a Nun*, version adapted for the stage by Ruth Ford, opens on Broadway January 30 after successful London run; closes after forty-three performances. Though not reappointed as writer-in-residence for the year, takes position as consultant on contemporary literature to Alderman Library at University of Virginia, and is assigned library study and typewriter. Accepted as outside member in Farmington Hunt and continues riding with Keswick Hunt. Fractures collarbone when horse falls at Farmington hunter trials March 14. Rides again in May at Rowan Oak despite slow and painful recovery; another horse fall causes additional injuries, necessitating use of crutches for two weeks. Works with Albert Erskine in New York on *The Mansion*, eliminating some of the discrepancies between it and *The Hamlet*. Writes preface to *The Mansion* explaining others. Completes purchase of Charlottesville home on Rugby Road, August 21. Attends four-day UNESCO conference in Denver late September. Harold Ober, long-time agent and friend, dies October 31. *The Mansion* published by Random House, November 13. Continues riding and hunting, suffering occasional falls.

1960   Divides time between Oxford and Charlottesville. Hospitalized briefly at Byhalia for collapse brought on by bourbon administered for self-diagnosed pleurisy. Accepts appointment as Balch Lecturer in American Literature at University of Virginia with minimal duties (salary $250 a year) in August. Mother suffers cerebral hemorrhage, dies October 16. Sees Charlottesville friends often, including Joseph and Yvonne Blotner. Becomes full member of Farmington Hunt. Establishes William Faulkner Foundation December 28, providing scholarships for black Mississippians and prize for first novels; bequeaths to it the manuscripts he has deposited in the Alderman Library.

1961   Hunts quail in Oxford in January. Reluctantly leaves on two-week State Department trip to Venezuela April 1. Receives the Order of Andrés Bello, Venezuela's highest civilian award; gives speech expressing gratitude in Spanish. Third grandson, A. Burks Summers, born May 30. Shocked by news of Hemingway's suicide, July 2. Returns to Rowan Oak. Begins writing *The Horse Stealers: A Reminiscence*, conceived years earlier as novel about "a sort of Huck Finn"; enjoys work and finishes first draft August 21. Returns to Charlottesville in mid-October. Novel, retitled *The Reivers*, taken by Book-of-the-Month Club eight months before publication. Checks into Algonquin Hotel to work on book with editor Albert Erskine, November 27. Hospitalized in Charlottesville, December 18, suffering from acute respiratory infection, back trouble, and drinking. Leaves after several days, but soon has relapse and is treated at Tucker Neurological and Psychiatric Hospital in Richmond until December 29.

1962   Injured in fall from horse, January 3. Readmitted to Tucker suffering from chest pain, fever, and drinking, January 8. Goes to Rowan Oak to recuperate in mid-January and hunts with nephew James Faulkner. Returns to Charlottesville in early April; intends to make move permanent. Travels to West Point with Estelle, Jill, and Paul, April 19, and reads from *The Reivers*. Turns down President John F. Kennedy's invitation to attend dinner for American Nobel Prize winners. Accepts Gold Medal for Fiction of National Institute of Arts and Letters, presented by Eudora Welty, May 24. Returns to Oxford. *The Reivers* published by Random House, June 4. Thrown by horse near Rowan Oak, June 17. Endures much pain, but continues to go for walks, and negotiates purchase of Red Acres, 250-acre estate outside Charlottesville, for $200,000. Pain and drinking increase; taken by Estelle and James Faulkner to Wright's Sanitarium at Byhalia, July 5. Dies of heart attack, 1:30 a.m. on July 6. After service at Rowan Oak is buried on July 7 in St. Peter's Cemetery, Oxford, Mississippi.

Note on the Texts

This volume prints the texts of *The Town, The Mansion,* and *The Reivers* that have been established by Noel Polk. All texts are based on Faulkner's own typescripts, the texts of which have been emended to account for his revisions in proofs, his typing errors, and certain other errors and inconsistencies that clearly demand correction. Underlying typescript and holograph drafts of the typescript setting copies have been consulted regularly throughout the editorial process and have supplied the editor with numerous solutions to problems in Faulkner's final typescripts. By the time these novels were written, Faulkner composed almost entirely at the typewriter rather than in longhand, as had been his practice up through the third book of *The Hamlet* (1940); although there are occasional holograph drafts of certain passages, most of the editorially significant preliminary materials for the novels in this volume are typescript.

Comparison has been made of all relevant extant forms of these works, published and unpublished, to determine the nature and causes of variants among the texts. The goal of these labors—to discover the forms of these works that Faulkner wanted in print at the time of their original publication—is sometimes elusive. Although thousands of pages of typescript and proof are available to the editor, it is not always completely clear what Faulkner's final intentions were, or even whether he had any incontrovertibly "final" intentions regarding some of the individual components of his novels.

Copytexts for all three of these novels are Faulkner's own ribbon typescripts (now on deposit at the Alderman Library of the University of Virginia), which were used by the typesetters of the first editions. Faulkner typed all of these pages himself, with different degrees of care; they contain both authorial and editorial alterations of varying extent and seriousness. Faulkner was in some ways an extremely consistent writer. He never included apostrophes in the words "dont", "wont", "aint", or "oclock" and very seldom used an apostrophe to indicate a dropped letter in a spoken dialect word, such as "bout" or "runnin". He never used a period after the titles "Mr", "Mrs", or "Dr". The editors of the first editions generally, though inconsistently, accepted these practices, but compositors often made mistakes, and many periods and apostrophes slipped in. More serious problems also frequently occurred, mostly attendant upon the editors' and Faulkner's indifferent proofreading and upon the editors' general lack of understanding of what Faulkner was trying to do. Although the original editors of the novels in this volume did not make the kinds of wholesale alterations that were made by the editors of *Absalom, Absalom!*, for example, or alterations as significant as changing the title of *If I Forget Thee, Jerusalem* to *The Wild Palms*, they did intervene in hundreds of ways that affected the capitalization, punctuation, and wording of the published texts.

Faulkner's attitude toward such intervention is neither consistent nor entirely clear. Almost from the start of his career, he was a supremely confident craftsman; he was at the same time aware of the demands his work would make not merely on the reader but also on the publisher, editor, and proofreader. He seems to have been indifferent to some types of editorial changes, and he acquiesced to them; he seems not to have cared whether certain words were spelled consistently or whether certain of his archaisms were to be modernized, and he seems to have expected his editor to divine from his typescript whether each sentence was punctuated exactly as he wanted it—that is, whether or not a variation from an apparent pattern was in fact a deliberate variation or merely an inadvertency he expected an editor to correct. Thus while some of his marks on galley and page proofs were genuine revisions of his own, many others were clearly attempts to repair damage of one sort or another made by someone else on the typescript setting copy.

With the benefit of decades of intense scholarship, we are now perhaps in a better position to understand Faulkner's intentions, although clearly many of the original editorial problems remain. The Polk texts attempt to reproduce the texts of Faulkner's typescripts as he intended them to be originally published, insofar as that intention can be reconstructed from the evidence. For the most part, only those revisions on typescript or in proof that Faulkner seems to have initiated himself in response to his own text are accepted, and not those he made in response to a revision or a correction suggested or inserted by an editor; this is a conservative policy that may reject some of Faulkner's proof revisions in favor of his original text. Every effort has been made to preserve Faulkner's idiosyncrasies in spelling and punctuation. Even so, certain corrections of unmistakable typing errors and other demonstrable errors in the typescripts have been necessary.

Faulkner began writing about the Snopes family early in his career. In late 1926 or early 1927 he wrote about 18,000 words of *Father Abraham*, an unfinished novel that begins with Flem Snopes already established as a banker in Jefferson and then continues with a flashback depicting his rural origins and his auction of the spotted horses in Frenchman's Bend. Faulkner continued to use members of the Snopes family as characters in his fiction, and they appear in several novels and stories he published in the late 1920's and the 1930's. In the fall of 1938 he began writing a "Snopes book," using the title *The Peasants,* and in a letter written in December to Robert Haas, an editor at Random House, he outlined plans for two more novels about the Snopeses, *Rus in Urbe* and *Ilium Falling.* By October 1939 Faulkner had retitled the volumes in the trilogy *The Hamlet, The Town,* and *The Mansion.* Although *The Hamlet* was published on April 1, 1940, Faulkner did not begin work on the second Snopes volume until 1955, having written *Go Down, Moses, Intruder in the Dust, Requiem for a Nun,* and *A Fable* in the intervening years, while confronting serious financial and personal difficulties.

He began writing *The Town* in late November 1955, incorporating into the novel two short stories from the 1930's, "Centaur in Brass" (*American Mercury,* February 1932) and "Mule in the Yard" (*Scribner's,* August 1934). On August 22, 1956, he wrote to his friend Jean Stein: "Just finishing the book. It breaks my heart. I wrote one scene and almost cried. I thought it was just a funny book but I was wrong." Faulkner finished the first draft on August 25 and went to New York in September, where he completed work on the revised typescript in the Random House office of his editor, Saxe Commins. The setting copy of *The Town* was sent to the printer on October 22, 1956, and the novel was published by Random House on May 1, 1957. Copytext for the Polk edition is the ribbon typescript setting copy at the University of Virginia.

Faulkner began concentrated work on *The Mansion* in January 1958 and finished a first draft in January 1959. He incorporated into the novel revised versions of the short stories "By the People" (*Mademoiselle,* October 1955) and "Hog Pawn," an unpublished story he had probably written late in 1954. In early February he sent a revised version of the "Mink" section of the novel to Albert Erskine, who had become his editor at Random House following the death of Saxe Commins in 1958. Erskine noted a number of discrepancies regarding names, dates, and events between *The Mansion* and the earlier novels in the Snopes trilogy and reported them to Faulkner. In response, Faulkner wrote that if changing *The Mansion* to match *The Hamlet* and *The Town* in instances where they conflicted would cause *The Mansion* to "suffer," he favored either changing his earlier work in future printings or ignoring the discrepancy altogether; but he said that if the necessary changes to *The Mansion* simply involved "a matter of a word or a date," then the changes should be made in the new novel. Faulkner finished revising the last two chapters of *The Mansion* on March 9, 1959, and sent them to Erskine. In his accompanying letter, he proposed coming to New York in late March to work on resolving the discrepancies within the trilogy and expressed his desire that *The Mansion* be considered "the definitive" volume, adding: "Unless the discrepancy is paradoxical and outrageous." On March 14 Faulkner broke his collarbone while horseback riding, and his slow and painful recovery from the accident delayed his trip to New York until June, when he spent two weeks working with Erskine on the revised typescript at Random House. At this time he wrote a short prefatory note (printed on page 331 of this volume) concerning the unresolved discrepancies and contradictions within the Snopes trilogy. (At Erskine's initiative, Faulkner and Erskine met in the autumn of 1961 and made further changes in *The Hamlet, The Town,* and *The Mansion* in order to establish greater consistency within the trilogy; these changes were incorporated into *Snopes: A Trilogy,* a three-volume boxed set published by Random House in 1964, two years after Faulkner's death.) Faulkner then returned to Mississippi, where he finished correcting galleys for the novel on July 21. *The Mansion* was published by Random House on November 13, 1959. Copytext for the Polk edition is the ribbon typescript setting copy at the University of Virginia, with the exception of the prefatory note referred to above, which is printed from the first edition.

In a letter to Robert Haas of May 3, 1940, Faulkner outlined the novel that became *The Reivers,* writing: "It is a sort of Huck Finn— a normal boy of about twelve or thirteen, a big warmhearted, courageous, honest, utterly unreliable white man with the mentality of a child, an old negro family servant, opinionated, querulous, selfish, fairly unscrupulous, and in his second childhood, and a prostitute not very young anymore and with a great deal of character and generosity and common sense, and a stolen race horse which none of them actually intended to steal." He began writing the novel in the summer of 1961, using the title *The Horse Stealers: A Reminiscence,* and completed three chapters by early July. Faulkner finished his first draft on August 21 and sent a revised typescript of the novel, now titled *The Reivers,* to Albert Erskine in late September; he then went to New York in late November to work with Erskine on the revised typescript. *The Reivers: A Reminiscence* was published by Random House on June 4, 1962. Copytext for the Polk edition is the ribbon typescript setting copy at the University of Virginia.

By preserving Faulkner's spelling, punctuation, and wording, even when inconsistent or irregular, the Polk texts strive to be as faithful to Faulkner's usage as surviving evidence permits. In this volume, the reader has the results of the most detailed scholarly efforts thus far made to establish the texts of *The Town, The Mansion,* and *The Reivers.*

Notes

In the notes below, the reference numbers denote page and line of this volume (the line count includes chapter headings). No note is made for material included in standard desk-reference books such as Webster's *Collegiate, Biographical,* and *Geographical* dictionaries. For more detailed notes, references to other studies, and further biographical background than is contained in the Chronology, see: Joseph Blotner, *Faulkner, A Biography,* 2 vols. (New York: Random House, 1974); Joseph Blotner, *Faulkner, A Biography, One-Volume Edition* (New York: Random House, 1984); *Selected Letters of William Faulkner* (New York: Random House, 1977), edited by Joseph Blotner; Calvin S. Brown, *A Glossary of Faulkner's South* (New Haven: Yale University Press, 1976).

THE TOWN

3.1   salted goldmine]   A barren mine into which gold has been surreptitiously introduced to make it appear rich.

.3   Chickasaw]   Indian nation forcibly relocated from northern Mississippi to Indian Territory (present-day Oklahoma) in the 1830's.

.25–26   E.M.F. roadster]   Open automobile with a single bench-seat for two to three passengers, manufactured by the partnership of Byron Everitt, William Metzger, and Walter Flanders from 1908 to 1912, when the firm was bought out by Studebaker.

.19   bib]   Faucet with nozzle bent down.

.24   old . . . girth]   Had an illegitimate child. Cf. Sir Walter Scott, *The Fortunes of Nigel* (1822), ch. 32.

.5   quicked]   Drove into the sensitive inner hoof.

.38   Bilbo and Vardaman]   Theodore G. Bilbo (1877–1947) and James K. Vardaman (1861–1930). Both served terms as Mississippi governor and U.S. senator and advocated white supremacy.

.2   Gayoso]   Once fashionable hotel on a street of the same name, much decayed by the 1920's.

.2–3   Mulberry street]   Street known for illicit activities, including prostitution.

.11   gee dee]   God-damned.

64.1   Professor Handy] W.C. Handy (1873–1958), blues composer.

70.37   fish-grabblers] Fishermen who catch fish with their hands.

74.3   boom logs] Manipulate logs by means of chain and derrick.

80.14   palped] Felt.

101.24   swivelling] Shriveling.

107.27   ks] Quais.

111.7   hipering] Hurrying.

111.30   turnrow] A strip at the end of a field for turning farm equipme around.

117.11   trigger-set covey] Group of quail ready to take flight.

165.23   tolling] Luring.

180.35   Pistol] Cowardly braggart in Shakespeare's *Henry V, The Mer Wives of Windsor*, and *2 Henry IV*.

187.32   *grüss Gott*] German idiom, here "thank God."

233.5   rieved] Stolen.

262.25   ambeer] Tobacco juice.

323.22–27   We . . . as if] In the 1961 Vintage Books printing of *T Town*, Faulkner made some minor revisions to the final episode involvi Byron Snopes's children's visit to Jefferson and the efforts of Claren Snopes to keep them corralled. Most of the revisions simply chang "Clarence" to "Doris" Snopes, but he changed these lines to read as follov

> We all knew Doris Snopes. And even if we hadn't, we would have recognised him at first glance since he looked almost exactly like his older brother Clarence (Senator C. Eggleston Snopes, our—or Uncle Billy Varner's—Ratliff and Uncle Gavin said—member of the upper house of the state legislature)—almost exactly alike, with (this is Uncle Gavin again) the same mentality of a child and the mutual moral principles of a wolverine; younger than Clarence in years but not looking younger or more innocent so much as just newer, as the lesser-used axe or machine gun looks newer—a big hulking animal about seventeen years old, who like his brother Clarence was all one gray color: a grayish tinge already to his tow-colored hair, a grayish pasty look to his flesh, which looked as if . . .

THE MANSION

334.11   woods-colt] Bastard.

337.17   Bluetick] Bearing blue markings.

58.36   standers]   Hunters placed in a position where game will pass.

87.27   banloo]   Hinterland or suburbs, from French *banlieu.*

00.5–6   Argonne, Showmont, Vymy Ridge, Shatter Theory]   Sites of World War I battles in France: the Argonne, Chaumont, Vimy Ridge, Château-Thierry.

14.25–26   drag dust . . . middles]   Cultivate the crop.

47.9   EMF roadster]   See note 12.25–26.

76.8   Silver Shirts]   North Carolina–based fascist organization of the 1930's and early 1940's investigated by the House of Representatives for its ties to German National Socialism; its leader, William Dudley Pelley, was tried and convicted of sedition.

476.10   Bilbo]   See note 33.38.

480.14   kit-and-biling]   Group.

494.17   Hardshell Baptist]   Member of the fundamentalist Primitive Baptist Church.

497.12   East Lynne]   Melodramatic novel (1861) by English author Mrs. Henry Wood, adapted and often performed on the American stage.

502.6   R.F.C.]   Royal Flying Corps.

507.7   burked]   Balked.

580.14   p.c.]   Platoon commander.

582.25   Top Soldier]   First sergeant.

592.19   cooter]   Turtle.

608.4   ruptured ducks]   Honorably discharged veterans of World War II, named after the small lapel pins issued upon discharge.

611.33   Four F]   Selective Service classification for those excused from military service on medical grounds.

THE REIVERS

730.6   *entendre-de-noblesse*]   Gentlemen's understanding.

744.35   EMF racer]   See note 12.25–26.

805.15   "drug my foot."]   To drag the right foot to a position behind the left while making a ceremonious formal bow.

821.13-14   bird dog trials]   The National Field Trials held annually at Grand Junction, Tennessee.

842.23   lick-log]   A log with troughs for salt for cattle.

859.8   steamboat-gothic]   Highly ornamental style used on wooden homes and steamboats.

859.13   Horace Lytle]   Wealthy sportsman, author of books on hunting dogs, and judge for the National Field Trials.

859.14   Mary Montrose]   Cumbrian pointer and National Field Trial champion.

859.15   Paul Rainey]   Millionaire owner of Mississippi's largest game preserve.

860.6   dog-trot house]   House or cabin with two rooms linked by an open breezeway.

861.11   McClellan saddle]   U.S. Cavalry saddle with modified western pommel.

868.4   Uncle Remus and Lord Fauntleroy]   Fictitious characters created by Joel Chandler Harris and Frances Hodgson Burnett, respectively.

873.18   Morgan]   An American breed named for the first of its sires, Justin Morgan.

881.31   George Peyton]   Dog handler for many years at the National Trials.

913.7   Earl Sande]   Popular jockey who won the Triple Crown in 1930.

913.7   Dan Patch]   Famous horse, a harness pacer, that set records for speed in 1903 and 1904 and toured the country in popular exhibitions; brands of tobacco and gum were named after him.

933.34   Stanley Steamer]   Record-breaking steam-propelled automobile manufactured by the Stanley brothers of Newton, Massachusetts, in the first decade of the century.

934.18   scafells]   Mountain peaks.

955.6   Gaines's Mill]   Civil War engagement won by Confederate General Wade Hampton, June 27, 1862.

Library of Congress Cataloging-in-Publication Data

Faulkner, William, 1897–1962.
 [Novels. Selections]
 Novels, 1957–1962 / William Faulkner.
     p.   cm. — (The Library of America ; 112)
 Contents: The town — The mansion — The reivers.
 ISBN 1–883011–69–8 (alk. paper)
 1. Yoknapatawpha County (Imaginary place)—Fiction.   2. Snopes
family (Fictitious characters)—Fiction.   3. Mississippi—Social
life and customs—Fiction.   I. Title.   II. Title: Town.
III. Title: Mansion.   IV. Title: Reivers.   V. Series.
PS3511.A86A6   1999
813'.52—dc21
                                                    99–18348
                                                      CIP

This book is set in 10 point Linotron Galliard,
a face designed for photocomposition by Matthew Carter
and based on the sixteenth-century face Granjon. The paper is
acid-free Ecusta Nyalite and meets the requirements for permanence
of the American National Standards Institute. The binding
material is Brillianta, a woven rayon cloth made by
Van Heek-Scholco Textielfabrieken, Holland.
The composition is by The Clarinda
Company. Printing and binding by
R.R.Donnelley & Sons Company.
Designed by Bruce Campbell.

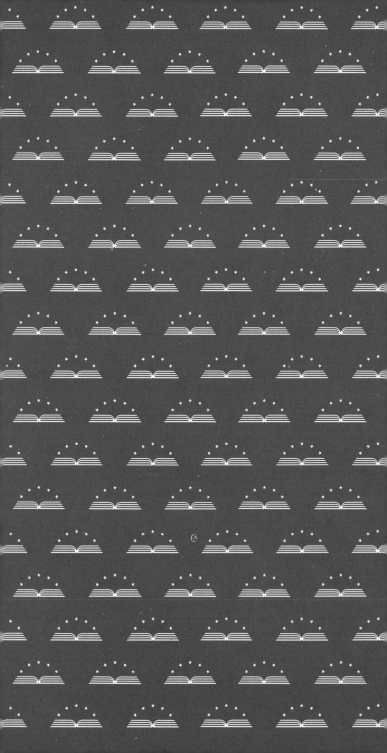